ALSO BY ELSIE SILVER

Chestnut Springs

Flawless

Heartless

Powerless

Reckless

Hopeless

Gold Rush Ranch

Off to the Races

A Photo Finish

The Front Runner

A False Start

Rose Hill

Wild Love

Wild Eyes

Wild Side

OFF TO THE RACES

ELSIE SILVER

New York · Amsterdam/Antwerp · London · Toronto · Sydney · New Delhi

OFF TO THE RACES
First published in Australia in 2024 by
Simon & Schuster (Australia) Pty Limited
Level 4, 32 York Street, Sydney, NSW, 2000
First published in the United States in 2021 by Elsie Silver

10 9 8 7 6 5 4 3 2

Sydney New York Amsterdam/Antwerp London Toronto New Delhi
Visit our website at www.simonandschuster.com.au

The authorised representative in the EEA is Simon & Schuster Netherlands BV, Herculesplein 96, 3584 AA Utrecht, Netherlands. info@simonandschuster.nl

A catalogue record for this book is available from the National Library of Australia

ANZ ISBN: 9781761634239
UK ISBN: 9781398551060

Cover design: Books and Moods
Internal design: Sourcebooks
Printed and bound by CPI Group (UK) Ltd, Croydon CR0 4YY

For my parents, who spent hours upon hours driving me to and from the barn.

PROLOGUE

Billie

TEN YEARS AGO

LIGHTS FLASH ALL AROUND ME, FORCING ME TO COVER MY EYES with my forearm. I can still hear the camera bulbs popping as I surge forward. The thrum of bodies around me is oppressive. They threaten to close in from every side.

I just need to get to the car.

"Wilhelmina! Wilhelmina!"

I move faster, butting up against security guards as I flail blindly toward the waiting town car, a beacon where I might finally relax. Where I can let the facade slip. Where I can put my head in my hands and cry.

I can see the open door beckoning me to slide in and escape.

I'm so close.

I'm jostled against my shoulder and feel cool crosshatched metal press up against my lips. Dropping my arm, I face eager eyes and too-white teeth.

"Wilhelmina, can you tell us if you've seen the videos of your father?"

All I hear is the steady beat of my heart pumping in my ears. I feel borderline feral in my need to disappear into the waiting car. The one I can see just beyond her perfectly coiffed blond hair.

I'm functioning on instinct. It's fight or flight now.

All I hear are gasps around me when I look right into the camera and say, "How about you go fuck yourself?"

I choose *fight*.

CHAPTER 1

Vaughn

I MOAN, HANGING MY HEAD IN MY HANDS, DEFEATED. "JESUS Christ."

The emails won't stop coming. The inquiring reporters. The never-ending questions.

I've been sitting at this desk for hours every day listening to the nonstop pinging of messages coming through while I turn my grandfather's office upside down looking for *something*. Scouring page after page of farm financials, digging through filing cabinets, looking for a clue. I've even gone so far as knocking on the inner walls of his desk drawers, like this is a movie rather than real life and a hidden compartment will pop open and show me exactly what I am looking for.

What am I missing?

I have to prove he's innocent. I can't let this be his legacy.

As the family business marketing whiz, I know I have a heaping pile of shit to clean up. That's what I should do right now. Paste on a winning smile and smooth things out. Nail down a plan to move forward. Reassure the media, apologize to fellow industry members, and rub our shareholder's backs.

I can't let the scandal here at the ranch seep into anyone's trust about how Gold Rush Resources operates. Sure, they're both our businesses, but one makes all the money while the other basically just continues to break even. And deep down, I know the only way to inspire confidence in the mining company is to throw my grandfather, one of the most important and influential men in my life, under the proverbial bus.

On a heavy sigh, I click the mouse to open my inbox.

Statement Request Re: Race fixing

Stubble rasps under my fingers as I scrub at my face. I don't want to make a statement, but it's been two weeks. I need to stop hiding out at the farm, banging my head against the wall.

Two weeks ago, our grandfather, Dermot Harding, the man who practically raised me when everyone else had tapped out, died from a massive heart attack. He keeled over right here in this office, and a day later, newspapers across the country splashed our family name and his photo on the front page, accompanied by a story about how he'd been the ringleader behind one of the biggest race-fixing scandals in thoroughbred racing history.

A fucking disaster, to be sure.

Rationally, I know the man was in his eighties—not an unusual time to die. But somehow his sudden loss has shocked me to my very core. Maybe his death hasn't hit me yet, because all I can think about is clearing his name. He's been slandered—his entire legacy—and he isn't even here to defend himself. There's just no way the man who practically raised me would have done this. I can't wrap my head around it.

My phone vibrates, drawing my attention away from the

email in front of me as I watch it dance across the desk's surface. The name *Cole* flashes on the screen with a picture of a G.I. Joe toy—an image that usually makes me smile. But not today. Today, I'm not in the mood to talk to my big brother.

I can't peel my eyes away from the phone but can't bring myself to pick it up either. I let the call ring through to voicemail, and within moments of the screen going black, it lights back up with another call. Cole is relentless, and I'm too obedient where my family is concerned to ignore two calls in a row. Something could be wrong.

I swipe the answer button and lift the phone to my ear. "What?"

"You done playing *Little House on the Prairie* yet?"

I roll my eyes. Cole is such a dick.

Everyone has their own idea of how I *should* act in the wake of my grandfather's death and the exposure of the scandal. My brother. My mom. The board of directors.

"Is there something you need that doesn't involve mocking me?"

"You need to get your ass back here. There are expectations, Vaughn," he grumbles, knowing this won't go over well.

I'm accustomed to being the face of the company, but they need me to put on a totally different show than usual this time, and I guess I'm not quite meeting their expectations for marketable grief. They want that devastation, sprinkled with a hint of shame, and they want it where everyone can see it.

And this time? I'm not buying.

"I know what the expectations are, Cole. I just don't care."

I can hear him groan on the other end of the line. I'm the one thing he can't check off his to-do list, and that's probably keeping him up at night. He's not worried about how I'm doing; he's worried about keeping things clean and tidy. Just the way he likes them.

"How long is this little stint going to last?"

I feel my jaw tick as I consider the best way to answer that question.

It makes him and everyone else involved uneasy that I shut them down and fled Vancouver for the tranquil mountains and valleys of Ruby Creek. I'm not mourning solemnly, toeing the company line about being shocked and disappointed, and "acknowledging my feelings" appropriately. Which is apparently achieved by holding press conferences, parading around with an appropriate date, like I'm some sort of glorified escort, and then penning an emotional editorial for the newspapers to print.

Too bad for them, I'm not sad yet.

I'm angry. Angry that the man I love more than almost anyone died alone in his office after being delivered such a shocking blow that his heart gave out.

And that anger? It makes the people around me uncomfortable, and if I've learned anything in my twenty-eight years on this earth, it's that most humans will do almost anything to salvage their own comfort. They'll grasp at it with white knuckles and sweaty palms and hold on to it with absolute frantic desperation. Destroy relationships with family members, endure shitty marriages, stab friends in the back—you name it. Comfort is king.

And for now, I care little about how I appear to the media or how my lack of comment reflects on the company. I've been their darling for years. I got the right education and then let them trot me out and parade me around like a fancy show pony.

"As long as I need it to," I bite back before hanging up. I'm done bending over backward to accommodate everyone else. I need some time for *me*.

I've suffered the company of people I can't stand, laughed at jokes that aren't funny, and rubbed shoulders with some of Vancouver's most influential people to satisfy my obligations to the family business. I've been the poster boy and most eligible bachelor of the elite scene in this city for years now. Without complaint. So as far as I'm concerned, they can all just buck up and deal with me feeling edgy for a few weeks.

The world won't stop turning if I take a break from smiling. Or if I take a step back from Gold Rush Resources to salvage the ranch.

Even just floating that idea went over like a lead balloon though. Cole hit the roof. Something about flushing my career and future down the toilet, followed by some advice about how perseverating on the farm isn't healthy or productive to the *main business*. According to Cole, in the wake of my grandfather's funeral, I should focus on my job and take some time with family. *Grieving.*

I snort. That was rich coming from him, the man who took off last time tragedy struck. Which I told him just before adding that I was in fact going to be taking a leave of absence to run the ranch. Then I'd spun on my heel and stormed out of our lavish downtown offices.

Good fucking riddance, concrete jungle.

I packed my bags and moved into my grandfather's farmhouse that very day, comforted by the closeness I felt here. Full of happy memories from my childhood.

Gold Rush Ranch has been in our family for generations. Once my grandmother Ada's family cattle ranch and now one of western Canada's premier racing facilities. This place had been my grandmother's dream—or at least that's what Dermot always told me. She died when I was younger, and my memories of her are less vivid. But I know that she's why my grandfather stayed out here and focused on the ranch while letting other people run the downtown offices for the mining company. And I know their love was one to rival a fairy tale.

So just because my brother and mother don't understand my attachment to the place doesn't mean it isn't true. Neither of them know me that well anyways, haven't ever really tried. Haven't ever gone out of their way to be there for me. Sure, we talk. But unless we're talking about running the family businesses, it's brief and superficial. I only tolerate my mother's meddling because it's the only attention I get from her. Which sounds pathetic—*I know* (hello, abandonment issues!).

Plus, if Cole can duck and run to the army in the wake of our father's death, I can duck and run to the ranch. Fair is fair.

I don't care what he thinks about it. Unlike everyone else, I'm not afraid of him. His holier-than-thou asshole attitude doesn't scare me. He never stuck around to take care of me before, and I will not let him do it now.

My grandfather spent decades building his empire from scratch. I owe him this.

Between the two companies, his blood, sweat, tears, and a little luck glued our entire family legacy together. Grandpa Dermot turned his full attention to the ranch in the depths of his mourning. And it has garnered accolades, prestige, and a hell of a lot of wins under his management. This whole place is a living, breathing ode to his late wife and son.

Reminiscing about my family history… I shake my head and stretch my arms out in front of me. *That* is not a productive rabbit hole to fall down.

Pity parties are for chumps.

Giving each sleeve a tug and adjusting my cuff links, I lean back and sigh deeply. I've been doing a lot of that lately. Big, heavy, hopeless sighs. The sound annoys me.

Looking out the office window, I feel… overwhelmed. I admire the perfectly arranged white fences in precise squares, each square a home to one horse. I appreciate the organization of the layout. One object arranged into one tidy box. So uncomplicated. So logical. The simplicity soothes me, and I repeat my grandfather's words to myself like a mantra. "You can only control what's right in front of you, Vaughn."

God. I sound like I've been reading lame self-help books. Something that my mother, bless her, has recommended. Right before she offered to set me up on *another* date. Like getting married off and pumping out grandbabies will make me as happy as it would her. She's a rich city girl through and through, one who fell in love with a farm boy, and I think Cole and I have never quite known where we belong. She loves me, but she doesn't understand me at all—doesn't even try.

"Well meaning. But so goddamn misguided."

"What was that, son?" Hank barks breathlessly, making me spin quickly in my chair. He's grasping the doorframe to pop his head back in, like he almost made it past without hearing me.

I really need to stop talking to myself.

"Nothing," I respond, more dismissively than intended. Kind of the norm for me these days, to be honest.

"You sure you're doing all right?" It's hard to sneak anything past old eagle eyes.

"Yup. See you at eleven." I try to make up for my tone by offering him a wave and a forced smile, but I'm not sure it works. It probably just makes me look feral. It doesn't feel natural. I'm just… numb.

Hank grins, winks, and continues on his way, completely undeterred by my shitty attitude. How the man is always in such a good mood is beyond me. He's so unflappable that it's borderline unnatural.

I need a few of whatever he's on.

The first thing I did when I got to the farm was clean house. Some people might say I burned the whole house down, but I couldn't rebuild this place's reputation surrounded by untrustworthy people or even people who were happy to look the other way.

Gold Rush Ranch is under new management, and that comes with a new moral code too.

I made it my mission to track down and hire Hank Brandt, the man who'd been Dermot's best friend when he moved to Ruby Creek all those years ago. A man who knew and loved this valley but who also knew racehorses. He went on to manage one of the East Coast's most successful racing and breeding programs before taking an early retirement and moving back out this way.

When I reached out to him about stepping out of that retirement, he'd been keen to return to the place where it all began, and to his credit, he wasn't even put off by the farm's declining success at the track and now tainted reputation.

He said he was "looking forward to the challenge" and flashed me his signature megawatt grin, like he knew something I didn't.

Hank and I agreed to a partnership where he would take the reins, so to speak, on all the horse-related tasks while I manage the business side of things. We agreed to hire everyone together. I wanted to ensure we were creating a work environment that we could both live with. I wasn't ready to relinquish control of my grandfather's legacy.

At least not before properly restoring it.

Which is why we're interviewing a new trainer this morning. Some guy named Billy Black who Hank met and worked with out east, who he raved about being young and cutting-edge. Trained in the United Kingdom under the tutelage of someone renowned over there who I didn't know at all and "brimming with new ideas and strategies," he said.

The guy didn't sound like the safe and reliable choice I'd like in place for this shit show, but I'll humor the old man. An interview can't hurt, and a person completely unknown to the industry in this area may just be the fresh start we need.

That *I* need.

Out the front window of my office, I can see the perfectly paved circular driveway. Just beyond the driveway, a fountain shoots arching streams of water in front of a bronze statue of my father in his jockey silks, poised over a galloping horse.

There are so many memories here. So many places for my mind to wander, to trip and fall into a daydream. So much to reminisce about.

The sound of rubber quietly rolling over sticky asphalt jolts me from my reverie, which is good because I don't have time to let myself turn into a sentimental sap right now. We are interviewing the new trainer in twenty minutes, and I really don't need any interruptions.

I watch the black SUV pull into the parking lot and feel frustration burn in my chest. I don't feel like dealing with people right now.

The driver's side door opens, and one polished black loafer steps out. It has interlocking horse bits across the top, accompanied by a long slender leg in slim-fit burgundy dress pants. My gaze travels up that leg, taking in the woman as she exits the vehicle. Bright spring sunlight glints almost blindingly off the thick chestnut braid that hangs down her back.

Standing to both feet, she gently smooths the collar on her black blouse before propping a hand over her brow and rotating slowly to take in the scenery. I can't help but let my eyes linger on the spot where her waist nips in between her curves.

A wistful smile touches her shapely lips as she stands there, all doe-eyed and serene looking.

She looks like a doll. She also looks altogether too smug. Like she knows she's here for her chance at bagging Vaughn Harding. I've seen that look a thousand times before, social climbers in their element. Gold diggers ready for their kick at the can. Women are constantly looking at me like that, and it has lost its appeal.

She's *beautiful*. Of course she is; they always are. But this woman is attractive in a classic and wholesome kind of way—a change in strategy, apparently.

I shake my head, feeling frustration bubble up in my chest, fast and hot. These games and charades are the last thing I need right now. Why is nobody *listening* to me? My fuse is short, and I'm ready to blow.

This time, I will not smile and nod. This time, I'm going to send a message. Loud and clear.

This time, my mother has gone too far.

CHAPTER 2

Billie

This.

This is my happy place.

No drama. No faking it. Just me and horses.

No human as far as the eye can see. Just the way I like it.

Anywhere with horses has always been my sanctuary, and this property is no exception. It's *immaculate*. Idyllic white fences outline the perfect green grass stretching out before me. And within each wooden square, a home to a beautiful shiny horse.

All layered with that comforting horse farm aroma I love.

I close my eyes and take a deep breath. No matter how pristine a farm is, you can't escape it, even outdoors. You can spend all the money in the world to keep your over-the-top, swanky facility spotless, and it will still smell like horse shit.

Makes me smile every time. Horses—1, humans—0.

I'm reveling in that score when a door slams behind me. I jump and turn around, hoping it's Hank, coming to wrap me in the best bear hug in the world. I peer through the fountain, centered in the driveway, expecting Hank's familiar frame, but it's not him. I'm met with an absolute vision far better in person than any of the pictures I found online.

Tall? Check.

Dark? Check.

Handsome? Check.

Looks like he wants to kill me? Also check.

I run my teeth over my bottom lip as his tall lithe body, wearing the hell out of a dark fitted suit, stalks toward me. Dark chocolate hair, longer on the top and a little disheveled, like he's been running his fingers through it, frames his annoyed face. Stubble blooms below razor-sharp cheekbones as he stops in front of me and peers down a straight nose almost too masculine for the shapely frowning lips beneath it.

Good thing I'm not one to cower, because at what has to be at least six foot three, this man is imposing.

Fiery mahogany eyes bore down on me. "You need to turn your sweet ass around, get in your car, and leave. Now."

Wow, what a greeting.

I tilt my head and search his face for some trace of humor. Finding none, I bark out a laugh. Because who talks to a person they've just met this way?

Okay, it was really more of a loud snort, but snort laughs make normal people laugh. Right? I even giggle a little at myself and think, *Hey, maybe he'll join in!* But no, not this fire-breathing dragon. He crosses his arms over his broad chest and continues to glare at me like I'm dirt beneath his expensive shoes. *Typical.*

"Pretty and slow to follow directions. Seems on par with every girl she's been serving up to me on a platter lately. This whole natural look is a fresh angle," he says, waving one arm up and down me like I'm a broodmare, "so I'll give her that. Do pass my kudos on in that regard when you report back to my mother about your failed attempt to lock me down into some breathtakingly boring arranged relationship. I'd rather date a blow-up doll."

I rear back slightly at that last bit. Date a blow-up doll? Oof. Did he really just say that? The man practically handed me an alley-oop. I could make so many jokes here, but I remind myself to keep it professional. Steeling myself, I take a deep breath, because this is about to get awkward. He clearly does not know who I am, but I've done a bit of homework and know exactly who he is.

Vaughn Harding.

I've missed Hank like crazy. When I showed up on his doorstep looking for a job ten years ago, he took me in and gave me a lot more than employment. Work, advice, a place to live, even a good talking to when I needed it. He was the father figure I always dreamed of. So when I heard I could be working beside him on the West Coast of Canada, I couldn't get on a plane fast enough. I mean, my working visa was up so I had to leave my training position in Ireland anyway. At least I knew where I was going and the name of the farm so I could do some research.

My internet stalking skills are so next-level I almost added them as a bullet point to the skills section of my résumé. In putting those skills to good use, I found two types of photos of this man populating the internet. Half of the images were Professional Vaughn, looking suave and serious in relation to his family's business ventures. The others were of Party Vaughn, looking charming and polished, usually at some glitzy event with a beautiful woman beaming on his arm.

Never the same woman from what I could find. And trust me, I *looked*.

An animalistic growl pulls me from my thoughts. "I said leave."

Is this fucking guy for real? As a general rule, my brain-to-mouth filter is a little relaxed. I've been an agitator since childhood and am well-versed in navigating situations where someone is ticked off. But this? This is new. Which is probably why I'm standing here silent and dumbfounded, staring like an idiot.

Before I can say something polite to defuse the situation, he holds his arms out and widens those molten eyes at me as if to say, "Hello? What the fuck are you doing?"

And then… He. Stomps. His. Foot.

Like a toddler.

A soft giggle bubbles up out of my chest. I don't even try to hold it in. I am well acquainted with men like Vaughn Harding. Few truly dependable things in the world exist, but trust fund babies being douchebags is one you can count on.

Holding one hand up to stop him, I launch in. "Okay, first of all, I am downright fascinated by your blow-up doll preference. Can we table that for now but revisit it someday?"

A sneer touches his lips. Ha. Didn't like that one.

"Second, I'm a grown-ass woman. Don't call me a girl. And third, when you're finished having this epic man-child meltdown"—I wave my hand up and down his body like he did to me—"can you please let Hank know that Billie Black is here for her job interview?"

And then I beam at him with a big old cheesy smile.

In his defense, he visibly pales while smoothing his suit jacket down and standing straighter.

He repeats back to me, "Billie Black?"

"That's me."

"I..." He shakes his head. "But you're not a man?"

"An astute observation, Mr. Harding," I reply with a smirk.

This is familiar territory for me. My name frequently confuses people; it doesn't bother me. It's a nickname, and I could go by something else if I wanted, but I kind of enjoy people's confusion over my name. And this encounter is no exception.

"Hey, Billie girl!" a familiar deep voice calls from over my shoulder. "You made it!"

Hank Brandt. Man, just hearing that voice makes me smile. I turn immediately, leaving Vaughn there gaping, to take in the face of the warmest, gentlest man I know. Broad shoulders, close-cut sandy hair, and a ruddy, deeply lined face, a face that's spent decades working out in the sun, rush toward me.

I've missed him. Sometimes you're born into a family, and other times you choose them. And when you choose them, you know in your bones that they're right for you. And that's Hank for me. The family I've chosen.

Almost jogging, Hank goes right in for a big old bear hug. And I soak it up. "You're even more beautiful than the last time I saw you," he says, holding me back by my shoulders and taking me in.

I go pink in the cheeks and roll my eyes at him. "Stop sucking up, old man. You already got me here. Now, show me around."

Hank has been a pillar of support in both my childhood and in my professional career: a friend, a father figure, and hopefully now an employer.

Assuming I haven't completely blown it with moneybags back there. Anxiety flutters in my stomach. I have my work cut out for me and will have to rise above that awkward introduction if I really want this job.

"Never lose that spunk, kiddo," Hank says, shaking his head and slinging an arm over my shoulder.

Hank leads me back toward Mr. Handsome and Crazy, who appears to have regained some composure.

"Billie, meet Vaughn Harding, the new owner and operator here at Gold Rush Ranch. He's a busy man, between this farm and the family mining business, but he'll be around for the foreseeable future managing our business operations."

Vaughn stares down at me now with an unreadable expression.

"He's going to sit in on the interview today to provide a second opinion. Hope that's okay with you."

I feel my throat bob as I swallow. *That's great. Just great.*

Stepping out from under Hank's arm, I extend my hand forward into Vaughn's strong grasp. I search for any signs of embarrassment on his part and find none. His face is stony and locked down now. All traces of the fiery passion he spit mere moments ago have completely disappeared.

Naturally, I test the waters by tossing him a quick wink while reciprocating his firm handshake. And by *handshake*, I mean *death grip*. I squeeze the hell out of his hand right back. Years of handling and riding powerful horses means I'm stronger than I look. I think I might even hear him grunt under his breath when I clamp down around his fingers. "The more the merrier," I say. "It's a pleasure to meet you, Mr. Harding."

He nods as he drops my hand abruptly and then switches his

focus to a spot over my head. "I'll be in my office when you're ready," he says to Hank before spinning on his heel and walking away, head held high, like he didn't just embarrass himself.

When I glance back at Hank, I see a twinkle in his eye as a slow Cheshire cat grin spreads across his face. Tutting and shaking his head, he says, "Billie, Billie, Billie. What did you do to that poor boy?"

At that, I throw my head back and laugh. Poor boy? I'm well acquainted with men like Vaughn Harding. I grew up immersed in that culture. Rich and spoiled men like him never outgrow their arrogant entitlement. Instead, they wear it like some sort of badge of honor.

My dad is exhibit A in that kind of behavior, followed by all the boys at boarding school and the men who mingled in our circles. Carbon copies of each other, the lot. Polished, calculated, and unfeeling.

Not to mention boring.

And fake, fake, fake.

Fake smiles, fake friendships, fake family. And that last one is the real kicker. I felt my pretty, perfectly curated life crash down around me the day that scandal broke.

Surprisingly, being a shitty, misguided person isn't enough to make a little girl stop loving her dad. But it is enough to make me lose respect for him. And that is a heart-wrenching combination… loving someone you can't respect.

Even a decade later, years into adulthood, it hurts in a way that has the power to take my breath away.

My father's word might not mean anything anymore, but mine is still good. I kept the promise I made to myself—leave and never darken the door of that lifestyle again.

I went out in a real blaze of glory, and I've been in rebuilding mode ever since. My sole focus has been my career, and this opportunity is the perfect next step.

As I watch Vaughn, the embodiment of everything I ran away from, enter the building, I admire the physique within his tailored suit pants. Trim waist. Incredible ass. Ten out of ten, would grab.

But I won't. Because I know this type of man. An absolute nightmare to interact with, dangerous to get involved with. But still fun to ogle. I am only human after all, and the man is hot as sin.

Yes, I will enjoy the hell out of this view, but from a safe distance. Because men like Vaughn are a trap I will never fall into.

CHAPTER 3

Vaughn

WHAT A FUCKING DISASTER.

I flop down in my desk chair and stare at the ceiling, wishing the floor might swallow me whole.

I can't help but shake my head at myself.

Marching out there like I had no self-control? Flying off the handle like a petulant child? What was I thinking? My mother's increased meddling in my love life is turning me into a goddamn wrecking ball.

She keeps dropping women on me like it's my birthday and they are perfectly wrapped presents for me to unwrap. I know being married to my dad made her happier than anything else, and she just wants that for me. I also know my brother, Cole, is a lost cause in that department, which means I get to play all her silly dating games alone.

Lucky me.

Even if it *had* been a woman my mother sent over with her insane scheming, my behavior would have been out of line.

The way I acted was so much worse because of Hank's excitement about the possibility of hiring this girl… woman.

One side of my lips quirks up at the way she bit back about being called a girl.

Whatever. She looked young and definitely nothing like the man I expected to interview.

Billie, not Billy.

Who would have guessed?

I suppose if I'd actually looked at her résumé, I might have noted that minute difference. Not that Hank really threw me any bones in that regard. He could have warned me. Instead, he was all, "I know this trainer who I think we should interview. Good international experience but not stuck in a rut. Might be a nice fresh option. Managed to take a stable in Ireland from relative obscurity to a mainstay in the winner's circle over there."

He seemed so excited, and his description sounded good to me. Most of all, I trust him, so I just gave him the go-ahead to set up an interview without asking much more.

Thinking back, I almost feel like he intentionally left out mentioning if we were discussing a he or she. Not that it matters. I have no problem hiring a woman. She's just young. Which means inexperienced. Too inexperienced for this high-stakes game.

And too mouthy.

That mouth. Sultry, soft, heart-shaped.

Yeah. *That* is not what I need.

I need someone dependable and organized who I can count on to take the success of Gold Rush Ranch seriously. This isn't a game.

The way she let me carry on like an idiot when she probably knew exactly who I was…

And then she had the gall to laugh at me.

Unbelievable.

I can feel myself getting worked up just walking back through the moment in my head.

I've elicited a lot of responses from women over the years: desire, lust, moans and whimpers, and even anger when our time together inevitably ended. No one ever looked me in the eye and laughed at me.

No, this is new.

Her glowing amber eyes widened so expressively when I told her to leave. Her full pink lips lifted at one side as a few stray pieces of dark chestnut hair blew gently across her cheeks in the breeze.

She looked wild and untamed at that moment. She looked like a challenge.

Under different circumstances, I'd have liked to grab that challenge firmly by her heavy braid and show her who is really in charge here. I'd tilt her head back and drag my teeth along the bottom of her jaw while whispering all the filthy ways I planned to wipe that condescending smirk off her face.

I huff out something that resembles a muffled laugh and adjust myself in my briefs.

Something tells me the only thing that scenario would get me is a swift kick in the balls. She has chutzpah; I'll give her that.

And she's a wild card, which is the very last thing I need in my life right now.

Racing season is about to be in full swing, and they have forced us to pull all the horses from the track. To retreat here to the farm in disgrace, suspended from all sanctioned events for three months. We won't be racing any of our string until halfway through the season at least.

I don't need a wild card; I needed a fucking miracle.

***

Light, feminine laughter filters through the hall outside my office door, pulling my attention from the full inbox in front of me. I've spent the last hour here staring at the screen, achieving nothing, and living in my head.

A place that no one wants to be right now.

"Ladies first," Hank announces as Billie rounds the corner.

I roll my eyes. Talk about laying it on thick.

I turn around to grab the files we'll need for the interview, assuming they finished with the grand tour.

"How'd it go?" I ask as I rifle through the drawer of folders.

"So good," Billie responds enthusiastically. "Your facility is truly world-class, Mr. Harding."

My cock twitches against my will at the way she says *Mr. Harding* with such admiration.

Vaughn, you're a fucking mess, bud. I manage not to chastise myself out loud this time—a minor victory for the day. But when I look at her now, she almost takes my breath away. She is positively glowing and so full of excitement she's almost vibrating in her seat.

I stare at her, struck by how genuine she is. So open and honest with her feelings. What must that be like?

I scour my brain but can't remember the last time I felt as happy as Billie looks in this moment. I feel like I'm looking at the sun, blinding but so deliciously warm that I just close your eyes and bask in the glow anyway.

"Yes, well, thanks. My grandparents transformed this place from a cattle ranch into everything you see here. Lots of family history," I say, dropping my gaze quickly.

"I want to extend my condolences about your grandfather. What a terrible loss," she says, hitting me with her best doe-eyed expression.

"Thanks. Let's carry on," I reply, brusquer than intended.

I'm prepared for battle with this woman, not decorum and innocent looks. She's giving me whiplash. Thankfully, Hank chooses this moment to jump in and save me.

"Okay, Billie. Let's get started."

Leaning back in my seat, I steeple my fingers and watch them interact. Hank asks pointed questions, and Billie responds eloquently even though she flaps her hands around like she's trying to take flight.

Of course, she's a hand talker.

They discuss training techniques, racing strategies, bloodlines, and god knows what else. To be frank, it's mostly Greek to me. As a child, I hung around the stables talking to people, lending a hand with farm chores, and doing schoolwork in the lounge, but it was more of social setting than anything—a way for my grandfather to keep me close, especially after losing my dad.

That's why Hank is here. I need his expertise. He's one of the best in the business with stable management, and I can tell by the proud look on his face he has practically already hired this woman.

I'll have to play this right. Anything short of diplomatic will be like taking away a kid's toys on Christmas morning. I'm not stupid. It's clear to me I can't afford to piss Hank off by raining on his Billie parade. I obviously missed the memo about how close they are. Come to think of it, I've missed a few memos from Hank where she's concerned, but that's a conversation for another time.

Either way, I'm not about to let this situation slip through my grasp. If Hank thinks he can pull a fast one on me and this woman thinks she can laugh in my face and still waltz into a cushy new job, they're both mistaken.

It's still my farm. I make the final decision.

"Why do you want this job?" I bark.

She gazes at me with intensity, a tinge of pink on her pale cheeks. I can see her thinking. I wait for her to scold me for interrupting her so that I can send her packing for a good reason.

Instead, she leans forward, rubs her hands down her slender thighs, and chews on her bottom lip. Fuck, I wish she wouldn't do that.

"To be frank, Mr. Harding…"

And now that again. How am I supposed to lead an intimidating line of questioning with her calling me Mr. Harding while innocently biting her damn lip? "Call me Vaughn."

"Okay, Vaughn. To be frank, I've earned a head trainer position."

I scoff. Talk about entitled.

"No. Listen, I don't mean I deserve one. I mean, I've *earned* it. I started on my own, with absolutely nothing, and I've taken every opportunity that has presented itself to me with a smile." She sighs and starts flapping her hands around again as she carries on. "I worked my butt off at low-end farms with low-end horses until I was good enough to work at mediocre farms with mediocre horses, and I kept my nose to the grindstone until I landed an internship as a working student at a world-class farm I had planned to apply for since I was fifteen years old. I made it happen. I worked with the best of the best in the United Kingdom. I learned the ropes and then got good enough they wanted to keep me around for actual paid positions. I've poured my blood, sweat, and tears into becoming one of the best so that I could apply that knowledge here, on home turf." Her hands land across her chest, and she looks at me so earnestly that I almost can't hold her gaze. "Give me a shot. I can turn this around for you. I know I can."

I have to hand it to her. That was an excellent answer. Not even a little contrived the way the story spilled from her lips, brimming with pride and grit.

I tap my pointer fingers together, assessing her from my position. She doesn't shy away from holding my eye contact in the moments that follow. My plan to trip her up has backfired because she blindsided me with so much confidence in her hard work, in her own ability, when initially she seemed like this was all some big joke to her.

Confidence and dedication are two things I probably respect the most in another person. I've worked my ass off too. I won't be the one who has to work with her every day, so if she's good at her job, what does it matter if she's also irritating?

"You're young," I say.

"I have energy," she counters.

"You're inexperienced."

"And I'm hungry to prove myself." She grins.

Is she intentionally filling her answers with innuendo? This woman is certifiable. Leaning forward, I toss the file folders I put together across the desk at her. *Last hoop, honey.*

"Okay, Billie, I've got five folders here, one for each horse that will make their debut at Bell Point Park, the track here in

Vancouver, next season. Why don't you look through them and pick a favorite?"

She eyes me with suspicion. "I mean, I'd have to see them run to make that kind of call. Despite what some people think, stats and bloodlines aren't everything. A horse needs a lot of heart to win. The right mindset."

Smart girl.

"For the sake of this exercise, just pick based on what you can see on paper."

She meets the challenge in my eyes with her own. I know she has an inkling I'm leading her to slaughter here. I see it written on her face. She's suspicious, but she's going to follow me anyway because if I can guess one thing about Billie Black today, it's that she's stubborn as fuck.

Hank starts in on me, not completely oblivious to what I'm doing here either, "Vaughn, I think that..."

Billie holds a graceful hand up in his direction while pulling the folders toward herself. "Hank, please. I can manage."

She leans over my desk and opens the first folder.

Each one contains a horse's Canadian Racing Club registration that breaks down several generations of their bloodline and notes physical information, like height and sex. I've also included information on each horse's dam and sire, which is often important in predicting a prospect's aptitude for success. Genetics and all that.

The part I've left out is each horse's report card in Hank's initial assessment. I had him take a small team through the barn and create a profile on each horse for me. If I'm being honest, the information I've provided her with is pretty bare bones. I know I'm making an unfair request.

But that's all part of my plan.

I examine her. Brow furrowed in concentration, eyes flitting back and forth, absorbing each line in each folder. Dark lashes frame golden irises with darker flecks throughout, like one of those tiger's-eye stones. The color gives her an almost feline look. I can spot mascara and maybe a little blush; otherwise all she's sporting is a smattering of freckles across her nose that you only get from time spent in the sun.

Studying her now, I'm not sure how I could ever have confused her for one of the women my mother handpicks. No chance they would go out with visible freckles on their nose.

Billie Black isn't a done-up kind of hot. She's just… naturally alluring. I'm sure men stop and stare at her but can't quite put their finger on why. At the risk of sounding like some sort of new-age chump, there's just an energy about her. Something gravitational.

She's now humming to herself and organizing the folders into three different piles. I realize that I've moved forward in my chair, trying to see what she's doing. With my elbows propped on the desk, I'm leaning toward her like a total creep.

She calls me out on it without even sparing me a glance. "Trying to steal the answers off my test, Vaughn?"

I clear my throat and sit up straight. When I chance a look over at Hank, he just lifts an eyebrow at me as if to say, "What are you doing, you absolute loser?"

My nostrils flare on a heavy breath, but Billie remains focused. She's lost in thought, tapping a pointer finger over her lips.

But I'm done waiting.

"Okay. Time's up," I bark.

Billie gives me the same lifted eyebrow look that Hank just did, and I already know that having these two working together is going to be a pain in my ass.

"Okay," she begins, "I've got these organized into three categories. This first stack, these three are all great high-quality horses ready to get started this year. They'll succeed, and we can probably get a few good races under their belt and then sell one or two as prospects for good money without pouring a bunch into them."

Yup. I like the sound of that.

"Second category is this mare, Brite Lite. I like her physical characteristics; she's young and has a nice early birthday, which will lend her a little extra maturity come race time. She's also beautifully bred, has a few famously consistent producers in her background, and could easily be a nice foundation mare for your breeding program in the future."

Hank nods his head and pipes in with, "I agree."

Her eyes flit from his back to me. "She *might* be my favorite."

I stare at her blankly, not wanting to give anything away.

Without breaking eye contact, Billie taps two fingers on the final folder. She hits me with a steely look and asks, "What's wrong with Double Diablo?"

I give her a deadpan look. "I don't know what you mean."

Hank groans audibly. *Fucking traitor*.

"I mean that he's three years old with zero starts under his belt. His pedigree is drool-worthy. Looking at his papers is like reading a list of the world's most famous racehorses. I know what breeding a horse like that costs. You must have at least a quarter million dollars invested in him already." Billie grunts and shakes her head, like she can't quite believe it. "Even with only a moderately successful racing career, he'd be your golden ticket to collecting big money on stud fees one day. He should have been running this year already, but he's done nothing." She flops back and pins me with her intelligent eyes. "So… what's wrong with him?"

Smart woman.

She looks at me like she expects an answer. But this is my test, and I refuse to give anything away. "That wasn't my question. I said, on paper, which one is your favorite? From what you've just told me, the answer is obvious."

She peeks back down at that final folder, nervously tucking loose strands of hair behind her ears.

"Is he injured?" she asks softly while flipping through the pages in front of her again as if she looks hard enough, more information might magically appear on the pages.

"No," I reply honestly.

I'm thoroughly enjoying watching her squirm. She looks so uncertain, and I know I'm taking far too much pleasure in knocking her down a peg.

She blows a dramatic breath out like I'm exhausting her and meets my gaze with a determined set to her face. "Okay, he's my favorite," she declares, tossing the folder back at me, like I had done to her, and then crosses her arms like a suit of armor.

Game. Set. Match.

I can't stop the sly smile that slowly spreads across my face. "Excellent choice, Ms. Black."

Hank is now shaking his head at me. I know I'm going to hear from him about this later, but I don't care.

My farm, my rules.

"I'm assuming I have Hank's blessing when I say I'd like to offer you the position of head trainer here at Gold Rush

Ranch. You can start as soon as you like. Take a few days to get settled. I'm including accommodations in the offer. There is a cottage down the road with your name on it. Our three-month suspension from competition ends on July first, and that gives you…" I trail off, assessing the calendar on my desk. "About three months."

Head tilted, she asks, "Three months for what?"

"To get Double Diablo in shape to win his first race of the season. He wins, we extend your contract to a permanent position. He loses, and you receive a glowing reference and an extra paragraph to beef up your résumé."

Billie blinks at me.

"Maybe we should talk about this first, Vaughn." Leave it to Hank to rush in and try to save her.

I understand this isn't the joint choice we agreed to, but this is the best way for me to appease him while also ensuring I won't have to deal with Billie Black's unpredictable attitude and boner-inducing face for long. It also gives me three months leeway to vet my own candidates and find the perfect fit for when our ban ends.

She'll do fine until then.

"No, Hank, it's a fair enough offer. I'm still untested in a lot of ways, and this will be the perfect opportunity for me to prove what I can do," she says with a determined set to her jaw.

Hank sighs audibly, and I grin triumphantly. A genuine grin.

God, I love winning.

"Well, it's settled then. Welcome to the team, Billie. Swing by tomorrow morning, and I'll go over the contract with you." I stand, rolling my shoulders back. The high of tying up a good business deal never fails to make me feel like a million bucks.

Billie looks me in the eye and takes my hand, just as firmly as last time. "Thank you for the opportunity, Mr. Harding."

"Billie girl, you have no idea what you've bitten off here," Hank warns.

She turns to shake his hand next. "Hank, I'm not an idiot. I can piece enough together here to assume that the horse is going to be a challenge."

Ha. A challenge is an understatement.

As they filter out of my office, I watch Billie go, sassy little thing that she is. I have to admit, the view from behind is equally as alluring as the front. The thrill of victory has me all worked up, and I can't help but let my mind wander to how good that perfect round ass would look with a pink handprint on it.

My handprint.

I imagine bending her over my desk, in complete control, yanking her pants down around her thighs, bunching up the back of her shirt, holding it in one fist, and giving her a few good smacks all while she moans and writhes beneath me.

She'd enjoy it; I'd make sure of that. My cock swells in my pants. *Good god.* What is wrong with me? I need to get my head in the game.

I turn back to my computer screen, resolving to do some actual work when out of the corner of my eye, I see that caramel mane pop back through my door with a mischievous glint in her eye.

"Sorry to interrupt, Boss Man," Billie says. "Forgot my purse!"

Boss Man? I roll my eyes and shake my head.

So annoying. My cock doesn't seem to care though.

She grabs the offending handbag and turns to leave but pauses at the door and looks over her shoulder, hitting me with a cocky smirk. "I also wanted to mention an amendment I'd like to make to my contract."

I scrub both hands over my face. This woman is going to be a lot of work.

"Go on."

"How do you feel about an extra ten percent on my base salary for my, what did you call it… sweet ass?"

Fuck my life. This is going to be a long three months.

CHAPTER 4

Billie

THIS IS GOING TO BE FUN.

I strut out of Vaughn's office, squeezing my lips together, trying to contain my laughter. The guy is too easy to rile. And no, I probably shouldn't be antagonizing my new boss. But I couldn't help myself. Stuffy rich dudes like him practically beg for it.

What dawned on me in that office is that our relationship here is rather symbiotic. He needs me as much as I need him. He needs a trainer who is new to the scene, and I need a job as head trainer where I can prove myself to be as good as I know I am.

Think I am.

I suppose I could fail. But believing that will get me nowhere. Best foot forward. Clear eyes, full hearts, whatever the fuck, can't lose—right? At any rate, I'm stoked. The facility is outstanding. Hank is possibly my favorite human. My boss is uptight eye candy. And my horse, from what I gather, is probably totally crazy.

Life is good.

I squint into the bright spring sun. It's low in the sky this time of year, so I hold my hand up over my brow and peer out into grounds looking for Hank. I haven't lived in Vancouver's Lower Mainland before, but what I know of it is that I should expect a lot of rain. But on days like this… man, Ruby Creek is breathtaking. Fresh air mingles with the aroma of pine and the mineral scent of the river rushing nearby, and lush green valleys butt up against the start of British Columbia's North Cascades mountain range. I feel like I'm standing in a picture book.

Someone nudges my shoulder, and I turn to see Hank standing with me, squinting out into the sun too.

"Beautiful spot, eh?"

I tilt my head slightly and raise one shoulder in agreement. The property itself is immaculate, tree-lined, and manicured. It almost looks like a golf course. All of which doesn't really matter if their actual racing program is in shambles. So yeah, it's beautiful, but troubled.

"Well," I say, gazing ahead, "why don't you introduce me to the new man in my life?"

He turns toward me slowly with a grave look on his face. "He's going to be a lot of work, Billie."

"Of course he is, Hank. Men always are."

At that, he snorts and shakes his head.

We walk through the lines of paddocks where Hank points out many of the horses to me. Some retired, some breeding stock, some just babies still. Most of the racing horses stay in their box stalls but exercise daily, sometimes even twice daily.

"When they handed down the suspension, it forced Vaughn to pull all the horses they had stabled at the track, so it's busier around here than usual."

I nod. There are a lot of horses on-site right now. "I read the gist of it all in the news. Is there anything else I should know?"

Hank sighs raggedly. "Dermot Harding was one of my best friends when I was younger. This was his wife Ada's family ranch. Never seen two people quite so in love as those two. Dermot was a good man who got embroiled in something he shouldn't have." He trails off. "Vaughn is struggling. His father was a jockey, you know. A good one."

I shake my head as we continue our stroll. "No, I didn't."

"He died on the track. His horse went down in the middle of the pack. Vaughn was only ten years old."

All the air leaves my lungs on a single exhale. This sport is not without its risks, that's for sure.

"Dermot practically raised him," Hank continues. "He was recently widowed at that point. I would have thought the loss of his son would be more than he could bear. But when everyone abandoned Vaughn, Dermot threw himself into giving that boy the best life he could. This is more than just a ranch for Vaughn. It's a legacy."

I blink rapidly, not wanting to feel bad for the man who just accosted me. "Gotcha," I say, grateful when Hank adds nothing more.

We make it to the far end of the paddocks where there is one larger pen tucked into the rolling green fields behind it. My new project is there, head down, grazing on perfect emerald grass. He looked impeccable on paper, but in person, he looks a little unkempt. Especially compared to the perfectly tended horses around him.

He's solid black. Classic looking. Not a single speck of white on his face or legs. He looks healthy, if lacking a little fitness.

He also looks like he's been rolling in the dirt. Dust covers what could be a shiny coat.

As we approach, I click my tongue at him, a noise we often use with horses to get their attention or signal that it's time to get going. He startles, head flicking up at me instantly, and I'm met with the most angelic little face. Dishy forehead, big innocent eyes, long lashes, and ears so pointy that the tips turn in toward each other.

All those features framed by a thick, unruly forelock, with a heavy tail at the other end to match, almost make him look like an oversize pony rather than a lean, mean racing machine.

I sigh. He is *adorable*.

I'm not sure he feels the same about me though, because those charming little ears whip back flat on his head, his soft little nose wrinkles up like there's a foul smell, and that big, luscious tail whips back and forth angrily. Then he drops his head and charges at the fence like a little warhorse.

Hank takes a step back from the fence, even though we aren't standing close enough to be in the line of fire. The horse isn't stupid; he's not going to bust through the fence. He's trying to scare me off or intimidate me. Sadly for him, it will not work.

I stand my ground.

Sure enough, he slams on the brakes as soon as he comes close to the fence and lunges his neck over, showing me the whites of his eyes and a nice set of pearly teeth as he bites at the air in front of me.

Charming. The men of Gold Rush Ranch are a lot of bluster.

I don't shy away, but I also don't want to threaten him by making eye contact, so I pull my phone out of my purse and start scrolling through my social media accounts, not giving him an inch.

Double Diablo stands there, staring at me, snorting so heavily I can feel the damp heat of his exhalations across my down-turned forehead. He eventually stomps his foot, which makes me chuckle. Seems to be an ongoing theme.

The young stallion eyes me warily as I say, "You remind me of someone else I met today."

He snorts again and then turns his butt to me. Yup, a total drama queen.

"And that," Hank says, pointing at the little black horse, "is why no one wants to deal with him. He's built and bred to be one of the best, but no one's put the time in to earn his trust so far. I haven't been here long enough to assess him, but the word among the staff is that he's just plain mean. They don't even bring him into the barn at night."

I snort and roll my eyes. "How much work has he had?"

"Not much. From what I gather, they started trying to get his training going early for his two-year-old year. People have tried intermittently since then. Apparently, he spends all his energy going straight up rather than straight forward, and he's proven to be dangerous in the starting gates. Throwing himself against the sides to the point no one wants to risk sitting on him in there."

I hum and tap my pointer finger against my lips. "So the poor boy is scared, and no one has taken the time to listen to him."

"Bingo." Hank points at me with a finger gun. "But don't underestimate him. He's a smart horse who's had a couple years of learning that he can get his way."

I scoff at that.

"I'm serious, Billie. You have to be careful. You need to create success for yourself, not end up in the hospital."

"Hank, the horse isn't some sort of evil mastermind." I sigh. "He's terrified. I clicked my tongue, and he jumped out of his skin. I'd be willing to bet my first paycheck that he hasn't had many positive interactions with humans. He needs a fresh approach. We both know traditional training techniques don't always work. You can ruin a sensitive horse and eventually injure an otherwise great one." Just thinking about the unfairness of it all agitates me. I cross my arms and shake my head, looking back at the beautiful animal before me. "He needs patience, confidence, and a new name. I mean, really. Double Diablo? It's like some shitty self-fulfilling prophecy."

I meet the incredulous stare of someone who clearly thinks I'm nuts. Hank barks out a laugh.

"You think his *name* is the problem?"

I smile sheepishly. "I mean, it doesn't help his case."

Eyes twinkling with mirth, Hank shakes his head. "I don't know about that. But the one thing I am sure of is that if anyone can bring this guy around, it's you. This horse needs some love. He just hasn't met anyone brave enough to give it to him yet."

Pride swells in my chest at his affirmation. Hank has never failed to make me feel like the world was mine for the taking. Sometimes all you need is one person's unwavering faith. Support that is absolute.

Looking back at Double Diablo, who is still sulking like a big baby, I decide that I'm going to be that person for him.

I pull a smooth white peppermint out of my purse and toss it over the fence to land beside him. Even at that one little movement, I see him flinch and flick one ear to the side where the mint lands. Other than that, he doesn't budge. *Tough customer.*

I turn to Hank, who is regarding me with those signature sparkly eyes. "Okay, what next?"

"Do you have all your stuff with you?"

What little I own, you mean?

"Yup. Figured I'd get a hotel out in the valley where all the farms are anyway. I'll have to deal with the rental car at some point though."

Hank nods decisively. "Let's get you settled in at your cottage. Then if you want to get anything, I can take you into the closest city to get what you need. Tomorrow, I'll introduce you around and see what we can do about the car."

I earn a head shake when I loop my arm through his to lead him away and respond with, "Sounds good, old man. Let's go check out my new digs."

We start back up the pathway toward the stables in a companionable silence. On one hand, I have so much I want to talk to him about, so much to tell him. On the other, I'm jet-lagged as fuck and just happy to be here with him.

A little way up, I sneak a look over my shoulder at the little devil horse, just in time to see him sniffle the mint on the ground. He stares at it for a moment, inhaling the minty scent, and then snaps it up quickly like he's stealing something and doesn't want anyone to catch him.

Then he turns his neck while chewing and looks back at me with ears pricked forward before storming off again.

The inside of my SUV is dead silent and awkward as fuck as Vaughn directs me down the back roads to a long gravel driveway that weaves through the trees. Why he insisted on showing me the place when he clearly can't stand me is beyond my comprehension.

"Left." He barks out directions like I'm his limo driver or something.

I take the left, biting my tongue, and come around a slight bend to see a charming pine A-frame house with a red tin roof.

If I'm being honest, it's more house than I need. It's definitely not what I was expecting when I heard "cottage," but I suppose this facility isn't really what you think of when you hear "ranch" either. People above a certain tax bracket enjoy doing this thing where they pretend they're just one of the commoners. Growing up, my mom loved to talk about our cabin like it was some sort of rural nature experience. Spoiler alert: it's a mansion on a lake.

Vaughn steps out once I've parked, every movement graceful and athletic. He strides up to the front door, taking every other step up the short staircase, and unlocks it before heading back to the rental vehicle. I move to the back hatch of the SUV to grab my bags only to feel his hand clamp down on my forearm.

The warmth of his palm, the firmness of his grasp—it has me thinking about things I shouldn't be.

"I've got these. You go ahead."

Cute. Now *he's going to be a gentleman?*

I just scoff and grab one anyway, walking past him with a smile so big and cheesy it makes my cheeks ache. I'm more than capable of carrying a bag. Haven't needed a man so far, not about to start falling over myself for this one, mind-numbingly sexy as he might be.

The inside of the house is beautiful and cozy. Open concept with exposed wood and vaulted ceilings, a kitchen island overlooking the dining table and living room. To the right is a staircase that I take up into a large loft bedroom and drop my bag.

From up here, the view is truly outstanding. Lush and green and so peaceful. This side of the house is almost all windows. It's built to face out over the farm's rolling fields. I'm fairly certain that if I headed straight out the back door and over the hill, I'd end up at the horses' paddocks.

I pinch myself. And I don't mean that as a manner of speaking. I literally pinch myself, thumb and finger gathering the skin on the side of my forearm. I've been rooming with other grooms and trainers in a male-dominated sport for years now, and the thought of having my own space feels downright luxurious. No stepping over questionable single socks or doing other people's dirty dishes. *Heaven.*

I let out a big breath and blow a loose piece of hair off my face. I want this so badly. This is what I've been craving my entire life. Roots. Family. A quiet setting. A secure job. A place to call my own.

"Billie. I'm ready to go," Vaughn hollers from downstairs.

My eyes roll so far back in my head they're at risk of staying there. "You can just walk yourself back to the farm, right?" I shout as I turn to head down.

He meets me by the door, chest all puffed out in some sort of *National Geographic*–worthy show of dominance that makes me giggle. Vaughn doesn't look quite so amused though. Instead, he looks pained. Like he's short on air, like he's holding one breath in and can't bring himself to let it out. He looks *uncomfortable.*

I quirk my head. "You all right?"

"Yup," he says brusquely, popping the *p* sound loudly. "Need to get back to work."

A ghost of the past flickers across his face as he spins on his heel and leaves. Good lord, this man is a puzzle I don't have the time or patience to figure out.

After a couple hours spent buying some basics, I pull back up to my new home. I drop my head back against the headrest and close my eyes for a moment. My eyelids are heavy. I momentarily wonder if driving in this condition was really my best move. Exhausted doesn't even cover it. But I know I have to keep pushing if I'm going to make jet lag my bitch.

I count to sixty and then force myself out of the car.

First, laundry. I'm looking forward to crawling into a fresh, cool bed at the end of this long-ass day. Nothing better than fresh sheets, that clean laundry smell wrapping itself around you like a comforting cocoon. One of the greatest feelings in the world, if you ask me.

Next most important point of business: coffee. I start a pot, hoping it will give me the boost I need to get settled in. Then I throw on some old torn jeans and a tank top, twist my hair up in a messy knot, and get to work cleaning and unpacking.

Upon closer inspection, I'm finding that the place isn't just dusty—it is plain gross.

I really have to put some elbow grease into scrubbing the stove top and cleaning out the unidentifiable sticky pools in the fridge. After finding mysterious yellow splatters around the porcelain toilet bowl, I close my eyes and spray bleach everywhere. Living in my filth is one thing; living in someone else's is downright scary.

I rifle through a couple closets and cupboards until I find a vacuum and all the mopping supplies I need. I mop myself right out the front door and stand on the front mat, looking around, feeling accomplished about what I've gotten done around the place.

With all the windows open, a breeze wafts through the house and slowly but surely pushes the stale odor out. Instead, it now smells overwhelmingly like cleaning products. Either way, it's a far cry better than bunking with other people, never mind the palatial dungeon I grew up in.

Amusement dances on my face as I imagine what my mother would say about this place, let alone her reaction to me scrubbing a stranger's dried piss off the toilet. Satisfying.

I take another step outside, looking over my shoulder at the still-wet floors that separate me from the coffeepot. I planned this poorly. Oh well. Onward and upward.

I turn away reluctantly and do a quick perusal of the property. Trees line the driveway heading up to the cottage. On the other side, the property opens up and faces toward the grassy rolling hills. A large wraparound deck juts out off the back door, overlooking what appears to be a hay field, and situated just to the left is a single empty paddock.

I'm trying to be as upbeat as possible, but I admittedly get grumpy when I'm hungry and low on sleep. Super grumpy. Hangry. Slangry? Where sleepiness, anger, and hunger collide into one terrible mood. And the more I stew, the more slangry I become.

Letting myself wander down a path to extreme agitation, I find a broom in a small shed and angrily sweep at the debris-covered deck.

Would it have killed Vaughn to have one of his million staff members come out here for a couple hours and make it even a little presentable? The lawn is mowed, so it's not like no one has been out this way. He knew he'd be hiring *someone*, so my arrival wasn't a total surprise. I don't need the red-carpet treatment, but a quick wipe-down and a roll of paper towels wouldn't have been overkill.

I try to imagine his reaction to arriving at a place this grungy. He strikes me as the type who probably expects a swan towel on the bed and a chocolate on his pillow. I envision those dark almond-shaped eyes narrowing to slits, those pronounced brows dropping low on his face, and the nostrils on that strong nose flaring in indignation.

I also imagine there would be foot stomping.

Which, to be fair, is how I feel right now. He didn't hire me to be a maid. I didn't work my ass off for years to become a trainer so I could do free favors for one more entitled rich prick in my life.

I got my fill of these types of guys at private school as a teenager and during obligatory owner meetings for certain horses at past farms as an adult. That's part of the allure of working somewhere with one owner rather than starting up my own stable full of independently owned horses. One owner to deal with, more horses to spend my time with.

The prick-to-horse ratio is favorable.

I've said it before, and I'll say it again: people suck.

I trudge back inside and kick my checkerboard-printed slip-ons off toward the mat. In my agitated state, I flick one more forcefully than intended, and it bounces off the wall, landing on the clean floor and dropping bits of grass and dirt around itself. I glower, like the shoe has somehow wronged me. Standing there, staring at the offending shoe, I force myself to take a few deep breaths.

In through the nose and out through the mouth.

"Let it go, Billie," I mutter, chastising myself for getting so worked up. I need to not let my temper get the best of me.

I know I fly off the handle too easily. I often feel like the ballerina in a music box, every irritable thought twisting inside me like another crank of the key. I know I do it to myself, and in the end, I'm the one left twirling around like an idiot with no way to turn that obnoxious twinkling music off.

On top of that incredible skill, I'm also a gold medal–level grudge holder. Forgiveness doesn't come easily to me. And right now, I'm acutely aware that leading myself down this path on day one of the most exciting job opportunity of my life isn't the best way to get started.

Luckily, I know exactly how to turn this frown upside down. I toss a bag of carrots and a wheel of brie into my backpack. I eye the loaf of French bread on the counter. It gets jammed in the backpack too. A girl's gotta eat, right?

My phone dings right as I'm about to pack it up. A text message from an unknown number.

Unknown Number: Billie, this is Vaughn Harding. Tomorrow morning we'll go over your contract. 7 a.m. Be there.

I can't help but laugh. This man has all the charm of a toad. How the hell am I supposed to respond to that kind of demanding bullshit?

I start typing.

Yes, Master.

Nope. *He's your boss*. Delete, delete, delete.

I settle on Or be square! ;)

Because Vaughn Harding is nothing if not square.

Smirking to myself and feeling very pleased with my level of wit, I swing a single strap of the bag over my shoulder with one hand while reaching for the bottle of red wine sitting in the middle of the island with the other. I march straight out the back door and into the buttery evening light with my eyes set on the hill ahead of me.

I need a glass of wine and some good company.

CHAPTER 5

Vaughn

Reaching out for comment…

Would you be willing to talk about…

Looking for confirmation that Dermot Harding was no longer involved at Gold Rush Resources…

I STARE AT THE PRESS RELEASE I'M ATTEMPTING TO DRAFT IN response to the endless requests from reporters until my right eye twitches with the strain. I don't know why I even continue to open the emails, to subject myself to this drivel. I have no intention of talking to anyone. The minute we present anything other than a united front is when these leeches will latch on and suck more out of us for a story than they already have. As it stands, the businesses have a good chance to recover, provided nothing else goes wrong.

"Like the loose cannon you hired today," I mumble, shaking my head while shuffling papers to clear off my desk.

Billie Black.

Probably not my most business-savvy hire to date. Unpredictable. Fiery. *Inappropriate.*

Not at all what I imagined for a nice, reliable trainer who could get us back on track. But I also know I had to find someone who has no connection to the questionable side of this industry, and Billie certainly fits that bill. Not only geographically, but I am almost positive that if anyone ever tried to solicit her in any way, she would tell them exactly where to stick it.

One side of my mouth quirks up at that thought. I can already imagine how that encounter would play out.

Pulling up the browser on my laptop, I do something I probably should have done several days ago. I google her. I know Cole will do a thorough background check when I hand all her paperwork over to him, but I'm still curious.

The first page of web results consists of news articles and racing results where she's mentioned or interviewed. I swap the top tab to only show photos and am met with a large picture of a bright chestnut horse wearing purple and white silk blinders over its face, with its head and neck tilted affectionately toward Billie's stomach. She's holding the reins in one hand, resting across its nose. Her face is barely visible, nuzzled in toward the horse's ear.

It's a sweet picture. Almost looks like they're giving each other a hug. The headline accompanying the photo reads *The Future Is Female: Young Trainer Taking the Track by Storm*.

I look for more photos, but that's the only one. "Huh," I mumble to myself.

"Huh, what?"

I jump a couple of inches out of my seat and slam my laptop

shut like a guilty kid who just got caught doing something he shouldn't be.

Billie stands in my office doorway, shoulder propped up against the doorframe. She crosses her arms over her chest, pushing her breasts up toward the neckline of her white shirt.

I slowly drag my eyes up her delicate neck, outlined by loose wisps of hair that have fallen from the mess twisted atop her head. A light shimmer of perspiration glistens over her collarbones, and a faint frown touches her full, pouty lips. She's sporting a big black smudge of dirt across her forehead. She looks fucking edible.

I work to maintain a blank expression, trying to keep my eyes from straying back down over her body as she crosses into my office uninvited.

"Talk to yourself often?"

"Why do you look like you've been playing in the mud?"

My shot must land because what was already a pouty face darkens into an angry one. Precious as it is, if I keeled over every time someone frowned at me, well, I wouldn't be where I am today—running a multinational company that makes money hand over fist.

"Well, Vaughn," she muses, "that's because you provided me a pigsty to live in."

What?

"I probably would have preferred to sleep in a stall with the horses than with the ants and piss splatters at the cottage."

I wish I could say I know what she's talking about, but I don't. And I'm not in the habit of apologizing to people for things I had no hand in. I haven't stepped foot in the place since I took over. Maintenance was low on my list of pressing things.

Shrugging, I say, "I have no objections to you doing that."

Now she's gone from glowering to gaping at me, mouth open like a fish out of water. I lean back and steeple my fingers, watching her lips move like she's saying something but can't get any noise to come out. I'll concede that I'm probably being too hard on her, but her level of insubordination and boldness irritates me. *Nobody* talks to me like this. And bad as it sounds, women are usually especially accommodating of my moods and opinions. I'm not sure what's wrong with this one, but it feels like she's intentionally trying to set me off.

"You are something else," she continues. "I spent all night on a plane to come help *you*, all morning dealing with *your* games, and now I've spent all afternoon playing maid and cleaning *your* house."

Images of Billie in a skimpy maid costume dance through my sex-starved mind.

"I am exhausted, and I am starving. Can you please just point me toward a knife so I can leave before I do something I'll regret?"

Short lace-trimmed skirt. Garters wrapped tight enough around each thigh that they create a slight swell at the top of the elastic. A feather duster in one hand. I imagine her quietly going about her job without disrupting and provoking me and realize *that* might be the real dream.

Her hostile attitude is a real boner killer. I lean back and take in her full form, standing here looking all sassy with both hands gripping her slender hips. Upon closer inspection, I realize she looks exhausted. Smudges of light blue are painted beneath her golden eyes, and where she carried herself tall and proud earlier today, her shoulders now sag with exhaustion.

No one informed me she came straight from the airport. *You haven't been informed of much where she's concerned.* Maybe I can throw her a bone, attribute a bit of her poor behavior to jet lag. I'm not a completely unreasonable man.

"Are there not any knives at your house?"

She sighs, shoulders slumping even further. "I walked back with a picnic to have out there and forgot to bring the one utensil I need."

I make my way around the desk in silence, striding toward the cabinet beside the door that is home to piles of Gold Rush Ranch promotional gear. I'm certain I saw a box of monogrammed Swiss Army knives in there when I tore the place apart looking for clues.

They don't jump out at me immediately, so I crouch down to rifle through the lower shelves. Still coming up empty-handed, I end up kneeling, trying to reach the very back of one of the lowest shelves. Leave it to this woman to come up with something colossally inconvenient for me to do.

In my annoyance, I chance a look up and see that Billie has switched back to leaning against the doorway and is watching me intently. Even though I've caught her staring, she doesn't drop eye contact. It's almost as though she's refusing to blink. I pause and stare back at her. Her throat moves up and down as she takes a big swallow. But unlike most people, she still doesn't look away.

Nah, Billie Black is a bit nuts and more than a little bold.

Two can play that game. "Enjoying the view, Miss Black?"

She tilts her head to the side and rests it against the doorframe. An almost imperceptible smirk touches her mouth. She lightly taps her pointer finger against the indent along her top lip. "Yeah, Boss Man. You look good on your knees."

I thought my comment would embarrass her, throw her off, wipe that obnoxious smug look off her face. But she comes back swinging. She was reaming me out not two minutes ago, and now she's back to spouting off inappropriate comments.

Absolutely nuts.

Dropping my chin and shaking my head, I grab the small box I can feel against my fingertips. Lifting one foot and pushing to standing, I roll my shoulders back. Billie is taller than most women, but I'm taller than most men and tower over her.

I hold one knife out toward her. She reaches for it, and her dainty fingers rasp lightly over mine as they wrap around the hilt. But instead of letting go, I yank it toward myself, causing her to stumble a couple of steps closer.

Uncertain eyes shoot up to meet mine, and I puff up a little at seeing her so off balance. I much prefer this look on her face.

Acting quickly, I run the pad of my thumb across my tongue and then reach forward to swipe it across the smudge of dirt on her forehead. Her golden eyes grow wide, like two glowing moons staring back at me. But not for long. No, if I hadn't been watching, I'd have missed that one uncertain moment before she reverts to shooting daggers at me.

She jerks the knife from my hand, spins on her heel, and storms out of my office into the darkened hallway, but not before muttering, "Fucking gross!" just loud enough for me to hear.

"You're welcome!" I call back as she propels herself out of my view.

I roll my lips together and swallow the chuckle bubbling up in my throat. God, I haven't laughed in weeks—maybe longer. Toying with Billie Black is *fun.*

I have to put up with her antics for three months before she'll be hitting the dusty trail, so I might as well enjoy it. If she thinks she's going to waltz in here, all alluring and sharp-tongued, and play this game unchallenged, she's in for a wild ride.

I don't roll over for anyone.

Fucking my employee is off the table. The farm is in too much trouble. But fucking *with* my employee… now that's another story altogether.

Off to the races, honey.

CHAPTER 6

Billie

What. A. Prick.

Who does that to a woman they've basically just met, let alone their employee? The guy's gumption is absolutely out of this world. Typical for a guy with a face like that and more money than sense. They're all the same. Altogether too confident, knowing there are no real repercussions for their inappropriate behavior.

As I head toward Double Diablo's paddock, I replay our interaction in my head. I'd be lying to myself if I pretended that his proximity didn't shake me. He stood close enough for me to know he smells like almonds. That alluring amaretto sort of smell, but not over the top, just the right amount. I expected something harsh and obnoxious—just like his personality. It didn't match up. I couldn't reconcile it.

It obviously muddled my brain. Because while I sniffed him like a bloodhound in heat, I couldn't help but check him out more closely. I blame the jet lag and the wine I already slammed back on an empty stomach before dragging my ass up there to find a knife. Like a brainless sap, I savored the way he filled out his suit. It was honestly criminal.

I've always had this theory that there are two types of men: the ones who look edible in a suit and the ones who look edible in their birthday suit. Suit guys are a little more slender than I like, naked guys a little too bulky to pull off that GQ suit look. I'm not saying I'd kick either out of bed if they knew what they were doing. It's just an observation. Like Goldilocks, my ideal man is somewhere down the middle. And Vaughn Harding is right down the middle.

I stood over him, gawking like a teenager, purely for research purposes, of course. I analyzed the way his suit sleeves bunched up around his broad shoulders and then let my eyes trace the line from his briefs on his firm ass in a completely clinical fashion. After collecting data, I can now conclude that under different circumstances, I would climb the man like a tree.

Reaching my spot in front of Double Diablo's gate, I sink onto soft grass, so thick it feels like a rug beneath me. I've opted to call him DD, like Deedee, because I really can't handle his name. He needs something as cute as he looks that I can whisper soothingly into his pointy little ears when he finally lets me close enough. His initials are short and simple and good enough for now.

I startled him when I came over the fence behind his paddock earlier, but he didn't race at me like a fire-breathing dragon charging out of its cave. Instead, he watched me walk to where I'm now sitting, gave me a suspicious look, and then turned his butt to me.

Upon my return, he's still facing away from me. The only recognition he gave me was a sulky little foot stomp and the flick of his right ear, pointing it back at me as a way of hearing what I'm doing.

Sitting cross-legged on the grass, I break off a piece of a carrot and toss it into his paddock. I cut myself a few slices of cheese with my shiny new Gold Rush Ranch knife and lay them on top of a freshly torn piece of French bread. I sip my red wine from the bottle because I also forgot a glass. The small victory in this day is that this bottle has a screw top, no corkscrew required.

Leaning back on my elbows, I stretch my legs out and try to relax while I watch day turn to night, twilight laying itself over the farm like a blanket. All in the good company of one grumpy little black horse.

A few small sandwiches later, DD finally turns his head toward the carrot I threw. Stubborn little bugger. He turns a little farther so I can spy his eyeball stretching in its socket to see me without giving away that he's actually looking at me. He looks like one of those guys who's trying to check you out discreetly but failing miserably. Except when he does it, it's cute.

The stallion looks back at the carrot and takes one small step toward it, drops his head, and brushes his lips across the bare patch of dirt where it landed to pick it up. Crunching away, he eyes me more openly now. I casually toss him another piece, enjoying watching the way his mind works.

He startles and flips to face me head-on while I take another sip from my wine bottle. After a moment of glaring, he continues crunching, a bit of orange-colored drool frothing on the sides of his lips. With brief hesitation, he drops his head again to pick up the piece of carrot.

"Good boy," I murmur gently, which earns me another flick of his little elf ears. I look up, taking in the white glow of the stars against the darkening sky. "DD, I don't think I'm off to a very good start with the boss man."

Big black doe eyes stare back at me with the strands of his thick forelock falling around them.

"You kind of remind me of him. You both have nice hair."

More staring and crunching.

"You know." I sit up straight like we're in the middle of an engaging conversation. "I raged all the way down here about what a prick he is. But with some food and wine in me, I feel like I'm ready to admit to you I haven't exactly been on my best behavior either. It's possible that I provoked him a little."

DD appears to have finished chewing, so I toss him another carrot, closer to the fence this time.

"Smart boy. Admit nothing. You'll only piss the girls off that way."

I watch his nose wiggle as he shifts his eyes back and forth between me and the carrot a couple feet ahead of him. One step. Two steps. And then he cautiously lowers his neck and stretches out the very tip of his top lip to pull the carrot toward himself.

"Good boy, DD," I tell him softly before continuing. "So, you know, the polite part of me thinks I should apologize for prodding at him so much. I know it wasn't very professional of me. And it's definitely not the ideal start to a new working relationship."

A slow blink. More contented chewing.

"He just ticks me off, you know? I'm painfully familiar with his type. All the same."

I marvel at what good listeners horses are. I can lay it all out, my deepest darkest secrets, and they never judge me or think less of me. In fact, the more I talk to DD and feed—ahem, bribe—him, the more he likes me. His eyes soften and the muscles along the top of his back relax.

"But then there's the childish part of me"—I toss a piece of carrot closer again—"that feels like he should apologize first. I mean, he's the one who flew out of there first thing accusing me of being some sort of paid date or something."

I watch the silhouette of the dark horse move ahead, with less apprehension this time, to claim his treat.

"You guys really are like the same person, DD. You can't continue to greet people that way either. It's unbecoming, you know? People will mistake you for being a mean boy rather than just a sensitive one."

We sit there staring at each other, no longer needing to avoid eye contact. I roll him another piece of carrot, which brings him right up to the fence line.

I smile and sigh with satisfaction.

"Guess I just answered my question, didn't I, big guy?"

The sound of footsteps on pavement has me shooting up and whirling around with speed that does not match my current level of sobriety. Looking up the slope of the hill, I see Vaughn standing beside his expensive black car. It's too dark for me to tell if he's looking at me or just pausing to admire the view.

My confusion clears quickly when he reaches one hand up to wave, his keys jangling in the quiet as he calls out to me, "Good night, Billie!"

I freeze and feel a flush creep up my neck and across my cheeks. *Fuck my life*. Had he just heard me talking about him? To a horse?

The parking lot is probably too far away for him to have heard me, or at least that's what I tell myself. Maybe he could have caught some general mumbling but not actual words. *Hopefully*.

Worst-case scenario, he'll think I'm a little nuts, and I can live with that.

I raise a hand up in his direction with an awkward "Night!" before bringing it down to scrub over my face when Vaughn drives away.

Facing DD's pen, both hands now covering my face, I peek through my fingers at him. Much to my surprise, in the time that I'd been facing the other way, he moved closer, bringing his chest right up to the fence with his neck and head now hung over the barrier.

I hum happily at our progress in just one night. "Are you laughing at me, DD?"

Bending down, I retrieve a whole carrot from the bag, the longest one I can find. I hold the thick end in my hand like a wand and reach out slowly toward his face, holding the carrot toward his flared nostrils. I stand stock-still and watch those big dark globes stare down his dishy forehead at the treat I'm offering him. It feels like minutes crawl by, even though it's probably only mere seconds.

In trying to stand still, I realize just how inebriated I am. Whoops. But I am no quitter. I stick it out, and it pays off in spades.

I watch as the whiskers on his nose twitch, his lips wiggle and smack against each other as he reaches out toward the tip of the carrot, making a hollow little popping noise. I feel the heat and moisture of his exhale as he stretches his face toward my hand and gently grabs the carrot.

He pauses for a moment and then pins his ears while stepping away from me. A sure sign he is unimpressed with what I just talked him into doing.

Baby steps with this one. Just like Vaughn.

CHAPTER 7

Vaughn

I ROLL OUT OF BED THIS MORNING, NOT FEELING RESTED AT ALL. *Again.* This seems to be my new normal. Work. Stress. Poor sleep. A vicious cycle. It isn't helping my mood either; I know I've been a cranky bastard. The overwhelming pressure I feel to succeed and the ever-present memory of my grandfather are combining to bring me down. To paralyze me.

Taking over at Gold Rush Ranch isn't just another challenge; it's downright daunting. I love the farm in a special from-my-childhood sort of way, but I was *thriving* in my role at the family mining company. I felt like I'd really found my stride. I liked the board meetings, the anticipation of drilling for new deposits, and managing something that was fiscally booming. Talking to the media about Gold Rush Resources was easy. It was *exciting*.

This? This is depressing. An absolute clusterfuck. And I'm not above admitting how grumpy I've been at having something my conscience won't let me walk away from dumped in my lap.

On my drive back to the ranch offices this morning, I replayed the events of the night before. Billie Black, talking way too loud as night fell over the quiet farm. I didn't mean to listen in on her, but the way the sound traveled up the hill made it almost impossible not to overhear. The gist of it was that I'd been such an ass that I drove a woman I hardly know to drink wine straight from the bottle and hash her day out with a horse in the dark.

That's a new low, even for me.

I knew she was a little nuts, but that scene was really just more depressing. And standing there listening, I felt a creeping sensation of shame swirling in my gut. I'd never tell her that though. Even if she was one of the trophy wife prospects my mom liked to send around, my outburst was a shit way to talk to a person. I've been told I can be cool or hard to get a read on but not downright rude. That's not who I am.

Apologies aren't really my strong suit either, but weaving down the back roads this morning, I know I'm going to have to extend some sort of olive branch. I should try to start fresh. I'm stuck in this small town working with the woman, and I know she's going to be grating, but I also know a business runs best when everyone is on good terms.

I can't afford to be on bad terms with her.

After pulling up to the farm, I step out of my Porsche, feeling the invisible pressure of running behind. Although for what, I'm not sure. It's only seven in the morning, so a light misty haze hangs over the back fields, contrasting against the vibrant green of the grass. I breathe deeply, feeling that cool, humid West Coast air slip past my lips and coat my lungs. It smells like spring.

I can hear the clip-clop of hooves on concrete around the corner. The farmhands and grooms will already be a couple hours under way. Horses don't much care about business hours.

Turning to head into the office, I catch movement out of the corner of my eye. Down by Double Diablo's paddock, Billie sits facing him, in a lawn chair this time, reading and flipping through sheets of an open folder on her lap while the horse happily munches his hay out of a feeder right next to her. I stretch my left arm out to check the time again, almost in disbelief that she's already here. And that she's sitting so casually beside a horse that everyone has told me is crazy.

A match made in heaven, those two.

I stride into my office to get the coffeepot going, because I really need the caffeine boost this morning. I slam the glass pot back into place a little too hard, agitation lining every movement I make. Luckily, it doesn't break. I fire up my computer and am met with what had me storming out of here last night.

The cursor blinks on the blank page of my Word document. Yesterday, I got as far as opening it and titling it *Gold Rush Ranch Statement*. That is what I have to show for all of yesterday. I shake my head, disappointed in myself.

"Big win, Vaughn. You fucking sad sack," I mumble to myself.

I've always been a hard worker, a high achiever. Not being able to buckle down and focus is messing with my head. I lean forward on my elbows, willing myself to type, but end up staring at the blank screen with my chin resting on steepled hands. Maybe what I need is scotch rather than coffee.

Or maybe just a change of scenery.

Five minutes later, I stand in front of Billie with a cup of peace-offering coffee in hand. She's either totally absorbed in what she's reading or ignoring me, because she hasn't acknowledged my approach. Even standing here, facing her, she doesn't glance up.

She looks cozy and relaxed. Natural. Like she belongs here, all curled up in the great outdoors on a lawn chair with one jean-clad leg folded underneath herself and a light blanket wrapped around her shoulders. There's a small bucket of crunchy horse treats in her lap, and her worn black Blundstone boots lie discarded carelessly beside her.

"Did you sleep out here?"

She snorts and quirks one eyebrow without looking up at me. "You said you wouldn't object."

I sigh. "Is the house really that bad?"

Feline amber eyes shoot like lasers to mine. "Not anymore, it's not."

I stare at her, honestly not sure where to take this now. "Do you like coffee?" I mumble.

Her gaze shifts down to my hands. "Is water wet?"

I reach one mug toward her, and she eyes me with suspicion. "I'll take the other cup."

I roll my eyes. "They're both black coffee, Billie."

"Yeah, but I feel you might be offering me the poisoned one," she deadpans.

"I—you… what?"

She presses her lips together, eyes twinkling with mirth. "I'm joking, Boss Man. If you wanted to kill me, you missed your chance with that knife last night."

I don't even know how to respond to her, so I just stand here, floundering. Like he can smell weakness, Double Diablo's head shoots up out of his feeder. He pauses before lunging toward me at the fence.

Little prick. Just because I've spent years wearing a suit doesn't mean I forgot how to be around horses. I give him an unimpressed look; his pinned ears and angry face are nothing new to me in the world of business. If nothing else, I feel like his angry face is just a reflection of mine these days. I lash out just like that too.

Billie gawks at me with a big smile on her face. "Not bad, fancy pants. You didn't even squeal."

Is she kidding? "I grew up on this farm, Billie. Horses aren't completely foreign to me, and I deal with assholes every day." I motion my cup at Double Diablo, who snorts and goes back to eating.

"Good boy, DD," she murmurs, tossing a small crunchy horse treat beside his feet.

I blink and shake my head at her. "What did you just call him?"

"Deedee. Like, his initials. His name sucks."

Inclining my head toward the little devil, I ask, "What would you name him instead?"

She wraps both delicate hands around the mug and takes a cautious sip of her coffee, looking over the rim to assess the horse. "I don't know." She snorts in a completely unladylike way. "Maybe Mister Black. Humans suck, so he's pretty much the perfect man for me. You'd take my name, wouldn't you, DD?"

I cough out a laugh. "My grandfather named him, you know."

She says nothing but pulls her lips back as if to say *yikes* and then promptly changes the subject. "Thanks for the coffee, but I take cream in mine."

Is she kidding right now? I must give her an incredulous look, because she smiles at me like the Cheshire cat.

"You know, for next time."

"You're incredible," I say, shaking my head at her.

"Thank you." She points behind me. "Grab a chair and chill out for a second. You're all uptight. It's making DD and me nervous."

"Did he tell you that?"

"No. He told you that when he snapped at you."

I shift my eyes to the horse. He stops munching and looks at me suspiciously, out of the corner of his eye, without lifting his head. Maybe she's right. I take a few strides toward the other lawn chairs she has leaned against the fence and fold one out beside her, facing the paddock. A breath I didn't realize I was holding whooshes out of me when I sit.

This is nice.

I attempt to look at Billie's profile without openly turning to stare at her. She's so unusual, so alluring, like a piece of art in a gallery I want to analyze, get lost in. She's like a splash of red in a sea of gray.

I realize she knows I'm checking her out when her cheek closest to me quirks up before her lashes shift my way. A mischievous look takes over her whole face as she says, "Hello, and welcome to my crib."

I can't help but laugh, and a low rumble rolls across my chest. "You're nuts. You know that?"

"Ha! I've been told they really broke the mold with me." Sadness flashes across her face but disappears as quickly as it showed up. She turns and looks at me, a small smile touching her full lips. "Thank you for the coffee. I'm jet-lagged as all get-out, and I may or may not have enjoyed a little too much wine last night after not eating properly all day. I really needed this."

She lifts her mug in a silent toast and appears so sweet and sincere. The carefree, sarcastic woman is missing right now, and I realize she's actually easier to take when she's being obnoxious. I don't know how to respond to this almost melancholy version of her.

I grunt and return the gesture with my mug.

Smooth.

We sit in silence, sipping our coffees and watching Double Diablo, or DD—insert eye roll here—as she's now calling him. The soft sound of him munching on hay mingles with snorts and whinnies from around the farm. The whole sensory experience brings me back to my childhood summers spent here. I close my eyes and tip my head back to rest on the chair. I'm not sure when I last sat outside and just enjoyed nature.

Life got too busy. Skyscrapers and busy traffic, the sound of phones ringing and printers pumping out warm sheets of paper usually fill my day. I have to admit, this is almost therapeutic. Extending an olive branch has been bearable so far. And Billie is being quiet now, which makes it even better.

But of course, she can't let it last.

"Are you okay, Vaughn?"

"What?" From this angle, I can really analyze her profile, lit by the early morning sun. She sniffs, and the end of her straight, upturned nose does a little wiggle. Thick caramel hair tucked behind her ear cascades straight over her shoulder like a waterfall.

"You heard me," she says, looking back out to the paddock.

She looks almost uncomfortable. Too still, like she's avoiding looking at me.

No one has asked me how I'm doing in the last few weeks. Not in a way that makes me feel like they *actually* want to know and aren't just asking to be polite. Billie doesn't strike me as the type of woman to ask me something just because it's the polite thing to do. It's unnerving to have someone I barely know—and barely like—reach out to me in this way. It throws me off balance, a feeling I'm not fond of. I don't want to share my inner turmoil, my inner shame, with *anyone*. Least of all Billie Black, who would probably find some way to mock it.

My goal of being passably nice to a new employee today is complete. I stand and shoot her a wry grin. "Peachy."

Her response is to stare at me and tip her head to one side. Her gaze makes my spine tingle, like she can see right through my charade.

I depart with a "Good luck today" from over my shoulder.

Yeah, I duck and run.

CHAPTER 8

Billie

THIS MORNING, THE FOLD-OUT CHAIR HAS BASICALLY TURNED into my throne, and I'm not complaining.

After my date with a grumpy black horse and a bottle of red wine last night, I quickly showered and fell into bed. I was dead to the world until about 3:00 a.m. when I jolted awake feeling totally disoriented. I tried to fall back asleep, but jet lag was still a bitch and wouldn't let me sleep anymore. After all, it was 11:00 a.m. in Dublin. I rolled out of bed, chastising myself, and let the shame spiral begin. How old am I? Draining a bottle of wine on a work night? Telling my new boss he looks good on his knees?

Cringe. Cringe. *Cringe.*

When I crawled out here for some fresh air and to peek in on how the farm runs in the morning, Hank walked up to me and said, "Billie girl, you look like death warmed over."

I grumbled back something about, "No, *you* do." Because I am very witty and mature like that.

He laughed and scrubbed my hair like I was a little kid.

Then he sent all the other staff down to introduce themselves and have a little chat.

I feel like a lazy queen.

DD seems pretty comfortable with me, the human vending machine, sitting here. So long as I don't move too suddenly and keep tossing the odd cookie his way, he's happy. I watch his reaction to each of the five men who came down to visit me. He ignores a couple, makes faces at one, and throws a total tantrum over the other two. I'm thinking he's a better judge of character than I realized.

None of them come very close except to shake my hand, after which they back away slowly. Or quickly, depending on how badly DD is behaving. It makes me chuckle inwardly. I feel like Daenerys sitting here with a dragon behind my back. Everyone is scared to come too close. Some more than others.

I think they're all being ridiculous. Sure, DD comes across as a real grumpy little bitch, but he's still just a horse. You work with them long enough and you get to know their different behaviors. And in my books, DD isn't that alarming.

I think he's kind of charming. I appreciate he doesn't have a silly, dopey little persona. I know that if I can channel his intelligence and spunk into a competitive instinct, he'll be winning Gold Rush Ranch an awful lot of races.

I just have to come at him from a different angle.

I'm still sitting on my throne making notes on each of the horse's files when I hear footsteps approaching. Looking up, I see a young woman with a serious look on her face walking toward me.

"Hi. I'm Violet Eaton," she says quietly, getting close enough to shake my hand.

"Hi, Violet." I give her a warm smile and look her up and down.

"I'm one of the grooms here. Hank has me assigned to the young horses, and I just wanted to come introduce myself." She stares past me at DD, wringing her hands.

"It's really nice to meet you," I say back. "It's also really nice to see some estrogen around this place."

At that comment, her round blue eyes shoot back toward me in shock. Her cheeks tinge light pink on her porcelain skin while she tries to bite back a smile. "It's kind of a sausage fest, isn't it?"

I bark out a loud laugh. "Welcome to the sport of kings, my friend," I reply with a wink.

She chuckles while nodding her dainty little head. She looks like a doll. Petite everything, topped off with a shock of icy blond hair rolled up into a tidy bun on her head. I feel like a slobby Amazon next to her.

"Tell me more about yourself," I say, waving a hand toward the chair beside me.

She hits me with a surprised look and then plops down.

My eyes immediately shift to DD, who startled at how abruptly Violet sat down. He stares at her with intelligent black eyes, then looks at me and pricks his ears forward. *Forward!* Which is basically the equivalent of a smile. Then he snorts and goes back to his fresh pile of hay.

I look over at Violet and bulge my eyes. She quirks one side of her mouth and shrugs in response.

"I don't think he's as bad as everyone makes him out to be. The rumor mill here is vicious, and so was the old trainer."

My mouth twists as I shake my head at her assessment. Pretty much what I figured all along.

"Sorry," she adds quickly, "I shouldn't speak poorly about someone who isn't here to defend themselves."

I roll my eyes at that. "Don't be. My responsibility is to the horses here, not some person I've never met before. Plus, I already came to the same conclusion."

And I mean it. A horse can't speak for himself. It's my duty to be his ally. Other adults can be accountable for their own actions and reputations. That isn't my job. I'm not here to hold anyone's hand and rub their back over how they trashed their own reputation. Either way, I like this girl. She's adorable, honest, and DD approved too.

I also need a friend. Everyone I met this morning was polite enough, but I could tell there were a couple exercise riders who might be a harder sell on their new boss. Older guys who've probably been around a long time, maybe friends with people caught in the cross fire of the scandal here.

As the new girl on the block, still only in her twenties, I know I'm going to be subject to some scoffs and silent treatment. Maybe even a little mansplaining, if I'm really lucky. That's my favorite. *Listen up, little lady. I been at this for a long time.*

I inwardly roll my eyes and look next to me where Violet still looks guilty for saying too much. Breaking our moment of silence, I ask, "Are you only assigned to the two-year-old horses?"

"Yes."

"Perfect. They're my main projects right now, which makes you my groom." I brush my legs off as I stand and stretch my hands above my head. Violet gives me another wide-eyed look. "You've really got that deer-in-the-headlights face down, huh?"

A shocked giggle escapes her lips as she grazes one hand over her cheek and stands. "I've been told I don't control my facial expressions very well."

"Ha. You don't, but I like it. It means you aren't full of shit. Join me for lunch at my house? I'm starving. Then we can get the horses out for some work this afternoon."

After enjoying tuna sandwiches on the porch swing, Violet and I walk back across the field to the farm. We had a nice lunch. The more relaxed she became in my presence, the more she talked.

"So where are you from originally?" I ask.

Violet rolls her eyes. "A small town you've probably never heard of. Chestnut Springs. It's just south of Calgary, Alberta."

"Sounds like a town in a cowboy movie."

"Looks like one too."

"Yeah? Hot cowboys and everything?" I waggle my eyebrows at her.

The apples of her cheeks bloom pink and she shakes her head, amusement dancing in her eyes. She's only a few years younger than me, but she comes off so innocent. For a farm girl, she's remarkably demure.

"Hang around with me long enough and you'll loosen up a bit, Violet."

"I'm a little scared by that statement." She giggles.

"I'm willing to bet that if I get a few drinks into you, you'll be swearing like a sailor and riding the mechanical bull topless at the local country bar. The quiet ones are always the craziest."

A strangled noise lodges in her throat as she turns her wide eyes on me once again.

I throw my head back and laugh as we round the corner back into the barn. But my amusement is ruined by Vaughn "the wet blanket" Harding when I crash right into his rock-hard chest and hear him say, "Why are you so loud then?"

He looks down his straight nose at me smugly, feeling all high and mighty about having overheard us no doubt.

What a dick.

I just roll my eyes and strike back, "Why? You hoping to catch me riding topless, Boss Man?"

I swear he growls as he shoulders past me, and I can't stop the small smile that tugs at the corners of my mouth. Antagonizing the boss shouldn't be this fun.

CHAPTER 9

Billie

The next week passes easily, and I fall into a comfortable rhythm. I'm kept busy working with the exercise riders who breeze the established horses first thing in the morning. Violet and I are becoming fast friends, having lunch together most days. Hank gives me the best hugs, and working on the day-to-day aspects of the farm with him has things running like a well-oiled machine. Even the most standoffish staff members are coming around. Sometimes, rather than speaking to me in grunts, they use words, which I'm counting as a win. Boss Man is still sex in a suit but also a typical crabby rich bitch who hides out in his office all day.

Now I'm doing what all the cool girls do on a Friday night: kicking back with my main man.

A horse.

We've come a long way in the last week. I walk over the crest of the hill every morning to find him waiting for me at the back corner of his paddock. I coo at him in a mushy baby voice as

I approach, and he doesn't even startle or pin his ears. He just looks at me expectantly because he *knows* I have the goods.

Apples, carrots, the odd peppermint. Yeah, he knows the drill.

He now allows me to sit on the top rail of the fence beside him, where I can pat his neck and scratch his ears. I sit by him and have one cup of coffee every morning, letting the early morning damp air wrap around me while watching the sun come up over the mountains. We sit in companionable silence as the farm bubbles to life. When I finish my coffee, I give him a kiss on his soft nose, and he stands there happily watching me walk up to the stables. It's honestly the best way to start my day.

The evenings at the farm are quieter. Everyone heads home, either to the bunkhouses on-site or into the small town of Agassiz nearby. I volunteered to do night check because, well, I have nothing else to do. So nobody knows it yet, but DD and I are making even more progress in the evenings when no one's watching. I can now walk right into his paddock and get up close with him. Consistency and cookies were key.

Tonight, my plan is to enjoy a few beers and groom DD to a perfect shine. After months of being untouched, the poor guy is looking worse for wear. Dusty black rather than shiny black. Tangled mane and dreadlocked tail. No wonder he hid at the back corner of the property. He looks like a lot of things, and an expensive racehorse is not one of them.

This time, he willingly dropped his head into a halter and let me tie him to the fence post. I grabbed a box of brushes from the stables and plan to groom him to a perfect shine. Plastic combs, rubber combs, soft-bristled brushes, moisturizing spray, special oil to paint on his hooves. Yes, DD is heading to the spa tonight. I take a swig of my cold beer and then get to work.

I zone out, departing into a happy place where I've always been able to lose myself, even as a child. I savor the sounds of his contented sighs and make sure I tell him what a charming boy he is. Standing by his shoulder, I peek at him out of the corner of my eye, watching his topline relax and his eyelids go heavy. I marvel at how far he's come in such a short amount of time—the ultimate validation that what I'm doing is working.

"Who is the prettiest boy?" I coo at the horse.

DD's head shoots up abruptly, knocking me out of my trance. I look over my shoulder to see Vaughn standing at the fence, arms resting across the top, looking pretty comfortable. And smug. Yup, he has that obnoxious, smug look on his face.

"Should I be concerned about how much you talk to this horse?"

I glare at him. No, I drink him in. He's been a hermit in his office, and I almost forgot how blindingly beautiful he is. I hate the way my body instantly responds to his presence. The uptick of my heartbeat, the hairs standing on my arms. "No, but you should probably be concerned about ruining your fancy suit leaning on that dirty fence."

He waves me off. "I can afford a new one."

Yup. Obnoxious. Comments like that are why I've vowed to stay away from trust fund babies. "Charming." I turn back to DD, starting with a soft-bristled brush to dust off all the loose hair I rustled up. "Can I help you with something, Vaughn?"

"I can see you down here from my office window and wanted to come check how this week has gone for you."

Great. So he's been watching me out here every night. It should creep me out, but my chest warms at the thought. *Don't act like an airhead, Billie.*

I continue brushing, moving around DD, who isn't helping me at all by ignoring Vaughn's presence. If he throws a fit, maybe Mr. Moneybags will feel uncomfortable and leave. Then I wouldn't have to continue staring so hard at the short black hair in front of me to keep myself from gaping at the handsome face beside me.

Admitting that I'm attracted to Vaughn Harding is annoying. Unsettling. But a fact all the same. A fact I am acutely aware of after barely seeing him all week. It almost seems like he wanted to avoid me after our last conversation. I've gazed up at his office now and then, wondering if he was going to bring me a cup of coffee again one of these mornings.

He's been out of sight and mostly out of mind. But now my brain isn't connecting to my lips because it obviously forgot he is insufferable. I realize I've been silent for an awkward amount of time and chance a peek up at him.

His cheekbones are still high and sharp, shoulders still broad and powerful, and those eyes are still dark and stormy—and trained on me. Boring into me with such intensity that I inadvertently lick my lips under the pressure of his attention.

His gaze narrows and drops almost instantly to my mouth. I swear the air around us crackles with unspoken tension. Yup, Boss Man and I have some crazy volatile chemistry. *Dangerous* chemistry.

"Good," I reply, in a much more strangled voice than I intend, dropping my chin and brushing DD more forcefully. It's safer to keep my focus on the task at hand. Obviously, my ovaries don't know what my brain does. Men like Vaughn are bad news.

Knock, knock, ovaries! It's brain here. Let me in.

"That's it? Good? Care to elaborate on how my horses are doing?" His voice is like velvet on my skin, like a soft caress in the low early evening light.

I stop brushing abruptly, shaking my head at myself, and sigh dramatically. "Can't this wait until Monday? I'm off the clock right now," I say, pointing at my beer, wanting him to leave now and stop interrupting what has been a splendid night so far.

His eyes follow my finger, and he looks back at me with a wicked glint in his eye. "No, you're not. You're doing night check," he responds while picking up my can of beer and taking a big long swig.

His gaze stays trained on mine, challenging me. And against my better judgment, I let mine slip and admire the way his Adam's apple dips with every gulp. His tan throat and dark stubble move against the crisp white collar of his dress shirt, sending a strike of electricity through my core.

I swallow in response. *Billie, what are you doing? This guy is a nightmare.* Tossing the brush back into the bucket and dusting my hands against each other, a little more forcefully than necessary, I turn to face him.

"Hope you can afford to treat the cold sores you'll be getting for the rest of your life now too."

"Nice try," he replies with a stupid smirk on his face.

"Guess you won't ever really know. From here on out, you'll wake up in the morning wondering if today will be the day you look in the mirror and see one marring your pretty face. You'll just be in a constant state of not knowing, and you'll forever regret stealing my beer."

One side of his smug mouth hitches up. "You think my face is pretty?"

I roll my eyes and grab the spray bottle and a rag, and resume grooming DD, who is dozing happily with one back hoof cocked and resting on the ground, somehow oblivious to the surrounding tension.

"Everything has been good this week." I launch into my explanation of what I've been working on and mention specific horses and staff. I tell him how impressed I am with Violet, and his only response is, "Who?" because the asshole is making me describe a bunch of strategies and people that he doesn't even understand or know, all while standing there looking breathtaking and enjoying his stolen beer.

The upside is that I'm ticked off enough to throw some good elbow grease into polishing DD, and when I finish my monologue, I stand back to admire my handiwork. The sunset gleams on his shiny flanks.

He'll probably go roll in the dirt as soon as I leave, but grooming him has been satisfying and therapeutic nonetheless.

"Sounds like it's been good then," is the very intelligent response Vaughn comes up with while also looking at DD. I'm so glad I gave him a ten-minute rundown of the week all for him to repeat back to me that everything was "good."

Removing DD's halter, I give him a kiss on his cheek and a good rub behind his ears, and then set him free before turning to climb the fence. I sit on the top railing like I do every morning, except tonight I'm right beside Vaughn. I like the height advantage this position gives me. From here, I can be the one to look down on him.

I feel DD popping his lips gently around my pockets, shaking me down for more treats, no doubt, as I take my beer from Vaughn's hand. Thinking I must look cool stealing it back, I take a long swig before I realize that what's left is basically just a warm mixture of our backwash and flat beer.

"Blech," I gag, shaking my head as if to dispel the taste and tossing the can toward my backpack lying on the grass.

I grip the fence and look down at Vaughn, whose eyes twinkle like he's at some sort of live comedy show. He intrudes on my peaceful evening, drains my beer, and now he's laughing at me for drinking his warm saliva? *Cool.*

That hot familiar fire licks up my throat, and I feel my head buzz with agitation. My will to play nice flies away into the pink twilight sky. "Has anyone ever told you what a smug dick you are?" is what I get out just before DD loses patience with his treat-thieving attempts and takes a more forceful shove at my waistband, sending me sailing headfirst toward the ground.

Except I don't hit the ground. Strong hands break my trajectory. Long fingers splay firmly around my rib cage, and before I know what's happening, I'm pushed up against a fence post with one of Vaughn's knees pressed between my legs to keep me from dropping like a stone.

Pinned.

Looking down at where his hands are resting on my thin shirt, I see his thumbs just crossing the boundary of my soft sports bra, grazing the side of each breast. I see the veins popping in his hands, somehow so masculine and alluring.

In his grip, I feel like my shirt could burn into ash, curl up, and float away on the evening breeze. Being surprised by my tumble has left my chest rising and falling more heavily than usual, and I'm completely entranced by his hands moving up and down with my ribs as my lungs heave.

His amaretto scent wraps around me like the softest silk. I feel like I've been dropped into a glass of him, all honeyed and manly. I drag my eyes away, chin tipping up slowly to meet his face. Bad choice. Very bad choice.

Under the thick dark fringe of his lashes, his eyes are hot molten chocolate, utterly focused on my body. He's staring, taking in the way his hands possess me, so big that they almost wrap right around my rib cage. His head snaps up to meet my gaze, his expression downright dangerous as he breaks our tense silence.

"No, Billie." His voice is dangerously low as he angles his head so close to my ear that I can feel his breath fan across my throat. "Women usually go out of their way to endear themselves to me. Not piss me off."

Time to teach this prick a lesson.

His words set me off, and without thinking, I reach out toward him and hook my index finger into his crisp white dress shirt, right between the buttons. I can feel the muscles in his abdomen clench under my touch as I gently trace the tip of my finger across his hot skin, feeling the firm ridges I knew would be there.

To anyone loitering at the stables, our silhouettes would almost look like he was a vampire going in for a quick taste with the way he towers over me. I send up a silent prayer that no one can see us and close my finger around the fabric that's brushing against my hand, pulling his torso closer to mine so that I straddle his thigh.

I hear his sharp intake of air and feel a familiar ache just below my hip bones. *This is such a bad idea.*

I look up, taking in the dark shadows falling across his brow and his almost pained facial expression. We hold each other in this limbo, facing off for a few seconds before I move so close

I can feel the scruff on his jaw lightly scratch my cheek. His hands squeeze my ribs, trying to hold me in place.

At the increase in pressure, my nipples harden and goose bumps bloom across my arms unbidden. *This is fine.* A totally typical reaction to absolutely anyone touching me like this.

Disturbed by the way my body responds to his, I opt to up the stakes, fingering the collar of his shirt with my opposite hand and gently running my teeth along the lobe of his ear. I'm pressed so close to him I can feel more than hear the grunt that breaks loose from his chest.

For a moment, I let myself imagine us together under different circumstances, all the delicious noises he would make as he moved above me, pressing into me so hard that our bodies would sink right into the mattress beneath us. Coming completely undone, just for me.

It's with that image in my mind that I slide my fingers up his neck and through his hair before grabbing a handful firmly. He stands stock-still, frozen.

"Well then, let me be the one to deflower you on this one, Boss Man," I whisper against his ear. "You are absolutely insufferable." I bite down on his earlobe again, a little harder this time, which causes the air to leave his lungs in a loud hiss. "Now get your hands off me. I'm not one of your playthings," I finish, essentially dousing us both with a bucket of cold water and firmly pushing him away.

I lick my lips as I watch him jerk his hands off me like I burned him. His absence leaves an arctic chill over places that had just been so hot, and I can feel my heart crashing around in my rib cage uncontrollably as we stand there staring at each other.

Shocked eyes bore into my wild ones. He looks stunned, and I can't help but notice how painfully beautiful he is standing here in the dim light with his hair all mussed. I did that to him. My chest pinches, and that ache snaps me out of my trance.

My god. I took this too far. Way too fucking far.

I think about all the goals I haven't yet achieved, all the shit men exactly like him have put me through. I remind myself of all the sacrifices I've made to get to where I am, and feelings of shame wash over me. Why even give him the power to make me feel like this?

The sensation of my embarrassment is so intense, it spills down my backbone like molten lava and hardens into rigid but brittle rock, lending strength to my frayed nerves. Strength enough to shove past a completely immobilized Vaughn, our arms brushing against each other one last time, as I scoop up my backpack and sling it over one shoulder.

"Recycle your beer can," I bite out, nudging it in his direction with the toe of my boot but not daring to look up.

He still hasn't said a thing or moved an inch.

I take off into the night, willing my feet to walk gently, my hips to sway confidently, and my shoulders to drop serenely, all to portray a level of confidence that's not at all a reflection of the conflict raging inside me.

CHAPTER 10

Vaughn

It's been exactly two weeks since Billie and I faced off. Not that I'm counting. Women throw themselves at me all the time. Either of their own fruition or at my mother's behest. It made no difference. One hundred percent of those encounters did nothing but irritate me, and I treated the lot of them with respect but a general lack of interest.

That night, with Billie pressed up against me, shouldn't have felt different—but it did.

I wish I could say I hadn't thought about the way she touched me. So confident and indifferent all at once. I'm not sure she even realized she had been slowly rocking herself on my leg as she brushed her soft lips against my jaw and bit down on my ear like the little vixen I hadn't seen coming.

No one has ever made me that hard and then pushed me away. She's a challenge now, and I am completely fixated.

I shouldn't be.

God, I really shouldn't be. It's like she's infected me with her recklessness, because I certainly should not be giving that interaction any thought at all. But I have been. That she can effortlessly rattle my grip on control is driving me crazy.

That night has been keeping me up. It's what runs through my head while I give in and grip my throbbing cock in the shower, spilling myself all over the tiles. I feel the swell of her breast against the pad of my thumb and her dainty fingers taking a fistful of my hair with a level of authority that does not befit her happy-go-lucky personality. But I can't stop and continually promise myself that each time will be the last as I jerk myself off angrily.

I hate it. I'm self-controlled and meticulous. I always have a plan, and now one of the most annoying women I've ever met has me shaken. I've been in a foul mood since our family scandal hit the papers, and I've been running on fumes trying to save my grandfather's crowning achievement, the farm he loved given to him by the wife he cherished. But this encounter has really pushed me over the edge. I know I'm snapping at people who don't deserve it. I'm distracted and agitated. I'm tired, and I'm tired of constantly thinking about bending my employee over my desk and having my way with her.

It's beneath me, and it's not even something I can just get out of my system and move on from.

Our family doesn't need more scandal. I'm aware of how I'm portrayed in the media. The Harding family heir with a new woman on his arm every time he steps out in public. I'm the playboy and my brother the cold recluse. Ask Page Ten (or whatever page it is). They would have an absolute heyday writing about me banging the new help.

I shake my head. Prime example. I know Billie isn't just the help. She's accomplished at her job. Despite what I initially thought of her, she's proving to be perfect for the position. At our management meetings, both she and Hank report to me that all the horses are running better than ever. It doesn't take a rocket scientist to see that all the staff around the farm love her. Some have even told me as much. I can hear the upbeat and playful way she interacts with everyone. That boisterous laugh constantly echoes down the barn alleyway and floats into my office like some sort of cruel joke.

She doesn't even give me the cold shoulder, like she's on some sort of holier-than-thou mission to be the bigger person. Every day, she waves a hand through my door as she walks past and gives me a "Hey there, Boss Man" as she continues past, completely unaffected by the fact that she almost ate me alive the other night. I can't even bring myself to tell her to stop calling me that ridiculous name. If only her professional facade would crack again, just a little, it would give me a good reason to get even with her.

I see her playing My Little Pony, or whatever it is she does with Double Diablo, who so far just looks like a shiny black hole that we've thrown almost a million dollars into for shits and giggles. Every morning, she has coffee by his fence, and every night, she brushes him until he shines like an oil slick. I can hear her talking to him every time I walk to my car, and I try to convince myself she's probably unstable, but truthfully, I can't help but admire the way she's turned the horse's attitude around. Even the grumpiest horse in the world likes her.

She is inescapable.

Which is why I'm here, pulling up to the farm late on a Saturday afternoon. The junior trainers do most of the training work early on the weekends, so it'll be a ghost town. And Billie doesn't work on the weekend at all right now, which means I don't have to hear her voice or breathe in that sunshine and lemon scent I associate with her now.

I worked out hard all morning and burned off my angst, and now I need to deal with month-end spreadsheets and compose an email to our public relations firm about how we should best approach rejoining the very public racing circuit in a few months. I need to focus.

Afternoon bleeds into evening as I hole up in my office, working. I take a break to eat the protein bar I packed for my dinner. It's not appealing at all, but cooking alone isn't either. I spin my desk chair around to face out toward the window, half expecting to see Billie down at DD's paddock.

I chide myself for feeling disappointment at not seeing her down there. What would I do anyway? Just sit up here like a stalker and watch her?

"Yup, pretty much," I murmur to myself. "It's what you do most days, Vaughn."

I shake my head at my foolishness and continue to gaze out the window. The longer I stare, I realize I can't see Double Diablo at all. I stand and peer out the window, hoping a higher angle will help me see him standing in the far corner of his paddock, probably chewing on company cash and swatting flies with his tail.

But it doesn't. He's not there.

I stride out of my office, calm but admittedly feeling a little concerned. I jog down to his pen, making that kissing noise that horses seem to love. It sounds sweet when Billie does it and just kind of lame when I do it. But it makes no difference. Here at the fence, holding the post I had Billie pushed up against, I can see that he is not in his pen. Not in a corner, not in his shelter, not lying down.

Blood roars in my ears, and my pulse thumps heavily against my sternum. Horses don't just go missing.

I scrub my hands through my hair and stare at the empty paddock. The gate is latched and all the fences are intact, which means he hasn't left on his own. But no one has been foolish enough to risk taking him out of that paddock in the time that I've been here, so I turn in a circle, hoping he might just be chilling in a neighboring paddock.

He's not.

A vise constricts my throat, because I don't know what to do in this situation. I work with files and papers. They don't have a mind of their own, and they usually just stay where you leave them. I'm out of my element here.

So I do the only thing I can think of—I run.

In a full sprint, I race back to my car, hop in, and speed down the back road to Billie's cottage, rounding the corner into the driveway with a spray of gravel. I'm driving like a maniac, and I know this. Unfortunately, I realize it a little too late as I come to a screeching halt by the front porch.

To the left of the cottage, I see Double Diablo standing up on his back legs, wildly showing the whites of his eyes. Billie, legs wrapped around his ribs with no saddle to hold her in place, gripping his mane in her hands, leans forward to meet his vertical motion, almost hugging his neck. She's glued onto him like a little fly on his back, gritting her teeth in concentration.

The pause at the top of his motion almost makes time stand still, and the surrounding sounds bleed into nothingness. Before I know it, his front hooves are lowering to the ground, and she has one rein away from his body, turning him in a tight circle. The sound of her murmuring to him in a low, soothing voice filters into my awareness.

I lean my head back against the headrest and close my eyes, running both hands through my hair. The breath that's been a hard knot in my chest for the last several minutes leaves my lungs in a shaky exhale. Relief flows over me like a cool shower on a hot day. The horse is here, and I didn't accidentally kill an employee in my moment of panic.

Lifting my head to glance out the window, I see Billie sitting securely on Double Diablo's back. His flanks heave with the weight of his breaths, and his head turns toward where her foot hangs at his side. She leans down to his face, rubbing his neck with gentle caresses.

Thank fuck.

I open the door and step out of my car. The inky black horse startles at the sound and swings his head up to look at me. Billie's head follows, but slower. Like a predator.

Beneath the shadow of her wide-brimmed black riding helmet, her lavalike eyes narrow. I know her well enough now to recognize her angry face. But two can play this game, so I stand in place and give it right back to her. I refuse to let her make me feel bad. She shakes her head and turns her attention back to the horse, slowly flipping onto her stomach to slide gently down his side, constantly running her hands over him and talking to him reassuringly.

Facing away from me, she takes the reins of the bridle and slowly lifts them over his head, like he's made of porcelain or something. I try not to check her out, but as usual, I fail. The thick brown braid hanging down her back is like an arrow directing my eyes straight to the way she fits in her skintight jeans. *Start here!* it says, pointing my focus to her slim waist, then the feminine curve of her hips, and finally to her firm round ass. It isn't one of those skinny flat asses either; she's sporting some curves. She isn't willowy and weak; she's slender and strong. I assume working on a farm and spending long hours in the saddle are to thank for that.

It cuts my perusal of her body short when she spins around and spits fire.

"What the fuck do you think you are doing? Flying in here like a bat out of hell? Scaring the bejesus out of my horse?"

"You must be confused," I bite back, resting one elbow on the roof of my car and trying to look more casual than I feel. "That is *my* horse. And you removed it from *my* property without *my* permission. I came to work to find one of our most valuable assets missing, and now I probably have dings in my Porsche from having to race around on gravel roads looking for him."

She sniffs haughtily and tips her chin up defiantly at me.

"Sounds like you should look into a more practical car. Minnie Mouse's slipper isn't exactly an ideal farm vehicle."

"I feel like I've said this to you before but… that's your takeaway here?" I reply, raw disbelief bleeding into my tone.

"Yeah, Vaughn, it is," she continues, absentmindedly holding a cookie out to Double Diablo, who is watching us intently with wide black eyes. "I have a phone. Presumably you know how to call and text people. That would have been a good place to start."

She has a point.

"This is still your property. I rode him through the pastures up to the house so I could work with him. *On my day off*," she emphasizes.

I cross my arms and look at the ground. "Okay," I grumble and give a pebble a swift kick.

She looks at me like I've grown extra heads and then launches back in, "Incredible! And now you've got the gall to stand here and sulk about your stupid car while accepting zero accountability for almost killing me?" She scoffs. "Typical trust fund baby behavior."

I. See. Red.

I hate that implication. It's one I've grown up having to shoulder. In my mind, I've worked my ass off to get where I am. I'm not completely naive though. I'm aware of the boosts my privilege has bought for me. The doors my family name has opened. The struggles I've bypassed. But I haven't sat back and coasted either. I don't need a participation medal for showing up, but I despise being lumped in with my peers who spend all day golfing at the country club and collecting interest payments on their investment accounts. I've put myself to use.

I can feel the heat of the ruby stain crawling up my neck. I hate that I'm offended, that her words have landed in the worst way possible. Full of tension, I turn to take a few clipped steps back to my impractical car when I feel something thump me right between the shoulder blades.

I freeze, facing away from her, and hear muffled giggling.

"Billie," I bark out, "did you just throw something at me?"

The giggling morphs into a loud snort.

I turn around in slow motion to find her laughing into the hand plastered over her mouth, reins drooping in the other. Her saucer-size eyes glitter with unshed tears.

"You are unstable." She is unbelievable. "Did you seriously just throw something at me?"

She nods her head, lips pressing together, obviously trying to hold back laughter.

"It was a treat," she chokes out. "Throwing them seems to have brought DD around."

I want to say I don't find this funny, because I shouldn't, but her amusement is infectious. And the aftereffects of all that tension make me feel giddy.

I smirk. "I'm pretty sure you haven't been throwing them *at* him."

She shrugs. "He doesn't make me as mad."

Point taken. Giving her a curt nod, I turn to leave.

"Vaughn," she calls out, "stop."

I keep going, opening my car door.

"Good lord, don't be such a bitch baby."

I can't help it. I bark out a harsh laugh against my will and turn back to take her in.

"Billie Black, did you just call your employer a bitch baby?" I say, giving her an incredulous look.

"Yeah, yeah." She grins as she walks toward the small pen beside the house. "Turn your fine trust fund ass around, and come have a beer with me. I owe you an apology."

This woman is absolutely astonishing.

Almost as astonishing as the fact that I am turning my "fine ass" around and waiting for her by the front steps. *What am I thinking?*

CHAPTER 11

Billie

After settling DD into the paddock just outside my back door and tossing him some fresh hay, I make my way back out front to find Vaughn sitting on the porch swing. He looks almost too big to be sitting on it, too broad, too tall, too *much*.

I've always thought he looked edible in a suit, if a little ridiculous on the farm in the middle of nowhere. But this jeans and a T-shirt look definitely tops the office candy one he usually has going.

A heathered gray V-neck leaves a lot less to the imagination than a dress shirt. I can almost see the lines beneath the fabric that I traced that night with my finger. The outline of his pectorals is square and stands out over his flat stomach and tapered waist. I wonder if he'd lift it up just a few inches so I could actually see what's under there. My working hypothesis is that there's a six-pack. Eight-pack is also possible. Those last two abs might just pop out because he's so uptight he's constantly clenching.

I breeze up the steps. "Come on in, Boss Man," I say, holding the door open for him.

He looks at me like I'm a grenade that could go off at any moment but follows anyway. Smart man.

I chuckle to myself. It makes sense Mr. Uptight would be nervous around me. I haven't exactly proven myself as cool and collected where he's concerned. But it's like he knows where my secret switchboard is and knows exactly which switch to flip to make me fly off the handle.

Waltzing into the kitchen, I open the fridge and grab two frosty glass bottles before turning back to face him across the island.

"Lager or pale ale?" I ask, holding up both options.

"Lager," he replies, pointing at the amber bottle.

I turn toward the cupboards. "Excellent. Bottle, glass, or sippy cup?"

I don't even need to look behind myself to know he is shaking his head since I seem to provoke that response from him frequently.

"Sippy cup it is." I wink over my shoulder with a sly smile.

"Bottle is good." He sighs and, sure enough, shakes his head.

I twist the cap off and slide the beer across to him before leaning against the opposite counter and taking a swig of my beer.

He looks tired. Like, exhausted. Hot, always stupid hot, but honestly a little haggard with disheveled hair and a tense set to his mouth. He sits on the barstool, shoulders slumped over the island. Guilt niggles at me, and I press my palm just above my breasts to push it away. With a dark lock flopped over his forehead, he looks like a lost little boy.

He stares at his beer bottle, silently picking at the label. I don't know what to say to him, so I let my typical instinct take over. I'm going to feed him.

"Do you have any food allergies?"

Dark chocolate eyes shoot up to mine. "No."

"Are you a picky bitch about eating anything?"

"No." He focuses back on his bottle again but quirks up one side of his sinful mouth.

I've been up close and personal with that mouth, so it's hard to forget. Some nights, when I'm alone in bed, I relive our interaction against the fence that night and kick myself for not just kissing the colossal idiot. My mind plays out what it would have been like, where we would have ended up. And then I usually flash to the hundreds of pictures of him on the internet with some new and expensive-looking woman draped on his arm, and I give my head a shake. No distractions and no rich playboys. Nope. No sirree. Not for this gal. Career goals and nice normal dudes are the winning ticket.

Without a word to him, I pull out a couple steaks from the fridge and walk out the back door to fire up the barbecue. I check in on DD. He looks happy in his new special digs, and I like knowing he's out there. The weekends have been lonely at the house all by myself, so I cleaned the pen up specifically hoping I could get him over here at some point. We'd been having a nice leisurely walk over until the man-child had to burn in here and ruin it. The good news is DD rebounded quickly; he didn't stay worked up. The little chicken pulled himself together. He's trusting me.

When I rejoin Vaughn in the kitchen, he hasn't really moved, except now he's tearing up the label and leaving little torn pieces in a pile.

I season the steaks and wash and chop the vegetables for skewers right in front of him, but he says nothing. His pile continues to grow until I can't take it anymore. "Are you building a baby bonfire there, Boss Man?"

He stops.

"Sorry. I kind of zoned out. I didn't really even realize what I was doing." He sighs and leans back.

"Something on your mind?" I probe, not looking up from cutting the zucchini into perfect coins.

"Too much," he responds on an audible exhale, piercing me with his dark eyes.

He's looking more and more like a storm cloud. It's easy to forget he's really my boss when we're being so combative with each other. My filter falls to the wayside, and I say regrettable things, often just for the sake of riling him up. Super mature, I know. But now his silence and contemplative looks are getting me worried. I chance another look up at him as I move on to boiling the potatoes. He's still staring at me.

"Look, I'm sorry. I owe you an apology. Maybe more than one apology, actually. I haven't been my most professional around you. I'll be the first to admit that you have a super special ability to just completely set me off. And I know I have a temper. It's not my best character trait," I ramble on, "but I love working here. The staff, the horses." I sigh wistfully. "The whole place is a dream."

He says nothing.

"And look!" I exclaim, pointing out the back wall of windows. "I'm even riding your devil horse with a modicum of success. He'll be ready to race this season! I promise you—"

"Billie," he cuts me off, "stop rambling."

"You just looked like… I don't know. Like you were coming up with ways to fire me or something."

Vaughn blinks slowly and massages his temples. "Some days, you're a lot of work. But no. I was trying to come up with a way to apologize to you," he grumbles.

Oh. Well, that's a relief.

"Is that why you looked so constipated?"

God, Billie, really? Yup. That's what I come up with. Even I impress myself sometimes.

He holds both hands up in front of himself and drops his mouth open as if to say, "Seriously?"

"Where did you learn your manners?" he asks.

"Private school. Where rich kids get away with behaving badly." I turn to get our steaks going on the barbecue.

"And here I could have sworn wolves raised you," he says to my back.

To be fair, he's not far off.

"Just call me Mowgli," I toss over my shoulder as I head out the door.

The rest of our dinner passes in peace. We sit at the antique dining table and make polite small talk as the evening sun slowly descends behind the mountains. He compliments me on dinner and even takes seconds. At one point, I tell him I accept his nonapology apology, which earns me a dramatic eye roll.

When I offer him another beer, he merely grunts and shoos me away while he takes over cleanup. While he does the dishes, I perch on the kitchen counter, enjoying the way his corded forearms flex and ripple as he scrubs the dishes. Has any man ever made doing domestic chores look this good?

Vaughn's frame is so large that even though I try to move away from the sink, we're not that far apart. Maybe a foot separates my thigh from his waist. And yeah, I'm looking. No man with a face like his should also be able to fill out a pair of jeans the way he does. It's almost criminal. All sharp masculine planes and dark brooding eyes paired with these powerful toned legs.

It's not fair. At least I can take comfort in the fact that his personality sucks. Or at least that's what I tell myself.

"I think we should try to be friends," I blurt out.

He snorts and continues scrubbing the plate in his hand.

"I'm serious. I'm tired of being combative. I don't want to walk on eggshells around you anymore. Water under the bridge and all that," I say, waving my hand dismissively. "Sitting here with you is better than sitting here alone all the time."

Okay, maybe that was taking it a bit far. But deep down, I know that even in his weird mood and with his sucky personality, having some human company is a pleasant change of pace.

"Okay, Mowgli," he replies with a faint smirk, still avoiding eye contact.

I swat his chest playfully and then dramatically pull my hand back to myself as though I'm cradling an injury. "Are you wearing a bulletproof vest under there?" I tease.

He finally graces me with a wry but forced smile. "Gotta be ready for anything around you, Billie."

We sink back into silence. He's unusually contemplative tonight. I haven't been able to find a single trace of smugness. And trust me, I've spent all night looking. I just gave him a perfect opening to lay a cocky remark down on me, and he let it sail right past his head.

After a few beats of total quiet, I sneak a peek at him out of the corner of my eye. He looks very serious. I can't help but wonder what's going through his mind. I lean closer, like I'll be able to see his thoughts floating around somewhere down in his ear canal. (I can't.)

I drink him in from this proximity. Dark stubble peppers his cheeks and neck, and a dusting of chest hair peeks at me from the lowest dip of his V-neck. The fresh smell of laundry detergent is a new addition to his sweet almond scent. He's intoxicating, and I breathe him in against my better judgment.

"Do friends sniff each other?" he asks.

Fuck. Busted.

I clear my throat and shift back away from him. "No, but they check in with each other when they can tell something is wrong," I reply, picking at something on my sweater that isn't there.

I think I've struck a nerve because he leans forward, gripping the counter, and drops his head.

I sigh. "Vaughn, are you okay?"

A strangled *no* escapes his full lips. Like it physically pains him to even respond to me at all.

My heart cracks a little at his broken tone, his defeated posture. I might not like him very much, but he sounds borderline distraught. He's been strength and confidence since I met him, and it feels just wrong to see him like this.

A tight lump forms in my throat, and I can't help but reach out to him. I pause when my hand gets close to his face. He shows no signs of distress at my proximity, so I push my hand closer, stroking a loose lock of his hair between my thumb and middle finger before reverently combing it back into place, dragging a few tips of my fingers against the scalp of his bowed head.

He doesn't move, and I'm emboldened to repeat the motion a couple of times. His eyelids flutter shut. The shadows from the porch light play across his profile, and I lick my lips. This brooding schtick is dangerous.

Get your shit together, Billie.

"Want to talk about it?"

He shakes his head.

My hand rests softly on the back of his neck when I whisper, "Do you need a hug?"

The silence in the house is deafening, and I shift awkwardly on the counter, already regretting my offer. I'm mentally chastising myself so hard that I almost miss his quiet, "Yes."

Vaughn rises and with one large side step moves between my legs. When he almost instantly wraps his steely arms around my waist, I can't hold back the sigh that escapes my lips. He feels so warm and solid pressed up against me—soft and vulnerable.

I snake both my arms around his neck, and we melt into each other. I've never hugged a person who needed to be held so badly. It should feel strange, hugging your boss like this, but wrapping myself around Vaughn Harding in the middle of my kitchen feels like the most natural thing in the world.

The air thrums between us as he burrows his face in my neck. My skin prickles with awareness at the feel of his stubble. I wish I could pry him open and figure out what's wrong, but I also know we only talk about our darkest thoughts when we're good and ready. God knows I have enough of my own secrets lurking beneath the surface.

Sometimes silence is what a person really needs.

I don't know how long we stand there holding each other. I'm zoned out until I feel Vaughn's thumb draw soft circles on the small of my back, just beneath the hemline of my sweater. Skin on skin. Arousal races up my spine, and my relaxed heartbeat crescendos. I don't want to ruin the moment, but I also can't help the way my body reacts to his touch. It's something deep and undeniable, a chemical reaction. Like pouring vinegar over baking soda.

I sigh and arch into his chest, feeling the hardness of his body rasp across my erect nipples.

"Billie." His voice is raw when he whispers my name against the shell of my ear. When he draws back to look at me, his eyes are hazy, more lidded than usual. Apparently, our embrace wasn't wreaking havoc on only my will.

I know I shouldn't, but I reach up and drag one hand through his dark hair. Vaughn's chest rumbles, and he drops his forehead against mine. My inner thighs clench his hips as I press myself closer. This is altogether too intimate, and I know it. He knows it too. But neither of us seem able to stop ourselves.

When he gently feathers the tips of his fingers up the side of my neck, goose bumps pour down between my shoulder blades. He strokes the bottom of my chin, and I tip my face up to bask in the heat of his gaze. My body follows the lead of his, like it's the most natural thing in the world.

And when his warm lips descend onto mine, I sigh, like we've done this a million times before.

The kiss is chaste. Reverent.

But my body doesn't care. It reacts like this is the most passionate kiss in the history of mankind. My breath stutters in my lungs, my stomach drops, the arches of my feet ache, and my core goes damp all at once.

This might be the best kiss of my life.

I pull away on a gasp. *What the fuck am I thinking?*

Vaughn steps back instantly, holding his hands up like I'm a scared animal. "I'm sorry."

"No. I'm sorry."

I press the tips of my fingers onto my lips, trying to erase the feeling of his imprinted on mine. We'd been yelling at each other not two hours ago. What is wrong with us? I slip off the counter, needing some space from his body—from *him*. Like space is what will somehow dull the intense tug I feel toward him now.

"Water. Want some water?" I offer as I round the island to grab a glass.

"Fuck, Billie. That was so out of line. I'm all fucked up. The hug was…" He combs his hands through his hair. His chest rises to full height and then falls on a whoosh of air, almost vibrating with tension. "I needed the hug. Thank you. But I took advantage." Dark, sincere eyes dart to mine. "I'm so sorry. It won't happen again."

I stare straight back at him. "It *can't* happen again. But you did not take advantage. We can chalk the whole thing up to temporary insanity."

The corner of his mouth tips up, but he looks melancholy as I move to sit at the kitchen table.

"Why don't you sit down?" I point to the opposite end of the rectangular table. "At that end, so there's no funny business, and tell me what's going on."

He groans and shakes his head. Apparently too fucking macho to talk about his feelings.

I hold one hand across my heart. "Vaughn Harding, I solemnly swear that I will go back to relentlessly taunting you effective

Monday morning. No one keeps a secret better than me." I look up at the ceiling momentarily. *If he only knew.* "Trust me."

His dark eyes dart around the house before landing on me. He looks like DD, avoiding eye contact. Scared of making a connection.

He sits across from me, hands flat on the table, and says, "I don't know where to start."

Less is more in a situation like this, so I say nothing. I know I won't be able to solve whatever is eating at him, but I also know that being able to tell someone, anyone, is cathartic. For me, that someone is horses.

His fingers trace the grain of the wood tabletop, swirling around every knot, gliding down every line. It's almost hypnotic.

"First, I was angry." Vaughn's voice is so soft that I barely hear him. "Now..." He looks away, out the dark window. "Now, I just feel overwhelmingly sad. Helpless. And I don't know how to get out from underneath it. I don't know how to stop."

Sounds familiar to me.

"Everyone keeps telling me how I *should* feel. What the proper stages of grief are," he scoffs, "or whatever. But it's not a fit, you know?"

I nod. I do know.

"I was only ten when my dad died. Of course, I was devastated, but it just didn't hit me the same. I didn't understand it the same. My brother up and left, my mom struggled, and my grandfather stepped in to fill that void through the most memorable years of my life. And now, I'm just..." His voice cracks, and he clears his throat to bat it away. "Really fucking sad. I keep hoping that I can prove him innocent, clear his reputation, but I don't think I can."

I trail my finger down the outside of my glass, watching the condensation trickle in its wake. "Maybe he's not innocent."

Vaughn's head shoots up to look at me.

"Maybe he's not, and, you know, that's okay. People aren't black and white; they're just shades of gray. Maybe he did some bad things, made some bad choices, but that doesn't make him *bad*. It doesn't negate all the wonderful things he did for you or the important role he played in your life. He can be both." I huff out a breath. This is a conversation I've had many a time. Except with a horse. Best listeners in the world. Telling another human is new, but I forge ahead. "You can feel disappointed and angry and sad and whatever the fuck else you want to feel. You can feel whatever you want. There is no right order or right way. You're entitled to it all. Because at the end of the day, he's not here to explain things to you, so it all just comes down to how much you can forgive. How much you can accept. And there's not a single other person in the world who can tell you what that threshold is." I look up at him now. "But you need to keep searching for it, no matter how much it hurts, because otherwise it will eat you alive."

"Jesus." Vaughn drops his head into his hands and mumbles, "Never thought I'd be getting good advice from crazy Billie Black. How do you know all this?"

"Because I'm still looking for that threshold."

CHAPTER 12

Vaughn

ONE MONTH LATER

I STAND AT THE TOP OF THE BLEACHERS, STARING THROUGH THE set of binoculars Hank just handed me. At the far corner of the track, I can see a little black bullet breezing around the corner, head and neck stretched out long, legs moving like a blur across the dirt track. Billie, long bronze braid flying out in the wind behind her, hunches down low on his neck, keeping herself light and aerodynamic.

I lower my hands and glance over at Hank. My look of disbelief meets his look of pure joy. I mean, the man is positively beaming. His smile threatens to crack his sun-worn face right open. I shake my head, like what I'm seeing is an illusion I can clear away with the motion. Once more, I lift the binoculars and peer back through the lenses to drink in the pair out on the track. They move as one. Like what they're doing together is as natural as breathing.

That's how Billie felt in my arms. She felt *right*.

I'm entranced by their faces when they turn down the home stretch and barrel toward us. DD—I've accepted he is never going to be called Double Diablo by anyone other than me and the track announcer—looks relaxed and determined. I'd almost say he looks like he's having fun. And Billie, my *friend* Billie, has a satisfied smirk on her face. She looks wild and free... and beautiful. Like she belongs up there. I can't hold back the genuine smile that takes over my face.

"Astonishing, isn't it?" Hank asks as I continue to watch them.

"She—they—yes, they are." I absently hand him the binoculars back and watch Billie stand up in the irons to draw DD up, slowing him down. He flicks one ear to her, in tune with every movement—the shift of her shoulders, the drop of her hips. He responds to the directions her body gives him almost instantly. No fighting at all.

The whole thing is impressive. Some horses take a good chunk of time to calm down enough to drop their speed and even more to relax after getting all hyped up. But DD seems perfectly amenable to all Billie's requests.

I reluctantly tear my eyes away from the dirt track to look at Hank again, standing in his signature jeans and polo shirt with that knowing sparkle in his eye. Like he knows something you don't.

"What? You want me to admit that you were right about hiring her?"

"No, son." His cheek twitches.

"Okay. So you're just taking pleasure knowing that my plan to get rid of her is looking like it might backfire?"

He lets out a booming laugh, slapping my shoulder on

his way past, rocking me back on my heels with his old-man strength. Smug prick.

I hate admitting he was right, but this was a show of force on Billie's part. I can't deny I'm more than a little excited. And relieved. Gold Rush Ranch desperately needs something to put us back on the map. I don't want to get my hopes up, but god, I hope Double Diablo is that something.

I don't even think I'd be sad about Billie sticking around anymore. She's grown on me. Enough that I've continued showing up on her porch like a sad puppy every Saturday, even though she never really extended the invite. She looked a little surprised the first time I knocked on her door, but she didn't send me away.

I like her company. I like her wacky sense of humor. I like the way her hips sway while she hums and cooks me dinner. I like the person I've become around her—unconcerned with the drama of the media and the country club crowd. I like the taste of her lips too, the little sighing sound she made when I kissed her, but I've been able to restrain myself from crossing that line again. Because that is the line that neither of us needs to blur. The farm can't take any more drama, and Billie doesn't need me thinking with my dick.

Sounds cliché, but hiding out in Ruby Creek has been almost healing for me. Leaving behind the office, the city, the pressure, is refreshing in a way I couldn't have predicted. I understand why my grandfather loved it out here. Tracing his steps around the farm gives me solace. I think I'm even working toward forgiving him.

Finding that threshold.

Finding a new rhythm.

Like getting to my office early every morning just to watch Billie ride DD bareback over the hill. Then I bring her down a cup of coffee. I even put cream in it now. Although sometimes, I try to put not *quite* enough in it just to see if there's a point where she'll lose it and say something. So far, all it's gotten me is a little sideways glare I try not to smile at. We drink our coffee at the paddock and have a little morning meeting about the farm and plans for the upcoming season. Hank often joins us, shooting speculative glances, like Billie and I getting along is truly suspicious to him.

Everything isn't perfect though. I'm still nervous about the future of the farm. About stepping back into Bell Point Park and being able to hold my head high considering the shame I feel over the scandal. Nervous about proving my asshole brother wrong. He wants me back in the office working at Gold Rush Resources, not wasting my time "playing Farmer Joe." Just thinking about it all is a bucket of ice water over a good mood.

I scrub my hand across my face, trying to wash all my worries away, and look back down at the track to see Billie has dismounted and DD is following her toward the gate like a lost puppy dog. It makes me chuckle. That horse is a total goner for her. I take long strides down the benches of the bleachers and head toward the gate to give Billie a metaphorical pat on the back. If her constantly babying that black stallion can save the farm's future, well, then Billie might just be my greatest asset.

I round the corner to find her hugging a small blond woman, both jumping up and down squealing while they embrace. Billie is so dramatic. You'd think they just won the derby. The blond's head shoots up with startled eyes when I clear my throat. She tries to extricate herself from the hug, but Billie has her tiny body tangled up in her graceful arms.

"Shh. Just ignore him. He'll ruin it," she whisper-shouts.

I place my hands on my hips and look to the sky, a silent prayer for patience.

"Billie, I was watching you guys out there. I came to reinforce you with some kind words so I can get back to work. Stop wasting my time."

She giggles like she's drunk into the small woman's shoulder.

"Hi, Mr. Harding," the blond says in a shaky voice while reaching her hand around Billie to shake mine.

"Nice to see you, Violet. Please, call me Vaughn." I shake her hand and then grip the middle of Billie's braid and gently pull her head back from where she's burrowed, forcing her to look up at me.

She might be tall, but I'm taller.

Untamed amber eyes flash to mine from under the brim of her black helmet, and Violet can finally step away. She finds something interesting to look at on the ground as Billie and I stare at each other in a face-off. Excitement courses through me. I like to compete, and we haven't done this in a while. Her breathing is slightly labored, but I assume that results from galloping a twelve-hundred-pound animal around in the warm spring sun. My gaze drifts over her flushed cheeks and delicate collarbones sprinkled with freckles before landing on her perfect bow-shaped mouth. Her tongue darts out to wet her bottom lip. And in a matter of seconds, Billie, *my friend Billie*, has taken me from exasperated to aroused.

God. I am pathetic.

"Congratulations. Double Diablo looks great. Very impressive." My words come out rigid and stilted.

She watches me with a knowing smile and hits me with a saucy wink. "Thanks, Boss Man."

"I'm going to go and get started on cleaning some tack," Violet interjects before basically sprinting away.

"That's my awkward little Violet," Billie says affectionately.

"You're incorrigible." I shake my head in disapproval.

"Okay, you can drop the private school vocabulary now. No one is here to impress. Your name alone is already a big enough testament to how expensive you are."

"Excuse me?"

"Vaughn Harding," she announces, pronouncing it with an English accent and rolling one hand through the air, folding into a bow.

I attempt to bite back the unwanted smile that's threatening to take over my face. I fail.

"Whatever, Mowgli" is my response. "We need to talk about jockeys for Double Diablo. The suspension lifts in July."

"Stop calling him that. He's a sweet, sensitive boy, and that name is stupid."

I ignore her. "I have a guy with an impressive record lined up for when you think the time is right."

She turns away to remove the saddle from DD's back. "I'll look at him. We're going to need someone special, Vaughn. It's going to take more than a winning record to get this horse to run in an actual race." She hefts the tack onto the fence and adds, "I don't think he should stay at the track. It's too stimulating, and I wasn't joking about him being sensitive. He needs peace and quiet. I'll trailer him the day of and then bring him home after the race."

"Billie, he's a racehorse, not a puppy. You know that, right?"

She shoots me a withering look. "You gonna hop on and take over his training?"

I look at the horse. He seems pretty docile these days, calmer than most stallions I've known, but she has a point. I take a step forward and surrender. "Okay, okay."

Her shoulders climb high and then fall on a big relieved sigh before she completely changes the subject. "I have a killer meal planned for tomorrow night. The veggie stand had the most incredible-looking asparagus so I'm going to make—"

I raise one hand to slow her down. "Actually, there's a fundraiser they have asked me to attend tomorrow."

Her hand freezes midstroke on DD's shoulder, and her eyebrows pop up. "No problem," she says.

Her shoulders droop incrementally from their typical proud spot, and she pastes a weird smile on her face. It's like watching a balloon deflate right before my eyes. *And you were the one to stick the pin into it, asshole.*

I take a step closer, wanting to comfort her without overstepping our tenuous boundaries. "Billie, I'm sorry. I should have mentioned it earlier."

She looks down and turns abruptly, horse in hand, to leave. "Have fun!" she shouts too brightly over her shoulder while hustling away to the barn.

Standing here, watching her leave, I'm tossed into a pool of total confusion. I didn't think our Saturday night dinners were so formal that I needed to let her know I wouldn't be there. I'm not accustomed to accounting for friends in my schedule.

My stomach hits me with a new flipping sensation, like I'm hurtling toward the ground on a roller coaster. A ride I want to get off. This doesn't feel good. I can't remember the last time I felt bad for letting someone down, let alone sick over it. But I sure as fuck do now.

CHAPTER 13

Billie

It's go time. I slam the door on the truck attached to the black trailer with the Gold Rush Ranch logo splashed across the side. Inside that trailer is the ebony horse that my career is banking on.

I'm nervous. Nervous as fuck. But I also *know* that DD is ready and up to the challenge. We have spent the last few months preparing for his first race. He's been on the practice track, in the fields and forest, and I've even let Violet breeze him a few times just to see how he'd handle a different rider. The last few weekends, I've trailered him down to the races just to desensitize him to how loud and busy it will be today. He's fit and mentally prepared.

Me? Not so much.

I know I shouldn't let myself think about it, but today's race is a qualifier for the prestigious Denman Derby. Go big or go home, right? I haven't vocalized my plan. That makes it too real—too ripe for disappointment. But I think we can do it. If we start off right, he only needs to win a couple races to qualify.

I don't want to run him into the ground; he's not the type of horse to go out and make money every weekend. He needs to do *just* enough and then kick back and relax until the big day.

I secretly have it all plotted out.

I paid the extra fee to register him late, which means our competitors won't see us coming. He is literally the dark horse, and I have everything planned out to a T. The only thing that's a minor unknown is the jockey. Vaughn's brother, Cole, has apparently made a huge deal about being half owner and having to use this guy because he knows him or some shit. It borderline enrages me he's using this horse and me to foster family connections for the Hardings. This "I'll rub your dick if you rub mine" mentality pisses me off. It's the garbage I left behind for a reason. But I know there's a time and a place to smile and nod, and, well, this might just be one of those times.

Vaughn and I have been distant since he bailed on our Saturday night dinner. I have no right to be angry with him, yet I can't deny the intense disappointment I felt. Or the twinge of jealousy that flared behind my solar plexus at the thought of him out with another woman on what was meant to be *our* night. It seems like he doesn't quite know what to say either, so shit is awkward now. Snark has been the lifeblood of our friendship since day one, but neither of us seems to have the heart for it anymore. The truth of the matter is I like Vaughn. More than I should. He might be a tad smug and broody, okay; he sometimes borders on pompous. But I know he's a good person trying to do his best. Maybe I didn't see it at first, but he's worked hard in the face of immense pressure and grief.

Aside from our first misunderstanding and a little verbal sparring here and there, he's never treated me (or anyone else) in any way that wasn't plain gentlemanly. So it sucks that our friendship seems to have fizzled. After he canceled a couple of Saturday dinners in a row, I kind of got the hint. We've been nothing short of cordial and professional—if a little cool.

I drive along the major highway, pulling DD in the rig behind me. It's raining now, not ideal for his first race. My stomach flip-flops nonstop. The feeling pools in my gut and crawls all the way up my throat. I couldn't even eat this morning. I suspect I'll be living on coffee today. Who knows? Maybe I'll even take up smoking. Seems like a good thing to do with my hands when I'm nervous. Plus, I'd look so much cooler puffing on a cigarette than wringing my hands.

The drive passes by quickly, and I focus on deep breathing and letting the constant swing of the wipers across the windshield lull me into some semblance of calm. It's borderline meditative. And when I pull into the stabling at the track, I feel a little relaxed.

I had my freak-out in private. Now it's time to put my game face on. DD doesn't need to pick up on my anxiety, and neither does the staff around me. I want to say there is no pressure, that this race is just for practice, but it feels like so much more. The farm's first weekend back at the track. My debut. DD's debut.

No big deal.

I drop out of the big truck in front of our bank of stalls here at Bell Point Park to see Violet already waiting for me. She looks stressed too. Wide blue eyes. Pursed lips. Bun so tight I wonder if her face hurts.

I wave at her and call out, "Hey, Vi! You ready to show these amateurs how it's done?"

That garners me a small smile. "So ready."

A firm grip lands on my shoulder, and I turn to see Hank grinning at me. My big old comfort blanket. "They're not going to see the little black bullet coming. He's like a secret weapon that you ladies have under wraps. I can't wait to see the race and hear the buzz."

All three of us grin at each other like loons. Stress does weird things to people, and I am not immune to the effects. The only thing that breaks up our creepy anxiety party is DD's loud stomp and snort summoning me, his slave, to get him out of the trailer and provide him with some food. We unload him without incident, make sure he's set with food and water, and then I go in search of my very special jockey, leaving DD behind with Violet to ensure he's the shiniest version of himself for his big debut.

On my stroll through the stables, I soak up the hustle and bustle of race day. The sounds of horses snorting, their aluminum shoes ticking against concrete, the whoosh of grain being added to a bucket. It's almost sensory overload behind the scenes in the stables, but to me, it's comforting to be back at the track.

I live for this.

Within a few minutes, I reach the main administrative building that is all offices on the main floor and boasts skyboxes and meeting rooms on the upper levels. It's about two hours to race time, and I'm due to meet Vaughn and our fancy new jockey in the owner's lounge upstairs. Make introductions, talk strategy, get everything set just right. I would have liked to talk to the guy earlier, paid him for a few practice rides, really hammered out the details of how specific DD could be. But apparently he's too busy. He gets thrown on a horse just before the race and then hops off at the end to go back to hobnobbing it with the suits.

As I climb the stairs, I hear the dull hum of dry conversation and the clink of ice against glass. I breach the doorway and take in the large room. Everyone else is crammed onto metal benches, drinking Budweiser from the can, but up here, it's all luxury. Floor-to-ceiling glass provides a completely uninterrupted view of the track. Plush brown leather couches and armchairs with nailhead details look out through the windows.

I continue scanning the room. I swear I feel Vaughn before I see him. Like a tug right at the solar plexus. We've spent so many of our interactions in the last month tiptoeing around each other that I feel especially attuned to his presence. When I finally turn in his exact direction, I find him already staring at me, head turned away from the conversation he's a part of, his deep chocolate eyes lasered in on me.

I drink him in like frozen lemonade on a hot day. Except it's cool and pouring outside.

What a specimen. He looks so good in this setting. If he looked happier, I would say that it suits him perfectly. But he looks predictably detached. Not at all like the man who would have a beer at my kitchen counter while I cooked for him. His perfectly tailored dark blue suit and signature white shirt contrast beautifully with his inky locks. They're gelled into place flawlessly, and all that makes me want to do is run my fingers through it and pull a few tresses free. Loosen him up a bit.

Under the scrutiny of his gaze, an unconscious shiver racks my body. I can't prevent it, don't even really want to—don't even try. I know I'm admiring him openly and he's scowling back at me. Which is a positive in my book. I still get high from rattling his control. Watching him lose his cool is basically a drug for me, and I know this look. It's the "pull yourself together" look, and it's meant to intimidate me.

But the joke's on him. All it does is set me on fire.

I flash him my best beauty queen smile and a secret wink as I head his way, which garners me an almost imperceptible agitated sort of head shake. *Ha. I win.* He thinks he's subtle, but I've spent the last decade of my life studying body language and using it to my advantage with horses. People are no different. Same shit, different pile.

I stride up to the group of three men just in time to hear Vaughn introducing me. "Gentlemen, I'd like you to meet the resident head trainer for us at Gold Rush Ranch," he says, gesturing toward me amiably, "Billie Black."

I reach forward to take the hand of a small middle-aged man with watery eyes and sandy-colored hair, who I'm assuming is our new jockey.

"Billie, this is Patrick Cassel, Double Diablo's new jockey."

"Nice to meet you, Patrick," I reply cordially, shooting Vaughn daggers as subtly as possible for still calling my horse Double Diablo. *What a dick.*

I shake Patrick's limp hand, the lamest type of handshake, and he gives me a flat smile. "How lucky for me. Canada's long-lost princess."

Panic suffuses me as I focus on schooling my features. I've always known this day would come. Someone was bound to recognize me eventually. After all, I've basically been hiding in plain sight. My plan all along has been to ignore it, and I will not deviate from that plan now. I see Vaughn's eyebrow quirk up out of the corner of my eye, but I just stare back at Patrick with a bored smile on my face.

I pivot to the other man in the group, wanting to move the conversation along. I would say I don't recognize him, except he looks an awful lot like Vaughn. Not as tall or refined, somehow coarser, more muscular. Cunning gray eyes rather than warm brown, but the same inky dark hair and the same facial features. If Vaughn is a soccer player, this guy is a football player. But the resemblance is unmistakable.

Vaughn's hand comes to rest on my lower back as he motions me toward who I'm sure is his older brother. "And this," he almost growls, "is Cole Harding. My brother and co-owner of Gold Rush Ranch."

Cole's icy gray eyes hit mine, and the differences between the two brothers multiply by the moment. This guy is cold as fuck. Where Vaughn is detached and smug, Cole is downright glacial. If I were a wimpier woman, it would intimidate me.

His handshake couldn't be more different from Patrick's. His long fingers wrap around my hand in an absolute vise grip of a handshake. He would have pulled me off balance if I were less fit.

"A pleasure to meet you," he says in the most obnoxious, sardonic kind of voice. Aha. Another rich prick. Condescending by nature.

I put on my debutante smile, pinch my shoulder blades together, and squeeze the living fuck out of his hand right back. "Oh, the pleasure is all mine. I've heard so much about you!"

His eyes narrow at that, and Vaughn's hand slides around my waist to squeeze my hip bone. A silent demand to please not lay the smackdown on his shithead brother, which is fine, but I'm not letting go first. Cole and I stare at each other, squeezing each other's hands to dust. I handle horses for a living, and this guy goes for weekly manicures and holds gold-plated pens. I'm really not worried about winning this pissing match. So I hold on and continue to stare with a fake-ass smile plastered on my face.

That fake-ass smile turns to my jaw swinging in the wind when Vaughn grumbles, "Jesus Christ, Cole. Don't break my trainer."

My head swivels to him as the big brute drops my hand. Did Vaughn just come to my defense?

I turn back to the men, smiling brighter than the sun, waving my fingers at them like jazz hands even though they hurt like hell. "Bah, nothing I can't handle."

The ice king continues to glare at me. What a riot. He seems like a fun guy. *Said no one ever.*

Vaughn clears his throat, eyes twinkling and lips pursed. I'm almost positive he's trying not to laugh. I can't stop winning today. That has to be a good omen?

"Okay, Billie," Vaughn starts back in. "Cole and I are going to leave you and Patrick to it. If you need me, I'll be in here. You're welcome to join us here for the race."

"No, I think I'll be good down at track level," I reply as Vaughn follows my gaze. "I want to be there for DD at the end."

He gives me the sweetest smile. Small but genuine. And it lights me up. It's like a balm to my nerves. A balm I'm going to need to talk to Patrick after that comment. Does he even know how lucky he is to ride on a horse like DD? Has no one impressed this upon him? He should be kissing someone's shoes in thanks. Instead, he's standing here smirking at me, trying to steer the conversation to places I don't want to go.

Tool.

"Okay, Patrick," I start off a little too brightly. "It looks like you have an outstanding record. I'm really excited to see what you can do with DD. He's a very special horse."

The brothers turn to leave, and I get a light squeeze on my elbow as they walk behind me, which I interpret as Vaughn telling me to behave. Does he have so little faith in me to conduct myself professionally? What a vote of confidence.

"Mothers always think their own children are special. I've been in this business long enough to know that a horse is just a horse until it proves itself," Patrick says. "Same can be said for a trainer."

Smiling in the sugariest way possible, because men like this are not a new phenomenon to me in this business, I say, "Well, call me Mother Hen then, Patty. Because you've never ridden a horse like this."

He sniffs and rubs his straight nose at that.

"It's Patrick, and I highly doubt that. I've ridden the best horses in the Pacific Northwest. I'm doing this as a favor to Cole, you know. Our families have been connected for years."

My fingers curl into my palms, nails threatening to puncture the skin.

"Congratulations. I've worked with some of the best horses in the world. You might be a big fish in a small pond, but I'm almost positive I didn't see any big-name derby wins anywhere on your record."

His eyes narrow. My aim for sore spots is exceptional.

"But this horse could actually do that for you. For *us.* So you're going to drop the attitude and listen to me. I don't really need you to believe he's special, but I do need you to execute my plan in a very precise fashion."

He lifts his hand, palm up, to peer down at his nails like he's found something interesting there. Avoiding eye contact he mutters, "I'm listening."

Relief courses through me. DD is depending on me, and I need this dick on board whether I like him or not. "Great. He's a nervous horse. So no whip."

"No whip?" he sneers. "It's just a tool. You are aware it doesn't hurt, right?"

"No. Whip. He doesn't need it, and it scares him."

He twists his face like I'm an idiot.

"Deal with it," I bite back, holding eye contact with him. "He doesn't like the gates. He's going to tense up in there, and I want to use that to our advantage. Off the start, hold him back. Let him own the back of the pack so that he can see the other horses running away from him, okay?"

A terse nod.

"Good. On the first straightaway…"

CHAPTER 14

Vaughn

THE GATES BURST OPEN, AND THE LINE OF HORSES FLY OUT. I CAN pick Double Diablo out immediately. Our yellow and black silks make it easy to find him. Under the amber glow of the overhead lights, the falling rain looks somehow suspended in motion, like this is a moment to pause and watch. Everything is about to be caked in mud, but still, DD looks outstanding. All lean muscular lines and gleaming coat. Even from here, I can tell that he's a cut above the rest of the horses out there. He's in his own class.

He leads the pack right out of the gate, surging ahead of the rest to take up an early spot on the rail. Keeping him on the inside of the track means less distance to run, making it a coveted position for a front-runner—which I didn't think this horse was.

They're on the first straightaway now, and Patrick has him absolutely flying. The other horses are eating their dust. I almost can't believe my eyes. To think that three short months ago, no one could get near this horse, and now he's leading the pack under the lights at his first race. It's bewildering.

I shake my head in disbelief and hear Cole beside me say, "Huh," as though he can't quite believe it either. He told me when we first arrived that he "couldn't wait to watch Patrick get dumped on his conceited ass by the crazy horse." It doesn't look like that dream will come to fruition.

Billie's unusual training regimen of trotting him up and down and around in the fields and over the hills and her unique approach of treating him like a lap dog really worked. The horse is spectacular and flourished under her hand. Pride wells up in me. It blooms in my chest and twines in my shoulders, flowing down through my elbows and fingers in a completely unfamiliar way. Like I am itching to hug her, to congratulate her. To tell her how wrong I've been.

I gave Billie what I thought was an impossible task. I believed I set her up to fail, and she gave me the middle finger in the most spectacular way possible. I'm not mad. She's an impressive woman. Smart, tough, kind, beautiful.

And maybe that's the most annoying thing about her. She doesn't annoy me at all anymore.

Watching the pack of horses come into the final bend, I feel a lump of nervousness in my throat. Double Diablo is slipping back. One spot. Two. Now he's lost position on the rail. I shove my hands into my pockets, jangling my keys, trying to give nothing else away with my body. On the final straightaway, I can see our team lagging, like they're losing steam.

Patrick reaches back and gives Double Diablo three hard thwacks with the whip, something I realize I've never seen Billie or Violet do in all the times I snuck around the back of the barn to watch them train.

But it works. It's almost as though the other horses drop into slow motion as Double Diablo flies past them like an avenging wraith. He drops his head and stretches out as far as he can, surging ahead with incredible power to cross the laser finish line a half a length in front of his next closest competitor.

I can't help but grin. I gaze down in wonderment at the little black horse. He's slowed down already, flanks heaving and body all splattered in mud. What a night. What a show. It was close, but a win is a win.

I turn my head slowly to take in my brother beside me. He's staring at the track, arms crossed, not a shred of emotion on his face. Typical. I get something right, and he can't even bring himself to grace me with a smile. I punch him in the shoulder playfully, just to irritate him, in the way that only a little brother can. He scowls at me.

"We did it," I say, smirking, nudging him with my elbow a few times.

He shakes his head and deadpans, "I would rather have watched Patrick get dumped in the mud."

I grab a glass of scotch and turn to lean against the bar, letting my gaze wander around the room in front of me. Cole is sullen, talking to some people he knows. He hates this shit. Always has. And lately I feel like I can't blame him. It's boring. But our dark horse was a winner at his first race, so I am on cloud nine.

A long swig of the amber liquid burns my throat. I feel content in this moment. I have to confess, the thought of this race made me nervous. I had pregame jitters, and this scotch feels both celebratory and soothing. I want Billie to come toast with me.

I see movement at the door and watch Patrick walk in like he's the king of the world or something. Some other owners in the booth who know him offer up light applause, and he takes an obnoxious little bow. As though he was the one who took that horse from zero to hero. The whole scene hammers a little crack into my contentment. I know he rode the horse, but I watched Billie slave over Double Diablo every damn day for months.

And now this tool is up here bowing like he's royalty, already changed out of his muddy silks and into his stupid khakis and polo shirt. Obnoxious little fucker. Billie is the one who deserves a round of applause.

The thought of applauding when she eventually walks in makes me smile. She would *hate* that, which is a great reason for me to do it anyway.

I turn back to the bar, tired of watching Patrick preen, and continue to smile privately over applauding Billie. The more I think about it, the more I really think it's a good idea. She likes it when I pick on her, enjoys the challenge. I know she does.

Zoning out at the bar, musing to myself, I feel the room go quiet. I turn back to the door to see Billie, wild-eyed and muddy. Covered in raindrops, her bronze braid looks darker than usual. Loose pieces of hair plaster against her forehead, and her eyes look like burning coals. Wearing a black pantsuit, she looks downright scary.

I'm standing here, hands held out like I'm about to clap, but her intensity stops me in my tracks. Focused on where Patrick is standing, she starts her forward motion again, prowling across the room like a panther in her formfitting suit, quiet and deadly. He's facing away from her, gesticulating, like he's recounting the most exciting story in the world. He's clueless about what is coming up behind him.

And within a few moments, I realize I am too. Because Billie stalks up behind the small man, and my brain is obviously a little slow on the uptake, because I am downright floored when she winds up one arm like she's the batter up at a baseball game, racing whip in hand, and gives him one sharp spank smack dab in the middle of his tiny ass.

I spit my mouthful of whiskey out, full spray. And then I gape at the scene in front of me. She just walked up and absolutely whaled on the guy. That is going to leave a welt. He lets out a high-pitched shocked scream and spins around to face Billie. He has to look up to meet her eyes, which gives the whole interaction this funny dynamic where he looks like a little boy who just received a public spanking.

Shock and disbelief course through me. I wipe my mouth across the sleeve of my suit jacket, not caring about the mess. I'm more captivated by the scene in front of me.

"You gonna scream like that," Billie says, gesturing the whip up and down his body in a condescending way, "and then try to tell me it doesn't hurt?"

Her tone is eerily calm and even. I'm impressed, because she is terrifying right now. I thought I'd seen Billie mad before, but now I feel like all I've seen from her mood is good-humored child's play.

Patrick's face is red. Red, like a dark cherry. Not a maraschino cherry with that bright vibrant dyed color. Like a black cherry. He. Is. Fuming.

"How… how dare you!" he splutters.

Pointing that whip right at his throat, Billie leans down just enough to be exactly at his eye level.

"How. Dare. You. You fucking rat bastard."

Patrick's hand falls across his chest in the most scandalized way. Every eye in the room is on Patrick and Billie. You could hear a pin drop.

"*You* work for *me*. I gave you explicit instructions. I brushed off your small-man-syndrome chauvinistic comments to forge a working relationship. And what did you do?"

"I will not allow you to talk to me this way, Wilhelmina. Though it shouldn't surprise me that Victor Farrington's daughter is just as trashy as he is."

Billie rears back as though someone has slapped her.

Wait. What? Victor Farrington. *Like former Prime Minister Farrington?*

Patrick huffs, puffing his tiny chest out and brushing his shoulder like there's dirt on it. He turns to leave, but she holds the whip out to stop him.

"I'm not done yet, Little Patty. I want to make myself clear, so look me in the eye before you run and hide." She bends even lower, her face coming within only a few inches of his, with the whip still resting on his shoulder. "You will never ride another one of my horses again. You will never come near Double Diablo again. The only view you're going to get of him is of his shiny black ass while you watch him cross the finish line." She lowers the whip and stands up tall. "And as for me? My family has no bearing on my professional life. I'm no mother hen. I'm a fucking mother bear. And you poked me. So when you see me around, I want you to turn and run the other way like the snively little bitch that you are."

From behind me, I hear a sigh and, "I think I'm in love."

I turn to see the bartender staring at the scene in front of her with absolute awe.

She shifts her gaze to me. Pointing over my shoulder, she says, "That lady right there is a stone-cold badass."

She's not wrong.

"And you..." Billie starts up again.

Oh god. Who's next? I spin around to see her pointing the whip at my brother, who is rigid like a statue. A soldier through and through. His gray eyes are cold and glacial, while hers are hot and molten. This will not end well for either of them.

"If you ever use me or my horses to win brownie points in your billionaire-baby sandbox, I will bury you there myself. Are we clear?"

Cole looks downright murderous. I move toward Billie to intercept the looming explosion.

"Ms. Black, that is not your horse," he says. "It's my horse. He's an asset."

"Give your head a shake. Before me"—she pokes her chest with her pointer finger—"he was an expensive lawn ornament, not a Denman Derby contender. He is a living, sentient being—not a pawn. And you put him in the hands of an asshole who has *your asset* so scared he can't stop trembling in his stall." She tosses the whip down at his feet, causing Cole to rear back ever so slightly, which is a bigger reaction than I've seen out of him in years. "I will *never* forgive you," she finishes, her voice breaking on the last sentence.

God, I need to get her out of here. Now.

In three long strides, I'm at her side, pressing my hand into her lower back, trying to guide her out the door.

"Don't fucking touch me," she bites out, shrugging me off and waltzing out of the room with her head held high. Like she's royalty. Like she fucking owns this place.

I follow her into the hallway. She looks around like she's unsure where to go and opts to head toward the fire escape at the end of the hallway.

"Billie, slow down," I call as she bursts out the door. She's like a tornado losing potency. I can see her facade starting to crack.

"Leave me alone, Vaughn," she shouts over her shoulder, blowing out into the dark rainy night.

I pause at the door. She's asked me to leave her alone, but I don't want to. I lean back against the wall next to the door, pinching the bridge of my nose. Trying to figure out what to do next.

"Is she okay?" I hear from down the hall.

"Hey, Hank." I drop my hand and look up at the ceiling, "I don't know."

"Did she put on a show at least?" he inquires with a smile in his voice.

A laugh bubbles out of my throat. "Did she ever."

"She's an impressive woman."

I roll the back of my head along the wall to look at him. "She is," I agree honestly.

Hank just smiles, that irritating, knowing smile of his, nods his head, and turns back down the stairs with a wave. I gaze back up at the ceiling, weighing my options, trying to figure out how best to approach her right now.

I reach my left hand up to the emergency exit door and knock three times. "Billie? It's Vaughn. I'll just wait here until you're ready for company."

"Man, you're like the clap. I can't fucking get rid of you" is her muffled response.

My lips quirk. Most women I know would be happy to have me following them around, but not Billie. Nope. To her, I am nothing but a painful STD.

"In that case, I'm coming out," I reply, pushing the bar across the door to open it.

She stands there on the landing of the metal staircase, holding the railing, looking out over the lit-up track. "Careful, Boss Man. I'm liable to murder someone tonight. And you're not exempt from my list."

I stand beside her, leaving a couple feet of distance between us. Just to be safe. I grip the railing and look out over the track. Silent moments stretch into minutes.

"Why didn't you go off on me in there?"

"Lost steam, I guess," is her quiet response.

"I have a hard time believing that."

"Because I know you well enough to know you'll be beating yourself up about it anyway. I don't need to say anything. You'll shoulder your family guilt and any guilt I give you like you're a modern-day Sisyphus or something. And you were probably too busy trying to bang the bartender to watch the race anyways."

That was a low blow, and my fingers clamp down on the metal bar. "Is that really what you think?"

"Sure is," she spits out while turning to rip the door open and head back inside. But not before I can turn and slam a palm down, forcing it closed from behind her. "Vaughn, I am so not in the mood for your trust fund baby temper tantrums right now."

"Billie, turn around."

She stands still, silent. All I can hear is the rain falling heavily on the metal stairs.

"Now." I use my boardroom voice.

She turns quickly then, one hand raised. "You know, go fuck yours—"

I capture her wrist in my hand, push her up against the cold metal door, and press my lips onto hers, interrupting her fighting words in one hard, punishing kiss. She doesn't respond or fight it, so I stop. I'm pinning one wrist above her head when I pull my face back to gauge her reaction.

Her molten eyes bore into mine. Absolute shock paints her feminine face. I cup the base of her skull, brushing the pad of my thumb across the high point of her cheekbone, and smirk back at her. The look on her face is endearing. I want to soften her up and work her up all at the same time. I've learned tonight that I like her like this, all feisty and wild and unpredictable. Her chest is heaving, and she looks cornered, a little bit scared.

"I'm sorry," I breathe.

I expect her to lash out, for more cutting words to fly past her bee-stung lips. Instead, she fists the lapel of my suit jacket and yanks me back into a kiss. Her lips move frantically against mine, so different from our first kiss, burning me up in a way I didn't think a single kiss could.

Raw emotions flow between us. Anger, frustration, tension, and yearning. So much yearning.

She turns from cold, hard stone to flowing lava beneath my hands. Her entire body relaxes under my contact. But our lips are still at war with each other. Nipping. Sucking. Sparring. How she and I have been since the day we met. I fucking love it.

I release her head and slowly trail my hand down to her neck and hold her there for a moment, giving her throat a gentle squeeze, making her whimper into my mouth.

"God. Billie. You drive me crazy," I rasp, desire coating my voice. Because it's true. In every sense of the word, she does.

She pulls back to meet my gaze, wet skin glowing in the low light. She looks beautiful. Painfully so. I watch a droplet of water fall from her hair and roll down to rest in the hollow just above her collarbone. I release her hand and bend down to kiss her there. Her eyes flutter shut and her head tips back. She moans. And it's like an instant blood rush to my already aching cock. We're fully clothed, and I can't remember the last time I was this painfully hard.

"Vaughn," she whispers, running both her hands through my soaked hair, "what are you doing?"

"Shutting you up," I murmur against her skin as I drag my teeth and feather soft kisses up her throat before giving her ear a good hard nip.

"Mmm," is the muffled sound she makes in response. "You're going to regret this tomorrow."

I stop at that, bringing my pointer finger to the dip just below her bottom lip. I press it there to tip her head back, and her exotic eyes flutter open to meet mine.

"No, I won't," I respond, dragging my finger up toward the seam of her puffy lips.

Eyes glued to mine, she parts her lips and then sucks my finger, hot tongue swirling around it.

"Fuck," I mutter, watching her suck on my finger and stare me down in the most sinful way.

I shift my hips closer, pressing into her so she can feel what she's doing to me. My hard length lines up exactly right with her pelvis. The way she looks right now is fucking criminal. Wet and hot and smoldering. My finger in her mouth is an image I'll never be able to scrub from my mind.

I pull my finger out with a wet pop. She presses her lips

together and drops her eyes, a shy blush staining her damp cheeks.

"Don't you dare look away from me, Billie Black," I say, gently tipping her head back up.

She looks down and to the side, all that brazen confidence seeping out of her now. I come back to cupping her head and kiss her gently this time, softly. Trying to coax her back from her retreat. Trying to tell her things through my touch that I've never said out loud. Our lips move together, slow and sensuous this time. Sweetly. Like waves lapping at the beach in a perfect rhythm.

She sighs into me, sliding her palms up the front of my dress shirt, exploring my body, running her nails down my back underneath my blazer. I open my eyes, like a total middle school creep, and watch her. She's pouring herself into our kiss, and the weight of it almost knocks the air from my lungs. Like a boy who's just been pushed off the playground equipment.

Eventually her hand comes up to my cheek, and she drops her chin, absently running her fingers through my tousled hair. She meets my gaze again, but not with the fire from a few minutes ago. Not the way I want. And in this moment, I know I'm not going to like what she says next.

She rests one hand on my chest and says, "Thank you, Vaughn," before turning and walking back through the door into the dark hallway.

I stand there at a complete loss to understand what just happened and adjust myself in my pants. The memory of her mouth on mine is burned into my body and something my aching dick is obviously not ready to let go of. And quite frankly, something my mind isn't prepared to let go of either.

And thank you? A fucking thank you? After we both just completely incinerated each other? With chemistry like that?

I don't think so, Billie.

CHAPTER 15

Billie

Wow. Monumentally stupid. Like, so fucking stupid.

Did I seriously just suck on the finger of the man who signs my paychecks?

Stupid, stupid, stupid.

But also:

Hot, hot, hot.

My panties are ruined. So is my job, probably, but I'll focus on that later.

I jog down the barn alleyways, trying to get back to DD's stall. I've been away longer than I intended, and now I'm feeling guilty for leaving him.

When Patty the Prick hopped off his back and left him with Violet, he'd been all right, but as soon as he got into his stall, he froze on the spot and trembled. We whipped his tack off and started cleaning him, covering him up with warm fleece blankets. Hank ran to get the track vet to come check on him, worried that maybe he had an injury. The poor thing was in shock.

And I tore out of there like a bat out of hell with a major bone to pick.

I almost couldn't believe my eyes when I saw Patrick all washed off and changed into some fresh douchebag outfit while his winning mount was melting down in his stall. It enraged me. All I saw was red and his shitty, smug miniature face.

I was clear with him. Precise. Forceful but specific. And he outright defied me, and now an animal who trusted us enough, against his natural instincts, to do what we asked of him was the one paying the price. That fucker was lucky I only hit him once. I was ready to turn him into a spit roast on that whip. Especially after spilling everything about my sordid past in a room full of people.

But I can't focus on that right now.

I finally get to our aisle and see Violet and Hank standing outside his stall, looking in. When I get there, I'm huffing as I come to stand between them and peer into the stall. DD is hooked up to an IV, and a young woman with a thick dark ponytail is checking his legs over.

"Is he okay?" I blurt out, breathless.

"I think he's all right. Just had himself a bit of a panic attack, I think. Legs all seem fine." She rises and gives him a soothing rub behind his ears. "Didn't ya, big guy?"

DD lets his eyelids droop and neck relax under her ministrations. He's not shaking anymore. But he looks exhausted.

"I've got him hooked up to the IV for some extra hydration. Nothing seems swollen or sore, but we haven't been able to get him out of the stall to see him move either. I think he just needs some TLC and rest."

A warm hand lands on my back, rubbing in small, sure circles. I peek over my shoulder and give Hank a watery smile, fighting the hot tears welling in my eyes. They threaten to spill out, but I'm not really a cry-in-front-of-other-people kind of gal. I'll save that for when I'm alone.

When I peer over at Violet, I expect to see puppy dog eyes and a tearstained face. But her eyes are like dark sapphires and her pouty lips are frozen in an angry frown. She looks like an angry little sprite, and it honestly lifts my spirits. She's such an enigma. There's still so much I don't know about her. But I like her. A lot. More than most people.

"Thank you so much for helping us out," I say, barely above a whisper, to the vet.

"Absolutely, any time. I'll give you my card, and I'll call for an update on how he's doing tomorrow." She returns a firm handshake and tries to force a comforting smile, but I can tell it's not really part of her natural persona. Her eyes dance with intelligence, but she's not the rub-your-back type of veterinarian. She's the facts-and-science type, which is fine by me. But I hug her anyway and she returns it woodenly, patting my back with quick slaps as she peels me off.

"All right then," she says, pressing her lips together.

"Thank you so much, Doctor…?"

"Mira Thorne. And you're welcome." She pulls a card from her pocket and hands it to me. "If anything changes, I'm on call tonight." She unhooks the IV from DD's neck, packs up her kit, and heads out with brisk strides.

Hank, Violet, and I stand in silence awkwardly. Like we don't know what to say to each other. We won tonight, and it was a big win. The points from winning this race mean if we pick our next race carefully and win, he could qualify for the Denman Derby, the crown jewel of racing on the West Coast of the continent and the first leg of the Northern Crown.

But at what cost? Would DD want to run again after this? Would it even be fair to ask him to? He was supposed to have a fun night, play around on the track, and get some experience. Not be traumatized.

Just thinking about it makes me feel sick and ramps my heartbeat back up, heats my blood. I am terrible at letting things go, and I can already tell this will be a night that sticks with me for years to come.

In more ways than one.

"I'm going to kill that arrogant little fuck," Violet spits out.

Hank and I both turn to look at her with jaws unhinged and flapping in the breeze.

"Vi… did you just swear? Are you sure you're old enough to talk that way?" I ask, trying to infuse some humor into the moment.

"That's rich coming from you, B," she barks back. "You swear like a sailor daily."

"She behaves like one too," Hank adds with a chuckle. "Or at least that's word on the street around here."

Violet arches one dainty eyebrow my way, shooting me a questioning look.

"Patty may or may not be nursing a big old whip welt across his ass," I explain with a cringe.

"You hit him?" she shrieks.

I tip my head from side to side and pull at the neckline of my blouse. "Yeah. Hard. Like… I whaled on him."

Violet stares at me, blinking slowly like she can't quite process what I've just said. Hank covers his mouth and laughs silently into his hand, shoulders shaking and amused shock on his face.

"Billie! That's assault! They could arrest you," Violet squeaks out.

I pull her into a side hug. "They could. But it would be worth it. You'll bail me out, right, little Vi?"

Her laugh is strangled, but she hugs me back. "I love your wild side, Billie."

With the mood lightened and with Hank and Violet's help, I manage to get the trailer all loaded up and DD ready to ship. After a little pick-me-up of sweet feed, a molasses-covered grain, DD started moving around again. We confirmed he was not in fact injured anywhere and loved on him as much as we could. Hugs, pets, massages, cold boots on his legs—full spa treatment. He loaded up into the trailer quietly, probably exhausted from a trying day.

I make the long dark drive home on my own. Both Violet and Hank offered to ride with me, but I need some space. Some quiet.

When I unload him at the cottage, I walk him to his paddock like he might break. I unlatch his halter and he stays right in front of me, so I wrap my arms around his big warm neck and hug him. I stroke his shoulders, and he drops his neck down to rest his head along my back. Like I even still deserve his affection. I should have fought harder to pick my own jockey, someone I knew I could work with. I could put a chimp on this horse and he would win. I know it in my bones. And the weight of my failure makes me almost nauseous.

I stand there for I don't know how long and cry. I cry so hard I feel like I'll never catch my breath. I cry for more than just tonight. I cry because I miss my family. I cry because I'm sure Vaughn will have to fire me after everything tonight. And I cry because this beautiful soul who is standing here, letting me rub snot and mascara all over his perfect coat, still loves me despite it all, which is more than I can say for almost anyone in my life. No one has ever *chosen* me. It's always money, reputation, or work, and then I'm somewhere further down the line.

Except horses. Their love in my life is an unwavering constant.

And I've never felt so undeserving of that love as I do tonight.

My broken sleep is short. I set an alarm to check on DD every two hours, and when I finally decide to just get up for the day, I catch sight of myself in the mirror and startle. I look downright scary.

I shuffle out the back door and rest my forearms on the banister of the back porch where I have the perfect view of DD's pen. I expect to see him standing by the gate, waiting impatiently for his breakfast, but he's not. My eyes dart around his pen until I finally find him in the back corner by his shelter. He's covered in mud and lying flat out on his side, groaning.

My heart jumps into my throat, beating wildly. Horses rarely lie flat on their sides, particularly nervous ones like DD. It's just not a good defensive position. When you've been around horses long enough, you know almost immediately what this kind of behavior can mean. Equine colic, which sounds silly and is common in babies, is emergent and deadly in horses.

My morning fogginess vanishes as I jam my feet into the slip-ons I leave at the back door. It's drizzling rain, but I don't bother with a coat and barrel down the few steps off the back deck, calling out to DD, trying to keep the panic I'm feeling from overwhelming me.

Grabbing his halter and lead rope off their hook, I duck through the middle part of the fence and am at his side in no time. He raises his head a few inches at my arrival before dropping it back down to the muddy ground with a groan.

"Hey, little man," I murmur, rubbing his big round cheekbone. "You gotta get up. You're gonna feel so much better if you get up."

Gravity doesn't work as well on their digestive tracts as it does on ours, based on shape. I drop my head to his stomach. Gut sounds would be good. Dead silence is not what we want.

But it's what we've got.

I gently lift his head into the black leather halter in my hand, attaching the buckle down beside his ear, constantly telling him what a good boy he is, rubbing him, patting him, covering myself in dirt and mud. I step away, gently tugging his head a few times before he lifts it and comes into more of an upright position. He's breathing hard now, uncomfortable. But I know the sooner I can get him up and moving, the sooner I can get him over to the farm for medication and veterinary attention.

Then we will walk. We will most likely spend the entire day walking. I'll walk him until I pass out if I have to. We just need to get that intestine straightened out.

I move to stand behind his back, pushing on his ribs and giving his haunches a gentle tap. "Up we go, DD. Come on, baby. You can do it."

He sticks both front legs out in an attempt but gives up and rolls back down into the mud. Sweat soaks his neck and chest, and I am having a hard time keeping my panic at bay. Worst-case scenarios race through my head. I want to keep a positive outlook, but I'm a realist, and this is not looking good.

I pull his head back up and get behind him again, pushing desperately now, pleading with him to get up. He's groaning and sweating but is stuck with his front legs out.

I'm wishing we were at the farm. There would be someone there to help me. The medication would be closer. He'd have a better shot. But I was emotional and selfish and kept him down here at my house instead.

Fear courses through me, and I give him a good poke between the ribs while shrieking, "DD, get up!"

And he does.

With a tremendous groan, he finally gets up.

I get moving immediately, opening the gate and heading straight toward the hills behind my house to cross the soggy fields leading to the stables.

I pull out my phone and dial as I walk.

"Hello?" a groggy voice answers.

"Hank, DD is colicking. Badly. I need you to call our vet and get him down here right away."

The sound of rustling sheets filters through the line. "Okay, Billie girl. Deep breaths. I'm calling him right away, and I'm coming to you. I'll be at the ranch in twenty minutes."

"Okay, great." My voice shakes.

"It's going to be okay. If anyone can take care of that horse, it's you. Just keep him walking. I'm on my way."

Hank hangs up, and we continue our slow walk across the field. Every time DD nips at his rib cage or kicks at his tummy, I urge him forward.

When we crest the hill, I see Violet in her pajamas, running toward us with a big syringe in hand. Obviously, Hank called her. The relief I feel at seeing her there ready to help makes tears spring to my eyes. My nerves are frayed, and my emotions are running rampant.

She reaches out to DD. "Hey, poor boy. Aunty Vi is here with your medicine," she coos, coming around to his neck with the needle.

I'm a tired, shaky, sad mess, and no one should trust me with a pointy object right now. Thankfully, Violet finds a vein, and I am so grateful for her at this moment.

"Hey, B." She turns to wrap me in a hug. "You look like shit."

I laugh, and it makes me cry. I drop my head into the crook of her neck and take a few centering breaths.

"Want me to take him while you go get some coffee or something?"

"No, I think I'll just head to the indoor arena and keep walking. I want to get him somewhere warm and dry. Could you bring some brushes and a fleece blanket though?"

"Of course," she replies, spinning on her heel and jogging to get our supplies.

We get inside quickly and begin our march. The more he walks, the better, so my plan is to walk in a big oval all day long.

"Billie!" Hank calls from the other end of the ring. "Dr. Thomas has been up all night with other emergencies.

He's still in surgery and won't be able to get here anytime soon."

Anxiety wells in my throat. I feel like the edges of my vision are blurring. There are only so many vets out this far. *Fucking fuck.* I holler back at him, "Okay. Call Dr. Thorne from last night. I know she's in Vancouver, but just see what she says."

"Got it!"

"And, Hank!"

He stops to look back at me.

"I don't want Vaughn here. I know you have to tell him, but I'm too mad at the Harding brothers right now to deal with their shit. Please, whatever you can do to make that happen."

Hank gives me a terse nod before he spins on his heel to leave. He doesn't like my request, but I know he loves me enough to respect it.

CHAPTER 16

Vaughn

I've spent all morning cleaning out my grandfather's house. Or trying to. How the hell am I supposed to throw any of this stuff out? What am I supposed to do with it all? And how do I make my mind stop fixating on last night in the rain with Billie?

Wilhelmina fucking Farrington. How on earth did I miss *that*? Probably because at that age, I was holed up on the ranch with my grandfather, sheltered from the news, and far too fixated on my own family's bullshit to care much about politics or someone else's pain.

But still… another person I've come to trust. Another lie. I must be naive to be continually surprised by this.

At first, I didn't care about her past. I mean, I *don't* care about her past. But it niggles at me she wasn't forthcoming about it. People I care about keeping secrets from me seems to be a recurring theme. It bugs me more than I let on that she kept that hidden from me. On a personal level and on a professional level. She didn't consider how her past baggage might affect me or my family business. The farm's reputation is already in tatters thanks to my grandfather's dishonesty.

Which is really what this all comes back to. Dishonesty.

And that's when it hits me. Cole never overlooks background checks on employees. He would have known this from day one, unless he's letting himself slip in his old age. Cole should have been able to tell me about Billie's hidden background. I jam my finger against the screen of my phone, pulling his number up.

The phone rings twice before Cole answers. "Little brother. You snuck out early last night." Amusement sprinkles his typically cool and indifferent tone. Or at least as much amusement as I've heard from him in over a decade.

I ignore his comment and cut to the point of my call. "Did you run a background check on Billie Black?"

"Crazy Billie?" he corrects me. "I did. Yes."

"Care to elaborate on that?"

"In what regard? Don't beat around the bush, Vaughn. Passive aggressiveness is a tactic reserved for hormonal teenagers and simple-minded adults."

I press my lips together to tame the inner dread that's creeping up my spine as I come face-to-face with what my brother isn't quite saying here. "Did you know about her past? Her former identity?"

He's downright apathetic to what I've just said. "As the daughter of our most scandalous and infamous prime minister? That came up, yes."

Air lodges in my throat. Betrayal sears through me. Deep down, I know I'm probably overreacting, but I hate that I'm constantly left out of the loop. The little brother, the new kid, still at twenty-eight years old. An afterthought.

After an awkward amount of silence, I say, "Didn't think that was worth mentioning to me?"

"Well, I didn't expect you to fall in love with the psycho."

I rear back in my office chair. *What did he just say?*

I'm not…

He's trying to get under my skin, but he leaves me speechless. Am I in love with Billie Black? "I'm not—"

He cuts off my protest. "Her tracks were carefully covered. It clearly wasn't some rash decision on her part. I didn't feel like it mattered much if she was good with the horses."

I just blindly trusted that Hank brought me the best. *Hank.* He was the next person I'd be grilling about this. He must have known too. Basically, everyone around me who I care about knew, and not one thought to tell me. Talk about a dagger to the back.

I'm still silent on the phone, because I'm so angry I don't trust myself to speak.

Cole sighs, quieting his tone. "Vaughn, you're taking this personally. But, and I mean this as kindly as possible, get the fuck over it. It's time to be an adult. You need to stop holding the people you profess to care about to these idyllic black-and-white standards. It's unrealistic, and the only person you're hurting here is yourself. Humans are complex." His voice hitches uncharacteristically. "Sometimes a person needs a fresh start. This wasn't my story to tell."

It feels like my brother just slapped me. Deep down, I know he's right. But I'm not ready to admit that. I need to grapple with the bits of wisdom he just dumped all over me. I need to lick my wounds privately.

"Okay, thanks."

I hang up on him but only get a moment's peace before Hank's number flashes across the screen.

I answer with "I have a bone to pick with you."

"Pick it later." His voice is gruff and commanding. "DD's been sick all day with colic, and Billie is unmanageable. She hasn't eaten. Hasn't slept. But she doesn't want you here. Not yet anyway, so don't push your luck, son. I'm handling it, and I'll keep you posted."

CHAPTER 17

Billie

I put my head down and trudge forward. I don't know how long I've been walking when I hear voices echoing through the alleyways that lead to the covered arena. Violet has brushed DD as he walks, at least enough to get the caked-on mud off him, and he's now wearing a yellow Gold Rush Ranch fleece blanket. Somehow Violet is calm and collected, and I'm the nervous wreck. She attends to him while I stare at my feet, watching each step and the imprint that it leaves in the sand. My shoe next to his hoof, in perfect sync. His head is low and sullen, but he's marching onward, trying his best for me.

Like always.

I don't deserve him.

"Billie girl, she's here."

I look up and see Hank with Dr. Thorne and what looks like a big toolbox. I head their way with a wave. "Dr. Thorne, I'm just so glad you're here. Thank you for coming all this way."

She enters the gate, walking with precise movements toward

me and DD. Her confidence is comforting. She's completely no-nonsense, and I love that. I feed off it, trying to leech some of her strength.

"Hey, big guy." She drags her hand down his neck a few times. "How we doing?"

She pinches his skin, checking to see his level of hydration. If the skin stays peaked, they're dehydrated. If it flattens back out quickly, then all is well.

It stays peaked.

"Billie, how are you doing?"

I stare at the spot on his neck as it slowly recedes into position.

"Billie, hon." She snaps her fingers in front of me. "You okay?"

"Hmm? Yeah. Just tired."

She gives my shoulder a tight, reassuring squeeze.

"And worried. I could barely get him up out of the mud when I found him."

"Okay, we'll take care of him. I'm going to grab some fluids. We're going to try to flush him out. We want to avoid surgery if we can. You just keep him walking." She looks me firmly in the eye, grabbing both shoulders. "You're doing great."

I nod my head resolutely and get back to walking.

I am beyond exhausted. My day moves along like one of those slow-motion montages from a movie, but a boring, shitty one. It's all cut scenes of walking in big circles, reassuring DD, and switching his fluid bags. Dr. Thorne has come and gone. She has set us up with all the medication and fluids we'll need, and she's of the opinion that if he isn't getting worse, he probably won't need surgery.

I want to be relieved, but I'll believe it when I see it.

She thinks his stress reaction triggered the episode, which makes me want to kill Patrick and Cole even more. And probably just maim Vaughn for being such a fucking pushover. Idiots, the lot of them.

I'm so busy staring at the ground, I hardly notice Hank walk up beside me and drop a hand on my neck in a fatherly way.

"Billie girl, it's been hours. It's almost dinnertime. You should go take a break. Let Violet and I walk him for a bit. Have some coffee, eat some food, take a nap, whatever you need. You look dead on your feet."

"I'm fine."

"I've known you a long time, and I know that you're blaming yourself right now. You shouldn't. You've always been too hard on yourself. None of this is your fault."

I scoff at that, sniffling and looking up at the roof, willing the pooling tears to leak back into my eye sockets where they came from. "Hank, I very much appreciate you being here. I do. But this is absolutely my fault. You should go home and enjoy your day off, spend some time with your family. I'm better off by myself right now."

And then, like he's trying to make me break down, he says, "You're my family too, you know."

I can't stop the tears then, and I turn into him, into the safety and comfort of his embrace, and rest my face on his chest. I'm engulfed by his large frame, his soft plaid shirt wrapping around me like an old blanket. One large hand holds the back of my head, and the other rubs up and down my back while he shushes me soothingly.

"Shh. It's going to be okay, Billie. We got this. Shh."

I allow myself a few minutes to seek comfort in his bear hug and to find solace in his words. I don't necessarily believe them, but it feels good to hear them all the same. When I pull back, I offer him a watery smile that doesn't reach my eyes. "I'm so lucky to have you."

He just smiles at me, rubbing my shoulders like he's trying to build me up, pull me up taller, shake me out of my funk. A soft nose nuzzles at my lower back, and I turn back to offer DD a kiss on his soft forehead.

"Stop crying. You're upsetting your horse." He winks at me. "You sure you want me to go?"

"Yes. I'll call you with any updates. I know you're just down the road if I need you."

"All right, all right," he replies, waving a hand my way. "Violet, it's your day off too, little lady. Go enjoy yourself."

Violet stares back at him, alarmed. "But that leaves Billie all by herself. What if something happens? What if she needs help?"

A conspiratorial grin touches Hank's lips. "She won't, but if she does, you'll be right upstairs," is his reply as he leads Violet off the benches at the end of the arena.

She looks back at me to confirm I'm okay with this whole scenario. I nod and wave a hand at her to skedaddle.

Finally alone, I look back at DD. He seems incrementally more chipper, like his head isn't hanging so low and like he's groaning less. Come to think of it, I haven't seen him kick at his stomach in—I check my phone—about half an hour now. He nuzzles at me, and I scratch his ears before moving toward his rib cage to listen for gut sounds.

And I hear them. Faint and fleeting, but definitely there.

Relief washes over me like cool rain on a hot day. I know we're not out of the woods yet, but this is concrete proof that his condition isn't worsening. That sense of relief is cathartic, and with no one around to see me, I burrow my face into DD's shoulder and let the tears come. I haven't cried this much in years. I didn't even cry when I left home. The fact that I have barely slept in two days is most definitely a contributing factor to the frazzled state of my emotional well-being. No sleep and a roller coaster ride of emotions have whipped me up and spit me out.

I'm a fucking mess.

I sob. Those bone-deep, body-racking kind of sobs. It's an ugly cry for sure. DD wraps his neck and head toward me, almost as though he's shielding me, as I rub snot and tears and second-day mascara onto his beautiful coat. Again.

"I'm so sorry," I weep into the little bubble we've created between us.

That's when I feel a hand cup my elbow, and a jolt of electricity runs up to my shoulder. A current that feels far too raw and far too recent for me to handle right now.

"Billie, come here."

I freeze in position.

"No."

"Yes. Now," Vaughn says, and it's a command, not a request.

He uses a voice that I've only heard him try to use a few times with me. Usually, it pisses me off. But falling apart here and now, it feels more like the direction I need. Like maybe all the strength in his voice means I can lean on him instead of propping myself up so poorly.

I turn around and look at him, biting at my lips to keep them from wobbling, wiping at my cheeks to try to cover up how hard I've been crying. Like he wouldn't have heard me or wouldn't be able to see what a hot mess I am right now. He doesn't give me a pitying look, and I could hug him for that alone. I don't want anyone to see me like this, and I especially don't want their pity. It's an affront to my pride, to my whole carefully concocted carefree persona.

He puts his arms out and glares at me. "Come here."

And I go to him.

Against all my better judgment. Against everything I know about him. Against everything my logical brain is telling me to do. I collapse into his arms. And he props me up, like I knew he would. He doesn't placate me or tell me it's going to be okay. He doesn't offer me fake words or try to console me, to fix me. He just lets me be. And as memories of all our quiet moments together bubble up in my mind, I realize maybe he cares about me more than I thought.

CHAPTER 18

Vaughn

Walking in to see and hear Billie sobbing into the horse's shoulder had been an absolute gut punch. Hank told me she wasn't in good shape, but he failed to mention the part where she was absolutely falling apart. Seeing someone as strong as Billie break down and sob her apology to a horse for something I am ultimately responsible for almost brought me to my fucking knees.

The guilt. The ache in my chest at the raw pain in her voice. I knew she was more sensitive than she let on. But this. This scene could crack my chest right open and leave my heart beating at her feet.

Yeah, this hurts.

She hiccups in my arms, head nestled toward my shoulder, arms resting low around my ribs. I'm holding her as firmly as I can without hurting her, trying to absorb all her anguish, letting it seep into me. I'm the one who deserves the blame. Her sobs slow as I run one palm over her messy chestnut hair.

I glance behind her at DD. He looks tired, closing his eyes and dozing now. Like he was just waiting for someone else to get here and take care of her.

I'm not a spiritual guy or into any new age energy kind of shit, but even I have to admit there is a special connection between Billie and DD. A connection you don't see very often, the kind in books and movies.

Her very own Black Beauty.

A tiny childish part of me is envious. What would it be like to have a woman like Billie love you, trust you, and believe in you? For DD, transformative.

"Thank you," she whispers into my shirt and gives me an extra squeeze around the ribs as she burrows her head further into my bicep. Like she's trying to hide there or something. Knowing Billie, she probably is.

"Of course," I reply softly, resting my stubbly cheek on top of her soft hair.

"You probably think I'm unstable. I shouldn't cry this hard over a horse."

"I actually do think you're unstable," I deadpan, which makes her laugh but also earns me a firm poke in the ribs. "Billie, some people celebrate Mother's Day for being a 'dog mom.' *That's* unstable. Crying over a sick horse that you love isn't." I pause a beat, trying to decide if I want to profess my culpability out loud. Hating how wrong I'd been to ignore her warnings about needing the right jockey.

"Don't judge dog moms, you dick. I plan to be one someday."

I chuckle, but it's half-hearted. She's trying to redirect an otherwise uncomfortable situation with humor. Jokes are her armor, and I know she's feeling vulnerable right now. "You can't beat yourself up this hard. I'm the one who fucked everything up in the last couple days. I'm sorry. I let both you and DD down, and you both deserved better from me."

"Wow."

"That's your response? *Wow*?"

She hiccups a laugh. "Yeah. Wow. That must have physically pained you."

I shake my head, rubbing it across the top of hers. "See? Unstable."

"Thank you, Vaughn."

"There's a sandwich and a bottle of coconut water on the bench for you. Go sit and eat."

"I'm goo—" she protests, but I interrupt her.

"Billie. I said go." I point back toward the entrance.

"What about DD?" She looks back at the dozing horse, running her long fingers gently through his forelock.

"I don't know why you continue to not believe me when I tell you I practically grew up on this farm. I'm more than capable of walking a horse around in circles."

She looks me up and down with narrowed eyes. "He might not like you."

"He's falling asleep. Hank updated me on Dr. Thorne's diagnosis. Has he improved at all?"

"Yes," she says, shoulders slumping.

I take the lead rope from her hands while pointing back at the bench. "Good. Now go."

A deep sigh rattles through her chest, and she relents, turning on her heel to walk back to the doors.

I give DD a gentle rub and get his attention with a gentle clucking noise. "Wake up, fella. We need to keep marching."

He groans but follows me without much protest.

I walk, and Billie eats.

As much as I hate to admit it, I spent all night and all day thinking about her. Her warm cinnamon-scented perfume intoxicated me. It lingered in my nostrils, made me hungry for more. I replayed our kiss, her touch, the way she'd dragged my finger through her mouth. She'd been bold and then shy. Mostly, she was confusing.

She wants nothing from me, which is a refreshing challenge since my money or my clothes or my car are important requirements for the women I've spent time around.

Should probably stop letting Mommy pick your dates, eh, big guy?

I round the corner of the ring, and my eyes find Billie immediately. She looks beat, but at least she's eating. Hank called me again a few hours after telling me not to come, saying that Billie wouldn't listen to him and needed someone who could handle her when she was being a brat. I laughed and told him *no one* could handle her then.

I glance back at her, catching her looking me over.

"Thank you for dinner," she says. "I needed that."

"You're welcome."

"And… uh." She clears her throat and looks away. "Thank you for driving all the way out here to help me. I know you were staying downtown for the weekend."

"I followed you back last night."

She gives me an astounded look, like she can't believe I would do that.

"Wanted to make sure you both got back okay. You were pretty upset."

Her cheeks flush pink, and I look away.

"We should just forget about what happened last night." Her voice comes out raspy.

That will never happen. But I'll play along for now.

"I don't think I'll ever forget you cracking Patrick on the ass in a room full of owners and sponsors," I reply with a chuckle, coming to stand in front of her.

She groans, covering her face with both hands, and leans back against the bench.

"And then you went off on my brother." I shake my head in disbelief. "Best thing I've seen in a long time."

She spreads two fingers and peeks at me from behind them. "Tell me the truth. Is your brother a robot?"

A loud, genuine laughs bursts out of me. I turn to DD, who is dozing again now that we're standing still, and chuckle to myself.

"I'm serious. I thought you were an uptight prick, but you're downright sunny next to him."

That comment hits me in a way I didn't expect. Did she really think that? I look back to check if she's joking. Her cheeks twitch in an effort to hold back a small smile, and I raise an eyebrow to let her know she didn't get away with that one.

"Are we going to ignore what Patrick said?"

A shield clamps down over her features as she schools them into perfect indifference. "Which part?"

I look her dead in the eye. "The Farrington part. In all our conversations, you conveniently left out that your father is the former leader of our country."

"Ha!" Her voice bites with sarcasm. "Oh yes. That's a title I just *love* to wear like a badge of honor. I have such fond memories of being paraded around as the dutiful, gracious daughter on his national apology tour. I especially enjoyed answering reporters' questions about whether I'd seen the videos of my dad fucking hookers. Which I had, by the way, and there's not enough bleach in the world to wash those images from my mind. So I guess forgive me for not laying it all out. I ran as hard and fast as I could as soon as I could. I worked my ass off to start fresh. I'm not Wilhelmina Farrington anymore. I haven't been for a long time."

Okay. Sore spot. My mind reels all the same. From what I looked up, her name was splashed over every newspaper in the country, maybe in the world, for weeks on end. I suppose this makes a lot of things add up. Her lack of presence online, her loathing of anything she considers to be elite. I laugh as a memory springs to mind.

"What?" She sounds accusatory, defensive—laid bare in a way she doesn't like.

"Remember that time you made fun of me for having a rich-person name?" I try to hold back my laughter, but my shoulders bob, and my eyes water under the strain. "Wilhelmina fucking Farrington," I blurt out before dissolving into uncontrolled laughter.

She tries to look offended but can't hold out. In a matter of moments, we're both laughing so hard we can't even talk. Tears stream down our faces. This is the type of laughter that only comes in the wake of tension and exhaustion.

"Oh god." She wipes the tears from her eyes as our laughter subsides. "It's true."

She gazes at me, shaking her head, and I turn to look at a calmly dozing DD. "You could have told me, you know."

She clears her throat. "I know." She wrings her hands and stares at her lap. "Are you angry with me?"

She can't be serious. Maybe I was angry at first, but how could I ever stay that way when all she wants is something different for herself than all that?

"Why would I be angry with you? I don't care who raised you, Billie. The only people I'm angry with are the ones who made you feel you had to run and hide."

She looks up at me from under her lashes, nibbling nervously at her lips. Like she doesn't quite believe what I'm saying.

"I wouldn't have—I won't—betray your trust with this though. It doesn't matter. I'm all ears when you're ready to talk."

She sighs, the look of relief plain on her face. "Thank you."

"You're welcome. And also, next time, you pick the jockey."

She sits up at that, surprised by the sudden change of subject. "Seriously?"

"Seriously."

"What about Cole Harding, the 'half owner'?" She uses her fingers to make sarcastic air quotes.

"I'll handle him."

She rears back, amber eyes wide.

"Don't worry about it. Relax for a bit. I'll keep walking."

She doesn't fight me on it this time, just leans back on the bench, slides her phone out of her pocket, and huffs out a deep breath.

I walk. And I think. I think about what Billie grew up in. About everything I read this morning. Videos of her dad, the prime minister of the country, having sex and doing drugs with prostitutes blasted out all over the world. *Jesus.*

I guess she really had an idea of what I was going through with my grandfather's scandal. She didn't bat an eyelash when I told her. She didn't make me feel guilty or pathetic for holding on to hope that he might be innocent. She just… let me feel. When everyone else around me wanted me to be a certain way, she just let me be me.

DD stops, jolting me from my realization. He groans and… he poops. I never thought I'd be so excited to see horse poop. The blockage has moved, and I turn to celebrate with Billie. But what I see is Billie curled up on the bench, out cold. She has one arm under her head like a pillow and her long legs bent so that her knees dangle off the edge. The sun has set, and one of the overhead lights is shedding its neon glow over her sleeping form.

Even in this moment of excitement, I can't help but notice how young she looks right now. No jokes, no sarcasm, no fighting words. She looks peaceful but sad. Beneath it all, she always looks a little sad. A surge of protectiveness washes over me as I make my way toward her.

Coming to crouch down beside her, I run a hand through her hair, pushing it back away from her face. This close, I'm truly entranced. The light smattering of summer freckles, the perfect bow shape to that puffy top lip, so soft and feminine. Until you pair it all up with one of the worst cases of trucker's mouth ever. Yes, Billie is all dichotomies and surprises. Hard and soft. Happy and sad. Hot and cold. And I like her hot. I like her every which way.

Her unpredictability used to make me nervous. Now, the feeling of being on my toes around her excites me. She's a live wire, and I am the idiot happy to see what happens when I pick up the loose end. When those walls come down, and I know they will, she and I will light each other on fire.

Our banter went from grumpy to funny to intense. Images flit through my head like one of those flip books that make an image look like it's moving. Billie on top of me. Billie on all fours in front of me. Billie gasping my name from beneath me.

Yeah, I have plans.

I just need to get Billie up to speed.

My thumb traces her cheekbone, thinking about all the sinful things I plan to do to her, causing her eyes to flutter open.

"How long you been staring at me, Boss Man?" she mutters.

"Since day one," I whisper in her ear.

"Take the sappy shit somewhere else, Vaughn."

I snort. "There she is."

She closes her eyes and tries to wave me away. DD nudges her hip and looks at her quizzically.

"I'll take over walking. Just give me five more minutes, DD. I know you're probably sick of him."

"Billie. He pooped."

Her eyes fly open, and she sits straight up. "Come again?"

I point out into the arena where the physical evidence sits.

"Ah! Oh my god!" She bounds to her feet. "For real?"

"I mean, you can go look at it if you want?"

Her hands shoot up in the air like she's just scored an Olympic goal. And before I know it, she's launched herself at me, causing DD to jump, and wrapped her arms around my neck.

"Thank you, thank you, thank you!"

And it's the best feeling ever. Seeing her this excited? It's addictive. I want to make her this happy all the time. Okay, maybe not all the time, because I kind of like her surly side. But more often.

Definitely more often.

I smile into her hair and rest my hand over the back of her head before she pulls back to look at me, one hand resting on each of my shoulders.

"Vaughn Harding, I could kiss you right now."

Fire licks at my core almost instantly at hearing her say that. My look must change, because she's promptly walking her comment back, wide eyes trained on my predatory ones as we stand here, suspended in time and space, holding each other.

"But I won't. Because you're my boss."

"I am." I take a step closer.

"And because you're everything I promised myself I'd stay away from."

I quirk my head at her as I step again, but she surges on.

"And because Gold Rush Ranch doesn't need to endure any more scandal."

"Who says we'd be a scandal?" I inquire, inclining my head toward her and dropping my eyes to her lips.

"Are you joking? Every woman you're seen with is splashed across Page Six." She steps back from me, pressing one hand into my chest. "It's hard enough getting people to take a twenty-eight-year-old woman seriously in this business. But one who's banging her billionaire playboy boss? I'd never live it down. I've worked too hard. Given up too much."

Her words are like a bucket of ice water over hot simmering coals. The steam burns me, and the smoke chokes me. And she stands in front of me looking completely unaffected.

I never gave much consideration to how the papers portray me. Truthfully, it never really mattered to me. It certainly has never been a black mark against me. But Billie is different. It's what I like about her, and it is also what's killing me right now. I can't undo my past choices, and holding them against me stings in a way I'm not prepared for. She's right though. And that's what bites the hardest.

There's wanting something you can't have, and then there's this—wanting something and knowing you'll ruin it.

I care about her too much to do that.

I step away and watch her hand fall from my chest. When I catch her big amber eyes looking at me with sadness, I hate it. I hate the pity. But most of all, I hate that she's providing excellent reasons I can't have her.

I revert to Spoiled Brat Vaughn and shove DD's rope toward her, shaking it. "You're right. Here. Take it."

She takes it but tries to capture my hand too. I yank it away.

"Vaughn, I'm sorry," she whispers, looking stunned at my reaction.

To be fair, I'm stunned too. Twenty-eight-year-old men aren't meant to throw tantrums when they can't have something. And I'm not sure I realized how badly I wanted *her* until now. I want to hide and lick my wounds, but I also know that DD isn't completely out of the woods, and she's going to need help tonight.

Eyes trained on the ground, I turn to leave. "Don't worry about it. Glad he's doing better. Let's go." I wave over my shoulder.

"Let's go?"

"Yeah. Back to your house so you don't have to sleep on a cold, hard bench. He needs a rest, and I can keep watch at the paddock you have there."

"You really don't need to do this..." she starts.

I just shake my head and continue walking. "Keep up, Billie. It's dark out."

CHAPTER 19

Billie

It's pushing midnight when we leave the barn and head out into the dark fields. It smells like rain and fresh- cut grass, and I can't see a single star through the clouds overhead. The moon is just a lighter spot in the overcast sky.

I'm tired, but I'm fixating on the tension between Vaughn and me.

Shit is weird.

Maybe I'm not firing on all cylinders—sleeplessness and high levels of stress will do that to a girl—but I am confused.

When I told Vaughn I could kiss him, his whole face and body changed, morphed into someone a lot more dangerous. It took me aback. He looked like a predator who was about to have me as his snack. And the worst part is, in that moment, I wanted to be snacked on.

If he wasn't my boss, that is. I mean, has everyone seen that man in casual clothes? Because it's pretty much criminal. Fuck suits. Vaughn Harding wears casual clothes like one of those sexy, scruffy Calvin Klein models. Like he's just rolled out of bed and wants to take you back there with him.

I volunteer as tribute!

Maybe for one night? We could probably handle one night with no complications. We're both mature adults… Haha. Just kidding. We are not. It would ruin our working relationship, which is often tenuous at best.

I peek at him from under my lashes and admire his masculine profile. He looks mysterious, all dark features set against the blackness of the night. But I also know him well enough to tell he's simmering, a bit angry, like he could manhandle the hell outta me right now. I like that side of him, how he took control of my body in the rain last night. He walked that line of power so deftly when he waited for me to come back and kiss him. Such a turn-on. My ruined panties were proof of that. And he's obviously scrambled my brain enough that I did it.

And fuck. Last night was hot. *Worth it.*

But then his reaction to me today? That was downright dangerous. Doing it again would make things complicated. Much too complicated.

He idolized his grandfather, and this farm was that man's legacy. His identity is far too tied up in it to let it flounder. This I know. He'd resent me if I were the reason it did. So I'll admire him—and his ass—from afar. I lean back a little to take a peek, but black pants in the middle of the night aren't very effective for creeping.

I settle for his face and nibble hungrily at my lip. It's a close second in the looks department.

"Billie, you're staring." His growl cuts through my musings.

"Yeah. Sorry." Why even deny it?

He just grunts.

The night is quiet, and our sneakers squelch across the damp grass intermingled with the clip-clop of DD's feet. He's so tired. I can feel him lagging behind.

"I'm sorry," I say again.

"You said that."

"No, not for staring. Well, I'm sorry for that too, really. But I meant that I'm sorry for whatever I said before that upset you."

"I'm not upset," he snarls, shaking his head.

"Oookay," I mouth silently up to the sky.

After a few beats, he adds, "I'm sad."

Hearing him say that absolutely winds me. Like I've fallen off the swing at the park, and hitting the ground pushed all the air out of my body. What the fuck am I supposed to do with that? If shit was weird before, now it's awkward as hell.

Sad? I didn't want to make him sad. I was being realistic. I honestly didn't even think I had the power to make Vaughn sad. As his annoying employee, I pick on Vaughn, and he picks back. It's part of our game, part of our push and pull. And even if I know he's the type of guy I should steer clear of, I don't dislike him for it. I wouldn't be intentionally hurtful or spiteful because of it. He's just not what I'd *choose*.

I don't know what to say to that, so I just reach out, yank at his wrist above where his hand is shoved into his pocket, and take his big warm hand in my own. He doesn't resist. In fact, after a couple minutes, his thumb rubs absently across my palm as we walk in silence, sending a wave of goose bumps up my arm that land right on my pebbled nipples.

This is fine.

After setting DD up in his paddock, I walk to the bathroom first thing and catch sight of myself in the mirror there. Wow. *Yikes.* The yellow in my eyes highlights dark smudges, and my hair looks like the little kid in elementary school who refuses to use a brush. It appears that I have cried off all traces of mascara (win!), but that win is balanced out by the fact that my entire face is puffy and pink from crying (lose!).

The good news is that this frightening look is an excellent way to deter Vaughn from whatever has been running through his head since last night. After seeing me in the light, he's probably already imagining all the fancy well-bred women he can invite on his next date. My raggedy ass just gave him the push he needed.

The thought twists in my sternum. Like that unending throb you feel when you hit your funny bone. Why the fuck do they call it that? There is literally nothing funny about it. Or what I'm feeling right now.

This isn't funny. It's fucking insane.

I brace my hands on the counter and take a few deep breaths. I almost feel like I could fall asleep right here, standing up.

I splash my face with cold water and rub vigorously before heading back out into the living room where Vaughn is waiting. He's rotated a chair to face out toward DD's paddock and is sitting quietly facing away from me.

"You could have told me I look like trash."

"You don't," he says.

I mean, yeah. But… harsh.

Walking into his view, I jut my bottom lip out. "This"—I point at myself, gesturing up and down my body—"is really bad."

He looks over at me, sighs, and closes his eyes. "You look like someone who saved that horse's life today. That's what matters. I already know you're beautiful."

If his eyes weren't closed, he would see my mouth hanging open. Does he realize he just called me beautiful out loud? Is he joking or not? I can't tell anything anymore. Down is up, left is right, and Vaughn Harding thinks I'm beautiful.

He cracks his eyes open a slit, his expression giving away nothing. "Billie, I can almost hear you thinking. Go to bed."

"Okay," is all I can muster as I turn and walk up the stairs, stunned. The word *beautiful* bounces around in my head, weaving between all the twisty lines of confusion.

I shower. And scrub and soap and shave off what feels like two days' worth of grime and emotions. It does nothing to lessen my confusion, but it makes me so dopey I crawl into bed and fall asleep with my damp towel still wrapped around me.

I startle awake at hearing my screen door close. Whatever time it is, it's still dark outside. I listen carefully and hear muffled footsteps downstairs. Logically, I know that it's probably Vaughn, but a seed of doubt lingers. As a woman who lives alone, there is always a level of fear about noises at night.

I drag my legs out of bed and plant my feet on the floor. Creeping toward the stairs, I ditch my towel and wrap myself in my thin black robe to combat the chill that runs down my spine. I peek my head around the corner as I tiptoe down the first few stairs.

Relief courses through me at the sight of Vaughn's dark form sitting in the same chair, illuminated only by the yellow glow of the patio lights. The phone he's scrolling through illuminates his silhouette. From here, I can see row after row of pictures

I recognize of him smiling for the camera, looking painfully handsome, with a beautiful date on his arm. I scrolled through these exact pictures when he canceled dinner at my place several weeks ago. Different suits, different women, and different events for each one. And if I'm being perfectly honest, I may have looked at them once or twice since. As visual reminders of why I shouldn't ever think of Vaughn as anything other than my very nice-looking boss.

Being around Vaughn reminds me of window shopping. I'm a woman, and I'd have to be blind to not notice him. But that doesn't mean I touch him or… uh… try him on?

Yikes. Okay. Different metaphor. I appreciate art all the time, but you don't catch me rushing in to buy it. I admire it and carry on. *Ooh, aah, nice painting! Look at those brushstrokes! The colors! Oh, wow, look at the time. I better get going. The end.*

The beautiful painting in front of me tilts his head to the side and rests his temple in his palm, elbow wedged against the big cushy armrest of the brown leather chair, and exhales. His shoulders take on an angle I'm not accustomed to, like he's folding in on himself. A part of me feels like I'm intruding, but the other part of me with very few boundaries doesn't care. I pad down the rest of the steps, which catches his attention.

He locks his phone quickly and turns to look at me. "Can't sleep?" he asks with a tired rasp to his voice.

"I did for a bit. But I heard the door close and got a little freaked out." I round the corner, giving his shoulder a squeeze on the way past, and lean against the windowsill in front of him.

"I just gave DD some hay and checked on him. Seems like everything is moving well again." He pauses and inclines his head a tad to show his confusion. "Freaked out how?"

Relief floods through me at his update on DD's condition. "Like maybe someone was in the house or something."

"But you knew I was here?"

"I know." I wave him off. "Sometimes living all alone out here means my imagination runs away with things. That's why I like having DD outside, for company. My guard horse." I force out a laugh.

His brow furrows, and his eyes pinch. "I'll have an alarm system put in for you."

I roll my eyes. "Vaughn, that's overkill. I'm fine."

"I'm doing it, Billie. I don't want you feeling that way in your own home."

What a caveman.

We stare at each other, my bitch face versus his. But he gives up earlier than usual, shaking his head and looking away. He seems tense, and after catching him googling himself, I know something must be up. He's been looking away for an unnatural amount of time, like he's intentionally avoiding my eyes.

"Vaughn," I start quietly, "I can tell I struck a nerve earlier. I'm sorry if I hurt your feelings."

"You didn't." His reply is curt.

"Don't bullshit a bullshitter, Boss Man. I saw you googling yourself."

He groans and scrubs his face with both hands at my admission. "I will not dignify out-of-context photographs on the internet with a response. I know what kind of man I am."

His eyes flit back to me before dropping lower. Super great. Now I've hurt and embarrassed one of the proudest men I know.

"Talk to me. We're friends, remember?"

"No."

"No? To which one?"

"Both," he says, settling his gaze back on mine now.

"Both?" I shimmy my shoulders taller, standing to lean against the window frame, trying to shield myself. I don't want to be offended by what he's just told me. But I am.

He stares at me with no hint of a joke anywhere. This isn't our regular ribbing; he's being very direct right now. And I hate that it's making my eyes sting.

Determined not to cry in front of him, I push off the window frame to move past him. "If we're not friends, then you don't need to be here. Go home. I'll see you at work tomorrow."

He grabs my wrist before I can escape past him, stopping me in my tracks. Memories of him pinning my wrist above me last night flood my mind.

I shiver, even though all I feel is heat. And when I look down at him, I'm hit with an overwhelming sense of desire. I hoped he wouldn't notice my physical reaction to his touch, but I know he did. It's so clear that we're both burning, and I don't know how to stop it. The look on his face takes my breath away—it hurts. Makes my chest ache.

Taking in all his hard angles, those intense eyes, I'm rooted to the spot. Frozen.

"I don't want to talk. We're not friends." His words are like a paper cut. They sting but don't produce any blood. "What I want is you, straddling me, and I don't let friends do that."

He's still staring at me, holding my wrist, rubbing small circles over my pulse point. All I can hear is my own shallow breathing and the rush of blood in my ears. I have no doubt my pulse is jumping wildly beneath his thumb, dancing to his tune.

"That's a bad idea, Vaughn," I rasp out.

"Tell me why."

"I already did. I gave you a whole list of reasons," I reply, panic seeping into my voice now. But my body is already moving to stand in front of him, responding in ways that my brain can't keep up with.

"Billie, I'm not the womanizer you think I am." He drifts his other hand up the outside of my robe, starting at my knee and landing on my hip. "I go on the mostly platonic dates my mother sets up to make her happy. Because I love her, and I know she means well." He pauses, pinning me with his glare. "And I have no reason not to."

His meaning hangs in the air between us like bait on a fishing line, shiny and undulating and enthralling. He looks up at me with eyes gone black with intensity. The question dangles between us, and all I can think about is how badly I want to run my hands through his mussed hair. Just one more time. *Don't give him a reason. Keep walking.*

I step closer to him and ignore the warning voice in my head. I reach out and drag my fingers across the hair at his crown, combing back that one dark curl that always flops onto the same charming spot on his forehead. The one that is always a dead giveaway for what type of day he's having. The one that always makes him look *just* disheveled enough to melt my panties.

His eyes never leave mine, that gaze holding so much promise. His hand trails across my hip and only stops where he can palm my ass and pull me closer. That hand travels farther down to my upper thigh where he squeezes his fingers. I can feel the tip of each one, wrapped around my leg, pressing into the delicate skin of my inner thigh just below where my panties would be if I were wearing any.

Those fingers send a jolt of electricity up through my pelvis and a rush of heat back down. And to make my body completely defy my brain, he leans his beautiful head forward and presses a kiss to that ultrasensitive spot just below my hip bone and whispers against the thin silk, "Give me a reason, Billie."

A whimper escapes my lips as he continues kissing me there, dragging his teeth along the bone, making me shudder. My aching body takes over, and before I even realize what I'm doing, I drop to my knees in front of him and pull frantically at the waistband of his joggers. I don't know much, but I know I want him in my mouth. I want to feel every ridge. I want to take back control, and I want him to lose his.

Firm hands grasp my wrists. "Billie, stop."

I look up, away from where his very impressive package is straining against his pants, and pull my hands back, scrambling away from him. "I'm sorry." The reality of what I'd just been trying to do to my boss hits me with full force.

His lips tip up at one side, and he beckons me closer with his hand. "Come here."

I take a tentative step toward him, and he holds both my wrists again.

"Sit," he says, dipping his chin toward his lap.

I comply, straddling him, exactly how he specified. His clothes are soft against my bare skin as I place one knee on either side of his trim waist.

We fit perfectly.

With both wrists still locked in his hands, I'm unable to adjust myself, and the front slit of my robe slowly falls open as I spread my legs around him, not leaving much to the imagination even in the blackness that surrounds us.

He groans, watching intently, eyes smoldering, and tongue darting out to tease the seam of his lips. Seeing him admire my body so openly is dizzying. I can feel the wetness between my legs, and I know he can see it too.

His quads are hard and unrelenting beneath me, but the erection pressing up into my ass is even harder. I grind down, rocking my hips against him, eliciting a growl from deep in his chest. He grabs my hips to stop the motion, and I let my hands come to rest on his pecs, whose solid definition I can feel through his thin T-shirt.

"Fuck," he says on a shaky breath while staring down at where I'm exposed before lifting his head to look me in the eye again. A look that smolders like hot black coals. Coals I'm probably about to get burnt on.

I bite at my lips nervously. "I'm going to regret this tomorrow."

"No, Billie." His hands stroke me. "I'm going to eat that perfect pink pussy and then put you back to bed. And tomorrow? Tomorrow all you're going to think about is how good you felt with my tongue inside you."

Breath hisses through my lips. Holy fuck. I am no virgin, but Vaughn just made my cheeks flame like one. Turned my entire body to flame, really. My brain too, since it seems to have melted into a puddle of poor decisions that I am about to happily roll around in.

Vaughn's hands slide sensuously up and down my back, leaving a trail of goose bumps and singed nerve endings in their wake. I can barely think. One hand moves up to grip a handful of my hair, and he pulls me into a kiss. A kiss I expected to be hot and rough, but it's soft and searching. He's masterful, playing my needy body like an instrument he's perfected over the years. And at this moment, I don't even care. Why mess around with a bumbling boy when I can play with an expert?

His tongue darts into my mouth. Teasing. Seeking. Asking for more this time rather than taking. His left hand has slogged its way up my stomach to my breast. His thumb rubs back and forth across my nipple while he grips my hair and explores my mouth.

I surrender, and not a single part of me objects to this right now.

"Say you want it, Billie," he rumbles against my lips with a nip.

So fucking bossy. Does he have to ruin this by giving me directions?

"Can't you tell?"

He tugs my hair so that I'm forced to look him in the eye. "No. I want to hear you say it. I want to be sure."

And with the way he's looking at me right now, I'd say anything. His eyes are like chocolate fondue. Hot and molten. I want to spread it all over my body and have him lick it off. His hair is wild and his five-o'clock shadow gives him that slightly rough look and feel I love.

Not love. Correction, that I'm a big fan of. I like rough Vaughn, more so than polished Vaughn. Actually, I like the dichotomy of his two sides and how quickly he can switch. Do I want it? Fuck yes, I want it.

"I want it." My body shudders at my admission.

"What do you want?" he muses with an evil glint in his eye and a knowing smirk on his lips.

I know he's trying to throw me off balance here. We're both constantly doing that to each other. I like the challenge, so I bat my eyelashes at him and lean in toward his ear, dragging my teeth along his stubbled jaw as I go. I try to speak low, but it comes out loud in the quiet early morning hours.

"I want your tongue inside me." I pick his hand up and drag it down my body, placing it right on the wetness between my legs.

His muscled chest rises and falls now, and his fingers move of their own accord, exploring my folds, brushing across my clit.

"I want you to eat this perfect pink pussy."

Almost instantly, he shoves one finger inside me. My body bucks as he curls it around to press right into that one spot.

My head falls back, and breath rushes out of my lungs. His hard cock presses into my ass as his firm hand coils in my hair, and that strong finger pushes inside me. The sensations collide. He overwhelms me. My nerve synapses sing. And before I know it, I'm wrapped into him while he grips my ass and carries me up the stairs, taking every second step.

I barely even have enough time to think. *What on earth am I doing?*

CHAPTER 20

Vaughn

I feel like a caveman as I carry Billie up the stairs. Or maybe a Viking who, after months of raiding, has finally gotten his hands on the treasure he wants the most.

I'm not even fighting this anymore. Fuck work. Fuck my family. Fuck what I thought I wanted.

I want Billie Black.

In fact, I've never craved a woman as much as I crave her. Her multiple personalities, her filthy mouth, her long legs and perfect round ass. I'm done pretending. Done holding myself back. Done sulking about it.

Tonight, I'm going to make her come harder than she ever has before. I'm going to own her body. Show her what she's missing. And then I'm going to tuck her in and make her yearn for more. I'll dole it out in pieces. Like little breadcrumbs on a path she'll have to follow. I will not rush and give her the satisfaction of thinking I don't take this seriously.

Because I do.

Those pictures? Those other women? They don't mean shit. And I'm happy to prove it.

I'm not stupid, and I know her well enough to understand that no matter what I do tonight, she's going to freak out tomorrow. I'm well prepared to get a different version of Billie in the morning. She won't be the molten, hungry, pliant version of her I have right now. But I'll enjoy this while I have it, and I'll prove to her this Billie should come out to play with me more often.

Because this is a game I intend to win.

I want to throw Billie down and ravage her, but I also want to treat her like porcelain. I don't want to break this tenuous agreement we seem to have arrived at. She puts up a tough facade, plays up her peppy personality, but I see the sad girl she hides under there. The shy, mistrustful one who's had to fight tooth and nail to get to where she is and will beat a stranger's ass with a whip.

I lay her down on the bed and move over her, resting my elbows on either side of her head. I kiss her again. Reverently. Her lips are putty beneath mine, open and eager. Her moans and sighs are like lightning strikes on dry grass. Fuel for my fire. I want more. I want to hear her lose control and scream my name. I want to imprint this in my mind. On my body… on hers.

I retreat from her lips to watch her face. Moonlight through the window showcases her delicate features, illuminating all the feminine angles and dips across her cheeks, at the base of her throat, and along her collarbones. I want to lick each one.

Her eyes glow amber, catlike in their color and shape, and they search my face with an openness I haven't seen before. Her full, heart-shaped lips are slightly parted, and I can't help but imagine pressing my cock there. Watching it slide between her lips. Watching those feline eyes go wide. Feeling her moan vibrate through me as she swallows my hard length.

Just thinking about it has me impossibly hard. She hasn't even touched me, and I'm about ready to explode. Across her face or those full tits. But I have a plan, and painting her with my come will have to wait for another time. Because I'm just getting started.

I stand up and look down, towering above her. Her beauty, the wanton look on her face, almost undoes me. My breath seizes in my chest. She's splayed out beneath me for the taking, all long lean limbs with that thick chestnut mane spread around her like a halo.

Like the most delicious dessert, ready for me to devour.

She doesn't shy away from my gaze as my eyes roam her body. The thin, black, poor excuse for a robe she's wearing doesn't leave much to the imagination. A deep V runs from her shoulders, just covering her nipples, to where it ties around her slender waist. From there, a mirrored V runs down her toned thighs, barely covering her.

I grab one end of the tie around her waist and yank. The knot unravels easily, and I hook a finger under each panel of the robe and drag it back, exposing her smooth moonlit body.

I know Billie is hard on her appearance. I didn't miss the self-deprecating way she referred to herself as an Amazon or acted like I'd be horrified to see her with unbrushed hair and a clean face. But she couldn't be more off base. Spread out beneath me, naked and wet for me, all I can think is *mine.*

Perky breasts. Just a handful. All I need. Toned shoulders and arms, flared hips, firm stomach and thighs, all from years of riding and manual labor on a farm. I'm not sure how I haven't found her completely irresistible since day one.

Was I blind? She looks damn near perfect to me.

She looks like no other man should ever enjoy this view again. If anyone ever made her feel anything short of stunning and supremely fuckable, they are idiots.

I kneel at the edge of the bed, right in front of her, ready to worship at her altar, and I don't miss the way she wets her bottom lip as I do.

I drag my hands along her calves and rotate them under her ass, right between her bare skin and the soft, thin fabric of her robe.

"Scoot down, Billie."

She lifts her head to look at me but says nothing. Her eyes say it all. Her breaths morph into pants that rattle her chest. Her pelvis pops up much too slow, and my impatience takes over. I grab her by the hips and pull her down, eliciting a gasp.

With her ass close to the edge of the bed, knees folded up, and heels pressed into the mattress, I rub a thumb over each hip bone and hold her there, exposed. "Tell me what you want."

"I... I want you to keep going," is her stuttered, breathy response.

Hearing her say she wants it, wants me, makes my cock swell and my heart quake in my chest. Billie is so guarded, so untouchable, this admission feels like something else altogether.

I press a gentle kiss to the inside of her knee. "I can do more." Don't have to tell me twice.

I hook my hands beneath her knees and spread them, kissing my way up the inside of her soft thigh as I hook one leg over my shoulder. Her pussy glistens now. This close, I can see that she is soaked. *I did that to her.*

"Fuck, Billie. You look edible."

She turns her head to the side, covering her face with one hand to stifle the moan she can't hold back. *Sweet girl, you don't know what you're in for.*

I place her other heel back on the bed and spread her wider for me. Driving myself wild. I am truly torturing myself here. Both of us, probably.

I run one thumb up through her folds, brushing gently across her clit at the top of my stroke. Watching her velvet skin move around me. Her hips buck off the bed. I rub again and watch her squirm and writhe. So responsive. So sensitive. I dip the pad of my thumb into her pussy and feel the leg that's now slung over my shoulder tremble.

"Vaughn. Please." She moans.

"Please what?" I ask, watching the top joint of my thumb pump in and out of her, slick and tight.

She pushes up onto her elbows, the wild look in her eyes reflected in my own. "I need more. Give me more."

Without breaking eye contact, I slowly drag my thumb back out of her and swirl it across her sensitive bud. Her head drops back as she cries out, pressing her round tits up into the air like the embodiment of ecstasy. I love watching her.

Focusing back down between her legs, I pull her closer and drag my tongue through her core. Slowly.

I faintly hear her: "Fuck, yes." Her entire body shivers around me.

That tremor is all it takes to snap the fragile grip on my control. And I'm pressing her legs open. Devouring her. Reaching up to manhandle her breasts. Rolling her hard nipples between my thumb and forefinger. She thrashes around me in pleasure. Her unfiltered words are a stream of consciousness, of desire, that stoke the fire burning inside me. "Keep going. Don't stop. Harder. More. I want you to fuck me, Vaughn."

I should have known she'd be just as vocal in bed as she is out. She's begging for it. And my cock is so hard. Harder than it's ever been. It hurts. And Billie tastes like heaven on my tongue. So I don't even care.

Both her legs curl around my neck, pulling me closer. Her hips gyrate, pressing herself into my mouth shamelessly. I fucking love it.

"Vaughn, I'm so close," she pants out at me, entranced by the show happening between her legs.

I stop and look up at her wickedly.

She whimpers. "I said, 'Don't stop.'"

I smirk and remove one hand from where it's been gripping her ass cheek. Then two fingers are there, and I thrust them in with one hard stroke.

Her head tips back again as she cries out, "Fuck."

Fuck is right. Fuck, I love watching that.

I focus back down on my fingers. Setting a rhythm. Pushing and pulling. Watching them move in and out of her wet heat.

"Oh god," is all it takes for me to add my mouth back into the mix, swirling my tongue around and pressing down on her bundle of nerves.

Billie's body is tight and writhing beneath my ministrations. She pinches her nipples. *Good girl.* I can feel the tension in her pelvis building. Like a coil waiting to release. To fire off. To explode.

And then she does.

"Oh my god. Vaughn! I'm—"

Everything around me clenches. Her legs. Her pussy. And her hands, which are now in my hair, pulling me into her.

Vibrations rack her body as I pump my fingers and lap at her, drawing out her orgasm for as long as I can.

Eventually, her body relaxes around mine. And the enormity of what we've just done hits me.

Time stands still. I'm wrapped up in Billie—her heavy breathing, her skin, her scent—and I realize this time, it's different. With Billie, it's *more.* My cock is about to self-destruct, and all I can think about is kissing her, holding her, and making her come again. And again.

Watching her fall apart all around me must be the most beautiful thing I've ever seen. Months of buildup, months of feelings, all toppling over into the single most satisfying sexual encounter of my life.

I am so fucked.

CHAPTER 21

Billie

Looks like Vaughn and I were both right.

It's six in the morning, and I'm wide-awake, freaking out about last night but also very fixated on remembering his sinful tongue. We took turns checking on DD every hour, and every time one of us would crawl back into bed, he'd pull me into the curve of his body and press a kiss to my hair.

I push the heels of my palms into my eye sockets before I look over beside me where Vaughn is still sleeping. He is breathtaking. Literally. My breath hitches in my chest when I study him lying there, looking like a god in the filtered morning light. *The god of pussy eating.*

I can't decide what's better: dangerous-looking Vaughn in the moonlight last night, cocky and panty-melting, or peaceful-looking Vaughn in the golden glow of the morning light, all warm skin and hard lines. Soft breaths, topped off with that signature amaretto smell.

Maybe that's why I feel drunk right now. I'm drunk on Vaughn and poor decision-making.

I'm usually adept at separating feelings from sex, but this is new, and I'm panicking a little.

Okay. A lot.

Over the years, Hank has implied I may have commitment issues. And the nosy fucker might not be all wrong.

Cheers, Mom and Dad! You sent me out into the world with something after all.

Last night, Vaughn, the epitome of every man I've ever avoided, strung me up and flayed me. Ripped my chest wide open. Made me come like a freight train. We didn't even have actual sex—though I vaguely remember begging for it.

Oh god. I *begged* for it.

Cringe. Cringe. Cringe.

He will hold that over my head forever and ever once we get back to our regular working relationship—because that's definitely happening.

One night only. Show's over, folks.

One night that will not wash easily from my memory. The way he touched me. Licked me. Bit me. *Owned* me. That will be burned into my brain and body for years to come. I've had good sex and bad sex. I'll even say that I've had great sex. (Irish accents just take dirty talk over the top, ya know?) But last night was otherworldly. I squeeze my thighs together just thinking about it. My skin burns at the memory of his stubble grazing my sensitive inner thighs. He was masterful.

Which is why I didn't give him the boot. He tried to leave, walk back to the barn and then drive home before dawn. Dumbass. I called him one too.

"Don't be a dumbass. You're not driving on dark country roads after pulling an all-nighter. Get in here." I held open the blanket and moved over to make space for him.

He seemed too big for a queen-size bed, but it worked. He looked at me suspiciously and said, "Okay, but I'm not going to fuck you," with a stupid cocky smirk on his face. *Prick.*

And then I watched him undress in the dark, with only the silvery light filtering through the windowpane. I knew his body was going to be good (I like to think that I'm a connoisseur of checking dudes out), and I copped a feel here and there.

But it was really something else.

He exceeded my expectations. I had ideas of what Vaughn did in his free time, which mostly involved boning every woman he comes across, but I'm thinking I might be wrong. Because no one looks that good without working out for at least a couple of hours every day. No. One.

Then he *cuddled* me. And I wasn't sure what to do. So I just lay there and took it like a champ. I expected him to just lie down and fall sleep. Not prowl into bed wearing skintight boxers, kiss me like we were exchanging souls, making me taste what we'd just done, and then wrap me in his arms while peppering soft kisses across my bare shoulder.

That part was a surprise. A pleasant surprise.

I soak him in again now, letting my eyes roam over his sleeping form. Trying to imprint the image in my memory. A fun story to tell my grandkids one day. Or whatever.

I'm overachieving. I bagged an Adonis for one night. Hard lines, impossibly broad shoulders, biceps I'd like to sink my teeth into, that V disappearing beneath the duvet, and a smattering of black curls. He is just plain masculine.

That growly, bossy voice rumbling between my legs.

Fuck. I am such a goner.

I drag myself out of bed, wrap my discarded black robe around my body, and pad downstairs. First, I check DD, who appears to be comfortably dozing standing up in a paddock with a couple poops in the corner.

Excellent news.

Second, I make coffee and plan out what I'll say to Vaughn when he wakes. While I am prepping myself to be cool and not just awkward as fuck, I hear vibrating and look around for my phone. Of course, I've misplaced it. I am a fucking mess after all.

Having checked over the kitchen, I end up in the living room, eyes landing on the offending chair from last night. Where my whole debacle started.

The black butt end of my phone is sticking out from between the seat cushion and the arm. *Hallelujah.*

I pull it up and go to open the screen, planning to send out a flurry of update texts. But my thumbprint doesn't work. Neither does my code. And as I reset to the phone screen, I realize this isn't my phone at all. It's Vaughn's. Makes sense that it might have fallen out of his pocket while I mauled him last night. I mean to leave it on the counter, but his waiting text message is staring me in the face. And when I tap the screen, the entire text pops up.

Mom: Good morning, honey. Just wanted to remind you that Emma Breland will accompany you to the gala next Saturday. I spoke to her at the tennis club yesterday, and she's looking forward to it. Sweet girl. She's planning to wear pink, so maybe you could wear something that will match?

Is this woman for real? Does she think they're going to prom or something?

And the really insecure part of me is also wondering why the fuck Vaughn would make date plans with another woman if he really wants to be more than friends with me.

He's your boss, not your boyfriend, you sad sap.

I shouldn't be surprised, really. This is what these kinds of guys do. I saw it growing up, and obviously my dad was exhibit A in obscuring the truth and philandering. Vaughn said all the right things last night to break down my guarded exterior, and I fell for it.

Hook. Line. And sinker.

Do I really think Vaughn is the man-slut I originally imagined? No. I don't think he lied about that. But I don't like being made a fool of. I've experienced enough public humiliation to last me a lifetime. Don't tell me I'm what you want when you've got other girls lined up a few days from now.

I do think he is a twenty-eight-year-old man stuck under mommy's thumb though. It's one thing for her to keep setting him up with random women and another thing for him to keep humoring her when she does it. She might mean well, but when someone is continually putting you in a position you profess not to like, the onus is still on you to tell them you don't like it.

Vaughn has no backbone with his mom, and I'm not here for it. I've got enough mommy and daddy issues of my own to work out without taking on someone else's. I don't need another project in my life. He can figure it out on his own.

I pour myself a cup of piping hot coffee. Dark roast. Lots of cream. And I lean against the counter to take that first heavenly sip. No other sip tastes as good as that very first one in the morning. I close my eyes and savor it, sighing and steeling my backbone, preparing myself to be mature but removed when he wakes. I'm a big girl. I don't have any expectations after one night of fooling around. We're not getting married. He doesn't owe me shit. So I'll smile at the memory and carry on.

I feel good about my conclusion and satisfied with my plan going forward. We're just an employee and her boss who fell into each other in a moment of weakness. A moment that ran high on emotions and low on sleep. Now, back to professional Billie. The Billie who's going to win herself a Denman Derby with the little black horse outside.

By the time Vaughn comes down the wooden stairway, completely dressed but still looking like a sex-mussed god, I've fed DD, tracked my phone down, and fired off all the messages I need to. I have a full cup of coffee in me, and I'm feeling more like myself.

Like smart, self-sufficient Billie.

"Hey." The corners of his sinful lips tip up as he prowls toward me, eyes roaming my body in a knowing way. In a greedy way.

Heat builds at the base of my spine in response.

I'm honestly pathetic. I can't even help myself around this guy.

"Hi," is my intelligent response when he cages me in against the counter with his arms. The scent of his skin wraps around me, plunging me back into the feel of him all over my naked body last night. The way he made me squirm and buck and beg.

His stubble brushes up against my jaw, and I shiver as he whispers in my ear, "Are you freaking out yet?"

I can't help the way my body responds to his. Especially now that I know what he's capable of. Which is why I overcompensate by smiling too cheerily and clearly state, "No! I'm great!"

His head tilts, assessing me. His intelligent dark eyes scan my lighter ones, clearly not buying my line.

"Billie..." His lips graze up over my cheek and brush against mine. "Don't lie to me."

He kisses me more firmly, and my traitorous body arches into him happily. I press one hand into the center of his chest and push him away, even though my body is screaming at me to pull him closer.

"I need to get dressed and head down to the barn. I'm meeting Dr. Thorne there in an hour." I brush past him, forcing my legs to move away from the sanctuary of his arms.

He turns to follow my retreating form with a confused look on his face. "Take the day off, Billie."

I wave him off from over my shoulder as I start up the stairs to get dressed. "Nah. It's all good. I'll sleep tonight. Your phone's on the counter. I found it in the chair." And then because I'm not as mature as I like to think I am, I toss out, "There's a text from your mom."

CHAPTER 22
Vaughn

FAN-FUCKING-TASTIC. A TEXT FROM MY MOM. I REACH FOR MY phone, dread creeping up my spine as I read the message.

Jesus.

Her timing is impeccable. I have to hand it to her. I finally start breaking down the walls around one of the most closed-off women in the world, and my mom sends a text about setting me up on a date with another woman.

A date I have no intention of partaking in.

Especially after last night.

It's no wonder Billie shot out of here with that too-sunny, awkward smile on her face. She was totally freaking out, and that text was the cherry on top.

Unfortunately for Billie, I won't scare off that easily. Her wounded pride over a silly text will not be enough to deter me. I've had a taste, and I want more. *A lot more.*

I'm a levelheaded, patient man. A pragmatic man. I may not be accustomed to being the one doing the chasing, but I've never been so set on any woman in my life. I'll play the long game with Billie.

She's worth it.

I poke my head into her room. "Billie, I'm running home to take a shower and change. And then I'm coming back."

"You don't need to do that! I'm all good. Bye!"

Her fake enthusiasm makes me roll my eyes. With her childhood laid out in the open, I'm on to her now. That bright, cheery facade is a cover, that much is becoming abundantly clear, and I'm going to pry it off, piece by piece. Get to the moody, temperamental woman underneath. That's the Billie who intrigues me. The Billie I want.

I'm barely buckled up before I'm barking, "Call Mom," at my Bluetooth system.

The loud ringing sounds through the speakers, followed by my mom's cheery greeting. "Vaughn! Such nice timing. I'm in the car with your brother. We're going for coffee. Want to join us?"

This is her new thing, intentionally ignoring the fact that I'm not living in the city anymore.

"Hi, Mom. Not today. I'm at the ranch, remember? I do need to talk to you though."

"Sure, honey. What's up?"

I opt to just blurt it out. "You're going to have to stop setting up dates for me. It's gone on long enough now. No more."

Awkward silence.

"I… Vaughn, I'm sorry. I was just trying to help."

I sigh. My relationship with my mother is strained at best. On one hand, I don't want to make her feel worse than she already does. I'm not oblivious enough to think that she doesn't live with intense guilt for handing me over to my grandfather and drowning herself in a bottle for few years in the wake of my father's death. But this making up for her years of absence by smothering me as an adult stunt has got to end. I have to confess, I'm worried that without it, we'll have no common ground. We'll be even more estranged than we already are. But that's a bridge I'll cross later.

"I know, Mom. But it's not helping anymore. Do you want me to call Emma Breland and cancel, or will you?"

I feel bad canceling. I've known Emma Breland for years. We've attended several events together as *friends*. It's not her fault my mom intrudes beyond what's normal. It's not her fault I've been too big of a pushover to put a stop to it either.

"You can't humor me one last time? She really is lovely, Vaughn. It's a good connection to make for the farm. I know you get along we—"

I take a deep breath. Is she serious right now? "Mom. Stop it. I said, 'No more.'"

I can hear my brother's evil cackle in the background.

"Am I on speakerphone?"

"Hello, brother," Cole responds, failing to hide the amusement in his voice.

"Mom, I have the perfect solution for you. Get Cole to take Emma to the gala. He's overdue for a date."

No chuckles this time. I smile inwardly, loving ribbing my older brother. He's made it through more than most people ever will, but he came back out the other side cool and removed. Unreachable. It's time he dips a toe back into the dating pond.

"Don't pick on your brother." And it's time my mom stops tiptoeing around him too. "I'll speak with Emma. I'm sure you'll see her there."

I roll my eyes. The woman is truly impossible. "Mom, I'm not coming."

"Why not?" She sounds truly aghast.

"Because I'm not ready yet. I'm busy. I'm happy out at the ranch. I need more time before I step back into the vipers' den."

She sniffles, not liking my answer but also trained to not ruffle feathers or make a scene. "Whatever makes you happy, darling."

"Great. Talk later," I say before hanging up and gunning it down the back roads to my house.

Billie has been avoiding me all week. Or that's how it feels, even though I know she's been spending her days driving to and from the track in Vancouver, training the horses we have down there now that the suspension has lifted.

I'm hiding out in my office at the farm. Totally failing at proving to her how badly I want her. That I'm serious about her. I had big ideas in my head about what I was going to do. Grand gestures I was going to make. But I realize I'm out of my depth here.

My feelings for her scare me. They've paralyzed me.

Basically, I'm a total pussy.

Close a high-stakes business deal? No problem. Fire someone? I'm your man. Talk to a girl I like and respect? I guess I'll just crumble instead.

People taking off on me when things go wrong is common. My mom. My brother. I've been here before. But somehow with Billie, it's worse.

I've seen her around the farm, always with that forced happy look on her face, but she's constantly armored up with someone else. Constantly with one of her sidekicks, Violet or Hank, and impossible to get alone. And I'm too chicken to just pull up to her house when she clearly doesn't want to be around me.

Short of groveling, I'm too inexperienced with relationships to know what to do next.

Plus, I don't grovel.

So when I get a text saying she has some things she wants to talk to me about, I breathe a sigh of relief. She's coming to me. *This* is familiar footing.

I fidget while I wait for her. Organizing my desk. Setting things just right. Running my hands through my hair. I'm nervous. Excited. Like a little kid.

Knock, knock, knock.

My head snaps up to meet her amber gaze as she stands in my doorway. Chestnut-brown hair and golden eyes. Everything about her is warm and sensual, like velvet.

"Come on in."

"Thanks for seeing me," she says formally, awkwardly.

"Of course," I say, like a total chickenshit. "What's up?"

"I've found a jockey for DD," is her reply as she comes to sit in a chair across from me.

"Okay." That's not what I thought we were going to talk about.

"It's Violet," she continues.

I take a minute to pivot, to realize we're talking about business rather than anything personal. Rather than *us*.

"Little country bumpkin Violet?"

"Don't be pretentious, Vaughn." She sniffs. "She's excellent with the horses. Gifted, really. And she's been working toward her license. All I have to do is sign off on her riding hours, and she'll be set."

Okay, she's got my attention now. I lean forward on my desk, steepling my hands beneath my chin. Trying not to be *pretentious.*

"Billie… she's… well, she's very young. Very inexperienced. Has she ridden in a single race? And you're just going to throw her up on a derby-contending horse to find her footing?"

"She is." She holds her hands up as though she's surrendering. "That's all true. But I've had her up on DD all week. He loves her. We can't take any chances with how sensitive he is. You know that as well as I do." Billie pierces me with a knowing look. "He's only got so many races in him. He's not a run-every-weekend horse. And she'll stay out of his way. Let him do his thing. You should see them together. It's… well, it's amazing."

I groan and rub my hands across my face, scrubbing, before pushing them back through my hair.

How did I end up here? Betrayed and abandoned by the man I admired most. Hiring a wild card of a trainer for his farm—his tarnished legacy. And now about to put a completely green jockey on my most valuable horse—this farm's only possible saving grace.

This is not the organized and logical approach I like to take to things. These decisions… they make little sense.

I am losing it.

"I… I don't know," I reply honestly.

She just stares back at me with determination painted all over her dainty features, and I know deep down that I won't deny her this.

"Do you trust me, Vaughn?" she asks with a quirk of her head.

Trust her? I more than trust her. Looking at her now, she's strong and resolved, saying what she wants and fighting for it. Not some giggling heiress amenable to everything I say or do. She's her own person. So thoroughly. So unapologetically.

I admire the hell out of her. Warm foreign feelings hit me like a ton of fucking bricks.

"Yes," I reply. My eyes search hers. It's true, but my mind is reeling with the realization that I would give this woman anything she wants, which is hilarious, because she might be the one woman I've ever met who wants absolutely nothing from me.

"Trust me with this. I won't let you down."

I remain silent, wanting to believe her but warring with my current frame of mind, which tells me people I love aren't always who I think they are. That they can't always be trusted.

I had my grandfather up on a pedestal. There's nothing I wouldn't have done for that man. Nothing I still wouldn't do for him to restore his reputation. And then he turned out to be so different from the idealistic image I created of him in my mind. I'd been so blindsided. How does one man misjudge one person so completely?

But Billie isn't him, and I don't want to spend my life wallowing in his betrayal. I don't want to be the sad, quiet guy with granddaddy issues.

So I leap and decide to trust the woman sitting in front of me, lit up with excitement. *I want that.* I want to feel like *that* again.

"Okay."

"Okay?" she asks, disbelief soaking through her voice.

How can I say no to her when my reward is *that* look on her face? That sparkly look, where she shines from the inside out. Where she glows. That special look she has that's reserved for all things horses. I want her to look at me like that. I want to bottle that up and drink it. Save it for the days when I'm feeling gloomy and generally unlovable.

She jumps up wearing a Cheshire cat grin on her face, doing small claps with her long elegant fingers. Fingers I want back in my hair and wrapped around my cock.

Fuck. Everything this girl does is a turn-on. *Her fingers, for crying out loud.* I mentally chastise myself. *Pathetic.*

She's like catnip for me. I lose my mind around her.

"Thank you, Vaughn," she singsongs, heading toward the door. "I'll get to work on updating his entry papers for the next race. You won't regret it."

"I know," I reply, because it's true. In the months I've known Billie Black, I've seen her grit and determination. I've seen her hard work in action. When she sets her mind to something, she makes it happen.

Watching her leave, I scramble for something to say to make her stay and talk. "Billie…"

"Yeah?" Her brow quirks up as she grabs the doorframe and looks back at me.

"Do you have plans this weekend?"

The psycho fake mask slips over her cheerful face. I cringe inwardly, realizing how badly that one brief text must have stung after our night together.

"I do."

I take a deep breath, steeling myself, wanting to find my own date for the first time in a long time. Not just any date either. I want Billie.

"Do you…?" I thump my chest with a fist and clear my throat. "Like you're going out?"

Her body stiffens. "Yup. Like I said. Plans." She walks away without looking back.

I feel heat flourish across my cheeks and my heartbeat in my ears. How the hell did she go from writhing beneath me, begging me to fuck her, to having "plans" in a matter of five days?

Have I blown my opportunity with one thoughtless text that was completely out of my control? I feel like I know her better than that. She isn't that thin-skinned, but she is skittish about men. She made that much clear. Which leaves me with one obvious alternative: sweet Billie is lying to me. Trying to push me off her trail. Trying to cover her tracks.

But she's too late. If I am the predator, she is my prey, and I already had a taste I can't forget. I'm coming back for more, whether or not she realizes it.

I'm not tiptoeing around her anymore.

CHAPTER 23

Billie

I'M AN IDIOT.

Why did I say that? Of course I don't have any plans. All I do is fucking work at Vaughn fucking Harding's fucking farm. I have no social life to speak of.

And now I've backed myself into a corner.

Like a big fucking idiot.

I hide in an empty stall down the hall from his office, scrubbing my hands over my face and trying to catch my breath, because until now, I've been able to avoid the thought of him out with some gorgeous, suitable girl in pink.

I'm mad at myself for lying, for acting like a total chickenshit. And I'm mad at him for asking me what I'm doing, totally rubbing it in. He has some serious nerve taking me to bed and still planning a date with another woman. And he hasn't said a word about that to me since he left that morning. He *knew*, and he hasn't said shit. Not that it should surprise me. This is par for the course with spoiled man-children like Vaughn Harding.

If I'm being completely honest, I'm offended he hasn't gone out of his way to talk to me this week. I know I've been in Vancouver at the track until late most days, but still…

I secretly want him to drive up to my front door, press me against a wall, and kiss me breathless. I want to see that manicured facade slip. I want all that testosterone lurking beneath the surface to spill over. I want him to *choose* me. I want him to work for it.

I need him to man up, and he didn't. And now I'm disappointed. Which is stupid, seeing as how he's my boss and one of Vancouver's most eligible bachelors. I have no good reason to be disappointed, no right to it. But here I am, lying about having a date just to spite him. And I just shot myself in the foot because of course, there's no date to speak of.

I need help. Professional help. But for now, Violet will have to do. I fire off a text message to meet me at DD's paddock. By the time I arrive there, she's already waiting for me, a concerned look on her dainty face, twisting her hands.

"What's wrong?" she blurts out as soon as I'm close enough to hear her.

"What are you doing tomorrow night?"

"What? Nothing. Why?"

"Great. Let's do something."

"You sure you want to hang out with a lowly groom?" she quips.

My cheek quirks up. I love delivering good news. "I don't… but the new jockey for local sensation Double Diablo will do."

Her eyes are round like saucers as she stares back at me, her serious little cherubic face frozen.

"All righty then, Vi. That's not the reaction I was expecting."

"This isn't funny, B. Are you joking?" she whispers, color draining from her face by the second.

"Why on earth would I joke about this? I'm evil but not that evil. Congratulations! We have promoted you. Vaughn and I just need to sign your papers. And you need to submit for your license. And probably start obsessively weighing yourself leading up to race day."

Her mouth opens and closes, but no sound comes out. She looks like a precious little fish out of water.

"I mean, you're still my bitch," I joke, "which is why you have to be my date tomorrow night."

"I... okay," Violet responds breathlessly.

I throw my head back and laugh at her. "That's all you have to say?"

Her smile cracks open, huge on her small face, and both hands come up to cover her mouth, muffling her giggles. Her shoulders shake with the force of her disbelieving laughter as it pours out of her. She looks so damn happy; it makes my cheeks hurt with the intensity of my smile.

I open my arms, offering her a hug, and she's there almost instantly, squeezing me right back.

"Billie. This... this is too much. I don't even know what to say."

I push her back and grab her shoulders. Her eyes sparkle with unshed tears, which is making my eye sockets burn in response. "Violet," I say as I shake her gently, "you deserve this. You've worked so hard. You're unflappable and calm. Something that both the horses and I need."

She chuckles at that.

"It is not too much. You're here before anyone else, and you leave after everyone else. You've put more blood, sweat, and tears into this career than almost anyone I know. Never, never sell yourself short. Take it, own it, and don't for a second think you haven't earned every bit."

Tears leak out over her long lashes; they're shimmering on the tops of her round cheekbones as she regards me.

I squeeze her shoulders. "We stick together, yeah? Sport of kings my ass."

She splutters out a watery laugh and reaches up to wipe her face.

"Now, stop crying. It's only one date. And look at me. I'm hot. It won't be so bad."

She barks out a laugh and shoves me back. "Good god, woman. Can you even be serious for a minute?"

"Never," I call out.

"Seriously though. Thank you, Billie. I'll make you proud. I promise."

"You already do, little Vi."

"Drinks on me tomorrow night! We'll go to Neighbor's pub."

"You're on. I'll drive," I say, feeling excited I might finally get off the ranch for a while in a social capacity. With one more quick squeeze, she's hustling away, practically sashaying up to the barn.

I feel a pang of guilt at knowing I'm using her as armor against Vaughn, but I also know she'll forgive me when I come clean. Violet is good people like that. Plus, I need all the armor I can get.

I style my hair in long chestnut waves. I even put on makeup and a gray T-shirt dress. It feels good to wear something other than jeans and boots, and I'm actually looking forward to going out and doing something that has nothing to do with horses. I drive to the barn to pick Violet up from her small apartment above the stables. She looks beautiful and distracted when she hops into the black Gold Rush Ranch truck.

"You doing all right?" I ask as she buckles herself in rather violently.

She looks straight ahead through the windshield. "Yup. But I need a drink."

And she isn't kidding. That night, I lose track of how many paralyzers Violet drinks. I switch to water after a couple of beers as I listen to her make vague comments about some guy she's been seeing who is clearly super unavailable. I don't know where she finds the time, but by the sounds of it, she finally told him to hit the dusty trail. Hence the voracious speed of her drinking.

She ends up telling me more about her family and childhood in Alberta. Her parents and her brothers. How stifling and overprotective they are. How she basically moved out to British Columbia just to see the world on her own. The more she talks, the more sluggish her words get, and as much as I'm amused by listening to her talk my ear off, I eventually suggest heading back to the ranch.

I watch her totter up the stairs to her apartment, wondering if I should have helped her up there, and breathe a sigh of relief when she closes the door behind herself. Poor little Violet is going to be in a world of pain tomorrow.

When I pull up to my dark cottage, tiredness hits me. All the commuting this week, getting to know new people around the track, listening to Violet, thinking about Vaughn—I'm feeling a little tapped out.

Which is why I'm instantly agitated when I see Vaughn sitting on my darkened front step.

"What are you doing here?" I sigh as I hop out of the truck.

"I came to talk to you." There's a bite to his tone that I don't like.

I walk right past him, shoving my key into the front door. "Don't bother. I'm going to bed. You should head back to your gala or whatever it is you're doing tonight."

He stands and takes a long step onto the porch. "You are so totally infuriating," he barks, surprising me with the volume of his voice, before quieting to an angry growl. "I'm about done with you running away from me."

He thinks he can talk to me like this? I spin around in the doorway, blood pumping quickly through my veins. "Speaking of running, how about you run back to your date in the pink dress now?"

A deep, sardonic laugh rumbles in his chest as he stalks closer. "If I didn't know any better, I'd say you were jealous, Billie. Where were *you* tonight?"

I rear back at that. "Are you fucking kidding me? I was out with Violet, for crying out loud! You, on the other hand, spent the night with me and then—"

"That mouth of yours," he cuts me off and presses his finger across my lips to silence me as he edges closer still. "I didn't go to the gala at all. I called my mom that morning when I left your place and told her to cancel it. I told her to stop trying to set me up, period. If you didn't purposely avoid me all week, you would know this by now."

I stiffen, and air whooshes through my lips. "Vaughn, you're my boss. I know we've blurred that line. But we need to define it again. I don't want this to be complicated. I don't want to keep tiptoeing around you. I just want to work and win races."

"I want the same thing." He growls and then pushes me back through the front door gently.

And locks it behind us.

CHAPTER 24

Billie

Vaughn yanks me to him, and before I know it, he has flipped me around and is pressing me back into the solid pine door.

His movements are confident, steady, authoritative, but his touch is gentle. I shiver as I watch him take total command of our interaction. He moves with the grace and surety of a mountain lion, and I stand before him panting and wide-eyed.

Like the most clueless prey.

My voice comes out shakier than I'd like. "I thought you just said you wanted the same thing?"

His hand glides up over my throat before he comes to grip my chin, forcing me to look at him, at his handsome face and his dark eyes searching mine, shifting between each of my irises, like he's reading an open book.

"I do."

Heat pools between my thighs at the deep rasp of his voice.

"Let me redefine that line you keep talking about. You are more than my employee, and I am more than your boss. I'm done giving you space that we both don't want. It's not at all complicated. You'll work with me during the day and underneath me at night. Every night. There will be no tiptoeing. There will be no running. There will be no one else."

Blood rushes in my ears. All my protests die on my dry tongue.

"I fucked up this week, backing off the way I did. What I should have told you is that I want *you* and to win races. I want it all."

He's nuts. So goddamn bossy. And he's never been hotter. My head spins with the weight of his confession.

"Tell me you don't want that, and I'll walk out this door. I'll pretend we never happened."

That last promise is like a spear to my heart. How could I ever pretend we never happened? It would be impossible, and the weight of that prospect is too much to bear.

My hands slide up the lapels of his suit jacket to grip the collar. It never fails to amuse me that he continues wearing suits while living and working in the middle of nowhere. He regards me silently, waiting for me to say something, to respond to his admission. My tongue darts out across my bottom lip as I scour his features, admiring him with no shame. His shapely lips, his strong brow, the sharp definition of his jaw, and the stubble that blooms out from there below his high cheekbones. His brand of beauty is harsh and overwhelming in its masculinity. He isn't smooth and shiny. His beauty *hurts*.

More than that, he's a good man. I know it in my bones. In my marrow. He's so different from what I expected. It makes my chest ache with longing, with the pain of my distrust.

I sound breathless even to myself when I blurt out, "This is such a bad idea."

His stubble rasps across my jaw as he presses a featherlight kiss just beside my mouth. Taunting me. Leading me down a path that I'm sure there's no coming back from.

"Lose the dress, and I'll prove to you otherwise."

He kisses me below my ear now, nipping gently there.

"But—"

"Billie, stop. Nothing else matters."

The man makes me crazy: hot, cold, excited, angry, comfortable, anxious, safe. He's chosen me, and I don't think that anyone in my entire life has truly chosen me or gone after me when I ran away. And here he is, invading my space in the most delicious way, demanding that I choose him back.

It seems like a small gesture, but to my twisted heart, it feels like everything. Right now, held by him, surrounded by his bulk and scent, all I I want to do is stop denying my feelings. To get out of my head for the first time in years and let his infectious heat thaw me out.

I'm *tired.* Tired of running, tired of planning, tired of pretending I don't want him. My resolve crumbles as my head races. He's right. Nothing else matters.

Trying to control my erratic breathing, I take a hold of the hem of my dress. Vaughn still has my chin grasped in his warm palm; his thumb is rubbing circles on my cheek reassuringly, only stopping as I pull my dress over my head and drop it unceremoniously on the floor. It pools by my feet along with all my inhibitions.

His sharp intake of air is loud in the quiet room as his hawkish eyes devour my body. I stand before him, naked save for my black lace panties and bra and a pair of brown wedge heels.

"Fuck, Billie. You are exquisite."

His hands drag down to my breasts, squeezing and caressing them, pulling them out over the top of my bra before discarding it. He holds one in each big palm before his head drops down to pull each hard nipple between his sinful lips. The feel of his mouth on my body is new and familiar all at the same time. Like we've been here before, like he's known my body for years. Like we were made for each other.

My head tips back on a moan, and I run my fingers through his thick hair, whimpering. "Please don't ever pretend we never happened."

He slides back up to look me in the eye, cupping my head with both hands. "You're even more insane than I already thought if you think I could ever forget us."

His lips crash down onto mine, and he pours his frustration into the kiss. His intensity is almost palpable, like I could reach out and run my fingers through it. He possesses me with his expert mouth, leaving me breathless and writhing up against the door. Leaving me damp and wanting more when he pulls away.

His hands drift down the gentle curves of my body before lifting me up and walking across to the kitchen island. "Sit on the counter."

He nods at the butcher block island beside me, and for once, I'm not annoyed by him being domineering. Heat coils at the base of my spine as I move to do what he's requested. I shift over on wobbly legs, and with his hands on my hips, I sit on the cold counter.

He steps away, putting space between us, as he crosses his arms and leans back against the opposite counter. I want him closer. I want his hands all over me. I want him inside me.

"If we're doing this, there can't be any more secrets, Billie. I can't take any more dishonesty in my life. Please don't hide your past from me."

His voice cracks with emotion, and my heart lurches. He's such a noble man, and the sting of his idol's betrayal won't be easily erased. But my promise to be better is a start.

"No more secrets," I whisper back.

He nods with authority. "Good. Now pull those skimpy panties to the side and show me how you touch that pretty pussy when you're alone and thinking of me."

Jesus Christ.

My breath catches in my throat. Shyness overtakes me as I feel unfamiliar heat creep across my sternum all the way up and to my bronzed cheeks. Vaughn Harding is not the square he appears to be. And looking at him now, the way he regards me with his hungry eyes, his sharp cheekbones stained pink, and his broad chest rising and falling like he's out of breath, I want nothing more than to please him. To make him happy. To dive into whatever this is between us. If he needs this to make him feel like I'm really here, wanting what he wants, then I'll do it. A thousand times over.

I look up from beneath my lashes, lean back slightly, and let my legs fall open. Peering down, I hook two fingers into the thin strip of lace at the apex of my thighs and drag it slowly to the side, eliciting a groan from across the room. I subconsciously praise myself for shaving and primping so thoroughly today. Vaughn's eyes are darting all over my form, like he can't choose which part of me he likes the most.

The corners of my lips tip up. Urged on by the plain desire I see all over his face, I circle my clit a few times with my opposite hand and let a small moan spill out over my lips, which makes his eyes settle on one spot. His posture is taut, and I see the bulge between his legs fighting against the fabric of his slacks.

While I have his attention, I drag two fingers through my glistening folds and then slowly press them in. I hum and close my eyes against the feel. The brazenness of what I'm doing, the arousal thrumming in my hips, makes me feel like I'm having an out-of-body experience. I put on a show, lazily pumping my fingers in and out of myself while he watches from across the room.

A growl tears out of his chest at the sight, and in three long strides, he's standing between my spread legs, towering over me, holding my sensitive inner thighs open. "Do you have any idea how hard you make me? How wild you drive me?"

"Show me," I huff out. And he needs no further urging.

His hands undo his belt, and mine attack the buttons along the front of his dress shirt in unison. I want to see everything that I've only been able to feel. I want him disheveled and undone under my hands. I want him to feel as out of control as I do.

His cock springs free from his briefs as he pushes them down. He fists the base of it firmly, pumping toward me a few times. I lick my lips and reach down to palm his steely length myself. Rock-hard, silky smooth, and warm in my hand. And Vaughn completely naked? He's an absolute vision.

"I… I want…" I'm speechless. I'm drunk on the smell of amaretto and the way he's looking at me. I want it all. I want him everywhere.

"Tell me what you want, Billie. Say it." His mouth lands back on the tops of my aching breasts, and the rasp of his facial hair tingles across my chest.

I grip his shoulders as I bring my head down toward his bowed one and place my lips and teeth right up against his ear. "I want you to fuck me."

He's upright and pulling a condom out of his jacket pocket like a flash of lightning, rolling it over himself like an expert.

"Of course you just happen to have a condom in your jacket."

His eyes flash at my jab. "I only brought it because I knew you'd be impaled on my cock before the night was through."

Okay. Yes. More dirty talk, please.

I roll my lips together and glower at him in response, loving his filthy mouth. He smiles back at me, gripping my chin again and running his thumb across my lips. His other hand lifts my thigh as he lines us up on the edge of the countertop.

I close my eyes, wanting to memorize this moment. The feel. The anticipation. I want to imprint it in my brain forever. So many months of longing, dodged advances, culminating in this. What could be better?

"Eyes open, Billie," he rumbles as he squeezes my chin and tips it down. "I want you to watch me fuck you."

He looks down, forehead leaned against mine, pressing into me, and I can't look away. Wouldn't want to even if I could. He fills me slowly, inch by inch, and I watch my body stretch to accommodate his girth. Our heavy exhales mingle between us as we hold each other's bodies and watch them come together in the most intimate way possible.

I feel impossibly full as he pushes inside, and once he's seated, I feel him throbbing within me. Seeing and feeling our bodies joined this way leaves me breathless.

He pauses there before he whispers, "Holy fuck."

My hands loop around his tense neck, and I shimmy my hips toward him. "Vaughn. Please move."

He thrusts slowly first, dragging himself out before sliding himself back in a few times, lost to the look and feel of our coupling. Then his lips find mine in a worshiping kiss while his fingers trail across my hip bones as we slowly move against each other.

But it's not enough. I want to *feel* it.

"I want more. Harder," I whisper across his skin, urging him on.

His feral eyes fly open, shining with approval. Hunger. Desperation. And that perfectly cultivated facade unravels right before my eyes.

Finally.

He unleashes on me. Each pad of his fingers presses into my ass cheeks as his hands grip me there. I wrap my legs around his waist as I cling to his muscled shoulders and latch on for the ride while he increases the intensity of his thrusts. His thighs slap loudly against the backs of mine as he plunders me.

He owns me. He possesses me. He *fucks* me.

His voice rasps desperately against my mouth, "Take it, Billie."

There's nothing gentle about the way our bodies clash. It's all teeth and nails. Sharp gasps and growls. Months of mounting emotions bubbling over. Pure, tangible passion.

We're explosive. Desire. Frustration. Longing. Anger. And something more that I can't bring myself to put a label on. My heart stutters at the thought, and my body shakes with the brutal force of his thrusts. Sensation overwhelms every corner of my body, the heavy thrum in my pelvis building with every delicious stroke.

This is what I want.

One of his hands slides down my body to land between us. His deft thumb brushes across my aching clit. Once. Twice. Three times.

"Come for me, Billie." His voice is deep and demanding. The words fall from his lips like a direct order to my body. Heat builds in my core, making that spot beneath my hip bones pinch. The heat pools there, and my legs tremble with the intensity of it.

"Oh god. Vaughn, I'm going to—" My orgasm hits me like a tidal wave. It burns and tingles like a surge of electricity spilling over me. My body shakes as I break apart in his arms. I know he's watching me intently, my body, my facial expressions, so focused on my pleasure—and I don't even care. I'm so lost in the moment, so lost in him, that nothing could distract me.

"So. Fucking. Beautiful."

Aftershocks of the orgasm rack my body as I hold him close, nuzzling into his neck, soaking up that intoxicating signature smell. I feel all gooey and soft, putty in his hands as he continues to pump into me. Good lord. This man is… so much.

"I'm going to watch you come all night long."

His dark promise makes my body break out in goose bumps, and a shiver runs across my shoulders as his thrusts hit peak force and speed.

I wrap my hands up in his silky dark hair and run my teeth along his jawline before whispering seductively in his ear, "Give it to me."

"Billie—" He snarls and bites down hard on my shoulder as he shoves himself deep in my body.

His hands squeeze my hips in time with the pulsing of his orgasm. We stay there, our ragged breathing perfectly in sync. Holding on to each other for dear life.

I'm trying to wrap my head around the enormity of what I'm feeling, sitting on my kitchen counter in Vaughn's strong arms. My head is buzzing, and every inch of my skin is hypersensitive. I feel like he's pried me right open, exposed all my soft and vulnerable hidden corners. My first reaction is to tuck them back away, to zip that side of myself back up. After all, being soft hasn't ever gotten me anywhere in life. But here, in his arms, I feel safe. Like maybe it's okay to embrace those feelings. Like maybe I won't fall apart if I do.

He trails the tip of his tongue across where I'm certain he's probably left a bite mark. He dusts my neck and cheek with gentle kisses as he comes to face me.

His dark eyes bore into my honeyed ones as he says, "What should we christen next?" It's a question as much as a request.

I garner an eye roll and an affectionate smile when I nod eagerly. "Everything."

CHAPTER 25

Vaughn

I've barely slept all night.

For starters, Billie is an insatiable animal. Her wild-child streak and jokes laden with sexual innuendo should have prepared me. But then, I've never been prepared for anything about this woman.

We spent hours rocking into each other. Exploring each other. We christened this cottage in a way I'm sure it never has been before. She's so carefree, so adventurous, so ravenous for me. I've never felt more desired and masculine as I do with her in my arms.

I knew I wanted her, but this… this is so much *more.*

Just looking at her now, naked and sleeping serenely on her back, one hand thrown possessively over my stomach, makes my chest ache in an unfamiliar way. I press a palm to my sternum, rubbing absently, trying to ease the mounting pressure.

I should be asleep too, but I can't tear my eyes away from her, can't stop soaking up her every feature. I want to commit everything about her to memory. I'm terrified she's going to duck and run as soon as she wakes up. Like everyone always does. I'm terrified that if I put a toe out of place, she'll throw in the towel.

She's gun-shy, and I can't blame her.

But her unpredictability scares me. The only predictable person in my life died and threw me for a goddamn loop. It feels inevitable that I'll be left in the lurch again. She's so guarded and has spent so many years putting up walls to cover big secrets. Maybe I should be angry with her for concealing her identity, but I'm not. In fact, I feel like I understand her better than ever.

If I could start fresh without my family's scandal looming over me like an ever-present storm cloud, I probably would. I can't hold that against her. I won't. It doesn't matter what her name was a decade ago. I want who she is now. Like, *really* want her.

She snuck up on me, planted the seeds, and I let the roots take over, wrapping themselves around every pulse point, filling up my darkest corners, squeezing painfully at my heart. We are intertwined now, and the thought of ripping her out—it's too painful to bear.

She rolls toward me, her slender hand dragging over my chest, sliding it underneath my palm. "That's a lot of staring. You plotting ways to kill me or something?"

Busted.

Her eyes close again as she snuggles into my shoulder. The weight in my chest is buoyed by the blooming heat her touch pours around it. "Nah. I tried to fuck you to death last night, and it didn't work."

A soft giggle spills from her lips. "That's probably the way to go out though." She wraps herself around me, one long leg resting over mine. I slide an arm under her neck and hug her close to me, loving the feeling of her naked body latched on to mine. "I'll be walking funny all day thanks to you and the monster in your pants."

I take a hold of her wrist and pull her hand between my legs. "This monster?"

"Jesus, Vaughn." She laughs as she palms my hard cock. "Good morning, Monster." Her confident grip slides up and down, and I swell even more, filling her hand.

I turn so that we're lying face-to-face, letting the tips of my fingers drift over the hills and valleys of her body, feeling the gentle dips and curves of her. Breast to waist to delicious round ass. I kiss her gently since her lips look puffy and pink from the way our mouths sparred all night. "I'm out of condoms. You're an animal, Mowgli."

Her hand continues to glide up and down my length as she whispers onto my cheek. "I don't need a condom for this…"

She moves over top of me and drifts down under the sheets, dragging her nails over the ridges of my abdomen. I feel her press a firm kiss into the crook of my hip before she drags her teeth along the line of my groin. My hips buck up as she licks her way across to the other side, sucking on a sensitive spot just beside the base of my cock.

Billie edges down farther, and I push up on my elbows to watch her. She holds my gaze with her glowing amber eyes and lets her lips brush against the tip of my cock. I groan and clench my molars. Her tongue darts out and swirls around the swollen head, lapping up the glistening drop of precum. *Does she have any fucking clue how sinful she looks right now?*

"Billie," I say, my voice thick with arousal, "what do you think you're doing?"

From between my legs, she gives me her best innocent look, lashes fluttering slowly across her cheeks as she licks my length brazenly from base to tip. "I'm trying to apologize to you for being… What did you call it? So totally infuriating?"

And then she takes my cock all the way into her mouth, straight to the back of her throat.

"Fuck," I rasp out, tangling my fingers in her chestnut waves, holding her hair back so I can watch her take me. Watch her cheeks hollow out as she bobs eagerly in my lap. "Best fucking apology ever," I growl, applying some pressure to the back of her head, feeling her go soft and pliant in my hands. Letting me move her how I want. So goddamn trusting, turning herself over to me this way. It feels like the ultimate victory. The ultimate gift. And it's like throwing gasoline on a wildfire. The animal instincts inside me buzz with pleasure, with wanting more. "Billie. I need to fuck you."

She pulls off me, wide eyes trained on mine as she daintily wipes a smudge of saliva off her bottom lip. "Okay," she breathes out. "I'm clean and on birth control."

I internally beat my chest like an absolute caveman. "I'm clean. I've never gone without a condom."

Her teeth press into that bottom lip, just like they did the first day I met her. So fucking distracting. "Good. I want you bare."

I jerk in her palm. Fuck me, this woman can talk about consensual safe sex and I'm raring to go. The thought of no barriers between us drives me insane. I pull her up to me and then roll her over so that she's underneath me. *Where she belongs.* My fingers swipe through her wet heat once.

My girl is so ready. I slide into her. Slow. Steady. Skin on skin for the first time. Wanting to be as close to her as possible.

Moving together, we share feelings that neither of us can put into words yet. She got hard and dirty Vaughn last night, but this morning, I feel off balance. *Sentimental.*

We fuck lazily. We kiss slowly. We let our hands roam tenderly. I whisper in her ear and tell her how good she feels, how incredibly beautiful she is. I tell her that our bodies fit together perfectly. And she moans her agreement as she topples over into another orgasm, her limbs trembling around mine as I pour myself into her body.

After soaping each other in the shower, I offer to cook Billie breakfast. She sidles up to the island, looking fresh in an off-the-shoulder white shirt. Just the sight of her shoulder and elegant collarbone peeking through makes my mouth go dry. The implication of no bra is downright distracting. I focus back on the cutting board. Can't keep mauling her if I don't feed her.

I slide a cup of coffee across the kitchen island to her waiting hands. She glances down into the mug, a small smile touching the corners of her mouth. I know she's checking the amount of cream I put in for her.

Her cheek twitches as a look of uncertainty overshadows the small smile. "What do we do now? What is this?"

My heart pounds in my chest. This is the conversation I've been dreading. The one where Billie the escape artist finds a way out of being *us*. I keep chopping vegetables for the omelet.

"We're together, Billie. I don't care what you name it. It's like I told you last night." I look up to her striking face. "You're what I want."

Her caramel eyes glisten with tears. "I want you too." Her voice is quiet. "But I'm concerned about how that works at the farm or around the track. It's hard enough dealing with douchebags like Patrick Cassel without being accused of banging my boss."

"You are banging your boss." I point at her. "And you love it."

She rolls her eyes, grinning. "I do. But can we just keep it quiet for a bit?"

I don't love the idea. I've never had a woman want to keep me hidden away. Usually it's quite the opposite. But Billie has a point. She's worked hard for her career, put a lot on the line to make it happen for herself, and I would never want to be the one to ruin that for her. Truth be told, I've become her biggest cheerleader. Whatever it takes.

"Of course," I say as I turn away to fire the stove up and hide my disappointment. It still stings, and I don't want her to see that it does. I don't want to push her too hard, too fast.

My phone rings on the counter, interrupting our conversation. Dread pools in my stomach when I see it's a call from a number I don't recognize. I never thought I'd be afraid to answer my phone, but this is my new normal.

"You gonna answer that?"

"I don't know who it is. I still keep getting calls from reporters asking about my grandfather. I'm tired of telling them I have no comment."

"Let me take one for the team then." She presses the answer button and turns it to speakerphone with a look of excitement on her face. Ever the shit disturber. Her fake sugary voice fills the room. "Helloo! Vaughn Harding's phone."

"Put me through to Mr. Harding." The voice is deep and sharp, slightly accented, as the man barks his order.

Billie is unfazed. "Unfortunately for you, I don't take orders from people whose mother didn't teach them to say please or thank you."

I cringe inwardly, stifling a laugh. She really has no filter. It's part of her charm.

"My mother is dead. Put him on. Now."

"I guess it's a blessing that she's not here to witness your bad manners firsthand then," Billie snipes back.

My fingers pulse and squeeze the knife in my hand. I don't want to police her behavior, but she is going to get me in trouble with that mouth one of these days.

"May I ask who's calling?"

"Stefan Dalca."

I pale. The man is an enigma, practically a recluse. A shady one who showed up in the area a year ago with too much money and no answers about who he was or where he came from. And in a small town where everyone knows everything about everyone else, his secrecy is downright suspicious. His land, his stables, his horses, he bought them all outright and then waltzed into the tight-knit racing industry in the Lower Mainland like he'd been a mainstay for years. Everyone in the community agrees, it's fishy as all get-out. I've intentionally avoided all connections to the man, which is easy to do when he's secluded on his property.

"Charming. You were far more polite last week when you were needling me for information at the track."

My eyes flash up to Billie. *Huh? She's met the man?* The line is quiet for a few beats too long.

Crazy Billie has left one of the area's most dubious businessmen speechless. If I weren't trying so hard to be quiet, I would laugh. I chance a look at her, assessing her profile. Yeah, she looks pleased with herself right now. She's just a cat playing with a mouse.

I shake my head. How did sensible Vaughn Harding end up with this smart-mouthed firebrand?

"Aha. Is this Miss Black? Or is it Miss Farrington?" His voice is more teasing now. It's almost like I can *hear* the smug look on his face through the phone. I want to punch it right off his slimy face.

"Miss Black," she replies, not giving away the momentary shock that flits across her face at him using her old name.

"Well, in that case," Dalca continues in his smooth voice, "Miss Black, may I please speak to Mr. Harding? I'd like to make him an offer on the black horse we spoke about last week."

Now it's Billie's turn to pale. Her whole body goes rigid, except for her mouth, which opens and closes without any words.

"Okay," she finally says, eerily calm. A lot calmer than she looks as her eyes dart to mine.

How the hell am I going to play this?

"Vaughn Harding speaking."

"Mr. Harding. My name is Stefan Dalca. We haven't officially met, but I had the pleasure of speaking with your"—he trails off suggestively—"trainer, Miss Black."

Billie turns away from me, looking out the window toward DD's paddock.

"This is a private number, Mr. Dalca. Care to elaborate on how you came to have it?"

"I have my ways." His tone is dismissive. "At any rate, as you know, I'm working hard to build an elite string of racehorses and thought we could work together as two of the big players in the area. I saw your black colt run last weekend, and I'd like to make you an offer."

Great. Just what I need. Another morally corrupt asshole trying to latch on to my business.

"My company email is listed on the website. You are always welcome to send me a written offer. Though I have to tell you, I'm not looking to work with anyone." Out of the corner of my eye, I see Billie's body relax on a long exhale.

His laugh is a deep rumble through the speaker, the kind of laugh you direct at a small charming child when they say something adorable. I don't like it. "Everything has a price, Mr. Harding. I knew your grandfather, you know."

Billie's head whips toward me now as I grind my teeth, making my jaw click.

"We had an excellent working relationship."

My voice comes out dark and dangerous. Now he's gone too far. This conversation is over. "How lovely. Thank you for your condolences. Have a nice day now."

"Keep your eyes peeled for my email. It's been a pleasure chatting with you."

I hang up, knuckles white, chest heaving, mind racing. *What a prick.*

"Well, that was… interesting," Billie muses.

I just grunt in response, not sure what to say.

"DD isn't for sale, right?" Her eyes are so clear and honest, focused right on my face. "I mean, I know horses come and go. I know it's part of the business but—" She cuts off, looking out the window and running her palm up over her throat like I had the night before.

"But you're attached to him?" I supply.

She clears her throat. "I mean, yes, I am. I'll be the first to admit I love that horse." Her voice cracks, but she continues. "Probably more than any horse I've had the pleasure of spending time with. But, Vaughn, he can win it all. I know he can. He's my—our—best shot at winning the Denman Derby. Hell, maybe even the Northern Crown. Horses like him come around once in a lifetime. You can't just replace that kind of prestige."

I give her hand a reassuring squeeze across the counter. "Don't worry about it. Dalca's the last type of person I plan to go into business with."

She places her other hand on top of mine, giving it a gentle squeeze, before she walks out of the house wordlessly to go feed her horse. A silent offering of her trust.

Stefan Dalca would have to make me one hell of an offer for me to ever even consider taking that horse away from her.

CHAPTER 26

Billie

THE RUBBER CURRYCOMB IN MY HAND MOVES IN SMALL AGGRESSIVE circles over DD's dusty black coat. The little pig rolled around in the mud and looks like an absolute swamp monster. Which, for once, is fine by me. I need to work out some angst.

Last night was *a lot*, but the phone call from Stefan Dalca had been something else altogether.

Vaughn fucked my brains out, but not all of them, so I didn't miss the fact that he didn't actually confirm that DD isn't for sale. Which is exactly why I held myself from jumping into the deep end with the man.

As my boss, he owes me no explanation about selling horses. My job is to train them, make them as successful as possible. His job is to run the business side, crunch the numbers, make deals with buyers and so forth.

But as my whatever-the-hell-we-are, well, that muddies the waters a bit, doesn't it?

I'm not quick to open the cage around my heart, but I know

Vaughn is close to getting there. If I'm honest with myself, he's consumed me since the day we met. I've gone out of my way to harass him. I accused him of being the little boy who pesters the girl he likes, but the truth is I am no better.

I constantly needled him, pushing the limits of his patience, all to see what he'd tolerate. To see if he'd snap. I've been hot and cold to the extreme. Because maybe, just maybe, if I couldn't scare him off, he'd be worthy of my trust. Maybe if I put my worst foot forward and he still stuck around, maybe then I could open up.

I need to sit down and explain this to Vaughn. I owe him an explanation. We probably should have talked about this already, but we were too busy giving each other delicious orgasms.

God, I've never had sex like that. Uncontained passion. Overflowing pleasure. There was no turning back. It's like something destined us to get that out of our systems. I don't know why I held back for so long, really. Vaughn is the perfect blend of gentle and domineering. Hot doesn't even begin to cover that first time on the kitchen counter.

He's addictive. Hazardous to my well-being.

I finish brushing DD to a shine and feeding him all the carrots I can find before heading to the stables to check in on the man I haven't been able to stop thinking about. The phone call with Stefan Dalca took the wind out of his sails, and while I was out with DD, he darted out of my house saying he was going to do a few things in his office. I'm intuitive enough to see that call rocked him to his core.

He said he was okay, but I'm not buying it.

I peek around the corner into his office, leaning against the doorframe. He's sitting at his desk, looking out the window with a thoughtful expression on his handsome face, fingers steepled in front of his chin. His body is tense, and I see the defined lines of concentration on his forehead.

"I recognize that look," I say as I tap gently on my temple. "You're hashing something out."

His chocolate eyes dart to mine, but his body doesn't move. "Yes." He huffs out a sigh.

I move into the room and drop myself into one of the chairs facing him, the same one I sat in on the day of my job interview. "You're a slow processor, you know?"

He quirks an eyebrow at me like I've insulted him.

"No, no, hang on. Let me finish. It's like… I feel, and it slams into me with such force. I feel everything so intensely. So… instantly." I rub my hands over my thighs as he regards me, not interjecting a thing. "Whereas you're so adept at keeping up appearances, you don't even realize something is influencing you until much later. You've buried it, and by the time you get around to uncovering it, it's necrotic. Practically eating you alive."

He sits still, looking at me from over the tips of his fingers. Seconds stretch out as we stare at each other.

"Maybe."

Ugh. Men. Why do I keep coming back for more?

"Tell me what's wrong."

"Dalca sent his offer."

I stare at him, hearing my heart beating in my ears. I'm scared to ask. "I'm so sorry. I had no idea who he was when he started talking to me. Is… is it…?"

His shoulders slump as he scrubs his hands over his face. "It's a lot."

I feel myself pale. "How much?"

"Not enough. Especially considering the way he roped Dermot into the conversation like he has something on him. Not wild about that implication. I don't even know where to start."

"Okay. I'll start. I want to tell you about my childhood."

He shuffles papers around on his desk, avoiding eye contact with me. "You don't need to do that."

"I grew up in Toronto, in a painfully ostentatious neighborhood called the Bridle Path—also known as Millionaires' Row. And yes, it's exactly as pretentious as it sounds. And no, I have zero intention of heading back that way, which is why the West Coast is the perfect place for me. Same country, opposite side."

"Way better weather."

"Way hotter bosses." I wink at him and then continue. "I spent my youth being groomed to make someone a gracious wife."

That garners me a chuckle. "Have your parents ever met you?"

I smile sadly at him. "That's just the thing, isn't it? My parents were so focused on curating everything about me, about our family, my appearance, my education, my extracurricular activities, my friends, that they overlooked pretty much everything about who I actually am. I don't think they really cared. If they could have had two point five kids just to achieve that perfect statistic, I think they would have."

His jaw ticks and his eyes soften. "I'm sorry."

I shrug. "I take solace in imagining their faces when they find out I'm an unmarried racehorse trainer with no postsecondary education."

"You don't talk to them at all? They haven't reached out?"

"Not even once. I was seventeen when the videos of my dad surfaced. I'm sure you've seen them. Pretty, young escorts, a pile of cocaine, and Canada's favorite prime minister. Naturally, I was expected to fall into line and come to my father's defense like a good soldier." I shake my head as I feel my tear ducts burn. I blink my lashes, trying to push the swell of water back down. "Nothing will ever be as humiliating as having to stand by him through that, watching my mother smile and nod at people like everything was fine."

Vaughn reaches across the desk to hold my hand in his. "So you left?"

I take a deep, ragged breath. "Yup. On my eighteenth birthday. My trust fund swapped into my name, and I stormed out of there in an absolute blaze of glory. Took a bus out of town and ended up on Hank's doorstep. I knew, even as a teenager, I wasn't ever going to fall on my own sword to cover up another person's mistakes. I was done." I let that long-buried anger seep into my voice now. "When you make shitty fucking decisions, you'll probably end up in a shitty fucking situation, and you don't force the people you love to sacrifice themselves for your reputation. It's unforgivable."

Vaughn's long fingers trace over the veins on the top of my hand as he stares at me. Like really stares at me. It's unnerving. I feel like he's looking right into me, right through my skin and muscle. Right through my bones. Right into my patchwork heart.

"Poetic." A dimple on his cheek peeks out, and I can't help but laugh. This man has been making me laugh since day one, whether it was at him or with him. Vaughn Harding is amusing.

"On a lighter note, I have an older brother. His name is Rich. He's the only member of my family I keep in touch with, and you'd probably really like him. Sometimes he fakes a business trip to come see me…" I trail off, thinking about how long it's been since I've seen my brother, since I've hugged him. "I miss him."

"He stuck around?"

"Oh yeah. That schmuck was born to be a politician. He'll stay out east, though he's not terribly tight with our parents either."

"That's…" He trails off, looking for the right words.

"A lot?" I huff out a tired laugh as I squeeze his big warm hand. "Sure is. But now you know my whole sordid past. The point of the story is people almost always disappoint me, but horses don't."

Vaughn's eyes burn with determination and something more when he says to me, "I don't want to disappoint you."

I shrug in response, not ready to get my hopes up in that department. Not yet.

"Then don't."

I launch myself at Vaughn the minute we push through the front door of my little log house. I hear his breath leave his chest in a whoosh as I crash against him, wanting him to wash away the memories I just dredged up.

He rumbles against my lips, "Bed. Now." His palms grip my biceps as he gives me a gentle shove toward the stairs.

A telltale spark dances around in my pelvis as I walk across the room. I love this version of him.

I lift my shirt over my head, dropping it on the floor. I unclasp my bra, dropping it on the steps. At the top of the landing, I shimmy out of my jeans and look over my shoulder at him as I head toward the bed wearing only a thong. I feel like he's hunting me as he prowls behind me, covering the ground more quickly with his long strides.

With one hand on my shoulder, he spins me around to face him and palms my breasts. "This body is *mine*."

I stand at the edge of my bed as his hands slide all over me. His lips follow in their path. Down my throat, across my collarbones, onto my nipples where his tongue darts out as he sucks and nips. I can't stop the wanton moans that spill from my lips.

The man sets me on fire.

His mouth travels down my body as he drops to his knees before me. He looks up from where he's kneeling, and I run my hands through his silky strands, soaking in his handsome face. The sharp masculine planes, the deep, dark eyes dancing with sinister intentions. Just looking at him kneeling before me makes me squeeze my thighs together in anticipation.

He hooks two fingers into the strip of fabric covering me and pulls it to the side. "This time when you beg me to fuck you while I eat this pussy, I might actually indulge you."

My teeth drag across my bottom lip as I sigh out, "Fuck."

Vaughn moves in. His expert mouth tortures me with every swipe of his tongue, every graze of his teeth, every well-timed suck. From above my heaving chest, I watch his head move against me.

I pant and try to put off begging. I really do. But I'm weak. "Please." It comes out strangled. "Please, Vaughn, I want more."

He doubles his efforts as his fingers dig into my hips and ass.

"P-please fuck me."

He sucks hard on my clit, making me cry out. He is both impressive and forever infuriating.

"Vaughn Harding!" I scold him. "Get that fine ass up here and fuck me. Now."

His chuckle is dark as he rises to stand eye-to-eye with me. "That's not how I remember you begging that night."

"You're impossible." I close my fingers in his hair and pull his face to mine. I can taste myself on his lips as he kisses me back. It feels intensely personal, and all I want to feel is his skin on mine. "Please." I tear at his shirt while he grapples with his pants.

When we're naked, he turns me around, fisting my hair and shoving me down onto the bed. Goose bumps bloom on my arms in anticipation.

His hard body covers mine from behind as he lines his bare cock up, whispering in my ear, "You're so wet for me, Billie."

"Yesss," I hiss out as he licks the spot on my shoulder where I'm sporting a red mark the exact shape of his teeth. I grind my ass back against his steely length, aching for him.

"Tell me what you want, baby. Hard or soft?"

"Hard."

He slams into me, fully seated in one thrust. Breath rushes out of my lungs in one breath as my body adjusts to his size.

"And then soft."

His dark chuckle rolls across my skin like static electricity, snapping at my nerve endings. "Whatever my girl wants, she gets."

We sink into each other, ravenous. Two broken people, damaged by the ones meant to love them the most, finding solace in each other's arms.

CHAPTER 27

Billie

Violet is already up on DD by the time I get down to the dirt track. She's in the saddle walking him around the grass infield. The sun has barely risen, but Violet is ready to go.

We already talked about testing the waters with him after his colic. Luckily, it wasn't very severe, and he's pretty much recovered. My hysterics may have been *slightly* over the top. But this horse is special, and I won't take any chances with him.

"Morning!" Her hand shoots up in a terse wave as I flip a leg over the white fence and sit on top of it. DD raises his neck and whinnies at me in greeting.

At least one of them is happy to see me. The duo walks toward me, and DD's petite head swings back and forth happily. He looks relaxed with his ears perked forward and back stretched long, and it warms my heart to see the anxious little horse looking so content. He just needed time and a gentle hand—and a metric fuck ton of treats. *Greedy little jerk.*

"Who pissed in your Shreddies, Vivi?" I ask as they approach me now.

"Har-har-har."

DD reaches his head out once he gets close enough, shaking me down for cookies. I blow a raspberry on his soft nose and boop him on the forehead. "After your workout, piggy." I lean back and take in Violet's wide blue eyes and the pinched expression at the corners of her mouth. "You okay?"

"Mm-hmm." She looks down and fiddles with the reins in her hands.

I swear, if it's that guy still, I'm going to kill him myself. "Don't quit this gig to become an actress."

"Don't tell her what she can and can't do."

I turn to see Vaughn walking down the gentle slope away from the offices. He's holding a steaming cup of coffee, and he gives me a knowing smirk as he approaches. My spine tingles at his heated look. Images of how I've spent the last couple nights flash through my mind. Filthy. And delicious. The man is turning me into a mindless bimbo. He's fully dressed, it's first thing in the morning, and all I can think about is dragging him back up to his office and locking the door.

Alas, I've got horses to train and races to win, so I ignore the blush that creeps across my cheeks as he leans in to hand me the cup of coffee and quietly says, "Should I make you beg for this too?"

"Prick," I huff out. I look down and see the perfect coffee-to-cream ratio in the hot mug and wrap my palms around it, letting the heat seep into my skin in the cool morning air. "Thanks, Boss Man. I'll keep you posted on how it goes at the track today."

He chuckles as he turns to leave, knowing I've just dismissed him. We're supposed to be keeping our relationship on the down-low around the barn, but when I look at the skeptical look on Violet's face, I have a feeling that we might already fail in that department.

I clear my throat and take a sip of coffee. "Planning on telling me what's up now that he's gone?"

She quirks an eyebrow at me and nods her head up toward the barn. "I don't know. You planning on telling me what's going on with you two?"

I lift my mug toward her to acknowledge her point. "Good talk. You ready to take that little psycho for a light breeze? See how he feels?"

She sighs and her shoulders relax. Her relief at me dropping that line of questioning is clear. "Yes. So ready."

"Good. Let's see what you've got."

DD breezes beautifully for Violet. She stands up in her irons and just lets him run. Her gentle squeezes on the reins hold him back, and her perfectly still torso allows him to move how he likes. When they round the top corner of the track, she presses the reins at him, and he shoots forward like a bullet. His stride lengthens, and he eats up the ground. Effortless.

If she can get him in position next weekend, the other horses won't stand a chance. And we'll be qualified for the Denman Derby, leg one of the Northern Crown. Bucket list, here I come.

Back at the barn, Hank is standing in front of a tack stall chatting with one of the grooms who is prepping Brite Lite for her turn on the track. Her sweet friendly gray face turns to me as I approach.

"Billie girl!" Hank greets me with his warm smile. "How ya doing this morning? How'd DD run?"

I shake my head at him, grinning like a lunatic. "That horse will win it all, Hank. He's primed."

His smile grows to match mine. We both know horses well enough to know how exciting a horse like DD is, how infrequently they come along. His big hand squeezes my shoulder as I lean into him for a hug. "You've worked magic with that little black horse. I'm proud of you."

I rest my head on his shoulder and sigh. "All thanks to you, old man."

"I don't think I can take all the credit for the woman and trainer you've become. Hard work pays off, and I don't think I know anyone who has worked harder than you. You deserve this."

His approval makes my chest ache with what I've missed my whole life. The praise my own parents most likely will never give me.

"Thanks, Hank," I say, not trusting myself with any more words than that.

The weeks fly by. I spend mornings with the young horses on the ranch and afternoons at Bell Point Park in Vancouver. Hours are spent commuting between the two, but it's worth it when I fall into Vaughn's strong arms every night.

All I can think about is this coming Saturday, the race that counts for everything. If DD can pull off a win, he'll be qualified for the derby. Because we let him start slow, this is the final qualifying opportunity. The dream I've dreamt for years now is within reach, and in my gut, I know if I can just get him there, he'll pull it off. He's a competitor. He'll know what to do.

I'm nervous about keeping him healthy. I'm nervous about putting a completely unproven jockey on him. I have moments when I wonder if I'm qualified to do my job at all. Impostor syndrome is a raggedy-ass bitch, and I know I'm not doing a great job of hiding my anxiety.

In bed, under the shroud of darkness, I confess my worries to Vaughn. He listens to my fears. He soothes my body with his. He's the rock I need. The rock I've been searching for my entire adult life. He doesn't coddle me, but he doesn't let me beat myself up either.

To be honest, he's too good to be true. Which is why I'm here at his house, just down the road from the barn, snooping through his bathroom. I came in here to clean up after a marathon sex session and couldn't help myself.

I'm terrible, *I know*.

I quietly open the drawers. Toothpaste. Deodorant. Shaving cream. Razor. Condoms. I huff out a sigh. "Boring. Boring. Boring."

"Looking for something?" He's leaning against the doorjamb, toned arms crossed across his chest, chocolate hair all mussed—just the way I like it.

I make eye contact with him in the mirror. "Yes. I'm trying to figure out what's wrong with you."

"I'm sorry, what?"

"You heard me." I turn to face him now and wave a hand in his direction. "Ever since you got me naked, you've been *nice*. And just the right amount of dirty."

He smirks.

"And so fucking gentlemanlike."

"Okay. And this is a problem?" He looks incredulous.

"It's just—" My teeth dig into my bottom lip as I look back into his dark eyes. "I'm waiting for the other shoe to drop. People are notoriously good at letting me down, so if I can find some proof of you not being this… this perfect, of this being an act, then I can prepare myself for when shit will inevitably hit the fan. I'll know what's coming."

Vaughn's smirk fades, and he looks back at me softly, like I'm a cornered wild animal. "Billie. This isn't an act. We're not an act. I'm not going to let shit hit the fan." He steps into the bathroom and wraps me in his arms. One hand strokes my hair soothingly as he presses a kiss to my forehead. "Just focus on winning the races you need to. You've worked too hard to be distracted by me. You've got too much on your plate. I'll be here when you need me, waiting for you. I'm not going anywhere. I'm in this for the long haul."

I relax in his embrace and run my hands down his back. "See? It's not normal to know the perfect thing to say."

"Plus, I keep all the body parts in my freezer," he adds.

I can't help but laugh into his chest as I feel my anxiety melt away in the safety of his embrace. "You do have that handsome serial killer vibe about you."

"Speaking of handsome, tell me more about how I'm perfect."

I groan as he laughs and lifts me up. I wrap my legs around his waist as he walks me back to bed where, despite my doubts and fears, he holds me tight in his arms all night long.

Race day is here, and I'm a wreck. I've given up *everything* to get to this day. It's do or die. There are no other qualifiers, and next year, DD will be too old to qualify. The pressure is weighing on me, and I'm letting it get to me.

I could be sick. Everyone else seems fine, perfectly happy. Like they trust that I'm leading them down the right path. At my log house this morning, Vaughn told me as much. Hank is all chipper. Even Violet doesn't seem that nervous for her debut race—a qualifying stakes race, no less—which is probably because she knows she'll be sitting on the most horsepower out of the entire group. I've talked her half to death about strategy. I think I'm at the point where I'm annoying her now with the whole mother-hen vibe.

So I'm hiding from everyone in DD's stall, brushing him to a perfect shine even though I'm wearing a beautiful pantsuit. But it doesn't matter. Breathing in that comforting scent and trying to find my center while he munches happily on his hay is what I need right now.

Hank's head pops into the stall. "You should head up to the VIP lounge soon."

I don't look up; my hand continues brushing the rubber comb in circles on the pitch-black coat. "I don't think I'm going to watch the race. I might just stay here at the barn. Can you record it for me? I'll analyze it after."

"You're not really going to send your baby out there alone, are you?" He strokes DD's forelock as I look into the horse's big intelligent eye.

My chest pinches at the thought of missing the race, but my head swims with the pressure of it all. "I'm freaking out," I whisper to the man who might as well be my father.

"I know you are, Billie girl. You don't have to go up to the lounge, but make sure you watch it. Find a quiet spot along the rail or in the stands where no one will know who you are. You will not want to miss the feeling of watching your boy win. What the two of you have is too special."

"Yeah," I mumble.

I know he's right. He just smiles and leaves, thank goodness. A hug would have had me falling to pieces in his arms.

I spend the next hour alone with DD, methodically getting him ready, wrapping his legs perfectly, placing all his tack just so. It's almost strange that no one talks to me, but I'm pretty sure Hank has warned them off bothering me, and to his credit, Vaughn knows me well enough to know I need to be alone right now.

It still unnerves me how easily he understands me, how he accepts me—my paranoia and colorful vocabulary too. He doesn't even try to change me. I'm thinking he might just like me for who I am. And the thought of letting him in completely terrifies me. I literally pinch myself sometimes to make sure I'm not dreaming.

Right now, I pinch myself to make sure this day is really happening. I step back to look at DD. His dishy head, his dainty legs, how handsome he looks in his yellow silks. He's getting antsy. He knows what's coming.

I press a kiss to his muscular neck. "I love you, DD. Be safe out there."

He's ready to go.

CHAPTER 28

Billie

The gates fly open, and the ten horses explode onto the track.

The loudspeakers crackle to life. "And they're off!"

I'm standing at the far corner of the track facing the finish line. I'll see them through the first turn and then, if everything goes to plan, I'll have a head-on view of DD making his final move.

My heart pounds in my chest as I watch Violet execute our plan to perfection. She's light and still in the irons and gently holds DD back. He shies away from the pack all on his own, so this is a simple task off the start. They thunder toward me, and the ground trembles beneath my feet. The front-runners round the first corner, flying past, fighting for that coveted spot along the rail. Burning all their energy—exactly what I want them to do.

DD is galloping steady, not too far back but not crowded either. Just the way he likes. He's a blur of shiny black and yellow as he passes the end of the oval moving into the clubhouse turn. Rounding out of the second bend, heading into the straight, I see his ears shoot forward. His head drops imperceptibly, and his ears flatten in that signature pissy fashion of his as he looks through the maze of horses ahead of him and realizes he's not winning.

Attaboy.

A lane opens up, and Violet moves in, easing into the middle of the pack. Exactly where DD doesn't like to be and exactly where he'll want to get out of as quickly as possible. They steadily move down the straight, passing the horses that are tiring.

Hours on the trails and trotting hills have given DD an edge where stamina is concerned. He's not at top speed yet, and he's got lots left in the tank. My fingers squeeze the rail of the fence as the pack moves into the far turn. He's dragging Violet now, leaning down into the bit—he knows what needs to be done. This is where they need to make their big move out of the middle of the pack. This is where they come from behind.

DD flies out of that final bend looking like a small and mighty warhorse. His face is vengeful, and his ears are so far back they're downright aerodynamic. But when Violet's arms press forward, his ears perk, and they're off.

In sync, they move up like they've just been shot out of a cannon. The other horses look like they're running in slow motion. All I can hear is blood thundering in my ears as I watch them move past horse after horse.

With only two horses ahead of them, Violet doesn't bother with moving close to the rail. She sets their sights on the finish line and pushes her hands at him, urging him on. I see her lips moving, talking to him, as dirt sprays up around them.

My hands move up over my mouth as they barrel down toward me. I want to scream, to cheer, but I can't tear my eyes off them as they eat up the soft ground and sail past the leaders. Right into first place and more. They blaze across the finish line easily six lengths ahead of the next horse.

It's not even close.

I feel wet heat on the apples of my cheeks as they gallop toward me, relaxing into a slower gait as Violet leans back a bit and murmurs at DD. He snorts and tosses his head, looking awfully pleased with himself.

I can't help but jump up and shout, "Violet Eaton, you are a rock star!" as they come into the bend where I'm standing. I swear one of DD's pointy little ears flicks toward me in recognition. Violet hears me too. I'll never forget the smile she gives me. So big it looks like it might hurt, like her cheeks are swollen.

I give her a matching one, and my heart soars with the reality of what's just happened. She leans down as DD slows in the bend and wraps her petite arms around his sweat-slicked neck, hugging him.

I can't believe it. We did it.

A no-name jockey, a freshman trainer, and a horse that no one wanted to handle.

We fucking did it.

I hustle to the winner's circle, not wanting to miss a moment of this. I'm going to soak it in. Revel in it. Kiss my little black horse. Shit, maybe even kiss my boyfriend. That's how crazy I am feeling.

People swarm the pen where they hand out the plate and take photos, and I push my way through. When I get close,

I can see Vaughn's perfectly coiffed hair, a head above most of the people around him as he moves toward the circle.

"Vaughn!" His head snaps back toward my voice as I walk briskly his way.

He stands still, hands in his pockets, letting the crowd part around him. He's shaking his head at me, lips pressed together, trying to hold back a smile. When I get close enough to look up into his warm chocolate eyes, I squeal and throw my arms around his neck. He laughs into the curve of my shoulder and lifts me off the ground. He hugs me so hard, with so much pride.

He kisses my cheek and whispers, "You did it."

I feel like I could burst. I squeeze his biceps through his suit jacket and lean back to look at his handsome face. "No. *We* did it."

And then I kiss him. In full view of everyone around us, and I don't even care if they see. I don't want to keep us secret. *Us* feels too good. He grunts in surprise, but his palms cup my jaw, and he kisses me back. Sweetly. Stroking my cheek lovingly with his thumb.

My icy heart melts in his hands. Everything feels so right today.

After mauling DD with kisses, almost knocking Violet over with the violence of my hug, and crying a few happy tears in Hank's comforting embrace, we pose for photos. Vaughn is presented with the trophy for the win, but he hands the trophy over to me almost instantly, and then they drape DD in the championship blanket. I feel Vaughn's presence beside me the whole time, like a rock, his hand often resting on the small of my back as people step forward to talk to me.

Cole shows up too, and despite my best efforts to ignore him and just enjoy the moment, I don't miss the way he gawks at Violet. The way he leans in toward her and whispers something. And the way her face drains of all color and excitement as she stares back at him slack-jawed. Violet doesn't look like a woman who's just been congratulated; she looks like a woman who's seen a ghost. Now *that* is something I'm going to have to come back to later.

I feel like I'm just spinning in circles, thanking people for their congratulations and answering their questions. Questions about DD, questions about my training methods, questions about how we chose Violet to get the ride.

One member of the press stretches her phone toward me. "Can you comment on the rumors that you were in a physical altercation with a well-known jockey here at the track?"

The pads of Vaughn's fingers press into my hips as I let a small smile touch my lips. "That doesn't sound very professional," is all I say before turning away.

Vaughn leans in, his voice rumbling across my neck and sending a shiver down my spine. "Sounds like word's gotten out about what a naughty girl you are."

I mutter under my breath, "I'll show you naughty tonight."

His hand trails down over my ass, and his voice is like silk against my skin. My cheeks heat as I look around. It's too busy for anyone to notice where my boss's hand is roaming.

"I'm holding you to that," he says, looking around now. "But I'm going to duck out for a sec and see if I can find Cole. Meet us up in the lounge for a drink when you're done here?"

"You bet," I say over my shoulder, already greeting the next person who's approaching me.

With a squeeze of my elbow, he's gone, and I turn my best smile back on the people hovering around, even though all I want to do is take DD home and fulfill my dirty promises to Vaughn.

★★★

Back in the quiet of our row at the barn, we dote on DD. He gets a cool bath, ice boots on his legs, and a lot of tender loving care from Violet, Hank, and me. We haven't used other grooms with him so far, and I'm not sure why we'd start now. Our ornery little champion only likes certain people, and I don't blame him one bit.

"He felt perfect out there," Violet says in awe as she towels him off.

"You guys *looked* perfect," Hank adds.

I smile. "He's right. You were both perfect. Beautifully ridden. Beautifully run. There isn't much more I could ask for."

Violet points at me. "It was your plan. Your training. Your strategy. I just hopped on at the last moment and executed it the way you wanted."

"She's right." Hank squeezes my shoulder.

"That may be true, but we aren't going to have it this easy at the Denman Derby. We don't have much time to prepare. We'll have to be perfect *and* lucky to win that one."

Violet nods solemnly, but Hank just laughs.

"Girl. You are too serious for your own good. You just won! You're qualified. Get outta here. Go make moon eyes with Harding Junior."

I gawk back at him. *How the hell did he know?*

"Billie, for Christ's sake. I may be old, but I'm not blind yet. You two have been circling around each other for months."

"He's right," Violet adds as she tosses a blanket back over DD's damp coat.

"You couldn't have picked a better one," Hank says. "Go act your age. Have some fun for once."

"I don't—"

"Git," he cuts me off, waving his hand, dismissing me. "I won't leave your horse's side until you get back. Don't worry."

I give in and walk down the long alleyway, past countless other stalls, toward the grandstand and VIP lounge. I'd really rather share a drink in the barn with our staff who actually played a part in today's success, but I also know there's a time and place to schmooze. So here I am, ready to schmooze. For the business and for Vaughn, because I know he secretly likes this shit.

I round the corner but stop short when I hear Stefan Dalca's cool authoritative voice. "I've been waiting for a response to my offer."

The voice that replies is icy, and I know it well. "I've already informed you that the horse isn't for sale."

I step back into the alleyway and peek my head around to see Vaughn's back to me as he faces off with Dalca.

"Everything has a price."

"So you've said. The horse just qualified for the derby though. He isn't going anywhere."

"You're right. It's probably worth more than the ten million dollars I offered last week."

Fuck me. Ten million? Is he serious? It's not unheard of for a stud who could go on to make a lot of champion babies. But DD is still relatively unproven.

Vaughn's posture is rigid as he faces off with the other man. He's not intimidated by Dalca's dangerous vibe. He's got a few inches on him, maybe a bit more, as he draws up and says, "I don't care what your offer is."

Dalca's smile is sly as his eyes dance over Vaughn with unbridled amusement. He's clearly enjoying this encounter, throwing his money around without a care in the world. He isn't the sunny media darling that Vaughn is. He is the shadows moving in the dark. Backroom deals and threats are his currency. He's wily, like a fox, not to be trusted. I want to jump in and tell him to hit the dusty trail, but this is Vaughn's battle, not mine.

It probably isn't appropriate for me to be listening in, but hey, no one ever accused me of being appropriate. Why start now?

"I almost get the feeling that you don't like me, Mr. Harding."

"I don't."

This is the Vaughn I met that first day when I pulled into the parking lot at Gold Rush Ranch. Cold and dismissive.

"Twenty million."

I cover my mouth to muffle the sound of me choking. That's an insane number, and the business side of me knows it's also not an offer to turn down. That amount of money could go a long way, buy a lot of nice horses. But the sentimental side of me? No, DD is too special. He could be worth one dollar, and I'd feel the same. He's priceless. The thought of him leaving makes my eyes sting.

"It's not about the number. It's about the future. The horse isn't for sale. End of story."

I am going to worship the hell out of that man tonight.

He turns to leave, but Dalca stops him in his tracks when he says, "The future, hmm?"

Vaughn angles his broad shoulders back toward the shady businessman.

"Twenty million and I go to the press with irrefutable proof that your grandfather wasn't involved in any illegal gambling schemes. I'll clear his name."

Everything goes still. I swear the birds stop chirping. The world feels like someone hits pause, save for the knowing grin spreading across Dalca's face. It's a calculated smile, like he saw the open chink in Vaughn's armor and aimed right for it.

It feels like a spear to my gut just watching it all play out.

"Are you telling me that my grandfather wasn't involved in your scheme?" Vaughn's voice is brittle, almost breathless, now. He still looks impenetrable, but his voice is a dead giveaway that Dalca just delivered an absolute knockout punch.

Dalca snorts. "It wasn't my scheme, Harding. And no, I'm just telling you I can make it look that way. He did what he's been accused of."

Vaughn goes white like a sheet, the truth of Dalca's words hitting him like a wrecking ball. The silence that follows is so heavy I feel it like a vise on my lungs and can't help the loud gasp that escapes my lips when Vaughn nods his head tersely and says, "Send me the paperwork."

That head of wavy dark hair, the one I love running my fingers through, whips around in my direction. Alarm shines in his eyes as he takes me in, the way I'm peeking out around the end of the building. I know that I'm intruding, but truthfully, I don't give a fuck. I stare back at him in absolute disbelief. The man I admire for his morals—his judgment—just sold off my hopes and dreams, his farm's redemption, all to salvage the reputation of a dead man who fucked everyone over.

I shake my head, begging to wake from what feels like a bad dream.

"Ms. Black, how nice of you to drop in." Dalca's voice drips with sarcasm. "No need to hide back there. I have a proposition for you as well." He waves me forward with a smug smirk.

I walk toward them on wooden legs, avoiding meeting Vaughn's eyes. I can't look at him right now. I'll either kick him in the balls or start crying. That's the tightrope I'm walking right now. *I wish I had that whip for both these assholes.*

"Congratulations on your big win today," Dalca says.

I make sure I don't stand too close to Vaughn, who is still staring at me.

"I've followed this horse since they started trying to make him run. I know what a challenge he's been. I also know that you've forged a special relationship with him. You're very talented, and you've done incredible work."

Now he looks earnest, genuine, but I just stare at him with no emotion. How could he possibly know all this? Am I supposed to swoon at his compliment?

Fuck this guy.

"When the horse arrives at my facility, I can assure you he'll be treated exceptionally well. Nothing but the best. That said, I'd like to offer you a position as his trainer. Head trainer. The compensation would be more than competitive."

Double fuck this guy.

I still say nothing. I pop a hip and cross my arms as I glare back at him, rage simmering in my gut. The *gall.* The absolute balls on this asshole to blackmail Vaughn into selling the best horse his farm will ever have and then turn around and solicit his employee right in front of him. It makes me want to rearrange his striking face.

Dalca's intelligent eyes skim my face, looking for an answer in my expression. But my face is an unreadable mask. I mastered this look as a teenager when my dad sold his family down the river to save his political career.

"Listen to me, Gangster Gary, and listen to me carefully." My voice is almost a hiss, trembling with barely contained rage. "I'm well acquainted with macho sleazebags like you. Overgrown children who think they're smarter than everyone around them."

Vaughn cuts in now. "Billie, be caref—"

I hold a palm up and swivel my head in his direction. "Don't you dare interrupt me. I have some choice words to share with you as well, but I can only handle one spoiled asshole at a time, so you just wait your fucking turn."

He presses his lips together. Vaughn's no pushover, but he's also smart enough to know which battles are worth picking—and apparently this ain't it. *Smart boy.*

My attention whips back to Dalca. His strong features are set in what looks, remarkably, like surprise. "No one ever talks to me like this."

"Well, maybe it's about time they start."

He rears back with a small amused smile on his face. Which honestly just pisses me off even more.

"I've spent enough years of my life catering to powerful men with no moral compass, whose priorities are all jumbled, whose loyalty lies only with themselves, and I'm not about to jump into that pool again. Do I love that horse? With all my fucking heart." My voice cracks with the emotion of it. "But I'm also a professional. Horses come and go. It's all a part of the sport. I'm a big girl, and my life will go on. But I will never sacrifice my integrity for money. And I will never, *never* work for a man like you."

He tilts his head at me, like I'm a puzzle he's trying to piece together. I don't like it, not one bit. I turn to leave.

To my back, he says, "Among the Romani people, we would say that Double Diablo is your heart horse. Your equine soulmate. A horse you understand like no one else can."

Emotion clogs my throat. My chest burns. Leave it to this manipulative prick to deliver a fatal blow like that. I know I can't look back; I can't handle seeing the pity written all over Vaughn's face or the victory on Dalca's. So I just call back over my shoulder, "In that case, good luck at the derby with my heart horse."

CHAPTER 29

Vaughn

Fuck. *Fuck.*

I spin on my heel and take long strides after Billie. From behind me, I hear Dalca say something about sending the offer via courier this week. I don't know. I can't even focus on him right now. All I can see is the utterly broken look on Billie's face when she heard me accept his offer.

I've come to accept that Dermot was probably guilty of fixing races, of defrauding the sport. But hearing confirmation of that stung. But even so, it was an offer I had to accept. To clear my grandfather's name would mean so much, not only for the business but for my family. It could mend the rift he created with this whole scandal. I have to make her understand, make her see that this is the best way forward.

With twenty million dollars, I can buy multiple champions for her to train *and* restore the farm's reputation. Obviously, this is not how I wanted her to find out. I would have liked time to figure out how to put this to her gently. If I could just get Billie to sit down and talk to me, she'd understand.

My pulse thrums in my throat as I follow her down the bustling stable alleyway toward DD's stall. Her heels clack as she speeds away from me. I'm impressed by how quickly she can walk in her heels, but then I'm reminded that Wilhelmina would have had plenty of experience with that. She hasn't always been the casual horse girl I know and love.

Watching her walk away from me, feeling those ripples of rage pour off her, I realize I do in fact love her. I didn't want to piss her off or hurt her, but the offer Dalca made was too much for me to ignore.

"Is the trailer packed?" she barks into one of the stalls.

"Yes," Hank responds, looking confused as he pops his head out of the stall. "Why are you back already?" He looks beyond Billie to see me storming up behind her.

Having finally caught up, I grab Billie around her upper arm. "Outside. Now."

She spins and shakes her arm out of my grip. "Don't lay a fucking hand on me, Vaughn Harding. I'm working right now. I'll talk to you later."

"No, Billie. We're talking right now."

DD, Violet, and Hank all stare back at me wide-eyed. Billie looks downright wild with flushed cheeks and her chest heaving.

"Let's go have a celebratory drink, Vi." Hank ushers her under the rope across the stall doorway, giving me a stern look and Billie a fatherly rub on the shoulder as he leaves us to face off. Violet scampers along behind him, looking back over her shoulder with concern in her wide blue eyes.

"Very professional," Billie mutters as she ducks into the dark stall next to the little black horse.

"You think I care about being professional right now?" I lean against the doorway and watch her crouch down and wrap the fluffy shipping bandages around DD's dainty legs.

"No. I definitely do not." Her voice drips with sarcasm. "I think you care about yourself, and that's about it. Today, you made that abundantly clear."

"Are you kidding me right now? Taking that deal is what's best for everyone. It's *business*, Billie. Twenty million dollars and the farm's name out of the mud? Do you know how many promising horses we can add to the string for that amount of money? How much work we can do around the farm? It's a no-brainer."

She snorts. "No brain. That's for sure." Her hands flatten the cotton wrap over the pillowy base, every movement sure and quick and edged with agitation. She runs her palm up DD's leg and stands. Her fingers scratch at his withers, making him twist his neck toward her happily. Her smile in his direction is wobbly, and then she turns those feline eyes on me. "You really don't get it, do you? It's not about selling the horse. It's about *why*. This horse just ran his heart out for us and qualified for one of the most prestigious races in the world. He came out of nowhere and overcame a lot of shit to put your beloved farm on the map. But that's not enough, is it? Because this isn't about the farm's reputation. He just put you back on the map, and in return, you traded him away on a shady deal."

"So what if I did? Twenty million is twenty million, Billie."

"So what? If he keeps winning, he'll make you that in breeding fees in his first year at stud." Her voice is shrill as she looks at me in utter disbelief. "Time to face facts, Vaughn.

Your grandfather *did* break the law. He did everything they have accused him of. That snake in the grass just confirmed it. Covering it up will not change a goddamn thing!"

"How about a little support? This is important to me. You know how hard this has been for me," I roar back, hating everything that she's saying.

She huffs a breath out as she rears back slightly. "So important that you're willing to trample all over my career? Violet's career? Our relationship?" Billie's head shakes back and forth, her disappointment almost tangible. "Imagine thinking that your desperate need to cover up a legitimate crime—one that undermines the respectability of our sport—trumps everyone around you. Real living beings are going to suffer for this. And that's all an acceptable sacrifice to polish up a dead man's reputation?"

I just stare back at her, grinding my teeth.

She huffs out an incredulous breath. "Unbelievable. Reality check, Vaughn. He was exactly as crooked as his reputation suggests. It's okay for him to have been both a fabulous grandfather and a shady businessman. Reconcile it. Deal. With. It."

I keep staring, at a loss for words. Deep down, I know that it's not an acceptable sacrifice. It sounds downright ludicrous when she lays it out like that. But I've spent so many months wishing and dreaming of a way to make the gossip and whispers stop. To make everyone see the wonderful man who I got to know. I can't turn my back on that goal, can't even fathom it.

Her eyes sparkle in the dim light of the barn, and tears build up over her honeyed irises. "You said you wouldn't disappoint me." Her chin trembles as she sucks air in.

Seeing her pain up close like this, it's killing me. I feel like my chest is about to crack open, like my beating heart might fall into the wood shavings in the stall right at her stiletto-clad feet.

"This is a business decision. I have to stand by my choices, even when employees don't like them."

As soon as the words leave my lips, I know they're the wrong ones. But my adrenaline is rushing. I'm pissed off that she doesn't understand, and I'm on an emotional crash course that I can't seem to stop.

"Employee?" she snaps at me.

"Yes, Billie. Trainers don't usually decide about the sale of horses they don't own. I know you feel like this horse is yours, but he's not. He's mine."

She draws herself up as a steel door slams shut over her face. All expression is gone as she stares back at me, lips pressed together in a thin line. "Thanks for the clarification, Mr. Harding." Her tone of voice is one I've only ever heard her use on people she's about to verbally eviscerate. "Hope that knowledge keeps you warm at night, because I definitely won't be." Her voice is cold as ice when she finishes by saying, "I'm not going to sit pretty on the arm of someone whose dubious decision-making skills are based solely on public perception again. I deserve someone who will choose *me*. We're done."

It's been almost twenty-four hours, and I still haven't heard from Billie. I miss her already.

After she told me we were done, I shrugged my shoulders coldly, spun on my heel, and stormed off. All I could hear as

I walked away from the woman I love was the swoosh of blood in my ears. Rage simmered in my gut, but it coiled and intermingled with shame too. I knew I shouldn't have spoken to her that way. Even now, a day later, I know I sounded like a total asshole. Yet I can't bring myself to apologize. It's not my fault she doesn't understand.

I stare out my office window at the paddocks, at DD's empty one. Billie obviously kept him down at her house last night. She looked so broken at the thought of the little black horse leaving. I hate to think that I hurt her by making the decision I did, but it's not unusual for horses to come and go. Especially ones as promising as Double Diablo.

I'll give her time to cool down, and then I'll lay my line of thinking out more clearly. She'll come around. I know she cares about me, even if she's been reluctant to accept those feelings. This is just a bump in the road. Couples fight all the time. We'll work it out.

I have to work this out. I can't lose her.

A firm knock on my office door pulls me out of my head. Billie stands in the doorway, hip cocked and arms crossed. I let my eyes drink in the way her blue jeans hug every sensual curve of her body, but when I get up to her face, my breath hitches in my throat. Her silky chestnut hair is pulled up in a high ponytail, her pale skin is makeup free, and her typically bright whiskey eyes are dull, puffy, and red.

You did that, asshole.

My chest constricts at the sight of her. She's obviously been crying. A lot. Which is not what I was expecting. I thought tough, sunny, optimistic Billie would win out. Sure, she'd take some time to herself—I know she doesn't like to be smothered—and then she'd come back out swinging. But this… this is not what I saw coming. She looks devastated.

"Hi," I say.

"Hi." Her voice comes out soft and fragile. "Do you have a minute?"

I shift in my seat, immediately uncomfortable with how formal she's being. "Yeah, yeah. Of course." I gesture to the seat across from me. The exact seat where she sat across from me a couple weeks ago and told me about her family, about her father and what he'd put her through. The exact seat she sat in when I hired her.

"Thanks." She folds herself into the chair, avoiding eye contact with me as she drops a piece of paper between us.

I clamp my teeth together at the sight of it, leaning back in my leather chair and steepling my fingers beneath my chin. "What is that?"

She glances up at me nervously. "It's my two weeks' notice."

I blink at her slowly, trying to process what she's saying to me. "You're… you're quitting?"

"Yes." Her teeth clamp down on her bottom lip, and I can't help but remember what it feels like to suck that lip into my mouth while my hands roam her toned body.

"Why?" My shock bleeds into my tone. I know I upset her, but this is blindsiding me.

"I…" She looks away out the window, sucking in a deep shaky breath. "I just can't do this." We stare at each other wordlessly, a stream of emotions in our eyes. "It just hurts too much to stay. I'll find somewhere… less complicated to go."

Is she kidding? "That's it? You're just going to quit on me?"

Her eyes are watery, and her smile is sad when she looks at me. "You quit on me first."

I rear back. "Is that really what you think? You can't bring yourself to see my side of things at all?"

"Oh, I can see them just fine. I just don't like what I see."

I scoff, but she continues.

"If it's all right with you, I'd like to spend one more day with DD. After that, you won't see me around the farm. I'll finish out my two weeks down at the track instead and will move out once I have everything wrapped up. I don't know how things are going to proceed with DD and"—her voice breaks—"I can't be here when he leaves."

A lone tear slips out of her eye and trails down over the apple of her cheek. I want to wipe it away. Kiss it away. Fold my arms around her and absorb every hurt.

But I don't. Instead, I guard my heart and focus on the thread of anger building in my chest at the thought of her leaving. The least I can do is make it easy on her to go. I should comfort her, I should tell her I'm in love with her, but I'm not one to grovel. Instead, all I want to do is lash out.

"And us? I thought you weren't running anymore." My comment comes out snide, and I instantly hate the childish approach I'm taking. She deserves better than this type of behavior.

She pushes to stand and reaches a hand across the desk in my direction. "Thank you for the opportunities you've afforded me." Her long lashes are wet and clumped together as she gazes into my eyes. "I can't tell you how much I appreciate everything you've done for me. I hope you'll be happy."

Her meaning is clear. She hopes I'll be happy with my decision. And why wouldn't I be? All I've wanted for the last year is to clear my family name. This is something I had to do, and if she can't understand, then so be it.

I stand and wrap my hand around hers. Her handshake is just as firm as I remember, her eyes just as emotive. I can see everything there. Betrayal. Anger. Confusion. Sadness. Absolute devastation.

You did that, asshole.

I should feel good about my decision. Instead, all I feel is sick as I watch her turn and walk out the door.

CHAPTER 30

Billie

"Are you sure?" Hank is sitting at my kitchen island, eyes full of concern, while I lean on the counter across from him scrubbing my face with my hands.

Am I sure? No. I'm not sure of anything right now. Vaughn Harding rocked the very foundation of everything I thought I knew about myself.

I put him up on some sort of moral pedestal, so not only did he rip my heart out, but he also added insult to injury by stomping all over it. I knew I shouldn't have gotten involved with him. Workplace entanglements always end up being clusterfucks. And this was a clusterfuck to end all clusterfucks.

"Yes, I'm sure," I say from behind my hands. "Why did I do this, Hank?"

"Because I begged you to come work with me," he offers with a hesitant chuckle, trying to make me feel better.

I drop my hands and look up at the ceiling. "Not the job. This is the best job I've ever had. I mean Vaughn. What is it about me that is so undesirable? Why does no one ever choose me? Like really *choose* me. Even when there's nothing in it for them. Even when it's not convenient."

I hear the strangled grunt he emits as he moves to stand before me. He puts his palms on my shoulders, and I peer up into his kind, open face. Silent tears stream down my cheeks as he gives me a gentle shake.

"I chose you, Billie. And I'd choose you again and again. You're like a daughter to me. I'm so proud of you. And I can't speak to your family and the choices they've made. To be frank, they sound like a bunch of assholes."

I can't help the small hysterical laugh that spills out over my lips. He's not wrong on that front.

"But Vaughn." He sighs and looks up at the ceiling. "He's a good man who's making a misguided decision. He's had a hard year, but you're right that it's not your job to fix this for him. He has to figure it out on his own. If I know him at all, I suspect he'll come around. I just hope he's not too late."

I blink rapidly and press my lips together. "I don't know if I can forgive him for this even if he does."

Hank hugs me then, cocooning me in his big heavy body. Everything about him is soothing and warm, steady and sure.

"That's your prerogative, Billie girl. But don't forget that if you want people to choose you, you'll have to give them the opportunity. I know you've been burned, and I know you don't trust easily, but you'll never find what you're seeking if you're not at least open to being chosen." His big hand smooths the back of my hair down. "It's a delicate balance. You're an exceptional young woman, so don't sell yourself short, but don't lock yourself away either. Somebody worthy will earn your trust."

"Okay," I whisper into his shoulder.

"Promise me you won't let this make you gun-shy."

"I promise." I say as I sniffle and nuzzle in harder. I'm pretty sure I've soaked his shirt in this spot with my blubbering.

"Did you just wipe your nose on me, kid?"

I laugh now.

Hank has always had the ability to make me feel better while also setting me straight. He gives me the kick in the ass I need and rubs my back all at once, which is something you do for people you love. You're honest with them about their shortcomings, but you're still on their side. No matter what.

"I think I might have. But I'm done now." I pull back and give him a shaky smile. "I'm not going to cry anymore. I can't cry anymore. It's dehydrating. And exhausting." Major understatement. I'm positively dead on my feet. I didn't sleep at all last night, and the emotional toll of the last couple days is catching up with me, hard. "Both of which will lead to premature aging, which I just can't have." I wink at him, trying to lighten the mood a bit.

He grins back. "There she is. My little fighter. I sure missed you while you were traipsing around Europe." His fingers squeeze my shoulder reassuringly.

I roll my eyes at his description of me. "Missed you too, old man."

★★★

I lean on the fence of DD's paddock. His head snaps up from his hay net, and he greets me with a gentle nicker before plodding over for attention. And cookies, let's be honest. It's probably cookies.

"Hey, boy." I run my hand over the big round plate of his cheek as he blows warm air into my ear. His head goes right over my shoulder, like he's about to hug me, but instead, I feel the brush of his sneaky little lips at the back pockets of my jeans.

Searching for cookies.

"I'm just your meal ticket, aren't I, big fella?" I press a kiss to his shiny ebony neck and then hand him a cookie, because I'm a sucker like that. Wrapping my arms around his neck as he crunches happily, I whisper, "I'm going to miss you, DD."

My eyes well, and that telltale ache at the back of my throat springs up.

Images of Vaughn moving over top of me spring up into my mind. I can almost feel the way his fingers trail possessively up over my rib cage. The way the scratch of his stubble beneath my ear can shoot goose bumps across my chest. The way the arches of my feet ache when he pushes me right to the edge so relentlessly.

But I shake it off. Thinking about those days and nights isn't productive, and they're damn near impossible to escape. Every time I let myself wallow in those memories, it's like being tossed around in the surf during a storm. Grasping around for something—anything—to hang on to until the realization hits me that there's nothing to save me. That I'm destined to sink into the black water.

I get back to brushing. This will probably be my last day with DD before he leaves for Stefan Dalca's facility, and I won't waste it wallowing over a man.

Instead, I spend the afternoon exploring the trails around the farm, relaxing into the gentle sway of DD's rib cage beneath the saddle, soaking in the feel of the warm sun on my back, on my face, and marveling at how relaxed DD is as he strolls along the trails with his head slung low and tail swishing.

I scratch at his withers often. I lean down over his toned neck to hug him too. I do my best not to cry, but silent tears stream down my cheeks as we turn back up toward the barn. A heavy pit forms in my stomach as we get closer. This is it. *Goodbye.*

I've said goodbye to plenty of horses in my career, but this feels different. And it's only made worse because my relationship with Vaughn has blown up too. Everything between us was fast and new and exciting. When we were together, it felt promising. We spent months getting to know each other, talking, sharing secrets—sharing quiet moments. Our gazes held unsaid words, and our touches lingered just that little bit too long. It was no wonder other people saw what was happening while we were both still in denial.

We were a head-on collision that neither one of us saw coming.

I can't help but wonder if I'm making the wrong decision. Have I overreacted? Would it be worth looking the other way to keep at least one of them? At least then I wouldn't be left with nothing.

A sigh rattles out of my chest. No. My pride won't let me do that. I've compromised my dignity one too many times to cover up the scandal of a powerful man. It left me feeling dirty, bought... cheap. I'd take a broken heart over that feeling any day.

Even if it means losing the man I love.

I've spent an awful lot of time denying my feelings about Vaughn Harding. Shielding myself, cracking jokes, ignoring the telltale signs of losing myself in him. But here I am, living proof that I am very much in love with him. I didn't even realize it until I lost him.

Maybe I should have told him. I keep circling around in my head. Maybe he would have handled the whole thing differently if he knew. But then, if he loved me back, he wouldn't be doing this, would he?

If he loved me, he wouldn't be selling DD off to clear a dead man's tarnished reputation at my expense.

At DD's stall, I shower him in kisses and slide my hands across his silky coat. I cradle his head and look into his big black eyes, reminded of Vaughn's dark irises.

"You be a good boy for your new family." My voice cracks brokenly and tears rush out, unstoppable in their flow. I tap his forehead, making him blink quickly in confusion. "You win it all for me, little man. Do you hear?" His pointy ears tip forward, and I stand on my tippy-toes to whisper, "Run your little heart out. Leave the rest of 'em in the dust."

Then I sit down on the floor of his stall and let the sobs I've been holding back all afternoon rack my body.

★★★

The floral tang of gin spreads out across my tongue as I look around the busy patio. Neighbor's pub is the quintessential small town dive bar: grizzled bartender, suspect carpet on the floors, and filled with either locals or people stopping in on their way to or from Vancouver. The patio is basically just a parking lot filled with picnic tables.

I love it.

Violet decided that a girls' night out is what I need. Apparently, finding me crying on a dirty stall floor was too much, even for her. So here I am, at a small-town bar, sitting in the sun, sipping a gin and tonic with Violet and my favorite vet in town, Mira Thorne, both looking at me like I'm a ticking time bomb.

"So help me, if you bitches don't stop looking at me like I'm going to break, I'll waste my drink on your faces. I'm *fine*."

Mira, the ice queen, smirks. "You're entertaining."

Violet's big blue doe eyes bore into me, concern etched all over her dainty little face. "Billie, I just want to make sure you're okay. I'm sad you're planning to leave Gold Rush, but more than that, I'm worried about you. You're always the glass-half-full one. And now you're not. It's stressing me out."

"Vivi, don't stress about things you can't control. You're about to be one of the most sought-after jockeys in the business. No way will Dalca switch up a winning combination. He's a lot of things, but stupid is not one of them."

Mira snorts as she takes a big glug of her cocktail.

I incline my head toward her. "Care to elaborate, Dr. Thorne?"

She smacks her lips and turns her cunning eyes my way. "The man is a goddamn snake in the grass. But you are right that he isn't stupid."

"I didn't know you had any experience with him."

"I'm a track vet. I know everything about everyone. Every rumor. Every hookup. Every backroom deal. He's been after me about coming to work at his farm exclusively."

I wrinkle my nose in distaste. "Gross."

Violet's cheeks go pink as she leans in and whispers, "Well, I mean, he's not *that* gross. He's actually pretty yummy."

"Yummy, Violet? Really? How old are you?"

Mira's eyes light with amusement. "You mean *fuckable*, Violet." Violet blushes, and Mira cackles.

As far as Stefan Dalca goes, I can't see past my pure rage to look at him that way. Never mind his physical attributes, I'd throw the whole man in the trash and slam the lid. "You're both fucked in the head." I turn to Mira. "Careful with that. He's scary manipulative."

"Don't I know it," she says, leaning back and sighing. "But I need to explore my options. I'm going to have to find something more consistent than just the track. Getting laid off during the offseason isn't ideal for paying back student loans. Or other things." She trails one dainty finger down the condensation on the glass before her. Head shaking, she adds, "Not nearly enough."

"Talk to Hank. We were literally just discussing hiring an on-site veterinarian. Ruby Creek doesn't have a local practice, and you know firsthand how bad DD's colic could have been if you hadn't been close already."

Mira strokes her chin as she muses. "You might be on to something. I'm dead sick of commuting downtown." She snorts. "And I'm dead sick of living with my parents on their dairy farm. I need a change."

I almost spray them both with gin as I struggle to contain my shock. "You still live with your parents?"

Pink smudges pop up on her round cheekbones. "It's a long story."

"This is great, you guys." I hold my glass up to cheers them. "Hearing about your fucked-up lives is actually making me feel better."

Mother hen Violet gives me a disapproving look, but Mira cracks a sultry smile and taps her drink against mine. I swear the woman just oozes sensuality out of every pore without even trying. Beauty and brains—what isn't to like?

Feeling the gin go to my head after not eating properly for days, I blurt out, "If I wasn't so into dicks, I'd be into you, Mira."

Violet chokes on her drink, laying her hand across her reddening chest, downright scandalized. But Mira just winks at me. "Don't knock it until you try it."

"Speaking of dicks, Vi… what's good with you and G.I. Joe?"

Mira quirks her head to the side in question.

"Vaughn's brother," I explain. "The two of them are weird as fuck around each other. I don't need a college education to figure that much out." I turn my gaze back on Violet, who is now taking very unladylike gulps of her drink.

Yikes. Looks like I struck a chord.

She takes a deep breath and then looks out across the busy patio, avoiding eye contact. "I plead the Fifth."

"Oh god. This has to be *so* good, Vi. You are killing me."

Mira smiles and pats Violet's shoulder. "Everything comes out in the end, Violet."

Violet looks like a deer in the headlights when she turns to the other woman and says, "In this case, it better not."

Our night continues much the same. Good laughs, good ribbing, and good company. On a lot of levels, I feel more settled than I have in years. But that could be the gin buzz too.

Later that night, when I walk into the empty cabin and look out at the darkened paddock, I don't even cry.

CHAPTER 31

Vaughn

I STARE AT THE COMPUTER SCREEN, NOT EVEN REALLY SEEING IT. All I can see is Billie riding up to the barn, a devastating repeating loop that I can't escape.

Earlier, I watched Billie and DD walk to the barn. She looked achingly beautiful in the tack, so natural and at ease. There's nothing fake about her when she's with a horse. Her hips swayed in perfect sync with his languid gait, and the sun glinted off the long chestnut braid that's slung over one shoulder from beneath her helmet.

I stood entranced by the sight of them until I looked at her face. Tears. They glistened there on her defined cheekbones.

I did that.

I rest my head in my hands and rub at my eyes, hoping it might help me see the way forward. It's impossible not to ask myself if I made the right decision. I look back up at the screen in front of me and the contract Stefan Dalca sent over yesterday. The one I've been avoiding signing for almost twenty-four hours now.

Twenty million dollars.

An insane number, to be sure. But is it worth it? I know what Billie said about making that in breeding fees if DD were to win the derby is true. People pay a million dollars a dose for winning studs, and if he produced winners, possibly even more.

I know it's stupid, but at this moment, I don't care about the money. I have more than I need. I don't even specifically care about the horse right now. He's a good horse, but in my mind, there are lots of good horses.

There's only one Billie.

I *love* Billie, and I lost her by my actions. She spilled her guts to me about her family. About her feelings. She told me flat out what kind of behavior she couldn't abide. And then I turned around and did just that.

I keep hoping I can think of some way to make her understand, to turn her to my side. Some way to keep her *and* clear my grandfather's name. Some way to have it all. Usually, I can work these kinds of things out. I turn on the charm and present a plan that's appealing to all parties involved. But that's not working for me here. No matter which way I spin it, I'm coming up blank.

Billie doesn't fit into the box I can usually push people into. She's a psycho kangaroo that jumps all over the goddamn place. And I love her for it.

What a fucking mess.

Rather than sitting here like a lovesick creep, watching her through the window, I should have talked to her. But I didn't know what to say or *do* to fix this. I don't have experience with *this*.

Hank walks past my office door without stopping.

"Hey," I call out. "Hank, come back for a sec."

A moment later, he pops his head into my office, looking downright grim. "What's up, boss?" His hand taps the doorframe.

"I..." My resolve falters. What do I even say here? "I need some advice."

He grunts in response and narrows his eyes at me. "Let me stop you right there." He takes a few steps into the room and closes the door behind himself before pinning me with a frightening look. "Billie is the closest thing I've ever had to a daughter. And she's out there right now *sobbing* in that horse's stall. I know horses move on. Billie does too. But this isn't about the horse. It's about *you*."

His index finger jumps in my direction, and for a moment, I see Hank as the stereotypical farm dad sitting on the front porch rocker with a big gun on his lap.

And I'm the poor fool who broke his daughter's heart.

"Listen, Vaughn. I'm proud to work here at Gold Rush Ranch. I respect you. But I *love* Billie. So right now, watching my girl's heart break, I can't say that I like you very much. I'll get over it. So will she. But you..." He shakes his head solemnly and says, "Well, I'm afraid that it'll be too late when you finally come to your senses, and then she'll be the one you never get over. All you'll have left is more money that you don't need and the memory of a dead man who wanted nothing but the best for you."

My chair creaks as I lean back and run my hand through my hair. "Thanks, Hank," I say on a ragged exhale. He just knocked all the excuses straight out of my head.

He gives me a quick salute before leaving. "Anytime, boss."

I'm reminded of taking a baseball to the chest as a teenager. That's what this feels like. A sharp, deep ache that takes my breath away. Followed by shame. Shame that hits me hard and fast, like a wrecking ball. It threatens to knock me right off my feet. I grip the edge of my desk to keep myself upright. I swear I feel her pain lance right through me.

I did this.

But I'm out of my depth. I drop my head onto the desk and stare at the floor beneath my feet, trying to put the pieces together. I've been solely focused on fixing my family's reputation. I think of my mom, my brother... *my dad.* All people who deserve better than what my grandfather left us with. The ability to fix all that is within my grasp.

But at what cost?

I turn the music up loud and drive straight to downtown Vancouver, to my brother's office. I've been putting off going over financials with him for days, and it seems like the perfect mindless thing to do. And with the perfect person. Cole is a former soldier, so he isn't going to sit me down and talk about my feelings. He's going to talk numbers and respond to my questions in grunts and dirty looks.

Which is exactly what I need.

Pushing through the glass doors of the lobby, I give Mack, our longtime security guard, a wave and head up to the top floor.

Everyone at the head office is happy to see me—unlike at the farm. Smiles. Waves. Even a handshake or two, followed by a "Good to see you!"

Their kind greetings just make me uncomfortable.

I don't deserve this kind of welcome. Do they have any idea what I've done? What kind of person I've become?

My inner guilt rears up, and I try to shake it off as I stride through the modern office toward my brother's door.

I waltz right in without knocking, something I know will agitate him. Little brothers have to still be little brothers, you know? It doesn't matter that I'm twenty-eight. Poking the bear can still make me giggle like a child. Internally now though. Not out loud. Plus, I feel like shit. Have to get my kicks in where I can.

Cole's perfectly coiffed black head snaps up in my direction. "Sure, Vaughn. Come on in. It's not like I could be doing anything."

I flop into the comfortable chair facing the big imposing desk. A smile touches the edges of my mouth. "What could you possibly be doing in here that requires privacy?"

"Maybe my secretary is blowing me under this desk right now," he deadpans. Cole hardly ever makes jokes, and when he does, they're shocking and meant to make you feel uncomfortable.

That shit doesn't work on me. "Great. I'll let Mom know that her recluse of a son is one step closer to making her one of those grandbabies she wants so badly."

He shakes his head at me and stacks up the pages in front of him.

Knowing I've got him there, I press on. "Let's go over those financials you've been bugging me about."

Cole says nothing as he continues to organize the top of his desk with military precision. I swear to god he cleans this thing with a toothbrush or whatever it is they make them do there. Unlike my desk, which I sometimes like to refer to as a "creative space," his office is spotless and neurotically organized. Nothing out of place.

He's still giving me the silent treatment a couple minutes later, forcing me to sit here and watch him in silence. I can never tell if Cole is unbothered by the quiet or purposely doing it to give himself the upper hand. It's like he knows it makes me twitchy.

My knee bounces as I watch him methodically organize his space and ignore me. I hate it when he does this power trip shit. It makes me feel like I'm at the principal's office. I guess this is my repayment for not knocking.

With an exasperated sigh, I huff out, "Cole. We crunching those numbers or what?"

He gives me a disapproving look, but he doesn't look away this time. He really *looks* at me, and I swallow under the intensity of his gaze. His cunning gray eyes scan my face and trail down to my collared shirt and jeans. After enough ribbing from Billie, I've finally given up the dream of wearing a suit around the ranch, and Cole doesn't miss this change. He's analyzing me, and it's fucking unnerving.

"You know how I stayed alive in Iraq?"

"Bored your enemies to death?" I quip, trying to lighten the mood. He almost never even references his time in Iraq. But he doesn't take the bait.

"Attention to detail." His eyes narrow as he gives me a finger gun. "And you, brother, are acting and dressing fucking weird."

I scoff and look away. "I'm fine."

"You expect me to believe you showed up here willing and eager to go over financials? *In jeans?* I usually have to chase your pretty-boy ass down and force you to go over this stuff with me. Stop lying."

A breath I didn't even realize I was holding rushes past my lips on a deep exhale. I run my fingers through my hair and look up at the ceiling. "It's that fucking horse."

"The twenty-million-dollar one?"

"One and the same." I steeple my hands under my chin as I look back at my brother. "It's just proving to be complicated."

"Why?" Suspicion seeps into his tone.

"I may have failed to mention there was another condition of his purchase. One that Billie is aware of and… not impressed by. Now I'm all turned inside out and second-guessing myself." I shake my head. "Over a woman."

"Vaughn. We both know Dalca doesn't play by the rules. What's the condition?"

My heart pounds in my chest. Having to say it out loud feels different from just knowing about it. Presenting the idea to one of the most moral men I know makes me feel greasy. Dirty. "Twenty million and he goes to the media with proof that Grandpa wasn't actually fixing races."

Cole gives me the glare he gave me when we were kids, the one he'd only pull out just before he beat my ass. The way his broad frame almost vibrates now makes me think he might do it again, and while I might have a couple inches on him in height, I still know I won't stand a chance.

His voice is quiet, and his words are sharp and perfectly enunciated when he finally speaks. "Why the fuck would you make a deal like that? With a snake like Stefan Dalca?"

"To clear Grandpa's name—our name."

"Your sense of duty is ass-backward."

I groan and lean back in defeat. Not a single person seems to agree with me, and when you're the only constant in an equation, consider the fact that *you* might be the problem.

And it's looking more and more like I'm the problem.

"Lose the rose-colored glasses, kid." His voice is louder now, rougher. "Time to stop living in pretty fairy-tale land where everything always turns up Vaughn. We all loved Dermot, but the man fucked up. He made poor decisions. Consciously. You think I spent years in special operations not to do a little research on what went down with him? He did it. Plain and simple."

"I know," I mutter.

He barks a disbelieving laugh. "You're telling me you know he's guilty, but you still dove headfirst into a shady backroom deal to fabricate his innocence? In exchange for a boatload of money and the only good thing that's happened to that business—and you—in years?" He's shaking his head at me now, incredulous at my confession. "I know you've spent years perfecting the shiny veneer of this family's reputation, but good god, Vaughn. This is real life, not a PR fix."

Jesus.

"When you put it like that..." I trail off. What the fuck have I done?

Cole must miss the shell-shocked look on my face, because he just carries on berating me. "You're going to blow the most genuine relationship you've had in your entire adult life to stage a cover-up?" He laughs cruelly, and in this moment, I hate him for how right he is. "Billie Black might be the most insane and annoying woman I've ever met in my life, but at least her moral compass is intact."

"Fuck." I lean forward and cradle my face in my hands. "Fuck, fuck, fuck."

"Yup." Cole leans back in his leather chair, still shaking his head at me, like he can't believe what an idiot I've been. He barks out a laugh. "I thought I had the market cornered on being emotionally stunted. Stop trespassing, little brother. You're supposed to be the sweet one."

"Funny. Like… hilarious." All I can hear is the sound of blood rushing in my ears. *What have I done?* "What do I do?"

"You tear that contract up, and you *beg*."

After Cole laid me out with that verbal ass-kicking, he still forced me to go through the financials for the farm with him, sadistic bastard that he is.

I venture into my downtown condo, thinking I might stay the night. But it feels too modern and sterile compared to the warm wood and dated appliances that fill the cottages on the ranch. It feels wrong. Too excessive for one person. I don't belong here anymore. So I leave. It's late, but I don't care. I have to talk to Billie. I have to apologize.

But not before I stop at the bank of mailboxes. It's been months since I've come here, since I started hiding out at the ranch, and there's a notice saying they've started leaving my mail with the concierge. I unlock the box and groan at how full it is.

Carrying the stack with both hands, I plop down on the tufted bench in the lobby to sort through it before I leave. There's junk mail, bills, a wedding invitation from some-one I barely know, and then I pause. An envelope with my grandfather's neat, slanted script addressed to me is the last piece of mail left.

My hands tremble. It suddenly feels too heavy to even hold up and far too daunting to open. I rest my hands on my legs and bounce my knee as I stare back down at the envelope, frozen by indecision. Why would my grandfather send me mail? I talked to him on the phone all the time.

I consider throwing it away, cutting my losses, and forgetting it ever happened. And then I forge on, tearing at the envelope and shaking my head at myself for considering being such a goddamn wimp. I pull the folded paper out, and it shakes in my hand as I read.

Vaughn,

I've always been better at explaining myself in writing. So here goes nothing.

Watching you grow up has been one of the greatest joys of my life, playing a part in your story—an honor. I cherish the years we've spent together, just the two of us, no matter the circumstances that got us there.

I admire the man you've grown up to be. I see a lot of your dad in you, all the best parts mixed up into an absolute blessing of a boy. When he died, becoming your caregiver was my salvation. And when your grandmother Ada passed, the ranch was my escape, my focus. A goal. She always dreamed of winning big prizes with her thoroughbreds. Derbies, cups, plates, and in her wildest dreams, she'd muse about winning the Northern Crown. I still remember the night we lay in the back of my old pickup truck and I promised her we would do it. That if we worked hard enough and stuck together, we could make anything happen.

But as you know, cancer had different plans. She didn't get to see her dreams realized. A damn shame if you ask me—a crime. And even though she was gone, I spent every day working to make her dreams come to fruition.

I was seeing my years fall away. My time to deliver on that promise I made in the truck bed all those years ago was slipping through my hands like sand. I got scared, and what's worse is I let my fear steer me toward choices that have betrayed her memory more than honored it.

I guess that's why I couldn't think of a way to tell you this to your face. I guess I'm too big of a coward. I don't want to be there to see the disappointment in your eyes or hear it in your voice. Because what I've done is a betrayal.

In the coming weeks, you're going to see my name—our family's name—in the news. I've made some bad choices, Vaughn. I've been around too long, made too many connections, become too sure of what money can do for me. Of what it can fix. But I can't buy my way out of this one. And even if I could, it wouldn't be the honorable thing to do.

Trying to play god with the sport that I love, that my beloved Ada loved, is my crime. You'll find out soon that several big races in the past few years have been fixed. I made the play, and I benefitted. But not enough to make the moral lapse worth it. There is nothing that is worth sacrificing our family's dignity and reputation this way, and for that, I am deeply sorry.

I don't know if you'll ever be able to forgive me, but I ask that you take some time. Days, weeks, whatever you require, and then please come visit me at the ranch. I want to see you, to explain myself and my actions in person. To give you a hug if you'll still let me.

My door is always open.

I'll always love you, Vaughn.

Your grandpa,
Dermot

Billie's little log house is dark when I pull up. She's either asleep or not at home, but I walk up to the front door and knock anyway.

I have to talk to her.

I knock again. "Billie! It's Vaughn." When a light turns on, hope bubbles up in my chest. In the quiet night, I can hear her footfalls as she makes her way down the stairs. But the door doesn't open.

"What do you want?"

That spot just in front of my armpits aches with the need to hold her. To fold her slender body into my chest. Because

Billie needs protection. She's had too many assholes in her life, and I'm kicking myself for being one of them. Even for just a few days.

"Open the door, babe. I need to talk to you." My voice comes out strangled, and my fingers itch to touch her. I press a palm flat onto the polished pine door, wishing I could reach right through it.

She's quiet for a few beats. "You should go."

"Billie." I squeeze my hand into a fist and lean on the door. "I want to explain. I want to apologize. I want you… us."

She doesn't respond, but I hear her soft crying on the other side of the door and thump my fist on it again.

"Shit. Please. Open the door. I hate listening to you cry. I'm so fucking sorry."

"It's not enough. I can't do this again. I promised myself I wouldn't. You can't drag me into this now that I'm finally free." A broken sob bursts out of her like a gasp. "It's just cruel."

My urge to comfort her is so strong, I actually wonder if there's a way to rip the door right off its hinges to get to her. I crumple onto the deck, trying to stay with her even if we're separated by the slab of wood. "Tell me how to fix this. I'll do anything."

"You can't fix it. You broke my trust. I know this must be hard for someone like you to fathom, but sometimes when you break a toy, you can't just rush out and buy a new one."

"I just want a chance to prove how much I care about you, Billie."

She laughs sadly. "If you cared about me, you wouldn't be selling my horse. You wouldn't be making this deal. There's a reason they say that two wrongs don't make a right."

The lights shut off. I don't even know what to say to her parting words, so I just sit on the porch, looking out at DD's empty paddock.

She's a hell of a lot more than a toy to me. But she's also not wrong; I'm absolutely unaccustomed to not getting what I want. Which is exactly why I'm not about to give up.

I fire Hank off a text as I jog back to my car.

CHAPTER 32
Billie

I'm being petulant, and I know it. Hank has been on my ass all week about going to the derby, and I keep brushing him off, refusing to go.

I haven't heard from Violet since yesterday. I imagine she's focused on prepping for the race of her life. And I haven't heard from Vaughn either, not since he showed up at my house almost two weeks ago.

I imagine he's rolling around in a twenty-million-dollar pile of cash.

A sneer touches my lips at the thought. I've officially moved out of the crying phase of our breakup into the bitter phase. I'm almost glad no one has been around me lately, because I'm not good company right now.

Mira called me once to check in. I was snarky on the phone, and she told me she wasn't cut out for motherhood and to please call her back when I was done acting like a child. Then she hung up. It was a comment that actually made me laugh and also send her a text message to apologize.

I was giving myself until the derby was over. Once DD won the race, I'd be able to put that dream away. The one where I was the trainer of a horse that won a leg of the Northern Crown, North America's most historic thoroughbred race series. I wanted to watch, to feel it slip away, to let the emotions course through me and then lay them to rest.

Then I could start fresh.

Again.

And I will. I'm not a quitter. I'm strong. I've made it this far, and I'm not about to let a pretty man in an expensive suit set me back. I'll land on my feet. I always do.

Except for right now. Right now, I'm sitting on the floor staring at DD's empty paddock, drinking coffee after coffee like an absolute sad sack. Pathetic.

Which is why when I hear knocking at the door, I don't even bother to get up. It's derby day. Everyone should be busy doing something else.

"Billie! Quit your cryin' and get that scrawny ass out here."

Except Hank. Fucking Hank is like an old bloodhound with a scent that he can't give up on. The man has no off switch. He doesn't know how to give it up.

Deep down, I appreciate him not giving up on me. But I'm still annoyed. I want to wallow by myself, not deal with his pushy ass.

When I open the door, I'm greeted with a smile, but that smile slips away as he looks me over. I'm in a sweatsuit. Hardly derby ready, unlike Hank, who looks awfully dapper in his navy suit.

"Billie Black." His tone is scolding. "This is not the young woman I raised. And you know I pretty much raised you, so don't even start in on me. Your horse is about to run the biggest race of his life, of *your* life, and you're still moping around here like Eeyore personified."

I snort at the mental image and look down at myself. *I'm even wearing gray!* The thought makes me giggle, but Hank just looks at me like I'm a crazy person. Which doesn't matter. I've grown accustomed to people looking at me that way. I like to think it's part of my charm.

"Get. Dressed. Driving into the city on Saturday is a nightmare." Obviously, Hank isn't in agreement about my charms.

I begrudgingly trudge upstairs. Hank is a gentleman through and through, but I also know he's old school enough to pick me up and carry me out of here wearing my Eeyore-gray sweatsuit.

Twenty minutes later, I'm ready to go. I slide my feet into saddle-brown leather wedges at the front door, trying to tone down the dressiness of my outfit. I may not be the fancy girl my parents raised me to be, but this is a sport I love—a tradition I love.

You don't show up to derby day dressed like a slob.

In honor of that tradition, I paired wide-leg cream-colored dress pants with a lace blouse. Classy *and* sexy. You can see little peeks of my skin through the bare spots in the patterned lace. It isn't a dress, but this is as close as I'll get.

My hair is fresh, which feels like a feat this week. I only had time to dry it in loose natural waves, falling down past my shoulder blades, but it will have to do. My makeup is simple. I mostly used it to cover up the dark circles underneath my eyes, and whatever I didn't achieve with concealer, I'll fix with a nice big pair of aviators. It's a pristine, bluebird sunny day in Vancouver, so I can easily hide behind dark lenses.

It's the perfect day for a derby.

Hank parks near the Gold Rush Ranch bank of stalls, and I bolt away from there as fast as possible.

Childish? *Probably.* Necessary? *Definitely.*

I've been working at the track every day for the last week. I've kept my head down, shown up at the ass crack of dawn to breeze all the farm's horses that are stabled here, worked with our exercise riders, grooms, junior trainers, and shown up for every single race that one of ours has run in the in-between. I don't hang around to listen to track gossip and drama. I just do my job and then leave to mope around my house.

And that's another thing I'll have to address at some point. Hank informed me I'm welcome to stay there as long as I need. Presumably, Vaughn relayed that message to him. But I can't stay there much longer. The charming little log house is brimming with memories. Too many memories. When I look out the window, I see DD munching on a big bag of green hay in his private little oasis. Inside the house, I see Vaughn sitting at the kitchen island, barefoot and happy, peeling the label off a bottle of beer. Upstairs...

My eyes sting.

Upstairs, I see Vaughn's dark mop of hair between my legs. I still smell him on my pillows. I feel him sliding inside me.

No, there are too many memories in that little log house.

I've done my job to perfection throughout the last two weeks. No one could ever fault my professionalism on that front, even if most people think I'm a total basket case who quit over the sale of a horse.

Being here at Bell Point Park on the exact day I've spent the last several months working toward just feels… heavy. Like I'm being suffocated. I keep telling myself that heavy feeling is all to do with my dashed professional dreams. But deep down, I know it's more.

Deep down, I know it's Vaughn.

I feel his absence like a missing limb. Despite my best efforts at keeping him distant, he wriggled past my best-laid defenses. Looking back, I'm not even sure I realized I was falling in love with him. Did it happen when he purposely brought me coffee the wrong way? When we faced off in one of our verbal sparring matches? I mean, what kind of woman gets off on that kind of snarky bullshit?

Maybe it was one of those cozy nights that we cooked together and talked for hours? When he opened up to me about his father's death? His grandfather's death? Or was it the night he walked DD in circles for hours so I could rest?

I can't put my finger on when I fell in love with him anymore. It just feels like I've loved him forever. Like our hearts have been intertwined for so long that cutting his from mine is causing me to bleed out. So I hustle out of the barns, past the staging area, hoping I won't run into him, and then melt into the crowd gathering by the finish line. I want to be among the fans while I watch DD win, because I have no doubt he will. I want to dive right into that tension. That excitement. Lean into every turn with everyone around me. I want to enjoy this race like any fan would, not like someone who has a stake in it.

I want to feel something other than sad.

My mind wanders to Vaughn, who's probably schmoozing up in the VIP lounge. And Violet, who is probably looking like a nervous little fawn as she gets ready right now. My text to her yesterday was full of pointers and tips. I couldn't help myself. She responded with Thanks B. See u in the winner's circle.

I rolled my eyes when that text came through. I'm staying as far away from the winner's circle as possible. I'll celebrate with Violet on another day, in another place.

I push to the front of the crowd, standing my ground by holding on to the white banister before me. I wrap my fingers around the post and close my eyes. Buttery summer sunlight beats down on me. The ever-comforting scent of horses floats on the gentle breeze, mingling with the smell of fast-food stands and spilled beer. People talk animatedly around me, and old-fashioned horn music bellows from the speakers in the infield.

A smile touches my lips. Yup. This is race day.

The announcer's voice crackles over the sound system, droning on about the odds on each horse as the board in the infield reflects the changing numbers. I see Double Diablo up there. He's drawn number eight, which puts him in perfect position for a closer, the type of horse that likes to run at the back of the pack. The higher numbers would box him in along the rail; he'd get stuck exactly where he hates to be.

It's almost all too good to be true. Perfect weather. Perfect position. I can't help but shake my head. The universe is working in our favor today.

Their favor, I remind myself, right as the announcer's voice starts up again.

His odds are worse than they should be. Nine to two, which means for every two dollars someone bets, they're going to be paid out eleven dollars.

I shake my head. Not terrible, but not great either. They're still underestimating DD. An inexperienced jockey and a relatively unproven horse who likes to come from behind at the last moment—who could blame them, really?

But the punters are wrong. Someone ballsy is going to win a good chunk of change today.

The loudspeaker crackles to life above at the top of a pole. "Five minutes to race time!"

The horses file out onto the track. I press one hand to my stomach to calm the flapping butterflies and lean out over the fence, straining to try and see a small black horse trotting out onto the track. I catch sight of Stefan Dalca's colors, black and lime green. Perfect for a venomous snake in the grass like him.

But the horse is a flashy bay. Brown body, white legs. Does he seriously have more than one horse running today? Shady motherfucker.

Finally, I see DD being led out by a nice calm pony horse. Some horses like to go for a quick gallop before the race, but the name of the game with DD is keeping him calm and steady. He's got nerves enough for the lot of us and needs to preserve that energy for his final burst. He's so shiny that he looks like an oil slick, almost purple and blue in the sunlight.

And he's wearing black and yellow.

CHAPTER 33

Billie

I BLINK FAST, TESTING MY EYES, TRYING TO FIGURE OUT WHY Violet is sporting the golden Gold Rush Ranch silks, the silks that look so pretty against the coal-black horse, rather than the bright green.

The speakers buzz back to life. "Ladies and gentlemen, we've had a somewhat unconventional change to our lineup today."

The pulse point in my neck throbs, and I wrap my hand around my throat to feel it pulse beneath my fingers as I stare out at the track.

"Number eight, formerly raced under the name Double Diablo and owned by Gold Rush Ranch, has just submitted a change in name and ownership."

What the fuck? I thought this was done already.

"Please note in your programs that number eight is now registered under the name Mister Black."

My mouth goes dry, my tongue like sandpaper. That's what

I jokingly told Vaughn I'd name him *months ago*. What the fuck kind of sick joke was this?

"And the colt is now both owned and trained by Miss Billie Black."

Despite all the noise and people around me, all I can hear is the sound of my breathing. All I can do is stand here, frozen in shock, while the world continues to spin around me. All I can look at is *my* horse heading toward his gate.

This has to be a joke.

The hand I have wrapped around my throat feels clammy against my sensitive skin as I turn to look around myself. I want to tell someone. I have *questions*. But no one here knows me. No one around me understands what just happened.

Turning back toward the track, I feel a familiar sting across the bridge of my nose as I sniffle and press my lips together.

Owned and trained by Miss Billie Black.

This must be a mistake. Because I sure as shit have not purchased any twenty-million-dollar horses lately. How could this happen? Even if I accessed my long-forgotten trust fund, I couldn't make this happen, not even close.

I feel hot, even though the air beneath the shadow of the grandstand is cool. I can't peel my eyes off the starting gate as the horses step in one by one. It feels like everything is happening in slow motion. Like this is some sort of insane dream that I will wake from any moment now.

Who am I kidding? My subconscious couldn't have come up with a scenario like this on its best day.

The crowd goes quiet, and I'm still in a confused daze when the bell rings out and the gates fly open. "And they're off!"

I stand rigid, gripping the white fence railing for dear life as

I watch the black bullet I've spent the better part of this past year pouring my heart and soul into. He draws back off the line, like always, shying away from the sounds and rush of horsepower all around him.

All twelve teams thunder past, and I see Violet's gloved fingers offer a small reassuring scratch at his neck as they find their pace toward the back of the pack. She's cool in the irons, calm like a rookie jockey has no business being.

They're off to a good start.

They hang back through the clubhouse turn and move forward through the second stretch. But they get stuck. There's no path through the middle of the pack, and the horses are running wide, rallying for position down the straightaway.

"Fuck," I mutter. There's nothing open. Nowhere for them to go. Unless...

Violet stands taller in the irons, shifting her weight imperceptibly to the left. She wouldn't really take him in on the rail, would she?

DD's inside ear flits forward like an arrow in response to her change in balance. He sees the opening that she's shown him, and he's already heading that way. Picking up speed. Pushing in toward the rail.

I want to look away, but I can't. He's completely boxed in. Anxiety clogs my throat. There are no other options, but this isn't ideal. Far from it.

Heading into the far turn, there are four horses ahead of him, he's running three wide, and there's a whole pack behind him. I bite at my bottom lip and tap my fingers against the railing. He's going to be stuck there, right to the finish line. *Fuck.*

This isn't good.

But as soon as they start to round the second bend, Violet leans low and shoves her hands forward at him. She hits the gas. My instincts say it's too early, but nothing about this race has been perfect from a strategic standpoint.

DD flattens his ears like a small but mighty warhorse and launches out of that corner like a cannon, toward me.

My hand shoots up to stifle a small gasp as he blows past the horses beside him. Violet takes him wide around the four front-runners. It's cost her some ground to give him a clear lane to the finish line, but provided he doesn't run out of gas, he should be able to sprint down the final stretch.

My left hand joins the right, over my mouth, as I watch DD fly down the track.

Stefan Dalca's flashy bay horse is in the lead, but DD is gaining on him rapidly. Where the other horses are starting to tire, DD's fiery attitude is pushing him harder. Faster.

He smokes them all.

He and Violet fly toward the finish line in sync, both laid out flat, wild eyed and determined.

I feel the ground shake beneath my feet as they thunder past. The flash of the camera momentarily blinds me as I watch them blow past.

They did it!

The next closest horse is a couple seconds behind. Violet and DD outclassed the field in every way possible.

My god. He won!

My chest aches, and the sting in my nose comes back in full force. But this time, it's accompanied by wetness streaking down my face, over my hands that are still plastered over my slack-jawed mouth.

The crowd is loud, some cheering and some booing, but that doesn't stop me from hearing, "Congratulations, Miss Black."

I spin around to face that voice I know so well. Deep and smooth. The voice I've played in my head and that's haunted me in my dreams.

"Your horse ran beautifully," Vaughn continues, looking downright edible in a gray suit.

I drop my hands and hold them wide in shock. "But… how?"

"I sold him to you," he says, stepping closer. Like it's the most obvious thing in the world.

"I don't have that kind of money, Vaughn."

He smirks at me, looking cocky. "I found a dollar in your grooming stall. I took that in trade."

"You sold *me* a derby winner for *one dollar*?" Disbelief seeps into my voice. *Is he fucking crazy?*

He shoves his hands into his pockets and rocks back on his heels. "Yup."

I stand there, gaping at him, utterly bewildered. "Why on earth would you do that?"

He takes another tentative step toward me, coming almost toe-to-toe. "You told me I couldn't fix this unless I didn't sell your horse. So that's exactly what I did… or didn't do. Whatever. The gist of it is he's yours." A tired sigh whooshes out of his chest. "I couldn't bring myself to sign the contract. I knew that while I had already broken your trust, I didn't have to break your heart by selling your horse." He reaches toward my waist before thinking better of it and snapping his hand back. His eyes dart down before meeting mine again. "I want *you*. And there's no price on that. The money. The horse. None of it matters so long as you give me a chance to earn your trust back."

I scoff, not prepared to let him off so easily.

He runs his fingers through his dark hair with that edge of agitation I get off on before he sighs. "I love you, Billie. And I'm an idiot. I obviously don't know much, but I know that both of those statements are true."

Did I just hear him right? "You"—I point at him—"love me," I say as I point back at myself.

He barks out a disbelieving laugh. "Yes. I love you. I'm pretty sure I've loved you since that day you marched onto my farm, dressed me down, and then demanded extra pay for having a great ass."

"Huh," I say, propping my hands on my hips. I'm honestly at a loss for words. We stare at each other in awkward silence for several seconds before I blurt out, "I can't believe you actually named my horse *Mister Black*. It makes me sound like a total nut."

He blinks once slowly. "That's… what you have to say to me?"

He's so good looking, and he looks so bewildered right now. It's an excellent combination, I think. I can't help the smile that touches my lips as I look away across the crowd and say, "Kiss me, Boss Man."

That hand that stuttered moments ago shoots out to palm my waist as he pulls me toward him. There's no hesitation now. And he's like the sun. I can't help but be pulled into his orbit.

His thumb strokes my jaw while his fingers grip my neck. I sigh and lean into the feel of his hands on my body. In public, with clothes on, it feels like sparks dancing across my skin no matter what.

When he drops his head toward mine, I lick my lips, wetting them, so I can feel his breath dance across my mouth as he moves in.

When he's close enough that it feels private, when his broad shoulders envelop me, I whisper my own secret against his lips. "I love you too, Vaughn Harding."

The edges of his shapely, wicked lips tip up in satisfaction. And then he kisses me. With one hand on my hip bone and the other gliding down over my throat, he pours all that love right into me. I can feel it in the way he moves against me. His lips tease mine in the most careful and delicious way. In a way that makes my cheeks burn and my thighs press together. In a way that sends shivers down my spine and tingles across my hips.

I hang on to the lapels of his jacket for dear life, letting his passion soothe my tortured soul like a balm. Like an antidote. Wishing we were somewhere more private right now. That we didn't have a winner's circle to get to.

Because *my* horse won the derby. Somebody fucking pinch me.

When he finally pulls back a bit, he holds me close and rests his forehead against mine. We're both a little breathless as he looks me in the eye and promises, "I'll always choose you, Billie."

And I smile.

Because I believe him.

After the whirlwind that is the winner's circle and never-ending interviews, I feel like I'm drunk. The kind of intoxication where your vision goes wonky and time flies because you just feel like you're spinning in circles meeting people and talking. I can't even tell you what I've said.

The entire day has officially broken my brain. I am mush.

Which is why when Vaughn slides his warm hand down my forearm and then grips my trembling fingers in his, I don't protest. I let him lead me away from the media circus, away from the throngs of people and reporters loitering around. I expect him to take me up to the stuffy VIP lounge, but he turns left and heads toward the Gold Rush Ranch bank of stalls. His thumb draws small reassuring circles on my palm as he walks me down the aisle toward where DD usually stays.

He pulls a rectangular hay bale down off a stack of them and plops it right in front of *my horse's* stall and then points at it. "Sit."

I'm too dumbstruck from the day to even argue with him. I take a couple of steps on wooden legs before sitting on the bale and exhaling. I put my head down low between my knees and try to take some cleansing breaths, try to get my bearings a bit. I feel like I'm in the fucking twilight zone.

"Here." I look up to see Vaughn holding out a folded piece of paper to me. His hand shakes slightly as he does.

"What is it?"

"Just read it." His voice is soft and vulnerable, even though he looks like pure masculine power towering over me in an expensive suit.

I press my lips together and take it from him, gently unfolding it on my lap. And then I read.

One hand falls across my chest as I read the letter from Dermot Harding. Basically, a love letter to his family. Intensely personal and intensely reflective. My throat feels thick, and my lashes go wet as my eyes trace the beautiful words the man penned to his grandson, the intense tragedy of his life almost more than I can take while I'm already feeling so vulnerable.

"Vaughn..." I look up into the eyes of the man I love and run my hand up over my throat.

His jaw ticks as his eyes blink quickly, trying to shut down the emotion building there.

I stand up, going toe-to-toe with him, placing one palm on each stubbled cheek and then looking him straight in his deep chocolate eyes. "Vaughn. I know I never got to meet your grandfather, which is a damn shame, but I can tell you two things." I give his head a reassuring little shake. "Dermot Harding was a good man, and he loved you deeply. How incredibly lucky are you?"

Vaughn doesn't say anything. His glistening eyes search mine, like he might find the answers to the world in me. Like I'm precious beyond compare.

"I love you, Billie Black," he says and then wraps me in his arms. A tight, bone-crushing hug, like the handshake he gave me on the first day we met. Like he'll never let me go.

We're still holding each other in the busy barn alleyway when Hank, Mira, and Violet walk up leading a freshly bathed DD.

"Back off, Harding. I need a turn," Hank quips as Vaughn chuckles and nudges me toward him.

Hank congratulates me and tells me he's proud, Mira gives me a full report on DD's postrace health before offering me quick congratulations, and when Violet and I hug, we basically just squeal and then cry like the emotional messes we both are right now. I see Mira roll her eyes, which just makes me laugh.

I put DD into his stall, showering him in praise and kisses while the others talk. I cradle his pointy little ear in my hand and lean in toward him so I can whisper, "We did it, boy. We showed them all." He nickers and shakes his head before pushing his head around my side to check my pockets for treats. *Some things never change.*

When I step out of the stall, Vaughn has procured a bottle of champagne and some red plastic cups. He pops the cork and pours each of us a cup of the celebratory bubbles before dragging me down onto the hay bale beside him.

I tilt my head toward Vaughn's ear, not wanting to interrupt the story Hank is telling now, and I whisper, "We're going to deliver on that promise your grandfather made, you know. We're going to win it all."

He squeezes me closer to him, letting the corner of his mouth quirk up as he responds, "I know. You'll do anything you set your mind to." He lifts my hand and drops a gentle kiss on the back, like a seal on the promise we just made.

I lean into the heat of his body, resting my head on his shoulder and sipping my champagne, as I listen to my friends—no, family—recount the race. Everyone is grinning ear to ear. Everyone is beyond happy. And I realize I am too. The happiest I've been in a long time, possibly ever. Maybe I've finally found what I've been searching for.

These people. This place. That horse. Sitting together on a hay bale beside the man I love. What could be better?

EPILOGUE

Vaughn

BILLIE WOKE ME UP BY CRAWLING ON TOP OF ME AND WHISPERING, "I need your cock, Boss Man," in my ear before dragging her teeth down my neck and fisting my length roughly. I have a real love-hate relationship with that nickname.

But this morning, it's working out well for me.

She's straddling my waist, hips rolling seductively. Golden morning sunlight fills the room, highlighting the matching streaks in her chestnut hair like a halo. I watch her body move, her hands roaming her breasts wantonly.

Fuck. She's looks so good touching herself while she rides me. Like an angel. A pain-in-the-ass angel with a trucker mouth, who I love.

"Come here, baby," I rasp out, urging her to lean forward. When she does, I wrap my hand around her throat, and she moans, letting her eyes flutter shut.

I can't help but smirk as I squeeze lightly around her slender neck. My dirty girl loves this.

She slams herself down harder on my length, and I feel a bead of sweat roll down the back of my neck as I strain to watch her.

When I reach my other hand up to circle her sensitive nub, her panting starts to sound more like mewling. "Oh god, Vaughn. I'm going to come."

I thrust up into her wet heat, swirling my fingers, excited to watch her come apart. It never gets old. This woman can crawl on top of me for the rest of my life, and I'll never tire of it.

When I squeeze that delicate bundle of nerves, she cries out and writhes on top of me. Her lips part, and her loose hair sticks to her damp forehead. The view paired with the way she's pulsing around me is too much, and I roar my orgasm into her body and growl, "Take it all, baby. Every drop."

"Yesss," she hisses out before falling forward onto my heaving chest.

We lie together, letting our breathing slow, letting our heart rates return to steady beats, for several minutes. Our quiet moments together are still some of the most intimate we share.

She eventually presses a gentle kiss right over my heart. "Thank you. Now coffee, please."

I laugh as she rolls off me and flops onto the mattress with a satisfied smirk on her face. "That's all you want me for. My cock and my coffee."

She bites down on her bottom lip with a mischievous glint in her eye. "Don't forget your tongue."

I shake my head as I toss on a pair of sweats, shooting her a wounded look over my shoulder as I jog down the stairs. If my girl wants coffee, she gets coffee. With cream. Just the right amount. Exactly how she likes it.

Down in the kitchen of the log house, I hit the button on the coffee maker and then slide on a pair of shoes to head outside.

DD nickers at me when he hears the back porch door open. I imagine that he's saying something like, "Bring my hay, peasant!"

So that's what I do. What the king wants, the king gets.

I shove a few flakes of our best into a net and toss it over the fence to him before giving him a few sound pats and shaking my head.

The little horse that could.

The horse that nobody wanted to work with. The horse that saved me—who brought Billie back to me. I'd never be able to repay him. So the best hay that money can buy and the odd peppermint for the rest of his life it will be.

Back up on the porch, I realize I missed the newspaper that someone left there. Hank or Violet, hard to say which. Stepping into the house, I shake the paper out and read the headline.

LOCAL STALLION TAKES THE NORTHERN CROWN IN ANOTHER STUNNING WIN

Pride bubbles in my chest. I can't take credit for any of this. It's all Billie, and I couldn't be more proud of her. Her work ethic, her drive, her passion. I've always known she's an inspiring woman. A force to be reckoned with.

A force I have every intention of locking down for the long haul. I pat my sweatpants to make sure the little black box is still there, where I planted it last night.

Coffee in hand, I head back upstairs. Billie is lounging in the sunny bedroom wearing my T-shirt in the charming little house we've both come to love and call home over the last several months. My city apartment is a glorified closet at this point.

Setting the coffees down on the bedside table, I drop a kiss on her forehead, trying to hide the shaking of my hands. "Coffee for my love. Just the way she likes it."

She giggles happily and sits up, propping pillows behind herself. "I'm amazed you didn't bring it black just to piss me off."

"I would never do that," I deadpan.

"Mm-hmm." She looks at me with accusation in her eyes.

I place one hand across my chest like I'm about to take an oath. But with the other, I pull the velvet box out of my pocket and hold it out to her. "I promise to make it just the way you like it for the rest of your life."

She shakes her head like she's testing her vision and then points at my outstretched hand. "Is that…?"

I drop to my knees beside the bed. "Billie Black, I choose you. Over and over again. Every time." My voice cracks with emotion, but I forge ahead. "Will you marry me?"

Her eyes are glassy and her cheeks are the prettiest pink as she stares back at me with earnest intensity on her face. It feels like minutes pass when it's really only seconds.

"Vaughn Harding, I'll choose you back every damn day."

"Is that a yes?"

One tear spills out and trails over her cheek as she whispers, "That's a hell yes."

I launch myself at her on the bed, wrapping around her, soaking up her feel, her smell. Our joy.

I can hardly believe it. I get *this*.

Forever.

How the hell did I get so lucky?

She sniffles and nuzzles into my neck. And then she says, "Do we have to name DD Mister Harding now though?"

I can't help but laugh as I lean back to look at her. "You're insane, you know that?"

She tilts her head and smiles shyly. "Yeah, but you love it."

And I smile.

Because it's true.

BONUS SCENE

Billie

DD's SLENDER BACK BUMPS AND SWAYS BENEATH ME. I CLOSE my eyes and relax my back and hips to let his motion lull me into a temporary place of calm. His black coat makes touching him like sitting on a big black rock that has been soaking up the sun's warmth all day.

His inescapable dusty horse smell mingles with the coconut scent of the moisturizing spray I use on him. His aluminum-clad hooves make a dull *clip-clop* sound against the lush grass, and the birds sing sweetly overhead as he plods along the path we take home every day.

This is peace. This is happiness. This exact moment is pretty much heaven. Who needs therapy when you can have this?

DD is like me in that way. We like the simple life. He'll be much happier away from the hustle and bustle of the track, away from the other horses and trainers and all the unspoken tension that inevitably floats around places like that.

Horses are simple to understand if you're listening. If something scares him, he tells me. If he's busy eating, he tells me. If he doesn't like someone, he tells me that too. He is honest, direct, and reliable. There are very few surprises with a horse's personality once you get to know them.

After spending every day together for almost three months, I have come to know DD very well. I know his body language, his moods, and I know that he can feel my inner turmoil right now when he stops and looks back at me to gently nibble the boot of my toe. I lean forward and give him a little ear scratch behind the leather strap of his bridle. My "What a sweet boy" comes out so much weaker than I want it to.

But it doesn't matter. DD won't judge me.

Not like Vaughn, who must currently think I'm totally erratic. Okay, more erratic than he already did. My reaction smacked me up the side of the head, like a dodgeball I didn't see coming. I sure as shit didn't dodge. And then I ran away from him like a huge crybaby. Like he owed me something. Talk about an overreaction.

He canceled our regular Saturday night dinner to go to some glitzy fundraiser. That's allowed. And he's probably got some smoking hot date to take with him. That's allowed too. Even though the mere thought makes my chest pinch painfully.

I blow a raspberry out through my lips.

My emotional control is somewhat lacking. I'm aware of that character flaw. But this. *Yikes.* This was new. I should not be disappointed over one missed casual dinner where I make boring small talk with a person I barely even like.

And since I don't like him, I definitely shouldn't care that he's probably going to spend the night with a completely different type of woman than me. She'll be beautiful and glamorous and probably not avoiding her family name and her gigantic untouched trust fund. No, Saturday's girl would probably be perfectly at home in that lifestyle rather than hiding out with her temperamental equine boyfriend.

It's his loss. My plan was to make the best asparagus risotto. I'll still make it. I'll just force Violet to hang out with me. I don't have to be a lonely hermit if I don't want to be.

And who Vaughn bangs in his free time is less than none of my business. In fact, I don't even want to think about it. It makes me feel a little bit nauseous to let my mind wander over to that image. *Why would it make you feel nauseous, Billie?* Because he's gross and all wrong, that's why.

He's a quintessential trust fund baby, exactly what I fled. He cycles through women like I cycle through trashy paperbacks. He's uptight and has a terrible sense of humor. And he's my boss at a job that I love and value and don't want to lose. Essentially, he's good enough friend material and terrible anything else material. I hardly notice his dark brooding eyes, defined jaw, and toned shoulders.

I'll admit to noticing his exceptional work ethic and his butt, and that's it. Because I'm only human and that butt is glorious. I get the best view of it when I piss him off and he storms away. Double win.

Basically, other than that ass, I am so not going there. I've got horses to train and races to win.

I start prepping dinner early so I'm not still cooking while Violet is here. Housing is limited in Ruby Creek, so she lives in the apartment over the barn.

I've been in a funk since Vaughn canceled on me, and the sting of not having any long-term friends or family around hurts more than usual. Which is why I'm calling Rich while stirring my risotto for the next few minutes.

"Hey, Little Willie!"

I roll my eyes at my brother's greeting even though he can't see me.

"Shut up, Dick."

He cackles. This has been an ongoing point of amusement for us throughout our lives. How two people as proper as Victor and Miranda Farrington managed to name both their children names with penis-themed nicknames would forever be beyond me.

"How is slumming it going for you?" my brother prods. He's such a priss.

"I'm not slumming it, princess. I'm living life like a normal person does. And it's great, thank you very much."

"I know, B. I'm just bugging ya. You know how proud I am of you."

His approval makes me feel all warm and gooey inside. A flash of guilt hits me for not being a better sister to Rich after everything he's helped me do. "I'm sorry I haven't called lately. The new gig has been keeping me busy," I say guiltily.

"Figured as much. Don't stress it. Busy around here. More of the same. Dad wanted me to ask if you were good for money. Your accounts are all still here. He says you haven't touched them."

He always has to go and ruin a perfectly nice conversation with this shit. "Don't plan to," I bite out.

"Okay, okay. Don't shoot the messenger. Just thought I'd ask. They worry about you, you know."

I snort. "Little late for that, don't ya think?"

"Yeah, yeah, B. I know. How about a visit sometime this summer? I'll come play cowboy for a few days or whatever."

"Never want to see you in chaps, bro. Never. But yes, absolutely. Let me know when you're thinking, and I'll take a peek at my work calendar. I'll be down at the track in Vancouver a lot more by then, so maybe we can keep you in your natural concrete habitat." I pause, hating that I even have to ask him my next question. "They don't know where I am, right?"

His responding sigh is an exhausted one. "No, B. They don't."

"Okay. I'll talk to you soon."

"Don't be a stranger," he says right as my timer goes off.

I hear the line click and look around the empty house, feeling a little less alone after talking to Rich.

With dinner prepped, I take a quick breeze through the house to make sure it's up to snuff for company and then I hit the shower. Violet will probably appreciate seeing me without sweaty helmet hair for once. With time to spare, I decide to style my hair for the first time in, I don't know, possibly years. It's too long right now. I haven't had it cut since I was in Ireland. Not enough time and not enough reason. Usually a braid or a bun is sufficient, especially when most of my days are spent with a helmet or cap on.

But today, I use a large-barrel curling iron to create some loose shiny waves. The nostalgia of primping like this hits me like a ton of bricks. These are things that mattered before I left my parents' home. High-society pressure told me that it did. That I represented my family reputation in some way, and the care I took in getting ready was somehow a reflection of my pride in that.

My parents would have had something to say if I tried to walk out of the house looking anything short of put together. I'd spend over an hour every morning getting ready for school, like how I looked mattered while I was trying to get an education. And the unspoken part of it all was that it did matter in those circles. No one cared what kind of professional I could become or how smart I was. They cared about what connections I could make through marriage.

Welcome to the 1800s! What a joke.

I pair my shiny chestnut locks with something plain and casual, a silent middle finger to my upbringing. Torn light denim jeans and a thin white crop sweater are just lowbrow enough to do the trick. I'm just finishing up with a quick spritz of perfume when I hear light tentative rapping on the door.

Ha. Violet. So predictably timid. If Vaughn thinks I'm a bonkers, then I'm pretty sure Violet must believe I've escaped an insane asylum. But we work well together. She has become the yin to my yang. The horses love her, our gentler handling methods align well, and even though she's softer than I am, she isn't a pushover. Which is also good because this industry will eat a flaky woman alive.

I swing the door open to find diminutive little Violet standing there with a bouquet of flowers in one hand and a bottle of white wine in the other.

"You're already the best date I've had in years."

Her shoulders rise up to her ears, and she squeezes her lips together to avoid smiling.

"Vi, has anyone ever told you how adorable you are?" I say, grabbing the flowers from her outreached hand and taking them to the kitchen to find something that could pass as a vase.

"Yeah, you. Almost daily." She snorts sarcastically.

"There she is! Violet the paradox. Never change."

"Yeah, yeah. Where's your wine opener? I need a drink."

I eye her speculatively and hand her a corkscrew.

"Something you want to share?"

"Nope," she replies, popping the *p* in an ultra-sassy way so I know that she's lying.

"Is it a guy?"

Her bright blue eyes assess me from over the wineglass she has already filled and is all but chugging from.

"Yikes," I say, forcing my lips back into a toothy grimace. "Would you like to speak with the resident therapist? His office is just out that door." I point to the back corner of the kitchen. "He's the strong, silent, dreamy one with shiny black hair."

Her cheeks suck in to keep from spitting out her full mouth of wine.

"Made you laugh!" I cry out, pointing at her.

She giggles and daintily dabs at her lips. I think I successfully made her lose a few drops of wine. "No, I think I'm good to just drink and chill out for tonight… unless you want to go over that hair-pulling episode with Mr. Harding yesterday?" Her brow quirks up quizzically.

"All right!" I reply a little too brightly, rounding the corner of the island and slinging my arm over her miniature shoulders. "Come sit with me on the patio, and we can talk about not-guys all night long."

★★★

The asparagus risotto is delicious, just like I knew it'd be, and when we're finished, we lean back in our patio chairs, looking out over the back field and rubbing our overly full stomachs. We're polishing off another bottle of wine, because why the fuck not?

"I think I have a food baby," Violet groans.

"Just make sure you tell everyone that I'm the daddy," I quip back. Leaving out the part where I too feel like I might have a food baby.

She groans. "Seriously, Billie. Why did you feed me so much?"

"Trying to make you grow, Vi. It's like you're stunted. You should become a jockey really."

"That's the plan."

My eyes shift over to her at that, but I'm too full to actually move to look at her.

"Really?"

"Yup. All my hours right now count toward the licensing requirements."

"I had no idea," I say thoughtfully. "Why haven't you asked to do any riding?"

"I don't know," she says, stretching out her sprite-like little legs and sighing. "I just haven't wanted to step on any of the exercise rider's toes, you know? I have to sort of wait my turn."

I muster the energy to sit up, turn toward her, and look at her intensely. "No, Violet. I don't know. Life doesn't just happen to you. You make it happen for yourself. Especially as a woman in this business. Say what you want. Say it every damn day. Step on those toes. Bathe in their tears. Achieving your goals"—I give her a good, firm, somewhat tipsy poke in the middle of her chest—"through hard work, dedication, and natural talent is not crossing a line. Take what you want. Do it honorably, but do it unapologetically."

She stares back at me, all big blue eyes and mop of silvery hair, and gives me a forceful nod. It's like I can see the determination flicker in her chest and blaze up across her facial features.

"That's some deep advice for someone who seems like they're joking around all the time."

"I'm two speeds. You just haven't seen me angry yet, little Violet," I retort with a wink, trying to keep my facade up, not wanting to show how solemn I'm feeling beneath it all tonight.

She shudders at that. Like she already knows she probably doesn't want to see me angry. *Smart.*

"Go get some sleep," I say, waving my hand at her dismissively. "You start riding some of the young horses on Monday."

"But who will groom for you?" she responds, looking alarmed.

"We'll tag team it. I didn't get to where I am by not knowing how to take care of my own horses. I can do grunt work just as capably as you."

She looks shocked, pert pink little mouth hanging slightly ajar. In her defense, most trainers wouldn't ever consider doing a groom's job. But then plenty of them don't even get on their own horses. They just set the program and have exercise riders do the work while they critique on the sidelines. I'm not saying that kind of system can't work, but it's not my style. If I'm not willing to get my hands dirty, how can I expect Violet to want to do it for me?

I cough out a laugh. "Violet, stop giving me that look. You're going to catch flies in your mouth, and then I'll have to start calling you flytrap, and everyone will want to know why."

She slams her mouth shut and rubs her hands down the tops of her thighs as she pushes up to stand.

"Okay, Boss Woman." She says it so quietly that I'm not even sure if I heard her correctly.

I tip my head all the way back and groan very dramatically. "Violet. Don't ever say that again."

She's full-on laughing at me now. "I think I will. And then I'll bathe in your tears over it."

"Jesus. What have I done?" I chuckle into her hair while wrapping her tiny frame in a tight hug.

"Thank you, Billie," she says earnestly.

I step back and look her in the eye, holding her shoulders at arm's length with a faint smile tugging at the corners of my lips. "You're welcome, Violet."

She beams back at me and then turns to leave, walking through the field toward the stables in what is not a very straight line. I'd be willing to venture a guess that my little Violet isn't in the habit of polishing off an entire bottle of white wine. So I stand there, chuckling to myself and watching her traverse the hill in the fading light.

With Violet gone now, it's just me, myself, and my thoughts again. And sometimes I hate living in my own head. I fixate on my past, I grapple with self-doubt, and I overanalyze the future. I feel tired of myself tonight. I need a holiday from my own brain.

So I open another bottle of wine.

Vaughn

I don't know what I'm doing here. It's a magnificently bad idea.

My night has been a typical represent-the-family sort of schtick. Smile for a few pictures, answer some reporter's soul-sucking questions about my grandfather and Gold Rush Ranch, and then make meaningless small talk with a bunch of strangers.

The only thing out of the ordinary is that I actually had the gonads to tell my mom I'd be attending alone. She grumbled about it, but I didn't care. I wasn't in the mood for women or entertaining one or whatever else came with a night out on the town with a date.

I'd be lying if I said there weren't nights over the last several years when I hadn't at least sampled the goods. When I was in the mood, it felt good, and it was convenient. That sounds cruel, but I was always very up-front with my dates. One night. No strings. Back to work. Long-term entanglements just aren't for me.

Which is why showing up at Billie Black's cottage at 10:00 p.m. is a terrible idea.

I cut out of the fundraiser early and started the long drive from Vancouver to Ruby Creek. I want to say that I couldn't tell you why I was doing this, but deep down, I know that I could.

Watching Billie's face fall yesterday afternoon was a punch to the gut. She'd been ecstatic after her ride. Positively glowing. Seeing her then was like looking at the sun too long and then trying to look elsewhere but having those big bright spots marring your view.

I waltzed in and tarnished her glow.

She's a tough cookie. She covered the slip of her features quickly but not quickly enough. I saw it. And then she marched off with this fake ultra-perky persona that didn't suit her at all. I liked it better when she was giving me hell. At least I knew where I stood then. For her to be frank, cheerful, amenable Billie creeped me out.

So maybe I could say I'm only driving out here to make sure she's still herself. To have her dress me down, swear like a sailor, prove that she's okay in her own unique way. But then I'd have to admit that I missed having dinner with her.

Sitting at a big round table full of people I only know in passing and don't really like has always been an easy sell for me. But tonight, knowing that I could instead have been perched on a stool enjoying a cold beer at Billie's kitchen island made it almost unbearable.

I pull up, relieved to see that there are still lights on in the cottage. I have no idea what I'm about to do or say, but I stride up to the door and knock swiftly three times. And then I wait.

But I don't hear or see any movement. I knock again a couple of times and then splay my fingers against the wooden door, leaning closer.

"Billie? It's Vaughn," I call out, hoping that she'll hear me.

I soak in the quiet for a few beats before I hear, "Sorry, I'm busy with my therapist!" from around the side of the house.

I follow the sound of her voice around to Double Diablo's paddock and find her lying flat on her back on a blanket beside his paddock.

"Is this where you sleep now, Mowgli?" I venture apprehensively, not sure her response was really an invite to join her.

Standing above her, in an area only lit by the dim warm glow of the exterior cabin lights, I can see that she looks more introspective than usual. I gaze down, drinking her in. Her skin glows against the brightness of her white shirt. Riding outdoors has left her looking kissed by the sun. Her chestnut hair is splayed out around her feminine face, styled in waves reminding me of the ripples you see in the sand at the beach.

She hums quietly, as though she's actually contemplating sleeping here. And then she shivers almost imperceptibly.

"Are you cold?"

"No," is her simple response as she continues to gaze up at the stars.

I shrug off my tuxedo jacket and lay it over her body like a blanket, as though I'm tucking in a small child, and take an apprehensive seat on the grass beside her, not wanting to invade her space but not wanting to leave either.

I sit quietly, taking in the stillness of the night, and watch her reach up to run one long finger across the collar of my jacket. I'm entranced and realize I have no clue to what to do or say next.

"Your jacket smells like perfume" is how she breaks the silence.

I don't want to have to explain myself—it's probably from my mother anyway—so I try to resort to our comfort zone and come back with, "You smell like wine."

She snorts at that before retreating into her head and looking all contemplative. I decide that giving her some space to sit in silence is the kind thing to do, not to mention I'm still not sure what to say to her or how to explain why I'm here in the first place. The moments stretch out, and I can feel my eyelids start to droop, forcing me to lie back. The dampness of the grass seeps through my white dress shirt, and I contemplate leaving when Billie whispers, "Do you ever feel like you're lonely even when you're in a room full of people?"

Jesus. I turn my head to look at her and let my eyes linger on her profile. Her face is serene, but her eyes look turbulent under those long lashes.

"All the time," I say on a sigh.

"Huh" is her only response.

"Are you lonely, Billie? If you need time off to visit family or something, you just need to ask."

She lets out a loud "Pfff!" before turning her head to look back at me. "I'm not in contact with my family."

"Why not?"

She closes her eyes gently for a beat before looking back into mine. "They disowned me. Or I disowned them. Probably depends on who you ask."

"How come?" I ask, open curiosity on my face now.

"Snoopy, snoopy," she says with a small curl to her lips as she reaches forward to boop me on the nose.

A laugh rumbles in my chest. "Billie Black, you are drunk as a skunk."

"Your date smells like she was sprayed by a skunk," is her very witty retort.

I scoff and shake my head at her. I interlock my hands behind my head to gaze up at the stars. They're so clear out here. Away from the neon glow of the big city, they aren't dulled at all.

She's still staring at me when she says, "You're so obedient. Do you ever just want to shirk your responsibilities? Stir the pot a little? Do things your own way rather than constantly worrying about how it will reflect on your family name or what people will think?"

God. Why does drunk Billie have to be all deep and full of questions? I know she's talking about my mother's well-meaning but bizarre fixation on matchmaking me. I know being married to my dad was the pinnacle of happiness for her, and that's what she wants for me. But she's never really stopped to ask me what *I* want. The whole schtick makes me feel sleazy enough as it is without having to discuss it with someone whose respect I value.

"I've never said that I worry about that."

She follows my line of sight, looking up at the night sky. "I can tell you do."

Am I really that transparent? Most of my employees, coworkers, and dates have compared me to Fort Knox in some way, shape, or form. A ragged sigh escapes my lips. "It would be hard for you to understand."

"The only thing that's hard for me to understand is why you put up with it," she replies with a bit of bite.

We turn to look at each other then. Really look at each other. I soak in her wild untamed beauty, trying to ignore how intensely I feel her gaze. It's like a weight on my ribs. I can see her chest rise and fall with each breath. Her typically upturned mouth is pinched with tension, and her intense amber eyes are glassy from a few too many drinks. She looks more broken than usual, and the urge to fix her is overwhelming.

Seeing her all laid out and tortured looking like this makes my cock swell and breath quicken. I lick my lips—I can't help it. The forlorn authenticity of the way she looks right now speaks to my primal side, the one that wants to comfort her in the most primitive way possible. The one that wants to press her cheek against the grass and claim her. The one that wants her riding me so I can watch every emotion play out across her face when I slide into her. So I can watch her head tip back in ecstasy while I roll her nipples between my fingers until she cries out and shatters with me inside her.

I want Billie Black. And it's the worst fucking idea I've ever had.

"You should go," she whispers hoarsely, yanking me from my reverie.

I blink a few times before pulling myself together. She's right, of course.

"I'll get you some water before I go," I say, shooting back up to my feet and heading quickly toward her back patio, adjusting my swollen cock now that I'm facing away from her.

I stop in my tracks as I take in the outdoor dinner table where we usually sit together on Saturday nights. Except I wasn't here tonight, and there are still two wineglasses sitting out beside the bottle of wine. Through the back window, I can see a big bouquet of white roses on the counter.

Suddenly I feel like I've intruded on something that wasn't meant for me. A night that wasn't meant for me. I've intruded on an employee, on a *friend*, by showing up completely uninvited to say absolutely nothing. And I blew off an important networking event to do it. All I had to show for my night was a raging boner and a harsh reminder that romantic entanglements were an unnecessary distraction from my career goals and a potential threat to the family reputation.

Billie was an especially bad idea. She couldn't possibly understand my world and the pressures that go with being a Harding. Tonight was proof of that. The woman basically had a personality for every occasion. Hot, cold, indifferent—*complicated.*

So in what I will admit is not one of my bravest moments, I walk around the other side of the yard, get into my car, and drive away.

Billie can get her own water.

Acknowledgments

I did it! My first novel. And I would not have made it to the finish line without the help of so many people.

First, my husband, who patiently listened to me hash this story out (and okay, sometimes cry about it) even though it doesn't include any dragons or lightsabers. My son, who is the best reprieve from writer's brain. Nothing like playing dinosaurs when I can't shake that fog. And my parents, who have been telling me that I should write for years now. Love you guys. And look! Skipping most of high school English worked out all right after all.

Paula, my editor and fairy godmother, you turned a pumpkin into a princess-worthy carriage. I would be lost without your keen eye and thoughtful critique. I pretty much live for your notes in the margin. It's hard to believe that this is the very first book we did together, who could have known that we'd go on to do another eight or nine? And more to come, because you are stuck with me!

My agent, Kimberly, who believes in me so thoroughly, and who's so good to me even when I'm not at my best, I'm so fortunate to have you on my team.

My editor at Bloom, Christa (and all the other amazing members of team Bloom!), thank you from the bottom of my heart for loving my books and for giving my debut series this kind of love. When I wrote this book I *never* thought this is where it would end up and it is truly such a thrill to be working with you all.

Lastly, Melanie Harlow, I don't know how I'll ever really repay you for your kindness, generosity, and feedback. Your truth bombs always land in just the right place, at just the right time, and I could not be more grateful for you.

Thank you, everyone, for reading. I really can't believe I published a book.

Someone pinch me.

OUT OF THE GATE

A Gold Rush Ranch
Prequel Novella

For all the girls whose best use for flowers was braiding them into their horse's mane.

"Why are you so sad?"

"Because you speak to me in words and
I look at you with feelings."

—LEO TOLSTOY

CHAPTER 1

Ada

I HIT THE HARD DIRT WITH A LOUD THUD THAT ECHOES THROUGH my bones. My teeth rattle at the impact and I feel a small rock pressing into my right shoulder blade. I close my eyes and groan at the sound of galloping hooves rumbling across the ground.

Again. She tossed me again.

I'm a farm girl; we're raised hardy. But good lord—my eyes flutter shut—this filly is going to be the death of me. All I want to do is spend my summer break away from university, training my new project horse. I want to be the one to sit on her for the first time, maybe walk around in a small circle. My expectations are pretty low. But she is not having it.

Footsteps approach and I still don't open my eyes. I know all the ranch hands think my project is a great joke and, frankly, I don't want to hear about it.

I'm probably fine. Bruised to hell and sore tomorrow, but fine. Right now, if I don't move, nothing hurts. So maybe I'll just stay here? Live out my life lying in the field.

A noisy sigh rushes past my lips as I take an inventory of my aching body.

Toes and fingers still wiggle.

Head still turns side to side.

"You alive, Goldilocks?"

Heart stops beating.

Eyes squeeze shut even harder.

That voice. I'm pretty sure my blood stops pumping and pools in my beet-red cheeks.

"Coulda sworn I taught you better than that."

My lungs empty painfully, all the air rushing out in a gasp.

Dermot Harding.

My heart slams back into action, rioting behind my ribs as I lift my hands to scrub my face. Not wanting to even look at him, because I know what I'll see. The single most attractive man I've ever known, older and out of my league. The man I've spent the last three years trying to get over. The childhood crush I've never outgrown.

The man I've loved since I was a ten-year-old girl.

When I finally decide to pry my eyes open, he's looking down over me, blocking out the direct sun but wearing its rays like a halo. Smirking.

My body melts into a pathetic, speechless puddle of a lovestruck girl right at his feet. I forget about my horse. I forget where I am. I just stare at him, thinking that I could probably just lie here under his glow and be happy.

And then the anger hits. *Three long years.* Not a letter. No word. *Nothing.* I latch on to that feeling, knowing I'll need it to maintain my strength. That inner fire and fury will be the only thing that keeps me from falling down the same rabbit hole as before. I haven't worked this hard at moving on to end up there again.

"You're back." *Obviously, Ada. You idiot.* I blink like I can't quite believe he's here. Standing over me, in the flesh, after so long. "When did you get back?"

He reaches one broad palm out to help me up. "A couple months ago."

I place my hand in his and struggle to swallow a small whimper when we make contact. Instead, I just make an awkward gurgling noise. I swear my entire body comes alive when he's around; it's like an electric current shoots up my arm. Touching him is akin to resting my finger on one of the live fences around here—it always has been. For me anyway.

His eyes widen imperceptibly as he pulls me to standing and then he yanks his hand back, as though I'm diseased or something. Like he can't stand touching me. Like *that* night all over again.

Clearing my throat, I dust my jeans off and roll my shoulders back, then jut my chin up proudly. I refuse to crumble around him. I have nothing to be embarrassed about. I'm an adult now, a university student—I've lived my life. Had boyfriends. Grown up. *Moved on.*

We all make regrettable choices when we're lovesick teenagers.

From the corner of my eye, I see my filly, Penny, grazing happily by the fence. Not feeling the least bit bad about bucking me off. Apparently, she's glad to be rid of me and *that's* the exact energy I need to channel too.

He's been home for months and hasn't thought to come see us? Feelings of inadequacy sour my voice when I finally respond with, "And you're just stopping by now?"

Dermot shoves his hands in his pockets and kicks at the ground. "I needed some time to get right after my tour. To unwind."

The gravel in his tone has my eyes snapping up to scour his form before me. Here I am acting like a petulant child, not even considering how his time in the army may have impacted him.

I drink him in like a cold soda on a hot day. Annoyingly, he's just as delicious as I remember. With a dropping sensation in my gut, I'm forced to admit he might be even more stunning than ever. He looks more densely muscled, broader, more mature—he must be thirty-one now. Dark shadows move behind his fathomless eyes, like a man who's seen too much.

But that doesn't matter, because he's more painfully irresistible than ever before. Hawkish dark brown eyes and even darker hair, strong masculine features that still somehow manage not to look too coarse. The perfect dusting of scruff over shapely lips.

Lips that didn't move at all beneath mine that night.

Big hands that could circle my entire waist. Dermot is tall and imposing, a farm boy through and through, and I feel like a delicate little bird next to him. A bird that has been chirping around his head, seeking attention for years.

A bird that he batted away three years ago before leaving the ranch—the country.

I stood on his balcony, eyes shrink-wrapped in tears at the knowledge he'd be leaving, and a voice thick with longing. I told him I'd miss him. I told him I loved him. And then I stood up on my tippy-toes, slid my hands over his muscular shoulders, and pressed my lips against his while he stood there completely frozen.

"Ada, you can't do this, you're too young," he said with pity in his eyes as he gently pushed me away.

The memory still makes me cringe. Makes my throat feel hot and dry. It could still make me cry, if I let it. But I finished crying over Dermot Harding a long time ago. I've moved on.

"Why are you here?" My voice sounds wobbly even to my own ears, and I cross my arms to hide my shaking hands.

"Your dad asked me to come down and break some youngsters for him." He grins at me, melting my panties. *You're still pathetic, Ada.* "He says no one starts a horse better than I do."

I scoff with forced amusement, meeting the warmth of his eyes. A soft, alluring brown, like the saddles I spent hours oiling on a fence while watching him break the young horses every summer. The perfect contrast against the bright green valley of Ruby Creek that leads out to the steep North Cascades mountain range.

"And after watching you just now, I have to say… I might know why he thinks that." He winks, always cocky and joking. Like nothing monumental ever happened between us.

"Yeah, yeah." I shake my head as I turn to walk toward Penny. "It's great to see you too, Dermot," I add from over my shoulder, not able to look at him any longer.

"You want help with the filly?" I stop midstep, surprised by the offer.

"Do you have time?" I call back, trying to act casual as I continue my approach toward the beautiful copper-colored filly.

"Spending a few weeks, so yup."

My breathing goes shallow. *A few weeks?* I'm going to have to deal with my haywire hormones, years-old embarrassment, and fluttering stomach for *a few weeks*? "Okay, great!" It comes out a little too brightly, making me wince.

"You're a twenty-one-year-old woman, Ada, get your shit together," I mutter to myself as I grab a hold of Penny's bridle and turn back toward where Dermot is still standing, looking at me quizzically.

"Tomorrow afternoon? I'll work the others in the morning." He nods toward Penny. "Then you can tell me all about Big Red here."

I just give him an awkward thumbs-up and turn back toward the barn, feeling his eyes roam my retreating figure like a spray of warm water across my back.

Time alone with Dermot Harding? Lord, help me.

"Your very own racehorse, huh?" Dermot drawls, the river babbling quietly behind him.

I trail my fingers over Penny's silky forehead, nodding and admiring her intelligent eyes—maybe a little too intelligent for my own good. I know deep down it will all be worth it when I can convince her to give me a shot. My daddy didn't raise his only child to be a quitter. But hitting the dirt day in and out is demotivating, not to mention painful.

Dermot chuckles. "Can't fault you for knowing what you want. You've been on about wanting to get into racehorses since you were a little kid. Picked yourself a hell of a challenge to start with."

"That's what everyone keeps telling me," I say, unable to tear my eyes away from where he's tightening the cinch on my saddle. The way his tanned forearms ripple and flex as he ties the leather off there is like dirty talk for the most primal parts of my brain. My tongue darts out, wetting my bottom lip as he pats the filly's neck and I let my eyes trail the veins that run down the top of his firm hand.

For crying out loud, Ada. You're lusting after a man's veins.

I promised myself I was going to play it cool today. But I obviously lied, because I'm not playing it cool right now, and wasn't first thing when I woke up this morning and imagined him moving over top of me, inside of me. Our movements jerky, hard, and fevered in my mind's eye.

Yeah, I imagined hate sex with Dermot Harding for the first time in a long time and now I'm a nervous wreck around him. Knowing he's sleeping across the driveway in the little laneway house after all this time apart? It's almost too much.

We left so much unsaid between us, and now everything feels awkward and strained. For me, anyway. He seems completely unaffected. Like the same easygoing, unflappable Dermot I've always known. But that's probably how most responsible adults react to an eighteen-year-old girl kissing them. For him it was probably a funny, teenaged blip in the radar. The bubbling over of wild hormones for a young girl stuck on a ranch for too long.

But for me it was the memory that still had the power to make me blush, the hot lance of disappointment that kept me up at night to this day. One of my greatest mistakes.

His hand lands on my shoulder, and I startle. "You ready? I'm going to hop on Solar and then pony Penny into the water. Once I get her knee-deep in the river, you can get on. In the water she won't be able to turn into a bucking bronco, and hopefully having an experienced horse beside her will help her stay calm."

The heat from his body seeps into mine, making me almost too hot under the high summer sun. I give him a terse nod, steeling myself. We lead Penny and my dad's favorite ranch horse, Solar, down to the river behind the small guesthouse where Dermot lives when he stays on the ranch. His family farm in Merritt is just far enough away that staying on-site makes the most sense.

I take a deep breath, determination clear on my face as I approach my thoroughbred filly. Dermot swings one powerful leg over Solar's broad back with Penny's rope tight in his hand and coaxes her into the gentle current. Once they're deep enough, I walk in, feeling the cold bite of the mountain water against my ankles. "Hey, little girl." I rub my hand along her flank reassuringly. "How about we try this again, huh? I'll be good to you if you're good to me."

Dermot snorts and my eyes narrow.

"Something funny?"

"Yeah. You're going to spoil this horse even if she's not good to you."

Does he even realize what he just so casually implied? I shake my head and turn away, chest searing with indignation. "I guess you'd know," I bite out as I lift my boot into the stirrup at her side.

"Ada..." He trails off, but I ignore him and step up, leaning against Penny's back. I feel her go rigid beneath my weight, anticipating my leg swinging up through her peripheral vision.

"Easy, girl," Dermot coos now, his voice all deep and soothing as I run my hand up her neck, just waiting a few moments to let her hopefully relax a bit. When I hear her loud snort, I decide to take my chances and ever so slowly lift my leg over the saddle.

I squeeze my core, trying to sit down as gently as possible. Letting my body hover before I come to rest on her back, softly. I feel her start and then go still.

I lift my head slowly, not wanting to break the tenuous agreement we seem to have come to, and look up at Dermot as a wide genuine smile takes over my face. It's been at least ten seconds and I'm still sitting on her. Her ears are flicking back and forth uncertainly, and her body is tense—but I'm still here!

Dermot's perfectly white teeth glint back at me as he gives me a proud shake of his head.

And then, with a squeal, Penny rears straight up. Her neck fills the space in front of me as she stands on her back legs. Her reflexes are so quick that I don't even feel it coming.

Before I can even grab her mane, I'm unceremoniously dumped into the freezing river water.

CHAPTER 2

Dermot

"Ada!" At first, I want to laugh. Her face went from shit-eating grin to unadulterated shock so damn fast. But then she toppled backward into the water. And now all I can feel is pure panic coursing through my veins. She has to be okay.

I tie the filly's rope around the horn of the saddle and jump off my horse, the sound of her scream still lingering in my ears. My steps feel heavy and awkward as I trudge through the river toward the other side where she fell.

"Fuck!" Her open palm lands on the water with a loud slap, and I see the horses startle behind me.

Ada is kneeling on the riverbed, chest-deep in the water that's surrounding her petite form. She's soaked from head to toe, her golden hair dark with wetness and slicked down against the elegant curve of her neck.

"Are you okay?" I keep moving toward her. I have to make sure she's all right. Much like yesterday, I can't force myself away from her—even though I should. I can't stop scanning her doll-like face, comparing it to all the nights I lay on my cot and tried to recall the way she looks. Imagining Ada's face, every curve, every freckle, was like therapy—a distraction from the much more violent images running through my mind every night.

Ada's fresh face, replaying that kiss; it all became my only lifeline to the real world during a time when I was knee-deep in blood, gore, and depression.

"I don't think I've ever heard you swear before," I say, falling onto my knees in front of her and resting my hands on her shoulders.

She scrubs her hands across her face and back over her head. "That's because you haven't known me since I was eighteen! And yeah, I'm *fucking* sick of falling off."

Okay. So, she's mad. Even someone as emotionally numb as I am can figure that much out. "Does it hurt anywhere?" My eyes dart all over her body, looking for signs of distress. My hands flutter down over her toned arms, feeling for possible broken bones. *Mr. Wilson will kill me if she's injured.*

"I'm fine." She sighs. "I mean, I hurt everywhere. That's what falling off every damn day gets you."

I grip her by the ribs. I can feel the thick strap of her bra through her thin wet shirt as I pull her toward me and stand us both up. She comes to stand easily and everything seems to be in working order. I rake my gaze up over her curves, prepared to make a smart remark about how if she doesn't want to be sore, she should stop falling off, but I stop when I get to her soaked tank top.

The one plastered onto her body, leaving absolutely nothing to the imagination. The taper of her waist, the swell of her breasts, the hard points of her nipples so clear through the wet fabric.

My throat goes dry and I groan, squeezing my eyes shut and looking away. Nothing good can come from admiring Ada like this. That kiss three years ago woke a sleeping giant inside my mind, opened my eyes to possibilities I *never* considered. Ada had always been just another farm kid to me—until she wasn't.

I've been almost constantly reminding myself that she's still the young daughter of a man I've known and respected for years. A man who has become my friend, almost family. She's still the girl all of Ruby Creek knows and loves. A girl that same town would whisper about if something were to happen with the older ranch hand who's been hanging around since she was a child. There is absolutely no way around how inappropriate that would seem, and I refuse to torpedo her reputation like that. I've had three years to mull over the options, and the only feasible one is that I need to stay the fuck away from her.

Plus, a woman like Ada deserves better than me. So I tear my eyes up and away from her body, only to be met with the equally tempting heart shape of her slightly parted lips, the spray of soft freckles across her bronzed cheeks, and those wide emerald green eyes.

The green eyes in which I watched a heart break three years ago. The green eyes that have haunted my dreams every night since. The green eyes that have looked at me like I hung the moon for years.

And now? A look full of longing and promise that a man like me shouldn't get used to.

Ada Wilson out of bounds.

I trail my hands down over her hips, relishing the feel of her body in my grasp. Wanting to pull her closer. I settle with inclining my head in toward her, seeking that signature scent that I've spent three years trying to commit to memory. My fingers pulse, squeezing her waist, and my words come out rough. "Are you sure you're okay?"

"Yes." Her voice is soft and slightly breathless. A raspy whisper that feels like silk on my skin.

She stares up at me with a fire that wasn't there before, like she can't decide between mauling me or drowning me. Her eyes twinkle as she drinks me in. And I let her—because fuck, does it ever feel good to have a woman like Ada Wilson look at you like *this.* Her hand comes up, and she trails her dainty fingers delicately over my cheekbone like she might break me or spook me. *Like last time.*

"Dermot… I—" Her voice cracks a little, and damn if I don't feel a guilty pinch in my chest at her show of emotion. I should put a stop to this, I really should.

"Ada. You shouldn't look at me like this."

She presses a finger to my lips to silence me and quirks one shapely brow up in challenge as she bites back, "Why would you care how I look at you?" The pads of her fingers brush up over the bridge of my nose and then across the peak of my brow, as though she's reading braille. Like my features might tell her a story, give her some answers. She drags her nails across my scalp, sending a spray of goose bumps down the back of my tense arms. "You've made it very clear how you feel about me." Her hands fall away and she looks me straight in the eye as she delivers her killing blow. "And anyway, I've moved on."

Then Ada pushes off of me as she moves past my immobilized form. I feel the heavy thump of my heart against my sternum. *Made my feelings clear?* Of course that's what she thinks. I've never told her otherwise. Nor will I.

In the months since I got home, I've tried to prepare myself for eventually seeing Ada again. I've worked hard at talking myself into believing that the chemistry I keep recalling from that night was all in my head. A shocking memory riddled by my intense longing to be back somewhere safe, away from the sounds of whizzing bullets and pained screams. My plan was to be cool, calm, slightly removed. But then I laid eyes on her, flat in the grass like a flower in the sun just begging to be picked, and my resolve started to crumble.

Now I'm constantly reminding myself that she's the ranch owner's daughter, and that I'm just the ranch hand who comes by to break his young horses every summer. *That's it. That's all.*

"Let's go," I grumble, and it comes out more harshly than I intend. But a rough tone is going to hurt her a lot less in the long run than thinking a man like me will ever be able to give her what she needs. What she deserves.

She unwraps her filly's reins and takes off up the riverbank, her stride stiff and her head held high.

"You can't be doing this, Dermot." I mutter as I grab Solar's reins and follow in her footsteps, lost in thought. It's safe to assume she's not listening by how far ahead she is. At the very least, she doesn't look back. Which is a good thing, because I know I've got desire written all over my face.

I shake my head and kick a rock as I forge ahead. I'm too old, too set in my ways, and after the things I saw on tour, I've retreated too far into myself to ever truly share my life with someone—especially someone as vivacious as Ada. She deserves to see and do it all, not be stifled by someone who hits the ground when he hears a loud noise.

I need to stay away from her. For her, and for myself. I've got a habit of sending people running. My parents could hardly wait for me to turn eighteen before they packed up and moved somewhere warm. They never visit and barely call. Girlfriends never last. And even friends I made in the army have either fallen out of touch or just plain never made it back. Everyone leaves, and Ada would eventually too.

Gold Rush Ranch is a slice of heaven. The Wilsons' vast swath of land here in Ruby Creek sits in a picturesque little valley where tourists visit to seek a hairy mythical creature on Sasquatch Mountain. It's bright and sunny here, just like Ada.

My farm up in Merritt is cold and stark, and the mountain peaks are so high that I feel almost claustrophobic sometimes, especially when the place gets snowed in. It's what my parents left me after they retired and moved south. None of my siblings wanted it. Apparently I'm a sentimental sap, because even though I'm not actually doing anything with the land, the thought of handing it over to someone else is more than I can bear.

And it's definitely not the place for Ada.

Which is fine, because I'm definitely not the man for her either. No matter how she looks at me or how my cock twitches against my jeans when she touches me.

After storming to the barn, we untack wordlessly beside each other. I sneak looks at Ada as she moves around the filly, brushing her a little more vigorously than necessary. It almost makes me chuckle. Leave it to Ada to want a racehorse when her dad has fields full of top-end ranch horses. She always was one to want something she shouldn't.

I pull the saddle off of Solar and manage to bite out, "Same time and place tomorrow. I'll get on her though."

She bristles and rolls her shoulders back. "Take a hike, Dermot. She's my horse. I'm breaking her. Help, don't help, I don't care. But you sure as hell will not waltz in here and take over *my* project." Her hand flails up above her head. "I've had it up to here with people telling me what I can and can't do." She spins on her heel then, and storms off with the fiery little filly prancing along beside her.

As I watch her leave, I realize that Ada Wilson is not the same girl I left on that porch three years ago.

"Okay, give me a leg up," Ada says, turning her ass toward me. I take a deep swallow, feeling my Adam's apple bob in my throat. Giving someone a leg up onto their horse isn't special, but it doesn't fall squarely into my *Don't Touch Ada Wilson* plan either.

I step up behind her, breathing in the scent of her tangerine lotion. It suits her, bright and citrusy—intoxicating. She lifts one leg and waits for me to help her. Bending down, I wrap my palm around her slender calf, willing myself not to trail my hand up further.

She looks back over her shoulder at me, probably wondering what the holdup is, and for a moment our eyes lock. I take a deep dive into the emerald depths of her irises. So wide and expressive, and for once since I got back they don't look angry. I hold them with my gaze, just enjoying looking at her.

Bad idea.

I shake my head and clear my throat. "One. Two. Three." On *three* I toss her up, but am slow to let go of her leg. I can't seem to tear my eyes away from the way my hand looks on her. The contrast, the compliment. Soft and hard. Sunny and dark. Young and old. *Older.* I refuse to consider myself old at thirty-one.

Either way, nothing about us matches. Ada and I are a dichotomy, opposites, like two ends of a magnet that can't seem to stay away from each other no matter how fucked up it is.

"Dermot?" she asks, her expression quizzical. "You okay?"

I yank my hands off her leg and step back abruptly, offering an, "All good," over my shoulder as I duck out of the round pen and turn to lean on it as casually as I can manage.

Ada ignores the awkward moment and gets to riding. She looks so damn pleased with herself as she trots around on her leggy filly, and pride swells in my chest. This girl is tough as nails, not a quitter's bone in her body. We've spent the rest of the week working on Penny—a chestnut mare through and through. She pulls out an awful lot of acrobatics, but Ada sticks on every time, and after one week she's got her walking and trotting in the round pen unassisted. Not half bad.

Where the filly has flourished, interactions between Ada and I are strained. She can barely look at me since that day in the river and I'm so busy trying not to stare at her body, the way her hips sway in the saddle, that I feel like all I do is make things more awkward by staring at her face instead.

The way her tongue darts out to wet her lower lip, the ways she purses her mouth when she's concentrating, the small genuine smiles she gives Penny that make the corners of her eyes crinkle.

Everything about her is downright distracting. Maybe I'm better off only looking at her ponytail? I stare at it, watching it sway. I could wrap it around my hand, give it a good hard tug, and…

My forehead falls onto the top fence panel in defeat. *I am fucked.*

I've known Ada since she was a buck-toothed, knobby-kneed ten-year-old. She used to burn around here on her bike, getting messy and getting into trouble. A true ranch rat in every sense of the word. The only child of one of the most hard-working, loving, and respectable couples I've ever known. It didn't surprise me at all when I came back summer after summer and saw her growing into a remarkable young woman.

I would have expected nothing less. But she was still just little Goldilocks to me. I still saw tangled blond hair and cheeks smudged with purple from feasting on wild blackberries when I looked at her.

Sure, her obvious crush was a running joke around the ranch when she was little. She'd follow me everywhere, make excuses to do things with me. Chat my ear off about horses, so full of questions. I was a twenty-year-old man, and I was awkward as all get out, especially when the other staff and even Mr. Wilson would rib me about it. It was endearing, really. But eventually everyone stopped talking about it, and I assumed she'd outgrown it. A childhood crush to look back on fondly.

Until she kissed me.

She shocked me into stillness when she cupped my jaw and pressed her plush, heart-shaped lips against mine. Clearly, with age, she'd just gotten really fucking adept at hiding her feelings.

"Be safe, Dermot. I love you," she said. And I pushed her back from me like it meant nothing and told her she should go. The look in her eyes that night? The way they welled up as she traced her fingers across the bow of her top lip? *Fuck.*

That look haunts me to this day. I can feel it like a weight on my chest.

I never wanted to hurt Ada. In fact, I've always known I would kill anyone who did. But that night, she planted a seed of possibility in my mind. And its vines grew fast and reckless, altering my sense of right and wrong, warping my memories, and changing everything I was supposed to feel about Ada Wilson.

That seed has left me battling myself for the last three years. Battling against wishing I'd fisted her hair and kissed her back. Hard. Shown her what a man could do, what a man could make her feel.

But I couldn't. Ada belongs firmly in the *My Friend's Daughter* column and also in the *She's Way Too Fucking Young for You* column.

Which is why, as we're wrapping up on Friday afternoon, I try to make casual conversation after a week's worth of tension between us. "She's looking good, Ada. You should be proud of yourself. Penny's not an easy horse."

She smiles as she strokes the filly's forelock lovingly and muses, "The payoff on something easy never feels as sweet though, does it? I like a challenge."

I clear my throat. I must be obsessed, because everything this woman says sounds like a metaphor to me.

"Next week we gallop?"

She turns and grins at me. "Next week we gallop."

And then I'm down on the ground. A loud bang flattening me almost instantly. I drop so quickly that I barely remember getting here. I wrap my arms around the back of my head, waiting for another bang to come. Another explosion. More screams.

The *tch-tch-tch* of bullets spraying everywhere. All I know is that I have to protect myself so that I can get home safely.

It's only when I feel a soft hand stroking soothingly between my shoulders and Ada's soft sugary voice saying, "I'm right here. It was just a truck backfiring. You're okay," that I start to realize where I am and what I've done. The flashes like this come hard and fast. There's no predicting them. And there's no avoiding them.

"Dermot?" Her hand moves up to massage the back of my neck as I pant into the dusty earth beneath me, trying to calm the erratic beating of my heart. "What can I do for you?"

"Nothing," I whisper raggedly, still unable to move. "Just give me a couple of minutes."

I expect her to walk away, but instead she ties her filly up and then lies down right on the ground beside me, going back to stroking my back quietly. She doesn't ask me questions, she doesn't rush me, she just stays with me.

After a few minutes, the anxiety of the moment passes, and I feel my breathing normalize again. I peek over at her, facing me with her head propped in her hand, wide green eyes regarding me carefully. She might be acting calm, but she looks scared. *This is why you're no good for her.*

"I'm okay."

"Are you sure?" Her brows knit together in concern.

"Yes." I roll onto my back to look up at the sky, remind myself of where I am. Ada does the same, but reaches between us to wrap her small hand around mine. She squeezes it tightly. Once. Twice. Three times. A simple enough gesture, but one that has a line of electricity buzzing up my forearm into my inner elbow. An ache. A dangerous current flowing between us.

I pull my hand away, resting both of them on my stomach, and try to lighten the mood. "We've got to stop meeting like this."

She chuckles, but it's a little brittle. A little forced. So I look over at her and try again, not wanting to talk about what just happened. "Friday night. Big plans, Goldilocks?"

She presses her lips together. "Actually, yeah. Meeting up at Neighbor's pub in town."

"Meeting up?" I waggle my eyebrows jokingly. "Like a date?"

She turns her head, eyes like beams straight into mine. Something sad shining in the sage-colored highlights of her irises. "Yes, Dermot. Like a date."

And then she gets up and walks away. Leaving me alone with an entirely different and unfamiliar type of green-eyed monster.

Maybe it's time to catch Ada up on the torture she's put me through for the last three years.

CHAPTER 3

Ada

My date sucked.

I buckle my seat belt and turn the key in the ignition. Shaking my head as I pull out onto the road that heads home. Ready to berate myself the whole way back.

I spent the entire time thinking about Dermot, wishing it were him I was out with but also wanting to kick him in the balls for ditching and then coming back like nothing happened. And then wanting to wrap him in my arms and fend off all the demons he's been living with. Just thinking about Dermot, strong and proud, cowering on the ground makes my eyes well with emotion—makes my chest ache for him.

I still want him, demons and all. And I hate it.

What's worse: that day in the river, he didn't even deny that he's made his feelings about me clear. He's supposed to feel nothing for me, except maybe some sort of brotherly love. But I'm not a virginal teenager anymore, and I didn't miss the way his eyes burned across my skin, the way his firm hands pulsed around my waist as he drank me in. This desperate little part of me thought he'd maybe change his mind and spill words about how badly he wants me, like in one of those books my mom hides under her mattress. *Talk about tragic.*

I've been telling myself that I'm over him, that I've moved on. But apparently my heart missed the memo. I've tried. I've had boyfriends at university. But they never last, and they never make my heart pound. They never keep me up at night, thinking about how their hands would feel gliding over my fevered skin. And even when we get to that point, it's fun but… lacking. There's no fire. No passion. No knocking the art off the walls. I want that messy, desperate, gasping-for-air kind of sex.

Travis, my date from tonight, is a nice enough guy, but we've been friends since before we could talk and we still feel like just friends now. We've been out a few times, but I know it's not going anywhere. Pickings are slim in a small town like Ruby Creek, and as I drive back to the ranch, I find myself wishing I could settle for a guy like Travis Bennett. Wishing I could be interested in cattle ranching. It's the family business, after all.

But instead, I spend my days dreaming about Dermot Harding and thoroughbred racing.

My parents drive us in to Vancouver every summer for the Denman Derby. A full day to watch the races. I look forward to that one special day every year, to the anticipation I feel when the bell rings and the gates flash open. To the rumble of hooves that shake the ground as the horses thunder past. There's just *something* about the whole sport.

I want to be a part of it.

And I want Dermot Harding. Stupidly, obsessively, pathetically—the feelings are seeping out through the seams of the carefully constructed box I tucked them away in. For the past three years, I've easily contained them in the *Never Gonna Happen* section of my brain. But that was before he touched me, before I knew what his calloused palms felt like sliding across my arms. Gripping my waist.

Before he hit me with a look so full of tortured longing that it took my breath away and made me flee. A look that has been living in my head for a week, bouncing around like a pinball in a machine. Giving me a goddamn headache.

So I went on a stupid date. Thinking I could clear my head, but boy was I wrong. Now all I am is agitated that I wasted my own time and possibly gave a friend false hope for something more. "Great work, Ada," I mutter as I pull into the ranch and park in front of the main farmhouse. Slamming the door harder than I should, I round the back of my car toward the path that leads to the front door.

Which of course takes me right past the small laneway house that my parents built for guests. The one that Dermot stays in when he's here. The one with *the* porch.

"You trying to injure that car, Goldilocks?"

He's sitting on the weathered swing that looks out toward the mountains with a glass of amber liquid in his hand. The mellow glow of the outdoor lights highlights the strong planes of his masculine face, the inky shine of his hair, and the brightness of his fresh white T-shirt. I imagine the shirt wet like in the river earlier this week, remembering the way it clung to the defined lines in his chest and hung suggestively over the deep V that disappeared beneath his waistband.

My mouth goes instantly dry at the memory.

I stop and face him, sick of holding my tongue. *Sick of feeling so lovesick.* "Better than injuring you, wouldn't you say?"

"Ada—"

"No. Don't *Ada* me. I'm not in the mood."

I move to keep walking, wanting to put distance between us before I say something I'll really regret, but he stops me in my tracks when he says, "Okay then. How was your date?"

There's a bite in his words that I don't entirely appreciate, not considering the way he's all but disappeared for the last three years. Now he's going to waltz in and act like he has some sort of claim on me? Nah. He's not entitled to that tone where I'm concerned.

I storm up the two steps toward him, hand gripping the railing so hard that I feel the edges of the wood bite into my fingers almost painfully. "It was great." I lie through my teeth with a confidence that doesn't match my inner turmoil. "Travis is great."

Dermot swaggers across the porch, all confidence and maturity, while I feel like I'm shaking in my boots, holding myself up on the railing like a crutch. So I step up, refusing to back away and give him the win, pressing myself against the vertical beam for support, gripping the railing that carries on around the deck.

Braced and ready for battle.

He comes close, too close, invading my space and stealing all the surrounding oxygen, like he just absorbs it with his presence alone. "Travis…" He rolls the name around in his mouth like he's tasting it, examining the flavor. He's close enough that I feel his breath fan across my collarbones, a small reprieve from the heavy mugginess that pervades the night air.

I watch him swirl his drink casually, ice clinking against the heavy glass. "Does Travis send goose bumps up your arms just by coming close?"

I glance down to confirm what he's talking about. *Dick.* I jut my chin out defiantly. "Travis is good for me."

"Anyone would be better for you than me."

An unladylike snort escapes me. "No shit."

He chuckles, stepping forward again, eyes searching my face as I press my back into the timber post behind me. "You weren't nearly this mouthy when I saw you last."

Rational thought flees my mind at his proximity.

"Things change." My voice comes out soft and raspy as I soak him in. His imposing frame, the way his Adam's apple bobs in his throat as he swallows. Suddenly I feel very young and very out of my depth. I squeeze my thighs together, noting that telltale spark at the base of my spine, that deep thrum in my pelvis.

"They do." Dermot grips my chin firmly and my breath leaves me in a quick exhale. I stand stock-still, chest rising and falling in time with his, not wanting to break whatever tenuous connection we have right now. He places his drink on the porch railing behind me and trails his index finger over my lips possessively. The top one, and then the bottom one as he muses, "You're too young for me."

I swallow audibly in response, and smirk with a confidence I don't feel. "Guess that makes you too old for me, something you've made very clear now."

His intelligent eyes dart around my face, analyzing me. Like he's making a tactical calculation. "I'm not sure I made myself all that clear, actually." He leans toward my ear to whisper, "Not very clear at fucking all."

I can feel the hard points of my nipples rasping against my bra as his toned body moves in, completely invading my space. His chest presses against mine as we face off, making me feel competitive. Or cornered. Like I want to lash out at him. "What the hell is that supposed to mean?"

"It means nothing should ever happen between us. It would be a mistake."

Good god. This man gives me whiplash.

"Thanks for clearing that up," I spit out. "Now get your hands off—"

"And yet…" He cuts me off abruptly, his hold on my chin tightening as he does. "Fuck it."

His lips crash down onto mine and this time he moves against me almost frantically. Hungrily. I moan into his mouth, trying to kiss him back, but he just holds my head in place, taking what he wants. What he *needs*. The kiss is brutal, primal, like a punishment more than a reward. Like a volcano that's been waiting to erupt. And this lava? It's probably going to burn us both.

But I must have a death wish because I arch my back toward him, pressing into his hard chest. I fist his shirt, wanting to pull him even closer. Wanting to crawl into his embrace and never leave, wanting to memorize the feel of his arms around me and the clean soap smell on his skin. The taste of whiskey on his tongue and the rasp of his stubble against my skin is a combination I'll never forget.

His kisses turn languid, reverent almost, as he cups my head and trails his thumbs over my cheeks. His mouth moves in their wake, peppering kisses over my earlobe, into the crook of my neck, and across the base of my throat. Shooting arousal straight between my legs. I turn to putty in his arms.

This. *This* is what I've spent years dreaming about. But no dream could do the real thing justice. Dermot Harding is powerful, exacting in every touch, experienced in a way I didn't anticipate, in a way that makes jealous feelings bubble to the surface as his hands roam my body and his mouth lays claim to mine. You don't learn how to own a woman this way without an awful lot of practice. He just didn't want to practice with me.

The realization is like a cold bucket of water over my head. Everything that was molten and hot quickly turns to brittle stone.

I freeze in his arms and panic comes rushing in. Memories of him turning me away in this exact spot—something I refuse to feel again. He tries to pull me back in, resting his forehead against mine. "Ada…" His lashes flutter shut, and he shakes his head. "What am I going to do with you?"

His eyes bore down on mine, burning with need as he rocks into me. I can feel his hard length through his jeans against my hip bone, a torturous teaser of what I could have had. Of what I want.

"Nothing." I almost don't recognize my own voice, so cold it's downright arctic. But what I do recognize is the survival instinct flaring inside of me. Doing *this* with Dermot is dangerous for my heart. Maybe it's easy for him to walk away and waltz back in. But for me? This is torture. Borderline cruel.

He sighs and steps away from me, almost trembling with the self-control it takes. "I'm sorry, Ada." His eyes are earnest and gentle as the heat of his body leaks away from mine. "This is just…" His hands rest on his hips and he looks toward the sky, as though he might find guidance up there. "I don't know how to explain what I'm feeling. I don't know if I should—if I can."

He laughs sadly. "It's been three years and I still can't make sense of it myself."

His voice is kind, but his words feel like the cruel lash of a whip. I can't believe we're here *again.* Except this time, it's worse. This time he kissed me back, practically knocked me over with the weight of his desire. This time I know the feelings aren't one-sided. And him pushing me away now because he's too scared to talk to me? It teaches me something I never knew about Dermot Harding.

I spew venom, not the shy teenager I was last time this happened. "Never took you for a coward, Dermot."

I know my blow lands with force because I see the hurt in the depths of his dark eyes. I feel bad for him momentarily until the humiliation hits. I spin on my heel, needing to get away from him and whatever the hell that just was.

Away from that goddamn porch.

I avoid Dermot the next day, opting not to do any work with Penny. I sulk around the house and offer to help my mom with prepping dinner. Which seems like a great way to clear my mind until she says, "Oh perfect! I could use some extra hands. Your father invited Dermot for dinner tonight so we can catch up with him."

Great, just what I need right now. I can't even bring myself to respond.

"Nice to have Dermot back, isn't it? I hear he's been a big help with Penny," she supplies lightheartedly, trying to stir some response out of me.

I just grunt.

"You always had the sweetest little crush on him as a girl. Like his shadow around this place." She chuckles good-naturedly, "I think you'd have followed him to the ends of the earth for a while there."

"Sounds creepy," I mutter, not looking up from the tomatoes I'm dicing.

"Aw, no." A wistful smile touches my mom's round face, and her eyes glaze over as she recalls the past. "Dermot was a good boy then, and he's a good man now. One of the best I've known. I think you could sense that even as a little girl."

I feel an aching twinge in my chest because as much as I want to throw this tomato at his stupid handsome face right now, I know she's right. Sighing, I let my shoulders fall on an exhale. "I know, Mom. He's been a big help with Penny. I think we're going to head out into the fields and gallop next week. See if I can stay on." I wink at her, trying to prove that I'm not sulking as badly as it might seem. Plus, everyone seems very amused by how often Penny has turfed me.

She claps excitedly, so genuine in her response. "I just know you're going to do great things with that little spitfire. She's the start of something new and exciting for you. I can feel it in my bones."

We sit around the dinner table that night making small talk. My parents love having Dermot around; they've always had a soft spot for him. I know they took him under their wing when he had no one else around. I also know they'd have had more children—they'd have filled this whole place up with a herd of Wilsons to take over the ranch for them one day.

Instead, they got me. Just me. One girl who has no interest in cattle ranching. But they don't care, just want me to be happy.

My cheek quirks in amusement. It's an ongoing joke that maybe I'll marry a rancher to keep the tradition alive. My dad says it and then winks. Yes, Thomas Wilson knows he broke the mold with me, and he loves me for it.

"So, Dermot," my dad starts in, "what are your plans for your land? Do you have anything going on up there?"

"I'm not sure, sir. A company that wants to buy it contacted me, actually. They seem to think the area is rich in mining resources. But I don't think I can bring myself to sell the family farm, no matter what's on that land."

My father stares down at his plate, spearing a piece of chicken and chewing exaggeratedly, like he's really mulling something over. "Don't sell it, son." He sits up and looks at Dermot seated across from him, next to my mother. "That land is valuable, and if they're out hounding you about it, they know there's something good on there. Might be the perfect opportunity for you start something for yourself."

Dermot looks genuinely shocked, like starting his own business isn't something he's ever considered. His dark heavy lashes flutter across his cheek bones rapidly as he tries to process what my dad has just said to him. "I—"

Tom holds a hand up to stop him. "Just think about it. You know that Lynette and I want to see you succeed. As much as I love having you down here every summer, I also know you're destined for bigger things. You've been through a lot, so if we can help you in any way—connections, financials, whatever—you just say the word. We'd be happy to help."

He looks at my mother now and she nods in agreement, eyes shining with emotion. An unspoken agreement, like they know each other so well there's no need to use words. That the two of them still look at each other like this after thirty years never fails to blow my mind. It used to gross me out, but I've come to realize how special what my parents have is. How precious.

I want that.

When I look back at Dermot, he's pressing his lips together, assessing my dad. His voice is rough, full of emotion, when he looks down shyly and says, "I'll look into it. Thank you, Tom. But first I'm helping Ada get that filly to the races."

I pipe up now, excited by the prospect of his help. Because past drama aside, Dermot is one of the best horsemen I've ever met. His help would be invaluable. "Really? You promise?"

He stares back at me sincerely, quieting the room with the intensity of his look. He nods once, decisively. "I promise."

"Good!" my dad barks, breaking the spell. He tosses his napkin down on his plate and leans back in his chair as he turns toward where I'm sitting beside him, like he's totally oblivious to the current between Dermot and I. "So, Ada, what are your plans for Saturday night in Ruby Creek? You going to paint the town red?" He winks.

I know that *moping and drawing hearts with mine and Dermot's initials in them* isn't an appropriate answer. But really, I have no plans. Which sounds far too lame to say out loud in front of everyone. Why couldn't he have just let me skulk upstairs after dinner without flinging me into the spotlight? Sitting across from Dermot, watching his easy smiles, his hands flexing as he cuts through his chicken, his softly mussed hair flopping across his forehead—this entire dinner has been torture enough.

I suppose that's why I blurt out, "Probably going to head into town for a drink or something."

"With who?" *Why is he doing this?*

I bulge my eyes in agitation. "I don't know, Dad. There's almost always someone I know there. It's a small town, I'm not too worried about it."

He just grunts in response and I look down, fiddling with the edge of the tablecloth in my lap. Dad's obviously not wild about the idea of his little girl going to the bar by herself for no good reason. I wish I could tell him I don't really want to go either, but now I've backed myself into a corner.

"I'll go with her." My head snaps up. Dermot just shrugs casually, not looking at me. "I could use a little civilization. Haven't been out much since I got back."

"I don't need a chaperone," I seethe. This is not what I want, and I don't care if I sound like a petulant child. I want to be alone, or at the very least just not anywhere near Dermot.

Lately all he does is make me angry and then horny. It's a terrible combination, and I need some damn space, but he's around every corner, his voice echoes around the stables all day long, and I swear I get whiffs of his clove-scented aftershave when he's not even nearby. The man is driving me to distraction, which is why I hid out in the house today. I'm fed up with his hot and cold behavior. *I'm over it.*

Or at least I thought I was until he came waltzing back onto the ranch and tossed me right back into the deep end of my obsession.

"Ada..." my mother scolds me. I know she's going to make some comment about manners and me being better than this.

But Dermot cuts her off. "Of course you don't. I'll just give you a ride and then leave you to your devices with your friends."

I glare at him before shoving my chair back and storming upstairs.

CHAPTER 4

Dermot

ADA PULLS HERSELF UP INTO MY COBALT BLUE PICKUP, HUFFING out a breath as she slams the door much harder than necessary. She shoves her seat belt into the buckle roughly before leaning back and crossing her arms, eyes trained straight out the windshield.

Okay, so she's pissed. Again. I guess I can't blame her. I'm a mess. I've *made* a mess.

"Are you going to drive or just sit there staring at me?" Her tone is biting and her jaw is set stubbornly. She still refuses to turn her eyes my way.

Shaking my head, I shift the truck into reverse, looking over my shoulder as I back out onto the long driveway. "You used to be cute, but now you're a mouthy pain in the ass, you know that?"

I swear she almost growls in response. Her mouth purses like she's eaten something sour, the tip of her dishy nose twitches, her chest flares an angry red, and she literally turns her entire body away from me to look out the window. "Good. That's what you deserve."

Her words don't hurt. I'm a grown man. It takes more than a shot-from-the-hip insult to wound me, but the physical act of her turning away from me, that she can't even look at me—that aches like a rusty lance to the heart.

My poor behavior, my inability to control my urges around her, or really even just communicate, has hurt one of the few women I've ever truly cared about. The woman I've spent the last three years dreaming about, writing letters to that I never had the balls to send. The woman I feel *more* for, but can never pursue.

Agitation blooms within me as I run through the last week in my head. Every time I've put my hands on her body when I should have kept them to myself. All the words that have spilled from my lips, that I should have shoved back down when I felt them bubbling up.

The last thing I ever want is to hurt Ada. Which is why I make a pact with myself, right here and now, as we drive in tense silence along the quiet dirt road.

I need to talk to her. I need to explain. I need to show her the letters so that she doesn't go on thinking that this thing between us is one-sided.

Impossible? Yes. But one-sided? Definitely not.

She jumps out of the truck almost before I've put it in park, like the cab is on fire and she can't get far enough away, and takes off through the heavy wood door of Neighbor's pub. The only watering hole around Ruby Creek.

I sigh heavily as I lock up and then trudge toward the entryway of a bar I don't really want to be at. I'm tired. I only volunteered to go out tonight because I could see the worry etched on Tom's face over his only daughter going out by herself. And I couldn't blame him, or at least that's what I was going to tell myself.

That's right—I'm only here tonight to do a friend a favor. It has nothing to do with the fact that I'm obsessed with his daughter and can't stand the thought of her out with another man.

Striding into the dark little bar, it takes my eyes a moment to adjust. Ada has already found herself a spot at a table just next to the bar with a few friends. Two guys and one other girl. It gets my hackles up that it looks like they're on a double date now. I have no right to feel this way, and yet I pull out a stool up at the bar, near their little square table, pathetically hoping that if I listen hard enough, bits of their conversation might filter over to where I'm sitting.

That's where one week around Ada Wilson has gotten me, a thirty-one-year-old man. Trying to ignore the frequent boners I get from just watching the way her ass fills out a pair of jeans as she walks around the farm and hoping I can eavesdrop on her conversations with friends. *Pathetic.*

Someone slaps the glossy bar top in front of me and I startle before looking up into the kind, wide face of the man behind the bar. "What can I get ya?"

I clear my throat as I look down the back shelf, full of glass bottles. "Just a beer is good."

The man grabs a pint glass and steps over to the taps, cranking the handle toward himself to let the golden liquid spill out. He's got a big farm boy build about him, and dark blond hair. I'm willing to bet he's only a year or two older than Ada. "You new around here? Don't think I've met you before." He drops a coaster down in front of me, plunking the frothy beer on top, and then offers me his hand. "Hank Brandt."

I squeeze his hand back. "Dermot Harding. Nice to meet you. I live up near Merritt but come down in the summers to help Tom Wilson with some colt starting."

He claps his hands as he leans against his side of the bar, making himself comfortable. "Right on. The Wilsons are good people."

I glance over at where Ada is sitting, nursing a bottle of beer and staring off into space. Clearly not interested in whatever conversation is happening at her table. "The best," I say absently.

"You bring Ada out tonight?"

I scoff and shift my attention back to Hank. "Yeah. Tom wasn't wild about her coming out alone, so I offered to join. Don't think she much appreciated my offer."

The young man waves his hand dismissively. "No need to worry about Ada. She's a good girl. If a little oblivious."

I quirk my head. "What do you mean?"

His lips tip up and he shrugs. "I mean… look at her."

I do, and this time she's glaring at me. Trying to incinerate me with her gaze, burn me to the ground. She might be a good girl, but right now she looks about ready to kill me.

"Every eligible guy in town is interested in Ada, but she doesn't notice. She comes in here, has a polite drink or two with friends, gently turns down offers for dates, and then goes home. I've heard some guys say she's had boyfriends at university, but here at home? I think this is the first time I've ever seen her hang around someone."

"Hm?" I ask as I tip my beer back. The cool fizz spreads across my tongue, soothing the fire I want to breathe at the thought of Ada having plural boyfriends at university.

Hank points. "Travis there"—my chest tightens—"the one with his arm around her chair. They were in together the other night too."

I sneak a look out of the corner of my eye, and sure enough, the lanky, sandy-haired boy has his arm slung casually over the back of Ada's chair. My first thought is that I want to break his arm, which is swiftly followed by intense shame. Shame that I, for even a moment, would think I have a right to feel that way.

She deserves that. Someone young and vibrant, not brimming with baggage, who can keep up with her and not worry about the implications of his relationship with her. Someone promising and carefree. Unlike me.

I just grunt, hunch myself low over the bar top, and take a big swig of my beer. More people filter in around me, and Hank moves on quickly to help the other patrons. I'm grateful to be out from under his assessing stare. The man may be young, but he was looking at me like he had me all figured out. He was making me squirm.

I'm not alone for long though. A shrill squeal assaults my eardrum from the same side as Ada's table. "Dermot Harding! Is that really you?"

My body goes rigid as I feel long nails drag across the blades of my shoulders and a body press against my side. Tara Bennett, a few-nights fling from just before I left, rubs herself up beside me. "It is! How are you, honey? It's been too long!"

"Hi, Tara," I say graciously, "long time no see."

I don't need to look at Ada to know her attention is on me now. I can feel the weight of her stare like a fiery brand on my bare skin. Like a heavy pulse in my bloodstream.

Tara trails her hand over the small of my back and I try not to cringe. What felt good three years ago feels downright wrong now. I turn toward her on my stool so that she's forced to remove her hand. But she just drops it onto my knee and steps toward me. She's wearing a Neighbor's pub T-shirt with a jean skirt and a black apron. "You working here now?"

"Sure am." She smiles proudly, eyes searching my face excitedly. "I'm off in a couple of hours if you want to catch up. You can buy me a drink." She winks flirtatiously. "For old times' sake. We had some good times, didn't we?" She slides her palm up my thigh boldly, and all I want to do is recoil.

Tara is a pretty girl, no doubt. But all I can think as I stare back at her is that she's not Ada. That's not the face imprinted on the backs of my eyelids. Lips a little too thin, hair a little too blond, makeup a little too thick, scent a little too sugary. Ada is soft and natural; she smells like the marmalade she has for breakfast every morning mixed with freshly cut grass—that sweet and fresh smell. I love that smell. I love... *Don't even think it, Dermot.*

The loud screech of a chair against the floor crashes through my awareness. I turn toward the sound, startled, to see Ada shooting up out of her seat. Face bright red like a perfectly ripe apple. Like a poisonous apple.

She marches up to me, swipes my keys off the bar top before I can connect the dots, and storms out the door like a twister on a path of destruction. Through the window, I watch her jump into the driver's seat of my beloved blue truck, crank the ignition, and gun it out of the parking lot. Leaving a spray of gravel behind her while everyone looks on in utter confusion.

Except for me. I'm not confused at all. She just overheard every word Tara said.

CHAPTER 5

Ada

I TRY TO SLEEP, BUT THE FARMHOUSE IS TOO HOT, MY BODY AND mind too restless. The air coming in through my window provides no reprieve, and even if I could get comfortable, my overactive brain won't give me any peace. It makes me miss the air-conditioning at my university residence hall. I switch the bedside lamp on and look at my clock. *Midnight.*

I heard the crunch of tires on the gravel driveway a couple of hours ago. I heard Dermot when he said, "Thanks for the ride." And as much as I wanted to run to the window to see who drove him home, I was too chicken. I couldn't bring myself to do it. If it was Tara, I didn't want to know. Having to watch her paw him so boldly, so publicly… well, that was more than enough torture for one day. Her suggestive words were the catalyst for my eruption.

I was ready to scald them both before I decided the safest course of action would be to just leave. And ditch Dermot. He deserved that. He had to know that letting another woman do that right in front of me would hurt. And I mean *hurt.* The ache in my lungs was very real. The mental images racing through my mind… god, I'm not sure I'll ever be able to erase them. Suspecting and seeing are two very different things.

I know I'm being immature. Dermot is a grown man, with years of experience on me. Logically, I know it's not like he's been chaste. He's tall, dark, and handsome in the most mouthwatering way. He's funny. He's a perfect gentleman. What woman *wouldn't* turn into a puddle at his feet? But seeing it firsthand was something else. I didn't want to face what his years on me really meant.

Worse than that, I like Tara. Correction: I *liked* Tara. In this moment, I'm not sure I'll ever be able to forgive her for having had a taste of what I want. The unfairness of it burns in my throat and lurches in my stomach.

My fist slams into my soft mattress. I'm far too keyed up to sleep. Too angry. Too *irrational.* I'm tired of feeling like this.

Sighing in frustration, I grab a towel off the back of my door and creep down the creaky old stairs, trying not to wake anyone. I've been doing this for years when I can't sleep. A quick dip in the cool river when it's this hot never fails to help me find peace. I know it's just the mental reset I need right now.

I slide my feet into a pair of sandals and walk across the backyard toward the riverbank, shooting Dermot's laneway house a dirty look as I walk past. The sound of crickets fills the air like a small symphony over the rush of water in the distance. Everything is so perfectly peaceful. It's dark and clear but the moon is full, shining like a spotlight over the entire valley.

I drop my towel in my usual spot. A deep bend in the river where the current is almost nonexistent, where the water is still and deep and cold.

Standing on the towel, I scoot out of my sleep shorts and rip off my tank top, dropping them both on the rocky ground. This is the best part about living in the middle of nowhere—no prying eyes.

I walk to the edge of the water, talking myself into making the plunge. Even though I know how it's going to feel, it takes a lot of internal convincing to throw myself into the icy water, every damn time.

With a small smile, I turn away from the water toward the walls of the riverbank, spread my arms wide, close my eyes, and fall backward into the deep pool.

I hold my breath and tread water below the surface, turning myself over to the rush of cold and the breathlessness that follows. The weightlessness of my body and the silty taste of the water that slips past my lips refreshes me. It's peaceful down here, dark and quiet, like time stands still. Like everything about my world is so inconsequential when the river and the rocks around me have been here for centuries. Weathering the storm.

My problems feel like a speck of dust when I think about the vastness and timelessness of the surrounding land.

Noise filters in, warped by the water around me. "Ada!" I kick my legs toward the surface to see what's going on. "Ada!" The voice is louder as I breach the water. "Ada! Oh my god! Are you okay?"

Dermot is perfectly illuminated by the bright silvery moonlight, calf-deep in the water, shirt torn off on the rocky bank, eyes wild and chest heaving like he's about to rescue me. From what, I'm not sure.

I smooth my hair back off of my face as I tread water. "What are you doing, Dermot?" I ask coolly.

He fists his hands on his tapered hips as he regards me, eyes scanning me clinically as if to confirm I'm actually okay. "I was sitting outside, heard a splash." He still sounds out of breath.

I take a moment to admire him, to weigh my response. Where he was still lanky and boyish three years ago, he's filled out now. I let my eyes follow the trails of his defined abdomen, his cut chest, the tempting hollows just above his collarbones, and the way his biceps bunch into a tight ball beneath his broad shoulders. I lick my lips, tasting the earthy river water that's dripping down my face.

Dermot Harding is a boy no more. He's now a clear and present danger to my heart. To my sanity.

"Okay. That doesn't explain what you're doing here." I try to keep my voice even, removed. Wanting him gone. "I'd like some privacy, please."

"You scared me. I thought you were—" He scrubs one broad palm over the dark scruff adorning his jaw. "I don't know. Not thinking straight. In trouble."

My jaw falls open as I realize what he thought I was doing. Shock, followed by indignant fury. "You think I would kill myself over your dumb ass, Dermot Harding?" I shout breathlessly as I move my limbs beneath the dark water, bringing me closer to the shore, just to where my feet can touch.

"I—"

"You're an idiot. That's what you are." I scoff before launching back in. "I mean the gall. The absolute gall. Get over yourself."

"I know you're mad about Tara," he says sheepishly, unmoving on the moonlit shore.

I bark out a laugh. "Well, hey, at least you know something. Hope she gave you an eventful ride home."

"What was I supposed to do, Ada? Be rude to a perfectly nice girl? And the bartender drove me back, because *you* stole my truck."

He had me there. The tiny petty voice in my head wanted him to be rude to her. But I also know he wouldn't be the man I've loved all these years if that was something he'd do. Dermot is brimming with integrity, which unfortunately, I like—even though it keeps biting me in the ass.

"Ugh." I look away, toward the shadowed stand of trees down river, not wanting to meet his eyes. Not wanting him to see how badly I want him. An urge that's only gotten stronger the more time I spend around him. The beat of a drum that started out quiet and is now so loud I can hardly think over the overwhelming rhythm of it. It isn't fair, wanting something this badly that you can never have.

"That was three years ago, Ada. She means nothing to me."

I think he's trying to be kind, but his comment just angers me instead. "So you can only fuck women who mean nothing to you?"

He doesn't like that comment; his voice changes, and so does his posture. Where before it was gentle and coaxing, it's now hard and commanding. "Get out of the water, Ada. You must be freezing. And we need to talk."

I stare back at him, letting the corners of my mouth tug up just slightly as our eyes meet in the dark. I'm not following his orders. "Why don't you come in for a swim, cool off a bit?"

"I don't have a swimsuit," he bites out, voice trembling with barely contained agitation.

I can tell his control is hanging on by a thread. I can almost feel the heat of the fire growing inside of him as I stand there weighing my next move. I can either throw gasoline on that fire, take a chance, push him to the edge. Or I can drench it with cold water and retreat again, preserving my pride.

Maybe it's the heat, maybe it's my exhaustion, but I go for the gasoline.

"Neither do I," I say as I take a deep breath and lie out flat, letting my body float on the surface of the river. Letting the soft white light from the moon illuminate the shape of my body against the black water, letting it highlight the hard points of my nipples and the gentle swell of my breasts that lie exposed for his eyes.

It feels like long minutes drag by as I stare up at the twinkling stars against the dark blue sky, schooling my breathing, trying to play it cool even though my heart is rioting beneath my ribs. Really, I'm sure it's mere seconds before I hear the steady sloshing of water. Sloshing that fades into quieter swishes before I feel the press of a finger pad on my chin.

"Ada..." The finger trails down the front of my throat gently, like a whisper, pausing momentarily at the dip between my collarbones. I suck in a ragged breath, scared to burst whatever bubble Dermot and I are in right now.

I chance a look at him; the water doesn't come up as high on him and his eyes are locked on my body. Burning across my skin, I swear I can feel the heat of his gaze, the weight of it as he takes me in for the first time. His other palm flattens against the small of my bare back under the water, easily keeping me suspended before him as his finger moves again.

He drags it through the valley between my breasts, sending shots of electricity to my core. Even the cool water between my legs feels like a caress; the way it sways and laps at me under the quiet blanket of night feels downright erotic. Every nerve ending is firing under Dermot's attention.

His lips press together in concentration and I see his jaw tick before his eyes flit up to mine. I can see the desire in his eyes, the indecision. The fire. And it almost knocks me over with its intensity.

It's so obvious. How I ever convinced myself this man didn't want me is beyond my comprehension right now. It's written all over his beautiful face.

His hand flattens and his fingers splay out over the lower curve of my breast. Our breathing goes ragged, heavy, and my mind goes blank. It's like all I can hear is our mingled breaths and the rasp of his skin against mine as he palms my breast, squeezing firmly. When he rolls my aching nipple between his thumb and forefinger, I arch up into him, letting my head tip back, like offering myself to him is the most natural thing in the world.

I can't even stop the guttural sigh that tears itself from my throat. Years of longing packaged up in one needy noise.

His hand presses harder into my back as he drops his head to my opposite breast. Latching his lips onto my pebbled nipple while squeezing the other one. *I can't believe this is really happening.* I whimper at the feel of his tongue circling there, before nipping at me—sending a wave of tingling goose bumps across my chest.

I feel hot and wet between my legs as I try to squeeze them together against the ache building there. It's a lost cause, of course. The ache is only starting. It's on the upward trend of a crescendo. If he stops, I'll probably sink to the bottom of this river, devastated and unfulfilled.

But that's all before he slides his lips across my wet skin and cups my cheek possessively. "Do you know why Tara means nothing to me?" he whispers roughly.

"N-no," I stammer out, not wanting to talk about her.

And then he steals my breath with his admission.

"Because no woman has meant a single fucking thing since that night you kissed me."

My heart pounds erratically as I'm lifted out of the water and into his arms. Chest to chest. Pelvis to pelvis. Mouth to mouth.

Dermot's lips claim mine and his fingers dig into my bare thighs as I wrap them around his waist. We pulse together, like one heart beating in tandem. I can feel the erection straining against his wet jeans. I grind my naked sex against the rough denim desperately—wanting more—before tangling my hands in his thick hair and challenging him.

Even if this is just for tonight, I want it all.

"Prove it."

CHAPTER 6

Ada

We crash through the front door and tumble into the small laneway house. Dermot's fingers are digging into my ass with the strain of keeping me close while carrying me here from the river. There will probably be bruises tomorrow. I *hope* there are bruises tomorrow.

He doesn't struggle. All that military training is really paying off where carrying me is concerned. "Hang on, Goldilocks," he said as he gripped me and marched us back to his quarters.

My mouth hasn't left his skin. I'm going to take my liberties while his hands are busy holding me. The heady scent of his aftershave surrounds me as I trail my tongue over his shoulder and up over the hollow of his throat. He kicks the door shut behind us and groans when I bite down and suck on his neck. *Hard.*

I want to leave a mark.

He turns us and grips my jaw as he pushes my head back against the door. "Ada, you're playing with fire, showing your teeth like that."

"Good. I want to get burned." I watch his eyes widen and nose flare in the dim light of the small house. I lick my lips, soaking up the dangerous look on his face. He looks almost feral. Wild. Like a man who's lost control.

"I don't want to hurt you." His fingers pulse on my face.

"You already have."

His chest rumbles with a deep growling noise. "I mean with all the things I'm about to do to you. Are you…?"

I smirk, knowing he will not like the answer to this question. "You're not the only one who's spent time with people who mean nothing to them. I'm not a little girl anymore, Dermot."

His face darkens and his hips thrust forward into me roughly. Pinning me. "That's done now." He lets go of my chin and looks down between us, where my naked body wraps around him, where he stands between my spread thighs, as he trails his fingers through the folds of my pussy. "This is mine."

I nod absently, alarmed by his words but unable to look away from the sight of his fingers on me. I'm entranced.

"Say it, Ada. Tell me you're mine."

My top teeth press into my bottom lip almost painfully as I watch his fingers circling over my aching core. My legs tremble anxiously, but my voice comes out clear and sure. "I'm yours, Dermot. I've always been yours."

My confession seems to be his undoing. He sinks to the floor right where we are, taking me with him. Lying back on the hardwood floor as I hover over him, shock coursing through my system over the fact that this is really happening right now. This man I've longed for—for as long as I can remember—stretched out before me, saying that I'm *his*. It's almost more than I can process.

When he angles his hips up, I grab his wet jeans and drag them down his legs, discarding them beside us, exposing muscular thighs and the outline of his rigid cock straining against the front of his boxers. My tongue darts out as I peel those off too, mouth going dry at the sight of him bobbing before me, impossibly thick and ready.

He's pushed up on his elbows, looking wide-eyed and uncertain, cheeks pink with arousal, dark waves disheveled from my fingers. I pause, soaking up every glorious inch of his body. Every line, every scar, every freckle. I want to memorize it all. Stamp it into my mind. I want to remember this moment for the rest of my life.

My chest aches with the beauty of him laid out before me. The sizzling burn of anticipation covering my skin. I push my knuckles to the floor, feeling the bite, wanting to make sure this is real. The words spill breathlessly from my mouth before I can stop them. "I've wanted this for so long."

His length jerks in response and he reaches for his jeans, pulling a condom out of his wallet and offering it to me. "Show me."

Our fingers touch as I take the wrapper, that same electricity I've always felt coursing through my veins like a storm. "I'm on the pill. Are you clean?" He nods once, his eyes wide and honest and totally heart-melting. I can almost feel my anger at him seeping away, dissolved by the droplets of water sprinkled around us. The intensity of my desire taking its place. I toss the foil wrapper across the floor and swing one leg over his body to straddle him. "Good. I want to feel you."

He groans and drops his head to the floor with a thud. His hands trail up over my hip bones to circle my waist. "You're going to be the death of me, Ada Wilson."

Good, I think to myself. *A little taste of your own medicine.* I reach down between us, fisting the smooth, steely length of him. Loving the sensation of it in my palm, feeling supremely powerful, like for once I might have the upper hand in this game of push and pull between us.

I line the swollen head of his bare cock up with my slick entrance. I should be cold, but instead my skin is burning. The feeling of him notched just inside of me sends a tremor down my spine. And after years of waiting, I drop myself down onto him. I impale myself on his girth and tip my head back on a strangled whimper.

"Fuck, Ada. Fuck..." He trails off, sitting straight up and pulling my breasts flush with his chest. The rasp of my nipples against the dusting of hair there has me mewling in his arms. It's all so much. So many emotions. So many sensations. I feel like I'm puffing more and more air into an already overfull balloon, like if I keep going, it's going to burst right in my face.

But I don't care, I can't stop.

I circle my hips on him, grinding down, loving the stretch of him inside me. Dermot's big, and I've never felt so deliciously full. He growls against the skin of my neck, the scrape of his stubble only adding to the blend of sensations coursing through my hypersensitive body. His fingers comb through my wet hair roughly, ending in a gentle tug at the base of my skull as he pulls my face right up to his. It forces me to look into his eyes, which somehow feels more personal in this moment than the knowledge that his bare cock is throbbing inside of me.

"Ada..." His thumb brushes reverently across my lips. "Do you have any idea how fucking good you feel? How many nights I've dreamt of this? The months I've spent trying to stay away from you? To convince myself this was all in my head? Fuck." He dips his chin and squeezes his eyes shut. "The things I want to do you…"

Tears spring up in my eyes. This confession… the time away, the years between us, the reasons this can't go anywhere, they all melt away in the wake of his confession. All the years I've spent feeling embarrassed, thinking I was the crazy one.

None of it matters.

Here. Now. Joined with the man I've always wanted. *Always loved.* This is all that matters.

I cup his cheek tenderly and echo his words. "Show me."

And then his lips are on mine, but it's different this time. It's leisurely and sensual, rather than hard and frantic. Our hands roam and we rock together in a steady rhythm. I feel every ridge and vein as he slides in and out of me, the rasp against my clit just adding to my frenzy with every thrust. My hips ache with the pleasure, that electric ball of tension building at the base of my spine with every thrust, with every brush of his fingers, with every lingering look.

God, the look in his eyes.

I grind down on him harder, moaning into his mouth. Whimpering against his skin. And when I'm bucking and writhing on top of him, lost to the sensations of having him inside of me, he lies down flat. His thumb goes straight for my clit, and he says, "Ride me, Ada. Come for me."

The words alone are almost enough to do it. I slam myself down on him hard a few times, taking his full length, feeling the bite of it and loving it. His thumb circles lazily, slick with the wetness of my arousal. And suddenly that building ball of tension snaps.

"Dermot!" I cry out as I grind on him harder. A single bead of sweat trickles down between my breasts like an arrow for the hot lance of pleasure surging through me as I ride the waves of my orgasm. And he doesn't stop touching or thrusting as I come apart around him. In fact, he picks up the pace, pushing me even further until my feet cramp and my thighs shake. Relentless in his taking until he joins me with his own release.

I feel him go rigid beneath me and growl possessively as he spills himself inside me. I feel my heart swell inside my chest, knowing that nothing has ever felt more right.

I fall forward onto his dampened torso, and he pulls me tight against him. Kissing my hair and trailing his hand up and down the indent of my spine. Our breathing is heavy and perfectly in sync, the only sound in the quiet house. I twirl a finger absently in the splash of hair on his chest, suddenly feeling like a little girl who finally got the thing she's always wanted.

Speechless. Breathless. Sated.

Overwhelmed.

But that's before Dermot whispers into my ear, "Time for a shower. I'm going to wash every inch of your body. And then I'm going to make a mess of you again."

An excited tremor courses through me, and I smile into his chest. "Let's go get messy then."

I fall back into the plushy feather pillows with a satisfied sigh. Dermot has spent the last several hours between my legs in one fashion or another, and I am positively boneless. I can die a happy woman now.

In my fantasies we'd been good together, but this was beyond. The chemistry. His skill. My hunger. It made for better sex than I've dared to dream about. If I'd known it could be like this, I would truly have lost my mind when he turned me down three years ago.

Saved by my own obliviousness.

But then I get to wondering if it would be like this at all if we hadn't been forced apart. If we hadn't had years to simmer and stew and *imagine*. I still can't believe that he's thought of this with me—that this might not be completely one-sided after all. And if I hadn't tried a thing or two in the dark, under the covers, with inexperienced boys at university, would I even be able to fathom the enormity of the last few hours with this man?

I don't think so.

I reach out to interlace our fingers as we lie beside each other, staring at the ceiling, watching shadows take form across the wood-beam ceiling as the early morning light reaches into the room. Snatching the safety and cover of night from us, or at least from him.

"You should get going."

My heart stutters and I go still. "I'm sorry, what?"

He rolls onto his side to look at me, head cradled in his palm. "I just mean back to the main house so that your parents don't find out."

I blink rapidly. Trying to catch up. Trying to wrap my head around what he's saying. "Dermot, I don't care if my parents find out."

He stares down at me intensely, with a sad smile on his face. "Ada… your dad—your parents—they've become friends to me, family almost. Taken me under their wing. Provided me with good, consistent employment. I can't just walk out my door in the morning with their only daughter on my arm. And everyone here, or in town, what would they think? I've known you since you we're a child. I never thought of you like this until that night on the porch, but no one else will know that."

Dread coils in my stomach. I hate the idea of keeping us a secret. Like there's something dirty about us being together somehow. But I also don't want to scare Dermot off. I need to figure out a way to strike a compromise.

I gaze back at him as I pull the sheet up over my naked body, uncertainty buzzing in my head now. "Okay but are we…? Is this…?" I groan and roll onto my stomach, burying my face in the pillows. I hate how I sound even asking. I hate needing him to reassure me that this is *more.*

The heat of his body presses beside me and I feel the drag of his teeth across my bare shoulder as he pulls the sheet back down. "Don't hide from me, Goldilocks. I told you. You're mine. I just… We need to think about this. I want you to be sure you know what you're getting into with me. I have a hard time believing you'll want me if you realize how fucked up I am."

"Are you talking about when the truck backfired the other day?"

His eyes go distant, to another place, as he carefully mulls my question over. "It's more than that, Ada. I'm not the same man I was when I left. I've seen too much. Been left behind too many times. I don't even think I like this new version of myself."

My heart thuds heavily and my chest aches, struck by the deep sadness in his voice. I don't know what to say to his assessment of himself. I wish he could see himself through my eyes. Strong and patient, with a wicked and addictive mouth. I feel safe when I'm around Dermot and all I know is that I want him any way I can have him. Walking away after last night would be… I can't even think about it. So instead, I lean into his broad chest and press a kiss right over his heart. "I like every version of you, Dermot Harding."

And then I wrap myself in a sheet and scamper back to the main house.

CHAPTER 7

Dermot

I'm dragging today. Which is saying something, because I haven't slept a full night since my tour. Usually, colt starting gets my adrenaline pumping; it's exciting to see the young horses get a good foundation. I live for long days on the ranch. It's where I feel most like myself—most at ease. But after a stressful first half of my night followed by a very active second half of the night, all I want to do is crawl back into bed.

With Ada.

There's no denying my feelings for her anymore. What I was convinced was merely a broken man's fixation on something innocent and unsullied, a comforting memory, is clearly so much more. I shouldn't have let things go that far, should have stuck to my plan and kept my distance. Because after last night, all my carefully built walls are mere rubble scattered at her feet.

I scoff at myself as I pull the saddle off the tired buckskin colt. I crashed through those walls like a goddamn bull in a china shop without considering the consequences of our relationship.

What would people think of me? A man in his thirties, who's known this girl since she was little. Who's taken a vow of honor, promised to protect people. Now… it feels wrong when I run through the scenario in my head. It feels worse when I consider how betrayed her parents might feel. How her reputation in this small town might suffer.

But when I'm with Ada, everything feels right. Last night, my mind felt quiet for the first time since I left the army. With her, I wasn't just going through the motions. I was *present.*

And I want that every day. At what cost though?

Since my parents took off, Tom and Lynette have become like family to me. I don't want to lose them. But now I've put myself in an impossible situation. Keep Ada and fess up to her parents—who I love and respect, but who will no doubt want to castrate me. Or give Ada up and… well, I can't even bear the thought of it now.

You are so royally fucked, Dermot.

I give the young quarter horse a light brush before walking him back out to his herd. Taking deep, calming breaths of the warm summer air. Until my eyes land on Ada's jean-clad ass, and then the wind is knocked out of me all over again.

She's walking out toward Penny's paddock, spinning the lead rope in her hand and humming tunelessly as she goes. She doesn't look worried at all. And like she can feel my gaze on her, she turns her head back over her shoulder, looking directly at where I'm standing.

I'm immobilized. I just stare back, slack-jawed, unable to process the fact that an angel like her would ever choose a damaged man like me. How could she possibly know that she likes every version of me? She saw me crumple that day when the truck went off. How can she throw caution to the wind like that? How can she forgive me so easily for pushing her away, for breaking her heart? It all seems impossibly naïve on her part.

That's why it's my job to warn her off.

And how the fuck am I supposed to get anything done with her around when all I want to do is strip her down and bend her over?

She's practically glowing, and the smile she gives me now? It's like looking into the sun—downright blinding.

A hard clap on the back knocks me right out of my daydream, and I try to will the swelling sensation in my jeans away as I turn to face... Tom Wilson.

"Morning, sir." I tip my head nervously, color draining from my face, hoping he didn't notice me ogling his little girl. Hoping he doesn't notice my uncontrollable erection.

"For crying out loud, Dermot. Why do you insist on still calling me sir? It makes me feel old."

I chuckle. "Sorry, Tom."

"That's more like it." He waves me along as he turns to walk back toward the barn. "Tell me how the horses are coming along before I head into town."

I give him a brief rundown of how each horse is doing, assuring him they'll all be broke and safe to sit on by the end of the week.

"You've always had a special way about you, Dermot. The horses know it, and so do people. It's hard not to love you."

My throat drops into my stomach like a stone. *If he only knew what I was doing to his daughter last night, he might not feel so sentimental.* "Thanks," I choke out awkwardly, looking away, unable to hold his gaze.

He barks out a laugh as he hops up into his pickup truck. "Hell of a mosquito bite you've got there, kid." I look back at him in confusion, realization only dawning on me when he smirks and taps his neck.

Ada's teeth left a bruise.

I'm trying to help Ada with Penny, but everything about her is driving me to distraction. The way her breasts bounce while she rides, the way her golden hair trails in the wind behind her when she gallops, the way she swung her leg over the saddle like she swung it over me last night.

Essentially, I'm a horny mess who can't stop envisioning all the ways I could corrupt a perfectly sweet twenty-one-year-old girl. *I want to corrupt her and only her for the rest of my life.*

Which is an alarming thought, a monumental realization, and truthfully more than I'm equipped to deal with.

"We galloped!" Ada singsongs from ahead of me as she slides down Penny's sweat-slicked flank, her entire body vibrating with contagious excitement.

My boots hit the ground as I step down off of Solar, grinning back at her. "You look excited."

Her emerald eyes rake down over my body suggestively and one eyebrow quirks up when she gets past my oval belt buckle. My body won't stop reacting to her mere proximity, no matter how much my brain begs it to stop. "So do you."

"Not here, Ada," I chide her, turning away, not wanting to hurt her feelings. But also not wanting to get caught by the other staff around the ranch. I hate that I have no control where she's concerned. I thought if I waited a few months after getting home, that if I could force myself to stay away from Gold Rush Ranch even though it was only a couple of hours away, that I'd be able to resist her draw—the imaginary connection I built up in my head overseas.

I didn't even last a full week. And god knows I didn't keep my hands to myself in the days leading up to last night either. For a soldier, my self-control is truly atrocious.

Back in the barn, we tie up and untack our horses silently. There's an unspoken tension between us. I know Ada doesn't understand my resistance and I can see the agitation in her every movement as she takes care of her little red mare. Even Penny seems nervous in Ada's presence. Like she can feel the storm brewing beneath her innocent-looking exterior.

We're walking past the hay shed after turning the horses out when she unexpectedly grabs me by the elbow and drags me into the darkened building. Before I can even protest, she's fallen to her knees and is grappling with my belt buckle, yanking my jeans down and fisting my cock like she's out for revenge.

"Ada—"

"Shut up, Dermot. I don't want to hear your excuses. Being around you has always been painful, but being around you and knowing what it's like to have you? It's downright unbearable."

She flattens her tongue, licking the head of my cock like a lollipop, and my mind goes blank. All my rational reasons to protest what she's doing fly right out the window. My hips buck toward her face when she wraps her lips around my girth, and when she slides her head toward my pelvis, I grab hold of the old plywood wall beside me to keep myself upright. Her tongue swirls and her cheeks hollow out as she works me, running her hands up over my thighs, squeezing my ass. Rolling my balls in her petite hand until I feel like I might lose control and finish right here and now.

But I'm not done. As much as I'm enjoying this, I want more.

I fist a chunk of her hair and pull her off of me, reveling in the way her eyes go wide and her lashes flutter as she looks up at me from the dirt floor of the shed. Reaching down, I scoop her up and turn around, sitting her on a stack of square bales as she squeals in surprise.

"Three bales high, the perfect height to taste what's between these thighs."

"Oh god." Her cheeks are stained the prettiest pink as she shimmies her hips to help me get her skin-tight jeans pulled off.

I toss them to the ground but put her beautifully stitched leather boots back on. "This is a good look for you, Ada," I murmur as I take hold of her thighs and spread her open before me. "You look fucking edible."

Her only response is the silent parting of her lips in the sweetest little *O* shape. She may have experimented with other men, but I can tell she doesn't have that much experience, and I am thriving off the quiet but needy way she reacts to me. I like that I can shock her with my mouth, and I know she does too as I watch her body tremble under my gaze.

I swipe a thumb through her folds and watch it come back glistening. I pop it into my mouth with an audible "Mmm," as I taste her, watching her eyes go wide and doe-like in response. "Tastes like..." I lift her legs higher before I growl, "Mine."

And then I dive in. Starting off slow and gentle with my tongue but ending up hard and fast. Urged on by her writhing and moaning, by her fingers raking through my hair.

Her legs shake, and she clamps them around my neck, but I don't stop. I add a finger, sliding into her wet heat while I continue to work her with my tongue. "Oh my god, Dermot. Please don't stop," she murmurs as I coax the orgasm from her body.

When it hits, her back arches and her hands turn to fists in my hair, yanking rhythmically, lost to her own pleasure. And I grin, loving making her fall apart like this. For me.

"Thank you," she sighs, breathlessly.

I pull away and quirk an eyebrow at her. "Oh, baby, I'm not done with you yet."

She just smiles as I pull her down off the stack of hay bales. Grabbing the twine of the top one, I chuck it onto the ground beside us and then spin her around. One hand on her hip and the other flat between her shoulder blades, I lean forward and whisper into her ear. "Two bales high, the perfect height to bend you over."

She moans as I press her chest down onto the bale of hay and add, "Legs wide, honey." I watch her step each boot-clad foot further apart, loving her eagerness. Groaning at how she looks bent over, bare legs disappearing into her boots.

It's fucking criminal.

I lean over her back while lining myself up, feeling her flutter against the contact. "You love this, don't you, Ada?"

And I slide into her.

"Yes!" she cries out, clenching around my girth and rocking her hips back toward me.

I tut at her playfully as I pull all the way back out. "Needy girl," I growl as I slide back in to the hilt. Pumping into her with a steady rhythm now, hearing my thighs slap against her bare ass, smelling the musky hay around us in the quiet shed, feeling her soft body moving beneath mine.

This—us—it's everything.

I stand up tall to watch from above and am struck by the depth of my feelings for her. By the enormity of them. How they've crept into my mind over the years no matter how hard I've tried to keep them at bay. I grip her hips, thrusting harder, driven wild by the fact that this woman wants *me,* when she could pick any man in the world. My control has gone up in a puff of smoke where she's concerned. And in this moment, I don't even care.

When she spasms and cries out my name beneath me, a blush spreading across her lower back, hitting that high for the second time, it's almost more that I can take. And knowing that she's been taken care of means I can chase my release with abandon.

"My turn," I say gruffly, just as sensations and emotions collide, shoving me right over the edge after her. As the tension between us ebbs, I lean back down to cover her body with mine, to press a kiss just below her ear. To tell her we're going to make this work. That I'm *never* going to give her up.

But then I freeze. The shed door swings open, and a voice growls through what was previously a private, safe space.

"What the fuck is going on here?"

I scramble to cover Ada. I don't even care that my jeans are around my ankles; she doesn't deserve this. Prying eyes. I recognize the voice as one of the farmhands, Gord. It's not news to me that these guys are ultra-protective of Ada. They always have been. But being righteous enough to announce yourself this way takes some serious balls.

I know I'm in trouble.

"Get out!" I bark angrily. Mind spinning with what this means for me. For her. For *us.*

When I hear the door close, I stand up and mutter, "Fuck!"

Ada stands and spins to face me, reaching for her jeans. She's still flushed from her orgasm, but her eyes are wide and alarmed. She rubs my arms as I do up my pants. "It's okay, it's okay..."

"No, Ada. It's not." I scrub a hand over my face. "If he tells anyone before I get a chance to explain... You don't understand."

"Explain it to me then."

"I've been around here as an adult since you were a lanky little kid with a rat's nest for hair. The things they'll say about us... People won't understand that I never thought of you this way even once until that damn kiss." I rake my hands through my hair and look up at the corrugated tin roof.

She tips her chin down to button her jeans before hitting me with the most innocent, trusting look. Like a shot to the heart. "We're both adults now, Dermot. Who cares what people will say?"

"Your parents are more than just friends to me, they're the family I never had. My own took off and haven't come back to see me. I can't do this to them. Disappoint them like this."

"Why would making me happy disappoint them?" She sounds genuinely confused.

I knew this would happen. I knew this was a bad idea. I've known all along that I should stay away from Ada Wilson. That giving in to my confused and fucked up daydreams borne of an innocent kiss years ago would only lead to trouble. I should have been stronger, because now this will hurt more than just me.

I grasp her face and kiss her forehead reverently before turning and walking out of the shed. If Ada doesn't care about her reputation—her future—I'll have to be the one to do it for her.

Gord's leaning up against the far corner of the building, a big wad of tobacco tucked into his lip, picking at his nails. He barely spares me a glance as I walk up. "The way I see it, one of us tells him or you just hop in that truck and head back up to the mountains."

I sigh. Hating the decision but refusing to be the thing that messes Ada's life up. I can give up the Wilsons if it means that Ada gets to go on and live life without a black mark against her name.

"I'll leave."

CHAPTER 8

Ada

I RUSH UP TOWARD THE OLD FARMHOUSE, LOOKING FOR Dermot. Needing to find him. That kiss on the forehead felt different. It lacked the heat and grit of our past several interactions.

It felt like goodbye.

He finally comes into view, jogging down the front steps of my parents' house. His shoulders are tense and tall as he marches across the driveway, that military training peeking out like it does sometimes now.

"What are you doing?" I ask, dread coiling in my gut. It's like my body already knows what my mind refuses to accept.

"I just went to let your mom know that I'm leaving. She'll pass the message on to your dad." He continues walking right past me, toward the little laneway house. Alarm bells ring in my ears.

"Where are you going?"

"Back home, up to Merritt."

I chase after him, like a sad little puppy on his heels. "For how long?"

He swings the front door open and I follow him through before he finally turns to look at me. His eyes are all steel. Cold and determined. The way he looked at me the night before, while I straddled him, right in this exact spot? All that warmth is gone.

"For as long as it takes." His words are like ice on my skin.

"For as long as *what* takes?"

"Sorting myself out. I can't do this to you."

I gasp, but he just turns and starts shoving stuff into his duffel bag. "Seriously, Dermot?" Anger bleeds into my voice, making it wobble. "You're going to run again?"

"I didn't run, Ada. I joined the army, served my country. Learned some tough lessons about life and myself. It's time you did the same."

"Oh yeah? Tell me, Dermot, what lessons am I supposed to be learning right now?" I cross my arms, digging my nails into my skin so hard it will leave marks.

He looks up at me. Dark eyes boring into mine, not unkindly, as he says, "That girlhood crushes are just that. Best left in the past."

I rear back as though he's just slapped me. This man made love to me, right here, last night. And now all of that is just a girlhood crush? I'm speechless. Frozen. All I want is for the floor to open right here and swallow me whole, but he continues talking as he drops his bag by the door and straightens the kitchen.

"I'm too old for you, Ada. I'm too broken. I've never had a long-term relationship, don't even know if I can manage one. I haven't slept through the night even once in almost three years. Loud noises scare me. I've seen things I can't get out of my head. I'm a mess, and you have the entire world in the palm of your hand. You deserve so much better than to be stuck limping along with me." His voice cracks with emotion and he tips his head up to stare at the ceiling.

My chest aches, the kind of ache that shoots right into my throat and threatens to transform into that all-consuming type of nausea. My cheeks feel hot and my eyes sting, but I refuse to cry. Dermot doesn't need me to feel bad for him. He needs a swift kick in the ass.

My finger shakes as I lift my hand to point at him accusingly. My voice comes out steely and eerily calm. An absolute bluff. "I have a dad, Dermot. He teaches me lessons, not you. You're just an asshole who's too self-absorbed to realize what he's got staring him in the face. You'll never be happy because you're too busy feeling sorry for yourself."

His jaw ticks, like he's swallowing words he wants to say. I hope the taste of the apology he owes me is bitter. I hope it turns his stomach.

"You should go," is all he manages to bite out.

The finality of his words lands like the lash of a whip. I try not to flinch, but I fail.

"So should you," I say, turning on my heel and storming out of the house.

I've been here before. I should have known better.

I don't want to face my parents and I don't want to face the staff. So I go to the only place where I know for a fact I won't face any judgement: Penny's field.

I duck through the wooden fence and head toward where she's grazing. The summer sun is beating down on her slender back, and her tail is swishing back and forth, keeping any bugs at bay. She looks shiny and healthy, bright copper—like a brand-new penny.

She's come along so quickly with Dermot's help, and the realization that I'll always have to attribute some of her progress to him stings like whiskey on an open wound. There's not a single place, or thing, on this farm that won't forever remind me of him. This is *my* home, *my* safe haven. And he waltzed in and stomped all over it. *Again.*

How could I have been so gullible?

I get close enough that Penny's head snaps up. She knickers her greeting, wide, intelligent eyes blinking back at me innocently—like I don't already know that this little chestnut mare has a devilish streak. I smile at her sadly. I like her sassy side; I wish I could be more like her. Tougher.

Because right now, I feel downright fragile.

And when I finally run my hands up around her silky neck, when I feel her warm, damp exhale on my shoulder, my carefully curated game face melts. The ache in my chest breaks through every barrier I've erected, hitting me with full force.

Taking my breath away as I burrow my face in the filly's neck and break down.

I don't know how long I stand there crying. But Penny's patience with me wears out, and she eventually steps away, a wet spot on her neck, to get back to her grass.

I don't know what to do. I feel like I'm living in a waking nightmare. The sky is perfectly blue, the fields are bright green, the birds are chirping happily, and yet my world is crashing down around me. How can such a perfectly pretty day feel so utterly ugly?

How did I come so close to having everything I've ever wanted, only to be left here with nothing in the blink of any eye? How am I supposed to come back from knowing what having him felt like?

I plunk down on the grass, lying out flat, feeling too dizzy to go anywhere else, finding the sound of Penny's teeth ripping at the grass rather soothing. The puffy white clouds above me float peacefully, and I'm taken back to my days as a child on the ranch. Playing in the dirt all day long, jumping onto horses with no saddle or bridle, cloud gazing and daydreaming of Dermot Harding. I'm pretty sure I even pulled petals off of daisies. *He loves me, he loves me not, he loves me...*

Now all I see in the clouds are meaningless white blobs. A manic giggle erupts from my chest. Talk about a grim outlook for a twenty-one-year-old woman with her entire life ahead of her.

"Should I be worried about you?"

My dad's voice wraps around me like a warm hug. I hear him give Penny his signature loud pats on her muscled shoulder.

"No."

"Ada, you're lying sprawled out in the field, staring at the sky, laughing. I've been watching you. I don't even think you've blinked. I love you, but this is creepy."

I smile at the image he just painted. It is pretty creepy when he puts it like that. "Love you too, Dad," is all I can think to say back right now.

"Your mom's been looking for you. It's dinnertime." How could it be dinnertime? How long have I been lying here for?

"Oh, sorry," I mumble, still fixating on the fact that I've been lying in the field for hours now.

He mumbles something that sounds an awful lot like, "I'll fucking kill him," before taking a seat on the ground beside me.

He picks up a blade of grass, eyes it warily, and then places it in the corner of his mouth. A rancher through and through. "You all right, my girl?" he asks without looking at me.

I sigh. I don't want to lie to my dad, he's been a pillar of support in my life. My biggest fan. I don't want to think he'd be disappointed in me now. But Dermot has planted a seed of doubt with the intensity of his shame.

So I settle on something truthful that also gives nothing away. "I will be."

He just grunts and picks at the soil between us.

"Of course you will. You're my daughter."

CHAPTER 9

Dermot

I'VE ALWAYS FOUND THE MOUNTAINS THAT SURROUND MY FAMILY farm to be oppressive. But these past two weeks they've become downright depressing. Too tall, casting too long of a shadow, and way too fucking cold.

I miss the warm sunshine and rolling hills in Ruby Creek. I miss the camaraderie of being around other people at Gold Rush Ranch.

I miss Ada.

The further I drove away from her, the less my reasons for leaving seemed to make sense. Last time I *had* to leave. The army was waiting for me. But now? There is absolutely nothing waiting for me. An empty farm and a traumatized mind are all I have for company.

With nothing else on the horizon, I finally got an independent geologist out to check my land for mining deposits. It appears I've hit the literal gold mine in that department. My reward for being the last Harding standing on this farm. When everyone else had the good sense to leave and start something new, I hunkered down. Too sentimental to part with it.

Too sentimental to do anything—to even move, apparently. Which is why I've spent my last several days walking and mapping the perimeters of my land. Checking the fences in the morning and then sitting on the front porch of the run-down house, staring out at my land in the afternoon. With over eighty thousand acres, I should be able to keep busy for a while.

The cows are long gone, sold before I left on tour. The chickens, too. No crops to speak of. The only signs of life here are the wildlife that passes through, the wildflowers that have taken over the valleys in my absence, and the squirrels that I'm pretty sure are now living in the attic.

And me. But I'm not living. I'm going through the motions. I sleep in fits and starts, often woken up by flashes of my time overseas—but that's not new. What is new is being woken up by deep regret over leaving Ada, rather than sweet dreams about one innocent kiss.

The memory of what we could have had under different circumstances haunts me. The way her ears went red and the tip of her nose twitched to hold back the tears when I told her I was leaving again.

The way I held her heart in my hand and crushed it into dust. All because I'm too big of a coward to fess up about how I feel and face whatever the repercussions might be. And maybe even more so because I'm fucking terrified to need anyone who might leave me. Who might move on. Every person in my life has been so impermanent. My parents, my older siblings, the friends I made in the army. Why would it be any different with Ada?

She's young. She's at university. She's going to run a racehorse business one day; I know it in my bones. Because Ada Wilson is smart, and strong, and an absolute go-getter. The last thing she needs is a broken-down man holding her back.

This is the best course of action for both of us. Even if it doesn't feel that way right now. Or at least that's what I keep telling myself.

I take a deep swig of my beer and rest my head on the back of the porch swing, giving it a good shove, hoping that maybe it might rock me off for a few minutes of peace. Where I could let myself remember the feel of Ada's silky skin beneath my fingertips, the press of her tongue into my mouth, the sound of her moans as I moved inside her.

This is a good dream.

I can feel myself drifting until the sound of tires rumbling over gravel cuts into my consciousness. Cursing without opening my eyes, I feel my body go rigid. I just want to be alone right now.

When the hum of the engine gets close enough, I open one eyelid.

And when Tom Wilson steps out of his truck, I open the other and straighten myself. Alarm courses through me. *Why the hell would he drive all the way up here?*

I sit up, blinking at him, rubbing my eyes to make sure I'm not seeing things. His truck is parked beside mine, except he's got a two-horse trailer attached to his, and by the way it's swaying, I'm thinking there's probably a horse or two in there as well. I'm so damn confused.

"You look like hell, son," he says good-naturedly as he climbs the steps up to the front porch.

"Wasn't expecting any visitors." My voice cracks after days of not speaking to anyone.

"Wanted to come for a visit. Felt like a trail ride in the mountains." He looks out over my land appreciatively.

I just blink at him in confusion. "You could have called."

He waves me off. "We both know you wouldn't have answered."

I just grunt. *He's not wrong.*

"You gonna offer an old man a beer, or just keep sitting there like a sulking bump on a log?"

"Sorry." I shoot up off the swing, realizing how rude I've been in the wake of his arrival. *Way to welcome a man you profess to love and respect, Dermot.* "Here." I point at the swing. "Take a load off and I'll grab you a cold one."

He gives my shoulder a brief squeeze as I slide past him into the messy house. In the kitchen, I hold the edge of the counter and bow my head, trying to figure out what the hell Tom Wilson is up to. If he knew about Ada and me, and was angry with me, well, I couldn't tell. But there's only one way to find out.

With two fresh beers in hand, I step back out onto the deck. "Beautiful farm you've got up here, Dermot. I can see why you didn't want to let it go."

I hand him his beer and take a seat in the big Adirondack chair across from him. "Seems like I made the right choice."

Tom takes a long pull of his beer and looks back at me inquisitively.

"I did what you said and had somebody out to survey the land, drill some holes and all that."

He leans forward to rest his elbows on his knees, his watery blue eyes regarding me with a knowing look. "And?"

My eyes scan the scrubby, rocky land around us. "We're basically sitting on a gold mine. Seems that big mining company was sniffing around for good reason." I shift my eyes back to Tom. "Thanks for pushing me to look for myself."

His eyes twinkle, and he shakes his head, leaning back to look out at the craggy landscape. "How much?"

"A lot. A metric fuck-ton."

"Well, I'll be… What are you going to do with it?"

"Start a business, I suppose. Though I have no idea how to do such a thing." I look up at him, properly meeting his eyes for the first time since he pulled up. "Your offer to help still stand?"

"You've been through a lot for a man your age, Dermot."

I don't respond. What is there to say to that?

"I want to see you succeed. So yeah, of course the offer still stands. Some startup capital and my support for five percent of the company. What do you say?"

I feel a pinch across the bridge of my nose, a thickness in my throat that I will away. "I don't know why you've always been so good to me."

The sad smile he gives me barely touches his eyes. "Had a soft spot for ya since that first summer you came to work for me. Twenty years old and a total idiot. Good with the horses though."

I bark out a laugh. "To be honest, Tom, I'm not sure much has changed. I think I'm more jumbled than I was then."

He just nods at me knowingly, tipping the brown bottle back and swallowing. "Nothing a night out on the range can't fix. Let's pack up and hit the trails so we can set up camp before it gets dark."

"We can just go for a ride in the morning, Tom. We really don't have to do the whole shebang."

He slams his empty beer bottle down on the small table beside him. "You never used to complain about campouts. Plus, I can see the inside of your house through the window. I'm too old to sleep in a messy bachelor pad."

I look through the window. *Messy* doesn't even begin to cover it. I've been a zombie living in a war zone; the place is a disaster. It makes me want to take a match to the old house, burn it to the ground and start fresh.

"Okay, give me ten minutes."

I settle into my sleeping bag, feeling more relaxed than I have in days. Fresh air, a change of scenery, a few sips of whiskey with an old friend. I feel like I'm twenty all over again.

My eyelids feel heavy instantly, and under the bright stars, beside the crackling fire, I drift off into a dreamless sleep.

When my eyes finally crack open, it's already light out and Tom is up making coffee over the fire. "Good morning, Sleeping Beauty."

I scrub my hands over my face and sit up, shocked that I slept through the night. "Sorry. I haven't been sleeping much lately."

"How long is lately?" he asks, forehead crinkled in concern.

A ragged sigh pries itself from my chest as I look up at the pillowy clouds drifting in the bright blue sky. "It's probably been almost three years."

"Oh, Dermot…"

I hold a hand up to stop him. I don't want his pity, and I don't deserve it after what I've done to his daughter. "It's okay, Tom. I don't need you to rub my back over it. I'll get better, eventually. It's always worse up here. It's too quiet. Too much time to think about… everything."

"Well, come back down to the ranch then. The laneway house is yours for as long as you need it."

I rake my fingers through my hair, tugging at it in frustration. "I can't."

He pours me a cup of strong black coffee and hands it over. "Why's that?"

"I just…" Shame coils in my gut. *If he only knew.* I take a sip of coffee to fill the silence.

"I know about you and Ada."

And all that coffee gets sprayed over my sleeping bag as I look at him. One side of his mouth quirks up, but he doesn't look all that amused.

I blurt out the first thing I can think to say. "I'm sorry."

His wise eyes narrow as he takes a deep inhale of his own coffee. "For what?"

"For betraying your trust." My heart is pounding in my chest. Anxiety coursing through my veins. *He's known all this time and acted like we were just going to hang out?*

"The only person you've betrayed is Ada. Me?" Tom lifts his shoulders and then drops them dramatically. "I'm just confused."

I feel my entire face go red. *Betrayed Ada?* Just the combination of the words makes me angry with myself. That's the very last thing I ever wanted to do. "Confused about what?"

"How the man I know could leave behind the woman he loves."

I startle. It feels like he's punched me in the gut. "Did she…?" I stare into the inky black liquid in my tin cup. "Did she tell you that?"

Tom just snorts. "You weren't kidding about still being an idiot." We sit in silence for a few moments, both lost in thought before Tom adds, "Any old fool with two eyes can see that you love that girl. And her?" He scoffs, shaking his head in disbelief. "She's always loved you. Right out of the gate. She never stopped. Not even for a minute. And that"—he wags his finger at me—"that is a gift most men will never know."

His words hit me like a wrecking ball. They knock the air right out of the valley, like the mountains have finally succeeded in suffocating me. I feel hollow.

"So you… don't care?"

Tom stands and starts packing the camp up, clearly agitated by my line of questioning. "Why? Because you're older than her? Because you've been around for years? I don't care, Dermot! And if you love her like I think you do, what other people think shouldn't matter either!" His voice is quiet, simmering with protective rage as he huffs out a deep, centering breath. "I love you like a son. I want you happy, just like I want Ada happy. And if that's together, then as far as I'm concerned, it's just the best of both worlds."

He shoves our things into bags, obviously done with our campout. I hear him mutter something like, "Ya'll are thick as bricks," as I stand to help him silently. Properly chastised.

Our ride back to the house is quiet. But not awkward. Maybe it should be, but I can't help but feel like Tom shed a lot of light on the situation. I also feel like a dog with his tail between his legs, like I should have known better, like I should have trusted myself.

Like I should have trusted Ada.

And now I'm going to have to prove to her she can trust me again. Knowing Ada, it won't be easy.

When we arrive at the homestead, I help Tom pack his trailer up. Years of working together have lent us knowledge of one another, meaning we move around in sync. Getting shit done quietly and efficiently.

When he pulls his truck door open, he turns around to look at me, holding his arms wide. I step into his fatherly hug, feeling his big, comforting slaps against my back—unable to stop the small smile they elicit. This man pats everyone like they're cattle.

When he pushes me back, he looks me dead in the eye, hands on my shoulders. "I can't make personal life decisions for you. But you promised that girl you'd help get her filly to the races. And I know you're a man of your word."

I offer him a decisive nod in response. "See you soon."

I'm going back to Gold Rush Ranch, and I'm going to get the girl whether I deserve her or not.

CHAPTER 10

Ada

I REGARD MYSELF IN THE MIRROR, MAKING SURE MY MAKEUP IS perfect. Today is the Denman Derby and I'm going to enjoy myself, like I do every year. I've got a new floral print dress on, I've curled my hair and painted my nails—you wouldn't know I'm a total ranch rat unless I told you.

Feeling satisfied with the girl looking back at me, I take a deep breath. "Time to woman up, Ada," I murmur to myself, rolling my shoulders back. "This is your favorite day of the year. Who needs Christmas?"

The girl staring back at me looks beautiful and strong, totally ready to take on the world. And I am. As painful as the last two weeks have been, I've also learned a lot about myself. I feel like I walked through the fire and came out the other side, turned over a new leaf, realigned my vision for my future. I'm sure of myself, of my strength, in a way I never have been.

I think I'll always love Dermot Harding, but I have other dreams I need to achieve, and I know his dumb ass wouldn't want me to sit around moping. I think I've come to know that Dermot loves me in his own way.

In a way that's not good enough for me.

Because Dermot needs to love himself first. He's so paralyzed by what everyone will think of him, by feeling like nothing is ever permanent, that he can't give himself over to anyone or anything.

The realization hit me one night during a midnight swim in the river. He can't put himself first because he doesn't love himself enough to make it a priority. That was the night my tears switched from being for myself to being for him. A man too scared to accept the love I wanted to give him.

An absolute shame. And not something I can fix for him. Lucky for me, I don't suffer from that same insecurity.

So this is the new Ada, forged in fire, soon to be a university graduate and future owner and trainer of Canadian racehorse champions. Dermot Harding had a chance to get on board, and now he can get out of my way.

I trot down the stairs toward the front door, sliding my feet into the strappy heels I picked for today with a small smile on my face. I feel *good.* In fact, I feel great. Until I step out onto the front porch and see a metallic blue pickup in the driveway. Dermot is sitting on the tailgate, swinging his legs, with a bouquet of roses laid across his lap.

His head snaps up at the sound of the door slamming behind me. "Ada—"

Butterflies flap in my stomach, but I cut him off. "No. I don't want to hear it." I march toward my dad's truck as I hear my parents lock up behind me.

"Five minutes, Ada. I brought flowers."

I bark out an incredulous laugh. "Do you know me at all, Dermot Harding? Flowers? Try harder." I pull myself into the back of the cab and slam the door on anything else he has to say. Today is *my* day.

My mom gives him an apologetic pat on his knee and my dad tilts his head and shrugs as if to say, "Women." But within moments, my entire family is loaded up in the truck and Dermot is nothing more than a slouched-over figure in the rearview mirror.

★★★

Our day down at the track is a dream, as usual. The buzz of Derby Day never fails to stir something inside of me. I want to be there, with a horse of my own, running in the Denman Derby. I know now, more than ever, that it's what I'm meant to do with my life.

We had a beautiful dinner, wine, placed some bets—came out even. And now on the drive home we talk about all the horses we saw.

"I want to buy another one, Dad."

"Another what?" he asks, eyes flitting back to me through the rearview mirror.

"Racehorse."

He just chuckles, the apples of his cheeks all round with the width of his grin. "One thing at a time, Ada. Maybe as your graduation present. You only have one year left at university."

I look out the window, into the darkening landscape, and press my lips together to hold back the huge grin threatening to break across my face. I can't wait to get started.

The closer we get to the farm, the quieter we all become. No one dared to bring up Dermot's appearance when we drove off, but now the unspoken weight of his arrival is filling up all the empty space in the truck.

"Do you think he's still there?" my mom asks as we turn off the highway.

I just shrug and look away. Probably not. Staying power isn't exactly his forte.

"You know that boy is head over heels in love with you, don't you, Ada?" she presses.

I roll my lips together, trying not to bite back too hard. My mom means well, and I know they both figured out what happened between us too easily for them to not have been on to us before. I knew they wouldn't care. Why couldn't Dermot have just believed me?

"He's not a boy, Mom. He's a grown-ass man."

"Ada Wilson! Watch your language!" My mother sounds scandalized, but my dad just laughs. He knows me well.

"It's a fact. He's an adult. And if what you say is true, he's got a funny way of showing it," I add before staring back out the window.

No one can argue with what I've just said. And when we pull up to the house, the truck is dead silent as we peer out into the darkened driveway.

Until my dad groans. Dermot is still here, sitting on the back of his truck. Waiting. It doesn't look like he's moved all day, and even though I just went off about him being an adult… right now? Looking at him? He looks like a lost little boy.

I feel a tug at the center of my sternum, that invisible string that's always drawn me to him, trying to pull me toward him again. The accompanying pinch in my chest makes me want to hug him, to soak up all his pain and disappointment. To lend him my strength.

But I can't yet. I'm still too pissed off. Too hurt. "Don't let him stay here," I say as I hop out of the truck, sniffling. I give him a once-over, then dart into the old farmhouse. Knowing that if I stare at him too long, if I get lost in those dark eyes, my resolve will disintegrate completely. The man is like a big vat of acid for my willpower.

I kick my shoes off and head up to my room to get ready for bed, not wanting to talk to anyone. Ditching my dress, I slip into pajamas and then scrub my face clean until it hurts. I'm about to crawl into bed when I hear the front screen door creak open. I'm up and looking out my window so fast it's embarrassing.

Pulling the lace curtain back ever-so-slightly, I watch my mom walk out to Dermot's truck with a pillow, a blanket, and a sandwich. *Traitor.* Then I hear her say, "She'll come around." *Double traitor.* She pats his shoulder before she turns to walk into the house and I fall into bed, squeezing my eyes shut hard until I finally drift off into a fitful sleep.

When I wake up in the morning, I'm dreading looking out my window. If I see Dermot sleeping outside my house, I'm going to fall apart. I wanted him to come back for me, and he did. So why isn't it enough?

The only thing I can think of is the fact that he thought he could just waltz out here with a handful of roses and I'd run back into his arms. It showed a total lack of understanding—of reflection. The only thing I've ever done with flowers is braid them into my horse's hair.

I drag my feet across the oak floors toward the bathroom but am stopped short by loud metal clanging. *What the hell?*

I pull back the curtain, just like last night. Dermot's truck is still there, but he's moved out into the field next to the barn and is using a mallet hammer, jamming what looks like a bunch of metal fencing together.

I have to admit, he's piqued my curiosity, so I shove on some jeans and head out.

He doesn't look up when I approach the paddock fence. He just keeps working calmly and steadily. I admire him openly, the way his hands flex with each strike, the sweat beading on his forehead. I imagine running my tongue along the bead of it that slips down over his defined cheekbone. And then, realizing where my mind has wandered, I start to get antsy with how long he's been ignoring me.

"What are you doing?" I blurt, unable to take it any longer.

He just smiles and runs his arm over his forehead, brushing away the perspiration. "Woulda thought you'd recognize this, Goldilocks."

My eyes scan the combination of bars he's put together, but I must be thick because I can't tell what it's supposed to be. "Okay," I huff out, agitated at not being able to pass this test. "Pretend I don't recognize it."

He chuckles, the dimple on his cheek peeking out playfully, and turns back toward his project. "It's a present."

"For what?"

"For you."

I rear back. I know I didn't want flowers, but I'm not sure I want this either. "Okay… why?"

He comes back to the fence and leans his forearms against it as he regards me. I can't help but look down at the way this position tugs his jeans tight over that very round ass. Being this close to him? It's like being offered water for the first time after spending two weeks in the desert.

He notices. And his cheek twitches, but he has the good sense not to comment. Instead, he says, "Because I made you a promise."

I just tilt my head, a silent signal for him to continue.

"To get Penny to the races. This is your new training gate. You only have a couple more months to race her as a two-year-old. And apparently the gate can be a challenge."

I look back at the gate. My mouth is moving, but no sound comes out. *This* is what I was talking about. I don't want flowers. I want *this.*

"Ada, you look like a fish dropped into a dry bucket. Go get your horse. I'm almost done here."

I nod mutely and walk away on wooden legs. What does this mean? Is he only back to help with Penny? Or is he back for me?

I'm standing beside Penny's shiny, coppery coat without even knowing how I really got here. Like my mind has been somewhere else entirely. She drops her head into the halter and we walk back toward Dermot, who is shifting the panels around so it's finally looking like a sort of chute.

"There are more attachments, but apparently the key is to get her comfortable in there. Walking through so she trusts you enough when you eventually box her in."

I raise an eyebrow at him, wondering if he's talking about Penny or me, but carry on anyway. We spend the morning working together. It's torture, feeling him so close to me and yet thinking he might only be back at the ranch on a professional basis. His body heat seeps through my clothes, and his form hovers close to mine as he moves around me, showing me the gate, breaking down how it works, but he never touches me. Not so much as an accidental brush of the leg or nudge of the elbow.

And after a few hours, I'm going insane. I want him to touch me. Kiss me. Throw me against this stupid gate and have his way with me. My entire body is thrumming with need and he's hardly looked me in the eye.

I know I need to leave. I've embarrassed myself far too many times by throwing myself at this man, and I can't let myself go there again. So I busy myself around the farm and Dermot goes back to sitting on his stupid truck. Like a lost puppy. A sexy lost puppy I want to kick and then kiss.

When I'm about to head into the house for dinner, I catch sight of him sitting there, casually looking through some sheets of paper, and my patience snaps. I storm toward him. "What are you doing?"

He looks genuinely shocked by the bite in my voice. "I wanted to show you these."

"Not that!" I knock them right out of his hand and watch them flutter to the ground. "I mean *here*. What are you doing here? You gave me the gate. If that's all you wanted, you can now go."

But then I look down and catch sight of the papers near my feet.

Dear Ada…

I bend down and pick up the closest sheet. Feeling the beat of my pulse stronger in my throat.

Dear Ada,

Just got to basic training and everyone here has someone to write to. I'm not sure who else I could send a letter to that might actually want to hear from me, so I guess you're stuck with me.

Yours,
Dermot

P.S. I should have kissed you back.

I look at Dermot, his face completely unreadable where he sits. My hands start to shake and I sink to ground, right on the gravel driveway, desperately grasping at the other loose sheets. *Good god. There are so many.* The papers rattle in my hands as I lift them up.

Dear Ada,

You know that feeling at the end of a long day on the ranch? You've been up early, worked your ass off all day, your legs feel like jelly, and you just crash into bed and have the best sleep? I'm so much more tired than that and I still can't sleep.

Instead, I avoid replaying my days by lying awake thinking about the night you kissed me. Analyzing it every which way I can. Trying to commit it to memory. Why did you do that? Plant a seed in the mind of a man you knew was leaving? A man who never saw you that way even for a moment? Now I don't know what to think about it, about myself, about you, and I don't even have the balls to ask. It's better this way anyhow.

Yours,
Dermot

P.S. I should have kissed you back.

A ragged whimper bursts out of my chest as I riffle through page after page. Letter after letter. "Dermot…"

Dear Ada,

Everything here is dark, and sad, and depressing. The days blend into each other and the only thing that ties me back to home is you. Your sunny blond hair, your carefree smiles, the scent of your tangerine body wash that wrapped around me that night when you stood closer than you ever have. The way your hands felt on my shoulders when you leaned in. What I wouldn't give for a simple gentle touch right now.

The longer I'm away, the more I remember things differently. The more I think that maybe there is a connection between us. Is it new? Has it always been there? I don't know. You're so fucking young. You're better off without me.

Yours,
Dermot

P.S. I should have kissed you back.

A tear falls onto the letter in my hands, drawing my attention from the pages. "Dermot," I say, coming to stand. "I… I never got these letters."

"That's because I didn't send them. Never quite worked up the courage." *All these letters. All this time…*

His jaw ticks as his eyes sear across my body, pausing momentarily on my heaving chest before moving back up to my face. "That's not all I wanted. To give you the gate, I mean."

I come back to standing and hold the pages out wide in tearful exasperation. "Then for crying out loud, Dermot, use your words and tell me what you want."

He doesn't even hesitate. "I want you. I want us. I'll sleep in this truck for as long as it takes. If I'm relegated to being your assistant trainer for the foreseeable future, I don't even care. I just want to see you succeed, to see all your dreams realized. And I'll do anything in my power to make that happen for you. I'll love you even if you don't love me back."

My heart riots in my chest. Almost ready to burst with years of unspoken truths and unfulfilled wishes. I almost can't believe what I'm hearing. *Did he just say he loves me?*

I step in closer to him, grasping his knee with both hands and looking up into the depths of his chocolate eyes. "You're a fool, Dermot Harding." The muscles in his thigh tense beneath the tips of my fingers. "Don't you know?" I say more quietly now, feeling him lean down closer to hear what I'm about to say, his breath fanning across the sensitive skin below my ear. "I can't remember a time in my life when I haven't loved you. It's always been you."

Dermot's throat bobs with emotion as one calloused hand comes up to stroke my cheek. I see his eyes sparkle in the late summer sun as a secret smile touches his shapely lips. Lips that are moving closer to mine, lips that I can't wait to feel against my own again.

So I stand up on my tippy-toes and kiss him as his broad frame leans down over me, as he grips my head possessively, protectively. We kiss, and the world stands still, and everything feels so suddenly right. So hopelessly fated. Like no matter what either of us did, we'd have ended up here, today, in each other's arms.

I'm breathless when he pulls back and smiles at me, his thumb stroking my cheek softly. "I'm never leaving you again. If you'll let me, I'm moving into the laneway house."

I just wink through the tears spilling over my lashes, my voice tearful but happy. "I'll think about it."

Much later that night, we lie out in the bed of his truck on a blanket. For the last hour I've made Dermot read me his letters out loud. I've cried, we've kissed, he even stopped at one point to strip me down and show me how much he loves me. And now I'm tucked safely under his arm with my legs slung over his as we look up at the stars. They shine like a string of twinkle lights over the farm, not at all diluted by the glow of the city. It's almost like looking at a painting, never quite the same depending on the day. And today there's a meteor shower.

"Right there." Dermot's hand shoots up to point out the falling star. "Make a wish, Ada."

An airy laugh floats out from my lips as I snuggle in closer. "What am I supposed to wish for? I have everything I've ever wanted."

He presses a sweet kiss to my temple and whispers, “Pick something.”

“Okay. I want to win the Denman Derby. I want to win it all. Maybe even the Northern Crown. Doesn’t that sound crazy?” I shake my head, grinning.

“No, Ada. It doesn’t.”

“Oh yeah? You going to promise to make that happen too?” I laugh, nudging his ribs with my elbow, thinking he’ll laugh along with me and my lofty dreams.

But instead, he’s completely sincere when he looks down at me and says, “I promise.”

Then his lips find mine, and I know deep in my bones that the world has a funny way of making wishes come true.

EPILOGUE

Dermot

Bells ring and the horses surge out of the gate. I feel Ada's nails digging into the palm of my hand. Her entire body is vibrating with anticipation—with nervousness.

This is Lucky Penny's debut race, and we both know we're out of our league. Two country bumpkins pulling up with one lone little racehorse. But everyone has to start somewhere, and Ada is determined.

Tom had to call in some pretty serious favors to convince a jockey to take the ride on Penny. But here we are, close to the end of the season, watching her blaze across the dirt track in the black and gold Gold Rush Ranch silks that Ada made. I wrap my opposite hand over the top of hers, feeling the center stone of the ring I put there a week ago dig into my palm. She smiles faintly but doesn't tear her eyes away from the track.

Ada and I happened fast, and yet we didn't. We both had three long years to be sure about one another. And when you know, you know. I wanted Ada, and I wasn't about to wait any longer. Or give her time to come to her senses and pick someone better. We're planning a spring wedding at the ranch, and her parents are over the moon.

Almost as over the moon as when I showed Tom his five-percent ownership contract for Gold Rush Resources. I swear the grizzled old rancher teared up at me extending the name of his beloved ranch to our new venture. Ada rolled her eyes, but I didn't miss the way she wiped at her them either.

"Oh god." Her voice is shrill, snapping my attention back out to the track. Penny is in the middle of the pack but is slowly losing position. Her ears are flicking all over the place. The poor little thing looks nervous. Most racehorses end up living at the track during the season, so the competition is desensitized to the sights and sounds here today in a way that Penny isn't.

But we knew all this coming in. Ada doesn't care if Penny wins; she just loves that lanky, sassy mare and everything she represents. The catalyst that brought us together on more than one occasion. Our very own lucky penny.

"Dermot," Ada laughs, "I don't think we're going to win." Her voice is light and amused, and she's shaking her head lovingly as she watches Penny fall to the very back of the pack.

I pull her into my side, hugging her and dropping a kiss on the top of her hair. "No, Goldilocks. I don't think we are. Not today."

But one day we would. After all, I made her a promise.

For Violet and Cole's story, read *A Photo Finish*, book two in the Gold Rush Ranch series.

For Mira and Stefan's story, read *The Front Runner*, book three in the Gold Rush Ranch series.

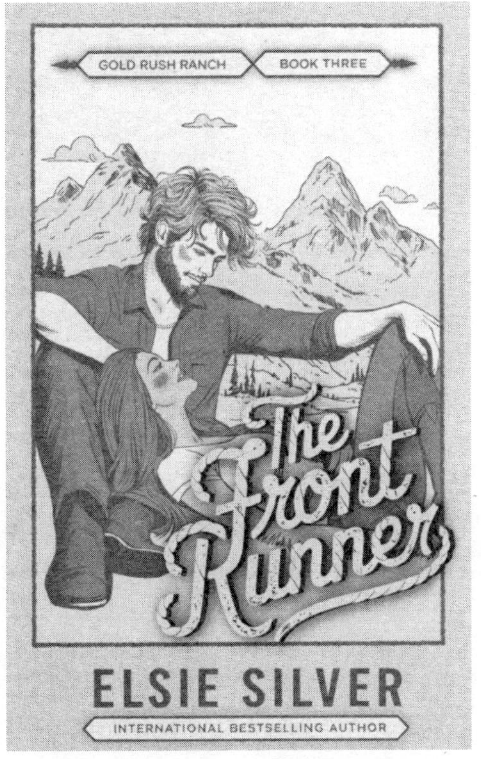

For Nadia and Griffin's story, read *A False Start*, book four in the Gold Rush Ranch series.

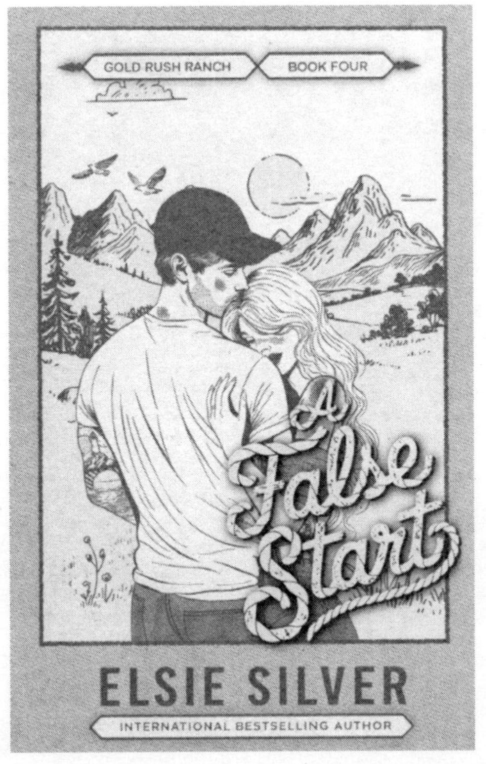

About the Author

Elsie Silver is a Canadian author of sassy, sexy, small-town romance who loves good book boyfriends and the strong heroines who bring them to their knees. She lives just outside Vancouver, British Columbia, with her husband, son, and three dogs and has been voraciously reading romance books since before she was probably supposed to.

She loves cooking and trying new foods, traveling, and spending time with her boys—especially outdoors. Elsie has also become a big fan of her quiet 5:00 a.m. mornings, which is when most of her writing happens. It's during this time that she can sip a cup of hot coffee and dream up a fictional world full of romantic stories to share with her readers.

Website: elsiesilver.com
Facebook: authorelsiesilver
Instagram: @authorelsiesilver
TikTok: @authorelsiesilver

A PHOTO FINISH

ELSIE SILVER

SIMON &
SCHUSTER

New York · Amsterdam/Antwerp · London · Toronto · Sydney · New Delhi

A PHOTO FINISH
First published in Australia in 2024 by
Simon & Schuster (Australia) Pty Limited
Level 4, 32 York Street, Sydney, NSW, 2000
First published in the United States in 2021 by Elsie Silver

10 9 8 7 6 5 4 3 2

Sydney New York Amsterdam/Antwerp London Toronto New Delhi
Visit our website at www.simonandschuster.com.au

A catalogue record for this book is available from the National Library of Australia

ANZ ISBN: 9781761634246
UK ISBN: 9781398551077

Cover design: Mary, Books and Moods
Internal design: Sourcebooks
Printed and bound by CPI Group (UK) Ltd, Croydon CR0 4YY

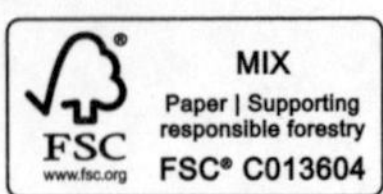

For my husband, Mr. Silver. I love you, but please stop following me on TikTok.

"No hour of life is lost that is spent in the saddle."

—WINSTON CHURCHILL

Reader Note

This book contains adult material, including references to PTSD, anxiety, and sexual harassment. It is my hope that I've handled these topics with the care they deserve.

CHAPTER 1

Violet

Did I really just win this race?

Everything around me moves in slow motion. The pointy black ears ahead of me leading to the shiny black mane down the neck that rocks in a steady rhythm beneath me. My fingers tangle in that mane, holding on for dear life.

I look over my shoulder to ensure I actually crossed the finish line. That I didn't just black out and miss a chunk of the race. Maybe there's another lap left? Maybe I've absolutely blown it like the total rookie I am.

But all around me, other horses and jockeys are slowing, pulling up. Pony horses go around us to grab excited racehorses. I even hear congratulatory words coming from my competitors. Which is nice because I have no business being here on a horse like this, winning such a prestigious race.

This is my first race *ever*, and I just qualified for the Denman Derby. That's pure dumb luck. That's unheard of.

I shake my head, trying to clear my thoughts, and the sounds from around me come rushing back in. Cheering from the stands, horn music over the loudspeakers, the number on our saddle pad flashing across the board in the infield.

We really did it.

I flop down onto his shiny black neck, wrapping my arms around him and nuzzling into his sweat-slicked coat. My throat clogs with emotion, and my eyes water as I murmur, "Who's the best boy?"

When I sit back up, we slow to a walk. Once the race is over, he doesn't stay keyed up for long. DD is a big old teddy bear, though he hasn't always been. It wasn't so long ago that nobody wanted to go near him. But his new trainer, Billie, brought him around, and somehow, I lucked into getting the ride on him.

I sit back and give DD some rein as we walk casually off the track toward the winner's circle. I think that's what I should do. Alarm courses through me as I realize I don't really know what to do here. I know my way around Bell Point Park, but I've never won a major stakes race before.

A moment later, Hank, the barn manager at Gold Rush Ranch, is at my side, patting my leg and looking up at me with pure contagious joy. His heavily lined green eyes twinkle with emotion. "Congratulations, Violet. I could not be more proud of you."

I blink rapidly and look away. Hank has that quintessential dad vibe going on. Or grandpa vibe? I'm not sure really. He's old enough he should be retired, but here he is, working on the farm every day like he's some sort of spring chicken.

The smile I return is watery. The reality of everything is sinking in, and it's overwhelming. "Thank you, Hank."

He reaches up and grabs the reins close to DD's bit. "Whoa, boy." He pulls us off to the side under the shade of a tree. "You two just take a moment before you head up there. A few deep breaths to get your bearings."

I could hug Hank at this moment for knowing what I need right now, even though I'm too shell-shocked to realize it.

"Thank you." I smile down at him and then close my eyes to take those deep breaths he recommended.

Until just recently, I was a groom at Gold Rush Ranch, sometimes an exercise rider when my friend and head trainer, Billie Black, would ask me to help. Imagine my surprise when she announced I would be the new jockey for one of the most talented racehorses I've ever seen. One bad race with local favorite Patrick Cassel as jockey was all it took for her to blacklist him and replace him with me.

So I dumb-lucked my way into this and am now certain everyone will notice and call my bluff.

When I feel like I've stopped spinning, I roll my shoulders back and jut my chin out. DD's breathing has slowed, and I can hear him chewing on the bit in his mouth, a sure sign he's feeling more relaxed as well.

Fake it till you make it, Vi. It doesn't matter how I got here. I rode that race, and it wasn't an easy one. DD and I deserve this win, and I'm going to accept it with grace rather than beat myself up about not deserving it.

"Okay. I'm ready."

With a sure nod, Hank clucks, urging DD forward, and we head for the circus that is the winner's circle.

Billie is there, big sunglasses on to cover what I'm sure are tearstained eyes. Vaughn, one of the two brothers who now own

Gold Rush Ranch, is there too, arm snaked around her waist possessively.

I can't help but grin. Obviously, something is happening there. I shoot Billie a wink right as she rushes forward to hug DD and me. She blubbers something about loving me and being proud of me. And I'd be lying if my eyes didn't start to sting and water furiously too.

"Thank you for this," I whisper into her mess of chestnut hair as I lean down to return the hug.

Vaughn steps up next, opting for a firm handshake in lieu of a hug. His smile is wide and genuine, his chest puffed out proudly. "Congratulations, Violet. Beautifully ridden."

"Thank you for the opportunity," I say, grinning back like a total maniac. Because seriously, who puts a completely unproven twenty-six-year-old groom on a horse like *this* for a race like *this*?

My eyes dart over as someone else steps up to us just beside Vaughn. I feel my eyes widen as he does and scold myself internally. My poker face leaves something to be desired. This is something I know and still can't control. My feelings are constantly written on my face. Like a big flashing neon sign. And right now is no exception.

The man is clearly Vaughn's older brother, Cole. I've heard plenty about him, mostly Billie ranting about what a dick he is and making jokes about him being a robot, which I can kind of see, looking at him now. Where everyone else is elated—celebratory—he looks downright murderous.

Murderous and delicious.

I don't know if the endorphins coursing through me right now are making me giddy or if being this happy kills brain cells, but I can't look away from the gorgeous man. Even though he's scowling at me, I drink him in like the champagne I can't wait to guzzle when this crazy day is over.

He looks like Vaughn yet totally different. Harder, more imposing. Where Vaughn is tall and lean, his brother is strong and broad. His shoulders push against his suit jacket, like they might tear through it if he flexed hard enough. My eyes trail down to his trim waist and powerful thighs. *Pull yourself together, Violet. You're practically panting.*

When I imagined the reclusive brother who spends all his time at their downtown office, the one who never sets foot on the farm, *this* is not what I envisioned.

"Hi!" I say a little too brightly. *Cringe.* "I'm Violet." I stick my hand out toward him while people and cameras crowd in around us.

He doesn't return my smile though. His shapely lips stay pressed into a flat line, and his gray eyes sear me from where I still sit on DD's back. When his hand wraps around mine, I can't help but realize how big the man really is. My hand and wrist practically disappear in his grip. The warm rasp of his palm starts softly; then he squeezes and steps close to the saddle. His opposite hand rises between us, and he crooks his index finger.

A silent order to move closer.

I feel my heart rattle around in my chest as I lean in like a total sucker. Like a moth to a flame.

I expect him to congratulate me.

What I don't expect is for him to send me reeling into past mistakes.

"Nice to see you again, Pretty in Purple. I almost didn't recognize you with your clothes on."

All the air in my lungs rushes out in an audible gasp as I jerk back away from him.

No.

I peer down at him, scouring his features, feeling all the blood drain from my face as I try to reconcile my memory of a man I've worked so hard to forget.

No fucking way.

There is only one person in the world who would ever know to call me that, who would ever have the gall to say it that way. My cheeks heat as memories from the last year come at me rapid-fire.

That youthful experimentation part of my life was supposed to be a bump in the road on my way to total independence.

That part of my life was supposed to have stayed anonymous and in the past.

When I ghosted him without a word, he was supposed to stay where I left him.

He wasn't supposed to matter to me.

But as I drown in his gray eyes while the circus rages around me, I realize he still does.

CHAPTER 2

Cole

ONE YEAR LATER

I DON'T WANT TO MOVE OUT TO GOLD RUSH RANCH.

I hate it out here. And I'm not just saying that either. It's that deep spark of revulsion in my sternum that lets me know I don't belong here. That inner instinct that kept me alive overseas flares up every time I get near this place. But here I am, hurtling down the highway that will take me straight there anyway. If this were Iraq, I'd turn my truck around and get the hell out of here.

But this isn't Iraq.

It's Ruby fucking Creek, which honestly might be worse. I'm quite sure all they've got is a gas station and a corner store and a bunch of gossipy old biddies. I hate small towns. I hate how friendly they are, that you're expected to stop and make small talk with people you don't know and definitely don't care about. And I hate that everyone knows your business.

Most days, I think I might just generally hate people, but even I don't want to be that far gone. That dark.

I like my privacy. I like my space, quiet and tidy. And I don't like being asked probing questions. All of which I know are going to be tested the minute I step foot onto the family ranch. Vaughn was bad enough, the perpetual little brother constantly nipping at my heels, but now he's engaged to and living here with Billie Black. Also known as the most obnoxious woman in the world.

Don't get me wrong. I'm happy for them. As much as it makes me roll my eyes to admit it, they're kind of sweet together. And Billie is good for my little brother. But the two of them are just so much fucking sunshine and rainbows that you almost need sunglasses to be in their presence. And earplugs. The talking never stops.

I groan just thinking about how little peace I'm going to get at Gold Rush Ranch.

I think about riding along the trails with my dad. I think about the way we laughed together, the way he smiled at me, and his passion for horse racing. How happy he always looked when he saw me up on a horse, how happy I always was to spend time with him. And then, as I make the turn onto the side road that takes me there, I think about *her*.

That's going to be trickier to deal with than the rest. I should have kept my cards closer. I shouldn't have lost control like that. I could have maintained my anonymity. But when I saw the face that's haunted me every night for the past year, the one I'll never forget, all beaming and pure and carefree, I did what I always do.

I ruined it.

Pristine white paper, and I purposely knocked ink all over it. Black liquid oozing out, marring the unmarked page.

I've spent an entire year since that race avoiding her at all costs. I dropped an atomic bomb on the girl and then walked away. Very on-brand for me. *You're such a fucking dick.*

My fingers pulse on the steering wheel, and my molars grind against each other as anxiety builds in my chest. I see the Gold Rush Ranch sign swaying on its chains just in front of the manicured tree-lined driveway. I snort. This place isn't a ranch anymore. It's a world-class horse racing facility and a far cry from what my grandparents started out with.

So much history.

I shouldn't be coming out here to this place filled with memories that haunt me and people who don't understand me and never will because I don't plan to let them.

But I promised the board of directors at Gold Rush Resources, the other family company, that I would take the new acquisition we picked up in the next town over and turn it around. I told them I wouldn't come back until it was running a profit. And in this moment, I can't fathom why I'd have made a promise like that.

I pull into the circular driveway and look around at the property. I have to give it to Vaughn; the place is immaculate. The horses, the fencing, the flowers even. He took over a year ago now, and the place has flourished. I hate to admit there's a little part of me that wishes he'd come back to the offices in downtown Vancouver. I kind of like having him around.

Instead, he started a whole new life for himself out here, and I'm almost envious of his ability to just completely recreate himself while I keep living in the same rut, snuggled up in the mud that spinning my tires has created.

My eyes flutter shut, and I take a deep, centering breath, the heel of my hand digging into my right thigh as I try to find some inner calm. Deep breathing is something my therapist recommended. I told her it sounded like hippie, new age garbage. She just gave me a blank look—she knows me too well. Which means she probably knows I've secretly been trying it, and it's working, so we won't have to talk about it as a coping mechanism again.

Knock, knock, knock.

"Hey, big bro! You taking a nap? I know you're old, but this is a bit much."

If I pretend that Billie Black isn't here, will she disappear? Like an annoying figment of my imagination I can wish away on command?

I pry my eyes open and slowly turn my gaze on her. I give her my best withering look, one that sends most people running. She just smiles back at me even bigger.

Billie barks out a laugh and turns away, waving me along. "When you're back on your feet, Vaughn's in his office."

I already hate working at Gold Rush Ranch.

★★★

"You look like you're going to kill someone."

I scowl back at Vaughn across his desk as I flop into a chair. "I feel like I might."

He quirks an eyebrow. "Why?"

"You know I don't like it up here."

"I do. But the new mine is in Hope. Why didn't you look for a place there?"

I scrub my hand across my face. Vaughn has always been so full of questions. I remember him trailing after me asking them incessantly, and with seven years between us, I wasn't much into explaining things like why the letter *c* so often makes a *k* sound.

It seems unnecessarily cruel to tell him I tried every option available to me, only to find there's not much in the way of long-term rentals in the small town. Seems like you either live there or you don't. And I wasn't about to buy a house in a shitty town or stay with the cockroaches at the motor inn just to satisfy my promise to the board.

"This commute is pretty short. You've got an empty office here. Seemed like the obvious choice." That should appease him.

Vaughn smirks. "Just admit it."

I cross my arms over my chest, the only armor I have these days. "Admit what?"

"You missed me."

His cocky grin makes me want to lay him out and remind him who's stronger. Instead, I just glare at him—my default expression.

He holds his hands up in surrender. "Okay, okay. You missed Billie."

This time, I groan and look up at the ceiling. *I love my job, I love my job, I love my job. Working in the spare office down the hall will be* fine.

"You're right. That's not it… Oh! I know." From the corner of my eye, I can see him lean forward on his elbows and steeple his hands in front of his mouth. "You missed Violet."

Suddenly, the sound of my heart beats loud, like an overbearing drum pounding in my ears. It thumps through my entire body. *Why the fuck would he guess that?*

Years of military training mean I can look like I'm not reacting when I am. Which is why I stare back at him and deadpan, "Who?"

His intelligent gaze scans my face, amusement dancing in those eyes that remind me so much of our dad. He got the dark ones, and I got our mother's light ones, and we both somehow lucked into our height. Maybe that's from Grandpa Dermot.

He stands abruptly, and my shoulders drop incrementally when he completely changes the subject and says, "Well, let's get you settled in then."

Vaughn leads me out to the parking lot and steps into his flashy Porsche. He may have given up on wearing suits every day, but he hasn't gotten rid of this yet.

"Why do you still drive this thing? You live in the middle of butt-fuck nowhere on a bunch of gravel roads."

He hits me with his signature boyish grin. "Because it pisses Billie off." And then he slams the door, and I'm left to keep up with him on the back roads. He drives like a maniac.

It's always seemed to me that everything is all fun and games for Vaughn. He's twenty-nine now and still gets a kick out of spraying gravel around the turns.

When we pull up to the blue farmhouse, I have to say I'm surprised. I expected to be relegated to the guesthouse, not the main house. The house our grandpa Dermot built. The house my dad grew up in.

My flight instincts kick in again. *I should get out of here while I still can.*

Stepping out of my black truck, I ask Vaughn, "Why aren't you and Billie living in the main house?"

He fumbles through an overfull key chain. The disorganization of it makes my eye twitch.

"Billie likes the guesthouse. We started out there and just

never left, I guess. You'll have more room to storm around in here anyway."

He means the jab to be funny, but the blow lands with some weight. I hate that I come off this way.

When he slides his hand along the door and swings it open, I'm surprised to find the space updated from when I last stepped foot in the house. Light and airy, like it belongs in a *Country Living* magazine. All white and blue and exposed wood. And it smells *clean.* Like properly clean. Clean in a way that I don't think my little brother can achieve.

I lean across the threshold and take a sniff of the lemony scent. Maybe even a little bleach. "Did you hire a cleaner?"

Vaughn just snorts. "No. Billie insisted on cleaning it for you."

I quirk a brow at him as if to say, "Crazy Billie did this for *me*?" But really, my chest pinches at the thought that someone whom I haven't tried very hard to endear myself to made the space this nice for me.

My brother just waves me off and walks into the house. With his shoes on. My teeth grind.

"Apparently, her house was a mess when she moved out here, and she's never let me live it down. Plus, she's been slowly updating this house as a side project. Said it needed a fresh start."

I know he's referring to the fact that our grandparents lived here until each of their respective dying days. I loved them too, but Vaughn and our grandfather Dermot had a connection I couldn't hold a candle to. One he almost blew his relationship with Billie over.

So while this house reminds him of Dermot, it almost painfully floods me with memories of my dad, my idol, who

I watched fall from a horse midrace and never get back up. Vaughn was too young when our father died to tie memories of him to this place, whereas every damn thing at the ranch reminds me of him.

I clear my throat, forcing myself off that train of thought. "She's done a nice job."

Vaughn's eyes bug out a bit, like I've shocked him by complimenting his fiancée. *Am I really so bad?*

"I'll let her know," he replies with a funny look on his face. "And, Cole, if you ever want to… I don't know, get a beer or something, let me know. I'd be game for that. You don't have to hole up alone out here."

I stare back at him, seeing the forlorn kid I left behind when I boarded the plane and took off for basic training. I've never known how to apologize to him for leaving, and maybe I don't need to, but feeling like I should has always left me uncomfortable around Vaughn. I'd like to be close with him, but that probably means hashing out things I prefer to avoid. *Pretty sure my therapist's ears are ringing right now.*

Speaking of which, I lift my wrist to check my watch. "I have a call I need to take right away, but maybe some other time." I don't miss the way my brother's shoulders drop as I turn to grab my bags from the truck. *Would it have killed you to say yes to a beer?*

He waltzes out behind me, that easy smile gracing his face again, and I'm momentarily jealous of his ability to recover quickly, the way shit just rolls off him while it seems to stick all over me.

"Catch you later!" he calls out as he slips his shades on and folds himself into his silly little car.

I grunt back and offer a terse wave, feeling acutely aware of how growly I am. How different we are.

With the door closed, I walk upstairs to the master bedroom to unpack, and I won't lie, I'm relieved to find it just as meticulous as downstairs. They painted the room in soft grays and warm whites. It's a little feminine, but it feels fresh. I even crack a small smile when I see the way Billie has turned down the covers and left a chocolate on my pillow. She is truly ridiculous.

I fold my clothes into the dresser carefully and lay everything out in the en suite specifically how I like it. Straight. Organized. And a bit obsessive about placement. Some habits you pick up in the military never leave you.

When my phone rings, I sink onto the oak rocking chair in the corner and swipe to accept the video call. My therapist's small, heavily lined face fills the screen like she's peering through a pair of binoculars or something. The lenses of her bifocals are so thick they look like magnifying glasses over her eyes as she furrows her brow at the phone as though it's performing some sort of sorcery. A stack of silver bracelets jangles on her wrist as she tries to hold it out in different positions.

"Cole, I'm not so sure about this. I don't look good from any angle on this thing," she muses distractedly, poofing her hair with a small wrinkled hand.

"Hello, Beatrice," I reply, not caring about my seventy-something-year-old therapist's *angles*.

She tuts at me as she settles back in her chair. "I've been talking to you for two years. I'm tired of telling you to call me Trixie."

I stifle the shudder that runs down my spine. There's just something about calling a grown woman Trixie that feels wrong to me, and I kind of enjoy ribbing her, to be honest.

One side of my cheek quirks up as I stare back at the screen. Her office differs from every other therapist's I've seen over the years. She sees patients in the comfort of her early-1900s-character home. Persian rugs blanket the old oak floors, plants thrive on stands in every corner, crystals dangle in the big windows, and art from her decades of international travel covers the walls. I swear I can smell the patchouli oil she diffuses through the screen of my phone.

Yes, Trixie Bentham is a funny old hippie. She couldn't be more opposite to me or my family. But she's also the only therapist I've ever had that has gotten through to me. So I keep coming back, because as detached as I might be, I also know I need this therapy. Which is why she agreed to do video appointments with me while I'm out being a country bumpkin.

"Want me to tell you how I'm doing? About how all I see out here are memories of my dead dad?"

She quirks her head and smiles. "I don't know, dear. Is that what you'd like to tell me about?"

Ah, the rhetorical question game. One of my favorites. I just stare back at her, which never works, but I do it anyway.

Except today she cackles, all raspy and amused, pushes her glasses up the bridge of her nose, and whispers conspiratorially, "Have you run into the girl yet?"

"What girl?" I'm intentionally playing stupid.

She laughs again. "The one you can't stop talking about."

CHAPTER 3

Violet

TWO YEARS EARLIER

AM I REALLY ABOUT TO DO THIS?

I nibble on my bottom lip and let my index finger hover over the mouse. On one hand, this is a colossally bad idea. This could backfire in so many ways. But who am I in the grand scheme of things? A twenty-five-year-old with little to show for herself—except a distinct lack of life experience and independence.

Growing up on a farm smothered by an overprotective dad and three older brothers will do that to a girl.

But now I'm here. On Canada's West Coast. New job under my belt, new place to live, lots of possibilities on the horizon. Now I need to get to know myself. To rack up some experiences and push my boundaries.

I'm not sure why posting a nude on Clikkit—an online forum with millions of users who dabble in a wide range of interests—is that thing, but it seems risky… a little bit exciting… and a lot out of character. Which is what I'm going for.

I'm tired of being sheltered. I want to feel exposed and uncomfortable without someone here to leap in front of me.

I want to do something young and stupid. Plus, I'm horny and lonely.

I click the button with force. The pad of my finger slaps against the mouse loudly. I immediately feel myself blush. It starts at my toes and creeps up my body. It pools between my thighs and crawls up over my chest before staining my face with its heat.

I can't believe I just did that.

The image stares back at me. It's taken from above as I lie on my bed. You can't see my face and I'm wearing my panties, so it's not too outrageous. Okay, you can see my small breasts, but in Europe, people go to the beach like this all the time. It's no big deal—or at least that's what I keep telling myself. The warm morning light is nice on my features, and it's sensual. Usually, I'm hard on my body. Usually, I think everything is a little too small, not what I'd consider "womanly," but in this picture… I feel sexy.

So fuck it! Look at my tits, world. See if I care!

I almost immediately consider deleting it. But the new Violet Eaton will not give in to that voice in her head, and my new internet alter ego, Pretty_in_Purple, doesn't give two shits about that voice either.

I slam my laptop shut, shove my feet into my paddock boots, and jog down the stairs from my apartment above the barn at Gold Rush Ranch before I can change my mind.

PRESENT DAY

My mental checklist is overflowing as I pack the last of what I'll need into my little Volkswagen Golf. The one with rust patches above the wheel well and the chewed corner of the seat from when my favorite ranch dog was a puppy. The one I packed up and drove away from my family home when I finally set out on my own a little over two years ago. Some people might see a car that belongs in a junk pile. Me? I see my golden chariot to independence. I love this little car and everything it represents.

I stand back to assess everything I've stuffed into the back seat and blow a loose piece of hair off my face. It's the first big race day of the season, and I'm trying—poorly—to keep my nerves at bay. This season is my shot, my chance to prove myself as a real jockey. To prove that my Northern Crown wins last year weren't just a stroke of freshman luck. This job is supposed to be fun. Hard work, but fun. But today it just feels overwhelmingly heavy. The pressure weighs on me like an invisible lead vest. Even getting air into my lungs feels like it takes concentration.

I force myself to take a mental inventory of what all's here and shake my head when I realize what I've forgotten. "Shit. Right. My silks."

How great would that have been? Showing up to the track in Vancouver—which is at least an hour and a half from the farm here in Ruby Creek—without my Gold Rush Ranch silks. The black and gold uniform I wear every single race.

Shaking my head as I march back into the barn, I head down the long hall of offices toward the laundry room at the end. I live in a small apartment above the barn, so I just do my laundry down here. I grew up on a proper ranch, in the dirt and snow, usually with hay in my hair, so the thought of washing all my clothes in the same machines used for the hairy horse laundry doesn't bother me at all.

I'm almost to the door when I hear it.

"Violet."

That voice. The low rumble of it. The threat woven into it. The man behind it. I swear my feet grow roots that shoot out and bind me to the ground. My heart knocks violently in my chest like it's trying to get out and run away. And quite frankly, I don't blame it. I want to get out of here too.

He wasn't supposed to be here yet. I was supposed to be gone down the highway by the time he showed up. He was supposed to be out of my life. I was supposed to have left him behind. Forgotten him.

But I haven't. I've warred with myself, wrestled and fought. Been with other men to prove to myself that I'm fine. But one word out of his mouth, and I seriously wonder if I am. I could run and hide, but that's not how the new me handles this. *The new Violet isn't a shrinking Violet.* That's what I keep telling myself anyway.

Maybe one day, it will feel true.

So I suck in as much oxygen as I can and hold my head up high. I refuse to let this man make me feel small or embarrassed. We have a shared past, but we're both adults. *This will be fine.*

Spinning on one heel, I turn and march back to the office I just passed, the one that has sat empty for years. I stop just inside the doorway, partly because I don't want to go any farther and partly because I'm reeling. All it takes is one look at Cole Harding, sitting behind a desk in a dark suit, spinning the cuff links on his shirt, for me to lose all the bravado I just puffed myself up with. I literally feel it roll right off me like someone has doused me with a bucket of cold water. My body's reaction to him has never been normal, and today is no exception.

The inky hair, the gray eyes, the square shoulders, the sad tilt to his mouth. He crosses his arms under my gaze, and I roll my lips together at the sight. Just the way he moves, so sure and so calculated, drives me to distraction. There's so much power coiled in every inch of his body. A soldier's body.

His biceps are where my eyes land and where they stay. They're incredible. I wonder how they'd look completely bare, how they'd feel wrapped around me. I hate myself for even going there. But I keep my eyes trained on them, because it's less unnerving than looking him in those soulful eyes. Silvery pools, deep and haunted and swirling with so much. The ones full of anger and pain and sorrow. Those are a much bigger problem for me. And for my heart.

"Violet."

He says my name like it's a sentence, a full thought. Like I should know exactly what he means when he says it. But I don't know *anything* where Cole Harding is concerned. I think I actually know less than anything. Other than the hair on my arms is standing up like there's an electrical current running over me, and my stomach is flipping like I just shot down off the high point of a roller coaster. Which is apt, because my history with Cole is nothing if not a roller coaster.

"Everyone calls me Vi." I hate how quiet my voice comes out. I hate the way my name sounds on his lips, too formal and too familiar all at once.

His eyes rove my body, but he doesn't smile. It's not appreciative. It's more like he's assessing me, like I'm a mess that needs cleaning up and he's trying to figure out how. Shame lurches in my gut. Flashes of the way he talked to me once and how it warmed me to my bones pop up in my head, but I do my best to will it away. I've worked too hard at moving on to go down that rabbit hole again.

"I'm not everyone," he says plainly.

I hiss as I suck air in, trying not to sound like I'm gasping for it. Trying not to give away the fact that he's just winded me with his words. Blood rushes in my ears and pools in my cheeks—like it always does. *You look so fucking pretty in pink.* He told me that once, and now it takes every ounce of my strength not to let my mind and body wander back to that day.

"What do you want, Cole?"

His eyes flash, and his body goes rigid right as his jaw ticks. Like somehow I'm the one who's annoying him when he's the one who called me in here. He could have kept his mouth shut, and I'd have been none the wiser. We could have avoided this entire encounter.

"I just want to make sure that we're on the same page. That we can continue to stay out of each other's way while I work out here. That you can keep things"—his eyes slide down my body and then back up—"professional."

Professional. Nothing between us has ever been professional. He's seen me naked, trampled my heart, and then showed back up out of nowhere with nothing but cool looks and mocking words, and now expects *me* to keep things *professional*?

Indignation flares up in me over the fact that he feels entitled to dictate how I should conduct myself. Like I don't come up against enough of that in this industry as it is. It's a sore spot, and he should know. I spent long nights telling him about my childhood. About how I struck out on my own. And now he's going to waltz in here and talk to me like *that*? No way.

"Let me be clear, Cole." This time, I don't let my voice waver, and I don't stare at his biceps. I stare right into his steely eyes. "This is *my* place of work, and I am nothing if not professional. The way you're talking to *me* right now? It isn't professional. So I'm going to continue doing exactly what I have been for the past year, and *you* can stay out of *my* way. Think you can manage?"

His body snaps back slightly, and his eyes go wide. Like he didn't see that coming. Didn't see *me* coming. And he lashes out at me for it. I see the flash of insecurity on his face right before he spews his words back at me. And it's that hint of sorrow that takes the bite out of them.

"Pretty in Purple was so sweet. What happened?"

I shake my head at him sadly. Because when it comes down to it, that's what I feel when I see him, when I think of him. Sad.

"Seems like you mistook Pretty in Purple for a doormat."

I look at him just long enough to see the forlorn look on his face, the crack in his cold exterior, before I turn and walk away. The spear to my damn heart. Golddigger85 is just as lost as he was before, just as complicated. Just as broken. And I've already decided I won't tolerate the way he lashes out. *We all make choices.* That's what he told me once, and he wasn't wrong.

It's why I moved on. It's why I disappeared without a word. It's why this awkwardness between us now is on him, not me. My head knows exactly what choices to make where Cole Harding is concerned.

But my heart?

It's not so sure.

CHAPTER 4

Violet

"Cole moved in today."

I shove my foot into my boot harder than necessary, grunting as I do, and then busy myself polishing it with the rag from the step stool beside me. Basically, I'm trying to ignore Billie, who is grinning at me like a maniac.

"You're not going to say anything?"

I side-eye her and shrug. Because the answer is no, I'm not going to say anything. Billie Black, my boss and the head trainer at Gold Rush Ranch, has become one of my best friends over the past year. And I've come to know her well. She's like a bloodhound with a scent, she's smart and intuitive, and anything I say she'll stock away in her crazy memory vault until she unpackages it and extrapolates her data. And then she'll figure out how I know Cole.

Which means I won't be able to look her in the eye without turning fire-engine red.

"Nope," I say, popping the *p* sound as I stand up in front

of our tack stall and reach for the black and yellow Gold Rush Ranch silks.

"Viiiiii," she moans, "this is *killing* me! It's been a year. I saw your face that day. What did he say to you? Give me something."

I feel the light sprinkling of heat crawling up over my chest. She is relentless. "Okay. We met online a couple of years ago. Chatted a bit."

She rubs her long fingers over her chin as she regards me. "Like some sort of veteran pen pal thing?"

"Something like that." I wave her off. "Now leave me alone. I need to go weigh in and get in the right headspace if you expect me to win."

"Okay, okay. Come find me when you're done, and I promise I won't ask about this again." She waggles her eyebrows as she stands to leave. "Until after the race."

I roll my eyes as I walk down the barn alleyway toward the track offices. Toward the Bell Point Park winner's circle. The very place where Cole Harding waltzed back into my life.

I remember sitting up on DD's back, overwhelmed by our qualifying win, when a man who was clearly Vaughn's brother approached me. I remember thinking he looked like an ominous storm cloud hovering over such a bright and joyful celebration. I remember the way his huge hand engulfed mine, the heat of it, the weight of it, as he crooked a finger for me to come closer. And I remember the warmth in my body evaporating and all the sounds around me fading to white noise when I leaned down to hear him say, "Nice to see you again, Pretty in Purple. I almost didn't recognize you with your clothes on."

Just recounting the memory makes me blush. But I am also still agitated by the way he took one of the happiest moments of my life and tainted it with *that*. The way he threw it in my face when he knew he had the upper hand.

You see, Cole Harding knew exactly what I looked like. What every inch of me looked like. And I still had no idea who he was—a real sore spot for me—until that moment.

Turns out he's my boss's boss, Billie's future brother-in-law, and now he's moving to the one safe space I've created for myself over the last couple of years. A place where I can be a successful and independent version of Violet Eaton with no one coddling me. I'm not the same girl I was two years ago when I responded to that message. And what happened between Cole and me? It's never going to happen again.

I don't think my heart could take it. And definitely not my pride.

Which is why I pasted a wobbly smile on my face and told him to go fuck himself before sitting back up and forcing myself to enjoy the win.

When I accepted his chat request, I didn't expect to spend months getting to know the man. And when I ghosted him in that chat room a year later, I didn't expect to ever come face-to-face with him. Me anonymously pushing my own boundaries and living a little turned out to be a whole lot more. And now my entire house of cards is about to come crashing down around me. Because he's here, at the ranch, threatening that buffer that I've tried so hard to preserve.

I keep my head down as I get prepped for the evening race. I may have a Northern Crown win under my belt, but I still feel like the new girl on the block, inexperienced and out of my depth. I still feel stuck in the mindset of living at home under the watchful eyes and overbearing involvement of my dad and three older brothers. I still feel like a little kid who doesn't belong.

Once I've weighed in, I head back to DD's stall and shove my headphones in my ears. A little Shania Twain never fails to get me in the right headspace. Reminds me of my childhood.

Before I became the in-house rider at Gold Rush Ranch, I was a lowly groom. A girl who moved out to British Columbia from her small-town home in Alberta with not much more to show for herself other than a good work ethic and a lot of desperation to pave her own way.

The thing is I liked being a groom, but I've always wanted to be a jockey, and I lucked into the right body type to pull it off. Sometimes, I miss the quiet moments that came with working behind the scenes. Those times when it was just the horses and me. It's why I still live above the barn in my tiny apartment up that long narrow flight of stairs. I like walking through the stables at dusk, hearing the quiet munching on hay. I like taking care of my own horses. I like the soothing rasp of brush bristles across their coats rather than the loud buzzers and speakers as I blast through mud, trying to make it across the line first.

So I try to create those quiet moments for myself. And this prerace ritual has become part of that. No one bugs me—Billie makes sure of it—and I get a bit of time to go inward and just be with my horse.

Right now, that horse is DD, our little black championship-winning stallion, with long legs and an intelligent disposition. Once I've put the finishing touches on his grooming, I lead him out into the bright sunshine—something we don't see much in Vancouver in April. This area brings a whole new meaning to

April showers bring May flowers. At this time of year, we pretty much live in a mud puddle, so even though it's sunny, the track is wet.

When DD's hooves clop loudly onto the asphalt road that leads down to the track, Billie pops up, seemingly out of nowhere. She's always ready and waiting for me. We talked strategy earlier in the day, so at this point, we can just walk together in a companionable silence.

She comes to stand beside me, bends down, and cups her hands behind me, ready to give me a leg up. "Up we go, Tiny Soldier."

I feel my cheek twitch; Billie's terms of endearment that reference my size never end. Where she's tall for a woman, I'm petite, and where she's curvaceous, I'm… well, flat as a board.

I drop my knee into her waiting hands, and she hefts me up into the tack, gives my knee a squeeze, and sends me on my way. The rest of my journey into the starting gate is a blur, as usual. The pony horses, the stewards, the other jockeys and horses around me,they all blend together, and I focus on DD and getting us to that finish line safely and quickly. When our pony horse steps up, the rider gives me a friendly nod. The pony rider is completely different from a jockey. They ensure we get to the gate safely, like a security blanket for a nervous horse. An important member of the team.

At the gates, he sends me off with a "Good luck."

DD is a great stallion, reliable and smart, talented beyond compare, but claustrophobic. And when they close the gate behind him, I feel him coil up like a ball of energy, like an elastic pulled back too far, ready to explode out of the small space.

This is where my vision narrows. All I see is what's between his long pointy ears. The rest of the world seems to go soft and blurry as we both settle into our focus.

Until I hear a voice that sends a slithering sensation down my spine. "Hey. New girl."

I ignore Patrick Cassel. He's one of the most sought-after jockeys in this area. He rode DD in one race last year, but he defied Billie's instructions on how to ride the race, and well… let's just say that didn't end well for him. Now he's on Gold Rush Ranch's blacklist—we all basically pretend he doesn't exist. And when he sees Billie coming, he promptly turns and walks the other way.

Looks like that level of avoidance doesn't apply to the quiet little blond though.

"Dinner after this, and I might let you win. What do you say, Princess?"

I try not to shudder at the thought. Patrick is slimy and entitled and makes me feel like I have bugs stuck under my clothes. Based on Billie's retelling of their encounter, he's condescending and sexist to boot. I want nothing to do with the man.

"I'm pretty sure princesses only kiss frogs in fairy tales, Patrick," I mutter. "I'll pass."

And before he can say anything, the bell rings, and the gate flies open. DD and I are off, and that interaction with Patrick disappears from my mind as we thunder down the track, staying toward the back of the pack through the first turn. Exactly where the little black horse likes to be.

I stay low and light on his back, mostly letting him do his thing. This horse was bred to run, and he loves it. When we push out of the clubhouse turn, everything is going according to plan. Now is where we move up.

Until I feel a dark bay horse move in beside me. From the corner of my eye, I see Patrick Cassel's lime-green silks. As he pulls ahead, I try to ignore him and reserve my focus for DD.

Until he shouts over the pounding of hooves, "Time to learn a lesson, little girl."

My instincts shift into overdrive as I watch his hands move ever so slightly to change his path. Dread courses through my veins. And before I have a chance to react, he's cut us off sharply, bumping DD's shoulder with his harsh angle, killing our forward motion. And on the slippery footing, the results are disastrous.

With his head and neck already slung low and legs stretched out in a gallop on a slippery track, DD stands no chance.

I feel our motion shift downward, and before I know what's happened, DD and I are both down in the mud.

"I'm going to kill him." Billie paces at the bottom of my hospital bed. "Like, literally murder him."

I'm in too much pain to react much to her meltdown. My leg is swollen like a tree trunk, and they won't give me any painkillers until they have time to look at my X-rays and MRI scans. Like you need a medical degree to confirm that it's fucked up.

"You need to tell Vaughn that I love him and to get the bail money ready. Because I'm going to tear Patrick limb from puny limb."

A ragged sigh escapes my lips as I look around my room. The walls are that signature pale mint color, a color I imagine they produce solely to paint hospital walls, and all I can smell is that harsh, sterile scent that permeates every single hospital

I've ever been in. Which is a lot because my brother Rhett is a walking disaster. A rodeo prince with no fear. And even though I'm a year younger than him, I was always the one stuck playing caretaker at the hospital while he was treated for one injury or another. It was the only way my dad could run our farm and keep us afloat enough to take care of the four of us.

So I *hate* hospitals. I don't care about Patrick. But I am worried about DD. He came down on my leg but didn't walk off without a limp either. I scrub my hands over my face and force a deep breath into my lungs.

It could have been so much worse.

"Any word from Mira on DD?" Mira Thorne is our friend and our newly hired farm veterinarian. She takes care of all the horses in the Gold Rush Ranch program, both at the track and at the farm.

Billie nibbles at her lip nervously now and shoves her hands into her pockets, obviously worried about our boy too. "She said he's fine" is her quiet reply. "She'll call as soon as she knows anything more."

"You should have gone with her."

Billie rolls her eyes. "And what? Left you all by yourself? Mira's got this."

I let my lashes flutter shut and sink back into the lumpy pillow. It's like they want you to be uncomfortable in the hospital. With my eyes closed, all I can see on the back of my eyelids is this entire season swirling down the porcelain bowl with a loud flush. My chance to prove I'm good at this rather than just the girl who got the ride on one of the world's most exceptional racehorses and struck gold.

This fucking *sucks*.

"Okay, Miss Eaton." A middle-aged man with a white coat over his slacks and dress shirt breezes into the room. "I have good news for you today."

I furrow my brow. Nothing about today screams *good news* to me.

"The imaging we had done tells me that nothing is badly broken."

I stare at my black-and-blue leg. It looks pretty broken.

"Are you sure?"

He laughs good-naturedly. "Very sure. There's a lot of bruising. Soft tissue trauma in the knee. And a small fracture in your fibula."

I continue to stare at my leg, still not fully convinced that it's not totally shattered.

The doctor takes my silence as an opportunity to keep talking. Looking down at the clipboard in his hands, he continues, "No surgery required. But you need to take it easy for at least a month. Crutches at the start, at least until the swelling goes down. Try to keep off any stairs. And definitely no riding."

I snort. *Yeah. That's not going to happen.*

"Miss Eaton, I'm serious. I know how athletes can be. But if you fracture the bone further or tear something in your knee, you will require surgery. And the rehabilitation timeline for that is much longer. You're lucky it's not worse. Don't squander that."

Lucky?

Billie steps in now, no doubt reading the look on my face. "No problem, Doc. I'll keep her on the straight and narrow."

The man barely looks at Billie. Instead, he raises his eyebrows and inclines his head toward me, obviously seeking some sort of affirmation. I wave one hand in the air dismissively before crossing my arms. He won't know what I do once I leave this place.

"Got it," I mumble, dropping my eyes and sighing, feeling more than a little chastised.

"Good. Let me grab you some painkillers, and then we'll get you discharged."

I force my cheeks up into some semblance of a smile, too sore and pissed off to do much else. I'm ready for some pain relief and my own bed. He turns on his heel and strides out of the room.

"Don't worry, Vi. We'll find you somewhere comfortable to stay."

"What?" I look at Billie, confused.

"You're not doing those crazy stairs up to your apartment right now. And back down?" She shudders. "I don't even want to hear about it."

"Okay, Mom. Where are you planning on putting me then?"

Billie scrubs her face, clearly stressed, even though she's trying to play it cool and hold it all together for me.

"I'll get Vaughn to stay with his brother at the main house, and you can stay with me at the cottage."

"In the love shack?" I blurt out just as a nurse walks in with a small white cup and hands it to me.

"The love shack?" Billie looks confused as I eye the two pills in the paper cup, toss them back, and then chase them with the water from the table beside me. I almost spit it back up. City water tastes all wrong.

"Yeah. I'm not staying at the love shack and splitting you two up."

"Is that what you call our house?" she barks out, clearly amused.

I can't help but smile now. She and Vaughn are living in some blissed-out bubble. "Billie, that's what everyone at the ranch calls it."

She blows out a tired breath and drags her hand back through her chestnut hair. "I'm not gonna lie. I kind of love that. You're still staying with me though. Vaughn will survive."

"Billie, there's not even a bathroom on the main floor of your place."

"Shit." She looks instantly deflated. "Right. Okay… why don't we move Cole into your apartment and let you take the house. Just for a few—"

Yeah, that can't happen. "No. He's not going in my apartment. That's *my* space."

"Okay then, Violet. What's your solution here? Wanna go back to Alberta for a few weeks? Stay with your dad? Or I don't know…" Agitation seeps into her voice. "You gonna go live at the farmhouse with Cole? Because there's a spare room and bathroom on the main floor."

I can tell that she's joking. But that's looking like the best option at this current juncture.

Yup, today is just full of good news. I'm so *lucky*.

CHAPTER 5

Cole

I GROAN AS I STARE AT THE SCREEN OF MY PHONE. AM I REALLY ABOUT to try this again? It's so fucking pathetic. I'm so fucking pathetic. Just because I've decided I can't show myself to anyone doesn't mean I don't still want things.

And the photo is so… ethereal? I don't know. I could get lost in it. I can't look away from it. It's so different from living in my head. Light pink nipples on flawless pale skin. I imagine running the palm of my hand up her body, right up the centerline from belly button over sternum, before coming to rest on her throat and thumbing those pouty, soft lips.

The way they'd part as I rasped my thumb over them, the little sighing noise that would escape past them.

It's been way too long, you old perv. You're getting hard just imagining touching a woman's lips. The ones on her face, no less.

Not to mention a girl who looks like that isn't going to be interested in me and what little I have to offer her.

But what the fuck? Why not? What have I got to lose? I look around my lonely West End apartment. The place is basically a shrine to a grown-ass man who's let every opportunity for the past several years slip through his fingers. A living shell.

I haven't even tried to be better. To get past my hang-ups around my body. To do more. I want all the things. The white picket fence. The 2.5 kids. The wife who kisses me with a little tongue every morning when we part ways. But I haven't done shit to get there. And it's probably too late for me now.

It's just me, myself, and my protein shakes. And my creepy fucking internet persona. Might as well embrace it.

My thumb taps the message icon, and I quickly type before I can change my mind.

Golddigger85: I have a proposition for you.

Then I walk away and get in the shower to wash away how fucking dirty I feel. But I can't stop thinking about that creamy skin sliding against my own. I imagine running my tongue up the inside of each thigh. Really taking my time to taste her, to feel her writhe beneath me. My hand curls around my cock, but I pretend it's her pillowy lips, opening up wide for me. Wrapping around me. Her cheeks hollowing out as her silky blond hair bobs in a steady rhythm while she sucks me off. Then she'd look up at me. Fuck, *I love that. Big wide eyes and my dick in her mouth.*

I wonder what color her eyes are as I spill myself against the cold tiles.

For a moment, I wish I wasn't alone.

Something that I'll never let happen.

"Hey, big bro." Billie stands under the yellow glow of the porch light above my front door, hands on her hips, and blows a strand of hair off her face. I don't know what she's doing here. But I know I don't like it.

It's 11:00 p.m. on a Saturday night. Is this what people do in small towns? Invade each other's privacy? I'm about to ask her as much when I see another set of headlights turn down the driveway. Vaughn parks beside her truck, and I notice now that she's left the back door open. A shadow shifts inside, and I lean forward a bit to peer past her.

"Is someone lying in your back seat?" I ask.

She glances over her shoulder. "Oh. Yeah."

My eyes shift back to hers. "I don't like you enough to help you bury a body."

Billie grins, her teeth coming off a little vicious in the dark of night. "Fair. I won't come knocking once I kill Patrick Cassel."

"Patrick?" I ask, confused, as Vaughn bounds up the stairs. I already hate Patrick's smug ass. If I had to help her with a body, it would be his. Maniacal laughter streams out of the truck, pulling me away from that thought. "You guys, what the fuck is going on?"

"She might actually kill him, you know?" a hysterical voice cackles out of the dark back seat.

"Is she okay?" Vaughn asks, slightly breathless as he comes to stand beside Billie.

"Yeah, yeah. She's just really high," Billie replies casually.

My teeth grind. This is so like them. Talking a lot but saying nothing at all.

"You. Guys," I bite out. "What. The. Fuck. Is. Going. On?"

"Patrick Cassel took Violet and DD down tonight, and her leg is all mangled."

Adrenaline courses through me as Billie's words process in my head. If I didn't already hate Patrick Cassel, I would now. I see dirt. I hear hooves. I taste bile. I rub at my leg anxiously.

"What do you mean, *took her down*?" My molars grind against each other as I'm transported back in time. To another day entirely. To a seventeen-year-old boy watching his dad ride a race he'd never finish.

"Cut her off and bumped DD's shoulder. It was muddy." Billie sniffs. Her voice sounds brittle, and I don't miss the hand that my brother snakes around her waist.

I feel like I could suffocate on my tongue as I forge ahead. "And can you elaborate on what a 'mangled' leg means to you?"

Vaughn's eyes dart up to me, going slightly wide. Usually, that means my tone is too brusque. Trixie is always asking me how I think other people perceive me. I keep telling her I don't care. She just ignores that and tells me to look at body language for clues. I think this wide-eyed look might be one thing I'm meant to watch for. Vaughn doesn't like the way I'm talking to his fiancée.

"Hairline fracture on her fibula and a strain in her knee. It's mild, but she's kinda beat-up. Recovery won't be that long. A month if she's lucky."

I force a deep breath down into my lungs, willing them to fill and empty evenly so that I don't start gasping with the ache of my memories. This could have been *so* much worse. I've seen worse. I was seventeen when I waved goodbye to my dad, my idol, as I clung to the railing at Bell Point Park. I watched him load up into the gates. I cheered and whistled and yelled until I was sure my voice would be hoarse the next day. I watched him closing in on the lead horse. I saw the grin on his face. And then I watched him go down. A simple trip and the crush of his mount's body over his. I watched the horse get up and gallop away, its eyes wide with terror.

I watched my dad's still form on the dirt track. I willed him to get up. But he never did.

This could have been so much worse.

"Is she okay?" I keep my voice cool, but even I can hear it brimming with rage, pain that's had years to fester.

"Yeah," Billie replies. "But she's not supposed to do stairs. Which means she can't get up to her apartment above the barn. We were going to let her stay at our cottage, but the bathroom is on the second level, and the whole place is pretty small for three people..." She trails off, shooting big wide eyes up at me like a little kid who's about to ask for something they're not supposed to have.

I guess this is body language that I can read as well. This look has *pleading* written all over it—seen it before. I'm just not sure why she's giving it to *me*, other than to irritate me and make me want to put Patrick in a choke hold more than I already did for the stunt he pulled last year.

So I fall back on my default expression. I stare blankly at my brother and his fiancée, not sure what it is they're expecting me to do or say here.

Vaughn groans and drags a hand through his hair. I don't miss him mutter something about me always making things difficult. *The feeling is mutual, little brother.* "Can Violet stay at the farmhouse with you? There's a spare bedroom and bathroom on the main floor. It'll just be a few weeks."

They can't be fucking serious.

I keep my fists shoved under my biceps, hoping that if I look angry enough, they'll both back off and come up with a different solution. My chest rises and falls heavily as my agitation grows, snaking out into every joint and muscle. They both just keep looking back at me expectantly. Like puppies.

And no one likes a guy who kicks puppies.

Violet bursts out laughing in the truck. She's laughing so hard she can barely breathe, let alone get her words out. I can hear her gasping for air between guffaws. I often wondered what her laughter would sound like. A year of talking and then another of forcing myself to recall her dainty little face… I didn't imagine the hyena howl she's currently emitting.

"I told you guys he would never go for this," she blurts out. "Look at his face!" She dissolves into another fit of giggles. "I *know* him. This will never fly!"

Okay. I need to put a stop to this. Now. The last thing I need is Mr. and Mrs. Bigmouth knowing my personal business. And the path of least resistance to ending this interaction is… *Fuck my life.*

My legs move before I process what I'm doing. I shove myself between Billie and Vaughn and approach the truck. Violet is laid out across the back seat, feet toward me and back propped against the opposite door. Her leg is wrapped in a plastic walking cast and is supported by rolled-up horse blankets. Her pupils are dilated, and fat tears of laughter stream down her muddy cheeks.

"Hey! It's Butterface!"

I growl as I reach into the truck. "Violet. Shut up."

She throws her head back and bursts out laughing again. Like spilling our personal history is the most hysterical thing in the world. *Comedy gold, everyone*. My jaw pops under the pressure of my bite. All I can think about is getting her away from prying eyes and ears, so I lean in and reach for her waist. I don't miss the way my hands wrap almost the entire way around her as I pull her across the leather seats toward me.

When I slide my arm under her knees, she winces.

"Are you okay?" I rasp so only she can hear me. I should have been more careful with her.

"A bit sore." Her glassy eyes gaze up into mine unsteadily, wide and lost and so fucking pretty. My lungs constrict at the sight of her, the girl I haven't been able to shake.

Never mind Billie. *I'm* going to kill Patrick Cassel.

I move slowly now, less agitated and more concerned, and wrap my other arm around Violet's narrow back. She feels small and vulnerable against me, and for all the times I let myself imagine meeting her, it was never like this.

Her head lolls drunkenly into my armpit as she announces, "Isn't he so strong!" One tiny fist knocks against my bicep. "Look at these arms!"

I blink once, slowly, working hard at keeping my cool as I carry her limp body up to the front porch. No one this small should feel this heavy. I fight the dread crawling up my spine, the memories of carrying my friends' limp bodies under the cover of darkness. The weight. The dry heat.

I take a deep inhale of the thick, humid air to remind myself where I am. "What the hell did they give her?"

Billie pulls a small orange container out of her back pocket and offers it up. "I don't know, but they probably should have given her a child's dose instead."

I just grunt. I'll look at it later. "I've got this," I bark as I push past them and into the old farmhouse with Violet held firmly against my chest.

"He's so romantic!" Violet giggles, and I roll my eyes. In the past, Violet was one of the few people I actually enjoyed talking to. But that girl is definitely not here right now. This girl is high as a fucking kite.

"Violet, are you okay with this?" Billie looks concerned, but I kick the door shut behind me, right in her face, done talking about this.

"Isn't he rude?" Violet shouts back through the closed door. "All those times you complained about what a dick he is—"

Now it's Billie's turn to shut her up. "I'll bring you your stuff in the morning, Vi!" Billie calls back. "If you need me, just call!"

My cheek twitches. Take that, *sis*.

"Don't worry about me, B! I told you. I know him!"

A deep sense of dread fills me. All I can see is my privacy slipping away. A part of my life that was always meant to be kept separate is now going to be sleeping in the bedroom below me and probably blabbed about with my brother's fiancée. Which will inevitably get back to my brother. Never mind the fact that I've been pining for her—a girl I've basically never met—for the last couple years.

Nothing good can come from this kind of forced proximity.

I groan as I carry Violet to the spare bedroom, feeling my meticulously organized life slipping through my fingers like fucking sand, and I haven't even been in Ruby Creek for twenty-four hours. This place is cursed. It took my dad down, and now it's going to take me down too.

The room is dark, but the spare bed is already made. Like it's been ready for her this whole time. Like this is some sort of huge cosmic joke.

Leaning down, I gently place Violet on the bed, not wanting to hurt her. She's even more beautiful than I remember, soft and feminine and soothing without even trying. Getting to know Violet was like discovering a medicine I didn't even know I needed.

"Why are you staring at me?" she asks quietly from where she's sprawled, her voice not so giddy anymore.

"I'm not," I grumble, jumping back into action, not wanting to talk. I pull a pillow from the headboard and prop it under her braced knee, how I know it feels best. When I lean over her to pull the covers down, I sneak a look up at her face, something I've avoided doing since that first day I saw her at the track, but I can't seem to stop staring now. It's like the mere sight of her has short-circuited my brain, opened the floodgates to me gawking at her like some sort of slack-jawed Neanderthal.

I expect those almost too-big blue eyes to be staring back at me, but her long lashes are casting shadows over her high cheekbones, and her heart-shaped mouth has fallen just slightly ajar, shallow quiet breaths whispering past her lips.

Knocked right out.

Which means I can really look. I stare at her openly—every line, every angle, every heavy rise and fall of her chest—my eyes adjusting rapidly to the low light filtering in from the living room, knowing she won't catch me now.

Is her breathing too light? Too slow?

I lean in closer to listen, a little concerned with how hard these painkillers are hitting her. Another thing to worry about. *Just what I need.*

Shaking my head, I leave the room. How did I get roped into this? I should pay someone to run the new company and head back into the city. Fuck the board. I'm a thirty-six-year-old man who can barely take care of himself. I need a woman to take care of like I need a fucking hole in the head.

Back in the kitchen, my hand shoves at the tap, making water shoot out as I reach up to grab a glass from the cupboard above the sink. The water out here stinks. Vaughn swears it's safe. Something about no added chemicals like in the city, but one of the first things I'm buying tomorrow—provided this water doesn't kill me first—is a flat of bottled water.

Turning to walk back to the room, I see my phone light up on the counter. Missed calls from Vaughn and Billie litter the screen. Must have missed those while I was working out. Before this all went to shit. I stare at my phone so much all day for work that I like to turn it to silent in the evenings. Then no one bugs me.

Except now.

Apparently in Ruby Creek, if someone doesn't answer their phone, it means you show up at their door.

I swipe my phone off the counter and flick through my notifications. Most recently, there's a text message from Vaughn.

Vaughn: Billie is really worried about Violet. We can work something else out going forward. Just bear with me for tonight. And take good care of her.

I roll my eyes. You'd swear Violet was a child on her deathbed or something. Is this level of micromanaging normal for adults?

Cole: Tell Billie that Violet is a perfectly capable adult. I'm sure she'll figure something out for herself when she's awake and not high as a kite.

I'm not even going to dignify his implication about me taking care of her with a response. Does he think I'm not capable? I don't know when Vaughn became so totally pussy-whipped, but it's definitely new.

I toss my phone back down onto the counter, trying some of that deep-breathing shit Trixie is always going on about, and head back to the spare bedroom with the glass of water I poured for Violet.

I set it on the bedside table, letting my eyes trace over her sleeping form again. Soaking her in, warring internally over how I should feel about this. About *her*.

There's a part of me that wants to crawl in beside her, to hold her and watch her all night. To run my fingers through her hair. Make sure she's okay, ease the tension in my gut, and assure myself that she's really all right. But the other part of me knows she wouldn't want that. That it would be way over the line, especially considering how we ended things.

So I walk out of the room, leaving the door slightly ajar, and sink to the floor against the opposite wall. "Only for a little while," I mutter to myself, shaking my head as I settle in to keep watch.

Deep down, I know that's not true. I know I won't be able to walk upstairs and leave her tonight. But I've been lying to myself and everyone else for years.

Why stop now?

CHAPTER 6

Violet

*H*OLY SHIT. *T*HIS IS A LOT OF MESSAGES. *I* SCROLL THROUGH THEM, *blushing as I go, feeling glad I already promised myself I wouldn't respond to anyone. I'm only here to look.*

Hey, baby… Hey, honey… I'd like to suck on… Don't be nervous…

Jesus. Who knew there were so many pervs in the world? I can't even read them all. It's too much.

I spent all day busting my butt at the ranch, trying to forget the fact that I put a naked picture of myself, titled "(25F) New and nervous," *on the internet. Since I've finished, I've come up to my little apartment, made myself some macaroni, and pretended my laptop doesn't exist. I even watched an episode of* Gilmore Girls *that I could barely focus on before I finally caved and opened the browser.*

This forum has tens of thousands of subscribers. How forty-seven of them found me and sent a message is beyond my comprehension. I wring my hands as I imagine what these men have been doing while they look at my picture. This was a bad idea. Very poorly thought-out.

A notification for my forty-eighth message pings in the top right corner of my screen. And out of morbid curiosity, I click it.

Golddigger85: I have a proposition for you.

I nibble at my lip. This message isn't like the other ones. What's just one message? It wouldn't be so bad, would it?

Plus, I'm too snoopy to walk away from an open-ended statement like that. What would the proposition be? I flex and release my fingers over the keyboard, itching to type back. If the person says something terrible, it's not like I'm obligated to respond.

Ah, fuck it. I'm going for it.

Pretty_in_Purple: Oh yeah?

I see the dots pulsing on the screen, showing that they're typing. My knee jiggles rapidly, tapping the wooden bottom of my too-small table. Is this person writing me a novel?

Golddigger85: I'm looking for someone I can pay to send me exclusive photos (like the one you posted) or do live videos with. I'll send you $2,000 US every two weeks, and we'll talk 2–3 times a week for 20–30 minutes. I'll give you directions, and you follow them, within reason of course. But I stay completely anonymous. Take your time to think about it. No pressure. Your photo is lovely.

I rear back. Daaammnnn. What the hell? *What a bizarre and clinical proposition. As good as an extra four thousand dollars a month sounds, there's no way I would do this. It's not that I consider myself above it; it's more that the whole thing completely defeats my goal of not living under another person's thumb. I don't want to follow another person's directions. Even as I try to do the conversion to Canadian dollars in my head.*

Pretty_in_Purple: Why?

My cheeks heat. I should just say no. But now I'm intrigued. I have questions.

Golddigger85: Why what?
Pretty_in_Purple: I don't know. Why me? Why do this? What's the point?
Golddigger85: Do you always ask so many questions?

Okay. Sore spot. Maybe I wouldn't like being interrogated about my sexual preferences either.

Pretty_in_Purple: Probably. I'm not going to do it. I'm just curious.
Golddigger85: Why did you post your photo if it makes you nervous?

I think about walking away right now. I don't owe this guy an explanation. But being forward and direct with someone I don't know from Adam just feels easier.

Pretty_in_Purple: Because I wanted to feel nervous. It's totally out of character for me, and quite frankly, I've been living in a bubble. This seemed like a good way to pop it.

Golddigger85: In that case, I do things this way because I'm quite fond of my bubble. Of my private identity. I work a lot. I don't have time to date. I like things done a certain way, and this ensures that. It's worked well for me in the past. I chose you because I liked the picture. You look natural. Real. That's what I like.

I feel my cheeks pink a bit at the compliment. The man may be a total stranger, but his words still land in a way that makes me feel soft and gooey. It's been too long since you last had sex, Vi.

Pretty_in_Purple: Well, thank you for considering me?
Golddigger85: Are you going to think about it?
Pretty_in_Purple: Probably not.

He doesn't respond after that.

I want to open my eyes, but they feel so heavy that it's borderline not worth it. I try to pry them open; I really do. But they're just so. Damn. Heavy. I give up, sigh, and roll over.

Pain lances through my body. From my toes all the way to the tops of my ears. I'm like one big ball of pain. My eyes shoot open easily now as I gasp, "Ah! Shit!" and opt to stay exactly where I am, flat on my back.

I squeeze my eyes shut and focus on breathing through my nose. If I don't move at all, nothing hurts. The perfect solution. Except with my eyes closed, images flash through my mind. Patrick Cassel. The mud. DD. *Oh god, DD.*

The stream of consciousness won't stop. We went down. My leg. The hospital. The drive back to the… My eyes snap open, and I look around the unfamiliar room. "Mothereffer."

Cole Harding.

I groan and pull the covers up over my face as I sift through my hazy memories, dying a little inside when I get to the one where I openly commented on his biceps. How am I going to face him after *that*? We were doing so well at pretending the other doesn't exist. It was the perfect solution. That strategy has been an absolute success for a year now. I hoped we could just continue it, even though he was going to be living out here. That was my plan. I like having a plan.

But now it's trash. Because I'm sleeping in his house, and my season is down the toilet.

I'm pretty much living my nightmare.

I shake my head at my misfortune and click my tongue against the top of my mouth, trying to get some saliva happening in place of the dry, cottony feeling. I need a drink, and I need to brush my teeth. Looking over at my bedside table, I see a full glass of water. I want it so badly that I decide it's worth moving. Even though I feel like one huge bruise, I shift myself over and up to lean against the headboard. It almost takes my breath away, the weight of the pain pressing in on me. It's everywhere, and it throbs.

But when I put that glass against my lips and taste that first drop of water, I know it was worth it. No pain, no gain. But seriously, where are my painkillers?

I want to stay in hiding. I don't want to face Cole with his stupid, handsome scowl and big biceps that do funny things to my stomach. It's not fair. I'm all broken, and now I'm supposed to face off with the man I've been avoiding for a year.

The universe is cruel, but this full body ache I have going on is worse.

The allure of painkillers is stronger than my desire to hide out in the bedroom all day to avoid Cole, so I slowly flip my legs over the side of the bed, gasping a little as I go, and then hobble out into the main living space on my walking cast, wincing with every step.

I limp to the kitchen island, hoping to see a bottle of painkillers somewhere. It doesn't even look like anyone lives here. Everything is sterile, every countertop perfectly clear, not even a wallet and keys tossed down or a water glass left behind. Maybe he left? My heart soars at the prospect. That would be ideal. Then I'd be able to have a full-blown meltdown about not being able to ride for a month by mys—

"Why are you up and walking around?"

Cole's cool voice is like a spray of frigid water against my back. Shocking and unpleasant. It leaves me breathless. So I freeze, not wanting to turn around and look at him. Because I know what I'll see. And I hate that I'll like it. *Just focus on his lack of personality and you'll be fine. Don't be a baby.*

I turn rigidly, slowly, while keeping one hand on the counter. I basically prop myself up. I need something to hold on to if I'm going to look him in the eyes again. Intelligent eyes, like granite almost, a mosaic of grays and silvers, rove over my body as though he's measuring me to see what size box he'll need to pack me in to ship me off.

"I... I need some painkillers."

Cole snorts and crosses his arms. He's standing in the front entryway of the house, door flung open and sun shining in from behind him. The way its rays wrap themselves around his brutish form makes him look like a glowing silhouette. He reminds me of a solar eclipse, and I know you're not supposed to look at those. It's *dangerous*.

I turn my head away, blinking and trying to find some equilibrium. Trying to focus on the throbbing in my leg that, in his presence, has dulled to a low thrum because my body is focusing on all the other feelings he brings up. Embarrassment, sadness, longing. I hate that he can still do this to me, so I concentrate on the pain, trying to pull it back up and wrap it around myself like a shield. I want to feel better, but I don't want it to be because I'm looking at Cole Harding.

This is living proof that the man is a drug I can't resist. But I dropped the addiction once before, and I'm stronger now. I'm on a different path, one he can't join me on. There would be far too many complications. Even more than before.

I pinch my shoulder blades together and jut my chin out. "Where are they, Cole?"

"In the cupboard above the fridge."

I turn to hobble away from him, wishing I were wearing something other than a pair of too-big sweatpants that say *Vancouver* across the ass and an oversize T-shirt with an orca whale across the chest. I traveled by ambulance to the hospital, and needless to say, my clothes were mud-soaked. And this sweet little getup is what Billie bought for me at the gift shop. *At least it's clean.*

I stare at the fridge, and then I look up at the cupboard

above it. Did he intentionally put the drugs somewhere I wouldn't be able to reach?

"I can't reach that," I grit out through clamped teeth, intentionally not looking at him. My composure is fraying rapidly, and agitation mixes with dread. *A whole month of this. Maybe more!* Now that they've given me the chance, all I want to do is compete. Win. Prove myself. Not take a month off to live in the same house as Cole Harding.

"I know," he says simply without a trace of humor in his tone. *Jerk.*

My head snaps toward him, and I feel my eyes widen in their sockets, my lips rolling against each other almost painfully. I *hate* feeling coddled like this. "Take them down. Now."

He's leaning casually against the doorframe, still staring at me coolly, but now his eyes are focused on my lips. Not exactly jumping into action to help me, which is even more infuriating. Being made to feel helpless is the worst feeling in the world, and men have a bad habit of doing it to me. I don't know if it's because I'm small or quiet, but it fires me up. My dad and brothers did it to me without even realizing that putting baby sister up on a pedestal was some real patriarchal bullshit. Even if they meant well, it wasn't doing me any favors, and it's ultimately why I struck out on my own. But Cole… he's just doing it to be a dick. To make a power play. And I loathe it with every fiber of my being. I won't stand for it.

"I don't know how Vaughn turned out to be such a gentleman when you turned out to be *this*." I wave my hand over his body dismissively, watching his eyes flare and his jaw tick as he clamps his teeth down. "I'll get them myself." I take one limping step toward the big farm table, planning to drag a chair back to the cupboard and stand on it to reach the medicine.

But before I can even get there, he says, "Violet. Stop."

When I look up, he's taking sure strides across the airy farmhouse and rounding the opposite side of the island before he comes to stand beside me. At what must be six one or six two, he can, of course, easily reach the cupboard.

He pulls the small orange pill bottle out from where it sits, surrounded by what looks like a bunch of bottles of vitamins and supplements. I crane my neck to see what they might be, trying to read the labels, before I blurt out, "Grab yourself some happy pills while you're up there."

He turns to me slowly—almost too slowly—before placing the painkillers on the butcher block island. I expect him to slam them down, but his movements are soft and quiet—a little unnerving if I'm being honest.

Just because I spent a year writing back and forth with the guy doesn't mean I know his mannerisms. In fact, I know little about him. He was never forthcoming, and I've realized, in the aftermath of permanently logging out of my account, that he mostly just played along with a lonely young girl who needed someone to talk to. And to get off. *Once.*

"If I'm going to live out here, I might need to invest in some."

Was that… a joke? I honestly can't tell. I peer up into his face, scouring his features for some trace of humor and finding none. What I find is a fine white scar that cuts through his thick right eyebrow and points up to his hairline. Something I've never noticed before because I've never really had the chance to admire him up close. And I am admiring him, because he's flipping hot. The kind of man who has been—as they say—designed by women. Rugged and harsh, masculine to his core. He looks like he could manhandle the hell out of a girl. A thought that makes my pulse race.

"I'm sorry. I know this… We…" I fumble around with my words, feeling a blush stain my cheeks. I look away, out the front window toward the green hills, and take a deep breath. This can't be my reality for the next month; it just *can't.* "I can understand why you wouldn't want to live with me. I'll find somewhere else to stay for the next little bit."

He turns away to grab a glass. "Go sit down."

I want to tell him to take a hike, but sitting sounds really appealing, and I decide this isn't my hill to die on. Not today anyway. Not when all I want is some water and some pain relief.

I move gingerly around the island, knowing I'm supposed to use crutches but not knowing how I'll do that when my ribs and shoulders hurt the way they do. Once I've heaved myself onto the simple wooden stool at the counter, I watch him turn the tap on and fill the glass.

I try not to look at his ass, but I fail. It's not sweatpants weather, but he's wearing them anyway, and wearing them well. Tapered at the ankle and snug around the waist. When he faces me again, I roll my lips together and pull my hair over one shoulder so that I can run my fingers through it.

I swear he lifts the glass and sniffs it before saying, "Here," and sliding it across the island toward me. His hand engulfs the glass. It looks like a child's cup in his grip.

I take the water once he's completely let go, not wanting to risk a brush of his fingers against mine, and then reach for the bottle of pills. I read the directions on the bottle. It says two pills every six hours. "I think I'll go with one," I mostly mumble to myself.

"Probably a good idea."

My eyes flash up to his. *Dick.* Now I want to take two just so he doesn't get the satisfaction of seeing me do what he says.

I twist the top off roughly and toss the lid down on the counter. "Didn't really ask your opinion, did I?" I shake one out onto my palm and toss it back into my mouth.

"Nope. I'm just here to provide the biceps," Cole deadpans, and I freeze. The bitter taste of the chalky pill dissolving on my tongue fills my mouth as I glare back at him.

Embarrassment flares up in my chest, and I force myself to choke back some water before whispering a quiet "I'm sorry" as my eyes dart around everywhere but in his direction.

"For what?" He leans back against the edge of the opposite counter and stares me down like he's trying to incinerate me on the spot. His gaze is… unnerving.

But I don't want to let him know I think as much, so I sit up tall and flatten my hands out on the wood counter. "For last night. I wasn't myself. I just… don't like being told what to do."

A smirk graces his full mouth now, and his look flicks from cool disinterest to something else as his eyes roam over my body, leaving a trail of heat in their wake. "That's not how I remember it."

My fingers pulse around the glass of cold water. *Do not throw this at him. You're an adult. Walk away.*

"Like I said." I glare at him now, pushing to stand and trying not to wince, keeping my voice as even as possible. "I'll be out of your hair before you know it."

And then I turn and hobble back to the safety of the spare room. I want to mope in private.

CHAPTER 7

Cole

I HEAR MY PHONE BUZZ BUT PUSH THROUGH MY FINAL SET OF DEAD lifts before picking it up.

Pretty_in_Purple sent you a message.

Maybe the girl changed her mind? Probably not, and I don't blame her. I feel greasy, like I need a shower after every time I send a message like that. I know I sound like a sleazebag, and I hate that. I also know there are creeps on the internet, and I like to think that I'm not one of them. But this arrangement works for me. It ensures me the privacy I want and provides me the companionship I crave.

Sort of.

I swipe the notification open.

Pretty_in_Purple: How many girls have you done this with?

Good god, does this girl have a lot of questions.

Golddigger85: A few.

Pretty_in_Purple: So... three?

Golddigger85: Something like that.

Three dots roll across the screen as she types, and then her message pops up.

Pretty_in_Purple: Guess they didn't stick around for the conversation.

I can't help but chuckle. She's not wrong. I've never been accused of being a great conversationalist.

Golddigger85: No, they stuck around because I talked them into the best orgasms of their life while I watched.

The dots roll and stop. Roll, stop. I wait a few beats before they roll again.

Pretty_in_Purple: Oh.

Golddigger85: Yeah. Oh. Still not interested?

Pretty_in_Purple: In internet orgasms? No, I'm good. I manage those just fine on my own.

I groan. The thought of the pale silky skin in that photo, what's hidden beneath the pretty pink panties, wedged just slightly between the lips of her pussy. The thought of her fingers slipping beneath the triangle of lace.

I adjust myself in my sweats. It's like this girl is totally clueless about how sexy she is—something I like even more.

Pretty_in_Purple is a tease, and she doesn't even know it.

I shove my AirPods into my ears angrily. I've already worked out today, but I'm going for another one. I dig my thumb into my quad muscle and drag it down, trying to relieve the building soreness. Exercise is the only coping mechanism I have for whatever this feeling is. Trixie would tell me to give it a word, but talking about your feelings isn't really part of what the military drummed into me as a special operator.

So with no gym in sight, I run. I do push-ups. I do sit-ups. If I can find some bricks or something, I could probably wrangle myself some weights. The gravel crunches under my feet as I hit the back roads; the air smells fresh and unfamiliar, like the silty rocks down at the cool river that runs through the property. Like the snow that hasn't quite melted off the top of the Cascades, even though it's already April.

I tell myself I miss the smell of exhaust and the sound of car horns blaring that I usually face when I'm downtown. But I think I might be lying. It's hard to tell anymore. What I know is that movement is a gift, freedom that we can never take for granted. Your body, no matter the shape or size, is a workhorse that does incredible things for you. Simple things that you don't even realize until you can't do them anymore.

Which means I also know that Violet is feeling trapped by her injury. Maybe she doesn't even realize it yet. But I do. And rather than being wise and understanding about it, I was… me.

After she stormed off, I went and got a step stool out of the storage shed so that she could reach that cupboard, even though I'm pretty sure the damage is already done. She thought I'd do that to her intentionally, so I'm going to go out on a limb and guess that I'm not in Violet Eaton's good books.

I pump my arms and run faster, eating up the ground beneath me, breaking into a sweat. Even I want to run away from my personality.

How can I make this up to Violet? I know I don't owe her anything, but the truth of the matter is she's the closest thing I've had to a friend since… I can't even remember. Hilary and I were certainly never friends. We were rich-kid fuck buddies. And then I was a soldier getting ready to deploy. And then we were engaged.

And when I came back for good? We were poison.

I stewed in that poison for *years*. I scoff at myself as I round the corner onto another completely unidentifiable road. *Nice try, old man. You're still stewing. You're saturated.*

Violet doesn't deserve to be tainted by my bullshit. She didn't ask for any of this, and it wouldn't kill me to make her life a little easier after hurting her feelings. Because I *know* I hurt her—not intentionally—but I couldn't give her more. I couldn't give her what she wanted. I wasn't brave enough to take my clothes off in person, let alone on a video chat. That night she told me to take over, to tell her what to do, it was *hot*. So fucking hot. Hotter than any other time I'd done it, probably because we'd gotten to know each other. Her trust meant something to me in that moment. I was feeling things for Violet that I couldn't put my finger on.

But that was all it was: a moment. For me anyway. So the least I can do now is not be a dick to her. I haven't even been trying to. It just always comes out that way, whether or not I want it to. And usually, I don't care how I'm perceived. It's beneath me. I can try to be helpful though. It won't kill me, and Trixie would definitely approve.

My breaths come out in huffs, and I hate to admit it, but my body is tired from my first workout. The midmorning sun is hotter than I expected this far inland, so I stop, linking my hands behind my head to stretch out my chest as I turn around slowly, taking in the heavily treed ditches. All the leaves are a vibrant, almost neon green at this time of year. All fresh and new before they grow bigger and take on a darker shade.

With a deep sigh, I force my body into action. Mind over matter. And feeling tired doesn't matter. So I carry on, forcing myself to run back even though I'd rather walk.

As I hit my stride, Violet's face flashes into my mind. The one she made when she realized she couldn't reach that cupboard. The pink stain on her cheeks. The way her round blue eyes sparked like a live wire. The stupid sweatpants she was wearing all rolled over to fit her tiny waist. The evil part of me wants to laugh because she looked like a scrubby little Tinker Bell stomping her foot, but the good part of me absolutely cringes. I didn't mean to do that. I didn't even think of it. I just put the pills where they belong, with the rest of my vitamins and supplements. I didn't need the counters cluttered with random shit.

I run harder until I feel my lungs and quads burn. Until my mind goes blank.

I don't need my *life* cluttered with any of this shit.

The minute I walk in the door, I see Violet scowling at me from the stool where she sat earlier. Her mouth is moving, but my music is so loud in my earbuds that I can't hear her. It's kind of glorious if I'm being honest. I'll have to remember this trick for later.

I remove them, holding one hand up to stop whatever tirade she's going on about right now. A bead of sweat trickles down between my shoulder blades as I calmly ask, "What is it you're going off about?"

Her bottom lip pouts out, and her shoulders drop on a sigh. Agitation flows off her in waves. "There's no coffee in this place."

"I know," I say, removing my shoes and placing them on the shelf before wandering into the house for a glass of water. "Coffee is a crutch. It tricks your body into thinking you have energy."

Her knuckles go white from gripping the counter so hard. "I want to be tricked. No. I *need* to be tricked." She slides off the stool gingerly. "I'm going up to the barn to get coffee. I need to figure out where I'm going to stay," she rants on, "because out of everything wrong with staying with you, the fact that you don't have any coffee is the most offensive."

Hands on my hips, I groan and tip my head up to the ceiling. "Violet."

"A crutch. Is that some sort of pun about my mangled leg?" she continues, hobbling away.

"Violet."

With her back to me, she tries to slide her foot into the flip-flop she got dropped off here in and mumbles something that sounds an awful lot like, "So fucking high and mighty."

So I opt for something that might actually get her attention. "Nice sweatpants."

She spins on me so fast you'd never know how injured she is. "Are you kidding?"

I cut her off. "Violet. I'll take you to get a coffee. I need to get some groceries anyway."

Now she just blinks at me, her expression straddling the line of rage and disbelief. When her dainty chin drops in a terse nod, I move near her, grab my keys off the hook, and usher her out the front door.

"Do you want your crutches?"

She takes the front stairs awkwardly, with one leg set straight in the cast, and leans against the railing to accommodate the motion.

"No." She almost growls at me. "You going to lecture me about that too?"

"Nope." I jog down the stairs and head to my black truck, leaving her behind. "You're an adult, and you know your body best."

I swing the passenger-side door open and wait there.

Violet regards me suspiciously as she walks forward, clearly still sore. "What are you doing?" Her tone is accusatory.

"Holding the door open for you." I honestly almost roll my eyes. *So many questions.*

She sort of grunts as she approaches the truck, assessing how she'll tackle getting in, and if she doesn't ask for help, I'm not going to give it to her. She's made that much abundantly clear. If I learned anything about Violet from the year we spent corresponding, it's that she's stubborn. I gave her almost nothing, and she kept badgering me, coming back for more, until it forced me to relent a little bit. She wasn't put off by my persona back then.

And don't I know it. She scrambles into the truck. It's not graceful, and I end up getting an eyeful of her round ass with *Vancouver* printed across it as she pulls herself up into the cab. My fingers pulse at my side, itching to reach forward and give her a boost. Watching her struggle makes tightness twinge in my chest.

When she's finally seated, I slam the door and round the truck, getting into the driver's side and firing the engine up so that we can get this over and done with. As I peel out of the driveway, I don't miss the way she reaches up for the oh-shit handle, like she doesn't even trust me to drive her down a gravel road.

It grates on me that she thinks so little of me now. I'm fairly sure that at one point, we were on good terms.

When we hit the main road, I chance another look at her, but she's turned her head away as she looks out the window, gazing at the green fields whipping past as I speed down the road. Her hair has a silvery quality to it, like a cool sunlit stream trailing down her back. Complete with mud from her fall, but I don't think it would be a wise thing to bring up when we're already on such tenuous footing.

Plus, I kind of like it. Violet just walked right out the door in hospital sweats, no makeup, and with mud in her hair because she wanted coffee. She didn't spend hours primping to go out in public, and she still looks beautiful. She's feminine, graceful, elven almost.

I remember noting that about her hair when she sent a shot of her head with bird shit on it. "Got a big old dose of good luck today!" she said.

The memory makes my cheek twitch. At the time, it made me laugh, and then it made my chest ache. I still can't remember the last time I smiled like that. She had literal shit in her hair, and all she could do was laugh and comment on the good luck it might bring.

That is a glass-half-full kind of attitude I can only aspire to. But I didn't need to knock her glass over in the process. That was just a dick move. I don't want to be a dick. I want to be *better*.

"You don't need to move out." I break the silence abruptly and stare out the windshield, hard, like there's something interesting out here in the middle of a field. Spoiler alert: there's not.

I feel her eyes on me even though I'm doing my damnedest not to look her way. Her gaze pierces me like a tattoo gun. A sharp needling sensation, followed by warmth that flows deep.

"You don't want me there though."

I sigh audibly and pulse my fingers around the leather steering wheel. What I don't want is all the feelings she stirs up in me. I don't want to have to look at her every day and wish I could touch her or let her touch me, because it's pure torture wanting something that you won't let yourself have. "That's not true."

Her head tilts as she regards me. "This is a weird situation. It's awkward. You're mad. I get it."

I don't need to respond to that. We both know she's right. Weird and awkward don't even begin to cover it. The girl I solicited anonymously on the internet to send me nudes became my pen pal and friend. (I never told her that.) She ghosted me, and now she works for my brother at the family ranch.

It's fucking bizarre is what it is.

Am I mad? Yeah. I'm mad at myself.

"I'll stay out of your way. Short of going home, I'm not sure where else to go. You won't even know I'm there."

I somehow doubt that, but deep down, I also don't want her to leave. It's a relief to not be alone all the time. "Okay."

"Okay." She sighs, relaxing back into the leather seat with a small smile on her shapely lips.

She's only quiet for a few moments. It seems like our tenuous peace treaty has paved the way to her inquisitive side.

"Why Golddigger Eighty-five?"

I try to act casual, but I'm not sure I'm ready to talk about that. About what happened between us. It's too… well, it still fucking hurts. So I try to play dumb, praying she might drop it.

"Huh?" I grunt distractedly as we turn onto the main street of Ruby Creek. It is literally called Main Street. One sad little street in a place that seems to be stuck in some sort of time warp. A bar, a coffee shop, a grocery/liquor/hardware store, a bank, and a few other stores line each side of the road. You can drive farther and have access to everything you need and more, but this is Ruby Creek. Not a single thing has changed since I was a child. *That's* weird.

"The screen name."

I can see her peering up at me from my periphery.

"Why'd you choose it?"

Why is the speed limit so damn low here? I want this to end.

"Because I run a mining company. We dig for gold. I was born in 1985."

"Huh." She taps her index finger against her lips, a loose piece of platinum hair resting against her rosy cheek.

"Why 'huh'?"

"It just sounds like you're after money or something. You know, like the Kanye song. It's kind of funny."

I try so hard not to smile, forcing my mouth into a straight line. For some odd reason, the name made me chuckle when I created the account. Now all it does is remind me of her.

"Why'd you pick… your name?" I ask, not wanting to say the name out loud.

She flushes and looks away at the stores as we roll past them. "Purple is just kind of my color."

I only look at her for a moment. It's all I can stand before blood rushes between my legs. But as I turn my eyes back to the road, my mind fixates on that blush. The memory of the way she blushed for me. *More like pretty in pink.*

My god. I need to get the hell out of this truck.

Finding parking is easy, so I pull into an angled parking spot in front of the Country Grind, the local coffee shop. Violet has her door open and is sliding out before I can get over to her side. I hear her whimper and then gasp when she hits the ground. I cringe. *So fucking stubborn.*

I stride up to the entryway and hold the door open instead of picking her up and carrying her.

She limps past me with one eyebrow up. "This gentleman's act is cute."

Cute? I can't remember ever being called that. *Distant. Grumpy. Creepy* even. I shake my head and follow her in.

"Hi, Macy!" Violet says.

"Honey!" the curvaceous redhead behind the counter booms back. "What have you done to yourself?"

"Oh, this?" Violet nibbles on her lip as she looks up at me where I stand beside her. "Minor spill. Nothing major. I'll be back in the tack in no time."

"Oh, baby," the middle-aged woman continues, "let me get you a cookie and a coffee. That will help. What about you, darlin'?"

These pet names. They're brutal. Thankfully, Violet jumps in and rescues me from this line of questioning. Or maybe she rescues Macy from me. Who knows?

"Oh, never mind him. He doesn't believe in coffee."

Macy looks genuinely horrified as her hand falls across her collarbone in mock shock. Her eyes rove up and down my body appreciatively, making me squirm, before she holds one hand up beside her mouth and leans into Violet conspiratorially. "There are certain flaws I'm willing to overlook for a man like that."

Violet gasps out a small giggle, and her porcelain cheeks instantly pink *again* as her eyes shoot up to me nervously, visibly as uncomfortable as I feel inside. I just stare at them like I'm bored, wondering if they're done yet. I hate it when people look at me too closely; that's why Vaughn is the face of the family mining company.

"Tough cookie, that one!" Macy cackles and then turns away, busying herself preparing Violet's order.

Crossing my arms, I look around the place, taking in the rustic decor. An older woman sitting with a newspaper smiles at me, her skin crinkling around her eyes when she says, "Good morning."

I carry on with my assessment, hating to admit that there is a certain charm to the place, when I feel a poke in my ribs and glance down to see Violet's furrowed brow looking straight up at me.

She whisper-scolds me, "She just said *good morning* to you."

I lean down toward her. "I know."

"But… you just ignored her."

"I don't know her." I don't like small talk. Or strangers. Or how small-town people don't know how to mind their business. If I don't invite that type of behavior, my time here will be less irritating. I've established myself as unapproachable before, and it really doesn't take long to accomplish if you offend people thoroughly enough.

Violet's bottom jaw drops open like I've just said something shocking. "You have better manners than that, Cole Harding. You've been opening doors for me all morning."

"Are you scolding me?"

She crosses her arms and raises one eyebrow at me in challenge. Her hip juts out as her slender arms fold beneath her breasts, and I focus on the mud in her hair so I don't sneak a peek at how her stance might press them up.

Her body still haunts me.

"Do I need to?"

She nods.

I groan inwardly while outwardly smiling in a way I'm sure looks more like a wild dog showing its teeth as I turn back to the woman at the table. "Good morning," I say clearly before turning back to Violet, whose eyes are dancing with amusement.

She rolls her lips together like she's holding back a laugh before she hits me with a full, blinding smile. A genuine smile. "Was that really so bad?"

All I can think is that I can't remember the last time someone looked at me like *that.*

CHAPTER 8
Violet

Yesterday, he stopped responding after I turned down his offer for… whatever he does. Watches you masturbate while he calls all the shots?

Sounds bizarre. Then why are you squeezing your thighs together just thinking about it?

How does he even know he'll be attracted to me? Or I him? Why would anyone do this with a stranger? Is this guy really some sort of orgasm magician?

I pull my phone out, determined to get to the bottom of this.

> **Pretty_in_Purple:** Why does anyone sign up for this arrangement?

I throw my phone down on my bed and get dressed for the morning, trying to work out why I'm so fixated on figuring this out when it has no bearing on me. It's not like I'm going to do it.

When my phone buzzes, I practically throw myself across the bed to grab it. Smooth.

Golddigger85: Still thinking about me, huh?
Pretty_in_Purple: What if I'm a total butterface?
Golddigger85: Butterface?

I roll my eyes. Who doesn't know that saying?

Pretty_in_Purple: But-her-face. You liked my picture, but what if I'm a total butterface?
Golddigger85: I wouldn't expect you to show me your face.
Pretty_in_Purple: Okay, Captain Literal. What if you're a total butterface? Maybe faces matter to me. I don't think I'd like showing the goods to some nameless, faceless person on the internet.
Golddigger85: Are you sure about that?

Arousal zings through me, pinging around in my pelvis as I imagine myself doing what he's asking. Touching myself on camera. What would his voice sound like? A shiver runs down my spine as my thumbs hover over the screen of my phone. I'm not sure, but I'll never tell him that. I'm just sex-starved. That's all.

Pretty_in_Purple: Yes.

Dots roll across the screen as he types back, and then a photo pops up on the screen. A selfie.

Golddigger85: Okay, what about now?

I tap the photo and take in the manicured dark scruff on the man's perfectly square jaw. He's wearing a hat that shadows the top half of his face, obscuring what sits above his straight, pronounced nose. I can't even see the color of his eyes, no matter how close I zoom in. It's dim wherever he is and almost looks like a basement or something.

Probably where he keeps all the bodies.

As I zoom back out, my eyes snag on his mouth, almost a little too shapely for the strength of his other features. He has nice lips, that perfect bow shape on the top one. And as I let my fingers fall away, I realize he has lots of nice other stuff too, because he's not wearing a shirt. A strong neck, with a pronounced Adam's apple. Big round shoulders, the bulge of one bicep visible where his arm is outstretched holding the phone. The shot cuts off before I can get farther down his chest, but I can see the sprinkling of hair and a line between his pectorals.

My mouth goes a little dry. Golddigger is cut. And suddenly I feel awkward. Flustered. So I deflect, just like I did when my brothers would start inquiring about boyfriends.

Pretty_in_Purple: Even a butterface looks good in a hat.

Golddigger85: You saying I look good?

I exit the app quickly and shove it in the back pocket of my jeans.

That's not a question I want to answer.

"Okay, spill." Billie leans forward, shoulders to her ears, with a mischievous look on her face. "What's it like living with the beast?"

Billie and Vaughn live in a cottage on the opposite side of the property, and it is the epitome of cozy. Open concept, exposed wood, big loft bedroom. It's small and simple, but they love it, and it suits them perfectly. Plus, there's a paddock right out the door where she can keep her horse, DD, close by. He's fine. The fall stung him, and he was a little jumpy afterward, but he's healthy—thank god. Billie says he's not racing until I'm ready to go again, so we'll make up for lost time then, even if it means running races closer together than we might otherwise. In the interim, he's happily enjoying some downtime and training with his favorite rider, Billie.

I can't hold a candle to what the two of them have. I'm just lucky he lets me hang on for the ride now and then and that Billie is way too tall to be a jockey.

She's been harassing me about coming over all week. She plied me with wine, and now we're on glass number three. And *this* is why. I finally gave in because it's Friday, and I'm bored of reading the steamy romance novels she left on my front porch. And now *this* is what I get.

I roll my eyes and mutter, "Snoopy bitch." She just laughs, and I ask, "Does that make me Belle?"

"I don't know. Are you going to have a snowball fight and fall in love with the big brute?" She cackles like it's the most ridiculous thing in the world, and I try not to cringe. If you'd have asked me that same question a year ago, I'd have sighed like a lovesick teenager and gone on dreaming about meeting Golddigger85 one day. I was so certain I was special to him, not just another girl he met on the internet, or I never would have taken it that far. Cheek-burning levels of far.

So imagine my surprise when he reminded me I was just that. My heart aches more at the memory than I like to admit. He hurt me, and it was all my doing. I asked for more than he could give.

I shake my head and take a sip of the red wine Billie poured for me, tucking my mixed feelings down behind the big crystal bell. Hopefully.

"I've barely seen him all week. He works long hours. And I have nothing to do, so it's not like I wake up early."

"That's not true. You came and hung out at the barn with me a few days."

"In a chair with my leg propped up on a bucket. Where I was forced to watch everyone else have fun while I sulked on the sidelines."

Now it's Billie's turn to roll her eyes. "Think of it this way. You're one-quarter of the way through your recovery. That's not so bad!"

I glare back at her where she's curled into the corner of the big plushy couch opposite me, legs tucked underneath herself, looking comfortable and carefree. I've been trying to put my best foot forward, to stay positive, but I must confess… I'm floundering. I'm bored. I'm sad. And I'm feeling a little resentful—angry, maybe. This was supposed to be my season to prove myself.

"You okay, Vi?" The skin between Billie's brows pinches together.

My breath rushes out of my body on a huge sigh. "Yeah."

She's not buying it. "What's wrong?"

I don't want to stress Billie out. I don't want her to worry about me, and she's such a mother hen that I know she will. "Nothing," I say, pasting a fake smile on my face.

She stares at me, hard. I hate it when she does this. It's like she's digging through my brain without permission. "Did Cole do something?"

I look down and snort as I trail my index finger around the rim of my wineglass.

"Violet," she whines, "are you ever going to tell me what's up with you guys? I'm trying to be a grown-up about it, but it's literally killing me. Being a grown-up is really hard."

My eyebrow pops up skeptically. "You look fine to me."

She groans and looks up at the wood-beam ceiling.

I roll my lips together again, weighing my options. I could talk about Cole, or I could talk about my intense level of sadness and disappointment and probably start crying. For once, talking about Cole feels preferable.

I take a big swig of my wine. Liquid courage.

"Okay, Cole and I met on the internet."

She hunkers down, leaning forward slightly, like a little kid getting ready to listen to a campfire story.

"On a… um…" Oh god, saying this out loud is harder than I thought.

"Dating website?" she prods.

I almost laugh. The thought of Cole on a dating website. "No, more of a… um… forum?"

"Okaayyy." Billie looks confused now, and my cheeks heat.

I just blurt it out and get it over with. "A forum where people post nudes," I say quickly before shoving my wineglass in my face again.

Her brows knit together. "Cole posts nudes on the internet? If he weren't my future brother-in-law, I wouldn't be averse to see—"

"No, I did."

Billie's feline eyes bulge out as she chokes on her mouthful of wine. With one hand across her chest, she gasps for breath. "You?"

I nod.

"My sweet little Vi?"

I go beet red. Head to toe, I'm sure. I hear a click but can't look away from Billie.

"You posted naked pictures of yourself… on the internet?"

And somehow, because I have the worst luck in the world, this is the moment that Vaughn waltzes in through the front door.

He looks at Billie and me, his dark features intentionally blank, and holds his hands up in the air. "I was never here."

"It was one picture! One time!" I announce to the room, trying to clarify myself and cringing so hard at the thought of people I know and respect finding this out about me. Billie is one thing. But Vaughn? *Ugh.*

"I heard nothing!" he calls back a little too brightly as he heads upstairs. "And even if I did, I'm all for women taking charge of their sexuality!"

I rest my head against the back of the plushy couch and groan. Maybe the cushions will swallow me whole? Envelop me into the down stuffing so that I'll never have to see anyone ever again.

"Sorry." Billie winces. "He went to Hank's place to go over some stuff. I thought he'd be gone longer."

I close my eyes, pretending I can rewind time to about five minutes ago, when my dignity was still intact.

Billie pats my knee. "Don't worry, Porn Star Patty. Your secret is safe with me."

A strangled noise lodges in my throat. I still refuse to look at her.

"Come on, Vi," she laughs. "Want me to tell you some crazy sex stories to even the playing field? Because Vaughn can—"

"Please don't." I hold one hand up to stop her.

"Okay, then stop being a baby and tell me the rest. You posted the picture… and?"

I hear the shower turn on upstairs, and I figure I'm safe to spill for a few more minutes.

"He contacted me." I decide that even if I don't really owe Cole anything, I don't want to betray his confidence with the details of that first message. His offer of payment never struck me as anything other than honorable. A fair exchange for a product—almost clinical, really. Like it made him feel better about what he was asking. And the more I got to know him, the more I realized it was exactly that as well as a way to maintain his precious distance. Something I went and threw a wrench into.

"And we ended up talking." She waggles her eyebrows. "As friends." Her shoulders droop in disappointment. "For a year."

"What! A year?"

I nod.

"What did you even talk about?"

I run my free hand through my hair. What *did* we talk about? It was mostly me asking questions or monologuing. But he always responded, and when I thought he was bored or tired of talking to me, I'd pull back, only to see a message from him pop up a day later, like that was his threshold for when he'd reach out. Something I took to mean more than it obviously did. Sometimes, we'd watch a movie at the same time and type back and forth about it. It was companionship in the most basic sense of the word.

"Everything and nothing," I say, because it's true. We talked about books, television, current events, our families in vague generalities, but we never talked about specifics. Shared nothing that might give our identities away. It was always entirely anonymous.

"So you guys never…" She holds her hand up in a rolling motion, implying *stuff*.

I bite down on my lip and look out the window into the dark rainy night. "Once."

"Once." Billie grips her wineglass with both hands, sitting up cross-legged now and nodding, like I'm telling the most fascinating story in the world.

I steel myself, wanting to get this part over with as quickly as possible. "Yes. Once. And it was very one-sided. Which resulted in the end of our… whatever it was." I feel so hot that I'm sure you could fry an egg on my cheek right now.

"What do you mean one-sided?"

Agitation roils around in my gut. This part still bugs me, no matter how hard I try to get over it. Embarrassment is tough to hurdle. "I mean, things got carried away one night. I ended up losing all my clothes on video because I thought I trusted him enough to do that after a year of corresponding. Had the best orgasm of my life. And then Cole refused to reciprocate. He left his screen black the whole time and said he would never partake. All things he had told me in the past.

I just thought…" I shake my head with a sad laugh. "I guess I thought I'd be different. Turns out I wasn't. I deleted the app and never talked to him again. Until the qualifier last year when he figured out who I was."

From upstairs, I hear, "Ow, fuck!"

"Were you eavesdropping on us, Vaughn Harding?" Billie shouts to the open loft bedroom while I look around for a spot to dig a hole and crawl deep inside it.

"Nope!" he calls back, popping the *p* with surety. "Just stubbed my toe."

"I hope it hurt!"

I groan and scrub my hand over my face. "Okay, that's my cue to leave." I set the wineglass on the oak coffee table in front of me and push myself up, feeling pretty used to the walking cast now. I can't get out of here fast enough.

"Vi," Billie says with a breathy giggle, "don't worry about it. He won't say anything."

I know that what she's saying is true. Vaughn is a good guy, an honorable one. But that doesn't mean I'm keen on him knowing about my sex life. About his brother's sex life.

Good god.

Cole. I should probably tell him about this minor mishap. Just in case. I can already imagine the blank expression he'll give me, the way his jaw will tick as he crosses his arms.

I limp to the door, and Billie follows. "Let me drive you home."

I'd come here with her after hanging out at the barn all afternoon, which also means I have no independent way of getting home.

"No, you've been drinking. I'll walk."

I hike my bag over my shoulder and slide my good foot into the rain boot I wore over as Billie holds the front door open for me.

"Let Vaughn drive you home."

"Ha!" I bark out a laugh. "I think I'll pass on that for now. I need a couple days before I can look him in the eye again, thanks."

"You sure?" She nibbles on her bottom lip nervously. "It's raining pretty hard."

I reach into my bag and pull out a small umbrella. "I'm all set. It's not that far."

Billie doesn't look convinced, but she doesn't stop me either—something I appreciate. I don't like being babied, and I don't need people treating me like porcelain because I have an injury. My brothers would have been back up on a bull with a tiny fracture like this, and here I am wallowing around like a wounded princess.

I step out into the dark, damp night and sigh. Raindrops pelt the top of my umbrella, the pinging sound loud all around me. The smell of dirt and rain permeates the air. It smells fresh, like new growth. The perfect night for a walk to clear my mind and cool my cheeks.

Walking was a bad idea. The heavy April rain has washed away all the charm of the night rather quickly.

My leg hurts, I'm cold, and this shitty little umbrella leaks. If I wasn't been such a wuss, I would have just accepted the ride from Vaughn. What's a five-minute drive for him is more like a twenty-minute walk for me. Probably longer with my limp. And I'm not even halfway.

"Motherfucker," I mutter as I hobble down the gravel road in my stupid walking cast—which is also not waterproof, which means my sock inside is getting soaked. And cold. I rarely swear, but now and then, a situation warrants it. This situation is one of those. This night is one of those. Actually, this week is one of those.

Tears sting at the backs of my eyes. The bridge of my nose tingles. I'm not a crier, and this isn't an unmanageable situation. But right now, everything feels heavy. Like more than I can bear. My career, my leg, my personal life. Sometimes being an independent grown-up is exhausting.

I stop and stare up at the sky, trying to force a deep breath into my lungs, but my frustration wins out, and I end up screaming to no one at all, "Fuck my fucking life!"

Which is right when headlights turn down onto the road, illuminating me like the Broadway actress that I am not, like the universe is just dying for someone to witness my meltdown or splash me as they drive by. But when the truck gets closer and slows, I realize I recognize it. A window rolls down, and a thick forearm shoots out, waving me forward.

"Get in!" Cole shouts.

I feel like under different circumstances, I would say no. But at this moment, all I feel is intense relief. Like I don't even care who's here to save me as long as I'm being rescued.

He reaches across the front seats and throws the door open before I even get there. A simple gesture, but I still feel like I could hug him for it. I fold down my umbrella and haul myself up into his big truck, hating how high off the ground it is but loving how dry and warm it is all at the same time.

I say nothing as I slam the door and buckle myself in. I can sense that Cole is looking at me. I can feel anger radiating off him in waves, like when you sit too close to a space heater. But I don't care. I just drop my head back against the headrest, close my eyes, and sigh, suddenly very exhausted.

"Are you *trying* to make your leg worse?" His voice is precise—I can hear his military background in there. He sounds authoritative, and I like it. It's not a question so much as a demand. It reminds me of the night we went too far.

"Thank you for picking me up" is all I say back, instantly feeling a little dopey. Wine, cold, and strapping yourself in on an emotional roller coaster will do that to a girl, I guess. And I assume Billie is behind this—something she'll pay for later.

He just grunts and drives. I sense him moving around beside me and squint from under my lashes to see what he's doing. One big hand reaches over to my side of the dash, and I watch his heavily corded forearm flex as he presses the seat warmer button for me. Is he worried about me being cold? I follow that arm up to his fingers as he rotates the knob to maximum heat, not missing the way his veins bulge over the top of his strong hand.

Everything about Cole is hypermasculine, something my body can't help but gobble up, even though my mind screams at me to ignore him. His body, his features, his *voice*. God. His voice. All deep and gravelly. He could make a killing as a phone sex operator if that was still a thing. And if he ever said more than a few words at a time.

As a pen pal, he was been slow to come around. But in real life? He was like squeezing blood from rocks. Next to impossible to get talking.

Which is why I don't bother making small talk. I let my eyes close and revel in the heat pumping out of the vents all around me. If he's not going to talk to me, I won't waste my energy talking to him about what may have come to light at Billie and Vaughn's house. *Want my trust? Earn it.*

When the truck finally slows and comes to a stop, I open one eye and peek at him. He's staring at me, completely closed off but staring at me nonetheless.

"Stay there," he clips out in that bossy voice.

I'm too bone-tired to argue, and I watch from under heavy eyelids as he hops out of the truck. He may have upset me, but I'm not above watching the way his jeans stretch across his ass and thighs. The man is huge, a wall of muscle. He could crush me if he wanted to.

A shiver runs down my spine as he rounds the front of the truck and opens the passenger-side door before announcing, "You're going to let me help you out of here."

I roll my head along the headrest to look back at him, quirking one eyebrow in response. That wasn't a question.

He crosses his arms, widens his stance, and glares at me. He looks like a bouncer at a club, about to deny me entry. A small hysterical laugh bubbles up out of me at the mental image. But Cole doesn't join in. He continues glaring at me, his mouth set in a thin line, his eyes burning across my skin, threatening to set me alight—like the strike of a matchstick.

Ugh. I need to drink less wine. *And have an orgasm.*

"Okay," I whisper, my voice small and unsteady. My leg really hurts. Not like it did last weekend, but walking around a bunch probably wasn't my best-laid plan. So I flip my legs out to dangle off the seat. I look like a little kid trying to get out of here. "'Why does your truck need to be so big?"

He ignores me as he steps forward. "Why do you have to ask so many questions?"

"You compensating for something?" Yup, that's the wine. I feel my cheeks heat at my boldness as I watch his jaw tick.

I expect him to plop me down on the ground, but he growls and scoops me up in his arms, one slung underneath my knees, the other right across the strap of my bra.

"Oh." I breathe out. "Okay."

He takes long, ground-covering strides toward the house, like he can't wait to drop me. I can feel his biceps bunching against the side of my breast, and with the golden cast of the porch lights, I can admire the definition in his arms, thickly corded and hard. *No wonder I commented on them before.*

I expect him to drop me on the front porch, but he keeps going, crouching slightly and easily snaking the hand from under my knees out to twist the door handle. I know I'm light, but the man isn't even struggling. At all. He kicks the door open and carries me in. I peek up at his face, the harsh slashes of his cheekbones, his heavy brow, the stubble across his jaw.

"What's the scar on your eyebrow from?"

His eyes shift down at me like I'm an irritating child.

"From my time overseas," he says.

I know that means during his time in the military. Something must have happened if that's all the explanation I'm going to get, and now I feel horrible for even asking. It's not my business. I feel like I crossed a line.

"It suits you. I like it," I say, trying to smooth things out. Except I'm sure that was a dumb thing to say by the way he's looking at me, those gray eyes pinning me in place. His chiseled chest rises and falls in a more pronounced fashion, and his breath fans across my throat as he regards me intensely.

That look only lasts a moment before he deposits me on the couch gently. Then he steps away quickly, like I might be on fire.

CHAPTER 9

Cole

I woke up to a message from Pretty_in_Purple. It said, "Good morning, Butterface," and I laughed. For the first time in a long time, I laughed. It felt foreign in my mouth, and I looked around like someone might have seen.

Except I'm alone. I'm always alone. It seems like this is how my life will be. I think it started out that I wanted it that way, but now I'm not so sure. I'm smart enough to know what people say about me… the recluse who runs the family company and is a total dick.

The role comes to me naturally, but I think I'm tired of it. Tired of my own company. Tired of the same fucking thing every fucking day.

I write back. I'm not funny or witty. I don't know what to say. So I just say what I'm thinking.

Golddigger85: Take off your clothes.

She replies a few minutes later.

Pretty_in_Purple: You first.

Yeah. That sure as shit isn't happening. Just the mention of it makes me nervous. I say nothing back, but a couple hours later, I check our chat again and reply this time.

Golddigger85: No chance.
Pretty_in_Purple: Guess we're stuck talking. We could be pen pals!

Pen pals. That's so far from what I had in mind when I first messaged this girl. How old is she?

Golddigger85: No.
Pretty_in_Purple: Come on! I'm lonely. You obviously are too. Let's just be friends.
Golddigger85: Why am I obviously lonely?
Pretty_in_Purple: Do I really need to answer that?

Touché, internet girl. And no. Please don't rub my nose in how pathetic I've become. "Does having a pen pal make me more or less pathetic?" I ask myself out loud as I rub a hand over my stubble and stare at the screen.

I would ask her, but that involves admitting I think I'm pathetic. I refuse to go there. Deflect. Redirect. That's what I'll do.

Golddigger85: Maybe I'm just a control freak.
Pretty_in_Purple: Maybe you're both?

I snort. Touché, internet girl. Tou. Ché.

★★★

I'm getting mighty tired of carrying Violet out of a truck. It's like she has no regard for her own well-being. At least this time, she doesn't feel limp in my arms.

I rip open the freezer and pull out one of my ice packs, agitation lining every movement. I was already annoyed when I walked in after a long week of working at the clusterfuck that is our company's new investment to find her shit *everywhere*. Water glasses abandoned around the house, shoes tossed carelessly by the front door, dishes piled in the sink, and a sweatshirt draped over the back of a chair almost made me go nuclear.

I'm the bachelor. I'm supposed to be the messy one. But instead, I have a twentysomething-year-old living in my space, a now world-famous athlete, who can't put simple things back where they belong. My feet stomped on the worn hardwood floors the entire time I cleaned up the place. Not what I felt like doing on a Friday night, but then I don't know what else I'd do in Ruby Creek.

With the ice pack in hand, I grab a water bottle from the fridge and walk back over to Violet. "Here." I hold the water out to her before I come to kneel by the couch.

I undo the Velcro straps on her air cast as she crinkles the plastic water bottle and regards me curiously. "What are you doing?"

"Getting ice on your leg so that you can get on a horse again one day." The mere thought of that sends a lance of anxiety through my chest, but I push it away. This is her journey, not mine.

"Did you know that plastic water bottles are bad for the environment?"

My god. She really doesn't stop with the questions. I don't respond, which she apparently takes as a sign that she should keep talking.

"They don't decompose. Instead, they end up in the oceans—"

I roll my eyes. Has she tasted the tap water here? "Why did you try to walk home on a leg that you know you're supposed to be resting?"

I know something is up. It was my job for years to sense when something was off.

Violet is ranting about water bottles, and Billie acted weird on the phone. The strained, tittering laugh when she suggested Violet might need help seemed panicky. I could feel the unspoken words, the tension.

She rolls her lips together nervously, and her crystalline blue eyes go wide. They only look brighter next to the pink blooming on the apples of her cheeks.

"Why are you blushing?"

"Now who's the one with all the questions?" she replies with fake bravado. A little tremor in her voice gives her away. The woman is an open book. No poker face to speak of.

"Violet," I scold her, pulling the cast away to assess her ankle below the hem of her leggings. Swollen. My teeth grind.

Her sigh comes out loud and ragged, her voice a little too quiet. "Okay. I just needed to get out of there. I didn't think it through."

"Why?"

Her eyes dart away, and I cup her heel delicately, the smell of her vanilla body cream in the air as I press the ice pack to her swollen leg. She hisses and gives her attention back to me—which is what I was going for.

"I'm just…" Her voice quivers, and she strokes her fingers through her golden locks. Her tell. She does it when she's nervous. "You know. Really disappointed. Really bored. Really… choked up about the current state of my life. I didn't want to talk about it."

She pauses, and I sit back on my heels, moving my hands down onto my thighs to listen, not wanting to touch her any longer. Her eyes are sparkling with unshed tears. I could tell that she was crying earlier, just like she's close right now.

"So I told them about us instead," she rushes out, looking at me pleadingly. "I'm sorry. I'm so, so sorry."

I go still. Stuck in place.

"I swear it was all just really general."

"*Them?*"

She flinches at the bite in my tone, and I'm instantly filled with self-loathing. "Okay. So I really only told Billie. I didn't know Vaughn was listening."

My skin crawls with embarrassment, like that feeling when you have a bug inching its way up your spine but can't quite reach it. My leg aches, like it often does. This was never supposed to happen. My sex life was supposed to stay perfectly compartmentalized on the internet where no one gets to see me. Violet was supposed to stay firmly removed from my real life. She was never supposed to crop up as a mainstay in the family business.

Panic courses through my veins as I see my perfectly laid facade crumbling. Just one little crack in the corner is going to lead to more questions. When one brick falls, the others will follow, torn down by questions I don't want to answer.

I know I'm fucked up. The last thing I need is everyone around me knowing too. And this bombshell is more than I'm equipped to handle. I get up woodenly, not saying a word, and walk away.

That's enough of this shit for one day.

***

The phone is silent for several beats, and then it fills with a raspy, maniacal cackle. "The woman is *living with you*?" Trixie gasps out, making me bang my head back against the brass bars of the bed frame. This place is like a fucking dollhouse.

"I don't pay you to laugh at me, Beatrice." I pay her because I *need* her. She's the first call I made this Saturday morning when I woke up after a shitty, fitful sleep. A sleep full of dreams about all my deepest, darkest secrets being spilled to the world. Dreams about Violet's naked body spread out before me. Dreams I can't afford and don't deserve.

"And she told your brother and future sister-in-law about how you both met?" She may not be laughing, but I can still hear the amusement in her voice.

"Yes," I grumble.

"And then she told you?"

"Yes."

"Well, you can't fault the girl for her honesty."

"I think I would prefer a little dishonesty in this case."

"Oh no, you don't need any more of that in your life."

I look out the big window across the vast field toward the barn.

"Why don't you let me—"

My eyes snag on something in my periphery. I jump out of bed and take a few hops over to the window, gripping the crown molding with one hand. *Why the fuck is there a horse in my yard?*

"I gotta go. I'll call you later." I hang up, but not before I hear Trixie say something about not being at my beck and call.

I get myself ready, throwing on the same T-shirt as yesterday before heading downstairs and out the front door, straight to the paddock that has been sitting gloriously empty until now. I eye the scrawny brown horse inside and then notice the paper rolled and shoved into one ring on the halter that's slung over a hook.

I pull it out, confused and annoyed.

Hey Vi,

I know this isn't how you saw your year going. I know setbacks are frustrating. So does Pipsqueak here. Do you remember her from a couple of years ago? Apparently, she was a preemie foal that was touch and go there for a bit. Anyway, she's two now, and she's a fighter. Small but mighty, just like you.

I know you can't ride right now, but that doesn't mean you can't work. I'd like to see what she's got. Mind getting her started for me?

Love,
Billie

No. No fucking way am I living with Violet *and* with a horse. I'm not above admitting this is thoughtful of Billie. I can't fault her for that. For me though? This can't happen. I turn and storm back up into the house, note in hand.

The door slams behind me. "Violet! Get up!" My voice is sharper than I intend, but my life is completely out of control, and I'm panicking. That ends now.

I hear a small squeal from the other side of her door, followed by a thump, and I instantly feel like a dick for not keeping my cool. When the door opens, she's already dressed and pulling an earbud out of her ear. "What? What's wrong?"

I shove the note at her as if it will clearly explain what's wrong. Violet takes it from me, one dainty hand reaching out to remove it from mine. Her eyes are wide until she recognizes the writing, and I watch her feelings dance across her face. She's so expressive, it's like she could tell me a story without saying anything at all.

Tears spring up over her irises, usually the color of the sky and now more of an indigo as they darken with emotion. Her long lashes blink rapidly, as though she could sweep the tears away with them. One side of her perfectly heart-shaped mouth tips upward sadly. And then slowly the other side pops up to match. The smile is small, but the impact on me isn't.

I feel like a little boy again, one who just fell off the tire swing and winded himself, the thud of my bones against the packed ground rattling through me. My breath is caught somewhere beyond my reach.

Violet doesn't even look at me though. She doesn't see my struggle. She just limps over to the front window, pressing a hand to it like a child at the zoo, like she's never seen a horse before. I watch her body from behind. Her round ass, the taper of her waist, the slender curve of her neck beneath where all that pale hair is piled up on her head in a loose bun.

"What's the issue?" she asks quietly on a deep sigh without looking back at me. Her spaghetti-strap-clad shoulders go from tight and high to slowly dropping, like the tension is melting right off her and flowing away on a warm, gentle current.

And I know.

I know at this moment that I don't have it in me to make her get rid of the horse. After watching that physical reaction, how could I? I'm not a cruel man—not intentionally anyway. Everything Violet feels is so plain to the naked eye, particularly to that of a man who's spent his entire adult life reading people and situations. If there was something that could soothe me the same way that Violet relaxed at the prospect of having some plain brown horse to play with, I would have done it.

And I would have resented anyone who tried to stop me.

Instead, I just resent myself for being stuck in a rut. Something I don't want for Violet. Because no matter what she thinks, the days I spent messaging with her were some of my brightest in recent memory.

She turns to look at me over her shoulder, her wide blue eyes full of emotion, her cheeks flushed with excitement. Life courses through her so vividly and almost tangibly—like I could reach out and touch it, bottle it up and drink it, or just keep it, possess it, knowing I have the option to consume it whenever I want. Money can't buy this brand of vitality. This is bone deep—soul deep. She shines like the sun, golden and bright.

What a man like me wouldn't give for *that*.

"No issue," I say huskily. "I'm just not taking care of it. That job is all yours."

Violet tilts her head almost imperceptibly. "Who knows, Cole? You might come around."

I cross my arms and widen my stance, wanting to make it clear to her that I'm serious. Although I'm getting the sense I don't intimidate Violet as much as I thought. She's tougher than she comes off. More resilient. "I don't like horses," I say plainly, pinning her with a serious look, choosing to leave out the part where my most vivid memory of them is watching my father fall to his death beneath their hooves.

Her body jolts ever so slightly, like I've just slapped her. And then a gentle smile spreads across her mouth. "We'll see about that."

She looks far too knowing for a woman her age. She's looking at me like *I'm* the project rather than the scrawny horse in the yard.

I'm already dressed for a run, so that's what I do.

I turn and run.

CHAPTER 10

Violet

I'M PRETTY SURE MY SURLY PEN PAL, GOLDDIGGER, HAS BECOME ONE of my only friends. We've been talking daily for a few months, and I've grown accustomed to it. I'd even go so far as to say I look forward to it. Some days, I wake up and fire off a message to him saying, Good morning, *or something equally chipper. And other mornings, he messages me first. Like today.*

Golddigger85: Hi.

My lips tip up at the one-word note. He's not a big talker—this much I've learned—yet he's always there. He always writes me back. If I were annoying him, you'd think he'd stop responding. I think he needs this as much as I do.

The quiet, grumpy vibe is just part of his charm, and I take it to mean he likes me enough to keep me around. So I always write him back too. Otherwise, all I do is work at Gold Rush Ranch from sunup to sundown. New girl on the farm means no clout, no seniority—grunt worker. And I like it. No one treats me like I need coddling. They throw me in the deep end and expect me to swim.

Pretty_in_Purple: Good morning, Butterface. How was your sleep?
Golddigger85: The usual.

I know what that means. It means he didn't sleep well. He's told me he wakes up a lot. He's also told me he's a veteran, so I assume those two things connect. I haven't asked because he hasn't seemed like he wants me to, and I've come to know that Golddigger is an intensely private man. That he likes my… Do you call what we have company? *I don't know. He likes my reliability but isn't about to tell me his deepest, darkest secrets. Which is fine. I don't expect him to.*

But it doesn't stop me from sharing about myself. I think he likes that too.

Pretty_in_Purple: I had a great sleep. Like a baby. I work outside all day, so by the time I get back to my apartment, I'm beat.
Golddigger85: I don't remember what it feels like to sleep through the night.

I wince. Sounds like my brother when he came back from Afghanistan.

Pretty_in_Purple: I have a brother who had a hard time sleeping for a spell.
Golddigger85: How did he fix it?

I roll my lips together at his question because I don't know the answer to that.

Pretty_in_Purple: I'm not sure he ever did.
Golddigger85: Reassuring, thanks.

Oh, jeez. I need to flip this script.

Pretty_in_Purple: Have you tried masturbating before bed? That always helps me.

The dots roll and stop.

Golddigger85: You offering to lend me a hand?

"Ha!" I bark out a laugh into the quiet room.

Pretty_in_Purple: A for effort. Never gonna happen.

This is our running joke. But the more I get to know him and feel comfortable around him, the more I wonder… Would it really be so bad?

I don't know where Cole went, and I don't care. The only thing I can focus on is the little bay filly eating her hay quietly outside my front door. She's small, yes, but the way she's built is all correct. Ideal, really. Billie has such a good eye for horses, no doubt she picked up on that too.

I hobble over to the front door and sit on the wooden

bench in the front entry to slide my good leg into my rubber boot I kicked off as Cole carried me in through the front door.

Again. Except this time, I remember it clearly. The way his hands gripped me, strong but gentle. The lines of his abs as they rippled along my rib cage while he held me close. The sheer power of him as he carried me through the rain effortlessly.

Every point of contact like a tease.

I wanted him before I ever knew he looked or felt like *that.* I wanted him even when I knew he'd never want me back. When he was just an avatar on my screen. *Stupid.* And that is something I've come to terms with. Something I've moved on from the day that I vowed to never look at our chat again. And I haven't. I never logged in again. I deleted the app. Were there messages there waiting for me? Did he wonder where I went? Or did he just assume my silence was a dismissal? I'll never know because I'll never check.

Having a soul-consuming crush on a stranger on the internet was a phase. And I closed the door on that phase of my life. I pushed my boundaries. I tried something new. And it's done.

I'm in a whole new chapter. Older, wiser, more independent.

I chuckle at myself as I head out the front door toward the paddock. Living with the man and falling asleep thinking about the hard lines of his body doesn't exactly scream *wise* or *independent. Great work, Violet.*

"Hey, pretty girl," I coo as I approach the fence.

Pipsqueak's head snaps up, but she doesn't startle. She just flicks her ears toward me with a joyful look on her dainty face, not the least bit perturbed by my arrival. In fact, when I get close enough, she forgets about her hay completely and comes to the gate, eager for attention. Not unusual for a horse that has probably been handled extensively for her entire life because of health complications.

As soon as I reach the gate, she drops her head over the top post and nuzzles into me like she's demanding a hug. Her warm, damp breath flows over the light hairs on my forearms as she snuggles her face into my embrace.

A genuine laugh bubbles up out of me. It's like she thinks she's a puppy. Her eyes flutter open and closed happily as I stroke my hand over her broad forehead, right over the bright white star in the middle of it.

I love this horse already. I don't even care if she runs well. This kind of contact is therapeutic, and once I can be sure the gesture won't bring me to tears, I have every intention of thanking Billie from the bottom of my heart for knowing this is what I needed. Horse therapy.

She was always rambling on about DD being her therapist. Maybe Pipsqueak can be mine?

"What do you think about that, Pip?" I ask, rubbing my cheek against the firm round plate of hers, basically bunting her like a cat. But I don't even care. Once a horse girl, always a horse girl.

The smell, the dust, the rasp of her ungroomed coat—it doesn't bother me at all. It comforts me. My very own little paper-bag princess.

Excitement at the prospect of her makeover courses through me, and when I look down near the gate, my eyes catch the pink grooming box that Billie left out. It's loaded with every brush and spray I could need. Hoof oil even. Did Billie pack up the trailer to get her here? Or walk over? I decide I don't care about that either. "You ready to hit the spa, girl?"

Pipsqueak snorts and gives her unruly black mane a shake. As close to a nod as I'm going to get. I grab the handle of the box and let myself in through the gate. I don't bother putting the halter on her. If she wants to walk away, she can. For now, we're just getting to know each other. No pressure.

I start with a big rubber currycomb at the top of her neck, brushing in tight circles and watching all the dust and loose hair come up to the surface as I work my way down to her shoulder. When I get to her withers, she sighs and lets her eyes fall shut, like she's getting the best massage. I continue, getting lost in the rhythm of the circular motion and working my way around her body.

By the time I get to the other side of her, she's so relaxed she has one hoof tipped and resting on the ground casually. She is *loving* this. And so am I. I'm completely blissed out. Zoned out.

Which is why I jump when I hear a car pull up. I turn to see the old blue truck, the one Hank got from Dermot and has kept running. It always warms my heart the way this place has stayed in the family, the way Dermot and Ada's legacy has tied everyone together—even when things got turbulent.

"Hey, Vi!" Hank hollers as he steps out, looking a little stiff. "How do you like your present?" His grin is infectious, all the lines on his face deepening around twinkling green eyes. Hank is wise and kind and comforting, and I've come to love him over the last couple years we've spent working together. He's been a surrogate father to Billie since she was a teenager, but I feel as though he's taken that role over with the rest of us at the farm as well.

"Like? I don't like my present. I *love* her!" I beam back so wide that it almost hurts my cheeks.

He reaches back into the truck and pulls out a bouquet of pink tulips before marching over and holding them out to me over the fence. "Sorry I haven't checked in on you since your accident. I've been getting regular updates from everyone else but didn't want to crowd you."

Taking the flowers from him, I hold them up to my nose and inhale that fresh grassy smell, the hint of honey. "Thank you for the flowers. And don't worry about it. I haven't been the best company."

Pipsqueak does the same, running her nose over the soft petals curiously.

Hank doesn't push the subject; instead, he just chuckles and reaches a firm hand out to pat the filly. "She's a funny little thing, isn't she? So curious about the world. I'm quite fond of her myself."

I sigh contentedly before looking back up at the man. "Me too. I think we're going to get along well."

Hank nods as he presses his elbows into the fence. He looks over at the blue farmhouse, a flash of sadness streaking across his features. "How are you getting along with Cole?"

How am I getting along with Cole? We communicate mostly in grunts and glares. We ignore the awkward vibe between us. I try not to stare at his body as if it's a cold drink on a hot day. It's basically torture. So I just settle on, "He's no Pippy."

Hank barks out a laugh. His head tips back, and his chest rumbles. "That he's not. He reminds me of Dermot. The kind of man who would do almost anything for the people he loves but hard to get to know. Strong. Silent. Sensitive."

Sensitive? I almost laugh. If we're going with *s* words, I pick *surly.* But my dad always told me that if I have nothing nice to say, it's best not to say anything at all. So that's what I do. I say nothing and just give Hank a small smile.

But I'm not fooling him. I can tell by the look on his face.

He tips his head back toward the house. "You know his dad grew up in that house?"

I look at it too. I know his dad died in a tragic racing accident but not much else. "I didn't know that, no."

Hank nods. "I think it might be hard for him to be out here, even though he'd never admit it. I'm sad about your leg, but I'm glad he's not alone. It's hard not to worry about all you kids." He chuckles good-naturedly. "May not have had any of my own, but I feel like you're all mine anyway."

My chest pinches at the thought of the ghosts Cole might live with, and my eyes sting thinking he could be as sensitive as Hank is saying. Maybe I've been misinterpreting him this entire time? I blink and change the subject, trying to keep my mind from focusing on the puzzle that is Cole Harding. "Didn't want any kids?"

He smiles sadly. "I'd have loved to have kids. Guess it just wasn't in the cards."

"Good thing we're all here to fill in for you then," I say with a wink, trying to lighten the mood.

Hank gives my shoulder a quick squeeze. "I'm lucky to have you all. But I won't bother ya. Just wanted to drop the flowers off and see your smiling face. If you need me, you've got my number. Take care of the boy, will ya?"

I smile and roll my eyes. The *boy* can take care of himself. "Thank you for the flowers, Hank." I limp out through the gate, wrap my free arm around his torso, and give him a quick squeeze. "Don't be a stranger."

"Deal," he says as he strides off with his signature wink and grin, firing up the old truck.

I wave back at him as I enter the house to get the flowers in a vase of water. I set them on the counter. They really are pretty, and they bring some much-needed life to the place. And then I head back outside and get back to brushing Pippy's fuzzy coat.

I feel more than hear Cole arrive back from his run, like a low-pressure weather system blowing in. I only peek at him before I realize it's not a good idea. His shirt is damp with sweat, clinging to his body in an almost erotic way, and his cheeks are flushed pink, making him look younger than I now know he is. It's probably too warm to be running in sweatpants, but that's not my business. He has a mom. And every other thought I have about the man is distinctly un-mom-like.

I bite down on my bottom lip to distract myself. Our eyes meet briefly before I turn back to Pippy, focusing on using a soft bristle brush now to sweep all that dirt and dander away. Cole and I say nothing to each other, and that's fine by me. He's probably still mad about my big mouth—and I can't blame him for that. I betrayed what little trust I owed him. Something I feel bad about but have no idea how to fix.

I can only fix what's right in front of me, so I focus on the ratty-looking little filly and promise myself I'll clean her up as best I can. My arm aches with the elbow grease I put into her, but by the time I'm done, she looks… better.

Standing back to admire my handiwork, I prop my hands on my hips. Maybe she's not shiny yet, but I thinned out her light bay winter coat, and I'm sure it will glow bronze once I get her on a better feeding regimen. Her four white socks are actually white now rather than gray, and her hooves are shining with the moisturizing oil I've applied. She's going to be a work in progress—after all, she just got pulled out of a back field—but I feel accomplished. Hopeful.

And for the first time in the last week, I don't feel quite so sorry for myself.

I'm sitting on a hay bale facing Pippy when I hear the door slam behind me. I've spent all day outside, and it's not even that nice out. Heavy clouds and the smell of impending rain permeate the thick air, making my skin feel almost damp. I don't care. It feels like one of the best days in the world to me.

Pippy's head pops up at the noise, and I turn around to see Cole in a fresh pair of sweatpants and a T-shirt. The image of him all sweaty flashes into my mind unbidden and almost instantly makes me blush. *Am I ever going to outgrow this reaction?*

"Where are you going?" I call out, trying to be conversational. I'm not an idiot. I know he was on the verge of telling me we weren't keeping a horse at the house. I don't know what changed his mind, but I thank my lucky stars he did.

His gait looks stiff as he hops down the stairs, and at my question, his body goes still, his head rotating toward me as his mouth twists into… I'm not sure. Maybe it's supposed to be a smile.

"For a run."

"Again?" I know running is good for you. To a point. It's never been my cup of tea, but two runs a day seems excessive.

"Yes. Is that a problem for you?"

Okay. We're grumpy again. This man needs one of those happy pills I bugged him about. "No," I venture carefully. "I'm just… Well, I'm in a great mood. Wanna grab a drink instead?"

His entire body turns toward me now, and his hand gestures between the two of us as he says, "You and me?" Like it's the most horrifying prospect in the world.

"Am I so bad?" The words spill out on a laugh.

Cole visibly winces, apparently not quite prepared to laugh with me just yet.

"I don't know." His hands rest on his narrow hips as he looks around himself on a sigh, like he's searching for an escape route.

"Come on," I pester him, because this man needs a little pestering. He reminds me of my oldest brother in that regard. Too serious for his own good. "I know you're old, but we'll be back before your bedtime. Before dinner even. It's…" I pull out my phone to check the time. "It's four o'clock. That's happy hour."

He just stares at me.

"Which means you have to be happy." I try to hold back the smile at my own cheesy joke, but I'm failing.

"Violet."

"Yes?" I bat my eyelashes with exaggerated innocence.

"Calling me old *and* grumpy is your plan to make me happy?"

Okay, jokes really fall flat around here. "Come on! I want a drink and to be around some other humans rather than locked up on the ranch. I'm feeling a bit squirrelly. If you don't come, I'll go on my own."

"Yeah? You going to drive with a big walking cast on your right foot?"

"No." I smile slyly. "I'm going to walk."

Cole groans and looks up at the sky like he's hoping some aliens will come whizzing by and beam him up out of this conversation. If they needed a magnificent male specimen, I could see why they'd choose him. "Give me five minutes."

"For what?" I quirk my head.

"To change into something appropriate."

I bark out a laugh. "Cole, have you been to Neighbor's Pub before?"

"No," he says with a slight wrinkle in his nose.

"Okay, well, you don't need to change. It's very casual."

He grunts at me and walks back inside, only to return a few seconds later with his keys. Our drive down the country roads is quiet but not tense like in the past couple of weeks. I almost feel like we've settled into a sort of companionable silence. Or at least on my end. Yes, we have an awkward history, but we're working with it. Plus, I'm only going to be living at the house for a couple more weeks. Once I get the all clear, I'm outta there. We can go back to pretending the other doesn't exist.

"Turn here." I point to where the old pub sits, rustic and full of character—just the way I like it.

I'm so excited that I bounce a little in my seat as I look out the window at the dark painted exterior with a big flashing sign over heavy oak doors and a parking lot patio lit by outdoor lights strung up over picnic tables.

"This?" Cole asks skeptically as he pulls up and looks at the building.

I haven't been off the farm in what feels like forever, and he clearly doesn't share my excitement. Which I don't get. Isn't he bored too? That's what running twice a day says to me: bored.

"Are you scared?" I grab the handle and crack the door. His head flicks instantly at the sound.

"Don't get out," he huffs before hopping out his side and rounding the front of the truck in what looks like only a few long strides.

The man is so big and authoritative, I feel a flash of nerves as he storms over to me. He's got that law enforcement vibe, like I might be in trouble for something. I squeeze my thighs together at the thought of being in trouble with Cole. It wouldn't be so bad. *You're so sad, Violet.*

"What's that look for?" he asks, standing before me now, one hand holding the top of the open door, stressing the rounded lines of his bicep against the sleeve of his T-shirt. It looks like it might unravel under the strain, especially when I take too long to answer, and his fingers squeeze the door harder, making that bulge grow right before my eyes.

Eyes that go wide and then snap back to his stormy face. The harsh slashes of his cheekbones, the square jaw covered in stubble that would rasp against my…

"Violet."

I startle. "Yeah? Yeah! Nothing. Let's go." I look toward the back of the truck, feeling my cheeks burn from the rabbit hole I just let my brain go down. Such a bad idea.

He doesn't even ask this time. His huge hands slide across my ribs and wrap around my waist. I thank my lucky stars I'm wearing a loose cable-knit sweater that hides the little goose bumps dotting my arms. Everything about him is so… almost aggressive that the gentleness of his touch never fails to startle me. I don't think I imagined the careful way he lifted me out of the truck that night Billie brought me to his house or the way he held me close and quietly asked if I was okay.

"You smell like a horse." He grunts as he places me gently down on the ground and yanks his hands back to his sides. His reaction to touching me is not quite a match for the memory I just lost myself in. "Let's go."

I watch his broad back ripple beneath the fitted T-shirt as he walks stiffly toward the front door of the pub.

Obviously, he *really* needs a drink.

CHAPTER 11

Cole

Golddigger85: Do you live near your family?

I SHAKE MY HEAD AT MYSELF. THIS IS MY PATHETIC ATTEMPT AT making conversation. We've been talking for several months now, and I'm not oblivious to the fact that she's been carrying most of the conversation. To be frank, I'm not sure why she sticks around.

I give her almost nothing, and she keeps coming back. Most people have friends because they enjoy their company. I have this friend because knowing she deserves better reminds me how badly I'm failing. I'm a fucking masochist, and I can't even stop myself.

Every time she's chipper and sweet, I feel more like a shit bag. But I can't walk away from her. I live in the shadows, and she's like this ray of light that brightens my day. I'm so fucking greedy.

Pretty_in_Purple: No. I moved to get away from them.

I don't want to pry, but that sounds brutal. So I settle on:

Golddigger85: Oof.

Pretty_in_Purple: Haha. No. That sounds bad. I love my dad and brothers. And they love me too, just a little too fiercely. Like... smother me fiercely. And in a small town? Forget it. I couldn't put a foot wrong or stay out too late. Even dating was brutal. They were constantly meddling, even when I was old enough to handle myself. So I had to get outta there. Fresh start. Fresh me. Naked on the internet was a step for me. Tragic as that sounds. They would HIT THE ROOF. But I did it anyway. Once. I'm good now.

Golddigger85: You showed them.

Pretty_in_Purple: Something like that.

Golddigger85: What about your mom?

She takes a few moments to type even though I can see that she's seen the message.

Pretty_in_Purple: She died having me.

This is why I don't try to make conversation. The fuck am I supposed to say to that? My thumbs hover over my phone, and I feel my heart rate increase, pounding against my ribs. I know a thing or two about dead parents. I settle on the most cliché thing I can think of.

Golddigger85: I'm sorry.

Pretty_in_Purple: Ah. Don't be. People get all weird around me about it when the fact of the matter is

I have no frame of reference for what I missed out on. I had a good childhood. I was well loved. I mean, I am well loved.

She's so forthcoming. So honest. I have the sudden urge to spill my dad's whole story. About that day. About watching it happen and about how my life was all downhill from that moment. It would feel so good to get that off my chest, to say the words that have solidified and gone stagnant there. Like when you don't quite swallow that pill, and it's just sort of lodged there in your throat.

But I don't.

Nobody wants to hear about my shit, and I don't want to scare her away.

This place is terrifying. I've seen some scary shit, but Neighbor's Pub might top that list. Who puts carpets in a pub? I watch my feet as I walk into the dim bar, and I swear I can feel them sticking slightly to the carpet with each step I take. I peek over my shoulder to make sure that Violet isn't entirely stuck to the flooring.

Instead of frowning at the interior, I see a small smile touching her lips as she looks around the place. With her silvery hair still in a big bird's nest and her petite body swallowed by an oversize cream sweater, she looks altogether too bright to be in such a dump. But based on the look on her face, she doesn't seem to agree.

"Where do you want to sit?" I ask her, eyeing the dark wooden tables suspiciously.

"Keep going. There's a table at the back beside a fireplace."

In a few more steps, the table—small and round with

two mismatched captain's chairs and a tacky green and brown stained-glass light dangling over top of it—comes into view.

I huff out a laugh, disbelieving that I'm actually doing this. "Trixie would love this place."

"Who is Trixie?" Violet asks, coming to stand beside me.

"My therapist," I blurt out before I realize what I'm saying. *Motherfucker.* Since when do I overshare? What else am I liable to blurt out around Violet? I'm getting comfortable around her—which is a problem.

"Cute name. I like it," she says cheerily before charging ahead and grabbing the seat that faces the front door.

That's it? No questions or interrogation? I expected judgment about being in therapy. Instead, she makes an offhand comment and sits down. Right in the seat I prefer. My PTSD is mostly under control these days; it's the image of a lump on the track and hooves pounding past it that keeps me up at night now. It's taken years of hard work, but my deployments don't haunt me like they used to. I still like to assess the room though, see my way out, know if there are threats looming. I hate the idea of having my back to the room, the danger it could put me in. The danger it could put Violet in. I know I'm not in Iraq anymore, but these are the things that stick with you. The training that sticks with you. You're never *just* a civilian again.

I sit down stiffly, feeling all wrong about what I'm doing but not wanting to reveal any more than I already have.

"How ya doin', hon?"

I startle when two plastic menus are tossed down on the table between Violet and me.

The waitress beams down at me, and I lean back in my chair, gripping the armrests, as I grind out, "I'll have a water."

Violet gives me a flat, unimpressed smile, a silent scolding for what I'm sure she sees as inappropriate behavior. Chastising I don't need or want—which is why I prefer to spend my time alone. Less explaining. Fewer expectations to fall short of.

Her look brightens as she smiles up at the waitress. "I'll take a Guinness, please." Her eyes dart over to me briefly before adding, "And thank you. Never mind my friend's manners."

"Sure thing!" The girl darts away, and I glance over my shoulder to watch her head back to the bar and get our drinks.

"A Guinness?" I ask Violet. I expected her to order a margarita or at least something that came with an umbrella in it. Not a thick dark beer.

"Yup." Her eyes dance with amusement. "Not what you would have guessed?"

I check over my shoulder and reply absently. "No."

"I grew up on a ranch with a single dad and three older brothers. Once I could drink, beer and whiskey were the only options in the house."

One side of my lips tips up. "You don't strike me as a whiskey girl."

Violet smiles shyly. "You might be surprised then."

I look back up at the bar, wanting to make sure I'm not startled by the waitress again. I can feel my pulse jumping in my wrist—I can see it even.

"Want to switch seats?" Violet leans across the table. She asks so quietly that I almost don't hear her.

"What?"

She pushes her chair out and stands. "Switch seats."

I want to say it's fine, but the truth is I'm utterly relieved by the prospect. Now she's standing beside me, looking down and waving her hand like she's shooing me out of my seat. So I go and don't ask questions. I just let myself accept the way I'm feeling rather than beating myself up about it. Trixie would approve.

"Better?" she asks as we both settle into our new chairs.

I look away like it's no big deal. It is. Not a single person in my life has ever picked up on anything like this before. On my nervousness around adjusting to civilian life. On how I avoid pieces of garbage on the ground, just in case. My refusal to let anyone else drive. I liked to think I didn't have post-traumatic stress disorder. Instead, I would say the military trained me to be ultracautious. Trixie didn't agree.

"Yep." I look away, feeling a little… I don't know. Vulnerable maybe?

"My brother is a veteran, you know."

"Really? I didn't know that."

She winks playfully, but her tone isn't a match. "You never asked."

That blow lands. She's right. I asked almost nothing about her personal life in the year we spent corresponding. It started out that I didn't care to know. And then it turned into me knowing that if I asked, I would care. But I cared anyway. I kept telling myself that people don't fall in love on the internet. They don't develop *real* feelings. But looking at her now, I feel sure that what I'm feeling is pretty damn real. And it's also a pretty damn terrible idea.

"Do you know Billie calls you G.I. Joe?" she blurts out, obviously trying to fill the space.

I can't help but laugh at that. A low, deep rumble that feels warm and unfamiliar in my chest. Billie is a funny duck, and her ranting has come to seem endearing to me. "I can totally envision her calling me that."

Violet laughs, her eyes all wide and shocked looking.

"What?"

"You… you just laughed. I don't think I've ever heard you laugh."

My head quirks as I lean in a bit. "I laugh."

Violet crosses her arms and leans closer across the small table. "Did it hurt?"

My lips twitch. But I don't want to give her the satisfaction of making me laugh again. Mostly, I want to thank her for ditching the veteran talk. For not looking at me with pity. For just throwing me a fucking bone without starting the Spanish Inquisition into my past.

But I don't. I shake my head instead.

"Get a drink." Her eyes are twinkling now.

"Beer is fattening."

Violet busts out the most unladylike snort. I had no idea someone so small and dainty could honk like this. And then her face is flaming as she slaps both palms over her mouth and dissolves into a fit of giggles.

I stare back at her, trying to look unimpressed, even though her amusement is contagious. Even though she's so fucking beautiful that it hurts.

"I think your abs will survive to see another day," she gasps from behind her hands. And then she clamps them down harder over her mouth, and her eyes bulge out of her head, like she can't quite believe she just blurted that out. She looks *mortified.*

And I can't help it. I laugh. A genuine laugh. It erupts from me like an animal that's been caged up for too long. Like a racehorse shooting out of the gate.

I watch her face transform from embarrassment to pure glee. The look on her face? It heats me from my core. Like a spark on dry grass that sends flames dancing across arid land. Fast and out of control. After all, wildfires are dangerous.

The waitress finally makes her way back over. You'd swear this place was packed, and she had to collect my water out of Ruby Creek itself. She slides Violet her dark frothy beer just as Violet quirks one eyebrow at me.

"I'll..." Ugh. Am I about to get roped into this? "I'll have one of what she's having."

I'll work out twice tomorrow.

I barely feel the waitress's hand land on my shoulder. Unsolicited touching is something that would normally annoy me, but right now, looking at the woman across from me, I hardly even notice. I vaguely hear her say, "No problem, hon."

Violet presses her lips together so hard it must hurt, except she doesn't look in pain. She looks like she's going to break right open and beam at me and is trying not to. She looks like she did that day after she won the Denman Derby qualifier. *Happy*. And for once, I don't want to ruin it. For once, I don't want to lie down and bask in my own shit.

Right now? I want to enjoy it.

But not *too* much.

"What? The water in this town is poison. Have you smelled it?"

Violet nibbles on her bottom lip and shakes her head at me.

"I'm only having one."

She nods.

"*What?*"

"A girl could throw her panties right in your face, and you wouldn't pick up on it, would you?"

I rear back. Why would a girl throw her panties in my face?

She takes a small sip of her beer, smiling knowingly into the creamy top of it as she does. "Our waitress. She's into you. Didn't you notice?"

My eyes shoot up over Violet's head to look back at the bar, and—sure enough—the girl is staring straight back at me as the bartender places my Guinness on her tray. I didn't notice because my mind has been fixated on the same girl for two damn years.

I roll my shoulders back and sit up taller, feeling a little less comfortable. "I don't think so." Eyes on me, even appreciative ones, have a way of making me squirm. I'm terrified that if someone looks too close, they'll see what I'm hiding. *You're half the man you were when you left.* That's what Hilary said to me that night. That's the sentence that's stuck with me, that's made me want to hide myself away.

But when the girl comes back to drop my beer off, she winks at me and taps my hand lightly before departing. And I almost can't believe it myself. "Women are never into me," I grumble as I look down at the carpet.

Violet leans back in her chair with her eyebrows pinched together and points at me. "She is."

"No chance. I'm too old."

She snorts. "You're not."

I finally look up and shrug. "I have to be at least ten years older than her."

"You're ten years older than me."

"And?" I take a sip of the malty black beer and sigh inwardly. It tastes so fucking good. I can't remember the last time I let myself enjoy a beer without worrying about taking optimal care of my body.

"It didn't seem to bother you with me."

I freeze, placing the pint glass back down. I don't have that much experience with navigating women and their feelings, but I know a field full of land mines when I see one.

"That was—"

She cuts me off before I can finish what I wanted to say to her, waving me off with her hand. "Don't worry about it. How's work going?"

Work. I can talk about work.

"It sucks. We bought a company full of fucking idiots."

"You're a regular ray of sunshine, you know that? I think your swearing might be worse than Billie's." She pulls her good leg up onto her chair, resting her socked foot on the edge and bending her knee. Looking supremely comfortable—a way that most people don't look in my presence.

I groan and scrub at my stubble before taking a long pull of my drink. "People swear in the military, Violet. This is why Vaughn is the happy shiny face of the family company." I spin my glass in my hands. "And the new company? It's just disorganized. Financials are a mess. Safety standards are fucking terrifying. Nobody knows what they're doing. Basically, there's a reason we got a rock-bottom deal on the place."

She shrugs. "I'm sure you'll turn it around."

My cheek twitches at that. "How can you possibly be sure of that?"

"I don't know. You just don't strike me as a quitter."

I grunt, mind racing with what she could mean by that statement. How much does she know? Maybe she saw my last messages? The ones I tried to delete, but the damn app wouldn't let me. The ones I sent when I realized she wasn't coming back. That I'd fucked up beyond repair. I wanted to be mad at Pretty_in_Purple for ghosting me, but when it came down to it, I couldn't blame her.

I'd leave me too.

I clear my throat, not wanting to go down that rabbit hole during what has otherwise been a surprisingly enjoyable outing. I also don't want to think about the bouquet on the kitchen counter. About some shmuck bringing them to her, doing nice things for her, when I've done nothing but be growly and awkward in her presence. I see red at the prospect. The truth is I don't know how to act around Violet, how to handle the feelings she pulls up in me. Feelings that make my dick twitch and my possessive side rear its ugly head.

So I change the conversation to work. The number one conversation boner killer next to the weather. "How about you? What's the plan for everyone's favorite jockey?"

Violet looks around the room in response, and I wonder if maybe she didn't hear me. I'm pretty sure the country music playing isn't *that* loud.

"I don't know." Her tongue darts out, wetting her bottom lip as she looks back at me. Her entire body heaves with the weight of her sigh. "I'm kinda pissed off, you know? Last season was like a dream come true. Like I just fumbled my way into this once-in-a-lifetime situation. Billie. DD. Hank. Just the whole thing was so... *perfect*."

I nod, remembering a time when my life felt the same. The perfect family. The perfect girlfriend—according to everyone else. My future set in stone and paved in gold. And then my dad died, and everything went to shit. I let it.

"But I still feel like I need to prove myself. The other jockeys…" She gestures down at her leg. "They obviously don't like me. I waltzed into those wins. I didn't earn them. I *want* to earn it. I don't want to be coddled and set up for success. I've had that my entire life. I want to struggle and come out better on the other side. You know? I want to prove that I can overcome and still be the best. And only for myself. I need to know that I can do it. My success so far just feels…" Her face squishes up, and her eyes go distant as she searches for the word. "Incomplete. And now I'll be behind. I'll have lost fitness, hours in the tack." Her shoulders droop, and she looks down into her beer like she'd like to drown herself in it.

"I can help you work out."

Her head flicks up. "Really?"

"Sure." That's an offer I shouldn't make, but I can't stand seeing her look so downtrodden over an asshole like Patrick Cassel. "There's lots you can do that doesn't include using your leg."

She blinks rapidly at me, as if she thinks I might be some sort of illusion. And to be frank, I can't quite believe myself either.

"Okay," she breathes.

"Patrick is going to pay for that move he pulled."

Violet rolls her eyes. "That's what Billie keeps telling me. It's under review right now. But who cares? He's out there riding, and I'm here. Doing"—she waves a hand over the table—"this."

My mouth quirks up in response, the odd smile feeling more natural every time I do it. I double tap the table with my fingers as I lean back with my pint in hand and shrug. "This isn't so bad."

***

It's dark out and pouring rain by the time we leave Neighbor's Pub.

"Wait here," I say to Violet as I duck and run to the truck.

No point in both of us getting soaked. I jump in, turn the key, and hear it roar to life as I immediately drive to the front door to pick up a very confused-looking Violet.

She pulls herself in awkwardly and wipes away a drop of rain from the tip of her nose. "You didn't have to do that."

I shrug, pulling away from the bar. "I know." But I'm in a good mood, and I wanted to. I'm internally shocked I had a great time tonight. I even ate chicken wings in that questionable establishment. They might be the death of me, but I must admit they tasted pretty good. I hardly go out anymore. I mean, nobody asks me, but I don't welcome the invites either.

My mom drags me out for coffee now and then, which always strikes me as a way to soothe her guilty conscience rather than to spend time with me. I let her do it anyway. Vaughn got pimped out on her dream dates with country club girls, and I got awkward coffee dates with Mom. As far as I'm concerned, I got the better end of that deal.

She went off the rails when Dad died, lost herself in the bottom of a martini glass for a while—or so I hear. Something she hasn't forgiven herself for, obviously. I wasn't here for that part. As soon as I could, I put a ring on my girlfriend's finger—because that seemed like the right thing to do—and then enlisted. I joined the army and got the fuck out of Dodge.

I stayed in for twelve years and kept myself safe and unscathed until the last month of that final tour.

Then an already numb existence went blank. Flatlined. But tonight, I've felt the odd blip of a beating heart, like maybe I'm not entirely down for the count after all.

"Thanks," Violet says quietly. "That was fun."

"It was."

Her smile is shy as her focus moves away into the distance. I wonder who else gets to soak up those smiles when I'm not around, and it makes me irrationally jealous. Enough so that I say, "Nice flowers you got today."

The moment the words leave my mouth, I hate myself for even saying them. I shouldn't care if some guy is bringing her flowers. And I definitely have no right to be jealous about it. But I'd be lying if I said it hasn't been niggling at me all evening.

Her lips roll together like she's trying to clamp down on an even bigger smile. "Yup. Hank is a sweetheart."

"Hank?" Now I officially look like a psycho. The longest-standing friend of our family brought her flowers, and I'm acting like a possessive tool about it.

"Mm-hmm" is all she says. But I can hear the trace of humor in her voice. Like she sees my comment for exactly what it is.

My fingers flex on the steering wheel, and we fall into an awkward silence. Where conversation flowed pretty easily in the dingy little pub surrounded by the hum of local regulars in for their daily happy hour and the twangy music playing through the cheap speakers, it feels more strained in the quiet of my truck. Like there's too much left unsaid between us. It's too intimate. Too dark.

Too much.

I nod and retreat into the silence as we travel down the dark side roads back toward the ranch. When we pull up to the house, I shoot Violet a look that garners me an eye roll. But she doesn't move to jump out of the tall truck on her own.

The minute my door slams, the brown horse whinnies loudly to me from her gate, looking like a drowned rat. A happy drowned rat with her ears all flicked forward.

I ignore it and jog around the front of the truck, yanking the passenger-side door open to get Violet out before I get totally drenched. The rain beats steadily across my shoulders as I look down at her in the dimly lit cab. Each drop feels like a pinprick on my skin as she looks up at me without turning her body. She hesitates, like she doesn't quite want to face me. Her blue eyes darken somehow in the low light, going almost indigo, and her hair looks more golden in its shimmer. I watch as her tongue darts out across the seam of her shapely lips.

We stand in limbo, her in the dry warmth of the truck, me out in the rain drinking her in like I've been stuck in the desert, parched.

My body pulses in time with my heart as she spins herself toward me slowly, one hand on the handle and the other on the edge of the seat, lifting the cast gingerly. I run a hand over the top of her injured leg to hook my palm behind her knee and pull her closer. She shivers, like she's cold, so I slide my eyes back up to her face. "Are you—"

She cuts me off this time. "Thank you again for tonight. I know you don't like me. But I still had a good time with you."

My chest fills with heavy air and self-loathing as I step in and feel my knees bump against the truck, my waist centered between her slender thighs. My fingers lock onto the back of her knee as I ask, “Why would you think I don’t like you?”

Violet looks over toward the horse, avoiding my eyes, stammering as she does. “I... I...” Her sigh is a harsh emptying of her lungs through that distracting heart-shaped mouth. “Because I ghosted you? Because I’m in your house? Your life? I’m not stupid—I know I’m invading your space. I know you like your privacy. I’m an inconvenience. I can tell you don’t like me. And you know, really, that’s my issue. It’s not my problem if people don’t like me. Not really. But it bugs me, you know?”

I almost want to laugh at the absurdity of the statement. She thinks I don’t like her? *If she only knew* is what runs through my head as I lean in closer.

CHAPTER 12

Violet

Pretty_in_Purple: Cats or dogs?

These are the questions I've resorted to asking to keep Golddigger engaged. I can't figure him out. Some days, he seems talkative, and other days, he's quiet and withdrawn. On those days, I usually let him be and then wake up to a message from him the following morning.

But tonight, I've cracked a bottle of wine by myself, and I want someone to talk to. The ranch has been launched into turmoil, and they finally hired a new trainer. And she's awesome. I tried to play it cool around her, but I'm pretty sure I just got all quiet and weird.

Either way, I'm excited. Because my days just got a lot less lonely.

My phone dings, and I snatch it up.

Golddigger85: Pussy.

My cheeks flare. Now and then, he throws out something super sexual. Something that makes me squeeze my thighs together and wish we were more than just avatars to each other. I wonder what his voice sounds like. What his mannerisms are. Does he have an accent? I wonder what color his eyes are. Does he do this with other girls every day too?

That last one makes my chest pinch uncomfortably.

I spend a lot of time imagining the details of Golddigger's appearance, trying to piece him together with the few puzzle pieces he occasionally drops. Mostly, I imagine his muscles.

Every man I've been with has been lanky and boyish, but based on that one photo of him, that's not the case here. I've had nice boyfriends. I've had nice sex.

But I'm tired of nice. What I really want is for someone to manhandle me. Cross that consuming type of lust off my bucket list.

Pretty_in_Purple: Huh. Never would have guessed. How many of those do you have on the go?

Golddigger85: One. I'm a solo pussy kind of man.

Pretty_in_Purple: Oh really? What's her name?

Golddigger85: Not sure. All I know is that she looks good in purple.

Pretty_in_Purple: Okay. Sorry. Innuendos aside. Are you meaning to tell me I'm the only girl you chat with on here?

Golddigger85: Yes.

Pretty_in_Purple: Why?

Golddigger85: Because talking to you uses up all my free time.

I read that sentence over and over again. Coming from anyone else, it wouldn't sound sweet. But coming from him, well, I can't help but smile and stifle a laugh on a sip of wine.

Golddigger likes me.

He leans in closer and glares at me, big fat raindrops rolling down his masculine face. His gray eyes bore into me from underneath thick lashes and then skim down to my mouth. He looks mad, like every muscle in his body is held taut. Like a predator coiled and ready to strike. But I haven't been afraid of him before, and I won't start now.

I keep rambling to fill the space. "Don't worry about it. Billie has talked to me about this too. Not everyone is going to like me, and that's *fine*." I edge forward to turn myself so he can lift me down the way he has in the past. The way he demands. But his hand pulses on my leg before lifting it higher and dragging me toward him. And I don't resist. We're like two opposite ends of a magnet, naturally drawn to each other.

His waist takes up all the space between my thighs. I almost lose my balance or swoon—I'm not totally sure which—but I let go of the handle above me to catch myself, my palm landing in the middle of his hard chest to brace against him.

His opposite hand shoots forward and captures my chin, the pad of his thumb pressing gently on the cleft there. The intense gray eyes scouring my face freeze me in place. He's so close I can feel his breath fanning down across my throat. His cologne wraps around me like a comfort blanket, all spice and cinnamon and warmth.

"You are not an inconvenience." His voice is rough, low, a growl. "Anyone who doesn't like you is an idiot. Do you understand me?"

I nod, feeling a bit breathless at his nearness. At his words. The way he overwhelms me. The way he's holding my thigh.

My fingers grasp at the fabric of his T-shirt, not wanting him to pull away. Wanting him closer. Even after everything.

I angle my face up at him, watching the shadows play across his features. The glow of the headlights highlights all the prominent ridges and sharp lines. His jaw ticks as he stands frozen, staring me down. But somehow the meaning behind that glare has transformed. I'm not sure what it is, but it's different. The flicker of desire reflected from my own eyes, maybe. Because I would have to be a blind idiot to pretend I don't want Cole Harding. I've wanted him for years—before I knew what he looked like—when he was just a faceless avatar providing a lonely girl company. The friend I needed as I set out in the world. The hand giving my bike a push as I took off on my own for the first time.

"Okay," I whisper, blinking once to give my eyes a rest, even though I don't want to take a break from looking at him. And holy hell, am I glad I opened them back up in time because his stony gaze goes straight to molten lava as he lifts that thumb from my chin and rubs it across my slack lower lip almost possessively.

The rumble that breaks free of his chest is like a shot of electricity to my core. My entire body tingles, goose bumps and intense awareness shooting out through every limb. Emboldened by his touch, I reach up with my spare hand and run it across the scar that cuts through his thick brow. I trace the raised tissue and hear his sharp intake of air as I trail my fingers over the line, reveling in the feel of his skin under my fingers, of his hands on my body. The leg he has nearly wrapped around his waist. The way we're just *almost* lined up perfectly. The soft pattering of rain around us. It's like we're frozen in time, in this tiny bubble of curiosity. Because that's what I see on his face now.

And it makes me brave. I fist his shirt tightly between my fingers and yank him to me, wanting to feel the swell of him against my thin pants. I sigh when I do, right as he groans, right as he drags that thumb across my lip again.

Jesus. I like that.

I lift my good leg and wrap it around his other side, wanting him closer. Our heavy breaths mingle wordlessly between us in the cold, damp air. His eyes devour me, confusion written all over his face now. I don't even want to think about what's written on mine as he hikes my thigh up higher and presses himself against the apex of my thighs, making my eyes flutter drunkenly. Pure lust, I imagine.

I let my other leg trail down the back of his, rubbing against him right as he rocks against me. But then he freezes and steps back abruptly, holding me at arm's length, panting into the night air, his breath like steam rising between us.

I want to launch myself back at him. I want to beg him to keep going. But I know Cole isn't the type of man who bends. I know he's complicated. I know he has rules. Rules that he doesn't break.

"I'm sorry." His voice cracks as he sets me down gently and brings his trembling hands back down to his sides.

I'm sorry?

Everything that was hot goes cold. Cold with dread. I shake my head. I've been here before. This is so like him—so like *me*. To let myself get carried away where he's concerned. To think something is there when it's not.

I can't even look at him as I feel myself go bright red. I send up a silent *thank you* that it's dark out as I stare out at Pippy's paddock. And like she knows this moment needs to be broken up, she whinnies. Long and loud and shrill, like an alarm bell that makes us both jump.

"Can I take your truck for a minute?"

Cole shakes his head as if to clear it, trying to keep up. "What for?"

"I need to run up to the barn and get her a rain sheet. She's getting soaked. No blanket. She doesn't even have a shelter in there."

He steps back quickly, putting space between us as he looks over at the little filly. "Horses have survived for years without waterproof coats."

Frustration surges up in me, fueled by our interaction. Fueled by my embarrassment. I can't be this close to him right now. "Can you just throw me a fucking bone and not tell me what to do?"

Now it's his turn to stare back at me wide-eyed. Dropping an f-bomb always does that to people. When you don't use the word much, it certainly packs a different punch.

He holds his keys out, looking adequately chastised and more than a little shocked. *Good.* I swipe them and walk away to the other side of the truck, leaving a motionless Cole behind me.

"Drive carefully, please." His voice is all gravel with a pleading tone to it.

I snort and continue to the driver's side. At least he knows better than to get in my way. My legs propel me, even though my head is spinning. It's like that night at Billie's. I just need to get away. And my new horse needs a blanket. I start the truck and pull out of the driveway, only sparing Cole a glance as I drive past where he's still standing like a statue in the rain. He looks shocked, and I don't care.

I need some fucking space.

***

Bang. Bang. Bang.

I peel my eyes open and look at my clock. It looks bright out. Ten a.m. I never sleep this long. But then, I hid out at the barn for a while, trying to get my bearings before coming back to the house and hanging with Pippy, who is now privy to some of my deepest, darkest secrets, including the fact that Cole still gets under my skin.

Once I tracked down a small enough rain sheet, I drove back to the farmhouse. With my left foot. It was a short, slow drive, and my left foot worked fine, though it's definitely not something I plan to make a habit of. Sitting on top of the fence in the rain, I stayed with Pippy until I was soaked and cold to the bone. She rested her chin on my lap, like the dog she obviously thinks she is, and let me braid her forelock. The best company I could ask for as I grappled with whatever the hell happened between Cole and me in the rain last night.

I genuinely thought he didn't like me. And I assumed the attraction was one-sided. But the rock-hard bulge in his pants that he pressed against me told another story. I just couldn't reconcile the cool, removed man I know with the person he was last night. None of it makes sense. Laughing, the odd reluctant tip of the lips, and then the way his hands gripped my body. The way I melted for him.

Bang. Bang. Bang.

The noise finally registers. Is that the door? I roll out of bed and strap the walking cast on my leg. I almost feel like I don't need it anymore. The pain is gone, as is most of the swelling, and only the yellow remnants of the bruising remain. After grabbing my robe from the back of the door as I head out into the main living space, I move toward the front door, hoping I don't run into Cole on my way.

When I yank it open a crack, because I don't feel like I'm appropriately dressed to be answering the door, I'm met with Billie standing on the front porch with her palms cupping her eyes like blinders.

"What are you doing?"

"Open the door, Porn Star Patty."

"Ugh." I groan and tip my head back. "It was one picture. One time!"

She pushes the door and shoves herself through frantically, almost tripping in the process. "Holy shit. Let me in already. And close the door!"

"What's going on?" I'm so confused.

"I'm trying not to check out my future brother-in-law. You're going to need to put up some sort of neon sign on the driveway if he's going to waltz around shirtless like that. Smoke signals would be effective too."

Wait. What? It's my turn to almost trip pushing past her, but I'm going in the opposite direction—back out the door. And holy *hell.* She's not joking. I swallow hard and feel my mouth go dry.

Cole is just outside Pippy's paddock, unloading lumber and setting up sawhorses, and he is gloriously shirtless. His body ripples in the bright sunlight. No rain today; instead, it feels hot, damp, and muggy. Apparently, Cole is a "sun's out, guns out" kind of guy. And irritated as I am with myself for last night, I'm not about to complain.

"Like… couldn't he just put some shorts on and call it a day? A glass of cold water does wonders to cool a person down."

I look over my shoulder to see Billie leaning against the wide-open doorway. "I thought you weren't looking."

"I'm engaged to the love of my life, not blind."

I laugh. That's so Billie. Turning away from the mouthwatering masterpiece on the front lawn, I usher her back into the house.

"What do you think he's doing out there?" she inquires, now moving to watch out the front window.

I roll my eyes as I head to the kitchen. "You're such a perv, B."

"I know." Her eyebrows waggle as she walks to the kitchen island and starts making coffee like she lives here too. "Go get dressed. I'll make some coffee. I don't know what kind of internet-sex-nudist commune you two are starting, but I'm not here for it."

I look down at myself. "I'm wearing a robe."

"What's underneath?" she asks before she hits the coffee grinder, effectively cutting me off.

Okay. She has a point. I turn and walk to my room. Cutoffs and a T-shirt so old and broken in that it's almost see-through are my picks. Perfect for a lazy Sunday. All I have planned today is spoiling Pippy and practicing some basic groundwork with her.

By the time I've brushed my hair and teeth and twisted my hair up into a bun, Billie has a cup of coffee ready for me on the counter.

"Okay." I slide up onto a stool and wrap my hands around the old clay-work mug. "Why are you here banging on my door and absolutely not checking out your fiancé's brother?"

Before she can answer, the front door swings open again. "Can we have our coffee on the front porch?" Mira, our veterinarian and the other member of the girl squad, waltzes in like she owns the place.

"We just came to visit our favorite little Por—"

"Billie," I warn, widening my eyes at her and knowing exactly which new nickname she's going for. Not that I wouldn't tell Mira. I mean, she probably would have been a better choice to confide in anyway. Cool and collected, the woman is almost impossible to get a read on. It took me a while to figure out that she's actually nice. It's just hard to tell with Mira. She keeps her cards close. So yeah, I should have told her instead.

"Oh, Vi. You should see the pictures I send Vaughn."

I clamp my eyes shut and let out a dramatic sob. "Billie!"

Mira, all shiny black hair and intelligent almond-shaped eyes with a smirk on her face, raises one shapely brow without inquiring and pours herself a cup of coffee before changing the subject completely. "How's Pipsqueak, Vi?"

I sigh, and I'm sure hearts pop up in my eyes. "So good. The best. Exactly what I needed." I shoot my gaze up to Billie and quietly add, "Thank you."

Her hand lands on my shoulder, and she gives it a firm squeeze. "Don't mention it." Billie seems like she's joking around all the time, but you'd be a fool to underestimate the size of her heart. She knew exactly what she was doing when she trailered that filly over here for me.

"When you get her going, let me come check her out a couple of times. Just make sure she's doing all right. No soreness or breathing issues."

I nod and sip my coffee, watching Mira meander over to the front window again.

"Come to the races tonight. You need to get out. Leave the farm. See some humans, not just the cyborg you live with."

"He's not so bad," I snap, a little more defensively than I intended.

Billie rears back a little, letting the corners of her lips tip up as she silently mouths *Okay* before adding, "That's good, because you'll have to catch a ride with him. Mira and I are heading down there for the early races right after this little visit."

I glance down at my coffee cup, trying to hide the pink stain I feel spreading across my cheeks. I hate how easily I blush; it's so blatant. I can't pull a fast one on anybody because I blush like a teenager at the drop of a hat.

"I think he's…"

I look over at Mira's form as her head tips to one side.

"Building your horse a shelter?"

"What?" I almost shout. "No chance." But I also don't want to go look. If she's right, it will confuse me even more about where I stand with Cole Harding.

Billie hustles over to the window, peering out beside Mira. They look like two snoopy old women watching the hot pool boy.

"He is! He's right in the paddock. Vi, come look."

All my joints lock up as I try to wrap my head around what they're saying. There's just no way. Cole hates horses. He wouldn't do that for Pippy. He couldn't even understand why I wanted to get her a blanket last night. Why would he go get wood and spend his spare time building her a shelter?

"Oh. He sees us."

"How can you tell?" Mira asks, neither of them looking away. No shame.

"See?" Billie points out the window. "He's scowling at us."

"Huh. I wasn't looking at his face, I guess." Mira waves at him, like this is perfectly normal.

I groan. "You guys. Time to go. Out!" I march over to the front door and swing it open.

They don't argue; Billie cackles, and Mira winks at me knowingly. *Mothereffer.* They're both totally onto me.

"See you tonight?" Billie asks as she pulls me into a bear hug.

"Yeah, yeah. I'll be there," I reply as they file out like little kids in trouble.

Billie keeps her head down as she heads back to her truck, but Mira gives Cole a long and thorough once-over before grinning at me over her shoulder and giving me a discreet thumbs-up.

I roll my eyes and blush all at once.

As they both pull out, I finally spare Cole a glance from where I stand on the front porch and feel my heart stutter as I watch him duck between the fence posts with a drill in his hand. He's like every construction worker porno I've ever watched rolled into the perfect package. And the fact that

Pippy is following him around happily is just the cherry on top. When he stops to look down at the setting on the drill, the little filly wraps her neck around his side and sniffs the tool.

He gives her an absent scratch under her chin, and I almost implode. Hot guy with a horse? It doesn't get better. He walks over to the boards, and she follows on his heels, observing, like she might learn how to make a shelter if she focuses.

"What're you doing, girl?" he grumbles as he reaches down, and I can't help the quiet swooning sound that bursts out of my throat.

Not quiet enough though. Because Pippy hears.

Her head shoots up, and she bobs her head in my direction with an ear-piercing whinny. *Little traitor.* Her signature hello just threw me right under the bus because Cole stands up, looks over his brawny shoulder, and pins me with those gray eyes.

"Hi!" I shout a little too brightly, not knowing what the normal thing to do here is. I've had the odd relationship over the years. More since leaving my overbearing dad and brothers behind, but nothing with the intensity of whatever this is. Whatever last night was. Nothing where I feel like a mere look from the man might make me burst into flames.

"Hey," he says a little cautiously.

My inclination is to run and hide back inside the house. But that's not the new me; that's not how adults handle this kind of situation. *Fake it till I make it.*

I force myself to walk toward him and try even harder to keep my eyes from roaming his body. I mean *seriously.* The guy is ripped, so it's hard not to stare. I guess that's what working out multiple times a day gets you.

When I get to the fence, I rest my arms against it. "What are you doing?"

One hand on his hip, he holds the drill up to me like I've just asked the most obvious question in the world. "Building a shelter."

My brow wrinkles as I hear him confirm what Billie and Mira guessed. "I thought you hated horses?"

"I don't hate horses."

Pippy snorts and bats her eyelashes at him. Another one down, apparently.

"Okay. You said you don't *like* horses."

"Yup." He grunts as he turns his back on me and crouches down to line up two boards. "But I like you."

And then he silently gets to work while I stand there watching him. Dumbstruck.

CHAPTER 13

Violet

Golddigger85: Like a full-blown cattle ranch? You're a farm girl?

I'm lying on my bed, in pajamas, chatting. As usual. I just told Butterface that I grew up on an honest-to-God ranch, and he seems horrified.

Pretty_in_Purple: Cowboys, lassos, and rodeo, baby.
Golddigger85: What about whips?
Pretty_in_Purple: More of a spurs and chaps kinda gal.
Golddigger85: Jesus. You should be careful talking like that.

My cheek twitches. If he can say suggestive things, I don't see why I can't do the same.

Pretty_in_Purple: Why is that?

Golddigger85: I have a vivid imagination.

I nibble at my lip and consider my next move. He's in a good mood. I think he's even flirting with me. It makes my chest feel all fluttery.

I laugh and look up at the ceiling. Sad, Violet. I've got that new-love-interest, giddy feeling over a stranger on the internet. I'm too old for this. I know better.

Pretty_in_Purple: Tell me more.

Oh god. I shouldn't have said that. I roll up onto my knees and stare down at my phone screen like I'm waiting for big news when really, I'm just watching those dots roll across the screen as he types. I wonder if he's lying on his bed doing the same thing as me.

Golddigger85: Turn on your camera, and I'll tell you in detail.

Jesus. My finger hovers over that little video camera icon. What would it be like to just throw caution to the wind and do it? Could I handle it? I don't know anymore.

Pretty_in_Purple: No chance, Butterface.

My response sounds resolute. But I'm feeling anything but. I'm confused. Tempted. Horny. Instead of giving in, I pull my favorite toy out of my bedside table and pretend I said yes.

I look around the expansive owner's lounge at Bell Point Park. As a farm girl from Alberta turned groom turned brand-new jockey, this isn't somewhere I've been privy to until now. Usually, I'm covered in horse manure and sweat down in the stables. And to be honest, I think I prefer that.

I put on my nicest dress, and I still feel like I'm out of place. One ballet flat, one walking cast, and a pretty, flowy floral dress that's perfect for a hot day and maybe less so for the amount of icy air-conditioning pumping into this room.

"Here." Cole comes to stand beside me by the tall windows and holds out a drink with an umbrella in it. I don't miss the way his cheek twitches when I look up at him.

Now we're joking around? Cole Harding gives me whiplash. Cold and agitated. Hot and handsy. Friendly and joking. How many versions are there? And why do I like them all?

"Cheers," I say with a small chuckle as I take the drink and clink it against his glass of water.

I have no clue where we stand right now. I spent all afternoon grooming Pippy in the sun. Practicing picking up her feet. Throwing brushes over her back so she gets used to seeing something out of the corner of her eye when I eventually swing a leg over instead. It's probably time for me to get some tack down at the house so I can mess around with trying the saddle and bridle on her. Because she is downright unflappable. Everything is just a fun game for her. Nothing startles her. Even Cole, drilling and hammering away on her shiny new shelter all day, didn't bother her.

In fact, she often went over there to check out her new digs and to give his elbow a little nuzzle. And I pretended not to see when he'd swipe a wide gentle palm over her forehead.

Doesn't like horses, *my ass.*

I have yet to meet a better judge of character than a horse, and Pippy wouldn't be hanging around him if he gave off that vibe. As much as I hate to admit it, she might even like him more than me.

Or maybe he just needs her more than I do.

A thought that makes my chest ache.

"Do you usually watch from up here?" I ask, trying to make conversation and fill the awkward void between us.

I sneak a look up at him. The bump of his Adam's apple bobs in his throat as he opens his mouth to answer me without returning eye contact.

"I don't—"

And then I see a perfectly manicured hand slide over the shoulder of his suit jacket.

"Cole." A woman's light feminine voice comes from the opposite side of him as she pulls into view, standing just a little too close to be a passing acquaintance. She's petite, like me, but that's where our similarities end. She's dripping in expensive jewelry, and her perfectly painted red lips are a match for her sleek hair. "Long time no see."

Cole shifts toward her, essentially blocking me out of the conversation by covering my body protectively with the bulk of his. "Hilary."

I can tell by the way he's holding himself—shoulders rolled back, neck held high, chin tipped up proudly—that all traces of the humor from before have dried up almost instantly in this woman's presence. Over the past few weeks, I've been privy to what Cole looks like happy and relaxed.

And this ain't it.

His knuckles are white around the glass in his hand, and I see his opposite one clenched into a fist at his side. His tells may not be as blatant as my flaming face or bulging eyes, but this is what Cole looks like when he needs rescuing. I can see that he's struggling, and suddenly I'm feeling very protective of him. I put my drink down on the table beside us as I step around his broad frame. My hand slides over his fist, and I push my fingers between his tense ones. They both look down at me, equally surprised by my appearance. But where Hilary looks irritated, I feel Cole's hand soften in my own and hear the breath that rushes out between his lips in relief.

"Hi. I'm Violet."

She stretches one hand toward me politely with a fake smile plastered on her face. "Violet. I've never heard of you before. But what a pretty name. I'm Hilary."

I almost snort, because I've spent enough time around my brother's past girlfriends to know fake nice when I see it. To know words laced with venom when I hear them. Hilary isn't fooling anyone with her polite act, and I know she's not fooling Cole by the way his hand pulses around mine.

I return her false tittering laugh with one of my own. "Well, that's too funny because I've heard *so* much about you!" I haven't, but my guess works.

Her face clamps down almost instantly as her eyes shoot up to Cole, seeking some sort of invite to stay but not finding any. "Well, it was nice seeing you again. It's been too long."

She rests her hand on his bicep, and I want to rip it off. White-hot jealousy shoots up my throat. Instant nausea. And instant self-loathing. I have absolutely *zero* claim to this man, yet here I am getting my panties in a twist over someone touching his arm with a familiarity I envy. *Pathetic.*

He nods sullenly as she turns and walks back across the room. We both watch her go, hand in hand, my gut churning with a deep sense of dread.

"I need some fresh air," I squeak as I set my sights on the door and dart away. Or as close to darting as I can muster with this damn walking cast. I'm so beyond ready to ditch this thing and get back to my life. My job. My focus. This hiatus is messing with my brain.

I sigh in relief as the stairs out of the godforsaken building come into sight. I need to be down on the ground with the dirt and the noises and the beer-drinking gamblers. I don't belong up there.

One more set of stairs comes into view as I round the corner. Except the exit is not clear. Far from it.

"Fancy meeting you here," Patrick Cassel drawls with a stupid, smug smile on his face.

I recoil but jut my chin out and keep walking, deciding the best way to handle a child is to ignore their attention-seeking behavior.

"Shame about the cast."

"Mm-hmm," I say, keeping my eyes peeled on the door ahead, on the bright white sunshine pouring into the dark landing, shining like a beacon on where I can get away from both Cole and Patrick.

But then his arm shoots out in front of me as he grabs the railing at the base of the stairs to block my forward motion.

"Trying to leave so quickly?"

"Move your arm, Patrick." I glare back at his manicured features and too-thin lips made especially ugly by the snide look on his face.

"Most new girls on the scene would bend over backward to have my attention. Forward too." He winks, and my skin crawls.

I know that this kind of shit happens behind the scenes. The sex. The drugs. The drama. And it's part of why I prefer hiding out in Ruby Creek on the ranch. I don't want to be down at the track every day catching whatever ride I can with whatever trainer I can. I *like* my bubble.

"Move. Your. Arm."

"You might enjoy yourself, and I might give you a little more space the next time I pass you out there."

My throat goes hot with rage. It's one thing to think he cut me off on purpose, but to hear him confirm it is something else entirely.

But a dangerous voice takes over my train of thought from behind me. "Nobody enjoys fucking you, Patrick. Now move your arm before I remove it completely."

I turn my head to look over my shoulder and find Cole standing at the top of the stairs like some sort of dark avenging angel. He often looks grumpy, but right now, he looks downright deadly. All those years in the military have scored every hard line in the body that stands over us. He looks relaxed. *Too* relaxed. Like this is an easy default mode for him. And Patrick, idiot that he is, doesn't pick up on the danger at all.

He *laughs*. "Harding Senior. Nice to see ya, buddy."

I don't even spare Patrick a glance, mostly because I can't tear my eyes off Cole. He looks like he could tear the other jockey limb from limb, and I'm alarmingly turned on by the prospect. I know they know each other from some intertwined family business, and Cole had him ride DD at his debut race, which went poorly. I also know Cole is not looking back at Patrick like they're friends.

"We're not buddies," Cole bites out. "You're a slimy little fuck who I would love nothing more than to set straight. If you think that episode with the whip hurt, you have no clue what you're in for. What I'm trained to do."

Patrick, who is clearly missing some sort of survival instinct, scoffs at him. "Dude. You're not seriously worried about this barn brat, are you? Our little conversation is just part of how things run around here. There are loopholes to working your way up in the world. Violet just needs to learn them."

"Touch her, and I'll kill you." Cole's voice is downright arctic.

Patrick just smirks in the face of the threat. He steps right up to me and defiantly places his spare hand on my shoulder. Like I'm too simple to understand his implication—like it's perfectly normal to talk about another person like they aren't even there. Like touching a woman without her permission is acceptable.

From the corner of my eye, I see Cole spring into motion, but not before uncontrollable fury lances through me. My season is in the toilet thanks to this sleazebag, and the realization makes me snap. I do to Patrick exactly what I'd have done to one of my shithead brothers when they picked on me too much.

I knee him right between the legs. Hard. And then stand back to watch him double over in pain.

"Serves him right," Cole says from behind me, surprise lacing his tone.

His hand lands on my shoulder, but I shrug it off. I don't want anyone touching me right now. I feel angry and scared and like I just narrowly missed what could have been a very scary encounter.

"Are you okay?"

I press my shaking hand against my chest to feel my heart racing there, to feel my ribs heave as I struggle to catch my breath.

"Let me help you."

His voice is soft, but I don't want this side of him. I don't want to be coddled. Especially not by him. It makes me feel things I shouldn't. And Patrick? I want to get as far away from him as possible.

"I'm good." I take that final step onto the landing, striding around a groaning Patrick, desperate to get out that door and away from whatever that was.

The worst part is, deep down, I want Cole to follow me.

CHAPTER 14

Cole

I'M WAY TOO ATTACHED TO PRETTY_IN_PURPLE. IT'S BEYOND MY COMprehension. A fucking internet pen pal. And I live for her messages.

Some nights, we type back and forth until I drift off with my phone in my hands. I wake up clinging to the device like it's a fucking lifeline. Maybe it is. Maybe she is.

Maybe that's why I check our chat first thing every morning, hoping she'll have written to me. Anything, even just an emoji from her, is enough to start my day off right.

I thought jerking off to girls on the internet made me pathetic. So what does getting attached to one make me? I only have that one photo of her saved. I should be tired of jacking off to it by now.

But I'm not.

And beyond that, I imagine meeting her in real life. I imagine holding her, whispering my deepest, darkest secrets into her ear and then feeling her arms wrap around me as I slide inside her.

It's gone beyond wanting to fuck her to… whatever that would be. I've gone so far as wondering if she's with someone in real life.

So fucking pathetic. Of course she is! She's sweet and she's beautiful—what guy in his right mind wouldn't want that? But it doesn't stop me from sending a message asking her.

Golddigger85: Any lucky guys in your life these days?

She takes a long time to respond. It's the middle of the day. I know she's working. I'm supposed to be working too. But here I am, obsessing over a random internet girl. Agitation builds inside me, something I take out on a few low-level employees like a total dick. Like a kid who can't control his emotions.

When my phone finally pings a few hours later, a deep sigh surges out of me. I flop down in my leather office chair and lean back as I pull my phone out of my suit pocket.

Pretty_in_Purple: Only one.

My brows squeeze together, and my forearms go tight. I knew it.

Golddigger85: Does he know about me?
Pretty_in_Purple: I don't know. Does he?

I rear back as I do some mental gymnastics to figure out what she's just implied. My chest puffs up a bit over a girl I've never met and never will.

Does she mean me?

★★★

I have no idea where Violet went. All I know is that I got a text saying she had a ride back to the farm. But she's still not here. So I'm just sitting on the porch step, nursing another tumbler of scotch, with the brown horse staring back at me like I owe her something. Attention, food, who knows. It's getting unnerving.

I can't believe I'm letting a fucking horse make me feel bad.

As if I don't already feel bad enough. I wanted to follow Violet when she took off, and I started out that way until I saw she was heading straight for the track—not for the stables. Then I pussied out.

The track is such a dichotomy for me. The place that holds all my best and worst memories. On one hand, I grew up there. My dad was a popular and successful jockey at Bell Point Park. We spent a lot of time there together. On the other hand, I watched him die on that track.

The booth up top is the perfect compromise. Trixie's idea—exposure therapy. A removed view, no sound of pounding hooves, no crackling loudspeaker, none of the triggers that take me straight back to that day. Never mind the war, *that* day is my tipping point.

I know Violet doesn't want anyone taking care of her, but goddammit, I wanted to. I wanted to grind Patrick to a pulp and then whisk Violet as far from him as possible. The sight of his hand on her shoulder made me see red.

I shake my head.

I almost combusted on the spot. I almost turned into the soldier that I haven't been in six years now.

Which is exactly why Violet is a weakness I can't afford. I've worked too hard to combat my outbursts and my down days, the ones where I can't even muster the energy to smile. Against all my best instincts, even when I know I'm nothing but a hot mess where she's concerned, I wanted to be there for her.

To chase her down and fix things for her. Which is a terrible idea. Colossally stupid.

And exactly what she doesn't want.

I want to call Trixie, but it's too late to be doing that. I hang my head in my hands and mutter to myself, "Good work, Harding."

The horse nickers from across the driveway and bobs her head at me with a long blink of her thick lashes. I can't help but chuckle. She is relentless. No quit in that one. I leave the tumbler on the deck and walk across to the fence where the horse is waiting.

She's kind of hard not to like. Her ears prick forward at my approach, and her head rises just a little taller in excitement. I swear if she had the right kind of tail, she'd be wagging it.

"Hey, girl," I whisper, running my hand down her neck and feeling the heat of her exhale against my stomach as she nuzzles in.

She's the first horse I've touched since my dad died. I've barely allowed myself to admit this, but it feels good. Therapeutic maybe. The soft prickle of her coat under my fingers… I wonder if I'm having the same tactile experience that my dad might have had when he was still alive. If I'm feeling the same thing as he did once.

Her excited whinny every time I pull up to the house almost makes me smile, and the way she followed me around quietly while I worked out here earlier made me feel… I don't know. Worthy of attention.

Like maybe I could be likable after all.

I walk down to the corner of her paddock where there is a stack of square hay bales under a blue tarp, and she follows.

Lifting a corner of the tarp, I pull a flake off the top bale and inhale the dusty, grassy smell as I carry it back over to her feeder.

The hay is all over my suit, but I don't care. Material shit hasn't mattered to me in years. I guess that's why I live in a small and dated condo in a four-story walk-up in Vancouver's West End neighborhood. It's a clean place to lay my head at night while I go through the motions of my day-to-day schedule. My days of feeding into my mother's elite lifestyle died along with my engagement to Hilary.

I'm leaning against the fence, listening to the horse's contented munching, lost in a memory, when lights turn down the driveway. I recognize Billie's truck, but it's too dark to see inside.

Violet jumps out and lands on one foot, obviously not wanting help to get out anymore after I dry humped the hell out of her last night.

I cringe internally at the memory. Thirty-six going on sixteen, apparently. Next thing I know, I'll be asking her to play just-the-tip.

Which is a terrible plan. Because like I told her, I like her—and I shouldn't. I like her as more than a friend, and that's all we can be. I haven't touched a woman in years, never mind had one touching me. I haven't let anyone get close enough. It feels insurmountable now. Pathetic as it sounds.

But after two weeks in the same house as Violet, it's all I can fucking think about.

"Hi," she says shyly as she walks over to me. "What are you doing out here?"

"Just feeding the horse."

Her head tilts imperceptibly. "I fed her before we left."

The brown horse's black globes for eyes flit up momentarily like she knows I'm a sucker for giving her more. Then she gets back to grinding her teeth and shoving the hay around. She looks happy, so who cares?

I just grunt and continue to stare at the little horse, expecting Violet to leave. Instead, she comes closer to the fence, a full post length away from me, and leans against it. I can feel her gaze on me, like hands roaming over my body—soft and searching.

I don't want to look back at her. To see that pale blond hair shining in the moonlight, those wide indigo eyes boring into me, so full of unasked questions. I don't want to think about Patrick's hands on her, the way he cornered her, the things he said to her. He deserved the extra twist I gave his arm, the threat I whispered in his ear before I headed back upstairs. He deserved a lot worse than that.

And Violet? She deserves a man better than me. More honest than me. A hell of a lot more available than me. But the more time I spend around her, the less I care and the more I want.

"You sure you don't like horses?" Amusement infuses her tone.

I scoff and keep staring at the brown filly.

"Not even a liiiittle bit?" She holds her thumb and finger up with little distance between them.

My cheek twitches, and I sigh, feeling the tension in my shoulders drain out to nothing. "Okay. If I had to like a horse, it would be this one."

"Ha! I knew it."

I shake my head. She looks far too pleased with herself. I shouldn't give her any more ammunition to run with, so I clear my throat and change the subject. "Are you okay? I didn't know where you went."

The victorious smile on her face melts off, and now it's her turn to look away from me. "Yeah. Just needed some space. I don't know if you noticed," she chuckles sardonically, "but I don't really belong up in the skybox."

What? "Why not?" I ask, genuinely confused.

Her eyes roll as she continues to focus on the horse. "You saw me in there. I'm a different breed, Cole. I'm not a Hilary, and I don't want to be."

"Thank fuck for that," I mutter as I look down between my arms, which rest on the top of the fence. We stand in silence, so much still left unsaid. "I was engaged to Hilary. When I was younger."

Violet's body goes rigid as she turns her entire frame toward me slowly. She says nothing, which I take as her giving me the opportunity to keep talking.

"We dated in high school. Our families ran in the same circles. It was… easy. It made sense to me. And then my dad died, and nothing made sense anymore."

I chance a look at Violet, who is standing stock-still, like I'm a wild animal she might spook if she moves or says anything. And it must work because my lips keep moving.

"I proposed, and she said yes. Everyone was happy. And then I enlisted, and everyone was distinctly *not* happy. But I didn't care. I needed to live in another world for a while. So I left. We'd write to each other and see each other when I was home, but… well, let's just say distance didn't make the heart grow fonder. And one tour turned into one more, which turned into one more. And I kept putting off the actual wedding. I always wonder if maybe I knew subconsciously that she was a bad idea. That she loved the image of me more than anything else…" I trail off thoughtfully, looking down again. Another age-old wound that still causes phantom pains. I press the heel of my hand in against the indent just below my thigh, something I've found that helps when the burning sensation strikes.

"At any rate, when I finally came back for good, I wasn't the shiny perfect husband she hoped to have anymore. So that was that."

"Because you came back with PTSD?" Violet's voice is brittle, a current of anger lacing it.

I scoff as I stare back at her. "Who doesn't? But nah, I'm sure I was grappling with that before I even enlisted. Apparently, watching a parent die as a teenager can do that to you. Or that's what my therapist keeps telling me. I guess I'm double fucked up."

She rolls her lips together, searching for the words, and settles for moving closer to me and resting her arms exactly as mine are.

Her forearm is so petite next to mine. She elbows me gently, not a shred of pity in her tone. "I think we're all a little fucked up in our own way."

I just hum my agreement. She's not wrong.

"I mean, you're clearly *a lot* more fucked up than I am, but…"

My eyebrow quirks up at her, the small smile playing across her face right now making me join her with a grin of my own.

"Okay, Pretty in Purple."

She groans dramatically and drops her head. "Am I ever going to live that down?"

"Probably not," I chuckle.

"You know I've spent the last year terrified you'd tell someone or out me somehow? Fire me even."

All traces of humor drain from my body. "Why would you think that?" I ask, standing up straight. "I'm the one who should be embarrassed."

She still doesn't look up at me. "You just seemed so angry when you approached me that day at the derby." Her tongue darts out over her bottom lip. "You're like... my boss's boss. I just didn't know what it all meant. I still don't."

Irritation courses through me, not with her—with myself. "Violet, look at me."

She peeks up at me from beneath the dark fringe of her lashes.

"No. Stand up and look at me."

She does it almost instantly, and the depraved part of me gets off on it. I'm transported to that night when she did everything I told her to. Even when it made her cheeks go bright pink. My cock twitches, and I berate myself internally. *You're really fucked up, bud.*

She tips her head up and rolls her shoulders back with fake bravado. I can tell she feels vulnerable; it's written all over her face.

"I'm sorry I did that. But you need to understand that I will never, *never* tell anyone. That will forever be between us... and apparently Billie and Vaughn."

She winces visibly at that part.

"I'm not angry with you. I'm angry with myself."

"Why?" she asks, pure confusion on her face.

"I don't even know where to start with that question. It feels like I've been furious for a very long time at nothing in particular. And definitely not with you."

Did it hurt when she disappeared from our chats? More than I ever imagined. But could I blame her? No. Wanting me would be like choosing a vial of poison to quench your thirst. A slow and painful way to get dragged down into the dark. And no one wants that. Not anyone sane. I know I'm damaged goods, which is why I like to keep my relationships at a safe distance. Fenced off. Something Violet wiggled her way under over the course of a year.

I run one hand through my hair and look away, not knowing what else to tell her. What I do know is that I'm tired of lying. Tired of obscuring the truth. Presenting myself as someone I'm not. Tired of hurting the people closest to me—or those who get as close as I let them. The ones who don't scurry off when I growl and bark at them.

She steps in closer to me, tilting her head to catch my eye again, seeking some sort of connection. One I'd rather pretend we don't have. It's less intense that way.

"Why are you angry with yourself?" Her voice is gentle, and her small hand snakes out and latches itself on to mine. Her dainty fingers wrap around my wrist, like she's feeling for my pulse point. The one that's pounding under the pads of her fingers. The one that riots every time she comes near or touches me. The only woman that's touched me like this in… a really fucking long time. The only one I've let get close enough to try.

And maybe it's that. That she's somehow poked and prodded at me enough that she's broken holes into my shell that are big enough for her to slide in and get at all my dark, sensitive spots. Or maybe it's just the fucking scotch. But I decide right here and now she deserves the truth. Even if it makes me feel nauseous to say it out loud.

"Because I scared away the only real friend I've had in—" I scoff. "Well, maybe ever."

Her thumb rubs in reassuring circles on the back of my hand. She's calm, like water lapping at the shore. Gentle and even, continuous, and I can't help but want to lie down in that shallow water and let myself get lost in the rhythm.

Violet soothes me. Even if she might be the most oblivious woman in the world.

"Who is that?" Her eyes are wide and shocked, scanning my face for more information.

I chuckle. Serves me right to say it out loud. "It's you, Violet."

"Me?" Her thumb stops moving, and her lungs empty on a gasp.

"Listen… I'm sorry." I reach out and touch a lock of pale gold hair that has slipped across her cheek.

"You're sorry?"

I groan. "Are you trying to rub this in?"

"No!" One hand falls across her chest in shock. "I just… You considered me your friend?"

Her eyes twinkle in the dark of night. With the light of the moon, everything around her is more of a dark blue than black, deep and sparkling, like the river I can hear faintly running behind the farmhouse. The moon's glow highlights her features in the most alluring way. I should tell her she's so much more. The thing that got me out of bed most mornings. My bright spot. My sunshine.

I run my thumb along the highest point of her cheekbone, watching the way the light plays up the coarseness of my hand against the silkiness of her cheek. Such a contrast between the two of us. Dark and light. Rough and smooth. Big and small.

The things I want to do to her. I shake my head, silently scolding myself for even letting myself go there. She's young, driven, bright—full of promise.

And I'm the opposite in that regard too.

I lean down toward her, hand cupping her lower jaw, and press a gentle kiss beside her mouth. "I still do."

I hear a sharp intake of air from between her lips when I pause there. I want to swallow that noise and taste her mouth. Claim it. I want her to never kiss another man again. But that's not practical. Not realistic.

I'm all about the realities of life. I know them well. And the reality with Violet is that as badly as I want her, I'm not sure I'll ever be able to open up enough to take that chance. Especially not with what she does for a living. The fact of the matter is I've worked too hard on my mental health to put myself through that kind of agony. Falling in love would be bad enough. Falling in love with a jockey would be downright impossible.

***

I gasp and sit straight up in my bed, blankets tangled around my legs like I've been kicking or maybe running. Running from my past, most likely.

I can feel the perspiration soaking the back of my shirt, can feel the strain in my lungs and the burn in my leg. I flop back down and run my hands over my face, scrubbing at the stubble there. Feeling myself so I know that it's real, where I am, that I'm safe. It's been so long since I had a dream like that, one that takes me back overseas. There were so many bad days, so many gruesome ones. But only that one stands out.

I remember the sun. The way it beat down on my dark uniform, the way I'd sweat under my heavy kit. The way you could gasp for air, trying to catch your breath, but all you'd get was hot, stifling oxygen and grains of sand. It would coat your tongue, scrape your throat, and stick in your nostrils.

It fucking sucked. But not so much as dragging your friend's body away from a blast. Checking his pulse, shouting at him to wake up. No, that was the part that sucked the most. That's the part that has my hands shaking right now.

The survivor's guilt. Why him and not me? *Why him and not me?* If I had a penny for every time I've asked myself that exact question, I could probably end world hunger.

A light knocking on the door snaps me out of the memory.

"Cole?" Violet's voice sounds small and uncertain. *What is she doing up here?* "Are you okay?"

"Yeah." My voice cracks uncharacteristically, so I clear my throat, not wanting to sound as choked up as I am right now. "Why?"

"Can I come in?"

My heart pounds hard in my chest, trying to silence my mind. My rules. It's too dark. Too quiet. She's getting too damn close. And my heart wins out. "Yeah. Yeah, sure." I pull my sheets over myself, lifting the duvet to use as an extra layer of coverage.

I see the shape of her as the door creaks open, a dim silhouette of the body that has consumed me for the past two years.

"I heard you shout," she says quietly.

I sigh, giving in just a little bit. I hate sharing this part of myself. This broken part. It's why I like my solitude. I don't need to explain my shit to anyone when I'm alone. "Sorry. I didn't mean to wake you up."

"It's okay," she whispers, taking a few small steps into the room. "Are you all right?"

A sad laugh escapes my lips. "Probably not." Because it's true. Some days are good, some aren't. Mostly they're good now. Lonely, but good… or good enough. But am I all right? I doubt it.

She doesn't press any further. The questions and inquiries don't come. She just says, "Do you want me to stay with you?"

And before my head even catches up to the question, my heart seizes hold of my vocal cords, forcing a raspy "Yes" from my throat.

With no hesitation, her feet pad quietly toward me, and she crawls onto the mattress, lying down on top of the covers a short distance away. I feel her proximity like a tug on a fishing line, like she's latched herself on to me and I can't get free. I could struggle, I could fight it, but she's hooked in. And I'm not even sure I want to get rid of her anymore. I'm not sure I want to hide myself from her anymore.

I'm not sure of anything anymore.

Except that when she reaches out to squeeze my hand, I squeeze back. And that when I wake in the morning after one of the best stretches of sleep in my life, I'm sad that she's already gone.

CHAPTER 15

Violet

Golddigger85: What are you doing?

I SMILE AS I WALK UP THE STEPS TO MY APARTMENT OVER THE BARN. It's been a tiring week. DD had a bout of colic after a bad race, and now Billie and Vaughn are acting super weird around each other. I feel like the kid whose parents are going through a divorce, like I'm tiptoeing around them both. Basically, I'm relieved to be alone in my space for the night.

Pretty_in_Purple: Just getting home now.
Golddigger85: You work too hard. Your boss must be a dick.

I chuckle as I walk in the door.

Pretty_in_Purple: I have great bosses. But I am beat.

I strip off my sweaty, dust-covered clothes. Everyone thinks horse racing sounds so glamorous. They think enormous hats and mint juleps, not wood shavings in your jeans and dirt under your nails.

Golddigger85: Want me to help you relax?

I shake my head as I walk naked to the shower.

Pretty_in_Purple: No, thanks. I've got a hot shower for that. Be back soon.

The response comes out so quickly I don't even have time to put my phone down.

Golddigger85: Are you telling me you're naked right now?

A smile touches my lips. Poor Butterface and his one-track mind.

Pretty_in_Purple: Yes.
Golddigger85: Fuck. Let me see.

I ignore that last message and step into the shower, my mind suddenly fixated on him and his offer. Something that has been taking up more and more space in my head. Something that's becoming more and more tempting with my total lack of consistent sex life stowed away on this farm.

My hands roam my body, slippery with soap, and I let myself imagine that they're the hands of the man I've talked to every day for almost a year. The first person I talk to in the morning and the last one I talk to before bed.

That counts for something, right? I may not know him, but I do feel like I trust him. A tiny voice inside my head yells, "Naive!" *but as one palm slides over my breast and the other trails down between my legs, I feel emboldened.*

And when I get out of the shower, I grab my phone and snap a photo before I can change my mind.

I'm going to kill Cole Harding.

"One more," he barks at me like I'm the one in the army here.

I'll definitely kill him—as soon as my arms stop shaking. And as soon as I stop daydreaming about his lips so close to mine. The scrape of his stubble against my cheek. The sheer power of his body as he towered over me that night a week ago.

That's right. It's been one week since Cole Harding called me his friend and kissed me on the cheek, and I'm a bumbling mess around the man. One week since I crawled into his bed and held his hand in mine like I had a right to. Every touch, every look, every gentle word, it's like a slow-motion reel that won't stop playing through my mind. I'm so far gone, it's not even funny.

Things were awkward before because we left so much unsaid between us, and it's awkward now because I can't stop thinking about banging the guy. Doesn't help that he's been *nice* to me. Like… normal nice. He's still quiet, but he doesn't grumble so much. He's even cooked me dinner most evenings this week. Like he wants to take care of me. He said he was sick of watching me eat mac 'n' cheese. That I'm an athlete, and I need to treat my body like one.

Which is why I'm here, on a yoga mat in the living room, working out with him.

Riding a horse feels natural, but *this* does not. This feels like torture. Double torture because it's obviously physically exhausting, but being this close to him is emotionally exhausting too. Every nerve ending stands at attention. Every time a warm palm lands on my body to position me, goose bumps race out over my arms. My breathing hitches. My stupid cheeks turn pink.

It's like every part of my body is in a competition with the others to out me as a total goner for the surly soldier who is currently nudging my hip bone with the tips of his fingers.

"Don't let your core sag. Your lower back will get sore."

I do the last push-up from my knees before flopping down onto the floor, feeling like a beached whale who's given up on life. Given the choice between moving and death, I choose death. After an entire week of working out with Cole Harding the super soldier? I. Choose. Death.

I hear the rumble of his deep chuckle from above me. "That wasn't so bad, was it?"

"It's been nice knowing you," I reply as I pant into the floor.

He laughs again and drops a palm onto the center of my back, rubbing up and down, his hand catching on the strap of my bra.

"Are you sore?"

"Not if I don't move."

"Dramatic," he grumbles as his hand moves again, fingers pressing in and massaging my aching muscles.

"Oh god, yes," I murmur, resting my chin on my forearms and letting my eyes flutter shut. His hands always feel good on my body, but this? This is ecstasy.

I hear a quiet grunt, but he keeps massaging me. His fingers move to the right places every time. Like he knows exactly which spots to hit.

"Where are you sore?" His voice is thick. It sends a chill down my spine.

"Everywhere."

"Violet."

He cups one of my elbows and flips me over so I'm flat on my back and forced to look up at him where he kneels beside my vulnerable form. I stare at his broad shoulders and biceps filling out his T-shirt in a way that just isn't fair. At his throat, which bobs as he swallows and looks down at me. At his eyes, which are locked on me like I might be his last meal.

Am I imagining the look on his face? The rise and fall of his chest?

"Where are you sore?" he repeats his question.

Transfixed by the sight of him kneeling over me, oozing raw masculine power, I lick my lips. It's like a shot to my core. What I wouldn't give to watch Cole Harding move above me with *that* look on his face.

"My neck and shoulders," I squeak out, trying to play it cool and failing miserably.

He leans over me, the sheer width of him casting a shadow over my body as his hands slide across my collarbones and rub at my shoulders, digging in so hard that it almost hurts, an ache that blooms into a burn that blooms into pure consuming heat.

I close my eyes, not wanting to watch him anymore. Not wanting to see the harsh look on his face though I can still smell him. That faint clove scent mingling with my perspiration and baby powder deodorant. The whoosh of his exhale feels like a cool breeze across my dampened sternum. My yoga shorts and tank top suddenly feel sticky and altogether too tight against my body, like they're constricting around me and stealing my breath.

I try not to focus on the caress of his hands on my bare skin, the flutter of his fingertips, the overwhelming press of his body looming over mine. But I can't. Even closing my eyes isn't working. He's *everywhere*, smothering me, weighing me down. It's like I'm suddenly being suffocated by him.

I can't breathe around him.

"Okay, that's enough!" I push up onto my elbows, breathing hard. "I can't do this anymore," I say as I look down over my body, noting the way my nipples have pebbled through my unpadded sports bra.

His eyes follow mine, those gray irises going molten as they scour their way down and land on my breasts. They momentarily flick back up to my lips, causing my tongue to dart out nervously. Any words I could say die in my throat as I peer up at the man I've fantasized about for two years, who is currently looking at me like he might have the same fantasy.

"Violet."

"Yeah?" My voice is weak, breathy.

Cole leans closer, inhaling deeply as his mouth hovers near my throat. "Tell me you don't want me to touch you."

My heart stops. Lurches. Freezes. I look up into his eyes, so full of uncertainty and longing. So tortured. So *pained.*

I search his face, looking for some clue as to what he really wants me to do here. A hint, a tell, *something*. But that military training is shining through, so I opt for the truth. "I'm not a very good liar."

A strangled growl tears free from his chest, right as his head drops down onto my body. I feel the tip of his tongue trail up the center of my sternum, sending a jolt of electricity straight to my core. My vision goes fuzzy, and my head spins. I fall back flat on the mat. *Is this really happening right now?*

Cole devours me like a man starved—like an expert. His lips dust kisses over each collarbone as the tips of his teeth scrape against my skin, followed by a soothing swipe of his tongue.

"Tell me to stop." His voice vibrates across my skin, spraying goose bumps out in its wake.

I whimper and run my hands through his thick hair, wanting to keep him close. Wanting him to keep going and never stop. "Cole…" I trail one trembling hand down over his neck, fisting his T-shirt at the shoulder and pulling him in.

He slides his hand up to cup the base of my skull as his thumb presses softly to the very top of my throat, holding me like it's his right. His body looms over mine, mouth moving up toward the hand that grips me. He nips gently just beneath my ear, and I arch up into him, my back coming up off the ground, my nipples rasping across his hard chest, wishing he was lying right over me so that I could grind up into his length again.

"Tell me," he whispers into my ear.

"Don't stop" is my pleading reply.

His teeth trail across the line of my jaw, his lips hovering close to mine. So, so close. I can't tear my eyes from them. I want to watch this all and commit it to memory.

"What are you doing to me?"

I can feel his breath on my lips, smell the mint on his breath. I want to taste it too.

It seems rich, him saying that, when there hasn't been a day in the last two years when I haven't thought of him. When my fingers haven't itched to log in to our chat and ask him an innocuous question or beg him to give me another one of those mind-altering orgasms.

I've *missed* Cole, and I've only dreamt of this. His lips on me, his hands roaming freely, while I turn to putty beneath him. I want so much more.

"We need to stop."

My eyes flash open as his mouth hovers just over mine, soaking up words that make little sense. Inches apart. So close and yet so far away. He pulls up and sits back on his heels, panting. His hands shake with the strain of holding himself back as he scrubs them across his face.

"Okay," I huff out. "Why?"

"Because I don't do this."

I'm breathing like I just ran a hundred-meter dash. "Do what?"

"Physical contact. Relationships. Any of it."

My eyebrows knit together. "Like… at all? Ever?"

"Not for… a long time. Years." He trails off as he stands, and the enormity of his confession hits me like a wrecking ball. *Years?* "Not since…"

He doesn't need to finish that sentence. I already know he means since Hilary. My throat burns with jealousy. Sad, pathetic jealousy. Such a wasteful and pointless emotion.

"I'm sorry," he adds as he turns to walk away stiffly toward the kitchen.

I stay here on the mat, trying to get my bearings and figure out what the hell just happened. He didn't seem hung up enough on Hilary to be pining for her to this extent. In fact, he didn't seem to like her at all. But… *years?*

What the hell am I missing?

My cast is finally off. The follow up X-rays were all clear, and the first thing I did after getting that go-ahead was march over to Billie's house and get on DD.

I wanted to gallop.

To feel the wind against my cheeks and have my shirt billow out behind me as I hunch down over a horse's back. To let the rhythm of his hooves and strong legs move beneath me like the drumbeat that gets stuck in your head. The beat I've been marching to since I was a little girl.

I've been good. Rule abiding. I stayed off the horses, even though I didn't want to. God knows there are plenty of riders out there who wouldn't have. Without Billie and Cole in my face, I probably wouldn't have either.

So I went out for a breeze around the practice track. And now I can't stop grinning. Or wanting to ride. I would get on every horse in that barn all night long if I could. Who cares about Cole Harding licking my chest when there are horses to ride? Who cares about the brush of his stubble or the sound of his ragged breath? Who cares about the fact that I let my hands wander in the shower while I recalled it?

Not. Me.

Now I have a *good* reason to avoid him. I can officially move back into my apartment. I can drive again. With my doctor's blessing that is. My first race back is in a couple of days. I can finally get my career back on track and stop obsessing over a man who is complicated beyond what I'm equipped to handle.

He's not my project; Pippy is. And I'm determined to get ahead with her as well. I pull my old Volkswagen Golf up to the farmhouse, feeling light for the first time in weeks. Like I have direction. That's what horses are for me. Purpose. There's no finish line. It's never good enough. There's always more. After each line I cross, I just want to keep pushing harder toward the next one, the next horse, the next win. It's *consuming*.

When I step out of the car, Pippy—sweet thing that she is—whinnies her hello at me. I pull my favorite saddle out of the back seat and walk to her fence, slinging it over the top board to rest.

"Hey, sweet girl," I murmur as she speed walks toward me, her dainty little head swinging with each enthusiastic step.

Once she's close enough, I glide my hands over her cheekbones, one on each side, and plant a big loud kiss on the tip of her nose. Her soft lips flap around near my neck as she does whatever this is. With most horses, I'd think this might lead to a quick nibble, but not Pippy. With her, it almost seems like a gentle kiss.

"You're a little weirdo, you know that?" I run my hand down her neck to give her withers a quick scratch, right at the base of her mane. She stretches her neck out and twists her head, enjoyment written all over her. "That's the spot, huh?"

I chuckle at how expressive she is. And as I stand back and take her in, I can't help but notice how different she's looking in just a few weeks. She's shed her spring coat and, as I suspected, is getting that bronze shimmer her coloring lends itself to. I've pulled her mane to a perfect straight line down her neck, and she has her first pair of horseshoes on. The farrier fascinated her. All the smoke, all the noises—none of it fazed her.

I can't tell if she's goofy or just totally bombproof. She might not have the regular competitive edge we look for in a racehorse, that eye-of-the-tiger vibe. But only time will tell.

Maybe she's smarter than I'm giving her credit for. Maybe she's an evil genius. After all, she brought Cole around. He thinks he's playing it cool, but I've seen him. I don't know what kind of special operator he was, but I think he's out of practice because I haven't missed that he throws her a couple flakes of hay every morning before doing some sort of jail yard workout in the driveway with tires and bricks.

I know he keeps a bag of carrots in his truck and gives her one after work every day. It's no wonder she practically runs to the gate when he pulls up. I've even spied him late at night, leaned up against her fence, holding a rubber feed tub full of the omega-3-rich feed I've been giving her, stroking her forelock while she chows down.

Basically, the man who swore he doesn't like horses—and who said he wanted nothing to do with Pippy—is feeding her three times a day. And try as I might to not find it endearing, I do. *God*, I really do. It makes my chest pinch and my core throb. That little bay filly has softened him up, and I'd be lying if it didn't almost make me jealous.

Things have been *awkward* since our last workout. Friendly but strained. Bordering on sad. The way he looks at me, talks to me… it's different.

I shake my head. I've never been boy crazy. Horse crazy, yes. But boy crazy? Nah. And I will not start now. Especially not with one so impossible to break through to.

I turn to grab the saddle and look at her. "What do you say, Pippy? You ready to take your maiden voyage?"

I swear she bobs her head in response, and I roll my eyes as I get to tacking her up. She's been the easiest horse I've ever started so far. Even at home in Chestnut Springs as a kid, I worked with young horses on my family's ranch, and not a single horse has *ever* been as easy as Pippy.

I cinch the girth, and she stands happily in place. She's not even tied up. Plenty of horses would walk away, but not her.

I've spent the last several days lying across her back with my stomach on the saddle so I could easily slide down if things went sideways. But she hasn't flinched. I think I even noticed her eyes flutter shut one time when I stayed there a bit longer, just to see what she'd do.

Fall asleep is apparently it.

So here I am, sliding the metal bit into her mouth—another thing that didn't faze her at all—ready to get on an unbroken two-year-old with a freshly healed leg and no one here to help. At the back of my mind, I know it's not the smartest idea, but it feels right. It feels like my moment to revel in freedom.

The sun is setting, the birds are chirping, and the cool mineral breeze off the river feels refreshing after an unseasonably hot day. I realize I'm happy. Happier than I've been in a long time. I have the perfect amount of distance from my dad and brothers—who I love but were smothering me. I have the job I've always dreamed of. Friends. My independence. My *body*. Something I will never take for granted again. Just being able to walk barefoot is such a gift, such a blessing.

I lift my boot into the iron hanging down Pippy's side, pressing down onto it twice to be sure that she's prepared for me.

And then slowly, so slowly, I lean across her and swing my leg over her back, letting myself sit on the leather seat of the saddle. Her ears flick out to the sides, like a little donkey, and I feel her back go slightly tense as I settle into the seat.

But any tension in her is momentary before she turns her head and neck to nibble at the toes of my leather boots. Right back to her goofy, in-your-pocket persona. Like she's been here and done this before.

Even when the crunching of gravel comes down the driveway, she doesn't startle or spook. Her head flips back toward the noise, and she watches calmly as Cole's black truck pulls up to the house.

When he gets out, wearing a suit with the top two buttons of his shirt undone in the most appealing way, I can't help but admire him. I wish I could crack him open and figure him out. *I really need to get back to my own space.*

Pippy whinnies, loud and shrill, and then walks to the corner of the pen, not at all concerned with my presence on her back. Simply happy to see the big grump who's now walking toward us.

"Hey, pretty girl," he murmurs as he reaches the fence and slides a big palm down her forehead.

I know he's talking to Pippy, but it doesn't stop my stomach from doing a flip. He's like the dad who never wanted the dog but ends up being best friends with it. It's like Pippy knows he didn't want her and proved him wrong. She tried extra hard to endear herself to him. To break through that tough exterior.

And it worked.

He looks up at me now, his eyes glowing and something like wonder on his face. "This is new." His eyes trace down my body, pausing momentarily on my castless right leg. He tips his chin at me in question.

"Got it off today."

"And you're already back up on a horse." It's a statement, not a question, and his voice goes a little chilly.

"Yup. No fracture means no fracture."

"Is this the first time you've been up on her?"

"Yes."

He rolls his shoulders back. "Alone?"

"Yes…" I say, not liking where he's going with this.

"Is that your best plan?"

He had to go there, didn't he? Trying to tell me what to do after I've been perfectly careful and patient for the past month. Now I'm supposed to keep acting like I'm injured when I'm not?

"It's *my plan*. I don't require your approval to get on a horse that I've been put in charge of."

One of Pippy's ears flicks back at me, like she can feel the tension, and then she takes a step closer to Cole, dropping her head over the fence and nudging him.

"Violet."

Agitation courses through me. The way he says my name like I'm a child. *Violet.* Like just huffing my name with that scowl on his face is actually saying something at all.

"No. Don't. Don't *Violet* me. I don't need your permission to do this. I have races this weekend. I'm riding in those too. I have a dad and three overprotective brothers. I don't need another one. You *know* this. So get on board, or get out of my way."

Cole shakes his head at me as he turns stiffly to walk away. I hate that he doesn't say anything.

I hate that I can't provoke a reaction out of him when he does nothing but make me react.

CHAPTER 16

Cole

I BLINK AT THE SCREEN OF MY PHONE AS THOUGH IT MIGHT CHANGE what I'm seeing.

The corner of one long-lashed eye, looking straight up at the camera. Like she might look up at me if she were down on her knees at my feet. Wet blond hair, plastered to small round perfect tits, the valley between them glistening with droplets of water. I imagine one rolling down her body, over her stomach, to the mound between her legs. Getting caught in that small pale patch of hair before dripping right over her clit.

Fuck. What am I supposed to do now? This girl has firmly friend-zoned me for the last year and then drops the sexiest fucking nude I've ever seen. Fresh out of the shower, wet and ready. She took it for me. Without me even paying her. Because she wanted to. And somehow that just hits different.

Golddigger85: Is that an invitation?

Pretty_in_Purple: Yes.

Jesus. My cock twitches, and my pulse thunders in my ears. I swear I look around my condo just to see if someone is going to jump and out and scream about me being punked or something. This whole scenario just seems so fucking unbelievable.

But she didn't send me that picture for me to be a shrinking violet. It's time to play.

Golddigger85: Good. Prop your phone up, swap to video, and kneel on your bed.

The chat is silent for a minute, and I wonder if she's changed her mind as I adjust myself in my pants. Maybe she'll back out. That's fine too. Whatever she wants. But fuck. I hope she wants this. Because I do. To see the real thing rather than imagining her while lying around with my cock in my hand.

Her face fills the screen, and I feel like someone just suctioned all the air out of my lungs and left me on the ground gasping. She's incredible. Fascinating—ethereal almost. Eyes a little too big, cheeks a little too full, chin a little too sharp.

"Hi, Butterface." A small smile touches her mouth, and her cheeks turn the prettiest shade of pink. I love that. She's genuine. She's brave.

She's fucking beautiful. The kind of beauty that makes you stop and stare. The kind of beauty you want to study. I don't draw, but suddenly I'm overcome by the need to sketch her face. Her rosebud mouth. To document her. She's like a porcelain doll.

Yeah. And you're going to fucking shatter her.

I brush my intrusive thoughts aside. I wouldn't. I can be a gentleman. I liked her long before I knew she'd make my heart seize up in my chest. We were friends first.

This is fine.

I turn my microphone on but don't accept the app's request to access my camera. That can never happen. Not only am I probably too recognizable, but I hate the thought of opening myself up again. To be ridiculed and made to feel less than. I won't ever do that again. That took me too low, and I have too much baggage to dip down into that headspace again.

"You are fucking beautiful," I say, hating how gravelly my voice comes out. I sound downright emotional.

She looks away with a quiet "Thank you." Her legs are squeezed together tight, and she holds her arms over her torso like a shield.

"Are you uncomfortable?"

Her eyes roll, and her laugh comes out as a nervous titter before she looks straight into the camera, pinning me with her gaze, crystalline like the water in the tropics. "Of course I am. I've never done this before."

Does it make me a douche for wanting to beat my chest over that? Probably. But I don't care. She hasn't done this with anyone before, but she's doing it with me. My sad, tattered sense of self-worth latches on to that knowledge with a death grip. "What can I do to make it better for you?"

I watch goose bumps rise across her forearms as she rubs her biceps as if that might comfort her. "Turn your camera on." She rolls her lips together, her expression implying that she already knows I'm going to deny her request.

I'm hit with an overwhelming sense of shame that I can't do this for her. The one thing she wants. I just can't. My voice cracks when I admit it to her. "I can't."

One small dip of her chin later, she drops her arms, baring her naked body to me. "Okay. Then talk. You promised me the best orgasm of my life."

My cock jumps again as I watch her mouth make the O *shape that goes with saying* orgasm, *and I pull it out of my pants, gripping it tightly, jerking it a few times. Pretending it's her soft hand instead of mine.*

"Do you have a toy you like?"

Her tongue darts out over her lips, and her voice is breathy as she replies, "Yes."

"Good. Get it out, but don't use it yet. I want to watch you fuck your fingers first."

My palm rasps over my steely length. I'm sure she can hear me fucking my hand while I watch her, but I'm beyond caring.

"Jesus," she mutters as she leans over toward the bedside table, trying not to show too much. Like she's going to be able to avoid that.

"Now lie back on your pillows and spread your legs."

She flushes deep crimson as her legs slowly part.

Holy fuck. *I growl and pump harder at my dick, feeling my balls tighten at the sight. Never has someone looked so perfectly made for me. The teeth digging into her lip, the pretty pink that applies to what's between her legs as well. The only thing that's missing is my come on her tits.*

I wish I were there to touch her. To press her knees wide open and then run my fingers through her wet heat. To feel her pussy twitch and squeeze and go slick around me. I'm panting at the thought, trying to keep myself from blowing already. I need to slow down.

"On all fours. Let me see that tight ass." I watch her raptly. So eager to please. "Good. Now look over your shoulder at me. Fuck me. You are incredible." I say it, and I mean it. Wide blue eyes, slightly parted lips, hair plastered against her cheek, and that perfect round ass. It's almost more than I can take.

I have so much planned. So many positions to put her in. So much pleasure to give her—as much as I can without sacrificing myself. Tonight, I'm going to see every square inch of Pretty_in_Purple's tight little body.

What I don't realize is... I'll never get over it.

★★★

Violet isn't at the house. Her car isn't here. All her stuff is gone. I can tell because usually it's all the fuck over the place, and now it's mysteriously not. I even poked my head into her room, and it looks like it did the day I moved in. The only thing of hers that's left is Pipsqueak, who still whinnies loud enough to hurt my ears every time she sees me.

I started out worried when I couldn't find her. I spent all day at work beating myself up for being an overbearing asshole last night. I couldn't help it. The thought of her falling off and getting hurt had me tied up in knots. I know how wrong that can go because I've seen it firsthand.

But now this? It feels even worse. I didn't wanted Violet living in my space. I was annoyed, and it had nothing to do with her and everything to do with the level of privacy I like. I've grown accustomed to having her around in the last month though. From the smell of the coffee she makes every morning to the quiet murmur of her voice when she calls home every few nights to the random shit she leaves all over the place.

I think I've actually started to *like* it. To crave it. To look forward to it. And now I've gone and been such a dick she packed up and left without saying a thing. *Again.* Not that she owed me an explanation. Her leg is better. Why would she stay anyway? I'm terrible company, and I know it. And once people get to know me, they rarely stick around. Why would Violet be any different?

I've done nothing to endear myself to her. Quite the opposite, in fact. I've acted like a total jackoff and mauled her a couple of times when I couldn't help myself. And then I turned and walked away like the fucking coward I've become. That day on the floor, she basically told me she *wanted* me to touch her. Her blue eyes all soft and alluring. Her soft lips parted, just begging to be kissed.

I wanted her, and she wanted me, and somehow, I still couldn't figure it out.

March into enemy territory? No problem. Face the girl you haven't been able to stop thinking about for two years? No fucking chance.

I am such a pussy.

My fingers dance across the phone in my pocket, itching to call Trixie and ask her what I should do. But I know what she'll tell me. She'll tell me to stop being such a baby and to use my words. Okay, maybe not so colorfully, but still. Trixie is over my mopey self-hatred. I can tell because she recently started pushing me a little harder, cutting into my streams of consciousness with those annoying rhetorical questions that make me reflect on myself.

I hate those fucking questions. I hate how fucking wrecked I am right now over Violet leaving. And I hate how I'm grabbing my keys to march back out the door and confront her about it.

I pull up to the barn, park beside her death trap of a car—one more thing for me to worry about concerning Violet Eaton—and get out of my truck. I march up the stairs to her apartment and knock loudly, probably a little too aggressively.

"Coming!" I hear her call from the other side of the door as I look out over the horizon. The low sun casts a golden glow over the farm. With all the white fences and rolling hills, it's kind of beautiful.

I shake my head. The water out here really must be poisoned. *Beautiful.* I almost roll my eyes, but the door opens, and instead they bug out of my head as I stare back at Violet in tiny cotton short shorts rolled down at the waist and a white ribbed tank top with no bra.

"Did you change your mind…?" She stops talking when she realizes it's me and not whoever she was expecting. "Oh. Hey. I thought it was Billie."

"Hey," I reply, like me showing up on her doorstep is perfectly normal. Except I can't tear my eyes away from her body, from where her nipples have gone instantly hard underneath her tank top. Just like that morning on the living room floor. The sight of them poking through her sports bra sent me over the edge. As if I hadn't been struggling hard enough to keep my instant hard-on at bay every time we worked out, every time I touched her to correct her position or give her a little support. I'd worked out with women in the military. And it had always been just that—working out. Helping a fellow soldier.

But Violet is not a fellow soldier. I don't know what she is anymore, other than firmly entrenched in my life and in my mind.

She must notice my gaze because she looks down quickly, squeaks, flushes pink, and then hides behind the door before narrowing her eyes at me. "What do you want, Cole?"

"You moved."

"Yup. My leg is better. So…"

I blurt out the part that's really bugging me. "You didn't tell me."

Her head quirks slightly as she grips the door in front of her like it's a shield. "Didn't know I needed your permission."

"You don't. I just..." I groan and run a hand through my hair, lost for the right words. I just what? *I want her to come back.* "I was worried. I didn't know you'd left or where you were." I cross my arms and look down at her. "I was worried. And you left your horse behind."

I watch her face soften as her eyes scan me, framed by the pale blond waves that spill down over her shoulders. The golden sunlight tints her eyes more of a turquoise color tonight; they're a like a mood ring—constantly changing.

"Okay." She nods. "That's fair. I'm sorry I didn't say anything. Friends don't do that to each other."

Friends? After I sucked my way up her chest and came close to totally losing control and fucking her bare on the living room floor, she's referring to us as *friends*?

"Want to go on a hike with me tomorrow?"

"A hike?"

"Yeah. I'm ticking things off my bucket list. Time to take life by the horns again. Sasquatch Mountain is one of them. Billie is too scared to go with me."

I raise one eyebrow, having a hard time imagining Billie Black fearing much.

"She thinks the Sasquatch might be real. You know, because of all the 'sightings,'" Violet clarifies, holding one hand up to do air quotes.

My cheek tries to tug itself up a bit at the thought of finally having something to bug Billie about.

"I'll go. I know the mountain well."

"You do?" Her voice perks up at the prospect.

"Yeah. I know a good trail and lookout. I used to run it when I was trying to get fit for the military. Should only take a couple of hours."

"Okay!" she says brightly, looking so happy I almost smile back at her before turning away.

"I'll pick you up when I get back from work." I wave over my shoulder, both wanting to stay near her and to get away from her as quickly as possible. I feel happy too, and it's throwing me for a loop.

Maybe I didn't run her off after all.

"You're late."

"Pfff." Violet waves me off as she climbs into my truck after making me wait for fifteen minutes. She wasn't even done working when I pulled up at her place. "It's just a few minutes."

I imagine myself trying to tell a superior that in training and cringe. "If you're not early, you're late." And being late in the military can cost lives. Violet doesn't live with these pressures, these memories.

She straps herself in and slaps her bare thighs with excitement, ignoring me entirely. "Let's go!"

Of course, she has to wear those tight fucking shorts again. The ones that leave absolutely nothing to the imagination. They hug every curve, including that tight round ass I'm dying to put a handprint on. Something she probably wouldn't like—I'm sure Hilary only pretended to. She did a lot of pretending though. Until she didn't. And her truths cut like a knife. She left me with wounds I wouldn't let heal. Wounds I pry open every morning when I look in the mirror and every night when I get ready for bed.

"I'm so excited!" Violet gushes as she looks over at me. Wearing that sports bra again too. This woman is a walking, talking memory. "You look hot."

My arms stiffen on the wheel as we head down the road toward the nearby mountain. *What?* My eyes dart off the windshield in her direction just in time to see her go beet red and look all flustered.

"I mean your clothes! It's warm out! The pants!"

She's scrambling to undo calling me hot, and I can't help but laugh at how awkwardly she's covering it up.

"Ugh." She drops her head back on the seat and throws an arm over her eyes. "Every time you laugh, it's *at* me!"

I chuckle because it's true. "Yeah, but I laugh with you more than I've laughed in years."

Her arm drops, and her head rolls in my direction as she looks at me. Really looks at me, like she can see right in through all the shields I've erected. All the walls, all the protection, it all goes to shit around Violet, and I'm thinking that might be okay. Maybe she wouldn't be disappointed if she found out I wasn't whole.

"That might be the nicest compliment anyone has ever given me," she says sincerely.

I just grunt back, not sure what to respond with. I've shocked myself into silence, and we drive the rest of the way just like that. In a companionable silence.

When we pull up and walk past the little wooden sign that says, *Lookout This Way*, the silence continues. I lift one arm, ushering her onto the narrow path ahead of me, something

I almost instantly regret, because all it gives me is a completely uninterrupted view of her ass in tight shorts, the bottom crease of each cheek taunting me with every step.

I've done this path a million times, but never with the added challenge of a raging hard-on.

"This is beautiful," she says, slightly breathless with the strain of climbing straight uphill.

"It is," I reply, mostly breathless from trying not to stare at her ass but figuring out that even her ankles turn me on. Everything about her is driving me to distraction. The way her calf muscles flex with each long stride. The way her ponytail sways as she walks. I've spent a lot of time thinking about Violet, wondering who she really was, what she was doing, if she's ever read those messages, if she found someone else to chat with online—or maybe even a boyfriend in real life. But obsessing over her body this way is new to me.

"How much farther?" She looks back at me over her shoulder with some stray hairs plastered to her damp temple, her cheeks flushed—not with embarrassment but with life. With the rush of a new experience, a new place. Violet is *living*, and fuck, does it look good on her.

It makes me want to live too. To stop being such a hermit. To take risks, make friends, maybe even leave a vitamin bottle on the counter now and then—because who the fuck cares if everything is in perfect order all the time?

Life is messy, something I know *well*. But when did I decide that the solution to that was to stop living?

We're so close to the top now, and I can't wait to see what her face looks like when she gets to see the lookout over the lake.

But I hear a loud snap. And I fucking crumple.

CHAPTER 17

Violet

He wasn't kidding about the best orgasm of my life. The only time I've ever felt so out-of-body is when I'm on the back of a horse with the wind whipping my face so hard it almost hurts. When all you can hear is that whooshing sound in your ears and the hoofbeats that reverberate through your bones.

Except this time, it was my heart beating and my blood rushing. Rushing to every delicious spot. Responding to every direction he gave me—coming to life for his words. For his attention.

Can you fall in love with someone you've never met? Never seen? I spent the day mulling over that question. Because this morning, I was nothing but one big bundle of complicated feelings.

We fell asleep talking to each other. Actually talking. And his voice. His. Voice. It's so deep and commanding. I don't know how anyone could ever deny him anything if he talked to them like that.

Never mind the sound of his heavy breathing, the rasp of his palm against the silky skin of his cock. The odd tortured groan that would slip out when I knew he was trying so hard to keep them in.

I could hear him pleasuring himself, but I couldn't see it. And it was so fucking hot.

We weren't even in the same room. I couldn't even see him. Yet last night catapulted itself firmly into the hottest, most unforgettable sexual experience of my life.

I want more. I want him.

I race up the stairs to my apartment, feeling so sure that I can convince him to join me on the video chat. I want to do more than hear his pleasure. I want to see it.

Pretty_in_Purple: I want to celebrate!
Golddigger85: Oh?
Pretty_in_Purple: I just got a HUGE promotion at work. Huge, huge. Like... FUCKING HUGE!

Billie pulled me aside and told me I was the new jockey for the best racehorse I've ever seen. I still can't believe it. I thought she was joking when she told me. Groom to jockey is a gigantic leap. An unheard-of leap. We're going out to celebrate tonight, but I thought I could fit some playtime in with Golddigger first.

Golddigger85: Ha! Congratulations. I've got something huge for you too. ;)

I smile. I bet it is. He looked like a big man in that one photo he sent.

Pretty_in_Purple: Butterfaces usually do. ;)
Golddigger85: You're so mean to me.

I can't help my smile. He's so playful today. Maybe we've turned a corner?

Pretty_in_Purple: I want to be really, really nice to you.
Golddigger85: Oh?
Pretty_in_Purple: Let's video chat again.
Golddigger85: Greedy girl.

I swear it's like I can hear him chuckle. The sound of it in my head makes my chest flush with the memory of last night.

Pretty_in_Purple: I am. I want you on there too.

The chat goes quiet. He goes from responding almost instantly to silence. Anxiety simmers in my gut. Maybe I pushed him too far?

Pretty_in_Purple: Please?
Golddigger85: I thought we cleared this up?

Okay. That's not the response I was hoping for.

Pretty_in_Purple: I thought you might... I don't know. Change your mind. I thought you might trust me enough to try it.

A several-minute wait again. I pace. I brush my teeth just for something to do.

Golddigger85: Well, I don't. I don't trust anyone. It's never going to happen. Never. I've been very up-front about that from the start of whatever this is.

I don't need him in the same room as me to feel that punch to the gut.

Pretty_in_Purple: Whatever this is? We've been talking to each other every day for a year. How many more years would I need to go? I've always said no to it too.

Golddigger85: We all make choices.

I suddenly feel embarrassed. Deeply embarrassed. He has been adamant from day one that he'd never show me more than that one photo. Yet I somehow convinced myself I'd be the one to change him—that I'd be the exception to the rule.

The realization that I've just been totally vulnerable with a man who would never reciprocate, even though I was naive enough to convince myself he might, hits me like an avalanche. It takes me right out. I compromised my values, my morals—fuck, possibly my career—all because I was horny and hopelessly obsessed with a stranger I met on the internet. The faint taste of bile burns my throat and sours my mouth.

I need a drink. Or two.

Or ten.

I see the crest of the mountain ahead when I hear a thump and a pained "Fuck!" I spin around to see Cole down on his knees, head bowed with his strong hands splayed out on the dirt path beneath him.

"Are you okay?" I hustle back, instantly concerned about what could take a man like Cole Harding down.

"Yes," he bites out harshly, making me pull back the hand I was about to rest on his shoulder. "Just go to the lookout. I'll be there in a sec."

I glance back up the hill before I recall how Pippy has softened him up by just being relentless in her affection. A strategy I've decided to adopt because, for as little as I know about Cole Harding, I *know* he is starved for attention. I know he has his shields up. I know he's been hurt. And I know no one has stuck around long enough to prove to him he's worth sticking around for. Pippy has taught me that much.

Which is why I moved out. I knew he needed his space, and he needed to see that even without being forced to live under the same roof, I would keep coming back for him. For no other reason than I want to spend time with him. I planned to invite him on this hike. He just made it easier by storming up my steps last night.

"No. I'm not leaving you behind," I say simply. Because I'm not.

"Violet." He still doesn't look up at me. "Please just go."

My heart races. This is weird. "Are you hurt?"

"No."

"Okay. Well, I'm not going." And then he looks up at me with so much pain in his icy gray eyes that I fall to my knees in front of him, feeling the tiny pebbles and grit digging into my bare knees as I come eye-to-eye with him. I watch his Adam's apple bob and his lower lip tremble slightly on a heavy exhale.

"Cole, you're scaring me. What's wrong?"

He presses his lips together again and rolls over to sitting, right in the middle of the path. "It's my leg."

"Okay. So you're hurt. What part?" I crawl around beside him so he can't keep facing away from me and then sit back on my heels. "Want me to check?"

"No, no." His arm darts out across my chest to stop me from moving down to his feet. And then he sighs. An exhausted sigh that lurches out from somewhere deep inside him. A sigh that takes his tall broad shoulders and makes him slump forward in defeat.

A sigh that leads him to pulling up his pant leg roughly, angrily, to show me the black prosthetic hidden beneath his pants. A sock covers his knee and disappears down into the plastic leg.

He points jerkily down at the high-tech-looking appendage and reiterates, "It's my leg."

I nod once, mind racing for how I could have missed this. We lived together for a month, and I never noticed that he's an amputee? What the fuck is wrong with me? And how hard has he been trying to hide it? That had to be damn near impossible. "Okay, so how do we fix it?"

He snorts dismissively. "We don't. It's probably something in the pinlock. I felt it go."

I don't know what that means, but I assume that someone closer to him will. "Okay… Want me to call Vaughn?"

"No," he almost shouts. "He doesn't know."

I widen my eyes as I look back down at the prosthetic. *His own brother doesn't know?* "Who knows?"

"My mom. But there's no reception up here." He looks away from me, avoiding my eyes as he shakes his head. The pain in his body right now—the shame—it almost kills me.

I rest my hand on his broad back, feeling his muscles ripple and tense beneath my palm as I rub small circles there. "Tell me what you need me to do."

He grinds his teeth, making his jaw pop as he looks ahead, avoiding my gaze. "You'll have to hike back down and get my spare from the house."

I glance around at the fading light over the peak. "But it'll be dark by the time I get back."

He just grunts and bends his knee, making the prosthetic fall onto the packed dirt with a hollow thud. "That's fine. You can come back for me in the morning."

"What? I'm not leaving you here overnight."

"I've done fine without your help so far. Don't need you to get all sentimental now. It won't be my first time sleeping outside, and Sasquatch Mountain is a hell of a lot safer than Iraq."

He has to be kidding. No way am I going back down there without him. I wouldn't sleep knowing I left him up on a mountain alone. "I know you can take care of yourself. I'm not worried about that. I wouldn't leave *anyone* I care about behind. I'll hike down in the morning and bring you the spare myself."

"No." He looks at me fiercely, but he doesn't scare me.

A lot of my missing puzzle pieces concerning Cole Harding fall into place. Plus, I already promised myself I'd stick around for him.

"Well, that's just too bad for you," I say, pushing to stand and dusting my hands off while looking around the densely forested path, "because I'm sleeping over with you."

"Violet."

There he goes with that again. I know I'm pissing him off, but frankly, I don't care. Maybe getting angry would be good for him. That blow-your-top-off type of explosion that consumes you but also leaves you with some startling clarity. Yes, that's what Cole Harding needs. Some clarity.

"Let's go." I reach my hand down to him. "I'm a farm girl, remember? It won't be my first time sleeping outside."

After helping Cole off the path, he sits on a log and tells me how to build a lean-to shelter. I know how to build one, but I feel like letting him dictate how I put one together will give him some semblance of control in this situation. Something I don't mind ceding, considering he still won't look at me.

I search for branches, pine boughs, everything I can find to build us a safe spot for the night. Yeah, the day was warm, but it's still May in Canada. It's going to be cold tonight. Something Cole obviously knows based on the way he's had me cover up so much of the space and leave only a small opening for us to get in through.

I stand back, hands on my hips as I blow a loose piece of hair off my face and admire my masterpiece. Twilight is setting in now, and it's cooling off. I shiver at the prospect of how cold I'll probably be tonight.

"Okay, I think that's as good as it's going to get," I say, slanting Cole a curious glance. He's still brooding on the log, the lighter version of him nowhere to be found. It's clear he didn't want me—or anyone else for that matter—to find out about his leg. Like I would care. *That's because you're more interested in what's between his legs.*

"Why are you blushing?"

Motherfucker.

I rub my cheeks. "I'm not."

He pins me with a glare that I assume means he's not buying my denial.

"Okay. Well, I'm heading into Casa del Violet. You know where to find me when you're ready."

I turn toward the shelter just as he lashes out, "What? You're not going to offer to help me get over there?"

Stopping my forward motion, I turn back to look at him. He's sitting tall and rigid now. He's trying to look strong and proud, but his words are insecure and petty. I could take his attitude personally, but I know him well enough to know that tone means nothing where he's concerned. In fact, I usually think it means he's angry with himself, not me. And right now, he doesn't need my pity. He's already drowning in his own.

"Do you need help?" I prop my hands on my hips and tilt my head in question. "Because it strikes me that you're one of the strongest men I know. Presumably, you've been getting around fine for years with no one's help. Am I right?"

He blinks at me, face blank. I think he might be shocked. But I have brothers, and I know when a boy needs coddling—and this ain't it.

"Hop on over when you're ready." And then I leave him. Big tough Mr. I Sleep Outside needs my help? I scoff to myself as I crawl into the dark lean-to, leaves crunching underneath me as I come to sit.

Only a few minutes later, I hear Cole making his way over. He kneels in front of the entryway and crawls in beside me. What felt spacious before his arrival feels downright claustrophobic with his bulk taking up space beside me. Taking up *way too much space*. I feel my heart race at the proximity of him, at the idea that I have nowhere to retreat to. Nowhere to hide from him and the intensely confusing feelings he stirs up inside me.

"Did you seriously just tell me to *hop on over*?" The light is dim in the shelter, but I can see the amused tilt on his shapely lips.

"I..." God, that sounded kind of bad, doesn't it? "I did." Might as well own it. "Seemed preferable to 'crawl on over.'"

The laugh he barks out is so loud that it startles me. Like it leapt out of nowhere and surprised us both with its power. I laugh uncertainly and eye him skeptically. Like... is this okay? Am I allowed to laugh at this? But Cole doesn't seem to have any such qualms. His shoulders shake, and his body curls in, his hands resting across what I know are rock-hard abs. He laughs so hard that when he looks up again, I see his fingertips swipe away a stray tear.

"What the fuck, Violet?" He gasps, still trying to catch his breath. "I never knew that amputee jokes would hit quite like that."

"I'm sorry!" My hand flies up across my mouth.

"Don't be." He shakes his head with a grin plastered on his face.

It's weird. He never smiles at me like that, with true amusement. Maybe the odd peek of contentment or care. But not like this. This is unnerving. This is... He looks downright edible like this. All dark hair and glowing eyes.

"Are you okay?" I venture, because I'm honestly a little disturbed.

He leans back on his hands and looks up at the roof of the shelter. "Am I okay? That's a loaded question. I'm..." He trails off, and I watch his chest rise and fall, his throat move as he swallows, his cheek twitch momentarily, and I feel my core thrum.

The tiniest things he does set me alight—that cheek twitch and the dimple that pops when he does it? Gah! Delicious. Everything about the man is delicious. Dark and chilly on the outside, soft and gooey on the inside. Far too experienced for a girl like me, but so damn tempting.

I lick my lips as I soak him in, staring at him and suddenly not really caring if I get caught.

"I'm relieved," he finally says.

"Relieved?"

"Yeah." He lifts his stump up and drops it back down in explanation. "It's like a weight off my chest that someone knows about this. Keeping it a secret is exhausting."

I mean, no shit.

"How did it happen?"

He sighs deeply and crosses his arms over his chest the way he always does when he's trying not to look vulnerable. "I was so close to finishing my third tour. So fucking close. It's not even a good story. We were outside the wire, no live fire or anything. We drove over an IED. Junior, who was with me, didn't make it. And my leg took the brunt of the shrapnel. There were nails in it. I didn't even realize how bad it was. I got Junior and carried him to safety before it completely gave out on me."

I swallow. That's more detail than I was expecting. "So why keep it a secret? No one would care."

"Hmm. Trixie asks me that too. I tell her it's because of Hilary. She cared."

"I'm sorry, what?"

"I wasn't easy to deal with when I came back. I had a lot of shit to work through, even beyond the amputation. But finding the right prosthetic isn't a quick process. The shape of your stump, it all affects your comfort and the fit. Not to mention the change in balance that comes with it. The phantom pains. We'd grown apart already, and I was a growly motherfucker. But apparently, the physical aspect of my recovery really wasn't working for her."

I feel a chill roll down my spine, like when my brother would drop that fluffy, dry Alberta snow down the back of my shirt. I probably shouldn't press, but he already knows I'm snoopy. "What does that mean?"

"You and your questions." He snorts and then angles a look down at me as if to confirm I'm not backing down. "Okay. Well. When I finally got my body and mind sorted out enough to fuck her, it just wasn't what it once was. She liked when I was aggressive and dominating. But I couldn't be that anymore. Especially because my heart just wasn't in it. At any rate, I lost my balance, everything felt different, and I fell over partway through." He shakes his head, lost in the memory. "Right on the fucking floor. It's where I wanted to stay too. So I decided I was done for the day. It embarrassed me, you know? It more than embarrassed me. It *ruined* me. I barely knew her anymore. And she got frustrated. Had some choice words about me being a *half man* that resulted in the end of our engagement. I wasn't the shiny whole trust-fund baby she latched on to a decade earlier. So that was that. The end."

I imagine Cole, proud and dominating and so fucking broken, fallen on the floor. And then I imagine a woman who professes to love him making him feel anything less than loved in that moment. And then I feel fury. Fury that spews right out of me.

"Okay, so Hilary needs to die." I slap my hand over my mouth. I didn't mean to say that part out loud. But I feel fierce. I feel protective. Like I want to crawl into his lap and use my body as a shield for him from anyone who would talk to him that way—wound him that way.

Cole laughs a sad laugh but doesn't look at me.

"So that's what you tell Trixie. But what's the real reason you don't tell anyone?"

"Picked up on that, did you?"

I can't stop looking at him. I want to touch him so badly that holding myself back is utter torture. My hands ache to even just hold his forearm, to feel the pulse of his veins under my fingertips.

"I guess I don't want anyone's pity. I don't want to be treated like I'm incapable, like I'm weaker somehow. I don't want those words, those looks. That's probably why I liked your crawling joke."

I turn my body, wanting him to look at me or at least know that I'm looking at him. "You are not weak, Cole. I said you were one of the strongest men I know, and I meant it. Your leg doesn't matter to me, and if it matters to anyone else, fuck them. They suck."

His eyes dart around my face as if he can't quite decide where to focus, and I wish—not for the first time—that I could figure out what is running through that beautiful head of his. I wish I could open it up and rummage around in there. Cole is such a closed book. And even though he's talked more to me tonight than he ever has, I'm greedy. I want more.

Which is why I'm blindsided by the frustrated growl that tears out of his chest and the hand that darts out to grip my head and pull me to him. His other hand moves to my jaw, cupping my face reverently as he stares down at my lips. Like he's tortured by them, entranced by them.

I don't move. I don't want to break whatever tenuous hold I have on him right now, sharing whispered truths in the dark. I want him to do it. To devour me. To take a piece of me and keep it.

I want him to want me as badly as I want him.

The smell of him mingles with the pine boughs around us and wraps around me as his chest heaves and his heavy breaths heat my cheeks.

"Do it," I whisper, taunting him. "Please," I add, begging him.

And this time, he doesn't deny me. "Fuck it," he rasps right as his lips descend onto mine. Hard and fast, strong and relentless—just like him.

My hands coast up over his chest and flutter over his throat nervously as he kisses me senseless. I don't even know what to do with my hands. They tremble as I let them trail through his hair while the rest of me turns to putty in his lap.

Everything about Cole is masculine. So powerful. I feel small and inexperienced and so damn hot. I swing one leg over his waist, wanting to be closer to him, and he groans into my mouth as I settle down on him, feeling his steely length grow beneath my ass when I do.

His tongue finds the seam of my mouth as he tastes me, lips moving firmly—like a command to open for him. I rock my hips in response, pretty sure my panties are already ruined just from the skim of his calloused hand over my neck. The way he holds me there, it's consuming, it's… liberating.

He wants me. He brought me to him. I can feel proof of it pressing against my aching core. I grind down again, brazenly riding him and loving the feel of his hands constricting on my body while he teases my mouth so expertly. His hands slip underneath my shirt, tracing the indent along my spine and burning across my skin.

We kiss. A tangle of tongues and hands and moans. We don't rush; we explore. And I sigh into him, a little overwhelmed by how right it feels to be here with him. By how little everything else matters when he takes me in his lap and claims me like this.

I roll my hips again, my mind wandering down a path where we're doing this exact thing but with no clothing between us.

"Jesus Christ, Violet. I'm going to blow in my pants if you keep riding me like that."

His voice is shaky, and I pull back—only slightly—to meet his wild, lust-drenched stare with my own. "Sorry."

"Don't be sorry. Stop apologizing." His eyes take on a faraway look, and he hesitates, fingers fluttering over my body uncertainly all of a sudden. "This is, well, it's just that this is—"

I want to rise up and cut him off. I want to make him stop what he's about to say because deep down, I'm terrified he's going to tell me to stop again. Something I'm not sure my body can take, let alone my heart. "Don't. Just... Can you just not ruin it? Save that for tomorrow. Let me just revel in how hot that was."

I don't want to hear him say that this is a bad idea. That we shouldn't do this. He's already put his mouth on my body and walked away once. I don't think I can bear it again. How many times do I need to get turned away by this man before I learn my goddamn lesson?

This time, I'll beat him to the punch. I kiss him one more time, hard, and then end it there, knowing that now isn't the time or place to push him. "It's fine. Let's sleep."

He regards me silently, a deep wrinkle in his forehead as I crawl off his lap and eye the ground, trying not to think about how many bugs are going to be down there with me tonight before shaking my head at myself. I'm a farm girl. Bugs don't scare me. I flop down, feeling the dirt and pine needles against my bare skin and hearing Cole's heavy breathing from somewhere near my feet.

He eventually lies down beside me. We're not touching, but we might as well be. I can feel his heat along my back and smell that spicy cinnamon and clove scent I always pick up on him, but I can't hear him anymore. His breathing has gone soft and quiet. I'm hyperaware of everything about him, his nearness. I could fold myself into his big warm body and fit perfectly.

I get lost in my head, remembering all those messages we swapped. All those nights I stayed up late talking to him. Saying good morning to him as soon as I grabbed my phone the next day. The dorky jokes we'd tell each other. How were we so compatible for so long only to be so damn confusing now? I know he's not an open book, not a clear communicator, but this not saying anything is driving me insane. I can't tell up from down where Cole Harding is concerned. Do I not live up to his expectations in real life? His dick felt like it was attracted to me, but maybe that's the reaction he'd have to any woman? If he hasn't had physical contact in years, that's perfectly feasible. Is he really so insecure about his leg he'd keep me at arm's length even now?

I shiver, thinking about the feeling of his calloused palms scraping up my bare back, about how I'd like him to press me down hard with that palm and—

"Are you cold?"

I look down to realize I'm hugging myself and have my knees tucked up tight, and yeah, I am cold. "A little," I confess quietly.

With no warning, his arm comes over me and pulls me back into his body, tucking me against him safely. I can still feel his hard-on against my ass, but I force myself to ignore it, relieved to feel his heat around me.

He surrounds me, chin on my head, arm draped over my ribs possessively, and legs tucked up underneath mine. The perfect fit.

"Cole?"

He sighs audibly. "Yes, Violet?"

"Do you think the Sasquatch is real?"

He doesn't answer. Instead, he pulls me closer and holds me tighter. The feel of him wrapped around my body soothes me, lulls me off into a light sleep where I'm resting but still intimately aware of every part of him. Every point of contact hums with possibility, something I can't quite stop thinking about, something that won't let me drift off completely. Which is probably why I don't miss his quiet whisper several minutes later.

"What I was going to say is that this is perfect."

CHAPTER 18

Cole

We all make choices.

The message that fucking haunts me. What a dickbag thing to say to a girl you care about. A girl who just put it all on the line for you to, what? Jerk off?

I shake my head.

We all make choices.

Don't I fuckin' know it. I should take my own implied advice.

She hasn't messaged me back, but she's seen the message. That was last night, and there's still no message this morning. That's probably not a good sign. Fuck. Leave it to me to ruin the one good thing I had going in my life. The one thing I actually looked forward to in a monotonous, lonely fucking day. Because she was right all those months ago.

I am lonely. Actually, I don't even know if lonely *really covers it.*

I'm numb. By choice. And talking to Pretty_in_Purple was like the one pinprick that was getting through, making me feel something. And I couldn't even bring myself to fess up about my leg, just put it out there in the open. I was too fixated on keeping it secret. Something that doesn't even make sense to me, yet I can't bring myself to change it. Maybe if she'd have known, she'd have been more accepting of my not wanting to go on video. Maybe if she knew I ran a multinational company and couldn't be recognized as the guy jacking off on the internet, it would make a difference.

Maybe she'd understand. Maybe letting someone in on my secret would be a good start? Someone whose face I couldn't see when I told them. The pity. The disgust.

This cloak-and-dagger game I play with my leg is fucked up, and I know it. I never intended to let it get this far. It started out as something I just wanted to process on my own. After all, when I came back from Iraq, I had a lot to process. Apparently, watching your friends get blown to pieces will fuck you up. Never mind coming to grips with losing a limb after spending your entire adult life defining yourself by how physically capable you are. But the longer I went without sharing with anyone, the lower I let myself go. The more I focused on Hilary and her cruel words, the more it just became something I never wanted anyone to know about. The more I believed them.

Hiding it became integral. Like breathing. And now when I think of it, I don't even know why I do it, but I can't quite bring myself to stop. I'm stagnant like a swamp.

I pick up my phone and fire her off a message, determined to fix this.

Golddigger85: How are you?

Smooth, Cole. You've really got a way with words, pal.

After a few hours, she still hasn't responded. She hasn't even seen it. I tell myself she's probably busy. It seems like her job lends itself to long hours without set weekends. But as the day wears on with no response, I get worried. In a year, we haven't gone a single day without at least popping in to say hi or mentioning that things are busy. Not because we owe each other an explanation but because we like each other enough to do it.

Golddigger85: Is everything okay?

Still nothing. I spend the evening closing the app and rebooting it. Uninstall and then reinstall. Hoping that it's a technical error. Technology fucks up all the time. It's probably that.

But when I wake up the next morning with my phone in my hand and still nothing from Pretty_in_Purple, dread takes up residence in my chest. I fucked up, and there's no clear-cut way for me to fix it. Or something terrible happened to her, which is a thought I can't even handle. I'd rather feel like the shithead I am than imagine her injured—or worse.

I can't even let myself go there.

All I want to do is make this right.

Golddigger85: Listen, I think you're probably angry with me. I'm sorry if I hurt you. That was never my intention. I just... I'm complicated. It's a long story. One I'd like to tell you if you come back.

My misery grows with every passing day that she doesn't respond. I feel pathetic continuing to message her. But I can't stop. Talking to Pretty_in_Purple has become part of who I am, a thread leading me back to the man I want to be. A thread I decide I will not let go of. I'll keep going even if she's not here to partake.

Golddigger85: I think I'm just going to keep writing to you, even if you never come back. I need this.

After all, I am exceptional at avoiding reality.

★★★

I've held Violet in my arms all night long. It doesn't take a rocket scientist to know that her telling me *it's fine* means that it's not fine at all. But I keep holding her anyway.

I've barely slept. I'm exhausted but also buzzing. Kissing Violet last night was fucking *everything*. It really was perfect. Until she freaked out and shut it down. The way she asked me not to ruin it. It's like she already knows I ruin everything.

And then holding her? Her warm body pressed into mine? It was like clinging on to a teddy bear for comfort. But I've never wanted to fuck a teddy bear.

I'm also freezing, but I couldn't care less, so long as she's warm. She fell asleep quickly, quietly, lulled into a dream world where soft little sighs slipped past her lips, where she snuggled in closer and turned into my chest.

It was heaven. Just holding someone—someone who knows *everything* and doesn't look at me with disgust. I haven't felt that level of relaxation in years. In the middle of a forest, in a shitty little shelter, I'm the most relaxed I've been in years. All because Violet is here in my arms.

Yeah, I'm royally fucked. Because not only do I want to rip all her clothes off and use her body in every way imaginable, I want to cook her breakfast after, make sure she takes her vitamins and works out. I want to take care of her body once I'm finished desecrating it.

What's worse, I want to talk to her. In the dark, in the quiet, I want to let it all out. My dad, my mom, my time overseas. All those stories bubble barely controlled beneath the surface. When that pin on my leg snapped, so did the reservoir of everything I've held in for so long. It came surging up like water out of a dam, and now I'm struggling to keep it in.

Trixie is going to be obnoxiously pleased.

I look down at Violet now, snoring softly, snuggled into my chest with one leg slung over mine. The warm drops of morning light filter through the porous roof of the shelter, speckling her cheeks and hair. Her long lashes cast a shadow, and her lips are a pale shade of pink, the same color as her pert nipples. Something I'll never forget. Violet has *perfect* tits.

She looks small and weak, but if I've learned anything about Violet in the last month, it's that she's strong. So damn strong.

I knew she'd yanked her independence away from her family and set out alone, determined to be her own woman. I just didn't realize how thoroughly she'd succeeded. How intensely herself she'd become. Her confidence isn't loud or brazen; it's subtle and natural, intrinsic almost in how well it suits her. She isn't hard or crass; she's just steadfast.

When our online conversation wasn't serving her anymore, she was done. I spent a year desperately hoping she'd log in and see my last messages. Hell, I still have our chat open on my computer and check it daily. If she would just log back in, she'd know I wasn't done with her. She'd know what I haven't been able to say out loud.

I admired that about her. Envied it. When life didn't go my way, I retreated, but Violet? She kept on trudging. With a smile. Eternal sunshine.

Her lashes flutter before her lids pop open. She looks around the shelter. Mostly she gets an eyeful of my chest as the gears in her head spin. When her chin turns up to look at my face, she startles. Obviously, she didn't plan on me being awake.

"How long have you been up for?"

"A while," I lie. "Hard to sleep with your snoring."

Her face flushes pink as she moves away from my chest. I want to pull her close again, but I don't. I'm not sure how I'm supposed to act this morning.

"I was not." She looks horrified.

"You were."

She scrubs her face with her hands as if doing so will make her cheeks less red.

"It was more like… purring. Like a kitten," I continue.

"Oh god."

"Hey. I'm missing a leg, and you snore like a kitten. It's all good."

Her hands shoot down off her face so fast I can't even react to her pointy little finger jabbing my chest. "Missing a leg isn't embarrassing!" She just went from embarrassed to all fired up in under one second.

I hold my hands up in defeat and roll away from her. "You're right. The only embarrassing thing here right now is your breath."

Her little mouth flattens as her already big eyes widen at me. She sits up slowly, shielding her mouth with one hand, muttering, "Cole Harding, you are such a prick." Once she's brushed herself off, she looks down at me. "Okay. Tell me where the leg is, and I'll go get it. I'm starving."

"Bottom left drawer of the dresser in my room."

She nods before turning away, and my hand shoots down quickly to adjust my cock. The thought of her in my room is not helping with my morning wood. And neither is the view of her ass in those goddamn shorts crawling out of the shelter.

"Make sure you sing or something on your way down. Make noise. Keep your eyes peeled for wildlife. There are bears out here."

"Good god, Cole. What do you think I am? A city girl?"

She brushes her ass off, wiggling it just a little as she does, and within a few minutes, I can hear her singing some god-awful country song about riding a cowboy—completely off tune.

I've made my way back out to the log I sat on yesterday. It's a good log, in the perfect position to see the path. The brush behind me is so thick it would be impossible for anyone to sneak up. I feel as relaxed as I ever would, sitting in the middle of nowhere, missing my leg from just below the knee.

I'm trying not to worry about Violet, but it's not working. I know she's perfectly capable of walking down the mountain, but I can't keep my mind from straying to her. The same way it has for two years.

Zoned out as I might be, Violet clearly has no military training. I can hear her coming from a mile away. How someone so small can be so heavy on her feet is beyond me.

"Got it!" Violet waves the prosthetic overhead like it's a flag, but her movements are jerky. Her face is pinched. Sure, I pestered her about the snoring thing and kissed her senseless last night, but she didn't leave with body language like this.

"What's wrong?" I ask as she approaches me.

She almost flinches as her eyes dart to mine before lowering again. "Nothing." She drops to one knee, swings the backpack off from over her shoulder, and zips it open.

"How is the brown horse? Did you feed her extra? She was probably starving."

"For crying out loud, Cole. She has a name. You can stop pretending you don't like her around me." She shoves a black fleece jacket at me, agitation lining her every movement. "And of course I fed her. Hard to forget with that loud-ass whinny every time one of us pulls up."

I can't help but smile. It really is kind of annoying, yet I look forward to her greeting every day. The soft brush of her lips against my palm when I offer her a carrot. The way she nuzzles her dusty little face against my dress shirt, like she's bunting me. I'm not used to someone being so happy to see me all the time.

"Okay, good. Thanks for the coat."

"I figured you were probably cold." Violet is bundled in a lightly quilted Gold Rush Ranch jacket now and looking… uncomfortable. Nothing like the way she looked this morning or last night, when she straddled my lap and ground herself down on me. What the hell is going on?

"Thanks." I eye her speculatively. "You sure everything is okay?"

"Yup!" she says a little too brightly, popping the *p*.

I'm not buying it, but I also hate when people pry—so I won't.

Instead, I focus on fastening my spare prosthetic. It's not as comfortable as my regular one. It's not customized in the same way, and I know it's probably going to rub my stump. It's definitely not made for hiking.

I look down into it, and my leg aches. My leg that isn't even there. Phantom pains. They're not as bad as they once were, but sometimes the reality that my leg is *really* gone just lands differently. It's like I can feel it there. The pain of the day it was blown off. The pain of my recovery. The pain of my loss.

It rarely bugs me, but shoving my leg into a prosthetic I know is going to be uncomfortable gives me pause.

I shake my head and push it in anyway. No point in crying about it. Gotta get down this hill somehow. With my socks pulled up comfortably, I tie my shoe before looking up at Violet, who is staring at my foot with her brow furrowed.

"Do you have another question?" I ask, half joking.

She sighs, her shoulders squeezing up high and then falling as she does. "No. It's just amazing. I had no idea. I couldn't tell at all—the way you walk, the way you work out, the way you"—she waves her hand over my body—"look."

I bite back a smile. I'm not sure of much where Violet is concerned, but I know she likes my body. I catch her checking me out all the time when she thinks she's being discreet, and relief hits me like a blast of AC on a hot day because she's still giving me *that* look now that she knows what I'm hiding in my pants. Or, well, one of the things I'm hiding in my pants. I almost feel bad I assumed she'd look at me differently, but that's been my experience, hasn't it? I have little else to go on because I've been so busy hiding it from everyone.

"Okay, let's get the fuck off this mountain." I stand and press a little weight onto the prosthetic, feeling it out. It sucks. But it'll have to do for now.

Violet turns and starts walking back down the path. I follow, pretty sure my walk isn't as even in this prosthetic.

People would notice now, but as Violet slows to match my pace, she says nothing.

The silence is fine by me.

Only when we pull up to the barn does she talk. “Thanks. See you at the track tonight?”

I wrinkle my nose. “Tonight?”

“Yeah. I’m riding tonight. That’s why I’ve got to get going.”

Maybe that’s why she seemed so off? Was she focused on tonight?

“Is that safe?” I ask before I can stop myself. But really, she just spent the night sleeping poorly and hiking up and down a mountain to help my crippled ass. Running around at breakneck speeds on a thousand-pound animal being anything short of perfectly alert seems dangerous to me.

One shapely brow quirks up as she crosses her arms back at me. I feel like I’m looking at a small blond elfin version of myself with that pose and facial expression.

“Friends look out for each other, Violet,” I grumble at her. I know she doesn’t want people telling her what to do, but this is serious.

And she just scoffs, “Yeah. *Friends*,” and rips the truck door open before slamming it with nothing more than a wave over her shoulder as she stomps up the stairs to her apartment.

CHAPTER 19

Violet

My head hurts, and I feel like death warmed over. I can barely move. I'm not sure if it's the copious number of drinks I downed in front of Billie at Neighbor's Pub last night or that I've made myself feel sick over a goddamn internet pen pal.

My stomach roils, and again, I can't differentiate the cause.

I'm so mad. At me. Not even at him. Because he's right. He was nothing but up-front with me about his limitations. About his rules. Yet I barged ahead, thinking I'd be the one he'd change for.

I shake my head and press the heels of my palms into my eye sockets, trying to dull the throb in my head. I can hear my oldest brother, Cade, giving me dating advice—and there was a lot of it—but this bit stands out as exceptionally pertinent right now.

Don't pick a man who needs fixing—or changing—to meet your needs. He either wants to, or he doesn't. And if you need to convince him, he doesn't love you the way you deserve.

I hated the way my brothers meddled in my love life. The three of them practically put me up in an ivory tower, but I guess they knew Mom better than I ever did. They lost our mom and didn't want to lose me too. So instead, they smothered me and drove me away. Because I couldn't stay there. But right now, I ache to go back. A hug from my dad, a noogie from Rhett, an easy smile from Beau, and some deep poetic advice from Cade. Good men, all four of them.

And I'm not sure I truly realized it until now.

I know what they'd tell me this morning, and I know what Billie told me last night.

It's time to move on. I deserve more. I deserve better.

I delete the app from my phone and go lie on the floor of my shower, where my quiet tears blend and wash away with the spray of lukewarm water above me.

The sounds of the track filter in around me as I tack Brite Lite up. It's my second year riding her, and she's a solid racehorse with a good head on her shoulders and a fair number of wins under her belt. But today, the pretty gray mare is antsy. Just like me, raring to go, right back where I was a month ago. I shove my earbuds in and get to work on zoning out, humming to try and soothe her nerves as well as mine. Except where I usually play the race through in my mind, I'm instead replaying the last twenty-four hours.

The walk down the mountain and subsequent drive home were quiet. Awkward. I didn't know what to say to Cole, and my mind was so busy piecing it all together that I couldn't have come up with small talk to fill the space anyway.

When I went into his room to get his leg, I tried not to take my time looking around, but I did a little bit. I'm only human, okay? And it doesn't matter. The place is military clean. Everything laid out just so, everything spick-and-span clean. I wondered if he polished the floors with a toothbrush like you see in the movies, but I couldn't even bring myself to ask him that.

Because when I shoved the sticky drawer closed on the dresser that was home to his spare prosthetic, it moved the mouse next to the laptop plugged in on top. The one that was still open. The one that was open to our chat. Our messages from over a year ago were sitting right there, looking me in the eye.

And I was very, very human at that moment. Because I couldn't look away and definitely couldn't stop myself from scrolling through. I wondered why the hell he would have our chat still open on his laptop when I haven't responded to him in a year. Until I came face-to-face with my answer.

Golddigger85: How are you?

Is everything okay? Listen, I think you're probably angry with me. I'm sorry if I hurt you. That was never my intention. I just... I' m complicated. It's a long story. One I'd like to tell you if you come back.

I think I'm just going to keep writing to you, even if you never come back. I need this.

Talking to you has been the most healing thing to happen to me in years. Please respond. I'll reciprocate. Sharing much about myself terrifies me. But I'll try.

I don't think you're coming back. But if you do, my offer stands. I want us, or whatever this is, back.

Sometimes I daydream about meeting you in real life. The things I'd do to you.

I miss you.

He's been messaging me ever since I ghosted him. Even since I moved in with him. Like a diary dedicated to me.

My breath left my body with a hollow whoosh. My heart pounded in my ears.

Tonight, I carried your limp body into my house. I know you're just knocked out from the painkillers, but I felt sick all the same. I've carried limp bodies before, and the thought of one being yours is almost more than I can take. I fell asleep in the hallway listening to you breathe.

Today you talked me into going out for a drink at some shitty little pub. I had the most fun I've had in years.

Today you moved out. I didn't expect it to hurt this badly.

Tears spring up in my eyes just reading them all, each one like a pin in my heart. The most aloof, closed-off man in the world turned my heart into a fucking pincushion with his words, and I don't even know how to tell him.

I am well and truly speechless. I've spent a month in close quarters with this man. A man who I thought didn't even *like* me, when the entire time, he's been writing me notes. I've been beating myself up over wanting Cole Harding, over going against every fiber of logic in my body that tells me he's just going to let me down again. Embarrass me again. And all this damn time, he's been writing me love notes he knows I'll never see while I try to be his *friend*.

Some girls might swoon. The notes *are* sweet. So sweet that my teeth ache. But I feel agitated. He could have just told me. It's not like we haven't talked about our pasts. Now I feel like a juvenile fool for crushing on him secretly this whole time, tiptoeing around his moods.

If I'd have known he missed me, wanted me, I'd have crawled in his lap and kissed him earlier.

I unbuckle Brite Lite's halter, and she instantly drops her head into the bridle as I easily slide the bit into her mouth. She's usually so polite, but today it's like she chomps down on the bit. Goes after it. Takes it, just like we're going to take this race.

It's time to put the big brooding soldier out of my mind and focus on kicking Patrick Cassel's ass in round two. Brite Lite is ready too. I swear she knows this is a revenge round. A rematch. Us girls have a keen sense for that—especially with tools like Patrick.

We walk out into the bright sunshine, very unlike that soggy day just over a month ago. The conditions are perfect.

Billie slinks out from who knows where with Mira in tow.

"All good? How's Brighty?" she asks, shrewd golden eyes assessing me like she just *knows* something is up. No one reads a person better than Billie.

No one.

"Yup. Let's do this." I nod, yanking up that competitive spirit that comes with the territory of being the only girl and youngest sibling of four kids.

Billie gives me a well-practiced leg up into the tack before pinching the side of my butt playfully. "Break a leg out there."

"Billie." Mira stares at her, unimpressed. Which, to be fair, is her go-to expression. "Really?"

Billie cackles and walks ahead but freezes in her tracks when we hear a smooth, slightly accented voice say, "Good luck out there today, Miss Eaton."

Stefan Dalca. The other big player in the horse racing scene out near Ruby Creek. Everyone thinks he's sketchy, and Billie hates his guts after he tried to bribe Vaughn into selling DD. Which would have been a huge mistake. Not only because the ranch would have been without our championship stallion, but Vaughn would have been without Billie.

"Dalca, you piece of..."

I sit up poker straight, a little worried that Billie might go off. She's a bit of a live wire that way, but Mira steps in front of us and turns her unimpressed expression on the suit-clad man in question.

"Stefan, walk with me." She crooks a finger and heads in the opposite direction without even looking back. Like she just knows he'll follow.

To his credit, the usually perfectly curated man looks a little shaken. He tugs at the lapels of his suit jacket and clears his throat before spinning on his heel and striding away.

Billie makes a gagging noise, and I giggle. I know how much she detests the man, but I'm thinking he should be a little more scared of Mira at this current juncture. Billie might be the unpredictable firecracker of the three of us, but Mira is smart, cunning, and wily. Billie you'll see coming because she'll burn it all down around herself to take you out. But Mira? I think you'd be down for the count before you even knew she was there.

Tonight, I am going to channel my inner Mira. Sweet and quiet Violet isn't here right now. Patrick Cassel is going down in the only way I can take him down.

On the track.

I pull into the driveway and park right in front of Pippy's paddock. I couldn't sleep because I was too excited about my win. Too high on adrenaline. So I snuck out of the barn apartment, slid my feet into a pair of sandals, and threw a long cardigan over my floral sleep shorts and matching tank to keep the chill out. It's dark out now, past my regular bedtime, and I hoped to keep my arrival on the down-low, but she's pretty much a guard horse at this point, sounding the alarm as soon as I pull up.

Little traitor.

"Hey, sweet girl." I jump out of my car with a pocket full of peppermints and head her way. "We won tonight. Left everyone else in the dust. It felt so damn good." She nickers and rubs her lips against my pocket, homing in on the minty smell. I pull one out and let her chomp away at it. White foam forms on her lips from the chalky candy. "I was going to go to bed, but I couldn't sleep. Figured I'd come celebrate with you."

I peek up at the darkened farmhouse before I shake my head at myself. *Cute, Violet. Pretending you're not here to spy on Cole. Pretending thinking about him and wondering where he is isn't what was keeping you up.*

I still don't know what to make of what I read on his laptop. I have even less of an idea of what to say to him. I'm half in love with the man, and the other half wants to shake some sense into him. He's so damn broken, so full of fake bravado.

Everyone sees cool, calm, and collected. Emotionless. I think I might have at one point too. But now all I see is sad. Closed off. Lonely. I'm scared he'll break me, but suddenly I'm more scared I'll break him. Loving him feels like a big responsibility.

"Violet?"

The sound of his voice sends a thrill down my spine. Deep and gravelly, a tad sleepy sounding.

I turn slowly to take in his dark form on the front porch of the little blue house. "Hi." I let my gaze trail over that perfect triangular upper body, strong thighs. "Did you see my race?"

"No, sorry. I didn't make it down."

Disappointment lurches in my chest. I wanted him to be there. "Did I wake you?"

"Yeah, but it was time."

Huh? I walk closer to the porch and realize he's only wearing formfitting boxers and a T-shirt. "Did you sleep all day?"

He runs a hand through his hair. "Yeah. I was pretty tired."

I come closer, gripping the porch railing. "I thought you were joking about my snoring keeping you awake."

He laughs. Deep and smooth. Like honey. And I want him to drizzle it all over me and then lick it off.

"It wouldn't have been safe for both of us to sleep. I kept watch."

"We could have taken turns!" I hate feeling helpless, hate that he didn't even bother to include me in that decision. "I don't need you to coddle me. I'm perfectly capable of taking care of myself."

He pins me now, his gray eyes sparking with fight. "That's what you keep telling me. But, Violet, letting me help doesn't make you weak. It just means I care. I know you don't *need* me, but I want to be there for you. Let me care for you in the only ways that I can."

"Is this where you tell me that's what friends do?"

He swallows. I watch his throat bob as his intelligent eyes regard me carefully. "No."

That one word. He doesn't say more, but he doesn't need to. It's his confession.

My tongue darts out to wet my bottom lip as I gaze up at him, his body towering above me, just a few steps away. I swear the air between us heats by the second—like I can feel his energy from several feet away.

"I saw the messages," I blurt out. "On your laptop."

He blinks a few times, but his face stays predictably blank. He shows so little emotion sometimes. It's almost impossible to get a read on him. But when he turns away from me and limps back into the house, I feel enough emotion for the both of us. Walking away, *again*.

I boil over. Fiery hot. Jilted, frustrated, *tired*. I storm up into the house I called home for a month, hot on his heels as he makes his way through the living room.

"Would you just talk to me already!" I shout. It comes out louder and more forceful than I think I've ever talked to anyone in my life. My cheeks heat, and I initially feel a little bad. It's out of character, but I am so done with not saying anything to each other. I like quiet, but this is beyond. Cole is downright uncommunicative.

He turns, jaw popping and the veins in his arms pulsing with tension, all highlighted by shadow with only a floor lamp shedding dim light in the corner. His hands fist and then let go as he raises his voice right back, shouting, "What do you want me to tell you? I never open up to anyone. You think everything between us just started and finished with a photo for me? Like it was easy for me to lose you? To not know if you were okay? To miss you so much it physically hurt? You broke me!"

His words wind me. My chest empties, hollow and throbbing with the weight of his confession. Both my hands creep up over my chest, my fingers wrapping around the base of my throat to stem the growing flow of nausea. *He missed me. I broke him.*

"You broke me first," I whisper. But the admission feels loud in the quiet room. Like I shouted it at him.

His smile is pained as he looks up at the ceiling. "You're not broken. You're perfect. And I'm a shitty fucking patchwork quilt. I've spent years picking up the tattered pieces of myself, every life event, every heartbreak, and slowly stitching it all back together. But I'm not good at sewing, Violet."

His eyes find mine across the room, raw and anguished. All I want to do is wrap my arms around him, but I'm stunned into stillness with his next words.

"And now the edges are starting to fray. I'm coming apart at the goddamn seams, and you're the one holding the thread that could undo it all." Cole groans and runs a hand through his already disheveled hair, agitation and heartbreak lining every limb. "Don't you get it?" His eyes are wide and pleading now as he shakes his head. "You have the power to completely unravel me, and I *hate* feeling like that."

I can feel my pulse jumping in my throat as I stare back at him, swallowing audibly under the weight of the responsibility I'm feeling. "I promise not to unravel you, Cole. It wasn't easy for me either. You hurt me. Being that vulnerable… I need to know what this is between us, once and for all."

His chest rumbles, but the tone is different. And when his eyes pin me in place, he says, "I'm not good at talking. I think I should just show you."

And with that, he grips the back of his shirt and pulls it off over his head, his smoky gray eyes not leaving mine for a single beat. His thumbs hook into the waistband of his boxers, his eyes still homed in on mine.

"What are you doing?" I pant out, suddenly feeling breathless and completely immobile, entirely unable to look away from his body in the warm glow of the darkened room.

"Evening the playing field. You need to know what this is between us? It's fucking everything."

My breath catches in my chest as he pulls his boxers down. My lips part on a sigh, and I stare at him like a total voyeur, dumbstruck. *Is this really happening?* Watching him undress before me. My mind is blank. I feel like I'm having an out-of-body experience.

He kicks the boxers off, and I watch his cock swell under my gaze. Thick, long, and veined, and growing harder every second I spend staring at it.

"Staring is rude, Violet."

My head snaps up to his face, and I bite down on my bottom lip, feeling my body pulse and my pussy go slick. "Sorry."

A smirk flits across his mouth. "No, you're not."

He's right, of course. I've never been less sorry in my life.

"Tell me what to do next."

"What?" My heart beats in every limb, right into the tips of my fingers. They itch to touch him.

"You read the messages." His voice is like gravel. "I told you I'd reciprocate. Tell me."

I feel like my throat could close on me. Like I could choke on all the things I want to say to him. How the hell am I supposed to do this? This man—this Adonis—naked before me. His length is rock-hard and jutting out in my direction now.

Knowing what I know, watching him undress in front of me, it's the ultimate in vulnerability. The ultimate in trust.

I take a step closer, tongue darting out to wet my lips. "Fist it."

His hand wraps around the thick base of his shaft as he says, "Fist what?"

I have a hard time dragging my eyes up to his face. "Your cock." Excitement coils at the base of my spine at my boldness. I've thought a lot of dirty things about Cole over the last couple years, but saying them out loud feels foreign.

I take another step, wanting to get a closer look. He's so well-endowed. It matches everything else about his body. Strong and thick and tempting.

My voice comes out as a hoarse whisper. "Now stroke it. I want to watch you stroke your cock."

His hand slides slowly over the silky skin of his cock, and he looks down briefly, causing one lock of dark hair to flop down over his forehead. He looks disheveled and completely at my mercy. Utterly delicious. My heart aches in perfect unison with that spot between my legs.

When he looks back up, eyes meeting mine, I know I'm a goner. His cheeks are pink, his eyes are wild, his body is tense, and all I want to do is touch him. To make him feel good.

"Cole." His name spills from my lips like a prayer.

And then I shrug my cardigan off and let it pool on the floor around my feet along with the rest of my inhibitions.

CHAPTER 20

Cole

My chest seizes as her sweater drops to the floor. Her flowery little pajamas leave little to the imagination. I want to rip them right off her, to lay her bare right along with me.

I feel so fucking vulnerable. So far out of my element. She knows about me, about everything—that I'm messy—and she's not running.

She's getting closer. Every nervous step she takes is like a shot to the heart. She's not looking at me like I'm pathetic. She's looking at me like she can't get enough. I can't remember the last time a woman looked at me like this, and it's waking up a side of me that hasn't come out to play in a very long time.

I keep my hand moving, stroking myself as she approaches me slowly, like she might scare me off. She has no idea what will happen if she gets close enough for me to touch her though.

I'm fucking done shutting down this thing between us.

"Violet. If you don't want me to completely lose it, stop right where you are."

Her voice is small, and her cheeks are pink. "What if I want you to lose it?"

It's hard to catch my breath when she talks like that. So effortlessly sexy. So innocent. "You don't know what you're getting yourself into."

"Don't I?" she muses with a quirked head. "It's like being small and quiet gives people the impression I'm a prude." She nibbles on her lip, eyes raking down over my body like I'm her favorite snack. "Would it shock you to know I've closed my eyes and imagined being fucked by you for two whole years? You're my go-to fantasy, Cole."

"Violet."

She's not dissuaded. Another step forward. "With my hands. With my toy. With other m—"

"Violet," I bite out. "I don't want to hear about that."

"Jealous?"

I nod because I am. The thought of her with any man other than me tints my vision red. I give my cock a rough jerk in her direction. She's so close now.

A small pleased smile touches her lips. "Good."

"Little minx, it's all fair game if you're going to taunt me like that." And then my spare hand darts out, hooking into the elastic waistband of her tiny shorts, yanking her to me easily.

Her wide, startled eyes stare up at me as she cranes her neck back, and my hard cock juts into her stomach. She repeats herself. "Good."

My heart races. I don't even know where to start. I want all of her. Every square inch. I want to kiss away past hurts. I want to bend her over and give her delicious new ones. I want to watch her come over and over again.

My fingers find the thin strap of her tank top and gently brush it off her shoulder before doing the same to the opposite one. Violet's breath comes out heavy and ragged as I lean down and press a kiss to her cheek.

I pepper them along the line of her jaw, up to the shell of her ear, nipping at her lobe and then smoothing the indent away with a gentle suck before I whisper, "Get on your knees."

She turns her head and kisses me square on the lips. Hard. Both her dainty hands wrap around my head, and her tongue pushes in between my lips. She tastes like mint toothpaste and cherry lip balm. She's fucking delectable, and I can't wait to taste what's between her thighs.

She pulls away, hands trailing over my chest and abdomen as she drops to her knees before me. The sight of her looking up at me with those wide blue eyes. *Fuck.* It's everything I've dreamed of. My cock twitches, and I can't help myself. I reach down and pull her tits out over the top of her tank top, liking the look of her disheveled and exposed on the ground in the middle of my living room.

"So fucking pretty," I murmur.

Her gaze shifts to my throbbing cock, and her lips part as she leans in and licks the drop of precum from the head. And then she fucking hums. Like it's a lollipop. Like it's the best thing she's ever tasted, and I swear I almost blow right here and now.

With one hand on my thigh and the other cupping the back of my knee just above my prosthetic, she slides my cock into her mouth, not once looking away from my face.

I'm not sure what I've ever done to deserve this. I'm not sure I even do. But the sight of Violet on her knees for me will live in my mind until the end of my days.

Her tongue swirls, and her cheeks hollow out as she sucks.

"Jesus, Violet." One of my hands finds her silvery hair, gathering it together so it doesn't impede my view, and the other cups her jaw as my thumb brushes across her cheek. Her head bobs eagerly, gliding over my length, taking me so deep that her nose bumps into my stomach. *What. The. Fuck?* "You are so fucking good at this."

She hums again before pressing a chaste kiss to the tip of my cock. And I lose it. This might be the best blow job of my life, but I need more before I finish.

I give her hair a gentle tug. "Up. In that chair." I nod toward the large armchair beside us and gently direct her there by the elbow.

She moves swiftly and sits down before looking back up at me like a little girl in trouble, her hands pressed between her knees, tits squeezed together between her arms.

"You gonna get shy on me now?" I take a step, wincing at the pain in my stump, but not caring.

"No," she whispers back. "I'll take my shorts off if you take the prosthetic off. I can tell it's hurting you."

I groan. That's a level of honesty I'm not sure I'm ready for. But when she adds, "I'm not wearing any panties," I bend down and get to work peeling the sock down so I can remove it. The minute it pulls free, my leg feels better, but my brain doesn't.

I feel exposed. Completely naked, right in front of the most beautiful woman I've ever laid eyes on. Young. Vivacious. Whole.

"You are so fucking hot." The words rush out of her as she licks her lips, and I realize she's not even looking at my stump. Her eyes are bouncing around my body hungrily, like she can't decide which part she likes best. Pure lust. Pure desire. And suddenly I don't give a fuck about my leg. If Hilary was the poison, Violet is the antidote.

I lean down, resting my hands on the arms of the puffy chair, as I come to kneel before her. She leans back and yanks her shorts down, and when they get stuck around her thighs, I lend her a hand, savoring the feel of them sliding over her skin, of the flex of her calves as I pull them off her feet. And then with one hand covering each of her tiny knees, I open her legs.

So much fucking better in real life.

I slide my palms up her inner thighs, giving her a tight squeeze there before letting one hand continue up over her mound.

"Oh god," she huffs out, looking down at me, at my hands, blue eyes gone dark with yearning.

"Is this what you've been dreaming about, little Violet?" I ask as I hold her spread open for me.

"This… this is beyond."

I can't help but chuckle. "I haven't even touched you yet."

Her hips buck in response, and I beat my chest internally. She's so damn eager. For *me*.

I trail a thumb over her seam, and she whimpers. So I do it again, more firmly this time, parting her lips. "Violet. You are so fucking wet for me."

"Always," she whispers, and I groan at her confession.

Why did I take so long to get here?

I slide my thumb into her up to the first joint, and she sighs, her eyes fluttering shut. She looks so fucking good that this time, I sink two fingers into her wet heat, feeling her stretch around me.

I gaze up at her, watching those perfect pink nipples turning to hard points, watching goose bumps spray over her arms. "I wonder how a pussy this pretty tastes."

Her eyes fly open, just in time to watch me slide those same two fingers into my mouth.

"Jesus Christ," she mutters, watching me with rapt fascination as I savor her.

And then I pull her down toward me and dive in.

CHAPTER 21

Violet

I'M HAVING AN OUT-OF-BODY EXPERIENCE. I'M BATTING SO FAR out of my league. Cole Harding is so fucking hot. I thought he was from that first day he came storming toward me in the winner's circle. Older. Richer. Better looking. But the sight of his disheveled, inky hair between my legs is something else.

It's primal. It's delicious torture.

The way he wraps his arms around my legs. The rasp of his stubble against my inner thighs. That goddamn tongue.

I feel so small with him holding me open. So exposed. But not like last time. This time he's *here*, and the way he looks at me—dark and possessive—makes my stomach flip.

I moan, making a sound I'm positive I've never made before this moment. A sound that would normally make me blush. But I'm beyond blushing. My entire body is on fire. I'm one big blush.

I roll my hips up toward his face, and he pushes back in harder, devouring me, propelling me higher. Tongue, lips, teeth, everything in perfect proportion. The man is a master.

"Cole…" I tangle my fingers in his dark hair and give him a gentle tug.

He pauses only long enough to pepper a few sweet kisses right along my inner thigh.

"Don't stop."

He chuckles, and it rolls across my skin like electricity. So deep and so private. Every time he laughs with me, shares that pleasure, it feels like more. He doesn't just hand out laughs like they mean nothing. With him, it's a true sign of affection. And I eat it up.

When he slides two fingers into me again and curls them *just* right, I fall apart.

"Cole!" My legs shake as I clamp them around his head, and my fingers twine in his hair, squeezing in time with the pulsing of my body. Pure heat surges through me as my orgasm overtakes me, making my back arch to its limits.

I swear I see stars.

But as I come down, I don't feel boneless. I feel ravenous. I want more. I want to watch Cole hit that high. I want to see him come apart for me.

I want him inside me.

My fingers dig into his toned shoulders, trying to get purchase, but they're clammy and just end up sliding over every muscle. "Get up here. I need you."

He looks up at me from between my legs, lips glistening, eyes wide and dark like coal. "Violet, it's okay. We can go slow." He unwraps his arms and slides his hands up the tops of my thighs, gaze flitting down to my pussy again.

I grab his wrist and pull him toward me right as I lean down and capture his mouth. He groans as my hands roam his shoulders. I can't get enough of his shoulders. Big and round and broad.

Holding him close, I whisper against his cheek, "I think I'm done going slow. I've wanted you for long enough."

With a deep growl, he grabs me as he pushes himself up into the chair and flips our positions. Now I'm straddling him just like I was last night in the forest shelter. Except this time, there's nothing between us, and the length of him is pressing right against me. I can't help but rotate my hips, to slide myself on him, to finally feel his skin on mine.

He stares at his hands wrapped around my waist and lets his gaze trail up over my body. "Lose the tank top." His voice is all heat now. Any hint of uncertainty has fled his tone.

I pull it off instantly, not feeling shy about being completely naked in front of Cole. Not at all. I've been here before. I knew less about him then—less about the type of man he is. Because if I've learned anything in the last month, it's that Cole Harding is a *good* man. Broken and sensitive and so fucking good.

I also didn't have the benefit of seeing the way he's looking at me right now, which is with pure awe. Unadulterated lust. Intense hunger.

"I don't have a condom." He doesn't even look up at me as he says it.

I push up on my knees, hovering over his lap, feeling the head of his cock bobbing against my inner thigh.

"I'm on birth control. I don't care. I want to feel you inside me."

"Jesus Christ, Violet." The pads of his fingers pulse on my waist as he lifts me to line us up perfectly. "I'm going to watch you take every inch," he mutters as he lowers me back down on him.

I feel the stretch, the overwhelming fullness, as I glide down the length of his cock slowly, his fingers digging into me tightly. I gasp with the feeling, with the knowledge that he's really inside me, with the brazenness of his words.

"Good girl. Every fucking inch."

His voice is raw, and my nerves are frayed. I want him to undo me and never put me back together again. We both look down at where we're joined. Nothing between us. Just the two of us. Together.

Finally.

His grip finds my chin, and he kisses me roughly, with so much passion that it winds me. I taste myself on his tongue as it swipes into my mouth, and I move my hips in time with the pace he sets.

Every pass of his tongue matches the swivel of my pelvis. His spare hand roams my body, leaving a trail of blistering heat. I feel every ridge of him, every thick inch, as his hips buck and meet me, shoving his length into me with growing abandon.

We clash. We melt. We heal.

I don't need poetic words or grand apologies from Cole. That's not the man he is. Just this. Opening up to me like this—loving me like this—it's how he shows me. The phrase *Actions speak louder than words* has never applied to another human more aptly.

Cole Harding wouldn't be fucking me like this if he didn't care about me, and I know it. I feel like a queen writhing in his lap as he pulls his mouth from mine and drags it down my throat and over my collarbones.

"You are so fucking beautiful," he whispers as he captures my nipple in his sinful mouth. His teeth graze, and I hiss. "And so fucking precious." The flat of his tongue soothes the sting. And then he glances up at me, looking completely and utterly blown away. He looks like he's worshipping at my altar in this darkened living room. His hands hover shakily over my ribs. "You are so fucking precious to me."

I can't keep my hands from fluttering over his face, my fingers from tracing that scar that cuts through his brow, as I look back down at him, knowing I'll never want to let him go after this. "Don't let me go this time."

His throat bobs, and I think his eyes might sting, just like mine, as he nods back at me. "I won't."

"Good. Now make me come again."

He moves hard and fast in me, gripping my hips and manhandling my body in the most dominating way. My thighs slap against his as he lifts me and slams me down on his length over and over again.

Perspiration dampens his chest, and his cheeks are ruddy when he puffs out, "Let me see you rub that clit, Violet. Come on my cock."

My hand darts off his shoulder as I lean back a little. I think his words might be enough to push me over the edge, and all it takes is a few slick swipes with my fingers to have me hitting that crescendo again. Heat pools at the base of my spine as my orgasm roars to life.

"Cole!" I cry out just as that spot below my hipbones aches and the arches of my feet cramp up.

I collapse forward onto his chest, damp and spent and completely at his mercy as he pumps into me a last few times, hitting every tender spot as he does.

And with one powerful thrust, he freezes.

He clamps his arms around me, caging me in as he holds on for dear life and pours himself into me.

Chest to chest.

Heart to heart.

A hot bath has never felt so good. Partly because my body is gloriously sore from the best sex of my life and partly because I'm sitting across from the most deliciously sexy man I've ever known.

After our time in the living room, we were both a sticky mess. Boneless, breathless, sticky messes. I didn't know what to say after sex like that, but I knew his stump was rubbed and sore from the spare prosthetic, so I got up and ran us a bath.

This bathroom has the best deep claw-foot tub. I thought it was big before, but looking at Cole sitting at the other end, it doesn't look so spacious anymore.

Steam wafts up from between us. It smells like eucalyptus from the Epsom salts, which has the added benefit of being good for soreness—and for perfectly clear bath water.

And yeah, I can't stop sneaking peeks at the monster between his legs.

Cole's hands are wrapped around my calves as they rest across his thighs, and his head is tipped back against the tub, eyes closed. I am positively bursting with questions, but I also can't stop admiring his body. It's like a piece of art. A testament to long hours spent healing, adapting, and surviving. Living proof of his strength and resilience.

A goddamned treat.

My eyes wander over his leg, the one that ends just below the knee. The angry red scar at the end of the stump, the puckered skin all pulled together to close off the leg they couldn't save. But mostly I stare at his huge dick. In fact, I have a hard time looking away from it.

Yeah, I'm perving hard, and I don't even feel bad. The man looks like a well-hung Ken doll, and he's somehow magically into *me*. A scrappy ranch rat from a small cowboy town. Scrawny little Violet Eaton.

"Are you sure you haven't had sex in years?" I blurt out, because I can't reconcile this hot, rich, successful older man being interested in me or keeping it in his pants for *years*.

He doesn't look up, but I see one cheek quirk and feel his thumb rub in a circle on my calf.

"I knew you had questions. It's like I could hear the gears in your head turning."

"I mean, *come on*. Look at you. You really mean to tell me you haven't had sex since—" Ugh. I don't even want to say her name. I'm jealous, and it's so unlike me. "Since what's-her-face took off?"

His shoulders shake on a silent laugh, but he still doesn't open his eyes. "There were a few off the start. Random encounters with a stranger where I wouldn't have to take my clothes all the way off. Like just bent her over and—"

"Okay. I've got the gist."

He chuckles again and peeks one eye open at me and catches me nervously chewing on my lip. He knows I'm jealous, but he doesn't call me on it. He just says, "All that taught me is that I don't like casual sex."

"Okay... but years? You could have anyone you want."

He grunts. Like he doesn't quite agree with my assessment. "Maybe I don't want just anyone. I think I like being in a relationship. It's probably why I rushed into an engagement before. But she didn't want me; she wanted the idea of me. The status." He sighs and sits up straighter. "You..."

My heart lurches in my chest. *I what?*

"You stuck around when you knew nothing about me. Like you enjoyed my company or something—and no one enjoys my company. Not anymore. But you were like a moth to a flame, knowing it would burn you eventually. Beautiful and innocent. And strong. And I was so fucking scared of letting you get too close, of opening up. But you never forced my hand. You just quietly made me need you." He scrubs at his stubble with one hand. "And then you left, and I told myself I was right all along—that everyone leaves me. Until the universe laughed in my face and shoved you right back into my life."

I let out a breathy laugh and blink rapidly, turning his words over in my mind. "It sort of did, didn't it?"

"And then you were just yourself. You didn't miss a beat. You came back for more. Forced me out of my shell. So relentless. So fucking consuming. It's like you've seen all my darkest corners and don't give a shit about them. You're not scared. You don't look at me like I'm tragic. You look at me like we're inevitable."

My throat aches, and my eyes go glassy. I look at him with a watery smile because I don't trust myself to speak. What I don't say is... *that's* what scares me.

We are completely inevitable.

CHAPTER 22

Cole

FOR THE SECOND MORNING IN A ROW, I WAKE WITH VIOLET snuggled into my chest. She's curled into me like she can't get close enough, little hands grasping at the white T-shirt I'm wearing, fisted into it to keep me close.

I smile, liking how it looks. Liking the thought that she wants me close. Liking waking up next to her, the smell of her on my sheets. Even the purring doesn't bug me. Someone so small and dainty making that noise is just plain charming.

The sun filters in through the windows of the room, casting a sparkly glow over her pale hair. She looks downright angelic. With those pouty, rose-petal lips parted slightly, I can't help but think back to sliding my cock between them, the way she kneeled before me and looked up into my eyes.

I feel myself swell. *Fuck.* That was something I'll never forget. She might have been the one on her knees, but it felt more like I was the one begging. Even this morning, I feel like I should pinch myself. A woman like Violet wants me. And I can't wrap my head around it.

She asked why her, when I could have anyone I want, a comment that still makes me shake my head. I'm a thirty-six-year-old man with nothing to show for my years on earth except a company that was handed down to me and a nice lingering dose of PTSD from a dead dad and a blown-off leg. No house. No friends. No kids. I've always wanted kids, but here I am without a single one of those things on the horizon.

And in walks Violet, every one of those things readily available to her, and she wants what? *Me*? I just can't reconcile it. I haven't even tried to pretend I'm something else. I've been surly and unreachable, and the odd time I've given in to her allure, I've ended up shoving her away like she's nothing.

I realize she might be everything.

The light at the end of the dark tunnel. The sunshine my dark existence so desperately needs.

I can't stop myself from brushing my lips across her temple. She feels so precious wrapped up in my arms right now.

"Hi," she murmurs quietly, nuzzling against my chest.

"Sorry. I didn't mean to wake you up."

"I'm glad you did. That's a pretty good way to start the day."

My heart thunders against my ribs. *Is she serious?*

This time, I press a kiss to her hair and cup the back of her head, still amazed she's even letting me touch her. She's so fucking precious.

"What time is it?" She doesn't even poke her head out of our little cocoon.

I look over at the bedside table. "Eight."

She groans. "I need to get going."

"For what?"

"Into the city. I've got rides today on some of the younger horses early on. And then DD in the stakes this evening. You coming to watch?"

Her voice sounds so hopeful. I swallow roughly. I don't love watching the races at the best of times. But now? After this? Having to watch Violet on a horse, running at breakneck speeds, over the ground where I watched my dad die? It feels impossible. Terrifying.

It feels like I need to call Trixie and confess some shit.

"Sure," I say woodenly as I trail a hand over her slender back, feeling it rise and fall with each breath, something that feels reassuring as I try not to fixate on the thought of her getting hurt out there. Or worse.

She slides a hand over my ribs and squeezes. "I'll be fine."

"I know," I murmur back.

The lie tastes sour on my tongue. I don't know that she'll be fine. I can't predict that kind of thing. The words feel cheap, but I say them because I know they're what she wants to hear.

★★★

The traffic heading into the city is obnoxious. I guess after over a month of living out in Ruby Creek, I've grown accustomed to getting anywhere I need to go in mere minutes and without encountering a single other person.

Something I appreciate. Not having people everywhere all the time is preferable to the noise, the mess, the ant-colony feel of downtown Vancouver. Just a bunch of mindless little worker ants scurrying off to their jobs so they can overpay for rent or—god forbid—a mortgage. The housing market in this city is downright criminal.

I could afford one if I wanted, but it's the principle. A run-down bungalow on a small lot shouldn't cost a person over a million dollars. I've seen how people live in other parts of the world, and the excess of this city grates on me. It's wasteful.

Maybe that's something I've come to appreciate about country living and small-town residents. They live well within their means. Hardworking people who aren't trying to keep up with the Joneses. It's like another world. A smaller, quieter, more real world where people work to enjoy what they've got rather than working to afford something that might impress their friends.

Just a completely different mentality. One I like—that I might align with more than I initially thought.

Since traffic doesn't appear to be going anywhere—on a fucking Sunday afternoon—I decide I might as well bite the bullet and call Trixie. Something I've been avoiding doing because truthfully, I don't know how she's going to react to everything that's transpired.

Have I gone off the deep end? Is this happening too fast? It feels fast. We haven't even talked about what we're doing. Violet kissed me sweetly, deeply, when she left my house this morning and then hopped in her car and drove off.

All she said was, "See you later," and I'm so fucking out of practice with women that I don't even know what that means.

I blurted out more to her last night in that bathtub than I've said to anyone, other than Trixie, and she didn't run screaming for the hills. So where does that leave us? I feel like a teenager all over again. Can I just leave her a note like I would have back then?

Want to be my girlfriend? Check yes or no.

I scoff as I jam my finger at the screen of my phone and hear the ringing filter in through my Bluetooth system.

Trixie's voice booms through the cab of my truck, making me wince and adjust the volume. "Cole. It's a Sunday."

"I had sex." That should change her attitude.

The speakers are quiet for a few beats. "Real sex? Or internet sex?"

Why does everyone keep calling it that? "Real sex."

She lets out a long whistle. "How was it?"

"Jesus Christ, Trixie. Is that something therapists ask their patients?"

"Ha! I don't see why not. If you're going to call me on a Sunday like I'm a guy friend, then I might as well ask the same questions someone like that might."

I groan. Trixie is anything but your average therapist. Of course, that's actually what I like about her. Sad as it sounds, she's also one of the closest things I have to a genuine friend. And I pay her.

"It was... overwhelming."

"Overwhelmingly... good?"

"Yes," I bite out, feeling uncomfortable even though I'm the one who called her.

"Okay. And where did you meet this person?"

"It was Violet."

I swear I can feel Trixie smile through the phone. She's spent the last year telling me I needed to bite the bullet and reach out to Violet. Say something. *Anything*. Rather than pretending she doesn't exist. That even if it didn't go anywhere, I might feel better just getting everything off my chest.

But I kept putting it off, telling myself I'd do it eventually. All I'd have to do is drive out to the farm and talk to her. But no, instead I hid out in the owner's lounge and scowled down at her during every race she ran. I haven't missed many since I figured out who she was. The one where Cassel took her down, because I was busy moving out to Ruby Creek, and yesterday, when I was just too tired and too sore from our adventure up on the mountain to make it. It felt wrong not being there. Like I've been in this secret relationship with her for the last year that she had no idea about.

Because I have. Writing her in the chat, watching her from the skybox, getting updates from Vaughn, who always eyed me suspiciously as he did.

"I'm happy for you, Cole," Trixie says. Like she doesn't think I've fucked up at all.

"That's it? No words of wisdom? No advice? No scolding?"

She hums. "What would you like me to tell you?"

"I don't know. Something. Anything? She's young. Maybe I'm a creep."

"Is she of legal age? Did she consent?"

I want to feel you inside me, that's what she said, and Trixie knows Violet is well into her twenties. She's only asking to prove a point.

"Yes."

"Then I don't see the issue," she says simply.

"She's just so vivacious. Really going somewhere, you know?"

"And you're not?"

I groan. She always does this. Spins it back around on me.

"I don't feel like I am."

"Okay. And have you asked her how she feels? Do you think that a woman who you've described to me as intelligent and going somewhere would saddle herself down with someone she perceives to be deadweight? What would that say about her?"

My brain backflips to follow her logic. But I see what she's saying. If Violet is who I've told Trixie she is, then she must see something in me I can't see in myself.

She takes my silence as an answer. "Presumably, she knows about your leg now?"

"Yeah." I scrub at my face, remembering how I felt like my world was falling apart two days ago on the mountain. How I felt like I wanted to dissolve into the dirt path to avoid her knowing about it. "My prosthetic malfunctioned on our hike. She knows about it in graphic detail." I spit the last part out, still hating how incapable it makes me feel.

"And what was her response?"

I think back on the hopping and crawling jokes she made and sigh. "She didn't seem to care at all."

"I've been telling you for two years that no one cares about your leg except for you."

I can't help but chuckle as I recall the few times Trixie has told me this. *You're not a special snowflake. Stop acting like one.*

"I guess I needed proof. The universe forced my hand with this one."

"It has a funny way of doing that, doesn't it?"

Traffic crawls toward Bell Point Park as I mull over those words. All the ways I've woven Violet into the fabric of my reality. How inescapable she's become.

"Guess so," I muse. "I just don't want to hold her back."

"But you want to keep her?" Trixie sounds far too hopeful. I almost hate to confess this to her.

"Yes," I reply, because I do. I've avoided admitting this to myself, but it's true. I want Violet as way more than a pen pal or friend and definitely as more than a one-time thing.

"Then don't hold her back. Bolster her up. Be her biggest fan."

All that hope sprouting in the dusty wasteland that is my heart shrivels. Can I bring myself to support her when I can barely stand the thought of her out there on the track? And why the fuck would the universe put her in my path when I can barely stand the thought of kissing her goodbye to go do the very thing that killed my dad?

"And, Cole," she adds, "talk to her."

Right. Talk to her.

I stand in the owner's lounge beside my brother, looking down over the track. It's almost time for the stakes race, and I feel like I might barf. I cross my arms over my chest and squeeze, trying to push the panic clawing its way up inside me back down.

"You look like you're going to kill somebody." Vaughn takes a sip of his scotch and shoots me a playful glance. Always joking around. What must it be like to feel so carefree? I wish I knew.

I just grunt. I'm okay with looking like I might kill someone. It means my poker face is still intact because I definitely don't want to look like I might break down. Or worse, like a lovestruck idiot. And even more, I don't want to talk about my past with Violet now that he knows about it. In fact, I'm a little surprised he hasn't cracked a joke about it yet.

"Gentlemen," I hear from behind me and turn around, coming face-to-face with a man I've never met before. Dark blond hair, crooked nose, expensive suit. He looks like a total chump.

"Dalca," Vaughn says, his voice going chilly after teasing me mere moments ago. "What can I help you with?"

Ah, this is Stefan Dalca. The man who almost took my little brother for a ride. The man who employs Patrick Cassel, the shithead who made Violet fall. I want to kill them both.

"I just wanted to apologize for Patrick Cassel's behavior. He's no longer employed by me."

Okay, I want to kill him a little less now. Maybe just maim him. Break that nose again. "The person you owe an apology to is Miss Eaton."

The man turns his hawkish eyes my way. They're intelligent, scanning—altogether too confident. I don't trust this guy as far as I can fucking throw him.

"I'll track her down." His lips tip up into a sly smile that I want nothing more than to wipe off his face.

But instead, I nod. My days of flying off the handle are behind me. I've got different problems now.

"Good luck today." He sticks his hand out as though I'll shake it.

I look at it and then shift my gaze up to his face. I'm not shaking this guy's hand. All I'm giving him is an unimpressed look. Vaughn does the same.

"Okay. Tough customers," he says with a chuckle before he swaggers away. I can see why Billie hates the guy. She's nothing if not an excellent judge of character.

"Nice. I love it when you go all glacial like that. It's fucking terrifying." Vaughn drinks again with a big goofy grin on his face. "Violet is a braver woman than I am."

There it is. I shift my eyes over to Vaughn, who looks like a kid on Christmas morning, far too excited to see my reaction to that comment.

"And Billie is a more patient woman than I."

Vaughn barks out a loud laugh that has people looking our way as his shoulders shake. "Thank fuck for that," he says, looking back out over the track. "There they are!"

He points toward Violet, sitting atop a shiny dark horse in matching black and gold silks, her champagne hair plaited straight down her back. I feel instantly nauseous at the sight of her out there but swallow it down.

I don't want to be that guy. And I don't want my snoopy little brother knowing that I feel like that guy.

DD prances beside the pony rider that leads them along the track, and I'm glad that someone is there to escort them safely. Some horses are really riled, jumping around, but not the little stallion. He prances along slowly, like he knows he's fancy—perfectly confident. Violet looks that way too. Still and quiet, one hand smoothing up and down the horse's muscular neck.

I shouldn't be nervous about this race. It's not a huge deal. It's a qualifier. But I am. My chest is tight, and I feel like my throat is trying to crawl up out of my mouth.

I cross my arms over my chest again as they load up into the gates. I know DD gets nervous in there because I've heard Violet talk about it. I also know jockeys can get injured in there if things go sideways. My fingers wrap around my thumbs underneath my biceps and squeeze tightly. Maybe if something hurts, I'll be able to get a handle on my anxiety, focus on something else.

The bell rings, the gates fly open, and the line of horses surge out in a mass of pounding hooves and flying dirt. Violet and DD hang back predictably. This is their play, their move.

My teeth grind as I watch her sink into the tack. So in sync, moving in time with the horse as he stretches out underneath her. He's a finicky stallion, but Violet doesn't get in his way. She lets him be quirky and uses it to their advantage, making it a winning feature rather than forcing him to be a type of horse he isn't.

They keep to the back—but not too far behind—down the first stretch. But when they move into the first turn, their focus changes. Violet shifts down lower, pushes her hands farther up his neck, and he surges up through the middle, making his way into the pack.

Exactly where *it* happened. The slip. The fall. The hooves. And a still form in the dirt as the pack continued to head away toward the finish line. Like a man in the dirt was nothing.

It's been *years*, and that image is still burned into my mind. No one stopped. No one went back. In the army, we *always* went back. Even if it was just for pieces.

A gray horse moves out in front of Violet, and I suck in a breath. Vaughn notices, but he doesn't say anything. He just peeks at me out of the corner of his eye. Violet backs off, playing it safe, looking for an opening. And when she doesn't see one coming out of that final turn, she takes him wide. It means they'll be forced to cover more ground.

But if anyone can pull the move off, it's going to be this team. Even I know that much. Murmurs roll through the skybox as she flattens out and pushes her arms at DD while his stride eats up the ground. I know he's not a large horse, not even especially leggy by racehorse standards, but the little spitfire doesn't let that stop him.

It is truly a sight to behold.

As they near the finish line with a wide-open lane, I feel my icy dread morph into something warmer. Excitement. She's about to do it again. And I am so damn proud.

Hard work, sweat, and her fierce determination are paying off in spades. A little country bumpkin with a no-quit outlook and infallible positivity is making her dreams come true. And I admire the hell out of her for it.

They fly across the finish line, and it's tight with DD and the other horse pretty much neck and neck. To be honest, I can't tell who won, but I don't care. All I want to do is see Violet. I realize in this moment how badly I need her—want her. I want to run my hands all over her body. I need to feel her. To know she's okay. I haven't felt this level of anxiety since right after my discharge, when I couldn't even hear a car door slam without jumping. *You're fucking losing it, man.*

"A photo finish," Vaughn mutters as he shakes his head and jangles his keys in his pocket.

I'm not the only nervous wreck, it would seem, but he stays up here because Billie gets anxious. She doesn't like him in her space when she's working, which is something I can appreciate. Suddenly, I realize I don't know what Violet likes. Would she want me down there? Are we going to be a thing where that's even an option? I'm not sure if I could handle it. What about now? After the race? Do I wait until tonight, back at the ranch? Tomorrow? Follow her around like a sad little puppy dog? *So fucking pathetic, Cole.*

I groan, hating how uncertain I feel about this whole thing. I hate feeling out of control. This is when accidents happen. Missions go wrong. People get hurt.

Hearts get broken.

"I gotta go," I say to Vaughn as I turn to leave before he can see my face. Because as good as I am at hiding my emotions, I feel like they are probably written all over me right now. I don't care about the photo finish results; I just need Violet.

I shoulder through the crowd in the skybox, heading to the exit, down the stairs, out the door, and into the muggy heat. Rather than turning toward the track, I head in the direction of the barns.

I'm going to see Violet because it feels right. And if I think about it too much, I'll let my uncertainty talk me out of it. God knows the woman has put herself out there enough times for me, to get to know me. And I've been a closed-off dick about it, taking far more than I give.

What's the worst that could happen? She tells me now's not a good time? She's busy? Seems to me I've faced bigger disasters for less reward.

I stride into the barn and turn down the row of stalls with the Gold Rush Ranch sign at the entryway. Mira, the vet, is at one stall going through what looks like a big toolbox.

"Where's Violet?"

She turns and looks up at me slowly, like she has all the time in the world. "Excuse me."

"I said—"

"No," she cuts me off, "I know what you said. But you missed saying it politely."

My jaw ticks. What is with all the insanely lippy women at Gold Rush Ranch? Has Vaughn made it a job requirement?

Even Violet isn't as mild-mannered as she used to be, which is good. Billie and Mira are good for her. But man, getting called on my shit all the time is tiring. It's like I'm living among a bunch of young Trixies.

I sigh dramatically as I try again. "Excuse me. Have you seen Violet?"

"I knew you weren't as bad as Billie makes you out to be," the black-haired woman singsongs. *Fucking Billie.* "And also no. I imagine she's weighing in. Head out that way, and you'll probably run into her." She points to the opposite end of the darkened alleyway.

"Thanks." I wave as I head in that direction.

She just winks at me. Like she knows I'm a total fucking goner. But as I round the corner, all I can think about is Violet. On her knees. In my lap. In my bed.

It's like she broke down all the walls around me, and now I can't stop myself from spilling everywhere. I'm oozing out all over the fucking place.

When I walk out into the sunlit road, I catch sight of Violet walking toward me, wearing a simple blue wrap dress that matches her eyes perfectly. Her hair is drawn up tight in a bun, and her smile is blinding when she catches sight of me.

"Hey, you!" she calls out with a small wave and a little skip in her step. "I'm so glad you're here! We won!"

And then I go full caveman.

CHAPTER 23

Violet

When I see Cole marching out of the barn, I can't help but smile. When I get close enough to him, I look away. He's so beautiful it hurts. He looks like a storm cloud, dark and menacing and problematic for my panties. But I know better. He's a big puppy d—

I lose my train of thought when he wraps his hand around my wrist and drags me back toward the barn.

"What's wrong?"

He pulls us into the darkened shed row and then straight into an empty stall. When he turns me to face him, he's all steely eyes and hard lines. He prowls forward, and I back away. Not because I'm scared. More because I don't trust myself not to combust under a gaze like that. I can't believe I was about to call the man a puppy dog. My nipples rasp against my bra, and I press my thighs together as I bump into the wall.

I hold one hand up to stop him. "Cole. What's wrong?"

"What's wrong?" His voice is low. "What's wrong is I can't stop thinking about you. And those perfect tits. And that tight little cunt. And those pretty little lips."

I moan and feel my face go pink. He may have been vulnerable last night, but *this* is the Cole I remember. Gruff and filthy and so damn hot. The man who could push me to my limits—exactly where I want to go.

I try to say something, but my lips just open and close like a fish out of water. Like a girl out of her league.

"Do you have panties on this time?" His intense eyes scan me, leaving a trail of sparks in their wake.

I go pure red, from head to toe, and look around us. The stall is lower than the alleyway, with no bedding in it, just rubber mats, and we're pushed up into the corner behind the front wall. No one would see us unless they specifically came into the stall.

I roll my shoulders back and look him square in the eye, refusing to be Shy Violet. I shed that skin a long time ago—at least in my head I did. "Yes."

"Turn around."

"What?" I feel my eyes bug out of their sockets.

"I said turn around."

My blood hums through my veins as I take a shaky breath and turn to face the wooden wall of the stall.

"You drive me crazy. Do you know that?" He steps in close, and I feel his heat along the entire length of my back, his breath across the nape of my neck.

"Good," I reply honestly. "Serves you right."

His breath hisses out, and he finally puts his hands on me, right where my waist nips in. And then he's taking fistfuls of my dress, pulling it up, the hemline tickling the backs of my bare thighs as he does. "I should spank you for talking like that."

I moan and shimmy my ass, brushing it up against the hard bulge at the front of his pants.

"You'd like that, wouldn't you?"

"Yes," I breathe out.

One minute, I'm in my element: galloping toward the finish line, winning a race, waiting on results, and weighing in; the next, I'm bent over and rubbing up on the man I can't stop thinking about, getting spanked for being mouthy. His palm lands swift and sure against the bare cheek of my ass, and I can't help the needy whimper that spills out over my lips. The sting blooms into heat, and I love the feel of it.

Today is a good day.

One of his palms presses between my shoulders, and he kicks my feet apart with perfect authority, complete control. Over himself and over me.

A thrill races down my spine, and I submit under his touch, allowing him to bend me forward. Is it okay for me to be fiercely independent everywhere except when his hands are on me? Because right now, all I want to do is exactly what he tells me and just let go for a little while, to not try so hard for a few minutes. It's addictive. Freeing.

My breath comes in choppy spurts as he lays my skirt across my lower back and hooks his fingers into my lacy panties, dragging them down, leaving them stretched between my thighs. He runs his hands over my ass, giving me an appreciative squeeze. "You look downright edible with a little bit of pink on that ass, Violet." His voice is quiet, but I feel it in my bones. Like his body is speaking right to mine. "But I'll save that part for when I get you home. Back in my bed where you belong."

"Fuck yes" is all I can manage before going completely mindless as he slides a couple of fingers between my legs. I usually feel scrawny when I'm naked, unfeminine, but with Cole's hands on me, I feel like a different woman.

He groans and I shiver as he slides a finger inside me. "You're wet already. Dirty girl. You do like that, don't you?"

"You have that effect on me," I rasp out as I look over my shoulder.

His eyes hold mine, dark and frantic. "Tell me what you want."

I don't even need to think about my response. "More. Always more."

One hand shoots out to grip my chin roughly. His lips crash into mine as he fumbles with his belt and zipper. He shoves his tongue into my mouth. He's not searching or asking—he's taking.

And I'm giving.

I feel the blunt end of his cock slide against my seam and moan into his mouth. Suddenly I'm ravenous. Everything is taking too long. Time is moving too slow. I'm greedy.

I arch my back and push myself on him, feeling him slide inside me. Hard and fast. Just like the kiss. Relentless and unforgiving, that's what we are in this moment. Two bodies joined. Two people running at each other without the sense to stop before they crash.

Our mouths part, and I turn back toward the wall, dropping my head as he slams into me. One of his hands grips my hip, and the other slides firmly up over my back. His calloused fingers hover over my neck, right to the base of my skull, before his grip wraps gently around my throat, essentially holding me in place.

Like I might leave him.

I want to tell him that there's nowhere else I'd rather be than here. But my mind is mush, and my body is burning. The words don't come.

When his hand slides across my hip and over my stomach, he pulls me tight to him, shoving me forward into the wall before his fingers move down and press on the perfect spot. I rock in his arms as his fingers circle, driving me higher and higher. Right toward a cliff. I should know better than to jump from such heights, but I'm past the point of caring.

I leap and plunge right over the edge with him inside me. And he follows. I feel him twitch and go still as he covers my body with his. I sigh when he relaxes over me, his lips replacing his hand at the nape of my neck as he peppers kisses down my spine. His breathing is heavy in my ear.

"That was..." I can't put it into words. Inappropriate? Unprofessional? Super fucking hot?

"Yeah," he replies, sounding just as breathless as me as he leans down to pull my panties up and smooths my dress back down over my bare legs. His touch is warm and reverent as he sets me to rights. And when he spins me around to face him, he kisses me sweetly, longingly.

Cole is a man of dichotomies. Hot and cold. Rough and soft. Intense and relaxed. Confident and uncertain. He's multifaceted. And in the weeks I've spent around him, I've come to realize that I like every facet. Love them? Maybe. But that sounds like the ramblings of a lovesick girl swept off her feet by a rich older man who she's been lusting after for years. And I don't want to be that girl. So I don't let myself go there.

Instead, I kiss him back with all the feeling I can muster. All the longing, the affection, the acceptance—I want him to feel it all. That I'm here for *him*. Just the way he is.

When he smiles against my lips, I wonder if I've succeeded.

"Can I come to your place tonight? Once I finish up down here?" I ask quietly.

He offers me one of those rare soft, panty-melting smiles as he cups my head in his palms and gives me one of his quintessential one-word answers. "Yep."

I let out a giggle as he pulls me into his embrace, wrapping me inside his steely arms, and presses a soft kiss to the top of my head.

Cole Harding is way more romantic than he lets on.

"Open the gate."

Cole stares back at me, bulging biceps twisted together across his chest, legs wide. I chuckle internally. When Billie calls him G.I. Joe, this is what I envision. Army green joggers and a black T-shirt that is being downright abused by his muscles.

Just like I have been for the last couple of weeks. Every time we're not working or in public, we're naked. Together. I like to think of it as making up for lost time.

"Are you sure?" he asks, enunciating his words carefully. I know he wants to tell me no. I know he worries about me riding. I know his father's death haunts him. He doesn't need to have told me explicitly for me to have pieced it together. You can't live in fear of these unexpected tragedies though. And the only way I can prove this to him is to have him hang out with me and *the only horse* he likes. I want him to see the fun—the joy—riding a horse can bring to his life.

I'm sitting on Pippy's back, and he is being a literal gatekeeper. He doesn't want me to take her out into the fields even though I've spent the last couple weeks getting her started in the arena. She's walking, trotting, and cantering under saddle now. The steering still leaves something to be desired, but that will come.

Plus, steering doesn't matter much in a big open field.

"Very sure." I give him my best serious look, trying to instill confidence, though I'm sure I just look like a mischievous child trying to pull a fast one. The fact is, I'm not *very sure*. You can't be sure of anything in life. That you won't die having baby number four. Or on horseback. Or in an IED explosion. There aren't any guarantees. I mean, hell, if someone told me two years ago I'd be the jockey for the world's most popular racehorse, I wouldn't have believed that was possible either.

But here I am. Living. Taking life by the horns. Exactly like I promised myself I would. My dad couldn't stop me, or my brothers, and definitely not Cole. I want him around me for the long haul. And I need him on board if that's going to happen.

He still doesn't look sure, but he unlatches the gate and holds it open so I can steer Pippy onto the driveway. The hills near the barn look so lush and green this time of year. I love running races on the track, but galloping across an open field takes me back to my roots. Back to Alberta's foothills, where I grew up kicking cow ponies across the range. British Columbia is beautiful, but I miss that prairie feeling sometimes. Less polished, more country, endless flatland.

I walk past him as Pippy's ears flick around. Her neck comes up higher now as she looks at her surroundings. She's sweet and calm, but even she can feel that something else is happening right now. That's the biggest question mark with this filly. Is she too mellow to run?

"Good luck," Cole bites out, every part of him tense as he watches me go.

I look over my shoulder, wink, and blow him a kiss, trying not to let myself linger on his ashen face, the way it matches his gray eyes. He looks sick, and if I let myself stare at him for too long, I'll hop off and hold him instead. So I turn my game face to the field ahead of me. Time to find out what this little filly has under the hood.

Once I hit the edge of the grass, I give her ribs a gentle squeeze, urging her into a trot. Her head is still swiveling around, and when she senses we're heading out of her bubble, she lets out an excited whinny.

I wince. Such a pretty horse. Such a terrible sound.

We go down a gentle slope, and then all that's before us is the freshly cut hayfield with a big hill at the end of it—same one that Billie conditioned DD on. In case my brakes fail, my plan is to use that to slow down if needed, like one of those runaway lanes for semitrucks on the highway.

I run the leather reins through my fingers, shortening them, and adjust my feet in the irons, wanting to be as stable in the tack as possible before I let Pippy gallop for the first time. At my change in position, her back comes up, and I feel her haunches go tight. Like she knows what's coming.

When I slip one leg behind the girth and give her a little nudge, she breaks into a comfortable canter, still feeling a little uncertain. Like she doesn't know what I want from her. She's such a people pleaser. It doesn't surprise me at all. It's like she doesn't want to put one hoof out of place.

I move up in the tack, getting off her back, and loosen my elbows, letting my hands float higher up her neck. Her ears flick back in question, so I give her a squeeze with my legs and a firm cluck. She bursts forward almost instantly. And then I smile.

Because I've got a racehorse on my hands.

CHAPTER 24

Cole

Violet stirs in my arms, rubbing herself against me, and my cock instantly stands at attention. But I squeeze my eyes shut tighter, wanting to stay exactly where I am and savor it for a little bit longer.

My mind wanders to the day at the track when I outed myself to her as Golddiger85. I could have said nothing. And she would never have known who I am. Who I *was*. We wouldn't be here. *Together*. My rash decision in that moment has completely altered the course of my life, and for once, I'm not beating myself up about it.

It's been several weeks of sleepovers now. We don't spend any nights apart, and I wouldn't want to anyway. When Violet's with me, I know she's safe, and as much as I hate to admit it, she makes me feel safe too. Someone who knows everything I've been hiding for so damn long and still wants me. Someone who just looked at me like, *Yeah? And? Who cares?*

My leg, my PTSD, my anxiety around horses, she just lets it all be. Like it's my shit to deal with. Shit she's happy to put up with for some godforsaken reason. A reason I can't explain—or maybe I don't want to.

It's been bouncing around in my head lately. That four-letter word. I often wondered if I was in love with this beautiful, sweet, funny woman who kept talking to me for an entire year. Like I had something to offer her—like she enjoyed my company. But now, spending almost every night with her, inside her, it's a thought I can't shake.

I'm definitely in love with Violet Eaton.

The problem is admitting I'm in love with Violet means my carefully plotted-out existence is about to topple. I've spent so many years feeling undeserving of love, hiding myself from the mere possibility of it, that it feels bizarre to think that I might have found it now. With Violet, no less.

My hips push toward her ass of their own volition. I can't get enough. I feel like I'm in my twenties again with her around. Insatiable.

"Good morning." Her voice is warm and dopey as she pushes herself back at me, always equally eager. *Because she* is *in her twenties.*

I always feel weird about our age difference, a feeling that Violet doesn't share at all. Mostly she looks at me like I hung the moon. A look that makes my heart constrict, even if it makes me feel uncomfortable. I've spent so long hiding from view. Having someone admire me as openly as Violet does is a little unnerving.

"Good morning, beautiful," I murmur as I drag my teeth up the side of her neck suggestively, watching a slow smile spread across the top side of her face. She's practically glowing in the golden morning light. She looks like an angel—my angel.

"I'll play if you go start the coffee."

Yes. Now I stock coffee. I don't know what it is with these women's reliance on the stuff, but it seems to make Violet happy. And I'm all for that.

I sit up and slide my stump into my new prosthetic, happy to have that custom fit back. And so damn fortunate that I can afford the state-of-the-art one I have. I like that Violet doesn't jump out of bed to make her own coffee because of my leg. She doesn't baby me, because she knows I'm perfectly capable. I smile over my shoulder at her, watching her stretch out like a cat in a sunbeam, all fucking pleased with herself.

I hum to myself as I jog down the stairs to the kitchen, feeling lighter than I have in years. I press the button on the coffee machine and then slide some sandals on at the front door, heading out to feed Pippy. The other girl in my life.

A chuckle rumbles in my chest when I open the door. She's waiting at the closest corner of her fence, too-long ears pricked in my direction and nostrils vibrating with the shrill hello whinny she's known for.

I never would have guessed it, but this little filly makes me smile every day. Another thing that hasn't happened to me in years. I pull a few flakes of hay off the bale and toss them over the fence for her, something she completely ignores until I've given her a few good scratches behind the ear.

"More concerned with lovin' than eating, huh?"

Her head twists toward me, and I admire how she's grown into herself. At two, her haunches are still a little higher than her wither, but she's filled out with muscle and a glowing bronze coat. Between her feeding regimen and Violet's elbow grease, she doesn't look like the same ratty filly who showed up at my house a few months ago.

"Guess we've both undergone a bit of transformation, haven't we, pretty girl?"

She snorts and bats her long lashes at me, her eyes like deep black pools. I swear she gives me a knowing look. Like, *Yeah, you fucking idiot. We both needed a fresh start.*

I shake my head and stroll back inside, leaving her to eat but mostly eager to get back to Violet. And when I make it up the stairs to the master bedroom, I go to announce my arrival, "I'm back—" but I stop short when I see Violet kneeling at the end of the bed, golden hair streaming down over her pert breasts, just like that day on the video chat. Except today, she's giving me that heartrending shy but willing look she pulls off so effortlessly.

"Let's try this again, Butterface." Her fingers pulse, squeezing at the bedspread beneath her. "But this time, we don't quit on each other."

My mouth goes dry instantly. "Violet. We don't need to do this."

"No." She wets her lips. "I need you to do this. Rewrite the memory for me. Don't leave me this time."

"I don't think I could leave you even if I wanted to. I'm so fucking sor—"

"Don't. Just tell me what to do."

Every muscle in my body goes taut. This is so fucking hot. She's so fucking forgiving. I don't fucking deserve her. But I'm going to spend every damn day trying. The thought invigorates me.

I start like I did a year ago, "Lie back on your pillows and spread your legs."

And just like the time before, she flushes pink. A whole-body blush.

"You look so fucking pretty in pink," I say as I stalk to the bed, feeling my knees butt up against the brass footboard. And when she lets her legs fall open, I groan. "You're going to be the death of me."

"Good," she says with a slight smirk. A small sign of her strength.

She might be gentle and soft-spoken, but Violet isn't weak. She can't be if she's going to withstand a man like me.

She settles back into the pillows, and I admire her body splayed out before me like an all-you-can-eat buffet. I plan to sample every inch. I let my gaze linger between her legs, glistening already. I can see it, but I want to hear her say it. "Are you wet already?"

Her chest rises on a small gasp as she looks down over her body and confesses with a small hiss, "Yesss."

"Of course you are." My prosthetic clangs against the bed frame, and my cock throbs. I don't know who I'm torturing more here—her or myself. "You love this, don't you?"

She just nods this time, cerulean eyes wide like pools of deep water. Like the river I can hear rushing behind the house.

"Why don't you touch yourself and show me?"

Her hand finds her pussy almost instantly while the other tangles in the sheets below her. Like she's holding on for dear life. I'm transfixed as her fingers trail through her folds, her eyes closing and head tipping back on a moan. Most men would probably be engrossed by what's happening between her legs right now, but I'm staring at the way her elegant neck extends, her exposed throat and the way it moves as she swallows.

"Two fingers in, baby."

She whimpers but follows my directions. I don't miss the way her thighs tremble as she does it though, the way her toes curl and clench. She pumps in a few times, making the most delicious fucking noises as she does.

"Now show me how wet you are."

Her eyes flick open, and her jaw drops. Still so damn shocked sometimes. *Oh, honey…*

Right as she holds her fingers up to show me how wet she is, I say, "Now suck them."

"Jesus…" she mutters, momentarily looking away with a small smile on her mouth. Like she loves it but can't believe she does. It makes me smile too. Until she puts them in her mouth and moans around her fingers.

Fuuucckk.

She giggles, which makes my cock jump painfully in my boxers.

"No toy to play with this time."

"I'm looking at him." She sounds out of breath now. Wet, breathless, and blushing.

I live for this version of Violet Eaton, and I can't wait another minute to dive in. I'm over the end of the bed and crawling toward her, yanking my boxers down and moving straight in between her spread legs before she can get another word out.

"I don't remember this part from last time." She laughs, and it's fucking music to my ears. I'll never get sick of making that up to her.

★★★

I'm ready to crawl back into bed and sleep after an early morning marathon sex session with Violet. I haven't had this much sex in, well, probably ever. Unfortunately, we're both gainfully employed and have jobs we need to get to today.

"See you tonight?" she asks, sliding into a pair of skintight riding pants that has my mind wandering places it should be tired of going by now. We've been sort of sneaking around for a few weeks. We don't go out. We work and fuck and then talk until we fall asleep in each other's arms. She's met up with Billie and Mira the odd time, but she never invites me to come—even though I know Vaughn is often with them.

I sometimes catch myself wondering if she wants more. I should just ask her. I should take Trixie's advice and talk to her about my anxiety around my dad, the depth of it. Around horses. And the fact that she rides them for a living. But it's so pathetically insecure, I haven't talked myself into it.

At least I'm consistent.

"Of course." I swipe her wet hair off her cheek and cup her head just below her ear as I press a kiss to her cheek. I love how dainty she feels in my hands. Precious.

We get ready quickly, quietly, running behind after having to take another shower. And when I lock the door behind us, she stops and spins around, launching herself at me, wrapping her arms around my neck and planting a big kiss on me. I'm a little surprised, but I catch up, pulling her close with one arm around her waist and letting the other take a nice big handful of that ass in those tight pants. This is the morning goodbye I've always dreamt of.

And then a throat clears loudly. "Is it weird for me to say that was pretty hot?"

Billie.

Violet laughs, her shoulders shaking as she buries her head in my armpit and whispers, "I'm sorry."

What? "Did you know she was there?"

She nods, her forehead against me, her body still shaking.

I laugh too. It's always contagious with her. I'm also relieved she doesn't seem horrified by being caught kissing me, and I can't help but let my amusement show. "Do you think that if we ignore her, she'll go away?"

Her laugh turns into a loud snort as she wheezes out, "No. Definitely not."

"I heard that," Billie shouts. "Really cute. I came to bring you the farm financials."

I look up as she waves a folder over her head and then sets it down on the gravel driveway.

"But I'm not getting any closer to that house. God knows what kind of filthy shit has been going on in there."

"Billie," I warn, knowing it won't make a difference. The woman has no filter.

Violet chortles in the most unladylike way, squeezing in tighter like if she gets close enough, she can hide inside me entirely.

"I'm leaving them right there." Billie points down before holding her hands over head and stepping away slowly, like this is some sort of hostage situation. "For what it's worth, I'm just glad people will stop talking about *my* cabin being the love shack now. See you up at the barn, Porn Star Patty!"

She grins and winks at me as Violet melts down into my arms. Billie looks far too pleased with herself and, to my surprise, not upset at all. I don't know why… but I expected her to be weird or protective or something. I expected a scolding for scooping up someone so young and normal. I expected Billie, of all people, to see how I don't deserve the woman in my arms.

But she just looks amused.

When she finally pulls out of the driveway, Violet gasps out, "I'm… I'm sorry." She looks up at me with tears of laughter pouring down her face. And I feel like I'm in some sort of upside-down world. Why is no one mad about this? "I shouldn't have done that to you."

"Let me get this straight." I lean back to look down at her with a furrowed brow. "You kissed me on purpose. Because you knew Billie was there?"

She swipes at her face, trying to catch her breath. "Yes. I–I'm sorry. I wanted people to know about us but didn't know how to bring it up or ask you or tell them. I saw her truck there out of the corner of my eye, and it seemed like the simplest solution. We are an *us*, right?" When she says *us*, she peeks up at me from under thick lashes shyly.

I blink at her, scanning her face for some sign that she might be joking. Because in what universe does *this woman* want *me* to be an *us* with *her*? I literally shake my head and count my lucky fucking stars. And then I kiss her hard, hold her to me tight, and show her how badly I want to be an *us*.

"We are definitely an *us.*"

I pull up to the farmhouse and close my eyes, dropping my head against the seat. Work was shitty, and that's saying something considering the mood I arrived in. Between hot morning sex and Violet staking her claim on me in front of her friend, I was in a great fucking mood.

I don't feel like I'm getting anywhere with the new acquisition. Which means I'll be stuck out in Ruby Creek for longer, getting things organized and running smoothly before finding someone else to take it over. I wasn't supposed to like it in Ruby Creek. I was supposed to hate it. But I'm not hating it at all.

I don't want to leave because I know Violet won't be leaving. And that agitates me. I spent all day working out the ways we'd see each other once I move back to the city. She can stay with me on the days she races at Bell Point Park, and maybe I can get out to the ranch on the weekends.

But I don't like that option. I want Violet in my bed every night. Where I can see her. Hold her. Keep her safe. Not an hour and a half down a major highway doing a dangerous job and living alone.

No. I don't like that at all. And what I like even less is the possibility I'm subconsciously making the new business out to be worse than it really is, all so I can stay here. *I'm a fucking head case.*

When I get out of the truck, I expect to hear Pippy whinny, something that usually makes me smile. But today, smiling feels like work. My muscles don't fire right. I feel a cheek twitch, but my body doesn't quite comply. The smile feels half-hearted. Even this horse deserves better.

And anyway, a whinny doesn't come.

I look at her paddock, feeling blue to my bones, wishing I could nap. Sometimes these moods hit me for a day or two. Everything feels heavy, and I feel low—downtrodden. I know I haven't been in touch with Trixie enough for my own well-being. One more thing I can beat myself up about.

I've been so high on Violet in the past weeks, I haven't had time to wallow. She's not here. I don't see her car, which means she's probably with Pippy up at the barn. I'd usually wait for her, but today I need to see her. I'd face Billie's mocking, Vaughn's smirk, and Hank's knowing twinkle if it meant getting to see Violet.

I jump back in my truck and take the road up to the barn. When I pull into the parking lot, I can tick off who will be here by looking at the cars. Everyone is here. Something I'm dreading already. There's a reason Vaughn took up the mantle as the face of Gold Rush Resources. Partly because he's pretty and partly because I hate that shit. Too many people and too much attention makes me feel like I'm an actor up onstage. Fake. With a big bright spotlight on me, highlighting every flaw while everyone stares, slack-jawed and horrified. A man who's killed people, who's watched people die, and who's been handed a multinational company with no experience. That's what I'm sure they must see.

I walk past the offices, not wanting to talk to Vaughn, and head down the vaulted barn alleyway. This facility is so ridiculous. *Ranch.* I snort.

A young man with a wheelbarrow full of dirty shavings gives me a friendly nod.

"Do you know where Violet is?" I ask.

"My guess is down at the track. Saw her and Billie head down there not so long ago."

"Thanks," I bite out, not really wanting to go to the track but wanting to find Violet more.

Back in the fresh air, under the oppressive cover of heavy cloud, I walk down the paved path toward the dirt oval, running the pad of my thumb over the teeth of the key in my hand, pressing it into the soft skin until it bites.

When the path angles down and I clear the stand of trees that gives the track a private feel, I see Violet on Pippy and Billie up on her black stallion. They're chatting amiably, trotting toward the gates at the far end of the track. Vaughn and Hank stand in the covered viewing booth, and I head that way.

I take the few small steps up onto the platform, and Hank turns to greet me, stopwatch in hand. "Cole! Good to see you, son. How you been?"

"Good." I try to muster a smile, but I know it's a sad attempt. Hank deserves better. He's been a mainstay in this town for years. My grandfather Dermot hired him and got him into the horses. I don't know him as well as Vaughn does, but he always gives off that warm, fatherly vibe—the one that makes me squirm with discomfort. The one I miss from my own dad.

"Hey." Vaughn looks me over the way he always does. A tad uncomfortable, like he's trying to gauge what kind of mood I'm in, and I hate myself for making my little brother feel that way. Like he needs to walk on eggshells around me.

I feel like I've sufficiently killed whatever good vibe they had going in here and jerk my chin out toward the track. "What's going on?"

"They're going to try the filly up against another horse, see how she handles the competition."

"Is a stallion the best choice?" My voice comes out steely, and Vaughn raises an eyebrow at me, though this time he spares me the teasing about my "military voice."

Hank steps in. "DD is a mellow stallion and very experienced. With Billie on him, it's the best choice for sure. If she needs to pull him up, she'll be able to. He's got a level head like that."

I try to ignore the anxiety roiling in my gut. I should go back up to the house, spare myself the stress of being here. But I've always been a glutton for punishment, so I stay, forcing myself to face it. Wanting to not be such a royal chickenshit about this.

I'll need to get a grip on this if Violet and I are going to be an us. I watch her and Billie guide their mounts into the slots. No gates are up today; it's just an open lane. I guess that part comes later.

"On your marks!" Hank shouts, his voice booming in their direction. "Get set!"

Pippy prances on the spot, like she knows something is coming. Like she's ready to explode.

"Go!"

As Billie and DD fly out of the gate, completely well practiced, Pippy startles. Her eyes roll slightly, showing the whites, and rather than surging out and running, the little bay filly goes straight up, standing tall on her back legs with her front hooves flailing ahead of her. I watch in frozen horror as Violet attempts to slide her arms around Pippy's neck and hang on. Her stirrups are set too short for her legs to provide any support.

Time moves in slow motion as her mouth sets in a grim line, concentration painted all over her face. I know Violet isn't new to a young horse's antics, but it doesn't stop pure dread from filling my chest.

And when I watch her topple off the back of the filly, I'm running. Down the stairs, across the bank of grass, vaulting the fence, as though I could get there in time to catch her. Billie sees me and pulls up, finally looking behind herself. Pippy lopes toward me, away from the gates, confusion in her eyes. Dirt flies out behind my feet as I scramble across the track.

I feel bile rise in my throat and stop a few meters away from Violet's still form, trapped in my worst nightmare.

I can't be back here again.

I can't breathe.

My vision blurs. The ground sways beneath me. And I bend over, pressing my hands into my knees as I drop my head and try to force my body to work again. I feel like an old car that needs a jump, a spark. I'm too fucking broken to even help her when she's on the ground.

But I can't get my body to cooperate. I heave, one hand coming up over my mouth to hold it in. If she's hurt. If she's dead. It can't happen. I only just found her. I only just found us.

"For fuck's sake!"

I look up just in time to see her fist hit the dirt and her small feet kick the ground like she's having a temper tantrum. And suddenly, I can get air back into my lungs. With a few more steps, I fall to the track at her side, kneeling in the dirt, fingers hovering over her body while tears spring up in my eyes.

Relief. Relief so intense. Like I've never felt before. "Are you okay? Are you okay?" I can't stop saying it. The question pours out of me repeatedly, as though I'm short-circuiting. Stuck on a loop. Suddenly, I'm transported to the dry heat of Iraq and to that day on the track all at once. It feels like I'm breathing sand again. It scratches my throat; it weighs on my lungs. Checking pulses. Ears ringing.

But Violet's eyes aren't dull and vacant. They're clear blue pools, reflecting the puffy white clouds above us. Her expression changes from looking pissed off to looking concerned as she takes me in.

"Hey, hey. I'm fine."

She tries to sit up, but all my first aid training kicks in, and my arms shoot out to hold her down. *What if she has a spinal cord injury? A brain bleed? She could be in shock.* When I watched my dad fall, he never got back up.

"Cole. Let me up. I'm fine. I was just winded."

Her lung could be collapsed.

I feel a nudge against my shoulder and look back to see Pippy standing behind me with a sheepish look on her face, black eyes staring at me with such kindness. Billie is just behind her with a sad look on hers. She's seen how fucked up I am, and now she pities me. *Great.*

"Just take a minute, Violet," Billie says so that I don't need to.

I'm intensely grateful that she's not just throwing me under the bus, telling me to chill out. Instead, she's helping me, something most people don't do. Especially people I've been as growly with as I am with Billie.

"You guys!" Violet shoves my hands off and sits up, frustrated. "If I tell you I'm fine, I'm fine. I don't need to be handled with kid gloves just because I'm the same size as one."

I flop back, sitting on my heels as Violet brushes herself off and comes to stand. She places one gentle hand on my shoulder before offering the other to pull me up.

"Cole. Babe. It's nice to see you. But I'm working right now. I'm coming to your place when I'm done. Billie, let's go again."

Her tone isn't cruel, but it is matter-of-fact. She's not in shock. But I think I might be, even though she's fine. I feel my hands tremble. I feel like I'm having an out-of-body experience. Like every square inch of me is numb.

Except for my heart.

That part of me aches. I can feel it, see it. The damage there, like an inconsequential ding from a rock that quickly splinters the glass and spiders out across the entire windshield uncontrollably. *Ruined.*

I stand and nod, keeping my eyes trained on the ground as I move away from the gates.

"Cole! Wait up!" Vaughn calls after me, but I wave him off and pick up my pace.

I flee.

Everyone saw me freak out. That goddamn spotlight I avoid is on me. *They all know.*

But I can't focus on that right now. My mind is reeling with two thoughts:

I need to be alone.

I can't be with someone who does this for a living.

CHAPTER 25

Violet

"I don't think you should be mad at him, Violet. You didn't see him. He was..." Billie trails off with a faraway look in her amber eyes. They pinch at the sides. "I think it would have made him feel better if you'd have just taken a minute to show him that everything was in working order."

"Why?" We're wiping down our tack together, and I rub the saddle soap–covered sponge over the reins of Pippy's bridle roughly. I'm aggravated. "I'm doing my job. I don't need him here micromanaging me and telling me what to do. Can you imagine if I waltzed into his office and did the same?"

"I know. I *know*." Billie squeezes the water out of her sponge with a loud sigh. "But sometimes, when we care about someone, we make their priorities our own. You didn't see him, Violet. He sprinted. I thought he was going to hurl right on the track. I don't think Cole's priority is to micromanage you—it's keeping you safe. Your safety is important to him. So throw the guy a bone and just, like, wiggle your toes and catch your breath next time before you jump right back on."

"Didn't know you were on Cole's team." I instantly hate myself for saying that. Childish.

"I didn't know you were twelve." Billie arches one shapely brow at me, successfully chastising me without saying more. She squeezes my shoulder and drops a sisterly kiss into my hair. "See you later, tough cookie."

But as soon as she goes, the sentence that runs through my head as I finish my chores in silence is the one about shared priorities. I'm still mulling it over when I pull up to his house, knowing that we need to hash some things out. Because if I'm going to make his priorities my own, he needs to make mine his too.

I'm about to open the door and walk in when nervousness hits me. Was I too hard on him? Snappy? I was miffed I fell off because I wanted to give Pippy the best experience possible, and that didn't happen. I was being hard on myself, and I think that spilled over into being hard on Cole. Based on Hank's and Vaughn's faces, I feel like I might have been harsher than necessary. Unintentional as it might have been.

I opt to knock instead, feeling the distance between the two of us already and not wanting to intrude.

"Come in." His voice is ragged, tired sounding.

I twist the knob and step into the pretty farmhouse. So light and airy, painted in whites and blues. It reminds me of delft pottery—the kind my dad still keeps in a china cabinet in the dining room from my mom's family in the Netherlands. I remember pulling them out as a child, running my sticky little hands over a plate or a bowl and making up stories in my head to go with the scenes painted on the sides.

Cole is in the corner, sitting in the cushy armchair where we first made love, looking like a dark shadow. Pure turmoil. I must have missed how insanely handsome he looks today when I was lying in the dirt. Gray dress pants with a bit of a sheen to them, black dress shirt with beautiful pearl cuff links. His elbows are braced on his knees and his head is dropped, his eyes fixed on where he spins one cuff link near his wrist.

He doesn't bother looking up at me. He's always looking at me like I'm the sun and he's been living underground for years. The way he looks at me warms me to my toes. I want him to look at me like that forever. So this—him avoiding me altogether—stresses me instantly.

"Hey," I say cautiously, unzipping my paddock boots and setting them neatly on the mat by the door. He likes it tidy. *See? Here I am. Sharing priorities.*

He mumbles something in response but doesn't change position.

"Cole? Are you okay?" I pad across the floor, onto the Persian area rug in the living room, and kneel before him, trying to get his eyes on mine, seeking that warmth.

I fold myself onto my knees, butting up against his feet. One flesh, one plastic. I wrap my hands around each of his calves. One flesh, one plastic. "Hey. Look at me."

When he finally does, my heart lurches in my chest. He looks tortured. Broken. So lost. His eyes are glassy, his longer hair on top disheveled and flopped over his forehead. His face looks more lined than usual, showing our difference in age, the difference in how our lives have played out. Sure, I've had my challenges, but Cole… It's like he got dropped in the middle of the mountains at seventeen and has been forced to survive on his own.

I feel guilty. Like I haven't really wrapped my head around just how much he's been through. I've been so focused on wanting him, on showing him, that maybe I missed seeing just how lost he is. *Has he been pretending to be fine this whole time, for my sake?*

I think back to his nerves around me riding Pippy in the fields, the fact that he never watches any races from ground level, his vocal dislike of horses—save for Pippy, who seems to have completely won him over—and realization dawns on me.

Dropping my head, I kiss his knee. "I'm sorry I scared you. It wasn't my intention. Is this something that's been bothering you for a while?"

"Yes," he says, looking at the ground again. Not touching me back. Zero reassurance in his body.

"Okay." My hands rub up and down his calves, silently begging him to look at me. "We can work on that. Figure out a happy medium. I don't want you worrying about me like this."

"Then stop."

"Stop what?"

"Making me worry."

I chuckle sadly. It's such a sweet sentiment. "Tell me how. I'll try."

I feel his heavy sigh over the tips of my fingers as he finally pulls his head up and looks at me. The sigh is defeated, and so is the look in his eye. "I can't do this."

I lean back, away from him, like he just slapped me. "What?"

"This." His voice has transformed to the cold, unfeeling version of him I started out with a couple of months ago. His defense mechanism. "You and me. *Us.* I can't do it."

My pulse throbs in my throat as I try to keep up with what he's saying. Seems like an extreme reaction to a simple spill off a horse. Not my first. And definitely not my last.

"Why?"

"The riding. The horses. The racing. It's more than I can handle. Day in and day out. Every weekend. My dad died on that fucking track. I'm both drawn to it and repulsed by it. You deserve someone who can be there for you. You deserve someone who will be your biggest fan. And I can't do that."

I reel. First, I'm devastated, and then suddenly I'm furious. "Are you telling me if I found a new job, we'd be fine?"

His eyes shift away and his jaw ticks, like he's too ashamed to admit I hit the nail on the head. I let my hands fall away from his legs and flatten them on the carpet to ground me, breathing deeply and taking in the low-pile threads, the way the dark blues and creams and whites blend. Him and me. Dark and light. I feel like he just plucked my thread right out and tossed me away.

"So you kept this going, pursued me even, *knowing* the job I've always dreamt of and am finally making a name for myself at would be a deal-breaker for you?"

He groans and runs his hand through his hair, tugging at the ends angrily.

"And now you have the gall to ask me to quit for you?"

He looks at me quickly now, his eyes blazing. "I would *never* ask you to quit for me."

I push up to my feet, shaking my head as I go. "Ask it. Imply it. What's the difference?"

"Violet—"

"No." I hold both hands out to stop him. "Nah. Don't. I don't want to hear it. You've always been clear about your boundaries. And now I need to set my own. I spent a whole year thinking I might be the exception to your rule. That maybe, just maybe, I would be the one to change your mind. Which is stupid, right?" I laugh tearfully, knowing I'm losing the grasp on my control, and move swiftly toward the door. "I'm never going to force you to change, and twice now, you've proven that I'm not worth changing for. Fool me twice, shame on me."

"Violet, please, you have to know it has nothing to do with—"

I spin and stare back at him. One tear spills out on my cheek. "I know, I know. It's not me, it's you. Except it's not. You're so much more than you give yourself credit for. I wish you could see it in yourself. What I see in you? So much strength. So much love. But I can't make you embrace it. That's on you. I don't believe for one second that you don't want us. But you're stuck, Cole. You can't see past one moment of your life. One terrible moment. And you're letting it define your entire existence." I jam my feet into my boots, hating walking away from him when he looks like he needs me more than he ever has before. "When you're ready to make other moments just as important, let me know. This isn't me quitting on you. But I won't wait around forever, Cole. Figure your shit out."

I keep my eyes trained on the door as I say it. My escape route. Because if I look at Cole right now, I'll go back to him.

I'll wrap him in my arms. I'll kiss him.

I'll forgive him.

And that's not what either of us needs right now.

I haven't slept. I haven't cried either. I've just thought. I lay in my bed all night thinking. About Cole, about his scars, his insecurities, his trauma. And about me and mine too. About how mad I am at him and how my heart bleeds for him.

I don't want us to be over. But I need him to be the one to take that step. And if he can't get over my chosen career path, then we weren't meant to be. I'm not folding to make another overbearing man in my life happy anyway. It's not even on the table.

"That's not the new Violet," I mutter to myself, staring into my coffee cup in the staff room, wishing I could hook it up to myself with some sort of IV drip. I should talk to Mira about that possibility.

"Hi, New Violet," Mira says as she marches in, like I willed her into existence, and grabs herself a mug. She's obviously oblivious to what went down yesterday.

"Funny," I deadpan.

"What was Old Violet like?" She stirs her coffee with a smile on her full lips.

I groan. "Meek. A pushover."

"Maybe you're not new. Maybe you're just growing. Nobody stays the same. New goals, new experiences… they're all building blocks that put a person together. Constantly shifting."

"Are you a doctor of philosophy or veterinary medicine?"

She laughs and takes a sip of her coffee.

"You're in a good mood. What's wrong?"

Her feline gaze peeks over her mug at me as she grins. "I'm always in a good mood."

"You're not usually this talkative."

"Sometimes I learn more by listening."

"You scare me a little bit."

She throws her head back and laughs. "I'm in a good mood because I just came from a meeting with Vaughn and your boyfriend. They're going to be building a clinic here on the farm for me to work out of. Not enough quality facilities around, so apparently they're expanding into their own."

I smile, and it's genuine. I couldn't be happier for Mira. "That's amazing! Congratulations. But he's not my boyfriend."

She scoffs and tops her coffee. "He looks just as shitty as you. Actually," she says and peers at me closely, "worse. The man's got it bad. What did you do to him?"

"What did *I* do to *him*? Why is everyone taking his side?"

"No one is taking his side, Violet. I just know you're strong. And yeah, that man might fill out a T-shirt like it was painted onto him, and he could probably bench-press me, but he's in pain. It's written all over him—even before you guys had your little spat. I diagnose animals who don't talk for a living. He's basically the same thing. Trust me."

I laugh and then look at her seriously. "You think I'm strong?"

"I do. And you shine bright. Bright enough that a man like that might need you to light his way."

CHAPTER 26

Violet

THE FLANNEL BLANKET IS SOFT BENEATH ME, AND THE STARS ARE bright up above me. Most of the horses have been tucked into their stalls for the night, but we're still lying out among all the paddocks, down by the farthest one that backs onto the fields—the one DD used to be kept in.

"Is this really how you spent your first night on the farm, Billie?"

"Yup. Pass the wine."

The two of them have me sandwiched in between them. Their way of forcing me to come out for a girls' night. When I said I couldn't muster the energy to go to Neighbor's Pub, this was Billie's suggestion. What I didn't tell them was I didn't want to go to the pub because it reminded me of that night with Cole. When he finally softened up a little. When things got out of hand in the truck. That night, over pints of dark beer and chicken wings with a little too much batter, we came to a tenuous agreement. We turned a corner. The next day, he built Pippy her shelter.

"Wine straight out of the bottle and everything?" Mira asks from where she lies on the other side of me.

"Oh yeah," Billie says. "It's not the same with a glass. Less therapeutic that way, I think."

I giggle. "And the bread? You didn't cut it? You just ripped pieces off?"

"I'm fancy like that." Mira snorts in the most unladylike way, and Billie continues, "But it's way more fun with you guys here."

"I love you guys," I blurt out with a light slur.

"Violet, no more wine from the bottle for you," Billie says. "You're just drinking your feelings now."

"Seems as good a plan as any." I put my hands behind my head and continue searching for constellations up in the night sky.

I wonder if Cole is sitting outside looking at the same thing. He liked to sit outside with Pippy when he couldn't sleep. But I haven't taken her back over there yet—something I feel bad about. I left and took the one other living thing he enjoyed spending time with.

"Maybe try eating your feelings instead?" Mira holds a chunk of ripped French bread with a slice of brie on it over my way.

I take a bite right as Mira asks, "Have you seen Cole at all?"

"No," I mumble around my overfull mouth. It's been three days, and nothing. No call, no text, no smoke signals from his house.

"Well, go get on his case already."

"I don't know what to say to him. He told me he can't handle me being a jockey. What the fuck am I supposed to do about that? Quit?" I snort. "Screw him."

I look over to see Mira nodding. "The screwing must be pretty good for you to be this torn up about it."

My mind flashes to his hands on me, his gruff voice, his stubble between my thighs, me bent over in that stall for him. "You have no idea."

"Ugh! Gross," Billie says as she sits up to take another swig of wine. "You guys are both so stupid. He's scared of losing you, and you're scared of losing him. You both need to toughen up and get back to smashing. You're both in a better mood when you do. He's less grumpy, and you're less emo."

I can't help but laugh. Billie minces no words, and it's one of my favorite things about her.

"When I first met you," she says, "I thought you were like Drew Barrymore in that movie, *Never Been Kissed*. Virginal and awkward, but you're more like a secret freak. I respect the hell outta that. Channel that girl, and go make G.I. Joe pull his head out of his ass so I won't have to keep avoiding the offices when I know he's there."

"So this is about you?" I quirk a brow and point at her unsteadily.

"Of course! Everything is about me!"

We all dissolve into a fit of giggles and revel in the lightened moment.

Until Mira ruins it. "Speaking of egomaniacs, Violet, has Stefan Dalca spoken to you?"

My body goes tense at the mere mention of his name. I feel like I sober up instantly. "No. Why?"

"He said he was going to."

"About what?"

"Not my place to say."

Mira is like a lockbox. I know there's no point in pestering her. Where Billie might spill, she won't.

"Just checking," I say.

"Didn't know you and Dalca the Dick were buddies, Mira." Billie swigs again.

"Honestly, Billie. What is with you and the nicknames?"

"Way to deflect." Billie flops back down onto the blanket.

I feel safe between these two women. Coworkers turned friends—best friends. I've never had this before, and it warms me to my core. Without a mom or sisters and living on a ranch, I always felt isolated. Not cool or girly enough to feel like I belonged with other women. But Billie practically plucked me up and told me we were friends, and Mira just slid in. She started out cool, maybe a little standoffish, but we carried on like we didn't notice and now... "Here we are. Sisters from other misters."

I meant for that to be an internal thought, but the other two women don't laugh. They shift closer to me, elbows touching mine, feet flopped over against each other.

I've been numb for the last few days and have thrown myself into Pippy's training. We've got her running the track pretty comfortably after that first blip on the radar. I want to call Cole and brag about her. *My* project. Living, breathing proof I'm not just the lucky blond who got handed a championship horse. I'm an exceptional horsewoman. I want to crawl under the covers and tell him about it. I want his smell to wrap around me and the light dusting of hair on his chest to tickle my lips as they move, telling him about my day as we drift off together.

I want him with me. I want him there cheering me on. I don't *need* those things. But I need him to be mine. And I decide, as I'm lying here with two of the strongest, most accomplished women I know, that I'm going to make sure I tell him. I'm not going to be shy about what I want. I won't make it easy for him to walk away.

Because Billie is right. More than anything else, I'm terrified of losing him. And I'm going to tell him. Even if he can't tell me back.

I walk along the gravel roads with a flashlight in my hand. I'm too inebriated to drive, and I have, once again, underestimated how long the walk is. With every step I take closer to the blue farmhouse, doubt seeps in. And sobriety. Maybe I shouldn't be doing this. Does this make me seem desperate or brave? I can't decide.

On one hand, how many times do I need to tell this man I want him for him to believe me? On the other hand, if I don't lay it out to him in plain terms, face-to-face, I know I'll regret it. If I let this thing we have fizzle without trying, I'll never forgive myself.

Still, my feet feel heavy, like someone put lead in my pink-and-white-checkered Vans. It would be easy to turn around. A relief even. But I made it my goal a few years ago to take risks, to take chances, to *live*. And this is that. Staying true to myself. Or at least the girl I want to be.

I walk up to the house and pause at the base of the few steps that lead to the porch. It's after midnight, and there aren't any lights on. *Great, I'm going to wake him up* and *put him on the spot.* I blow out a deep breath and look up at the sky. A silent prayer for strength.

"Careful. I hear the guy who lives there is a real dick."

I start and spin, eyes scouring the dark yard until they land on his figure, sitting hunched over on the top rail of Pippy's empty paddock. He takes my breath away. His inky hair in the dark almost looks like it's alive above his glowing gray eyes.

"He pretends to be."

"He is."

"He's not."

Cole runs his hands through his hair. It's like he wants me to hate him as much as he hates himself. But I won't.

"You're stubborn," he says as he drops his elbows back onto his knees.

"Yup." I nod my head, struggling for what to say next, aching to rush across the gravel driveway and kiss him, hold him, run my hands over his neck, and tell him how I feel.

"I'm sorry." His eyes look pained as he trails them over my body. He looks uncomfortable.

I give in to my urge to move closer, wanting to get a better look at him in the moonlight. "Sorry for what?"

Only a few feet separate us, and my entire body aches with the need to touch him. But I don't give in because it would make walking away again that much harder. I'm like an addict. One more hit, and I'll be off the rails.

He breathes heavily for a few beats, and I watch his pectorals rise and fall in his signature black T-shirt. His closet is full of them. Different neckline shapes. Same color. Arranged perfectly on hangers.

"For messaging you two years ago. For being intrigued by all your questions and sticking around when we clearly weren't after the same things. For talking to you. Every day. All night sometimes. For coming to rely on a woman I'd never met to make me feel good. For embarrassing you to save myself. For the way I spoke to you on the day you won the qualifier—not sure I'll ever forgive myself for that one. For being a growly shithead when you came to live with me. For not being able to resist you. For being dishonest. For not telling you things you deserved to know. For not being what you deserve." He stops, panting under the strain of the extensive list he just recited, and looks down. "Fuck. I'm sorry because I fell in love with you somewhere along the way, and now I don't know what to do with that."

I thought I blacked out that day DD and I fell on the track, but that was nothing compared to right now. I sway on the spot, and I don't think it's the wine straight from the bottle.

"You love me?" My voice is high and uncertain. I sound like a child to my own ears. My chin wobbles.

"Yeah." His wobbles too as his eyes meet mine.

"Then get your shit together and start loving me!" The words burst out of me in a flurry of frustration that even I didn't see coming.

"It's not that easy. I'm…" A tense growl tears from his chest as he looks away. "I'm fucked up, Violet. There's hard work that I need to do. The shit in my head? It doesn't just get better because I want it to."

If he's searching for pity, this isn't where he's going to get it. He just told me he loves me, and he's still dicking around ignoring me? That's even worse than thinking he doesn't care about me enough to make this work.

"Do you want it to? Do you want to get better? Because from everything I've seen, you're pretty stagnant."

"Violet—"

"No. You are. Don't lie to me and pretend you're not. Take the demons by the horns. I don't need you *better.* What is better anyway? That's not a goal. That's not quantifiable. Pick something you can do, and *fucking do it.* I don't need you down at track level. I don't even need you at every race. I don't need you to love horses, but I *need* you to love me."

He starts, gray eyes wide and glassy, full lips rolling together like he's holding words in that he just can't quite bring himself to say.

"I know you see yourself as dark. But you aren't. You're swirling color, all different shades, a mosaic. You're complicated and beautiful. And I'm not quitting on you, so you better not quit on me." The words ring out between us like chimes on a windy day. The silence is heavy, and so is my conscience as I brace myself to put an expiration date on us. "Pippy has her debut race in two weeks. Tell me a plan by then. Or don't. At least I'll know how to proceed with my life."

"You're giving me a deadline?" He sounds borderline offended. Like no one ever lays down the law where he's concerned. Like they're so busy tiptoeing around his shitty moods and broken persona, they forget to treat him like he has responsibilities. Like he's capable of handling pressure. That his actions have consequences.

"Yeah. Two weeks should be long enough for you to decide if you're going to try or not. That's all. Not"—I hold my hands up in air quotes—"'better.' Not healed. Not different. I don't want you different. I want you with your jagged edges and your growly moods." I step forward and let my hands fall onto his knees, feeling the line of muscles beneath my palms. And I squeeze, urging him to look me in the eye.

Really look me in the eye. So he knows how serious I am right now. That I mean every word right down to my bones, to my marrow. "I know everyone else has let you hide away. No one has gone out of their way to check on you, to love you. Everyone around you has failed you so thoroughly, given up on you so easily." I shake my head, and tears spring up in my eyes at the injustice of it. It makes me want to fight even harder for him. "I want *you*. But you need to want you too. I can't want you enough for the both of us."

There are no more words to be said between us, and it feels like Cole knows that too. He just gives me a terse nod, one I return before turning and walking away from him for what might be the last time. I walk down the gravel road back to my apartment, mulling that possibility over.

And then the tears finally come.

CHAPTER 27

Cole

I LIE ON THE COUCH AND STARE UP AT THE CEILING. LITTLE rainbows dance across the flat expanse from the crystal prisms hanging in the window. Light and pretty. They remind me of the farmhouse, of Violet.

"Does this actually help? Or is it just something people do in movies?"

"I don't know." The stacked bracelets on Trixie's wrist jangle as she holds a hand up dramatically. "But I will say that I don't think I've ever seen you relaxed enough here to lie down. You can't even see the door from there."

"Maybe I've stopped caring."

She cackles a raspy laugh. "Is that what you're doing? Lying down to die? How very Shakespearean of you. Good thing you drove back in for a session."

I turn my head to glare at Trixie. Sometimes it's like she thinks I pay her to mock me. "You know that's not what I mean."

She smiles back at me, all the wrinkles around her lips creasing in a way that tells years of tales. "Then by all means, tell me what you intended to say."

"I need to figure out how to cope with watching the woman I love get up on a horse and ride away from me. I need to know how to be happy for her rather than terrified she'll never come back."

"Okay. Is this something that has come up between the two of you? What does Violet say?"

I'm grateful she doesn't home in on the *L* word, but it also feels good to admit it. Last night talking to Violet outside, the way she reacted, I don't know why I waited so long. I've loved her from afar for years and never said a thing.

I think she might love me too. She didn't say it. But I can *feel* it. What woman would wait around for a fucking mess like me if she didn't love me?

I think we might love each other.

She makes me feel safe, makes me want to take chances, makes me a better me, and if making someone a better version of themselves just by being there isn't love in action, then I don't know what is.

I want to do that for her too.

"This is where I fucked up."

I chance a look over at Trixie. Her face gives nothing away, and she just sits there, staring at me. She's not disappointed or joking. She's just waiting.

"She fell off a horse while I was watching, and I crumbled. I had a full-on attack like I haven't had in years. In the aftermath, I may have implied I couldn't be with her because of her job."

"And what was her response?"

There's no hint of judgment in her voice. For some reason, I was expecting a scolding for being such a self-centered prick. I'm always expecting people to see the worst in me.

"In much kinder words, she said something along the lines of *fuck you* and *get your shit together.*"

"I do like this woman." Trixie adjusts herself in her seat and watches me thoughtfully.

I can feel the old crone's eyes on me. I can hear the wheels turning in her head.

"Tell me, what do you like about her?"

"What are we doing? Making a pros and cons list here?"

Trixie gives me a look as if to say, *Are you done yet?* I sigh, feeling self-conscious waxing poetic about a girl on my shrink's couch. I'm a walking fucking stereotype.

"Okay. Most of all, I like how driven she is. She hit the road on her own to carve her own path and has worked her ass off to get it. I admire that. She's calm and quiet, soothing, but not a pushover. I don't feel agitated by her, even when she never stops asking questions. She's thoughtful. She lets me have my issues and doesn't look at me like I'm a puppy who's been kicked a few too many times. She just reroutes, like I'm not an inconvenience to her at all. She's just… she's like sunshine on my face. Warm and bright. I feel like I've been living in the shade, in a dark corner, and rather than dragging me kicking and screaming out of it—like so many people have tried to—she's just shifted over a little bit to share her light."

I watch the multicolored dots move across the ceiling from the prisms, the pattern swaying slightly as the crystals do. They're hypnotic.

My voice comes out hoarse. "I don't want to live in the dark anymore."

Trixie looks up at the ceiling too, her neck stretching out above the big wooden beads of her necklace. "Pretty, aren't they?"

I swallow audibly, trying to clear my throat before I say anything. "Very" is what I manage.

"It's fitting, you know. Those crystals in the window are called suncatchers."

I blink rapidly.

"They're good feng shui."

I snort, but Trixie ignores me. She knows I'm not into that kind of stuff but carries on anyway.

"They take the sun's energy and cast it around, breaking up negative energy. Positive light. Healing light. Brightness and color."

I know it's my turn to respond, but I'm too choked up to do it. I just make a gurgling noise. Caught up in what she's telling me without really saying it. What are the chances I message Violet? What are the chances we forge a friendship? What are the chances she ends up working for my family? What are the chances I think of her as the sun while I'm staring up at a fucking suncatcher? Everything about us feels so unlikely yet so fated. After all the bad things that have happened to me in my life, it's hard to wrap my head around the universe shoving a gift like Violet in my face over and over again. But it's too much to ignore.

"You fell in love with that woman's drive. Her passion. Her spark for life. Her *light*. What if, rather than throwing that all away, you became her suncatcher? Take that light and amplify it in every way you can. Bask in it. How wondrous to have found it!" Trixie claps her hands excitedly. "But light is tricky. It slips through your fingers. It's fleeting. It comes and goes. We never get to possess it; you can't hold it in your hand. We just get to enjoy it. And if you can figure out a way to just let go and *enjoy it*, well, Cole, you'll be one of the lucky ones."

Lucky. I've never considered myself to be lucky. My dad, my leg, my engagement, my mental health. Money doesn't matter when everything else around you is shit.

I can't hide the crack in my voice when I respond. "And what if something happens to her?"

"But what if nothing happens to her, and you spend the rest of your life missing out on all that light?"

One voice in my head screams out louder than all the other ones. All the doubting ones. All the hateful ones.

I don't want to live in the dark anymore.

One step I need to take in getting my life back is rekindling some sort of relationship with my baby brother. Trixie only confirmed this for me as our conversation went on this morning. Which is why I'm here, sitting on the front step of his cottage while he's not home, waiting for him to get back. I don't know what I'm going to say to him. *Hey, want to sit down and drink a bottled water while I tell you about how I've been pretending not to be an amputee for the last six years? Cool, right? Super normal, I know, thanks.*

I groan and cross my arms, kicking at a rock before me. I'm frustrated. I'm impatient. I want this all fixed now. *Yesterday.*

I want Violet back now.

How did I let this get so far out of hand?

I'm ready to jump into berating myself when Billie's truck pulls up to the house. *Great. Just what I need.*

"Hey, big bro!" she calls as she hops out, just perpetually in a good mood or something. "Good to see ya."

I eye her speculatively. I thought Billie would be mad at me for the shit I've pulled with Violet. But she's acting totally normal instead. Annoying. She's acting annoying.

"Do you call me that specifically to annoy me?"

Her brows knit together as she approaches the front porch. "No. I call you that because we're going to be family, stuck together until we're old and gray and wrinkly, and I'm going to soften you up eventually. I'm very likable. You'll see."

Her ponytail swings as she stomps past me in her signature Blundstone boots. She enters the cottage saying nothing else to me, leaving me with my thoughts about how she just automatically assumes we'll be family for the rest of our lives. Like it's a fact, an unavoidable truth. I wish I had that kind of optimism where permanence is concerned. Nothing feels very permanent to me most of the time.

"Here." She startles me as she reappears, dropping to my right on the step and handing me a cold brown bottle of beer.

I take it from her and trail my thumb across the condensation forming on the outside. "I don't drink much."

"Be a lot cooler if you did."

I snort. "Dazed and confused. That's me these days for sure."

She chuckles and takes a swig of her own beer, staring out at DD's paddock. The black horse is munching on his hay, swishing his tail happily. A multimillion-dollar pet. I shake my head.

"Beer isn't healthy," I continue, trying to qualify my statement and mostly just change the subject.

She outright laughs now, waving her hand over my body. "Neither is whatever you're doing to your blood pressure right now."

A sigh whooshes from my mouth, and I take a deep gulp of the beer. She's right. Billie is perceptive like that. She's smart. People smart. The kind of smart they don't teach you in school. I remember setting Vaughn straight when he almost blew it with her. She knows right from wrong, and she taught my little brother a lesson in that.

I like them together.

"You must think I'm a real dick."

"Nope." She still doesn't look my way. Thoughtful eyes stare at the hills beyond the paddock, the ones that lead to the barn—to Violet. "I think you're doing the best you can with the shit hand life dealt you. Just like the rest of us."

Okay. That's not what I was expecting. But then, I know Billie has her own share of family drama, her own set of daddy issues to contend with. Maybe we're more kindred than I ever realized.

She drinks again, looking thoughtful. "The shitty thing is Violet's out of your league."

I just grunt. And then drink. Because she's not wrong about that either.

"The good thing is she's too fucking angelic to see it that way." She inclines her head toward me and holds her beer up in a silent cheer. "So you've got that working for ya."

"Thanks for the vote of confidence, sis." I figure if she's going to dish it out, I might as well give it right back.

Her lips tip up in a small satisfied smile. "What you need to do is level up. It's not about Violet. It's about you believing you're worthy of her."

"You know I pay someone to help me with these types of revelations."

She doesn't miss a beat. "Okay. Cash or check is fine."

I chuckle. I can't help it. I hate to admit it, but Billie is funny.

"What would make you feel worthy of her?"

"That's a great fucking question. I… don't know."

"What's holding you back? This?" She taps her finger to my temple. "Or this?" She taps my prosthetic.

I pause, turning my head slowly to stare back at her. Bright feline eyes regard me inquisitively. "How did you know about that?"

"If you're asking if Violet told me, the answer is no. But I watch people and horses for a living. I think I see things that other people don't. Body language. Tics. Clues. Is a horse scared? Uncomfortable? Where can I diagnose a problem? I'm constantly assessing. And you… you hide it well. But your gait is just a *little* off. You always wear long pants and high socks, no matter the temperature. You massage your leg without even noticing. I put it together a while ago."

"And you just haven't said anything?"

Her nose wrinkles up in confusion. "Why would I say something? First, it doesn't matter to me. Second, it's not my business."

"Does Vaughn know?"

"Nope. You once told him that my secret was a conversation to be had between me and him. And my feelings on this are the same. That's for the two of you to talk about."

My chest caves in a little. "Do you think he'll forgive me?"

She shakes her head absently, looking back at her horse. "Forgive you for what? He's your little brother. He loves you."

My eyes sting with the simplicity of her statement. Like it's the most obvious thing in the world. The most natural. I hate how badly I've failed Vaughn.

"What about Violet?"

"Same question: For what? You plan on breaking her heart?"

I bristle. The thought of causing Violet pain causes me pain instead, like a heavy punch to the gut. Shrapnel to the leg. "Not if I can help it," I grumble.

"Okay, good. So what's the holdup?"

I tap my temple, mimicking the way she did it before. "Everyone thinks I'm fucked up from the war. But I've worked on that. I've got that part under control, for the most part. It's the sight of my dad falling to his death on the track that haunts me. It's what I see every time I watch Violet race. It's what I worry about every day when I know she's up on a horse. What if it happens to her too? It's the question that plays on repeat in my mind. I want to be her biggest fan in one breath, and in the next, I don't want her on a horse at all. Which I know is a dick thing to admit, but it's the truth. I need to figure out a way around that."

Billie spins the bottle in her hands. She looks like she's completely ignoring me, and she's quiet for long enough that I seriously question if she even heard me blabbing about my feelings.

"Okay. So… are you afraid of losing Violet, or are you afraid of horses?"

"I'm…" My knee-jerk reaction is to say that of course I'm not afraid of horses. I grew up around them. But something stops me as I mull over the question. "No one has ever asked me that before." Am I? Afraid of horses? Does my fear stem from not understanding what she does more than my fear of losing her? *Fuck.* "Can I be both? I used to ride with my dad, and I wasn't scared then, but I don't know anymore."

"Yeah, man. You can be whatever you want to be. Except her number one fan, because that's me. You'll have to fight me for it. But if you don't fight me for it, some other guy will. Is the risk of her maybe, possibly, improbably, one day dying worth having to watch that? The family, the wedding, the babies?" She groans. "Ugh. Violet will probably make the cutest babies."

What. The. Fuck? Leave it to Billie to drop the most devastating emotional truth bombs possible. I feel my cheeks heat and my heart pound. That blood pressure? It's right back up where it started. "No fucking way. No chance. That can't happen."

Billie smiles and leans her elbows back on the step behind her, looking so damn smug. "Good. Ready to put in some work? Because I have a plan."

A Billie plan? I am equal parts invigorated and terrified. As she lays it all out, that terror turns to dread. I'm not sure I'm up to it, but I'm sure as shit going to try. She only stops talking when Vaughn pulls up in his stupid sports car.

"Everything okay? Did someone die?" he asks, looking concerned as he steps out quickly.

I guess from his perspective, it's weird that Billie and I would have a beer together when we're usually like oil and water.

"Everything is great except for the fact that you continue to insist on driving that car out here. You look like a total tool. A hot tool, but still," Billie quips back quickly, earning a sly grin and brow waggle from my brother. As he approaches us, Billie stands and hands me her empty beer bottle. "I need to… uh… go talk to Mira about the construction on the clinic."

Bullshit. She's clearing out so that I have to talk to Vaughn. She saunters up to him, ignoring the suspicious look on his face—apparently, he's not buying it either—and plants a quick kiss on his lips before slapping his ass and continuing to her truck. These two are perfect for each other.

"Hey, man," he says to me as he approaches. "Want another beer?"

I see my micro and macro counts go out the window, but it's not every day you have this conversation with your little brother.

"Sure. Why the fuck not?"

CHAPTER 28

Violet

It's Pippy's maiden race day, and I should be excited. But instead I'm pissed off and a little sad.

I still haven't heard from Cole. It's been two damn weeks, and I *still* haven't heard from him. Billie keeps telling me not to worry about it, and I've asked her a couple times if she knows something I don't. Her answer is always no.

But for once, I hope she's lying to me.

I shouldn't have given him a deadline. I shouldn't have put this pressure on him. I shouldn't have fallen in love with him. But here I am, taking all that frustration out on Pippy's coat, trying not to feed her all my anxious energy and failing miserably. Everyone knows I'm in a mood. Billie, Hank, Mira, Vaughn—they're all ignoring me. Pippy though, she's just stuck with me. And luckily, she's the happiest, most laid-back little horse on the planet. She's like an eternal optimist. I guess when you're born as early as she was, just surviving is an accomplishment, something to be proud of.

I need that optimism to rub off on me because I feel like a storm cloud right now. The good part of that is my killer instincts are in overdrive. I want to win. I want to brutalize the competition. I want to prove to everyone I'm not a ditzy blond. I'm the woman who took a horse that no one thought would race and turned her into a winner.

All Pippy's breezes have been solid lately. Her health is excellent. She's unflappable. But you never *really know* until you get a horse on the track. Sink or swim.

I threw myself into the deep end a couple of years ago, and today it's Pippy's turn to do the same.

"Miss Eaton?"

I start and then turn with a scowl to face Stefan Dalca, who is standing at the entrance to our grooming stall. I have to hand it to him. The guy must have a real pair on him, showing up in the Gold Rush Ranch shed row with how most of us feel about him.

"Why do you insist on talking to me before a race? It's not a good time. Do you know nothing about this sport?"

He blinks at me, looking surprised by the way I lashed out. To be honest, I'm a little surprised too. Do I like the guy? No. But this is out of character for me. *Fucking Cole Harding.*

"I just wanted to come and offer an apology to you."

"You?" I point at him. "Want to apologize to me?" My thumb butts up against my chest.

"For Patrick Cassel's behavior."

I snort and get back to tacking Pippy up.

"I was completely unaware of his behavior, and he's no longer in my employ." When I look up at him, his jaw ticks and he pins me with his green eyes. His hawkish features leave no room to doubt his sincerity. "His behavior on and off the track is not befitting of someone who works for me and especially not befitting of any man I want aligned with me. I'm very sorry for all the discomfort he's caused you."

I could say something snarky. I could throw his sleazy move last year in his face, but he seems serious. He seems… chastised.

"Okay." I huff out a breath as I tighten the cinch around Pippy's ribs. "Thank you for that. I appreciate it."

When I look back at him, he looks shocked by my response. Like he was expecting me to tear into him or something. But that's not me. I don't like holding grudges. I don't like having enemies. I like being on good terms with people, and if I can't be on good terms with Cole, then I can be with Stefan. At least that's something.

"Okay. Well. Best of luck." He holds his hand out to me, and I stop what I'm doing to take it in my own.

"Thank you. Same to you." I see his body relax as I offer him a small smile, like he was genuinely worried about talking to me. It's kind of sweet for a guy who's been nothing but a total snake in the grass.

I let his hand go and turn back to Pippy with a renewed sense of excitement. If someone like Stefan Dalca can come around, maybe Cole can too? The day isn't over yet. But now, it's time to put boys and drama out of my mind. It's time to work, to get down to business.

It's time to win a race.

With all our silks on, we walk out of the barn toward the hitching ring. Billie pops out of nowhere as usual, wearing one of the pantsuits she always dons on big race days, gives me my leg up, and leads me down to the circus that is Saturday afternoon at Bell Point Park. Pippy looks around with interest but not with alarm or anxiety—something that is distinctly not normal for a two-year-old at her debut race.

Other horses prance around anxiously, frothing at the bit, but she just walks her big steady walk with a curious look on her face. It's like she's been here before. Like she's here to teach us all a lesson, and maybe she is. I'm just not sure what it is yet.

When we get to the hitching ring, Billie gives my knee a squeeze and sends me in with a "Go get 'em, tiger."

I'm handed off to the pony horse, and everything else falls away. The noise, the distractions. All I see is what's between those pointy brown ears. My goal lies straight ahead. All I need to do is reach out and take it. Billie and I talked strategy earlier. The basic plan is to take it easy and let her find her footing. This race is practice since it's not a qualifier. It's a test. There is no pressure, except for the heaping piles of it I've put on myself.

After one lap, we load up into the gate, and I can feel Pippy tense up a little bit—finally. Her big ears flop around like windmills on her head, making me chuckle, and I reach down to give her some gentle scratches.

"Good baby. You got this. Everyone ruled you out. They thought you were too small, too weak. We're going to show them though, aren't we? We're going to show them what that rosy little attitude will get you."

And maybe that's my lesson. Positive energy begets positive energy. A winning outlook, that's what Pippy has, and when the bell rings and those gates fly open, I smile. I feel it in my soul.

Pippy is going to win this race.

She drops her head and drives forward, hard. She doesn't hang back and take some space. She doesn't assess the competition. It feels like it's more likely that she'll run them right over if they don't get out of her way.

Gone is the sweet little filly. In her place is a competitor. She drops her head and pushes hard from behind. I try to hold her back a bit. She isn't all that fit yet, and I don't want her burning all her energy down the first stretch. Running flat out from start to finish isn't anyone's ideal game plan. Except Pippy's, apparently.

She takes the bit between her teeth and drags me down that first straightaway. I sit up, leaning away slightly, trying to ease her off. But she's not having it. She is full throttle and flying to the front of the pack. And me? I feel like a little kid on a runaway pony. All that time spent turning and stopping and going, all those little nuances that I thought she had a decent enough grasp on, go out the door. At her practice runs on the farm, she was fast. But not like this.

So I'm left with a choice. Fight with her or let her run the race in a way that feels natural to her. Let her take the lead and show me what she needs.

I barely need to think about it.

I press my feet into the irons, get low on her neck, and let her run away with the lead. She flows through the corner beautifully, and I can't help but smile. Being on a horse with the wind on my face, I feel alive. And based on the way she's not tiring, I'd say that Pippy does too. She uses that final turn to rocket herself into the straightaway. We are absolutely flying, and I'm glad this is a short race, because I don't know how long she can keep this up.

When I chance a look behind myself, I almost can't believe what I see. The other horses have to be at least ten lengths behind us. With a small shake of my head, I press my knuckles into her mane and get low. Might as well make it eleven lengths.

We thunder down the straight to the finish post on an even tempo. I can feel her tire beneath me, but by this point, the spread is so big that it doesn't matter. I don't need to push her.

We sail across the finish line. It isn't even close.

I let my arms slide down around her neck as I press a kiss to her mane and laugh. That was the most bizarre and most fun race of my life. Pippy is a total psychopath.

"You're nuts. You know that?" I sit up tall to slow her a little, scratching at her withers the way I know she likes, feeling my cheeks ache with the intensity of the smile I can't wipe off my face.

I see our pony horse move up out of my periphery, something I'm glad for because Pippy doesn't seem too keen to stop. Hopefully an older, calmer horse will get her head screwed back on right. I'm still looking around as the rider comes up beside us and reaches for the rein. Sad as it sounds, I'm still looking around, hoping I might catch sight of Cole somewhere. Wearing a beautiful suit and that growly look on his face. I love that growly look and the voice that matches it.

I love him.

I should enjoy this win. But I'm pining after a guy I fell in love with like some wishy-washy teenager.

"I knew you'd win," the pony rider says from beside me. But his voice is…

I look over, and my jaw goes slack. Because Cole Harding is on the sturdy quarter horse beside me. He's holding Pippy's rein. *He's on a horse.*

"Cat got your tongue?" He grins, looking so damn proud of himself.

My eyes prickle and fill as I work to pull Pippy up, wanting to slow down, wanting to stop—wanting time to stand still so I can crawl into his lap again. "You're here."

"Surprise."

His smirk is panty-melting. All I can bring myself to do is shake my head.

"Did you think I'd miss it?" he asks with a tilt of his head.

"I..." We slow to a trot and then a walk before coming to a complete stop in the middle of the track while other horses barrel past us to the exit gate. "I honestly wasn't sure."

"Both my girls in one race? No chance."

My girls. "I just..." My mouth moves, but no sound comes out. "It's been two weeks!"

"I know. Learning how to ride again with a prosthetic in only two weeks was almost a full-time job."

I scan his body in the big western saddle. He looks comfortable. "You look good," I say honestly. "How did you pull this off?"

He chuckles. "Billie." Like her name alone explains everything. "Something about horses being therapy. I honestly think she might be on to something."

"You're here. On this track. On a horse," I say dumbly, still having a hard time wrapping my head around it.

He looks around as if soaking in everything—the sights, the sounds, the horses—and a wistful smile touches his lips as he looks back at me. "I am."

"Why?"

"Because I don't want to live in the dark anymore."

My throat constricts, and I wish I could say something, but I'm too choked up. I wipe my eyes and look around us shyly.

That's what I wanted to hear. Not that he's only doing this for me but for himself.

"Come on. Let's get you off the track."

I nod, letting him give the rein a gentle tug as he leads us toward the gate and the winner's circle. I'm dazed. Elated. *Shocked.*

I watch him ride, and he looks so natural. He said he rode with his dad. It was something they liked to do together. Hit the trails and go on an adventure. I know he hasn't sat on a horse since his father's death.

"How does it feel? Riding again?" I murmur quietly as our horses' hooves clip-clop in unison on the concrete path to the winner's circle.

His Adam's apple bobs as he swallows, peeking at me from the corner of his eye. "It feels like this is what he would have wanted."

I nod, sensing he's had a bit of a breakthrough, and look back up at the crowd gathering at the winner's circle. It's not quite the frenzy it usually is with DD, but it might be even more satisfying. It might be the best race ever, to be honest.

Cole is about to hop off his horse, but I can't take it anymore. "Stop." I reach out and grab his elbow right as he looks over my way. "Does this mean you're going to try?"

He looks around us shyly, knowing that people are watching now. Probably wondering why the hell I'm having an intense conversation with the rider of my pony horse. He looks at me so sincerely, I swear I feel my heart squeeze in my chest. He reaches out, one hand on my cheek, thumb rubbing like he always does.

"Yeah, Violet. I'm going to try. More than that, I'm going to just fucking do it. Because you? Us? I think we're meant to be.

You found me, and I found you. Over and over again. If that's not a sign, I don't know what is."

A big fat tear rolls down my cheek. He catches it and wipes it away.

"I love you, Violet Eaton. I loved you before I ever met you. And god knows, I love you even more now."

More tears fall. I hear murmurs around us, but I don't care. I can't look away from his silvery moonlit eyes. He thinks he's dark. I think he just shines differently. The way the moon illuminates the world at night, soft and subtle. He doesn't shine—he glows. Especially when he looks at me the way he is right now.

And the thought that I could be the one to make this man glow? It takes my breath away. "I love you too," I whisper, eyes searching his, wishing I had more words for him.

He leans down, and his mouth finds mine.

And I opt to just show him how I'm feeling.

I pour myself into this kiss. The pain, the longing, the admiration—I lay it all out, and he soaks it all up. Every hurt, every triumph. He's there, and I know he always will be. His hands on my skin tell me so, his tongue against mine like a promise.

He pulls back and rests his forehead against mine. "Go. Savor your win. We'll finish this off in a stall later."

I giggle and blush at the memory, peeking around us, realizing we've got an audience.

"I'll be right here. I'm not going anywhere."

With one more swift brush of my lips, I turn and walk a very pleased-looking Pippy into the winner's circle, where she basks in the attention and pricks her ears up prettily for pictures. I soak it all up, knowing Cole is right there.

And he's not going anywhere.

EPILOGUE

Cole

ONE YEAR LATER

"Put. Your. Heels. Down. Do you not speak English anymore?"

I swear, if Billie didn't currently have my sleeping baby strapped to her chest, I would jump off this damn horse and give her the noogie she's so desperately asking for right now.

"It's my prosthetic," I grit out instead of, *Fuck you, it's my prosthetic*. I'm trying really hard to not swear so much now that I have another girl in my life. A far more impressionable one. Okay, she's only a few months old, but if I practice now, then I won't have to worry about *fuck* being her first word when the time comes.

Billie rolls her eyes dramatically, one palm resting gently on Lilah's bald little head. "Suck it up, buttercup. If our Paralympic athletes can manage, then so can super soldiers."

My teeth grind, but I push down on my leg as I trot around the ring, trying to find my center of balance and get that joint at the angle Billie requires. We're not doing daily riding lessons anymore, but we try to keep up two per week. Billie is busy, and so am I, but she never complains. Even if it's at the very end of her day, she'll come out and help me.

I'll probably never admit it to her, but I love Billie. I jokingly call her Little Sis, but the truth of the matter is, that's exactly what she's become. She gave me an ass kicking and then patted my back. And now, I'd say we're friends. *Family.*

"Yup. Now you've got it." Her hand swirls around on Lilah's head.

"She's not a dog, Billie."

"I know." She peeks down at the tiny human strapped in a carrier to her chest and smiles. "But she's soft like one."

I chuckle and slow to a walk, feeling the ache in both my legs from the no-stirrup work she just had me doing. Total fucking masochist. "I thought you didn't like kids?"

Her eyes narrow at me, and she cups her hands over Lilah's ears. "Shh. Don't tell her that. She's the only one I like, but I don't want to hurt her feelings."

Now it's my turn to roll my eyes. "You're a fuckin' piece of work, you kno—"

"Cole Harding. I know you did not just swear in front of our baby." Violet walks up to the fence of the outdoor ring in those tight riding pants I love so much with a teasing smirk on her face. Beside her, Vaughn shakes his head. They just gave a press tour of the newly finished vet clinic, something neither Billie nor I wanted any part of. Cameras. People. Attention. *No thanks.*

"How'd it go, pretty girls?" Billie quips, walking toward them. "Want your baby back, Vi?"

"If you wake her up and ruin my couple hours of freedom, I will kill you." Violet's eyes flash with humor and a smidge of desperation. She's joking, but only sort of. New babies are both wonderful and exhausting.

Turns out Violet got pregnant as soon as we got back together, after Pippy's maiden race—possibly in what's become known as the baby-making stall. Something that makes me cringe every time someone says it. The timing wasn't ideal for Violet's career, something that stressed her almost instantly, but with her doctor's blessing, she finished the season. (Something I spent many hours on Trixie's couch hashing out. There's no finish line where therapy is concerned.) But ultimately it was fine. Lilah was born in our farmhouse in April, and a month later, Violet was back up on a horse. Violet is happy. And that makes me happy.

I think my dad would have loved Violet. He'd have respected her. Just like I do.

"It was great. Vaughn is made for the camera. You should see him. It's like they hit a switch, and he just turns on. All charming and mature."

"I am charming and mature." My brother grins with that playful look in his eye, something I love seeing. It reminds me of when we were kids. A time I can now look back on fondly rather than with bitterness and longing.

"Ehhhh. You're charming..." Violet says, rolling her lips together and going pink at her own joke. *Fuck.* I hope she never outgrows that blush. It makes my dick twitch every time.

Motherhood has changed her in all the best ways. I knew as soon as we found out that she'd be an amazing mom, patient and gentle. I just didn't foresee the fierceness it would bring out in her. It's added a little spunk to her, a little possessiveness that I live for.

I watch Billie and Vaughn sometimes and feel like Violet and I missed out on the fun, playful part of our relationship. But I'm not sure we were ever that type of couple anyway.

"Where's Mira?" Billie asks, only for Vaughn to pipe up with, "Hey! You're supposed to defend me."

She just raises an eyebrow at him and gives him an unimpressed look.

Everyone laughs, even Vaughn.

"She got called out to Dalca's farm." Violet answers Billie's question warily, almost predicting the growl that she emits at the answer. "Billie. It's not about him. It's about the horses. You wouldn't have her ignore a horse who needs help just because it belongs to Dalca, would you?"

Billie sighs and whispers something in Lilah's ear. I already know she's going to get her into trouble once she's old enough. Aunty Billie is going to be a problem.

"Really mature, Billie!" Vaughn laughs at his own joke like a total dork.

I jump off my horse to plant a kiss on my wife's cheek. "Hi, sunshine," I murmur against her skin, only for her to nuzzle in and reply with, "Hey, Butterface. I'm hungry." A nickname that has stuck.

"For dinner?"

She smiles, and her eyes dance with mischief. "No."

And suddenly, I want Sunday dinner over with and Lilah put to bed as quickly as possible.

We all turn together and march back up to the barn to finish with the horses and then head over to Vaughn and Billie's place.

Sunday dinner is a tradition that Billie started, and it's now become a regular part of our week.

Especially since I never moved back into the city. I go back weekly, but the ranch is my home. I feel tied to the property in a way I didn't realize I could. It's the family connection, knowing that my grandparents met here. Lived here. Knowing my dad was born here. It feels right to be here. Like part of my feeling lost was just a complete lack of connection to my history—my roots. So that picturesque blue farmhouse is where I want to be, with all my girls, Pippy included. She still lives out front in the shelter I built her. A champion sprinter in the making and also the family pet.

Because we are a family now. In the very traditional sense of the word. In the way that I've longed for. Once Violet finished having her freak-out about being pregnant, I got down on one knee and let her freak out about marrying me. That was a happy sort of freak-out though. We traveled back to her family ranch, to a real cowboy sort of town in the prairies, and tied the knot with her entire family in attendance. They got to see the new Violet, the butterfly that emerged from the cocoon. And judging by the number of farm boys shedding a tear during our ceremony, I'd say they were impressed with her too.

"Hold up. Want help getting your horse put away?" Vaughn walks up quickly from behind me and gives me a quick shoulder shove.

"Dick." I shake my head and laugh at him.

Our talk on the front porch that night about my leg turned into a talk about a lot more. It turned into a pile of beer bottles on the ground and a big old shame spiral and headache the next morning. But it was worth it. Vaughn and I talked about our feelings—something I'm getting better at—and we reminisced. I've never felt closer to my brother, and my regret over pushing him away has slowly ebbed.

"What's for dinner?"

"Lasagna. Billie made it this morning, so the place has smelled like it all day. I'm only going to help you because I'm starving."

I can hear Billie and Violet walking up the path behind us, talking animatedly and laughing airily. Music to my ears. It doesn't even bug me anymore. The talking, the questions, that incessant chatter comforts me. It's the sound of my girl being happy.

"Charming," I say, looking at my brother, who grins happily back at me and claps my shoulder.

"Have a beer with me?"

I sigh. Why did this have to become our bonding ritual? "Okay, yeah." I can't say no. I'm too… happy. Too relaxed, too softened up from reflecting all this light that surrounds me.

I tie up GD, the old gelding I like to ride, and get to untacking him while Vaughn brushes him down thoroughly. I smile as I watch him talking to the horse and doting on him. Our dad would have fucking loved this. To see us like this. At his farm, working together, continuing his legacy. My throat feels thick at the thought. Maybe he can see us; maybe he knows. Wherever he is. I hope he sees this. I hope he sees us happy.

Violet once said something to me about wanting to earn what she gets. Wanting to struggle and come out stronger on the other side. It's a sentence that changed my perspective. It gave my day-to-day life a purpose. It made me want to come out stronger on the other side too. It made me want to get to the other side, period. To step out of the dark and the mundane and into the light. Life was bitter, and now it's sweet.

I pat GD firmly and pull off his saddle. "Thanks for putting up with me, old man," I grunt as I pat his back. A perfectly golden palomino that Billie found for a novice like me—one with a heart of gold to match and who I jokingly named Golddigger. Who is now the pony horse that leads Violet's mounts to and from each race. And so long as I'm not stuck at work, I'm the one riding. I'm the last one to wish her good luck and the first one to congratulate her. I may not be jockey material, but being out there on the track with my wife—where my dad loved to spend his days and where I'm starting to as well—it's special. Especially when I get a front-row seat to see the look of pure joy on Violet's face as she crosses that finish line.

Win or lose. She's always smiling out there. Smiling right at *me*. Lighting me up.

Because she's my fucking sunshine.

BONUS SCENE

Cole

"Do you, Cole Harding, take this woman to be your lawfully wedded wife?"

Violet looks up at me, head craning to see my face. Her eyes are the same color as the sky, and I can't believe she's about to be *mine.*

After everything we've been through, after the way our roads kept crossing and leading us back to each other… it's almost hard to believe that we're here. Making it official in the way I've always wanted.

I'm still not convinced I deserve her, but when has the world ever given me anything that I deserve? I'm taking her anyway. She's mine. She always has been. I feel like the woman on that IKEA commercial who gets a such a good deal that she acts like she's stealing everything. She runs toward her husband waiting in their vehicle, shouting, "Start the car!"

Start the fucking car is right.

"I do," I reply to the officiant, my voice more gravelly than I want it to be.

Violet beams back at me, eyes shining more than usual, and my heart constricts. I love this woman so damn much that it's almost painful looking at her sometimes. *She saved me.*

"And do you, Violet Eaton, take this man to be your lawfully wedded husband?"

Her head quirks slightly, and her eyes scour my face, like she's committing this moment to memory.

"I—I do." Her voice cracks, and she has to look away for a moment to regain her composure.

I squeeze her tiny hands, the ones she's placed in mine. Along with her heart, her life, her trust.

On one hand, loving Violet the way I want to feels like a heavy burden. On the other, nothing has ever felt more right. I fully intend to spend the rest of my life proving to her she made the right choice—for herself and our precious baby growing inside her.

I stare at her stomach. The swell is still so small that you can't see it beneath the simple Grecian-looking princess-cut wedding dress she's wearing—one that is going to look mighty fine on the floor in a few hours. But I stare anyway. Something she catches me doing a lot lately.

Just like now. A small watery giggle escapes her lips. And I look back up, melting into her soft smile.

I need everyone to get the fuck out of here so I can christen this woman as Mrs. Harding for the first time. Waiting until tonight is going to be torture. My eyes scan the crowd. Getting her away from her dad and brothers, the Three Musketeers, is going to be like a goddamn military operation.

They're staring at us now. Her dad looks choked up. The grizzled old rancher's cheeks flush, and his eyes are full to overflowing. He shook my hand so damn hard that he almost broke all the bones the first time we met. But the "Hurt her and we'll kill you" he whispered in my ear made me like the guy instantly. We were on the same page with that.

Her brothers are a little harder to read. They're all so different but are clearly all good men. My eyes trail over to them. The youngest, Rhett, with a handsome, cocky smile on his face. He just looks like trouble, like a little kid who's been caught with his hand in the cookie jar but knows he'll get away with it. The middle brother, Beau, swipes a tear off his cheek and looks around himself like he's hoping no one saw. He reminds me of Vaughn, charming and eloquent. Possibly the most presentable of the three. Definitely nothing like the eldest, Cade, who is staring daggers at me. He reminds me of myself before I sought Trixie out. Angry. Cold. Distant. You can see the turmoil bubbling beneath the surface. The only time I've seen the man smile is when he's with Violet or his son.

Violet's fingers pulse around mine, forcing me back into the depths of her baby blues as the officiant carries on.

"I now pronounce you husband and wife. You may kiss the bride!"

Fuck yeah, I may.

I tug Violet toward me, one hand instantly snaking out around her waist. I love the feeling of her body pressing into mine, the way she instantly fits herself to me. My left hand skates up over her throat, and I don't miss the way her eyes heat at that. My shy little Violet loves it when I grab her there, but I'll save that part for later. Instead, I cup her jaw and brush her cheek with my thumb and look down into the eyes of the woman who is it for me.

Mine.

"I love you," I whisper against her lips as I claim them. I leave my eyes open just long enough to watch her lashes flutter shut and hear her responding moan as she slips her tongue into my mouth. *No shame.* My chest rumbles with amusement and possessiveness.

This. This is what I've always wanted.

Her arms wrap around my neck as she pulls me down toward her and kisses me with so much passion, it almost bowls me over. I somehow thought she'd tone it down in front of a whole crowd of people, but no. My girl can't help herself around me.

I hear a loud whistle from behind Violet, and I just *know* it's Billie. The whistle turns into the sound of my brother, Vaughn, hooting behind me, which turns into cheers and laughter and clapping. And fuck. I feel like my heart could grow wings and just take off into the sky.

Violet bursts into giggles and tucks herself into my shirt, her fingers sliding down the lapels of my jacket before fisting them and holding me close. I wrap my arms around her tiny body and look around us at all the people smiling. Friends. Family. Friends who have started to feel like family. Whatever Billie is.

She smiles at me, wide and genuine from over Violet's shoulder, where she stands as her bridesmaid. I can't stop the enormous smile that spreads across my face in response. I owe a good bit of my happiness to her meddling, and that's something I'll never forget.

Violet's arms wrap around my ribs as she comes to rest her chin on my chest. She stares up at me with one small tear streaking over the apple of her cheek. "I love you, Mr. Harding."

My thumb rasps over her skin, clearing the tear. I'll wipe away her tears forever. "I love you too, Mrs. Harding."

Fuck, that sounds so good. I'm so fucking happy I don't even know what to do with myself. This is it. This is the life. This is the light.

And I'm so glad I chose it.

"I need a break." My lips brush across the shell of my wife's ear, and I see her smile.

I'm being a needy bitch, and I don't even care. I've been a good boy. I've made the rounds. I've talked with people. Shit, I've even smiled. My cheeks hurt from it. I'm going to have to scowl for a week straight to recuperate. But Violet wanted a wedding, and I'll do anything to make her happy. I would have married her in the middle of a swamp with only the mosquitos there to witness it. But here we are, doing the whole thing with what feels like everyone we've ever met.

"There are still guests here." Violet whispers as she gives me a quick poke in the ribs.

I look around the wooden dance floor set up under a sea of string lights. There are too many people here wearing cowboy boots with a suit. Chestnut Springs is something else. I feel like someone dropped onto the set of *Yellowstone*, a show that Violet keeps making me watch with her. She's even told me she had a childhood crush on Kevin Costner. After which she told me I should *thank* him for getting her into older men. I could see her cheeks twitching as she tried to keep the laughter in. Eyes glued to the TV, lips rolling against each other with amusement.

Joke or no joke, I'm still going to punch Kevin Costner if I ever see him.

"I don't care." I let my hand slide down from the small of her back and over the curve of her very delectable ass as we stand looking out over the dance floor. "Plus, I don't want to watch Trixie make her move on Hank."

The two of them are dancing and laughing and looking at each other in a way that feels like too much information.

She snorts. "God. That would be adorable."

"Ugh." I shudder. Trixie has no filter. I can already imagine the lack of boundaries that would come with that. The stories she'd subject me to. A growl tears itself from my chest. "I'll show you adorable." I bend down and scoop Violet up into my arms.

"Cole Harding!" She slaps my chest on a shocked gasp as I turn away from the party. "Put me down."

"Wave goodbye, Mrs. Harding."

She wiggles in my arms and laughs, waving goodbye over my shoulder to the guests who are now chuckling and shaking their heads as I carry her away like a total caveman.

I don't care. I'm done being paraded around. I hate crowds. I don't even know where I'm going. I just want to be alone with my wife.

My wife. That's going to take some getting used to, but fuck, does it sound good.

I walk out into the darkened pasture, pausing only when we get close to an old stone well.

"I want to stop here," Violet says quietly, the humor in her voice seeping away.

I place her on the ground, but she just tucks herself into my side, clinging to me as we both stand facing the well.

"Today is one of the first times I really feel the absence of my mom." Her voice is clear and quiet under the cover of the stars. "I've never known any different, but today I can't stop picturing how my wedding day would have looked with her here."

It's like she reached into my head and plucked out my thoughts. I've been joyously happy today, but the ache of knowing my dad wasn't here to share in that happiness is hard to escape.

"Same" is all I say. I don't trust myself to say more, so I just squeeze her petite frame into mine, reveling in the feel of her palm sliding across my stomach and her head resting against my ribs.

"This is where she used to bring my brothers. They'd bring coins and toss them in. Making wishes and waiting for the sound of them hitting the water."

My chest constricts as she continues.

"My dad renamed the ranch after she died. On one hand, I think it's kind of beautiful. On the other, a little morbid. Like when you're here, you can't escape her memory."

Wishing Well Ranch.

My eyes trace the cedar shake peak that covers the stone well, the vines planted on either side that crawl up the posts propping up the roof. It's like a tribute.

"I kind of like it," I say to her as I reach into my pocket, knowing I have one coin in there from tipping the bartenders tonight. I can vividly imagine a woman—a spitting image of Violet—seated on the edge, surrounded by a small throng of unruly little boys with disheveled hair, spending a sunny afternoon making wishes.

It sounds like heaven.

"Go make a wish." I guide Violet forward and hold my palm out across my body, the metallic shimmer of the coin catching the moonlight as her gaze drops. Her lip wobbles as we approach the wishing well, but she picks the coin up and takes a deep breath anyway. She steps forward to look down into the depths of the dark water. And I stand back, letting her have this moment, watching her slight frame, her glowing hair, the curves on the body that's carrying my baby. *I'm going to be a dad.*

Is there such a thing as too happy? Because that might be me.

She holds the coin up and drops it down into the well, leaning over slightly like she'll be able to see it under the cover of darkness.

When the splashing sound reaches us, I see the corner of her mouth tip up. A small satisfied smile graces her elfin features as she lets out a ragged sigh. She turns around to look at me, and it takes my breath away. Every damn time.

"What did you wish for?" I ask jokingly.

Violet just rolls her eyes at me. "Can't tell you, or it won't come true."

I just chuckle and fold her into my arms again, letting the heat of her body seep in through my tux.

"We need to go get another coin so that you can make a wish," she murmurs against my chest.

I just scoff, lifting her up in my arms again and turning toward our guesthouse. My strides cover the ground as she snuggles up against me, and I realize I'm never going to tire of carrying this woman around. Or other things. I'm never going to tire of all the other things. Other things that I am going to show her so hard right now. As soon as I get this woman behind closed doors, I am going to *thoroughly* other-things her.

I smile into the night just thinking about it.

"Don't need to, Mrs. Harding. I've already got everything I've ever wanted."

A Special Thank You

I'd like to note a special thank you here to Kelsi and Jay, both of whom so candidly shared their experiences with me. I know that each individual's experiences with PTSD, adjusting to civilian life, and living as an amputee are vast and varied. What I've written here represents but a sliver of what people are living with on a day-to-day basis, but these two individuals gave me a special peek into their personal histories, and I wouldn't have felt comfortable writing this book without their invaluable feedback. I feel so honored that they both entrusted me with their stories.

Acknowledgments

There are so many moving parts that go into getting a book ready for publishing, and I'm eternally grateful for all the awesome people involved in mine. Thank you to each and every one of you. Even the ones I've undoubtedly missed.

To my husband, thank you for your relentless support. Your pep talks are the stuff of legends.

To my son, who always asks me if I'm "working on my Kelsey Silvers stuff." You are my favorite human.

To my editor, Paula, this book wouldn't be what it is today without you. Your feedback is invaluable, and you are pretty much the ultimate hype girl.

My editor at Bloom Books, Christa Désir, thank you for believing in my very first books. It's such an honor to work with you.

My beta readers! Amy, Amber, and Christy: you ladies are awesome. Thank you for your time, energy, and direction.

My ARC and street team members, I am absolutely overwhelmed by all your support! It makes me a little misty-eyed to think about how much you have all done for me. I'm really not sure how I'll ever thank you all. I send hugs to each and every one of you.

Shannon and Laetitia, hats off to you both for your exceptional eye for detail and time spent poring over my words. I so appreciate your help.

Finally, the biggest thank you to my agent, Kimberly Brower, for being a constant source of support and wisdom on the wildest ride of my life.

For Billie and Vaughn's story, read *Off to the Races*,
book one in the Gold Rush Ranch series.

For Mira and Stefan's story, read *The Front Runner*, book three in the Gold Rush Ranch series.

For Nadia and Griffin's story, read *A False Start*,
book four in the Gold Rush Ranch series.

About the Author

Elsie Silver is a Canadian author of sassy, sexy, small-town romance who loves good book boyfriends and the strong heroines who bring them to their knees. She lives just outside Vancouver, British Columbia, with her husband, son, and three dogs, and has been voraciously reading romance books since before she was probably supposed to.

She loves cooking and trying new foods, traveling, and spending time with her boys—especially outdoors. Elsie has also become a big fan of her quiet 5 a.m. mornings, which is when most of her writing happens. It's during this time that she can sip a cup of hot coffee and dream up a fictional world full of romantic stories to share with her readers.

Website: elsiesilver.com
Facebook: authorelsiesilver
Instagram: @authorelsiesilver
TikTok: @authorelsiesilver

ALSO BY ELSIE SILVER

Chestnut Springs

Flawless

Heartless

Powerless

Reckless

Hopeless

Gold Rush Ranch

Off to the Races

A Photo Finish

The Front Runner

A False Start

Rose Hill

Wild Love

Wild Eyes

Wild Side

THE FRONT RUNNER

ELSIE SILVER

New York · Amsterdam/Antwerp · London · Toronto · Sydney · New Delhi

THE FRONT RUNNER
First published in Australia in 2024 by
Simon & Schuster (Australia) Pty Limited
Level 4, 32 York Street, Sydney, NSW, 2000
First published in the United States in 2021 by Elsie Silver

10 9 8 7 6 5 4 3 2

Sydney New York Amsterdam/Antwerp London Toronto New Delhi
Visit our website at www.simonandschuster.com.au

The authorised representative in the EEA is Simon & Schuster Netherlands BV, Herculesplein 96, 3584 AA Utrecht, Netherlands. info@simonandschuster.nl

A catalogue record for this book is available from the National Library of Australia

ANZ ISBN: 9781761634253
UK ISBN: 9781398551084

Cover design: Mary, Books and Moods
Internal design: Sourcebooks
Printed and bound by CPI (UK) Ltd, Croydon CR0 4YY

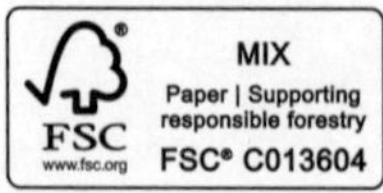

For all the women who've been told
they should smile more.
Fuck that noise. Frown all you want.

Reader Note

This book contains adult material including references to animal death typical with farm life as well as domestic abuse and sexual harassment. It is my hope that I've handled these topics with the care they deserve.

I'd also like to extend a special thank you to Anna P. for performing a very thorough sensitivity read to ensure that Mira and her family have been represented with proper care and accuracy.

CHAPTER 1

Stefan

SIX MONTHS AGO

"DALCA, YOU PIECE OF..."

Here we go. The woman who works for and is engaged to my biggest competitor is going to fly off the handle. Again. Billie Black is especially talented at this kind of behavior. She reminds me of my little sister. Entitled and impulsive. The difference is my sister likes me.

This woman does not.

It's a bold spot to make a scene. I'll give her that. We're in the middle of a public roadway at the prestigious Bell Point Park. Our horses are ready for their race. In fact, hers is standing right behind her with the petite fair-haired jockey they seem to use exclusively now.

I slide my hands into the pockets of my suit pants and quirk one eyebrow at her in challenge. I would be lying if I were to say I don't take some small pleasure in riling people up. File that away under the behavior of a child who didn't get enough attention growing up. Any attention is good attention, and this type of attention is especially amusing to me.

But the raven-haired veterinarian steps in front of the other two women, hitting me with a look that would make a lesser man's balls shrivel.

"Stefan, walk with me." She crooks a finger and heads in the opposite direction without even looking back, like she just knows I'll follow.

I'm not sure what's going on. It feels like I'm in trouble; it looks like I'm in for some sort of scolding. I smooth my hands over the lapels of my suit jacket and clear my throat by way of saying goodbye to the two women glaring at me and spin on my heel. Billie makes an immature gagging noise as I walk away, but I tip my chin up and keep walking after the woman who has piqued my interest since the first time I laid eyes on her.

Dr. Mira Thorne. My favorite equine veterinarian in the area for more than one reason. The woman is beautiful. But more than that, she's smart. Cunning. Thinks quickly on her feet. She's impressive in so many ways.

She's a *challenge.*

And I love a challenge.

I've seen her save more than one horse down at the track with her quick thinking. She may be younger than the other track veterinarians, but it strikes me that she could probably run circles around the rest of them.

Her impressive brain doesn't stop me from admiring the way her hips sway as she marches away from me, straight toward the barns. She takes a hard left near a tractor and moves to the other side where no one will see or hear us. My stomach flips.

What the hell is going on?

Dr. Thorne is an alluring woman, and I'm still human enough to admit that. There's an arrogant edge to her cool exterior, hawkish intelligence in her eyes. A spark that, with the right fuel, just might combust.

She spins on me, her dark eyes pinched as she homes straight in on mine. I like that she doesn't shy away from eye contact, and I meet it, even if there's a minor part of me that's concerned about what she's going to say next. Something feels off.

"How can I help you, Dr. Thorne?" I force my voice to sound smooth and confident, even though I'm brimming with questions.

"It's more about how you can help yourself."

I tilt my head at her, studying her face, admiring the straight line of her nose, the angle of her brows, the puffiness of her lips, and the stubborn set to her jaw.

"I'm going to give you a bit of advice, Stefan." I like the way she calls me by my first name—the way it sounds in her mouth. "The horse-racing business is a tight-knit industry in this area. This community is small, and Ruby Creek is even smaller. Making enemies of Billie and the Harding family is not in your best interest. You compete on the track, not off."

I almost want to roll my eyes. "Thank you for your input, Dr. Thorne. But unfortunately for Billie and the Harding family, I like to compete everywhere."

She nods at me slowly, turning my words over in her head as her arms come up to cross under her full breasts. They're magnificent. I've noticed over the past couple of years that she tries to hide them with layers. Sometimes, when it's damp and cold, she wears this big brown Carhartt coat, but today she's wearing a fitted, quilted vest over her long-sleeved T-shirt that does her nothing but favors. It nips in around her waist, and I swear she almost can't get the zipper all the way up.

But I don't stare. I'm not a total Neanderthal.

"Then you'll need to find another veterinarian to use."

I scoff. "You can't be serious. All because I made a perfectly fair offer to buy one of their horses?"

Her chocolate eyes are all fire now. "First of all, that was a very subtle attempt at blackmail, and we both know it. But bravo on walking that line so skillfully. This time it's different, Stefan. You've gone too far. I don't work for men who employ predators."

I rear back, ice racing down my spine and stiffening my entire body. "What did you just say to me?"

Mira drops her chin and offers me an unimpressed look. "You heard me. You're a smart man, so don't play stupid about Patrick Cassel. You've taken this vendetta too far by weaponizing your employee."

Every ounce of humor drains from my body as I stare back down at this woman, who is accusing me of something I would *never* do. Patrick Cassel is the jockey I've hired to ride my horses. Do I like the guy? Not particularly. But he wins, and I like to win.

"I would *never* do that. Not in a million ye—"

She cuts me off. "He intentionally took Violet down on that track. Purposely injured another comp—"

My spine stiffens as I fist my hands in my pockets and interrupt her right back. "That is still under review."

"Shouldn't be. I overheard him confirm it when he cornered her, terrified her, and told her he wouldn't do it again so long as she slept with him."

My throat feels tight as I blink stupidly at the veterinarian, trying to wrap my head around what she's just told me. Trying to keep the rage surging up inside me at bay. I can't let how distraught this makes me show.

"Is she okay?" is the first thing I think of, and I blurt it straight out. The thought of him doing something like what Mira just described makes me feel borderline murderous.

She blinks a few times, assessing me. "Yes. She's small but mighty."

My breath rushes out in a whoosh. Mira has no reason to lie to me about this. She's been nothing short of professional, even though her friends and employers have labeled me as the Big Bad Wolf.

But apparently, she's not done knocking me on my heels for today. "I also have my suspicions about what he's doing to the horses he works with."

"What is that supposed to mean?"

"I saw him inject one with something before a race last weekend."

"One of mine?"

"No. But it doesn't matter whose it was. He was acting off, looking around like he didn't want anyone to see. It just didn't seem right. Between you and me, you need to be careful. Both of these things could come back on you and your business."

"I... had no idea." *And Patrick Cassel is a dead man walking.*

She shakes her head, and her chest heaves under the weight of a tired sigh. "The worst part is I actually believe you. I don't think you're the devil everyone makes you out to be, Stefan. Here's your chance to prove it. Find a new jockey, and I'll continue working for you."

I almost laugh. She looks so serious, so deadly serious. "Isn't *that* blackmail, Dr. Thorne?"

The smile she hits me with now is pretty much a snarl. She reaches out and pats me on the chest, right over the front pocket of my suit jacket. It's almost condescending.

"No, Mr. Dalca. It's a *perfectly fair offer*."

I bark out a laugh as she spins on her heel and walks away. She just spat my words right back at me with a pretty smile. She knows she's got me by the balls, and she's absolutely delighted about it. On top of that, she's walking away with the last word.

I hate not getting the last word.

"Let me take you on a date, and we'll call it a deal. I'll fire Patrick," I call out—only half-joking.

It's her turn to laugh now. It filters back toward me, melodic and amused.

"No chance, Stefan. You'd fall in love with me, and then I definitely couldn't be your vet."

And with one sly wink over her shoulder, she's gone. Back around the tractor, melting into the race-day crowds at Bell Point Park, thinking I'll fall for her whole smart-mouthed, confident persona.

Challenge accepted.

★★★

FIVE MONTHS AGO…

Second place. Again.

The whir of the track immediately following a major derby rages behind me as I stand at the fence line watching the horses cool down after a hard-fought race. I'm disappointed. I hate losing, and I'm not above admitting I especially hate losing to Gold Rush Ranch and all their happy, sunshiny positivity and family-like vibe. I swear I can hear them cheering above the buzz.

I know it's petty—I know I'm jealous. But I really thought this was my year. I thought I had a horse who could beat the spunky little black stallion. My horse, Cascade Calamity, is well bred. He's an athlete—a competitor—but the Gold Rush horse is a force to be reckoned with.

They had two races in hand heading into the final leg of the Northern Crown, so while I knew I couldn't take the crown, I definitely thought I could prevent them from taking it again. Back-to-back crown wins with that horse will make Billie and her boyfriend so much more smug and obnoxious than they already are.

"He ran well." Nadia slips her hand into mine and gives it a tight squeeze.

I give her a curt nod, still looking out at the track. "He did."

"Maybe next year." She says it sweetly, but with a total lack of understanding.

Nothing is certain in this sport. Some racehorses have long, healthy careers, but the vast majority of them don't. They get sore, they get sour, and I'm not about to push my horses beyond what they're capable of doing. I'm not going to ruin an animal just to win a race, and it's my feeling this boy is about ready to retire. He's sound, he's happy, and he's had a very winning career. I can stand him at stud somewhere, and he can spend his days eating grass and making babies.

I respect him enough to let him walk away from the sport while he's still healthy. Could I run him into the ground for another season and make some cash? Probably. But I refuse to do that to an animal who has run his heart out for me and my business.

He deserves better.

And despite what Billie Black—who clearly hates me—likes to run around telling everyone, I am not a dick. Well, at least not to my horses.

"You know what you need to do."

I peer down into Nadia's mahogany eyes. She's grimacing at me because she knows how much I'm already dreading what I have to do next.

My shoulders heave under the weight of a heavy sigh, and I give her a terse "Yup."

A quick squeeze on her slender shoulder and I'm gone, pushing my way through the bustling crowd toward the winner's circle. I hate watching the race from the owner's lounge, surrounded by the sorts of people I can't stand, the types I turned away from when I left Europe. Money. Excess. Lack of sense. Obsessed with their image.

I hate it all.

So I watch down at track level, among all the regular Joes. It feels more real down here. More separated from how I grew up. And I'll do almost anything to distance myself from that.

I make my way through a sea of oversized hats and fancy dresses. Derby day is charming to be sure. The excitement is palpable. It's hard not to get swept up in the thrill. But right now, as I approach the winner's circle, all I feel is dread.

I need to walk in there and congratulate my competitors. The Gold Rush Ranch team. Billie Black. The Harding brothers. The little blond jockey who always looks at me like she feels sorry for me. That expression might be worse than the total distaste the fiery trainer aims my way.

With the circle in sight, my steps falter. Dr. Mira Thorne is also there with them, a sultry smile on her lips and a twinkle in her big dark eyes. My stomach flips at the sight of her, like it always does. I must be a glutton for punishment because getting turned down by her has become one of my favorite pastimes.

The crowd presses in around the circle—reporters, cameras, fellow owners, and jockeys. Everyone comes out of the woodwork to ask questions and offer their congratulations.

It's the classy thing to do, and I'm not about to play into their hand with what they think about me. I'm aware they hate me—more than the average athlete hates their closest competition. But I don't need to give them more reasons to.

Kill them with kindness.

Walking up with a forced smile on my face, I try not to stare at Mira. I have a good idea of how this is going to go, but it still needs to be done. I stop right in front of Billie, who hates me more than any of them. She's the ringleader in the campaign against me—that much is clear. And I suppose there's a part of me that can't blame her.

All is not fair in love and war where she's concerned. And that chip on her shoulder has proven impossible to smooth out.

"Miss Black." I thrust my hand out in her direction. "Congratulations on another crown win. Absolutely incredible."

And I actually mean it. Back-to-back wins are practically unheard of. An exceptional feat, to be sure.

But her shapely brow arches with pure disdain. "You think I'd shake your hand?"

I should have known she would make a scene.

I tut at her, replacing a fake smile with a smug smirk. "I thought you might value good sportsmanship."

She steps in closer toward my hand, looking around herself with a wide phony smile before whisper-shouting, "*You* are going to talk to *me* about sportsmanship?"

"I'm happy to let bygones be bygones."

She stares back at me, slightly slack-jawed. *If looks could kill.*

"I don't make deals with the devil, Dalca. Some people might look the other way where you're concerned, but I'm not one of them."

"Billie." Vaughn, her fiancé, comes up behind her, snaking an arm around her waist. He leans in close to her ear with a small smile, and I swear he says, "If you don't have anything nice to say, say nothing at all."

Her gaze flits up to his, and she gives him a small nod before turning away from me. He doesn't though. He stands there and glares at me.

If looks could kill.

"Don't suppose you're up for a handshake either?" I shouldn't say it, but they're all so childish. It's difficult not to stoop to their level.

He shakes his head and turns away from me with a disappointed sigh. I make a point not to look around myself. I'm not above feeling some level of embarrassment. And being entirely ignored by some of the biggest names in the business stings. Something I refuse to show.

Shoving my shoulders back, I turn to Violet, who is positively beaming on the back of the black horse. "Remarkable win, Mrs. Harding."

She looks down at me with a slight smile before placing her small hand in mine. She never has been as hard on me. Instead, she looks at me with pity—which is definitely worse.

"Thank you very much, Mr. Dalca. Your stallion ran well too."

From behind Violet, I can see her husband storming through the crowd, looking like he might take my head off. The man is massive and terrifying, and I'm probably out of my league where he's concerned.

"Stefan." Mira sidles up beside me, wrapping her hand around my elbow. "It's time for you to go."

I tilt my head in her direction with a quirk of my cheek. "But why, Dr. Thorne? I'm having so much fun."

Her lips purse together like she's trying to hide a smile. "Because Cole Harding will legit murder you for waltzing in here and making trouble."

She tugs me away from the center of the circle, other people already pushing in to take our spots.

I bristle a bit as she leads me toward the surrounding fence. "I'm not making trouble. I'm offering my congratulations like any good competitor would."

She stops with a sigh and hits me with her signature stern stare. "*I* know that. But them?" She hikes a thumb over her shoulder toward her closest friends. "They don't see it that way. The best thing you can do is leave. Send a card in the mail if you need to congratulate them. Please just don't make a scene. Let them enjoy this."

I shoot her a disbelieving look. Billie Black might be her best friend, but we both recognize I'm not the scene maker in this scenario.

"I know." She runs a hand through her hair. "I *know.* Please?"

"Please what?" That word sounds so damn good on her lips.

"Please, just go." Her eyes are wide and pleading. Absolutely distracting.

I tap at my lips and stare up at the sky dramatically like I'm considering what she's told me. "What's in it for me?"

"Stefan." Her tone is so scolding.

I pin her with my gaze. "Let me take you on a date, and I'll leave like you want me to."

She shakes her head, and this time she can't contain the smile that touches her mouth. "You're insane, you know that?"

Can't blame a guy for trying.

I wink at her before I turn away and call back over my shoulder. "Yeah, but that's what you love about me."

She groans, and I chuckle under my breath as I leave.

Yep. Just insane enough to keep trying.

CHAPTER 2

Mira

PRESENT

My breath comes out in puffs, white against the night sky, as I trudge down the steep stairs from my apartment. I had been warm. I had been dead to the world, blissfully floating through a deep, dreamless sort of sleep.

Until the alarm went off.

It only took one glance at the webcam set up beside my bed to tell me there was about to be another new arrival at Gold Rush Ranch.

The last one for the season—thank god.

This has happened every night this week. It's the end of February. Foaling season—at least for racehorses, who need to be born early in the year. And it seems as if every single mare at Gold Rush Ranch has gotten together over a bale of hay and discussed syncing up their births just to spite me. I imagine them like women, sitting around sipping a green smoothie, planning out how cute it would be to have their babies at the same time.

How they could all play together, go to school together. *Ha ha. Imagine if they dated one day! How precious.*

We wanted the foals this year to be born as early as possible to give them every advantage on the track. But back-to-back-to-back? This is just torture.

The night is quiet and wet. Rain mists down continuously, causing a chilly dampness that leaches the heat from your bones and creeps into all the layers you've tried to guard yourself with. Spring in Ruby Creek is a different beast from what you'd see in the city. The elevation change ensures that, and Canadian winters aren't known for how mild they are. We butt up against the Cascade Mountains, which means it's frigid even when there isn't snow. Cold in the winter and scorching hot in the summer.

My leather gloves wrap around the steel barn door and heave, the wheels screeching as I slide it open. A quiet nicker greets me as I head down to the last stall. It's lit with warm infrared lights and glows a sort of orange color in the otherwise dark foaling barn.

We have seven mares on the farm who were due this year, six of whom have already foaled out. Four this week alone. In the middle of the night, no less.

Sadly, the mare from last night didn't make it. Everything seemed fine. Baby was up and nursing—until she collapsed. It doesn't happen often, but it does happen. And it sucks every goddamn time.

I've wanted to be a veterinarian since I can remember. I'm well aware it's not all sunshine and rainbows, but it doesn't stop the bridge of my nose from stinging when I think about it.

Now we've got this beautiful red colt, with flashy white legs and a wide blaze over his face, who doesn't have a mom. What's worse is he's our first—and only—foal sired by the farm's celebrity stallion and two-time Denman Derby winner, DD.

He's the special foal we've *all* been waiting for.

For the past twenty-four hours, we've been taking turns bottle-feeding him. Every single person on the ranch has put out feelers looking for a mare who may have lost a foal because what this little orphan needs is a mare who will adopt him. A nurse mare. Without one, his chances of survival aren't great. He *really* needs that colostrum.

I peek into his stall, trying not to tear up at the sight of his tiny sleeping form, before moving on to the next stall. *One thing at a time, Mira. You can't save them all.*

"Hey, Mama," I coo at the dark bay mare, who is already down on the ground, sweat slicked across her neck. "How we doing, huh?"

I run my fingers through her thick forelock as she gives me a slight head bob, her eyelids closing under the gentle pressure of my hand. This isn't Flora's first rodeo. From what I understand, she's produced several nice foals for the farm and is the great-granddaughter of the first-ever racehorse at Gold Rush Ranch, Lucky Penny.

The interconnectedness of it all is almost saccharine in its sweetness. The two grandsons of the couple who founded this place are running it with their partners and making international headlines. Still breeding racehorses off that very first bloodline.

I'm not an overly sentimental woman, but even I must admit it's pretty adorable.

I crouch down behind Flora, lifting her thick black tail while rubbing at her haunch to watch for contractions, checking my watch to time them. The second one comes, but not so fast that I need to stay here and crowd her.

That's the philosophy I try to carry forward with the animals I treat. How would I want a medical professional to react in this situation? I haven't had a baby before, but I imagine having a doctor hover and stare at me would be stressful.

So I extend the same courtesy to Flora and head into the staff lounge attached to the barn. Might as well make some coffee. *Again.*

I flick the lights on, put a pod in the coffee maker, and then slump down in the cushy armchair, feeling the weight of my exhaustion. It's like the marrow in my bones has turned to lead. My entire body feels heavy. But I've always wanted this career, and I've worked too hard and too long to complain now that I'm finally here. *People have survived worse, Mira.*

Dragging my phone out of my pocket, I fire a text off to Billie as promised, and I wait for the hot water to flow through the pod and create a hot caffeinated drink for me. Billie is the head trainer here at the ranch as well as the owner's fiancé, but she's also become one of my closest friends over the last couple of years. We initially bonded over a close call with her stallion, DD. And then she was like a fly I couldn't shake off, hugging me and inviting me to girls' nights. Talking to me like we'd known each other for years. She's one of those people who just has a way of making you want to be around them. Her energy is as addictive as her language is colorful.

Mira: Ginger is foaling. I'm at the barn.

She's been sleeping with her ringer on, waiting for this final foal. Billie is usually cool under pressure, but she's nervous after last night. With a fresh reminder of how wrong it can all go, I can't blame her for feeling that way.

It only takes a few moments for her to respond, even though it's just after 2 a.m.

Billie: You really need to hire someone to help you.

Don't I know it. The problem is, I'm kind of a loner. As an only child, I take pleasure in my solitude. There are very few people in the world I can spend extended periods of time around without eventually feeling agitated by them.

Mira: Fucking tell me about it.

It's the only response I can muster as I shove my phone back into my pocket, grab the cup of steaming coffee, and wander back into the barn. I hear Ginger's labored breathing and soft grunts now, all normal. I peek in and time another contraction, which are slowly getting closer together. She won't be long now. Provided everything goes the way it's supposed to, it rarely takes long for a foal to be born.

As I sip my coffee, I move back over to the small orphan colt's stall and watch his tiny rib cage rise and fall where he's snuggled up in the straw. I'm worried sick about him. I grew up on a farm. I'm a scientist, so I like to think of myself as rational. But as much as I've trained myself to look at much of what happens to animals in this line of work as the natural circle of life, now and then, you get one that just kicks you in the gut for no good reason. Something so unfair that it clenches your heart in a fist and won't let it go. And this nameless colt is that for me.

I feel powerless to help him, and I *really* hate that. It almost makes me want to wake him and feed him again, even though I can see from the chart on his stall that Hank was here only a few hours ago and gave him a bottle then. He needs to rest, and I recognize that I just want to wake him to comfort myself. To convince myself that he really will wake again and stand on those wobbly, gangly legs. This shouldn't be how DD's first foal hits the ground.

It should be a moment of celebration, not sadness.

When my phone rings in my pocket, I don't even bother checking the number before I hit answer and say, "Go to sleep, psycho. I'll call if I need your help."

But it's not Billie's voice I hear. "Dr. Thorne? It's Stefan Dalca."

Stefan Dalca is pretty much everyone's least favorite person. He's solidified himself as enemy number one to most people at this farm for the arrogant shit he's pulled or for the arrogant shits he's employed. And to be honest, the only reason I haven't entirely written the guy off is because I kind of like him. He's a good client at the clinic. He takes meticulous care of his horses, he pays his bills early, and he keeps his appointments—in a lot of ways he's a good guy.

"Listen, if you're calling in the middle of the night to ask me on a date, the answer is still no."

Stefan is also relentless—and I kind of get a kick out of it. He asked me out six months ago as a joke. And now it is *the* running joke. He smirks and offers a date in lieu of paying a bill. He winks and offers a date in exchange for throwing a race. A woman with better sense would tell him to back off, but I've always been drawn to the man—against my better judgment—so he usually gets a headshake and an eye roll followed by an "in your dreams" with a small tip of my lips.

"I called the clinic, but—"

"That's because it's closed. You can't be calling me at all hours of the night, Stefan. I don't even know how you got my personal number. I'm not on call. We open at nine—"

He cuts me off with a crack in his voice. "It's an emergency. I need you at my farm as soon as possible."

I pull straight up to the big barn doors at Cascade Acres. My footfalls echo in the otherwise quiet barn as I run down the alleyway to where lights are on at the back.

"Stefan?" I call out breathlessly. "I'm here."

"Over here," he barks back from only a few stalls ahead, just as I see his wide-eyed barn manager, Leo, step out into the aisle.

The man presses his lips together and shakes his head at me as I turn down into the oversized foaling stall. Stefan is hands-on with his horses, and it's irritating that Leo, who is supposed to know something about this business, is standing here like a bump on a log while I've spent the drive over talking his employer through what to do to salvage a dangerous situation.

Stefan is down on the stall floor, kneeling beside a motionless foal, his hands braced on his knees and his head bowed.

His voice comes out quiet and lightly accented when he finally speaks. "I've been trying to resuscitate her the way you told me to. I think she's dead."

I step in and check the chestnut mare, who is standing above the foal's body, quickly. She looks tired but isn't bleeding excessively. Thankfully, nothing looks emergent with her—it's the foal that has me worried. "Mom looks okay for now."

"I burst the bag just like you told me to." His voice is thick, and blood covers his naturally tan arms and white T-shirt.

Red bag deliveries are dangerous, messy, and rarely end well. The placenta separates and the foal is born prematurely.

I take a deep breath and then kneel beside Stefan. "You did great. You did everything right."

He looks at me now, his green eyes almost mossy in the low light. There's no smirk on his face tonight. He looks genuinely gutted.

I drop his gaze, pull out my stethoscope, and listen for a heartbeat. Finding none, I place my hand gingerly over one of his. "I'm sorry, Stefan."

He nods, unable to meet my eyes. I hate this part of being a vet. The dealing with people part. The dealing with feelings part. Animals live their life in the moment. They are eternal optimists—they don't know any better. But people are complicated and traversing their emotions isn't my strong suit. I'm not a talk-about-your-feelings type of gal.

With my other hand, I awkwardly pat his back. I'm aware my bedside manner leaves something to be desired, but I'm good with the animals, and in my book, that's what counts. It's moments like this where my tongue ties in a knot, and my otherwise quite exceptional IQ short-circuits.

"Did I miss something?" he asks, his voice so thick it makes me blink away unwanted moisture in my eyes.

I sit back on my heels and heave out a sigh. "You didn't

miss a thing. This is just… nature. It's sad and gritty sometimes. But what you did saved your mare's life. In the wild or without supervision, they'd both be gone."

He nods but still doesn't look at me, so I opt to sit beside him in silence, holding vigil over the lost foal. What more is there to say, really?

The world is a cruel place sometimes.

CHAPTER 3

Stefan

DEATH SUCKS. THIS IS SOMETHING I ALREADY KNEW, BUT WATCHing something so young and innocent die is different. It's just *wrong.* It makes me feel almost nauseous. All the prepping, all the money, all the knowledge. None of it matters when the universe shits on you.

I stand and pat the sweet broodmare, whose eyes are fluttering shut with exhaustion. "You did good, pretty girl," I say as I slide a hand down her face. "You did good."

And then I walk woodenly to the bathroom to wash some of the blood off myself. I'm a goddamn mess. I look like Carrie on prom night, and as much as I hate to admit it, I feel like I could cry.

I haven't cried in years. I've become far too closed-off for that. And I'm sure as hell not going to do it in front of Dr. Thorne. It would probably just give her something to run back to all her annoying friends with. Something to mock me about.

I'm not stupid. I know they think I'm terrible. I'm not

oblivious to the fact that there are almost certainly jokes made at my expense around Gold Rush Ranch. Did I resort to questionable tactics to buy their championship-winning stallion out from underneath them? Yes. Did I hire a jockey who may have set out to harm their horse and rider? Yes. Did he also turn out to be a sleazy predator? Yes. But I had no knowledge that he was going to do that. And I *never* would have instructed him to do so. I might not describe myself as a "good man," but I'm not morally corrupt enough to actually hurt someone. Plus, I'm not finished with him. He'll get what's coming to him if it's the last thing I do. There's a special place reserved in hell for men who hurt women, and I plan to ensure he gets there. At any rate, the last thing I need to do is give them ammunition to take me down when all I want is to succeed in this business.

Making my way to the top has been my singular focus for years now. I've done what it takes to get ahead. To establish myself. I promised my mother on her deathbed I would take her dashed dreams and make them a reality. So here I am, trying my best and not all that concerned about making friends along the way.

I watch the dark-pink water swirl down the drain until it runs clear before drying myself off and heading back to the stall. Dr. Thorne is in there tending to Farrah, the mare who just lost her foal. She's hooked up to fluids and who knows what else. Mira has wrapped the filly in a blanket and moved her out of the stall.

"Is she going to be okay?" I ask as I lean on the doorjamb.

Mira's fathomlesss dark eyes shoot up to mine. She looks serious. She looks *tired.* Blue smudges beneath her eyes mar her beautiful face. Mira Thorne is alluring, and I'm not immune to it. Black hair and similarly dark, almond-shaped eyes. A slight smirk always on her lips, like she thinks she's smarter than everyone around her.

And she just might be right. Though I'm sure I could give her a run for her money if I wanted to, but I don't. Out in Ruby Creek, the pickings for veterinarians are slim, and Dr. Mira Thorne is damn good at her job.

"Yeah. I'm just going to get her hydrated, get some antibiotics through the system, just in case. We'll have to keep a close eye on her for the next while."

I just nod, feeling the sadness of the lost filly like a weighted blanket across my chest. I feel responsible. Like I could have done more. Should have hired better people. Should have called Mira sooner. Should have had my own on-site veterinarian. Should have done *something.*

Like she can see my turmoil, Mira looks at me, her expression perfectly sincere. No trace of that smirk she's usually giving me. "Hey, you did everything you could. More than most people would. This isn't on you."

In moments like this, I feel distinctly out of my element. I wasn't raised on a farm, and I don't have a background in this industry. I just waltzed in with a checkbook and a keen mind and set myself to learning, as well as hiring and buying the best. Maybe she's just being nice. Maybe I could have done more.

I watch Mira work quietly and gently beside the mare, mumbling things to her I can't quite make out. She has a way with the animals that I admire. I could use a little of her gentleness sometimes. I recognize that the way I've gone about doing things has rubbed some people the wrong way. But I don't concern myself with their opinions. Instead, I think of my mother, who, after years of protecting me, got taken out by the asshole she married. The one who got off on knocking her around. I think of her, hooked up to tubes and wires after that plane crash, telling me she never should have left Ruby Creek.

A place I'd never heard of.

Telling me she should have stuck around and trained racehorses.

A part of her life I'd never known about.

Then she dropped a life-altering bomb on me.

And then she died.

He died, too, but he took my mom with him. In his stupid small private plane, the kind that rich people have a bad habit of dying on. One final *fuck you* to the son he never liked. She never could quite leave him, so the plane crash took them both. So bitter and so sweet all at once. And I missed out on so many years with her while she shipped me off to private schools to keep me safe and away from him, my supposed dad.

She was battered and bruised and so damn injured. With her hand in my hand, she took her last breath, and I promised to bring her back to Ruby Creek. A small town on the other side of the world. And then with all the vast amounts of cash that asshole left behind, I set out to make her dying dreams come true.

Life isn't fair, and neither am I. Especially not when I have a promise to fulfill.

I storm through the barn and grab a shovel on my way out the door. It's dark and cold, and it's raining again, but I don't care. I'm a mess already.

Shovel in hand, I head down toward the small lake on my property. The one that separates my house from this barn.

The one where I spread my mother's ashes. And beneath the big weeping willow to the east of the water, I dig a hole.

This place is about to become a cemetery for everyone I can't manage to keep safe.

***

"Stefan, sit down."

I barely hear her silky voice over the rush of the rain falling. I shake my head and keep throwing dirt back into the hole. When I retrieved the foal's body, Mira looked at me sadly. I don't want her pity. I don't want her to look at me like that. I just want to bury the foal and then carry on with my day like this shitty fucking night never even happened.

I freeze when I feel her hand come to rest on my back again, her slender fingers lying across the expanse between my shoulders, heating the skin beneath through my soaked shirt.

Her touch is warm. But her voice is not. "Sit. Down."

"I can't. I need to finish filling this hole."

Her other hand shoots out and wraps around the wooden handle of the shovel. "No. It's my turn."

I stand up straight now and peer down at her. "This isn't what I pay you for."

She rolls her eyes at me but yanks on the shovel. "Don't I know it. But I'm going to do it. So back off."

"You look tired," I say, looking her up and down, her stern face peeking out from beneath the hood of her raincoat.

Her gaze scans me, and that signature smirk touches the edges of her lips. "I guess I'm in good company." I get distracted by her mouth for just long enough that she yanks the shovel right out of my hands. I expect some sassy comment, but she just turns around and starts shoveling scoops of heavy, wet soil into the big hole.

My feet root to the ground as I watch her work, misty rain falling around us as the sun comes up over the Cascades, casting a blue glow across the valley. It's eerie and beautiful all at once, and suddenly I feel just as tired as I accused Mira of looking.

I sink to the ground right where I am, not caring about how wet or muddy I might get. I'm past that point. It feels like I'm having an out-of-body experience—that's how tired and stunned I am.

"Why are you helping me?" I blurt out to the woman in front of me, who I could have sworn is completely indifferent to me but is going out of her way to help me right now. At the very least, her friends hate me. Helping me would probably be a crime in their books.

She doesn't look up. The shovel clinks and rasps against the small pebbles in the pile of silty dirt. It smells fresh and earthy between the soil and the lake and the rain.

"Because you needed help," she eventually responds.

"What are all your friends going to say about you doing this?"

She stops now, jams the shovel into the ground, and puts one booted foot on top of its edge as she looks down at me. Her eyes are intelligent, and her cheeks are pink, and her chest rises and falls with the exertion of digging. "Not sure. I don't usually ask their permission to do what I think is right."

I scoff and stare at the upturned tip of her nose, the way a droplet of water drips off it. Leave it to the woman who saves lives for a living to be all morally superior when I'm so clearly morally gray. I wonder what she really thinks of me.

"You know what they say about assuming, Dalca. And you definitely shouldn't make assumptions about me." Mira glares at me so hard that I drop my eyes. I'm not in the mood to face off with anyone right now. So I sit, lost in thought, getting soaked to the bone while my veterinarian finishes covering the grave. I don't even bother interrupting her to take the shovel back. She doesn't strike me as the type of woman who needs my help.

Plus, I'm probably no gentleman as far as she's concerned.

When she's done, she drops the shovel on the ground and comes to stand over me. Her warm breath puffs out in front of her as she speaks. "I'll be back later today to check on Farrah. You should get some sleep."

"Are those the doctor's orders?" My tone is condescending. It's kind of my default mode—I sometimes talk that way without even meaning to. I sound like a spoiled rich kid with mommy issues even though I'm thirty-four years old. *Adorable.*

She puts her hands on her hips and quirks one shapely brow in my direction, scolding me silently. "Never believed you were quite the dick people make you out to be. But when you talk like that, I can see it."

I clench my jaw, working my teeth against each other, internally berating myself. When I finally look up to offer her an apology, she's walking back toward her Gold Rush Ranch truck, hips swaying with a gait that defies how exhausted she must be right now.

I should have thanked her. She helped me. In the dark. In the rain. And I acted like a sullen little prick.

Her friends call me *Dalca the Dick*, but right now is the first time I've actually felt like one.

CHAPTER 4

Mira

Billie and I fall side by side onto the couch in the stable lounge. We let our eyes flutter shut while more coffee brews.

I'm so tired that I feel like I'm drunk. The kind of tired that pushes you past exhaustion right into giddiness. I need to sleep, but I can't. We've got a beautiful new filly on the farm that Billie delivered last night after Stefan called me away on the emergency.

Flora had a healthy, uneventful delivery and gave birth to a perfect doppelgänger filly. Dark bay with long eyelashes.

Seeing a happy, healthy foal was the lift my heart needed after leaving Dalca's farm this morning. Losing a foal is never easy, but seeing how hard he was taking it made it even worse. I'm well aware I'm not a comforting person. I'm not a hold-your-hair-back-while-you-barf kind of friend. I didn't get the nursing gene. But I do know how to make myself useful, and sometimes that's an okay way to comfort a person too.

"Thanks for taking over with Flora," I mutter quietly.

"Hey, no worries. It was kind of fun. It also never fails to kill any inkling I might feel about wanting to have a baby."

I snort.

"Seriously, Mira. Something that big coming out of something that small is terrifying."

"Vaginas are very elastic. You'd bounce back."

Billie groans. "Ugh. Why is everything so literal with you? You're like Amelia Bedelia."

"I loved those books," I chuckle.

"Speaking of idiot savants, how was Dalca the Dick? He sure kept you there long enough."

"His foal died," I say bluntly. Sometimes Billie needs to be sobered up a bit.

"Well, shit. Now I feel like the dick."

I peek over at her and see her amber eyes shrink-wrapped in a layer of wetness. That loss hits a little too close for her with DD's orphan baby lying in a stall by himself not a hundred yards away. "You should. Red bag delivery. It was a tough night."

She grunts and blinks rapidly. "Did the mare make it?"

"Yes..." I say, trailing off suggestively.

Billie turns her head and hits me with wide eyes. "Why did you say it like that?"

"Are you being intentionally dense because of the person we're talking about, or are you just so tired that you're not firing on all cylinders?"

Billie is whip-smart. To pretend the first place her mind went wasn't our orphan colt would be ridiculous. Just ten minutes down the road is a mare with no foal whose milk is in full swing.

The math is pretty simple.

She blinks and nibbles at her lip. "Would you believe me if I told you I'm just super tired?"

I huff out a laugh and shake my head as I get up to walk toward the coffee machine. "Better fix your attitude, Billie. Dalca the Dick just became your best shot at saving that colt."

I pull up to Cascade Acres with two coffees in tow. I basically *am* coffee now. My blood is straight-up caffeinated, and I need it to make it through the rest of this day. Not only am I physically tired, but I'm emotionally exhausted. Vaughn, one of the owners of the ranch, told me to close the on-site clinic and get some sleep. It still means I'm on call for emergencies, but at least I'm not dozing in the new state-of-the-art facility while I pretend to work. I don't even think I could safely treat a horse right now if I wanted to.

That's the side of this gig that people seem to forget about. Some days, you feel sad right down to your toes. It's hard to shake.

But at least there's coffee.

Sweet, sweet bribe coffee. Because somehow, I'm the one who must waltz out here and convince Stefan Dalca to let us borrow his mare for the orphaned foal. Probably because I'm the only one who is on reasonably good footing with the man. I tried to convince Hank, the sweet older barn manager, to do it. But he just laughed good-naturedly at me and said he's too old for the drama we "kids" are into.

A comment I resent. I avoid drama at all costs. Good thing Hank is so damn loveable, or I'd have pressed harder. Violet offered to go, but the scowl Cole gave me—like he might skin me if I sent her over here—had me turning her down. That motherfucker is scary when he wants to be. And Billie and Vaughn? That wasn't even on the table. They both *hate* Stefan, which is why this situation is going to require some finesse.

So I gave in and opted to take one for the team.

I walk in through the big sliding barn door and peer around. Usually, Gold Rush Ranch bustles with staff at this time of day, but this farm is pretty quiet. It's a much smaller operation. I still kind of assumed there'd be people working.

"Stefan?" I call out into the echoey alleyway.

I stop and wait for a response but hear nothing, so I keep walking toward the tractor with a trailer full of soiled wood shavings attached at the end of the barn. As I pass by the dark-stained wood Dutch doors on the stall fronts, I see the odd shovelful of waste flying out of one of the last stalls into the trailer—clearly someone is mucking stalls out down here. I'll get them to point me in the right direction.

Except when I peer down into the box stall, I don't see the staff member I was expecting to find. I see Stefan Dalca, wearing fitted black jeans, a black T-shirt, and a dark scowl on his face. AirPods are in his ears, and he obviously has no clue I'm here. So I watch him for a minute.

Dark-blond hair and golden skin give him a glow. Long limbs, corded with muscle, move with a confidence most men try to fake. But on him it looks natural. There's something alluring about his slightly dangerous vibe and the mysterious accent.

Everyone else sees Stefan all polished in an expensive suit at the track and thinks that's his go-to look, but they miss the version of him doing the dirty work at his farm. Stefan tossing hay bales off a truck in a fitted T-shirt and jeans is a memory I have stocked away for rainy days. The way his arms rippled and sweat slid over his temples. Away from the public eye, this man is a farm boy, with glowing skin from days spent working in the sun.

"Are you having a stroke, Dr. Thorne?"

My head snaps up, surprised by the sound of his voice. His smug veneer has slid back in place perfectly. This is the version of Stefan I'm accustomed to. Quick-witted and sarcastic. Frankly, it's easier to take than Sad Stefan. That was really doing a number on me.

I smile though. Because I absolutely got caught creeping. Something has inexplicably drawn me to the way this man looks. "No. But I think I might have fallen asleep."

He leans against the pitchfork in his hand, matching the way I'm leaning against the stall door, head tilting like he's assessing me. Stefan Dalca is a bright man; you can tell by the way his green eyes spark when he talks. *Nothing short with this one*, as my nana would say.

"What can I help you with?" He looks like some sort of farmer porn leaning on that pitchfork.

"Where is all your staff?" I gesture down the barn alleyway with one coffee cup.

"I sent them home. Needed to be alone."

"So. You're… mucking all these stalls by yourself?"

"Well done, Watson."

"Dick," I murmur, chuckling as I hand him the extra coffee.

"For me?" He reaches out for it slowly, eyeing me with suspicion.

"Yup."

"Is it poisoned?" His green eyes go bright as they dance with dry humor.

And I find myself laughing and joking back, like a total traitor. Like when he asks me out and I brush him off with a stupid giggle. "Nope. Just black. Like your soul."

His eyes drop as a wry twist takes over his mouth. I expected him to laugh at that, but it almost looks as if my words carried some weight. A heavy silence fills the stall, and I work to come up with something that might salvage this conversation. I can't afford to blow this. I really need his help. That foal really needs his help.

"You, uh, want some help?" I gesture down at the pitchfork.

His brows pinch together. "Why would you do that?"

"Because I'm a good person," I say brightly.

"Because you feel bad for me after last night?"

"Nope." I pop the *p*, trying to sound extra convincing.

His head tilts in an almost feline way, like he's got me totally figured out. "Because you want something from me?"

I sigh, frustrated with his ability to see right through my ruse. "Listen. Do you want the help or not?"

"Pitchforks are hanging by the feed room down the alleyway." His chin juts out in that direction. "You can take the other side." And then he gets back to sifting through the wood shavings and flipping the dirty ones skillfully into the trailer.

Saying nothing further, I grab the pitchfork and get to work. I grew up on a farm. My parents are blueberry farmers, but we still had some livestock. Chickens and goats, that kind of thing. So scooping shit isn't exactly new to me. I go inward and get lost in the repetitive nature of the job. The scrape, the shake, the toss. It's almost therapeutic. And I'm so tired that I'm pretty sure my brain departs altogether, letting my body and muscle memory take over entirely.

Stefan and I work silently and efficiently. I'd be lying if I said I'm not surprised by his work ethic. He always looks so polished and prissy, like a total square, when I see him. Expensive suit, perfectly coiffed hair, absolutely in control *always*. So these last twenty-four hours have been a surprise. My forehead wrinkles under the pressure of trying to reconcile the two different versions of this man. He's a walking, talking contradiction, and I can't help letting my mind wander to the golden manual-labor version of him.

This version is what I like in a man, and it's tripping me out. Thinking of Stefan Dalca as anything other than our competitor and a dick in general feels traitorous. If my friends could read my mind, they'd read me the riot act.

Especially when he hops up onto the tractor, turns the key, and lets his tongue slide out over his bottom lip as the machine roars to life beneath him. He drives it casually, inching forward down the alleyway so that the trailer lines up with where we're working next. His corded forearm ripples where it's slung casually over the wide steering wheel.

And I blame everything that I'm noticing about Stefan Dalca on the delirious level of exhaustion I'm experiencing today. With all my faculties about me, there'd be no way I would check him out.

His gaze moves over to me, and I drop my head quickly, raking through perfectly clean shavings like I missed something. Hoping upon hope that he didn't notice me staring at him. *Again.*

We finish the barn, fill the hay nets, and lead all his horses back in from their time outside. We don't talk, we just do.

He must be almost as tired as I am, and I figure I'm gaining some good karma points for helping him today.

I think? Probably not any good karma points with Billie. But whatever. She doesn't need to know what it took to soften the man up. She'll just be happy when she gets what she wants.

The metallic clang of the last stalls being latched echoes through the barn, and he finally turns to regard me. A light layer of dust from the shavings coats his dark-gold hair.

My fingers itch to brush it off for him.

"Now are you going to tell me what it is you want?"

I brush the shavings off my fleece coat instead, mulling over the best way to respond to him. It strikes me that playing dumb with Stefan won't be a winning strategy. So I smirk at him. "Yes."

He chuckles and stares up at the ceiling, shaking his head. "You must want it pretty bad to have spent the last few hours doing physical labor with me."

I wave him off. "I can handle physical labor. I need your help though."

He leans back against the stall and quirks an eyebrow, urging me on.

I take a deep breath and open my eyes wide. It sounds bad, but I've learned a few tricks throughout the years for bringing men around to my way of thinking. A well-placed doe-eyed look has brought many a gruff old horse breeder around to splurging on a lifesaving procedure. Does that make me a bad person? I'm not sure, but I'm willing to toe that line to save lives. As far as I'm concerned, it's just me doing my job to the best of my abilities.

Stefan snorts, hitting me with a smirk of his own. "Don't use that look on me, Mira. Just spit it out."

For crying out loud. This guy really is the worst. "Fine. I have a foal that needs a nurse mare. Without one, he won't survive."

He just stares, green eyes pinning me in place.

"And you have one..."

"Whom does the foal belong to?" His voice is calm, measured. He shows no signs of surprise.

Might as well just spit it out. "Gold Rush Ranch."

His lips roll together in thought, and I run my sweaty palms down over my jeans. He'd been a good enough guy to turf Patrick Cassell the very day I told him about what the jockey did to Violet. He marched straight back to the barn and fired the weasel on the spot. Pulled him from the race they were heading into and ate the entry fee with no questions asked.

Hopefully, he'll be good enough to do this too.

"Okay." His reply is simple. So simple that it almost confuses me.

"Really? Just... okay?"

His responding grin is wolfish. Boyishly charming. And the dark smudges beneath his eyes do nothing to detract from how handsome he is.

"Yes." He pauses. "Well, I have a couple of conditions."

Yup. There it is. Wiley bastard.

I roll my eyes. I can't help myself. And I flick my hand, motioning for him to spit it out.

"One, I want to keep them here on my farm."

Good god. That's going to be a hard sell. "It makes more sense to have them at Gold Rush with the clinic on-site."

Stefan waves me off. "It's a five-minute drive. You'll be fine."

My teeth grind at his dismissal, but I tamp my agitation down and focus on how badly that foal needs a mom. "Fine," I grit out.

"And two." The man looks downright gleeful. "You let me take you on a date."

Motherfucker.

He scratches his chin thoughtfully. "Actually, three dates."

Mother. Fucker.

"You can't be serious," I whisper-shout at him, watching his eyes flashing with something I don't recognize. I think he secretly gets off on agitating people, self-serving prick that he is. "You're really going to make that running joke part of this deal?"

His lips tip up. "That's rich coming from the woman who brought me a coffee, spent hours helping me, and tried to hit me with her best damsel-in-distress face to get what she wants."

I shake my head at him with wide eyes and fists propped on my hips. "I can't believe how thoroughly you outmaneuvered me. You're willing to use a dying foal to corner me into this? Man, I feel like I just got schooled."

"You did." He smiles smugly, looking altogether too pleased with himself. He knows I won't be able to say no. Not only because I want to save that foal, but because I won't let my friend down.

"Why three dates?"

"Because it's more than one."

My foot taps. "Why not two?"

"Because it's fewer than three?" He says it like a question.

"Okay, then why not five?"

"Are you asking for more, Dr. Thorne?" The smile he hits me with now is downright devastating.

"So basically you've taken your running request and added two punishment dates?" My voice is incredulous.

"They won't be a punishment for me." He grins, and I almost want to slap it off his smug face. I wish I didn't want to save this horse so desperately, or I would. I also wish I didn't admire his tenacity. I definitely wish my stomach wasn't fluttering over why Stefan Dalca wants to take me on a date so badly.

I am a smart girl who is about to do something very stupid.

"Fine. But they will not take place in Ruby Creek, they will be platonic, and you can't tell *anyone*." I turn and head toward the door before he can respond, looking forward to escaping to the safety of my truck.

"Whatever you say," he replies smoothly. "I just can't fall in love with you, right?"

I chuckle as I twist the doorknob to leave. "Oh, Stefan. I think you already are."

I smile into the crisp afternoon air at the sound of his laughter behind me. I may be stuck with the guy, but I don't have to make it easy for him.

Can't let him win every round.

CHAPTER 5

Mira

"No. No fucking way. No, Mira. No."

Violet looks between Billie and me with wide blue eyes, like she's trying to figure out how she can smooth this over. I've just told them about Stefan Dalca's stipulation but conveniently left out the date part for obvious reasons. There are some things the people you love just don't need to know. I will make that sacrifice in secret.

And I don't want to watch Billie full-on erupt either.

"I told him it was fine."

Billie is *riled*, amber eyes narrowed and her head shaking vehemently. "No chance am I sending DD's first baby into the lion's den. Over my dead fucking body."

"Well, it'll be your dead body or the foal's."

"Jesus, Mira. That's dark," Violet pipes up, running her hands through her hair.

Billie glares at me. She doesn't like what I've just said, but she can't deny the truth of it either.

"Man," Billie sighs raggedly. "He's such a dick. I hate this." Her hatred for the man isn't news to anyone. His tactics rub almost everyone the wrong way, but he almost ruined her and Vaughn—something completely unforgivable in her book.

"He isn't so bad." Violet is obviously more forgiving.

"Listen. It is what it is. Are we saving the foal or not? Because the way I see it, he's kinda got us by the balls. It's five minutes down the road. I can check on the foal daily and report back. In the fall, we'll wean him and forget this ever happened. Then we can all go back to openly hating Stefan Dalca."

Billie sighs.

Violet nods.

I think that's as close as I'm going to get to agreement from these two, so I slap my knees in closing and push up to stand. "Who's going to help me load up the trailer?"

Both women stare back at me with frustration and resignation in their eyes. But then they stand and follow me out to help anyway. It doesn't take us long to lift the foal and get him positioned in the trailer. He's still so wobbly and weak, it's definitely not ideal having to transport him. But it's close enough that I figure the reward outweighs the risk.

"I'm coming with you." There's a hard set to Billie's jaw but also a slight wobble. She's trying to be strong, but this is killing her inside. She feels so deeply—loves so thoroughly. She's got this boisterous exterior, but she's incredibly sensitive.

I grab her shoulder and stare back into her face. "Not today, B. Let me do this for you. Let me do my job and get them settled." What I don't say to her is that there's a chance the mare doesn't accept the foal. I don't want her there if that happens. "We can go together tomorrow and check on them. Let's keep it as quiet and private for them as possible today."

She nods once, tersely. We're talking about skittish animals, and she knows that sometimes what we want isn't really what's best for them. And she's willing to sacrifice her own comfort for that—it's part of what makes her such an exceptional horsewoman.

Violet scoots in beside her, fitting herself into Billie's side like a puzzle piece. The two of them are so cute together, it almost makes me gag. Soon to be sisters-in-law since they're each with one of the two brothers who own Gold Rush Ranch.

We're all friends, but I still always feel a bit like the third wheel. And that's not on them, it's on me. I've never been big on loads of friends or the whole girl-tribe thing. But these two just sort of claimed me and haven't let me go, and I'm not complaining. Billie and Violet are easily the best friends I've ever had. It just still feels weird to have these people that I'm accountable to after being a loner for so long.

I hop in the truck and buckle up, rolling down the window as I slowly pull out of the circular driveway in front of the main building.

"Wish me luck!" I call out to them with a wave.

Lord knows I'm going to need it.

"Who are you?"

The girl at the door is eyeing me like I'm yesterday's roadkill. Even she knows I shouldn't be here. She has headphones around her neck and is wearing an oversize T-shirt with tight shorts barely peeking past the hemline. I can see gum in her mouth every time she opens her jaw wide to chomp back down on it. The pink scrunchie that holds her blond hair in a high ponytail makes her look like a walking, talking attitude problem, complete with a bow on top.

The house itself is beautiful, like it's made for the land that surrounds it. All river rock and natural wood beams. A rounded front door with a wrought-iron-framed window at the top. It's big, but not gaudy. It's classy—just like Stefan.

"I'm Mira. The vet." I hike a thumb over my shoulder back toward the farm, where I left the unnamed foal in the trailer because Stefan is nowhere to be found and I need some help. "I'm looking for Stefan."

She looks me up and down, still chewing her gum like a cow would chew its cud. I can't tell how old she is, but she strikes me as young. Too young to be with Stefan.

I hope.

God. I hope he's not slimy enough to con me into three dates when he has a girlfriend.

"Stefan!" I startle when she turns and yells up the curved staircase behind her.

Within moments he's jogging down the stairs, torn jeans hugging his legs in an almost distracting way.

"Nadia, would it kill you to take a few steps and look for me?"

Nadia rolls her eyes and storms off. Stefan offers me a tight smile as he reaches down to slide his feet into a pair of worn work boots. This angle gives me the perfect view of the muscles in his back as they ripple beneath the plain white T-shirt. I figure if I'm going to be forced to go on fake dates with the man, I might as well enjoy the view.

I'm only human.

A human who is currently way overworked and way undersexed.

"Sorry about Nadia. Taking in my little sister is not the cakewalk I thought it would be."

I sigh in relief. *Sister.* Hallelujah.

He reaches into the closet and pulls out a shearling-lined brown jacket. There's something decadent about the way Stefan moves, confident and borderline hypnotic. My eyes trail down his body, watching the veins in his hands as his long, deft fingers button the jacket.

"Eyes up here, Dr. Thorne," he coos with a knowing smile.

I like this more playful version of Stefan Dalca. Not the uptight, almost too-smooth version of him everyone sees down at the track.

I decide to roll with it. "Why?"

"Because you might fall in love with *me* if you stare for too long." Even the light lilting of his accent is more pronounced here on the privacy of his farm. Like he's not trying as hard to project a certain image. He's comfortable and teasing.

It's weird. And what's worse is I live for this type of banter.

I scoff. "Pfft. Don't worry. You're not my type."

He holds one arm out, gesturing me down the front steps of his house up on the hill. The property is not as expansive as Gold Rush Ranch, but it just might be more picturesque. It overlooks a valley with a small lake at the base. The barn is just up the opposite slope, and there's a huge weeping willow tree right beside the gravel road that joins the two buildings. Everything nestled into the valley gives it an effortless cozy feeling that I like.

Our footsteps fall in time on the gravel road as we walk down to the stables.

"And why am I not your type?"

I sneak a peek over at him, hands slung casually in the pockets of his jeans. The way he carries himself—perfect posture and head held high—gives him an almost regal air. If anyone thinks he's practically royalty, it's Stefan Dalca. So why he's hung up on me saying he's not my type is beyond me.

"Blond hair." I laugh, watching my breath blow out in a white cloud before me, unwilling to admit that it's not *that* blond, really. In certain light you see the shimmery gold, and I bet as a child it was much lighter. But now it's this dirty color. Either way, it's not my usual dark vibe.

He shrugs. "We can dye it."

I can't help the big stupid grin spreading across my face. I feel like I'm living in the twilight zone. *What the hell am I doing? Are we being friendly? Are we flirting?*

"Okay. Also… you're arrogant."

He gives me a sly look out of the corner of his eye, one side of his sinful mouth tipping up into a cocky smirk. "You'll get used to it."

I shake my head. "You're just proving my point." He doesn't respond, but I see his body stiffen slightly as we walk past the fresh grave we dug last night. His eyes fixate forward on the barn. "Okay. What about the Mafia ties? Everyone says you have mafia ties."

Small-town gossip is vicious, and I'm not sure how or where this rumor started, but people around here spread it like wildfire. Probably the accent, the murky past, and the boatloads of unexplained cash.

As the daughter of an Indian farmer and his white hippie wife, I'm not oblivious to how judgmental rural towns can be. Having to always work harder to fit in or succeed isn't new to me.

He stops at my question, turning toward me slowly. The energy in the air shifts from laid-back to something more ominous. "And what do you think about that?"

Our eyes clash as I assess him. I swear I can see the humor drain out of them right before me. "I think you're all bark and no bite."

He huffs out a quiet laugh and starts walking again with a subtle shake of his head. "You are something else, Dr. Thorne."

I take a few long strides to catch up with him. "I'm going to take that as a compliment."

"You should," he replies with complete sincerity as we approach the Gold Rush Ranch trailer parked in the lot before us. Before I have time to ruminate on that last comment, he continues, "Okay. What do we do now, Doc?"

I blow a loose piece of hair away from my face. "I'm going to need your help walking him into the barn. He's very weak. Let's just get him into a stall on his own first. I'm going to need some of the mare's manure, and I've got some Vicks VapoRub."

His nose wrinkles. "For what?"

"The manure we need to rub on the foal. The Vicks is to block her sense of smell. Hopefully that will be enough. Is she a mellow mare? A mild tranquilizer is also an option."

"She's always been very calm. Why would you tranquilize her?"

I peer back at him as I pull open the trailer door. "She could react poorly. She could reject the foal. This isn't guaranteed."

Stefan presses his shoulders back stiffly, his lips pressing into a grim line. "I didn't realize that was a risk."

I step up into the trailer, muttering to myself, "Sometimes I wonder how you got into this business at all."

I feel him step up behind me, but he says nothing.

"Hey, little buddy." I run my hands over the foal, happy to see he's still standing. "Out we go. Stefan, just support his body in case he stumbles."

Between the two of us, we get the small colt out of the trailer and into a warm stall. Stefan stands in the doorway staring at him with a sad look on his face while I swipe some of the rub into the mare's nostrils a few doors down. Then with one gloved hand, I pick up a few pieces of manure from her stall before heading over to rub it along the foal's back. Right where she might sniff while he nurses. *Hopefully*.

To Stefan's credit, he doesn't even flinch. And when everything is as set as it's going to get, I turn back to the tall man waiting behind me. The grim expression on his face and red-rimmed eyes are a perfect reflection of my own face.

"Ready?"

He gives me a steady nod. "Yup. Let's do it." There's a hard set to his angular jaw now. Our time for joking has passed. He almost looks nervous.

"Okay. Let's get him up."

I'm not big on praying. But I send up a small prayer now.

I'll take all the help I can get to make this work.

CHAPTER 6

Stefan

My heart hammers against my ribs as we walk the tiny colt down the concrete alleyway, small soft hooves clopping quietly through the barn. I feel like a shmuck. Here I am, joking around and flirting with Mira, feeling all proud of myself for squeezing three dates out of the woman while a horse's life is on the line.

And this might not even work.

I'm usually comfortable with morally gray business decisions, but this time I just feel like a dick. Mira saves lives for a living, and I leveraged that passion for my own gain. Asking for the dates was a shot in the dark, just like it was the first time I did it and every time since. But her turning me down has me fixated. I want to know Mira Thorne in ways she can't even imagine.

Truthfully, I should probably feel worse. But watching her work, so steady and focused, just makes me more attracted to her. I've studied my ass off since starting this venture to learn as much as possible about the business. My closest friend,

Griffin—who I bought this place from—is my go-to source for horse information. But orphaned foals haven't come up in our chats yet.

Mira slides the stall door open and takes a deep breath. Her eyes meet mine over the back of the foal, and she gives me a decisive nod before we step into the stall.

I'm nervous. It's so unlike me. But, god, I really want this to work. I don't even care who owns the foal. The truth is, I'd have done this even if she said no to the dates. Plus, I don't dislike Billie Black or the Harding family enough to wish this upon them. Watching my foal die this morning was heart-wrenching. I've come to love these animals, and watching them suffer is torture in a league of its own.

"Hey, Mama. Meet baby. He's a real sweet boy." Mira's voice is deep and smooth. She doesn't use a high-pitched baby voice. It's almost like she could hypnotize the horses into acceptance with a tone like that. Or me. I'm a sucker for her sultry voice.

She flicks her head back at me, effectively dismissing me as she holds the small red foal and lets the mare walk toward it. Stepping back into the doorway, I watch raptly. I'm not a superstitious man, but I'm not taking any chances tonight.

I shove my hands into my pockets and cross my fingers. I think I'd cross my toes if I could.

The mare's dark globes for eyes assess the colt, and her ears flick around in confusion as she tries to sniff him. To the colt's credit, he may be weak, but his sense of smell is just fine. I watch his head snap toward her udder, ears pointing exactly in that direction, and spindly legs follow. His back moves right beneath her flared nostrils. They're glistening with the rub that

Mira smeared there, but she must catch some small scent of the manure because she gives him a small nuzzle on his bony haunch with her top lip.

I don't miss the small gasp that slips past Mira's lips. She holds her hands up off the foal like he burned her and steps back slowly. Carefully. Like she doesn't want to break whatever momentary connection the two horses seem to have formed.

My fingers hurt from how hard I'm squeezing them across each other. I don't move, even as Mira's body comes to pause only a few inches away from mine.

Within moments, the colt shoves his head beneath the mare's belly and nuzzles at the overfull udder. Trying to figure out something he hasn't quite learned how to do yet.

I glance down at Mira's tense body—raised shoulders and hands fisted in front of her breasts—feeling her heat seep into the front of my body. The only part of her moving is her chest, with the rise and fall of her deep breaths.

The stall is almost entirely silent. Until a noisy suckling noise fills the space. Followed by a ragged sigh from the woman standing in front of me. In wonder, I watch the content mare go back to the hay net before her. Mira's thick black ponytail flops forward as she drops her face into her hands.

The relief pouring off her bleeds into me, and I pull one hand out of my pocket and place it on the nape of her slender neck, giving her a reassuring squeeze. "You did it."

She just nods. She doesn't shake me off; she stands there, soft skin beneath my palm, watching the mare and foal accept each other like life meant them to be together no matter how tragic the circumstances.

"Fuck. What a relief." Her voice is hoarse, but I can't see her face to confirm how emotional she might be. I absently brush my thumb across the base of her skull, and after a beat she clears her throat and steps away. "Let's leave them for a bit." Mira turns to exit the stall but doesn't meet my eyes.

Usually, she covers her vulnerability with a smirk—but not today.

I shouldn't have touched her like that. I'm like a cat playing with his food. But all I really want is for her to see that I'm not a bad guy. I don't always play by the rules, but I'm not a *bad* guy. I grew up with one, and I refuse to become him.

I move away, letting her pass. Wishing my hands were still on her. I don't know why the woman intoxicates me the way she does. Her eyes, her lips, her cool exterior, the sensual hum of her voice—it's all driven me to distraction since the first time I met her down at the track. Her no-nonsense way of handling me while being perpetually gentle and sweet with the horses was a contradiction that fascinated me then and still does now.

She's an equation I'd love to solve.

Or maybe the broken little boy in me just wants her to treat me the way she does a horse. *With love.* I shake my head at myself as I turn to follow her. The thought of her softening up for me is the ultimate carrot she could dangle. I want nothing more than to watch her melt.

I don't love Dr. Mira Thorne. I barely even know her. I'm just fascinated though—inexplicably drawn to her. And I'm too damn accustomed to getting what I want to let it go.

"What now?" I ask as she marches toward the lounge area, complete with cushy brown-leather couches, a pool table, and a fully stocked bar.

She straight-up ignores me for a few beats before flopping down onto a couch with a loud sigh. "Now we wait a bit and see what happens."

I follow suit and drop onto the couch across from her, propping my feet up on the table and resting my hands across my ribs. "You look tired."

She hits me with an unimpressed look. "Charming, Stefan."

"Why don't you sleep for a bit, and I'll keep an eye out."

"No." Her head drops back, and her eyes close.

If she's half as exhausted as I am, she must feel like utter garbage. But I don't argue. Mira doesn't give off the vibe that says she wants to be coddled. So, if she wants to be dead on her feet, good for her. I'll support it.

"What's the accent?" she asks without opening her eyes.

"Romanian." I keep my eyes wide open. Truthfully, I can't peel them off her.

"You're Romanian?"

"I was raised there."

"You just look so… I don't know. Not Romanian?"

Yeah. I'm not sure how it took me so long to figure that out either. I'm about to ask her about her family's background, but after only a few moments, her fingers fall open and her pillowy lips part.

She's out like a light.

She looks younger and… softer somehow while she's asleep. More innocent. The sight of it stirs some instinctual part of me, and all I want to do is take care of her. Make sure she's comfortable. That she rests for a while.

I walk over to the large wicker basket at the end of the couch, pull out an Aztec-style wool blanket, and drape it over her gently. She stirs slightly, but only to nuzzle her cheek into the couch.

She looks so damn tired.

I figure I can sleep tomorrow while she'll probably have to work. With one final glance over her sleeping form, I walk back out into the barn alleyway to the stall with the mare and foal. I flip the latch and creep in. My chest warms seeing mom standing and dozing with sprawled-out baby sleeping happily beside her. They're a perfect match. Red and red. You would never guess they aren't related.

I step into the stall, closing the door behind me, and slide down onto the ground near the foal's head. With my back against the wall, I let my gaze travel over his spindly body, warm under the glow of the red lamp hanging above. He looks weak but peaceful.

I'm momentarily transported back in time to the horse I had as a child. The same color as this foal, but not with flashy white legs and face. An entirely different type of horse. But he was *mine.* He was my reprieve from the hell that was living in my childhood home.

I lean forward and let my hand trail over the sleeping colt's leg to his knee, where the white stocking blends into the coppery brown of the rest of his coat. My body moves of its own accord, coming to kneel beside the small horse. My palm rests over his rib cage, feeling it rise and fall in a steady rhythm. He may not be out of the woods yet, but his breathing is strong. I think he's a strong little horse.

A fighter.

When I move up to his head, cupping the round plate of his cheekbone, he nurses in his sleep. A sweet suckling noise that makes me smile. This guy knows what's up. He's not down for the count yet. And I'm going to make sure he succeeds.

I lean back against the wall, resting my elbows over my knees, vowing internally to make sure this is the healthiest foal anyone has ever seen.

"Wakey, wakey."

My foot wobbles from a kick, and my eyes flutter. The first thing I feel is stiffness as I try to get my bearings. Stiffness in my joints… and in my pants.

Mira's voice filters into my consciousness. Something that is definitely not helping the morning wood situation. "Up we get, Sleeping Beauty. I made you coffee."

And there she is, standing in the stall's entryway, looking a tad disheveled. How I imagine she'd look after a night spent in my bed. Soft and lacking the snarky smirk that's always plastered on her face.

I scrub at my stubble, trying to wake myself up. A small chestnut face moves into my periphery. The foal is looking at me like I'm absolutely fascinating. Farrah is just ignoring me—the weird guy who slept on the floor of her stall.

Mira steps closer, leaning down slightly to hand me the mug of steaming coffee in her hand.

I peer down into the mug. "Cream this time?"

Her eyes flit away shyly. "You didn't seem big on the black coffee, so I tried something else. How do you take it?"

I just don't want you to think my soul is black. It had been a joke when she said it, but I'd let it bug me anyway. I'm inexplicably concerned with what this woman thinks of me.

"This is fine," I reply gruffly, taking the coffee from her, willing my raging boner to disappear. *Hello, morning wood.*

"Okay, get up. I need to check these two over."

I take one thoughtful sip of the coffee before I calmly say, "I can't get up right now."

Mira scoffs. "Of course, you can."

I grin back at her, and after a beat, her confused eyes trail down to my lap and then go wide as she puts all the pieces together. "Oh." She clears her throat. "I'm, uh, just going to get a few things from my truck then." And then she darts out of the barn.

I can't help but chuckle as I bang the back of my head on the wall a few times. That's not the reaction I was expecting from her at all. She acts like a siren, but the mere mention of a boner, and she can't get away fast enough.

After a couple of minutes, I stand and lean back against the wall of the stall. I sip the hot coffee and scan over the mare and foal again. The foal comes closer, clearly curious about the person who spent the night sleeping with him. His soft nose rubbing against my jeans, nostrils flaring wide as he tries to take in my scent. Bulging black globes with chestnut lashes fanning down as he wiggles his lips against my shoulder curiously.

Damn. He's *really* cute. I reach my free hand out and rub the fuzz of his goofy little forelock between my thumb and forefinger before letting my palm slide down over the wide white blaze on his face. His eyes flutter shut, like he's enjoying the feel, and I can't help but smile at how sweet and trusting he is. How unmarred by the world—by life.

"He's pretty sweet, isn't he?" Mira's voice interrupts the dark turn in my head. She's standing in the doorway with a stethoscope around her neck and her ponytail slicked back harshly against her scalp.

"Does he have a name yet?"

She sips her coffee and shakes her head. "No. I think Billie didn't want to get attached, so she was pretending to have a hard time coming up with something… You know, in case he doesn't make it."

It's the perfect opportunity to take a jab at the other woman, but I can't bring myself to do it. "What's his breeding?" I ask, curious about the colt's lineage.

Mira continues to sip her coffee and stare at me. Her eyes flit momentarily to my crotch, and I swear her cheeks pink a bit, but I don't get long to think about that before she says, "He's the black stallion's first foal."

I blink at her. "The one I tried to buy?"

"Yup."

"Jesus. Did you have to tranquilize Billie to get him over here?"

"Don't be a dick. She's been sick over this foal. She hates you, but she wants him to survive more."

Feeling properly chastised, I hide behind my cup of coffee for a moment before changing the subject. "He needs a name. It's important he has a name."

"Why?" Her voice is quizzical as she steps in and holds the stethoscope over the nameless colt's ribs.

"Because he's going to make it. A name ties him to this world. It gives him an identity. Means we recognize his existence."

I see the searching look she gives me. It's quick, but it's there. Full of curiosity.

Every time I ran away as I child, I'd end up with the local villagers who lived nearby. I'd hide out in their homes and listen to their stories, their teachings, their connectedness. That immense sense of community—it all stuck with me. Rather than growing up to be a man who was afraid to fall into my parents' footsteps, I decided it was my goal to prove that I wouldn't. I'd have a wife, I'd have a family, I'd have it all, and I would treat them like gold.

She rolls her lips together but doesn't look up from where she's staring down at the foal. Her mouth moves silently as she counts his heartbeats.

"Then name him. He needs all the help he can get," she says as she steps away. "I'll be back later to check on him again. I need to go open the clinic. Can you make sure he's nursing throughout the day? I'm going to do a blood draw when I come back. I'm probably going to bring Billie—she needs to see that everything is good. So can you either keep your mouth shut or make yourself scarce?"

I nod, trying to hide my amusement over her thinking she can dictate my behavior or whereabouts on my property. My gaze follows her decisive movements as she packs up her kit and heads out. I shouldn't check her out the way I am, admiring the roundness of her ass in the pair of dark-wash Levi's she's wearing. But goddamn, she fills them out so well.

Her hand taps the frame of the stall door as she leans back in, tongue darting out over her bottom lip. "And, uh, thanks for the blanket last night."

"Next time I'm joining you." I wink, and she just rolls her eyes.

I should try harder to keep things professional and not let my curiosity about Dr. Mira Thorne take over my brain. I shouldn't think with the wrong head.

But the more time I spend with her, the more of a challenge that feels like. I like a challenge… but keeping my hands off Mira isn't one I'm sure I want to take on. The woman is not my biggest fan, this much I know.

But then I've got three dates to make her *want* my hands on her body.

CHAPTER 7

Mira

Nice Stefan is tripping me the fuck out. I've spent almost every appointment today trying to figure out what to do with my opinion of him.

I stare out the big floor-to-ceiling windows of the clinic as I wait for the X-rays I took to develop. Taking in the rolling hills around Gold Rush Ranch, I mull over the past thirty-six hours. I had Stefan neatly classified into a file where I put people I feel mostly indifferent about. He'd done some shitty things, but I'd also been witness to him being a decent human being. He was morally neutral. One experience sort of canceling out the other.

Past tense.

Now?

I don't know. Watching him these last couple of days threw a wrench into all my preconceived notions. Was he a cocky prick? Yes. But was he also charming and sensitive? Yes.

Should I be mad at him for forcing my hand on the dates? Ugh. Probably. But I'm not. And I don't really want to analyze why that is. I especially don't want to think about the possibility that he's using me to get at my friends.

I thought I'd be worried about leaving the foal there with him, but I'm not at all. He slept beside it, for crying out loud. I watched the way he ran his deft fingers over the colt's face—the expression of wonder on his own had been like a punch to the chest.

No, I'm not worried about the foal at all. I feel it in my bones that Stefan is going to name him and love him the way he deserves. It had been the look in his eyes, the gentleness in his touch. He was nothing if not determined.

For one mindless moment, I wondered how it would feel to have Stefan run his hands over me that way. It was *such* a bad idea. It would backfire spectacularly, especially with my friends. But it almost made me want it more. Under different circumstances, he'd be a fun onetime thing.

The door swings open, shaking me from my reverie.

"How's the baby?" Hank grins at me as his broad frame fills the front door, his cheeks and ears red with the bite of the cool air outside, and I marvel at how the barn manager still looks like he has a tan in the middle of winter. I guess years spent in the sun get you a perma-tan. People pay good money to look like that.

I smile at the older man who swooped in to help Vaughn run the farm when an alleged cheating scandal broke. The man who's been a mainstay in Billie's life since her teen years and a close friend of Dermot Harding, the founder of Gold Rush Ranch.

"He's good. The mare took him right away. It was amazing."

He stomps his boots on the mat at the door before approaching the front desk. "Well, you know how it goes. Sometimes it takes mere minutes, sometimes hours, and other times not at all. You should give yourself a pat on the back."

I reach over my back dramatically, patting my shoulder with a big grin on my face. I have to confess, I'm feeling proud of myself for working this out. I don't even care about the three dates I agreed to go on with Stefan. I can totally handle them. Maybe I'll get a good meal out of the deal. My stomach growls just thinking about it, and I resolve right here and now to make sure Stefan takes me for a super fancy meal.

He's gonna pay for this trick, and I'm gonna enjoy the hell out of some delicious food.

"You did good." Hank beams at me, his eyes crinkling at the sides as he leans over the counter. He's so sweet. A surrogate father to pretty much everyone at the farm now. It's probably close to time for him to retire, but I have a feeling Billie will have to drag him kicking and screaming off this property. It's never going to happen.

"Thanks. How's Trixie?" He tries to bite back a smile at the mention of the new woman in his life. They met at Cole and Violet's wedding and hit it off almost instantly. She lives in Vancouver, just ninety minutes down the road, and they take turns visiting each other when their schedules allow it.

It's freaking adorable.

"She's wonderful. So different from anyone I've ever met or thought I'd be with. She keeps me on my toes."

I can't help but laugh because the woman is a character. "I'm so happy for you. On your toes is a good thing!"

"Is it ever." He clicks his tongue and shakes his head. "Never settle, Mira. Sometimes what you want isn't what you need."

"You giving me dating advice, Hank?" My lips tip up at the thought.

"Yup. You spend too much time working for a woman your age."

I flinch. This is a sore spot for me. I've known I wanted to be a veterinarian since I was tiny. It was my single-minded focus through school and into university, straight through vet school. Did I miss out on social experiences to get where I am? Yeah, but it was worth it.

Unless you ask my extended family on my dad's side. They always have something to say about me needing to start a family. They mean well, and I know it's a cultural thing, but it gets old fast. And while my parents would never say that to me, they don't correct them either. It's like none of them completely appreciate how hard I worked to become a doctor of something, that I graduated at the top of my class, that I worked my ass off to do it. At twenty-seven years old, I'm more educated and more accomplished than anyone else in my family career-wise, and yet none of them seem to want to celebrate my achievement.

Basically, my love life revolves around the purple rubber boyfriend that lives in my nightstand and all the thirst traps I browse on TikTok. I don't have *time* for a relationship, even if I wanted one. So my silicone friend is perfect. He doesn't need anything from me, and he doesn't get in my way. I don't owe him anything except to charge him up now and then. And that's about the level of commitment I can handle right now.

"Hey, I didn't mean that in a bad way." Hank's brow crinkles in concern.

"Oh, nah." I wave him off. "It's all good. Just distracted today. Did you need something? I'm planning to close up shop soon."

I'm aware I come off a bit cool sometimes. I'd like to say I don't mean to… but I think I do. I don't like people meddling in my business. I'm not a spew-my-personal-issues type of girl. I've been told I'm intensely private.

I say I'm just independent with clearly defined boundaries.

Hank straightens, and I smile at him kindly, trying to show that all is well without having to verbalize it. I'm not big on explaining myself when I don't think it's necessary. That's one thing I like about animals. They judge you by your actions.

"Billie is meeting me here. I'm going to drive her to Stefan's. Consider me her… bodyguard? Or Dalca's, considering my job is probably to hold her back from killing him. I'm also her getaway car if she does."

I huff out a laugh as I shut down the monitor at the front desk. "Billie should hold it together. His willingness to help is what's going to save her foal."

One corner of Hank's mouth quirks up as his eyes scan my face, a little too curiously. "I wouldn't put it that way to her if I were you."

I wink at him. "Wouldn't dream of it."

The door swings open right at that moment. "Wouldn't dream of what?" Billie asks, stomping her boots on the mat and shaking out the thick chestnut braid from under her hood.

"Oh, geez. It's pouring," I say, trying to change the direction of the conversation.

"Yeah. Just started." She looks up with a smile. "We good to go see the baby?"

"Are you?" Hank asks with the quirk of an eyebrow.

Billie grunts and rears back, like she's offended by the question. "Why wouldn't I be?"

I cut in. "I think what Hank is trying to say without actually saying it is, 'Are you prepared to behave civilly?'"

Her amber eyes narrow at me. "Yes."

Hank and I both laugh.

"What? I am. I will be just as civil as Dalca the Dick." A knowing twist takes over her lips. "And don't worry, Violet just read me the riot act. She even said he's not as bad as I think he is."

She shudders, shoulders shaking dramatically. Hank's eyes flit over to mine, like he's a freaking mind reader, and I glance away, grabbing my keys, feeling grateful that neither of them actually is.

When I jump into my vehicle, I take my phone out and open a blank text conversation with Stefan. He only ever calls me, and texting feels more personal somehow. There's a casual familiarity that comes with texting that I'm not sure is a match for a client and me, but I need to make sure he won't pull some sort of childish shit once we get there.

Mira: Hi. We're on our way. Can you throw me a bone and just stay away for a bit?

He texts me back almost instantly.

Stefan: Maybe if you beg.

Ha. That'll be the day.

Mira: You'd like that, wouldn't you?
Stefan: Absolutely.

Perv.

Mira: Go fuck yourself.

Stefan: You shouldn't talk that way. It's unbecoming.

He's not wrong. I've been spending too much time around Billie. But would it really be so hard for him to be compliant this once?

Mira: Okay. Please go fuck yourself.

Stefan: I think I will. ;)

I shake my head, half-amused and half-agitated. He can't just give me a straight answer. It's so typical of him. Between him and Billie, I'm going to have to pray for some superhuman levels of patience these next several months.

We travel to Cascade Acres separately. There isn't a lot of spare room in my truck with all the equipment I have to haul around. And Hank isn't wrong. Having a way to get out of there isn't his worst plan. *God, I hope Stefan stays away.* He and Billie are like water and oil. Or gasoline and a spark.

When we pull up, I direct them where to go and unpack what I'll need for tonight's checkup. I'm working overtime right now, but the Hardings gave me a generous compensation package, including lodging. Sure, the apartment is a far cry from fancy, but it beats living with my parents to afford my student loan payments. They've done so much for me that I don't mind spending a few extra hours here and there, going above and beyond.

When I round the corner into the immaculate barn alleyway, I'm transported to the morning Stefan and I spent mucking out stalls together in quiet companionship and shared sadness over the lost foal. The truth of it is, I hadn't planned on doing that. I could have just asked him the favor straight out, but he looked so downtrodden. And I'm a sucker for a wounded animal.

"Mira. You saved him." Billie's eyes sparkle as she claps her hands together when I enter the stall. "He already looks so much better!"

Hank's palm lands on her shoulder, his green eyes glittering with the same grateful emotion as hers.

"Okay, well, let's not take this overboard," I say, prepping my tubes for the blood draw.

"No, I'm serious. Thank you. I know it means you have to spend time here with that asshole, but… well, I'm not sure how I'll ever repay you."

Oof. If she had any idea what it really cost me, I'm not sure I'd be so securely in her good books.

She hugs the foal's neck, planting a kiss on his little head before turning to the bright chestnut mare with the flaxen mane. "Thank you," she says, voice cracking as her hand trails over the mare's delicate face. "You're the best mama in the world."

"She's a special mare, for sure," I murmur as I shoo them out of my way.

Billie and Hank look at her with so much love my heart squeezes. If everyone could stop making me feel so emotional these last couple days, that would be great.

"Skedaddle, you two. You've seen he's fine. There haven't been any confrontations. Let's call this a win. I'm going to take blood and wait to collect a fresh fecal sample."

Billie wraps her arms around me. She's a hugger, and she has been since that first day I met her when DD had his bout with colic. I am not a hugger—public displays of affection are not my thing—but I let her do it. These are the sacrifices you make for your friends.

"Thank you. I'm so lucky to have you as my friend." She squeezes me tight enough that it dislodges all my traitorous thoughts. They swirl in my head, increasing my internal shame over my growing tolerance for Stefan Dalca.

On one hand, I don't owe anyone any explanations about my feelings or choices. On the other hand, even just knowing I agreed to three fake dates with him is making me feel guilty and traitorous.

"I need to get these done and out of the way as quickly as possible." I pat Billie on the back woodenly, hoping that will signal to her the hug is over.

She pulls away, laughing. "Love you, my Ice Queen."

I can't help but roll my eyes at her nicknames. Pornstar Patty for Violet, Bossman for Vaughn, Big Bro for Cole… Dalca the Dick for Stefan.

"Love you too, B. Catch ya later, Hank!" I wave casually before turning back to the horses.

I'm relieved when they finally leave—that's enough attention for one day. The compliments, the hugs, the intense levels of thankfulness… they're all nice, but I find them overwhelming and never know quite how to react appropriately.

So, while I wait for the foal to give me the sample I need, I pull out my phone to browse social media. I find one of those dumb personality-type quizzes and start typing in my answers. Essentially zoning out while I lean up against the frame of the stall door.

"What are you doing?"

A voice startles the hell out of me, and I jump, feeling my back press into a hard chest while two gentle hands slide beneath my elbows to keep me upright. *Stefan.* I'm too shocked to even move out of the embrace.

One of my hands flattens over my sternum, where I can feel my heart thumping. "You scared the shit out of me," I pant. It's after dinner, and the barn has been quiet and empty. "What the hell kind of stalking skills are you practicing?" I spin, feeling the chill of the air against every spot that has been warm pressed up against him. It almost makes me want to spin back around and sink into his embrace. *Almost.* "I didn't even hear you at all!"

His mossy eyes scan my face, the slight bump in his nose just adding to the intensity of his face. Most people would get a break in their nose fixed, but on Stefan it just adds to his look. His mystery. I hope he never fixes it.

He takes advantage of my shock and swipes my phone out of my hand. "Then you're definitely not Black Widow. She would know someone was approaching." He smirks, and it's both annoying and adorable all at once. "*Which Marvel superhero character are you?*" he reads the name of the quiz out loud, and I will my cheeks not to pink. I can take dumb quizzes if I want. "Sounds very scientific."

I roll my shoulders back. "You do it. I bet you'll get Thanos."

His nose wrinkles, and he throws a hand over his chest dramatically like he's offended. "The big purple bad guy?"

I offer him my sweetest smile and quirk my head to the side as if to say, *If the shoe fits.*

He just grunts and goes through the quiz.

"You have to answer honestly," I remind him.

He doesn't look up at me, but I don't miss the way his jaw pops at the comment. "I am always honest. I don't abide lying."

Well, that joke fell flat.

I step beside him to peer over at my phone right as he submits the survey. The wheel spins as "calculating" flashes across the screen. Like there's some legitimate process to matching this up.

Tom Hiddleston wearing horns pops up on the screen, and I burst out laughing. "Loki!"

He grins now, eyes twinkling with mirth, and hands me my phone back. "I'm going to have to get a hat like that."

"Oh, yeah. That would be hot." His head quirks almost instantly, and I try to cover the slip of my tongue. "The god of mischief," I say, nodding. "That's pretty accurate. Maybe their science isn't so bad after all."

He peers down at me, looking altogether too confident. It does funny things to my insides. Laughing with this man in a dim barn when I'm not supposed to enjoy his company at all is bad. *And did I just accidentally call him hot?* I should know better. I should *do* better.

But I've always been one to want things I shouldn't.

"Speaking of mischief," he says, eyes scanning my face in a way that heats me to my core. "You owe me three dates."

I smile back at him, meeting his stare confidently. "Yeah. I've been thinking about that. I think I'm due for a *really fancy* meal. I mean, I want to give that black Amex of yours a real workout."

"Charming." His mouth twists wryly.

I wink. "Cute coming from the guy who conned me into going on dates with him just to prove a point."

We smile at each other in the dark barn, a battle of wills raging between us.

"And what point am I trying to prove?"

"Oh, come on, Stefan. We both know this is just an obnoxious power play. That you're trying to prove you have the upper hand. That you have me up against a wall."

His smirk morphs now into something more feral as he leans in. He moves across me, his head coming to my ear while his opposite hand cups my elbow, holding me close. His proximity, the feel of his breath against the shell of my ear, it all makes the soft hairs on my arms stand on end. I desperately hope he can't feel it.

"Trust me, Dr. Thorne, if I had you up against a wall, *you'd* be the meal."

My breathing stutters, and I jerk my arm away from him. I have no clue what to say to that. I have even less of an idea of how to react to his level of confidence. I'm too out of practice. Hell, I'm too inexperienced. So I just hit him with my best unimpressed, glacial stare.

His responding chuckle is dark and sensuous. It feels like hot wax on bare skin. I want to hate it, but my tongue darts out over my bottom lip.

He turns to leave, and only now do I notice he's wearing gym clothes that hug his body in the most delectable way. I'm too confused to even stop myself from staring at his perfectly round ass as he strolls away looking completely unaffected.

And I'm too speechless to even respond to the parting remark he tosses over his shoulder. "Pick you up at six on Friday."

God. I'm in so much trouble.

CHAPTER 8

Stefan

Mira: You can't pick me up. Someone might see. I'll meet you at your place at six.

I READ THE TEXT A FEW TIMES. IT STINGS MORE THAN IT SHOULD, and it feels distinctly improper to not be picking her up—no matter how fake the date is. Call me old-fashioned, but I enjoy ringing the doorbell. Not being able to hold the car door open for her when she gets in has the gentleman in me twitching. I've been enough of a brute where Mira is concerned that I feel like I owe her that chivalry.

I've spent the entire week avoiding her because what I whispered in her ear a few days ago was crossing a line I shouldn't have crossed. And I didn't like the way she shut down afterward.

The worst part is, I can't actually say what it is I want from her. Am I attracted to her? Yes. But I don't think it can ever be more than that—even if there's a part of me that wants it. I really need her as a veterinarian. My horses do too. Risking that seems like a colossally stupid idea.

So platonic dates it is.

Friends.

I could try to be her friend so that the dates aren't just awkward disasters.

Or I could let her off the hook for the dates altogether.

But I shake that thought out of my head. I'd rather prove to her I'm not the bad guy she thinks I am.

And why does what she thinks of me matter?

That's the real question, isn't it?

Because I'm pretty sure I've made things awkward by reverting to the private school douchebag I grew into as a teenager. In fact, it seems an awful lot like she's avoiding me. I know she's been here to check on Farrah and the foal, but she comes at random times, and I haven't received a single message from her since that day when she told me to stay away while she had Billie here.

She hasn't even said anything about me naming the foal *Loki*. I put a tag on his stall, so Mira's seen it, but she hasn't said anything. I imagined a snarky text from her about it, but nothing came. The name makes me smile, and the more time I spend with him, the more I think it fits.

As he gets healthier, he keeps getting spunkier. When I go down in the evenings to hang out and brush him, he likes to play with my shoelaces. His toothless gums snap at them and pull the strings curiously. And then when he gets them apart and I move my foot, making them drag across the ground like a snake, he spooks. He jumps back all wide-eyed with flared nostrils like they might attack him.

It's nice having some company.

In the morning when I come to check on him before I go for my workout, his shrill baby whinny rings out through the barn. One morning, I figured I could leave the stall unlatched while I came back with extra grain for Farrah, but he pushed it right open and went on an adventure through the barn. The little prick had fun evading me, making me chase him around like a total amateur until I got a rope wrapped around his neck and led him back to his stall with a big grin on my face. I'm still glad no one was here to see that episode.

And I'm especially glad that dying horses don't pull stunts like that.

The lively rat is growing on me every day. It's nice having someone who needs me. And the moment that thought flits through my head, my phone screen lights up with Ruby Creek High Calling, and my stomach plummets.

Nadia moved here a year ago from Romania after being kicked out of her aunt and uncle's house. She's struggling—I can tell—but no one has ever equipped me to be the parent and guardian of a nineteen-year-old with a massive chip on her shoulder. Nannies and headmasters raised me, and I ran in a pack of poorly behaved rich boys—unfortunately, Nadia's upbringing isn't so different. She failed her senior year here, so she's back for a second try. And terrorizing all the teachers and administrators in the process. No one in this small town is equipped for her.

"Yup," I answer the phone brusquely.

"Mr. Dalca, this is Principal Cooper. Can you come down to the school for a conversation with Nadia and me?"

I sigh out in frustration. "Is she okay?"

"Yes." The man's voice is clipped.

"Okay. I'll be right there."

What's it going to be this time?

***

My mouth goes dry when I swing open the door. Mira is standing on the front landing wearing a gray cable-knit sweater dress with cream thigh-high socks beneath a pair of tall black-suede boots. A thick black-wool coat with oversized buttons and matching cream-plaid print falls open at her sides, like a present that has already been partially unwrapped. She looks cozy and sensual all at once, with her black hair smoothed out straight, a heavy mane spilling down over her shoulders.

She looks *edible*.

"What are you wearing?" Her face scrunches up as she looks me over from top to bottom.

"What do you mean?" I peer down at my clothes, checking for a stain or something.

She looks slightly flustered as she waves a hand over me. "Just the turtleneck. And the glasses."

I open one arm to usher her into the house. "What about them?"

She ignores the gesture and licks her lips, shaking her head as if to clear it. "Nothing." She laughs sharply. "You look like you were shooting a professor-themed porno or something."

I wink at her. "Maybe I was."

Mira rolls her eyes and dramatically tips her head back with a groan. I don't miss the way her cheeks pink at my joke. And as much as I should regret the comment, I don't. She's the most fascinating dichotomy. Confident and cool while being shy and awkward all at once. She keeps me on my toes. I just never quite know how she's going to react.

"Let's go get this over with." She hikes a thumb over her shoulder.

I ignore the punch her words deliver. "So, minor change of plans."

Her slightly upturned almond-shaped eyes narrow at me, and I swear if looks could kill, I'd crumple to the floor on the spot. "No. No change of plans."

"I don't think I can, in good conscience, leave my sister home alone tonight."

Her puffy lips roll together. "Why?"

"She had a bad day and could use some company. I promise I still gave my Amex a workout on your behalf. I have excellent wine and beautiful food, and if you come in, I will provide you with a perfectly platonic home-cooked meal."

Her eyes dart behind me into the house, like she's trying to gauge if I'm lying. A growl rumbles in my chest. "For crying out loud, Mira. Let me feed you and then you can turn around and go home. In fact, you are welcome to leave anytime you want. I'm not going to murder anyone in here."

She steps into the foyer begrudgingly and mutters, "No, you'll just be filming porn."

I laugh, closing the heavy door behind us before reaching out to take her coat and hang it for her. I try not to focus on the hum of the zipper as she bends down to remove her boots.

"Leave the boots."

Her eyes dart up to mine. "Inside the house?"

I just shrug. Trying to play it casual. "Yeah. You look nice." What I don't say is that those boots and socks are giving me all sorts of ideas that I shouldn't be having about her. What I don't say is that I'd like to see her in *just* the boots.

"This way." I saunter further into the house, leading her to the open-concept kitchen.

"Your place is so cozy. For its size, I expected it to be different."

"Thanks. I think?"

She chuckles as we enter the kitchen, my favorite room in the house. It's surrounded by floor-to-ceiling windows that slide open onto the patio overlooking the small lake out front. The living room and dining room all blend into the big open space with vaulted ceilings. Warm cream tones play off dark-stained wood and exposed stones.

Mira walks to the oversize island in the center of the kitchen and props herself up on one of the stools before looking over at me expectantly while I try not to stare at the expanse of creamy skin between the hemline of her dress and high socks. That small tease of bare skin feels particularly stimulating in the comfort of my home.

"Well? You promised me wine. I could really use some wine."

"Pfft, you and I both." I round the island and slide over two bottles of red wine. "Pinot noir or cabernet?"

She reaches out, dainty fingers wrapping around each bottle as she pulls them toward herself. Her lips roll together as she eyes the bottles. "Let's start with the pinot."

I chuckle. "Start with, huh?"

She smiles back at me. "Would be a shame to let these go to waste."

I shake my head as I reach for the bottle with the purple label. The tips of my fingers graze hers, sending a tingling sensation up through my joints, right into my wrist, morphing into an ache in the crook of my elbow. I drop my eyes and turn away quickly, trying to put the feeling of her nearness out of my mind as I uncork the wine.

I hate the way she throws me off balance.

When I turn back around to decant the bottle of wine, Mira is sneaking a furtive glance over at the leather couch, where Nadia, her wavy blond hair freshly washed and falling loose to her shoulders, is curled up reading a book with her sound-canceling headphones on. Under the glow of the floor lamp, with her doll-like face scrubbed free of makeup, she looks younger than she often does.

I don't love easily, but when I do, it's fiercely. Which is probably why my mother's betrayal stung as badly as it did. There may be fifteen years between Nadia and me, I may not know her that well, but she's all the family I've got left, and I love her with every bit of my soul. I've wanted to protect her for years, and now that she's finally back with me, I probably won't ever stop. I may not have been able to protect my mother, but I will protect Nadia if it's the last thing I do. Leaving her behind killed me, and I'm happy to have her here no matter the added challenge. I would burn the town to the ground for her, and today I almost did.

"Is she okay?" Mira asks.

I pour us each a large bell of deep-red liquid and slide her glass toward her. "No. But she will be. She's tough." I swirl the wine and inhale the cranberry scent, letting my eyes bounce between the two women before me. "People see that strength and try to tear her down. I think some people—men in particular—thrive off that. She's young now and has me to make them regret that type of behavior. But in a few years, she won't need my help at all." I smirk into the glass as I take a drink, letting the flavor of cherries and menthol pour across my tongue. "She reminds me a bit of you."

Mira takes a sip, snuggling further down into the upholstered stool, and looks back over at my little sister with renewed interest. "May I ask what happened?"

My molars grind against each other unbidden. "I received a call from Principal Cooper asking me to come down to the school. There were issues all last year, and this year is nothing new. She's nineteen now, but the transition to living in Canada hasn't been an easy one. Not to mention what our family has been through the last few years." Mira's eyes widen in interest, but she doesn't make a move to ask anything further. Something I appreciate. "She failed a few classes last year. She's retaking them, and it seems to me that she's got a target on her back."

I stare down into the wineglass, swirling it, trying to keep my agitation from creeping out and taking over. "Apparently, the principal saw her and felt her skirt was too short. So, in a hallway full of her peers, he made the girl who has already been singled out as the one who failed last year kneel on the floor to prove the skirt didn't meet their dress code by one inch." My lips press together almost painfully as I shake my head at the memory.

"Excuse me?" Mira leans forward, her eyes flaring with rage that is reflected in my own. "Did you flatten him?"

I chuckle darkly. *I wish.* "I'll admit I went nuclear. I don't know how I'll send her back. Or if it's even my place to. She's smart—too smart—but she's also proud, and this was a real blow to her pride." The memory of her tearstained face still has the power to set me off.

"No shit." Her words come out with a bite. "Stefan, you can't send her back to that school. There are other options, and she won't be missing out on the experience of being at school at this point in her life. Whatever you do, don't let her see that patriarchal assholes behaving poorly don't face consequences."

Her words land like lead in my gut.

But the fierce spark in her eye makes my heart race.

CHAPTER 9

Mira

Stefan oozes confidence in the kitchen, something I didn't expect to find so attractive. I watch him chop and stir and move around the industrial-style space with such ease that I almost wonder if he was a chef in a past life. The wine is delicious, just like he promised. It tastes expensive, but I also drink wine straight out of the bottle on girls' nights, so it's possible I'm not the best gauge for fancy.

He seems quieter, less jovial, since that conversation about his sister and the sexist pig of a principal. He's lost himself in cooking, and after my second glass of wine, I give up on trying not to check him out. Never mind porn—he looks more like my unfulfilled professor fantasies. The black rims of his glasses contrast perfectly against the bronze glow of his hair. The turtleneck makes him look uptight and proper, but I know better, and it just adds to his allure.

I shouldn't be looking, but I'm defiant. It's a character flaw. When someone tells me not to do something, it makes me want to do it more. I'm Eve picking the apple just to see what happens. Want me to settle down and have babies? I think I'll throw myself into my education and my job. Want me to hate Stefan Dalca? I think I'll start fantasizing about him instead.

It's not healthy. And I still have two dates to go.

He's standing at the stove right now, stirring something that smells unbelievable. His body sways gently with the motion of the whisk, and his ass fills out the dark jeans he's wearing in a way that has me gawking while quietly sipping my wine.

"Gross," Nadia huffs as she slides onto the stool beside me.

"What?" I say, pretending something interesting above the cabinets has caught my eye rather than her brother's ass.

But she's not buying it. She quirks a brow and gives me an unimpressed look. Yup, *nothing short with this one.*

"Men suck," she says, and I see Stefan stiffen out of the corner of my eye. "Be careful."

I lean forward and stare at my glass, watching the red liquid slosh against the sides as I swivel it on the white-marble countertop. "Some do. They aren't all bad. Principal Cooper sounds like a real piece of shit though."

She snorts. "On that we can agree." A small smile touches her pink lips. "Total pig."

"Have you considered finishing what you need to finish online? That's easily done now. I did that in university with a couple of classes."

"Really?" Her voice sounds hopeful as she fiddles with her fingers, elbows propped on the edge of the counter.

"Definitely. Grab your laptop. Let's look it up while he finishes cooking."

She bounds out of the kitchen almost instantly with a hopeful smile on her face, blond waves bouncing as she goes. When Stefan turns around, his eyes find mine, but I can't tell what he's thinking. Can't tell if I've overstepped. He leans back on the opposite countertop, palms against the edge of the marble, and stares at me like he's never seen me before this moment.

"What?" I ask, struggling to catch my breath.

His green eyes twinkle as they scour my face, tracing every feature like it's the first time. And then he shakes his head and turns back to the stove. "Dinner will be ready in fifteen minutes."

When Nadia returns, we search the web for what her options are while I polish off a third glass of wine. On one hand, I feel like I'm completely ignoring Stefan. On the other, I'm not sure I care. I'm having fun helping Nadia.

This date isn't so bad after all.

Once Stefan finishes cooking, Nadia and I set the table while chatting about her strengths and favorite subjects at school. Math and sciences are a breeze. It's the language arts and language-based classes that are killing her. She's fluent in French and Romanian, so English is her third language. I can barely speak two languages. According to my family, my Punjabi is an "embarrassment," so in my book, struggling with her third one is understandable.

The duck dish Stefan made is heaven. Crispy skin, served over a bed of creamy polenta with a fresh bitter-greens salad topped with blue cheese and walnuts.

"Oh my god," I moan. I'm feeling loose from the wine, and in the back of my mind, I identify the sound as almost sexual, but I don't care. It is truly succulent. "The only thing missing is a blueberry reduction for the duck."

"Yeah?" Stefan asks with a quirk of his head as he sips a glass of wine from the second bottle.

"Yeah. My parents own a blueberry farm. I'll hook you up when they come into season."

"Can I come pick blueberries?" Nadia asks excitedly.

I snort. The charm of picking berries has pretty much completely worn off for me. People actually pay my parents to come pick their own berries, something that never fails to make me chuckle. But I refuse to quash her enthusiasm. "Of course."

Dinner carries on much the same, but I still catch Stefan staring at me over the candle lit in the middle of the table. The flame highlights the blend of colors in his irises—the greens, the golds. His eyes are beautiful, and throughout the meal, I remind myself not to get lost in them. In *him*.

"That was incredible." I lean back and toss my napkin on the table beside my very empty plate. "Thank you." I smile at him, and it's genuine.

I've had a thoroughly enjoyable night. Relaxing even. I've felt my carefully placed walls crumble, and right now I don't feel like beating myself up about it. There's something distinctly intimate about tonight. Something sweet that I don't want to overanalyze.

But it doesn't mean I don't need to leave before I do something I'll regret.

"Nadia, do you have your driver's license?" I ask, staring at the glass of sparkling water before her.

She scoffs, sounding distinctly teenager-like in that moment. "Of course I do."

She hasn't touched the wine tonight. At nineteen, she's of legal age here, but she hasn't asked, and Stefan hasn't offered.

"Would you be willing to drive me home and then pick me up tomorrow morning?"

She shrugs. "Sure."

Stefan stares at me from over the flame. His pointer finger circling the top of his glass while he gazes at me. It's almost hypnotic.

He doesn't offer to drive me, but that's for the best. His eyes are a bit glassy, his smiles a little easier. We have both thoroughly enjoyed the two bottles of wine.

I break the spell when I say, "I'll help clean up."

"You absolutely will not. You're the guest," he replies smoothly, leaning back in his chair.

He oozes class and control. Looking like a dreamboat professor out for a glass of wine at some fancy lounge after a long day of fending off the advances of his overeager students. I can't help but giggle at the path my thoughts have taken after single-handedly drinking what equates to a full bottle of wine.

"Well, in that case, Stefan…" He quirks his head, one dimple popping up on his cheek as it hitches, hanging on my words in a way that not many people do. "Thank you for the truly outstanding meal. I had a delightful night."

"Yeah. I actually like this one," Nadia says absently, now browsing through her phone.

I burst out laughing, slapping a hand across my mouth to cover my guffaw.

"Nadia, go put your laptop away and get what you need to drive Dr. Thorne home."

She salutes from her forehead without even looking up at him as she replies with "Sir, yes, sir," and then slowly moves toward the stairs, eyes not leaving her phone.

I stand as Stefan ushers me toward the front door. His palm briefly presses into the small of my back as he guides me into the hallway, and I feel the imprint of his warm hand through my sweater like a brand. There's a catch in my breath and in my step at the feel—the familiarity of the touch. It sears me. I feel like if someone looked, they'd be able to make out the swirls of his fingerprints against my milky skin.

Words fail me as he holds the long plaid coat out for me to slide my arms into. The wine has my mind going places it absolutely should not, and the press of his firm body behind mine leaves me feeling heady. He's not even touching me, but I swear I can feel the weight of him against my shoulder blades, guiding them together and pressing on my lungs. His mere presence sticks to me like static cling.

"Thank you for coming tonight," he whispers, his accented voice endlessly deep, turning me to face him and smoothing down the lapels of my coat. Like we do this all the time.

He takes a hold of my wrist and presses a swift, featherlight kiss to the center of my palm. Something that feels intensely personal.

My tongue darts out to wet my bottom lip as I gaze up at his proud posture and the troublemaking glint in his eye. "Thank you for having me."

I smile, but it's watery and uncertain. The man has me completely off balance. My pulse beats in my stomach. Nice Stefan threw me for a loop, but Doting Stefan, who cooks and cleans and loves his little sister, is straight crushing my ovaries.

Any man could do those things and you'd find him attractive, my mind assures me right before he leans in and presses a kiss to the sensitive spot just below my ear.

Then my mind goes blank. Goose bumps crawl in slow motion, covering my entire body. The feel of him towering over me, the rasp of his stubble against my cheek cause all coherent thoughts to flee my mind along with the air from my chest.

Nadia's steps thump down the stairs, breaking the spell. I step back quickly, trying to even out my breathing and be strong enough to still look him in the eye.

"One sec," I whisper, my voice cracking in the most obvious way. "I'll be right back."

I dart into the kitchen and then return to wait while Nadia ties up her laces. I can feel Stefan's gaze on me as though he's trailing a finger everywhere he looks. My body hums as I recall the rough scrape of his stubble and the hot press of his hand.

I need to get the fuck out of here.

With a casual wave over my shoulder, I escape onto the front porch and start walking to my truck, sucking in deep breaths of cool air as I go. A few moments later, Nadia catches up and slides into the driver's seat.

Pale eyebrows knit together suspiciously. "All good?" she asks.

I pull out the carton of eggs I hid in my coat and smile at her with all my teeth. *The perfect distraction.* "Yup. Did I mention I'm well acquainted with where Principal Cooper lives?"

"Good morning, Dr. Thorne."

Stefan's voice used to make me roll my eyes. But now it just feels like someone is sliding silk around my neck. Probably to make a noose, which is what thinking about Stefan this way is going to get me.

A death sentence. At least where my friends are concerned.

"Hi, Stefan," I say stiffly as I check the mare and foal over carefully. Nadia just picked me up and drove me back to my truck at Cascade Acres, so it seemed like the perfect time to do my daily check on the horses.

"How is Loki today?"

I snort. I got a kick out of the nameplate when I saw it. My fingers itched to fire him off a text message about how he named a horse after himself. But for the sake of keeping our professional boundaries clear, I resisted.

"Full of piss and vinegar." I smile as I turn, but the grin quickly slides off my face as I take in the sight of him and the hunter-green bespoke suit he's wearing. The man wears an expensive suit like he was born in it. Like whoever came up with suits as a thing was looking at Stefan when the idea struck them.

It's borderline criminal.

The crisp white shirt underneath has a few buttons open, and a perfect V of tan skin at the top of his chest shows, just below where his Adam's apple bobs. It's not borderline, it *is* criminal. And me looking at him like this, dragging my tongue around on the barn floor, is even worse.

I don't even know if I can blame the wine anymore this morning.

"Where are you off to looking so dapper?"

"The police station and then the city." His voice dances with amusement as his eyes home in on mine.

I school my features. This is one of those situations where I'm better off listening than talking. "Oh?" I reply, turning to pat Farrah.

"Mm-hmm. It seems they have some questions for me. Someone egged Principal Cooper's car last night. Of course, we were all at my house having dinner. So I just need to clarify that for them. May I put you down as a witness?"

I should argue; I don't really want anyone knowing I was at Stefan Dalca's house for dinner. But I don't want to come off guilty either. "Of course." My lips tilt up in a grimace at the white lie.

He just stares back at me, and it unnerves me to my core. I seriously hope I'm not blushing, but I can't risk saying anything, so I blink and offer him an even bigger smile. *Enthusiasm, Mira.* "Hope everything goes okay."

"Everything is going wonderfully," he replies, his voice softening as his gaze burns across my face.

He doesn't sound mad. *Fuck. This is awkward. He couldn't possibly know.*

"Well, good luck." I sound lame, even to my own ears. "I'll be back tomorrow to check on them."

I beam brightly, grab my case, mouth, "Excuse me" as I squeeze past him, and try to force myself to walk with a confident swagger down the barn alleyway toward the parking lot rather than sprinting away like I want to.

"Hey, Mira?" he calls out right as I reach for the door handle.

"Yeah?" I toss back into the echoey barn, continuing my forward motion.

"You owe me a carton of eggs."

Well, shit.

CHAPTER 10

Stefan

Loki isn't acting quite right. While he has truly been living up to his name as the god of mischief, he seems lethargic tonight. Dopey. He was fine before dinner when I checked him, but now at 10 p.m. he isn't quite right.

I've been avoiding Mira this week, and I'm quite certain she's been doing the same. The tension between us is thick enough to cut with a knife, and I don't think either one of us has figured out what to do with that just yet. I should let her out of the remaining two dates. A better man would. But I'm greedy. I want to prove to her I'm not the evil dick they've made me out to be.

I just didn't predict craving her the way that I am.

I want her back in my house, laughing and smiling. All soft and warm. I want her in my bed—even though that would ruin a few friendships on her end. And that isn't fair.

But tonight, I need to contact her for purely professional reasons. My thumb swipes across the screen of my phone as I pull up her contact information and tap the phone icon. I watch Loki's little eyes grow heavy on his drooping head. He looks so small and vulnerable, and I can't stop myself from going into the stall to crouch beside him and rub his shoulder while the phone rings in my ear.

"Hello?"

It's loud wherever she is. It sounds like she's out having fun—after all, it is a Friday night.

"Mira, it's Stefan."

"Hi?" She's clearly confused about why I'd be calling her at 10 p.m. on a Friday.

"There's something wrong with Loki."

She doesn't even miss a beat. "I'll be right there."

Her heart is so damn pure. Far more pure than someone like me deserves.

Within twenty minutes, she arrives, bursting through the door looking like some sort of country goddess.

"I'm here!" Inky-black hair billows out over her brown-suede bomber jacket as she struts down the hallway. Her long legs are poured into a skintight pair of jeans, and the ornate cowboy boots on her feet click swiftly against the concrete. I'm still not accustomed to seeing her in anything other than her cargo pants and oversized Carhartt jacket.

She drops her kit and looks up at me, cheeks rosy and eyes narrowed. "Tell me what's wrong." She doesn't waste any time digging into the box that carries all her general medical stuff, only grabbing a small flashlight and her stethoscope.

Her level of seriousness alarms me. This is what poor Loki gets for having me take care of him. I'm a goddamn angel of death. I can't keep anyone safe.

"He was fine when I checked on him before dinner." She comes close, listening to his heartbeat and nodding, urging me on. "I came down to check on him before bed, and he seemed lethargic. I mean, look at him. He's been a bit of a terrorist lately. He's not himself."

"Diarrhea?" She looks around the stall and stands up straight, eyes landing on what looks like very liquified poop. *How did I not notice that?* She pinches the skin on his neck and when she lets go, it stays pinched together, not returning flat as it should with a properly hydrated horse. Next, she opens his droopy lips and presses her thumb against his gums, testing how quickly they pink back up under pressure. Her movements are efficient, not panicked, but prompt.

"Okay. He's dehydrated. Orphan foals are prone to infection if they miss out on colostrum—which he did for a few days. Just stick with him while I grab some stuff from my truck."

She darts out of the stall, and I'm left patting the small chestnut horse and murmuring to him. "You're gonna be fine, little dude. I'm sticking with you. And did you know Mira is the best vet I've ever known?" His eyes flutter, and his head bobs. "It's true. She's very impressive." My voice cracks.

I hear her steps behind me and feel her dainty hand land at the top of my back. Her fingers pulse against my spine in a light squeeze before she pulls an IV pole into the stall and gets to work, setting up a drip.

"Fuck," she mutters to herself as she struggles to find a suitable spot for the catheter. Her thumbs work, pressing down the line of his neck, trying to make a vein bulge. The only sign that she likes what she sees is a quiet grunt and then the precise movement of her hand sliding the needle into the spot she selected. "Good boy, Loki. Tough man. You're a fighter, aren't ya?"

Within a few moments, Mira has the gauge taped to Loki's neck and the line attached. Hopefully, whatever is in that clear bag hanging above us is what he needs. I don't think I can bear the thought of anything happening to him.

"What now?" I ask quietly from where I kneel beside her.

Mira's lips press into a thin line as she looks down at me and sighs so heavily her shoulders rise and then fall. "Now we wait."

"Coffee?" Mira is back, peeking down into the stall from between the bars. "It might be a long night."

"I thought you left?" I ask sullenly, feeling kind of low and introspective. I guess that's why I haven't moved off the stall floor. Again. I don't want to leave Loki. Just in case. So here I am, leaning against the wall once again.

"Nah. Figured I'd camp out with you for a bit." She kicks the stall door open and steps in with a steaming cup of coffee in each hand. "I think I might have gotten it right this time." She grins mischievously as she comes to stand before me.

The scent wafts off the hot liquid as she folds herself down about a foot away from me. "Is there booze in this?"

"Yeah." She smiles as she blows on her mug. "I found some Bailey's in the fridge. You look like you could use some."

I peer back at her, following the strong angle of her pronounced cheekbones down her perfectly straight nose.

"No Bailey's for you?"

"I'm technically on call. They generally frown on practicing veterinary medicine while under the influence. I take turns being on call overnight with a few other vets so the area is covered for emergencies."

"I didn't know that," I say thoughtfully.

"Of course not. You just call me directly when you need something." Her laughter is light and airy as she leans in to sip her coffee.

"Black coffee for you?"

"Like my soul." Her lips tilt up in a wry twist, but her eyes stay focused on the horses before us. Farrah hangs her head over Loki protectively. I marvel at the way she's taken him over, the way she cares for him when he's not even hers. Or maybe he is hers now.

While Mira stares at them, it gives me the freedom to stare at *her*. To let my gaze roam appreciatively. She looks beautiful tonight—fun—far too done up to be sitting on the dirty floor of an oversized foaling stall with the likes of me. "What's with the getup?"

She quirks a brow. "You asking if I was on a date?"

"You mean we're not exclusive?" I feign offense, even though internally the thought of her out with another guy makes me see red.

"Are you dating someone?"

I scoff. "No. Not for a while now."

"So you just… go without?" She sounds so curious.

"I didn't say that either, did I?" Mira shimmies her shoulders taller and looks away. "Things have always been pretty casual in that department for me since I moved here. Women aren't exactly lining up to date me in Ruby Creek, and having my sister in the house makes it awkward."

"But in the city?" She's still avoiding looking at me, picking at a piece of wood shaving on the rubber mat beside her.

"What happens in the city stays in the city. This farm is my refuge. I wouldn't bring just anyone here. Anyway, stop changing the subject. All dressed up tonight?"

"Girls' night at the country bar. Sober for me. Super fun." Sarcasm seeps from her tone.

"With who?"

She gives me a dry glance now. Like I'm asking a stupid question. "Billie and Violet."

I just grunt. What am I supposed to say? They hate me and have me pegged as a lot worse than I am.

"You know, I think under different circumstances you'd all get along."

I scoff at that. "And why is that, Dr. Thorne?"

"Because when it comes down to it, we're all just good people who love their horses."

"I'm not so sure I'm a good person."

"Hmm." She tips her head like she's mulling that over.

"Hmm what?"

"I disagree with your assessment."

"Oh yeah? You told them that yet?"

"No," she says quietly before hiding behind the big mug again. That stings worse than it should. It's one thing for her to tell me I'm a good person here in the quiet barn where no one else can hear her and another for her to say it to her friends. She might not think I'm so bad anymore, but she's not rushing out to tell anyone about it.

"How's Nadia?" Mira asks, effectively changing the subject.

The liquid drips into Loki's line as he leans close to Farrah, seeking her warmth. I consider lying to Mira but opt for the truth. "Not so good."

She nods silently, and I continue. "She's led a privileged but traumatizing life. I've done what I can to keep her safe. But I don't think it was enough."

"Why not?"

That's not the question I was expecting. "Because she's still sad and lost and desperate for love."

"Why?"

God. I forgot how brutally blunt she can be sometimes.

"Because we grew up watching our dad viciously beat our mother."

Her head bounces back against the wall, and she exhales. "Fuck."

"Yeah. He liked to leave the bruises where no one could see. That way he could still package her up in a fancy dress and tote her around to all his classy events. Everyone was spared the horror, except Nadia and me." My lips roll together, itching to spill it all, hidden down low in this warm stall encompassed by the quiet munching sounds of the surrounding horses with this woman who has slowly become something like a friend. "With the age difference between us, she got stuck at home while they shipped me off to boarding school in Switzerland. She was a baby when I left. But we got summers together, I guess." Now I know why I got the boot and she didn't. But I don't feel like going there right now. "As soon as I graduated from that cesspool, I went straight to university in London. I didn't want to go home. I was worried I'd kill him if I had to live with him again. So I stayed. I did my degree and then moved on to the London School of Business for my MBA."

"Did you kill him in the end?"

Not exactly. "No."

"I would have killed him." She nods her head succinctly, like she's very satisfied with her conclusion. Mira Thorne is kinda dark, and I like it.

"A plane crash did that for me instead. Unfortunately, his plane crash took my mother with him."

"Jesus. That's depressing. How long ago was that?"

"Four years ago."

Mira nods. "Right before you came to Ruby Creek." She doesn't miss a damn beat.

"Yeah. My mom grew up here. It seemed like a good way to be close to her at the time."

"At the time?" If she's shocked by that revelation, she doesn't show it. She just looks at me. Her dark eyes are soft as they slide over me like she can read my mind.

"Yeah. Sometimes it feels like I have no idea what I'm doing." I can't hold her gaze for long. I rest my head on the wall and stare up at the warm lights above us.

"I think we all feel like that sometimes."

I swallow audibly. She's probably right.

"And when did Nadia move here?"

"As soon as she could legally—about a year ago. She was stuck living with *his* sister until she turned eighteen. Then I got her on a plane straight here. It's been an adjustment for her. I wasn't there enough through her most important years. I should have gone back. There's a lot of baggage to unpack." My free hand presses down into the rubber mat of the stall floor to ground myself. The top joints of my fingers ache with the pressure as I grasp at the flat surface. It almost hurts. But I probably deserve that.

"You feel guilty." It's not a question, the way she says it. She knows. It's hard to get anything past Mira.

"Yeah." A ragged sigh escapes me, and I run my free hand through my hair. "And I don't even know where to begin on making it up to her."

I start when her hand covers mine, like a warm blanket over a cold soul. Her fingers slide between mine, prying them up off the floor. Tangling together.

With one squeeze, she carries on, like we hold hands all the time. "What's going on with school?" She sips her coffee, but I can't tear my eyes away from her hand on mine. She has elegant hands, long fingers, but they don't feel soft and manicured. Her nails are clean and natural, trimmed neatly, and I can feel the light callus on her palm against the top of my hand. Mira works with her hands, and I can feel the proof.

I can feel everything.

"Umm." I cough in an attempt to clear my throat, where my heart is currently lodged. "I told her I'd support whatever she wanted to do. I mean, she's a nineteen-year-old woman. She went back for a couple days, but it sounds like there were a lot of cruel jokes flying around." My teeth grind just thinking about it. "On one hand, going to school with a bunch of kids is probably really humbling. On the other hand, I'm not sure what she'll do all day if she does the online school thing for her last few courses. I'm worried she'll be lonely. Or, worse, bored." I groan. "God. A bored Nadia would be dangerous for everyone in a hundred-mile radius."

Mira laughs, deep and raspy. It's sensual. Her hand feels hot over mine. I swear I can feel her heart beating through her palm. Forcing mine to beat in time with hers.

"She'll be fine," she says with another gentle squeeze of my hand. "We womenfolk are smarter and stronger than you all give us credit for."

She means it in a joking way, but the tension between us as our eyes lock onto each other is anything but lighthearted. I've always been drawn to Mira, but this is torture. I feel like she's reached right between my ribs and wrapped her delicate fingers around my lungs. Like if she wanted to, she could squeeze too hard and cut my breath off entirely.

The moment drags on and feels like it lasts forever, but with a sharp inhale, she stands and brushes off her pants. She doesn't explain herself, just goes about checking Loki again before unhooking him and urging him to nurse with a few gentle pushes toward Farrah's hind end. I must admit he's starting to look more perky. Within moments, he's latched on and feeding. At the sight, Mira's shoulders drop on a heavy sigh, a small smile touching her lips.

This is a good sign. My heart hammers when she turns that pleased expression down on me. And suddenly, I wonder what it would be like for her to gaze at me like that between her thighs. I wonder how low her voice would go then—how my name would sound on her lips while she comes on mine.

"Better?" I ask, veering back into reality. Because getting between Mira's thighs is a bad idea. I'd probably never want to leave.

"A little. Too early to say," she replies as she slides down the wall.

But this time, she sits close enough that our shoulders graze against each other.

And after a few beats, she reaches for my hand again.

CHAPTER 11

Stefan

I NEED TO TAKE A BREAK. MY EYES ARE ABOUT TO CROSS FROM HOW long I've spent staring at a spreadsheet. I press my fists into the sockets of my skull and press gently until I see white.

On Friday night, I stayed in Farrah and Loki's stall, so afraid to disturb the tentative truce that Mira and I seemed to have come to. I sat there so long, feeling the press of her fingers between mine and the heat of her body so close, that we fell asleep. Her head tipped to the side and rested against my shoulder, and what was I supposed to do then?

I didn't want to disturb her, and I didn't want it to end either. I tried to stay awake as long as possible, but sleep overtook me at some point, and I woke up to the feel of cold air against my side and the sound of Mira shuffling around the stall.

She didn't say anything to me. She looked groggy, and it felt like she was avoiding looking at me.

I wanted her to come back and grab my hand again.

To snuggle up against me once more.

But I knew that was too much to ask.

And she clearly thought that would take it too far because she packed up and left with a quiet "See you later. I'll be back in the morning."

I didn't even bother going back to my house. I stumbled into the barn lounge and sprawled out on the leather couch there. And that's exactly where I've spent the last two nights so I can watch Loki.

The good news is the colt seems to be steadily improving. The bad news is I'm barely functional. If it wasn't for the one-on-one time with Mira, I think I'd feel an awful lot like I'm doing Billie Black a favor.

That's a thought I sweep away. I'm doing this to save the foal who's living in my barn. The one who deserves every fighting chance available, no matter who owns him.

With a deep sigh, I head to the front door, where I grab my favorite shearling coat and slip my feet into a pair of boots, hoping some fresh spring air will rejuvenate me.

I walk down the winding road from the house, past the lake where my mother's ashes are sprinkled, feeling conflicted about her, as is my new normal. It's a trip missing someone so deeply but also being so unforgivably angry with them. I'm still not sure how to make heads or tails of that, even after four years.

When the barn comes into view from around the far side of the huge weeping willow, I see Mira's black truck with the gold logo and canopy cover parked out front. In a paddock just next to the barn, Nadia leans against the fence looking down at the ground where Mira is crouching over a horse that is flat out on his side.

The hell are they doing? My heart races. Lately, every time Mira is here, it's because something isn't going right. I pick up my pace, cutting across the grass to reach the paddock as quickly as possible.

"That's *it*?" Nadia's disbelieving voice is what I hear first. "Just like: incision, yank it out, and then snip?"

"Yup." I can hear the smile in Mira's voice. "That's it."

"Huh." Nadia's blond curls bob with her head.

"So the next time those pencil pricks have something shitty to say to you, you can tell them in detail how you'll castrate them."

What the…?

I get to the fence beside Nadia to see Mira disposing of what looks like… Oh. *Oh god.* That's hard to look at.

I'm not especially squeamish, but I'm not keen on watching a fellow male get castrated. I know it's a horse, but still. It just hits slightly too close to home.

"Stefan, did you realize how simple this procedure is?" Nadia asks, sounding a little too excited by the prospect. "I really almost feel like I could do it myself!"

Mira hits me with a knowing grin as she stands and tosses her gloves into the same bucket as the poor horse's family jewels. This woman is terrifying. "I'll get you to help me next time, Nadia."

"Jesus Christ." I drag a hand through my hair and shake my head. "What are you two hellions up to here?"

"Turning a stallion into a gelding. And teaching Nadia how to handle all the immature teenage boys who think the best way into her pants is terrorizing her." Mira slaps her hands together with a satisfied smirk on her face. "I wish I could be there to see their faces."

"What happened now?" I turn to my sister, instantly concerned about what's going on in her personal life. I'm not involved enough. I don't know how to be. And every time I try, I get the distinct impression she doesn't want me to be.

She waves me off, looking happier than she has in a long time. "Don't worry about it. I won't need to deal with them anymore after tomorrow."

"Why is that?"

"Because tomorrow I'm cleaning my locker out and getting my distance learning packages. The next day I'm starting a new job."

Jesus, what poor sucker hired Nadia?

But I opt to be outwardly supportive. Maybe some responsibility would be good for her. A purpose is good for coping with trauma, and I want my sister to succeed in life. Even if the girl is like a hurricane that leaves chaos in her wake. I want her *happy.* "That's great. What's the job?"

Nadia's full lips stretch out over her face, and she looks genuinely excited. "I'm Mira's new assistant at the clinic!"

I blink, trying to wrap my head around that. And then I look at Mira, who softens her features and shrugs before grabbing her stuff from the ground near her feet. "I've been meaning to hire someone" is all she says. As though Nadia is a perfectly qualified and natural choice.

She doesn't act like she's going out of her way to help my sister. To help *me.* She doesn't prance around acting like she's doing us a favor or extending some great kindness.

But she is.

And after everything I shared with her on Friday night, this feels like more. It feels like someone caring about us—something that hasn't happened in a very long time.

"I brought your eggs," Mira calls into the barn the next morning.

She's been coming back to check on Loki every evening and first thing in the morning before the clinic opens. Twice a day she's been here, running herself into the ground because I'm a greedy prick who wanted to keep the upper hand in an imaginary war with her employers.

"Mira, I was joking about that."

I'm sitting on the concrete floor just outside the stall waiting for her, feeling like a full-blown shmuck for using a woman who would make a special effort to help my little sister.

"Trust me. You want these eggs. They're from my parents' farm. I collected them myself."

Now I feel even worse, if that's possible. But I still take them from her outstretched hand.

"I also brought you a coffee." She holds the paper cup out to me with an amused tilt to her shapely lips.

I'm going to hell.

"Mira. Honestly. You don't need to do this."

"I know. But I like watching your face when I try to guess what type of coffee you like. It's worth the few bucks that cost me."

She pushes it toward me again, urging me to take it from her hand. When I finally do, she moves past me into the stall to check on Loki.

"Good morning, sweet baby boy," she coos. "And you, pretty mama, how are you?" I hear a quiet kissing noise and know she just pressed her lips to the mare's soft nose. I've seen her do it before. And it made my chest pinch then too.

I conned a lifesaving, sister-helping, horse-kissing angel into going on dates with me just because I could. I feel like dirt, and there's a part of me wondering why it's taken me this long to get to this point.

When she finally emerges from the stall, she locks it behind her, drops her workbox on the floor, and comes to the other side of me. I watch her boots as she slides down the wall to sitting. This time, she's only a few inches away from me. I can't figure out why she's sitting with me when she could leave and carry on with her day.

"Seems like sitting on the barn floor is kind of our thing," I say.

She laughs, a soft chuckle. A noise I want to take and suck into my mouth. I want to swallow her whole. Devour her. I don't deserve her, but goddammit, I'm not sure I've ever wanted another woman more.

"How's the coffee?"

She quirks an eyebrow at me as I take my first sip.

"What the—what on earth is this?"

Her head tips back, and she laughs, a full laugh that warms me from the inside. One hand falls across her chest, and the press of her forearm against her breasts makes them strain against the plain gray T-shirt she's wearing beneath her open coat. "Yup. Worth every penny."

It tastes like some sort of caramel cupcake blended into a coffee. It's atrocious. But she bought it for me, and that makes me want to drink it.

"I'm going to drink this, but I'll put you out of your misery. I take my coffee black."

"Was that so hard? Why didn't you just tell me?" She shakes her head, looking amused.

Because I'm a greedy bastard who liked feeling taken care of.

"Because the coffee doesn't matter when I'm in your company." I meant it to come out teasing, but it doesn't—because I mean it.

I take another sip as silence settles over us like a heavy blanket. I can hear the hum of the heater and the soft munching from Farrah's stall. The smell of fresh wood shavings blends with the sweet smell wafting up out of my coffee mug.

"I want to end our deal. You don't need to do the last two dates. I'm happy to help Loki, no matter what. I should never have put you in that position."

Mira scoffs and waves me off. "It's fine." And then with a chuckle and slight shake of her head, she admits, "I had fun on our first fake date."

The word *fake* burns. Maybe it's accurate, but whatever I'm feeling for Mira feels… well, not fake. I nod, effectively plunging us back into silence.

"Thank you for hiring Nadia."

Her head tilts. "I like her. She's got spunk. And I really could use the help. Sounds like she excels in math and sciences, which is exactly what I need. She can do schoolwork and still get some socialization around the clinic. The girls are going to love her."

"Right." I snort. "Billie is going to love having my family around."

"Billie is a good person. She won't hold a single thing against your sister. Plus, she's probably the last person in the world who would judge a person by their family."

I grumble. "Yeah, maybe." Knowing Billie's background, I suppose it's possible.

"It's going to be great. You'll see."

I just nod. My throat feels thick.

"Where did you go to vet school?" I blurt out eventually, trying to fill the space with something. Unsure why she hasn't left yet.

"In Calgary." She smiles wistfully. "I loved it. Every second. The late nights studying. The classes. The stress. I thrived there."

I smile too. I can totally see it. There's an academic side to Mira. She's a bit nerdy. But in the best possible way. There's something about a woman who wields her brain like a weapon and her tongue like a whip that makes me want to worship at her feet.

Never mind physical chemistry, I need intellectual chemistry to hold my attention. Getting lost between the sheets with just any warm body has lost its appeal the older I've gotten. And I have no doubt that if I stripped Mira down, there would be a battle of wills. She would keep me on my toes, and I'd keep her on hers. And then I'd have her on her knees.

I shake my head, trying to clear my filthy mind.

"Did you always want to be a vet?"

She sighs now. "Yeah. I did. I was constantly tending to the animals on my parents' farm or finding injured animals. Birds." She snorts. "Rats."

"Rats?"

"Hey, man. Even rats need love." She winks at me. I'm pretty sure she just called me a rat in a very roundabout way.

"You've got a big heart. Your family must be very proud of you." It comes out teasingly, but I mean it seriously.

"Yeah. I think they'd be happier if I found a good man and pumped out some babies though."

"Really? But you're still so young."

"It's just a complicated dynamic. I'm the most educated person in my family. My dad is the child of Indian immigrants who have only ever worked the family farm. My mom is this free-spirit hippie who came to pick blueberries one day, found a man instead, and just never left. I love them dearly, but we have vastly different goals in life. I think the fact I'm permanently single stresses them all out."

"Are you?"

"Stressed?"

"No. Permanently single?" I try to keep my voice from going husky. I hadn't even considered the prospect that Mira might not be single, and suddenly I'm feeling a little jealous for absolutely no good reason.

"No."

My teeth clench, and my heart riots against my ribs.

"I'm in a long-term relationship with Mr. Purple."

My brow crinkles. "That's a weird last name."

"He's battery powered and made of silicone. I think it would be weird if I brought him home to meet my parents."

I bark out a laugh. I can't help it. Her delivery is so dry and not at all ashamed. Plus, I was momentarily jealous of a dildo. *Adorable.*

"You could try. But I would like to be present to see it, please."

She doesn't laugh at the joke. "Yeah." Her eyes take on a nervous glint as her lips roll together. "I was wondering if I could ask you for a favor."

Ah, there it is. The reason she's been hanging around all awkwardly. I sip the sweet coffee and realize I'm developing a taste for it. Or perhaps I'm just enjoying her attention.

"Shoot." I'm dead curious what this favor is.

What she doesn't comprehend is I'll do almost anything she tells me to at this point.

Her fingers twist in her lap. "Any chance you'd be willing to use one of those dates we have left to attend a family reunion with me?"

I feel a grin spread across my lips. "You want me to meet your family?"

"Ugh." She looks up at the roof, searching for patience. "No. But I don't want to spend another year being treated like an old spinster who has nothing but an education to crawl into bed with at night."

"Are you telling me you'd rather take me to your family reunion than your dildo?"

She laughs and shakes her head. "Consider yourself the front runner in that race."

"When is it?"

"Two weeks. Not this Saturday, but next." She nibbles at her lips nervously. As if I'd be able to tell her no.

"It would be my pleasure." I drop a hand onto her thigh and give it a squeeze.

She pats my hand gently before standing. "Thank you."

This is when Mira runs. When things get too comfortable, too intimate, she bolts.

"I'll be better company than a dildo. I promise."

She shakes her head again and swipes her kit off the ground. "Doubtful" is her reply as she walks away.

I can't help but appreciate the way her cargo pants hug the round globes of her ass. *The things I'd do to that ass.*

"Bet I can make you come harder too."

She laughs, a girlish laugh. Not her usual throaty husk. "I'd like to see you try."

Challenge accepted.

CHAPTER 12

Mira

I'M WATCHING HANK TROT BRITE LITE IN A STRAIGHT LINE AWAY from me, but I'm thinking about Stefan.

I'm supposed to be watching the pretty gray mare to see where I think the hitch in her step is coming from, and instead I'm replaying the feel of his hand when he wrapped it around my thigh. It's driving me to distraction.

He's driving me to distraction.

Exactly what I've always promised myself I wouldn't let a man do. Let alone a man like Stefan. It's complicated. His entire persona is sketched in blurry lines, and I'm worried I'm getting lost in that fuzz. When I took Billie to see Loki today, I found myself constantly looking around, hoping to catch even a glimpse of him.

I have a savior complex. You don't become a veterinarian or medical professional without that facet to your personality. And everything he's shared over the last several days about his mom, his dad, his upbringing… it's got a stranglehold on my savior complex.

He really is like an injured rat. He grosses everyone out. And I'm drawn in. I want to swoop in and bandage up his broken parts. Watch them heal.

Seeing animals, and people, heal is my catnip. It's what fills my cup. I've seen it with my friends over the last couple of years, and it never fails to make me smile.

I shouldn't want to fill my cup with Stefan.

But I do.

And now I feel like I'm drowning in a man who is only dragging me along in his game to one-up my best friend. I'm a pawn. And I'm smart enough to know better.

"So? What do you think?" Hank huffs over the sound of aluminum horseshoes clopping on the paved driveway out front.

Busted. And I'm making the old man work for it, no less, while I daydream about enemy number one.

"Just catch your breath. And then one more loop around the driveway. I think it might be up in her stifle." I was watching—sort of—but I still feel like a total asshole. "Take you for a drink after?"

Trixie is in the city working right now, so Hank is lonely sometimes. I can tell by the way he hangs around. By the way he pops into the clinic just to chat.

He flashes me one of his big grins, followed by a wink of a twinkly green eye. He has a distinct Robert Redford vibe going on that, if I were older, I would certainly appreciate. He's one of the good ones. That's for sure.

"I'm gonna need a cold one after this workout, Dr. Thorne." He turns the mare around to trot away again. But not before tossing out a casual "Try not to daydream this time!"

So busted.

I offer to drive into Ruby Creek's favorite watering hole, Neighbor's Pub. And we even manage to get my favorite table at the back near the fireplace. Spring is here in the valley, but it's damp and cool today. The weather just seems to swing back and forth this time of year, between a warm taste of summer and then a cold jolt of winter. Today is that, and I'm happy to be seated next to the crackling fire with a beer on the way.

Usually, I'm here with Billie and Violet, and sometimes they even bring Vaughn and Cole. Both of whom I like. A lot. But I feel distinctly out of place as the single friend who gets dragged along on those nights, so it's nice to hit happy hour with just Hank.

Hank folds himself into the seat across from me and looks around with a bemused smile on his face. "Love this place," he murmurs.

"Me too," I agree, picking up the plastic menu to figure out what I want, right as the waitress hustles over with our pints.

This pub is the quintessential small-town meeting spot. Stained-glass shades over the lamps, mismatched captain's chairs at every dark-stained table, and old-school burgundy carpets on the floor. There's even a jukebox in the corner.

"You eating too?" Hank asks.

"I think I might," I reply. "Cooking every night for just one person is kind of soul-sucking." I blurt it out without even considering that Hank has been doing exactly that for probably his entire life. "Sorry," I add on with a twist of my lips.

"Don't be. It's true. I'd be lying if I said I don't spend every week looking forward to Sunday night dinners with all you kids. A date at my favorite pub with Dr. Thorne isn't so bad either."

I laugh. "Maybe we should make it a regular thing. A special club for the only two people not totally shacked up on the ranch."

The waitress swings by and takes our orders. A burger for each of us.

"No men in your life?" he inquires gently.

I take a sip of the fizzy golden lager and smack my lips together. "Nope." I sound very sure when I say it, but inside I'm in turmoil. My arrangement with Stefan may not be real, but I don't like feeling like I'm lying to Hank either. "Too busy with work."

"I know how that goes." He sips his beer and nods his head. "Happy I've got Trixie in the picture now though. She's the best surprise in my life lately. You'll get one eventually too."

I grunt. "I'm not really a big fan of surprises, to be honest. I like a nicely laid-out plan. A clear path."

The older man chuckles kindly, like I've just said something desperately naive. "Oh, Mira. All the best things in my life have come as an absolute surprise. Didn't expect an eighteen-year-old girl to show up on my doorstep demanding I give her a job, but I'm glad I did. Billie is the daughter I never got to have. Didn't expect my best friend to scandalize the racing world and then die of a heart attack. But here I am, helping his grandsons run his farm." He shakes his head thoughtfully. "I mean, shit, I didn't even expect to have the job I do now. I used to bartend here, did you know that?"

I smile and rear back a tad. "I didn't. But I can totally picture it. I bet you were a real lady-killer in Ruby Creek."

A shadow of the past flits across his eyes, but he chuckles all the same.

"If Cole and Vaughn's grandfather, Dermot, hadn't waltzed in here on a wild-goose chase after a girl, I'd have never met him. I'd have never started working for him and Ada. I'd have never been out East to meet Billie. And I'd have never met Trixie at Cole's wedding in Chestnut Springs." Hank takes a swig of his beer. "Sometimes unexpected surprises change the course of our life in the most irrevocable of ways. In the best ways. Life is one big adventure, Mira. Don't let it pass you by while you're stuck on a boring old path."

I laugh, but it rings hollow. What he's just said hits a little too close to home. He didn't tell me I belong barefoot in the kitchen with a baby on my hip. He just told me to be open to new possibilities. I think he just told me to take my blinders off. But my blinders keep me safe and focused and achieving all the goals I set for myself as a younger woman.

"Thank you for sharing your wisdom, Hank," I say right as the server swings by with our burgers. "You want a good surprise?"

He nods, and his lips tip up when he winks at me. "Always."

"I hired Stefan Dalca's younger sister to work in the clinic."

His eyes go wide, and his beer goes down the wrong tube. He coughs and pounds a fist against his chest. I feel bad for making him choke, so I keep talking, trying to fill the lull. "Her name is Nadia. She's had a tough go. But I think you'll really like her. She reminds me of Billie. Well, younger Billie."

"Lord have mercy on us all," he coughs out with a laugh. And I join him too. "Listen, Mira, if you like her, I'm sure the rest of us will as well. You're a good judge of character."

God. Am I though?

We dig into our meal, and conversations about different horses on the ranch flow easily. But I'd be lying if I said my thoughts weren't constantly veering off the path. Heading in a direction that I desperately don't want them to go.

"Don't be such a baby."

Stefan has his arms wrapped around Loki's neck and is looking down at the foal like he's a stuffed animal, not a future athlete and animal that needs space to frolic and run.

"Are you serious right now?" I prod him. "I thought you were a big tough man, but you're too chicken to let this little guy romp around outside?"

"Mira. I'm not a big tough man. I'm just a dick. Remember?"

"Yeah, yeah." I wave my hand at him dismissively. Stefan is a lot of things, but the more I get to know him, the less I think a dick is one of them. "Let's go. Outside. Fresh air is good for everyone." I slip the leather halter onto Farrah's head and buckle it near her ear. She looks excited. Ready to get out of the barn.

"What if he hurts himself?"

"Can't live life that way, Stefan. Bad things happen all the time. Buck up. Let's go."

With a firm cluck, I walk Farrah out into the barn alleyway and head toward the big wide-open sliding door. Today was beautiful and sunny and dry. And now, under the quiet charm of the evening, it's the perfect time to let them take their maiden voyage outside with no tractors, no staff milling about, just calm and privacy for this colt and the mare who's taken him under her wing.

Within a few moments, I hear the clopping of Loki's hooves against the concrete and the scuff of Stefan's boots. I smile to myself. The big bad wolf has certainly developed quite the soft spot for Loki.

Out under the setting sun, we head toward the paddock that's already waiting and open. It's a big grass field on the opposite side of the lake from the willow tree where Stefan and I buried the other foal a few weeks ago. I pull Farrah's halter off, and she's through the gate. Loki follows her, like the sweet little colt he is.

Until Stefan lets him go.

Beneath the pink and orange sky, the sweet little colt blows a gasket. He's got his head down between his knees and is trying to buck. Mile-long legs fly out all over the place while Farrah takes off for a leisurely trot down the fence line. Loki goes with her but doesn't stop his antics. I shut the gate quickly and lean against the fence, chuckling.

Stefan steps up beside me and presses his elbows against the railing. "He looks like Elaine doing that godawful dance on *Seinfeld*."

I straight up cackle. That is exactly what he looks like. "He looks happy," I reply.

Stefan nods. "He does."

"You've done a great job with him, Stefan." I want him to understand what a huge difference he's made for this small horse. That even if everyone sees him one way, I see that they're all wrong. It feels like something he should know. This man is still clearly so broken up about his mother and trying so hard for the only family he has left.

His eyes flit to the side. "This is all you. I probably just made your job harder."

"Oh, you mean by using me as a pawn in your pointless war with my friends?" I joke.

Now his head turns to me. Slowly but sharply. Like a predator that's heard his prey fumbling through the forest. "Pawn?"

I roll my eyes. "Don't play stupid, Stefan. It's not cute. Making them keep Loki here rather than at Gold Rush Ranch. The three dates. I'm sure you're just desperately hoping Billie finds out about those so you can sow discord between us. I know it's all part of your plot to cut them down at the knees."

He unfolds his fingers slowly as he regards me. Turning his body to face me. And mine follows like the opposite end of a magnet, matching his movement so we stand facing each other under the golden glow of the evening sky. "You think that you're the pawn in my game?"

I scoff and roll my eyes in response. *How dumb does he think I am?*

He moves swiftly now, surely. One hand shoots out and slides between my coat and thin shirt. He palms my ribs there as he presses me back against the fence. We're supposed to be watching the horses. But suddenly, all we're watching is each other. My hands come up to push him away, but as soon as I feel the hard lines of his pecs beneath his shirt, my resolve withers.

"I'm going to tell you something, Mira." I can feel the rumble of his voice through my palms. I can't take my eyes off the sight of my hands on his chest. I'm not supposed to be touching Stefan Dalca, but my body must have missed the memo. Because my nipples rasp against my bra, and with each breath I draw, an ache coils just behind my hip bones.

"And I want you to listen very carefully." With his free hand, Stefan reaches up and drags the pad of his pointer finger over my collarbone.

My breath turns to stone in my lungs. I'm too shocked to move. And too far gone to stop him. He's standing so close I can smell his laundry detergent and the hint of pine that must be in his cologne.

"Because you are very confused."

He starts at the center of my chest, his eyes following his finger, watching goose bumps fan out across my skin in his wake. When his finger gets close to my shoulder and the neckline of my shirt, he slips it just inside. Just under the strap of my bra. And with one flick, that strap is pushed right off my shoulder. His grip pulses on my ribs and he steps even closer, forcing me to look up and hold his gaze.

A quiet gasp escapes me when I catch sight of the expression on his face. What I see there is primal. He's not just looking at me appreciatively… he's looking at me like he wants to devour me.

I'm positive no man has ever looked at me like this before.

A sinful smile touches his mouth as he leans in close. His free hand cups the back of my skull so his thumb can brush across the sensitive part of my neck, almost at my throat.

His whisper is warm and silky. "Do I have your attention now?"

I swallow and nod, feeling chills break out over my skin. There is not a single part of my mind or body that is not entirely focused on the man who has pushed me up against the fence.

"Good. Because I want to make myself abundantly clear." We're so close. I can feel the entire length of his body covering mine. He teases me with the lightest brush of his lips against my ear as he drops his voice and holds me captive. "You are not the pawn, Mira. You are the prize."

I reel, and I feel the burn of his lips against my skin as he presses a featherlight kiss to the spot his thumb had been rubbing. My pulse hammers, and I swear all I can hear is my blood rushing through my veins. The air crackles between us. No man has ever spoken to me like this.

I should put a stop to our interaction. And yet there's nowhere else I'd rather be. My body comes to life for him in a way it shouldn't.

He steps away, and I feel alarmingly bereft, like I want to yank him back toward me. Like I want *more.* I'm the biggest traitor I know because I want him to continue. I want him to whisper more forbidden secrets against my body.

His tongue darts out over his bottom lip, followed by his teeth, in a very intentional way as his eyes peruse my body. His gaze lands on the hand I now have slung over my chest in an attempt to slow my racing heart. The other one grips the fence post behind me, possibly the only thing that's keeping me upright at this moment.

"And I love to win," he finishes with a stupidly sexy smirk, and then turns around and walks away.

Leaving me with the perfect view of his firm ass and a jumbled mess of confused feelings.

CHAPTER 13

Stefan

The bell rings, the gate flies open, and I watch the new gray filly fly out with ears pricked forward. She has a sweet face, but the little demon can *run*.

She drops her head low and gets to work almost instantly. The season hasn't started yet, but she's going to be ready when it does. Jose is light in the irons, gently hovering above her, letting her stretch out and not overmanaging the way Patrick does during his rides.

Not that he ever shows up to practice days. If it's not race day, you don't find him down here at Bell Point Park. I imagine he's hanging in his mansion wearing one of those red crushed-velvet robes you see in movies, sucking on a cigar. The guy is just such a douchebag. I can't wait to bury him once and for all.

Jose and Silver thunder past where I stand, pulling my attention from my Patrick plans. And true to her name, she looks like a silver streak, a blur, as she gallops past with her dark dapples flashing under the sun. She's a beautiful mare.

Although, last time I spoke to Jose, he cackled and told me that she's "a bit of a bitch" and "her attitude will win her races." Her muscled haunches push her through the turn, and I can't help but smile. I told him we could just refer to her as a "go-getter" from now on. Call her what you want, but he's not wrong—that mare has *winner* written all over her. Plus, she'll make a hell of a broodmare one day.

Happy with what I've seen, I turn and begin my walk back to the stables, wanting to have a quick chat with some of the staff down here at the track. I pass the winner's circle—a place I'd like to spend more time—and then turn toward the barns. It's quiet here this time of year; there aren't any spectators, just staff working quickly and efficiently. Which is why I'm surprised when I hear Patrick Cassel's voice filtering out of the mouth of the first barn alleyway.

"You'd look a lot prettier if you smiled more, you know."

I roll my eyes while standing around the corner, out of sight. *Total douchebag.*

"I'll smile when you show me what you're hiding in your pocket."

My blood runs cold. Another voice I'd recognize anywhere. A voice that has me leaping into action because I sure as hell am not leaving Mira alone with a pig like Patrick. And truthfully, I'd intervene no matter who was here with him. The mere fact Patrick is at the facility on a day when there aren't races is suspicious.

With my hands slung in my pockets and my neck held tall, I turn into the wide-open end of the barn and lean a shoulder up against the frame before casually crossing an ankle over my shin. Mira's gaze finds mine almost instantly, while Patrick has no idea I tower behind him. His lack of awareness might be his most impressive quality.

"I think Dr. Thorne looks especially lovely when she's frowning." My voice comes out as a snarl, which makes perfect sense. Seeing Patrick alone in a barn with Mira has me feeling a bit feral.

He spins, cheeks reddening, lips curling into a vicious smile I don't trust at all. "Stefan, how lovely to see you."

His tone tells me he doesn't actually think it's lovely.

"Did you find your misplaced work ethic, Patrick? Putting in some extra hours? Not sure I've ever seen you here on an off day."

He sneers at me, and I see Mira worrying her lip behind him, her eyes darting down to the pockets of his bomber jacket where his hands are shoved in. It's not a stretch to say he looks like he's covering something. But I already know that.

"Fuck you, Dalca. You fired me, remember? The work I do now is none of your business."

My fingers curl into fists in my pockets. The problem with men like Patrick is they think they're much smarter than they are. He thinks he must be the smartest man in the room right now, simply because we haven't caught him.

Yet.

Mira pipes up now. "As the person in charge of these horses' health and well-being, you trying to enter their stalls *is* my business."

He scoffs as he turns back to face her. "I was doing no such thing. Just taking a shortcut through this barn."

He's a poor liar, and the way Mira arches her brow says she thinks so too.

"You were." Her eyes narrow, and if looks could incinerate a person on the spot, Patrick would be on fire right now.

"Okay, Mira, then get a search warrant," he chuckles condescendingly. "No one is going to believe the little country bumpkin with the worst case of resting bitch fa—"

That's not happening.

My hand snakes out, fingers clamping around the back of his neck, hard enough I hope it hurts. "That's *Dr. Thorne*. And it's time for you to leave. Now." My fingers pulse, and I feel him tense.

Being the weasel that he is, he tries to leave immediately, but my grip pulls him back as I lean in toward his ear and chuckle darkly. "A gentleman like you wouldn't leave without apologizing to Dr. Thorne, would he?"

"Of course not." His voice is thin with barely contained rage bubbling beneath perfectly enunciated words. But he's also not brave enough to do anything about it. "My apologies, *Dr. Thorne.* Now get your fucking hands off me, Dalca."

He squirms around like a slippery fish, trying to escape my grasp. I almost wish I had a bat to put him out of his misery. It's just pathetic enough to make me smile before I let him go. He marches out with his head held higher than is fitting for someone who is fleeing a losing match.

"He was up to something." Mira stares at me, dark eyes searching my face like she's looking for something.

"No doubt." I shove my hands back in my pockets to ease the urge to wrap her in my arms. To assure myself that she's okay. "But he's not wrong. Short of holding him down and frisking him, it would be hard to prove."

She grunts in dissatisfaction, jutting her chin out in the way of saying goodbye. "Thanks for running interference," she adds as her eyes dart down just before she turns to saunter back through the darkened stable.

"Of course." My eyes fall to her firm ass. No one should look that irresistible in cargo pants. "And Mira?"

"Yeah?" Now facing me, she continues to step backward, putting space between us, making the pull more powerful than ever.

"Only smile when you want to."

Her full lips press down, almost certainly hiding a small smile. And she gives me that look again. The one so full of questions and confusion.

I stand and watch her leave, like she can't get away from me fast enough. Since I came clean about wanting her, she's been skittish around me.

Shaking my head, I marvel at how the more confused she is about me, the less I am about her.

I tried avoiding Mira a while back, and it didn't work. And apparently, she's trying her hand at avoiding me now. I'm supposed to attend a family reunion with her tomorrow, but I've seen neither hide nor hair of the woman since our run-in with Patrick. She's been here checking on Loki; I can see her notes and initials on his chart hanging on the front of the stall. I just don't know when she's coming because she's ignoring my messages. Calling the clinic doesn't even work anymore because the person I now have to talk to is my endlessly lippy sister.

So now I'm going to sit on the barn floor and wait for her to show up.

Was I too forward the other night? Maybe. Do I regret it? Hell no. I refuse to let a woman like Mira walk around thinking she's anything less than the queen she is. She's not a tool; she's not a pawn. I don't have it out for her friends the way she thinks I do. Did I want to buy that horse? Yes. Did I resort to a less than savory offer to make it happen? Also, yes.

But I hold no grudge. That's just business. I'm well aware Billie hates me, and that's okay. She can hate me. She has zero bearing on how I feel about Mira.

Which is determined. I feel determined to prove to her I'm not the dick she thinks I am and that I'm definitely not playing with her. That I want her.

What started out as a simple attraction morphed into a curiosity. And then into a tentative friendship, which is when she showed me the woman beneath the cocky smirk and the unimpressed looks. And that woman?

I plan to take my shot with that woman. I just need to soften her up first.

Step one: talk to her.

Step two: woo her.

Step three: win her.

Mira is closed off and actually more shy than I originally banked on. Skittish even. She comes off like this confident siren of a woman, but when I press, she turns into a deer caught in the headlights.

I'll take it slowly. I'm a patient man, and I think she'll be worth the wait.

So I wait into the night, through dinner, for two hours before she shows up, closing the door quietly behind herself before she catches sight of me and stops in her tracks.

"Hi," I venture quietly into the private barn.

"Hi," she replies sharply, propping one fist on her hip, leaning one leg out to the side. Wearing that attitude and glare like a suit of armor. "Are you waiting for me?"

"Yes." No point in lying. "You've been avoiding me."

"Ha!" She barks out a laugh. "I wonder why?"

"Am I so bad?" My cheek quirks up, but there's a part of me that doesn't want her to answer. *If she only knew.*

"No, Stefan. You're not. I'm the one who's bad. Lying to my friends about the deal we made. Sneaking away to spend time with you. Do you know how shitty that makes me feel? I already couldn't win this situation, and then you had to go say what you said and throw an even bigger wrench into my dilemma."

"Dilemma? That means you're torn by something." *Good.* There's a petty part of me that wants her to be as confused as I am.

"Ugh!" Her free hand pulses into a fist and then lets go as she storms toward the stall. "Now I have to deal with you openly wanting to fuck me too."

I tut. "Such language, Dr. Thorne."

"Oh, lucky me. Mr. Cool, Calm, and Collected is here to lecture me about how he never swears."

"I swear."

She shoots me a disbelieving look. "I have never once heard you swear."

I stand up as she approaches and drops her toolkit on the concrete alleyway with a loud clang. Loki startles on the other side of the stall door.

"I do when the situation warrants it."

"Well, I'll wait with bated fucking breath for when that situation arises."

I chuckle. I like her all snappy and worked up. I like to think she's worked up *over me.*

She's about to go into the stall when she spins on me. "Tell me the truth. Are you connected to the mafia? People say that you are, and you haven't outright denied it. One day, are you going to be calling me to stitch up some guy in a back room here?"

I laugh. Small-town gossip is vicious. And wrong.

"I'm not. I don't know why that started circulating. Probably because I waltzed into a small town with a question mark for my past, a chip on my shoulder, and more money than I really knew what to do with."

"Where is all your money from? Most people your age don't just mope around their multimillion-dollar barns all day waiting for their vet to show up so they can accost her with sexually suggestive one-liners."

Oof. She's fired up. But while we're having a no-holds-barred conversation, I might as well give her the truth.

"I took my father's multibillion-dollar shipping company and ripped it up. I sold it for parts. He spent his life building it and beating my mother. He took what I loved most, so I took what he loved most and ran it through a chop shop. I dissolved the company. I ruined his life's work and took great pleasure in its disintegration. I also signed off on his DNR with a smile on my face. It was as close to killing the bastard as I could get."

She freezes, and I wonder if I've gone too far. Only someone with a tarnished soul would take pleasure in something like that.

But I continue, filling the quiet with my reasoning. "I took all that money and bought this place, and then I took the rest and started a shelter downtown for victims of domestic violence. I fund it and am on the board." I hold my hands up and look around myself. "My mother told me on her deathbed, before she succumbed to her injuries, that she wished she'd stayed in Ruby Creek and run a racing farm. So that's what I decided I'd do."

Mira swallows audibly. I think I've poured some water on her fire. "Good." Her head bobs as though my answer pleases her. And then she moves to unlock the stall. She stops, though, before she steps down to check on the colt and looks back over her shoulder. "Are you out to hurt my friends or their business?"

Her dark eyes are almost a perfect match for her black hair in the dim barn. Like flawlessly polished onyx. Her lips are rose-petal pink and so delectably soft. I could press her up against the wall right now and taste her. But that's not taking it slowly, and I don't want to blow this.

"No." The one word rings out between us as I hold her gaze, willing her to believe me. Willing her to see me as more than my past mistakes. "I promise."

Her lips thin as she regards me. "Okay. I'll be here at three tomorrow. Don't wear a suit."

My chest warms at the thought that we're still on for our *fake* date tomorrow. "Why not?"

"No one will believe I'd bring a guy who wears suits home. Just..." She looks me up and down. "Keep it casual. You already don't look like my type."

I almost laugh. *We'll see about that.*

As she brushes past me, I murmur conspiratorially, "Is it because I'm not purple and made of silicone?"

And I swear I see her blush.

★★★

"They're never going to buy this."

Mira is talking, but all I can focus on is her hands clamping down on the bare part of her thighs, just above her knees. She's wearing some white lacy dress with white Converse sneakers and a jean jacket. I should have my eyes on the road, but *goddamn*. Watching her hands grip her body beneath that hemline is practically pornography.

"Buy what?" I reply, forcing my eyes back to the charcoal road winding through bright-green hills.

After a rainy spring, it's an unseasonably warm day, and it feels like everything that was brown has suddenly popped into this vibrant green. I'm glad I have my sunglasses for the drive… and so I can creep on Mira discreetly.

"You. Me. That we're together. No fucking chance. I'm so screwed. And everyone will think I'm even more tragic for bringing a fake boyfriend. They're going to corner you and grill you. You have no clue what you're in for."

"Mira—"

"I'm a smart person. I was valedictorian of my graduating class at vet school. I have an IQ of one forty. People like me don't pull stunts like this and expect to get away with it."

Okay, she's really spiraling. "Mira—"

"And with you? God. What the fuck am I thinking?" Her hand closest to me jerks through her hair. "You're blond, for crying out loud. They'll know immediately. I've never batted an eye at a blond guy. Me having a type has been a running joke for years."

Yeah, joke's on you.

My hand darts out and clamps down on her thigh. Her skin is smooth and warm, and just the feel of her sends sparks up my arm.

"Mira." She stops ranting and stares down at my hand on her leg. "It's going to be *fine*. I'm good at schmoozing. I'll take care of you. I've got this. I'm not even that blond." She just sits there, frozen. Staring at my hand. The one that still hasn't let go of her leg. I could so easily slide it up her thigh and pull her panties to the side. A good orgasm would probably take the edge off. My dick twitches at the thought, and I force myself to focus on the road. "Do you trust me?"

She leans back in her seat and looks out the window. She doesn't make a move to withdraw my hand, but she goes quiet for an extended period.

If I wasn't listening carefully, if I wasn't hanging on her every breath, I might not have heard her say, "I think I do."

CHAPTER 14

Mira

We approach the front door of my parents' white bi-level split house, surrounded by a sprawling yard that butts up against flat fields filled with blueberry bushes. They keep it tidy, but the house looks dated. It's not something I've ever felt self-conscious about, but with Stefan here, I feel like I might barf.

His house is so opulent in comparison, his wealth so staggering next to the small working farm I grew up on. He's so damn polished next to my family. I told him to dress casually, so he wore a white dress shirt with a pair of navy-blue chinos. And somehow, I still don't feel like he looks casual.

He's cuffed the hem and put on a pair of loafers with no socks. I suppose for him, this is dressed down. But there's something about the way he just oozes class. He looks like he belongs in a magazine shoot for casual cool. It's tripping me out. How can he be so calm about pretending to a group of perfect strangers that we're dating?

I'm *tripping.* They're going to see right through it.

My hand wraps around the door handle, and I freeze. Once I turn this handle, there's no going back. Is this one of those moments Hank was talking about? A moment that can change the path of your life forever. One simple turn of a worn brass knob.

"Are you installing important updates?" Stefan chuckles from behind me.

How is he joking at a time like this?

He steps in closer, and his hand lands at the small of my back while the other lifts my free hand. His lips press against my palm just like the time before, and my body hums—just like the time before.

I wish he'd stop touching me. And not because I don't want him touching me. It's because I do. And I shouldn't. I can still feel the shape of his hand on my bare thigh like a brand. One I hope never fades or heals.

I'm so fucked up.

"Let's go Mira-bot. It's going to be fine. I've got you." His body presses in close to mine, and I internally chastise myself for melting toward him.

I'm not sure when Dalca the Dick became a comfort to me, but I'm too stressed to fight it right now. He feels like a wall of lean muscle behind me. Tall and firm and reassuring.

I twist the handle and swing the door open.

In a matter of seconds, the smell of cumin hits me, and moments later, my mom calls out, "Mira! You're here!"

She stands at the top of the stairs. Lines of gray streak her brown hair, and she's wearing some baggy cotton dress with feather earrings and a pair of very broken-in Birkenstocks. My mom is a hippie at heart, and while we're very different women,

I can't help but smile at the sight of her. Before I moved out to Gold Rush Ranch, I was still living at home, and as lame as that was for a woman in her mid-twenties, I'd be lying if I said I didn't miss my parents—and my nana, who lives with them too. When you go from seeing your family every day to a couple of times a month, it's an adjustment.

"Hi, Mama."

She hustles down the stairs and wraps her arms around my neck, pulling me into a tight squeeze. "Oh, my baby. It's so nice to see you."

I feel like she's suffocating me. Or maybe I just can't breathe with Stefan standing so close. She holds me back eventually and looks over my shoulder. "And who have we got here?"

My throat constricts, and I already know I'm going to blow this.

"Mrs. Thorne, I'm Stefan. Such a pleasure to meet you." Stefan reaches around me and extends his hand to shake my mother's. His other hand falls to the small of my back, where it always does. It feels comforting having him there, propping me up. My body never fails to come alive for him.

"Oh, please." My mother *blushes*. "Call me Sylvia."

Her eyes dart down to his hand on the small of my back, and her lips tip up. "Sunny! Come meet Mira's new boyfriend, Stefan!"

Boyfriend.

The word lands like a bomb, and I stiffen at the mention. In response, Stefan's fingers slide back and forth across my skin, making my eyes flutter as I swallow what I'm pretty sure is a moan. The fabric of my dress feels altogether too thin.

His hands on my body are making me absolutely insane.

I swear my brain is melting right down into my spinal cord.

I've officially turned into *that* girl.

My dad, black beard neatly trimmed, appears at the top of the stairs with his arms crossed over his chest. His thick black hair and almost-black eyes are the perfect match for my own. He's scowling at Stefan, and it makes me smile.

Sunny is one of those men who isn't frivolous with his words. But I know by his actions that I'm the apple of his eye. When he dropped me off at college, there was no tearful goodbye. No promises to visit. He helped me unpack and snuck an envelope with a thousand dollars cash under my pillow for me to find later.

He's never babied me or treated me like I'm less capable than I am. He's never given me the "if he touches you, he's dead" talk. He's a modern man who took my mother's last name when they got married.

But looking at him now? A small giggle bubbles past my lips. Looking at him now, descending the stairs with dark eyes perfectly narrowed, I'm going to go out on a limb and say my father isn't all that wild about his little girl bringing a boy home.

"Mr. Thorne, thank you so much for inviting me to your home." Stefan steps up to the stairs and sticks his hand out.

My dad just grunts and says, "Pretty sure Mira invited you," as he clasps his hand back in a death grip.

This is off to a great start.

"I'm sure glad she did." Stefan grins at my father, completely unperturbed.

We remove our shoes and head into the house together. Straight into the hustle and bustle of my father's family all together under one roof. He's a second-generation Canadian, and his siblings have spread out all over the country, which is why this annual get-together happens. Mostly, everyone convenes to see Nana.

At the kitchen table, my grandmother is folding samosas with a bored expression on her face. I'm pretty sure she could do this in her sleep.

"Hi, Nana." I bend down and drop a kiss to the top of her head and whisper, "Are you making enough that I can take some home with me?"

She shakes her head. "You think I'm so old I've forgotten you hoard these like a squirrel preparing for winter?"

I laugh. She's right. I always have them stocked in my freezer. "Nana. This is Stefan." Stefan is standing across the table, his eyes on her hands. "He's my…"

I don't know if I can lie to her about this.

"I'm her boyfriend," he says, like he's not concerned about pretending to be my boyfriend at all.

Nana looks him over and smirks. "He's blond."

Oh god. She totally knows. "He's not *that* blond," I reply, parroting what Stefan said earlier and trying to be casual as my eyes bulge out at him. Stefan just chuckles at me, shaking his head like I'm nuts.

"Can I help?" He pulls out a chair and sits down across from my grandmother, sincerity lining his every movement.

She shrugs but pushes a stack of the wrappers across the table and moves the bowl of filling into the middle. She doesn't give him any instructions; she just keeps going and expects him to pick it up.

I watch Stefan's keen eyes observing her closely, studying her movements. After watching her make a couple, he reaches into the bowl and takes a spoonful of the filling and then gets started on his first samosa. His gaze darts up and down when his fingers move. He mimics everything she does. Rises to the challenge. And makes a pretty damn fine-looking samosa.

I catch Nana assess it as she reaches forward to start her next one. She doesn't compliment him; instead, she just says, "He's fine, Mira. You can go."

Stefan doesn't even look up at me, already engrossed in making his next one. He looks so earnest about learning this, it warms my heart to him. The look of concentration on his face, the way he captures the tip of his tongue between his lips make my stomach flip.

But I've been dismissed.

I turn and grab two beers from the fridge and drop one in front of Stefan. As I walk away, I drag my hand across the broad expanse of his shoulders with my free hand.

I can't explain why I did it. I just felt the overwhelming need to touch him back. To thank him for doing this for me.

I still can't quite figure out why he's doing this for me.

You are not the pawn, Mira. You are the prize.

Try as I might, I've been unable to scrub that sentence from my mind. I feel like he went and carved it into my brain like teenagers carve their initials into a picnic table. There's no erasing it. The rut is there. And I'm stuck in it.

I walk into the living room and am met with a chorus of hellos, hugs, and backslaps. My cousins, my uncles, my aunts—it's nice to see everyone, but it's always so overwhelming. So loud and busy. I prefer to socialize one-on-one or in a small group. It's more relaxing, more intimate—less chaotic.

The get-together moves around me, and I chat when necessary from where I lean against the wall. But my eyes keep finding Stefan, hunched over a table, working quietly with my grandmother.

It makes my chest ache in a foreign way. And I give up all pretense of looking elsewhere and allow myself to watch his hands moving deftly, his toned forearms flexing below the cuffs of his dress shirt, which he's now rolled up. He really looks into it. And I'm finding myself entranced. It's right up there with watching him kiss Loki square on the nose. Or stroke Farrah's forehead with so much love and respect.

What if I've been wrong about him this entire time?

"Honey, you're staring." My mom nudges me with her elbow, shaking me out of my daydream.

My cheeks pink at once. "Oh shit. Sorry."

"Don't be sorry. It's nice to see."

I roll my eyes and take a swig of my beer, peeking at the table again. Which is right when Stefan looks up and catches me staring. A slow grin spreads across his face, and he lets his eyes trace my body. Heat pours through my bones, and I feel like they might melt entirely when he looks at me like that. Like he's undressing me with his eyes and plans to devour me.

He finishes his perusal with a sly wink, and I'm almost positive my panties combust on the spot. *Wink. Poof. Gone.*

I look away, blinking and swigging pointlessly at my empty beer bottle.

"No shortage of chemistry between you two. I bet the sex is sensational."

Here comes the free-spirit, Kama Sutra side of my mother. A couple glasses of wine and this is what comes out to play.

"Mom. Please, don't."

She turns to face me, and I see Stefan behind her, being dismissed by Nana with a wave of her hand. With only a few steps, he's closing in on us. Which is right when my mother adds, "Listen to me, Mira. Your father looked at me like that too. And guess what? The sex was sensational. It still is. A marriage is hard work, but great sex makes it easier."

Someone dig me a fucking hole.

"Wise words," Stefan says, folding himself into the spot right beside me. His arm snakes around my waist, hand splaying across my rib cage possessively as he presses a casual kiss to my temple. Like this is perfectly normal. Like this is real.

It's feeling pretty authentic right now. In my family home. Where he's being nice and polite and charming.

It's unnerving.

My mother grins and moves on to the next group of people, completely undeterred. In fact, I'm pretty sure in her mind, Stefan just promised her grandchildren.

"What are you doing?" I whisper-shout through gritted teeth.

He pulls me tight to his side and whispers against my hair, "Pretending to be your boyfriend. Like you asked me to. You do realize people in relationships touch each other?"

I scoff. "I wouldn't know."

I chance a look up at him to find blatant confusion on his face.

"Excuse me?"

"You heard me."

"Are you implying you've never been in a relationship?"

I try to drink more out of the empty beer bottle. I'm like a nervous toddler sucking on a soother for comfort. I absently wonder if beer bottles are the adult equivalent.

"Wrapping those pretty lips around a bottle like that isn't an answer, Mira."

On a gasp, I inhale whatever backwash I left in the bottle and end up coughing while he gently pats my back.

"You can't just keep saying things like that."

"Answer the question." His thumb swipes across my cheek, wiping away the tear my coughing fit elicited.

I take a deep breath. "I'm not implying anything. I'm *telling* you I've never been in a relationship."

"Why?"

"Because it's never served me."

His chuckle is dark and low. "Why is that?"

"Because the idea of being beholden to a man annoys me. I don't like having to report what I'm doing or why I'm doing it or where I am. They always have all these expectations, and I don't like feeling like I can't do whatever I want without running it past someone else."

"Why else?" His breath is warm as it pours down the side of my neck. If I turned my head, I could press my lips against his and get whatever this is out of my system.

God. Why are we having this conversation in the middle of my family living room?

To throw him off, I turn and whisper, "Because I can fuck myself better with Mr. Purple than any man ever has."

I don't know why I thought that would throw him off. The man is relentless. Like a dog with a bone.

The way his tongue presses into the side of his cheek thoughtfully drives me to distraction. I turn my head away, wanting to see if anyone can tell what's going on in our corner of the living room. But no one seems to be watching. They're all lost in their own conversations, happy and relaxed.

Unlike me. My feet go heavy, and a weight lurches through my gut when Stefan murmurs, "Challenge accepted. But I'm not going to fuck you until you're *begging* for it."

And then he saunters away to work the room, like he didn't just knock me into a complete tailspin.

CHAPTER 15

Stefan

This is fun. Not only am I having an absolute ball teasing Mira, but being in a house full of happy, loving family is making me feel like I'm living in a TV show or something. The space is loud, but it's full of laughter and camaraderie. It's the polar opposite from the house I grew up in, and I am reveling in it. It doesn't hurt that the food smells amazing.

I'm so hungry.

And based on the less than stealthy looks Mira is shooting me from across the room, she is too.

She's been dancing around the house and keeping her distance from me since I told her I was going to make her beg. The way her eyes widened—damn—that's a look I want to see, but from above her while I slide myself between her legs.

Her cheeks are pink, and she's smiling. She is stunning, and I'm spellbound. I'm trying to talk to her father about the nitty-gritty details of being a blueberry farmer, but my focus keeps slipping to his daughter.

The things I want to do to her.

If he could read my mind, he wouldn't be tolerating my presence in his home, I'm sure. He's gruff and intelligent and gives clipped answers. His eyes remind me of Mira's in color and the way they flash with a keen cleverness. I would be a fool to underestimate this man, but I am softening him up to me.

Over the music and hum of conversation, Sylvia shouts, "Dinner is ready!" from the kitchen and waves toward the huge family table they have set up for everyone.

I follow the crowd of people. I've met them all now, but I'd be lying if I said I can remember every name or relation. It's overwhelming.

Gravy dishes, fresh naan bread, and the samosas I'm super proud of making all look sensational. When I'm done staring at the food, I notice Mira is pulling a chair out at the opposite end of the table from me. Retreating like she usually does. Backing down. I like her when she fights back. She's a tough cookie when she's working, but this shy, softer side in her personal life is a new facet.

I suppose the fact that she's never been in a relationship could be part of that. I'm thinking her awkwardness around me can be chalked up to lack of experience. She's just mature enough to come off like she has more than she does. Either way, I'm happy to sit by Nana—I like the old crone.

"Mira, you're not really going to leave Stefan over there by himself?" her mother exclaims in front of everyone, and I wish she'd just left it.

The good news for Mira is that if she wants a man who is happy for her to go on having her own life and goals and ideas—I'm that guy. I couldn't care less if she wants to sit at the opposite end of the table. I saw how she's been looking at me all night. I'm pretty sure that where she wants to be sitting is on my cock.

"She can sit wherever she wants," I say, but Mira is already walking toward me with a tight set to her jaw. I pull out the chair next to me, and she sits down like she's made of wood. She's clearly annoyed. She's got that look on her face like she might gut someone.

I secretly love this side of her. The resting bitch face. Even when she looks at me like *that*, her fierceness is exciting. She's not afraid to let her claws out, and I'm not afraid to get scratched.

I tuck my chair in next to her, and she leans incrementally toward me. "Thanks."

She mumbles it tersely, and I offer her a gentle nudge of my elbow against hers. The meal carries on, and I get lost in the flavors. I answer the odd question about what I do—run a racing business. What my accent is—Romanian-ish. If the food is too spicy for me—no.

I love the whole thing. I only wish Nadia were here to see it. It might soften up that very jaded side of her. She grew up too fast, and I'm not sure how to slow her down now. A worry for another day.

"So, Mira, any plans to get married soon?" a woman from across the table asks. Her aunt, I think. Her father's sister-in-law. She smiles, but I can see what Mira mentioned. There's a level of judgment, and it makes me roll my shoulders back and sit up straight.

"Can you pass the naan bread, please?" I try to interrupt.

The woman hands it over as Mira leans into me. "Naan."

"That's what I said." I take the platter with a kind smile.

"No, you said naan *bread*. It's obviously bread. Like chai, you don't need to call it chai tea," she whispers to me, keeping the conversation between us with an amused curve to her lips.

"So, Mira? You never answered my question?" the woman cuts in, not taking the out I tried to provide her.

Mira rips off a bite of her *naan* and chews angrily. "Nope," she says through a full mouth. Like if she shoves enough food in there, she won't say something that she'll regret.

"That's a shame." The woman's eyes dart to mine before turning back on Mira. And I can already tell that what's going to come out next will be unnecessarily cruel. I slide a hand between us and take a hold of her thigh again. I'm pretty sure my hands belong on her thighs.

"You're so focused on your job, and you aren't getting any younger."

Mira goes completely rigid, and I let my thumb rub gentle circles on her inner thigh in an attempt to soothe her.

"You need to think about having babies at some point. You won't experience that fulfillment until you have one for yourself."

Mira's eyes narrow, and her mouth opens, but I cut her off. The part of me that has failed at protecting the women in my life up until this point rears its ugly head. "You know what's wild?" I announce to the entire table. "I've answered a lot of questions tonight. And it's been an absolute pleasure meeting every one of you. But not a single person has inquired about my family planning agenda or implied that I might be close to my expiration date on becoming a father."

The room is so quiet you could probably hear a pin drop. Have I gone too far? Some might think so. Others might think… not far enough. I smile and shovel a mouthful of lentils past my lips and chew thoughtfully, making sure I take a moment to meet the eyes of every single person who is staring at me.

My thumb never stops stroking Mira's inner thigh.

"I find it fascinating that no one has ever asked me that as a man, but somehow it's polite dinner conversation for a young woman with lofty career goals and an enviable level of focus."

No one says anything, but I see Sunny's lips twitch as he eats again.

I look back at the woman who started this whole conversation. She looks properly chastised, but I can't find it in myself to care. I have a vicious side too. A protective side. And just because I haven't been able to protect the people I care about in the past doesn't mean I can't start now.

"Maybe you can ask her about the premature foal she saved this month instead?"

I keep eating and feel Nana pat my leg gingerly before she gets back to her food. But it appears I was so busy glaring at everyone else that I missed looking at the beautiful woman beside me. The one who is currently boiling over. Tears glisten across the surface of her wide eyes, taking me completely by surprise. With a loud screech, her chair shoots back.

"Excuse me," she bites out before storming away from the table and heading toward the front door.

With her gone, I can let my fangs out. I can't help it—wolves raised me.

I dab at my mouth with the cloth napkin before placing it on the tabletop. "The next person to make that woman cry will wish they hadn't." I push my chair back calmly and turn to Nana. "Thank you for the beautiful meal. I look forward to meeting you again." Then I turn to Mr. and Mrs. Thorne. "Thank you so much for hosting me in your home. I had a lovely time."

I say nothing more because I'm spitting mad. I don't think I can come up with any additional nice things to say at this current juncture. Mira's father stands on my way past and shoves his hand into mine, shaking it with a firm nod. Sylvia looks like she might cry too.

It's almost exactly like Mira said. Lovely people, but so averse to confrontation they sit by for garbage like that.

Lucky for her, I'm not so lovely.

I stride to the front door and slip my feet into my soft brown loafers before heading into the humid spring air. It's sunny and warm, but it's raining. Fat drops of water fall from the sky, and I expect Mira to be waiting in my SUV, but she's not.

I scan the driveway, feeling the rain soaking in through my thin shirt. The urge to snap on someone is powerful right now. The look on Mira's face when that woman just kept going, even though she was clearly upsetting her niece…

Fiery rage burns through my bones as I recall it.

Never again.

A flash of white catches my eye on the far side of the yard. Mira is standing in the rain staring out across a field of low-growing shrubs. She looks tiny from this far away, fragile even. My feet move toward her before my brain even has time to catch up. All I want to do is talk to her. I want to whisk her away to the floor of a stall in my barn and stay up all night talking to her. Hearing about her hopes and dreams. I want to tell her everything.

I want my hands on her body. My skin on her skin.

"Hey," I murmur once I'm close enough I'm sure she'll hear me over the patter of the rain. Looking up above us, I see dark clouds circling the valley and the bright rays of sun stretching down through them, bathing us in their light.

"Stefan, please. Not right now."

"Mira—"

"Can you just not?" Her voice is tearful, and from behind, I can see her hands shoot up so she can press the palms of her hands into her eye sockets. She's trying not to cry.

She's so strong.

I step closer and touch her midback, right over the indent there. I can't explain why I find this part of her body so erotic, but I can't stop resting my hand on this indent. I trail my fingers up the column of her spine until they glide across the wet skin exposed between her shoulder blades.

"Stefan." Her voice sounds rusty when it breaks over the sound of my name. "You can't keep doing this."

"Doing what?"

The rain falls around us, muting any other sounds like a veil. A protective layer from the rest of the world. I watch a droplet of rain roll down the slender slope of her neck, tracing her body the way I wish I could.

"Making me want things I can't have."

My heart thunders against my rib cage. That's not the answer I was expecting. "I'm not."

She shrugs my hand off her body, but she doesn't step away or turn around. Instead, she groans and tips her head up to sky, loose locks of dark hair plastered to her face. She closes her eyes and lets the rain wash over her face.

"You are. You embody it. With you here charming everyone and then burning the place down to defend me… I feel like I could have it all. The career, the family—I could have someone like you. But that's not real. *This* isn't real. I can't have that."

"Mira, listen to me." I step closer to her. She smells like honey and fresh rain. "You can have that."

"People wouldn't understand. They wouldn't forgive me." Her chin drops to her chest now.

With the wild mass of black hair pulled over her shoulder, I'm stuck staring at the rain shimmering on her bare skin.

"Who cares?" My hands itch to touch her, and I don't fight it. I reach forward and grip her hips from behind as I drop my lips to the bone at the base of her neck. My tongue darts out over the droplets of water there, and she whimpers the second it does.

I pull away momentarily to watch goose bumps race out over her arms. A dead giveaway. "Tell me that's not real, Mira."

Her chest heaves under the weight of her breathing. With our height difference, I can see the globes of her breasts from over her shoulder. Full and round and covered in water. I can't take my eyes off her, and when she turns to look at me over her shoulder, her dark eyes aren't shrink-wrapped anymore. They are living fire, dancing with every shade of amber and burgundy and black. She looks almost otherworldly.

Her rose-petal lips part slightly as she scours my face, and I wonder if my eyes are the same. I wonder if I look like I'm starving the way she does.

"It's real." Her voice is thick and sultry, and I reach across her body and twist her toward me.

My eyes are fixed on her puffy lips. The way they moved as she said "It's real." I know in my heart, in my soul, that it is too. And I'm about done with pretending it's not.

I cup her neck and press my thumb against her jaw as my mouth crashes down onto hers. Her lips open for me instantly, and she goes soft in my arms. She discards all the resistance in her body like a piece of dirty laundry, dropped and forgotten on the floor.

We melt into each other. In a lush green field, covered in fresh spring rain, we give in to the pull between us.

I stroke my tongue against hers, and she matches my fervor as her hands roam my body. One shoots straight under my shirt, and her long fingers splay across the lines of my abs while she moans into my mouth. The other hand grasps at the fabric on my chest frantically, like she can't get a grip. Like she can't get close enough.

The world swirls around us, but we stand still, lost in each other. And, damn, it feels good. I knew we'd be explosive, but this is mind-altering. This is like a drug.

This is the best kiss of my life.

Frantic kisses turn languid and exploratory. I run my hands over her, luxuriating in the way they glide across her wet skin, and she wraps her hands around my neck like she never wants to let go.

I hope she never does.

I move my mouth over her cheek as I grip her head in my hands. The full length of her body presses against mine as she tries to move in closer. I pepper soft kisses up to her hairline and feel not an ounce of guilt over the scene I made at the dinner table.

This woman is about to be my undoing.

And I'll do almost anything to prove to her I'm deserving.

I'll burn it all down to make it happen.

"We shouldn't be doing this." She leans her cheek into my lips with need. "Someone might catch us."

I kiss her forehead and slide my lips down the bridge of her nose, cupping her jaw with both my hands as I tip her head up. "Good. Let them catch us." And then I take her lips again, swallowing the tiny whimpering sound she makes and committing it to memory.

I never want to forget this kiss. The feel, the smell, the sound of rain pattering while Mira whimpers into my mouth. It's one for the record books.

But then her hand slides down my back and disappears under my shirt. The tips of her fingertips trace the top of my boxers, sneaking just beneath the elastic.

This isn't one for the record books.

This *is* the record book.

CHAPTER 16

Mira

I WANT TO GRAB HIS ASS SO BAD.

How I went from wanting to get as far away from him as possible to now standing here, soaked, in a field, weighing the merits of grabbing the town bad guy's ass, I'll never know. It's a *great* ass, and I'm already drowning in a dunk tank of poor decision-making, so why the hell not?

I slide a couple fingers in between the buttons of his shirt to draw him closer. My other hand has been tracing the line of his boxers, but now I let my lizard brain take over and push it down between the back of his pants and the smooth fabric of his boxers. When I splay my fingers out and squeeze, he follows suit, fisting my loose hair and giving it a gentle tug. His ensuing chuckle is dark and velvety—thoroughly amused—like he knows I just bit off more than I can chew. I feel it rumble across my lips, and the corresponding shot zings through my core.

Our foreheads rest together as we breathe the same air. Suspended in the moment.

A shiver races down my spine, and he pulls me into a hug, muscular arms wrapping around me like a shield. "You're cold. Let's grab your jacket and get out of here."

"God. I really don't want to go back in there." The thought of facing everyone after pitching a fit and running out of the house feels like too much right now. Plus, I'm awfully comfortable where I am, and as soon as the cold seeps in from where we've spent the last several minutes plastered against each other, so will reality.

And I don't want to face the reality of making out with Stefan Dalca right now.

His hand strokes my back in soothing circles, and I almost want to purr under his ministrations. Because I am now basically a cat in heat.

"I'll go in and get it for you. Let's get you in the car."

When he steps back, I'm cold, just like I knew I would be. The damp air and cool water chill me to my core, and I wrap my arms around myself to conserve the warmth that Stefan's firm body left behind.

I want him to hold me again. It's a bad idea. We both know that it's a bad idea. That's why we walk in silence across the soggy grass toward the driveway. He opens the passenger-side door of his silver SUV, and I crawl into the seat. He doesn't even put his hand on the small of my back, nor should he. But my inner cat-in-heat wants him to. I love the way he touches me so casually. The way his hands linger on my body like I'm a piece of art worth savoring.

Before going to the house, he comes to the driver's side and starts the vehicle. He cranks the heat and shoots me a panty-melting grin before darting back into my parents' white rectangular house. His hand grips the wrought-iron railing on the front steps as he takes every second stair. His pants are wet and tight against his round ass.

I grabbed that ass.

It really is a great ass. And his upper body ain't bad either. Especially with a wet shirt clinging to every indent and hugging his broad shoulders in the most alluring way. I momentarily wish I was his shirt before scrubbing my hands over my face.

What am I doing?

When I drop my hands, I look down at myself and laugh into the quiet vehicle. I thought Stefan's clothes were leaving little to the imagination, but my white eyelet dress looks like a translucent slip. It's suctioned onto my body, and I'm pretty sure I can see my nipples through the fabric. And not because they're still pebbled from the way he devoured me. I thought this dress didn't require a bra, but I didn't account for the wet T-shirt contest we just had.

My head snaps up when the door across from me swings open.

"Got it."

I instantly grab the denim jacket out of Stefan's hand and cover my tits with it. He grins at me knowingly and shoots me a wink.

"Dick," I mutter as I turn to the window.

"What? I'm only human. Am I supposed to complain about my smoke-show fake date wearing a wet white dress? Because I refuse."

"Yeah. Yeah. Save it for the spank bank, Stefan."

His hand reaches across the back of my seat as he checks behind us before pulling out. "Oh, no doubt." He pushes the stick into drive and smiles. "I imagine you and Mr. Purple will have quite the time tonight."

Dick.

My cheeks heat, and I wish they didn't. I'm accustomed to acting one way around my girlfriends, but coming face-to-face with a man and talking about sex so blatantly is kind of new to me. There are things I want to do, want to try, but I've had such sparse and mediocre sex, I've never found someone I'm comfortable enough to try them with. Basically, my cool, confident exterior is a farce when it comes to that topic.

If I study anything hard enough, I can master it, and that's exactly what I've done. But I'm worried that Stefan is going to call my bluff.

"Are we going to talk about the kiss?"

"Nope."

"Dr. Mira Thorne caught kissing enemy number one in the middle of a field." He tuts me jokingly. "What would the girl gang say?"

I shoot him a dirty look because I don't need him rubbing my nose in that mess. I'll beat myself up about it enough later.

"How was it in there?" I ask as we turn onto the road and head back out to Ruby Creek.

"Fine."

I snort. "Very believable."

"It was. It was as fine as any of them deserve after that episode."

"Ugh. I'm sorry I put you through that."

He shrugs, eyes on the darkening road. "Don't be. I had a good time."

"Ha. No, you didn't."

"I did. Your parents are very welcoming, and I'm pretty sure I love your nana. The food was excellent. And the dessert was even better."

I laugh. I can't help it. He looks so damn pleased with himself.

"You have to understand, Mira," he continues. "The house I was raised in wasn't filled with laughter. I didn't grow up having family gatherings. There weren't relatives who cared about where my life was going. Are yours overbearing? Yup. Out of line? Absolutely. But they all care about you. If they didn't, they wouldn't say anything. I know because that's what I got."

Well, shit. When he puts it like that? "I'm sorry. My family problems must feel very trivial to you."

His hawkish eyes shoot over to me, glinting like emeralds. "Definitely not. Anyone who thinks they can speak that way to you in front of me is in for a rude awakening."

I swallow. For some reason, that sentence sounds very long-term to me. Like there will be future opportunities for someone to speak to me out of line with him in my presence.

"I know my mom loved me," he continues quietly. "She used to sneak into my room in the dead of night and wake me up to talk with her. Partly because that's when he'd be drunk enough to not notice or too asleep to care. It was also because under the cover of darkness, I couldn't see the bruises on her body."

My chest aches at his admission. That feeling where a crack fractures itself right down your sternum. What must that be like? To not have your mom there laughing and making inappropriate sexual jokes while making moon eyes at your dad. When I was younger, I thought it was gross. Now I think it's kind of inspiring.

I want to be making moon eyes at someone after thirty years of marriage.

"It always felt like a special time for us. A time when I could tell her anything while we huddled beneath my duvet. I felt safe with her on those nights. I felt like there were no secrets between us on those nights. It was in those moments she could be the mom I always wanted her to be."

My lashes flutter over full eyes. Stefan is confiding in me right now, and it's pulling at my heartstrings. "That's a beautiful and terribly sad memory all at once."

He laughs, but it's a bitter laugh. "It was." He shakes his head and presses his lips together. "Until she ruined it."

A part of me knows I shouldn't press him on this—it sounds intensely personal. But the scientist in me is constantly solving equations, and Stefan has quickly become the most challenging one of my life. "How did she do that?"

His eyes dart to me, and a look of vulnerability flashes across his face. He looks younger, more human, with a lock of golden hair plastered to his forehead and a pink flush to his sharp cheekbones.

"You don't need to answer tha—"

"No. It's fine. I trust you to not blab my history all over Ruby Creek."

I offer him a firm nod in response.

His chest heaves under the weight of a ragged sigh before he launches in. "He mostly ignored Nadia and me. There were moments when I remember thinking he was kind to us—as kind as someone like him can be. But one day, he turned on me. It had to have been the day it all came out. I don't remember when it started, but I remember the last time it ever happened.

My mother threw herself in front of me while I ran out to the barn and hid at the bottom of my horse's stall with my eyes squeezed shut. But not before he broke my nose. And when he found me cowered there, he promised to sell my horse. The stable hands marched the only thing that was truly mine onto a trailer that very day, and he was gone."

Stefan clears his throat and looks out the driver's-side window. "The next day, I packed a bag and started school in Switzerland. I was thirteen."

"Jesus." My hand falls across my mouth. "I didn't know you had a horse."

"He was mostly a pet. But he was *mine*. He was my best friend. My heart horse. My reprieve from my life. I could spend all day out in a field with that horse, pretending I was anyone in the world. A knight, a traveler—the options were endless so long as I didn't have to be a boy stuck in a violent home. On the bad nights, I curled up and slept on the floor of his stall in the small barn we had. When Constantin sold him to teach me a lesson… well, the only lesson I learned was that when a heart breaks, the pain never stops."

It's quiet in the vehicle as I absorb what he just said. I try to imagine a small blond boy sleeping on a stall floor, and in my mind, that boy morphs into the man I've seen over the past couple weeks. The one who will still sleep on a stall floor. The one who will hold my hand on a stall floor.

Stefan speaks again. "So I left at my mother's insistence. I left my baby sister behind in that house. Bandaged nose and suitcase in hand. At that point, it felt like a punishment. It felt like I was unwanted. And I suppose, in a lot of ways, I was. But now I can see it for what it was: a kindness. A way to save me."

His Adam's apple bobs in his throat as he stares out the windshield. I scan his profile, the subtle bump in his nose, and try to imagine him without it but can't.

"She met *him* when she was young and vulnerable. Naive and traveling for the experience of it. He was wealthy and alluring, and I imagine he put on a good show to lure her in. He excelled at manufacturing the perfect facade. She married him quickly. It was a whirlwind romance. She told me in her last hours he seemed wonderful until she signed the wedding contract. She told me..."

Stefan clears his throat, and his fingers pulse on the steering wheel, making the skin around his knuckles whiten.

"She told me she was already pregnant with me when she met him."

"Oh, shit."

He smiles ruefully. "*Oh, shit* is right. He needed a pretty young wife for appearance's sake, and she needed someone to take care of her. Pregnant out of wedlock, uneducated, and from a small town on the other side of the world. She did what she needed to do, I suppose. But it backfired when he found out I wasn't really his."

My god. How fucking sad is this? It sounds almost unreal. Like one of the daytime soap operas I would curl up and watch with my mom when I got home from high school. Stefan was hiding in a stall alone, and I was watching trash TV and laughing with my mom.

The world is a cruel place.

"And she didn't tell me any of this until she was on her deathbed, hooked up to wires and machines. That's actually part of the reason I came back here."

My head tilts. "What is?" I ask as the dark fields whip past us. We're almost home.

"She told me she wished she never left this small town. That she should have stayed and trained racehorses. I don't know… She wasn't making much sense at the end. It was whispers and broken sentences. Maybe I'm on a wild-goose chase." He huffs out a small disbelieving breath. "Just before she died, she told me my biological father used to be the bartender in Ruby Creek."

CHAPTER 17

Mira

"LISTEN." NADIA'S TONE IS SO CONDESCENDING THAT I FLINCH.

I'm jumpy today. I've barely slept for the past two nights. All the coffee in the world hasn't helped—in fact, I'm fairly certain it's making me worse.

"I can't read whatever kind of sign language these dirty looks are," I hear her say. "You're going to have to *talk* to me. Or write it down or something. Wait, let me grab my *crystal ball*."

I shove the swinging door open from the back room to stop her there. Nadia has been excellent her first week. She's a hard worker, a fast learner, and she has just enough of a backbone that the good ol' boy farmers and ranchers in the area don't walk all over her. Doesn't hurt that they're all too busy trying to impress her.

The girl is a looker.

But her charm appears to be lost on Griff. He's glaring at her from beneath his signature black cap. The man can wear a pair of Wranglers and cowboy boots like no one's business, but he's not chatty. He's a different dude, for sure. He trailers his horses to the clinic now and then for some work, spends a few days, and then heads back up to his cabin in the woods.

He's a mountain man recluse personified.

"Griff! Good to see ya. You got those samples we talked about?"

The man just nods at me, places a paper bag on the front desk countertop, and then struts back out the front door like he owns the place.

"Piece of work," Nadia mutters, rolling her brown eyes.

Brown.

It's all I can focus on for a moment. Stefan's eyes are green. Vibrant green. Like emeralds and bright spring grass and like… Hank's.

Fuck me. Now that I've seen it, I can't unsee it. Every time I close my eyes, I compare the two men on the backs of my eyelids. If it weren't for the bump in his nose, Stefan would be a dead ringer for a younger Hank.

Maybe I'm imagining it. No doubt, there have been many a bartender in Ruby Creek. But the horse-racing clue? I don't know. It just seems like too big of a coincidence.

"Do I have something on my face?" Nadia rubs at the corners of her mouth self-consciously.

"No. No. Sorry. Just tired. I zoned out."

"What the hell is wrong with that guy? He walked in here like he's some sort of celebrity, like I should know him. Wouldn't say a goddamn word. Manners leave something to be desired." She huffs out the last part like she's taking personal offense.

"Griff? He used to live around here."

There are lots of stories about Griffin, none of which I feel are verified enough to share. Small-town gossip can be unnecessarily cruel.

Nadia bristles and mutters, "Still a dick," before turning back to the computer.

She's been an immense help with organizing my schedule and keeping people paid up. It makes my life so much easier, and it doesn't hurt that I enjoy her company. Sometimes, I have to remind myself that she's only nineteen.

Stefan's nineteen-year-old *half* sister. Does she know? Man. I thought my family was fucked up. But my drama is minor league compared to the bomb Stefan dropped on me the other night.

And then there's the kiss.

This is why I keep to myself. Why I don't date. I dip my toe in the shallows, and suddenly I'm flung into the goddamn deep end. I'm at a loss for how to navigate this situation. What I know. My feelings. My body's memory of Stefan owning me the way he did.

I'm fucked up.

"I need to go check on Loki," I blurt out. Nadia looks at me like she doesn't understand why I'm running my schedule past her. "I, uh, won't be back. Can you lock up?"

"Of course." Her pale-gold curls shake with her head like I've asked her to do the most mundane thing in the world.

"Thanks." I grab my favorite brown coat off the hanger and shove my arms through as I head out the front door.

On the drive over to Cascade Acres, I mull over my best plan of action. For both problems: the kiss and what I think I might know.

The kiss needs to never happen again. I'll have to tell him that much. I can't handle it, and it's not fair to get involved with my best friend's nemesis. Perceived or not. Stefan and I can be friends. In secret. And he can be my client in public. That's what I'll offer him.

The next problem is less clear-cut. I could find out his mother's name and ask Hank. But that feels intrusive. He asked me not to share his story with anyone, and I won't betray his trust. I don't want to get his hopes up for nothing because I could be very wrong, and I don't want to drag Hank into something that might be nothing.

I think I just need to ask him more questions. Feel him out. Maybe we can chat in the barn. I'll make coffee, and we can sit on the floor.

I look forward to our barn floor dates. *Meetings?* Barn floor *meetings*.

When I pull through the gates, from the bottom of the hill I see his SUV parked at the house, so that's where I go. My palms slip on the steering wheel as the nerves creep in my stomach. I'm accustomed to having difficult conversations with people. It's part of my job description. But this knowing-and-keeping-secrets thing is killing me.

Having to keep him at arm's length is killing me too.

I pull up at his sprawling house up on the hill, and right as I step out of my truck, the front door opens and I'm met with the sight of a tall shapely blond in a tight pencil skirt and expensive heels, leaning in to kiss Stefan on the cheek. My stomach flips and threatens to push itself up my throat.

She's gorgeous. Standing next to Stefan in his expensive clothes, she's the perfect match. My baggy canvas coat and ponytail look downright grubby in comparison. I realize I know nothing about Stefan's dating history. Less than nothing, actually.

But this is perfect because I was drawing a line in the sand. *Right?* And I refuse to be the type of woman who lets this bother her. I'm good enough for him to kiss in a field, but in any other setting, we're completely mismatched.

"Just don't make me drive out to the boonies again. You can come to me next time," the woman says with a genuine smile.

My throat thickens, and my stomach churns. *I really am naive.*

"Thanks, Jules." Stefan chuckles and gives her a wave as she walks down the stairs before his eyes fall on me. "Dr. Thorne." His voice is warm and gooey, and I want to punch him for thinking he can use that tone on me after having another woman over to his house.

And then I want to punch myself for even caring. Maybe it isn't even what I think. Deep down, I have a hard time believing Stefan would do that to me. But I'm just far enough out of my league with him to feel insecure about it anyway.

"Hi. I'll only be a minute." I walk toward the front step and smile as I pass Jules. She smiles back kindly and gives a subtle dip of her chin. I don't have it in me to hate other women, so I tell her exactly what I'm thinking. "Killer shoes." There's one wide buckle across her foot and a matching one that wraps around her delicate ankle in a sensual-looking cuff. They really are hot. If I didn't work in a small town and spend most of my days covered in horse shit, I'd rock the hell out of a pair.

Her perfectly white teeth flash back. "Thanks! Just got them."

I reply with a small thumbs-up and continue my beeline for Stefan while she heads over to her sporty BMW parked around the corner. Of course she drives a BMW.

The sooner I can get this over with and get out of here, the better.

"Come in?"

"No. I can't. I need to check on Loki and then get back to the clinic," I lie.

He nods but can't hide the disappointment that takes over his features for a moment.

"Listen… I don't know how to phrase this gently, so I'm just going to say it. You can't kiss me anymore."

One brow quirks up as his arms cross, and he leans against the doorjamb. "Is that so?"

"It's inappropriate. I shouldn't have let that happen."

His jaw ticks, but he doesn't say anything. He just glares at me. Haunting me with those clear green eyes.

"I'm good with continuing whatever sort of friendship we've forged. But it needs to stay under wraps. And I'll honor my end of the deal. One more date."

"Mm-hmm." He sounds and looks pissed.

"You're not my type. And I'm not yours. And it will be better this way."

God. I'm rambling like an idiot.

"You're not *my* type?" Tension lines his body even though he casually crosses his foot across his shin.

"No."

"And I'm not yours?"

"Exactly." My voice comes out clear and concise despite the fact that I'm rambling inside. This feels *wrong.*

"And I'm not allowed to kiss you?"

"Really glad we cleared this up." I wave my hand with my truck keys and turn to leave.

He projects his voice across the driveway before I can hide in the safety of my truck. "Guess I'll be waiting for *you* to kiss *me* then."

Stefan Dalca is relentless.

★★★

The package Stefan had delivered to my apartment for our date tonight essentially gave me two things to do. And I'm not wild about people telling me what to do. Just ask my family.

But when I opened the shoebox, he put me between a rock and a hard place.

I already felt guilty because I didn't tell him my hunch about Hank. Instead, I turned and ran like the chicken I am. I was so unnerved by seeing a woman at his house and by his reaction to me dialing things back between us that my mind went blank. And now it's been a week, and I still haven't said shit.

The guilt is eating me alive.

It just feels like me sticking my nose where it doesn't belong. I'm good at listening, and I hear it all in this job. But I don't run around flapping my gums about it—especially when I don't know something *for sure.* I could hurt many people over an unverified hunch. It's just a hypothesis. I've done no research, and that's what I need to do. Find more information before I make a claim like that.

And then he bought me *the* shoes. The ones the woman leaving his house had on her feet. Hers were a nude color that matched her pretty flaxen hair. But these are black—a perfect match for mine.

I love the buckles. They're gold and chunky and feel so rich next to the soft leather. My inner teenager who wore heavy black eyeliner loves the classy punk style. I have no idea how he knew my size, but they fit perfectly.

A note accompanied the shoes.

> *Dr. Thorne,*
>
> *My car will pick you up at 5 p.m. on Saturday to attend the Next Chapter Thoroughbred Rescue Fundraiser. Our final "fake" date. It's a black-tie event. Wear the shoes.*
>
> *—S*

The defiant devil who lives on my shoulder says to send them back.

But I can't.

I'm going to enjoy the shoes. Because the only person I'm punishing by getting rid of them is myself. If I'm taking the shoes, I'm sure as hell not following his instructions to wait around like some sappy lovestruck date. This is *fake.* I'm more than capable of showing up at his place on my own.

So that's what I do. I hop in my truck and drive to Cascade Acres. Do I feel out of place driving my dusty work truck wearing expensive heels and an evening dress? Yes. But it makes me smile. Somehow, I feel very much like myself, a woman of contradictions.

When I arrive at Cascade Acres, heels clicking delicately on the rough concrete alleyway, the staff give me a few funny looks, but they continue with their tasks. It's almost quitting time for them, and I've become a regular fixture around here, so they wave and go about finishing up.

"Hello, little Mister Loki." I swing the stall door open and take in the two chestnut horses. "And you, sweet mama. How are you?"

Farrah bobs her head under my palm when I rub it across her forehead. She really is a sweet mare. And truth be told, I barely need to check on Loki anymore. I want to say he's out of the woods. But it's become part of my schedule. A habit.

What I don't want to admit is that I like coming here. The thrill of running into Stefan has become an addiction. I told him to stay away, and now I'm the one loitering around.

Stefan has stayed out of my way this week. I haven't seen him since that day on his front step when I told him we can't kiss anymore but can continue to be friends. Judging by the way his jaw ticked and his arms crossed over his chest like a shield, he wasn't happy.

But he also didn't seem deterred.

He hasn't been since that first day he asked me out, so I guess I don't know why he'd start now. He's been jokingly asking me out every opportunity he's gotten, and I've laughed and brushed him off. It's a running joke at this point. But it didn't feel like a joke last weekend. It felt like it could be the start of something with the power to knock me right off my track. Right off my wobbly high heels.

It's better this way, even if I secretly listen for his footsteps in the barn every day and my eyes dart up to the house every time I go to leave. I should be happy he's giving me the space I asked for, but I wish he'd go back to being completely relentless.

I think I might miss him.

Which is why the sound of dress shoes clacking against the barn alleyway sets my heart to racing. It doesn't sound like work boots or sneakers. It sounds almost like my heels sounded. I both dread and long coming face-to-face with him tonight.

My poker-face game is strong though. I just need to keep myself in a professional frame of mind, and I should be able to handle whatever Stefan Dalca makes me feel.

I set to work on checking Loki over, keeping my back toward the stall door so I don't have to face him when he gets here. I hear the stall door swing open even though the buds of my stethoscope are in my ears.

He doesn't say anything. I can feel him standing behind me. I can feel his eyes on my body, searing their way over my bare skin. Having him stare at me uninterrupted is unnerving. His presence is heavy. It presses on my chest and threatens to steal my breath.

And my heart.

I somehow count the heartbeats, even with the tall glass of distraction standing behind me. But when I turn to take him in, my mind goes completely blank. He's leaning against the frame of the stall door, hands shoved in the pockets of his bespoke midnight-blue tuxedo, doing that thing he does where his tongue runs across the inside of his cheek. His hair is slicked back perfectly, totally tidy, not a single strand out of place.

But his eyes are chaos. Brambles in the wind. Darker than their usual bright tone.

"You wore the shoes."

His voice is deep and sure—authoritative. Something I like about him. I don't have to be tough and independent around Stefan one hundred percent of the time. He doesn't think less of me for getting tired of being strong all the time. Last weekend in the rain was proof of that. He kissed me senseless and then still treated me like I was perfectly capable and not in need of excessive coddling.

"How could I not? They're beautiful. Thank you."

"At least you're walking through wood shavings and manure in them and showed up here all on your own. I'm not entirely disappointed. I fully expected you to wear a pair of sneakers just to put me in my place. But I still thought you'd maybe wear them one day."

One side of his lips tip up suggestively.

"Ah, yes. For all the fancy events this small-town veterinarian attends."

"Who said anything about an event?" He smirks. And then he winks. *Is he implying what I think he's implying?*

Loki chooses this moment to shove past me. With a small nicker he approaches Stefan and snuggles his head in between his body and his arm and rests there.

"Is he… snuggling you?"

Stefan smiles as he pulls his opposite hand out of his pocket and slides it up and down the young colt's neck. "Horses are an excellent judge of character, didn't you know?"

Loki nuzzles in farther. It's fucking adorable. Especially now that Stefan has confided in me about his horse as a child.

"We've become buddies over the last several weeks. Sometimes I sit out by his paddock with my laptop and work. He's so innocent, you know? My first foray into breeding wasn't exactly a success. I just want to soak this up with him while he's still here."

I swallow audibly. Stefan is so fucking misunderstood. Anger flares in me over how hard on him my friends are. If they could just see this side of him—the one who comes to my defense and snuggles baby horses—I just know they'd see him in a different light. It would be impossible not to.

He looks up just in time to catch me gawking, his eyes glowing in the most captivating way. "You are beautiful, Mira."

I glance down at myself, feeling like I could almost purr at his compliment. The way he looks at me makes my pulse beat in my throat. The wine-red slip-like dress does me an awful lot of favors. Slim-cut silk, it ends midcalf, and the cowl neckline gives me coverage where I need it—over my boobs, since a bra is a no-go in this dress.

I hold my hands over my stomach to still the lurching sensation. "Thank you. You don't look so shabby yourself." Which is to say, he looks fucking edible. Mr. Purple is going to get a hell of a workout tonight. "For a fake date."

His lips thin, and his jaw pops as he steps back from the stall, opening the door to usher me out. With one last pat for mom and baby, I step through the door into the quiet barn. The staff have now cleared out, leaving just the two of us standing facing each other in the stable.

Stefan's eyes coast down my body and pause at the floor. "Your buckle is undone."

I look down at the beautiful new shoes, grateful for the excuse he's just given me to stare at the ground and catch my breath.

"Oh, thanks," I breathe out. I definitely should not be breathless over a man who spent the night with another woman after kissing me the way he did.

"I've got it." With two long steps Stefan is right in front of me, one knee down and reaching for the strap. The sight of him kneeling before me unexpectedly takes my breath away.

His warm hand wraps around my ankle, and I shiver. His movement pauses, but his head stays down. I watch his fingers move deftly, gently tucking the strap back through the gold buckle. When it's back in place, he continues holding my ankle like he's entranced by the sight of my dark-red toenail polish.

But then his hand slides up the back of my calf, and he looks up at me, green eyes boring into mine with so many unsaid words, looking at me like I'm the most incredible thing he's ever seen. So much overflowing emotion.

My lungs seize, and I don't try to stop myself from getting lost in his emerald gaze. The seconds tick by as the pads of his fingers slide along the back of my calf. I feel the softest contact so intensely. The warm hum of electricity races up my inner thigh. I clench my core against the growing heat and roll my lips together to stifle a moan.

With a simple clearing of his throat, he stands, leaving my body begging for him to return his hands to my bare skin.

His fingers encircle my wrist like a bracelet. His lips press against my palm tenderly, and my stomach drops. Like it always does around him. "We should go," he says, letting go of my arm and walking toward the door looking completely unaffected. But me? I still need a few seconds to come back down to earth.

Something between us just shifted. I just can't tell for the life of me what it is or what it means.

All I know is that I wanted his hand on my leg to keep going.

I wanted his lips on my skin.

CHAPTER 18

Stefan

THE LONG RIDE DOWNTOWN TO THE VANCOUVER CLUB, SOME ritzy private hangout, is filled with tension so thick you can feel it in the town car. My intense attraction to Mira, paired with the lance of agitation I felt when she referred to our date as fake, makes me want to shove her flimsy silky dress up around her waist and bury my face between her legs—driver be damned.

I'd love to ask her how fake we feel after I make her come so hard she can't see straight.

But I won't. I said I'd make her beg. I said I wouldn't kiss her. Despite what she might think of me, I'm a man of my word. An honest man.

So we ride in tense silence on opposite sides of the black leather seat. At one point, the driver turns up the music to fill the space. I'm sure he thinks we're some couple who'd just had it out and hate each other's guts.

Little does he know the tension between us is because we both want to rip each other's clothes off. But Mira is pretending to be completely oblivious to our chemistry. She's smart enough to recognize what's going on between us; she's also masterful at avoiding it.

Maybe after tonight, it will be clearer to her what type of man I really am.

I tip the driver when he pulls up to the old stone building, and he beats me to Mira's door to open it for her. The man smiles at her and scowls at me, like I've been a prick—and I guess I have. Truthfully, I rage-played Mario Kart on my phone the entire way here rather than attempt to make small talk with her.

Mira just stared out the window.

I wish she'd tell me what she's thinking, but I know she's not the type of woman who spills all her deepest thoughts and feelings at the drop of a hat. That's part of what I like about her. She's like a vault, and once I figure out the code, I'll get that side of her.

I could keep her secrets. She could be soft with me. She could let loose with me, and I'd still stand back and let her be the fiercely independent woman she is. I don't want to tame her; I just want a front-row seat to watch her win the race.

She steps out of the car and thanks the driver with a gentle smile. I'm instantly jealous. I want her smiling at me, not ignoring me. I want her looking at me the way she did when I ran my hand up her leg.

I settle for letting my hand fall against the small of her back as we walk up the front steps of the opulent club. A small gasp spills from her lips when I touch her exposed skin. I'm accustomed to doing this when she has a shirt on, not a backless dress. And with nothing between us, my hand tingles and my thumb strokes the dip at the column of her spine of its own volition.

I can't help myself around her.

It's probably too cold outside for what she's wearing, and she presses into my side incrementally. I slide my hand farther, cupping her hip. The dress is so thin I can feel the lace strap of her panties through it.

We enter through the front door into the heritage building and take another small set of stairs toward the ballroom. Creams and golds line the crown moldings on every wall, and tall windows boast red-velvet drapes. Chandeliers drip with crystals and beads. The place screams money.

We stop at the door, and she looks up at me, slightly wide-eyed. Her makeup is heavier than usual tonight. Her hair is silky and shiny, like polished onyx. Whether she realizes it or not, she's the most beautiful woman in the room, and it's not even close.

"Let's go. Might as well enjoy this last fake date. There will be lots of familiar faces." The words are bitter in my mouth, and I try not to let the distaste show on my face.

Mira nods and gazes back into the room. "Then we need to keep a professional distance." I want to protest because I don't give a damn about these people. I want her right here, tucked into my side for everyone to see. But before I can say anything, she steps away, turning heads as she makes a beeline for the bar.

I watch the sway of her rounded hips, the swell of her firm ass, her dainty ankles in those heels. I want them propped up over my shoulders while I slam into her.

I roll my shoulders back and will my growing erection away. Something that's become a constant battle around Dr. Mira Thorne. I come to stand beside her at the bar in the corner, and the steady hum of conversation wraps around us, the quiet clinking of glasses, the odd round of raucous laughter.

People here are trying too hard. Unlike at Mira's family's house, where everyone was exactly how they are—even if that was meddling and overbearing. Every time I attend an event, it's a reminder of why I left this lifestyle behind me. Sure, I put a suit on for race days or for sponsorship meetings for the shelter, but generally, I live in jeans and sweaters so I can tinker around the farm. I feel safe there—like the version of myself I want to be.

Already I feel my youth kicking in. The schmoozing. The wheeling and dealing. The "I'll scratch your back if you scratch mine" chatter. Wealth impresses some people.

But I know better.

I'm here for one thing only. And I can see him across the room telling a story with animated hand gestures to a group of people who are pretending to be interested. A foot shorter than everyone here and a notch or two more obnoxious. The man is a predatory snake in the grass—precisely the type of man I have zero patience for in my life.

He plays checkers.

But I play chess.

A lesson Patrick Cassel is about to learn the hard way.

Mira steps up to the bar when the people ahead of us get their drinks. "I'll have a beer in a champagne flute."

The bartender, his brow knitting together, looks at her like she has two heads.

Her head tilts. "Did I stutter?"

The man jumps into action, shaking his head as he does, like he's offended by her request. A crack of a bottle later and Mira is reaching for her glass with a fake smile.

The bartender turns in my direction. "What can I get you, sir?"

I rub my stubble as I look over the fully stocked bar. "I'll have what the lady's having."

I swear the man rolls his eyes. Mira fails to stifle a giggle, and I find I don't care at all what the bartender thinks when she makes noises like that. When my eyes dart to her, amusement is written all over her face.

"Very classy, Mr. Dalca."

"I guess that makes two of us, Dr. Thorne."

I wink at her, and she can't help but smile as she looks around the packed room, taking in the women in fancy dresses and men in tuxedos, not missing a single thing.

"Lots of people I know here."

"Figured as much." I grab the glass off the bar and toss a tip down before taking a sip of my beer.

"It's kind of funny," Mira begins, though she doesn't look very amused. "There are several people here who aren't all that great to their horses. In fact, I'd say they're part of the problem with this industry. The reason so many young thoroughbreds end up injured and unusable. And yet here they are, opening their checkbooks like it absolves them of that responsibility."

She sounds so fierce. She isn't wrong. There is no shortage of questionable people in this industry.

"You must get tired of seeing that."

She takes a quick swig of her drink, chocolate eyes dancing with intelligence. "You have no idea." But now she's staring at Patrick across the room. For such a small man, he sure can project his voice.

I wrap my arm back around her, wanting to feel the line of her panties again, and usher her out into the crowd. My index finger absently slides across the thin strap. *Good god.* These panties must be barely anything at all.

When I rub down the line again, unable to stop myself, she leans into me. "Hands off. I'm not interested in joining your rotation."

She looks smug, but I'm downright confused.

"My rotation?"

She scoffs. "You know. Me on Saturday nights. The hot blond on Sunday nights."

"Hot blond?" I stop us in our tracks and, with a firm grip, spin her to face me.

Her eyes roll. "The one with the shoes." She points down at her feet. "Who was leaving on Monday morning?"

Her eyes dart behind me, and I turn to look at what she's signaling toward. Juliette Monroe. If Mira's assumption wasn't so absurd, I would laugh out loud. I stare back down at her fierce face. "Jules is my *lawyer*."

"Your… lawyer." She takes a huge swig of her beer and shakes her head as she looks out across the room. "You fucking idiot," she whispers to herself as her cheeks flare to match her dress. Although part of me wants to laugh, the other part wants to shake her.

I step in close to clear a few things up about us. About me and my intentions where she's concerned, but I'm cut off by one of the most annoying voices in the world.

"Well, well, well. Look what the cat dragged in. How's the offseason treating you, Dalca?"

I take a deep breath, eyes flitting to Mira's. She looks uncertain, but now it's go time. I turn and take one step ahead of her, trying to keep Patrick as far away from her as possible.

I smile, but it doesn't touch my eyes. This is the face I mastered as a child. "Patrick. Life is good. How are you?"

Patrick grins. His teeth are too white, and his hair too greasy. I can't for the life of me remember why I hired him. A winning record, I guess. *Too winning.* I've beat myself up about that enough.

Now I know what kind of man Patrick is, and I have no intention of letting him get away with it.

"Just great. Living the dream. Riding much nicer horses than yours these days. Guys like us always land on our feet. You bangin' the vet now?" He nods at Mira and grins at me, like he's begging for me to give him a nosebleed the old-fashioned way. A nice bump to match my own.

Mira moves beside me, her face calm and her head tilted at him like she's sizing him up and finds him entirely lacking. Condescension drips off her in waves. "Did you know that I can castrate a pig just as easily as a horse, Patrick? Even a little one like you."

Now there's something I'd like to see. I glance behind myself at where I saw Jules chatting someone up before. She's already looking in my direction and nods once.

I smile, except this time it's real. I'm going to enjoy this.

"Who are *guys like us*, Patrick?"

He chuckles like I'm being intentionally obtuse, but the truth is I hate the idea of being lumped with men like Patrick. It makes my skin crawl.

I roll my shoulders back and tug at the cuff links on my shirt before staring down my nose at the man. "I've often thought the best way to judge a man is by his actions rather than his words." Patrick's eyebrows knit together as people around us start to watch. "You talk like you've got it all. But the fact of the matter is you harass women with unwanted advances and drug horses to keep yourself in the winner's circle." His face goes white, and Mira's head snaps toward me.

Hushed murmurs break out around us. These people thrive on drama, and I'm about to feed the beast.

"Get a grip, Dalca." His tone goes frigid, and his watery eyes narrow, taking on a vicious facial expression.

"You're a disease, Patrick. A blight. And I've got all the documentation to prove it." A couple of officers appear from a back hallway. Just how Jules and I planned it. "You drug my horses, you face the music."

Patrick sputters but is cut off by the officer stepping in front of him. "Patrick Cassel?"

The officer explains the situation to him, reading his rights, suggesting an attorney. Probably a good plan. I'm going to love wasting my stepfather's money on burying this rat.

Patrick looks grim. White as a sheet. And then spitting mad when he meets my eyes. "This isn't over, Dalca."

"I trust it's not." I slide my hands into my pockets and smirk. "I'm just getting started with ruining you."

Patrick turns beet red as the officers lead him away in a shiny set of cuffs. They suit him so well.

"Unbelievable," Mira murmurs, mouth hanging open. "I was right?" She places her drink on a tall cocktail table and walks after him toward a darkened hallway at the back of the ballroom. A neon emergency exit sign lights the door at the very end of it. She looks stunned, entranced.

"You going to go to the station with him?" I joke. "Never took you for a rubbernecker."

"Are you kidding me?" She keeps walking down the hall, head craned to listen to the excuses falling from Patrick's twisted tongue. "You think I signed up for blood and gore as a career without being a rubbernecker? This is too fucking good. You don't even know how hard I'm trying to refrain from pulling my phone out to record. This is *gold.* I want to remember this night for the rest of my life. Best date ever."

When the door slams shut behind them, she flops against the wall with a satisfied sigh. And I don't miss that she didn't call it a *fake* date this time. "How did you pull this off?"

I smirk and puff my chest out, feeling proud of myself for how smoothly that went off. "The day you told me your suspicions, I had another vet draw blood from each horse I had living down at Bell Point Park. When they came back positive for performance-enhancing steroids, I hired a PI to find me the proof."

"Why didn't you have me do the tests? I could have helped!"

"Because I needed to have an impartial third party do the testing. You're too connected to Patrick to stand up in court. No chance was I getting you embroiled in this."

She rolls her eyes. "How honorable."

I take a step closer to her, knowing we're perfectly obscured at the very end of a dark hallway. "You know I'm right."

Mira looks at me, her eyes clear, with something like wonder painted on her face. "I think I might have been wrong about you. I think everyone might be."

Her head tilts back to keep eye contact as I take another step, leaving only a few inches between the tips of our toes.

"I think you've been wrong about me on a few counts, Dr. Thorne." I place one hand against the wall on each side of her, effectively caging her in. "The only reason my lawyer has been around so much is because she helped me organize this whole show."

"Oh." She breathes out.

"Yes, *oh.* But I do rather enjoy your jealous side. Do you think I've been asking you to let me take you on a date for the past several months just so I could pursue another woman after finally tasting your lips? Do you think I'd give up that easily?"

"No, I thought you were teasing me. I thought it was all a big joke. A game."

I lean down to whisper in her ear. "Absolutely nothing about the way I feel for you is a joke. And I'll keep telling you that until you believe me."

Her breathing quickens, and the silk covering her voluptuous breasts heaves beneath the weight of her gasp.

I lift my index finger and trace the spaghetti strap where it caresses her collarbone. "I'm just very, very patient. I know what I want, and I'm willing to wait for it. I don't mind biding my time until you catch up." My finger slides over the crest of her shoulder, and I feel her warm breath against my jaw as she tips her chin to follow. She's watching my every move, her eyes locked onto my finger. "It's a shame I'm not allowed to kiss you anymore. Because you look positively edible right now, Mira."

With one quick grab, her fingers twist into my dress shirt, and she yanks me toward her. Free hand wrapped around the back of my neck, she pulls my face to hers and kisses me with so much longing that my stomach drops.

The kiss isn't frantic. It's hard, and her mouth clamps onto mine like she's trying to steal my soul. It almost feels like an apology.

Apology accepted.

I use my tongue to trace the seam of her lips, and she moans. Her mouth falls open, and our tongues meet instantly. She jerks me closer still, and I revel in it. The event hums at the opposite end of the dim hallway, but here in the shadows, I feel like we're in our own little world.

Just the two of us.

Her soft breasts press against my chest, and I imagine sliding my dick between them one day, watching her round eyes go wide while her tits glisten. I let my hands trail down over them, featherlight. A tease. Her nipples harden through the thin silk while her soft lips move against mine.

Nothing about this feels fake. Our bodies. Our minds. Our hearts. Absolutely everything about being with Mira feels like one of the most real things I've ever had in my life. And I won't let her slip between my fingers now.

I'm going to make her come on them instead.

I pull away to nip at the lobe of her ear, and she whimpers in protest. "Do you remember what I said I was going to do to you if I had you up against a wall, Dr. Thorne?"

"What?" Her voice is pure lust, almost slurred.

"I told you that you'd be the meal."

CHAPTER 19

Mira

All the air empties from my lungs. The sound of my ragged exhale rushes through my ears, blocking out the sound of polite conversation and classical music playing in the ballroom. Stefan is smirking at me, like he knows something I don't.

And for the first time in my life, I think that might be true.

I wrack my brain, trying to think of the first time he asked me on a date. It's been so long that I can't even remember. It's become an ongoing part of our relationship, comic relief for the awkward tension that comes with doing work for my best friend's enemy.

Unprofessional? Maybe. Necessary icebreaker? Definitely.

I don't know why it never occurred to me that it might have been real. The way he looks at me. The way he touches me. The way he defends me. And now every interaction between us is hitting me upside the head like an awkward teenager with a dodgeball she never saw coming.

I've been dodging and deflecting for *years*, only to find out I was playing the wrong goddamn game all along.

The heat of Stefan's lips moves against my neck. Goose bumps spread across my arms, and I squeeze my thighs together.

"What do you say, Mira? Are you going to give me a taste? Would you like that?"

His mouth moves down over my sternum, a quick nip at the top of one breast before he crouches. My mouth dries at the sight of this perfect man working his way down my body. I usually have a quick quip or snarky comment at the ready, but right now, all the blood has rushed away from my brain to somewhere between my legs.

Every reason not to do this grows wings and flies right down the hallway.

"Yes," I say, throwing caution to the wind.

His teeth find my nipple through the thin silk of my dress, biting down gently before sucking, and a moan erupts from my throat.

"Quiet, Kitten," he murmurs, dropping to one knee. "I don't want to be interrupted."

My chin falls to my chest just as his second knee hits the ground. "Right here?"

He presses a firm kiss to my stomach before dragging his teeth across my hip bone. "I think I've waited long enough, don't you?"

My clit aches, and I buck my hips toward him. Stefan Dalca is kneeling before me, hands on my thighs, still looking so proud and polished—but just a bit undone. He yearns for me. I see it in his eyes. He does nothing to conceal his longing. And that feeling must be contagious. Or maybe seeing this man on his knees for me twice in one night is just too much to take.

"What if someone walks down here?"

He reaches forward playfully and undoes the buckle on my ankle. "Oh, look at that. Your shoe needs fixing. *Again.*"

Biting down on my lip, I check down the hallway one last time. We're fairly hidden here. And I'm already not feeling like myself tonight. My concern for the consequences slips away as I murmur, "Yeah, fuck waiting." And then I gather the silk of my dress in my hands, like I can't get it lifted fast enough.

And it must not be quick enough for Stefan either because he lifts what's left and disappears beneath a curtain of red fabric. Immediately, he pulls one leg over his shoulder and wraps his strong arm around it to pin me in place against the wall. His face is so close to my pussy that I feel the dampness of his breath against the front of my panties as his teeth graze my inner thigh. He clamps down, taking a quick bite that borders on painful but mostly drives me to tip my hips toward him again.

"That's what you get for making me wait so long."

"I'm sorry" spills from my lips, and I don't even care how out of character the words are for me. All I want is for him to keep going.

His spare hand trails up my thigh, and his deep chuckle vibrates across my core. "No, I'm sorry."

"For what?" I pant.

"For this." His top hand grips the waistband of my skimpy lace thong, and the other one reaches right toward the damp strip of fabric and pulls down. Hard.

The sound of my panties tearing echoes through the hallway, followed by my startled gasp.

"What the f—" The scolding dies on parted lips because Stefan doesn't waste any time putting his mouth on me. My head tips back against the wall, and the ceiling opens up in blackness and bright stars.

I'm officially having an out-of-body experience.

He starts slowly, keeping his tongue wide as he laps at me. There's no protecting myself from him with one leg slung over his shoulder. Every nerve ending fires, and I moan loudly before clamping one hand over my mouth and dropping the other onto the back of his head. Even the silk of my dress in my palm feels sensual. A match for the feel of his tongue sliding across my pussy.

"Delicious," he murmurs before gently nipping at one lip.

"Oh my god." My palm muffles my voice, and my eyes flutter shut at the feel of his lips and tongue and teeth between my legs.

He's a master, and I'm so far gone that my wanton hips keep swiveling, riding his face. All I can think about is how good this feels and how I don't want it to stop.

Which is right when he pulls away and trails his thumb over my seam with an appreciative groan. He presses down on my clit with firm, even pressure, and suddenly, all I want is to see his face. I pull my skirt the rest of the way up, grasping it at my hip, and watch Stefan's green eyes staring at me greedily. His fingers press into my thigh hard enough they might leave marks, while his opposite hand plays with my pussy like it's his to use as he sees fit.

I feel the heat from my cheeks clawing its way down my throat and across my chest.

His hair is disheveled, and his lips are glistening when he asks, "Are you always this wet for me, Mira?"

Good god. I don't think I've ever hooked up with someone so talkative. Maybe that's why every hookup so far has sucked. Maybe that's why I'm soaked.

"I don't think I've *ever* been this wet for *anyone*," I whisper back.

One side of Stefan's mouth tips up seductively as his thumb slides over to spread me open. He liked that answer.

Part of me wants to crumble because no one has ever looked at me like Stefan. So closely. But the other part of me wants to open my legs wider and give him all the access he wants. He doesn't give me time to think about it. His head tips down, and two fingers glide inside me.

"Fuck." My voice doesn't even sound like my own.

With Stefan's lips on me, I feel like a completely different woman. I feel like the woman I pretend to be, free of nerves and shyness. With his hands on me, I come alive, like I'm soaking up every spark that sizzles between us.

And right now, riding his fingers while he tortures me with his tongue, there is no shortage of sparks.

A familiar tugging sensation takes root at the base of my spine, and my legs shake. His fingers slide in and out of me rhythmically as his tongue works circles around my clit.

"Stefan," I whisper. "Stefan… I'm going to—"

He looks up at me abruptly and presses his thumb down over the bundle of nerves where his tongue had been. "Come for me, Mira."

One quick circle with his thumb and I'm gone. All the tension between us snaps as my orgasm overtakes me in a wave that crashes over my body. Stefan watches me. His fingers continue to torture me, but his eyes scour my face, my body, my every movement.

It's unsettling the way he's looking at me with so much pleasure. Like my climax was just as enjoyable for him as it was for me.

Shyness overtakes me, and I throw one arm over my face. My other arm hangs limp beside me, my dress still twisted between my fingers. "Stop staring at me!" I half laugh. I sound out of breath.

"I can't," he growls. Butterflies swarm my stomach as he leans forward and presses a soft kiss to my aching core, sending aftershocks through my body.

This man is going to be the death of me.

His fingers soften on my thigh and stroke soothingly before he removes it from his shoulder and leans away. His hand closes around my fisted one, softly, loosening my grip so the fabric falls back over my bare thighs and ripped panties.

"You owe me a pair of panties."

"I'll buy you an entire shipping container of them if it means I get to keep ripping them off you."

I roll my eyes and laugh. The nerves, the tension, it all leaves me in a girlish giggle. A sound I'm almost certain I've never made. "Maybe."

"Maybe?" He smooths the silk back down over my thighs and straightens my dress from where he still kneels before me.

"I mean, I guess I see what all the fuss is about now."

He rises, towering over me like usual, looking concerned. "Have you never had a man do that for you?"

My lips roll together, and my cheeks heat. He just put his mouth on the most personal part of my body, and I can barely look him in the eye or talk about sex like a normal adult. "No. No, I have. It was always just *okay*. Awkward. Even sex.

You know? Not a lot of it. Here and there. I tried hard to love it. But it just always felt okay. Mechanical maybe. Just not that exciting. Kind of boring."

Fuck, I'm totally doing an awkward ramble. He killed my brain cells like I knew he would.

His serious face slowly morphs into a cocky, panty-melting smile, and my words die in my throat as my eyes go wide. He looks almost predatory with that grin on his face. He leans in and kisses me slowly, softly, expertly. And I melt into him. I can taste myself on his lips, and it wakes something primal in me. When he pulls away, I try to move closer for more, but he chuckles and presses his lips to the shell of my ear.

"Boring? Dr. Thorne, haven't you learned by now that I love a challenge?"

No, it has definitely never been like this before.

"Let's get out of here." I grab his hand and tug him toward the emergency exit.

"What? You don't feel like networking out there?" His voice is thick with amusement and something more seductive.

"Do you?"

"No." He comes to stand beside me and drops his hand to the small of my back like he always does. I clench at the feel. It drove me to distraction before, and now it just straight up makes me crazy.

"Did I mention that this is a good look for you?" He chuckles and snaps the elastic waistband against my skin before leaning back to get a good look. The scraps of my ruined panties have apparently ridden up so they butt up against his hand. With a low growl, he tucks them back down and gives my ass a squeeze.

Perv.

I smile anyway. Reveling in his admiration.

"The only reason I brought you here tonight was so you could watch Patrick take a tumble off his glass throne."

A small laugh bubbles up out of me as we take the stairs down with a sense of urgency I can't explain. "How thoughtful of you to include me in your scheme."

"I've told you before… I'm not the villain you think I am."

"Or maybe you're exactly who I think you are and I like it."

His eyes sparkle and his grin turns wolfish as we hit the bottom landing and push out into the cool night air. "Maybe."

With our fingers intertwined, we search the pull-through for our town car. Something I can say I've honestly never done. Yellow taxi? Uber? For sure. Personal driver? It's kind of weird.

Especially when we find him and get in the car. Things between us were so tense before that the guy is shooting me skeptical looks through his rearview mirror, like he's worried about me—or my sanity.

I guess I can't blame him. We left the event early, and now I'm wedged up against Stefan in the middle seat rather than leaned against the opposite door staring out the window while he played Mario Kart. Yeah, I saw that. And he's fucking terrible. He obviously needed the practice, so I just left him to it so I could disappear inside my head for a bit.

We speed through the dark city, lights a blur outside the window. Twists and turns and bridges pass us by, but all I can feel are Stefan's fingers combing through my hair. His firm thigh pressed tight and warm against mine. The side of my breast against his suit jacket and the sticky remnants of our torrid hookup in that hallway between my legs.

The drive back to Ruby Creek is far too long for what I'm feeling right now. I thought it would cool the heat simmering in my veins. I thought I might come to my senses and change my mind about hooking up with my best friend's enemy, but the closer to home we get, the less in control I feel.

I drape my hand over his knee, fingers twirling nervously. If I could wish away all the fabric between us, I would. I want his skin on mine. His shoulders over me. His hands gripping my hips. I've never been so physically worked up over a person in my life.

Without even thinking of it, my hand glides up his inner thigh. My body knows exactly where it wants to go—where I want to be. The tips of my fingers trace the inner seam of his slacks. I can feel the hem of his boxer briefs beneath the expensive fabric, and I can totally understand how he felt the need to rip my panties the way he did.

How have I gone so long without realizing we weren't just business associates? It's so on-brand for me, immersed in books and work and taking care of everyone that I missed something just for myself.

No more. I deserve fun in my life too.

"Mira." Stefan's hushed voice is gravelly as his lips move against my hair. "If you don't watch that hand, I'm going to pull you onto my lap and fuck you right here in this car."

My lips part, and I suck in a harsh breath. I don't think I've ever heard him swear before, and I didn't expect it to make me instantly wet when he did. I peek down and am met with the impressive outline of his cock pressing against the front of his pants.

I'm definitely not going to be bored when Stefan Dalca finally fucks me.

CHAPTER 20

Stefan

Mira is driving me absolutely insane trailing her fingers up my leg.

The fields hurtling past the window of the town car are dark, and if we didn't have company, I'm pretty sure my inner caveman would come out to play and I'd take her on the spot. But I promised her I wouldn't fuck her unless she begged, and that's a promise I intend to keep.

"My place or yours?" I murmur against her hair. I can't stop touching it, so soft and thick.

"What about Nadia?"

"She told me she'd be out for the night, so she won't be able to hear you screaming while you ride my cock later." Her fingers pulse at my words. I love how flustered she gets when I say things like that.

"What if she comes home? She's my employee."

"Okay, then. Your place."

"We can't go to my place."

My muscles tense. "Why not?"

She shifts in her seat, shimmying her shoulders more upright rather than leaned in against me.

"It just doesn't seem right. What if someone sees you there?"

My eyes narrow. "Yes, how embarrassing for you."

She turns her wide chocolate eyes on me with a grimace. "I just don't know if I'm ready for that."

The practical part of me knows what she's saying is rational, and I'm not here to coerce her into sleeping with me. But the unwanted little boy who lives inside me feels a bit different about that sentiment. It feels like she's embarrassed. Like I'm a dirty little secret—and I don't like that.

Following suit, I straighten up and lean away. "Okay. Of course."

"I'm sorry," she whispers, turmoil flickering in her eyes.

I smile at her and weave our fingers together the way she did that night on the floor of a dirty stall. "Never be sorry for setting your own boundaries."

She nods and rests her head against my shoulder. "Thank you."

"For what?"

"For the best date of my life."

My chest warms, and I lean into her again, pressing a kiss against the top of her head as we pull in between the large gates at Cascade Acres.

"Just pull up next to that truck there. I'll walk up to the house."

The driver nods and does as I ask with a quiet "Yes, sir."

This time I beat him out of the car to open Mira's door for her. I feel like a dork for how quickly I rounded the car, but

I'm not letting this guy get his hands on her a second time. His sneaky looks through the rearview mirror happened just a few *too* many times on the drive to be merely coincidental. I'm not an idiot. I'm familiar with what's running through his head. I almost told him to keep his goddamn eyes on the road. A surge of possessiveness overtook me that signals how royally fucked I am where Mira Thorne is concerned.

Mira slips her hand into mine as she steps out of the black town car, and keeping her tucked close, I walk her toward her truck. She looks hilariously dainty and dolled up to be stepping into such a beast of a vehicle, but Mira is full of contradictions.

I don't want the night to end here—it feels unresolved—but I also know she doesn't need a man clinging on to her with a death grip. The crunching of tires on gravel filters in from behind us as the town car pulls away into the darkness. The floodlights on the barn are the only reason we can see anything as the clock nears midnight. Ambient light isn't a thing in Ruby Creek.

I look up at the sky while Mira digs through her small purse to find her keys. Every star is so bright against the blackness of the night, the constellations so clear, it almost feels like I could reach up and touch them. When Mira catches me staring at the sky, her head tips back, and I watch the ethereal shadows play across her features.

"Beautiful," she murmurs.

"Very," I say back. Except I'm not looking at the sky anymore. I'm looking at her, visually tracing the elegant slope of her throat. Her deep eyes, her full lips, and her glowing skin. She's downright enchanting. I've always thought so, but spending this much time with her and Loki has tossed me into turbulent waters I didn't see coming. I'm completely adrift with Mira. About to drown in her. And I'm not sure I have enough of a survival instinct to save myself. I'm not sure I want to.

I'm thinking I might be more than just enchanted with her.

My dick twitches, and I shake my head at myself. I've got a date with my palm in T-minus about five minutes.

She smiles at me now. I used to think it was a smirk, like there was something high and mighty about her smile, but now I recognize it as a defense. A facade.

I lean forward and kiss her cheek. "Thank you for the best fake date of my entire life," I say before winking and shoving my wandering hands into my pockets. Then I turn and take a quiet stroll up the driveway to my big empty house before I turn into the one begging her to give me a chance.

Still, I refuse to be dissuaded. I can handle hurt feelings, but I'm not easily deterred.

I know she's worth it.

CHAPTER 21

Mira

I AM STUNNED.

Did he seriously just call what happened between us tonight a *fake date* and then walk away like it was nothing? After I said it was the best *date* ever?

Fuck him.

His head shoved between my legs definitely did not feel fake. That line has been crossed. That line has been absolutely wiped off the playing board. And him lobbing that term at me like a grenade stung.

It stung worse than it should have.

I slam my truck door shut and fire it up. I need to get out of here before I kill someone. There are too many things in this truck I could use to commit a crime. And Stefan is far too close and unsuspecting to escape.

It's hard to make me angry. But when I do finally get there, I find it hard to come back down. My hands shake as I wrap my fingers around the steering wheel. Through the window,

I can see his dark figure swaggering up the driveway to his McMansion.

Looking completely unaffected, I might add.

Fucking prick.

Here I sit barely able to contain my rage, and he's all calm and polite. And I hate it. I feel like a fool, and I especially hate that.

I hit the gas and peel out of the driveway, sneaking one final peek before I turn out onto the road, and I swear his shoulders droop, his head tips forward. I'm not sure he meant for me to see that change in body language. Or the smirk slipping off his face.

But I did.

On the way home, my mind keeps wandering back to the sight of Stefan walking up the sloped driveway, the way his proud shoulders fell. The way he stiffened beside me when I said we couldn't go back to my place. The way he asked if he embarrassed me.

The ranch's circle driveway comes into view, and then it hits me.

I hurt him.

So he went on the defensive. And in his attempt to protect himself, he pissed me off too. All because we're both treading so damn carefully around each other, trying to keep things *fake* when they clearly aren't anymore.

For two smart people, we sure can be stupid.

He sure can be stupid. Too polite. Too patient. Too fucking perfect. It's annoying.

I take one loop around the driveway at the ranch and drive right back out into the dark. The back roads between Cascade Acres and Gold Rush Ranch aren't well lit, but I've been driving them so much over the last month that I feel like I could probably do it with my eyes closed. I speed. My lead foot presses against the gas like my heart thunders against my ribs as I pass through his front gates. This time, I drive right past his barn and straight up to his house. I jump out and pound my fist on his stately front door. It's cold now, but my adrenaline is pumping so hard I don't feel it.

The door doesn't open fast enough, so I bang on it again. I'm about to slam my palm down on it impatiently when all I'm met with is air. The door swings open, and Stefan stands there, brows knit together with a frown on his lips. He's so fucking hot I almost can't handle it. His cheeks are flushed, and his shirt is untucked. I almost just straight up maul him—but first I have some things I need to get off my chest.

His mouth opens to say something, but I cut him off. "You know what? Fuck you." His brows shoot up, and he rears back. "That date was not fake, and we both know it. So fuck you for saying that."

I'm worked up, and my chest rises and falls heavily. "And also fuck you for walking away like a perfect gentleman. Weeks of blatant sexual promises, and you walk away? You should have bent me over the hood of my truck and fucked me on the spot." I watch his bright-green eyes go dark. "Stop treating me like you'll break me. If I wanted someone to court me and bore me to death, I wouldn't be wasting all my free time with you." I stomp my heel-clad foot and feel completely juvenile as I demand, "Stop dicking around and show me what you've been promising."

His eyes roam the full length of my body, licking over me like a flame. And he definitely doesn't look confused now. He looks like he might incinerate me on the spot.

Stefan crosses his arms over his chest. "Is that your idea of begging, Dr. Thorne? Why would I sign up to be your dirty little secret?"

My tongue darts out over my lips. "You won't be."

His head quirks. "Doesn't seem that way to me. I thought I wasn't your type," he spits out, betraying his otherwise unaffected persona.

"Okay. You're mad."

His gaze flits between my eyes and my mouth. "I'm not mad. I'm… too invested."

The words hit me like a battering ram to the chest. "I'm sorry."

"Stop apologizing." His head shakes. "It's unnecessary."

I step forward. "I'm sorry I made you feel that way."

His jaw ticks, but he doesn't move, continuing to stand in the doorway like a sentinel.

"I'm sorry I took so long to figure this out."

I take another step, unable to resist his appeal. I've been moving toward him slowly this entire time. Since the first time I laid eyes on Stefan, I've been in his orbit. And suddenly, the pull is more than I can bear.

Right now, he's too close, and I'm too weak.

"I'm sorry you're too invested."

He grunts as I move into the entryway of his house. Mere inches separate us now. My teeth dig into my bottom lip as I weigh my next words. My fingers itch to touch him, and I follow their lead, reaching up under the tails of his dress shirt to his hastily buttoned slacks. The zipper is still open, and there's no doubt in my mind what I interrupted him doing by charging back up here.

I pop the button open and slide my hand down over his firm stomach and the front of his tight boxers where I can feel the swell of his rock-hard cock. "But not that sorry." I squeeze and feel my cheeks heat when he jumps. I meet his eyes now, but they give away nothing. He put himself on the line, and I turned him away, so I guess it's my turn to make it up to him. "Because I'm a little too invested myself."

I drop to my knees, feeling the smooth hardwood and the silk of my dress beneath them. "Let me show you."

With one firm tug, his pants and boxers slide down around his legs, and his dick springs free, bobbing in front of me.

"Mira. Get up," he growls.

"No." I palm his bare length, relishing the feel of his smooth skin against my hand. "I'm not done apologizing yet."

"I told you to stop apologizing."

I stare at him from beneath my lashes, feeling a strange type of power coursing through me as I kneel before him. *Is this how he felt on his knees for me?* Because all I want is for him to be thrusting into my mouth and whispering my name.

With one hand on each of his toned thighs, I let my tongue graze the drop of arousal glistening on the tip of his cock. He groans and tips his head back.

"Should I stop?" I ask with feigned innocence.

One broad palm strokes my head as he stares down at me. The night air is cool against my back through the open door, but the energy between us runs hot, crackling with electricity.

"No." His voice is so raspy, I almost don't hear his simple response.

But with that one word, I pounce, opening my jaw wide and taking him into my mouth. My tongue swirls and my cheeks hollow out as I suck. Stefan's hand is gentle against my hair while I bob in front of him, hoping to show him with my mouth how real this is. How badly I want this.

How badly I want *him.*

My hands roam his body. Fingers tracing the defined lines of his abs before reaching behind him to squeeze his ass. The ass I've been staring at far too much.

As I increase my pace, his fingers tangle in my hair, and his opposite hand scoops up my loose hair in a fist.

"Hard to have a good view of your apology with all this hair in the way, Mira." His fingers tense, tugging lightly at the roots, and my core vibrates.

I hum in pleasure at his corresponding moan. I tilt my head back and peer up into his eyes through my thick lashes, feeling his length bump up against the back of my throat and gagging slightly as I do. Heat flashes in his green irises, and I brace my palms against his thighs again before going soft in his hands.

He must feel the shift because he takes over, fingers gripping my hair to move my head in a rhythm that suits him, and I submit, loving the feel of him taking charge.

And excited about the way my body tingles, the way my dress feels too restrictive. Excited about the open door behind us—the thought that anyone could pull up to his house and catch me on my knees with his dick in my mouth.

Excited in a way I've never been until tonight.

His stomach and the loose ends of his dress shirt bump against my nose as he pumps into me, and my jaw aches in the most delicious way.

"You are so fucking beautiful, Mira. Down on your knees for me. Dark-red lips wrapped around my cock." I moan on his length, feeling myself melt for him, practically purring at the compliment and how undone he sounds. His fingers tug my head back, forcing me to look into his eyes. "But this is no apology." His eyes dance between mine as he stills in my mouth and brushes my cheek with his thumb. "This isn't even you begging. This is just you taking what you want." He leans forward, and his voice goes quiet. "This is instinct. This is *real.* And *you* want *me.*"

I blink a couple times but don't make a move. *I want him so badly.*

"I guess you're a lucky girl because I want you too. I have since the first day I laid eyes on you."

And then he moves, hips thrusting between my lips as his deft fingers cup the back of my head. My fist wraps around the base of his cock, and my opposite hand cups his balls, squeezing gently as we move together.

I press my knees down onto the floor, really leaning into him, wanting him deeper, even though it borders on feeling like too much. Too overwhelming. Like pretty much everything about Stefan Dalca already is.

His movements turn frantic, and within moments, he says, "Mira, I'm going to come." He tries to pull away, but I clamp a hand down on his ass and pull him closer. No chance is he pulling out now.

"Jesus Christ," he grunts, and then, with one hard jerk, he throws his head back and spills himself into my mouth. I feel every twitch, hear every garbled moan as he holds my head close to his body, and all it does is wind me up more. Is this what he felt like after what happened in that dark hallway?

Because this is addictive. Blow jobs have always felt like a chore, but that one felt like a drug.

I pull away and stare at his cock, feeling mindless with lust. "I want to do that again," I say without even thinking about it. I *need* to do it again.

The familiar sound of Stefan's responding chuckle makes my chest pinch as my gaze flits up to his face.

In one smooth movement, he drops to his knees, meeting my eyes and cupping my jaw lovingly. "No. Now it's my turn to take what I want."

He reaches behind me and slams the front door shut. The click of the latch sends a shiver down my spine.

It's the sound of going all in on whatever this thing is between us.

CHAPTER 22

Stefan

Being alone together in a quiet house, with no pretense of work separating us, feels intensely intimate. Mira's eyes widen slightly when the door slams shut. We're on our knees facing each other, and it's like she just realized she's in for one very long night. Sex has been boring for her?

Challenge fucking accepted.

I drop my mouth onto her puffy lips and kiss her. I taste myself, and I don't even care. It makes me feel like she's mine. I want her smelling like me, tasting like me, and looking at me with those round saucer eyes while I move inside her. I want her to be *mine.* Period.

The way she looks constantly surprised by our chemistry is such a turn-on. I hope she never stops looking at me like that.

Shocked awe. Lips slightly parted. Cheeks stained a pretty pink.

Her mouth moves against mine as our tongues tangle, and I slide one hand down over her ribs to where the dainty zipper holds her dress closed. I was happy to rip the panties, but this backless dress is going to make more appearances in our life. I'll find fancy places to take her just so she keeps wearing it.

Because she and I? We're just getting started.

Mira's fingers move against the buttons down the front of my shirt as we both undress each other. When I tug the dress off her shoulders, I lean back to get a better look. I always knew she had incredible tits, but seeing them bare right in front of me is a gift.

"Fuck," I murmur, tracing the feminine curve of her heavy breasts and the deep-brown nipples that are pointing straight back at me.

"Yeah," she says breathlessly, eyes roaming my upper body just as appreciatively.

I reach forward and palm one, squeezing gently as I flick a thumb across her nipple. "I'm going to fuck these one day."

"What?" There's the shy girl I've come to know.

I lean close again, kissing her neck and covering both of her breasts with my palms. "I'm going to watch you rub oil all over them." A ragged moan breaks out of her throat as I continue kissing along her jawline. "And then I'm going to slide my cock between them. Watch your gorgeous eyes go wide while I do." She whimpers, fingers shaking as they trail up over my chest, nails scratching slightly as she does. "And then I'll leave you with a pretty pearl necklace before I settle in for another taste of what's between these thighs. You'll never be bored with me, Mira. I can promise you that."

"Jesus Christ," she breathes out with a small tremble in her voice.

"I don't really care what you call me while I do it, sweetheart. So long as you spread those legs and let me worship between them."

She jerks back now, fisting my hair. "Stefan, so help me. If you don't shut up and get naked with me right here and now, I'm going to lose it."

A sly smile takes over my face. "Are you hungry, Kitten? I like it when your claws come out."

She shimmies the rest of the silk down over her hips, moving just enough to discard the dress on the floor, and sits back on her heels. Now she's kneeling in my fully lit foyer, wearing nothing but a pair of torn panties around her waist.

"I thought I liked the dress on you," I say, devouring the sight of dark hair tumbling over her shoulders and wild eyes boring into mine with so much hunger it almost knocks me over. "But now I think I might like it better on the floor."

"Lose the clothes, Stefan." There's an edge to her voice, an urgency.

I slowly remove my shirt, dropping it behind myself. "Is this your version of begging, Mira?"

She licks her lips and looks down at her hard nipples, the blush on her chest, the raised gooseflesh on her arms. Her voice is quiet when she looks up at me shyly and replies, "Yes."

My pants are torn off in a flurry, and I'm too ravenous to leave the hardwood floor of my entryway. Does she deserve better than being fucked on the floor? Definitely. But I'll make that up to her later.

I sit down and reach forward, yanking her into my lap, feeling her wet lips slide across the length of my erection. Her hips buck, rubbing against me again, and we moan in unison. My lips latch onto one nipple, and I suck.

"There's a condom in my wallet. Pants pocket." Then I dive back down onto the opposite nipple, sucking hard, swirling my tongue and then squeezing with my teeth. She's grappling with my pants, fumbling around with my wallet, chucking cards and cash all over the floor in a rush to find the aluminum wrapper while I feast on her breasts like a man starved.

"These are delectable," I murmur, wrapping my hands around her waist as the tearing sound fills the room.

"There," she breathes out as she pulls the condom out triumphantly.

I lean back onto my hands and watch her. She looks downright erotic, her heart-shaped lips all puffy and glistening, her eye makeup slightly smudged. And all I want to do is make more of a mess with her. She's a canvas, and I'm about to paint.

"You put it on."

"Me?" Her hands tremble as she looks around the room, but I don't think it's nerves. Mira's not a nervous woman.

"Who else would I want to put it on?"

The tip of her tongue peeks out between her lips, and she nods. Her hands are sure when she wraps them around my length and edges back a bit, carefully rolling the condom over my cock. Her hands look delicate, but with all those hours of professional training, she moves with confidence.

When she looks up, her long hair makes a curtain around her face. "Now what?"

The contrast of her vulnerability and confidence is such a goddamn turn-on. I can barely handle it. I reach out and grab her. Hands back on her waist, I move her onto my lap, my dick right up against the front of her pussy, resting on her stomach, giving us the perfect visual for how much room I'll be taking up inside her.

And both of us are watching. It seems like neither of us can look away.

I lift her slightly, feeling her nails digging into my bare shoulders, lining the head of my cock up with her slick entrance before I stare into her beautiful face. "Now you sit on it."

A small smile touches her lips as she eases herself down. What was frantic before suddenly feels in slow motion. She pauses after every inch with a small gasp. I've never seen anything sexier than the look of pure lust on her face as she takes me. At first, I watch her pussy, the way it stretches around me, but now all I can see is her face and the way her focus is fully on where we're joined.

Her lips are slightly parted, her eyes glazed with pleasure, and she looks downright fascinated. I'm not going to last if she keeps looking at *us* like *that*.

When she drops to fully seated, we groan in unison. I feel her pulse and clench around me. My head tips back and hers tips forward, her lips moving across my chest reverently.

Her hips swivel, and she moans. "Stefan." Her breath breezes against my nipple as her hands travel up the back of my head, and I can't keep my hands off her any longer.

Sitting up tall, I wrap my arms around her and drag her mouth into a gentle kiss. Mira's hips move in a soft twisting motion, and my vision blurs. I can't pinpoint what it is. The angle, the snug fit, the tense lead-up? All I know is that sex—two people coming together—has never felt so absolutely necessary as it does right now.

I've known I'm attracted to Mira for a long time, but my head is spinning with the way this feels like something else entirely. Her lips on mine, her hands gripping me at the same time as her cunt. Our kiss turns into just breathing each other's air while her hips pick up the pace. She rises and drops herself down onto me with abandon.

"Stefan, you feel..." She trails off, head back and fingers knitting around the back of my neck while she continues to ride me.

And for once, I'm speechless.

The sensual curve of her throat entrances me, the light sheen of sweat on her chest distracts me, and the way her tits bounce while she fucks me is my undoing.

In one swift motion, I pull her close and flip her over onto her back so I can be on top. "How do I feel, Mira?" My hand trails over her chest reverently as I push up above her. "Tell me."

I expect her to need some time to think about that. I expect her to balk. But her lust-drenched voice takes my breath away when she says, "You feel like this is how it's supposed to be."

I drop my head into the crook of her neck. The smell of her perfume is strongest here. It's intoxicating, something with licorice and honey. My tongue darts out as I pump slowly into her. "You are fucking delicious. And you are fucking right. Stuffed full of my cock is exactly how you're supposed to be."

A quiet chuckle filters into my awareness. "All that scolding about language, and you talk like this as soon as the clothes come off."

I smile against her collarbone and nip at her soft skin again. "You love it. And Mira?"

"Yeah?" she breathes, impatiently writhing against me.

I pull up, catching her gaze again, feeling the bite of the hardwood against my knees and the squeeze of her thighs around my waist, those hot-as-fuck spiky heels scratching at my back. "You feel like this is how it's supposed to be too."

She nods and rolls her lips together, but that movement blends into the shaking of her body as I thrust in hard. I rest one elbow by her head so I can watch her face while I drive into her. My other hand finds her clit and circles.

"Oh god," she cries out as I press down and continue with slow, hard strokes. Her pussy flutters around me. Soon, her legs shake. She's close.

Her legs clench, keeping me close, and I throw one leg up over my shoulder, needing to feel her deeper. My hand wraps around her ankle, brushing against the cuff of her stiletto. I turn my head and press a kiss to the delicate bone there. "I knew these would look good propped up on my shoulders."

Her top teeth bite down into her pillowy bottom lip as I slam into her, making her tits bounce with the force of it.

"Good girl, Mira. Come on my cock now." I give her clit one firm squeeze and she tenses, rearing up beneath me before dissolving into a tangle of trembling limbs and incoherent words. I can make out "holy fuck" and "so good," and it makes me smile as I brace myself above her and chase my own release.

Her hips move to meet mine even as she mewls and goes soft beneath me.

She's so wet and so warm, and I tell her as much. "You feel like heaven," I say as I slide into her body one last time.

And then it hits, and I drop my head onto her heaving chest as I spill inside her.

We're both sweaty and breathless as her hands circle around the back of my head to hold me close.

"Is sex always like that for you?" she pants out, awe bleeding into her voice.

And because I pride myself on being honest, I tell her the truth.

"No. It's never been like that. Not even fucking close."

CHAPTER 23

Mira

SORE AND GUILTY. THAT'S WHAT I AM.

My entire body aches in the best way. I've always seen that on shows or read it in smutty books—someone talking about being sore from having their brains fucked out all night. I thought it was fiction.

It is not fiction.

Stefan lies beside me in his spacious king-size bed looking exhausted after taking me over and over again until we ran out of condoms. Being a sex expert must be exhausting. The man is a fucking god. I'm a girl who lives inside animal science textbooks and peer-reviewed papers and uses a big purple dildo when the fancy strikes because I honestly don't think about sex that often.

Until him. Until his whispered words and searing glances. Now all I can think about is sex. This is a disease a condom can't save me from.

Obsession.

My eyes flit over his face. His cheekbones and defined nose. His dark dirty-blond hair all disheveled from where my hands spent hours hanging on for dear life. His lips swollen from me latching on to his face like a goddamn succubus. Or maybe they're swollen from the words that spill from them.

The man has a filthy mouth. His accent gets stronger, more sensual, when his walls come down. I'm pretty sure he could talk me into an orgasm if he tried, if he looked at me in the special way he does. Yeah, I'm almost positive I could orgasm on the spot from that alone.

Maybe if he played with my nipples too. The way he rolls them. I had no idea he'd be *so* into my tits or that covering up the way I do would drive him crazy the way he confessed to me last night.

He sighs and pulls me into his chest. Nothing about Stefan is simply what meets the eye. He's complicated and fascinating, and god, he's really not boring. He's beautiful—I've always thought so. The accent, the smirk, the mysterious background. Nobody prepared me for the fact he'd be equally alluring and beautiful on the inside.

He's addictive.

I snuggle in close, the smell of his mint soap from the shower last night wrapping around us as I try to escape the sense of looming guilt closing in on me. Not guilt for sleeping with him. I truly cannot bring myself to feel bad about that. Though I'm not looking forward to everyone inevitably finding out. That's probably something I'll put off for a while yet. I need to wait and see where this goes.

I feel the light dusting of hair on his chest against my cheek as I close my eyes. I can see his face above mine last night while he moved over me, giving me more pleasure than I've ever experienced.

I was mindless in the moment. But the memory haunts me. The green eyes. The knowledge he's looking for his biological father. Knowing I have a hunch and haven't disclosed it makes my stomach burn. I need to figure this out, and fast. It's a terrible secret to keep. But blowing up multiple people's lives when I could be wrong isn't ideal either. I need to stick to my plan, my hypothesis followed by a proper inquiry so I don't make an ass of myself.

He'll never forgive me if I'm wrong. Too many people in his life have let him down, lied to him. He talks about protecting the people around him, but it sounds to me like no one has ever protected *him*. I don't want to cause him pain. When I tell him about this, I want to be sure. And after lying here for the past hour mulling it over, I don't think anything less than sure is a risk I'm willing to take. Anything less is not what he deserves.

I need to play it safe with Stefan Dalca because I don't want to lose whatever it is that we've just found.

"Stop squirming or you'll force me to fuck you again." Stefan's voice is sleepy against the top of my head, and his legs tangle with mine, clamping them down into the memory-foam mattress.

I giggle quietly and feel his hips grind forward, his erection rubbing against my stomach. "You're out of condoms, remember?"

"Careful handing me a challenge like that, Mira. I'm full of ideas that don't require a condom at all. That's hardly a deterrent."

His fingers trail down my arm, and my skin pebbles beneath his touch. "Tell me about this tattoo." His voice is all gruff and sleepy, and butterflies erupt in my stomach. "What does it mean?"

I giggle quietly, watching his finger trace the outline of the black floral design on the inside of my forearm. "It doesn't mean anything. My parents told me I couldn't get a tattoo when I asked for one, so I went out and found someone who would give me one without their permission anyway."

He hums thoughtfully before lifting my hand and pressing a quick kiss to my palm before resting it against his cheek. "Fascinating that you still think it means nothing."

"What do you mean?" I look up at him, and his eyes glow with such intensity, his beauty is consuming—it steals my breath just to look at him this closely. This intimately.

That signature devil-may-care grin graces his lips, and then his mouth is against the ornate ink on my arm, lips and tongue tracing the lines in a way that has me squeezing my thighs together. "This right here is proof that you are your own woman," he says against my skin. "No one tells Dr. Mira Thorne what she can and can't do."

I try to change the direction of our conversation, feeling suddenly jumpy in the presence of someone who can turn me to putty in his hands while also reading me so damn easily. Someone whose vision is like a laser through every shield I've erected. Someone who appreciates my rebellious streak—encourages it even.

"What's with you always kissing my palm?"

His eyes meet mine once again, and his responding smile is soft and vulnerable; completely oblivious to my inner turmoil.

Instead of replying right away, he runs his fingers over top of mine, still watching his skin slide against my own with a look of quiet awe on his face.

"You have beautiful hands. Almost as beautiful as your mind and heart. Sometimes I find myself staring at them while you work, so elegant and strong all at once. Hands that heal. Hands that save lives." His voice drops. "Hands that belong in mine."

My heart races, and my body heats. I swear it's like he uncovered some secret button on me and knows exactly how to push it. He makes me feel treasured. I get this indulgent side of him that no one else sees. I feel like I'm in on a secret. One that I want to keep for myself—to revel in.

"See? You like that plan. I can tell by the little sigh you just made," he grumbles, lifting my palm to press a reverent kiss right to the center, his lashes fluttering shut as he does.

I didn't even notice the sigh. I must sound like a lovesick teenager.

"It's true. You promised me I wouldn't be bored, and I'm not."

One eye flicks open as he looks down at me. "You really thought sex was boring?"

"It was always… fine? Like… nice? But not something I felt like I couldn't go without. My mind would always wander somewhere else. Like a diagnosis I couldn't figure out or what was going to happen on the next *Grey's Anatomy*. It just wasn't a priority. I'm too busy to worry about sex. Still am."

He chuckles like he doesn't believe me. "Okay, Dr. Thorne."

"What?" I bristle. "I am. Better sex doesn't make me any less busy."

"Better? Is that all?" He lifts up to rest his head in his palm and smirks down at me.

If I were wearing panties, they would melt for a smile like that. Instead, we're both tangled up in each other, completely naked, and now I'm feeling like that was a colossally stupid idea. Even a single layer of protection would have kept his hand from gliding across my bare skin, from cupping my ass and sliding a finger through my slick core.

"You're awfully wet for someone who is just barely better than bored."

I say nothing as his fingers continue their exploration, spreading my wetness over my lips as proof of how completely full of lies I am.

"Do you often get this wet for men who aren't your type, Dr. Thorne?"

My head snaps to him. "Stop saying that." I don't like him saying that. I meant it to push him away, and now it's not true. It's so damn far from the truth. And I'm done pushing this beautiful, complex man away.

"Why?" His green eyes glitter as they move between mine knowingly.

"You know why." I roll my eyes, body wound tight.

Stefan flips me flat onto my back. "I don't think I do. You're like a safe, and I think I'm close to figuring out the combination. So don't worry, Mira. I'm going to get in there and learn all your secrets. I'll keep them for you, too. Especially the one about me being *exactly* your type."

And with that, he winks and disappears beneath the covers.

My walks of shame usually just refer to drunkenness. Smudged makeup. Maybe a broken heel on my shoe due to said inebriation.

A fancy backless dress and missing panties just slap a little differently, and I pray no one sees me as I race up the stairs to my apartment above the barn with my fancy stilettos in hand. Stefan offered some spare clothes or to "borrow" something from Nadia. Both options seemed even more obvious to my sex-addled mind.

I fumble with my keys, cursing under my breath as they drop to the landing. "Motherfucker." I don't even risk looking around myself. I pick up the keys and get through the door before slamming it behind me and leaning up against it. A deep sigh leaves my chest, and I let my eyes close as I lean my head back.

Once I get my bearings, I open my eyes and look around the tiny apartment. I'm home, but it feels very empty and very quiet. A bit lonely even. My friends are paired off, connected at the hip to their men and loving it, and I just left the house of the only man who has ever made me feel something for no reason other than I needed some goddamn space. Tearing myself away from him after one night of mind-blowing sex was already hard enough.

I need *space.* And to think.

My phone pings, and I pick it up.

Violet: Don't forget it's girls' night!

Goddammit. How did I forget? And why does it have to be after pulling an all-night sex-a-thon with the man they all hate?

Violet: I invited Nadia too. Hope that's okay!

Fuck. This is going to be awkward. My thumbs fly across the screen.

Mira: Of course that's okay. We going to Neighbor's?

The pub is our go-to hangout.

Violet: Nah. The Paddock. Nadia said she doesn't really drink, and I thought that might be more low-key. I'm tired, but I need a break. 7 p.m.? I won't last late.

I'm not sad that we're going to our favorite field to drink and chat. It's honestly my favorite meeting spot.

Mira: See you then, hot mama.

Violet: It's cute that you call me hot when we both know I just look eternally exhausted.

Violet loves this new chapter of her life. But being a full-time jockey and mom to a baby is hard work. She's lucky she has Cole, who might be the most attentive husband and father of all time. I absently wonder what type of father Stefan would be as I let my dress fall to the floor, shaking my head at myself. *Pathetic.* I crawl into bed, determined to catch some hours of actual sleep before I make an appearance and try not to seem super guilty around my closest friends. But when I close my lids, all I see is Stefan and his beautiful green eyes.

My new favorite color.

When I wake up, I'm distracted. Not feeling like myself. The problem is… I don't want to go to girls' night. I want to go to Stefan's house. I want to fall into his bed. I want him to wrap his arms around me so I can disappear into him. I feel like a child who's just gone through a developmental leap. I can firmly say I have *never* felt like this about a guy before.

Especially not one I shouldn't be tangling myself up with.

Especially one I'm keeping secrets from. Or whom I'm keeping secret.

It feels dirty. It feels like an injustice to a man who has done nothing but go out of his way to help me, to defend me, to soothe me.

It's a fucking trip, is what it is.

I lock the door behind me and jog down the narrow set of stairs to the ground floor. The ranch is quiet, the horses are in safely for the night, the ones who are prepping for the upcoming season are living down at the track for their training regimen, and all the staff have gone home for the day.

There's still a spring nip in the air this close to the mountains. I pull my oversize canvas coat tightly around my body and consider going back for an extra blanket, but when I round the corner of the barn and look down the grass pathway to the paddock where we meet up sometimes, a bright fire catches my eye. The three girls are already there, and it's looking like they've got a pretty cozy setup, which is new.

This whole thing started when Billie was hired as the trainer here at Gold Rush Ranch. According to her, she spent her first night on the farm lying on a blanket by her new project horse's paddock with a bottle of wine, a loaf of bread, and a wheel of cheese.

Now we just keep the tradition going. It's cozy, and as someone who hasn't had a lot of friends, I love the simplicity of it. Just good people and simple food under the open air of Ruby Creek. I hope we're still lying here drinking wine out of the bottle when we're old and gray.

Assuming they don't hate me when they find out I've been fucking the enemy.

"What have we got here?" I ask as I approach the group.

Violet smiles softly and runs her fingers through her hair. "I said I was cold when Cole walked me down here. A few minutes later, he pulled up to the barn with lawn chairs and a fire bowl."

Good lord. Cole Harding is such a goner.

"He carried this all down here for us?"

Billie laughs as she cracks open a bottle of wine. "Have you seen the guy? He's built like a tank. I think he enjoys carrying heavy stuff for fun in his free time. He's also totally pussy-whipped."

Chuckles erupt, and Violet's cheeks go pink as she rolls her eyes. "Vaughn is no better. Care to tell the class what he's doing tonight?"

I drop into the empty chair and wink at Nadia, who looks happy but a little out of place. "Let's hear it, B."

She takes a swig of wine straight from the bottle because according to her it "tastes better that way." With a deep sigh, she passes it over to me and says, "He's planning our wedding."

I almost spray wine out my nose. "He what?"

Trying to avoid eye contact, she rifles through the backpack at her feet and pulls out a loaf of French bread. "You heard me. He's planning the wedding because I don't care about our wedding and my parents and Vaughn do. So I told them to plan it and tell me where to be when the day comes."

My brow furrows. "Billie, I'm well aware you're not a weddings-and-babies type of person, but don't let other people tell you what your day should be like."

"I'm not." She shrugs as she rips a chunk of bread off before topping it with a slice of cheese from the plate in her lap. "I just don't care. I'd marry Vaughn tomorrow, right here in this field. And he knows that, but he has a better sense of duty than I do. He's also my mother's dream. Listening to them talk to each other makes me wish I could have fallen in love with someone who would have been a disappointment to them." Violet snorts, and Billie hits her with a grin. "Either way, he can handle her, and I can't. So he can taste the cakes and worry over invite fonts. I'd rather be here, doing this."

"Cheers to that." I hold the bottle of red wine up and then go to hand it to Violet.

She just shakes her head with a shy smile. I check to see that everyone is distracted with their food before quirking one brow at her. She nods and looks away, cheeks and chest going crimson.

Dang. Another baby Harding on the way already.

I give Violet's knee a quick squeeze before whispering, "I'm so happy for you."

She smiles so hard I think her face might crack open. No wonder Cole was out here setting up a whole fire and chairs for her. Papa Bear is feeling protective.

I hand the wine back to Billie since Vi obviously doesn't want this announced. "How about you, Nadia? How's life in Ruby Creek treating you now that we got that pesky principal off your back?"

She gives me a conspiratorial, pleased look. Her golden tresses pulled up in a messy bun make her appear younger than when her wild curls flow down to her shoulders. "That was fun."

"It was."

"What did you guys do?" Violet asks, leaning forward from under her blanket, looking all wide-eyed and innocent.

"We, uh…" I glance over at Nadia, and she shrugs. I figure if we were going to get in trouble for this, we would have by now. "We egged her principal's car."

Violet gasps, and Billie cackles before asking, "Why?"

"Because he's a sexist pig," Nadia bites out, clearly still miffed about her humiliating ordeal.

"Yes! I knew I liked you, Nadia," Billie says before holding her bottle of wine up over the fire in a cheer. "Here's to taking out all the sexist pigs."

Nadia raises her soda in response.

"Hear, hear!" I call as we all dissolve into a fit of giggles.

Silence descends as we all work on getting some food in us. Chugging wine on an empty stomach is a rookie move. And we're all too old for that shit.

"Speaking of sexist pigs… I was at the second-chance fundraiser last night," I tell them. "Patrick Cassel was arrested."

"What?" Billie drops her food onto the plate and stares at me, mouth agape. "What for?"

"Doping horses without their owners' consent or knowledge, among other things, I assume."

A low whistle erupts from Billie's lips. "Goddamn. I knew that guy was a piece of shit, but that's really just the cherry on top, isn't it?"

"Yeah. My brother has been slaving over taking that guy down for months," Nadia mumbles over a mouth full of food.

My eyes go wide, and Billie's head whips to her. "Stefan?"

She nods right as Violet pipes up, "You make him out to be a lot worse than he is, B. Your grudge-holding ability is next level."

All I can hear is my heart pounding in my ears. This is toeing the line awfully close to my secrets spilling out. And with a warm buzz coursing through me, I wonder if it would be so bad to just get it off my chest. Just blurt it out and get it out in the open.

"I hate that fucking guy," Billie grumbles as she rips at her bread again.

"Hey, hey, hey now, that's my big brother you're talking about," Nadia chimes in just as Violet scolds her with a whisper-shout, "Billie!"

I take a contemplative swig of wine. A really big one. "You realize he saved your horse, right?"

She scoffs, agitation lining her every movement. Billie *is* a championship grudge holder. Ask her parents. I appreciate that she's got her baggage, her reasons, but I'm feeling protective of Stefan. The Stefan I know doesn't deserve that kind of treatment.

"We'd have figured something out," she says. "The guy is a slimy fucking snake in the grass."

My cheeks heat with indignance. "No. That foal would have died."

She rolls her eyes and chuckles, trying to lighten the mood. "Okay, Mira. When you're done fondling Dalca's balls for doing us one little favor, let me know."

I take another large swig and then rest my head back on the chair, looking up at the darkening sky, feeling the heat of the fire soak into my bones. "I did a lot more than fondle his balls."

Violet spews water all over herself.

Nadia groans and shakes her head with a small smile. "Fucking gross. I knew it."

Billie stares at me, shock painting her pretty features. "Please tell me you're joking."

"Sorry, B. No joke."

"Okay…" She settles back in her chair, pressing her lips together. Clearly mulling over what to say next. She steeples her hands in front of her face, tapping her fingers on her nose before pointing them back at me. "Is this you going deep cover? Like when a CIA agent bangs the bad guy to uncover enemy secrets? Because I could probably admire your commitment."

I tilt my head to the side and smile at her with sadness. I recognize she's not going to like this, but when have I ever done things the way other people wanted me to? "No, B. It's…"

I worry my bottom lip between my teeth as I search for the right label for Stefan and me.

"It's real."

CHAPTER 24

Mira

I FEEL LIGHTER WALKING BACK TO MY LOFT APARTMENT ABOVE the barn. Actually, I feel almost giddy. Part of that is the wine, and part of that is just the general feeling of relief at ditching one of the secrets that's been weighing on me. I didn't like lying to my friends, and I didn't like treating a man who's been nothing but incredible to me like I was ashamed of him.

The fact of the matter is, I'm not ashamed of Stefan Dalca. *At all.*

Luckily, Billie sort of let it go after I dropped that atomic bomb on girls' night.

She tossed out a joking "Well, you know what they say: love is blind!" and then dropped the topic altogether. She probably needs to sleep on it. The conversation moved on easily after that, though I didn't miss the curious smiles Violet was shooting my way or the way Nadia chuckled and shook her head when she hugged me goodbye.

Everyone had something to say, but no one said a thing.

And now I'm back in my apartment. Alone and all amped up. Positively fixated on how badly I want to see Stefan.

Before I talk myself out of it, I pull my phone out and fire off a text to him. I'm tired of holding myself back.

Mira: What are you doing?

Text dots roll across the screen almost instantly.

Stefan: Plotting evil ways to ruin your friends' lives. You?

I snort.

Mira: Dork. Come visit me.

Stefan: At your place?

I scan the small space. Cat's out of the bag where my friends are concerned, so why the hell not?

Mira: Yes.

Stefan: Why?

Why? That's not exactly the response I was going for. Now I feel uncertain. Out of my depth.

Mira: Okay, don't. I'll be there to check on Loki tomorrow.

I toss my phone down on my bed, feeling a tad huffy. I'm terrible at asserting myself with Stefan. I'm too inexperienced. I take things too personally. I want him to pick up on all my innuendo so I don't have to admit out loud I want him more than I care to admit. Like a total sucker, I pick up my phone to check if he's said anything.

Stefan: Do you miss me, Dr. Thorne?

Groaning, I scrub a hand across my face. *Do I miss him?* It's been about twelve hours since I saw him. Missing him already would be so fucking lame.

My eyes spring open.

I am so fucking lame.

I reel with the realization. I've spent so much time at his farm, working with him, going on fake dates with him, he's become a staple in my day without me even realizing it. A nervous breath shudders through me as I type back my response.

Mira: Yes.

And then I sit and stare at the screen. The blank screen. No dots roll. No messages come through. My throat burns, and I squeeze my hand on it to stem the flow of embarrassment. I shouldn't have been so straight with him. He must think I'm fucking nuts.

I get up and walk across the hall to the small bathroom where I aggressively brush my teeth.

Yes. Why did I have to say yes? I'm officially that girl who had sex with a guy once and is acting like a clingy psycho. No wonder he didn't respond.

As I wash my face, I realize I wouldn't respond to me either. If a guy told me that after one night, I would run in the opposite direction with my career and independence clutched in my fists. So I can't blame him.

A loud banging on the door startles me, and I instantly dread the thought that Billie is here to tell me off for hooking up with the enemy. I'll have to tell her she was right. That I'm nuts and he was a bad idea.

But when I swing the door open, the person standing there is Stefan.

"Hi—"

The crash of his lips against mine cuts off anything I was about to say. He steals my breath and commands my body. His muscular arms wrap around me the exact way I wanted them to, his day-old stubble scratching against my face as he devours me.

His hands palm my ass, and he lifts me up, hiking my legs around him as he takes a few steps into the space before kicking the door shut behind us, and then turns to press me against it. My arms close around his neck as I kiss him back, all the worry from mere moments before disappearing with the way he's holding me—owning me.

I moan when he pulls his sinful lips away and presses his forehead to mine. "Hi." His breath tickles my damp lips, and I wish he'd just shut up and keep kissing me.

"Hi," I say back, *again*, letting my fingers trace the soft hair at the nape of his neck.

"You missed me?" His eyes are soft, wide—uncertain almost. A look I don't see on him often. And something about that look undoes me a little.

"Yeah," I breathe back quietly, feeling like we're in our private universe again.

Somehow, when his arms close around me, the world melts away. Everything that mattered two minutes ago ceases to exist now because he looks at me like I'm the only thing he sees.

His lips tug up at one side as he stares at me with so much warmth. "I missed you too."

My heart jumps in my chest, rattling against my ribs. The man with the shiny veneer, the mysterious past, and the impenetrable smirk *misses me.* Hearing him, of all people, say that to me feels like so much more.

I kiss his cheek, appreciating the feel of his stubble. I kiss his nose, right on the bump I've come to love so much. His eyebrow, the one that quirks up just after he says something inappropriate.

I rake my hands through the sides of his dark-gold locks, knowing exactly what I want from him at this moment. "Take me to bed, Stefan."

He hits me with a cocky smirk, and my core jumps in response. "Whatever you want, Kitten."

Within moments, I'm tossed on the bed and feel the crush of his body on top of me, caging me in. The only light is what filters in from the hallway. His arms frame my face as he pauses, watching me as I watch him. Our eyes connect, and I don't even try to look away.

This man. This look. It makes me want to dive deeper. I want to get lost in this connection, disappear into it, and never come back out.

I have never felt so desired.

And Stefan doesn't ruin it with words. Instead, his thumb traces the lobe of my ear, and his stern features soften. I love the way he's always touching me. A hand pressed here, a thumb grazing there. It's like he can't help himself where I'm concerned. Like he can't keep his hands off me even if he wanted to.

His lips find mine, searing my soul with their reverence. I'm not sure what's changed between us tonight. But where last night felt like fucking, like two people working out some tension and having some fun, tonight feels almost thoughtful. More profound. There's a shift in the air, in his eyes, in the way sparks dance across my skin when he touches me.

Kneeling above me, he strips me bare, working every piece of clothing off my body, gentle hands moving over every square inch of my body. We don't speak, the dirty talk doesn't come, we just watch, lost in each other's eyes. The gold flecks, the mossy hues, the dark forest greens. There are just as many facets to his irises as there are to him, and I want every one. I want to explore them all. I want to see them all, even the darkest ones—the questionable ones. Stefan doesn't scare me. I don't see him as a threat. He's not my enemy. And he looks at me the same way. He looks at me like I'm a dream come true.

Words aren't even necessary when a man looks at you like *that*.

His clothes fall in a pile around him. T-shirt, soft gray joggers… no underwear. My neediness obviously pulled him straight out of some downtime. But watching his cock bob before me, fully erect already, the lines that cut down from his toned abs, right over his hip bones—like arrows for where I want to go—I don't feel an ounce bad about pulling him away.

"You are so beautiful." My voice is breathy, almost desperate sounding. "Inside and out. Every last piece of you."

He crawls back on top of me, skin sliding against skin, and I can't keep the tips of my fingers from tracing the shapes of his defined muscles. Every curve, every sharp corner, they're almost like a map.

The winding road that brought us together.

Because who the hell would have guessed.

"No one has ever told me that before," he replies as he strokes my hair, eyes devouring my every feature.

My heart squeezes, and I rear up to taste his lips. He kisses me senseless while our hands roam each other's nude bodies. We learn each other, each hollow and dip. I want to memorize it all. There's something so innocent about it, something exploratory rather than rushed.

It's also stoking my inner fire, driving me absolutely insane.

"Condom. Bedside table," I breathe out between kisses.

Needing no further urging, Stefan pushes up and reaches beyond my head, into the drawer. But rather than grabbing for a condom right away, he pauses. I watch his lips take on a mischievous curl before a hand darts out. When his focus switches back to me, he smirks, looking suddenly playful.

And then he holds up…

"Look who I found."

Mr. Purple.

"Oh." The sight of him holding the big purple vibrator sets my heart to racing.

"I wonder who can make you come harder?" Stefan muses. "He is my top competition, is he not?" His head quirks in challenge.

I can't help but smile. "He is."

"Challenge accepted, Dr. Thorne." And with a cocky smile he clicks the bedside lamp on and slides down my body until he's braced between my spread thighs. "This is something I want to watch."

My top teeth bite down on my bottom lip to stifle a moan.

I fail miserably.

I arch my back as the low buzzing sound fills the quiet room. I feel the tip of the vibrator as he drags it through my folds with an appreciative grunt. I am *soaked*, something he has a perfectly clear view of.

The vibrator swirls around my clit, and my eyes flutter shut, hips bucking desperately. I am going to come fast playing this game with Stefan.

"Are you always this wet for him? Or is it me?" His voice is low and gravelly as he plays with my body.

"It's you." The words tumble off my tongue, almost a plea.

"Fucking right, it is." He pushes an inch of the length into me slowly, and my legs fall open wider. I love the way his crass side comes out to play in private. The rude words stoke my inner fire in a way I never knew they could.

"Oh god!" Another inch in, and it feels so tight; the vibrations feel so intense. It's an entirely different experience having someone else control the pace and the pressure.

"Sit up, Mira. I want you to see how pretty you look right now."

I groan. How such a simple request can seem so filthy is beyond me, and it sends arousal coursing through my veins. Most of my sexual experience has happened in the dark, an added layer of protection, with me squeezing my eyes shut and imagining things that might make it more exciting.

But Stefan Dalca has laid me completely bare with the lights on and has turned my mind to mush. I push up on my elbows and gaze down the valley between my heaving breasts. Stefan stays focused on my pussy, pushing the vibrator into me slowly, and I almost fall apart on the spot. His disheveled hair, his flushed cheeks, his eyes devouring me. It's too much.

"Jesus Christ," I pant as he slides it home. The vibrations rattle through my core, and my legs shake. The visual of him between my legs, completely engrossed—entranced—is more than I can take.

"No, Mira. It's just me." He smirks, eyes flitting up to mine, as he slides the vibe all the way out before pushing the length back in.

"Stefan." His name is a prayer on my lips. He's my new religion. Heat prickles out over my skin, and I'm ready to combust.

"You are fucking incredible." He pumps it in and out of me slowly, eyes getting hotter by the second. He looks like he might set me on fire with his gaze alone. "Do you have any idea how utterly irresistible you are?"

My entire body quakes under his ministrations. My fists clench the sheets, holding on for dear life, and I can feel my wetness coating my lips. He's making an absolute mess of me.

"I'm—"

The words die on my lips when he pulls the vibrator out and presses it to my clit. It's instant fireworks. They crackle across my skin, shooting down my inner thighs all the way to my toes. The arches of my feet cramp. My vision blanks.

I have never come so hard in my life. But I get barely any time to consider it before he tosses the vibrator across the bed and the tearing sound of a condom wrapper filters in through my jumbled consciousness.

I'm flat on my back when Stefan edges up beside me, peppering kisses along my shoulder as he twists me over and lifts my leg. From behind me, he wedges his rock-hard length between my legs and pulls me flush against his firm body.

"I can see why you like him so much." His voice is ragged against the shell of my ear as he lines us up, hand gripping my inner thigh possessively. "But I think you'll like this even better." He shoves his cock into me to the hilt, filling me so deliciously. "Or maybe we can work together more often?"

"Yes."

"You like that?" he growls.

"I love it."

That seems to be all the urging he needs as his hips piston into me, hitting a spot I've only ever been able to reach with a toy. The blunt head of his cock tantalizes the sensitive spot as he drives in. Our skin is slick, and I grind my ass back into him.

"More."

He fucks me harder, his moans echoing my own.

"Harder," I beg, feeling that telltale coiling sensation at the base of my spine. The one that swirls out around my hip bones and yanks on every nerve ending.

"Mira," he pants. "How do we feel this good together?"

The tension crescendos under the weight of his words.

He turns my head back toward him to claim my mouth as he pounds into me. "Who fucks you better?"

I don't even need to think about it. "You do. Always you."

His hips slap hard against my ass as I push back at him, and I snap. I tumble. I fall hard. "Stefan!" I cry out.

I feel him twitch and throb, spilling his release inside me as my entire body shakes. Our lips clamp together, like an anchor holding us together as we set each other adrift on a stormy sea. We clutch at each other desperately, perspiration mixing, limbs tangling. Joined in every way imaginable.

And I am so far gone I barely recognize myself.

CHAPTER 25

Stefan

"TELL ME ABOUT YOUR MOM."

Talk about a buzzkill. We just had the best sex of my life. The woman of my dreams is sprawled naked on my chest, and she wants to talk about my dead mom? The fingers I've been trailing down the indent of her spine stop in their tracks.

"If you want," she adds. "I'm just curious. You don't have to."

"Mira, take a breath. It's fine. You never need to feel like there's something you can't ask me or tell me. After what I've been through, honesty is important to me."

She stiffens, so I keep rubbing her back, wanting to go back to that blissful state of relaxation we were in just a moment ago.

"Nora was . . ." I'm at a loss for what to say about my mother actually. "Naive. Quick to fall in love. Starved for attention and constantly looking for more. And sometimes in all the wrong places. She grew up in a small town but had a wanderer's soul. I suppose that's why she started traveling." I try to imagine my mother living in Ruby Creek, and I can't. She doesn't fit here.

Mira drags a nail over the lines of my abs tenderly. My cock thickens, but I can take her again in a bit. I'm kind of enjoying the quiet solitude of talking with her, even about something I never say out loud. She has this way of making me feel safe, like she's really listening, not just humoring me to achieve some end. She genuinely enjoys our conversations, and somehow that's more flattering than anything else she's said or done. Her attention is healing.

"She was also strong and driven. Curious. She would pack up and hit different countries for a few months at a time. Traveling on a budget. Hitchhiking. Working odd jobs to make ends meet. And then when she depleted her bank account, she'd come back here and work whatever jobs she could find to replenish her account before taking off on another adventure. Until she went to Romania and met Constantin. Then her travels stopped, and that's when she was pregnant with me. He essentially locked her up and threw away the key. She should have hated him for it; instead she loved him to her dying day. Even against her better judgment."

"It's sad, you know?" Mira muses. "She sounds like a fascinating woman—a free spirit—the way you describe her. It seems a real shame to tie her down that way. I wonder what she could have done with her life under different circumstances?"

I take a deep swallow. I've been so angry at her for so long, so busy wallowing in my pity, that I haven't let myself consider how truly sad her story is. "I've never quite thought of it that way. Mostly I think about how badly they fucked up Nadia and me."

"I think your experiences have shaped you in ways you don't even see."

"Yeah, yeah. Morally gray. I know." I roll my eyes up at the ceiling and sigh, feeling tired of always being labeled the bad guy. "And they've shaped a crooked nose."

"I like your nose."

My heart seizes in my chest. "You do?"

I've left my nose as a sort of reminder. I could have had it fixed by now, but then I wouldn't be able to beat myself up over not keeping my mom and sister safe every time I look in the mirror.

Mira clambers her naked body on top of mine, looking straight down into my eyes. "I do," she says before delicately kissing the bridge of my nose. Her finger trails down in its wake, making me feel more self-conscious than I have in years. "I've always thought you were devastatingly handsome. Alluring." She kisses me again, more slowly this time. "The nose. The accent. The quick tongue. I've always been drawn to you. Even when I barely knew you."

I bask in her attention, soaking up her sweet words like medicine. Loving that this attraction wasn't one-sided.

She tips her head and presses a kiss to the center of my chest. "You're not morally gray. You walk the line of being intensely supportive without being overbearing perfectly. Look at Nadia. Look at me. Life gave you some sour fucking lemons, and you added the sugar and made yourself some lemonade. You love so fiercely. I think she'd be proud of you. Just like I am."

Love.

The word bounces around in my head. A perilous word to be sure. I love Nadia, absolutely. But the way Mira lumped herself in there felt a little too natural. My heart says she belongs on that list, but my head says it's too soon. My head says that everyone I love ends up hurt. Or dead.

Could I love Mira that way? Fiercely? I stare down at her elegant fingers, still skating across my skin. I think I probably could.

Possibly already do.

I grunt and palm her skull, silky hair sliding beneath my skin as I kiss the crown of her head. I pull her closer and chide myself. For a guy who claims that honesty is an important quality to him, I'm a fantastic liar. I shouldn't love Mira. Because everything I touch turns to shit. And when I love something too much, the universe takes it away from me.

"Good morning."

I turn around from the coffee maker to see Nadia sliding onto a stool at the island in the kitchen. This is my favorite room in the house. I love cooking. I especially love cooking for other people. It's an easy way for me to show affection without having to talk about my feelings.

When Nadia moved in with me, she looked me in the eye and told me to stop apologizing to her. My guilt over leaving her behind as a teenager is heavy, and the regret over not going back as an adult is possibly even worse.

So I cook for her. It's my way of saying sorry without uttering the words. Homemade fine dining. I slide a plate of smoked salmon eggs Benedict across the island toward her, followed by a cup of piping-hot coffee.

"Fuck yes." Her eyes light up, and she runs her finger through the hollandaise sauce before sucking it off with an exaggerated moan. My sister has no shame.

"You've been hanging out with those Gold Rush girls too much."

She laughs. "So have you."

I ignore the comment. I know Mira wants to keep us under wraps. And as much as I hate the feelings of inadequacy that come with it, I respect her decision. No matter how badly I'd like to shout it from the rooftops and not feel like I have to sneak over to her house under the cover of darkness. She asked me to stay last night after our heart-to-heart, but I knew she'd regret it in the morning when I would inevitably have to walk out to my vehicle amid a bustling farm filled with her friends and colleagues.

I put her on all fours and fucked her hard one more time—just the way she likes—and kissed her senseless before driving home in a haze of memories and complicated feelings.

Plus, I have work to do around the farm this morning. Racing season is almost upon us, and I've got some young horses that really need to get started training. Something I know nothing about. But luckily, Griffin does.

"Ready?" I ask as he rounds the corner after using the washroom.

He lifts his chin and grunts, hiding beneath the brim of his baseball cap. Nadia whips around, startled by the strange man standing in our house.

"Sorry, Nadia. This is Griffin. The guy I bought this place from."

She takes one look at him and places her fork down. "*That* is Griffin?"

My brow furrows as I load my and Griffin's coffee mugs into the dishwasher. We've already eaten and had coffee and are ready to go. The guy gets up at the crack of dawn, and I don't mind getting him acquainted with his new projects nice and early.

"Yeah."

"Your *best friend* Griffin?" Her eyes bulge in their sockets.

"Relax, Nadia. Adults don't have *best friends*."

Griffin snorts, rubs his beard, and walks to the front door to shove his feet into a pair of worn cowboy boots.

"I've already told you. He sold me this place, and we've just stayed in touch."

Okay, that might downplay it. I like Griffin, and he probably *is* my best friend. He's not invasive or annoying, but he's also the only person in this valley who didn't treat me like a leper when I got here. He moved up into the mountains once I took over. His new property is pretty remote, but I've been up a couple times. He's a private guy, but he's invited me hunting—a new experience for me—and I've helped him with some repairs to his cottage. Which is why he's here repaying me the favor. As a former bronc rider, he assures me he can get a few youngsters started up for me, and that's not a gift horse I'm about to look in the mouth.

My sister's face scrunches up in confusion as she whispers, "But… he's a total dick."

I bark out a laugh as I round the bar top toward the front entryway. "I'm glad you think so." I wink at her. "Then I won't have to worry about you scaring him off with your antics while he's here."

I swear I can almost hear Nadia roll her eyes. That girl has an attitude the size of Texas. And to be honest, it's part of what I love about her.

And Mira.

Fuck.

Not love. *Like.*

I toss a coat on and step into my work boots, shaking my head at myself as I head out the front to catch up with Griffin. It takes about an hour to get him all set. I show him the three youngsters that need a start, and I feel suddenly very overwhelmed by running the farm.

Needing the sunshine, I walk out to the paddock where Loki and Farrah now spend their days soaking up the rays and rolling in mud. His shrill whinny greets me as he trots across the pen with a real prance to his step, knees coming up higher than necessary just to show off. The older he's gotten, the more hilarious he's become. He's going to be a handful, that much is clear. He's smart and playful… and mischievous. I frequently catch him trying to undo the chain around his gate. He bucks and leaps around his pen like he's a world champion bucking horse.

Yeah. I don't envy the poor sucker who has to get on him for the first time. This horse will probably be reading full sentences by then. Either way, I'm beyond relieved to see him turning a corner. He's a healthy colt. No one would ever guess the shape he was in a couple months ago.

I've come to love him. There are a lot of horses on this farm and at the track in the city that belong to me, so leave it to the one horse that money can't buy to weasel his way into my heart. I haven't loved a horse like this since I lived in Romania.

"Hey, bud." I stroke the broad white blaze down his forehead, and he snorts his contentment. Wild as he might be, we've forged a special friendship. I told Billie once that DD was her heart horse, a horse she could understand like no one else can. A term I learned from the villagers in my hometown.

Looking into Loki's wide black eyes now, watching his soft lips nip at the button on my jacket—trying to pull it off, I might add—I wonder if I've met a second heart horse.

The thought of him leaving in only a few months makes my chest ache and my nose tingle. He's a pain-in-the-ass little horse. But he's *my* pain-in-the-ass little horse. The only reassurance I give myself is knowing at Gold Rush Ranch he will get the absolute best shot to live up to his potential. He'll receive top-of-the-line care. And he might even get to dump Billie Black in the dirt a couple of times.

I chuckle, scratching at his ears. "She's stubborn, but I think you might have her beat in that department."

With that, I grab a pitchfork and start picking out his paddock, tossing manure and loose hay into a wheelbarrow. I have paperwork I should do, registrations, endless emails to answer, but I'd rather hide out here with Loki, trying to avoid his snappy lips as I clean out his field. Physical labor is therapeutic in a way I never imagined. I never really did any until I bought this place. It was part of how I chose to recreate myself.

I didn't get my MBA so I could do farm chores, but I didn't get it to run a horse-racing empire either. I watch Mira, an absolute force to be reckoned with, going after everything she wants. Refusing to be deterred. And I'm just… adrift. Everything is so unresolved for me. I have so many questions about my background that are just *blank*. There's no one to ask because there's no one who knows.

I spent most of my life working my ass off to not become Constantin, to not give in to that part of my genetic makeup. A wife or family felt like a curse I wouldn't ever place on another person, least of all one I professed to love. After all, what if I became him?

And then I found out not a single part of me belongs to him, and my world unexpectedly unlocked. I wasn't beholden to that dark legacy anymore. It was freeing but also confusing. Without that vendetta, I knew nothing about what I wanted out of life.

The older I get, the more I ache for a family, for a connection, in a way I never knew I would. I'm a well-put-together facade. I'm a lost little boy, living his life based on a crusade. A promise I made to no one but myself.

And for what?

There are days where I have no clue what the hell I'm doing with my life—where I wonder if it matters. But most of all, there are days where it feels like I don't know where I'm going because I have no idea where I came from.

The only thing that's certain about where I'm going is that Mira will be with me when I get there. I'll make sure of it. I'm playing for keeps.

CHAPTER 26

Mira

My fingers twist together as I wring my hands and stare at Stefan's door. I haven't seen him in over a day, and I've had too much time to think.

Too much time to overthink.

On top of that, I'm meeting Hank for dinner tonight to do some further research. Questions and confusion are riddling my brain.

How is this all happening so fast? How is *he* interested in *me*? I mean, god. How am *I* interested in *him*? Am I about to ruin my life over a guy? Are we exclusive now? After years of having my nose stuck in a textbook and then throwing myself into a career, sex has always been just sex. I now know that I never experienced a true intimate connection when I fell into bed with a guy just because I felt like that was something I should be doing. Especially now that I realize what I've been missing.

And now Stefan Dalca has orgasmed me into confusion. Confusion about what we are, where we're going, and what this all means. Because it feels like it means more than just sex.

My phone vibrates in my pocket, and I pull it out, grateful for the distraction. Until I see that it's Stefan texting me.

Stefan: You planning on coming in? Or are you just going to stand out there and rub your hands raw?

I look around, trying to see if he's watching me out a window or something. When I see nothing, I text back, figuring he has some sort of security camera app on his phone.

Mira: You're creepy.

Stefan: Part of my charm. You love it.

Anxiety coils in my gut at the mention of the *L* word. The only thing I've loved in recent memory is my job. And my girlfriends at the ranch. Maybe the odd horse. Loving something is a distraction, a time commitment, a risk. And I'm not a big risk taker—especially not when everything I've worked my ass off for is in jeopardy. My career, my independence, my *sanity.*

I take a deep, centering breath and text back.

Mira: I'm coming in.

Stefan: Door's open. I'm in my office. Take a right at the kitchen.

With a small shake of my head, I twist the knob and step into the impressive house. I kick my boots off and walk back toward Stefan's office, which I peeked at last time I was over. My mouth goes dry when I enter his space.

He's leaned back in his chair, one foot casually slung over his knee as he looks through the contents of a brown folder with a wall full of books behind him. He's sexy wearing a simple white dress shirt with cuff links that glint in the light, the veins in his hands bulging in the most mouthwatering way. I sometimes get lost staring at his hands when he's fucking me, the way they flex when he grips the sheets and drives into me harder. I never knew such a generic part of a man's body could be so distracting.

I hear a low rumble, a chuckle, and my eyes snap up to his face. Which is honestly no less hot. He studies me with head quirked and his fingers in a loose fist pressed against his soft lips. And he's wearing those fucking glasses. Like he knows the whole hot professor thing has been an ongoing fantasy for me.

I'm instantly wet. I'm thoroughly ruined. I should tell him it's been nice knowing him and get the hell out of here before I spontaneously combust like the sex-crazed maniac I've become.

"What's going through that beautiful head of yours right now, Mira?"

"I haven't heard from you in almost two days."

"I had meetings at the track today. Was there something you needed me for?" One side of his mouth tips up knowingly. *Fucker.*

"No."

I engage him in some sort of staring contest. I refuse to drop his gaze, but it's doing funny things to my insides standing here, staring at him in the quiet office. Especially when he looks like *that.*

"Okay. So you're here because?"

"Are you serious?" I hiss at him, stepping close enough that my thighs butt up against the wide oak desk. "You fucked my brains out. Like, I am literally brainless now. You told me my hands belong in yours, for crying out loud. I can't stop thinking about it. And about you. And it's all driving me crazy. What am I supposed to do now? I haven't heard from you at all. And I just need to know what this is so I can organize my life accordingly. And that's what I came here to ask you, but you're sitting there looking like Professor Pornstar."

Stefan's face slowly transforms from amused to serious, his gaze turning heated toward the end of my rant.

"You've made it abundantly clear you don't want a clingy man-child in your life. Which is perfect because I don't want to be that. I love how fiercely independent you are. You were working these past two days, and so was I. I fully intended to call you when I finished what I was doing here."

I sniff, feeling foolish and realizing he's right. I have said that. I do want that kind of relationship. *Did* want.

But he ruined my brain. And now I'm obsessed.

"Well." I roll my eyes. "You don't have to go radio silent. Especially after everything that happened over the weekend. How am I supposed to discern what that means? How am I supposed to know you're not off dating other women?" I sigh and stare up at the ceiling, hating how completely inexperienced I sound. "This is fucking annoying. You've put a curse on me. You're all I think about."

He laughs and leans forward, elbows propped on the edge of his desk. "Mira."

I press my lips together, not wanting to look at him. But the silence stretches between us. He's waiting for eye contact. I give in, dropping my gaze to his. He's back to looking amused. Which honestly kind of pisses me off.

"What?"

"When? When on earth am I supposed to see all these other women? I've spent almost every free moment I have for the last several weeks with you."

I blink at him.

"I sleep. I work. I work out. I run the farm. I obsessively check on Loki. I try to keep my sister on the straight and narrow. And then I spend my free time either with you or thinking about you. You've put a *spell* on me. *You're* all *I* think about."

My heart lurches in my chest.

"I… I didn't think of it like that. Everything just feels so uncertain."

His grin turns wicked. Knowing.

"That's because I fucked your brains out."

I clench, not fully understanding why hearing him talk this way does it to me. The dirty words drive me crazy. The way he switches from all proper and businesslike to scorching hot and foul-mouthed. It's the dichotomy that gets me off. He pulls it off so well.

He stands and tugs open the top button of his shirt before turning his attention to the cuff links at his wrists. He rotates them slowly, his calloused fingers moving so deftly, it's almost distracting. The plunk of the metal as he sets each one on the desktop sounds loud in the otherwise quiet office.

The silence stretches between us before he says, "And now I'm going to pull those tight jeans down and fuck the uncertainty right out of you."

A small gasp erupts from my lips, and my heart rate crescendos as he ambles around the desk.

"You look pleased. I thought I wasn't your type."

I roll my eyes. "Men who gloat aren't."

Amusement rumbles in his chest as he rolls up his sleeves like he's about to get to work. "But are you bored?"

I wish he'd stop rubbing that in my face. He knows damn well I'm not bored. I'm not sure how any woman in the world's history could be bored with Stefan Dalca. Or how any of them had him and then let him go.

"Do you fantasize about your professor, Mira?"

My head snaps up as he adjusts the glasses on his face. *Fuck. Looking that good should not be allowed.* The forearms. The dress shirt. The glasses. Just… fuck.

My eyes widen as he draws closer. "My professor?"

"Yes." He comes toe to toe with me, forcing me to look up at him. This conversation doesn't make him the least bit uncomfortable, but I'm glowing pink. "You brought that up like it's something you've thought about before. Did you? While you were still in school? Do you now?"

What the hell? Was he taught to be some sort of psychic in Romania?

"It—" I roll my shoulders back. I will not be ashamed of this ongoing fantasy of mine. I refuse. I dig the dynamic, so what? "It is. So yes, I have."

The smile that takes over his face is far too greedy. A smarter woman would run with a man looking at her like this, but all it does is make my stomach drop and my heart race. I realize I trust Stefan. With my heart and with my body. So instead of running, I bite down on my bottom lip and hit him with my best wide-eyed look.

He picks up on the change instantly.

Hand darting behind me to grip my ponytail, he asks, "Care to tell me why you came to my office today, Miss Thorne?" He leans close, voice vibrating across the sensitive spot below my ear. "Are you concerned about your most recent grade?"

A small part of me wants to laugh. This is *so* unlike me. So out of character, it feels almost silly. But when he tugs at my ponytail, forcing my head up farther, I catch sight of his glowing green eyes. All traces of humor melt away. I'm not good at dirty talk, but I love listening to his. So here goes nothing.

"Yes," I whisper.

"Do you have any suggestions for how you'd like to make it up to me?"

I pant as his lips slide down the side of my neck and across my chest, the cool plastic corner of his glasses scraping against my throat.

"I was hoping you could tell me what it would take."

"Dangerous choice, Miss Thorne."

The change is subtle, but he's not calling me Dr. Thorne right now. I love his intelligence. Even during sex, Stefan is thinking. In one swift motion, he turns me toward the desk and bends me over it, my ponytail still wrapped around his hand.

He gently presses my cheek against the cool surface as his free hand roams the center of my back, all the way down so he can grab a handful of my ass. "How hard are you willing to work?"

"As hard as you want me to." My fingertips slide over the polished desktop as I try to get some purchase. I feel like I'm free-falling. Completely out of control. Completely out of my element.

"Fuck, you're perfect." His body looms over mine as he presses a gentle kiss to the back of my neck. "Now stay right where you are. If you move, there won't be any extra credit."

All I can muster is a whimper as I feel the heat of his torso leave my back. His hands glide down my sides, savoring every curve with reverence I've never felt before. When he reaches my hips, his arms encircle me while his hands do away with the button and zipper at the front of my jeans. He drags my skintight jeans down, savoring every rasp of fabric and inch of exposed skin. He unwraps me like a present he's always wanted and will never forget. He uses one dress-shoe-clad foot to nudge my feet into a wider stance, and then my panties are slid down, stretched between my thighs while I'm bent over and bared to him.

"You were made for me."

The statement is like an anvil to my chest. It feels an awful lot like that's true. Like we were made for each other.

I peer over my shoulder at him. The air between us is thick. I can feel it, the way it vibrates, the way it heats as his eyes scour my body. Bright and sparking with…

Love?

"I need to get a condom. I'll be back. Don't move."

I swallow audibly and nod, body humming with anticipation.

He leaves, and I do as he asked. I feel myself getting wetter and more worked up with each passing second I wait for him.

The longer he's gone, the more I want him. When he returns, his control has frayed beyond being patient. The jangle of his belt blends into the rip of the condom wrapper.

He steps up behind my bare ass and drags himself between my cheeks. "Next time you need to fix an assignment, I'm going to take you here."

My body trembles with need. I'm at the point where I don't care where he takes me. I just want him inside me.

Now.

"Okay," I murmur, looking over my shoulder again as he notches himself at my slippery entrance.

We lock eyes for only a moment, and I feel like the look we share says it all. It answers every question I've been wrestling with for the past forty-eight hours. A promise is made in that look, and then he impales me with one rough thrust and sends me reeling. His hands grip my hips hard enough I'm certain there will be bruises tomorrow. And I bask in the raw passion. The intense need. I love the way we bring out each other's most base instincts. The way we're both so proper in public and so improper behind closed doors.

"Take it like a good girl, Miss Thorne," he says, before his control snaps completely and his voice becomes a harsh growl. "Every. Inch."

The wet slapping noises of Stefan taking me forcefully fill the room, mingling only with his heavy breaths and my quiet, desperate moans. He eventually leans over my body and reaches beneath me, finding my clit with his fingers.

He rubs firmly while continuing to drive into me wildly, panting in my ear. "If there was any uncertainty in your mind about where we stand, let me clear that up for you now." He slows his thrusts, pulling out and then driving in hard, rattling my body with the force of his claim. "You are mine." My hands slip on the desk, and my legs shake. "And I am yours."

And as I fall apart beneath his firm body, feeling him move inside me, I know I'm exactly where I need to be.

There's no uncertainty now.

CHAPTER 27

Stefan

I'M SITTING AT THE KITCHEN ISLAND STARING OFF INTO SPACE, trying to pull all the thoughts running through my head together. Trying to pull *myself* together.

I wanted to go for another round. I wanted Mira upstairs, spread out on my bed, begging for more. I wanted my skin on hers and her moans in my ear. I wanted to live between her thighs.

Unfortunately, she had other plans. Something with Hank, their farm manager over at Gold Rush Ranch. So I let her go, as badly as I wanted to beg her to stay. Her independence is one of my favorite things about her. She's not clingy or obsessed despite how she might feel right now. She's just excited, and I am too. This thing between us feels new—like it's going somewhere. I don't have to worry about cramming our time together in because we have all the time in the world.

I have a feeling about her.

A smile tugs at the corner of my lips, and I lean my elbows onto the counter before me. Getting lost in the dark lines weaving across the marbled stone countertop, I replay our conversation. The one that took place almost immediately after I'd bent her over my desk and claimed her the way she needed.

As I tugged her pants up over her deliciously round ass, she asked me quietly if we were exclusive now. Vulnerability written all over her beautiful body.

I pulled her into my arms and assured her. "Absolutely."

"Are we dating? What do you call this?"

I laughed. She scowled.

"I don't give a fuck what you call it so long as you're mine."

That's what I'd told her. And I'd meant it. Because it was all so obvious to me.

Sitting here now, it hits me that I'm putting it all on the line for her. Pushing past all my fears about caring too much for another person. Trying to let go of my deep-rooted fear of betrayal. Ignoring the fact that the people I've loved the most in life have been ripped away from me. Acknowledging I have a terrible track record for protecting those very people.

But the look she gave me when I told her she was *mine* was worth the risk.

Over and over again. Worth it.

Because she looked at me like I was *her* prize as much as she is mine.

I feel like it's too soon to be in love. I feel childish even entertaining the thought. But maybe that's just it; maybe a child knows what they're feeling and freely admits it. They don't have years of baggage telling them to ignore what they already know to be true.

With a shake of my head, I pivot and opt to distract myself by showering the other woman in my life with some attention.

"Nadia!" I call up the stairs.

She came home shortly after Mira left, and I momentarily scolded myself for fucking her so publicly. Sometimes, it's hard to remember I'm living with another person. Nadia leads her own life. She is loving working at the clinic and doing her schoolwork in whatever free time she has left. In fact, I'd go so far as to say she's happier than I've seen her, well, ever.

I know she's out with boys. Possibly even *many* boys. But as her older brother who doesn't have a super close and personal relationship with her, I'm never sure what to say about that. I just hope she's being safe. I hope she's making good decisions. Because whether she recognizes it or not, she's a fucking catch. And I suppose that's one area I can find solace. The women at Gold Rush Ranch are an excellent influence—they don't take any shit. And that's the exact type of women Nadia needs in her life.

Strong women.

Something she hasn't had and something I can't do for her no matter how badly I'd like to.

"Yeah?" She jogs down the stairs, looking like a spitting image of our mother.

I'm always glad she didn't take after *him.* I don't really look like either of them, and my chest aches from the questions swirling in my head about whom I *do* look like.

"Wanna grab a bite?"

Her brow furrows. "Why? What's wrong?"

I bark out a loud laugh. "Nothing. I just want to hang out with my little sister. Is that a crime?"

She smiles back, looking amused. "Let me change real quick. I'll be right back."

Twenty minutes later, we walk through the grungy front door of Neighbor's Pub. Nadia's pick, not mine. Apparently, this is where the "coolest" people in town hang out. I eye the place suspiciously and wonder if we have wildly different definitions of cool. The place smells like stale beer, deep-fried chicken, and butter. The smell of popcorn wafts off the self-serve popcorn machine in the corner. The thought of shoving my hand in there to take a bowl full of cold popcorn that everyone else has touched holds zero appeal.

Nadia looks completely at home, and I realize this is probably where she's spent several of her nights lately. Even though she doesn't drink.

I can see a bit of the place's charm. Locals stooped over pints of frothy golden beer line the bar, and "Hotel California" blares through the speakers, mixing with the clacking sound of someone breaking a set of pool balls. It belongs in a movie. I guess I've never felt welcome enough in Ruby Creek to make my way in here. I constantly feel like the outsider and haven't gone out of my way to change that.

"Isn't this place great? So Canadian." Nadia smiles wide as she slides onto a stool at a high top beside a pool table. "Any chance you want to play?"

I marvel at my little sister, no longer the sullen young woman who stepped off a plane. She's strong, so fucking strong. My chest pinches at the thought of how she had to pull herself up by the bootstraps. About how I left her hanging to serve my own ends.

I hope she can forgive me one day.

"Yeah. Yeah, I'd love to." I shake my head and smile back, trying to clear the guilt of walking down memory lane.

"Great. I'll be right back. Drink?"

"Yeah, I'll have…"

"Don't say wine, Stef. I know you're a wine guy, but this isn't a wine place." She grins at me, ribbing me. Not treating me like the bore of an older brother I sometimes feel like with the age gap between us. *This is what I want with her.*

"How about a cosmopolitan?"

"Dear god," she huffs. "You are such a priss."

A deep laugh rumbles in my chest. "I'm joking. I'll take a beer."

"Are you though?" She quirks a brow at me before strutting away, laughing.

I watch her walk up to the bar, cringing at the way heads turn as she passes. I could take off a few heads for looking at my baby sister the way they are right now, but I haven't held that kind of role in her life, and it would be weird to start now. So I won't.

Instead, I glance away, scanning the rest of the bar. Taking it all in, until my eyes snag on an ass I'd recognize anywhere. An ass cupped by the denim I pulled down mere hours ago.

Mira is digging through that godforsaken popcorn machine with a scoop in one hand and a basket in the other.

I'll be happy to take care of her when she inevitably gets sick after this. That's how much I like this girl. I'm looking forward to holding her hair back while she hurls.

I find myself peering around the bar, wondering why the hell she's here when she said she had a meeting with Hank. She wouldn't be here with someone else, would she? After everything we've done together? Everything we've shared?

I can't imagine it, but it doesn't stop my gut from churning and my heart rate from ratcheting up. If Mira wasn't with me, what kind of guy would she be with? My eyes scan the bar, hoping upon hope that she wouldn't lie to me.

There's a lot I can tolerate. But lying isn't it. After my life, it's a hard line for me. Anxiety creeps up over my sternum as I let my paranoia run away with me. *Something* feels off. I just can't pinpoint what.

But then I find Hank sitting alone at a cozy two-person table beside a roaring fireplace in the back. My body relaxes as I watch Mira smile in his direction and head back that way.

She's almost at the table when she's intercepted by Nadia. Her body tenses. I see her lips moving, asking whom Nadia is here with, as she looks around nervously.

Something is definitely off.

Nadia greets Hank, and he smiles back with a quick wink. And then when Nadia points at me, Mira's eyes shoot in my direction. She smiles, but it's tentative. She waves, but it's small.

Not one to back down from an awkward situation, I stand and walk across the room, approaching the small table and watching Mira's eyes go more round with every step I take in her direction.

She has *never* looked at me like that. I feel like I'm watching my own life play out before me.

"Stefan. Hi." She pushes the loose strands from her ponytail behind her ears as she takes a seat. Across from Hank.

"Sir." I reach toward the man and offer my open hand.

He grins, looking between Mira and me as he shakes my hand.

"Oh, please. No need to call me sir, son. We owe you a big thank-you for taking on our little guy the way you have. Mira tells me you've named him Loki?"

The apples of Mira's cheeks pop up as she looks away shyly. Sounds like someone has been talking about me.

"Yeah. The name fits him well. He's a mischief maker. You're going to have your hands full with this one."

Hank shakes his head. "Not me. Billie. I'm too old for projects like that. She can play bucking bronco on her own." He grins. "Loki. The god of mischief. I like it. The funny part is… I think Billie will too."

We all chuckle, and then Mira says, "Hank and I have something of a standing date here on Tuesday nights. You know… as the two unattached people at the ranch." I don't know why she's acting so nervous. Like I'd be mad about her going out for dinner with a man old enough to be her father. "I've missed a couple times, so here I am. Making it up to him."

"You brought him to this dive to make it up to him?"

Mira's cheeks pink as she lifts her pint of beer to take a long swig.

My brow furrows as I take her in. Something passes between us, and I get the sense she wants me to leave. But before I can go, Hank pipes up.

"Aw, nah. I love this place. Did Mira tell you I used to bartend here?"

Mira freezes, pint glass held high as her eyes bore into mine over the rim. All the sounds around us blur to white noise as I drag my eyes off the woman I thought I trusted to take in the man sitting across from her.

His features hit me rapid-fire. Like bugs against a windshield. Eyes. *Splat.* Hair. *Splat.* Square jaw. *Splat.*

My breathing becomes labored. It feels like someone has doused me in scalding-hot water. Intense feelings of betrayal course through my veins. My layers of composure slough away. I turn back to Mira, her pint glass now placed back on the table and her eyes giving me a sad, pleading look as she nervously wipes at her lips.

She knew. *She knew.*

And she didn't tell me.

Never mentioned it.

The utter shock of it all lances through me. Hot and painful and nauseating. I need to leave. I need to compose myself before I say or do something I'll regret.

Hank's head quirks, the emerald eyes that match mine so full of questions. "You all right, son? You look like you've seen a ghost."

Son. The word fills my mind and blankets my vision. After all this time, he's been sitting right under my nose. And the woman I thought I might be falling in love with fucking *knew.*

I've experienced betrayal in my life, more than most people have. But this is different. Only people who had already let me down in some way have ever betrayed me.

Mira bowled me over by being perfect for me, and I didn't even have the sense to see it coming.

"I'm fine." My voice is brittle. "Enjoy your dinner." I spin on a heel and march toward the heavy front door of the dingy pub.

I need fresh air. I need distance. I need time to process. I can't do that with Mira's doe eyes pleading with me.

And I sure as fuck can't do that while I stare into eyes that are a perfect mirror image of my own.

Pushing into the cool night air, I keep my strides even and controlled until I get to my SUV. I round the front of it toward the grass ditch and heave. It's been hours since I've eaten, so nothing comes. Just silent nausea and the choked sounds that accompany it.

When the episode passes, I'm still bent over, hands on my knees, trying to catch my breath—trying to cool my head.

"Stefan?"

Her voice is quiet, pained. Uncertain.

"I don't want to talk right now." And I don't. At this current juncture, I have nothing to say to Dr. Mira Thorne.

Her steps don't falter as she approaches. "Let me explain." Her voice cracks.

I turn on her, eyes blazing. Heart throbbing. "Explain what, Mira? How, after everything I've divulged to you, you can't so much as mention this to me?"

"I—"

I cut her off, words coming out hard as I stand up tall. "I trusted you. I told you things I've never told *anyone*."

"I had a plan. I was going to tell you."

"How long?"

She blanches, her face going deathly white under the light of the moon, almost blue beneath the dark sky.

"How long did you know?"

"Listen." She holds her hands up in a gesture that tells me she wants me to slow down. But I can't do that right now. My head is spinning. I've spent years languishing over this secret, and she's had the power to put me out of my misery for… how long?

"Did you know before we got involved?"

"Define *involved*."

That's my answer. Rage churns in my gut, and I quirk an eyebrow at her, scoffing as I do.

"Everything between us has happened so fast. Just let me explain before you cut me off again."

"So now this is my fault? No, Mira. This was a simple conversation you could have had with me. It doesn't matter now."

Her face stays stoic while silent tears trickle down her cheeks. "What does that mean?"

"It means… I… fuck!" I shout as I run both my hands through my hair. This is not how this was supposed to go between us. "I'm not sure I can be with someone this dishonest. In fact, I'm almost positive I can't."

A hollow gasp erupts from her lips as she slams a hand over her mouth. "Stefan, just—"

I wave a hand to stop her. "Nah. No, thanks. I've already got one woman I loved who lied to me up on a pedestal. I don't have room for another. It's no wonder you wanted to keep us a secret." I shake my head and walk around to my driver's-side door. "I mean, really, Mira? Do you ever do anything that doesn't benefit *you* in some way?" The noise she makes in response is deep and guttural. "Tell Nadia I had to go."

I don't let my eyes anywhere near her as I get in and pull away. I can't. Because as angry as I am with her, I know one look at her face will kill my resolve to protect myself.

I watch the outline of her body shrink into the dark as I drive away and realize protecting myself is something I've already failed to do, considering I just admitted I'm in love with her.

CHAPTER 28

Mira

I FEEL LIKE I'M ON AUTOPILOT. FLOATING, BUT NOT IN A GOOD way. I walk back into the bar on wooden legs. I barely feel in control of my body, like a marionette on a string and the universe is having a good laugh as it walks me around. Hank and Nadia must be able to tell because she's taken my place at our table, and they're both looking at me with confusion written all over their faces.

I'm accustomed to tragedy, but I'm at a loss for what to say right now. I can't think of a way to cover this up. I don't know what to do.

"Everything okay, Mira?" Hank asks, concern lacing his voice.

Nadia looks at me sadly, her brows knitting together in concern.

"No. Not really." I wipe at my eyes, realizing that I walked in here with tears pooling on my cheeks.

"Here." Hank stands and pulls another chair up to our table, lining it up behind me and giving my back a quick rub as he does. "Take a seat. You look like you're going to topple over."

I sit rigidly, twisting my hands in my lap. Usually when I deliver bad news, I take solace in knowing I've done everything in my power to avoid this outcome.

Tonight, I can't say the same.

I could have handled this differently. But I'm not sure that would have been preferable. I don't know. I don't know anything other than I'm drowning in guilt. My chest aches with such raw pain, it radiates up my throat and steals my words.

I've been so unfair to Stefan. He's done everything he can to protect me, and I repaid him by withholding something he's been killing himself trying to figure out. I thought I was protecting him too.

A wave of shame hits me, soaking me, chilling me to the bone. "I've made a huge mistake."

"Well"—Hank shifts in his seat, eyes darting to Nadia—"let's see what we can do about solving that." He pushes my beer toward me, but I can't handle the thought of consuming anything right now.

"I… Hank, I can't. I still don't feel like it's my place to say anything. I had hoped to talk with you tonight. I had some certainty, but this… god. This really blew up in my face."

"Talk to me about what?"

I glance over at Nadia, white teeth nibbling at heart-shaped pink lips. I have no clue if she's aware of this whole thing. *How did I make such a big mess? How did I blow this so badly?*

I opt for a very general line of questioning, just in case.

"Did you know someone by the name of Nora when you worked here?"

Hank clears his throat and shuffles his broad shoulders around in his chair. "I did."

I nod, looking down at my hands again, rolling my lips together. I feel like I could hurl. My voice drops an octave and comes out as almost a whisper. "How well did you know her?"

A shadow passes over Hank's face, a memory maybe. I watch his proud chest rise and fall under the plaid shirt he's wearing. His head tilts, and a sad smile touches his lips. "Well enough that I still think about her often."

My heart cracks and tears spring up in my eyes again. *Fuck my life*. This whole thing is just painful.

I blink rapidly and grab Hank's knee right as Nadia pipes up, confusion lacing her tone. "Are you talking about my mom?"

My hand pulses over Hank's jeans as his eyes snap down to mine. Shock weaves its way between the different shades of green as the realization sinks in.

"You need to talk to Stefan. That's all I can tell you." I stand and wrap my arms around the shocked man's neck, squeezing him in a bone-crushing hug. I whisper so only Hank can hear me, "He really needs you."

The stinging in my nose overwhelms me, and without saying anything further, I turn to pay. "Come on, Nadia. I'll drive you home."

She says nothing but pushes to stand, clearly trying to piece things together. And when I get to the front door, I check over my shoulder to see Hank spinning his pint of beer, staring at the golden liquid. But he's not really there.

He's lost in a memory.

CHAPTER 29

Stefan

I woke on a pillow that smelled like Mira's honey-scented shampoo. I stripped the bed and threw everything in the wash—hot water and an extra pod—as though washing my sheets would help scrub her from my mind.

Now I'm sitting at my kitchen counter staring at the steam rising off my black coffee. The coffee that has done nothing to wake me up after a long, restless night. I've been fixating on the fact I've probably finally found my father. I don't know where to go now, and I don't know what to say. I don't even know *if* I should say anything or if it's best to let sleeping dogs lie.

I don't know if the man has a family. I have no clue what I'd be interrupting. *I don't know a fucking thing.*

But Mira did. She knew everyone's situation perfectly and opted to keep me in the dark. She let me spill my guts to her. She let me expose all my inner misery, and she did nothing to ease that.

She made me care for her. She wiggled her way into my life.

She made me want things I wasn't sure I'd ever want. And then she turned around and ruined it all with her dishonesty.

Letting her go should be simple. A clear-cut choice. An obvious answer. But I feel like I'm sitting here sawing off a perfectly good limb.

It *hurts*. More than I thought it would. More than I knew it could.

Quiet footsteps pull me from my moping as Nadia pads across the kitchen straight toward the coffee maker.

With her back to me, I say, "Sorry I left you last night."

"It's okay. Mira drove me back."

I sigh and scrub at my face. "I'm sorry I have such a terrible habit of leaving you behind."

My sister turns, her golden curls a wild mess in a bun on top of her head. "I wish you'd forgive yourself. Do you have any idea how much happier you'd be if you stopped blaming yourself for all the bad things that happened to us in our lives? They aren't worth it. Not even a little bit. Don't let them keep the power. I want you to be happy. I hold nothing against you. Yes, I was stuck with them for longer before I left, but you're still stuck there in that house even though you're standing here before me."

I swallow. I am. I live in that house every damn day. I relive it. I'm trapped there, and I've made it my life's mission to undo everything he did—but at what cost? Who am I really punishing? Constantin is dead in the ground on the other side of the world.

My mom is in the lake.

And Nadia is sitting here. Giving me advice that is wise beyond her years.

"I know we don't have the same dad."

"Pardon?"

"Look at us, Stefan. I'm a dead ringer for Mom. You look like you belong to the milkman. Or as it's currently looking, the barn manager down the road."

"Jesus. You have no filter, do you?"

She smiles, wide and cheesy, not looking the least bit upset about this conversation. "Unapologetic honesty. You should try it some time."

I groan, scrubbing at my face even harder. "Fuck."

"Oh, wow." She lifts the steaming mug up to her lips and bats her lashes. "Things must be bad if Mr. Proper is swearing."

"I'm sorry."

"For what?"

"For…" God, where do I even start? "The course your life has taken."

She scrunches her face and shakes her head like I've said the most ridiculous thing in the world. "I'm not. Not everything happens for a reason. Some things happen because we make the conscious decision to stop letting shit happen to us. And no matter what, you're my brother. We're family. DNA doesn't change a damn thing."

I swallow. My little sister is usually nonchalant. Carefree. A pain in my ass. But today she feels more like a big sister, hitting me with all the things I need to hear.

"Don't blow it with Mira."

Except that. I don't want to hear that.

"I'm not sure what you're talking about."

Her brow arches. "You spew an awful lot of bullshit for someone who goes on about valuing honesty."

"I—"

One hand shoots up to stop me. "Stefan, stop. I know you guys are together. She told us."

My stomach bottoms out. "What?"

"Yeah. Girls' night. Billie said something bitchy about you, and Mira wasn't having it. Told us all that you guys were a thing. Or whatever. I stopped listening because it was gross—you're still my brother." She shudders.

She told them. I was certain she planned on keeping us a secret. She's so hard to get a read on. She keeps her cards so close. Why wouldn't she have told me this? That was the night I showed up at her apartment because she missed me.

"At any rate," my sister continues, "don't let her get away. She's the best thing that has ever happened to you. And you have a bad habit of not letting good things happen to yourself."

The doorbell rings, effectively cutting off our conversation. Which works for me because I'm still irrationally angry with Mira. I'm still not ready to forgive her.

I don't know if I can.

But all thoughts of Mira flee my mind when I swing the front door open and stare back into eyes that are exactly like mine. I've never taken a very close look at Hank. The dark-golden hair swooped back off his face, the deep lines on his tan skin from years spent in the sun, his broad shoulders and trim waist. He's fit for his age—whatever that is. Strong in a way only a lifetime of manual labor can achieve.

"I have a feeling that you and I should chat."

He smiles, but it's a nervous smile. Not the typical happy-go-lucky grin that I've seen him sporting. The man couldn't be less like Constantin if he tried. Looks-wise, personality-wise, life-wise. It's something I instantly love about him.

I give him a nervous smile of my own. "Come on in." I hold the door open wide and gesture with my arm for him to enter. "Coffee?" I ask, walking away toward the kitchen, trying to catch my breath and looking for something to fix the dry throat situation I have going.

"Got anything harder?" Hank chuckles.

I've never heard a better idea in my life. Instead of reaching for the coffee, I reach into the cupboard above the sink and pull out a bottle of bourbon and two whiskey glasses.

"It's five o'clock somewhere." I hold them up and face the man who is most likely my father.

He chuckles again. It's warm and comforting and genuinely happy. I ache for that sound. The sound I missed growing up. And when he winks at me, my mind flashes with moments in my life when I missed that exact look. My graduation. Swim meets. I could have had *that.*

I clear my throat and will the emotion clouding my eyes away. "Living room is that way."

Once we're both seated on the plush leather couches with a healthy two-finger pour of whiskey in hand, Hank leans back, arm over the back of the couch, and lets his eyes soak me in. I can feel him analyzing me, cataloguing our similarities with a small sad smile on his lips. I wonder how this must feel for him.

I'm about to ask when he says, "So, Stefan, tell me about your life."

And I do. I start at the very beginning, and I leave absolutely nothing out.

I'm drunk. It's 11 a.m. on a Wednesday, and I'm drunk.

With my dad.

Talk about things I never thought would happen. We're both pretty sure he's my dad. The timing works out. We'll get a DNA test done to confirm. It all makes sense. Except my mom's decisions. Those will never make sense to me. Hank says he begged her to stay. He says he loved her.

That part was hard to hear.

Just like me, having to tell him what became of her life was hard for him to hear. I'm not above admitting that we both shed a few tears over the course of our two-hour conversation. We have that in common too, I guess.

And now, we're walking down the driveway toward the farm, both a bit tipsy, because Hank wants to see Loki.

"See that lake?" I point to the small body of water at the base of the valley. "Or pond? Slough? I call it a lake, but maybe it's too small."

"It can be whatever you want it to be." Hank laughs, hands in his pockets, strolling down the driveway with a tipsy grin on his face.

His smile melts off the minute I drunkenly blurt out, "That's where I spread her ashes."

His Adam's apple bobs in his throat as his eyes gaze out over the sparkling water reflecting the clouds on its still surface. "I think she'd have loved it here." His voice is thick with emotion, and I instantly regret saying anything. I immediately start beating myself up about it, staring at the ground, wondering why I would blurt that out. I'm so accustomed to walking on eggshells around people that I'm taken by surprise when a warm hand lands on my shoulder.

"Thank you for telling me." He smiles a real smile. "It's nice to know where she is."

I feel like a little kid. A sad little kid with daddy issues basking in the glow of someone with kind hands and a friendly face. I've spent so many years dreaming of this day, and somehow it still doesn't seem real. I feel like I'm hovering above, looking down at myself.

And it's not just the whiskey.

We walk side by side in a companionable silence until we reach the stable parking lot and come face-to-face with Mira's big Gold Rush Veterinary Services truck parked in front of the large sliding doors.

I go rigid and stop in my tracks. I'm not prepared to see her. I have too many feelings to process first. I said things last night I wish I hadn't said. Things I'm not ready to apologize for yet. To be honest, I'm still not sure they warrant an apology.

I still can't believe she kept this to herself.

I catch sight of her in Farrah and Loki's paddock, doing her daily check, stooped down over her workbox full of needles and bottles.

"You should talk to her," Hank says.

"I..." I get lost soaking up the expression of concentration on her face. The way her intelligent eyes dart around, her teeth worrying at her bottom lip while she looks for something. My first instinct is to rush over and help her.

I wonder if that need will ever wane.

"I'm not sure I'm ready."

"I'm not telling you what you need to say to her. Only that you need to talk to her. You both need closure. *If* that's what you want. She's a tough cookie. She's not an open book, but she has a good heart. She came to your defense on more than one occasion. That woman cares about you. Don't doubt that for a moment. Because we all only have so many moments left to live." He looks over at the lake thoughtfully before adding, "I'm going to go have a chat with your mom."

And with one final squeeze of my shoulder, he's gone, strolling away like giving fatherly advice is something he's been doing for me my entire life.

His movement catches Mira's attention, and she stands abruptly to stare at him before her eyes search the driveway for me. And when her eyes meet mine, emotion moves between us. There's always been a palpable tension between Mira and me—something that hasn't lessened just because I broke it off last night.

It might even be stronger. It feels like there's an elastic between us and I've pulled it taut by yanking myself away. I wonder if the more I pull away, the harder we'll collide.

I wonder if we'll survive the collision.

"Hi," she says tentatively as I move toward her.

"Hey." My voice is slightly slurred, and I stop a few meters away.

I don't trust myself to get any closer, and at least this proximity has eased the throbbing in my chest. As long as I don't get lost in her eyes. Her wide onyx eyes, the ones that give everything away lately. Every thought and feeling. Every insecurity.

Today they look sad. Devastated even.

We stare at each other stupidly. Awkwardly. Two intelligent adults who've shared one another's deepest, darkest secrets and still can't think of a damn thing to say.

"I need you to listen to me. I don't need you to respond. I don't even need you to understand. I just want the opportunity to present my reasoning for what I did. Then I'll leave. I promise."

All I can offer her is a terse nod.

With a deep sigh, she starts in, her hand gently scratching at Farrah's ear. "I didn't know Hank being your father was even a possibility until the night we drove back from my parents' place. When you told me what your mom said. The only connection I had to go on was that he'd been a bartender in town. I knew Hank had bartended before he started working here. But, Stefan"—she pauses, looking at me imploringly—"there has been a lot more than one bartender in town over the years."

I know she's right, but I just keep staring.

"I had no idea if there were more bars or restaurants in town back then. It didn't *have* to be Neighbor's. I suspected, but what was I supposed to do? Get your hopes up when it could be nothing? Tell Hank, who is almost like family to me, that maybe I was on to something?"

"Yes, Mira. Either of those options would have been preferable."

Her hands land on her hips, and her eyes swim with sadness. "And who should I have told first? Who is entitled to my completely unproven hypothesis? I asked you about your mom for more information. Even just her name. And then last night, my plan was to ask Hank if he knew her."

"Wow, you really had this all planned out." My voice is cutting. I hate feeling like she was plotting something behind my back.

She ignores the dig, but I don't miss the tears that spring to her eyes.

"This was *so* not any of my business. I was trying to make responsible decisions with big information. It's not in me to run around spouting a theory without any good evidence. My brain doesn't work like that. I didn't know how quickly things between us would"—she sighs and looks up at the puffy clouds overhead—"evolve. I didn't see you coming, Stefan. Not like this. And I couldn't tell Hank because that would break your confidence in me. And I couldn't tell you because I didn't want to be the one to hurt you if I was wrong." Her voice cracks on the last few words, and she looks away, foot tapping against the ground anxiously. "Believe me when I say that I was trying to protect you."

"You hurt me anyway."

Any happy buzz I had before has leached into the ground at my feet. Now, I feel monumentally depressed. I'd have to be an idiot to not see her point. But it doesn't change the result. She lied to me, kept a secret, and I can't get over that hurdle. But pain traces her every feature. I want to wrap her in my arms and kiss away every hurt, but my pride won't let me. The sad little boy inside me won't allow it.

I lean into that childish side of myself when I respond in a wooden tone, "I… I need some time to wrap my head around everything." Her lashes flutter in a failed attempt to stop the tears from spilling down her cheeks. "Thank you for explaining your line of thinking."

She sucks in air like she can't breathe. There's so much pain there, and I hate thinking I caused it for her. I never wanted to hurt Mira, but I'm feeling too fragile to save us both. I want to be able to let it go, but my mother's betrayal is a wound that's been freshly ripped open. The truth of the matter is, I'm not in the right headspace to make big decisions. And Mira might be the most important decision I've ever had to make.

"Thank you for hearing me out." Her broken voice is a searing lance to my heart, but I knock it away. I can't afford a killing blow right now. "I don't think Loki will require regular checkups anymore, so you won't have to worry about seeing me."

"Perfect" is my quick response.

And I instantly want to take it back. I meant perfect that he's better, not that I won't have to see her. That part stings in a way I didn't expect.

A few minutes ago, she asked me to hear her out, and hope welled in her eyes.

Now, thanks to me, it's spilling down her cheeks.

CHAPTER 30

Mira

It's been the longest week of my life. I'm a shell of myself, and I'm not even succeeding at hiding it. My heartbreak is on my sleeve for everyone to see. I thought foaling season sucked, but getting over what happened between Stefan and me is worse. It's truly a torment I've never known.

I haven't heard a single thing from Stefan all week. He hasn't called or texted. And I haven't either. Giving him space seems like the most grown-up approach at this time.

I wish I could make him see things the way I do, but I'm not one to force things on another person. If I were more like Billie, I'd march over there and browbeat him until he relented. I'm more live and let live though. If that's what he thinks of this, of me, then that's fine. I'll get over it.

Eventually.

But not soon enough. Because this hurts. I feel like we've spent months building a complicated puzzle together, and now he's taken one piece and hidden it on me. It's annoying to look at, no matter which way I spin it, what perspective I move to—the puzzle is incomplete.

I'm incomplete.

How it happened is beyond me. All those quiet nights on the barn floor, I guess. All the inappropriate jokes. All the times he asked me on a date. All the times I turned him down.

All the time I wasted when we could have been together.

If I'd said yes, I might have had more time with him before this happened. Maybe it wouldn't have happened at all. Maybe it all would have come out more organically if I hadn't been so fucking stubborn.

Instead, I'm here in the office replaying our interactions and nights together, feeling his hands sliding over my skin, hearing the filthy words spilling from his lips.

I'm missing him like crazy and trying to pretend I don't. Nadia eyes me speculatively now and then. We both know talking about my relationship with her brother would be weird. And he's *her* brother, so I fully expect she takes his side in this nightmare. If there are sides to be had at all. Plus, I know he loves her more than anything in the world, so it feels wrong to lament anything about him to her, even if she's become a friend.

If you ask me, it's just one big sorry situation. She asks me how I'm doing with a weird intonation that tells me she doesn't believe me when I say I'm good.

I am not good. I'm fucking sick.

"What are you staring at?" Billie says from behind me where I'm staring out the enormous windows at the front of the clinic.

I spin, startled by her presence. She must have come in through the back door closest to the barn.

"An eagle," I lie.

"Huh." She peers at the sky in an exaggerated fashion. "I must have missed it."

We both know she didn't miss shit.

"Must have."

"You holding up, Mimi?"

"Jesus Christ. Can you not?" I cross my arms and shake my head.

Her hand falls across her chest in mock alarm. "Not what?"

"Your nicknames. I've escaped them for this long. I thought I was doing okay, and now all of a sudden I'm *Mimi*?"

She snorts. "It doesn't suit you at all."

"Yes. Exactly. Thank you."

"But that's why I like it."

I groan and drop my chin to my chest. "Sometimes I wonder why I love you so much."

"Because I'm honest."

Ugh. I really don't want to hear about honesty. According to Stefan, I'm dishonest. And that hurts too. I don't think I'm a dishonest person. Not at all. I got tangled up these last couple months, but I'm not a liar. And I don't like being called one.

"Uh-huh..." I peek at Billie out of the corner of my eye, wondering what's coming next.

"I'm here to tell you to pull yourself up by the bootstraps. He's just a boy. And you are a fucking rock star."

This conversation is the epitome of what I don't want to talk about. "Thanks," I reply tersely.

She snorts. "Maybe Dalca the Dick really is a dick after all, huh?"

I know she's trying to make me laugh, but this doesn't feel funny right now. It feels like she's diminishing what happened between us. And the more time I spend away from Stefan, the more I realize what happened between us is love. Or at least something a lot like it.

"Funny." I don't laugh.

Her amber eyes dart over to mine. "I wasn't trying to be funny, Mira. I was right. The guy *is* a dick, and you deserve better."

What are the stages of grief again? Because I'm pretty sure my best friend just catapulted me into the anger phase.

"You know what, Billie? Fuck you. This isn't the moment where I need you to be right. I need you to be wrong."

Heat lashes at my gut, and I spin on my heel to walk away. I need to get out of here. But I come face-to-face with a wide-eyed Nadia. "Can you lock up, Nadia? I'll see you tomorrow."

It's only been one week since Stefan asked me if I only do things when they benefit me, and I'm still not over it. Still not over him.

And I'm not sure I ever will be.

"You're really out?" My nana is not buying my story about how I came to see her for more samosas. "Because you don't *look* like you've been eating."

I haven't been.

"Yup. Can we make some?"

Folding samosas with my grandmother is therapeutic. It's soothing. And right now, I need to be soothed. Even her lilting accent soothes me—until it reminds me of Stefan's and the way it's more pronounced when he's turned on. A shiver races down my spine.

She hobbles back into my parents' house, shaking her head. "Your parents are out right now."

She moved in here a couple of years ago after my grandfather passed. She tells me it's because I'm her favorite grandchild, but I'm pretty sure it's because my parents have a separate suite she can live in.

I follow her to the kitchen and try to pull stuff out, but I'm moping, and I keep getting in her way. I feel like Eeyore dragging his sad ass around just being generally brutal.

"You"—she points at me and then points at the table—"go sit down."

"Okay." I tuck my tail and drop into a chair, relieved to be resting and away from prying eyes, disapproving stares, and awkward conversations with Hank. *God*, are they ever awkward. He's trying so hard to be chipper around me while also not talking about the elephant in the room.

It's brutal, and I'm ashamed to say I've taken to avoiding him.

"Where is the blond boy?" Nana has her upper body shoved into the fridge, where she's pulling ingredients.

"Probably working."

"Did he break your heart?"

My throat constricts. But I don't respond.

"Yes?" She shakes her head as she bends down to pull a bowl out of the lower cupboard, her cotton sari draping with her every movement. "I knew he would."

"I thought you said he wasn't my type?"

She looks at me now, her eyes fierce, her index finger pointing straight at me once again. "Exactly. Your type wasn't working for you, so I knew he would. All smart and sexy and established, why wouldn't he?"

Did my grandmother just call Stefan Dalca sexy?

I clear my throat and pick at a dent on the dated wooden table.

"So?"

"So what?"

"Did he break your heart?"

I feel my bottom lip wobble. "Yeah."

"And what are you going to do about it?" she asks as she continues organizing ingredients and cooking utensils.

"I mean… nothing. I don't think he can forgive me. I'm not one to grovel. I'm still not even sure I did anything wrong. It's… complicated."

"Mira, Mira, Mira." Her head shakes, and she makes a tutting noise. "You work so hard for everything else that you want in life. School, career, your independence—you haven't cared about what anyone thought about all that. What makes this any different? What makes you think you won't have to work for this?"

"I…" I trail off.

I don't have a good answer. The only thing that runs through my head is Stefan asking if I ever do something that doesn't benefit me. Going after him with reckless abandon would serve me, but would it just upset him? I feel like I'm living each day with that one sentence haunting me. Do I really do that? I became a veterinarian to help animals, to be a voice for those who don't have one, and I know I've helped countless people along the way. As a general rule, people love their animals and appreciate my work.

But I'm paralyzed by the sentiment that I do nothing unless it helps me in some way. Do I only save animals because it makes me feel good? And if I do… is that even a bad thing?

"Do you want him?"

That's a question I barely need to think about. "Yes."

"Then take him. I saw the way that fool looked at you when you were here. You might have thought you were tricking us by bringing a fake date to fend off the questions, but not me. And nothing about that day was fake for him."

I think she's trying to reassure me, but it's not working. The cracking pain in my chest is sharp enough to take my breath away.

"Okay." My breathing hitches as my brain whirs.

What have I done? How have I so easily dismissed our connection as something fleeting? Why did I give up on him when I've never given up on anything that matters to me in my life? Maybe it's not so bad that I do things that benefit me.

Maybe my mistake is failing to make Stefan one of those things.

"Well?" She props her tiny fists on her full hips and gives me a suffering look. "Why are you still here pretending that you're out of samosas?"

Why does she know absolutely everything?

"Get out of here. Go get him. Nobody walks away from my favorite granddaughter unless she lets them."

I was so concerned about what everyone else would think that I failed to notice the way a great man worshipped me. The way he was *good for me.* And now I've hurt him. And it doesn't even matter who's right or wrong. There's no fault. My intention doesn't matter. None of that matters because I hurt a man who has done nothing but care for me in a way no one ever has.

I don't even respond. There's no point in denying that my freezer is practically overflowing with samosas. My plan was to pawn these new ones off on Billie and Vi. I nod, swiping my keys off the counter and striding out the front door.

My heart knows how I feel about him. But my head—well, my head is a complicated place to be sometimes. I exist in a world of absolutes and science. But there is nothing absolute about falling in love.

No, that's a matter for the soul.

The minute I hop in my truck, all fired up and feeling determined, my phone rings through the Bluetooth system. Nadia is calling. I press the button, expecting her to have some question about closing the clinic for the night.

What I don't expect is her panicked voice. "Mira! The barn at Cascade Acres is on fire!"

I've never driven so dangerously in my life. I know the back roads around these small towns like the back of my hand, so I cut every corner I can and break every speed limit. Nadia didn't have much information other than she'd gotten a call from the barn manager and was heading over there.

I got a hold of Vaughn to close the clinic for us, and I've made it back to Ruby Creek in record time. I can see the smoke billowing ahead of me like an omen. My stomach sinks at the sight of the dark clouds over Stefan's picturesque farm.

Inhaling deep breaths into my lungs, I try to force myself into the right headspace for what I might walk into. Barn fires aren't exactly unheard of. Unfortunately, hay and wood make for excellent kindling. But the outcome never gets easier. Burns, smoke inhalation—it's almost always ugly and heartbreaking.

Especially with the size of the smoke cloud overhead. This isn't some small spark.

I confirm my suspicions when I turn into the driveway. The scenic barn is covered in smoke, flames licking up the back side of the building. Lights flash in the darkening night, and I hear the firefighters shouting as I park and jump out of my truck—heading straight for the fire.

I see the barn manager, Leo, staring at the scene before him, mouth agape, standing with the glow of flames lighting his face.

"Are the horses out?" I ask him.

"I—no. Not all of them. We'd just put them all away for the night when it happened."

My heart lurches. *Loki. Farrah.* Rage courses through me. "And why are you just standing here?"

"What am I supposed to do?"

Absolute idiot. "Were you here when it started?"

He nods solemnly. The coward was here when it started and didn't do shit except stand here catching flies.

"Where is Stefan?"

"On his way."

"Where is Nadia?"

"She went in."

A chill starts from the ground, seeping up through my bones. "Excuse me?"

He points at the barn. "Just a couple minutes ago."

"Fuck, Leo. Has anyone ever mentioned that you're a pussy?" I storm toward the barn and stop near a fully outfitted firefighter. "There's someone in there, did you know that?"

"We just got here, ma'am. We're assessing the situation."

Not good enough. Nadia is in there. Stefan can't lose her. It will kill him.

Moments later, Nadia stands at the wide-open doors, eyes wild and searching. My relief is short-lived.

"I need gloves," she shouts. "I can't get the stalls open! The metal latches are too hot."

Then she turns and races back into the building. A firefighter runs to the door, trying to grab her before she disappears back into the smoke.

My stomach sinks as I stare at the barn. Her words haunt me as I watch the flames building on each other. Everything Stefan has worked so hard for. The redemption he's thrown himself into. His horses who he loves so quietly. Sweet souls who have no hope of helping themselves in this situation.

His sister.

The thought barely crosses my mind before I'm moving. I grab a pair of gloves sitting on the bumper of the fire truck and sprint for the barn before anyone can stop me. No chance I'll stand here watching a barn full of horses and a friend of mine burn to death while they formulate a plan. It's simply not an option.

I hear shouts behind me as I shove my hands into the big gloves and charge through the door. It crosses my mind what I'm doing is monumentally stupid, but I don't linger on that thought. Even if I can save a few horses and get out, I'll be happy.

Thick smoke fills the dark barn. The whinnies are loud over the crackling of the fire. I can almost *taste* the fear. And then I see Nadia, trying to grab a latch but jerking away when it sizzles against her skin.

Her eyes find mine, her voice imploring as she points down the barn alleyway to where the smoke is thickest. "Mira! Loki is down there! They're *all* in here."

She looks down at her hands, and it doesn't take a medical degree to see that she's burned them in her failed attempts to open the stalls.

"Nadia. Out. You need medical attention. I've got this."

"Let me help you!" She's in shock, tears streaming down her face.

"No."

"Mira. You don't understand. If he loses Loki, I don't think he'll ever forgive himself. That foal is proof that not everything he touches turns to shit. I have to get him out."

"And if he loses you, Nadia? Then what?" I grab her, sheltering her underneath my arm and walking her toward the open doors. "Go. I'll get Loki out."

The look she gives me is full of pleading as the emergency crews descend on her, but I'm back in the barn before they can grab me.

Moving quickly, I pull my coat over my nose and grab the metal latch of the first stall. I step in, slap the horse on its haunches, and watch it run for the door. Horses are flight animals. I just hope someone out there has the good sense to corral them off somewhere. Even if they don't, running free is better than burning.

I work my way swiftly down the barn, thankful that many of Stefan's horses live at the track and this is not a full stable.

The smoke thickens the farther I get down the alleyway. The heat is intense, but I push on. Luckily, the fire seems to be worse on the outside of the building than on the inside.

I feel like I've gotten almost all the horses out, but not the ones I desperately want.

I mutter into my jacket, "Fuck my life," as I trudge to the end of the barn where Loki and Farrah have been living.

I specifically picked the back because it's less drafty. A choice I now regret. Farrah is pacing nervously when I get to them. Loki huddles by her side, all signs of his spunky personality replaced with pure terror.

"Hey, guys. I got you." I swing the door open.

Farrah doesn't need any prompting. She bolts for the safety of the front door with Loki at her haunch, galloping to keep up.

I spin to follow them when a wave of dizziness hits me.

I need to get out of here.

That's my last thought before everything goes black.

CHAPTER 31

Stefan

I HAVE NO IDEA WHAT I'M WALKING INTO, BUT I KNOW IT'S NOT good. I could see the glow of my property from down the road as I sped back from a court date in Vancouver where I was really looking forward to burying that slimeball Patrick Cassel.

When I drive through the tall iron gates, with my heart firmly in my throat, I'm met with chaos. Lights flash and horses are loose around the property. I sigh when I see Farrah and Loki closed off in the paddock closest to the house. *Thank god.*

I'm relieved to see Mira's truck is here. I suspect we're going to need her help, and I'm willing to endure the pain of being around her if it means saving my horses' lives.

Nauseating butterflies erupt in my stomach as Nadia runs toward my car, waving bandaged hands, tears clinging to her mascara, leaving black smudges down her cheeks. For a girl who looks constantly put together, she is downright frantic.

I sit frozen, not sure I'm ready to face what I'm about to walk into. I'm watching my goal go up in flames. Literally.

I've spent the past several years chasing a vendetta. And here I am, watching it all turn to ash. I don't even know how to feel.

Nadia yanks my driver's-side door open. She's shouting frantically, but I can't quite wrap my head around what she's saying. I'm too lost in the flames, what they represent.

It's almost hypnotic.

Her hand lands hard and fast across my cheek, forcing my attention to her. "Wake the fuck up! Mira is in there! She hasn't come out!" She's screaming now. Distraught.

And in a blast, I absorb all her anxiety. Her horror. I'm in motion before I have a single second to think about it. I leave my door open as I jog toward the barn, the devastation of the fire dawning on me.

"Stefan! They said they can't go in. But *she's in there*! She sent me out and went in instead, promising to get Loki and Farrah! They both came out. They were in the last stall. But she hasn't followed!" The pain is palpable as it rolls off my sister in waves.

Everyone is just standing back, watching.

"Where is she? Where is Mira?" I hear Billie from just behind me, her golden eyes desperately searching the crowd while Hank stands at her side, his green eyes alight with pure agony as he wraps an arm around Billie's midsection to hold her back.

Word travels fast in a small town, and I'm certain they could see the fire from their property. They must have arrived mere moments after me, and I'm sure they overheard Nadia's shouting.

The lack of action enrages me. *I* enrage me. I told Mira she only ever does anything to benefit herself. Now she's in *my* burning barn. Saving *my* horses. Saving *my* sister.

And I said *that* to her. What I should have said to her is that I love her. That I needed some time to lick my wounds. That we would be fine. That I was going to come back. That I'd never felt this way about another person before.

That I never wanted to again.

The need to tell her overwhelms me. And instinct overtakes all sense. All I know is I *need* her.

I need to tell her I love her.

I take one look into my newfound father's eyes, and something passes between us. An understanding. An agreement. I only just found him, and now I might lose him. But if I don't at least try to get her out of there, I will lose myself. He nods at me, and with his blessing, I push through the line of firefighters.

"Sir!"

"Sir, stop! The structure isn't stable!"

A hand reaches out to grip me, but I'm stronger. My strength is coming from somewhere else right now. *Adrenaline.*

I shake the person off and hold an arm up over my mouth to stifle the smoke. Once I cross the threshold, I realize they localized the flames on the outside of the building but the smoke inside is suffocating. It's captured in here like steam from a shower in a closed bathroom. Deep down, I know I'm making a stupid decision walking into a burning building.

But even deeper down than that, I know it's the *right* decision. It's the *only* decision.

Every stall door is open as I rush down the hall, checking for where she might be located. Panic rises in me every time I check a stall and don't find her. It chokes me. The smoke I can handle. Losing her when I've only just found her is what

I won't survive. It's what's closing my throat and making my eyes sting.

Flames, spurred on by the hay stall at the back, cut through the smoke. The heat is borderline overwhelming, and the thought that I might have to turn back flits across my mind before I shake it away.

And then I see it, a dark lump on the floor. *Mira.*

I rush forward, shucking my jacket off and covering her head with it. The long tips of her hair are singed from the close flames. I pat them out over the top of my jacket before scooping up her limp form.

"Stefan..." I can barely hear her. "I got them out for you."

Her words cut me off at the knees. *I did this.* I told her something so cruel that she walked into a burning building to show me otherwise.

"Mira. I love you." But she doesn't hear me. Her body goes heavy in my arms.

Sagging. Lifeless.

She doesn't respond. But I chant my confession as I turn and run for the door.

"I love you. I love you. I love you."

All those months ago, in almost this exact spot, I carried a limp, lifeless foal out of this barn. And she sat in the rain with me digging a hole for that foal, even though she didn't need to help. I don't know why she did it. I don't know how she knew I needed her steady, quiet company that morning. But I fully intend to spend the rest of my life repaying her for it. For sticking it out. For not shunning me or hating me or thinking the worst of me when everyone else did.

For *protecting* me.

And now it's my turn to protect her.

I rush out of the barn, staying low and holding her as tightly as possible. Her limbs swing as I hug her to my chest and pray to whatever power is listening to please not let this be it for us. I tell her over and over again, hoping she can hear me through it all.

"I love you. I love you. I love you."

I stumble out into the fresh air, gasping to get it into my lungs. "Help!" I cough, moving as far away from the burning building as possible. "She needs help!"

Bodies surge in around us as I drop to my knees and place her on the gravel road as carefully as I can. "Mira." I smooth her burnt hair away from her beautiful face, smudges of ash trailing in the wake of my fingers. "Mira." I shake her gently and am met with the heavy feel of a body that offers no resistance. The firefighters descend around us, but I can't take my eyes off of her. "I love you."

What if the last thing I ever said to her was harsh? What if the last thing I ever did was make her cry?

"Sir, we need you to move." Hands grip at me, pulling me away from her when all I want is to cover her body with mine. To give her anything she needs. Lungs. Skin. Life. She can have it all.

I love you. I love you. I love you.

"Stefan, they need space." Hank's soothing voice filters in through the chaos as his hand squeezes at the back of my neck to urge me away from her. "Move back so they can do their jobs."

What if I never see her again? I don't think I'll ever forgive myself.

Nausea surges in me, and for the second time in a week, I get up and run toward the lake, where I can empty my stomach in peace. Paramedics surge past me in the opposite direction carrying duffel bags and oxygen. The surrounding noises are loud, but all I can hear is the whoosh of blood in my ears, the quickened thump of my heart beating through my body as I lean up against a tree and give myself over to the sickness.

What if she dies saving everything that she thinks is dear to me without knowing she *is* everything *to me?*

I love you. I love you. I love you.

The guilt eats at me, tearing at my flesh. I feel like I'm being ripped apart piece by piece. I gasp for air and stare out over the lake, wishing my mom were here when a warm hand slides over my shoulder.

Hank says nothing, but I know it's him. We have a connection and barely know each other. Deep down, I know he's my dad. Sure, a DNA test will prove it, but I already know it. I know it in my bones.

His firm grip on my shoulder soothes me as I try to recapture control of my breathing.

"She's breathing. She's got this."

I peek over my shoulder. Relief and regret pummel me with equal strength. "I can't lose her."

He gives me a solemn nod. "I know."

"I just can't."

"I know."

"I love her."

He sighs. "I know, son. I know."

I stare back out over the lake, silently begging my mother for some of her strength. Her strength to endure years of what she did to keep us safe. I need that strength to keep Mira safe.

"She'd be proud of you."

My breathing goes raspy.

"I know I am."

My eyes sting, and I wish I were man enough to properly respond to that. It's all I've wanted to hear for years. But my brain fixates on Mira.

I squeeze his hand back. "Thank you."

"Go be with her. She needs you."

I don't like the way he says that. It sounds far too final. It makes me feel like a shmuck for wasting precious time retching when I should have been with her. Even though what she needs is medical attention.

I rush across the grass, watching them load her unconscious body onto a stretcher with an oxygen mask affixed firmly over her delicate face. Billie and Nadia stand huddled close to each other, tears twinkling on their cheeks. The back doors of the ambulance open, and Billie moves to get in with Mira.

"No," I say. "I'm going."

She glares at me, her eyes bright like the flames as they rake over my face, assessing me and looking like they find me entirely lacking. "I'm not sure what she sees in you. I'm not sure what drives her to defend you, to choose you when she could have anyone she wants—to walk through fire for *you*." Her finger presses into the center of my chest. "But this is your chance to prove yourself to everyone. And if you ever make her cry again, I have a lot of land at my disposal to bury your body."

I've always thought Billie was a bit of a loose cannon, but her love is absolute. I love that Mira has friends like this in her corner. I've never had anyone like this in my corner. And her challenge is one I'm happy to accept. I nod, never dropping her eye contact.

"Who's with her?" one paramedic calls out of the back of the ambulance.

And I don't miss a beat. "I am!" I grab a handle and pull myself onto the small bench beside Mira's still form.

Moments later, I take one last look at the wide eyes looking on. Her friend. My sister. My dad.

And then the doors close, and it's just us.

I grip her hand and drop my head to my chest.

I need it to be us *forever.*

The hospital is a blur. I spend the night drifting off in an uncomfortable chair, too anxious to sleep but too exhausted to keep my eyes open. People I know or recognize flit in and out. And when Mira's parents rush in through the door, I stand.

Her mom envelops me in a full hug before she breaks down in my arms, her tears soaking through my thin dress shirt. "Thank you."

If she knew the things I had said to her daughter, she wouldn't be thanking me.

"You saved her. Th-thank you."

She holds on to me like I'm a lifeline. The hug more than just an embrace. Deeper than that. I feel her gratitude wrap around me as she clings to my body, vibrating under my arms. Her dad and grandmother stand behind her looking stoic.

When Sylvia pulls away, her father shakes my hand, tearing up, unable to say anything. Which works just fine for me.

Her nana, though, steps up close, gripping my chin tightly in her bony hand. And then she smiles. "How are you feeling?"

"Guilty," I reply honestly because there's no lying to this woman.

Her head quirks, eyes twinkling. "Why?"

My palm rasps across my face. "I can't help but feel responsible for her being here. Injured. God knows wha—" My voice cracks, and I look away.

She pats my chest and shakes her head. "Poor sweet fool. That girl was coming back for you. Don't you know her well enough to know she doesn't quit? She walked into that barn because that's the type of person she is. A little prickly, but as loyal as they come once you get her. And don't worry, you've got her. I rather think you're stuck with her."

Claws rake down the back of my throat. I know she's trying to make me feel better, but the guilt is still there. Magnified by the longing I feel. I just want to be with Mira.

I want to hold her.

When she wakes up, I'm never walking away from her again. I'm going to bask in being stuck with her.

No matter what it takes.

And I'm going to tell her I love her. Over and over and over again.

CHAPTER 32

Mira

Nothing makes sense.

A steady beeping sound filters through my consciousness. My eyelids are heavy like lead, and my body aches. I roll my tongue through my mouth, chasing away the dryness as best I can, but my throat feels like sandpaper, raspy and sore enough to make me whimper.

I feel a squeeze on my forearm and a firm hold on the opposite hand.

My eyelids flinch as I force them open. It feels like there's dirt inside them. I'm in a mostly dark room. Dim lights give it a sort of warm-yellow glow. It strikes me that it's probably nighttime.

"Hey." I glance over at my best friend, into eyes lined with anxiety.

"Hi. God." Her voice quavers. "It's really fucking good to see you."

I try to smile, finding comfort in the crass way Billie talks. It feels so normal. "Am I…?" Jesus, my throat feels terrible.

"You're in the hospital." Her hands stroke my forearm, and she nods to my opposite side. I slowly turn my head, realizing I can feel someone holding my hand, but it's not my friend. When I look down and to my left, I'm met with a slumped figure in a chair pulled close, a mop of beautiful dark-gold hair resting on the bed beside me.

He's here.

I sigh, my lungs burning and chest aching.

He's clutching my hand like I'm his lifeline while he sits in an uncomfortable hospital chair, face resting on the bed by my thigh. He looks exhausted, but I soak in his face like I haven't seen the sun in years. His sharp cheekbones, covered in more stubble than I'm used to seeing. His full lips slightly parted. The dark smudges beneath his eyes.

I feel confused about everything that is going on around me.

Except him.

I've never been so sure of anything in my life.

"He hasn't left your side," Billie whispers. "Nadia had to bring him fresh clothes because he reeked of smoke but refused to leave you."

Tears spring up in my eyes as I watch the beautiful man sleeping beside me. All I want is for him to hold me and tell me everything is going to be okay.

"He went into the burning barn—when everyone told him not to—and carried you out. If it wasn't for him, I'm not sure we'd be sitting here today. I mean, he literally walked through fire for you."

Tears roll down my cheeks.

Billie reaches up to wipe them away, drawing my attention away from Stefan. "The guy is a total nightmare." Her voice cracks, but she blinks quickly and forges ahead. "But not in the way I thought. Never mind his barn, I think he's been ready to burn this whole fucking hospital down to get you the best care available and what I'm pretty sure is like a twentieth opinion." Her laugh is tearful, and I smile back at her.

"Listen, Mimi." I groan and shake my head. Billie is insane in the best possible way. "I was wrong. And I'm sorry. Any man who loves you as much as he does is a winner in my book."

"Thank you," I rasp. I know I don't need my friend's permission, but knowing she accepts him—accepts us—well, that makes my heart happy. "Did he tell you much?"

She snorts and rolls her eyes. "That Hank is his daddy? Or that he named my horse?"

I scrunch my face up and nod, whispering, "Yeah. Kinda big news. I know Hank is like a dad to you and has been for a long time." Then I point at her. "And you know that name is a good one."

"Yeah. I have to confess, it is." She chuckles tearfully. "And man, Hank is so happy. It's downright infectious. I can't *not* be happy for them. The world works in mysterious ways, Mimi." She winks saucily, clearly getting hold of her emotions. "I mean, I need another dumb brother like I need a fucking hole in the head. But here I am with one anyway." She gestures across at Stefan's sleeping form.

He stirs, like his ears are burning. I give his hand a quick squeeze, and his head snaps up. Dopey eyes latch onto mine instantly.

"I'm gonna go," Billie says with a gentle squeeze of my arm and a kiss to my hair.

I don't even look at her. "Okay, bye." I can't tear my gaze away from Stefan, his entrancing green eyes, his slightly crooked nose. I drink him in, trying not to think about how I almost let him get away.

"Hi." I smile, unable to discern the expression on his face as the door clicks shut. Like he's almost angry.

"How do you feel?" His fingers push between mine.

"Sore." Why lie? Every part of me feels sore.

"You suffered smoke inhalation and a concussion from when you passed out. You've been out for about a day."

"Oh. Okay."

He's all business right now. "The doctor said your trachea and lungs should heal completely. But I've got a second and third opinion on the way." Rigid tension lines his body as his eyes rake over mine. "I'm not taking any chances they missed something."

"Okay." I'm sure I'll be fine. I'm capable of understanding any diagnosis I might have, but if micromanaging this makes him feel better, I won't interfere. "How are *you*?"

I brush my thumb across the underside of his hand, reveling in the feel of his skin on mine. In the way energy crackles up my arm with the simplest touch. This man sets me on fire. Maybe that's why I ran in there with no regard for my safety. I'd already endured the most intense heat I could imagine. That barn was no comparison for our chemistry.

"Mira, you shouldn't have gone into that barn." His jaw ticks with annoyance.

"Neither should you," I scold him right back.

"I couldn't leave you in there." His voice breaks as his eyes land where our hands are joined.

I reach up and run my hand through his hair, savoring the feel of the strands running between my fingers. Something

I never thought I'd feel again. "You love so fiercely. Just like I told you. Just like me. I didn't think twice about walking into that barn."

His sad eyes meet mine. They more than meet. His gaze plunges into mine. The way he looks at me is borderline invasive, like he's staring straight into my soul. "Love?"

My hand slides down his cheek, the feel of his stubble against my palm sending goose bumps up my arm. "Yeah. You love me."

He looks so intense, which emboldens me. A man who was done with me wouldn't be regarding me like this.

"Who told you that?" His eyes dart to the opposite side of the bed where Billie sat earlier, but I tip his chin back down toward me.

"You did."

"Did you hear me in the barn?" His voice is raspy, his accent shining through a little more than usual as his free hand lands on my knee and strokes me there.

I quirk my head, knowing I've struck a chord. "No… but have you walked through fire for any other girls lately, Stefan?"

I smile, but his facade cracks right before my eyes. His face falls and a sob wracks his body as he gives up all pretense of control and crawls onto the small hospital bed beside me, turning my body in toward him with the utmost care. With heartbreaking gentleness. I bury my face in his chest. Rejoicing in the feel of his hard arms around me and his warm skin against mine.

His breath shudders, and his hand shoots into my hair, lovingly cupping my head. "I can't ever lose you. I'm so sorry I walked away." His words rumble across my scalp as he burrows into me. "I love you too fucking much."

"I know," I reply, stroking his hair. "I love you too, Stefan."

"Nothing else mattered when I thought you might die. *Nothing.* There is nothing you could do to make me leave you behind. And I'll never forgive myself for doing it once."

I nod into the warmth of his chest, feeling my eyes leak again.

"I don't know if I'll be able to keep you safe. But I want to spend forever trying if you'll let me."

"Oh, Stefan. You already do." My voice is thick as I stroke my hand over the length of his broad back. "You saved me last night. You believe me. You listen to me. You protect me. You stood up to my family for me, Stefan. And Patrick? You took him out for me." I laugh through the tears. "I mean, shit. You lied to the cops for me when I egged the principal's car with Nadia."

"That guy fucking deserved it."

I laugh again, but it's cut short when he pulls away and tips my chin up. "I love you, Mira." His confession is quiet and deep. Private and just for us. Even though he's already said it, this time it really sinks in. "You make me a better man. A happier man. I said it once before, and I meant it: you are mine, and I am yours. I will drink whatever ungodly coffee concoctions you bring me. I will worship your body." His eyes drop to my lips, and even in a hospital bed feeling more roughed up than I ever have, when *he* looks at *me* like *that*, I feel more beautiful than I ever have. "I would walk through fire for you any day. Over and over again."

And then his lips descend on mine. Soft and searching. Perfect and panty melting. His hands cup me like I'm the most precious thing he's ever held.

And I melt. I melt into him. Into us.

I whimper, overcome with emotion. Soaking in the feel of him and how he surrounds me, feeling infinitely safe in his arms.

"Does it hurt?" He draws back, concern etching his handsome face.

I fist the neckline of his T-shirt, gathering it between my fingers as our legs tangle together on the small hospital bed.

"No," I murmur. "Please." I sigh. "Don't ever stop," I implore.

He drops his forehead to mine. "I love it when you beg, Dr. Thorne."

His lips press against one cheek, in the sweetest kiss. "I love you." Before moving over to the other, butterflies erupt in my stomach. "I love you." Our lips meet in a soul-searing kiss, the perfect fit, and he says it a third time. "I love you."

And nothing in my life has ever felt more real.

I love him. I love him. I love him.

EPILOGUE

Stefan

THREE MONTHS LATER…

I FEEL MIRA'S FINGERS DIG INTO MY THIGH FROM WHERE SHE sits at the dinner table beside me. Hank sits across from us, and we've just finished a beautiful dinner I cooked for two of the most important people in my life. Seared duck breast, complete with a special blueberry sauce Mira concocted. Just to remind me of our very first "fake" date.

I've just placed an envelope in the middle of the table. It holds the results of our DNA test. It's what I've been waiting for, except now that it's here, I'm not sure I want to open it. Hank and I have been spending time together as though he is my father. Making up for lost time. And I've been soaking it up. No matter how much time I spend with the man, it's just never quite enough. I always feel like I want more. I have so much to share with him in whatever time we might have left. My perception of making the most of the time we have has drastically changed since the fire. Some might say it was a wake-up call to stop living in the past.

"Is that what I think it is?" Hank asks, eyes glued to the yellow envelope.

Who knew something so life-altering could come in such a generic-looking package?

"It is."

He swallows, and I watch him, feeling Mira's steady presence beside me. The tips of her dainty fingers press into my inner thigh, making me think about things I shouldn't be at a moment like this. But then she's always had that effect on me.

"It's funny"—Hank's voice is all gravel as he smiles and looks up at us—"because I've been looking forward to this, and now that it's staring me in the face… well, I think I'd be happy to go on pretending that it's exactly as we think it is."

A silence descends over the table before Hank continues, "You know, Stefan, even if this envelope doesn't hold what we're both hoping it does, I'd… well, I'd like to keep doing what we've been doing. Everything I felt about your mom is still true, and I like to think she'd be happy to see us spending time together regardless of DNA."

I lick my lips and wish away the stinging sensation across the bridge of my nose. "I would like that."

"Do you guys want me to read it first?" Mira asks quietly, her thumb rubbing soothing circles against my jeans. Her head volleys between us, her shiny black hair brushing the tops of her shoulders. After the fire, she cut the burnt ends and went for a straight blunt bob, and it suits her to a tee. She is striking, and there's still plenty for me to wrap between my fingers when I take her from behind.

Hank and I make brief eye contact before both nodding. Her hand darts out, and I see the anticipation shining in her eyes. Feelings about this have been a bit of a roller coaster for me, but Mira is *so* certain. She's the only thing keeping me grounded.

In a flash, she tears the top of the envelope and pulls out crisp white papers. Intelligent eyes scan the first page, her practiced impassive face giving nothing away. She flips the papers onto the place mat before her, rolling her lips together as her almond-shaped eyes find mine. Like always, I could get lost in those eyes. I often do, but right now I'm staring at them looking for some sign, some tell. She's giving me nothing.

"Stefan…"

This is torture.

I can't even tell if she's taking forever to say it or if time is standing still. Her full soft lips tip into a smile. "I'd like you to officially meet your father."

Hank barks out a loud laugh, leaning back in his chair with an exaggerated clap. But I just reach for Mira and yank her to me, gathering her in my arms. Her hair smells like honey, and her T-shirt smells like fresh laundry soap.

I realize that without her, without the universe placing her in my path, without a sick horse, without a dead mom… without all of that, I may never have found Hank. Without Mira, I may never have met my dad.

"Thank you." I nuzzle into her neck, momentarily distracted by all the ways I plan to thank her later tonight.

"Always" is all she says before holding me back and smiling at me, eyes twinkling with unshed tears. "Now go hug your dad."

So I do. I round the table and walk right into Hank's wide-open arms. My *dad's* wide-open arms.

God. That feels good.

"Nice to officially meet you, son."

I hear the emotion in his voice, and to be frank, I don't really trust myself to respond. So I just squeeze him tighter. It feels like I've spent a lifetime looking for him. And now I've found him.

We spend the next thirty minutes talking, laughing, and just feeling immensely relieved. When the night winds down, he hugs Mira, and I don't miss the way he whispers, "Thank you for bringing me my boy."

I also don't miss the way she wipes at her eyes and nods.

I don't know how I'll ever repay her. Repay the universe for giving me her.

Actually, I do. I know exactly how I'm going to do it. Which is why after Hank leaves, I suggest a walk down to where the barn used to stand. They have cleared away the rubble, and now it's just a big flat space. Ready to be rebuilt.

Next to the lake, Loki and Farrah graze happily in their field. Loki whinnies when he sees me.

"Your heart horse is saying hello, my love," Mira says.

I wrap my arm around her and pull her closer, feeling endlessly grateful.

After the fire, Billie approached me with a deal. Half-ownership of the little colt for everything I'd done to help with saving him. The woman I thought hated me is now calling me her "brother from another mother" and giving me half of one of her most prized horses. The world works in truly mysterious ways.

We walk into the middle of the cleared space. Hand in hand. After the hospital, Mira moved straight in with me. I wouldn't take no for an answer. Life was too fragile to spend another moment not together. This much I have learned. Plus, since finishing her courses, Nadia has decided to attend a college in the city to become a veterinary technician. That's how much she loves working with Mira. She'll be moving to Vancouver to pursue that soon, leaving the house to just the two of us.

A companionable silence stretches between Mira and me. Today is already one of the happiest days of my life. And I'm about to make it a whole lot happier.

There's this part of me that thinks standing here in the aftermath of a fire that took so much should make me sad.

But I feel relieved.

This is where I almost lost Mira. This is where I roped her into my arrangement. This is where I spent quiet nights learning Mira. This is where I laid my life on the line to save her.

I believe my mom is overlooking this exact spot from where I sprinkled her ashes.

This spot is my whole world. This spot is fate. This spot is my future.

This is where I'm going to rebuild.

Mira and I? We're like a phoenix, born from the ashes. And I wouldn't have it any other way.

She's looking up at the sky, all pink and orange as the sun crosses the horizon of the mountains, when I drop to one knee.

Her head snaps down to me immediately. "What are you doing?" One hand lands across her chest.

I grin. "What does it look like I'm doing?"

"It—"

"Do you think I'm down here trying to fix your shoe again?" Her eyes widen as she looks down at her simple slip-on sneakers.

"Don't worry, Kitten. I can"—I wink at her—"fix your shoe later. First, I have something I want to ask you."

"Oh my god." Her hand slides up around her neck, and I can see her pulse jumping in her throat as I pull a small velvet box out of my pocket.

"I've never considered myself a particularly good man. I never thought I was a bad man either. I was just a man with a sad past and no one to love. And then I saw you. It only took one look, and I swear some part of me knew."

Her free hand cups my cheek lovingly.

"I knew my life would never be the same. You didn't treat me like I was a bad man. You didn't always treat me like a good one either. But you made me want to be a *better* one. You make me want to deserve you. And I have every intention of spending the rest of my life trying."

"Oh, Stefan." A tear trails down her cheek as I flip the box open to display the thin yellow-gold band with a sparkling teardrop-shaped emerald affixed to it. All she can talk about these days is how green is her favorite color because it reminds her of me.

"This fire almost stole you from me. I almost lost you. And that's a mistake I never intend to make again. I intend to cherish you like the treasure you are. This fire burned everything else away. My anger, my vendettas. The only things that mattered to me I pulled out of it. And so I'm taking this as a fresh start. Everything else is ash—dust in the wind. And now I realize that the only thing that matters is what made it out. You and me." I pause here, watching my love reflected at me in her eyes. "Mira Thorne, would you do me the incredible honor of being my wife?"

She falls to her knees before me in one swift motion, hands cupping my face. "Yes. Yes, yes, yes. Nothing would make me or my aunt happier."

The smile on my face is huge as I slide the vintage ring onto her delicate finger. And when I gaze back up into her eyes, all I can see is our future.

I love you. I love you. I love you.

"Green is my favorite color, Stefan." She looks down at her hand with a tearful smile. I laugh and brush the tears off the apples of her cheeks before I erase the space between us and press my lips to hers. The lips I plan to kiss for the rest of my life. *Mine.*

A better man would have let her out of our arrangement.

I am not a better man.

And I've never felt less sorry about anything in my life.

BONUS EPILOGUE

Stefan

TWO YEARS LATER...

"I'M NERVOUS," I BLURT.

Mira smirks. It's slow and full of amusement. "I know. But he's here for experience. The win doesn't matter."

We're standing right at the finish line at Bell Point Park, where the little horse who brought us together will run past the post for the very first time. His first race. His maiden voyage.

"How do you know?" I jangle my keys in the pocket of my bespoke brown suit. I had it made to match Loki for today. And I don't care if that's lame.

Her lips roll together. "I can tell."

I scoff. "How?"

She lifts our joined hands up. "Well, for starters because your hand is so clammy that I can feel mine starting to shrivel." My brow furrows, so she clarifies, "You know, like when you spend too long in the bathtub?"

My eyes roll, and I release her hand. She's not wrong about the clammy part, but when I flip her hand over and trace the lines of her palm with my thumb, the only thing I notice is gooseflesh creeping up her arm. "Kitten. Your hand is not shriveled… but I can see the goose bumps when I do this."

"Do what?" Her voice has dropped an octave. It doesn't matter that strangers are starting to press in around us. When Mira and I touch, the world falls away, and in two years that hasn't changed a single bit. I can get just as lost in her eyes today as I could sitting on that dirty stall floor.

So I trace her palm gently again, and this time I watch a shiver race down her spine as she looks away from me. Like she's annoyed with herself for reacting to me so unmistakably.

Now it's my turn to smirk. I lean down toward her, letting the tip of my nose graze the shell of her ear. "You love my hands on you."

A low groan erupts from her lips. "Only you could go from being stressed out to horny at the drop of a hat like this."

I laugh because if nothing else, this conversation has distracted me from how nervous I really am. "You love me for it though." I wink at her and bask in the glow of the full smile she returns.

"I do. Very much."

The loudspeaker crackles to life right as I murmur that she can sit on my face later and I'll show her how much I love her back.

Her cheeks flare, but our attention is drawn away to the dirt track where the horses are spilling through the gate. It's a weeknight, and this is in no way, shape, or form an important race.

Except for me.

This is the most important race in the world because the sick little colt that Mira and I saved—the one that had no business making it through what he did—is out there.

My eyes find him immediately, and I feel my wife's hand pulse in my own. He looks like a brand-new copper penny. He shines so brightly, he's not just brown; he's metallic.

He looks flashy as all get-out with his high white stockings and wide white blaze. He also looks like a hormone-filled teenaged boy at his first high school party.

That is to say, he is leaping everywhere like an absolute fool. Violet is stuck on his back like a little fly with a long blond braid down her back, and I can see her grinning from here—not the least bit put off by his antics.

No, the surly-looking frown is reserved for her husband Cole, who is riding the pony horse, GD, that's walking beside Loki. His job is to keep the racehorse calm, and GD does it well. If a horse could roll his eyes, I'm fairly certain that's what he'd be doing to Loki right now.

Cole gets them loaded up into the gate and then trots away. He gives us a quick salute as he rides past where we stand, and I can't help but notice the amused look on his face as he takes me in.

Everyone has been making fun of the suit. Mercilessly. And clearly he heard about it too. But I don't care. This suit looks killer on me. Mira even agreed. Of course, she then asked if Loki and I were exchanging friendship bracelets as well.

The announcer is talking, but I register little of what he says. My eyes are glued to the gate. I don't even hear the countdown. Suddenly the bell rings and the gates fly open, horses surging out like a tidal wave.

I lean forward eagerly, watching them thunder down the stretch. Violet and Billie's plan for this race is to keep him in the middle of the pack. Where he's possibly packed a little too tightly to goof off the way he likes, where he won't fall too far behind or tire too quickly to make a move.

Basically, this race is one big experiment.

As they move into the turn, I can see that they're exactly where they wanted to be. In the middle, but there's still this part of me that wants to see him right up at the front.

Billie is all about giving him a positive experience, which I love. But… deep down I'm still really, really invested in him winning. In proving to the world that he's the real deal, like his dad, DD.

The main group of horses turn the corner, heading toward the final straightaway. Some have fallen away toward the back now, and a few have pulled ahead.

Loki is still running even and comfortable in the middle of the pack, and as I take a deep breath, I resign myself to the fact that his first race might not be the one he wins. After all, he's just getting started. He's a playful young stallion whose focus leaves something to be desired. Champions aren't made overnight.

But that's the moment Violet opens one rein to move him over, just enough that he's now looking down a perfect open lane up the middle of the pack.

And I swear he goes from looking around at the other horses to the eye of the tiger, tunnel vision straight down that path. Like there's some instinctual part of him that just *knows* what to do with all that space.

Violet goes low on him and shoves her hands at his neck forcefully, urging him to take the bit and run.

And he doesn't hesitate.

He shoots up the middle like he's been rocketed out of a slingshot. To be honest, I wasn't aware he had a streak quite like this in him.

He's a spitting fucking image of his dad right now. That inherent competitor in him—the winner in him—just leaping out to play. It's truly incredible to see.

And based on the flash of teeth coming from Violet's petite face, it must be a pretty incredible feeling too.

They thunder ahead; the ground vibrates beneath me. Passing the third-place horse, then the second, and with only moments to spare, they really stretch out. Covering the ground with an incredible final few strides, they push out to the front. A full length in front of the next closest horse.

And with a flash of the finish-line camera, Loki is officially a winning racehorse.

"Ahhh!" Mira screams, and her hands shoot up into the air above her head like she's just won an Olympic medal or something. Then she launches herself at me. Nuzzling into my neck while her arms squeeze tightly. "He did it! He fucking did it!"

My eyes water, and I bark out a loud laugh. "I thought he was here for the experience and the win didn't matter?"

She's vibrating with laughter now, and when she draws away, I realize there are tears sparkling in her beautiful dark eyes too. "I lied. I wanted him to win so badly I could barely stand it. I was trying to play it cool for you."

We laugh and hug again, and my chest feels so full of happiness that I think I could burst.

"Let's go revel in the winner's circle!" She grabs my hand and tugs me in that direction. Where I know all of our friends will be waiting with equally big smiles. Friends I never thought I'd have. Family I chose. I only wish Nadia was back from school to soak it up too.

We round the corner, and sure enough, there they are. Waiting for us. Billie waving at me wildly as she calls out, "He did it, Stef!" Vaughn grins playfully as he adds, "It was the lucky suit!"

I can see Cole leading Violet and Loki down the path toward the circle, and I soak it up. There's nothing in the world that could make me look away from them in that moment.

"Daddy!"

Except that. That is one of my new favorite sounds. My son's voice and my dad's deep chuckle to accompany it.

Hank and Trixie walk up, grinning broadly. My dad holding my son, Silas, who is reaching his chubby little arms out in my direction while my wife clutches my arm.

And all I can think is…

How did I get so damn lucky?

Acknowledgments

All throughout junior high and high school, my parents would pull me out of school for one day every month so that I could go volunteer with my horse's veterinarian.

One day we were called out to a barn fire. Luckily, the worst of it was smoke inhalation, on the one young horse that was stuck inside the longest. Her breathing was worsening by the minute, so we rushed her back to the clinic. But by the time we got there, she could barely breathe at all. So this veterinarian pulled out a textbook, read for a few minutes, and then proceeded to perform an emergency tracheostomy on the spot—a procedure she had never done before. She saved that horse by winging an unfamiliar procedure, and I just remember thinking that she was a stone-cold badass.

She was beautiful, smart, funny, and kind, and completely took me under her wing. Major girl crush over here! My days with her are some of the most memorable from that time in my life.

My mom always said that not all learning takes place in the classroom—and boy was she right. I learned *a lot* on those days. That castration scene? It really happened… except the next time she actually did let me do it on my own.

For years I swore I was going to become an equine veterinarian when I grew up, but I think Dr. Mira Thorne is as close to that as I'm really going to get. Something I'm okay with because her character is so full of personal pieces of me and I just love her so much.

I hope you all did too.

This is my third book! One that really fell to the page for me. I'm very proud of it. On top of that, I'm eternally grateful to all the people who helped make it possible.

To my husband, who encourages me to lock myself in a room and hang out with fictional men, you are my rock. *My person.*

To my son, who has taken to telling people, "My mom is on a deadline," you are a procrastinator too; I'm pretty sure you got it from me. Sorry about that. But I love you to the moon and back anyway.

To my editor, Paula, I feel so blessed that I get to work with you. Your feedback is not only helpful, but it brings me comfort. I trust you so much with my words and my worries, and I still think you should charge me extra for being my therapist sometimes.

Krista Callaghan, I'm so glad we crossed paths! I can't even explain to you what a huge help you've been. You're a superstar!

Anna P., who gave this manuscript a very thoughtful sensitivity read for me. THANK YOU. Thank you for helping me do Mira and her family justice. I also promise to never call it naan *bread* again.

To Mary, I think our covers just keep getting better. I adore working with you and can't wait to make more beautiful covers with you.

Brandi, Shannon, and Laetitia, hats off to you for your exceptional eye for detail and time spent poring over my words. I so appreciate your help.

My beta readers, Lena, Amy, Amber, and Christy, thank you for reading my manuscript even when it still feels all jumbled. Each of you helps me see things more clearly.

My ARC and street team members, I am absolutely overwhelmed by all of your support! It makes me a little misty-eyed to think about how much you have all done for me. I'm really not sure how I'll ever thank you all. I send hugs to each and every one of you.

Melanie Harlow, who gives so much of herself and her knowledge to helping new authors, thank you for your thoughtful responses every time I harass you about something.

Sarah and Jenn from Social Butterfly, thank you for sharing your wisdom and offering me so much direction and encouragement. I absolutely love working with you both.

Finally, thank you to The Golden Girls. My partners in crime. My friends. I love you both, meaty balls and all.

For Billie and Vaughn's story, read *Off to the Races*, book one in the Gold Rush Ranch series.

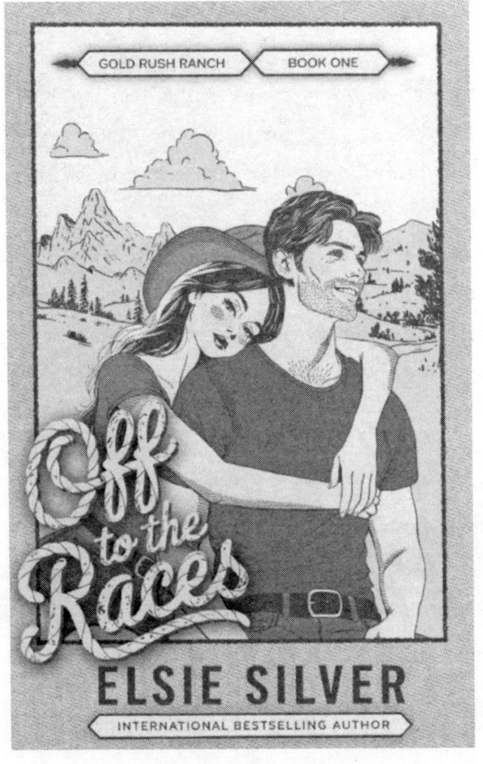

For Violet and Cole's story, read *A Photo Finish*,
book two in the Gold Rush Ranch series.

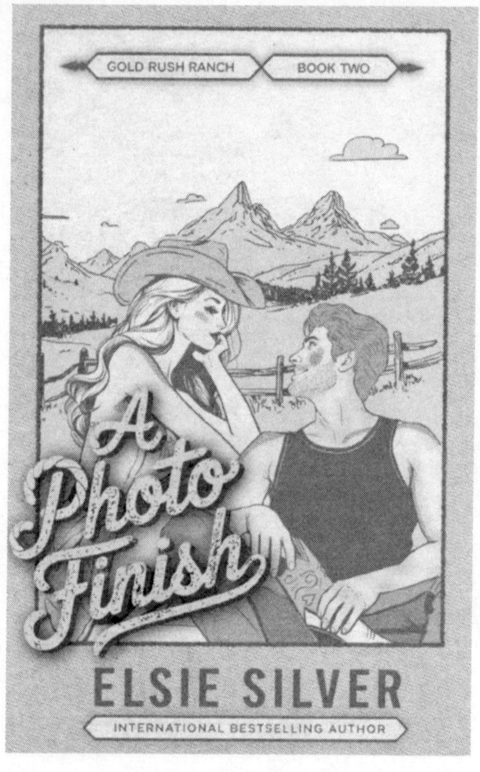

For Nadia and Griffin's story, read *A False Start*, book four in the Gold Rush Ranch series.

About the Author

Elsie Silver is a Canadian author of sassy, sexy, small-town romance who loves good book boyfriends and the strong heroines who bring them to their knees. She lives just outside Vancouver, British Columbia, with her husband, son, and three dogs and has been voraciously reading romance books since before she was probably supposed to.

She loves cooking and trying new foods, traveling, and spending time with her boys—especially outdoors. Elsie has also become a big fan of her quiet 5:00 a.m. mornings, which is when most of her writing happens. It's during this time that she can sip a cup of hot coffee and dream up a fictional world full of romantic stories to share with her readers.

Website: elsiesilver.com
Facebook: authorelsiesilver
Instagram: @authorelsiesilver
TikTok: @authorelsiesilver

ALSO BY ELSIE SILVER

Chestnut Springs

Flawless

Heartless

Powerless

Reckless

Hopeless

Gold Rush Ranch

Off to the Races

A Photo Finish

The Front Runner

A False Start

Rose Hill

Wild Love

Wild Eyes

Wild Side

ALSO BY ELSIE SILVER

The Chestnut Springs Series

Flawless

Heartless

Powerless

Reckless

Hopeless

The Gold Rush Ranch Series

Off to the Races

A Photo Finish

The Front Runner

A False Start

The Rose Hill Series

Wild Love

Wild Eyes

Wild Side

A FALSE START

ELSIE SILVER

New York · Amsterdam/Antwerp · London · Toronto · Sydney · New Delhi

A FALSE START
First published in Australia in 2024 by
Simon & Schuster (Australia) Pty Limited
Level 4, 32 York Street, Sydney, NSW 2000
First published in the United States in 2022 by Elsie Silver

10 9 8 7 6 5 4 3 2

Sydney New York Amsterdam/Antwerp London Toronto New Delhi
Visit our website at www.simonandschuster.com.au

The authorised representative in the EEA is Simon & Schuster Netherlands BV, Herculesplein 96, 3584 AA Utrecht, Netherlands. info@simonandschuster.nl

A catalogue record for this book is available from the National Library of Australia

ANZ ISBN: 9781761634260
UK ISBN: 9781398551091

Cover design: Mary, Books and Moods
Internal design: Sourcebooks
Printed and bound by CPI (UK) Ltd, Croydon CR0 4YY

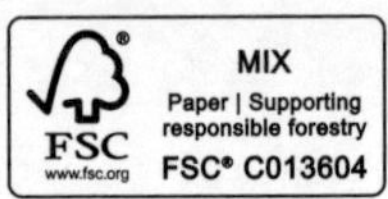

For my sweet little boy, who so proudly wears all the Gold Rush Ranch merch and tells people that his mom's work is called "Elsie Silvers" and that she writes books about kissing, which is "really gross." Just wait until you actually read one, Son.

I figure if a girl wants to be a legend, she should go ahead and be one.

—CALAMITY JANE

Reader Note

This book contains adult material including references to alcoholism, domestic/childhood abuse, and sexual harassment. Traumatic brain injury is discussed, and I fully understand that the impacts of this type of injury vary greatly from one person to the next. It is my hope that I've handled these topics with the care and research they deserve.

CHAPTER 1

Nadia

Tommy Koss is a terrible kisser.

He's mashing his lips into mine with zero finesse, and I wonder if a girl has ever taken the opportunity to tell him how utterly awful he is at this.

"You're so fucking hot," he murmurs between messy, slobbery kisses.

"So are you," I whisper back, arms slung loosely over his shoulders, rolling my eyes and wishing I could shut this running monologue off and just enjoy myself. His tongue tastes like cheap beer, and he's pawing at my breasts like a bear mauling a tree. The taste of alcohol in my mouth is an instant turnoff. A relentless reminder.

I had it in my head that making out with Tommy might make me feel something. It might be the cherry on top of an unusually wonderful day. Turns out, I only feel repulsed.

Maybe I'm outgrowing these antics?

His hands glide up under my tight tank top as he steps between my legs where I sit on the vanity in the men's bathroom. It smells like urinal pucks and whatever cheap body spray Tommy is wearing. I'm not so sure the scents are very different.

He yanks one of the slim straps of my tank top down and moves his lips to my chest. My head tips back, resting against the splattered mirror, and I stare up at the ceiling. The water stains on the foam panels are so old they've turned a rusty-brown color. Tommy's elbow bumps the hand dryer, and a loud blowing noise fills the small room.

My lips tip up in amusement, and I stifle a laugh. If this weren't so sad, it would be hilarious. At nineteen years old, making out with boys in the bathroom of shitty bars is supposed to be fun. Nineteen is when you're allowed to hit the bars in British Columbia. Going out is supposed to feel like living. But legal ages have never stopped me. It used to make me feel rebellious and excited. Now I just feel numb and bored. This idea that I'm missing something and hoping I might find it near some guy's tonsils is getting old.

Chalk it up to daddy issues, I guess.

My brother thinks I'm a wild card—reckless. Possibly even promiscuous. And I am, but what he doesn't understand is that I'm looking for something.

I'm just not sure what yet.

Tommy is about to pull my breast out over the top of my neckline. He's fumbling with it when the bathroom door swings open. I glance over at who walked in, but all I catch is a flash of dark eyes beneath the brim of a cap and a bearded jawline before the guy turns his back and makes use of the urinal like we're not even here.

Talk about big dick energy.

My lips part in a mixture of shock and glee, and Tommy gives me this sweet, boyish expression before shrugging and grabbing the nape of my neck, pulling me in for more unskilled face sucking. I should tell him to stop, but my body isn't attuned to him. For a few moments, I keep my eyes open, but I'm not looking at Tommy. Every ounce of my awareness is on the man taking a piss. The confidence. The sheer gall.

I'm honestly impressed.

I let my lashes flutter shut and pretend I'm kissing someone else.

The sound of a zipper closing draws me away from the wet smacking noises Tommy is making. And then the deep gravel of the stranger's voice makes me pause entirely. "Move."

The boy with his lips on mine pulls away and looks into the eyes of the man beside him. "My dude, just use the other sink. There are two."

The man's features are shadowed beneath the low-slung brim of his worn cap. Dense brows and deep-set eyes top off a strong nose. But mostly, he's too obscured beneath the brim of the cap for me to really make him out. Like he's hiding in plain sight.

The white mesh covering neatly trimmed brown hair has a faded brown panel at the front and the outline of a cowboy on a bucking horse. I lean in closer, inextricably drawn to the man, trying to make out the writing just beneath it.

Someone only wears a hat into that state if it's special to them. And I want to know more about what's special to a man like this. One who can take up all the space in a room without even trying.

"Go!" he barks, and I startle.

Raised voices always do that to me. I freeze, fire licking up my throat. I *hate* when anyone takes that kind of tone with me. All it does is make me combative.

Tommy just scoffs, totally oblivious to the steel in the man's voice, behaving like a boy who has seen nothing bad in his life and has no concept of the consequences. "Whatever, man. Let's go, Nadia," he says, moving toward the door without a backward glance. He doesn't stop and wait for me. He doesn't hold the door open for me. He just assumes I'll follow him back out into the bar where all our mutual acquaintances are waiting, where the other girls who I barely know will glare at me with envy in their eyes like Tommy is some great catch.

If they'd ever kissed him, they'd know the glares aren't necessary.

I don't follow. I sigh and lean back against the mirror, facing off with the mysterious stranger. The one glaring at me. I've always promised myself I won't respond when a man uses that voice on me, when they try to intimidate me, and today is no exception.

You're going to bark at me? I'll bite you back.

I give the man my best resting bitch face before peering down at my nails with disinterest. "I'm not well trained like that, so you really are going to have to use the other sink."

I gesture across the vanity, and he glares at me, irritation rolling off him in waves. The only part of him that moves is his broad chest as he breathes heavily and stares me down.

"And if you're going to talk to me like that again, I suggest you cup your boys to soften the blow."

He shakes his head and steps over to the other sink, flicking the tap, agitation lining every movement. A breath rattles past my lips, and the tension in the room begins to dissipate.

"I know. This is the men's room. I shouldn't be in here. Yadda, yadda, yadda. But you just pulled your dick out and took a leak without a second thought, so it's kind of hard to believe you're averse to washing your hands in front of me."

He says nothing. Just pumps a few gelatinous blobs of pink soap into his wide calloused palm. He looks older. He must be. The confidence, the thin lines highlighting the tense set of his eyes, the whole brooding act.

"You know," I continue, completely unprompted, just prattling on now, "I should thank you. That guy is the worst kisser. All teeth and saliva." I shudder dramatically as a small giggle escapes me, and I trace a finger over my puffy, ravaged lips while staring for too long into one of the pot lights above me. "Like, really bad."

Bright spots dance across my vision, and the quiet stranger just grunts, white T-shirt stretching across his thick chest, and then says, "Why?"

"Why what?" I ask, leaning in again, trying to get a view of his face. To make heads or tails of what this guy actually looks like. His light-wash jeans hug his ass, and his thighs fill them out just right, not too thick. His waist is trim, and a sea of intricate black tattoos that I could spend hours deciphering cover his arms.

His eyes flit to mine as he rinses his hands methodically. He swallows, and his Adam's apple bobs heavily in his throat. "Do that with him."

"Kiss him?" My head quirks, and he nods, stepping closer as his long arms reach across my lap to use the hand dryer. The loud whooshing sound fills the bathroom again, substantially less funny this time around.

I watch the way his hands fold over each other under the warm air, the odd droplet of water landing on my bare thigh just beneath the hemline of my jean skirt. When the dryer stops, he turns to me, and the weight of his gaze winds me. I suck air in through my nose, my shoulders coming up high as I do.

"I wanted to celebrate tonight. Found out I got into school today. I'm finally doing something for myself. I guess I just wanted to feel good for a bit."

He stares wordlessly, so I fill the space with words instead.

"Today I found out they accepted me into the program I applied for months ago. I'm going to be a veterinary technician. It's the first thing I can say I've ever really wanted to do entirely for myself. I was so nervous about applying that I haven't even told anyone I did—let alone that I got in. Not even my boss, who should probably know because she's going to need to hire a new receptionist by the time September rolls around."

The man hits the dryer again, as though to drown out my rambling. The warm air envelops my thighs, and I can almost imagine him palming them instead. To distract myself, I keep talking, hands gesturing animatedly.

"So I'm supposed to be celebrating my accomplishment tonight. Having *fun*. And if nothing else, Tommy has always been fun. Easy. A nice enough guy—if a terrible kisser. Best of all, he doesn't want any sort of commitment. Which is perfect because I don't have any commitment to give."

The dryer stops, and lights glint off the deep-brown irises that trace my face now, his nose wrinkling as he turns my words over in his head. This nameless man is studying me like I'm nuts.

A nervous laugh spills out over my lips before I lick them. *He is so intense.* "I don't know why I just told you all that."

His face is impassive, but he lifts one hand, hooking a finger through the strap of my tank top that is still pushed off my shoulder, making me feel just as disheveled as I must appear. But rather than pulling it down farther, like I hoped he might, he slides it up and places it back over my shoulder, the first knuckle of his pointer finger dragging across my collarbone.

My breath catches at the contact, goose bumps racing out in its wake, the man's dark-mahogany eyes fixed on where he touched me.

"Kiss me." I blurt the words out before I even think about them. His gaze snaps up, searing into mine. "A congratulatory kiss. A real kiss."

Here it is. My reckless side is out to play.

I swear I can see him thinking, weighing his options. Anyone could walk in at any instant.

"Why?" Suspicion taints his gaze.

I shrug. "Why not? Two perfect strangers who will never see each other again. What have you got to lose?"

He continues to stare at me for a beat, and I watch some of that wariness melt away. Within moments, his hand comes up underneath my jaw, his thumb pressing gently into the cleft of my chin as he pulls me to him, and like a moth to a flame, I go.

Up close, I get a glimpse of how ruggedly handsome he is. He turns his head to allow for the brim of his hat, giving me the perfect view of his stern face. This is a man who knows what he's doing. Knows exactly how to tilt his head, how to angle mine.

His face descends, and when his lips land against my own, I swear the world stands still. He smells like laundry soap and freshly fallen pine needles. His lips move with precision, with a longing I've never felt. And his mouth tastes like cinnamon.

I lean closer and sigh into the kiss, letting my palms press against his chiseled chest where the thumping of his racing heart beats against them. I find myself wishing he'd hold something more than just my chin. Wanting his calloused hands on me the way Tommy's smooth ones were minutes ago. I already know it would be better. This is the universe's cruel version of a side-by-side taste test.

And I already know who the winner is.

His mouth is firm, and I open for him, softening and surrendering as his tongue dances against the seam of my lips. His teeth don't clash against mine. His beard prickles at my skin, a sensation that sizzles over every nerve ending. I push closer to him. The unyielding pressure of denim sliding up my thighs makes me ache as he comes to stand between them. And when his hips press into the cradle of mine, I shiver.

I melt.

This kiss is like a dance with a man who knows how to lead rather than one who keeps stepping on my feet. It's effortless, and I want it to go all night.

But it doesn't.

He pulls away slowly, eyes raking over me, an almost confused expression on his face. My breathing is labored as I gaze up into his eyes, trying to figure out what's going on in here—in a dirty bar bathroom with a perfect stranger.

I want him to do it again.

Instead, he lifts his thumb and rubs it down over my slack bottom lip, sending a zing of arousal right between my legs. There's something possessive about the act. It's a filthy secret in a grungy restroom. It makes me want to follow him out of here and spend the night unraveling the mystery.

But his hands fall limp at his side, and he steps away, leaving me cold without his body heat. "Congratulations, Wildflower." His voice is so deep and so low that I almost don't hear it as he turns toward the door.

My eyes bounce back and forth between the blades of his shoulders, the ones straining against the fabric of his simple T-shirt. The expanse between them held taut.

"Again." I sound breathless, bordering on desperate. This can't be it for the dark stranger and me. Not when he just scorched the small bit of earth I'm standing on. Not when I feel like I might have just found *something.*

He doesn't turn around as he wraps one big hand around the door handle. He doesn't need to look at me to embarrass me, to make me feel small the way that most men in my life have. He only needs a few quiet, well-placed words.

"Once is an accident. Twice is a mistake."

CHAPTER 2

Nadia

I'M PMS-ING, I'M HUNGRY, AND I'M TIRED. IT'S A DEADLY COMbination, and I'm taking that deep-rooted anger out on the keyboard as I put together invoices for the month.

As it stands, I'm working part-time at the vet clinic and also taking my last few remaining high school courses by correspondence. So I sit at this front desk, alternately doing schoolwork or odd jobs that get handed off to me—something my boss, Dr. Mira Thorne, is totally fine with. In fact, it was her idea.

I answer the phone and greet people when they walk in the door. For those parts of my job, I'm supposed to be chipper and polite.

Both of which I'm not today.

I want to go home, curl up with a filthy book and a bottle of Midol, and play out that kiss with the hot-as-fuck stranger from the bar bathroom on the back of my eyelids. Apparently, orgasms are good for cramps. At least that's what my personal research has proven.

Which is why, when I hear the front door open, I stifle a groan and glance at the clock. One hour left. So close and yet so far away. Right now, I do not want to talk to a single person, and that's the only consideration in my mind as I swivel my chair around to face the entryway with a big fake, cheesy smile plastered on my face.

A look that freezes in place for a moment before transforming into one of utter shock, mouth hanging open like I'm about to say something. But then I just... don't. I literally can't because I especially don't want to talk to *this* person.

The dirty bathroom guy—that's what I'm calling him now—is here. At my place of work. Holding a brown paper bag and wearing a scowl that would scare most people. But not me.

Because I'm giving him an equally unimpressed look right back. I lean back in my chair, fingernails digging into the armrests as I force a grin onto my face. I don't want to be embarrassed around this jerk. There is nothing to be ashamed of because I am a modern, single woman. I can kiss ten guys a night if I want to.

But none of them would stick with me like this prick. And that's what really chaps my ass about him. I never let guys get to me the way he has.

"Hi. Can I help you with something? Do you have an appointment?" I take a mental note to scour the schedule and find out who he is so that I can google the hell outta him later.

But he doesn't respond. He just holds up the paper bag. Like that explains a single thing.

"Yes. It's a lovely bag. Do you have an appointment?" I grit my teeth. Pretty sure my forced smile is making me appear downright deranged.

His dark eyes narrow from beneath the brim of that same hat, and this time, he holds the bag up, shaking it at me. *Oh, hell no.*

"Dude. I don't know what that means. How about you use your big boy words?" Oh, yeah, my patience is absolutely shot.

I swear he growls at me in response, which just annoys me more. He talked enough to tell me I was a mistake or an accident or whatever the other night, but now he won't talk to me at all? Rich. Really fucking rich.

"Listen." I use the most condescending tone I can drum up. "I can't read whatever kind of sign language these dirty looks are using. You're going to have to *talk* to me. Or write it down or something." I hold up a finger and pretend to check under my desk. "Wait, let me grab my *crystal ball*."

It's at that moment Mira pushes through the swinging door and waltzes into the reception area with an accommodating smile on her face.

"Griff! Good to see ya. You got those samples we talked about?"

Dirty bathroom guy nods at her, but he doesn't take his eyes off me. It's honestly a little unnerving. I lick my lips and hold his gaze, refusing to drop his gaze. He drops the paper bag on the front desk countertop and then swaggers back out the front door.

"Piece of work," I spit out, rolling my eyes.

Mira stays suspiciously silent. When I glance at her, she's a million miles away, staring just past me.

"Do I have something on my face?" I rub at my mouth and wave a hand in front of her.

She blinks and shakes her head. "No. No. Sorry. Just tired. I zoned out."

"What the hell is wrong with that guy? He walked in here like he's some sort of celebrity, like I should know him. Wouldn't say a goddamn word. Manners leave something to be desired." I shake my shoulders out and scoff just thinking about it.

"Griff? He used to live around here."

I turn back to the computer screen and mutter, "Still a dick."

Again, Mira barely notes what I'm saying. "I need to go check on the foal," she blurts out, changing the subject entirely. "I, uh, won't be back. Can you lock up?"

She's acting totally weird. "Of course."

"Thanks." She grabs her coat and takes off, leaving me thoroughly confused, in a terrible mood, and stuck at work for another fifty-seven minutes.

Just great.

"Good morning." My brother smiles at me from where he stands at the coffee maker as I slide onto a stool at the expansive island in the middle of his kitchen. The smell of him cooking some sort of gourmet breakfast and making a fresh pot of coffee drew me out of bed early on my day off.

This man loves to feed people, and I am *here for it.*

Within moments, he slides a plate of smoked salmon eggs Benedict across the island toward me, followed by a cup of piping-hot coffee.

Best brother ever.

"Fuck yes," I groan, almost inappropriately.

"You've been hanging out with those Gold Rush girls too much."

He's referring to the swearing. "So have you." But he has to know I've noticed how much time he and Mira spend together. That I see them both staring off into space like lovesick fools. They think they're subtle. It's adorable.

I dig into the meal before me, savoring every flavor and just generally feeling happy and at peace for a hot minute. Things have finally started coming up Nadia in life, and it has me invigorated like I never knew it could. I have family, friends, and school, and I don't live with an abusive shithead.

Life is good.

"Ready?" Stefan asks, and my eyes flit open in confusion. *Ready for what?*

I turn, following my brother's gaze. And that's when I see him. *Him.* Hot bathroom guy.

Fuck this guy for showing up everywhere. Can I not just masturbate to him in peace?

I must look startled by his presence because my brother pipes up with "Sorry, Nadia. This is Griffin. The guy I bought this place from."

I swallow slowly and place my fork down carefully before pointing at him. "*That* is Griffin?"

My brother's brow furrows as his eyes bounce between us. "Yeah."

Blood rushes, the whoosh of it loud in my ears.

"Your *best friend* Griffin?"

The broad-shouldered man stops as he rounds the corner into the kitchen, going deathly still. I swear I can almost hear him thinking. And I definitely see his eyes bug out like he's just figured out who I am.

Oh. *No*.

My eyes widen as I connect the dots. Mira called him Griff, and I don't know how I didn't see this.

Fuck my life.

Heat slithers over my skin as my stomach bottoms out like I'm free-falling in an elevator, and I realize what I've done. The man's forearms ripple with tension beneath the black ink covering them, fists pulsing in a furious tic.

"Relax, Nadia. Adults don't have *best friends*."

Sure. Yeah. Especially not once they find out their little sister has been making out with them. Then that friendship would end.

Griffin snorts, rubs his beard, and walks to the front door to shove his feet into a pair of worn cowboy boots. Fleeing this endlessly awkward interaction.

"I've already told you. He sold me this place, and we've just stayed in touch."

Yep. Stefan has told me all about the one guy he hangs out with. The one who didn't treat him like a leper when he moved to town. The one he spent all his free time with. The one who is helping him around the farm here.

I think he may have even referred to him as the only true friend he's ever had.

I watch Griffin's toned ass and muscular thighs disappear out the front door, and try to think of something to say that will cover up what must be a perfectly stricken look on my face. "But… he's a total dick" is what I opt for, but in my head, all

I'm thinking is this one-handed obsession with the guy from the bar can't continue.

Stefan barks out a laugh as he follows his best friend out the front door. "I'm glad you think so." He winks at me over his shoulder. "Then I won't have to worry about you scaring him off with your antics while he's here."

Oh, brother. If you only knew.

CHAPTER 3

Nadia

TWO YEARS LATER

"WHAT ARE YOU DOING?"

"Nothing." I yank the floral-patterned journal back toward myself, slamming a palm over the page to cover it.

Mira's shapely brow lifts as she stares back at me impassively. "Yeah. Definitely seems like *nothing*."

Not only is Dr. Thorne my boss and the veterinarian who runs this clinic, but she's also my new sister-in-law. Additionally, she's kind of my idol. I've never told her that, but she is. She's smart, strong, and driven. She's everything I'm not—everything I've been told I'm not.

In the time I've been attending the local college, she and my brother got married and had a little boy named Silas. Hell on wheels, that kid. A mop of black hair from Mom and wild green eyes from Dad. The perfect blend. He's almost two and climbs everything he can get his hands on. Truthfully, it's terrifying.

I love my nephew, but he's also why I've now moved out.

With my diploma in hand, I was lucky enough to walk back into a job just down the road at Gold Rush Ranch. It's a prestigious racehorse training facility run by our good friends, and it's also the site of the vet clinic Mira runs. Which made moving into the small apartment above the barn a no-brainer.

It's convenient for a twenty-one-year-old fresh out of school. It's also included in my salary and about a two-minute walk from the front door of the clinic. Bonus points for not having to listen to Silas throw tantrums at 5 a.m. Truthfully, it felt weird to keep living with my brother and his wife while they were starting a new family. It felt like it was time for me to start my journey while they do theirs.

I sigh and lean back in the front-desk chair. "It's a list that I started in therapy." Since coming back from school, I feel like I have my entire life ahead of me—special shout-out to my therapist for that. After two years of chatting with her, I figured out that I've let enough life *happen* to me—the good and the bad—and I'm ready to continue taking the bull by the horns and going after what I want.

My college education to become a veterinary technician was my first step. Now I'm here, searching for the next steps. I feel continually lost but accepted that giving myself attainable goals mitigates that a bit.

Hence the list.

"What kind of list?" Mira leans up on the tall counter, propping her chin on her palm as her shiny black ponytail spills over her shoulder like an onyx waterfall.

I bite at the inside of my cheek, feeling a little young and foolish admitting this to Mira even though she's only eight years older than I am. "Like a to-do list for my life."

But she doesn't laugh at me. She never does. She's almost

like the mother figure I never got to have, always searching for a solution to my problems and offering to lend me a hand. Or a carton of eggs. The memory of egging my principal's car with her two years ago never fails to make me grin.

"So, a bucket list?"

I groan. A bucket list sounds so cliché. "No," I say, pulling my hand off the page to show her the title. "*Life To-Do List.*"

She laughs and gives her head a little shake, clearly amused by but also accustomed to my antics. "I think that's smart. Goal setting is important. Keeps a person focused." Her dark eyes trail over my face, and I can see that she wants to ask more.

I chuckle at the blatant interest painted on her face. "Mira, you look like you're going to burst. Just ask it."

"God. Thank you. I was trying to play it cool, but the suspense was killing me. What's on the list?" She leans farther across the counter, eyes lighting up like a kid at Christmas.

I clear my throat as I pull the pad back toward myself to read. "Number one is to build up my own savings account. I don't want to rely on *his* money anymore. I'll do something with it; I'm just not sure what yet. Something good, something worthwhile."

My late father has taken on an almost Voldemort-like presence in our lives. We don't talk about him often, and when we do, it's not by name. He exists in my mind. He haunts me. But if I compartmentalize him into a nameless, faceless box, he bothers me a lot less.

Mira just nods. "I think that's an excellent goal." She knows the full story. Stefan's version anyway. Which, as far as I'm concerned, is the sanitized version. He wasn't there for the worst years. He got out.

I didn't.

Until three years ago, I lived in my own personal hell, caged by an abusive monster. Even once he died, I couldn't leave his fucked-up family behind. Until I was eighteen. I took possession of my sizable inheritance, and then I fled Romania to the safety of my brother's farm as quickly as I could. I didn't look back. I don't miss it. And I've spent the last three years of my life recreating myself in a way that leaves no ties to that part of my life.

I've even completely erased my accent. Most of the time, you would never know I wasn't born here in Ruby Creek. Which is what I was going for.

"Yeah. I thought so." I drop her gaze for a moment, looking back at the lined sheet of paper before me. "I think… well… I think, at some point, I'd like to go to vet school." Heat rises in my cheeks. I wanted to be a vet tech, but now I'm finding I want more. "It's silly. I'm probably too late. I'm pretty sure I'm not even smart enough. Plus, I just got back to working here and wouldn't want to let you down."

Just saying it out loud ratchets up my anxiety.

Mira shoots up, shoulders pinned back straight. She's so regal looking, so put together. *Dignified.* I feel so young and lost around her sometimes. "Nadia. I never want to hear you say that about yourself. I swear I will spank you. Or dock your pay. Or something."

Of course, this is the moment that the back door of the clinic swings open. "Who's getting a spanking?" Billie calls out in the way of announcing herself.

Mira and I both laugh. Billie is the wife of one of the owners here at Gold Rush Ranch. She's also one of the world's most famed and respected racehorse trainers.

She's also very, very pregnant with twins.

My literal nightmare.

She waddles through the hall door grinning like a fool with a hand placed casually over the top of her bump. "I miss getting a good spanking. Vaughn handles me with kiddie gloves now that I'm pregnant. It sucks. I just want him to slap my ass and call me a whore." She sighs wistfully while I try not to crack up. "Does Stefan still do that for you now that you're a mom, Mira?"

Too fucking far. I stifle a groan as Mira rubs at her forehead with a small smile playing across her lips. Billie is forever inappropriate. I'm not sure if she ever had a filter, but it's missing now.

"We were just talking about goal setting. I was telling Nadia here to not sell herself short. And to answer your question, our sex life is better than ever. That's all I'm saying."

Mira winks suggestively, and I mutter, "Thank fuck for that."

Billie's hand lands on my shoulder with a gentle squeeze, and I'm so busy cringing over the visual of my brother that Mira just created that I leave my list open to being read from where she stands behind me.

"Well, Naughty Nadia." God, I hate that nickname. "I can help you with the learning-to-ride-horses one. Also, the getting-your-own-horse one. Tropical vacation! Girls' trip anyone?" Then she stops, lips quirking playfully. "*Making love*, not so much. What was that guy's name the other day? The one who popped in here to ask you out? Tommy?"

I snap the journal to my chest. My throat constricts, and my face heats. *Fuucckkk.* That was supposed to be private. I drop my head onto the desk, gently banging my forehead against the top of it.

"Not him? He was cute! But fine." She pats my back. "It's going to be okay, little one. You'll find someone to make love with. I sure didn't take you for a virgin. But no judgment."

"Biiiillllliiieee," I whine. "I'm not a virgin!" My head flops against the back of the chair, and my eyes flash open, ready to tell her to pound sand. But that's before my gaze snags on the man standing in the front entryway. Beside the door that's propped open to let a breeze in on this sweltering early-summer day.

Double fuck.

"Griff! You're here." Billie claps her hands together. "Excellent."

He's got a duffel bag in hand, and even though Billie is talking to him, he's watching me.

Griff Sinclaire. The man who kissed me stupid in a dirty bar bathroom and left me feeling irretrievably childish when he walked out. I thought that would be the last of him. But the joke was on me when a few days later he walked into this very clinic to drop off some samples and refused to talk to me.

Not. A. Single. Fucking. Word.

Which should have been infuriating enough. But imagine my surprise when I walked downstairs one morning shortly before starting school to find him hanging out with my brother. Not sure how I didn't put it together, but *Griff* is *Griffin*—my brother's best friend, whom I hadn't met since moving here from Romania.

My stomach bottoms out, like it always does around him, and the weight of his gaze presses down on me. The disapproval in his stare is front and center. The dismissal.

The grown-up version of me knows Griffin should not have kissed me in the men's room that night, that he made the right choice to walk away. But the childish part of me hates him for being such a dick about it. The immature part of me has blown that night up in my mind to be something that it wasn't.

The man hasn't said a single word to me since that night. And I know he can talk. I can still feel the low rumble of his gravel-worn voice against my skin.

No matter how hard I try to forget it.

He's too old for me anyway. He's got to be in his mid-thirties by now. Not to mention, I think Stefan would crucify him if he found out. He's probably avoiding talking to me because he values his life. *Smart.* The worst part is… he just heard that exchange.

"Right." Billie rounds the desk toward him. "A man of few words. Forgot that part. No problem. I'll talk, and you can just listen. Except to that virgin bit. Ignore Naughty Nadia over there. Let me show you around."

My stomach lurches as I close the journal and let my eyes drop. I wish I could fold myself in between the pages and just hide there. I knew I was going to run into him again eventually, but wearing faded-blue scrubs with my hair in a lopsided ponytail while exclaiming that I am not a virgin is not what I envisioned. I planned to look so hot that he'd be drooling.

And kicking himself for being such a dismissive prick.

"Where did you park? Let's get you settled first. Then I'll give you the grand tour," Billie prattles on, completely oblivious to the tension between us. Maybe there isn't tension between us. Maybe I'm the only one who feels it. Maybe I'm the only one whose world turned on its axis that night.

Maybe he doesn't even think about it.

That's probably what an adult does after he accidentally kisses a teenager. He compartmentalizes her into the "do not touch" category. He doesn't think about her, just like I don't think about my dad—because it's wrong.

I suck in a deep, centering breath and glance up just in time to see Billie leading him back out to the landing, hands flailing around in front of her. Major hand talker, that one. "Later, ladies!" she calls as they step out onto the wraparound deck.

Agitation coils in my gut. The guy is such a dick. He doesn't deserve my embarrassment. So right here and now I resolve not to be embarrassed. It was one innocent kiss two years ago. *It meant nothing.*

Mira flicks through a folder on the desk, reading a file while nibbling at her bottom lip. Not a care in the world. Completely oblivious. It's like both are so happily married that they miss this guy's incredible ass. He doesn't wear the jeans. *They* wear *him.*

"Why is Griffin here?" My hands are slick, the cool metal of the rings on the journal digging into my palm.

She doesn't even look up at me. That's how inconsequential this is for Mira. "Didn't Stefan tell you?"

Obviously not. "Tell me what?"

The folder flicks shut, and she reaches for another one. "He's moving into Vaughn and Billie's old guesthouse for the summer to break the young horses because obviously Billie can't. Something about a compromise that she and Vaughn came to. She keeps riding, but only DD. So she hired Griff."

"The *whole* summer?"

Mira's finger traces the line before her, lips moving as she reads to herself—something she often does. "Yup," she responds.

My eyes shoot to the front porch, through the big windows that overlook it. Billie is still talking at Griffin.

But Griffin is looking at me.

CHAPTER 4

Griffin

THE WOMAN IN FRONT OF ME IS TALKING A MILE A MINUTE, HANDS gesturing like she's conducting a goddamn orchestra. I wonder if this level of excitement is going to send her into labor. Would probably be fine since we're standing outside a veterinary clinic.

I should listen to what she's saying. After all, she *is* my new employer. But my brain is back in that clinic. It's stuck on the blond spitfire sitting at the front desk, looking at me like I'm a bug beneath her shoe.

My best friend's little sister.

Trouble.

And off-limits in the most absolute way.

When I took this job, I didn't think she was going to be here. I didn't know what she was studying at college, but I figured she'd be gone for four years. I figured that once a girl like that got a taste of freedom, she'd be gone for good. When I agreed to take this gig, I didn't account for having to deal with Nadia Dalca and her massive attitude.

I hold a hand up to stop Billie from talking. I don't know the woman well, but Stefan has assured me she's good people. I wouldn't have taken the job otherwise. I'd have stayed up in the mountains, where I've found some semblance of peace.

Ruby Creek is a double-edged sword for me. Home to my highest highs and my lowest lows.

"Just tell me where to put my stuff. My horse is still in the t—in my rig."

The woman's eyes analyze me a little too closely for comfort. "Sure thing. I'll ride with you to the cottage and help you unload."

I eye the full swell of her very pregnant stomach, but she points a finger at me and purses her lips. "Don't even try to tell me what I am or am not capable of. It will end poorly for you; ask my husband." I grunt in agreement, but she keeps going. "Let's get one thing cleared up before you start your job here. I'm pregnant. Not injured. Not sick. Not on my deathbed. Don't treat me like it."

"Wouldn't dream of it," I mutter, shoving my hands in my pockets and rocking back on the heels of my boots.

She nods at me before spinning and marching toward my truck and trailer, heaving herself into the passenger seat.

"Back out of the driveway and take a right. We have to go around the property, but if you're riding or walking, you can easily cut through the hills. I'll show you that too."

Another grunt is what I offer in affirmation as we turn onto the back roads I know so well. The roads I grew up on.

I sold the functioning part of my farm to Stefan Dalca when I needed a fresh start—something I knew I couldn't find if I stayed on the path I was on. I kept Cascade Acres as a home base near my parents. It was meant to be a place for me to retire. I just hadn't banked on retiring quite so early. But when it all came crashing down, I left everything I knew, loving parents included, and holed myself up on remote acreage in the cliffs above Garnet Ridge.

And then I got to work.

Idle hands are the devil's workshop has never applied to another person more aptly. I went from the town golden boy to the boy in town drowning in amber liquid. But building my home from scratch in the peace of the mountains gave me the purpose I so desperately needed.

"Turn at the mailbox." Billie's directions snap me out of my thoughts, and I steer into the winding, well-treed driveway that opens to reveal a cedar A-frame house in the middle of the clearing. Just beyond it are a few paddocks, complete with shelters that back onto the rolling fields that must lead to the main barn.

"Just pull around the house. You can park your trailer in the back."

Once I've parked, she hops out like she's trying to prove to me she isn't set to explode at any moment. "How many horses did you bring with you?"

I hold a finger up to her as I round the back of the trailer and pull down the ramp on the side.

"Okay, well, there are three paddocks here now. So, if you ever want to add to your harem, go ahead. If you want to take on extra horses while you're here, there is space. I've got hay stocked in that shed." She points just beyond me. "And unfortunately, there aren't automatic waterers back here, so you'll be hauling buckets."

"S'fine." I yank open the barrier and watch her step up into the trailer.

"Hey, kid. Welcome to vacation." Her voice softens as she steps into the open space in the center of the big rig. It's too much space for my one horse, but I love this trailer, love the layout, and refuse to trade it in for something more appropriate. Maybe I'll have more horses one day, and then it will make perfect sense.

For now, Spot is my only constant companion.

I unload him carefully, letting him take a good long look around while Billie opens a bale and tosses a few flakes in for him. I rake out the trailer, and she chatters away at my horse like she thinks he might talk back to her.

When I make it back to where she's standing, watching my horse chow down happily, she props her fists on her hips and blows her hair out of her face. "Cute. What's his story?"

My general silence clearly doesn't deter her.

I point at the deep-brown Appaloosa with a spotted blanket over his haunches—a real pretty motherfucker. "Rescued him from the meat auction." Not sure how he ended up where he did, but isn't that just the way life goes? Sometimes the best of us end up in the worst of positions.

"I love that. He's a pretty boy." She smiles softly at me, and I nod before she turns toward the house. I follow her up onto the deck as she pulls the keys out and swings the door open to a consistent beeping noise. "Security system," she says over her shoulder. "The code is six nine six nine."

She types the numbers in, and sure enough, the beeping stops, and she spins around to say something but must catch the expression on my face. "What? Are you going to tell me there's an easier number to remember?"

I already miss the solitude of the mountains.

★★★

Ruby Creek is small as fuck—one main street and one town bar. I push through the heavy front door at Neighbor's Pub. I know I shouldn't be here, but I keep coming back. Like a glutton for punishment, I do this every damn time.

It doesn't matter if I'm coming to see my mom and dad, visiting Stefan—my only friend—or getting something done at the vet clinic. I always force myself through the front door of this establishment. No matter how it turns my stomach.

Sliding onto a stool with a quiet sigh, my eyes catch on the wall full of liquor behind the bar. All the shapes of the bottles, the colors on the labels, all the dark memories, or complete lack thereof, at the bottom.

"What can I get ya?" A coaster slides across the bar and lands in front of me as I glance up into the slightly upturned blue eyes of the bartender. Her dyed-black hair lies poker straight over her shoulders, framing her huge tits, which sit like she's trying to push them up to her chin over the neckline of her tank top. I almost want to ask her if it hurts because I'm genuinely curious.

"Bourbon. Neat."

"A man after my own taste." She throws a wink over her shoulder and arches her back unnecessarily as she reaches up to the top shelf and pulls down something expensive rather than the Wild Turkey sitting in the well. "Upgrade is on me, doll. Not every day we get a future Hall of Famer in here."

Excellent. Someone who recognizes me still.

She pours the amber liquid into a single shot glass before dumping it into a tumbler, licking her lips as she places it on the coaster.

There was a time when I'd have slammed the drink back and offered to take her out back. I got off on people swooning over Griffin Sinclaire, quarterback extraordinaire, the small-town boy who made it to the big show. I'd say something rude, like *I'll fuck your cunt so hard you'll be walking bowlegged for days,* and she'd giggle as if she just won the lottery. And so long as I hadn't had too many drinks, I'd usually follow through on that promise. Never had any complaints in that department except that I never stuck around. Plenty of complaints about that. But I always moved on. To the next city. The next game. The next Super Bowl. Because I wanted more than the two that I already had. I was greedy and keen, and lived to win big, fuck hard, and party wild.

But these days I feel *old.* I feel a little used up. I suppose that's what becoming a functioning alcoholic in your twenties does to you.

I raise the glass with a silent nod as a way of thanking her. And hopefully dismissing her. I really don't need to fuck the twentysomething bartender on my first night in town. I haven't spent the past six years living on my remote property, trying to find some sort of purity among the filth in my brain, to give in just because she's got a great rack.

She smiles curiously and strolls away, swinging her hips like a pendulum. But I barely notice. I'm too busy staring down into the glass. Rolling it between my hands and watching the way the syrupy liquid splashes against the sides before slowly dripping back down.

I can still taste it if I close my eyes and let myself go. The malty flavor, the texture of it in my mouth, the pleasant warm burn as it slides down my throat. Sometimes I wonder if I liked the act of drinking more than the taste. But when it's close enough to smell like it is right now, I know that's not true.

For me, alcohol is addictive. The taste, the smell, the act, the way it made me feel like a fucking king.

I used to miss it. But I don't anymore.

"You moving back into town?"

The bartender is back, pulling my attention from the alcohol in my hand.

"Sorta." I don't even look up. I hate when people recognize me now. I used to love it. Used to take pride in locals patting me on the back and telling me they cheer me on every Sunday.

It only made my downfall that much more humiliating.

"Where are you staying?" She picks up a rag, polishing an already perfectly clean spot on the bar just so she can lean over in front of me. There's nothing subtle about this girl. And I remember being an age when I thought that was sexy.

I don't think I'm that age anymore.

"Gold Rush" is all I say. Because everyone is going to find out, and everyone here knows what that is, and I hate the way two *R* words in a row twist my tongue up.

"Fancy," she says, smiling. And I admit to myself that she's quite lovely while also acknowledging that it makes no difference to me. That's not why I'm here tonight.

I'm here to torture myself, not enjoy myself.

So I offer her a wry twist of my lips before ducking my head and hiding behind the brim of my hat again.

I do this every time I'm in town. I walk into my old stomping grounds, Neighbor's Pub, order a bourbon, and sit at the bar. Staring at it like it's a living, breathing nemesis. I let myself remember what it tasted like as I run my tongue across my teeth like it's actually in my mouth.

And then I throw ten bucks down on the worn bar top and leave, just to prove to myself that I can.

It's what I do tonight. Reach into my back pocket and pull a bill from my wallet, tossing it down beside the glass while the bartender converses with someone else.

And then I walk right back out that door. Feeling like the victor. Knowing that in my years away, I've grown stronger. Even if I haven't been able to heal completely, I make better decisions now. Except for the night I kissed Nadia, that night I headed back to take a leak before I left.

That night I felt just vulnerable enough to do something stupid, like kiss a girl who was barely old enough to drink.

CHAPTER 5

Nadia

"Hey, you. Just as hot as I remember."

Tommy is leaning against the railing at the top of the stairs that lead to my apartment with a wide boyish grin on his face. I dislike the familiarity of the way he talks to me, like we know each other well. The way his eyes rake over the floral off-the-shoulder shirt I'm wearing makes me want to squirm a little bit.

Sure, we made out a few times. Were a thing. Sort of. In the most casual sense of the word. But that was a couple of years ago now. And we haven't maintained a friendship.

"Hi, one sec." I dart back into the house when I realize it's just cool enough out that I want to take a sweater with me.

He's been relentless in asking me out, showing up at my work, saying we should give it another shot. That we're good together. Which is a bit of a stretch in my book. We were never exclusive, and seeing him hanging off one of the other girls in town never bothered me.

Not after that kiss with Griffin. Once I knew what a kiss could be, everything else just came up short.

Especially Tommy.

But Griffin isn't a reality for me. First, he speaks to me with growls and grunts. I'm pretty sure he hates me. Second, and most important of all, he's my brother's best friend.

Crossing that line would be frowned upon. No matter how heart-stopping the kiss was.

So here I am, taking Tommy to Sunday family dinner to see if we can be a thing for real this time. We're both older now, more mature—or at least trying to be. I went off to school, and so did he. Maybe a fresh start is what we both need.

"Okay, ready!" I round the corner and expect Tommy to be standing at the door, all golden-blond locks and twinkly blue eyes. Happy-go-lucky and laid-back are just what a girl like me needs to shine a little light on her dark past.

But he's not waiting at the door.

I step onto the landing and peer down the stairs to see him sitting in his truck. *Off to a good start.* I roll my eyes. Couldn't even handle waiting a couple minutes for me. I lock up and hustle down the stairs, already regretting agreeing to this.

He's on his phone, engine already running when I get in. Doesn't even look up.

Annoyance courses through me. I spent an entire lifetime in a house with a mother who believed a man every time he said he would change. I wonder if this is just part of my genetic makeup. Tommy says he's changed, grown up. He's going to business school so he can start his own company.

And I believed him.

So far, it seems like the joke is on me.

I don't need him to roll out the red carpet. But telling me I'm hot and then ignoring me isn't making me wet in the panties. The thought of locking myself down in a relationship is hard enough. Never mind with someone who annoys me within minutes of arriving. It seems like this is what I'm supposed to be doing though, so I forge ahead.

"Ready?"

He chuckles and shakes his head at his phone. Like there's something funny and I'm not in on the joke. And then, without a word, he shifts into drive and pulls out of the driveway toward my brother's house just five minutes down the road at Cascade Acres.

"Some of the boys are going out for drinks tonight." He reaches to roll down the window. "Let's meet them after dinner."

He's smiling. He looks happy and relaxed, excited to be home and off school for the summer, a perfect contrast to the stress coiling in my gut.

I don't drink, and it's a Sunday night.

"I have to work in the morning. I don't think that's going to work for me."

"Ah, come on, Nadi. Don't be a stick-in-the-mud. You're only young once."

My arms fold across my chest. The problem is, I don't feel that young after the shit I've lived through. "I like to start my week well rested. If that's what you'd like to do, I won't stop you. I can hitch a ride back to the ranch with someone else."

He snorts and rolls his eyes like I'm being ridiculous. "We'll see. I've got a couple of hours to loosen you back up again."

I turn my head, glance out the window, and say nothing. What I really want to say is *More like I only have to endure you for a couple more hours.* But I've worked hard at taming that spark inside me, the one that lights easily and races across everything I touch. My temper can be a wildfire, and I hate to think where that aspect of me comes from, so I tamp it down.

We pull through the gates at Cascade Acres, and I direct him up to the house, all river rock and exposed lumber. It's quite something, perched up on the hill overlooking the lake. Stefan sprinkled our mom's ashes in that lake. I still don't quite know how to feel about that.

Every Sunday, our friend group takes turns hosting dinner. I look forward to it every week. Our get-togethers have that family vibe I've dreamed about my entire life. The one that was not present with my much older brother gone and two alcoholic parents who fought nonstop. With a sperm donor who was heavy with his fists, something I escaped less and less the mouthier I got, the warm fuzzy feelings that most people attach to their childhoods are foreign to me.

It's been years since anyone has hit me. But I can still feel the burn across my cheek and the sting of tears across the bridge of my nose. I still have nightmares about cowering at his feet while he screams at me with my mother drunk and passed out on a couch somewhere.

I push those memories away once Tommy has parked and hop out without waiting for him. I just want to get into the safe haven that is my brother's house, to be surrounded by all the people I've come to love and trust. To get away from the guy who calls me *Nadi* like he knows me well enough to use a shitty nickname.

I suck in a deep breath as my hand wraps around the front-door handle. *I'm being too hard on him. Tommy is sweet. Relaxed. He will be good for me. I just need to lighten up and act my age.*

His warm palm lands on my shoulder and his friendly surfer-boy grin takes over his heart-shaped face. "Let's go, babe."

Babe.

I absently think to myself that Tommy is like a golden retriever. Cute and friendly, but just a bit dumb. Or a little too eager to please. But I stomp on those thoughts—the comparison is unfair to a golden retriever now that I think about it—and step into the house.

Music and laughter filter in from the open-concept kitchen, echoing down the hall. These sounds in a house still make me do a double take. Four years ago, I would have never heard these sounds.

"Hi!" I call out as I toe off my shoes and head down the hallway toward everyone. "We're here."

"Come on in, sweetie." Mira pops around the corner with a big bell of red wine in hand. "Your brother is cooking up a storm in here. I hope you're hungr—"

Her head quirks as she takes in Tommy standing behind me. "You brought someone."

"Yeah," I worry at my bottom lip, realizing I should have told them before now. "Sorry. I hope that's okay."

Her full lips curl up as she studies Tommy. "Of course, of course." She steps forward and holds her hand out to my date. "Hi, I'm Mira."

"Tommy." Even his voice sounds like he's smiling as he claps his broad palm into hers. "Nice to meet you."

She nods, but her head tilts, and her dark eyes dart between us. I love Mira. I love how she loves my brother. But goddamn, she is impossible to get a read on sometimes. "Come on in. I'll introduce you to everyone." Then she swaggers back through the wood-beam archway, waving us in over her shoulder.

"Nadia is here," she announces to the room as she slides herself onto one of the stools at the oversize island. "And she brought a date." My cheeks heat, and I momentarily inspect the ceiling, wishing the floor would swallow me up. *This was my worst idea ever.* "Everyone, meet Tommy."

Tommy steps up beside me with a wave and a breezy "Hey, gang."

It's a dopey thing to say to a bunch of people you've never met, but I can't pay attention to Tommy right now because I feel like there's a collar around my neck and someone just gave it a good, hard tug. I give myself over to that sensation, meeting the stony gaze of Griffin Sinclaire. He's sitting at the dinner table, dark eyes drilling into me like he could grind me into dust if he stares hard enough.

Everyone is staring at Tommy and me, but I can't take my eyes off Griffin. No hat, hair slicked back, looking fucking delicious. I'm immediately plunged back into our encounter in the bathroom.

Will that night never fade?

It's then that I notice Silas, my nephew, is sitting beside him coloring. In fact, so is Griffin. His huge hand holds a small purple crayon while they draw an underwater scene on a plain sheet of paper together. Silas is bent over the page like some sort of prodigy. Tiny chubby hand fisted around a blue crayon, so small next to the big mountain man seated beside him.

He must notice that Griffin has stopped coloring because his elbow juts out, nudging the inked arm beside him. "More fish," he says simply, in his sugary baby voice. "Do a biiiig fish."

It's then that Griffin drops my gaze and leans into the little boy next to him and hits him with a soft, playful sort of smile. One that jabs me right in the ovaries. "Yes, boss," he says, with more animation than I've ever heard him use. "How big? Shark big?"

Silas claps, grinning up at the man who has no business looking this good. No business looking this sweet. It's almost more than I can take.

I plaster a smile on my face and turn away before I turn into a total puddle, focusing my attention back on the rest of my friends spread throughout the living space. Billie, Violet, and Mira sitting at the island, Hank and Trixie playing with Cole and Violet's two little girls in the adjoined living room, and Cole and Vaughn sitting with Griff at the table. Everyone acts like family, although the relations are a little convoluted by marriage, by blood, and by choice. Either way, it's a tight-knit group, and what we all have in common is Gold Rush Ranch.

I offer a wave. "Hi, everyone." And then I walk into the kitchen, desperate for a drink to fix my dry mouth.

"Hi." My brother, Stefan, peeks up at me with a smirk while he dices fresh rosemary into tiny pieces. The man could have been a chef if he wanted to. It's the thing I miss the most about living with him. The gourmet cooking was hard to let go of when I moved out. "A date, huh?"

He keeps his focus down on the cutting board, but I'm not stupid enough to think he's not having a good chuckle right now.

"Apparently." I rip the fridge open and reach for my go-to flavored sparkling water. Pineapple.

"Come on, babe. Have a beer." Tommy reaches over me and straight into the fridge like he owns the place.

I sneak a peek back at my brother and instantly want to wipe the amusement off his face when he silently mouths, *Babe?*

Head shaking, I turn back to Tommy. "I'm good. I don't drink, remember?"

Beer in hand, he scoffs and leans against the island behind himself, blocking everyone else out of our conversation. "Still? I figured you'd have outgrown that phase by now." His thick fingers crack open the can of beer, and he holds it up to me. "Come on. One little sip won't hurt. Maybe I can whip you up something sweet instead. Margarita?"

My heart grows heavy, the hammering of it stretching out and pounding in my ears. I hate being put on the spot like this. There's always this tiny voice in my head—a negative voice—that tells me other people know better than I do. Maybe Tommy is right and I need to lighten up a bit.

Learning myself outside the confines of the house I grew up in is a constant struggle. I don't trust other people easily, and what's worse is I often don't even trust myself.

"She said no." A rusty voice caresses the back of my neck, and even if he's barely ever spoken to me, it sounds familiar.

"Joking around, man. I'm Tommy."

I turn just enough to see both men. Griffin doesn't look like he finds the joke all that amusing. A muscle ticks in his jaw. In fact, if looks could kill, I think Tommy might keel over on the spot.

Where Tommy is bulky, broader, Griffin is powerful, muscles bulging only where it's natural. Strength lines his limbs without appearing overwrought. He's not in the gym bench-pressing and doing deadlifts until his body shakes. He's tossing hay bales and pounding fence posts, and that's really working for him.

Tommy's features are soft. Griffin's are hard. Tommy is day. Griffin is night.

The two men could not be more opposite if they tried.

The older man tugs the yellow can out of my hand, cracks it open, and hands it back to me. All without saying a word. Then he shoves past Tommy and opens the fridge door in search of something for himself, effectively blocking us out.

I want to peek around the edge, get a better view of Griffin. He looks different tonight. No cap, inky hair styled, beard smoothed, white collared shirt rolled up just enough to show the black tattoos that adorn his forearms.

The man is an amusement park for my eyes.

"Who's the asshole?" Tommy whispers.

My forehead wrinkles. *I* think Griffin is an asshole, but I have good reason. It bugs me that Tommy thinks he does. But I don't go there. "Griffin. My brother's best friend" is all I mumble back.

"Griffin Sinclaire?" Tommy's head whips around, seeking out the older man, brow furrowing in concentration.

"Yeah." I shrug, confused about how he might know him.

"Like... *the* Griffin Sinclaire?"

"Uh, I don't know what that means." I sip my drink, sneaking a peek over at the big brooding ball of muscle at the table.

"Like the famous quarterback who grew up in this town? And then got injured and disappeared?"

I raise an eyebrow at Tommy. Because the truth is, I know nothing about the man. And where I grew up, football is soccer. So it's not like I'd know. Plus, no one has mentioned it.

"Okay!" I jump at my brother's loud clap. "Everyone at the table. Dinner is ready."

Tommy's hand lands on my back, and I force myself not to flinch. *Tommy will be good for me.* My eyes shift over my shoulder, sneaking one last peek at Griffin. My stomach flops when I see his eyes fixed on where Tommy is touching me.

I move to the beautifully set table, feeling nervous under Griffin's unwavering gaze. With its raw-wood edge, the dining table has an industrial vibe that's warmed up by bright-white plates and brass-tone flatware. I search the modern black chairs and grab a spot beside Tommy. Easy, bright, sunshiny Tommy. I need more bright days in my life.

Not more dark broody nights.

CHAPTER 6

Griffin

I'M CUTTING INTO MY SLICE OF PRIME RIB WITH MORE FORCE than necessary, still fuming over the big dopey Ken doll trying to force a drink on my best friend's little sister. No one else saw, and even if they did, it wouldn't bug them as much.

But as a person who steers clear of the stuff, it gets my hackles up. I don't know what Nadia's reasons are, and it doesn't seem like he does either. All that aside, a man should always take no for an answer. If you have to pressure a woman into doing something, you're a pencil prick with no manners. In my book anyway.

And this guy is one of those. Big talker, a shiny small-town showboat. I recognize it because that used to be me.

Minus the not taking no for an answer. My mama taught me better than that.

"This is so good, Stefan." The petite blond across the table, who introduced herself as Violet, smiles kindly over the quiet clanking of cutlery. Other murmurs of assent fill the space while everyone chows down.

"Glad to hear it. I love cooking for you guys." Stefan grins at his wife. A charged grin that almost makes me a little jealous. All these people seem so damn happy in each other's company.

I'm out of my element. I haven't been in the habit of meeting new people for several years now. I'm out of practice. Most of the people sitting here are new to me. Stefan and Mira I know well, but the rest not so much. I know Billie now, or at least she talked at me like we know each other.

For a few years there, it was just Stefan. He was the only person I spent time with, aside from my parents. When he bought this place from me, he was so fucking clueless. I couldn't figure out why someone who knew almost nothing about running a farm would want one. So I offered to help him in my free time. Teach him the ropes.

The only reason I offered is because when we met, his eyes didn't widen, he didn't ask for an autograph, and he didn't inquire about where I'd disappeared to, which meant he had no idea who I was.

A sincere *Nice to meet you* was all I got. And that sliver of anonymity gave me the freedom to be a completely new person around Stefan. Of course, my history eventually became known. But on my terms. Stefan liked me for me, the grumbly prick that I'd become. Our friendship foundation had nothing to do with who we'd been and everything to do with who we both were at that moment when we met.

Two lonely motherfuckers with pasts we'd rather leave, well, in the past.

Violet continues to carry the conversation. "Nadia, I heard Billie is going to give you riding lessons this summer."

The young woman beside me, who I've been trying my damnedest to ignore, stiffens ever so slightly. She places her fork down carefully, like every movement is planned. Intentional. Like she's playing the role of someone soft and demure.

The girl in the bathroom wasn't this reined in. She was wild. Demanding. *Again,* she'd said. The one word that pierced my shields. I almost did it too. Kissed her again. I was so close, but something held me back.

And now, spending the summer here in her general vicinity, I know I'm going to have to keep holding myself back. Pushing her away.

"Yeah. Yes, I think I'd like that. I'm pretty comfortable working with the horses. It seems like a natural progression to learn to ride."

"I'm happy to help when I have time. I'm not sure Billie understands how tired she's going to be once the babies arrive." She grins at her friend knowingly.

Billie just rolls her eyes. "I'm right here, you know."

It's under the din of laughter that I notice Tommy's hulking frame lean in on the opposite side of Nadia. He drops his voice, but not low enough. "Should we tell them you already know how to ride real well?"

Nadia stops chewing, her eyes shifting around the table to see if anyone heard. Her warm-brown irises flash to mine for only a moment before they drop back down to her plate.

She knows I heard what he said, and she can't even look at me because of it. He embarrassed her. *What a fucking dickhead thing to say to a girl at a family dinner.*

My teeth grind. I want to say something so badly—I want to smash his big dumb face into his plate—but I swallow my rage and carry on brutalizing my steak.

"Violet might be right, you know." Vaughn doesn't even glance at Billie as he says it, like even he knows his wife will injure him for trying to tell her what to do. "Just a thought." He snorts in a poor attempt to contain his amusement, obviously sensing her unimpressed stare on his face.

"Thanks, *Boss Man*." The words cut, and Vaughn's cheeks twitch. The few times I've been around these two have been enough for me to know they enjoy the push and pull of these confrontations. It's charming, in a way. "But I'm pretty sure I can decide what I can handle."

"I c—" I talk before my brain has enough time to shut it down, stopping on the hard *c* sound of *can*. My brain-to-mouth connection is questionable at the best of times, so I guess leave it to me to blurt something stupid out now. "I will. If you're not able."

Billie points her fork at me and narrows her eyes. "Thanks Griff. That'd be great. *I*"—she glares at her husband—"will let you know if I need you to step in."

I nod and turn my attention back down to my plate, wishing I hadn't risked talking in front of everyone. Especially by volunteering to spend more time with a girl whom I should stay far away from.

Especially considering the way she's looking at me right now.

***

"I love having you around." My mother smiles at me like she's worried she might scare me away.

We've always been close, my parents and I. But when things went to shit a few years ago, they let me retreat and lick my wounds. They didn't force my hand or tell me what to do, but they gave me an ultimatum and have never given up on me, even when I'm sure they wanted to.

When I was spiraling down the drain, they were the ones who picked me up and gave me the ass kicking I needed. They didn't judge me or make me feel like shit about my fall from grace. Their support—their love—was and still is unwavering.

I hate to think about where I'd be without them.

"It's nice being close enough to pop in." I lean close to my mother's petite frame and wrap an arm around her narrow shoulders. "I love you, Mom." My lips press against the black hair at her temple.

"I love you too, sweet boy. Thanks for joining me for a coffee date. Can you believe how different pour-over coffee tastes?"

This is my mother's new obsession. Pour-over coffee. Some fancy kettle. A scale to weigh the beans. Organic beans washed with love and positive energy or some shit. It all sounds a bit woo-woo to me, but she's so pleased with herself that it's almost impossible not to share in her fascination.

Plus, even I must admit the coffee is good.

"It was delicious." I stand with a gentle squeeze to her shoulder. "Let's do this again next t-t-t…" My lips thin, and I sigh, trying not to beat myself up. "When Dad golfs next."

She doesn't react. She knows me well enough to know how much the stutter pisses me off. Instead, she carries on like she didn't notice, even though I know she did. How could you not?

"That would be perfect." She claps her hands together softly as we walk to the front door of their spacious condominium. It's nestled up into the base of Garnet Ridge, just one town over from Ruby Creek. When I sold the ranch, the one I purchased with my shiny new contract all those years ago, I bought them this place in a fifty-five-plus community. Beautiful views of the valley and right on the golf course where my dad enjoys spending all his free time. I live on the mountain above them now, and Dad likes to joke that if he squints real hard, he can see me moping around.

They're happy, and that makes me happy. After everything they've done for me, I wish I could do more.

Feet back in my boots and arms slid into my jean jacket, I turn to give her one more hug.

"Any pretty girls on that farm?" She smiles into my neck.

Except *that*. I don't know if I can do *that* for them.

"Mom." My tone is warning but playful.

"Griffy, it's the grandbaby-rabies. I'm sick. I can't help it."

I shake my head with a small smile. "Seek treatment, Mom."

We share a look, and then I turn to leave, knowing I need to get back to Gold Rush Ranch to start my new job. A job among people and a community that I've spent years hiding from. I grew up riding. My grandfather was a bronc rider and would sit me up on many a horse. I spent my days following him around and learning everything I could about colt starting. Until I found football.

Football was my universe until it wasn't. But getting back into working with young horses has proven to be almost therapeutic for me. Taking on a few training horses up at my farm keeps me busy enough.

I cruise the winding roads under clear blue skies, the harsh sunlight bouncing off the brim of my hat. Just as I drop my concentration from the road to grab a piece of my favorite cinnamon gum, I catch a flash of gray out of the corner of my eye.

And then I feel a small thump under my front driver's-side wheel.

Fuck my life.

Doesn't take a rocket scientist to figure out I just hit something. My heart constricts as I pull over to see what I've done. Another thing for me to beat myself up about. Killed a fucking bunny or something.

But when I hop out of my truck on the quiet country road, I don't see a rabbit. I see a filthy pile of matted hair whimpering in the ditch. My pulse ratchets up at the sight.

"Whoa, boy." I hold out a hand as I scale the steep side of the ditch. "What are you?"

Small black eyes squint back at me, and I decide it must be a dog. A very worse-for-wear dog. It's trembling, and the closer I draw, the more rigid it becomes. "I'm sorry, fella." One of his hind legs is twisted at an angle that it should not be. "I got you."

I reach out for the little dog, alarmed by how skinny he is when I pick him up. He just shakes and whines, clearly in shock, as I race back to the truck with him in my arms. At least I know where to take him. Luckily, I'm friends with one of the best veterinarians in the area.

When I whip into the parking lot in front of the on-site vet clinic at Gold Rush Ranch, the dog is in much the same condition. I scoop him up, wrapping him in a towel from my back seat, and dart into the clinic.

Nadia is at the front desk, showing another woman something on the computer. Her face gives nothing away when she looks up at me.

"I need help."

"What is that?" She points at the mess in my arms, confusion lacing her tone.

"I hit a dog."

"Oh shit." She shoots up instantly and hustles around the desk, brow furrowed as she pulls the towel away to peek at the canine. "How long ago?"

"Maybe t—nine minutes ago?"

"*Nine* minutes?" Her nose scrunches up, like she thinks I'm fucking weird. But I don't care. I'm not going to stumble over the word *ten* in front of her. "Oddly specific. But okay, at least you talk to me now," she mutters as her eyes roll. But her hands are already reaching for him. She's not wasting a second. "I'll take him back. Let's just try not to jostle him too much."

Without missing a beat, she steps in close to me; her toned arms slide inside mine, trying to replace my positioning without moving the stoic little dog.

"Okay, got him."

She hits me with a terse smile. And then she's gone. Leaving me with the light scent of sweet roses that I still remember from two years ago.

The one I haven't forgotten to this day.

CHAPTER 7

Nadia

The little dog looks like shit. He's sedated because he was shaking far too hard to take a proper X-ray. I run my palm over his small skull while Mira takes pictures of the obvious broken leg. He's in rough shape, in more ways than one. Yes, the leg is broken, but his matted coat is worse than I've ever seen, and when I get my fingers beneath that layer of wool, all I can feel is bones.

This is not a well-loved dog. He's either lost or abandoned, according to Mira, who takes the entire scene in with perfect serenity.

The bridge of my nose stings, and tears well in my eyes.

"Why are you crying? He's going to be okay. I can fix this." She stares up at the scans hanging on the backlit board. The leg is shattered.

"I just feel bad for him."

Mira shrugs with her hands affixed to her hips, still assessing the imaging. "I feel happy that I can save him."

I sniffle. That's one way to look at it. Plus, Mira is kind of robotic with some of this stuff. Seeing suffering up close still tugs at my heartstrings. Maybe I'm projecting.

"Go tell Griff that the dog will survive but I'm going to have to amputate the leg."

I blink rapidly and smooth a hand over the dirty little body. *Poor baby.*

"Then you can scrub in and help me."

"Do you think he's still here?" The guy seems like a dick. My money is on that he left to cowboy it up or whatever he does.

Mira nods matter-of-factly, like there's no question in her mind that he's still out there, and then disappears through the doors into the surgical area to prepare. With just the two of us on-site and it not being a scheduled surgery day, we'll have to make do. It means we both pitch in.

I let my hand linger gently on the dog's emaciated body, sucking in a centering breath before I head back out to the waiting area.

Mira called it. Griffin is still here, sitting in a chair, legs spread wide, elbows propped on his knees with his head hung low. All curled in on himself, like the weight of what he's carrying on his shoulders is more than he can take.

His head snaps up, dark, mysterious eyes meeting mine without flitting away. He hasn't properly held my eye since that night, since before he knew who I was, and I find my steps faltering under the weight of his gaze.

He's so fucking hot. He oozes masculinity. It leaks out of his pores, and the effect on me is heady. There's no doubt I have a crush on my brother's friend. And I almost want to laugh at it. *How fucking cliché.*

"He's going to be okay." My voice breaks as I swallow my emotions—something I've become adept at over the past couple of years. I gave up being the broken, angry little girl in favor of setting a nice, normal life up for myself. "But we're going to operate. Mira says that hind leg is too damaged to keep."

"Amputation?" The brim of his hat shadows his heavy brow and strong nose, making it hard to see his expression.

"Yeah." I twiddle my hands in front of myself, like a nervous little schoolgirl, not sure what else to say. He's so intense right now that he almost makes me nervous. Smoldering, I can handle. Silent treatment, got that too. But this guilt-ridden body language has me off-kilter. He looks like he could use a friend right now.

"Are you okay?" I ask quietly as I come to crouch before him.

"Mhm." He nods, dropping his head again as his calloused fingers knit together between his knees.

"Okay. Um… do you want me to call you when he's done?"

He shakes his head without looking back up at me. "I'll wait."

I blink again, but this time it's not to chase away the tears. It's because I almost can't believe my own ears. For some reason, I didn't expect that reaction.

Without thinking, my palm falls over his hands. Like I just know he could use a gentle touch. God knows he's not being gentle with himself right now. "Hey, we got this. He looks like he's been on his own for a while. This isn't on you. Accidents happen."

He just grunts in response.

But he doesn't shrug my touch away.

I walk up to the clinic with a smile on my face. The sun is out. The birds are chirping. Life is good. I'm tired from checking up on the dog throughout the night, but I have my coffee mug in hand. I bounce up the low-slung stairs to the wraparound porch that meets the front entryway.

Something moves, and I jump. Spilled coffee burns against my hand.

"Ah!" One hand thumps against my chest when Griffin unfolds his long limbs from one of the wicker chairs on the front porch. "You couldn't have said hi before springing up on me like that?"

His lips flatten out, and his eyes roll beneath the shadow of his brim.

"I saw that." Moving past him and his wordless ways, I slide a key into the front door and almost miss the quiet "Hi," from behind me.

The alarm beeps as I enter the code and flick the lights on.

"How's the dog?" Griffin's boots thump on the floor as he follows behind me.

"Good. I've been checking on him all night. He seems groggy but fine. Wanna see him?"

His hands shoved in his pockets, stance wide, he nods at me as I drop my stuff at the front desk.

"Come on back then." I wave him along as he tails me. "Good morning, little pupper," I coo toward the metal crate at the back of the exam space. He sits up unsteadily, little head quirking as we approach. And the closer we get, the more excited he becomes. He's up and wagging, pressing a small black nose through the holes in the crate's door.

"He's bald," Griffin's rusty voice cuts through the room.

"Yeah. We had to shave him down. He was one big knot and crawling with fleas. Definitely has had no one taking care of him for a while."

"He's standing." Griffin walks closer, staring at the little dog with concern etched on his face.

"Nothing gets by you, does it?"

He glares at me, and I try not to laugh.

"So dogs don't really feel sorry for themselves. Not how we do. They just make the best of their situation and carry on. Luckily, they rebound pretty quickly after losing a hind leg."

Griffin grunts and steps next to me, my body humming with awareness as he draws close. He holds one hand up to the door of the crate, letting the excited dog lick at his skin. *Don't blame you, boy. Don't blame you at all.*

I smile at the sight. "He knows you saved him."

"I didn't save him. I hit him."

I lift a shoulder. "You could look at it that way. Or you could look at it like he threw himself in your path because he needed help. And you helped him."

His eyes shift down to where I stand beside him. "Young enough for rose-colored glasses, eh?"

I arch a brow and cross my arms. I don't think anyone has ever accused me of wearing rose-colored glasses in my life. The young bit? Well… he must have had a real fucking shame spiral when he put the pieces together about who I am. But rose-colored glasses? I almost laugh. I've lived with shit-colored glasses most of my life, until I *chose* to take them off and stop *letting* things happen to me.

"Old enough to choose the color of glasses I wear. Thanks."

Dick.

I turn to make the no-name dog his breakfast and cocktail of medication.

"Why don't you t-talk to *him* that way?" The motion of him turning away catches my eye.

"Him?"

He hesitates, and I swear his cheeks pick up a little color. "Barbie Doll Boy."

I laugh, measuring out a syringe of anti-inflammatories. "You mean Ken Doll?"

"Whatever." His fingers press through the cage.

"You can let him out." I mix the small serving of wet food and pills together, hoping he's the type of dog that won't pick them up and spit them out. "And I don't know what you mean."

"He shouldn't say shit like that to you." God, he's so vague. I'm pretty certain he means the *riding* comment, which was so fucking cringey. But I refuse to agree with him. My pride won't let me.

"Thanks for the input. I'll keep that in mind on our next date," I add because fuck this guy for telling me what to do. *Especially* with our history. I have one big brother, and I don't need another.

I slide the bowl across the floor toward the waggling rat-like dog that Griffin just freed from the crate, and he dives straight in. Poor thing has got to be starving, but we can only start with small meals.

When I stand back up, Griffin's eyes are fixed on the bowl and the quiet grunting noises coming from the dog. "He doesn't deserve a next date."

My eyes narrow at him. "Drop it, okay? I didn't ask for your opinion. You gave me your opinion of me two years ago, and that was quite enough, thanks. Accident? Mistake? Whatever. I heard you loud and clear." I rub clammy hands over my scrubs before crossing them over my body like a shield. *I just want to live a normal life—a job, a husband, a herd of happy kids—so that's why.*

"Just looking out for my friend's little sister."

I bark out a disbelieving laugh. *The fucking gall.* "Is that what you did that night in the bathroom? Looked out for me?"

"That was different."

"Why?"

He grunts. "Didn't know who you were."

I click my tongue, disappointed in what a chickenshit the guy who grabbed me and owned me is being right now. "Pussy."

"Nadia." His tone is a warning, but I've heard worse. Griffin Sinclaire does a lot of things to me, but scaring me isn't one of them. "I'm thirty-five years old. You're barely legal. We c—shouldn't even be talking about this. You need to forget it."

I roll my eyes. *Barely legal.* What is this, a porno?

When you've lived through the shit I have, age is just a number on a birth certificate. I feel like I've lived a few lives. Reinvented me. When you've seen what I've seen, what the hell do you have in common with normal, happy people your own age?

I pack away the food and medications, silently eyeing the small dog limping around the bowl clumsily, sniffing and searching for more.

When I finish, I catch Griffin's dark eyes tracing my body. They rise to my lips, and the hair on my arms immediately stands up. It unnerves me how attuned to him my body is.

In an attempt to recover, I plaster a practiced smirk on my lips. "Thanks for the input. I don't think I will. Forget about it, that is. I actually enjoy replaying that night in my head."

His jaw clenches, that one muscle jumping as his arms cross before him. He looks so fucking grumpy, I almost laugh. "Don't be a brat."

Everything about his body language is tightly wound, feral almost. Except his eyes when he hit that word. *Brat.* Those are pure scorching smolder.

And they tell a completely different story.

I wink at him, watching his tense body rear back like I just slapped him. "But why? Why stop when I can tell you like it so much?" And then I head back out front to open the clinic for the day.

He's right that I shouldn't let Tommy talk to me the way he did, but I'm not about to let him do it either.

Griffin Sinclaire can't ruin my good mood with his growly bullshit. My first riding lesson is this afternoon. I'm checking things off my to-do list and experiencing everything life offers whether he likes it or not.

CHAPTER 8

Griffin

Irritated. That's the word I'll use to describe what I'm feeling right now.

Nadia Dalca is like a sliver under my fucking skin, stuck a little too far in to get out. It's annoying.

Wildflower. She doesn't want to be tamed, and I shouldn't want to try this badly. I should steer her in the opposite direction and send her running.

It's been years since a woman sparked my interest beyond some nameless, meaningless exchange. My football days were a wild ride in many ways, and now I have a few women in the area I can call when the need strikes me. It will not give my mom the grandbabies she so desperately wants, but it scratches the itch.

And it's an easy way for me to maintain my privacy.

I storm up to the barn to start my day. The hours pass methodically, one young horse at a time, until all five have put in a good day's work. No one talks to me. No one bothers me.

Except Nadia.

She fucking bothers me. Her lips haunt me. Her words preoccupy me. And the fact that she's fourteen years younger, living on the same ranch, and so fucking off-limits almost makes me see red.

I should drive into town tonight and fuck Natasha. She doesn't ask questions or talk back. She doesn't run her sassy mouth, hit me with a challenging smirk, and make my dick hard without even touching me.

With her, I could get this out of my system. I could let loose and work out some tension. And then come back here and get to work without eye-fucking a girl I shouldn't even be looking at.

"Maybe another day," I mutter as I turn out the last of the horses with a firm clap on the haunch. I'm not in the right headspace for another woman right now. I mull over when I will be, when another empty fuck will fit into my schedule, and the fact of the matter is, I have free time galore. I could fit it in whenever… I just don't want to.

Something I'm turning over in my mind when I hear the low hum of wheels on the asphalt behind me.

Mira pulls up in a truck beside me, rolling the window down with an expression of urgency on her face. "Hey, Griff. You're gonna need to do Nadia's riding lesson."

Fuck my life.

"When?"

She glances down at her watch. "In about an hour."

My brow furrows. I know I offered. But I didn't really expect I'd be doing it. I was just being polite. "Why?"

"Because Billie is at the hospital. It seems like her water might have broken, but it's way too early. I'm headed there now.

She's the one who mentioned the lesson." Her fingers tap impatiently at the steering wheel.

"She's possibly in early labor and worrying about a riding lesson?"

She shrugs as if it's normal. "Yep. She also told me I need to get there because I'm the only doctor she trusts with her vagina."

I snort, shaking my head. "You chicks are fuckin' weird."

"Oh, absolutely." She nods, not offended at all. "So you've got the lesson?"

"Yeah, yeah." I wave her off. "Go deal with her… whatever. You know. Just go."

"Vagina." Mira laughs as she rolls up the window. "The word you're looking for is *vagina.*"

Walking back up to the barn as she pulls away, I close my eyes and wish for the calm of my acreage on the mountain.

"What are you doing here?"

Nadia sounds about as happy as I do about this situation. But I also know I'm the best man for the job. The only one with the time for the job. Time I could have spent getting lost in Natasha or someone else. Honestly, anyone other than the tempting blond standing in front of me.

"Billie is at the hospital. So c-call me…" I trail off, rubbing a hand over my face. You'd think by now I could work my way around the words that trip me up. But I'm just dumb enough to run into them full throttle.

At least I'm consistent in my life choices.

When I remove my hand, I can see Nadia's tilted head,

glittering eyes regarding me curiously as she leans up against the fence. "Call you Coach?" she finishes the sentence.

A nod is all I offer her. I'm already tired of talking. Missing the peace of my time alone.

"I've heard you do that before."

"Yup." I bark the word more harshly than I intended and don't miss the way she flinches.

"Do you have a stutter?" She just asks it. Straight out. No shame, no treading lightly, no backing down. Just out with it.

I like that about her. The way she just says what she's thinking. Wears her heart on her sleeve. It's why I was so pissed off watching her around that douchebag the other night, all demure and accommodating. I wanted her to tell him to go fuck himself. Because that's what he deserved.

Even if I barely know her, I know deep down *that's* who she is. And spending time with a person who you can't be yourself around is a tragic waste of time. So I don't bother lying to her. This is who I am now.

"Yes," I mumble, turning toward the gate. "Let's get started."

"Is Billie okay?" Her eyes are pinched with concern.

I sigh because I have little comfort to offer her. "I don't really know."

She nods with a bigger sigh than mine and then forges ahead. "Okay." Her tone is back to light and happy. "Just tell me what to do."

I almost groan out loud at her saying shit like that to me, and I have to remind myself that she's fourteen years younger. Just starting her life. She doesn't need someone like me—reclusive and damaged—and I can't betray Stefan's trust by pulling anything with his little sister.

"How much do you know? Have you ridden at all?"

"Nope." She sidles up beside me, eyes trailing over Spot appreciatively. He is a good-looking horse. I can't blame her. "What's his name?" Her chin juts out in his direction.

"Spot." I unlatch the gate and hand the leather halter over to her. "Go get him."

"*Spot?*"

I bulge my eyes at her. Silently asking, *Yeah, and?*

"It's just not a very creative name. What with all the spots on him." She marches into the paddock confidently and holds the halter out for the horse to drop his head into it. "It would be like calling me Blondie instead of Wildflower."

My molars clamp down at the mention of the pet name I called her, and it's obvious to me that making little comments like that amuses her. Her lips are rolling together in a pathetic attempt to keep her smile concealed.

"Nadia," I say her name like a warning, silently thanking the universe that her name doesn't start with a *k* or a *t*. Scolding her while stumbling over the letter wouldn't pack quite the same punch.

"Yes?" She shoots me the most innocent look, caramel eyes all wide behind the flutter of her thick lashes. *Brat.*

"Bring him into the barn and get him in the cross ties. Think you can manage that?"

"Yes, Coach." Her voice overflows with amusement as she saunters past me toward the pristine facility.

If she weren't completely off-limits, I'd take her over my knee. Age difference be damned.

I stare at her ass as she leads Spot into the barn. The way her jeans crease under the round globes is almost hypnotic. They curve up into a tight, narrow waist before flaring back out into her ample tits.

If you searched for *hourglass figure* in the dictionary, I'm sure you'd find a shot of Nadia Dalca's wicked body.

With Spot latched into the cross tie, we get him ready. I show her the pieces of tack she'll need, explaining the various parts and how to put each piece on safely.

The tip of her tongue catches between her teeth in concentration as she works to commit what I'm telling her to memory. The suggestive comments and flirting die off, and she makes an earnest effort to learn what I'm attempting to teach.

Something that makes her more alluring to me. She's smart, savvy, committed to figuring it out, and I can respect that. What's more, she doesn't look at me differently since the stutter came up.

No pity. No judgment. No wounded puppy routine. Just a blunt question. Followed by complete indifference. At her reaction, or lack thereof, I relax in her presence. The words flow easily, and I get lost in sharing things I could do with my eyes closed.

"Okay, grab your helmet and let's head outside."

"Oh, nah. I'm good." She walks toward the doorway like she thinks she's going to march that fine ass out of here without a helmet on.

"No chance. Helmet. Now."

She turns back to me, rolling her eyes and fisting her hands on her hips in a way that makes me acutely aware of her age. "You know I'm legal, right? A helmet isn't mandatory."

My eyes narrow. I didn't miss that dig. "If you're legal, stop acting like a child." I point brusquely to the room down the hall where I know they store the tack and riding apparel. Anger singes my every movement. This is non-negotiable for me. "No helmet. No lesson."

We face off, her eyes searching my face for answers that she won't find. Something she must realize because her slender shoulders heave under the weight of a deep sigh. "Okay. Quit your grumbling. You don't need to take the whole dad routine so seriously. I'll be right back."

Within minutes, she's striding back out of that room, fastening the strap beneath her chin. "If you had insane curly hair that takes forever to straighten, you'd understand," she mutters as she takes hold of Spot's reins and struts out into the center of the oversize sand ring.

Hair. She's worried about her fucking *hair* instead of her brain. My teeth grind and my head shakes as I follow her in, trying to keep my temper under control.

"Over by the mounting block," I snap, striding over to the big wooden step stool in the middle. "Now, before you get on, you're going to check the girth. Sometimes a horse will puff up when you cinch it the first go-round, which means it's loose when you get on. Rookie way to fall off." I internally pat my back for not tripping up the word *to*.

It's a constant running tally. A fixation I can't stop. It's exhausting.

Nadia nods, reaching under the flap of the saddle, pushing up onto her tippy-toes as she struggles to tighten the girth. Spot's ears flit back, unimpressed.

"You're not trying to suffocate him. Here," I step in beside her, close enough that her upper arm brushes against my bicep. The heat of her body seeps into mine as the faint scent of her lotion hangs in the air between us. But she doesn't move away from me. She watches my hands, still perfectly concentrated. But I'm distracted by the rosy tip of her tongue that's captured between her teeth again. "You don't need to squeeze him t-t-to death." My heart pounds in my chest as I try to ignore the slip. If I pretend it didn't happen, maybe she will too. The more I fixate, the worse the stutter becomes. The more nervous I am, the more it comes out to play.

I tug on the girth, testing for just the right amount of wiggle room. "About like that. Feel it."

"Okay." Her brow furrows as her slender fingers wrap around the girth, testing it the way I just did. "Got it. What now?"

Her face, all smooth, sun-kissed skin, heart-shaped top lip, and slightly fuller bottom lip, tips up at me, seeking direction. Eyes like warm leather, soft and free of judgment.

I clear my throat. "Now you get up on the block." She does so immediately. "Reins in your left hand." I hand them to her and close my hand over hers, wrapping her fingers around the well-worn leather.

"Good." My voice is quiet. "That hand here on the pommel, other hand at the back." As I position her body, we fall into sync. I direct, and her body follows. We inhale and exhale in unison, and an eerie sense of calm overtakes me. After years of hiding away from people, I never expected to feel this at ease in the presence of someone I barely know.

But there's something about her. Natural and comforting. It's like I already know her somehow. "Now just swing a leg over and see how you feel in the tack."

Within moments, she's seated up on my horse with a pleased smile touching her lips while I stare up at her. Breath stolen right out of my lungs, like it was two years ago, at a complete loss for what to say next.

I can't pull my eyes off her. I have one hand on Spot's muscular shoulder while the other hangs limp at my side. My eyes are glued to her face, fixated on the way she glows from within.

"I did it! I'm riding." Her grin could light an entire stadium with its brightness.

"I mean, you're just sitting there." I chuckle quietly. The excitement radiating off her is *almost* infectious.

"Get outta here, Debbie Downer." Her head shakes as she gathers the reins in one hand and slides a palm up over the crest of Spot's neck. "Thanks, buddy. I'm going to cross this off my to-do list with your help," she murmurs down at him. Like he's done her some huge favor by just standing there.

Like the simplest things in life bring her pleasure. It makes me desperate to know what else is on that list. What else could bring her happiness like what's flowing off her right now? Because, in this moment, I think I'd do anything to check those things off for her.

CHAPTER 9

Nadia

The scrappy little dog runs in circles around me the second I let him out of his crate. His tail is like a string bean now that we've shaved him down, and I swear that scrawny tail is wagging his entire body. He is positively vibrating with excitement. All because I brought him out and sat down on the clinic floor.

I smile so hard my cheeks hurt. I can't help myself. He just had a leg amputated, but all he cares about is that I sat on the floor and talked to him in a baby voice.

"Who's a good little boy? Huh?" The dog's head quirks with intelligence. "Who is it?" He presses his rib cage down toward the ground and wiggles his tiny bum up in the air, like we're playing a really fun game.

My palm slaps the ground in front of him, and he pushes up to standing, tail tucked between his legs, and tears around the clinic like he's the fanciest racehorse on this farm. Oblivious to the fact that he looks a little drunk with the way he's weaving around.

I laugh. A full laugh that fills my chest. "Do you have the zoomies, Tripod?"

The door behind me pushes open, and Mira's chuckle joins my own. "Tripod. I approve."

"It suits him." We smile at each other before Mira crouches down to scratch him behind the ears.

"How is Billie?" I ask eagerly.

Mira sighs as she sets her things down behind the front desk. "She's good. The babies are good. The bad news is they've recommended full bed rest, and that's going over about as well as you might think. Vaughn is in major overprotective mode, so I imagine there will be some battles there."

I snort. *Understatement*. Billie is a force to be reckoned with. Something tells me Vaughn is going to have his hands full. "Oof. Poor Vaughn."

My sister-in-law crouches beside me, and Tripod instantly ambles over, still wiggling his entire body. "I've contacted other clinics and the local shelter. I even put up posters in town. No one has come to claim him. Poor little fella."

A pinch squeezes my chest at the thought that no one is coming for this little dog. That no one misses him or wants him. Sadly, I can relate.

I have Stefan now. But he never came back for me. He got the fuck out of dodge the second he could and never really looked back. I understand why. God, at the time, I was more jealous than anything. I was a canary in a cage, and he was the hawk swooping around outside. So, while I can't blame him for putting as much distance as possible between our childhood home and his well-being, there's still always this tiny packed-away part of me that's sad I got left behind.

Angry even.

But I keep that part of me well hidden. It doesn't serve me, and it certainly doesn't fit into my plan to create a happy, *normal* life for myself.

My plan to erase my past and create a shiny new future. A secure career, white-picket fence, two-point-five kids. I want the whole thing.

I realize I've zoned out, watching Mira pet the orphan pup. "So what now?" I ask.

Her lips press together in a grim line. "Shelter, I guess? Maybe a rescue? If I weren't so busy already, I'd keep him myself."

I look down into the bulgy brown orbs of his eyes. I wish I could too. I want so badly to not leave him behind. The bridge of my nose stings as I lay all my trauma out on a perfectly happy little dog. But I've got this little voice at the back of my head telling me I'm not ready to settle down yet. That I've got a few things to do still.

"How was your riding lesson?" Mira changes the subject entirely, and I'm not sad to let my brain travel in a different direction.

A slow grin spreads across my face. "It was amazing."

"Yeah?" Her eyes light up, excited for me. "Griff was okay? I know he's not much of a talker."

I absently wonder if she knows why. Does Stefan know? Has anyone paid enough attention to Griff to even figure it out?

"He was great." I nod. "I rode his horse, Spot. He only let me walk because he's all high and mighty and shit." Mira laughs. "But it was still amazing. We're doing another after work tonight."

She rubs my back in a sisterly way and beams down at me. "I'm so proud of you, Nadia." I lean into her touch, thriving on it. I know people think Mira comes off a little prickly, but she's been nothing but warm and protective of me. Since the very first time we met.

I know she's my brother's soulmate. But more than that, I think she was meant to come into my life as well.

"Are you going to apply?"

"For what?" Am I being intentionally oblivious? Yes, yes, I am.

And by the way she rolls her eyes, she knows it too. "Vet school, dumbass."

I chuckle. "The window is open on my laptop, and I have spent a lot of time staring at it. Does that count?"

She nudges me. "Fill it out."

"I... I don't want to leave you in the lurch here. I basically just started again after ditching you to do my last program."

"Hey. Look at me." I do, and her fierce eyes bore into mine. "Don't you ever apologize for going after what you want. Don't you ever let anyone stand in your way. If they do, they don't love you the way you deserve. And me? I love you. Apply. You have to try."

That pinch in my chest is back, but for a completely different reason. I'm so lucky to have her and Stefan now. I may not have experienced unconditional love before turning eighteen and getting the hell out of Romania, but it's better late than never.

The door swings open again, interrupting our sisterly moment, and my chin jerks, following the sound.

Mira stands up immediately, but I'm stuck on the floor... at Griffin Sinclaire's feet. Struck too dumb to move.

I keep telling myself that kiss two years ago was just that.

A kiss. I've kissed a lot of boys. A lot of hot boys. But none of them have wriggled into my subconscious the way Griffin has.

Kneeling here, staring up at his unwavering gaze, not a shred of warmth on his face, I hate myself for still wanting him. I decide he's more like a tick. All I did was brush up against a bush one night, and he latched on. Now he's stuck under my skin, poisoning me.

The good news is, I've pulled my fair share of ticks off animals in this line of work. So that's what I'll do. I'll grab my imaginary tweezers and yank him out like a fucking bug.

Shiny new future doesn't include Lyme disease, thank you very much.

"Hey." I pat Tripod once more before pushing up to stand. Because over my dead body am I staying kneeling in front of him when he can't even spare me a smile. "What's up?"

His arms fold over his chest, and he scowls at me like he's unimpressed. I don't know what it takes to impress Griffin Sinclaire, but based on the way he goes all stony around me, I'm going to guess that I'm not capable of it.

"Here to check on the dog."

"Aww. Griffin, you're so sweet." Mira says lightly, walking back around the desk to sit at the computer. "As you can see, he's doing fine. Dogs handle amputation pretty well, actually." Her eyes scan the screen, and she clicks the mouse, probably breaking down the schedule for today as she continues. "I haven't been able to track down an owner. So once the incision heals, I'll start the process for placing him with a rescue."

Griffin visibly jerks back. The corners of his mouth pull down farther than usual. Mira doesn't notice; instead, she casually carries on. "Actually, I have a favor to ask you guys."

I arch a brow, not loving the sound of that. *Guys.* Plural. Griffin and me together. I'm already suddenly dreading the riding lesson I've been looking forward to since yesterday. It seemed like he and I had made some headway. Until he strolled in here and scowled at me like I'm an annoying teenager.

Griffin just grunts as a way of saying, *No problem, what can I do for you?*

Rude.

"I'm double-booked with what I had to reschedule after yesterday. Actually"—she worries her bottom lip against her teeth—"I'm more than double-booked. I have a lameness consult down at the track, but everything else is out here. Nadia, would you be willing to go take a look? Video call me so I can see what's going on?"

I shrug. "I mean, yeah. Of course. But I can do that on my own."

She turns wide pleading eyes to Griffin, and I almost laugh. She knows how to wield the doe eyes to get her way.

"Griffin, the owner of the horse at the track is… Well, I don't want to send Nadia in there alone. Go with her? I'll make it up to you with dinner at our place tonight."

"Hi." I wave an arm between them. "I'm right here. I don't need the crabby mountain man to accompany me."

Griffin snorts, but Mira turns pleading eyes on me. "Nadia, this guy is not one of the good people in this business. I don't even like going by myself, but at least I have a few years' experience handling him."

I turn on Griffin, his eyes dancing with amusement that isn't reflected anywhere else on his body. Aside from his eyes, the guy is like a fucking statue. "Fine, but you can just stand there with crossed arms like you are right now. I don't need you to hold my hand."

The brim of his hat tips down, his face disappearing behind it. "Wouldn't dream of it."

Mira's body noticeably relaxes now that we have agreed to her request.

"But I don't want dinner." Griffin is staring at the little white dog sitting on the ground, wagging his tail and staring up at all of us like he speaks English too. "I want the dog."

Mira's head tilts, and a soft smile plays across her face. "You mean you'd like to adopt Tripod?"

"Dumb name," he says, but he gives a decisive nod, signaling that, yes indeed, he would like to adopt the dog.

My face twists up in his direction. "You named your spotted horse *Spot*. Who are you to talk about dumb names?"

"My dog, my name." He doesn't even look my way. He's too busy staring at the dog. I wish I could see his face—his eyes—so I can figure out what's running through his head right now. This big gruff man staring down at a small fluffy three-legged dog. They're an odd pairing, that's for sure.

It's Mira's turn to laugh now, shaking her head as she regards the stray dog. "Consider him yours, Griffin. He'll need a couple more days at the clinic before you can take him."

"Yup," is all he says before he turns and strolls out of the clinic.

Like he just expects me to follow him.

"He's kind of a dick, huh?" I say to Mira, rolling my eyes and expecting her to join in with my complaints.

But instead, she appears contemplative. "I don't know. I think he's kind of sweet, to be honest."

I shake my head and roll my eyes at her before stomping out of the clinic toward his cocky swagger and killer ass topped off with proud broad shoulders.

Apparently, I'm the only person here who doesn't have heart eyes for Griffin Sinclaire and his quiet, gloomy persona.

"It's lame. Limping like it's broken."

I instantly hate the man standing across from me. The way he's dragging on a cigarette and then blowing the smoke in my general direction. The way he just referred to the horse tied up beside us as *it*. Not to mention the way his eyes linger on my body, the smirk, the lick across the lips. I'm fully clothed, but this fucking guy makes me feel like someone served me to him on some sort of platter.

Yeah. I hate him. I recognize his type. He's not new or original.

Suddenly, knowing that Griffin is standing behind me like some grouchy, unflinching sentinel doesn't seem so ridiculous. Suddenly, I'm really fucking glad.

Was the drive into the city awkward and quiet? Yes. Does Griffin listen to terrible twangy country music? Also, yes.

I tried to talk to him.

I didn't know you wanted a dog.

Yup.

Do you even like dogs?

Well enough.

Have you had one before?

Nope.

Do you have a name in mind then?

Nope.

Are you going to name him Snowy because he's white?

grunts

And that was the last of our conversation for ninety goddamn minutes.

But in this moment, with this man eyeing me and treating his racehorse like an object rather than a living being, I confess to myself that having Griffin here is a relief.

"His hind fetlock is very swollen." I crouch by the horse's back leg, running my hand over the joint. "Easy, fella."

The minute my hands touch the puffy area, I can feel the heat radiating from it. *Poor boy.*

"Have you been cold hosing this? Or icing?"

He sucks on his cigarette. "No."

I stand and brush my hands off on my scrubs as I come back to the front of the horse. "Dr. Thorne wanted us to video call her so she can watch him move. Then I'll take some X-rays, and she'll follow up with you."

"I'm not spending that kind of money on this horse. Racing career is about over. Made some good money. I'll ship him if that's the case."

My brow furrows. "Ship him?"

"Auction. Meat. Lawn ornament. Makes no difference to me."

Angry tears spring up in my eyes as my gaze travels over the beautiful horse's seal-brown coat, highlighted with dapples across his haunches. Blinking rapidly to maintain my composure, I run a palm over his velvety nose, the long white snip that covers it.

His eyes flutter shut at the tenderness of my touch, and my heart twists. "This could be something very minor. We could investigate further before you take such a drastic measure."

The man throws his head back and laughs. It's raspy, and he sounds out of breath. Hopefully, his cigarettes will take him out.

It's a cruel thought. But my mind is a cruel place some days. I should feel bad about it, but after all the shit I've seen assholes like this do—I don't.

My molars grind against each other as I struggle to maintain some professional composure. Two years ago, I'd have gone off on this guy. My temper would have taken over and made me say things I shouldn't. Obviously, I still think them though, and if thoughts could kill a person, this guy would be toast.

"Oh, little girl, you've got some things to learn about this business." He steps toward me as his eyes rake over my body hungrily. It makes my skin crawl. And then he props a nicotine-stained hand on my shoulder. "I could teach them to you sometime if you w—"

"Hands off if you plan on keeping them." Griffin's voice rumbles from behind me. Right now, it's gritty in a whole different way, almost like it's rusty from years of not being used. But still velvety, still full and warm. He's standing much closer than he was mere moments ago.

The man just smirks. He drops his hand but doesn't peel his gaze from my tits.

I hear two thumps of Griffin's boots, and then his hand is wrapping softly around my elbow, pulling me behind the shield of his broad body as he hisses out, "Eyes up here, asshole."

I want to be angry with Griffin for intervening when he promised he wouldn't. He was supposed to stand there and look grumpy. But now, with his body providing a wall of protective muscle between myself and the man with the greasy hair and wandering eyes, I sigh in relief.

I want so badly to be capable and brave and self-assured. But the fact of the matter is, deep down, men like this *scare* me. Men like my father, ones with anger that simmers just barely concealed beneath the surface. Ones who know there are infrequently consequences for their actions.

If I let my mind wander down that path, I would realize that, on a subconscious level, men scare me in general.

Talk about daddy issues.

"Easy, cowboy." The man cackles, amused and not deterred. "Just letting Blondie here know the realities of life. Racehorses come and go. The bottom line is what I'm focused on."

I watch Griffin's body go tense before me. A vein in the side of his neck throbs, and his fingers curl in on themselves.

He usually seems so unaffected, but right now, he looks like he's ready to explode. Without even thinking, I reach one trembling hand forward and trail it down the center of his lower back. I watch the gray fabric of his T-shirt fold beneath my touch, and Griffin's body goes still.

An ache crawls up my arm at the contact, burrowing itself at the inner part of my elbow. With a small gasp, I pull back, rotating my wrist to soothe the sparks. But Griffin is still staring the other man down, so I hook two fingers into the side loop of his jeans and give a sharp tug back.

His head flicks to the side, his eyes finding mine over the crest of his shoulder. Eyes that were amused earlier today but are pure chaos right now.

"Don't do something stupid," I whisper, imploring him to take it down a notch. On one hand, having someone come to my defense is a new experience. On the other, the glint of violence in his eyes scares me a little bit. "Please." I tug again.

He blinks in response. Which I subconsciously add to his range of nonverbal reactions.

"We'll let Dr. Thorne know," he bites out before turning around and shepherding me down the row of stalls. His calloused hand falls at the back of my neck, giving me a comforting squeeze, but he doesn't give up his position behind me, blocking the greasy owner from seeing me at all as we retreat.

I don't know if it's the adrenaline, someone swooping in to protect me, or the fact that poor horse is going to be sold for meat after giving all his best racing years to an asshole, but the tears I held back start to flow, silently trailing down my face and dripping off the apples of my cheeks.

When we hit the sun outside, I hustle away from Griffin toward the Gold Rush Ranch truck that's parked at the end of the alleyway. My escape vehicle. It's like my feet can't get me there fast enough. But when my hand wraps around the handle, I stop. My opposite palm lands against the glass of the window and I drop my head, trying to gather my composure before I have to spend another hour and a half in the small space with Griffin.

The man who kissed me brainless once and I was supposed to have forgotten.

"You okay?"

He's not touching me anymore, but he might as well be. I can feel that simple squeeze on my neck like a brand. Anytime he touches me, my skin hums with pleasure.

I hate it. I hate it because he turned me away and because he had to be best friends with one of the few people in the world I would *never* hurt.

I hate him for being the only man who's lit me up the way

he did. And I hate him even more for being the only man I really can't pursue.

And I *really* hate that I can't save that horse in there.

"No." It comes out as a sob despite my best efforts to control my voice.

"Guy is a prick." He spits the word out like he wants to hurt it.

"That horse. Griff—Griffin." My voice cracks over his name. "That poor horse."

I'm fucking falling apart, and I can't even explain why. I'm overwhelmed with crushing sadness. And anger.

"For fuck's sake," he barks out before I hear him spin on his heel to leave.

I'm too embarrassed to even turn around. Instead, I close my eyes and attempt to center myself, to get a grip on my emotions. *The girl you want to be doesn't crumble like this.*

The girl I want to become should be pissed that Griffin stepped in and went all caveman on that sleazebag.

But I'm not pissed. I'm relieved.

I don't know how many minutes pass as I stand there breathing in through my nose and out through my mouth, giving myself an internal pep talk.

All I know is that the uneven clopping of hooves pulls me out of the safe space I've created in my brain. And when I spin to see who's coming my way, I see Griffin.

Leading the beautiful and sore dark bay horse beside him.

"What are you doing?" I sniff as he struts straight up to me, holding out the tattered red rope that's attached to the gelding's leather halter.

"Here." He can barely hold my gaze. *Probably because I terrified him with my meltdown.*

I take the rope, confusion etched on my features. "Why?"

"Because he's yours now."

"What?" Disbelief paints my tone as my head swivels between the broody horse and the broody man who just handed him to me. "You bought me a horse?"

"He's sorta broken."

He bought me a horse.

My eyes flit down to the pink skin at the center of the horse's white nose as emotion wells up in me again, my brain stumbling along, trying to make sense of the last fifteen minutes of my life.

I don't know what to say to his comment, so all I do say as I stroke my new horse's nose is "That's okay. So am I."

CHAPTER 10

Griffin

We pull out of the barns at Bell Point Park in silence.

Truthfully, I've been sitting in silence for the past three hours. I left Nadia and her new horse at the Gold Rush row of stalls, and then I drove all the way back out to Ruby Creek to pick up my horse trailer because, of course, we didn't bring one with us.

Then I drove all the way back, trying for the life of me to figure out why I'd buy the girl a fucking horse and then spend hours of my day figuring out transportation for it. Aside from the fact that I personally can't handle the thought of a horse being sent to slaughter, it doesn't add up. I saved Spot from the same fate, all skin and bones and dull coat with dead eyes, like he already knew what end he was facing.

I wish I could save every horse at those auctions from that fate.

But none of that equates to a rational reason to buy Nadia Dalca an injured racehorse. I could have just bought myself a second horse.

But I know she wanted one. And I'm still not over her referring to herself as broken. Nursing Spot back to health made me feel a little less broken, and maybe this horse can do that for her too.

All I know is that when she turned around, I saw her heart crumple in her beautiful brown eyes. There's an innocence about her I can't quite figure out. Did she not know about the dirty underbelly of this industry? The number of horses that are tossed away when their moneymaking ability expires?

She was a sassy, lippy teenager two years ago, and now, she's transformed into someone buffed to a beautiful, fake shine.

Just now, there was a crack in the smooth surface she's manifested for herself. And I recognized the hell out of that sentiment. Of that look. I see it in the mirror, staring back at me now and then.

I hate that look on anyone. A dog. A friend. That friend's little sister.

I mean, shit. Even that horse was looking like he knew it was the end of the line. So saving him seemed like an easy fix. I'm a sucker for a horse that needs saving. Ask Spot.

Except now, Nadia is staring at me as we drive through Vancouver traffic toward the highway. I can feel her gaze tracing the lines of my face so heavily that she might as well be running a finger over them. I know getting a horse was on her list. I overheard that part of their conversation that morning, and I have the resources to do it. So why the fuck not? It was a nice, perfectly innocent thing to do.

At least that's what I tell myself.

"Thank you. For doing what you did earlier. Today. Just all of it." Her palm presses into the center of her chest. "I'm overwhelmed."

She was easier to brush off when she had the bratty little sister act down. This version of her is harder to keep from getting under my skin.

"Welcome." My fingers squeeze the steering wheel, and I force myself to keep my eyes on the road as silence stretches between us. Usually, I like silence. But right now, it's awkward because there's a lot to say and no one is saying a thing.

"How much did you pay for him?" Her fingers twist together in her lap, and she stares down at them.

"Doesn't matter. Don't bother t-t-trying to pay me back." I scrub one hand over my beard, grateful it covers some of the heat creeping up my throat. "Consider him a gift. My way of saying sorry." I let my eyes wander over to her. She's still staring at her lap. Her lips press together, and she gives a small shake of her head.

"Okay."

A quiet chuckle rumbles in my chest. An attempt to break the tension. "Expected a fight from you, Wildflower."

She lifts her molten-brown eyes, dark lashes providing the perfect frame for them. "I don't think anyone has ever given me a more thoughtful gift, Griffin." My lungs fill with thick air. Her smile is watery but sincere, and then she turns herself toward the window and watches the flow of traffic around us.

Anyone?

The word rattles around in my brain as I think about all the things I've received in my life, all the awesome experiences my parents have provided. The gifts, the vacations, the sentimental little trinkets along the way. I would never have guessed an injured racehorse purchased by *me* would rank up there for her.

It's not until we've made it out of the city that she speaks again. "Has Stefan ever told you about our family?"

"That they died in a plane wreck?"

She nods. "Anything else?"

I rack my brain and realize he hasn't. "No."

"My dad was a drunk."

I grunt. So was I. What am I supposed to do? Judge the guy?

"He beat the hell out of our mom."

Yes. I am supposed to judge this piece of shit.

"Stefan left for boarding school when I was a baby. He only came back in the summers. Then I had someone to hide in the closet with while it happened."

A strangled groan erupts out of my throat. But I say nothing. Nadia's head rests against the glass of the passenger-side window, and the words are flowing. Saying anything now would just be an interruption.

"Eventually Stefan went off to college. And then he never came back anymore. That's when my mom started drinking. I'm pretty sure he was her favorite—her reminder of a happier time in her life. Me? I was just a reminder of the monster she was locked in that fucking house with. From what I gather, she had a lot going for her before she met him. Plans. Dreams. And then it all just went out the window. I don't actually know though because I never really got to know her."

Horror washes over me. I spend an awful lot of energy feeling sorry for myself, and suddenly I feel like I have no right to that level of self-pity.

How can I feel bad for myself when Nadia has been through *that*?

She continues before I can say anything. Her stream of consciousness completely unfettered. "I think she became boring for him to beat up when she was passed out. So, eventually I became the new target. It happened the first time when I was fourteen. That's when I decided I would never be his victim. I would never be *her*. And I started staying at other people's houses because it was preferable to staying at my own."

"Where would you stay?"

"It started out with girlfriends. Ended up with boyfriends." Her voice is detached, in a faraway place. "For a few years there at the end, it was… a lot of boys."

My heart clenches thinking of someone so young and impressionable with no direction. No support. No love.

"Did your parents wonder where you were?"

She snorts.

It's almost cruel to not grab her hand, to lend a gentle touch to her after the way she just sliced herself open for me. But I also know that keeping my hands off her is in everyone's best interest.

So instead, I fill the space with a confession of my own.

"I didn't always have a stutter, you know." I slur the word *stutter* a bit. It always trips me up. It seems cruel to have made that word have so many hard *t* sounds. I'd like to kick whoever came up with that square in the balls.

Her head whips to me, ripped right out of the memories she's been immersed in for the last several minutes. "Really?"

I nod.

"How?"

"I used to play pro football. I was a two-time Super Bowl champion. A Ruby Creek sensation." My ensuing chuckle is laced with disappointment. I didn't just let myself down with my spiral—I let a whole town down.

She nods eagerly, entire body turning toward me, hanging on every word.

"I lived for football. Spent my life on the road, chasing wins, partying, and fucking every girl I could."

I chance a look her way. Her throat bobs with a thick swallow, pink staining her cheeks.

"A simple play went wrong. I failed to attach my chin strap, and when I got sacked, I went down hard. And my helmet went flying." I groan at the mere memory of how young and stupid I'd been.

"Oh shit." Her nose scrunches up. She's adorable. So enthralled in *me*.

"And all I remember is waking up in the hospital. My body was fine, brain not so much. Concussed as fuck. Spent a couple of weeks there. Probably took a few years off my parents' lives in the process."

"That must have been terrifying for them."

I just nod. I don't like to think about how hard I've been on my parents. I've been terrifying them since I was a kid, I'm sure. But these last several years have really taken the cake. Their only boy, spiraling while they stand back, powerless to help.

"Apparently, with some brain injuries, there can be the onset of a stutter. Sometimes it's short-lived; in other instances it sticks around." I shrug. "I'm almost certain there's a mental aspect to it as well. It's always the *k*s and *t*s that get me."

"What do you mean?" Her head tilts, curiosity lacing her tone.

"Like… sometimes I overthink it, and then it's worse. Stress and pressure make it worse. Some days are just better than others."

"Is today a good day?" Her voice is lilting and soft, and I can't help but turn my attention over to her beautiful face. All warm golden tones and chocolate-fondue eyes.

"Why?" My voice comes out more gravelly than I intend.

Her tongue darts out over her bottom lip, a subtle smile tugging at the corners of her mouth. "You've used words that begin with both those sounds in the last few minutes with no problem."

My mind races back, trying to pick out the spots where I said those letters. I was so lost in focusing between her and the road that I didn't tiptoe around my words for once.

"Maybe you just like being around me." Her smile grows, her body language changing. When our eyes meet, she pulls out a saucy wink. She thinks she's joking, but the truth is spot-on—I *do* like being around her. I just can't explain why.

"Nadia." I angle a disapproving glare her way.

"Oof." She flops back in her seat with a noisy sigh. "Tough crowd."

My cheek pinches with a lopsided smile. And then I blurt out something I should not. "It's because your name starts with an *n*. Just makes scolding you that much easier."

I laugh it off, until she turns to me and says smoothly, "I think you just like saying my name."

I swallow because I am so fucked where Nadia Dalca is concerned.

Yes, Wildflower. I like saying your name.

"Why don't we put him in the smallest paddock behind Griffin's cottage?" Mira points over the field from where we stand in the front parking lot. "The best thing for that horse right now is going to be a little peace and quiet. Not a busy barn. Stall rest, cold hosing, and unwinding are what he needs. Then we can figure out what to do with the leg. Probably surgery for what I'm assuming is a joint full of bone chips."

Nadia nods, looking strong and capable with her hands propped on the swell of her hips. I try hard not to let my eyes trail down over the curve of her ass.

But I fail fucking miserably.

I've never considered scrubs to be sexy, but on Nadia, it's like a whole new ball game. A man would have to be blind to not appreciate her soft curves and long limbs.

It's almost criminal.

She turns to me, and I drop my gaze onto the scuffed toes of my boots, feeling guilty as hell. "Is that okay with you? I'll have to pop in at your place regularly then."

Say no, you schmuck.

"Yeah, sure."

Griffin Sinclaire fails again.

"Get him settled in and then come for dinner," Mira says. "You guys have had a long day. We'll order in. Nothing crazy."

These women are running circles around me, making plans and getting shit done. I'm not accustomed to dealing with people this way. Accounting for their plans. Adjusting mine to fit them. Up in the mountains, I don't answer to anyone. I do my daily chores, work out, and train the few horses that get sent up to me.

I eat by myself. I read by myself. And when I do get lonely, I visit my parents.

"Fine."

"He means, *Thank you. That sounds lovely, Mira.*" Nadia pipes up with a laugh. "We'll be there soon."

Mira gives us a slow smile, eyes bouncing between Nadia and me. I swear, if someone were going to be a mind reader, it would be her. She probably knows I was eye fucking her husband's little sister.

Nadia and I hop back in the truck, and it strikes me that I am *very* tired of driving. All I want to do is relax. Soak up a little peace and quiet. My shoulders rise and fall under the weight of a heavy sigh as we pull out of the circle driveway at the entryway of Gold Rush Ranch.

I miss my place in the mountains.

I miss being alone.

I miss my privacy.

And I just agreed to let Nadia come over to my place daily rather than pushing her away like I should be doing.

You also bought her a fucking horse, sucker.

I groan aloud, and Nadia's eyes snap to mine.

"Are you growling?"

I shake my head and keep my eyes on the road, hauling the trailer carefully behind us.

"That's very feral mountain man of you. I went from thinking you didn't talk at all to realizing that you mostly speak in grunts and growls." She crosses her arms across her midsection and leans back in the seat with a pleased smile on her face. "A lesser woman would think you were nuts. Lucky for you, nuts works for me."

God, give me patience to endure Nadia Dalca.

"It's part of your charm. Sometimes people just talk to fill the space. I think they might just like the sound of their own voice. But you're so comfortable with silence. It's kind of peaceful, really."

I shoot her a withering glare. The irony of talking about people who fill the space with unnecessary chatter while she chatters away unnecessarily is not lost on me.

"Give me that look all you want, Sinclaire. I know you're a big softie underneath that hard shell. Like a turtle." Her voice is full of mirth. She's enjoying the hell out of this. And my mind wanders to all the filthy ways I could wipe that smirk off her pretty face.

I groan and bang the back of my head against the headrest. I want to say something about her terrible comparison to a turtle, but I don't trust myself to articulate it right now. Not with her attention fully focused on me.

It's fucking unnerving.

In a way that it should not be, considering our age difference and connection. I should feel brotherly toward this girl.

And brotherly is very, very far down the list of what I feel for her. But then I do have a special knack for fucking things up when they're going well for me. Maybe I'm destined to do that to the only real friendship I've had in years too.

CHAPTER 11

Nadia

I walk into my brother's home with Griffin trailing behind me. I swear I can feel his gaze on me. My skin hums for him.

Is he staring at my ass? I hope so.

My lips roll together as I try to shove that thought back down. I should not set my sights on my brother's friend, but that's getting harder and harder to stick to the more time I spend with him.

He says the horse is a gift and made it seem like he only bought him to rescue him. But I'm having a hard time not looking further into that. Why give him to me? Why not just keep the gelding for himself? Why be okay with giving me riding lessons and having me come around his place when he wants to stay away from me?

There are things that don't add up, and I'm smart enough to notice them. I'm just not sure what to do with them.

"Hi!" I call out right as the scent of pizza hits me, making my mouth water.

"Hey, guys." Stefan rounds the corner with his signature smirk on his face. He's not closed off like he used to be, so I'm not sure why he still hides behind that mask. Either he's just grown accustomed to that facial expression or Mira has made him happy enough that it's not a mask at all anymore.

I'd like to think that's what it is.

He ruffles my hair like I'm still a little kid before stepping just beyond me to clap Griffin on the shoulder. "How ya doin', man? Nice to have you around."

The two of them are honestly adorable together. Griffin grunts and I giggle as I walk into the house I called home for several years.

It's sprawling but cozy, with dark-stained wood beams and an industrial kitchen. Big windows lend incredible natural lighting, and the house has this way of matching the rugged landscape of Ruby Creek while also being just a little bit over-the-top. I try to imagine Griffin living here. I try to imagine Griffin being a professional football player too. I can't see either of those things, to be honest.

The two men chat about I don't know what, and I don't care. I have tunnel vision for food right now. They can bro out without me.

Padding into the open living space, I slide into a chair at the counter and assess the open pizza boxes on the counter. I'm pretty sure I'm going to eat them all. It's hitting me now that I spent all day wrapped up in the new horse and I haven't eaten a thing. Now, I'm famished.

I grab a slice of pepperoni. No plate. No cutlery. I fold it in half and start shoving it into my mouth.

"Very ladylike, sis," Stefan mocks. *Dick.*

"Whatever," I reply over a mouthful of food. "I'm starving,"

He chuckles and goes to pull out plates for us, and I'm pretty sure I won't be using one just to spite him.

"Where is Mira?"

"She fell asleep with Silas. They're so sweet all cuddled up together." My brother's face takes on this soft look that I never used to see on him before he met Mira. "I don't have it in me to wake her. She's been working so hard between the clinic and Billie and everything else. She overdoes it." He puts a few pieces of her favorite—veggie supreme—on a plate and covers it with plastic wrap. I bet he'll bring her a midnight snack in bed or something equally romantic. That's the type of dude he's become.

I shove another massive bite of pizza into my mouth. A deep chortling sound rolls in from beside me, and when I peek up, Griffin has taken the seat beside me and has his fist covering his mouth.

Unsuccessfully trying to smother his laugh.

"Yeah, yeah. Yuck it up, Sinclaire. You're the one who stranded me with no food."

Stefan leans back against the counter opposite the island with his plate of pizza. "He did what to you?"

"Did Mira not tell you that Griffin bought me a horse?"

My brother's eyebrows shoot up, and Griffin clears his throat.

I roll my eyes. It's not like I just told him we made out in the pub bathroom. *That would go over poorly for sure.*

"Sounds like a good story." Stefan takes a bite of his pizza, chewing thoughtfully as his eyes flit between the two of us sitting at the island.

"So there was this total asshole at the track. Mira made Griffin go with me because she knew what kind of dude he was—"

Griffin cuts me off. "He was going to send a perfectly good horse for meat and was gawking at your sister like she was a piece of candy." He wipes one hand across his mouth before looking back down at his plate. "I stepped in."

"I'm going to pay him back," I blurt out as my cheeks heat. I don't know why it feels like we're in trouble. It's probably because we're both sitting here keeping secrets from my brother. We did nothing wrong—not this time anyway.

Griffin's intense gaze catches on the side of my face for a moment, but then he turns to my brother and shrugs. He doesn't bother correcting me.

Another secret for us to keep.

"Well, Nadia, sounds like you've got your work cut out for you. Congratulations on your new horse."

I push more pizza in my mouth and smile as the two men talk about some hunting trip they're planning for the fall. Their conversation is full of laughs and inside jokes, and I listen to the words that Griffin uses. The ones he thinks he stumbles on but doesn't in the company of a good friend. An observation that both warms my heart and makes it clench.

I thought we could play it cool around my brother.

I was wrong.

Zoning out, I startle when my brother addresses me. "How's the boyfriend, Nadia?"

My shoulders tense. *Fucking Tommy.* "He's not my boyfriend."

Stefan chuckles. "Oh, yeah? Did you tell him that, man-eater?"

I suck in a deep breath. I hate that I'm perceived that way, whether or not he means it as a joke. Have I settled down with one guy? No. But that's changing soon. I crave the security of something more serious—I want what my brother has found—and I don't want it with Tommy.

Something I'm going to have to tell him next time we talk.

Instead of sharing that with my brother, I roll my eyes. "We haven't done a lot of talking."

Stefan guffaws, and my hand lands over my mouth. I peek over at Griffin, who has stopped with his pizza partway up to his mouth. Frozen. But only momentarily.

"That's not what I meant." The laughs keep coming from the opposite side of the kitchen, and my cheeks burn. "Stef! Shut up! I just mean we haven't been in touch."

He holds a hand up in surrender as he shakes his head. "None of my business. Just enjoying watching you get all shy about a boy. It's cute."

"You know what's going to be cute? How you look after I shave your eyebrows off in your sleep."

That makes him laugh harder. There may be thirteen years between us, but it somehow hasn't prevented my brother from falling into childish taunts now and then. But the joke is on him because I'm just crazy enough to shave off his eyebrows.

I rip another piece of pizza out of one box and dig in, avoiding looking at Griffin. I don't want him to think I'm with Tommy—and that's a problem. It shouldn't matter to me what Griffin thinks of my love life.

Stefan tries to pick up their earlier conversation about hunting. Something about target practice. He asks if I want to come, and I nod, but I'm not listening.

I'm too busy analyzing that brief pause in Griffin's movement. The way he didn't laugh at my brother's jokes. And the way he's gone from fully conversing back to grunts, nods, and one-syllable words.

★★★

"I want to say good night to my horse. I've never had a horse, and I'm excited. Just take me with you, and I'll walk back up here to my place."

"No."

I'm trying to convince Griffin to drive back to his cottage and then let me walk back to the main barn across the field. It's a nice night, so there shouldn't be a problem. Instead, he drove me straight up to the base of the steep stairs that lead to my little apartment above the barn, hopped out, yanked my door open, and pointed at the door.

Like I'm a child being sent to her room.

"Yes."

"Out." After a reasonably enjoyable day together, Griffin is being a full-blown cocksucker.

"Make me." I cross my arms and arch an eyebrow at him in challenge. No chance would he—

One long step and he's right up in my space with his hands wrapped around my rib cage. His grip is firm but gentle, and I swear he smells like the mountains, like a pine forest, and cinnamon gum, and it makes me want to lean in and run the tip of my nose up the curve of his neck.

His scent is intoxicating.

Even as he lifts me, like I'm a fucking bale of hay, takes a few long strides, and deposits me at the bottom of my stairs.

"G'night." He slams the passenger-side door. And never mind smelling him. Now what I want to do is kick him in the balls.

"What am I?" I shout at him, ire rising in my chest as he rounds the front of his truck. "A child?"

And I'm damn near positive he mutters, "Pretty much," before he jumps in the truck and drives out of the circular driveway into the darkening scenery.

Did he seriously just drop me here and take off? I flip off the back of his truck.

And then I smile as my eyes find the rolling field that leads to the private cottage on the far side of the property.

It's a pleasant night for a walk.

Within ten minutes, I'm ducking under the white fence that divides the hay field from the back part of the lot that the guesthouse sits on.

Try to tell me what to do again, asshole. See how it works out for you.

"Hi, boys," I whisper into the dusky night. Two heads pop up and stare back at me. One is Spot. Then there's *mine*.

His shiny coat matches the warm receding light that fills the valley right now. It's only shortly after 9 p.m. but the sun goes down quickly when you're sitting at the bottom of the Cascades. They jut out from the bright-green fields violently. All sharp points and rocky ledges.

Sometimes they feel almost oppressive. I turn my back to the mountains and instead walk to the paddock at the end of the row so I can spend a little time just gazing at my new pet.

"Hi, Horse." He hangs his head over the gate and closes his eyes beneath the stroke of my palm. I drag my fingers through his thick forelock and scratch him right between his ears. He nuzzles into my chest, and I swear he's thanking me. I swear he knows we saved him.

I may not know how to ride a horse very well—okay, at all—yet, but I've worked around them on the ground enough to know that they are intuitive. Incredibly sensitive.

My cheek drops onto his dusty forehead. He's clearly been rolling in the dirt, and I find I don't care at all as I wrap my arms around him. I'm not sure I recognized how tall he is, taller than your average racehorse.

"You're a very sweet boy," I murmur, hugging him. And he lets me, clearly loving the attention. "We'll get you feeling better soon. Mira has more of that medicine for you."

He snorts quietly, and I smile, feeling soothed by the contact. It's almost like he's hugging me right back. And some days, I could really use a hug.

When the back light of the log home flicks on, I drop my forehead against my horse's with a small smile. "Uh-oh. I think I'm about to get spanked by grumpy Griffin."

The back door slams shut, and I force myself not to jump. The man frays my nerves without even trying.

"Nadia." He sounds exasperated. I'm oddly pleased with myself for being the source of his frustration. Irritating someone should not be this much fun. "What are you doing here?"

I try so hard not to laugh. I don't want him to know what a kick I get out of this. "Visiting Horse."

"Horse?"

"Yeah." I finally turn around to see him standing at the top of the three steps that lead up to the sprawling deck off the back of the cabin, hands pressed into his hip bones. Wearing those goddamn jeans like they were made for him.

He looks pissed, heavy brows pressed low. Frowning just adds to the rugged edge of his beauty. He looks like he wants to do very bad things to me.

And I want to let him.

A small giggle bubbles up in my throat. I'm dead sober, but I feel almost giddy under Griffin Sinclaire's gaze.

"Yeah. This guy right here." I hike a thumb behind me at the leggy racehorse, who is still nuzzling against my back.

"You named him Horse?"

I run a hand over my mouth, trying to hide my smile. "Hardly seems like something a man who named his spotted horse *Spot* should criticize me for."

He glares at me. The seconds stretch out, and I seriously question if he might be having a stroke. I sigh and turn back to the gentle giant. "I just haven't decided on a name yet. All I know is that he needs a fresh name to go with his fresh start."

Griffin sighs and tips his chin up to stare at the sky like I exhaust him.

I ignore how clearly frustrated he is. "Do you have any brushes I can borrow?"

"You're exhausting," he huffs out before stomping down the deck to retrieve a bucket of brushes from where he's stashed them underneath the stairs. He drops them near me and then instantly retreats to sit on the stairs, back where he started.

"Thanks," I say brightly before putting a halter on Horse, tying him to the fence, and getting to grooming him.

I lose myself in the circular motion of brushing, watching his neck stretch and head twist when I hit the good spots. I smile up at his sweet face as he basks in the attention under the calm starry skies out in Ruby Creek.

I'm so engrossed with grooming him I almost don't hear Griffin when he says, "You're not paying me back. For the record."

"I know." I don't chance a look at the older man. I just keep my eyes on the soft coat in front of me.

"Then why'd you say that?"

Great question.

I sigh so deeply my shoulders come up to my ears before dropping back down again. "I don't know. I didn't want Stefan to suspect anything."

"Like what?"

Now I peer back at him, shooting a knowing look his way before going back to my task at hand.

"You have a boyfriend." The word sounds wrong on his lips. "Why would he suspect anything?"

"Good god. What is with everyone calling him my boyfriend? He's not."

Griffin casually props his elbows on his knees. "Well, you have history. He was there that night."

That night. He says it like something terrible happened. Best kiss of my life, but that was before I knew what a growly dick Griffin Sinclaire is. It wouldn't be that hot again, not now that we know each other.

"*That night* was the first time I'd kissed Tommy. I snuck out the back door once you left, and apparently, he left with another girl. That was that. Not that I cared. I didn't have high hopes for us. That's what most of my"—I hold my hands up to make air quotes with my fingers—"boyfriends equate to. With daddy issues like mine, the prospect of something serious is downright anxiety-inducing."

Griffin is staring at me, and he's mad. But I don't get the sense that he's mad at me, so I continue, filling the space between us with everything that's been running through my head for the past several years. "My brother and Mira are the first time I've seen two people truly love and respect each other. I want that too, but I'm not holding my breath. It seems fragile and unlikely, and I don't think I can handle getting hurt any more than I already have."

The words keep spilling, like it's somehow safer to say these things out loud under the cover of darkness. "So now I'll try for that too because it seems like what I'm supposed to do now. Right? I've got the education I wanted. The job I wanted. And I figure, hey, why not go for the trifecta? And so I bring a boy around *once*, who, for the record, is a massive disappointment, and I'm the butt end of every joke there is about having a boyfriend. All over a guy who I don't even like."

I toss a brush back in the bucket. The clank makes Horse jump a little as I rave on. "I'm just the silly little sister who can't settle down and gets around instead. And I fucking hate it. I don't want to be that girl. I just want a normal, happy life. Even though I'm realistically too terrified to go anywhere near that type of life. Self-sabotage is a good friend of mine, ya know? But I force myself to try anyway. And then it's just like... what am I supposed to do with a normal, happy person like Tommy? Normal, happy people don't want to hear about the shit I've seen, the shit I've endured. Normal, happy people like to be around other normal, happy people. Am I just meant to fake it for the rest of my life? I want all that"—I gesture in the general direction of my brother's house—"but I don't know if I'll ever be able to let myself really have it."

My chest is rising and falling rapidly when I finally turn my eyes back to Griffin, who is still sitting silently, a quiet witness to my insecurities, but now with a different expression on his face. Less angry and more something else.

"You're a good listener," I say, meeting his gaze pound for pound.

Our eyes lock for a few seconds and then…

Griffin bursts out laughing.

"Are you…?" My bottom jaw drops open as I watch him. The rich sound of his laugh fills the night air. "Are you fucking laughing at me?"

He covers his face with wide palms, body shaking under the intensity of his laugh.

"Griffin Sinclaire! I just poured my heart out, and now you're laughing at me!"

First, I'm incensed. I mean, how dare he? But the longer I stand there with shock painting my face, the more his amusement rubs off on me. Grumpy Griffin has the giggles.

And that's giving me the giggles.

It starts small. A little hiccup. Some tension drains out, falling away piece by piece, until the giggles turn into guffaws.

I cover my face with a hand when my eyes water with the extent of my laughter. I haven't laughed like this… *ever.* Griffin's raspy laugh twists together with my breathless one, and in the quiet darkness of the night we come together in a shared moment of levity. Something in us aligns. We're overcome with the same feeling, and we give ourselves over to it.

Something we've done before.

"My god," I wheeze out as I bend over and grip my knees. "What is wrong with you?"

He gasps out a last laugh before he says, "I guess I'm not a normal, happy person either."

My eyes find his. Mirth reflects between the two of us, and I click my tongue. "You sure as shit are not."

He leans back on the stairs again, looking seductive and delicious without even trying, filling out his T-shirt in a way that he has no business doing. In a way that has my tongue darting across my lower lip.

"You just t-t-told a man"—his chin dips briefly, but he keeps talking—"who barely speaks that he's a good listener." His eyes close and his head tips back, laughter spilling out of him once more.

And I love the sound. It's like a balm between us. I want to hear it more. I make it my goal right here and now, as I watch the ridge of his Adam's apple bob in his throat, to be the one who makes Griffin Sinclaire laugh more often.

He doesn't need to know. But I'm adding it to my to-do list.

I stand up and lean against the fence. "You are. You're a surly prick, but I can tell you're listening to me. Most people don't. Everyone is so involved with their own lives. They listen but don't absorb what I'm saying. But you don't just listen, you *hear* me."

His chest heaves as he stares back at me and his expression transforms. Almost stricken, but he nods quickly to cover it up.

Then he stands and leaves me there in the dark with a soft "Good night, Wildflower."

CHAPTER 12

Nadia

I'm halfway back across the field when I realize we didn't confirm a riding lesson tomorrow. We were too busy laughing about how fucked up we are.

Standing at the top of the hill that separates the barn from the guesthouse, I weigh my options. I don't even have the guy's number, and I'm right here. We just ended on good terms. There's no reason I can't walk back and ask for another lesson.

I'll say please and everything.

With a heavy sigh, I turn and walk back down the gentle slope toward the wooden A-frame. It's a beautiful little spot, the way it's nestled into the trees with the paddocks just out the back door and the gravel driveway that circles the entire way around it. So full of charm.

It has me wondering what Griffin's place up the mountain is like. Is it cozy like this? Or is it a sparsely decorated bachelor pad? Does he take women back there? Has anyone ever lived with him? Is he even single?

Those questions send a bolt of anxiety through me, but I talk myself down. I honestly can't really see him doing that.

He seems so self-conscious about the stutter. To be honest, I don't even notice it because I'm too busy gawking at him. That ass in a pair of jeans? The tattooed forearm porn he's constantly flashing? Dark hair and equally dark eyes and all the meaning-filled glares?

Wet dreams are made of him. He's the guy your mom tells you to stay away from. Lucky for me, my mom was about as absent as they come.

And even if she hadn't been, I probably wouldn't listen to anyone who told me to stay away from Griffin Sinclaire.

I'm not so sure about his personality, but the man is fuckable beyond compare. Which is fine because I'm not sure I'm equipped for much more than meaningless encounters. The therapist I saw while living in the city was pretty sure I wasn't—much as I'd like to be.

Back at the house, I tiptoe up to the back door, not wanting to disturb him if he's already turned in for the night. It's wide-open. He's just left the screen door to cover the opening.

It's a balmy night, and I imagine a small place like this can benefit from a little airflow between the doors.

I'm about to knock, my fist poised to tap against the thin metal beside the screen. But I stop in my tracks.

I freeze.

Because from where I'm standing, I have an uninterrupted view of the couch. The one in the open living space that Griffin is sitting on.

The one he's sitting on with his pants pulled down. The one he's sitting on while he fists his bare cock.

His knees are spread wide, and his shirtless torso relaxes back into the cushions. His eyes are closed, hair mussed, head tipped back, lips parted while he pumps his dick into his hand.

He's an Adonis. The definition in his body is insane. Broad, round, tattoo-covered shoulders that give way into his chest. His collarbones jut out over defined pectorals with just the right amount of hair to make him even more masculine than already he is.

My mouth waters or dries out—I'm not sure which—as my eyes trace the lines that extend up over his hip bones. The ones beside his chiseled abs, pointing straight down to all the action.

I lick my lips hungrily. It's very unladylike the way I'm gawking at him right now, the way I'm spying on him. But when his teeth sink into his lip to stifle a moan, his Adam's apple bobs beneath the light stubble that fans out beneath his beard, and suddenly I don't feel bad about spying at all.

He left the door open, and I'm not a lady anyhow. So this is fine.

The dry pumping sound of his palm against the silky skin of his cock is only slightly less erotic than the deep growling sound he makes when his hips buck forward, back arching with pleasure.

All I can think about is that I could go crawl on top of him. We could call it a riding lesson and he could teach me everything he knows.

I press my thighs together at the thought. He'd kill me. Scratch that, he'd say *Nadia* and drag out the last syllable in that distinctly crabby way he often does.

But it wouldn't deter me. Because clearly, I have no boundaries. If I were polite, I'd walk away and never mention this again. I'd forget about it.

Unfortunately, best-case scenario at this current juncture is that the mental image of Griffin jacking off on the couch becomes my fodder for doing the same.

Accepting the fact I'm comfortable being a Peeping Tom, I drop my hand and let it fall over my throat to cover the blush that's overtaking me right now.

I want to burn this into my mind so I'll never forget it.

The pearl of wetness at the head of his cock is a tease. My tongue darts out again as I imagine all the things I would do if I had the balls to push this door open and make my presence known. The man's cock is even beautiful. A big fucking weapon, and I'm not above admitting that I want him to hurt me with it.

His pace ratchets up, his chest rising and falling more rapidly as he nears release. Perspiration glimmers on his skin. Slickness forms between my thighs along with that familiar coiling tension just behind my hip bones. I'm riveted, absolutely getting off on playing voyeur to a man who is so out of bounds it's not even funny.

My heavy breathing falls into sync with his pants. His empty hand claws at the couch cushion until it finds the T-shirt that's been discarded there. And not a moment too soon because I can see him barreling toward his release and it might be the most sensual thing I've ever seen.

And then he proves me wrong.

"Fuck, Nadia." He growls my name, and it's like a shot of electricity straight to my core.

He covers his swollen cock with the spare shirt and empties himself with my name on his lips.

I can't help it, I gasp. And then my hand flies over my mouth, as though I can cover the sound in the otherwise quiet cottage.

His head flips my direction, startled. But instead of saying anything, he stares at me. Smolders. Glares.

I don't know what it is exactly, but it makes me weak in the knees. It makes me red in the cheeks.

It makes me wet in the panties.

"I… um… Riding lesson tomorrow?"

His cheeks are pink with exertion and his cum-covered cock is still in his hand, and *that's* what I say? I'm not nearly as smooth as I think I am, and just looking at Griffin kills my brain cells on the best of days.

This is not the best of days.

The way he's glaring at me right now is confirmation of that.

"Okaythanksbye," I rush out.

And with that, I bolt.

★★★

"Heels down." Griffin manhandles my ankle into the position he wants it.

We're back to the ornery version of him. The crabby face. The single-syllable words.

And definitely no laughter that warms me to the very tips of my toes.

I guess that's what I get for invading his privacy. That show was not for me to watch, and after sleeping on it, I'm feeling guilty about not walking away.

So we're not really talking. Instead, his gruff hands tell me what to do. I'm sitting on Spot, and he's criticizing my position—like I should know this shit—constantly.

He clucks at Spot and steps away, letting the length of rope attached to the bridle extend between us. I'm riding in a large circle around Griffin, attached to the line for extra control.

"You ready?" He's avoiding saying the word *trot.* But that's what we're working on, trotting. One gait faster than walking, and I want to gallop on the beach, so let's get this show on the road.

I nod and give Spot a squeeze with my legs. He's a well-trained horse, so he steps into a trot instantly. I try to keep my core tight, but I fall a little behind the motion—and I'm almost positive my heels come up.

I try to sit gently in the saddle, but I'm still getting bounced around like a rag doll. I sneak a glance at Griffin and notice the corners of his lips pulling up, confirming I do, in fact, look like a rag doll.

"Are you laughing at me, Sinclaire?" I ask, attempting to hold my hands still. How is riding a horse so much harder than it seems?

His mouth thins. He's trying way too hard to cover up that smile. "Whoa, boy." He holds his hand up, and Spot stops on a dime. *I am literally just a passenger.*

Griffin loops the rope around his hand as he approaches me again, face straining as he clearly forces himself to frown so that he doesn't laugh. *Stick-in-the-mud.*

"Alright. You're too rigid in your seat." He reaches up and grabs my hip bone, and I do my best to ignore the way his touch makes me ache, even atop my jeans. His hands on me are almost more than I can take. "This joint here"—he pushes on the bone—"is stuck. You need to loosen your hips so you can absorb the shock of the movement."

I turn wide eyes on Griffin and waggle my eyebrows in his direction.

He scowls. "Nadia."

I hold my hands up to prove my innocence. "Hey, you said it. Not me."

I swear he growls. But he doesn't feed into my leading comment. *Total stick-in-the-mud.*

The worst part is it doesn't deter me from soaking him up. Strong hands, inked forearms that ripple under the warm summer sun, and the two lines that form between his brows when he scowls at me. I want to see the lines near his eyes crinkle when he smiles. That's what my dreams are made of. Older, growly, protective men.

Especially one named Griffin Sinclaire.

Hearing him laugh undid something that was holding me back, and I swear all I dreamt about last night was being manhandled by him.

Dreaming about my big brother's best friend strikes me as a bad idea, but the more time I spend around Griffin, the more I wonder why I even bother trying to deny it. *Why is it so bad?*

I've never been attracted to someone the way I am to Griffin. The fourteen years between us aren't a deterrent for me at all. In fact, I'm almost positive they add to the fantasy.

A dull throb takes root behind my hip bone, right where the tips of his fingers just dug in, and in an attempt to clench my thighs, my heels come up.

His hand shoots out, cupping the back of my ankle and pulling down steadily. "I said down, Nadia." His voice is so authoritative, his entire delicious body filled with so much tension right now. With his broad chest puffed up, he's like an overfull balloon, ready to explode.

I get off on his intensity. It makes the lighter moments much more rewarding. Butterflies dance in my stomach when I look down and see his hand on my body.

And then he mutters, "If I didn't know any better, I'd think you just want me to force you into position."

His eyes shoot to mine from beneath the low-slung brim of his cap, a pink hue staining his tanned cheeks.

I should ignore it. I should really, really ignore it. That's the mature thing to do, but… the spirited twenty-one-year-old in me comes out to play.

A smile takes over my face. "Maybe I do."

His jaw pulses, and I can almost hear his teeth grind. "Go again," he bites out, completely ignoring my innuendo-drenched comment.

And then I'm back to riding in circles, practicing *relaxing my hips* while Griffin barks instructions at me.

I'm fucked up enough to kind of get off on it too.

By the end of our lesson, I'm exhausted. But not too exhausted to make a joke about how he worked me so long and hard that my legs are about to give out.

He tries to scowl at me, but I swear he almost smiles.

"I'm here to pick up my dog."

The door slams, and I glance up from where I sit at the front desk of the clinic. And I do a double take.

Because a cleaned-up Griffin Sinclaire is standing before me, and I literally feel my mouth dry out and my kitty flutter. And by *cleaned-up*, I mean hair slicked back, beard trimmed, white Henley, and dark-wash jeans.

The man is a fucking snack. And I let my mind wander back to how he looked with his cock in his hand. It's branded into my brain. Right where it belongs.

He doesn't try too hard to look put together, it's just the way he carries himself with confidence. Like he can make a woman come so hard that her vision goes black. It's effortless, and I'm sure he has no idea he gives off that vibe. Or maybe that's the athlete in him.

"Are you done with work?"

"Um..." I swivel around, like he's talking to someone else. Especially considering the man has all but avoided me for the last several days. Even when I'm at his house to groom my horse and cold-hose his swollen leg, he doesn't come out.

I'm sure he thinks I don't notice him peeking at me out his kitchen window, but I do.

Boys are dumb like that.

"Me?" I tap a finger against my chest.

He crosses his arms and sighs, like I'm the most exasperating person in the world. "Who else, Nadia?"

I mean, fair point. "Yup. Yes. I can lock up in..." I trail off and check my watch. "Five minutes." Griffin showing up here is throwing me off. I'm fumbling around. Like he can see what I've been thinking about when I use my showerhead in ways it's not really intended. Don't even try to tell me a woman didn't design a removable showerhead.

If he can tell, he doesn't show it. "Okay. I'll get my dog while I wait. Mira said I could get him t—now." *Today.* He wanted to say *today*. So we're both back to being awkward around each other.

"Wait for what?"

He pushes through the door toward the back where Tripod is. "Got something to show you."

He comes back with the small white wiggly little dog under one arm, carrying him like he's a football. And I swear I spend the next five minutes crumbling under the silence between us, staring at the watch on my wrist, and trying not to gawk at how insanely sexy Griffin is with the small rescue dog in his lap. The one trying desperately to lick his face. The one who isn't deterred at all by the gentle hand that continually tries to redirect his excitement.

Me too, little buddy. Me too.

"Okay!" I almost shout it, so relieved to get out of the too-quiet clinic. "I'm done. What do you need to show me?"

"We have to drive there." Griffin doesn't even glance up at me. He's too enamored with his new pet. All his features have softened, and he hugs the dog to his chest protectively.

My ovaries ache. I swear they do. This big grumpy recluse hugging a scrawny ten-pound dog? It's more than an animal-loving gal like me can handle.

"Drive where?"

"Don't worry about it." He glances at me. "Do you want to change?" My pink scrubs are clearly not appropriate for whatever secret field trip he has planned.

"Uh, sure? Do I need riding clothes?"

"No." He follows me out the door, still gazing down at Tripod.

I hate surprises.

"How long will this take?" I ask, entering the alarm code and locking the door behind us.

"Less long if you stop asking so many questions." With no brim to hide behind, I can see the amusement dancing in his eyes as plain as day.

I think Griffin Sinclaire just made fun of me.

CHAPTER 13

Griffin

We pull up in front of the building I know so well. I told Nadia to stop asking so many questions, and she has.

"I googled you."

But clearly, she's still going to make statements.

"What?"

"Oh, right." She winks at me. "Google. It's like a modern-day library where you can look things up. I'll demonstrate it for you sometime."

Cute. Another old joke.

I ignore the jab and hold the door open for her. "And what did you find?"

"A very enlightening poll," she says as I direct her into the waiting elevator while staring at her ass like a perv.

I grunt and arch a brow, signaling she has my attention before jamming the button to go up a few floors.

"I found I agree with eighty-two percent of people."

My brow furrows. "On what?"

The elevator dings, and we filter out into the hallway. I press a hand onto the small of her back, directing her to the correct door. She shivers beneath my touch, but I force myself to ignore it.

"If your ass looks better in jeans or those tights you wore to play football. There was a side-by-side photo and everything."

I stop, forcing a smirk off my face. This girl cracks me up. "And what did the eighty-two percent choose?"

She grins. "Jeans. Definitely jeans."

I scoff and shake my head as her eyes trail down me. I yank my hand off her back and knock on the door before delivering a blow of my own. "Ready to meet my parents?"

I smirk at the wide-eyed, uncertain expression Nadia is giving me now. It's a dead ringer for the one she was sporting when she watched me blow a load into my shirt with her name on my lips. I think we're both just pretending that never happened. Which works for me.

She smooths her palms down over the blouse she's wearing. "Seriously?" She leans in and hisses at me.

She's nervous. Unlike the dog, who is still wiggling under my arm, pulling toward her and settling for licking the air close to her face.

Me too, pal. Me fucking too.

Even nervous, Nadia is breathtakingly beautiful. Visually, she appears young, yes. But when I look into her eyes—really look into them—her soul stares back. And that part of her holds a wisdom, a weariness, beyond her years.

I've fixated on the years that stretch between us. The number of them. But her years have been filled with a lot more pain and suffering than most women her age.

The more time I spend with her, the more I'm struck by the fact that she doesn't *feel* like a twenty-one-year-old. Which is a dangerous fucking realization.

The door swings open, and my mother's happy squeal follows. "Griffin!"

She's already smiling when her eyes land on me. Then her gaze finds the dog, and I swear I can see cartoon hearts floating up from above her head.

When she turns her attention to Nadia, I realize I've made a grave mistake. Her coiffed dark bob tilts with her head, sweeping against the bright-yellow shirt she's wearing.

I swear those hearts in her eyes turn to fucking wedding bells.

"Hi, Mom." I grimace, trying to take control of this situation as early as possible.

"Griffy, who have we got here?"

She looks like that creepy goddamn Cheshire cat, staring at Nadia and the dog. Like I just walked up to her with a ready-made family.

Mistake, mistake, mistake.

"You know my best friend, Stefan? This is his sister, Nadia. She's a t-t-tech at the vet c—office and has been taking care of him." I hold the three-legged dog out to my mom, trying not to fixate on how nervous this meeting is suddenly making me. I'm stumbling over my words like a total idiot. "My new dog," I clarify.

Fuck. That clears nothing up at all.

"Nadia, this is my mom, Joan."

My mother takes the dog into her arms and smiles down at him, letting him lick her chin like the excited little spaz he is. "Well, this is just lovely. Come on in, you two." And then she spins on her heel, swaggering far too happily into the condo, all windows and patio space that open up onto the golf course.

We step in through the door, and Nadia nudges her slender shoulder up against mine. "Griffy." Her eyes dance with amusement, and I groan. All I wanted to show Nadia is that plenty of people have lasting, healthy relationships. It's not as rare as she thinks, and my parents are an excellent example. I was trying to be nice for once.

She drops her voice, and her breath fans out over my neck as she leans in close. "We kissed *once*. Don't tell me you're so wholesome that you think you need to introduce me to your parents now."

I can't help but chuckle and shake my head as I shuck off my boots. *Wholesome.* Don't think I've ever been accused of that. I lean back in close to her, using my height to tower above her. I don't touch her, but I drop in close enough to her ear that I could press my lips against her easily. Desire courses through me. The way she smells is a constant reminder of that one kiss. My brain has created a pathway based on that smell alone.

I'm fucking Pavlov's dog.

"Call me Griffy again, and I'll spank you like the little brat you are." The words are out before I can stop myself. They're suspended between us, and I wish I could grab them and shove them back in.

Nadia doesn't look as mortified as me. In fact, her warm-brown eyes are downright molten. "I'll keep that in mind, Mr. Sinclaire."

And then she fucking winks at me before waltzing down the hallway into my parents' home. "I love your condo, Joan. What a beautiful view."

I can hear them chat. But I need a few seconds to get a grip on the swelling in my pants. And also to beat myself up for thinking this was a remotely good idea.

By the time I've composed myself enough to join them in the kitchen, my mom has cornered Nadia and is talking her ear off about the dog and how he came to be as she gets started making a coffee.

"Has Griffin told you about pour-over coffee yet?"

Nadia smiles, and it's genuine as she drops her elbows onto the kitchen island to watch the painstaking process go down. "Not yet."

Each coffee is going to take like ten minutes to make, which means I'm going to be stuck here watching Nadia bend herself over the counter like she's fucking asking for it.

I don't need coffee. I need a cold shower.

"Griff, you didn't tell me you hit a dog." Mom's brow crinkles like she's concerned as she scans me. I know what she's thinking, and I feel like shit for giving her enough reasons in the past to think about it at all.

I give a brief shake of my head to help do away with her concern. "I took my eyes off the road to reach for my gum."

Cinnamon gum is my new whiskey. So I'm not sure it's any better than being drunk.

"Ah." My mom turns her focus down at the dog, who is drinking out of a small glass bowl she's put out for him. "Well, you never have done things the easy way, so why just go get a dog at a shelter when you can do it this way?"

I laugh because how can I not? She's one hundred percent correct.

"In a roundabout way, Griffin kind of saved him. When he brought him in, the dog was malnourished and matted. I think he'd been on his own for a while. In definite need of a little TLC."

Nadia smiles down at the dog, oblivious to the way my mom is looking at us. I can see the questions in Mom's eyes. I know it's killing her not to ask why I brought Nadia here. But I also know that she understands me well enough to know that if she asks too many questions, I'll pull away.

So I look at Nadia instead. She's not normal or happy. She's *so much more.*

"That's a lovely way to think of it, Nadia," my mom says, knocking me off my train of thought. But I still don't look at her. I can't peel my eyes off the girl bent over the kitchen counter. The curve of her ass, the swell of her breasts above the marble countertop.

I eye fuck the hell out of Nadia to keep my gaze away from my mother's. I'm a mess. This is why I live alone in the woods. Because it's never enough. Never enough wins—until I crash. Never enough whiskey—until I've pissed my life away. Never enough friendship—because the longer I stare at Nadia, the more certain I am that I'll let Stefan down eventually too.

"Yeah. Lucky dog. I had to hit him to save him. Just call me a hero." I roll my eyes and drag my hand through my hair, trying to lighten the mood. Trying to make these two women stop treating me like I'm a saint.

That's the exact moment that the front door flips open. "Babe, that coffee smells incredible." I don't need to see my dad to recognize the sound of him dragging his clubs and propping them up in the hallway. "I can't wait to—"

He walks in, his vast frame and barrel chest filling the hallway. He stops what he's saying as the dog runs up to him, body vibrating with excitement at another person to see. He's gonna be in for a shock when we head back up the mountain in a couple of months and it's just the two of us.

And then, in all his excitement, the dog pees at my dad's feet, yellow liquid spraying all over the floor. I drop my face into my hands and groan, but my dad's boisterous laugh fills the room.

"Joan, why don't you get this excited to see me anymore?"

My mom giggles. She *giggles*. "Because I'd be the one stuck cleaning it up."

At that, I hear Nadia laugh. It's melodic and laced with just a bit of disbelief.

This is what I wanted Nadia to see. That two people can be happy together. Gentle together. There can be trust and love, and she isn't too broken to have this.

She just hasn't met a man who deserves it with her yet. One who's willing to work hard enough to have it. Because this side of Nadia will have to be earned.

"Hey, little fella." My dad bends down and scoops up the small dog, chuckling as he does. He steps over the mess on the floor, like it's no big deal. "What's your name?"

"Tripod," Nadia pipes up.

I scoff as I push past her to get some paper towels, poking a finger into her ribs as subtly as I can. "I'm not naming my dog Tripod."

"I already named him. So you don't need to." She laughs, but everyone else is quiet.

"You call him what you want. I'm not going to name him something that's a joke. He deserves better."

"You named your horse Spot, for crying out loud." She stands up and holds her hands out wide.

"I didn't mean to," I grumble, searching for paper towels and a bottle of disinfectant spray in the cupboard beneath the sink. "It just sort of stuck." But everyone ignores me in favor of Nadia and Tripod. Whose name is clearly sticking too. And I don't hate that she's the one who named him.

"She brings up a good point," my dad interjects as I grab the spray and stand. "I'm not sure we've met. I'm Doug." He shoves his free hand toward Nadia, smiling as he takes her in.

"Nadia."

"She's Stefan's little sister," I grumble as I cross the floor and crouch down to wipe up the pee spot.

"Your friend?"

"Yup."

I wipe one more time until I'm satisfied it's clean and head to the garbage.

"Is he okay with this?" I turn back around, and my father is gesturing between us.

"There is no *this*," I blurt, wanting to clear any confusion.

Nadia rolls her lips together to cover a smile. *Brat.*

"We're just friends. I've been giving Nadia riding lessons."

My dad can barely hold back his guffaw as he says, "Is that what kids these days are calling it?"

Good. God. What was I thinking? It's like I completely forgot how ridiculous my parents are.

"Douglas," my mom scolds him with a playful slap to the chest before turning back to her coffee setup.

When my eyes land on Nadia, she has her fist pressed against her lips, and her body is shaking with laughter.

"Tell them, Nadia."

"Tell them what?" She turns her doe eyes on me, and I know I'm so screwed if I push this. Nadia is a lot of things, but shy isn't one of them, and I suspect she's not above revealing the things we've done that are better left unsaid.

"I don't know why I thought this was a good idea" is all I say back. I try to give her a serious glare, but she bursts out laughing.

"Me neither, son. Me neither." My dad continues to chuckle as he walks toward the living room. "This way, Nadia. Take a load off. Let's chat."

"I'd love that, Mr. Sinclaire." She pushes off the counter, bumping her hip against mine as she walks past, and I see the corner of her lips tip up as she does.

Brat.

Nadia and I walk silently down the hallway toward the elevator.

Coffee with my parents turned out to be nice. Once they both settled down a bit and everyone had their extremely involved cups of coffee in hand, the conversation flowed easily. The dog curled up on my mother's lap and was snoring happily in no time. And I didn't even stumble over my words, which was a nice change.

I expected taking Nadia to my parents' place would give her some perspective. What I didn't expect was for her to fit in so seamlessly. I didn't expect it to feel like something else entirely, like she's the missing piece of the puzzle.

My dad invited her golfing with him, for crying out loud. My mom is sending her links for where to purchase a special kettle so she can start making pour-over coffee too. She wasn't supposed to be funny and charming and make my parents welcome her into the fold of our family unit like she's some long-standing friend.

But Nadia *is* funny and charming. Her energy is infectious. It's like she makes everyone around her happier.

Even the dog is enamored.

Everyone except me is now officially calling him Tripod. And I'm pretty sure my parents are in love with Nadia and think grandbabies are on the way, no matter how many times I assured them we're just friends.

I tossed the word *friend* in everywhere I could as well as emphasizing our age difference a few times. It didn't stop my dad from whispering in my ear when he gave me a parting hug, "Methinks the lady doth protest too much."

Fuckin' dick. So I poked him in the stomach. "Getting soft, old man."

Then my mom went from whispering something in Nadia's ear to piping up and saying, "Hardly."

Gag. That was my cue to leave. I latched Tripod to his leash with one hand and grabbed Nadia's bicep with the other and dragged us all out of there, tossing a promise to visit again soon over my shoulder.

I always look forward to visiting with my parents, but I have *never* brought any woman home with me, and I severely underestimated their ability to play it cool.

We stand silently at the bank of elevators, and I watch the floor numbers light up as it speeds toward us. Nadia slants her head toward me, eyeing the place where I'm still holding her bicep.

Truth is, I don't want to let her go. I'm comforted by how well she rolled with the punches in there. My parents were acting fucking insane, and she seemed like she was enjoying the hell out of it.

"That's a firm grip you've got there." Her eyes flick up to my profile because I'm still trying not to look at her. "Am I in trouble, Mr. Sinclaire?"

"Nadia." My tone is full of warning. It makes me sound old and creepy when she calls me *Mr. Sinclaire.*

"What?" She stares openly now, and when those elevator doors slide open, I pull her into the blissfully empty elevator with me, eager to put as much space as possible between my parents and what I'm about to do.

She hums in amusement as the doors slide shut, clearly enjoying agitating me.

The minute the doors close, my hand with the leash darts out and slams into the red emergency stop button. And then I turn, drop the leash, and press Nadia up against the mirrored wall of the elevator, one hand still on her upper arm while the other slides across the taper of her waist. Her eyes widen, but she doesn't cower. In fact, she looks downright pleased.

"What, Griffin?" she taunts as my jaw pops under the pressure of my teeth grinding.

This woman tests every piece of patience I possess. I should step away from her, take my hands off her. I should keep this side of myself under wraps from her.

She's been roughed up enough in her life. The last thing she needs is me manhandling her. And I would manhandle the hell out of her. She'd love it. There's no doubt about that. I've had no complaints in that department. Quite the opposite, in fact. But gentle I am not. *Making love* I don't do.

"Say it." Her free hand lands on the waistband of my jeans, and my body goes tense. She slides her dainty fingers beneath the front of my shirt, trailing a nail over the ridge of my hip bone, forcing a low ache to take hold at the base of my spine.

If I don't get control of this and stop it now, I'll be fucking her against the wall of this elevator. Which is not what she needs.

I shoot back like I just touched a hot stove, pressing myself against the opposite wall, trying to put as much space between us as I can while being locked in this fucking box of temptation. My breathing comes in quick, frustrated pants. "Call my dad and me Mr. Sinclaire within a few minutes of each other again and—"

"And what, Griffin? You gonna spank me for that too?" Her top teeth press down into her pillowy bottom lip. "Or are you going to kiss me again and then tell me I'm a mistake?"

A low rumble takes root in my chest. My entire body is rigid, my will to stay away from her melting with every second I spend staring at her. The imprint of her fingers still burns on my abs.

I need to get the fuck away from her. The last thing I need to do is torpedo what little semblance of happiness I've created in my life by not being able to keep my dick in my pants around Nadia Dalca.

My hand slams into the red button, and we lurch back into motion.

CHAPTER 14

Nadia

Griffin Sinclaire is a prick.

Hot and cold. Left and right. Full steam ahead and full stop. I don't know what's up or down with that man. And I'm fed the fuck up. Which is why I stormed up to my apartment and hit send on that vet school application. I almost missed the late deadline. I'm probably not getting in, but I did it all the same.

I almost feel bad for my horse with how hard I'm brushing his coat, but based on the way his eyes are drooping, he isn't concerned. My fingers itch to pour every thought and emotion out into my journal. There are a lot of rude names for Griffin in there already, and I wonder if I can get even more creative with my name-calling later tonight.

My desire to hang out anywhere near Griffin's guesthouse was low. I journaled and scarfed a tuna sandwich and then forced myself to come over here while it was still light out because I'm a good horse owner and Horse needs his leg cold-hosed and his daily dose of too many apples. I want to give him all the love he didn't get before, which means showing up every day and proving to him I'm in this for the long haul.

"He told me once was an accident but twice would be a mistake. Me. A mistake. Can you believe that?" I scrub the brush in a circular motion over the slope of his shoulder down over his chest. He might be tied to the fence post, unable to go anywhere, but he's also a good listener.

"And then he takes me to his parents' house? Why? That's what I want to know. But apparently, we're back to the silent treatment now. So in the dark is where I stay."

Horse snorts, bobbing his head happily.

"I know, right? The guy is a fucking nightmare. He finally talks to me, but he doesn't *tell* me shit."

I hear another snort. But it's not an equine one. I freeze but don't turn around. Tripod comes whipping around the corner and throws himself down at my feet, begging for belly rubs. I can't deny the dog, but I don't want to turn around to face Griffin right now.

"Not in the mood, Cowboy," I mutter over my shoulder as I bend down to pet Tripod.

"Is that what you named him?" Griffin snorts.

I peer up at my horse's big shiny eye, the one reflecting golden evening sun back at me. *Cowboy.* A smile touches my lips. Cowboys are tough. They get bucked off and then keep going. Just like this horse and me.

"No. But it is now."

Another snort. I finally turn around to face Griffin, my stomach dropping the way it always does when my eyes land on him. "What do you want? I'm not really in the mood to chat."

One of his thick brows arches at me before he casually strolls toward the back steps where he seems to always end up sitting out here. Tripod takes off to sniff around the yard, like he's experiencing secondhand embarrassment and wants to put some space between us. "Can hear you chatting out here from my front porch."

Well, shit.

He lifts a mug of something to his lips, and I can hardly look away from the way his throat bobs when he swallows. The way his eyes narrow at me from over the rim. The way his lips wrap around the edge.

Never wanted to be a piece of pottery before right now.

I shimmy my shoulders back and swap the rubber comb for a bristled brush. "Eavesdropping, Sinclaire? Cute."

"Still mad about something I said two years ago, Wildflower?" He smirks, and I swear I could slap that cocky expression right off his beautiful face. I imagine that's the kind of hell he gave women before he retreated up into the mountains.

My teeth grind as I focus on brushing Cowboy. And I don't even know what to say to him. Obviously, I'm still mad about it. Obviously, I still think about it. Obviously, I'm still moderately obsessed with him despite my best efforts.

I don't know what to say, so I say nothing at all. It's kind of hard to talk around the foot lodged at the back of my throat. Griffin gave me the silent treatment the entire drive back to the ranch after whatever the hell that was in the elevator, so I figure I can give him the same right now.

I continue to work my way around my horse's lanky body, trying to lose myself in the beauty of my surroundings. The green fields that butt up against the Cascade Mountains, the melodic sound of birds chirping in the trees. I stare so hard at Cowboy that I observe the subtle way he's filling out. He's losing that ultra-slim racehorse physique with all the extra feed he's been getting. Retirement is looking good on him. His new name suits him.

It's not until I get to the other side of his long body that Griffin's raspy voice starts up again. "I brought you with me so you would see people who are happy. You'll have it one day. I know you will." He stares down into his mug, elbows propped on his knees, looking altogether too big to be sitting on the small steps. "You'll do anything you set your mind to. I just know it."

I suck in a big breath, eyes glued to the man in front of me. The man who acts like a real prick sometimes and then says things like *that.* Or rescues me a horse. Or shields me from creepy creeps who are staring at me like I'm their next meal.

"You're a piece of work, Sinclaire."

A dimple pops in one of his slightly pink cheeks as he stares down. He comes off almost bashful after being nice. "So I've been told."

Satisfied with the way Cowboy's coat gleams under the setting sun, I ditch the brush in my hand and lead him into his paddock. His hind leg swelling has come way down, although Mira is pretty sure he'll need surgery to remove some bone chips at some point if I plan to do anything more than treat him like a dog. Which I do. Cowboy and I are going to make something of ourselves.

"Good night, Cowboy," I say, before pressing a kiss to the wide heart-shaped snip on his nose.

"You're serious?"

I latch the gate where Cowboy is still lingering. He lives for the excessive attention I've been giving him. He waits for me every night. I know he does.

I turn back to the beefy, grumpy man sitting on the steps behind me. "About what?"

"Naming him Cowboy?"

Now it's my turn to smirk. "Yeah. It suits him."

A grunt is what I get in return.

I hang the leather halter on the hook beside the gate and am about to leave when Griffin stops me in my tracks.

"What else is on your bucket list?"

I turn and face him slowly. "Excuse me?"

"The list. With riding a horse on it. And…"

I quirk an eyebrow as he trails off. *Why the hell does he care about this?*

"The other part I ca-can't help you with." His knuckles go white on his mug. "But what about the rest?"

He won't even say it. Unfortunately for him, talking about sex doesn't make me nervous. Have enough of it, and it doesn't feel so taboo anymore, I guess. "Making love. You can't help with that part?" I cross my arms to shield myself and pop out a hip.

I expect him to back down, but his gaze finds mine and latches on. "No."

"Because I'm a mistake?" My lips thin after I throw those words from two years ago back at him.

He swallows, and his eyes rake over my body with enough heat to make me combust on the spot. "No."

"Because you're not attracted to me?" If he says yes, I'll know he's a big-ass liar. No man looks at a woman how Griffin is looking at me right now unless he wants to fuck them. I'm not new to this game.

"No." He shakes his head and only keeps his eyes on mine for a moment before he stares hard at a spot just beyond me, where Cowboy and Spot stand with their heads together like they're having some sort of meeting of minds.

"I limited my experience to a lot of fucking. That's what I have to give. And that's not what you're after."

Fucking. That word sounds so delicious in his mouth, wrapped in the deep dark depths of his voice. It sets my heart racing and the hair on my arms to standing. Truthfully, I'm not sure if I can surrender enough to feel like I'm making love to someone, no matter how badly I'd like to. And yet…

I tilt my head because I've got him in my crosshairs now. He should never have admitted this to me. Thinking this attraction was one-sided is one thing. Knowing it's not? That's a chance.

"And what if I am?"

I can see the full breadth of his chest rising and falling heavily now.

It matches my own. I'm out of breath, and all I'm doing is standing here staring at him.

His brows furrow, and he scowls as he holds one hand up between us, as if to stop me. I haven't even taken a step toward him, and he's signaling for me to stop. "No."

"Why?"

"Your brother."

"What about him? I don't need his permission, and neither do you."

Griffin scrubs a hand over his beard, squeezing his eyes shut for a moment. "Not that simple."

"Then simplify it for me. Clearly, I'm too dumb and young to make sense of your ever-changing moods."

When his eyes flick open again, the heat from before has turned into pure longing. The look on his face makes my chest ache and my core clench. No man has *ever* looked at me the way Griffin is right now.

I've shared plenty of lust-filled looks with other men. I've seen desire in a man's eyes. But this? This borders on desperation. *Pain.*

"You deserve someone normal and happy. I want that for you. And I'm not that guy."

I rear back, annoyed. "You've got it wrong, Griffin. I deserve someone who makes me *feel* normal and happy. Which is something else entirely."

With that, silence falls between us once again. My heart twists because I want him to say something and he doesn't.

Needing space, I turn and start my walk home across the darkening field, and he doesn't stop me. I want him to stop me. And I hate that I want that. I feel desperate, and I especially hate that.

It strikes me that Griffin is perfectly capable of making me feel normal and happy. He does sometimes.

But sometimes, he does the opposite.

Which means he also has the power to break me completely.

CHAPTER 15

Nadia

I MAY NOT BE READY TO HAND MY HEART OVER TO A MAN YET, but I don't need to waste my time with the likes of Tommy Koss either. Protecting myself doesn't mean settling.

I realized that on my walk home, which is why I'm here pushing through the front door of Neighbor's Pub. He's not answering his phone, and I need to talk to him now. Suddenly, getting rid of Tommy is like an itch I just *have* to scratch.

I can't wait. I need to clear my conscience.

Even if I can't have anything with Griffin, I don't *want* anything with Tommy. I know we're not anything—something that is confirmed by the girl snuggled up next to him when I walk into the bar.

Color me not surprised. I knew I'd find him here.

"Hey, Tommy," I say as I stroll up to the table where he sits with all his friends. Cheap beer and red plastic baskets from their wings litter the table.

"Hey, Nadia." He smiles up at me and doesn't even bother

to remove his arm from the back of the blond's chair. Can't say the guy doesn't have a type.

"Can I talk to you for a sec?" I nod my head to somewhere behind me. I don't need a lot of time or privacy to say what I have to say. Based on how cozy he seems with this other girl, I don't have to say anything at all. But I feel the need all the same.

This is part of what my therapist and I discussed. I can't control other people's actions. But I can control my own.

And I can control my reactions. My life, my choices. I don't live under anyone's thumb anymore.

"Yeah." His brow furrows. "Sure. Of course." He stands, and the other girl gives me a wan smile, and I give her a small one back. I almost want to wish her luck with the colossal idiot.

"Just over here is good," I say, right as I turn and smack into a solid wall of muscle.

"Easy, brother." Tommy's hand reaches over my shoulder and lands on the chest in front of me. The one clad in a denim button-down I recognize from earlier. The pearl buttons stare back at me. "Back on the sauce, huh?"

My head snaps back to glare at Tommy, who has a downright evil smirk on his face.

"Pardon me?" I ask, feeling the heat from Griffin's chest seeping into the front of my body.

"Ah, yeah. You didn't grow up here. Football star turned town drunk. Guess that didn't come up at dinner the other night, huh?"

I swear my heart almost stops beating as I turn slowly to gaze up into Griffin's beautiful face. *Drunk.* He wasn't drunk that night, was he? He didn't taste drunk. I want to get lost in his eyes and see the truth of it, but he's not focused on me, he's staring right past me. At Tommy.

And my god, if looks could kill.

A muscle in his jaw jumps, and my words grace his lips. "Not all of us are normal, happy people." I blink, hearing him in a way that no one else can.

Then his hard eyes turn down at me. A war rages in their depths. There's so much to unpack—shame, desire, humiliation, anger. A man with eyes like that should send me running after what I've lived through. But if Griffin is a flame, I'm a moth, destined to dance in his flames. My sense of self-preservation goes out the window when he looks at me like *that*.

If Griffin Sinclaire told me to jump off a bridge, I just might.

"Good night, Wildflower," he says, his hand cupping my elbow and giving me a gentle squeeze before he turns toward the back exit. His touch is so sweet, it aches all the way up into my shoulder.

And then he's gone, walking away. His normally broad shoulders slump under the weight of whatever he's carrying with him.

I can control my reactions.

Spinning on Tommy, I hold up a hand to stop whatever dumb shit he's about to say. I'm mad, spitting mad. "That was rude. That was *cruel*. And my life is full up on cruel men, Tommy. This? You and me?" I gesture between us. "Never going to happen. Never."

Before he can respond, I'm gone, jogging across the bar to the darkened hallway that leads out back, letting my heart drag me out of this place without a backward glance. I need to be near him right now.

"Nadia! Wait!" Tommy calls, but he doesn't come after me. Thank god, he's consistent in his flakiness.

I pass the men's room where whatever this is between Griffin and me began.

Romantic, Nadia.

My heart aches. I don't know what his story is, but I know Griffin is a good man. A deeply good man. A man who doesn't want to betray his friend, a man who is killing himself to resist this thing between us because he thinks it's a mistake.

And maybe it is.

But maybe it's not.

Letting him leave this place, thinking that I'm in any way aligned with what Tommy just said, would be a mistake.

I poke my head into the men's bathroom and am met with a "Get the fuck out!" from a man who is not Griffin.

Which leaves me with the rear exit. He could be gone by now, but I feel a pull in that direction I can't ignore.

It's dark out back, and it smells like grease. I look left, and there's nothing but huge garbage bins and some employee vehicles in the otherwise sparse gravel lot. I look right, and there is Griffin, leaned up against the stucco wall, hands pinned behind his lower back as he stares up at the navy-blue sky twinkling with bright constellations.

He doesn't move to recognize my presence, but he knows I'm here. And me? I stand and watch him. He reminds me of a cornered animal. Wild. Feral. Distressed.

With a few small steps, I'm standing in front of him, his gaze still trained on the stars.

"You gotta stop coming after me." He swallows audibly.

I nod because he's probably right. That would be the smart

thing to do. But I've already established that I don't do smart things where he's concerned.

So I take a deep breath and shoot my shot. "Okay. I'll stop tomorrow." I step in closer. My breasts press against his firm chest as I snake my arms around his ribs.

I tuck my head under his chin, and I hug him. I grip him. We don't talk because we don't need to. I feel the tension leaving his body, seeping out slowly. And I'm happy to absorb it all. Taking someone else's pain is a hell of a lot better than stewing in my own.

Eventually he rasps, "You shouldn't be out here with me when your boyfriend is in there, Nadia."

I roll my lips together and inhale deeply through my nose, wanting to wrap myself in his scent. Pine and laundry soap. "I came here tonight only to tell him we would never happen. I think I made myself clear."

Griffin's body heaves beneath mine, like he's relieved by what I just told him. And then his arms come out from behind his back. He drapes them over my shoulders and drops his bearded cheek onto the top of my head.

He nuzzles me. Wrapped up in his strong arms… it's heaven.

If I were a cat, I'd straight up purr right now.

"Good. You can do better." His voice is quiet, but that doesn't matter when we're pressed up against each other like this. I can feel him breathing, I can feel his heart beating. If he's the ocean, I just want to ride the waves.

"I can," I murmur back, fisting the back of his denim shirt in my fingers.

In Griffin's arms, I'm more at peace than I ever have been, and I can't explain why.

"I'm not better." His voice cracks.

"Okay." I'm not going to argue with him. That's not what he needs right now. He needs someone to lean on, not pretty words.

"I'm an alcoholic. Haven't touched a drop in years. But I'll still always be one."

"Okay."

"That should send you running." His voice picks up a sharper tone.

"Okay." I snuggle in closer. If he's trying to scare me away, it won't work.

"I've been with more women than the number of years you've been alive."

I snort. "Okay." Then I press a chaste kiss to his sternum, right over his heart.

A growl erupts from his chest, and he spins us, pressing me up against the wall, his arms above my head, caging me in. I'm certain he's trying to intimidate me, but I've felt nothing short of safe around Griffin, and right now is no exception.

I know how the air changes when a man wants to hurt you. I know how he looks at you—with disgust, with contempt—and for all his grumbling, Griffin has *never* looked at me that way.

"Jesus Christ, Nadia." His gaze frantically roams my face. "Don't you get it? I'm bad news. I'm profoundly unavailable. I've got nothing to give you," he whisper-shouts.

I've got nothing to give him either. "Okay," I murmur. His entire body vibrates, and his pulse jumps in his neck. I can see it. I lick my lips as I watch it, getting lost in the rhythm.

"Nadia. This can't happen."

Even hidden behind the pub, it feels like we're sneaking around. I want to point out that I'm not the one keeping him here. But I just stare up into his fathomless dark eyes. Everything about him screams raw masculinity. He makes me weak in the knees.

A small smile touches my lips. A smirk. A challenge. "Okay."

One of his hands slides through his dark hair, tugging at the ends in frustration. "Fuck." He checks over his shoulder, one arm still plastered to the wall above my head, protecting me. I can tell he's agitated. He looks mad, but not at me. In an instant, his face snaps back down to mine, and his breath dances across my damp lips when he scolds, "You drive me c—"

I quirk a brow. "What?"

His jaw pops, and he draws imperceptibly closer.

"C-c—"

"Say it. I dare you." I move my face toward him, the tips of our noses brushing together. He looks like he could kill me, in the best way possible.

A sigh leaves him in a ragged whoosh. Goose bumps dance across my arms under the muggy night air. His voice is like a feather dragging across my skin as we face off. "You drive me crazy."

And then he kisses me.

His free hand cups the back of my skull, and he crushes his lips against mine. For a second, I freeze. I wanted him to kiss me, goaded him into it, but I'm not sure I thought he would give in.

I catch up fast, kissing him back with every bit of emotion I can dredge up. He won't believe me if I tell him he's good for me. Instead, I'll have to *show* him.

My lips move against his frantically, fingers grappling with the hemline of his shirt. All I know is that I want my hands on his body. I want to feel him. I want more than he's willing to give me.

I tug at the tails of his shirt in frustration and then pull until I hear the sharp snapping noise of those pearl clasps pulling apart. I moan against his mouth when my palms slide up over his bare abdomen, tracing the lines of that delicious V that disappears beneath his jeans. The one I've fantasized about since I saw him on the couch last week.

A moan slips out between us. I can't even tell whose it is. His skin pebbles beneath my touch, and his cock swells against my thigh.

"Fuck. Nadia." He breathes my name against my lips, raspy and full of awe. It's so clear to me that whatever this connection is, it isn't one-sided.

His teeth press into my bottom lip with a firm nip, and I arch into him, urging him on. Wanting more. Every nerve ending in my body buzzes as my body bows into his. My head tips back, and Griffin takes that as an invitation to move his mouth onto my neck as my hands slide up to wrap around the back of his.

First a kiss, then another bite. I jump at the pinching sensation, but then his tongue is there, soothing the sting and driving me crazy. I hold his head close, desperate for more. He moves to the other side and bites me again, right where my neck slopes into my shoulder.

"You are fucking delicious. So responsive for me." His fingers curl into a fist in my hair, and he pulls, forcing my head back farther and opening my chest up to him like a platter to feast on.

And he does.

Teeth drag and lips press searing kisses in the wake of his mouth. The tip of his tongue dances over every aching spot, twirling and teasing as he works his way down to the tops of my breasts.

"These..." His nose trails over one peak as he bends over my heaving body, one hand still completely entangled in my hair. "Are fucking perfect."

Then his free hand darts down and yanks the neckline of my tank top down, taking the cup of my bra with it.

He sucks a breath in right as all the air whooshes out of my lungs. Like he stole the breath right out of my body. We stare down at my exposed breast, the swell of it pushed up by the clothing pulled beneath, my nipple pointing upward, right at him.

Griffin raises his eyes—dancing with flames and an utter lack of control—to mine. I love this expression on his face. I love what it does to me. We stare at each other for a few seconds, the sound of our mutual heavy breathing loud in my ears.

Something passes between us. A question. An answer. An agreement. And then his sinful lips latch on to my nipple, and I moan, letting my lashes flutter shut as I get lost in the feeling of his mouth on my body.

The way my body makes him lose control.

He pulls his hand free of my hair and uses it to yank down the opposite side of my shirt so that it props up both my tits for him.

"Fucking look at you, Wildflower." His hands squeeze firmly, bordering on too firm, but then he pulls back, always brushing away a hard touch with a soft one. The perfect balance. "So fucking smooth and pretty." He moves to the other breast, leaving the other nipple wet and achingly hard as the night breeze flows over my skin.

He sucks my nipple in and then lets it go with a loud pop before pulling a couple inches back and staring at my exposed breast like he's having some sort of religious experience. "So willing. So eager to please."

God. Damn.

I try to squeeze my thighs together to ease the throbbing between them, but he shoves his muscular leg between them, keeping me pushed up against the wall, and I grind myself on him instead.

The relief that motion gives me is addictive. I do it again, feeling delicious heat bloom at the base of my spine.

"Nadia." He says my name like a threat. I sigh in pleasure, loving the way his deep voice rumbles around in his broad chest. It's so intense with his shirt unbuttoned, I can almost *see* his body vibrate when he does.

I swivel my hips, rubbing myself on him, getting lost in the sensation of being surrounded by him. Of holding his attention in this way.

His calloused fingers dig into my breast. "Do that again and I won't be accountable for what I do next."

My eyelids feel heavy, but I drag them up from his bare chest all the same. My tongue darts out, wetting the seam of my lips. And then I whimper, knowing I'm about to set him off and not really caring.

I look him dead in the eye and grind myself on him again.

"You're impossible." His voice is deadly quiet.

Then one hand shoots up, wrapping around my throat, pushing me against the wall. Firm but gentle, completely in control. The other grips my bare breast as he clamps onto the skin there with his teeth.

"Ah," I cry out, the bite startling me. But the pain doesn't last. Not when he uses the hand on my throat to push me down onto his leg. And I let him. I surrender to the motion and feel my slick pussy sliding across damp panties.

I'm mindless with *him.*

The way he manhandles me is like nothing I've known. I have experience, but none of it prepared me for Griffin Sinclaire.

"Are you going to come grinding on my leg, Nadia?" His words are almost taunting, but I have little time to think about them before he moves over and gives my other breast the same treatment.

The press of his teeth—it's addictive. It's savage and unhinged and out of control and makes me feel more alive than I ever have. More desired than I ever have.

When he removes his mouth to admire his handiwork, I let my eyes travel down over myself. My pink nails tangle in his messy hair, the perfect match for the marks glowing on the soft flesh of my breasts.

"Fuck," I breathe out. "That's hot. No one has ever bitten me before."

He goes rigid in my hands. I swear he stops breathing. And then he's drawing up, flying backward like someone shoved him away from me.

The hand that was just gripping me in the most delicious way wipes across his mouth. "I'm so sorry."

He looks like he's going to be sick. It's like a switch flipped in him.

"I'm so fucking sorry."

My heart rate ratchets up as I watch him spiral, my arms limp at my sides as I use the wall behind me to keep myself upright. All that arousal knits itself into regret.

"You don't need to apologize."

"God." He swallows deeply, eyes still trained on my exposed breasts. The ones I'm too shocked to tuck back away where they belong. "I really do."

"Stop it," I spit, my annoyance building. "Just stop. Don't make that seem cheap when it wasn't."

His eyes finally meet mine. The flash of sadness in them is hard to miss. "Okay." One hand drags through his hair, and he takes a few tentative steps toward me.

He gently runs an index finger over the mark on one breast before pulling my shirt up over it, like he can't stand to look at it. He does the same to the other side before turning his attention back to my face, namely my lips. The ones that are still swollen from the way he kissed me. *Owned* me.

"Nothing about you is cheap, Nadia. You're a fucking catch. You deserve so much more than a man who kisses you in dirty bar bathrooms or beside grease-filled dumpsters. Someone who leaves marks on your body… fuck." He shakes his head. The heaviness that momentarily evaporated when we disappeared into each other is slinking back.

He can't even make eye contact with me.

And I'm not having it. I reach up between us, capturing his chin in my fingers, gently turning his handsome face back to me. I wait until his eyes meet mine and let my thumb rub over his bearded jawline, reveling in the feel. He's so unlike any man I've ever given myself to. I've been playing with prissy city boys, and Griffin Sinclaire is the Wild West.

I want him right down to the tips of my toes.

"You know what I deserve?" His irises dance across my face. "Someone who needs me badly enough to take me without apology. A man who knows what he wants. A man who wants *me.*"

He nods, pulse jumping in his neck.

"And do you know what you deserve?"

"What?"

"A woman who feels like a goddess when you leave a mark like this on her. A woman who doesn't want a goddamn thing from you other than to be worshipped anytime, anyplace." The intense way he's staring at me almost makes me squirm. "You deserve a woman who drives you crazy every damn day and nothing less."

Silence stretches between us. My words hang in the air, suspended, until his deep sigh blows them away. An opportunity dashed.

I stand on my tippy-toes and press a soft kiss to Griffin's lips. He kisses me back, but it's not the same. It's chaste. Innocent almost. The heat is dampened.

There's something heartbreaking about the kiss. And now, I'm the one who can't hold his gaze.

Suddenly, I feel infinitely less experienced. Colossally foolish. Who the fuck do I think I am going after a grown-ass man like I'm some kind of siren? Like I'm not just his best friend's sad, troublemaking little sister?

A dejected small laugh bursts from my lips when I pull away from him, my eyes trained on the ground as I roll myself along the wall away from him.

"I hope you find her."

And then I slink away to my car, ready to lick my wounds in private.

CHAPTER 16

Griffin

ONE MONTH LATER

The fields whip past as I make the five-minute drive down the road, clenching the steering wheel hard enough that I could almost rip it right off. Tripod sits on my lap, happily looking out the window, my new constant companion. I swear the floofy little dog just follows me everywhere all day. I'm not mad at it either.

It's the weekend, and we're supposed to go up to my place to do some maintenance for a few days so I don't go back to a total disaster when my contract is up at the end of August.

But first, I told Stefan I'd come to his place early to help him with the massive load of hay he just received. Then he'll come help do some things around my place for a couple of days. Even told him we could do some target practice to prepare for hunting season. A fire, some food, bring the wife—basically camp out for a couple of nights. A fair trade if you ask me.

Seemed like the least I could do, seeing as how I've been avoiding him. And avoiding his little sister. My plan to be a huge enough dick to push Nadia away has worked. In spectacular fashion.

Except now, I'm not so sure it was a good plan at all.

It's been a month since I devoured her behind the local pub. Since she rode my leg while I put my marks all over her tits like an out-of-control caveman. I roughed up the twenty-one-year-old girl who has *making love* on her fucking bucket list like she was just some eager jersey chaser waiting behind the stadium to turn a head.

Total douche. How selfish can I possibly be?

Obviously selfish enough to send her packing. Mission accomplished. So why do I feel like total trash about it?

Within a few days, she moved Cowboy to her brother's farm. Probably because she caught me staring at her out my back window while she worked with him. When my only friend showed up with a trailer, he was all excited that his sister would be hanging around and he'd get to see her more often.

I had to pretend to be happy for him. Deep down, I was jealous. The petty part of me felt like he was taking her from me.

But I'm old enough to know better. I'm smart enough to know that I'm what sent her packing. That girl looked up in my eyes and gave me the perfect opportunity to tell her I'm fucking obsessed with her.

And I didn't take it.

I'm a coward.

She told me she'd stop coming after me, and she did. I just didn't expect it to gut me the way it has.

This thing between Nadia and I should *not* have me this keyed up after a month. I shouldn't still feel bad. I've been the king of no-strings hookups for my entire adult life. It's not something I'm especially proud of at my age; nevertheless, it's not like this is unfamiliar territory for me.

The problem with Nadia is that there are a lot of fucking strings. So many strings. And I've completely tangled myself in them. Tied myself up in knots over the girl.

Usually, I'm tying someone else up. So I guess that part is new.

The vision of winding my rope around Nadia's slender wrists takes root in my mind as I turn into the driveway at Cascade Acres. The way she'd squirm in pleasure against them. All the things I'd do to her if I had her at my mercy. All the things I could show her.

I'm yanked from my filthy train of thought, the one that has me thickening in my jeans, when I see Nadia's parked car in front of the barn and her brother standing outside the big sliding door waving at me. Smiling at me.

Because he has no idea what I was just thinking about doing to his little sister.

I grind my teeth, willing the swelling in my jeans to ease. It's easy to do with Stefan acting like he's happy to see me. Shame is a real boner killer.

I adjust myself quickly, taking a deep breath before offering him a quick nod and pulling the brim of my hat lower on my face, fully intending to hide underneath here today.

Hopping out, I offer a gruff "Hey."

I slam the door of my truck harder than necessary, and Tripod takes off somewhere. Probably to eat horse shit. I guess after starving for however long he did, his palate isn't very discerning because he fucking loves the stuff.

The sun already beats down overhead, heating the cool morning air. We're hitting the dog days of summer where we're close enough to fall that the nights are cold but the sun still chases the chill away. When it's high in the sky, it's almost insufferably hot.

Truth be told, I prefer the heat of summer. I hate bundling up. I hate how stuck I feel when we get a heavy snowfall on the mountain and can't go anywhere. The only thing those colder nights have me looking forward to is hunting season. It's how I stock up on food for the days when I can't go anywhere.

On one hand, I love the solitude. On the other, the longer I spend up in the mountains, the lonelier it gets. Something I haven't been able to admit to myself until this summer spent on Gold Rush Ranch. I know I can be a grumbly prick. I know I don't talk much. But it's been nice having people talk around me.

Or talk *at* me the way that Nadia did. I miss that. The charm of her chatting away and not expecting me to interject but enjoying my company all the same. Most people treat me like I'm a letdown on the days I don't talk much.

But not her.

I didn't need to talk for her to enjoy my company.

"You ready for this?" Stefan pulls on a pair of leather gloves and nods toward the flatbed stacked with square bales.

Goddamn. We're going to be here all day. I almost forgot the sheer scale of running this place. Up on the mountain, I only ever have a few horses at a time for training, plus Spot. It's manageable enough, but this… this is a lot. Stefan has the money to pay people to do the work, but I think he likes to feel useful.

A deep sigh rushes out of me as I peek out at my friend. "Let's go."

He claps me on the shoulder. "I owe you one, man."

I flinch. *Owe me one.* Jesus. Not even close. "All good." I pull my gloves from my back pocket, ready to dig in. It's when I'm sticking my second hand in that I feel it.

Electricity prickling across my skin. The sensation like I can't suck enough air into my lungs. My eyes shoot up, right into the warm pools of bourbon that are Nadia's. The only bourbon I crave these days.

She's standing in the open door, holding Cowboy's lead rope. But she's not smiling. Her lips are parted, and she looks like she lurched to a stop after seeing me. She looks like she's wishing I weren't here.

And fuck. I wish I could say the same, but she's a welcome sight. We've kept our distance for weeks. I've kept my head down and worked the young horses. I've visited Billie to update her on their progress, and honestly, I've enjoyed working with her, chatting about the youngsters in my care. That's what's kept me busy.

But now, taking Nadia in, I realize I've been going through the motions. Cowboy's back leg is bandaged, and I roll my lips together to keep myself from asking her if he's okay, if he had his surgery. I want to talk to her so fucking bad. Just being in her presence makes my chest ache in a completely unfamiliar way.

After mauling her, I told myself I was going to call up one of my regular booty calls, but I sit at home every night jerking myself into a towel on the couch while I imagine her standing at that back door.

Except she doesn't just stand there in my fantasy.

She joins me. She crawls onto my lap and kisses me. Straddles me and slams herself down on top of me.

I snap my head away, not wanting Stefan to see me standing here staring at her like a horny teenager. Or, in Nadia's case, like she's annoyed with me.

My cheeks burn as I climb up onto the flatbed, feeling like a bigger piece of shit than I have in years.

"Ready?" My friend claps his hands with a wide grin.

I nod and then throw myself into tossing bales of hay off the truck. Hoping upon hope that losing myself in physical labor will numb the sting of the expression on Nadia's face.

But I'm not that lucky.

We're only a few minutes in when Stefan shouts, "Hey, any chance you want to come help?"

"No, thanks. I just had my nails done." Nadia's cool voice floats up from behind me. I don't need to look at her to know that she doesn't want me here—let alone to work with me.

Stefan laughs, clearly not picking up on her brushing him off. "Grab some gloves from the barn. Just for a bit. We're supposed to head up to Griffin's place for the night. Mira's got Hank and Trixie lined up to stay with Silas. I just wanna get this done."

I hear Nadia sigh. It sounds loud even though it's not. That's the thing about not talking very much—you hear more. Every little noise is more pronounced.

"Okay, fine." I hear her stomp off, clearly not happy about being talked into this but doing it anyway.

"You're the best sister a guy could ask for," Stefan shouts, chuckling and shaking his head. Then he turns to me, laughter lining his tone. "Man, she's grown up so much. But she's still got an attitude the size of Texas."

I just grunt. I like her attitude.

"I hope she finds someone who can appreciate her. I'd hate to see anyone drum that wild streak out of her."

I snort. "She'd eat 'em alive first. Women like her aren't

meant to be tamed," I blurt out before I even have time to obsess over the *t*. And I immediately worry I've said too much.

"See?" Stefan pants, running a forearm over his sweaty brow. "You get it."

I turn back to the bales. Talking about this with Stefan is precarious territory.

"Okay. Where do you want me?"

On your fucking knees.

I clamp my eyes shut. I can't see her, but even her goddamn voice sets me off. I'm fucking losing it. I haven't had a drop of alcohol, and yet I feel downright intoxicated around her. Like I'm completely out of control, and after spending years working on regaining it, I *hate* that feeling.

"Just swap spots with Griffin. Hand the bales down and he can get them set under the coverall. That work for you, Griff?"

Nope. "Yup. Sure." Stefan's brow rises at the bite in my tone, so I force a wolfish smile.

He rolls his eyes and gets back to grabbing bales from the top of the stack like he's grown accustomed to me being a grumpy bitch and isn't all that ruffled by it.

When I turn around, Nadia has one booted foot on the bumper of the trailer and is pulling herself up. I offer her a hand to help, but she waves me off and moves right past me, leaving me in a dazed cloud of her signature rose-petal scent. The one that gets me every time I walk past the flower section at the grocery store. The girl is driving me nuts.

The breeze of a bale flying past me cools my skin, the scent of dried grass mingling with that floral smell. "Get to work, Sinclaire," she says before turning to grab the next one while her brother laughs at me from the other end of the trailer.

I don't know how long we work like that. An assembly line of sorts. Stefan handing a bale down to Nadia from the top of the pile and then Nadia handing the bale down to where I stand on the ground.

She avoids looking at me, and to be fair, I do a pretty good job of hiding my gaze beneath the brim of my baseball cap. Now and then, our gloved hands make contact. Her leather-bound fingers, wrapped around the twine, brush against mine. It feels forbidden. It feels *right.*

It feels like fucking torture.

But when she announces she's done helping and has something else to do—when she leaves?

That feels even worse.

CHAPTER 17

Nadia

"Come with us! It will be like celebrating you getting into vet school."

Mira looks so excited at the prospect. And truthfully, I've been pretty over the moon since I got that email welcoming me to the program—celebrating sounds pretty good. Which means I'm about to be a total hag because I'm turning her down. The entire weekend up at Griffin's cabin in the woods? While she and my brother sneak off to do god knows what and leave me with the one man I don't want to be around? I'd rather sit here alone and write in my journal.

Liar.

I tamp that inner voice down. It's much healthier for me to pretend I don't like him.

"No, thank you. I'm going to stay with Cowboy. Make sure he's okay and everything."

I stare down at the gravel driveway as we make our way back to the farm. We just had lunch with Hank and Trixie, where they all gushed about me being accepted into the veterinary medicine program at Emerald Lake, and then we sent them off with Silas. Something Mira played cool about but was clearly struggling with.

Mira's dark eyes plead with me. "Please? I promise he'll be fine. His surgery went perfectly. It's been a week; he's fine. The staff are more than qualified to take care of him."

She has the sad-puppy face down pat.

"I'd rather not. Just in case. I want to keep doing what I've been doing. I would never forgive myself if something went wrong."

"Nadia. I'm leaving my *baby* behind. For one night. It's the first time, and I'm terrified. I'm pretty sure you can leave a horse at a full-service stable."

She's not wrong. But I'm not about to admit that.

"It's not even that far away! If you need to come back, you can be here in, what? An hour?"

One side of my mouth quirks up. "You telling me that? Or yourself?"

Mira huffs out a laugh and runs a hand through her hair. "Snarky little bitch."

I laugh too, right as we round the curve of the lake at the base of the valley, right beside the barn.

"Sorry, sis," I say, still looking at the lake.

A dreamy sigh is her reply. I glance back at her and instantly recognize the look on her face. It's the same one she made the first time Stefan had her over to our house for dinner. The one she made while staring at his ass while he cooked for her.

It was gross then, and it's still gross now.

But when I follow her gaze, I'm pretty sure I make the same face.

The temperature has shot up since earlier this morning when they started unloading the hay, and I guess that's why my brother and his friend have lost their shirts.

In exchange, I've lost my ability to talk.

Wranglers.

Sweat-slicked abs.

Leather gloves.

And that glorious, bearded face.

Everything about Griffin oozes sex appeal. And I am very much *not* immune to it.

"Wow," my sister-in-law whispers as we slow to a standstill at the base of the driveway.

"Yeah," I breathe out, sounding like a total idiot. "But not about my brother," I add quickly. "That would be gross."

She snorts, eyes flitting over to me. "I'm not related to either of them. So I can really enjoy the full experience."

I bark out a laugh.

"What? Look at them. I didn't know Griffin was so… *cut.*"

"Yeah," I say again, having lost the ability to use many words at the sight of him working without a shirt, sweat trickling down his throat. His inked forearms ripple in the sun, the muscles in his back bunching every time he heaves up a bale.

"Damn, girl. You look like you're going to eat him alive."

Mira isn't eyeing them up anymore. She's eyeing *me* up. Irises dancing with knowing amusement.

"No. He's too…" I trail off. *Too what?* Manly? Strong? Comforting?

"Old?" Mira supplies, like a bucket of ice water over my head.

I swallow deeply and nod, trying my best to not look like a starstruck idiot. Which, coincidentally, is how I'm feeling.

Pretending I don't feel inexplicably drawn to Griffin is a hell of a lot easier when I don't have to see the man. Shirt or no shirt, I'm a total goner where he's concerned.

Mira squeezes my shoulder, hitting me with her signature stare, which is almost indecipherable. Smug and amused, like she knows a secret you don't.

"Age is just a number, little Dalca. And the only number that counts is eight." She points over to where Griffin stands, panting and glowing under the scorching sun. "Because that's how many abs I can count on him."

"Jesus Christ, Mira."

She throws her head back and cackles as heat spreads across my chest. Her laughter draws the men's eyes. And then the fucking traitor shouts, "Great news! Nadia is going to come keep me company while you guys do whatever man stuff you have planned."

My brother lifts one gloved hand and offers a firm thumbs-up.

Griffin just scowls.

The property is breathtaking. There's something about being high enough up that you can see the entire valley that just feels so otherworldly.

Down in Ruby Creek, the heavy presence of the tall rocky peaks can feel oppressive. Like they're weighing down on you. But up here, I almost feel like I'm flying.

I stepped out of my car and walked onto the front lawn,

thinking I'd take a quick peek at what the small house overlooks, but now that I'm here, I don't feel much like moving.

The hot sun is making its way across the sky, but there's a cool breeze up here. With a hand held above my eyes, I scan the horizon, still not over the beauty that this part of Canada possesses.

I take a deep breath, letting the clean mountain air pour through my lungs. A fresh pine scent that is heart-wrenchingly familiar floats on the wind. A scent reminding me of Griffin and how it felt to be captured beneath his arms. How I felt surrounded by *him* when he kissed me.

I shouldn't want him this badly. I've never wanted a man this badly. Usually, it's the other way around. They chase the hell out of me. I like that part, and then I give in. We have lots of hot, fun sex. And then I get bored with them. Then it gets mundane. Then I feel trapped, destined to follow in my mother's footsteps. Get knocked up, get tied down, be stuck in some dark, miserable spiral. There's this part of me that thinks I want that and then this other part that is terrified to go down that path at all.

So I move on to the next boy, keeping my insecurities close and my heart closer.

Without even trying, Griffin has ripped all that safety from me. He hasn't wooed me. He hasn't chased me. In fact, it feels an awful lot like he's done everything in his power to push me away.

Truth be told, I'm not sure the man likes me. *Likes me.* Not just wants to fuck me, because I'm accustomed to that approach. I'm accustomed to men's eyes on me—appreciative looks aren't new to me. When your boobs fill out early and you're a dead ringer for a woman like my mother, well, male attention hasn't been scarce.

Some days, I ache for a man who sees more than the way I look on the outside. A man invested enough to peel back all the layers. But most of them stop the chase as soon as they peel off my clothes. Like that's the final destination for them with a girl like me.

I want *more.*

"Beautiful, isn't it?" My brother comes to stand beside me, scanning the horizon the way I did.

"It's perfect," I say, sounding a little awestruck.

"We've had some good weekends up here, Griff and I."

I nod, words fizzling out on my tongue.

"Haven't been up as much since Silas. Hell"—he palms the back of his neck—"since Mira. I almost feel bad."

I tilt my head in question and watch him swallow.

"I helped him renovate that house." He gestures toward the home behind us, the one covered in cedar shakes with a bright-red door to match the tin roof. "We spent a lot of time together before you arrived. He helped me get the farm set, and I helped him up here. We both had our demons, but neither of us forced the other to talk about them. We just took solace in one another's company, and neither of us expected the other to talk about whatever haunted us. He liked that I didn't know who he was. Didn't recognize him at all."

My stomach sinks, and I bat my eyelashes, willing the building wetness away. I know my brother was in a dark place for a very long time. I'm aware he carries around a lot of guilt over how things played out for me and how they played out for our mother.

It's a burden he doesn't need to carry.

But I've watched him do it all these years. Until Mira. She lit him up in a way I've never seen before. And then a baby? I've never seen my brother happier. And god knows he deserves to be happy after the shit he's been through.

"I'm really glad you had him, Stef." I smile over at my brother, but it doesn't touch my eyes. It's been too easy to disregard the fact there's more than just Griffin and me at play in this game between us. Causing a rift between him and my brother would gut me.

"Me too. But I feel a bit like I've left him behind. Like we were so kindred in our misery. And now… well, I'm so far from miserable it's not even funny."

This time, the smile touches every corner of my face. There's something about seeing a tough, protective guy like my brother all mushy and happy. It warms me. It gives me hope for myself.

"I hope Griff can be this happy one day." He glances over his shoulder, like he's worried the other man might overhear his wish for him.

The sound of my swallow fills my ears. "Me too." Because I do. No one deserves to be as deeply unhappy as Griffin seems.

"Are you happy?"

His question catches me off guard. I'm not sure where this heart-to-heart is coming from. If it's having his dad in his life or if it's becoming one himself.

I nod and tip my head onto the top of his bicep. "Yeah, big bro. Happiest I've ever been."

Which is true, but what I don't say is that *happiest I've ever been* is more like *happy enough for now.* Or *better than I was.*

"Thanks for joining us. I like having you around. And Griff… He's not as bad as he seems, you know?"

I nudge my elbow into his ribs as we stand taking in the view from the mountaintop. "I know."

CHAPTER 18

Griffin

Stefan is like a little kid—way too excited about target practice. Especially for a guy who is about to miss every shot.

My friend is good at a lot of things, but shooting guns is not one of them. I took him hunting last year, and he did two things exceedingly well: kept me company and made delicious gourmet sandwiches. Beyond that, I might even go so far as to say he was a bit of a burden. Not that I'd ever tell him. Beggars like me can't be choosers when it comes to friends. Plus, he's got the bug now. After big city living, he's settling into country life and seems to think hunting is one of those things he needs to master.

Enter me, the best friend who's been hunting since he was a kid.

I set the cans up on the log. "Alright, Stefan." I stand back to check the spacing of the five cans before walking back to where everyone is standing, trying not to look at Nadia. "I think that's about set."

She's been a distraction all day without even trying. Just having her up here in my space, in my safe haven, is driving me crazy.

And not in a bad way.

More because I can imagine her up here. With me.

She leans back against a tree, wearing a pair of my earmuffs, sipping a pineapple-flavored sparkling water, looking completely amused as her brother explains to Mira how to hold the gun.

Nadia isn't as prissy as she appears. I don't know what I expected her and Mira to do all day, but getting into the few flower beds around my place and pruning the hedges wasn't it. I watched her on her knees, digging through the soil with her bare hands. Marveled at the way she propped them on her hips as she scanned the area, not caring at all about the mud it smeared on her clothes.

From where I was repairing a spot on the roof, I watched her let herself into the back field, the one full of wildflowers. Pinks, yellows, purples, every shade of green imaginable. I watched her prop a hand over her brow and scan the horizon.

Fucking wildflowers as far as the eye can see.

I swear I forgot how to breathe for a few minutes as I watched her, all long limbs and flowing golden hair.

For years, I've stared at that field and tried to figure out a way to get rid of the flowers that run rampant in the alpine valley. I can't let the horses out to graze back there, but I'm not wild about blanketing the field in herbicide. The alternative is stripping the top layer of the plants and soil, and well, that's a big job I haven't gotten around to yet. I bought this place in the winter, in desperate need of the isolation it offered. I didn't ask or care about what was in the field.

But now, every spring, more flowers crop up, their seeds spreading in the wind, their roots lacing themselves down into the soil. Hardy as all get-out and almost impossible to get rid of.

So instead of me dealing with the issue, that fucking field has sat there for years, taunting me.

Just like Nadia.

"Okay, now gently squeeze the trigger." Stefan is standing behind Mira when she pulls the trigger on the rifle she chose.

Bang.

I can hear Tripod going postal in the house. Yappy little motherfucker. I roll my eyes but can't stop the small smile. That little dog follows me everywhere. Sleeps in my bed even though I swore I wouldn't let him. I'm not even sure what he's barking at right now. The sound of the gunshot or that I locked him away and he's miffed about it.

Bang.

She tries again. And misses. Again. And again. But she doesn't care. She and Stefan are laughing. The city boy and his bookish wife giggle over shooting a rifle for the first time, and I'd be lying if I said it wasn't a little bit adorable.

"You wanna try, Nadia?" Mira turns to her, asking a little more loudly than necessary over the plugs in her ears.

Nadia holds up the can in her hand, ankle crossed over her shin where she leans casually against the trunk of a tree. "I'm good, thanks." She smiles, but it's strained. I glance back to see if the other two notice the discomfort seeping into her previously relaxed expression.

"Try it, Nadia. It's fun. Even if you don't come close to hitting a can. Right, Kitten?" Stefan winks at his wife, who rolls her eyes and playfully nudges him in the ribs.

"Griff can show you how. He's a pro. Right, Griff?"

My friend juts his chin out at me, and my eyes dart over to his little sister. I try so hard not to stare at her, to let my eyes rove over every hill and valley of her body, but it's goddamn impossible. The girl is temptation personified without even trying. And maybe that's why I'm such a goner.

She doesn't care about impressing me. She's still got mud smudged on her hips, wavy hair up in a high ponytail, the skin stretched across the rounded tops of her breasts light pink from too many hours in the sun today.

She's not even trying, and I'm driving myself crazy. What would happen if she said it out loud, gave life to this enormous question mark between us?

I wouldn't be able to stop myself. That's what.

"Only if you want to." I shrug, wanting to hear her say yes. Wanting to know what this discomfort I'm picking up on is.

She sighs heavily, giving me a slightly wide-eyed look that I just can't place. "Yeah. Sure."

"Any preference?" I gesture toward where the different types of guns are laid out.

Without moving, she shifts her gaze to the cases set on the rickety wooden table beside her. Top teeth scraping against her bottom lip, she regards the firearms. She stares at them for so long that I wonder if she's even going to say anything. Out of the corner of my eye, I see Stefan and Mira look at each other in question.

"The handgun."

It's not what I expected her to choose.

I shrug again. "Okay."

She places the yellow can down on the table and steps up to the line we've been shooting from. I grab the gun and walk up behind her, placing it into her hand. If I turn to Stefan right now, who is standing behind me, I'm going to look guilty as fuck. All I'm doing is showing his sister something completely platonic. If I start acting like an anxious bastard, he'll figure it out.

Figure out that I fuck my hand every night while imagining it's his sister.

"Like this." I wrap my fingers around hers gently, placing the gun in her dominant hand. "And on this side"—I step behind her and lift her opposite hand so that her petite palm wraps just under the butt of the pistol—"like this."

My fingertips trail over the top of her hand, and I watch goose bumps rush up her forearm. *Fuck.* The air in the few inches between our bodies crackles, and we both suck in a breath, trying and failing to hide our reactions to each other.

"Okay..." The scent of my cinnamon gum tangles with the scent of her rose cream and something more distinctively her. The smell of sunshine on her skin. "Let your eyes follow that line on the barrel." I peek around at her face to check but end up staring at her lips, recalling the feel of them pressed against mine, so soft and hungry.

I clear my throat. "This elbow up." My fingers drag along the underside of her arm, and I hear her breath catch. Her throat works as she swallows and forces herself to keep her eyes on the soda can.

I need to get away from her. "Safety off, right here." I tap the spot softly and note her small nod.

Stepping back, I say, "Now lock your arms and press softly. This one doesn't take any muscle."

A few seconds pass, and again I wonder if she's going to

make a move. I swear I can almost *see* the gears in her head turning.

It happens in slow motion. The deep breath she takes sends relaxation snaking out through her limbs, her feet sink into the ground, and a ferocious expression overtakes her face.

Her fingers move so, so softly.

Bang.

The tinny noise of a can hitting the packed dirt beneath the log draws my attention down. *She hit it.*

Shock has me moving slowly because the next bang almost startles me. I jerk my eyes up to catch the second can falling through the air toward the ground.

Bang.

She hits the third can. I stop staring at targets and instead let my gaze find the woman holding the gun.

Bang.

The one who doesn't look surprised at all.

Bang.

She shifts imperceptibly, takes aim.

Bang.

Five in a row, with ease. I'm not sure I've ever heard the forest this quiet. Nadia doesn't meet any of our eyes, she just drops her chin and slips the safety back into place. Based on the way all the color has drained from her brother's face and the look of heartbreak on Mira's, there's a story here.

One that hasn't been told until just now.

She finally turns, a fragile smile wobbling across her beautiful face. "Thanks." Within a few steps, she's at the table, placing the pistol back in its case. "That was fun." Her pink fingernails trail over the black metal reverently, but none of us say a thing.

Usually, I'm the one who makes things awkward with my silence. But this time, it's everyone.

"I'm going to go take a shower. I'm a mess." She gives her brother's bicep a gentle squeeze on her way past, sneakered feet padding across the dirt and pine needles as she goes.

Leaving an awful lot of unanswered questions in her wake.

★★★

"I'm not sleeping in the house with you guys."

We sit around the picnic table polishing off what remains of the dinner Stefan put together on the barbecue. Steaks, fully loaded baked potatoes, and local corn that doesn't get any better than at this time of year. The perfect dinner after a long day spent doing manual labor.

My body is tired, which means my mind feels still. Having something to do with my hands has been what keeps me out of trouble for the past six years. It's one thing to be tired at night, but being physically exhausted after a full day of putting your body to use is the best feeling. I'm relaxed from head to toe even though the muscles in my back ache after tossing hay bales.

"Why not?" Stefan takes a sip of his wine, looking genuinely confused.

Nadia's whiskey-colored eyes widen, and she stares at her brother like he's stupid. "This"—one finger lands with a thump on the tabletop—"is your first night away and alone in almost two years."

Mira shifts in her seat, a pink blush blossoming on the apples of her cheeks.

"And I don't want to be stuck in there listening to you call her *Kitten.*"

Nadia shudders dramatically, and her brother bursts out laughing, smiling and shaking his head at her.

Earlier, they spoke quietly while he stood over the grill. I watched my best friend's mouth turn down into a sad frown while Nadia offered him a tight smile. I watched their eyes fill with unshed tears. I watched them hug tightly. They exchanged words between them that erased the awkwardness of Nadia making us all look like amateurs during what I meant to be a fun and lighthearted round of target practice in the forest.

"Do you have no filter?" Stefan asks.

I snort. I can't help it. Kinda rich coming from my friend, who truly calls his wife that pet name an awful lot while looking at her like he could burn away her clothes on the spot with the power of his mind alone.

His brow quirks in my direction. "Got something to say, Griff?"

I take a swig of my soda, cheeks tugging up as I do. "I have"—I hold up two fingers, not wanting to risk back-to-back *t* words—"tents I can set up outside for Nadia and me. The house is small." I swallow a chuckle because Mira looks like she might dive underneath the table and hide from such a blatant conversation.

Stefan has no such qualms.

The night wears on, and we move over to the big fire pit , which Nadia stocked with kindling earlier today. Surrounded by three people who know me, who don't consider me a disappointment, who treat me like I'm just one of them, the words flow freely. I hardly stumble. I hardly even think about it.

I enjoy myself in other people's company more than I have in years. Especially with Tripod curled up in my lap. My hand trails over his back, where his hair has grown back in curly.

I, Griffin Sinclaire, a man's man and former football god, have a fluffy white dog as a pet. It's hilarious, but I don't care. I fucking love this dog.

When the light dims and the sky blazes pink, Mira yawns. "I'm sorry." She slams a hand over her mouth. "Toddler schedule means this is past my bedtime."

Slapping my palms over my knees to stand, I say, "Let's get everyone set up then."

"What can I do?" Nadia asks as the other two wander toward the house. She's all fresh-faced, the bridge of her nose and high points of her cheeks touched by the sun, hair falling in soft waves over her shoulders.

"Just grab bedding from inside the closet beneath the stairs or whatever is on the sofa. I'll pitch the…" She stares at me, waiting but not pushing. "Tents. Won't take me long."

She nods, eyes flitting over my face, and I wish I'd put my cap on after my shower. At least the brim gives me a place to hide from her scrutiny. Right now, I'm completely exposed to her gaze. It's unnerving.

Her eyes drop to my lips, and I wonder what's running through her beautiful head. After a few beats, she turns slowly, like it takes some effort for her to peel herself away, and wanders up the path to my house like she's spent day after day here with me. Like she knows this land.

I watch *her* walk into *my* house like she belongs here. And it makes my chest ache.

In the shed near the driveway, I pull out the two small tents that I last used when Stefan and I went hunting. I've put them together so many times that I could do it with my eyes closed. By the time she returns, arms loaded with sleeping bags and pillows, I already have one set up.

I point at it. "Yours."

She snorts, tossing the rolled sleeping bags down and placing the pillows on top before shaking out the gray wool blanket she must have grabbed off the couch. "You have an impressive vocabulary, Sinclaire. Will you say something if I make a joke about you pitching a tent?"

I chuckle, reveling in the way she can gently poke fun at me. There's no bite, no cruelty—just a friendly sort of teasing.

"People don't like me for my words, Wildflower."

She stills but doesn't look at me. She doesn't need to. Her aim is effortlessly accurate even as she turns away. Her quiet words are a fucking shot to the heart as she wraps the blanket around her shoulders and ambles toward the rocky ridge overlooking the valley.

"I like all your words, Griffin. It's what you don't say that kills me."

CHAPTER 19

Nadia

I CAN FEEL THE COOL AIR DESCENDING OVER THE MOUNTAIN, the elevation chasing all the late-summer warmth away as the sun falls over the Cascades.

I'm addicted to the view up here. The sweeping green valley, the little square properties below, all different colors, making the stretch of land appear like a pixelated image. Each square with a different shade of green. The way the roads wind through the perfect squares, the lights that are twinkling under the magenta sky.

It's a visual I want to remember. I close my eyes and sigh deeply, as though I can imprint it into my mind by sheer will.

A single inhalation has the scent of pine and fresh mountain air swirling around me, and before I can even hear his approach, I can *feel* him.

Since that first night, it's been this way. Some sort of invisible link between us. Like our connection is bigger than who we are, where we're from, or how old we are. All of that is just background noise when he looks at me—touches me.

Anything that might be wrong melts away with the rightness of us.

A twig snaps beneath his gentle footfalls, and I shiver. A thrill races down the column of my spine just as the smell of cinnamon sluices through my senses.

The man has ruined an entire spice for me. I'll never smell it or taste it without thinking of him.

I'm not sure I'll ever stop thinking about him.

I pull the soft wool blanket tighter around my shoulders as though it might protect me from how flayed open and vulnerable I feel around him.

I've been far more exposed with other men in my life, but I've never felt more powerless than I do around Griffin. The way he looks at me and sees more than I want him to…

I *hate* it.

"Hi." A simple one-syllable word, and a chill blooms out across my chest.

I tug the blanket tighter. I'll strangle myself with the damn thing if I have to.

"Hi." My voice is barely a whisper as I focus even harder on the valley and sunset that stretch before me, trying so hard not to show my hand as he comes to stand beside me.

I've already said too much tonight, been all emotional and bitter when the man merely tried to make a joke with me about how he doesn't talk much. My molars clamp down as I think about what I said to him before disappearing to this spot to chase a little privacy. A little room to breathe.

Could I have been a more precise embodiment of a whiny baby sister if I tried?

"Pretty good aim you've got, Wildflower." He shoves his hands into his pockets, a suitably safe spot for them.

I sigh. "Yup. Once Stefan left for good, I realized I needed to be prepared to defend myself if things took a turn for the worse."

A pained choking sound jumps from the thick column of his throat, and he goes entirely still.

"So that's what I did. He turned his fists on me *once*. And I knew in that moment that I wasn't going to become his punching bag for long. I knew I'd find a way out. I learned how to shoot a gun. I didn't just get good; I got *great*. So that when he came to my room, I could pull it out from under my pillow and turn the situation around. And I did. I never pulled the trigger, but I aimed it at him and seriously considered it. I was just young and stupid enough to think it didn't affect me. That I could spend long hours at a shooting range and feel safe again. That I could move across the world and feel safe again. That he could go down in a fiery crash and I'd feel safe again. But I only stopped sleeping with a gun under my pillow a year ago."

I shiver, even though I'm not cold, and his head snaps in my direction. This time, I can't stop myself from taking him in. Messy, manly perfection, with his hair looking disheveled after putting our tents together and a few locks flopped over his forehead. My stomach flips at the sight, a perfect contrast to the heavy aching in my chest.

"Hey, hey," he says tenderly, stepping closer to me and instantly wrapping a comforting arm around my shoulders. His opposite hand comes up to cup my face as his calloused thumb brushes across my cheek, smearing wetness in its wake.

I'm crying.

"Do you have any idea how strong you are?" His cinnamon breath warms the air between us as he cranes his head down to capture my gaze. "How much you've overcome? How determined and inspiring you are?"

I press my lips together against the ache in my throat and tilt my head, more tears falling as I do. "I don't feel strong." My voice cracks.

A deep rumble takes root in his chest. It vibrates straight through my body as he pulls me into a crushing hug, wrapping his muscled arms around me and pressing a kiss to the crown of my head. My eyes hook on the spot where his black tattoo peeks up over the neckline of his white shirt in the most enticing way.

"I haven't lived through half the shit you have. And I took off up here to hide from my life. The first sign of adversity and I fucking crumbled. Partied so hard that I almost lost everything. And then locked myself away up in the mountains where I could wallow in my shame."

"We all do the best we can with what we've got. Trauma is a tricky bitch," I say as I clutch his white shirt in my fists and nuzzle into the warmth of his firm chest, allowing myself to soak up the safety in his arms—even if it won't last for long.

"Living with shame is different from living with trauma. You? You come back stronger every time." I glance up at him shyly, and he gently brushes my hair back, tucking it behind my ear. "Like a wildflower." His smile is soft as he gazes down at me like he's looking at something more precious than words. "Me?" The strands of my hair move through his fingers as he combs his hand down their length. "I'm weak."

His words are a punch to the gut. I hate that he sees himself as weak. If he's weak, then why do I feel so safe with him?

I pull the blanket loose from around my shoulders and wrap it around Griffin instead, tugging him against me as I reach up and push the loose locks of hair off his face. I trace the tips of my fingers over the lines in his forehead and trail them down over his temple until I hit the coarse hair of his beard.

The one I dream about being between my thighs.

He doesn't make a move to stop me. It's like we've called some sort of truce between ourselves for the moment. One where we spill our hearts' darkest secrets to each other and allow soul-warming touches to guide us back into the light.

The tips of our noses graze. This is dangerous territory, and we both know it.

"I don't think that trauma and shame are so different, Griffin." His dark eyes glow in the fading light as the crickets chirp around us. "One happens to a person, and the other is a choice, a feeling. The real difference between us is that I don't pity you. *You* pity you."

I'm pretty sure I've shocked him into silence. The look he's giving me is so intense my knees threaten to give out and drop me right at his feet. An altar to worship at.

Instead, I press a gentle kiss just beside his mouth, the roughness of his beard against my lips the cruelest sort of tease. And then, before I can say or do anything else embarrassing, I drop my eyes, pull the blanket tighter around him, and make my way back down the path to my tent.

The first thing I do once I've zipped that flimsy divider shut is pull out my journal. Some people go to confession. Me? I spill that shit on the pages of this notebook.

I hear Griffin's heavy footfalls as he approaches the tents, Tripod merrily hopping around with him. They pause outside. He set our tents up right beside each other, just around the side of the house, near the fire that's still burning low and throwing enough light to make my orange tent look like it's glowing.

My heart jumps in my chest. He's been standing still out there for way too long. I exhale loudly when I hear the zipper on the tent beside me hum.

The worst part? I wanted him to charge in here. To give the fuck up on depriving us of each other.

But I don't know what I have to give. I'm not sure I can keep sex and feelings separate where he's concerned. I'm not sure I want to. And that terrifies me.

I write that down, listening to the pen scratch across the paper, a sound that's almost hypnotic for me. Therapeutic, really. I suppose that was the whole point of this exercise when my therapist suggested it to me.

I scribble down every thought and feeling until the day's light is so far gone I can't clearly see the strokes of my pen anymore. Then I set my notebook down beside me and slip into the simple leggings and oversize crewneck I brought as pajamas, aiming less for aesthetic than comfort, but I'm suddenly wishing I had something pretty to wear.

My body hums, knowing Griffin is in the tent a few feet away. The air between us always holds a charge, and the thin layers of nylon between us do nothing to negate that. It seems more like they might melt away under the heat of our connection rather than keep us apart.

The shields here are too flimsy, and I'm not strong enough to keep my own walls standing. Tonight, I'm *tired.*

Hidden between the layers of my sleeping bag, I let a shaky hand travel down, slipping underneath the wide elastic waistband of the black leggings. My finger trails through the wetness at the apex of my thighs.

Only someone as fucked up as me would go from crying on a man's chest to getting wet at the mere knowledge he's sleeping a few feet away.

I swipe again, circling my clit, feeling it swell as I imagine a hand that isn't my own. I press one finger into myself and clamp down around it, wishing it were thicker, more calloused. And then pretending it is.

I pump in once. Twice. Add a second finger as I reach up under the sweatshirt and pinch one aching nipple.

My head tips back on the pillow that smells of laundry detergent and *him.* And I moan. Surrounded by his scent, an image forms of his disheveled hair between my thighs, and I play with my body until I'm panting, completely lost to the sensations and bunching of nerves under my skin.

If I was cold before, I'm certainly not now. I'm fucking burning.

And I'm so deep in my head that I only absently hear the zipper of my tent. My reaction time is slow, so by the time I drag open lust-heavy eyelids, I find the hulking silhouette of Griffin Sinclaire on his knees, taking up almost the entire entryway of the small tent, lit only by the dying embers behind us.

"Are you trying to make me lose it?" He looks downright primal—broad shoulders and heaving chest, hands shaking with how tightly he grasps the tent flaps.

I don't know what I'm thinking. In fact, I'm pretty sure I'm not thinking. All I know is that I'm *tired.* Tired of being scared and tired of pretending that he isn't the most real thing I've ever had.

My hands move again. I hold his gaze, cupping my heavy breast as I grind my hips up onto my fingers again.

"Jesus fucking Christ, Nadia." He sounds out of breath. He's eerily still, muscles bunched tight, like he's ready to pounce. And I just don't give a fuck about guarding myself against him right now.

I want him to take me and unmake me, fucking ruin me. If I'm as strong as he thinks, I'll bounce back.

So I keep going. Willing him to lose his precious control. Willing him to charge in here and use me the way I know he wants to.

The way *I* want him to.

I hear his signature rumble, and I sigh. My eyes flutter shut when I hear him growl, "Fuck it."

CHAPTER 20

Griffin

I YANK THE TENT SHUT BEHIND ME, CROWDING NADIA IN THE small space and pulling the zipper down as promptly as I can.

Fuck staying away. Fuck ignoring her. Fuck everyone. Fuck forgetting what I want. What I *need.*

I could hear her from my tent next door.

If this woman is a test, I just fucking failed, and I couldn't care less.

With the flimsy tent shut at my back, I kneel at the base of the sleeping bag, loving what she's doing to herself underneath there.

I crawl over top of her, and she still doesn't fucking stop. Up close, I can see the way her eyes have gone glassy with pleasure.

"You do not know what you're in for, Wildflower."

"Show me." Her words are a plea as I reach over her to unzip the sleeping bag and flip it open, proving myself right. One hand shoved up under her shirt, the other stuffed between her wide-open little legs.

My cock was hard before, but the sight of her playing with herself has me straining against my jeans painfully. Something I'll have to endure for a while longer. Because I don't plan to make quick work of Nadia Dalca.

No. I'm going to savor this beauty.

I hover over her slender body, letting that sweet rose scent wrap around me like a balm as I straddle her legs. Fisting the hem of her sweatshirt, I yank it up, exposing her soft round tits and pert nipples.

Just as incredible as I remember.

Her eyes fly open, wide and golden. Sweet like honey. But she doesn't shy away from the way I'm looking at her.

My wildflower isn't shy.

I let a blast of my jealousy out from behind the impenetrable wall I've created around my inner feelings. "You know what I thought that first night I saw you? Sitting up on that counter, kissing some careless little boy?" Watching her give that asshole even a minute of her attention has been pure fucking torture.

The highlights in her irises flare at the bite in my voice.

"What?" Her voice is thick, her tongue darting out over her bottom lip as she continues palming her breast.

I put my hands on her, starting at where her waist nips in, firm and narrow. Sliding them up, I admire how soft and smooth she looks beneath my sun-worn skin. When I hit her ribs, she shivers, and the hand fondling her breast drops onto my forearm, fingers stroking, urging me higher.

An invitation.

"I thought..." My hands hit the lower swell of her breasts, that tempting crease, and I groan. Palms enveloping the heavy flesh, I give her a gentle squeeze and flick my thumbs against her hard nipples, watching her jump beneath me. "I thought you looked too fucking good to be wasting your time with someone like that."

She sucks in a sharp breath as I lean down, tracing the shape of her jaw with my lips and relishing the texture of the goose-flesh erupting across her tits. "I thought you looked like you needed to be handled by a real man. By me." I nip at her ear, loving the feel of her fingers tangling in my hair, like she wants to keep me close. "I thought you looked like you were supposed to be *mine.*"

She whimpers and clamps her lips together. How hard she's trying to play it cool makes me smile.

"It's okay, Wildflower. You don't have to say anything. You keep your cards as close as you want." I kiss her neck slowly, holding back the urge to bite her again and leave my marks all over her bewitching skin. "Your poker face is pretty good. But I know what we both felt that night. And I think I'm about done pretending we didn't. You can show me your hand when you're ready."

Her responding chuckle is raspy and deep as she tugs at my hair. Something I think she likes just as much as I do.

"And what if I'm never ready?" The question is laced with teasing but also with insecurity.

I rear up above her, letting a playful smile touch my lips, feeling just a tad like my old self gazing down at the beautiful woman beneath me. The wild child. The quarterback. The man who could fuck as well as he threw a ball.

I move down her body, leaving her question hanging between us until I'm able to grip the waistband of her thin leggings. "Then I'll wait."

The good humor seeps out of her features. "Don't say that."

"Don't tell me what to say, Nadia." I yank her leggings down and groan when I realize there are no panties between her pussy and me. Just bare pink perfection staring back. "That's not the game we're playing right now."

She licks her lips nervously, eyes never leaving my face. "What game are we playing?"

I drop her gaze again, pressing a thumb against the seam of her, dragging the slippery wetness up over the hard bud, making her hips buck up into my hand.

So responsive.

"We're playing the game where I fuck your tight little cunt like I've dreamed about since the first time I laid eyes on you. We're not making love. I'm not being gentle. We're fucking. And you're going to take it like the good girl you are."

Her eyes light as she whispers, "Yes."

What I don't add is *tonight.*

Tonight that's all we're doing. I'll stay in familiar territory for us both because that's all she can handle right now. I can tell by the panicked look she gave me when I told her I'd wait.

God knows I have no clue what I'm doing beyond meaningless fucking, but I'm going to try. I'm crossing off that goddamn bucket list of hers if it's the last thing I do.

I run my thumb through her wetness again. Watching her squirm. Feeling my dick pulse. And I realize that even just simple fucking with Nadia won't be meaningless. It can't be.

"Do it." Her eyes dance now. I see them twinkling with excitement in the soft glow of the tent.

"Do what? Why don't you tell me what you want?" I swipe up and press down on her clit, making her moan.

Right before she says…

"Make me take it like the good girl I am."

With that, I scramble back and rip at her leggings, wanting to see her smooth, bare thighs spread wide for me. Once they've cleared her ankles, I sit back on my heels to appreciate the view. Pale-pink sweatshirt pushed above her collarbones, round globes and hard nipples highlighted by the glow of the fire outside. The flare of her hips that leads down into toned limbs.

"Spread your legs. Wide. Let me see it."

She does it instantly, and I groan at how willing she is. How confident. It's my undoing.

"Now fuck those fingers, just like you were when I came in here."

"Like this?" she asks, batting her eyelashes and sounding far more innocent than she is.

And fuck her fingers she does. Two of them glide in and come back out glistening with her wetness. *Fuck.*

I reach over my shoulder and pull my shirt off before standing crouched over in the small space to do away with my pants and boxers. Then I'm hovering over her body, spread out for me like a fucking feast. One of her hands plays with her tits while the other pumps slowly between her legs, her hips tipping up as she grinds against it.

When I drop to my knees between her legs, she whimpers, and I catch the flash of her white teeth biting into her puffy bottom lip.

"Touch me." Her eyes glow with arousal.

I chuckle and roughly fist my cock, jerking it in her direction like I've been dreaming of for the past several weeks. "I don't think I will. That's not the game, remember?" My palm slides over the length of my shaft, and I let my gaze trail down her firm body until it lands on her pussy again. The way it's stretching around her two fingers as they glide in and out.

"Add a finger."

Her eyes flutter shut, a stuttered moan erupting from her lips as she obediently adds a third finger, stretching herself so eagerly. My cock swells in my hand as her hips swivel to accommodate the fullness.

"Oh goddamn. That's a girl." My voice is a raspy growl, still acutely aware that we need to keep it down in here. "How do you feel?"

She whimpers, voice thick. "Full."

I'm certain I've never been harder in my life. My cock aches, and wetness glistens on my crown. If I don't tear my eyes away from Nadia riding her fingers for me, I'm going to blow all over her right here and now.

"That's it. Lose the fucking sweater."

She makes a quiet whining sound as she tears her hands away to pull the sweater over her head, but before she can even finish, I dive and run my tongue through her soaked core. Just once.

"Oh, god!" She curses as she chucks the shirt across the tent and then pushes up on her elbows to stare down at me.

"Do you have any idea how delicious you are, Wildflower?" I can't stop my eyes from roaming her bare body as I kneel above her. "How delicious?"

She opens her legs even wider, breasts heaving. I love how bold she is. How unashamed.

"Greedy girl."

"I am."

Her pussy glistens before me. "You're fucking soaked. And you taste like candy."

Her fingers curl into the sleeping bag beneath her, the sound of her nails sliding across the nylon loud in the otherwise quiet tent. The corners of her heart-shaped lips tip up as she smirks in my direction and shrugs lightly. "I could be wetter."

Brat.

I run my tongue over my teeth, lower my head, and then spit on her already slick pussy.

"Fuck." She gasps as I shove one finger into her roughly.

"Is that better for you?" I add a second finger and her silky heat clenches, wrapping around them.

"Yes!" Her legs tremble under the strain of holding them open so wide. I add a third finger and feel her pulse, working to fit me in.

I pump into her and smile. "I'm going to be so fucking good to you, Wildflower."

"You better," she says breathlessly, a shadow of emotion flitting across her face.

And with that plea, I throw one of her legs over my shoulder and make myself comfortable between her legs, watching my fingers disappear into her body, setting a leisurely pace.

"First you come in my mouth. Then you come on my cock."

CHAPTER 21

Nadia

Griffin says he trips over his tongue. I say he has it *mastered.*

His tongue glides between my legs in a way I've never felt in my life. Most men I've been with treated going down on me like a chore, like the lead-up to the main event.

But Griffin? He's treating my pussy like it's the star of the fucking show.

Every lick. Every nip. Every suck. He pushes me higher. He curls his fingers inside me, stroking a spot that has my legs shaking uncontrollably.

When I said I could be wetter, I *lied.* I lied so goddamn hard. And then he spat on me, which just drove me crazy. Who knew I'd be so into that?

"How are you so fucking good at this?" I flop back on the pillow, one arm flung over my flaming face, the other tangled in his hair while I revel in the feel of his lips on my pussy as his beard scrapes against me. His fingers dig into the thigh that he has shoved up high and wide, and I keep my other one wrapped around the back of his bare shoulders, clamping him to me while I grind down on him.

He shoves me close to the edge and then yanks me back from it. Practically torturing me. Dragging this out in the most delicious way. *Hello, sensory overload.*

He pulls away for a moment. "You like this, Wildflower?"

I feel like I might finish to the sound of his voice alone, the slight burn of his cinnamon breath against my core.

"I love it."

"Fucking right you do," he says, before dropping his head back between my legs.

This filthy, confident side of him is new to me. It's like it's been lurking there under the surface, always dancing in his eyes. But now he's brought it out to play, and I am so here for it.

Sex is familiar territory. This particular territory is better than any other I've explored, but it's familiar all the same. Every nerve ending in my body is humming, coiling. Like they're being stretched to the point they might snap.

To a point where I might come completely undone in a way that doesn't feel familiar at all. He plays my body like an instrument. No one has mastered me this way.

And when he sucks hard on my clit while twisting his fingers into me, filling me so well, I come apart. I see stars.

"Griffin," I cry out as my orgasm washes over me like a wave of hot water spilling over me, burning me. Every corner of my body heats, every toe curls, and my nails dig into his scalp, desperate to keep him in place.

His assault doesn't stop. He pumps his fingers harder, his teeth graze my sensitive nub, and I go completely boneless under his attention.

"Fuck. That was hot." He licks my seam once with a satisfied growl before pushing up to kneel and tower over me. He wipes his hand over his beard and then smiles down at me. Wickedly.

And I swoon. I swoon so fucking hard.

"You are so hot." He fucked me stupid. That's the only reason I would blurt something like that out.

The asshole just smirks. "Are you on birth control?"

"Yes." I try to pull myself together, not wanting to sound like a love-drunk loon. "But we should probably call it quits there." My eyelids are heavy. That was hands-down the best orgasm of my life.

"Oh, yeah?" Griffin licks his lips, drawing my gaze to the way his tongue works across his skin.

"Yeah. I don't think I can come any harder than that. It's all downhill from here."

His eyes flash. He looks like he's ready to devour me. And a less reckless woman might quake under the intent in his gaze now.

Me? I just smile.

"Turn over. Get on your fuckin' knees."

My heart rate skyrockets, and I consider refusing just to see what he does. But the sight of his huge thick cock bobbing between us is too tempting.

I roll over slowly, noting that even the brush of the slippery sleeping bag fabric against my skin feels good. As always, I can sense his gaze on me. I push up onto my knees and elbows and arch my back before I turn and look back at him over my shoulder.

"Like this?"

His eyes are on my ass and the suggestive way I've presented it to him. He palms one globe, giving it a firm squeeze.

"Almost," he growls, and then his knee is between mine, shoving them farther apart, positioning me exactly how he wants me.

I shiver when the thick head of his cock rubs against my pussy. Teasing across my oversensitive clit. Making my head bow down in response. It's almost too much. *Too* intense.

"Griffin."

"Yes, Wildflower?" Another swipe, and then he notches the crown of his bare cock inside me for just a moment before withdrawing again.

The cruelest, most delicious type of torture.

"I don't think I can come again. And that monster between your legs? I don't think it's going to fit."

His responding chuckle is low. It breaks me out in goose-flesh. So heavy with promise and desire. He palms my ass and holds me open as he places his cock right at my entrance. "You can take it." He swipes it across me again, and I tremble with anticipation. "You can. And you will."

And then he shoves himself inside, to the hilt.

"Oh my god." I drop my face into the pillow, feeling like I might melt into the ground as his hands slide over my hips, gripping them like handles.

Truthfully, I think it's the only thing keeping my ass up the way he wants. I'm so full. And he feels so delicious, stretching me the way he does.

I've waited so long to have him move inside me; I can't stand waiting any longer.

"Please, move," I beg, not caring how desperate I sound.

"I need a minute, Nadia," he rasps. "You are so fucking tight."

I wait, impatiently.

He presses a soft kiss to the center of my spine. "You feel so fucking good."

Another kiss a couple inches higher, the tip of his tongue trailing behind.

I shiver.

"And you look so fucking pretty on your knees for me."

A kiss lands on my shoulder blade as the delicious heat of his body seeps into my back.

His hand lands in front of my face on the pillow as he stretches out above me, claiming my body as his own while his cock throbs inside me. I wiggle my ass, trying to rid my body of the pressure that's building again.

This time, he kisses my neck just before he whispers in my ear. "I'll fuck you how you want me to, and I'll take every shred of what you're willing to give. But Nadia?"

"Yeah?" It's a pathetic little sound, but it's all I can manage right now.

He nips at my ear. The rasp of his beard against the sensitive skin there is a straight shot to my core that has me clenching hard around his girth.

"If you think I don't want more, you're out of your goddamn mind."

I gasp, but he moves so quickly, wrapping my hair around his fist to hold me in place as he surges back upright, sliding himself out before slamming himself back in.

"Ah, god." I go with him, pushing up onto my hands, my body rattling under the strength of his thrusts as I push back to meet him.

"Look at you, taking me so well."

"More," I moan.

He growls and fucks me harder. A small smile touches my lips before I fall back into a series of sighs and pants. The sound of his thighs slapping against mine is just as erotic as the feel of him moving inside me.

"Harder."

He chuckles darkly and slows down, running one hand up the column of my spine reverently before pushing me back down into the pillow that smells like him and forcing my ass higher in the air.

"I said *harder*, Sinclaire." Using his last name sounds wrong, but it also gives me a little distance. A little thread of control in the face of being consumed by him in a way I should have seen coming but didn't.

"Don't tell me what to do, Nadia." He releases my hair and trails his hands all over my body, his length resting inside me while I squirm, trying to force him to move, trying to move myself on him. Basically, rubbing myself on him desperately to dull the ache building inside me again. "And don't talk to me like I'm your teammate while I'm riding your pussy."

His warm, calloused hands graze my shoulders, slide around my torso to cup my breasts, and briefly squeeze my nipples so hard that it's just this side of painful before continuing their path. He explores me gently, in such contrast to everything else he's ever done with me that I feel a tickle at the bridge of my nose.

He's not fucking me; he's learning me. Tracing me like braille in the dark. His filthy words are just a distraction for what's really going on here.

My fists squeeze the pillow roughly, and I swivel my hips, feeling his steely length grinding inside me. "*Harder.*" My voice holds a crazed edge to it. I really need him to stop whatever this is.

I want him to bite me, use me, manhandle me. That's fucking. This… this is not.

"Quiet, Wildflower."

Gooseflesh covers my body. His voice is so deep that I swear it makes the ground rumble. I swear it trembles in my bones. He speaks straight to my body.

I raise my voice, feeling completely out of control. "Please!"

Griffin pulls out of me instantly, but his hands never leave my body. "Someone is going to hear you if you can't shut up, Nadia." The words should be harsh, but he says them so gently they send another jolt to my core.

"I don't care." The words tumble out before I can stop them. *Do I care?*

I'm not so sure. I'm not thinking straight right now, with Griffin's hands here worshipping me like I'm something special.

I'm not myself.

One of his big hands shoots forward to cup my chin and I push up onto my palms, turning my chin over my shoulder. My gaze crashes into his, even though it feels safer to keep my eyes trained on the pillow before me.

He raises his opposite leg in a show of power, his foot flat on the ground while his hand grips my ass.

He thrusts into me once, and I make a needy little moaning noise. "You keep your eyes on mine."

I nod, feeling the tips of his fingers flex, gently pressing into my jawbone.

He thrusts again, slowly gliding in and out now. "And you keep quiet."

My eyes flare. "No."

The smile he gives me now is pure sex, pure challenge, and it sends a jolt of electricity to my core. His tongue darts out, followed by his bottom teeth scraping over his full lower lip, drawing my gaze away from his.

"Fine then." My eyes snag on one dimple, and I stare at him dreamily. *He's so fucking hot.*

It's a testament to how lost I am in him that I barely notice when he shoves two fingers into my mouth. Hooking them into my cheek.

And then he unleashes.

One hand grips my waist, the other fills my mouth, all while he pumps into me. His thrusts are rough inside me; his hands are steel on my skin. He's like some dark avenging god using my body in any way he sees fit. Golden skin, a light smattering of dark hair across his defined chest, perspiration glistening over every hard ridge of his chiseled body.

But his eyes? His eyes glow with softness. And I get lost there. In that look.

My thighs shake as I meet him thrust for thrust. Pressure builds and coils. The tenderness in that look wraps around my heart like vines while he plays my body so capably.

A smarter girl would realize what a goner she is right now. But I'm not her. I'm a survivor. So I push those feelings in my chest aside and focus on the flames engulfing my body, on how good Griffin Sinclaire makes my body feel.

"Fuck. Nadia. I'm… I'm going to fill you up so good."

God. I whimper. We topple over that cliff in perfect unison. He curses under his breath as he shoots his release into me, and I cry out, the sounds muffled by his hand. I shut my eyes as I turn myself over to the turbulent waters of another orgasm, feeling the sensual slide of his skin against mine, coming apart beneath the hands of a man who fucks me like he doesn't care but looks at me like he does.

He looks at me like he cares an awful lot. And *that* is absolutely terrifying.

CHAPTER 22

Griffin

I STARE AT THE POLE ALONG THE TOP OF MY TENT, HANDS propped across my chest. I've been lying here like this for hours. It started off as me staring up at pure darkness, and slowly, as dawn broke, the blue glow of morning seeped in, and now I can see the silhouettes of every pole that makes up this tent.

I'd rather be in the other tent.

But Nadia didn't want me there. And I think that might be a first for me.

I fucked her like a savage, and then she told me to leave. The girl who has been chasing me down and watching me squirm for months is now pulling back.

Right when I decided maybe resisting this pull between us isn't the right move at all.

Shit, maybe I even *want* to be around her. That's a scary realization for someone who has spent the last several years alone. I think I've enjoyed being alone. Usually I grow tired of company, the small talk, the smiling. I like the peace that my spot up here in the mountains provides me. I like the solitude.

The idea of sharing that space and time with someone doesn't feel quite so off-putting right now though.

But only if that someone is Nadia.

I groan and scrub a hand over my face as my dick swells again at the mere memory of her. The way she looked over her shoulder at me, right into my soul, while I pounded into her.

I tried hard to make it just sex. I even turned her over, thinking that might help me keep a little distance. But with her, it's just impossible. Her eyes taunt me like those couple ounces of bourbon I like to torture myself with at the pub.

At least I've come to the point where I can resist that.

Nadia's warm coppery eyes?

Fucking irresistible.

I could get lost in those eyes. I'd hit the bottom, and it still wouldn't be enough. I've spent months—fuck, years—telling myself I need to stay the hell away from her because of Stefan. Because I couldn't do that to him. Because she deserves better than the disagreeable washed-up jock, the town golden boy fallen from grace, the man with a major loose end he has yet to face.

She shines so bright, so golden. She deserves someone to match.

I'm wondering if the beauty is in the contrast. Nothing makes gold sparkle quite like black.

Poetic, you head case.

I shoot up, frantically pulling my clothes on out of the pile I left them in before I fell into my sleeping bag last night. I gasp a little as the cool morning air hits me. A reminder that my days down at the ranch are drawing to a close. At the end of this month comes the end of my contract. And then it'll be Spot and me sequestered in the mountains.

Alone.

I unzip the flap and burst from my tent, feeling like I need space. Air. *Perspective.*

I turn away from Nadia's tent, but then I face the field of wildflowers. Which is no better. She's everywhere.

I'm a thirty-five-year-old man, for crying out loud, all fucking tied up over a twenty-one-year-old with her entire life ahead of her.

A good guy would walk away and spare her the heartache of a man like me. The things I've done. The mistakes I've made. She would hate me if she knew. I'm sure of it. She grew up under the thumb of an alcoholic. The last thing she needs is to tie herself to one.

"Good morning." Mira's smooth voice pulls me from internally berating myself.

I spin the opposite direction and see her sitting on the back porch of the house, wrapped in a blanket, and sipping a mug of steaming liquid.

"Hi," I huff, too agitated to say much more.

A smug smile stretches across her facial features. She's always looking at me like that. I like Mira a lot. But I feel dumb around her. It's fucking annoying.

"Sleep well?" One eyebrow arches, and she takes a sip, eyes scanning my face. Like if she stares hard enough, she might pry my brain open and see the filthy things I did and said to her sister-in-law last night.

I just grunt and start striding toward the house.

"Not really a morning person, huh? Long night?" Her eyes sparkle, and I work my ass off to school my features. *Does she know anything? She can't. She can't possibly.*

"Just been up for a bit." I can't be a total dick to her, even though there's this raging part of me that wants to tell everyone to leave. That I need space.

I hear a zip and soft steps behind me, but I don't stop. I need coffee. I need to get on a horse and ride out into the mountains as far away as possible from temptation. For years, I've been riding away from alcohol, but this time it's the tall drink of sexual temptation standing behind me saying good morning like nothing happened.

"How'd you sleep?" Mira asks her as I take the steps up to the house two at a time.

"Great." I can hear the smile in Nadia's voice. She's not struggling to keep it together at all.

And it hits me then. Am I mad because I gave in to something I shouldn't have, or am I mad I want more and she doesn't?

***

"I hate to do this to you," my friend starts, looking sheepish as we all share the amazing gourmet breakfast he cooked us, "but I think we're going to head back down to the farm today instead of tomorrow."

It's barely 9 a.m. and we're all sitting at the picnic table on my back porch, the three of them carrying the conversation like this has been a fun little getaway while I sit and mope beneath the brim of my hat.

If any of them notice, they don't say anything. Which almost makes me laugh. I guess I'm a grumpy bastard often enough for this to not seem out of character, even if the running monologue inside my head is different this time.

"Okay." I cut through the thick-cut piece of farm bacon without glancing up.

"Sorry, man, I know you have a couple more things to do and I said we'd stay another night." I see my friend's cheeks soak up some color before his eyes shoot over to his wife, who is smirking at him.

"I just… I just miss Silas. Why doesn't anyone tell you that once you have a kid, you'll want to escape them but then also hate being away from them?"

Mira bursts out laughing, and Stefan rolls his eyes.

"He spent weeks convincing me a night or two away would be good for us. And now… " She shakes her head and smiles, eyes sparkling with so much love it's almost hard to watch.

"Don't worry about it," I say around a mouth full of food.

"Nadia, you don't mind giving Griff a drive back down to the farm tomorrow, do you?" Stefan asks.

Her eyes widen slightly before she plasters a smile onto her face, and all I can think is that I shouldn't have let my friends talk me in to carpooling up here. I could really use my getaway vehicle right now.

"Of course not."

"Okay, great." Stefan beams, looking relieved. But Mira still has that expression on her face. Her keen eyes flit back and forth between Nadia and me, making me wonder if she overheard us last night. I get the sense we aren't fooling her.

I should have shoved my fingers into her mouth sooner.

"Great!" Nadia says, too brightly, and Mira smirks at me before pulling her mug up to her lips to cover it.

Nadia and I tidy breakfast up wordlessly and let the two nervous parents get their shit together so they can drive an hour back down the mountain. We stand a safe distance away from each other on the front porch as they pile into their truck, waving at us as they pull out of the driveway and disappear into the trees around the bend, and then the silence stretches between us.

My eyes trace Nadia's profile, and she rolls her lips together, standing just a little too still to be relaxed.

I might be fourteen years older than her, but somehow, I can still be awkward as fuck around a girl I like. That she grabbed my clothes and practically shoved me out the door last night is seriously messing with my mojo. Especially considering I haven't been with a girl I really care about in, well, ever.

The sex was hot as fuck, but I also liked the way my hands looked on her bare back. The way she squirmed beneath me. The way she moaned my name.

I want her moaning my name again, and my name only.

"Stop looking at me like that," she snaps as a few loose tendrils of golden hair blow across her full lips.

A gentleman would do as she just asked, but I've never professed to be any such thing. So I keep staring. I'm not sure I could pull my eyes away from her even if I tried.

"Like what?"

Her eyes roll and her arms cross, and all that achieves is to push her tits up in a really fucking distracting way. I stop staring at her face, just like she asked me to, and let my gaze drop south.

She cants her head in my direction with a snarky little smile, like she knows how badly I want her and gets off on it. "Like you want to eat me for breakfast."

I chuckle. I can't help myself. The girl is direct, and I love that about her. "Don't be ridiculous." Her brow goes low, all scrunched up like I've offended her. "I've already eaten breakfast."

I brush the brim of my cap and give her my best polite golden-boy smile. A tip of the hat, a flash of the white teeth. Straight out of a goddamn movie. Works every time.

This one is no exception, and I can't help but puff up as I walk away. Because I may have been looking at her like I wanted her for breakfast, but she wasn't doing any better.

I toss a few parting words over my shoulder as I swagger to the back of the house with Tripod hopping at my feet.

"But I'm ready for dessert when you are, Wildflower."

CHAPTER 23

Griffin

My private oasis in the mountains is suddenly my personal torture chamber as memories of the night in that tent pummel me nonstop. We spend the day working on fixing the front steps and replacing a few boards on the back deck. Nadia is helpful and a hard worker. We behave cordially, if a little stiffly, around each other. For Nadia, *stiffly* means keeping a safe distance away. For me, *stiffly* means my fucking dick twitches every time I catch sight of her ass in the cutoffs she's wearing as she kneels on my deck.

When we finish, she takes off into the field of wildflowers, saying she wants to explore the property. I watch her stroll away, journal in hand, until she finds a spot among the flowers and seats herself right on the dirt before flipping the canvas-bound book open and putting pen to paper.

If it weren't totally creepy, I'd take a photo of her, sitting peacefully among a field of flowers that do nothing but remind me of her. Weeds at worst, a miracle at best. Something I can't get rid of no matter how fucking hard I try.

I groan, mocking myself internally for turning into a total sap after one night with the girl. It's so unlike me that I'm not sure what to do with it. So I opt to break shit.

To winterize, I always make sure I have enough wood and kindling to get me through a storm. While Nadia looks all angelic in the field, I decide to pull my axe out and get to work on chopping wood.

I've always found physical labor to be therapeutic, and this is no exception. Line the stump up, raise the axe, drop the axe. Break shit. Rinse. Repeat.

The simplicity of the motions is easy to get lost in, and that's what I do. I only stop to pull my shirt off once I've already soaked through it and it becomes downright uncomfortable. I'm not sure how long I chop. I lose track of time. The only proof of how long I've been going is the growing pile beside me.

Definitely more than I need.

But I keep going until the muscles in my back ache and my arms shake with exhaustion. I only stop when I feel it. *It*. The way it feels when I know Nadia's eyes are on me. I can't explain it, but there's this pull between us, an energy, and there has been since the first day in that dirty bathroom in the back of an outdated bar with that absolute loser shoving his tongue down her throat like he lost something down there.

I hate that fucking kid.

I stop, tossing the axe onto the ground, panting as a droplet of sweat trails down the indent of my spine. "I can feel you staring at me, Nadia," I say, without even turning around.

"You have no business looking that fucking good, Griffin Sinclaire."

Her voice sounds better after her time in the field. More like herself.

I turn, grinning. I can't even help myself. Hearing her say I look good is a weight off my shoulders. Like maybe she's not disappointed about last night after all.

"You're gonna make me feel like a piece of meat, Wildflower."

She winks, all sassy and playful with her journal wedged underneath her arm. I'm so dead curious what she wrote in there. Something that turned her mood around, to be sure.

"You hungry?" I ask, wiping my brow with my forearm and trying to ignore the way a pink blush is crawling up over her cheeks or the way she shifts her hip and looks away quickly like she doesn't want to even recognize the dual meaning of what I've just asked her.

When she peeks back a me from under the fringe of her lashes, she points at me and raises a scolding brow. "For dinner."

"Mind out of the gutter, Junior." I laugh, tossing my gloves down on the stump and striding toward her.

"Can you put a shirt on?" She waves a hand over my bare torso, taking me in just a little too appreciatively to be truly offended.

"Why?" I pretend to be oblivious.

"Don't play dumb, Sinclaire."

Busted.

"Nah, I'd only be playing dumb if I pretended not to notice you eye fucking me while I unloaded hay bales yesterday."

She barks out a laugh, walking back up to the house beside me. Coming closer than she has all day. "I was not!"

"You absolutely were. And I felt very scandalized about it."

I feign offense, pressing a hand to my chest. "If I didn't know any better, I'd say you only want me for my body."

"Who says I don't?" She shrugs while forcing her face into a neutral expression, not missing a beat.

I point a finger at her sparkling brown eyes. The pools of truth that give her away every time. "They do."

She blinks in confusion.

"You look at me like *that* too, Wildflower."

She stops in her tracks, a little stunned. "I hate you, Griffin Sinclaire!"

I laugh at her feigned outrage and keep walking. Gotta feed the girl before I make her my dessert. "What is it they say? Hate and love are two sides of the same coin?"

"Huh. Must be a *really old* saying. I've never heard it."

"Brat." I grin but don't turn around as I march up the back stairs.

"I'll teach you a lesson later after dinner, Wildflower!" I call back, hearing her musical laughter filter in behind me as I stomp into my house to make her dinner.

She sounds so good here with me.

The night is warm, and Nadia can't stop staring at the view from the back porch. I'm not entirely sure if she's enjoying the scenery or if she's just avoiding looking at me, but I'm not overly concerned about it either way. It's giving me the perfect opportunity to take her in without getting caught.

And by *take her in*, I mean stare. Gawk.

I'm here. In my space. With the woman who has occupied her own little corner of my mind for the last two years. I shoved her in there, thinking some dark corner in the recesses of my fucked-up mind might keep me from obsessing about her.

Now I realize how wrong I was. How monumentally stupid that was. I've forgotten and ignored a lot of mistakes I've made. I thought I'd be able to do the same with her.

The problem is, Nadia isn't a mistake.

The night we met. The riding lessons. The horse I bought her. The fucking dog. It's all one big cosmic joke, shoving her in my path at every turn.

"I want to go watch the sunset from the flower field."

She's trying to kill me.

"Alright," I say, never wanting to stop her from doing anything she wants. Plus, I love watching her in that field.

With no further words, she stands and saunters toward the long wooden gate separating the field from the rest of the yard and paddocks. The small red barn to her left and the simple post-style paddocks to her right. This place isn't quite Cascade Acres. I bought Cascade when I was all about glitz and glam and show. This place is… *me.*

It's simple; it's cozy; it possesses a wild and unruly sort of beauty.

She fits here perfectly.

I watch her go and feel a jerk at the center of my chest, like she's got me by a leash and just gave me a tug. My lips quirk up. This girl has me by the throat, and I'm not even sure she realizes it.

Shit, I'm not even sure she wants it.

Up here is one thing. We're in a bubble away from the realities of all the reasons we can't be together. But it might be different once we get back down into the valley.

And if I only have tonight, then I shouldn't waste it sitting here watching her. I should experience it. I've spent a lot of years watching my life pass me by, but with Nadia around, I want more.

I want a dog. I want friends. I want *her.*

My legs are moving toward her before I even have time to realize what I just figured out. I stop only to grab the gray blanket out of my tent, the one that I shoved into a corner last night to escape the way she smells. Those fucking sweet roses taunted me all night long.

Ducking through the fence, I take the quickest path in her direction. She turns, eyes finding mine over her shoulder, and my breath dies in my lungs.

She's so beautiful, it almost hurts to look at her sometimes. The soft smile paired with her warm, wild eyes. Eyes that have seen too much for a woman her age. The dichotomy between how sweet she looks and what a spunky little devil she is gets me.

My little vixen in disguise. The girl with the innocent face who can handle a gun like some sort of fucking undercover assassin.

Hot.

And her looking over her shoulder at me like she did last night?

Hotter.

That's going to be my favorite thing for the rest of time.

"It's just so beautiful out here." She sighs as her eyes flit across the field. "We overuse that word, you know. *Beautiful.* Beauty. Full. I think lots of things are appealing or pleasing to the eye. But this spot is truly beautiful. I'm not sure I've ever seen anything like it. It's just so untamed or something. Utterly peaceful. I can't get enough. I don't even want to leave."

She's trying to kill me.

I swallow, my throat suddenly extraordinarily dry as I come to stand beside her. I haven't felt this smitten with a woman in, well, ever.

"You match this spot perfectly."

She makes a small, deprecating laugh and peeks up at me. "Yeah?"

"Beautiful and untamed. It's what I love about this place too." I look away, suddenly shy, and spread the blanket in front of us before taking a seat, staring up at the sky splashed with gold and coral and hot pink. Dark blue creeps in around the edges.

After a beat, Nadia takes a seat beside me. Her bottom lip trembles as her eyes find the sky too. "But not peaceful. I don't feel peaceful. I feel so untethered. Like I'm lacking direction or purpose or my own family. I have Stefan, but… he has everyone else. And now he even gets Hank. I still get that asshole as my dad. And I feel behind somehow. I see all these people my age knowing what they want out of life, and they go to school, and they do it, and they get the job, and their life just carries on. And then there's me, just sort of swimming in circles."

I grunt and lean back on my palms. I know that feeling well. "Didn't you get into vet school?"

Her responding smile is tentative. "Yeah."

"Then get in there and crush it."

"I don't know if I can. Maybe I should just use my inheritance to start up a rescue. For retired racehorses like Cowboy. I think I'd like that."

I quirk an eyebrow at her. "You can do both."

Her nose wrinkles, like she knows she has the money but finds it unsavory. Can't say that I blame her really.

"I don't know if I'm up to it."

"You are."

"Just like that?"

"Yeah, Wildflower. Just like that. It's almost like that asshole who raised you made you think you aren't worthy of more than whatever shit he left you with. But you'll show him. I know you will."

Our eyes meet, and something passes between us… a feeling, a look. I can't put my finger on it, but it's heavy enough that it forces me to drop her gaze, staring at her manicured fingers instead.

"Did you always know you wanted to be a football player? American football player, that is." When I peek up, she winks. Really gets a kick out of that.

"Shit no. My path is a real curvy one, Wildflower. Truth be told, as a younger child, I always figured I'd want to be doing what I'm doing right now. Living a simple life. Working with horses, just like my granddad."

She lies back on the blanket, folding her hands beneath her cheek as she turns those big brown eyes on me. "Tell me about it."

"My parents aren't horse people. I'm not sure if you picked up on that with the fancy coffees and golf obsession."

She laughs, and it's light and airy. And fucking music to my ears.

"I learned about horses from my grandfather, my mom's dad. He grew up on a cattle ranch in the area with his family. He got me on a horse early. Taught me everything I know. I loved my days with him—until I threw a football and got a taste of everything my life could be with that. I did a few rodeos. Sat a bucking horse or two. But then I lost interest. My throwing arm became too valuable. Success became addictive."

I sigh. Hashing out my childhood makes me feel like an even bigger failure than I already do. I have no good reason to have fallen into the shit I did. Greed and ego.

"Before my accident, I was a real douchebag. I don't think you'd have liked me very much. I don't like that version of myself very much either, to be honest."

"How come?"

"Because I took everything for granted. My good fortune. My family. It was never enough. I wanted to win more, fuck more, buy more. I had it all, and it was never enough. I was greedy and cocky. I thought I was untouchable. The universe has a fascinating way of putting us in our place though, and I think that's what happened to me. I made a lot of really stupid decisions."

"I think you're too hard on yourself."

"That's because you don't know all the shit I've done."

"Okay."

"Why do you always give me that out?"

She shrugs, looking up at me from where she lies on the blanket, hair fanned out around her like a halo. "Because me saying you're wrong won't make you believe it. I'll save my breath."

I chuckle and lie back beside her. "Sounds like a line from therapy."

"It is."

"Is this where you tell me I need therapy?" God knows my parents have tried.

"Would it make you go?"

I turn my head to meet her curious gaze. "It hasn't in the past."

She smiles, but it's somber. "Then I'll save my breath on that too. You'll know if you need it. I did." I snort. "I still do."

Rolling toward her, I mimic her position, folding my hands under my cheek. "How did you know you needed therapy?"

"Because I kept sabotaging every potentially good thing that was happening to me. Because the voice in my head that told me I was worthless was louder than the one that told me I deserved to be happy."

"I have that voice too," I murmur.

"I know you do."

"How do you know that?"

She laughs, but there's no amusement in her tone. "Because I swear, I can see it in your face, in your body, when you're listening to it. It's like I can hear it too."

Our eyes lock for a few moments, and the air crackles between us. Her lips part, like she's about to say something more, but she sighs and flips over on to her back, letting the cool air rush in between us like an invisible wall.

"Let's watch the sunset. Then I'm going to bed."

I should pull her back toward me. I should tell her I'm what she needs, that nothing is too complicated in the face of a connection like this.

But I think that would probably be a lie.

CHAPTER 24

Nadia

Griffin lay beside me in the field, and a companionable silence stretched between us. He may have flirted back with me, finally rising to my bait, but he didn't take it any further. He didn't put his hands on me. He didn't crawl on top of me and take my clothes off, but he didn't just disappear after getting naked with me either.

He looked at me like I fascinated him. Like I was a treasure, like I held value to him. He lay there with me, not touching. Just talking. He listened to me, and I could see him turning my words over in his mind. I could see he wanted more, but he was respecting my space. I guess I made myself clear when I handed him his clothes and said good night.

I kicked him out because I was tripping out. The complicated feelings crashing through me after having sex with him were totally consuming and complicated, and I didn't know how to handle that. I don't want to be consumed by a boy. A man. Whatever. I don't want to be that vulnerable to another person. Period.

And he gets that. Respects that.

But now I'm lying here in my tent wishing he were far less of a gentleman. A growly, rude, dirty-talking gentleman. Go figure.

He tried to fight me on staying out here rather than in his house. But I wasn't having it. Staying in that house with him would be too tempting.

The way he claimed me last night. His gruff words, his sensual touches. God, his rough touches. I'd never had sex like that. Sex where it felt like the other person knew exactly where to put their hands. When. How hard. Knew to say something that would light me on fire. Followed by something sweet that would make me swoon.

Sex with Griffin Sinclaire was filthy and romantic all at once.

It was also addictive. I realize as I lie here, replaying it over and over again. His fingers in my mouth while he filled me up, the tenderness in his eyes, the reverence in his hands. The way his face had momentarily filled with disappointment when I all but told him to leave.

Usually guys were all for that, but Griffin had looked downright wounded. Like he would have stayed and held me all night long. And I hated that look on his face. I hate that I want nothing more than to be lying in his arms.

I pull the sleeping bag up over my face and let a quiet, frustrated scream out. My plan was to stop having meaningless sex with meaningless men, and I figured I could break my rule for one night. I thought I could scratch that itch.

The problem is, Griffin is right. Nothing between us feels meaningless. And sitting here journaling until my vision blurs has brought me to that exact conclusion.

Catching feelings for a guy has always scared me. It ruined my mother's life—almost ruined my life in the process—and keeping feelings and sex separate has been a sadly easy line for me to walk.

Until Griffin fucking Sinclaire waltzed in with his growly moods and bristly fucking beard and ruined my streak. Never mind the shirtless lumberjack routine. That was just cruel temptation.

I wasn't sure I was ready to have sex that meant something, but I went and fucking did it. And now I'm tripping balls.

My brother's best friend. A man a good handful of years older than me. It's bizarre that something so outwardly wrong can feel so damn right.

I flip the sleeping bag down and force a deep breath into my lungs, weighing my options. After a full day of working around this gorgeous goddamn oasis, I should be exhausted. But I'm jittery. Confused. Frustrated.

Horny.

So. Fucking. Horny.

I either need to be close to him or get as far away as possible from him. I know it in my bones. My options are jump in my car and abandon Griffin up here, which would make me a huge dick but might salvage the course my love life seems to be taking, or walk up to that house, bang on the door, and tell him everything.

Lay it all on the line. Risk him treating me like I'm a tragic little girl who he got what he wanted from on the off chance that he wants to bang again.

He won't. I know it.

Deep down, I know he won't turn me away. I saw the shift. I *felt* it. And that's the scariest part of it all. If I open myself up to him, will it ruin me? Will it make me want to quit school? Give up my dreams? Hide away in the mountains with him?

It almost sounds appealing, but I'd never forgive myself if I gave up on everything just to do that.

My heart rate jumps, and my breaths turn to anxious pants as my mind races through all the worst-case scenarios.

Only one way to find out.

I flip the sleeping bag off myself as I stand and burst through the tent flap. I don't even bother with shoes. The damp grass tickles the bottoms of my feet as I jog up to the front door of Griffin's beautiful little mountain house.

My knock is tentative. I glance over my shoulder briefly, wondering if I should have jogged to my car parked mere feet away from where I currently stand. Two options so close together and yet so far apart.

The door swings open, and Griffin fills the space, an expanse of bare chest and bulging biceps covered in scrolling black patterns. His dark hair is loose and disheveled, and I can still feel it running between my fingers. All he's wearing is a pair of simple gray shorts and a concerned scowl.

I love that scowl.

"What's wrong?" He's peering around behind me, like an axe murderer chased me up here.

"I'm scared," I blurt out, squeezing the wrist cuffs of my oversized sweatshirt between my fists.

"Of what?" He's still staring beyond me, like there's something out there, one thick arm wrapping around my waist and pressing into the small of my back, pulling me into the protection of his house while he steps out past me. My breasts brush against his bare chest as he switches spots with me, like he can just waltz out there and slay my inner dragons while I curl up in the safety of his home.

I wish it were that simple.

"Nadia." He turns, gripping my shoulders and crouching down just low enough to look me in the eye. "Did you hear something out there? See something?"

I blink, trying to find my nerve again.

"Fuck." He runs a hand through his hair, turning out to face the dark yard again. "I knew I shouldn't have listened to you about staying out there by yourself. You don't have to be so fucking tough all the time."

He reaches for the rifle hanging by the back door, and my fingers find his bicep, stopping him in his tracks. My pink nails are a perfect contrast against the black ink there.

It's true. I had been absurdly stubborn about staying in the tent rather than in his house. I felt like I needed the space.

"No," I breathe. "I'm scared of this." I can't even look at him. I keep my eyes trained on his chest, searching madly for the words that this beautiful man deserves from me.

"This." I wave a finger between us. "I'm scared of this. Us. You." I turn my face up at the ceiling, tracing the lines of the doorjamb as I shove my fingers through my hair. "I'm scared of myself."

I wait for him to say something, and I don't know why. Griffin is a man of few words. I should have seen this coming. I should have known I wouldn't be what he needs. He's a man who knows what he wants out of life, and I'm the girl who's flitted from guy to guy like she's pollinating fucking flowers. "You know what, never mind. Forget I said that." I laugh, but it's a dark laugh. "I should have realized you'd be after something else."

I move to shove past him. Fleeing. *A-fucking-gain.* Am I being childish? Maybe. But he's got my head all jumbled. I'm not making a lot of sense, and I know it.

But his forearm wraps around my waist, and he yanks me into his body, my back pressing against the warmth of his chest as his heavily corded arms wrap around me like a vise. "Don't tell me what I'm after, Wildflower." His voice holds an edge of danger now, like I've said something that pisses him off. "Any man not after you is a fucking idiot."

My heart thunders so loudly I can barely hear his deep, growly voice over its beat.

"Then why do you keep pushing me away? Or letting me push you away?" I sound small and sad and a little bit broken. My eyes flutter shut, as though that can block out the embarrassment of giving voice to that question. Why hasn't he burned the world down to have me?

His beard rasps against the side of my neck as he cranes to catch my eye. "Why the fuck do you think?"

"Because I'm your best friend's little sister who's been out with half the guys in town? Because you got what you wanted from me now?" That's a gross exaggeration and a sad attempt at sarcasm. It's also possible that I'm being angry and combative—it's my default mode.

His arms clamp down on my body even harder, one hand gripping my chin and turning me back to him. Pure fury dances in his eyes, but not the kind of fury I've seen before. This is different. He's incensed. "Who told you the only thing you have to offer is what's between your legs?"

My shitty dad and every shitty guy I've met since.

He rakes his fingers through his hair in agitation. "I could honestly tear apart every man who has ever made you doubt your value."

I scoff and try to look away, jerking my head sharply and failing. His fingers bite into my jaw. "Fucking look at me when I tell you this, Nadia." I blink rapidly but hold his wild gaze. "I don't give a flying fuck who you've been with. You could have ridden every dick in the entire city of Vancouver, and I'd still want you. I'm happy to wait for you. Do you know why?"

"No," I grit out. I genuinely cannot fathom why he wouldn't care about that.

A feral smile touches his lips as he glares down at me. "Because my dick is the last one you're ever going to ride."

Shock courses through my veins, along with a disbelieving laugh. "You can be one cocky motherfucker, Sinclaire."

His lips twitch, but he's still perfectly intense when he says, "It's true." His thumb strokes my jawline as he stares down at me like I'm the night sky, full of complicated constellations, dark spots, and bright flashes of pure light. "I push you away because I'm fourteen years older than you. I've lived a lot of life that you haven't yet. There are days I feel so fucking washed-up that I hardly think I'm worthy of your attention. I've got baggage inside my baggage. But I care less and less about that all the time. I'm trying so damn hard to be good, Nadia. I want to be good for you."

His arms soften around me, and I turn in the cage of his embrace, feeling every point of contact as I do.

"I don't care what other people think of me. I'm long past that, and I'm not asking your brother's permission to take the one thing that has breathed life back into me since everything fell to pieces. I'm trying to be mature. I'm trying to give you space to figure yourself out. God knows, I've got some shit I need to figure out. And it's the hardest fucking thing I've ever done. But I care what you think of me. I want to be worthy of you. I'm afraid I'm not there yet. I *know* I'm not there yet."

His hands cup my skull like I'm the most delicate piece of glass, his thumbs rubbing across tears I hadn't even realized I'd spilled.

"I'm scared too." His breath whispers across my wet cheeks, and his forehead rests against mine as our eyes fall closed in unison. "I'm scared because I want to give you the world and I know I can't. Not yet."

My hands go from fists to sliding across him, exploring the hard lines of his abdomen. "Just give me right now. Give me one day at a time. With you, they're always better, and I just want more of the better days."

He swallows loudly, and neither of us moves. My words hang in the air, suspended like they're about to shatter on the floor between us if he doesn't reach out and take them. *Then* this interaction will be what I feared, never mind my angry outburst before. If he turns me away now, I might never recov—

"I'll give you all my right nows, Nadia. Every fucking last one. I'll give you anything you want. I've been powerless since the first time I laid eyes on you." His deep voice, what he's just professed, sends gooseflesh racing over my body even though I'm warm in the cradle of his arms, and when his lips press against mine, every fear melts away.

He kisses me like he did that night. Not desperately, not roughly—reverently. He kisses me how I know I deserve to be kissed. The comforting rasp of his beard on my face sends a low throb between my legs, and the soft swipe of his tongue against my own has me whimpering and turning to putty in his hands. Like my body knows that the two of us together are just right.

"That noise. You have no idea what that noise does to me."

"What noise?" I whisper right as he presses me up against the doorframe and takes my mouth again, his tongue teasing mine with just the right amount of pressure as his fingers push a lock of hair back behind my ear. His touch lingers, and I whimper.

"*That* noise. Fuck this." He pulls away, taking me in with furrowed brows. "You're *mine*, Wildflower."

He hoists me up, and my legs instantly wrap around his waist as he kicks the door closed behind us and carries me farther into his house. I giggle in surprise and clamp on to him, loving the feel of his hands on my ass and those words on his lips.

Mine.

No one has ever said that to me before. No one has ever made me feel wanted the way Griffin does—wanted in the most complete way.

"Say it again."

He storms across the little bungalow toward what I'm certain must be a bedroom. His eyes flash up to mine, the curtain of my blond hair between us making me feel like we're in some private bubble.

"Mine." He growls and kisses me just beside my lips as he strides into the bedroom. He tosses me down onto the king-size bed before standing over my body, looking over me like he's a conqueror and I'm land that's ripe for the taking.

The pure desire in his eyes takes my breath away, especially when they flash with possessiveness as he says, "You got that? You. Are. Mine."

I nod eagerly, speechless, as he undresses, dropping his shorts to the floor. The room is lit by two bedside lamps, and I have a far more generous view of him than I had last night. Every hard line is more exaggerated as the light plays out across his mouthwatering body.

His body is *perfect.* Bulky in all the right spots, his calloused hands a result of how hard he works, the fine lines beside his eyes a testament to days when he might have laughed more.

I want to make him laugh more.

Within moments, he stands naked before me, in many ways. He's shed his clothes, but he's shed so much more. His insecurities, his restraint, he's completely undone all for me.

He tugs at the ankles of my leggings, but his eyes never leave mine. He looks at me so closely that I almost can't stand it. Like he sees every insecure corner and still wants to make me his.

"Prove it," I say. My tongue whips out across my bottom lip, and a fountain of nerves bubble up within me as he tosses my leggings away. "If I'm yours, prove it." I tip my chin up, not wanting to appear as vulnerable as I feel.

He falls to his knees at the end of the bed, letting his gaze move between my legs as his fingers grip my inner thighs and spreads me wide. "I thought we'd been over you not telling me what to do."

"Really? I don't recall—"

The movement is quick but unmistakable. I gasp. The burn that follows is unfamiliar but not at all unwelcome. I push up on my elbows, panting. "Did you just slap my pussy?"

The look he gives me from beneath a crooked brow is completely devilish and so fucking hot. "This?" He takes two fingers and twists them into me, torturously slow, and my head falls back. "Is mine."

I whimper right as his lips follow his fingers. He's slow and intentional, every thrust, every kiss to my inner thighs. It's the perfect symphony composed to drive me insane.

"Please," I moan.

He pauses only to press a kiss to my knee and ask, "Please what?"

"Please…" I trail off. *Fuck me* is what was at the tip of my tongue. But saying that right now feels wrong, and yet I can't bring myself to say the other thing. I've put too much of myself out there tonight already. I'm not ready to give this that type of label yet.

"Please…" My mind races. *Please what?* The kisses he's trailing up my inner thigh while he waits for me to find my words are so goddamn distracting. "Show me what gentle is like."

His fingers flutter against my skin as he pauses, lips on me, and my heart aches with the confession. That I just want someone to hold me, to use their hands on me with something other than anger or messy, crazed lust.

"Anything you want, Wildflower," he murmurs as he works his way up my body, taking my sweatshirt with him as he goes, peeling back the layers until all that's left is him and me. Bared to each other. His eyes tell me as much, all traces of his growly indifference erased.

He kisses my stomach. "Mine." He kisses my sternum. "Mine." He kisses my temple. "Mine." And then he holds me.

All our scars melt away as our hands trail over one another's bodies.

All our restraints dissolve as he nudges the head of his hard length between my legs.

And all our hope for not falling head over heels for each other washes away as he pushes into me slowly, savoring every inch and whispering how incredible I am against the crook of my neck.

And as we rock into each other quietly, slowly—gently—a perfect tangle of limbs, I'm pretty sure I cross something monumental off my list without even trying.

CHAPTER 25

Griffin

I WAKE WITH HAIR IN MY FACE. BEAUTIFUL GOLDEN STRANDS crisscrossing my line of vision with Nadia's naked limbs entwined with mine. I'm not sure where I end and where she begins, and I realize that's how I like it.

My eyes clamp back shut. I'm not ready for this night to be over. Not ready to face the day and all the realities it might bring. I'm happy here, suspended in time up in the mountains with a woman I didn't see coming and don't deserve.

Last night was…

I sigh. Last night was something else entirely. When I inhale, her sweet rose-petal scent filters in, and I smile. Her feel, her smell, the fucking whimpering sounds she makes. This girl is *it.*

After spending the better part of the last several years alone, I know what it is to feel at ease around someone. To not just like them but feel like they belong with you and you belong with them. Sure, I can manage around most people. But I'm never sad when we part ways. Aside from my parents, I don't really *miss* anyone.

But the mere thought of spending the winter up here while Nadia spends her winter in the valley has my chest clenching. It literally makes me flinch, which she must notice. Because now she's nuzzling into my chest and pushing herself closer to me, even though I'm pretty sure there's no extra space to take up.

Her hand slides over my chest, and she presses her palm against my cheek, letting her fingers rake through the thick stubble. Then she makes this adorable little sighing noise before walking her hand back down my torso.

I force my eyes open when her path doesn't change. Her lashes stay shuttered, but her lips turn up in a playful little smile as her hand disappears beneath the sheet.

"Good morning, Wildflower." I chuckle, pressing a kiss to the crown of her head.

"Good morning." She drops her lips onto my pec, letting her tongue dart out over my skin before nipping at me.

"What's that for?"

She stares up at me, her honeyed irises sleepy and warm and full of mischief. Her fist clamps down around the girth of my cock, and she licks her lips. I swear I almost come on the spot. Blow my load like an overexcited teenager.

"That's for all the hickeys you left on me after that night behind Neighbor's."

My lips roll together. That was admittedly not my finest moment, but she doesn't look disappointed about the encounter.

"I shouldn't have done that."

She climbs up on top of me, straddling my hips and pressing

the slickness between her thighs against my raging hard-on. Her full tits practically glow in the golden morning light. My mouth dries out. She's so fucking beautiful.

"I guess you'll have to make it up to me." She sticks her bottom lip out dramatically, and I bark out a laugh.

My arm wraps around her waist, and I flip her underneath me as she squeals with happiness. Fuck, that sounds good.

"Has anyone ever told you what a brat you are?" Our gazes collide, the heaviness of last night having transformed this connection between us into something surer, stronger.

"Never." She says it, but we both know she's lying. She can hardly hold her laughter in, those top teeth digging into her bottom lip as her cheeks twitch. But she fails, dissolving into a fit of giggles.

We both know she's full of shit. But I kiss her anyway, loving the feel of her soft lips against mine, loving the way she's opened up to me and silently convinced me to do the same with her. It feels like she knows me better than I know myself.

Her light laughter continues against my lips, her arms looping around my neck as she bucks her hips into me.

"You done giggling yet, Wildflower? I've got some making up to do." My teeth sink into her lip, and she moans. And then we spend the morning sinking into each other.

Until Tripod finally wakes up and starts leaping through the covers like we're playing a really fun game. *Asshole dog.*

★★★

We tidied the property quickly and quietly this morning.

Except that time I yanked her away from whatever chore she was doing to fuck her brains out on the stairs.

But after that, we got the place locked up, and now we're in her car driving down into the valley. She insisted on driving, and I'm not gonna lie, it's terrifying.

I wonder if this is what it's like in her brain. Just no speed limit and lots of sharp turns, leaving a trail of dust behind herself on whatever dirt road she's flying down.

"Are we in a race that I don't know about?" I ask, looking over my shoulder. "Is someone in hot pursuit?"

She snorts. At least her hands are at ten and two. Hot little psycho driver that she is.

"Are you even old enough to drive this thing?"

Her head turns, and her eyes narrow. "Fuck you, Griffy."

"You already did."

Her goddamn lead foot sinks down, and she smirks out the windshield like she's proving something to me right now.

She's not. Other than she's just as crazy as I already know.

I let out a sigh of relief when Nadia finally slows. What I don't expect is for her to pull over. "You drive."

"Why?" I ask.

She just grins. "Because you look like you're going to have a heart attack."

As she flips her door open and unfolds herself, I ask, "Is that some sort of old joke?" Nadia barks out an amused laugh as she rounds the back of the car and comes to yank my door open.

With very wide, very serious eyes, she says, "I would *never*."

I can't help but chuckle and shake my head as I get out of the car. I snake my hand around her waist and capture her mouth on the way past, unable to stop myself, or keep my hands off her. I could spend hours tracing this body. Kissing this body.

Feeling her lips move softly against mine, that cool little rush of air when she sighs into my kiss like she did just now.

She steps in closer to me, and I'm like a teenager with hearts in his eyes. Her warmth, her scent wraps around me like a comfort blanket. I push her up against the pearl-white car and claim her mouth, angling my head over hers, one hand clamping on her ass while the other cups her cheek. The little hairs at the base of her neck tickle my fingers. The brim of my hat lends an air of privacy, like we're locked into a fantasy world on the side of the road.

She smiles against my lips, a light, airy giggle escaping her as I nip gently at her bottom lip, giving her a soft, private smile of my own.

"Careful, Sinclaire. You're gonna make me climb you like a tree right here on the side of the road."

I smile even bigger. I love that she doesn't want anything from me. She doesn't care about my money, my past, my fame. She wants a quiet, simple life. And I think she might want it with *me*, which is the most incredible feeling. To know that someone wants you for you, not for what you can do for them. It warms me in a completely unfamiliar way.

She squeals when I scoop her up and place her into the passenger seat. And my goddamn heart races at the sound. So sweet and playful. Nadia grins up at me when I grab the seat belt and pull it gently over her shoulder, and when I lean across her body—eyes catching on the rise and fall of her full breasts—she presses a kiss to my neck. She trails a hand over my spine and reaches behind me to squeeze my ass.

When I make a deep rumbling noise, she just laughs again, before leaning close and nipping at the lobe of my ear. All while

I struggle with a fucking seat belt buckle. Distracting me from day one.

"Wildflower…"

Her hand slides up beneath my T-shirt right as the latch clicks tight. "It's not my fault you're strutting around, teasing me with a body like this."

I shake my head, almost uncomfortable with how genuine the compliment is. How hungry her voice sounds. Gripping her chin with my fingers, I gaze straight into her eyes with a knowing smirk. "Behave yourself."

Brat that she is, she just winks. And I kiss her again swiftly, tongues tangling briefly, but as her hands start to wander, I pull away. I'll never leave this goddamn mountain if we keep this game up.

When I hop back in the car, she gives me a mischievous look. A look I recognize. A look that haunts me.

Again.

She said it that night. And her eyes say it right now.

I swallow as I adjust the seat and mirrors, avoiding turning my eyes on her right now, because if I do, I'm worried about where my head might go. Suddenly, this thing between us feels so monumental.

So monumentally right.

I pull back out onto the road as she fiddles with the radio, trying to find reception that doesn't exist. When she finally gives up, she flops back in her seat and places a hand casually over my thigh. It starts out innocent, but after a couple of minutes, one finger strokes. Her thumb joins in, rubbing in a firm circle. Hand sliding down and in toward my swiftly swelling cock.

I keep my eyes trained on the road in the quiet car, but I can sense her gaze on me. And out of my periphery, I see her smile.

A troublemaking smile.

Which is right when her hand slides up to the button on my jeans and flicks it open.

"Nadia." My tone is warning, but my desire betrays me. My voices oozes longing. She has that effect on me.

"Yes?" She blinks innocently as she makes quick one-handed work of my zipper. And then her hand slides into my boxers and wraps around my steely length, chasing all the words I was about to use right out of my head.

She pumps me and quirks her head innocently. "Was there something you wanted to say to me, Griffin?"

I give her a quick look with one eyebrow arched, but don't take my eyes off the road for long. We're not driving fast, but my track record with safe driving leaves something to be desired of late, and Nadia is the most precious of cargo.

Focus on the road.

I just grunt at her, seeing her lips tip up in pleasure as she reaches for her seat belt.

"That stays on," I interrupt her movements.

She rolls her eyes playfully and adjusts it without removing it before pulling my dick right out of my jeans.

A small sigh escapes her. "You have some nerve looking the way you do and also having a cock like this."

I chuckle. I can't help it. I love her compliments.

"No dick will ever compare. I'm ruined."

My shoulders go tight right as my cock throbs, bobbing lewdly in my lap. "God," I bite out, and she just giggles. She licks her lips and stares down at me.

And I pray I don't crash.

Because within moments her head is dropping, tongue swirling around the head as she laps at me and hums in pleasure.

"You have the perfect cock," she whispers before sliding my length into the back of her throat. My fingers clamp around the steering wheel, knuckles going white as I chance a look at the mess of blond hair now bobbing between my legs while I drive down the bumpy gravel road. The vibration makes it that much better.

The sight of her working me, sucking me so firmly, has me groaning and willing myself to focus on the drive.

When she pulls back, eyes trained on my cock, I feel a surge of precum, and she instantly licks it away. "Mm. I love that."

"Jesus Christ." I steer the car to the side, knowing it's not safe to keep going. Not when she says things like that in her sugary-sweet voice.

She looks up with an evil smirk as I reach over her to put the car in park. And then she dives back down. I quickly scoop her golden locks into my fist, lifting just enough to lean back and watch her work me. Watch her cheeks hollow out, her pretty pink lips suctioned on to me as she slides up and down.

Even the way her lashes flutter and cast a shadow over cheekbones drives me crazy.

Eyelashes. I mean, goddamn.

She hums, sending a throb through me and an ache twinging just behind my hip bones. I brace a hand on the roof of the car, wanting so badly not to take over. Just wanting to watch her take care of me. To revel in it.

A light graze of her teeth has my hips bucking, and I curse. "You love this, don't you?"

She tries to meet my eyes and nod with my cock still wedged between her lips. I swear I almost blow at the sight.

"Good girl. You suck me so well."

Her lips tip up at the compliment before she slides her soft mouth back over my length. On the way back up, her teeth graze gently, and I feel the telltale pressure building in my pelvis. "Oh, fuck yeah. Like that again."

She repeats the motion, and my head falls back against the headrest as my heart races and my lips part. A truck drives by, and I suspect the passenger may have seen what we're doing.

On one hand, I feel like I could beat my chest. Look at this beautiful girl blowing me. *You see that, asshole?* But mostly I feel like I'm going to track him down later and kill him.

But when her teeth graze again, my murder plans evaporate. All I can think about is the tight squeeze of her fist around my hilt, the warm, wet heat of her mouth, and my cock butting up against the back of her throat as she takes me all the way back.

Suddenly, I can't hold back any longer. My pelvis tips up a couple times as I fuck her mouth. "Fuck!" I bark out, surging forward and shooting my release over her tongue.

She keeps sucking—twisting and licking me like I'm a goddamn Popsicle. Swallowing like she loves the taste.

I sag back against the seat, stroking her hair and basking in the feel of her taking care of me this way. So eagerly. So playfully.

And when she sits up and smiles at me while daintily wiping the corners of her mouth, I swear I almost have a heart attack. She's just too fucking much. A special brand of kryptonite made exactly for me.

I never stood a single chance at resisting her.

"Best blow job of my life."

"Really?" She sounds genuinely excited by that compliment, smile widening and eyes twinkling.

Hand cupped around the base of her skull, I tug her forward, dusting my lips over her puffy, ravaged ones as I say, "Hell yes. That's one I'll think about for the rest of my life. I can't wait to repay the favor."

When I pull her close and claim her mouth, she shivers. I can taste myself there, but I don't give a fuck. Kissing her is a privilege that I'll never take for granted.

"Ready to go, Wildflower?"

She rubs her lips across my beard and smiles against my skin before kissing the bristly hair. "Yes."

We both take a moment to right ourselves, and then I'm pulling back out onto the road. I place her hand back onto my leg and link my fingers through hers, wanting to maintain whatever contact I can. Like she might slip away from me if I don't.

Like this is just too good to be true.

When we hit the stop sign where the dirt road joins up with the paved one, Nadia takes a deep breath, her shoulders rising and falling with the weight of it. "I wish we were just staying at your house."

"Me too."

"I can see why you like it up here so much. It's peaceful."

"It is." I nod and let out a deep sigh.

"Can I come back up here again?" She peers out the window with a little too much interest, like just asking me that makes her uncomfortable. It's a failed attempt at being casual.

I swallow. "Yeah. Anytime."

Her head tilts in my direction. "Do you only speak in sentences with more than two words when you're on your own property? Just revert to single-word answers and grunts the minute you leave?"

I grunt. I'm lost in my head right now.

She laughs.

I roll my eyes, folding my arms across myself. "You're the one who told me I'm a good listener."

She nods as I flip the signal light on and check the road again. Even though there's hardly ever any traffic up here.

"I don't want this to end." Her voice is so small that I barely hear her. The confession makes my heart twist. "This weekend, I mean."

Right.

"Wanna go for a stupid coffee and hear about how riveting playing the same golf course every damn day is?"

Her smile is soft as her car accelerates beneath my foot.

"Yeah. A stupid coffee sounds great."

CHAPTER 26

Griffin

I KNOCK ON THE DOOR AND WAIT, RIGHT AS I REMEMBER MY mom whispered something in Nadia's ear last time we were here. Right before we left.

"What did my mom whisper to you last time you saw her?"

Nadia looks up at me, her pinky finger grazing against mine before she steps just a little farther away from me, clearly not ready to waltz in there acting like we're an item. "She told me I'm the only person she hasn't seen you stutter around."

My mind reels as I try to think about it. Have I tripped over a single goddamn word in her presence in the last couple of days? I can't seem to drum up the memory. But surely, I must have. There's just no way that—

The door swings open. Tripod yaps once at my feet and then takes off into the condo like he owns the fucking place.

"Hey, Mom."

"Tripod! Griffy!" My mom's arms shoot out wide as she wraps them around me. Then the volume of her squealing increases, which means she must have spotted Nadia standing behind me.

"Nadia, honey! How nice to see you again." I swear my mom shoves me out of the way so she can hug Nadia, which makes her laugh and mouth, *I think she loves me more,* over my mother's shoulder before she pulls away to take us both in.

"It's nice to see you again too, Joan. Griffin hasn't stopped talking about how much he loves your pour-over coffee, so we just had to swing by."

Brat.

My mom smiles wide, giving me a skeptical glance. She knows Nadia is full of shit but likes that she's giving me a hard time. "It's the flavor, isn't it, darling?"

"Yeah, Mom. It's really good," I say right as my cap is ripped off my head and my dad's huge mitt of a hand lands to ruffle my hair.

"Hey, kid. And Nadia! What a pleasant surprise." My parents exchange a look that is far too excited. I guess when you haven't brought a girl around in thirty-five years, twice in a row seems like a big deal.

Nadia catches my eye and winks.

I swallow. She's a huge fucking deal.

"Okay, to the living room we go. Preseason is on Griff. You wanna stay for a game?"

I almost groan. Watching professional football since the demise of my role in it hasn't been very high on my to-do list. I love the game. I *miss* the game. And watching it is like twisting a knife into my chest. But my dad is so genuine in his excitement. He put so many years into supporting me, showing up to my games, watching game tape with me, and so much more.

It's almost cruel to him that I made it big and now hardly even recognize the sport still exists.

"Yeah, Dad. That sounds great."

He claps his hands together, and we all make our way down the hallway to the open living space.

"What's your team, Nadia?" he asks as she curls up in a large armchair across from me. I scowl because she belongs in my lap, not across the room.

"Sorry?" she asks, tucking her legs underneath herself. Tripod hops up, spins a quick circle, and then presses himself against her. I sigh contentedly at the sight of the two of them there together. A dog I ran over and a girl who ran me over.

"Football? Who is your favorite football team?"

"Oh, gosh. I don't know. Where I come from, football is what you call soccer."

My parents heads both shoot up, like she's said something blasphemous, and I cover my mouth with a fist to keep from laughing.

"Are you telling me you don't like football?" My dad sounds more alarmed than offended as he pauses the game and bathes the room in awkward silence.

Nadia just rolls with the punches. "Well, I wouldn't take it that far. I'm sure I'd like it. I just don't really know anything about it."

"So," my mother pipes up, "when you met Griffin, you didn't know who he was?"

I don't know how I stop my body from shaking under the strain of keeping myself from laughing. Know who I was? That sounds so lame.

I think of the girl in the bathroom that night, all big dick energy and sultry smiles. Calling me out on being the prick that I often am. Nah, that girl had no fucking clue who I was—or who I'd been. Not that she'd have cared.

"I knew he was a total asshole," Nadia deadpans.

And the dam breaks.

The laugh comes out of me in a painful-sounding wheeze as I double over, just after seeing Nadia's lips twitch and eyes flit to me.

My dad barks a loud laugh, and within moments, I hear my mom join in too.

Nadia chuckles, watching us as she throws her hands up and adds, "What? It's true!"

It makes me laugh harder. Only Nadia Dalca would sit here in my parents' living room and tell them their beloved only child was a *total asshole.*

"I like you, Nadia," my mother says from where she's still standing at the kitchen island, shaking her head with a twinkle in her eye. "Griffin needs more people like you around him."

"What kind of people would those be, Mom?"

She turns, pinning me with a pointed index finger. "The kind who don't put up with your shit."

"Ha!" Nadia points at me, looking triumphant. "See? She knows what I'm talking about."

I grin and shake my head. The mood is so fun and light, I just want to soak it up. Nadia feels right here too, with me and my family.

"Okay then, Nadia." My dad moves to the other end of the couch to sit closer and starts in on her, explaining the game as it plays across the huge flat-screen again.

I sit and watch her, entranced by the sloped line of her nose, the bright twinkle in her eyes, her soft lips, and all that flaxen hair. She scoops it behind her ear and peeks across at me as she listens to my dad go on about a sport she clearly has no interest in. We exchange a look so sweet my heart twists in my chest.

"Griffin. Come help me with the coffees." My mom's face is completely unreadable as she beckons me forward with a folded hand.

I can barely tear my eyes off Nadia. We opened the floodgates last night, and now I'm feeling a little obsessed. Uncomfortably so, like it hurts to put space between us.

"Yeah. Of course." I slap my knees and unfold myself, moving into the kitchen, where my mother clearly doesn't need any help.

"What's up, Ma?" I flatten my palms against the marble countertop and take in all the contraptions before her, still not entirely sure why she wouldn't just grind her coffee, fill the coffee maker, and then press a button.

"The first time was a coincidence." She's weighing ground coffee on an honest-to-god scale, not even looking at me as she talks. "But a second time? I've got questions, Griff." She says it quietly enough that she can't be heard over the announcers blaring in the living room.

I run my tongue over my teeth as she begins to pour boiling water into the funnel.. "Kinda figured you would."

"So, she's Stefan's sister?"

"Yup."

"How old is she?"

Too fucking young.

"Twenty-one."

She doesn't react to that little tidbit. Bless her. "It seems like you two make each other happy. I don't know when I last heard you laugh like that." *Before Nadia? Years.*

"Mhm." I watch the coffee drip into the glass carafe.

She pours the boiling water out of this dainty little kettle, spilling the steaming liquid out in slow circles over the filter, not missing a fucking beat. "Have you heard from—"

"No."

"Does she know about—"

"No," I growl, a protective streak I didn't even know I possessed leaping up and rearing its ugly head.

My mom turns to me, her eyes narrowing on me. *Now we're in touchy territory.*

"Don't you growl at me. You need to tell her. And you need to tidy that up. It's way overdue. You can't keep running from your past, or it's going to bite you in your very stubborn ass."

"I know," I whisper harshly—hardly better than a growl—good mood evaporating right before my eyes.

"Don't drag your feet." She pours the coffee into the waiting mugs.

I press my hands to the brim of my hat, squeezing the edges in as I stare down at the countertop. "I *know*. I'm trying. I have been trying for years."

Her eyes narrow as she glares down her nose at me. "Try harder, Griffy. And grab the other two." She gestures with her chin at the two mugs closest to me. And then her face morphs into a smile as she scoops her two up and walks into the living room.

"So, Nadia, tell us about your plans. Last time, you said you were thinking about going back to school. What for?"

Nadia takes the coffee with a warm smile, wrapping her dainty fingers around the mug. "Well, I got into vet school." She looks my way from beneath the thick fringe of her lashes, suddenly shy. She clears her throat. "I actually start in September. They took me as a late application."

"That's just great!" God, why does my dad always sound like he's shouting? I smile into my coffee mug.

"Close by?" Mom asks.

Nadia nods. "Yeah. At Emerald Lake Veterinary College."

"Will you come back and work where you're at now when you graduate?" My mom is not so subtly trying to figure out if she's sticking around, and it takes everything in me not to roll my eyes.

"I… don't know." Nadia's cheeks go pink, and she stares down at her coffee. "I think I might like to do some sort of rescue work, actually." Her eyes find mine, swimming with an emotion I can't quite put my finger on. "I've really enjoyed rehabilitating Cowboy, the horse that Griffin bought me. The racing industry can be hard on horses. I know some end up in less-than-ideal circumstances. I think I could do something with that… I don't know…"

She shrugs, trailing off and looking up at the ceiling like she's said something silly. But nothing about what she said sounds silly to me. With her soft heart and spunky side, she'd be perfect doing something like this with horses.

"I have a bit of an inheritance. I'd like to put that money toward something good. Something helpful."

My throat constricts as I try to swallow. How someone like her has even looked my way, someone who's risen above her circumstances so fearlessly—I just don't get it.

I really need to get my shit together.

"That sounds like a lovely idea," my mother says kindly. But she doesn't get how incredible this woman is. How pure. How strong. How inspiring.

Because never mind myself, all I want is for Nadia's dreams to come true. And the prospect of hurting her makes me almost physically ill.

Which means I've got one major loose end I need to tie up. The one woman in the world I manage to find all the right words around deserves that much and more.

CHAPTER 27

Nadia

I wake up in Griffin's arms and have the strangest sense of belonging somewhere for the first time in my life.

I feel safe. I feel treasured. I feel like my home is held tight between his rock-hard arms.

And those aren't the only thing that's rock-hard this morning. His bulge is wedged between my ass cheeks, and he's got me clamped in his arms like I might run away from him, given the chance.

And nothing could be further from the truth. In fact, I'm feeling like I might just live here. Wrapped up in *him*. All cinnamon and pine, hard body and soft hands.

After coffee with his parents yesterday, we took Tripod for a walk, and he told me all about growing up here in Ruby Creek. He also told me more about Griffin Sinclaire, quarterback extraordinaire, and how much he loved the sport. How much he misses it. And how hard his parents worked to see him meet his every goal.

I hate to admit there was this tiny part of me that was envious. Sure, it all went to shit, and he's been facing down demons every day since. But the rest of it? The parents? The support? The love?

I wanted that. I still do.

We came back to his place, and he ran me a bath while he stepped outside to feed the horses. I could hear him talking on his phone but tuned it out as I sank into the bubbles. When I got out, I only meant to lay myself naked on the bed.

My plan was to become an all-you-can-eat buffet for Griffin Sinclaire. But I fell asleep. And rather than wake me up to indulge in that, he tucked me in. Like a perfect gentleman. He crawled in beside me, and I woke up partway through the night, realizing what had happened.

Then I snuggled back in and passed back out. I didn't swipe my hand beneath my pillow to check for a gun. I just fell back into the most peaceful sleep of my life.

From across the room, his phone trills, the sound of his alarm filling the formerly quiet room, and he groans. A deep, masculine sound that makes the cage of his chest vibrate against my back.

I smile. The sun is shining through the slatted blinds, and I have the manliest man of all time holding me. What could be better?

He kisses my hair and runs a calloused palm over my bare arm before climbing out of bed and padding over to the dresser to hit the alarm. I roll over, tangled in the sheets and feeling thoroughly blissed out. My eyes fall to the round globes of his ass as he walks away.

Best view in the world.

I love that he sleeps naked. Love that he feels confident enough around me to walk around without a stitch of clothing when he seems to be riddled with so many insecurities most days. It warms my heart.

When he turns, he smirks at me. Probably because my eyes went from his ass right to his dick. "Good morning, Wildflower."

I return the smirk. "Lookin' good, Sinclaire."

He shakes his head in a knowing way, but his lips tip up all the same. I expect him to come back to bed—I *want* him to come back to bed—but he opens a dresser drawer and starts pulling clothes out.

"Where are you running off to?" My brows scrunch together in confusion.

"It's supposed to be a scorcher. Gonna get the horses worked before it's just plain too hot for them."

"Oh." My heart sinks. Guys always pull away after sex, so that's where my head goes.

"Hey. Hey." He crosses the room as he pulls a gray T-shirt over his head. When he gets to the edge of the bed, he drops to his knees and stretches one inked arm over me, stroking my hair as he stares into my eyes. "This means nothing more than I need to go to work. I..." He trails off, face falling just a little bit. "Come over tonight. When you're done with work. Okay?"

I search his face for any clues as to what might be going through his head. On one hand, things have evolved between us kind of quickly. On the other, it seems like we've been circling each other for years, ignoring feelings that have always been there.

I'm anxious all the same. "Okay" is my quiet reply.

His heavy brow presses down over his stormy eyes. "So help me, Nadia. If you're questioning a single thing right now, rest assured, this is very real for me too."

My heart rate quickens, and I let out a breath I didn't know I'd been holding at hearing him say that out loud. "Okay. Here. After work. It's a date."

He smiles, but it doesn't quite touch his eyes. "It's a date."

And with that he kisses me quickly and is gone out the door. The voice I've worked so hard to get rid of asks if I'm *sure* he'll be back for more.

★★★

I walk over the field at the end of my day, not sure how to feel. Aside from hot, sweaty, and agitated. Work was busy, and that kept me mostly occupied. Though I did spend a huge amount of time thinking about Griffin and wondering why he was acting so restrained this morning after not holding back the last couple of days.

Something was wrong, and that inkling keeps cropping up, twisting my thoughts and feelings into something uglier than I want where Griffin is concerned. It makes me think of my mother and how thoroughly she was swindled by my dad. By his endless amounts of money, by the sophistication of an older man. She had the world at her fingertips, and she gave it all up to be locked into a lifetime with a man who turned out to be a monster.

I constantly wonder if I'll fall into the same trap. Even though the sane part of me knows Griffin is nothing like my sperm donor.

Something that is reaffirmed when I get to the top of the hill and gaze down over the small yard attached to the guesthouse.

There is Griffin. Reading a book in a beach chair. Swim trunks and nothing else. Just patterns painted over his endless muscles. Another empty beach chair sits beside him, and his long legs are stretched out before him, feet soaking in a small blue plastic pool. His Bluetooth speaker is blaring some sort of Caribbean-sounding music, and he has a bucket full of…

I walk closer, heart crawling up into my throat and eyes wide.

A bucket full of my favorite pineapple-flavored sparkling water.

Moving toward him, a blush creeps up over my cheeks. It's too hot out for anyone else to notice, but I can feel it all the same.

When he glances up and grins at me from beneath the brim of his hat, I trip. I mean, goddamn. The man should not be allowed to look this good. All tanned skin and black tattoos that give him a slightly threatening edge.

"What's all this?" I call out, drawing closer.

"As close to a tropical vacation as I could reasonably get you right now."

My stomach flips over on itself and my chest aches as I look over the setup again. Towels beneath a big sun umbrella. A stack of trashy magazines. A skimpy pink bikini. The man has literally thought of everything.

"Well, shit. This is pretty romantic, Sinclaire."

He tips his chin at the bikini a little sheepishly. "Go get changed."

"I could change right here…" I trail off suggestively.

He presses his lips together. "As good as that sounds, let's not risk someone seeing you."

"Right." His point is so valid, but it stings all the same. I don't want to hide this thing between us. "I'll be right back."

I head to the house to change, but I can tell something isn't quite right. Something is off with him today. Who the hell turns down the girl they're into when she wants to get naked in front of them? The chances of someone seeing us are practically zero. I slept here last night, for crying out loud.

I slip into the bathing suit, and it fits perfectly because of course it does. Griffin is like this growly, dirty-talking, romantic dickhead that I can't get enough of.

As I march back out to where he's sitting, I get more and more annoyed. Blame it on the heat, my hormones, whatever. I walk right up to him, cock a hip, and cross my arms the way he likes. His eyes always fall to my breasts when I do this. And I'm willing to use every weapon at my disposal to find out what the hell is wrong with him.

"You're acting weird."

I can see him fight to keep his eyes trained on mine, but they eventually drop, and I try hard not to look smug about it.

He scrubs his beard with his free hand; the other is wrapped around a can of my favorite drink. "I know."

"Why?"

His eyes are wide and clear, and I can see the hesitation in them. The *pain* in them. "Something from my past. Something I've been running from. Actually, more like neglecting to deal with."

Anything but that. Anything but that because *that* I can empathize with. Not wanting to talk about it. After all, we don't know each other very well. There are dark parts of my past I haven't told him about. Things I'm sure will come out over time as our trust grows. Tidbits of my story here and there that I'll tell him when the time is right.

So instead of giving him shit, I just sigh, looking back over the field briefly. "You wanna talk about it?"

His lips roll together as he regards me. "Not really. I'd rather just sit here with you. Just being near you makes the world feel like a better place." He swallows, and I watch his Adam's apple bob beneath the stubbled skin on his throat. "You make me feel happy."

Even the way he swallows has me pressing my thighs together.

"Okay." I nod and flop into the chair beside him, and I swear I can feel the relief flowing off him.

He cracks a yellow can and hands it over to me, and I sink back into the beach chair. I'm tired, I'm overwhelmed, and I'm overthinking the hell out of things.

But when he reaches over and takes my hand in his, everything feels better. Actually, for the next several hours, everything feels a little bit better. I revel in his company, soak in the cool water, and read bullshit news about celebrities.

It's actually bliss.

Until he ruins it all.

CHAPTER 28

Nadia

GRIFFIN HASN'T FUCKED ME IN FIVE DAYS, AND I'M LOSING MY mind. Which is why I'm gawking out the clinic windows at his perfect ass as he walks a horse up and down the driveway while Mira watches for any signs of lameness.

All I can confirm is that he can wear the hell out of a pair of jeans and that he's so much sweeter than I ever banked on.

Even though I'm pissed at him right now.

When we were about to go our separate ways after the annoyingly sweet but fake tropical vacation, he told me he needed a bit of time to work something out. When I asked what that something was, he said he'd tell me once he took care of it.

When I asked what a bit of time was, he told me he couldn't say for sure.

He promised me over and over again that this wasn't the end. *Don't misunderstand me, Wildflower. This isn't the end. This is just the beginning. When I told you you're mine, I fucking meant it. But to keep going with you while I have this hanging over my head feels wrong. You deserve better.*

Honestly, his vagueness pissed me off. Which is why I told him not to come around until he's ready to talk honestly with me. I hate secrets. I hate not knowing. I hate being kept in the dark like I'm a child or something. And even all that raw pain in his eyes wasn't enough to convince me otherwise.

But I still want to fuck him. Because nobody—and I mean *nobody*—is better at sex than Griffin Sinclaire. Plus, I really do understand having things you're not ready to talk about.

And if I'm being honest, it's a lot more than just sex with him. I wouldn't have done it otherwise. I promised myself I wouldn't have casual sex to fill some void inside me, and I haven't.

The problem is, I'm getting obsessed. With his dick. With his moody growls. With his commitment to my to-do list. With the soft looks he gives Tripod when he bends down to scratch him behind his ears. Is there anything hotter than a man who's a total softie for animals? Because I'm pretty sure there's not. And watching Griffin take in the dirty, malnourished, three-legged mutt and love him so completely could make me cry.

He stops to talk to Mira after trotting the horse back to her, and when she moves along the filly, running her hand over her ribs as she goes, Griffin's head snaps up. He glances my way, like he just *knew* I was scoping him out. Our eyes find each other like it's the most natural thing in the world, like we're opposite ends of a magnet. Drawn together in the most intrinsic of ways. Even if we shouldn't be.

When he looks at me like this, none of that other stuff matters. It feels like the world put us in each other's paths that night. It feels like my brother bought his farm so we'd be a part of each other's worlds.

At the risk of sounding like a woo-woo sap, there's something about us that feels written in the stars.

I don't look away, and neither does he. He just scowls at me, and it makes me smile. He might act like a grizzly bear, but I know what's underneath. I've felt him soften beneath my palms. I've heard the loving things he whispers in my ears.

I'm smart enough to know there's something holding him back, something he's embarrassed about. Some demon from his past. But his demons don't scare me. They call to my own. Our wild sides match, our shadowy parts twirl together so easily. Our demons spill out and dance together, like dark plus dark makes light.

I told him once that I didn't know what I'd have in common with someone my age who's lived an average life. That I'd feel like I was darkening their bright, shiny aura with my shadows.

But with Griffin it doesn't feel that way at all. He doesn't treat me like I'm damaged. He takes all my little broken bits and mixes them with his own.

And I want more of that. He must see it in my face because his brows drop lower, lips tipping with what someone who doesn't understand him might see as a bad mood. I just see anxiety. I see all the things he wants to say to me but can't bring himself to voice.

I wink at him and turn away, checking the clock as I grab my bag and walk toward the front door.

A week of space is enough for him to freak out. And me, for that matter. I'm also tired of pretending my vibrator is him.

It's time to poke the bear again.

"You off?" Mira calls out.

I wave, grinning. "Yeah. I think I'm gonna grab a horse and go for a trail ride."

"Good for you. Between this guy"—she hikes a thumb over at Griffin—"and Violet, you've come along quickly." Since day one, this woman has been my biggest fan, and I love her for it.

"Well, you know me. Not afraid to work for what I want." My gaze flits over to Griffin, who stiffens, his scowl only deepening even though I didn't think that was possible.

"I'm so proud of you." Her eyes twinkle.

Earlier today, I told her my plans about starting some sort of racehorse rescue or rehabilitation program after I finish vet school. Between Mira's excitement for the idea and the votes of confidence from Griffin and his family, I'm feeling like this dream is possible. Like I really could do it, like I have a growing number of people in my life who genuinely want me to succeed. And that support warms me in a way I've spent years searching for.

Mira looks like she could cry as I stare back at her. Having a baby softened my sister-in-law, and I'm not mad at it. I'm happy to soak up any motherly attention that comes my way. Sometimes, I think about the fact we almost lost her. My life would be a lot less bright without her in it. Which is why I wrap her up in a hug and whisper in her ear, "I love you so much."

She squeezes me tight. "Love you too."

When I pull away, Griffin's scowl has washed away, swapped with an expression I can't quite place.

"Later, Sinclaire," I mutter as I turn to leave.

"Who are you riding with?" he bites out as soon as I've taken a few steps away.

"No one. I like my space."

"Not safe."

I peek over my shoulder because I don't want to miss this reaction from him. "Thanks, Dad."

I almost laugh when that one spot on his jaw pops. I'm sure he's grinding that cinnamon gum to absolute shit between his molars.

"Meet me at my house. You can ride Spot. I'll take one of the young ones that I have over there right now."

I stop, turning back to them, not missing the ways Mira's eyes move between us, no longer sparkling with emotion. Now it's amusement.

"I just said I like my space." My tongue swipes against the back of my teeth, trying so hard not to crack a smile.

"Heard. Just don't care." He shrugs, horse in hand, and walks away with the last word, annoyed masculine energy radiating from his shoulders.

But me? I'm not annoyed, I'm grinning because I just won myself some alone time with Griffin Sinclaire.

Mira brushes past me, doing a poor job of smothering the smile that's playing across her face. She puts a good chunk of space between us before she mutters just loud enough for me to hear, "My God, Little Dalca. I daresay that man has it bad for you."

And all I can think is *Good.* Now we can have it bad for each other. I hope he's as fucked up over me as I am over him.

***

"You saddled my horse for me." Griffin gives me an impassive look as he stares at the paddocks behind his house.

"Do you want to check that I did it properly?" I lean up against the fence and quirk an eyebrow at him. "Ruin my alone time *and* boss me around?"

His lips twitch, but he doesn't smile, just dusts his hands together and heads toward the leggy bay thoroughbred in the paddock beside Spot. "No. I taught you how. I know you did it right. Ready?" he asks, tossing his cap on the ground and pulling a helmet on.

I nod and turn away because if I don't, I will seriously fucking throw myself at the guy, climb him, tackle him to the ground, and have my way with him right here and now.

Save a horse, ride a cowboy and all that.

"Yup." I chicken out on that and bridle Spot before lining him up with the fence and hopping on. I urge him forward with a gentle squeeze without looking behind me and head down the driveway. The only way I know Griffin is following is because I can hear his horse's hooves clopping behind me.

"This way." He gestures down a wide path that winds between the trees, pulling up beside me as we head out for a leisurely walk. Spot's head is slung low, swaying back and forth in a relaxed fashion. Griffin's young colt is clearly nervous, his head held high, eyes bugging out of his skull, ears swiveling all over the place.

"Your horse is tripping balls, Sinclaire."

"Stop calling me Sinclaire. That's what the guys on my team called me."

"So?" I shrug.

"I've been inside you. You're not one of the guys."

I shrug again. "Might as well be. You've been treating me like one."

"Nadia." His tone is warning, but I don't care. "Don't say that."

A bird swoops past, and his young horse flinches.

"Well, stop acting like a grumpy old man."

"I told you I had something I needed to work out."

"For what? You really didn't tell me shit. And I'm just supposed to sit around here twiddling my thumbs, all fucking confused and horny, waiting for you to do whatever cryptic bullshit you're doing?"

He growls and hops off his horse when we hit a long metal gate that leads into a big open field, unlocks it, and swings it wide.

"Are we back to not talking? After *everything*?" I scoff, agitation rising in my chest as I urge Spot into the open field, not a clue where we're going. Based on the sun's position, this must be the land that separates Gold Rush Ranch from my brother's farm, Cascade Acres.

Griffin gets back onto his horse as it skitters sideways. His big palm slides up its neck, and I'm momentarily jealous. I want those hands on *me*. But he needs a couple of weeks for *something*.

He murmurs gently to the horse, taking me back to the night we spent together. The words he murmured against my skin. The way he claimed me as his. *Mine*, he said. But now he's pushing me away? Again? Ignoring me.

And it enrages me.

"Did last weekend not mean anything to you?"

His head shoots up like I've just slapped him.

"Just tell me! I can't stand not knowing. I mean, I'm supposed to be the immature one here, right? Can you just fucking tell me something? Anything? You? Me? Us? This land? Are we fucking *trespassing*?" I wave a hand as I shout the last word, my agitation boiling over.

And it's that flailing motion that sets his horse off. The bay rears on his hind legs before scooting to the side, and I distract Griffin just enough that he's caught off guard. His body topples to the ground with a heavy thud. I swear it rattles my bones just watching it happen. I hear my scream, but it doesn't sound like mine. It sounds distant, drowned out by the pounding hooves of his horse taking off and blood rushing through my ears.

He's flat on his back when I jump off Spot and race to his side. I know barely anything about his head injury, but I suspect that a good thump to the head is not what he needs. I think of how adamant he was about wearing a helmet and am immensely grateful he's been a stickler for safety.

"Griff. Griff." I fall to my knees beside him, hands clutching at his shirt, feeling his firm, warm skin beneath my hands. "Griffin!" I sound shrieky and frantic as I check him over, straight into his dark eyes.

He bursts out laughing.

"Are you okay?" I pant out, trailing my hands over his beautiful body as though I could heal whatever hurts just by running my fingers over it.

And the asshole just laughs harder.

"Griffin! Are. You. Okay?" I swing a leg over him, straddling his waist. Because clearly the idiot is fine. Unless he doesn't stop laughing. Then I'm going to be the one to hurt him. Why does someone so fucking annoying have to be the only person I've ever been so consumed with?

"No." He laughs, scrubbing a hand over his face. "I'm in love with a fucking crazy person."

I still. His body shakes beneath me as I struggle to wrap my mind around the words that just spilled from his lips.

"What?" The blood drains from my face.

He sighs and places his hands over mine, which are now braced against his pecs. He gives me a little tug, clamping me onto him and forcing me to meet his eye. "I'm not telling you anything because I'm embarrassed about what I've done in the past. And I don't know what to say. You deserve so much fucking better than me. I'm still trying to wrap my brain around it all."

He shakes his head, huffing out a disbelieving breath. "I've spent years scaring people away by being a growly asshole. And then you waltzed in, and even when I'm on my worst behavior, when other people back away slowly, you just sit there smiling. Looking at me like I hung the fucking moon. I want to *deserve* that look. And right now, I don't. Right now, you wouldn't look at me like that. I want to lay it all out for you. I want to make a plan to show you I'm serious. Because *that's* what you deserve. So just let me work this out in the only way I know how, okay?" He rolls his lips together, no doubt taking in the shell-shocked expression on my face.

"And also, I own this land. I held on to it when I sold the main farm to your brother. So we aren't trespassing."

The scent of sweet grass swirls around me. I gaze out over the beautiful rolling hills, the greens, the golds. There is so much about this man I don't know. He's so secretive, so restrained in so many ways. So accustomed to doing everything on his own. But my heart doesn't seem to care. It practically beats out of my chest for him.

I should be more scared about what he's just told me. Whatever shit he's hiding sounds problematic. But I'm a little hung up on another part of what he just told me, and deep down, I know there's very little he could do to scare me off. "Can you back up to the part before that?"

His full lips quirk up. He looks so fucking good when he smiles. Younger and more carefree. It's worth waiting for, worth all the grumpy glares in between when I get a peek at this version of him. This version that only *I* get. It feels so good to have something all my own.

I want Griffin to be all mine. *Mine.* All the scowls and growls and smiles. All the hickeys. A streak of possessiveness flashes through me as I let my mind wander to other women who have gotten those things from him in the past. I want to claw their eyes out. Few people have truly loved me in my life, and I'm so desperate to be told that. To *feel* that. If I get it, I'll never let it go.

"The part about you being a crazy person?"

Dick.

"Yeah. That part."

His fingers squeeze mine, and his length thickens beneath me as his gaze rakes over my body, the way I'm straddling him, before landing back on my face. He looks at me with such heart-wrenching softness that I almost turn to a puddle right on top of him.

"I must be a crazy person too… because I am head over heels for you, Wildflower. Please be patient with me."

In that moment, I realize I'd wait around forever for another look like that followed by another confession like that. My heart swells in my chest, and the bridge of my nose tingles as the thumping of his heart dances beneath our joined hands. It's like, as unbelievable as it may seem, I can feel how much he loves me.

Lord help me, I am so far gone for this man. I swore I wouldn't give anyone the power to take me down. But Griffin Sinclaire has been making a liar out of me since the first day I laid eyes on him.

CHAPTER 29

Griffin

I WAKE IN MY HOUSE ALONE. HIDDEN AWAY IN THE MOUNTAINS. I only have a few weeks left to work at Gold Rush Ranch, and I know we just spent a weekend up here prepping for winter, but after that trail ride with Nadia, I needed some space. To think. To figure out what the fuck I'm doing. Because it seems like everything I've been running from is about to hit me full force.

My lawyer has warned me it will.

Anxiety coils in my chest. Digging my grave and lying in it never really bothered me, but with Nadia around, I'm suddenly overwhelmed. I should have dealt with this years ago.

The urge to drive to the local diner and order a drink surges inside me. *That's* how I've washed my issues away for years. Well, before I started hiding from them.

But I'm turning over a new leaf. I'm thirty-five years old. It's about goddamn time I pulled myself up out of this pity party.

I'm lonely in my bed for the first time in years. It seems impossible after nearly a week, but I swear I'm still getting whiffs of Nadia's scent on my sheets. I fisted my cock last night thinking of her soft skin, her tempting moans, the way our souls wrap around each other at the same time as our bodies. And then I spent my night dreaming about her, all the things I want to give her, and the type of man I want to be for her.

I know connections like ours don't come along very often in life. And that fucking terrifies me.

So I'm starting with coffee rather than liquor. I throw my duvet back and push my messy hair out of my face. *I really need a haircut one of these days.* I pad across the rancher to the kitchen, where I make my shitty plain coffee in my shitty plain coffee maker.

My lips tug up as I watch it pour out of the machine. I'm pretty sure coffee will forever remind me of my mother now. My sweet mom, who has stood by and watched me spiral but always lends her support. That scolding last weekend was the most incensed I've seen her over the state of my life in a very long time. Not since she picked me up at Neighbor's Pub one night has she put her nose in my business. I'll never forget that night. You'd think being as drunk as I was it wouldn't register in my memory, but somehow it does. It's fuzzy and warped, but a turning point all the same.

"Griffin Sinclaire, get your ass up. Now." Her eyes flash with anger. My mom has never looked at me like this, and I recognize I've disappointed her so thoroughly that I've forced her to look at me with a level of contempt she never would have otherwise. Her head swivels, regarding everyone around us.

She's embarrassed.

"Yup." I wave a hand at the bartender whose name I currently can't remember. "I'll take one for the road."

He shakes his head at me, a delicate blend of annoyance and pity taking over his face. A look that truthfully just pisses me off. "I'm a paying c-c-c-customer!"

The thing about being drunk is that my stutter is worse, but it's also easily blamed on being intoxicated, which is less embarrassing in my twisted mind, where all that matters is how you're perceived and how good you are at your job and how much money you make. Playboy quarterback. Super Bowl champion. Highest-paying contract in the league.

That's what I was once upon a time. Now I'm a stuttering fucking mess.

The man polishes a glass and stares at me impassively. "A paying customer who has been cut off. Go home, Griffin."

Home. *A big empty house on a big empty farm. Turns out all that money and fame and notoriety doesn't buy you happiness. It buys you people who you think are friends until they realize your star is no longer rising. Then they jump ship.*

And your mom comes to pick your drunk ass up from a shitty small-town bar. Oh, how the mighty have fallen.

"Griff," my mom says, slinging her arm around my ribs, as though a woman her size could truly support me. "Let's go. Your dad is waiting in the car."

Great. Perfect. As if my humiliation wasn't complete for the evening already. I groan and let my eyes flutter shut heavily. The room spins around me, and I waver in my seat.

Fucking pathetic.

I force my eyes open and hold my unsteady hands up in surrender as I push to stand. "Okay, okay. It's past my bedt-t-t-ime anyway."

The bartender nods at me, his shoulders dropping, like the prospect of me leaving is a relief to him.

"I'm really sorry," I blurt out, sounding a little teary.

Fucking pathetic.

I'm not an angry drunk. I'm just a sad one. I save the anger for when I'm sober, for when I really have to face the turns my life has taken.

I try not to lean too hard on my mom as she leads me out of the bar. I stare down at her petite face as she does. The pink stain on her cheeks—she's really mortified. I've humiliated my mother in her hometown, the woman I love more than pretty much anyone else in the world.

Shame hits me again. How could I do this to her? How could I rise so high only to fall so far? One hit to the head and my life is in shambles. It's all so unfair.

She pushes me into the back seat of the waiting car, door already open and ready for me. My dad doesn't even turn to look at me. Instead, he stares at me through the rearview mirror. I wish he were angry. But even in my current state, I can tell he's disappointed.

Which is way fucking worse.

My mom gets in, and they drive. Neither of them spares me a glance or talks to me. They just let me stew in the back seat. I'm hammered enough that I feel like I'm watching it play out from above us all somehow, like I'm watching my own life happen to me. I look like a chastised little kid in the back seat of his parents' SUV.

They don't acknowledge me until we pull up to their house in town. Then they both turn back to me. And I'm not too drunk to recognize the gavel is about to come down. I may be a football star. I may have a pile of money sitting in my bank, but I'm not above recognizing when the jig is up.

"This shit ends now, son." My dad's voice is cool and level, but my mom's lip wobbles, and her eyes glitter with unshed tears.

"You've been dealt an unfair hand. But drowning your sorrows like this ends now. You have the resources to access all the help in the world, and starting tomorrow, that's what you're going to do. Rehab. Therapy. A fucking remote cabin in the mountains. I don't care. But drinking yourself to oblivion? The bartender calling your parents to pick you up as a thirty-year-old man? That ends now."

The car spins around me. I'm strong. I'm a fucking athlete. The idea of asking for that kind of help is just counterintuitive.

A cabin in the woods though. The image of it spins in my head, and my stomach lurches. Maybe I could do that. I think.

And then I hurl all over the back seat.

A knock on the door pulls me out of the memory. I shake my head, still cringing over that night. My parents left the car a mess and told me to clean it in the morning when I got up sober.

I bought them a new car instead.

And if that isn't a metaphor for how I've dealt with my life, then I don't know what is. No responsibility. And now, taking it back feels downright daunting.

The knocking sounds again, but this time it registers. No one knocks on my door up here. No one visits me up here. What the fuck is going on?

I eye the hunting rifle and length of rope I leave mounted by the front door, just in case, but decide against grabbing it. That's for cougars and wolves or if a horse gets loose, none of which knocks at the door. As I inch my way across the room, I peek out a window and recognize the pearl-white car in the driveway.

Nadia.

I pull the door open, and there she is. Looking a little ticked off. I can't help smiling down at her. I love the little ragey streak in her. Firecracker that she is.

"Hi, Wildflower."

"What are you smiling at?"

"You."

"Well, knock it off. I went to see you and couldn't find you. I called your phone, and you didn't answer." Her hands find her hips, like that might make her look tougher.

"I came back up here for the weekend." I stretch one arm up the doorframe and clamp my fingers there to keep from touching her.

"Didn't think to mention that to me?"

"Well, I didn't think—"

"Exactly." She points at me, cutting me off. "You didn't think. You didn't think that I might be worried about you? You didn't think that telling me you love me would change anything? Sometimes you make it really fucking hard to love you back."

I stare at her. "I know I do."

"You're a real dick sometimes," she huffs out, looking away. Wildflowers blow in the breeze over her right shoulder.

"You're not wrong."

"You can't just keep hiding up here when the going gets tough. There are people who care about you. Including me. I'm people."

Gut punch. My voice drops along with my eyes. "I know. I'm sorry."

"It scares me when you won't tell me things." *Double gut punch.* "I've spent the last several years of my life promising myself I would choose a simple life. That I didn't need fireworks and longing and that consuming sort of love so long as I had a safe, honest partner."

I just grunt. That sounds fucking terrible. It also sounds distinctly like not me.

"And then you waltzed in and fucked everything up."

I bark out a laugh and scrub my hands over my face. "Yeah. I'm especially talented at that, it would seem. Throwing a football and fucking everything up."

"Also eating pussy." She cracks a smile, always tossing something in to lighten the mood. *Where have you been all my life, Wildflower?*

"I'll add that to my résumé."

We stand on the front step, smiling at each other. But there's a tightness. Her smile doesn't touch her eyes, and I'm certain mine doesn't either.

"Want to come in? I'll make you a shitty coffee and tell you everything."

Here goes nothing crosses my mind as she nods.

But as I watch her pad into my house, her acid-wash jeans creasing beneath her perfect ass and waves of blond hair trailing down her back, I realize it's more like *There goes everything.*

Because deep down, I know she's not going to stick around now.

CHAPTER 30

Nadia

I WALK INSIDE GRIFFIN'S COZY HOME, TRYING TO FORCE MYSELF to look calmer than I feel. Because I feel distinctly *not* calm. But I'm putting my big-girl panties on and playing it cool.

If he can bring himself to sit down and tell me whatever has been eating away at him, then the least I can do is handle it maturely.

Unless he murdered somebody. Maybe there's a body on his land. Maybe he's secretly in the mafia? Maybe we're somehow related?

My mind runs rampant as I head toward the big kitchen table and plop into a chair. I take a really, really deep breath and stare down at my hands flattened on the tabletop. I've seen some shit, some terrible shit, and this can't be as bad as that.

I gaze up at Griffin, who follows slowly behind me. There's just no way. I know in my heart that Griffin is a *good* man. He's not my father. He is gentle and considerate, and whatever he has to tell me will be completely surmountable.

I need it to be.

I check him out while he pours us each a cup of coffee. The way his shoulders bunch beneath his T-shirt in the most mouth-watering way, the hem of that shirt resting along the curve of his ass, his hair all mussed like he spent the entire night running his hands through it.

"Here." He slides the coffee across the table and pulls up a chair opposite me before turning it around and sitting on it backward, the backrest pressing into his broad chest like some sort of shield.

His big brown eyes rest on my face, and he drinks me in. There's a finality in his eyes that I absolutely *hate*.

"Stop looking at me like that," I snap. "Out with it. You're going to give me gray hair with all this waiting."

His lips quirk up. "You'd still be hot with gray hair."

He's stalling.

"Griff." I give him a pleading look. I know he's trying to lighten the mood or whatever, but it's not working for me.

He stares down at his coffee cup as silence stretches between us. He trails the pad of a finger over the handle of his mug, delicately, thoughtfully, and the veins on the top part of his hand bulge and ripple, almost hypnotically. His touches are always hypnotic. With purpose—with meaning. Never sloppy or rushed.

I love his hands on me.

"I've never admitted this to anyone except my mom. Not even my dad. I c-c—" He groans, running a hand through his hair and tugging at the tips. My heart lurches as he stumbles over the word. *He's nervous.* "I c-c-couldn't stand the thought of how he might look at me if he knew. Him and my mom, their relationship? It's what I've always wanted. What I know they've wanted for me."

I nod and wrap my hands around the mug before me. Not wanting to interrupt him but hoping the heat from the coffee might seep into me and chase away the chill that's creeping through me.

"The day of my accident, I was drunk."

Drunk. I hate that word. I hate it anywhere near Griffin. Hate to think of him that way.

"I was partying a lot. T-t-too much money. God c-complex. Surrounded by yes-men. Bad mix." His throat bobs, and his cheeks go pink. He still won't meet my eye.

"Hey. Hey." I reach across the table and capture his hand, hating watching him struggle. "You got this."

He nods abruptly but doesn't meet my eyes. He knows what he'll find there. The muscles in his hands relax at my touch though, and I watch his shoulders drop just a little when they do.

"I was still drunk from the night before, I'm sure. We were on the road for a game in Vegas, and the temptation was just… a lot. My decision-making was consistently getting stupider. I often wonder, if I'd been sober, would I have made the play I did? Would I have seen the play coming? Would I have forgotten to strap my helmet? Everyone saw this wholesome superstar, the media's version of shiny, perfect quarterback Griffin Sinclaire. But that's not how things looked from where I sat."

God. I had no idea. He said he partied too hard. He referred to himself as an alcoholic. But I did not know he tormented himself like this, no idea he's hidden his struggle and buried himself in the shame quite this thoroughly.

Suddenly, a lot of things about his behavior make a lot more sense. I squeeze his big warm hand in mine, lending him whatever strength he needs.

"That night." He growls and glares up at the ceiling. I see his Adam's apple bob in his throat, and I just wish he would look at me. "That night I got married."

All the air leaves my lungs in a heavy whoosh. "You're married?"

He snorts. "On paper. She was some jersey chaser who came to Vegas to cheer the team on. I'd never met her before then, and I haven't seen her since."

My heart is pounding so loudly I almost can't hear his words. *Married. Married. Married.* That one word is like a cruel fucking echo in my mind. Not that I'd been thinking about getting married to Griffin, not yet. Maybe I absently mused about spending my life with him.

"You're married?"

He looks at me now, eyes drowning in pain as he wraps his other hand around mine. He looks fucking devastated. "Listen to me. I didn't even know it had happened until I got a letter from her lawyer over a month later with a copy of the license, pictures of us with a fucking Elvis officiant, and a demand for a monthly stipend. According to her, there was a tape, a threat to release it. I mean, literally it was out of a bad movie. Less funny when it's your own life."

My tongue darts out over my lips as I try to piece everything together that he's telling me, that little spark of rage I recognize so keenly growing in my chest. "Like a sex tape? She came for your money? She blackmailed you?"

"Nadia, I lost so much in that one trip. My career, my speech, my fame. Everything I used to define my value in life was swept away in a matter of seconds, and anger and sadness consumed me. And just this overwhelming sense of shame and guilt. Because there was no one to blame but me and the universe and just pure bad luck. And I wanted someone else to blame so badly. But all I could come back to was *me.* And I was stuck with my own company, with this deep sense of self-loathing. And that manila envelope from a woman whose name I didn't even recognize was a nail in the coffin. It's what tipped me over the edge because not only was my career gone—everything I'd ever worked for—but I'd spat in the face of my parents' values and everything they'd instilled in me. The last thing I cared about was money or that contract. I didn't want any of it coming out. My biggest goal at that point was to not entirely humiliate my parents. Or myself. That's all I cared about."

His other hand lands on top of mine so that we're practically clinging to each other over the top of the table. "Until you. I want a fresh start with you. I don't want to drag this shit around with me. I've been sending her divorce papers for years with no response, and it never bothered me. The money. The legal implications. I just didn't care. I had no reason to. It was easier to hide. But now… well, now, it really matters to me."

"You can't shoulder this all, Griffin. It's not fair." My eyes scour his face, his strong features, the fine lines from years of pain and suffering that he just doesn't deserve. Self-inflicted pain and suffering. "You don't deserve this kind of misery."

"You should hate me."

I tilt my head and stare at him. Hard. Trying to pierce through the haze of shame in his eyes. "No."

"You should." He takes a harsher tone with me, no doubt trying to push me away. I know because I recognize that spark in his eyes. The anger. *He looks as angry as I felt on the inside. Except I'm not angry anymore.*

I dig my nails into his skin, hard enough that he shifts in his chair. "I could never hate you, Griffin Sinclaire. I tried, and I failed. You hate yourself enough already. I hate that this happened to you. I hate that you didn't tell me sooner. I hate that you feel you can't tell anyone. But I do not hate *you*."

"I'm sorry." His thick lashes flutter down, pushing away the moisture building there. My entire body aches with the need to wrap him in my arms and show him this changes nothing for me, but something holds me back.

It doesn't change how I feel about him. That much is true. My heart pounds to the same beat as his. That's why it hurts like it does right now. But there's an inkling of my survival instinct creeping in, words from my therapist, words from my journal, thoughts of desperately not wanting to become my mother.

Attached to an unhappy man, who, in turn, makes everyone around him unhappy. Griffin is *not* my father, but sometimes I worry that I'm my mother.

"I'm so fucking sorry. I tried so hard to stay away from you, to keep you away from me. And I failed at that too."

I smile sadly, pulsing my fingers on his. "I'm persistent, Griffin. You never stood a chance."

He smiles back, but it's forced. "She's apparently finally going to sign the papers, my lawyer told me last night. Then the divorce would just need to process."

"Did you pay her off?"

"No. I decided I didn't care if she wanted to run her mouth about it anymore."

I nod in approval. "Good. I'm thrilled for you."

He laughs, but it's angry. "You have no business being this mature about my mess, Nadia."

"In my head, I'm not being very mature. In my head, I really hate that bitch. It's more like *Good riddance, you money grubbing whore. Come around, and I'll kick you in the box.*"

He stares back at me, shaking his head, lips pulling up a fraction. "You're vicious, Wildflower."

"Is there really a video? Did you sleep with her?" I blurt it out before I can even stop myself. I guess my maturity knows some bounds after all. Obviously, he slept with the woman.

Griffin grimaces, looking physically uncomfortable. "I don't know. I've never spoken directly to her, and I don't remember that night at all."

A pained sound escapes me as I lean back, untangling my hands from his. The air is cold against my skin, and what I really want to do is crawl across the table and curl up in his arms. My mind is telling me to sit back and take some space though.

"What will you do if she releases it?"

His eyes slam shut, and he sucks in a raspy breath. "Pray you never see it."

Heaviness lodges in my throat, and my stomach drops. I feel like I might be sick, so I promptly change the subject, not wanting to think about seeing him with someone else or having the world see him so exposed.

"Did you ever go to rehab?"

His hands lay limp on the table before him, and he looks completely flayed open. I fucking hate it. I hate seeing him hurt. Because I recognize it so perfectly. The pain, the anger, the sadness—it was me a few years ago. Before I worked on myself.

"No."

"Therapy?"

"No." He winces, like he knows those aren't suitable answers.

I pick up my coffee cup and sip it, but I don't taste it. I turn this all over in my head. His story. His sadness. His growth.

Leave it to me to want someone normal and happy but to end up head over heels for one of the most complicated men in the world.

"Why didn't you tell me?"

He groans. "Old habits die hard. And I've buried this secret for a very long time. I'm so embarrassed. I wanted to be a normal, happy person for you, and I thought I could just…" He drops his head into his hands before speaking straight into his palms. "I don't know. Get this all dealt with and then tell you and I'd be the fresh slate you deserve. It sounds really dumb now that I say it out loud."

I chuckle. It does sound dumb. Well-meaning but dumb. Dumb and impossible. "We're not normal, happy people, Griffin. Remember?"

He leans back with a heavy, ragged sigh, letting his arms go limp at his sides in defeat. "Yeah. I know."

Does he?

"I need to go for a walk." A panicked expression crosses his face as I push the chair away to stand. "I'm not leaving. I'm not quitting. I just need some processing time."

Griffin nods, schooling his face back into that unaffected look as his lips thin and press together. He's totally freaking out. And as I walk out that front door, emotions warring inside me, I realize we're both faking.

Because I'm freaking out too. School. Family. Life goals. I see them all slipping away right before my eyes.

I'm in love with Griffin Sinclaire, but I refuse to give up everything I've wanted in life just to hear him say he loves me back.

CHAPTER 31

Griffin

I CAN'T MOVE. UNABLE TO GET UP FROM WHERE SHE LEFT ME here at the table, I spin the mug between my hands. I can't even enjoy my coffee.

Nothing is as good without her around. The air isn't as soft. My heart doesn't race, and I don't look forward to catching sight of her. Just a flash of her blond hair or the sound of her laugh can turn my entire day around.

Having Nadia in my orbit for the past months has made me realize I was living before, but I wasn't *alive*. I was existing. Her presence resuscitated me, and now I've overwhelmed her with the weight of my baggage.

I take a sip of my coffee as I stare at her still-full cup. It's lukewarm and really tastes bad. This cup of coffee and I have more in common than I care to admit.

Her car door slams, and the sound makes me flinch. *She's leaving. And I can't fucking blame her.* She's a smart woman, and smart women run for the hills when they stumble across a man like me.

But the sound of her car engine revving never comes. I'm met with silence and the grinding sound of my cup spinning on the table. It grates on me. I'm annoying myself.

I'm also torturing myself by not getting up to see what she's doing. Finally, I give in, abandoning my chair, placing the cups in the sink, and striding through the living room to the front window. Her car is still parked outside. A deep sigh of relief rushes out of me as I move to the side window.

The one facing the field of flowers.

She's sitting in the very middle of it, head down, furiously scribbling in her journal. I wish again that I could take a photo of her sitting out there, so immersed in doing what she knows she needs for herself.

The wildflower I can't get rid of no matter what I try.

She glances up, and even though she's far away, I swear we lock eyes. She bites her lip, and I stumble back, suddenly feeling like I'm intruding on a moment she needs to herself. So I sit on the couch and wait.

I brace my elbows on my knees, drop my head into my hands, and wait. I run through every scenario in my head, including losing her, which makes me feel physically ill. I didn't make it through as much as I have to find the one and then lose her.

I just didn't. That's a fate I refuse to accept.

I'm not sure how long I sit here spiraling before I finally hear footsteps on the front porch. My heart beats harder, and I go still when the front door opens. She leans against the jamb and stares at me. I can't tell what's going on in her head right now. Her face is carefully blank.

"I think I'm going to head back home. I need to get ready for school."

My stomach flips. She's running from me, and I can't blame her one bit.

"Okay." I nod and let my hands fall limp between my legs. Defeated.

Her eyes flare, and she bristles, arms folding beneath her breasts, journal in hand. "Fuck you."

I sit up taller, pressing my hands into the couch on either side of me. "Pardon?"

"I said *fuck you.*" She really enunciates it this time.

My molars grind against each other. "I'm sorry. I really am. I tried to spare us both from this."

She rolls her eyes, looking her age. Looking like a total brat. "Boys are dumb, you know? I don't give a flying fuck about your meaningless marriage. Do I irrationally hate a woman I've never met? Yes. Could I get sick just thinking about you with someone else? A big fat yes. Am I pissed off you didn't tell me? Yeah, *Griffy*, I am. But mostly I'm pissed off you're too big of a pussy to fight for me."

I glower at her, hating how right she is.

"Too scared of my brother? Too scared of hurting me? Too scared to work on yourself so that you can be worthy of something good? Fuck you for being such a coward. You said I was *yours,* and now you're going to sit there and let me walk out?" She scoffs. "Yeah. Pardon my French but… fuck. You."

I go deathly still, letting the truth of what she just said hammer me. The competitor in me is wide fucking awake now. The buried athlete? The one who works his ass off to get what he wants? To defy the odds? To win the games? She just tapped that guy on the shoulder.

No.

Kicked him in the balls.

Something I should have done a long time ago. A flare of frustration burns in my chest as I stand and close the distance between us with a few long strides. One hand shoots out to wrap around the back of her neck while the other rests above her on the doorframe, caging her in. "You *are* mine."

Nadia's eyes widen with how quickly I moved, but her lips tip up. Like she's amused by pissing me off.

She walks her fingers up my heaving chest. Beauty and the Beast facing off in a remote mountain cabin. "There you are. Been wondering when you were going to man up enough to take what you want."

My breathing is slightly labored as I lean down to whisper in her ear. "Are you trying to piss me off?" I watch the gooseflesh race down her arms.

"No." Her voice comes out breathy, and I see her nipples pebbling beneath her shirt. "I'm trying to wake you the fuck up."

"Mission accomplished, Wildflower."

Her chin juts out in challenge, not the least bit intimidated by me. She never has been. I wouldn't want her to be. "Good."

"Get your ass back to that table so we can talk." I gesture over my shoulder toward the kitchen.

"Make me." Her eyes flash, irises shifting earth tones, like living flames. "I'm not much in the mood for talking, *Griffy*. I'd rather you bend me over tha—"

With one arm, I reach down and heft her over my shoulder, quirking a smile at her delighted squeal. Should have known she wanted to work out the tension this way. I swat her ass firmly with my free hand before reaching for the rope hanging beside the door.

"What did I tell you about the next time you called me Griffy, Wildflower?"

She squirms as I storm across the house before depositing her on the chunky wooden farm table and pushing myself to stand between her spread thighs. I toss the rope down beside her, not missing the way her tongue darts out across her lips as her eyes flit to it.

"I'm having a tough time remembering." She taps a finger over her lips. "It was so long ago." *Bullshit.* She's been trying to goad me since the second she stepped foot on my front porch.

"We should really talk. And I'll tie you to a chair if you try to run off again." My gaze bounces back and forth between her eyes, looking for a sign that she's uncertain or confused. But all I find is pure heat and longing.

"Later." She tosses the floral-print journal onto the floor before reaching down to pull her shirt over her head, letting it fall to my feet. "Right now, I want you inside me. I want to feel like I'm yours and you're mine. Not anyone else's. I need that."

There's hurt written in her words. And all I want to do is erase it. If this is how she wants me to do it, I'm hardly going to deny her. Especially not with the sight of her soft breasts straining against the pale-pink cups of her lace bra. There's no padding, and the translucent effect has my cock straining against my jeans instantly. Her dusty-pink nipples tease me.

I reach out and twist one between my thumb and forefinger, watching her full lips pop open with a surprised gasp.

"You jealous, Wildflower?"

Her jaw pops as she stares up at me, feral and turned on. The prettiest blush stains her bronzed skin. "Yes," she grinds out, like it physically pains her to admit it.

"Don't be. You're all I want." My eyes race over her skin, watching her heartbeat jump in her neck and the blush creep down her chest. "You're all I think about." I lean over her, hands against the tabletop, and lick that pulse point. "You're all I dream about." She makes a mewling noise, and I clamp my teeth into her neck hard enough to leave a mark. *My girl likes that.* "You're all *mine*. You're it for me." I pull back to take her in, to make sure she hears me clearly. "Now lose the fucking pants. I want you naked and begging for it."

She stands instantly, chest pressing against mine as she shucks off her jeans. I groan when I catch sight of the matching lace panties.

This girl is going to be the fucking death of me.

She moves to turn away from me and bend herself over the table, but as much as I love fucking her from behind, I want to see her face today. "Nuh-uh." My hands wrap around her waist as I spin her back toward me and lift her onto the edge. One palm to the center of her chest, I press her down flat across the width of the table, reveling in the quiet gasp the cool surface against her back elicits from her pretty mouth. She hits me with a hungry look, a flash of nerves in her eyes. I know she's not quick to open up. Shit, neither am I. But if we're going to make a go of this, then we're both going to have to try. "Like this, so I can see your face when I fill you up."

I press a thumb against her clit through the thin lace and watch her body buck beneath me.

"Fuck," she breathes out, fingers trying to dig into the wood beneath her.

"Are you wet for me, Nadia?" I ask as I stare down at the beautiful body laid out across my table. *Right where she belongs.*

"Yes," she whispers as she looks up at me through heavy-lidded eyes.

I already knew the answer. I can feel her wetness through the triangle of lace that's doing a very poor job of covering her up.

"I'm going to tie your wrists. Would you like that?"

Her top teeth sink into her lower lip. "Yes."

With one more press to her clit, I move away to the opposite side of the table, grabbing the rope as I go. She moves her wrists up above her head, and I quickly wind the rope around them before tying it to the ladder-back chair at the opposite side of the table. I give the rope a tug and smirk when it holds fast. You don't grow up on a ranch and not learn how to tie a good knot.

I stride slowly back to the other side of the table, watching her chest rise and fall with the speed of her panting. Her nipples poke through the lace as she squeezes her thighs together, clearly trying to ease the ache between them. I move to stand close, brushing against her knees where they dangle over the edge.

"Do you trust me?" My voice drops an octave as I ask the question. This is important to me. I want her to trust me.

"Yes," she breathes with perfect sincerity.

I swallow the lump in my throat before reaching up and hooking my fingers into the waist of her panties, sliding them down over her shapely hips and firm thighs, leaning in to press a kiss to her knee as I drop them on the floor with the rest of her discarded clothes.

"I can't even decide what I want to do to you first," I muse, trailing a finger up her leg, dipping into the hollow beneath her hip. Teasing her.

"Fuck me." Her voice is edged with desperation as she squirms against the rope, testing its fastness. "Please. Just put me out of my misery and fuck me. I want you so bad. I love it and hate it all at once."

I can't help but smirk, feeling more like my old self by the minute. I know *exactly* what she means. Because I feel it too.

"No chance, Wildflower." I kiss my way back up her body. Her pulse pounds beneath my lips when I get to her throat, and I revel in how vulnerable she is for me right now. "I'm not going to fuck you. I'm going to savor you. I'm going to make you fall apart for me."

"You already have," she whispers. There's a hint of sadness in her voice. Like she's figured out something I haven't.

"Not even close," I rasp, reaching down to cup her sex and pressing the heel of my hand against her throbbing clit. She squirms and moans, the light sounds of her panting seeping in around the sound of blood rushing in my ears.

When we're together, it's like nothing else exists. The world dissolves around us. Our breaths sync—our hearts pump in perfect unison.

Dragging my lips back down her torso, I cup her breasts, tugging gently at her nipples. Lick the small dip between her hips and stomach. Watch her buck beneath me and hear the rattle of the chair as she tugs helplessly at the rope.

I don't pay her pussy any attention, even though I can tell she's shimmying toward me, wishing I would. "Agony, wanting something you can't have, isn't it?" I ask as I ghost my hands over the tops of her thighs.

"Touch me."

"No." I stand up tall with a smirk, crossing my arms over my chest.

"Please touch me, or..." She's begging now.

"Or what?"

"Or I'm going to freak out." Her voice holds a desperate edge to it now. "This is torture." Her fingers clench and release over her head.

"You are the very best kind of torture, Nadia. My special brand of hell. But I want you so badly I don't even mind the flames."

Her tongue darts out as she regards me. Chest heaving. Clearly struck speechless by my confession.

I take a step back, gaze raking over her. "Now spread your legs for me."

A shiver races through her, and she obeys, slender thighs parting on a quiet whimper.

My dick hurts, it's so hard. "Do you have any idea how pretty you look like this? I've never been harder than I am right now with you trussed up and spread out on my dining room table like a fucking five-course meal."

She giggles, sounding a little unhinged. "Only five?"

I step closer, and her body trembles. Running a hand over her inner thigh, I press one finger into her wet heat, watching it disappear inside her. I groan. She is too fucking much.

When I glide it out, her head flops from side to side. Nadia isn't a patient woman. I know the anticipation is killing her as much as it's killing me, but that's what our relationship is—brilliant, cruel, torturous anticipation.

Her eyes flare with heat when I slide that finger into my mouth, sucking on it before pulling it out with a lewd popping sound, never dropping her gaze. "You're right, five courses won't be nearly enough."

"Griffin. Hurry up, and f—"

I stop her right there as I drop to my knees before her spread legs. "If you call this *fucking* one more time, I'm going to flip you over and redden your perfect ass." My fingers dig into her thighs as I prop them over my shoulders.

"I'm scared to call it more. The timing feels all wrong," she confesses, and my heart constricts.

"Then I'll wait for the right time." I hold her gaze for a beat, wishing I could force her to understand how all in I am on her. And then I drop my mouth between her legs and get to work on showing her instead.

Her thighs shake as they wrap around my head, squeezing harder the closer I push her to orgasm. Every lick, every kiss, drives her toward the edge. Sometimes I press hard; then I'll pull back and slow my licks, opting for a featherlight touch that makes her snarl at me in frustration.

I just smile and carry on, driving my girl wild.

There's something about this moment that feels like a beginning and an ending all at once. Like everything is on the table and neither of us is sure what it all means. But I think we both know this thing between us is monumental.

When I drive two fingers into her, she screams my name and thrashes on the table. "Griffin! I'm going to come. Please don't stop!"

Fucking right, you are is what I want to say, but she said *don't stop*. And I don't intend to. I push her harder until her entire body goes rigid around mine, legs clamping down and pussy pulsing in my mouth.

It's fucking heaven.

When she finally goes soft, I stand and shuck my clothes off, watching her eyelids flutter as she struggles to catch her breath.

She hasn't even opened her eyes when I run the crown of my aching cock through her seam.

"Do you want my cock, Wildflower?" My voice rumbles through the quiet room as our eyes finally meet. She takes my breath away. Warm eyes. Rosy cheeks. Sated look on her face.

This is how she looks in my dreams. How she should look every day.

"I want..." Her throat works as she falls silent. Which is very unlike her. I figured she'd beg for cock like the adorable little vixen she is, but she finishes by saying, "I want *you*. All of you."

And fuck me, that is so much more than I banked on. So much more than I deserve.

I slide into her with one firm thrust as I lean down over her body and claim her mouth, swallowing her whimpers and feeling the press of her lace bra and swollen breasts against my bare chest as her tight sheath milks my length.

"It's not enough. More," she murmurs against my lips, and I know she's right. I want her closer. I want even more from her. More than she can reasonably give.

Reaching up, I tug the rope off and sigh in relief when her arms wrap around me, holding me close. Her legs clamp around my waist, and my hips rock into her violently. The table makes a dull screeching sound with every hard thrust that drags it across the floor.

"I want this so badly," she whispers, tangling her hands in my hair. We kiss each other frantically. Cheeks, chins, ears, throats—we cover each other in kisses as I pound into her with reckless abandon. Her back arches to meet every thrust.

"Me too, Wildflower. Me too."

I push away the little voice in the back of my head that's popped up to remind me that when I want something badly, it doesn't work out.

I wanted a long celebrated career. I wanted a marriage like my parents have.

Wanting this with Nadia is the kiss of death.

But I make love to her all day long anyway.

And later, while she sleeps, I pick up her journal and cross that off her to-do list for her.

CHAPTER 32

Nadia

The closer I get to Ruby Creek, the heavier the sense of dread in the pit of my stomach. Up in the mountains, everything feels right—just the two of us in a perfect little bubble having mind-blowing, toe-curling sex.

But down in the valley, reality sets in. I watch the bumper of Griffin's truck in front of me as I follow him back to the ranch. Back to complications.

While we were holed up in his house, it felt like nothing could touch us. We spent the entire day and night tangled up together, only stopping to eat or bathe, both of which turned into more sex. We barely talked; we literally just disappeared into each other's bodies. Hid there, where it was safe and felt good. Like we both knew if we came up for air, certain realities would come crashing back in.

School. Baggage. Divorce. Opinions. Sex tapes. Judgment.

It doesn't bother me he's fourteen years older than me, but I'm not stupid enough to think other people might not have opinions about our age gap. Not that they matter. I've never much cared what other people think of me, but the thought of anyone making Griffin out to be something he's not makes me see red.

And beneath all the anger is sadness. I need to prove to myself I can do all the things I've ever wanted to accomplish. And what's more is that Griffin does too.

We turn onto the winding, tree-lined driveway leading to the A-frame guesthouse at Gold Rush Ranch, but as I come around the last bend, I'm not met with an empty parking lot.

Quite the opposite, in fact.

My brother is here, leaned up against the front door, looking really pissed off. There's a red Audi parked beside his gray Jeep, and when Griffin pulls up and hops out of his truck, another person steps out of the crimson car.

Perfectly straight bottle-blond hair swishes around her waist as her toned, tanned limbs fold out of the vehicle. She turns a practiced smile on Griffin, and my heart stutters, slowly puttering out in my chest until it feels like it's going to stop altogether.

Stefan is watching her like a hawk until his gaze snags on me. His head tilts in question, but I only spare him a glance before I stare back at Griffin as he approaches the real-life Barbie doll in skinny jeans and stilettos. She strides toward him like she owns the fucking place.

I don't even need to get out of my car to know who she is. I don't even have to meet her to hate her. It doesn't matter that Griffin spent the last day worshipping my body and professing his love for me. It doesn't matter that he doesn't know her or want her.

All that washes away as I watch his *wife* lay a hand on his forearm. The one crossed over top of the other as he scowls down at her. The arms that held me tight all night long.

That forearm is *mine,* and seeing her drag a French-manicured nail over it like she has a right has me shoving my door open and storming up the driveway. I can't hear what she's saying, and I don't even care. She just needs to keep her fucking hands to herself, or I will seriously kick her in the box.

"Don't fucking touch me." Griffin's voice cuts like a hot knife through butter. Quick and absolute.

She rolls her eyes and cocks a hip. "Who's this?" She nods her head toward me, eyes sparkling with venom.

The feeling is mutual.

"That's my sister." Stefan shoves past her, eating up the ground to stand beside me.

"Adorable." She turns back to Griffin with a pout on her frosty-pink lips. She's overdone, but you'd have to be an idiot to not notice how stupidly fucking hot she is. Which is honestly just worse. I take an inventory of my current appearance, feeling self-conscious in a way I never have before in my torn acid-wash jeans, flip-flops, and concert tee.

I feel childish and messy standing next to this woman. And I despise myself for letting her make me feel this way without even trying. She doesn't deserve it after what she's done to Griffin.

She reaches out to touch him again, but he steps away, regarding her like he'd destroy her on the spot if he weren't such a gentleman. "Let's talk inside," she urges him.

"No."

"Without an audience?" His gaze follows hers to where Stefan and I are standing, and I'm intensely grateful that my big brother is here. He's like a shield against what's happening in front of me. He's always protected me in his own way, and right now is no different.

"You c—" Griffin reaches his hands up and squeezes the brim of his worn baseball cap down on either side. I know he was about to stumble over that word, which means he's stressed. And I hate that for him.

I hate *her* for him.

"Say what you need," he simplifies.

"Yeah. I'd love to hear why you were skulking around his house and looking through windows." Stefan's voice is all bite, his stance foreboding. He is protective with a capital *P.* Something that has only become more pronounced since he became a father.

She sighs and lifts the manila envelope in her hand. "I told my lawyer I'd sign, but this version doesn't include any financial compensation. Your lawyer won't budge, so I figured I'd track you down and talk some sense into you."

A deep rumble sounds from Griffin's chest. He's a gentleman, but the threat is clear, and he doesn't like it.

"We're estranged. We never had a relationship. There's no basis for it. I only paid you so you'd go away."

The woman bristles and has enough sense to look a little embarrassed in front of us. "Well, if you want to keep your problem under wraps in the press, then you'll be adding to this." She slaps the envelope against his chest with a flourish. "It would be a shame for that video to see the light of day. Not that I'd mind showing that off. We look good together. Or we did before this beard happened." She waves a hand over him, and I instantly want to break it. I *love* his beard. "And we really had a spectacular time, didn't we?"

Then the bitch has the gall to wink at him.

"This has gone on for t-t-t-too long. It ends now." My heart twists, and I am so damn proud of him for not giving up on the exact words he wanted to use.

"T-t-t-too bad," she mocks, with a practiced smile that makes my skin crawl.

And I see red. "Leave. Now. You're trespassing." I point at her car, stepping toward her, hand shaking with rage.

She just rolls her eyes, and I suddenly want to get my gun out of my car and do a little target practice on her plastic nails. I've always promised myself that I'd never resort to violence after what I grew up with. But I am seriously considering it right now. It's the glare my brother gives me that holds me back, like he knows I could probably kill a bitch.

"Not until I get what I came for."

"Griffin, don't you dare give her a single thing," I blurt out, even though it's none of my business. He'll never get out from under the shame of his past if he keeps burying it. I don't want that for him. I want a fresh start for him—for us. Video be damned.

Plus, she doesn't deserve shit from him.

He looks over at me, his harsh gaze softening as I stare back at him. A look specially reserved for me. And when our eyes meet like this, I know it doesn't matter if I'm standing here wearing scrubby clothes with wild, freshly fucked hair. What's between us isn't skin-deep. It's soul-deep. We understand each other in a way that no one else can.

Based on the way he's looking at me right now, he feels the same.

He steps away again, giving her the full force of his glare, letting the envelope flop down onto the packed gravel at their feet.

His eyes swivel back to me as he sucks in a deep breath. "See you in court."

We share a small smile as she storms back to her car, head held high, like she didn't just try to blackmail a man into giving her money by exploiting the lowest point of his life.

"I hate her with a fiery, fiery passion," I grit out, right as she revs her engine and blows past Stefan and me, just a little too close for comfort. I watch her brake lights glow as she rounds the bend and speeds away.

Hopefully for good. But I think I know better.

"Someone care to tell me what's going on here?"

I swivel back to face the two men, eyes widening when my brother's attention turns on me, an accusatory glint in his green eyes.

When neither of us jumps to explain, he turns his back on me, focusing his attention on his best friend. "Because I can't think of a single good reason why my best friend would be spending his days off with my little sister."

"Frankly, Stefan, that's not your business." He stiffens at my words.

"It is when everyone has been trying to get a hold of you to tell you that Billie had her babies." He turns on me, and I finally recognize how distraught he is. "No one knew where you were! I've been going crazy trying to find you."

Fuck. Now I feel like a dick. "I'm sorry." I roll my lips together. "There's no reception up at the mountain house, and my phone is dead. Is Billie okay?"

"Yes. Everyone is healthy and happy. But going back to the mountain house. Can we elaborate on why you were up there at all?"

I blink, not ready to give a name to what we were doing up there. Especially not in the wake of the whole scene here.

"Griff?" my brother asks, with a note of pleading in his voice.

Griffin shrugs. "I'm not going to speak for Nadia."

Stefan runs a hand through his hair like we just announced the worst news of his life. "Seriously? She's fourteen years younger than you."

Griffin's eyes flit to mine again. The look he gives me is like he's about to throw caution to the wind, jump off a fucking cliff. And he doesn't disappoint when he says, "Yeah. Well. I'm in love with her anyway."

CHAPTER 33

Griffin

My best, and possibly only, friend stares back at me with pure shock written all over his face. I always knew I was going to tell him. I just didn't imagine it happening like this.

"You're in love with my sister." He says the words like it's a new language to him, confusion etching every syllable.

I just offer him a stern nod.

"Stef," Nadia cuts in.

He turns his gaze on her. "Nadia, please don't interrupt. This is between Griff and—"

Rage flares in her eyes, and her pointer finger shoots up at her brother. "Don't you dare finish that sentence, Stefan Dalca. Don't you fucking *dare.* This is between me and Griffin. You? You are a nonfactor. You think you get to hightail it out of my life the first chance you get and then waltz back in and gatekeep my relationships? My body? Well, have I got news for you."

Stefan visibly pales, clearly still haunted by their past.

"I'm not sticking around for this pissing contest. I'm too angry with both of you right now." Her body shakes with the energy coursing through her, and I realize what a tenuous hold we had on our relationship. I suspect that seeing Tonya waltzing around like she's royalty broke whatever weak agreement we came to last night. I'm married, and that debacle clearly will not get better before it gets worse.

Nadia marches away, and neither of us makes a move to stop her. She turns around when she gets to her vehicle, gripping the top of her door until her knuckles go white. "You two Neanderthals are best friends. Don't be stupid about this. I'll see you both at family dinner tonight."

With a disappointed shake of her head, she gets into her car, pulls a three-point turn, and burns out of the driveway. Leaving us both standing in a cloud of dust, staring at each other a little sheepishly.

Stefan breaks the ice. "I think my sister just gave us both a spanking at the same time."

"She's a force to be reckoned with," I agree. Because she is. She takes no shit, not from anyone.

The two of us stare at each other, awkward silence swelling between us. "Listen, I should have told you."

Stefan shakes his head and scrubs a hand over his face. "No. She's right. It's none of my business in the grand scheme of things. I'm just shocked. Surprised. Mira mentioned she could see there was a spark between the two of you, and I laughed it off. I couldn't see it, but maybe I just wasn't looking."

I suck in a deep breath. "We actually met before I knew she was your sister. Two years ago, at Neighbor's."

"Well, shit." He cups his hands behind his neck. "I had no idea."

"Yeah." It's all I can think to say because Nadia *is* right. We don't owe him an explanation or any details. Most of this is between her and me.

"Well… I like you a lot better than that Tommy guy."

"I fucking hate that kid," I growl back. Just the mention of his name makes my jealousy levels spike.

Stefan chuckles, still regarding me like I've grown a second head or something. Like he can't quite reconcile the whole thing. And really, who can blame him? It's out of left field for someone who didn't know.

"Listen. All I want for Nadia is the best. Love. Happiness. For every single one of her dreams to come true. We have a unique relationship, and I know I've made mistakes where she's concerned, but I don't want to make any now. If she loves you and you love her? If you make her happy and you can make all her dreams come true, well, I already love you like a brother, Griffin. It wouldn't be hard to adjust to having you around. I want nothing but the best for both of you."

"Fuck, Stefan." I wasn't prepared for how this conversation would be.

"But… Griffin…" He hits me with a penetrating stare. There's no cruelty or challenge in his expression, just pure honesty. "If you think any of this shit"—he waves a hand behind himself at where Tonya stood and proclaimed she was going to drag me through the mud—"is going to blow back on her, then that's something you need to think about. I know you have your demons, and I know one of the most valuable things about our friendship is that we never pick on each other about those things. But my sister? She needs no more demons."

What he says rings true. It's painful to hear, but he's not wrong. I struggle to find any words to respond. Words aren't my strong suit at the best of times, and right here in this moment is not the best of times.

So I just meet his thoughtful stare with a patient look of my own. A stony nod is all it takes for him to know I understand what he's saying.

He claps me on the shoulder and strides away to his Jeep, peeling out of the driveway, leaving me standing alone.

Well, not alone. With my demons.

CHAPTER 34

Nadia

I'm hiding out in Cowboy's stall at Cascade Acres. He's all tucked in tight for the evening. The swelling in his leg is all but gone. I've brushed him to a perfect shine, given him a massage, done the stretches with him that Griffin showed me, oiled his hooves, kissed his soft nose, and held his head as he snuggled up against me in a bid for even more cookies than I already spoiled him with.

I turn in toward him, nuzzling against his shoulder and wrapping my arms around his neck. He's like the biggest, warmest, most comforting teddy bear. I told him everything that happened today as I worked on him. He sighed and let his long lashes fall shut. No judgment, no opinions, just a nuzzle against my pockets because he knows I am the ultimate bearer of treats.

Who knew this horse would become the friend and confidant I've never had? I mean, I've always liked the horses, but Cowboy is different. We're kindred. Both discarded, both underestimated, both with so much potential and more to do.

My plan is to give him the next few months off while I start school and have Billie do some work with him. I'll only be an hour down the road, but I know my days will be full with my courses and studying. I'll still take a lesson every weekend. But hopefully by the time my spring semester wraps up, those riding lessons will be on Cowboy.

Maybe we'll jump; maybe we'll spend our lives doing trail rides. I don't really know. I just know he and I are in it for the long haul. I'll follow his lead.

Peeking down at my watch, I realize that I'm officially late. I've cooled off since earlier, but I'm still dreading facing everyone. After one more kiss pressed to my horse's dark-mahogany neck, I leave the stall, locking it behind me and trudging up the sloped driveway, straight to the chaos that is Sunday dinner.

Except tonight, I'll be facing both men I spent the afternoon avoiding.

My mind flashes back to when Griffin told my brother he's in love with me. My heart flutters at the memory, but my stomach drops like I'm being ripped in opposite directions. I want to explore whatever this is with Griffin. I want to be able to tell him I love him back. But I know—*I know*—the timing isn't right.

I can still see the way my brother gaped at him right as my jaw fell open. It was one thing for him to whisper it against my skin and another entirely for him to profess it to my brother in such plain terms.

Truthfully, it's huge. Epic. But I still have this niggling feeling that it isn't quite right. Like we deserve a cleaner start than this. Like we both still have a metric ton of shit to work out and maybe neither of us should bring that into a new relationship. Like we were damned if we did and damned if we didn't.

Seeing that beautiful, conniving woman threatening him was living, breathing proof of that.

But my days of running away from my problems are over. I can face this because I know I'm strong. I know I'm capable. Or at least that's what I keep telling myself.

I reach out to grab the handle, but the front door is jerked open before I can apply any pressure. Mira stands in the entryway, smirking at me. "I was just coming to look for you."

I give her a closed-mouth smile. "Here I am. You found me."

She snorts. "It's fucking awkward in there. Come join the fun."

I groan and tip my head back as she wraps an arm around my shoulders and tugs me into the house with her, enjoying this way too much.

"Come on." She squeezes me. "It won't be so bad. Everyone here *loves* you."

My chin dips to my chest, and I try not to laugh at the ridiculousness of the way she emphasized that word. "Good god, does Stef tell you everything?"

She chuckles, eyes twinkling with amusement. "Literally everything. You know he's a stickler for honesty."

I roll my eyes but follow her into the open kitchen and out onto the back deck where my brother is barbecuing. Violet and Cole's two girls are frolicking in the yard with Silas, peering into a mesh cage while squealing happily about the bugs they've captured in there. Cole and Violet are sitting beside each other, chairs pressed impossibly close. "Why don't you just crawl into his lap, Vi?" I joke as I step through the sliding doors.

Violet's cheeks flush, but Cole hits me with a wolfish grin. "Great idea," he says as he picks up his petite wife and drags her onto his lap, completely ignoring her weak protests and surprised squeal.

They're fucking adorable.

My eyes snag on Griffin, sitting at the head of the table spinning a can of soda water between his hands, watching me. But his expression isn't a happy one.

I offer him a shy smile. He winks back from beneath the brim of his hat, and I realize that it's a tell for how he's feeling. On days he's feeling confident and like he could take on the world, he's got his hair slicked back, looking like a hot young bearded Keanu Reeves. But when he wants to hide from reality, that dirty old cap gets pulled out, the brim shadowing his eyes like it did the first night we collided.

"Hey, Stef," I call to his back. "Smells amazing."

"Hey." His reply is stiff.

Super fucking awkward.

"That's my nana's tandoori chicken recipe!" Mira calls from the kitchen.

"Nice!" I call back, genuinely excited to try it out. Because everything her nana makes is incredible. "How's Billie?" I ask as I flop down in a chair at the wrought-iron table. Mira slides me a soda water. Pineapple. My favorite. I can pretend I'm on a tropical vacation.

"She's good. Babies are good. Long labor that ended in a C-section. They're resting up at the hospital in Garnet Ridge for now. Hank and Trixie are there with them."

I smile as I sip the bubbly liquid. This little family out at Gold Rush Ranch is really something to behold. My heart squeezes at the thought of Billie showing up on Hank's front step, looking for a job as a runaway teenager. And now she's here, living her happily ever after with her hot husband on her beautiful farm, with Hank acting as the father she never had.

My eyes prickle at the beauty of it.

"Did you go see her?" I ask.

Violet pipes up. "Not yet. Giving them some space."

Cole cuts in to add, "I called to congratulate them, and all they did was bicker about what names they were going to pick and whether Vaughn was going to trade in his 'bitch baby' sports car for a safer option." He huffs out a laugh and rolls his eyes. "Like they haven't had nine months to figure these things out."

Everyone chuckles, and even my brother's shoulders shake.

Mira leans back with a sigh, staring up at the sky. "I think I'd be worried about those two if they *weren't* at each other's throats. It's like foreplay for them."

Cole groans and hides his face in Violet's icy-blond hair. "Pass."

Violet giggles and changes the subject. "How's Cowboy, Nadia? I peeked at him yesterday. He looks incredible."

I grin, preening under the compliment about my horse. "Thanks. He's good. I'm hoping to get some training on him this winter so maybe he'll be ready for an amateur like me next summer."

She nods. "It's a good plan. Giving him this time to unwind. Why not send him to Griffin? Some time up in the mountains and on the trails would be perfect for him."

Stefan goes still and glances over his shoulder at the table. The first time he's done so since I arrived. "Well, I don't know. I thought maybe—"

"I think that's a great idea, Violet." Mira smirks before taking a sip of her wine, and now my brother turns all the way around to give her the full weight of his scowl. She ignores him. "Don't you, Griff?"

He nods with a forced smile. "For sure. Happy t'help." He bridges the words together.

"Nice. We've got a room full of big talkers here tonight," Mira announces with a laugh.

Stefan's shoulders drop and his expression softens as he takes his wife in, throwing her a bone and tossing out a joke. "Almost makes me miss Billie." He winks, and everyone laughs, knowing there is no replacement for the space Billie's personality takes up.

The night carries on in a similar relaxed fashion. Stefan and Griffin are quiet, and the rest of us carry the conversation. Even the usually quiet Cole steps up to fill the void because easy as the company is, not even one of us is oblivious to the unspoken tension. When we finish eating, Stefan shoots out of his chair and flees to the kitchen, insisting on cleaning up—as he always does.

But this time, I follow him because I hate this strain between us. He's the only true family I've got, which means the big dummy is stuck with me.

"Are you going to keep ignoring me?" I ask as I stride straight into the kitchen with an armful of plates.

"I'm not ignoring you." He flicks the tap, letting steaming water fill the sink.

"Don't be a dick. You're my only family. I can't handle you being mad at me."

He turns then, looking at me a little sheepishly. "Every single person here tonight considers you family. I hope you know that. And I'm not mad at you." He runs a hand through his hair, eyes flicking around the house like he's searching for a word hidden in one of his bookshelves. "I'm worried about you."

I blink at him, not having expected that response.

"I love Griff like a brother. But he's got some matters he needs to attend to before I'm going to look kindly upon him *loving* you." He spits the word out, clearly a little wounded because we kept this from him. "I don't want you to get tangled up in that. And most of all, I don't want you to get hurt. You've been hurt enough for one lifetime. I've *let* you be hurt, and I'm trying to figure out a way to prevent that from happening to you again without being an overbearing fucking douchebag."

I laugh. I can't help it. He barely swears, and it cracks me up every time he does.

"Stop laughing! It's a hard fucking balance!"

I fall back against the edge of the counter and flatten my hands against my face, shoulders shaking with laughter.

"God. You're such a pain in my ass. I love you so goddamn much. It's almost annoying." That sobers me a little. Stefan and I have a lot of years between us. In many ways, we're united by our upbringing. In other ways, I've only come to truly know him recently because he was lucky enough to escape the hellhole that was our childhood home while I was still younger.

"I love you too."

He groans and then closes the space between us, folding me into a firm brotherly hug as he rests his chin atop my head. When he pulls away, he holds me by the shoulders, green eyes pinning me with their sincerity.

"I want you to be careful. I want you to put yourself first. I want you to consider the implications of getting involved with a man this much older than you, one with demons big enough to rival your own. One who is about to get dragged into the media. And I really, *really* want you to go to vet school. I want to watch you walk across that damn stage at your graduation, a huge fuck-you to the monster who raised us. I want the world for you. Every dream, every goal. I want you to have every opportunity our mom never got."

His fingers tighten, squeezing my shoulders in a way meant to be comforting. "You got that?"

I nod, trying to keep the tears at bay.

I got it all right. He has no idea how perfectly aimed that shot was. *Becoming my mother.* A perfect strike to the spot that makes all my defenses slam straight back into place.

CHAPTER 35

Griffin

Gold Rush Ranch is beautiful. Everything here looks flawless. The rolling hills and perfect white fences. The shiny horses and pristine buildings.

I don't belong here.

The pebble in my hand rolls across my fingers as I sit on the back step of the guesthouse. I toss it, watching it clack across the ground and bounce off another rock.

Flawless I am not, but I'm not stupid either. I saw the way Nadia regarded me when she came back out on the patio tonight. The tension was written all over her face, the anxiety—the questions. Questions she doesn't deserve to have to ask.

She deserves a love that's simple. Natural. Easy like breathing. Exactly what she wanted. Not this treacherous path we've started down. It's reckless, thinking we can come out on the other side unscathed.

Maybe I am stupid.

Not stupid enough to think I won't see her cresting that hill in the next couple of hours. We have unfinished business, things we need to say. And as much as it pains me to admit it, I hope her brother talked enough sense into her that I won't have to be the one to break her heart.

I'd break my own heart a million times over to spare hers. I'll shoulder the pain of what needs to be done if it means she sheds one fewer tear.

I'll take the blame, the hate, the disappointment. She can put it all on me, and I'll still come back for more. Because Nadia Dalca is it for me. And if I have to wait for the right moment to present itself, then I will.

Because she's worth the wait. I've told her that before, and I meant it.

I reach down to grab another rock, rolling the smooth weight of it against my palm, transporting myself to the feel of her smooth skin beneath my hands.

A tugging sensation in my chest has me looking up, seeing Nadia walking down the slope of the hill that divides the farm from this little oasis.

Just like I knew she would.

I'm beyond pretending I'm not staring at her, so I lean my elbows back on the step behind me and take her in. I try to commit her to memory. The sway of her hips, the curve of her neck, the unruliness of her hair. *My wildflower.*

I soak up every inch of her, not wanting to forget a single thing. Because I have this sinking, devastating notion that soon, I won't be seeing her very much.

"Hey," she says with a sad smile as she approaches, rubbing her hands on her jeans as if she's nervous.

"Come here, Wildflower." I lift an arm and nod my head to the space beside me.

Her eyes water, and her nose wrinkles up, like that might stop the tears that are about to fall.

Her glossy lips roll together, but with a few small steps she's in front of me and folding herself down onto the step beside me, snuggling up under my arm, so small and fragile tucked against my body. When her head tips against my chest, I take a deep draw of rose-scented air and nuzzle against her hair.

I'll never forget the way she smells. The way she feels. Like redemption. Almost too good to be true.

"You okay?" I breathe against her, pulling her in tighter.

"No." Her voice cracks, breaking a line through my heart that matches the sound. *Me fucking neither.* "Did my brother give you a spanking?"

I chuckle, hand coming to rest on her thigh and giving her a quick squeeze. "Not the good kind." She laughs softly. "Really, though, our conversation was fair. He only has your best interests in mind."

Her head brushes against me as she nods. "I want you guys to still be friends. You were all he had for a long time."

"I'm very confident that we will always be friends. No need to worry about that."

We fall into several moments of silence, gazing out over the landscape as the sun dips low on the horizon. I'll never watch the sun set again without thinking of her. That view over the cliffs at my house is going to haunt me every damn night. I try not to think about the possibility of being friends with Stefan for the rest of my life and *not* having Nadia. Of having to watch her move on with someone else. Just thinking about it shreds me up inside.

She eventually breaks the silence. "I need to go to school. I need to prove to myself I can do something big with my life. Something more than I ever thought I could. I need to rise above that little voice and do something that makes me truly proud of myself."

I can't stand not seeing her right now. I drag her into my lap, clasping her chin in my fingers and forcing her to look up at me. "You absolutely do. And I can't wait to watch you climb that mountain. I already know you're going to k-k-kick ass and t-take names. I'm so proud of you."

Her bottom lip wobbles, and my thumb brushes against it, not giving a fuck about my stutter with a girl like *her* looking at me like *that.*

"I need to do it on my own." Her arms wrap around my neck, fingers stroking soothing lines down the back of my skull.

"I know you do." I shift my hand to cup her cheek. This time my thumb brushes a tear tracking down the apple of her cheek. She's so young, has so much to do. And I never want to be the thing that holds her back.

"For now." Her eyes twinkle, and she stares at me desperately. My eyes sting at the sight of her damp cheeks.

I nod. "For now."

She nods in return. "I want you to be proud of yourself too."

A ragged sigh tumbles past my lips. I swallow, hoping it might pull the building tears back down where they came from. Back in the depths of my soul, where they've been hiding for years now.

"I want to see the man you can be when you get out from underneath all that shame, all the pain you've buried. You deserve a fresh start, Griffin. You deserve to be happy, and I can't be the only thing that does that for you. I don't want to be your antidote. I want to be your reason. The reason you put the work in."

I nod, drowning in her eyes. Wishing I could live there. Spend all day, every day memorizing every little fleck, every color. But I know she's right.

"This isn't goodbye forever. This is goodbye for now. A clean break for now. I can't do any in between. I don't expect you to wait for me. Okay?"

Hasn't she been listening to me? I'll be waiting for her no matter how long it takes. One tear spills over my cheek, and I fight the urge to run and hide. If I can fall apart in front of anyone in the world, I know it's her. "Okay." My voice sounds rusty, like I haven't used it in years. And I guess I haven't. My throat aches as I swallow the words trying to claw their way out. The ones that want to beg her to stay. The ones that want to explain away all the excellent reasons for us to hit pause. The ones that want to tell her I can make everything better for her if she lets me.

But this thing deserves more. It deserves two confident, capable adults. And she needs this time as badly as I do. I'd never forgive myself if I were the reason she didn't check every fucking thing off that list.

I'd give this woman anything she wants. A limb? An organ? A clean break.

But not waiting for her? That's not even a consideration. That's not even possible.

Her dainty hands cup my face, thumbs stroking the stubble on my cheeks. "You've got your own mountain that needs climbing. Yeah?"

"Yeah." My stomach lurches, and I swear if I looked down, my heart would be beating on the ground somewhere. Ripped out and torn apart. Because she's right, I've got a lot of fixing to do.

She presses a tender kiss to my lips, so many emotions flooding out between us. Spilling out of me, drowning my system. Her forehead tilts against mine, the tips of our noses brushing together. "Meet you at the top, Sinclaire?"

My fingers pulse around her ribs, and I know that this is the moment where I let her go.

It makes me nauseous. But I choke out the words she needs to hear anyway.

"Meet you at the top, Wildflower."

CHAPTER 36

Nadia

WHEN I GET BACK TO MY APARTMENT, I REACH FOR MY JOURNAL, needing to write in it like a plant needs light and water. My fingers itch as I huddle under my blankets, ready to crumble under the weight of them, ready to fall apart in the privacy of my own space.

Floral journal in one hand, blue ballpoint pen in the other, I prepare myself to bleed on the page for the man I just walked away from. I flip it open and look at the first page—the list—like I do every time. It usually brings me peace. A sense of purpose. A way to manifest the things on my list into reality.

But this time, it brings a crushing ache to my chest and hot, stinging tears to my puffy eyes. Because Griffin has crossed off and initialed the one thing he swore he never could. *Make love.*

And what hurts the most is he's not even wrong.

CHAPTER 37

Griffin

THE PAST TWO WEEKS HAVE PASSED AS A STRANGE OUT-OF-BODY experience. I work with the young horses who have come so far. I'm certain they don't even need me. At this point, I'm just fulfilling my contract and exposing them to as much as possible. Tractors, traffic, trails, rain, dark… you name it, these youngsters have seen it. When they get to the track this winter to start their training, they're going to be beyond prepared. Even the scaredy one who dumped me in the field.

I pat that exact horse on the neck as I lead him into his paddock, let him loose, and lock the gate behind me. When I turn, my eyes snag on the building that houses the clinic, just on the other side of the property. The one where Nadia spends her days. Until now.

I've seen Nadia since our chat on the steps that night, but mostly in passing as she goes to or from the clinic. I took Tripod in for a checkup with Mira and hoped Nadia would be there. But she wasn't, and I know Mira caught me peeking around behind her like I might catch even a small glimpse.

I'm not above admitting I'm heartbroken. Or that Tripod snuggles me every night in a little spoon position and I'm endlessly grateful for his three-legged company.

Doing the right thing feels like absolute shit. I'm supposed to be the mature one, but today is the day Nadia is leaving, and I'm in a terrible fucking mood over it. She was supposed to live here and commute to school in Emerald Lake. But suddenly, she's found a condo to rent and is moving. I want to go say goodbye to her, but I don't know if I'm strong enough to watch her leave. I don't even know if she'd want me there.

Seeing her depart across the darkened field with so many pieces of me was cruel enough. Seeing her *really* leave might do me in entirely.

I grunt, shaking my head, and make my way back into the barn, trying to find something to do that will keep me busy. Keep me from crawling to her place and acting like an idiot. I turn into the tack room, grabbing a bucket of water, a sponge, and a puck of saddle soap before getting to work on every stitch of leather hanging on the wall.

I get lost in the motion. In the process. Scrub. Wipe. Dip. Squeeze. Rinse. Repeat. I don't know how long I work on the tack, letting my mind wander to my days on the field, all the friends I had—the ones who are nowhere to be found since my fall from grace. I fixate on the fact that my future ex-wife is going to splash our wedding story and sex tape across any magazine or newspaper that listens to her, hoping to get whatever money I won't give to her. Regret pierces me in the chest, like a fucking spear to the heart.

"That why they pay you the big bucks?" Violet smiles at me from the doorway as she steps into the room and hoists a saddle up onto a rack.

"Something like that," I grumble back, sounding like a total asshole but not caring. I've been a growly prick ever since Nadia walked over that hill and out of my life.

I thought I knew suffering. But I didn't.

"You're missing her something fierce, aren't you?" Violet's voice is gentle, even though I don't deserve that tone. It also bothers me that everyone knows about what went on between us but it's not really spoken about. It's like it never happened, and I hate that more than anything. There's no proof *we* ever existed.

A low grumble sounds in my chest. "Yes," I clip out the single word. No point in lying.

"You sound like my husband when he's in a bad mood." She's not the least bit deterred; in fact, she's smiling. A small smile. But still.

"He's ten years older than me, you know."

I glare at her longer this time. "Yeah? Is this the 'age is just a number' pep talk?" She doesn't deserve me lashing out at her. "I'm sorry," I add quickly, shaking my head as I stare down at the leather reins in my hands.

She shrugs. "I think in some cases, age is just a way to measure the number of years you spent without the person meant for you."

Fuck. That's poetic.

"You can grow together, but taking the time to prove to yourselves that you can grow on your own is wise." I swallow heavily as she continues. "What I know about Nadia is that when she wants something, she goes after it." She takes a few steps across the room, squeezing my shoulder as she passes. "If you want her, you need to be ready for when she comes after you. If she grows, you grow. Don't let her down by stagnating."

And then she's gone. Leaving me with an ache right in the center of my chest. I crush my palm there, like if I press hard enough, it will go away.

It doesn't. It just gets worse all the time.

And I tumble. Straight into a deep pit of sadness and self-loathing. The itch to leave and go drown myself in a glass of amber liquid is so sharp, so present, that I crumble.

I toss the sponge into the bucket, stride out of the barn, and head straight to Neighbor's Pub, dying to see if I'm still strong enough to come face-to-face with a big pour of bourbon and turn myself around. I'm out my driver's-side door and pushing through the heavy front doors before I can think twice. Sliding onto a stool at the lacquered bar top and ordering a drink before I can think at all.

The bartender slides the drink my way, and it lands between my fingers with a familiar weight and smell. Her eyes don't linger. My cap is slung low, and I smell like horse shit. Clearly, today's staff doesn't recognize me.

I watch the amber liquid as I spin the tumbler, a syrupy outline of every splash dripping down the sides of the simple bar glass. I don't even have to taste it to remember the flavor.

Or the dark fucking place it took me.

I stare at the glass, feeling the tug-of-war raging in my head, in my heart. So familiar. A vicious cycle. Find something, drown in that something, *need* that something, let myself get to a place where I've convinced myself I need that something to function. That just a sip might cure me, might make me feel better.

I don't want to be your antidote.

It made little sense to me when she said it because I was too busy trying not to fall apart. But now, face-to-face with a whole different type of temptation, the clarity of her words almost bowls me over.

I want to be your reason.

I push the glass away hard enough that liquid sloshes over the edges and pools on the bar top. Suddenly, I'm repulsed by the sight. By my weakness. By how sad it is that I come here and do this to myself.

I pull my phone out and dial. When he answers, I sigh in relief. "Hey, Dad? Do you still have the names of those rehab programs you looked into?"

This shit ends here and now. Because I've never had a better reason.

CHAPTER 38

Griffin

ONE MONTH LATER

"HEY, MAN!" STEFAN CLAPS ME ON THE BACK AS WE LOCK ARMS tightly. I don't need to look at him to know that he's grinning like a maniac. "It's so good to see you."

I huff out a chuckle. "Thanks for giving me a ride. My parents were seriously talking about postponing their winter stay in Mexico to be here to pick me up. Couldn't have that."

"Of course. Not a problem at all. Just the one bag?" He glances around me in confusion, since I asked him to bring a pickup truck today.

"Oh, yeah. Let me toss it in. There's something else just inside I need your help with."

He nods a bit suspiciously, his eyes never leaving me as I ditch my bag in the back seat and head back in his direction. I've been in rehab for a month. Checked into the first place that would take me and didn't look back. I knew if I had too much time to think about it, I'd back out and come up with an excuse to avoid treatment.

After years of avoidance, I've become adept.

But no longer. Now I'm facing things head-on. My days of hiding are over. Hiding from society, my past, or the truth. Because even after weeks away from her, I am still head-over-fucking-heels in love with Nadia Dalca.

Even more because she walked away from me. What a woman. Goddamn, I'm just so proud of her.

"What are you smiling about?" Stefan asks as I stroll back toward him with my hands shoved into my pockets.

"Nadia."

He blinks at me, like he didn't quite expect me to just say it point blank. Yeah, we've talked on the phone pretty regularly since I checked in here, and I haven't stopped asking how she's doing. I've made no secret of the way I feel about her, and I don't plan to start now.

I have an entirely different plan.

When I wave a hand over my shoulder, Stefan falls into step beside me. "She's doing really good, you know."

"Yeah?" The sliding doors open for us, and we step inside to grab the big slab of wood wrapped in a sheet. I point at it, and confusion paints his features, but he doesn't ask anything more. We're still working on this new phase of our friendship. One where we talk more about things rather than just mutually ignoring them.

It's fucking hard. Talking about your feelings. I've got a real love-hate relationship with it. Even after a month straight of practicing.

He hefts up one side, and I take the other. "Yeah. I mean, sure, she's stressed and a little overwhelmed, but she's working so hard at it. She's so focused. It's just crazy to see, considering the wild child she showed up in Canada as. A few short years and boom. She's really transformed herself." He shakes his head with a small smile as we approach the open truck bed. "I mean, she's like a whole new person."

I swallow. Hopefully not *too* new. Not so new that she won't want me anymore. That she'll realize I'm washed up and weighed down and that she wants some normal, happy fucking Ken doll.

I'd respect her decision if she did. But I'm pretty sure I'd never get over her. She's it for me.

And who am I kidding? I'd kill that fucking guy.

We heft the piece of wood into the back of the truck, and once it's slid into place, Stefan gestures his chin toward it. "Listen, I'm trying not to be too snoopy. But what is this?"

I feel suddenly shy. Like maybe I'll never show it to anyone, even though that's been my plan all along. "It's something I made. You can take a look at it."

Offering him a tight smile, I hop off the back of the truck and head toward the passenger seat. Through the rearview mirror I see curiosity get the best of my friend. He hops up and crouches down, peeling away the sheet. His brow pinches as he stares down at it, and I swear I watch the color drain right out of his face.

His head snaps up, and he meets my gaze in the mirror. I don't pretend I wasn't watching him. That wouldn't be honest. I hold his green eyes with my own, and he nods at me. It's firm, it's precise—it means something.

And when he gets back in the truck and pulls away from the facility I've called home for the past month, we don't talk about it at all.

Instead, he breaks the silence with "You're not trending on Twitter anymore."

I can't help but laugh. What a fucking joke. As soon as that gold digger realized I wasn't going to shell out any cash to her, she dragged her greedy ass straight to the first tabloid that would listen to her.

I scoff. "Not sad that I didn't have social media access in there. Easier to ignore it when looking isn't even an option."

"For sure. The good news is, I don't think there's a tape. If there was, she would have released it by now."

I rest my head back on the seat and blow out a breath. "Yeah. That's what my lawyer thinks too." Which is honestly something I'm very conflicted about. Relieved that there's no tape that can be leaked but enraged I spent years running from an outcome that was a venomous fucking lie.

When I told my parents the full story that night I called to talk about rehab, they'd been stoic. I wanted them prepared. As usual, they were painfully supportive—but I'm not dumb enough to think it didn't gut them.

Preparing the people you love to be publicly embarrassed by you is a hard pill to swallow.

Luckily, for once, things are coming up Griffin.

"The only thing I've seen are the wedding photos with Elvis," Stefan continues, eyes on the road. "And hilariously, the general response to those has come in two camps." I lift a brow at him to go on. "People who think you look hot and people who think she's, and I'm quoting here, *a manipulative bitch*."

I cringe a little bit. I obviously don't like Tonya, but I'm still the drunk idiot who did it. That said, I'm not mad that this campaign has blown up in her face.

The only person I'm mad at is myself. For doing this to myself. But even that is getting better. After a month spent with daily therapy, counseling, and even speech therapy, I'm feeling like I know myself better than I ever have.

I'm feeling motivated.

"I guess that's why she's agreed to mediation rather than some big court drama. Tucking tail."

"Good." Stefan's knuckles go white on the steering wheel. The only clue that she pisses him off more than he lets on.

A companionable silence stretches between us as we drive down the main highway back out to Ruby Creek until he breaks it.

"Is that special cargo in the back for my sister?"

I swallow and roll my lips together before quietly replying, "Yeah."

"Is that why you had me bring the truck down there?"

"Yeah." My heart twists. I hope so fucking badly that this works.

"I'm sorry this has been such a bumpy road for you."

I clear my throat and suck air in through my nostrils, trying to keep it together. "She's worth it."

My best friend just smiles. "You really love her, don't you?"

"So much it hurts" is my honest reply.

His smile grows. "Good."

That's when the greenhouse shows up in the distance on the right-hand side of the road. I point at it. "Pull in there, you fucking sadist."

He laughs as he signals.

I pull out the list in my back pocket, praying like hell my plan will be enough to win her back.

Or at the very least, make her smile. So I can live my life knowing that all her dreams came true.

CHAPTER 39

Nadia

I TAP MY PEN AGAINST THE TEXTBOOK LAID OUT IN FRONT OF ME. Vet school midterms are already upon me.

I feel accomplished. I feel challenged. I feel over-fucking-whelmed. *What was I thinking?* I had a nice, safe job. Was on the path to make a great living. I had a man who loved me.

And I gave it all up for *this.*

Stress. Never-ending reading. And late nights spent with that dickwad voice who lives in my head and tells me I'm not good enough. He sounds suspiciously like my dickwad father, which makes me want to crush him even harder.

I lean back in my chair and press the heels of my hands into my eye sockets. Swear I can't even see straight anymore. I'm about to hit that point in studying where you think *If I don't know it by now, I'm probably not going to know it at all.*

For a change of scenery, I grab the stack of mail I pulled from the little locked cubby in the lobby of my building. I lucked out getting a furnished place near campus on short notice. I could have commuted the forty-five minutes to and from Emerald Lake, but with traffic I could have potentially added almost two hours into my day—two hours I'm now glad I have to study.

Burying myself in my books here means three things. One, I don't run into Griffin Sinclaire around town. Two, I don't read any tabloids that might discuss Griffin Sinclaire or his divorce, which, according to my brother, has become a popular tabloid story—even without the existence of a sex tape. And three, I spend slightly less time obsessing about Griffin Sinclaire.

My blood still boils at the memory of that woman. That spark of anger I've worked so hard to control dances in my chest. *I really hate that bitch.*

Right around when I got here, Stefan called to tell me Griffin had checked himself into a twenty-eight-day rehab program and that they were pretty sure she didn't have a tape at all. When I hung the phone up, I cried. I missed him, like some part of me was left behind. But more than anything, I was *relieved.*

He owes himself so much more than he's been giving. I wanted that for him so badly that it hurt. I wanted him to know in his bones what I already do—he's worth it. He's worth *everything.*

I shuffle the envelopes.

Bill.

Bill.

Junk mail.

I stop with a pink envelope clutched in my fingers. The blocky all caps scribbled across it not a match for the feminine color.

My heart races as I stare at it, already knowing who it's from, even with no return address. I feel the hum of his touch on the paper as I slide a shaking finger beneath the fold and rip it open. On a shaky inhale, I pull out a small slip of paper and a smaller envelope with a photograph of a white flower that had light-pink stripes on the wide petals adorning it. I open the smaller envelope, but it's empty. I'm sure it once held seeds for the flower labeled *Spring Beauty.*

I flip the paper, where the blocky scrawl continues.

Spring Beauty

Alpine wildflower. Comes up right after the snow melts. Blooms within two to four weeks. Can use energy reserves to produce heat and melt through the last of snow. Strong as fuck. Reminds me of you.

A tear drops onto the page, and I panic, wiping it off frantically. Not wanting to mar the note. I don't know what it means, but I know he's called me Wildflower since the first day we met. And the nickname has become incredibly meaningful to me.

That night I sleep with the note clutched in my hand and pretend that Griffin is here with me.

I miss him.

It's been two weeks since midterms. The midterms I absolutely slayed. I've shed a good chunk of that self-doubt I've been toting around with me for years, and I'm thriving.

I wipe the sweat off my brow as I walk into my building after a run. My new hobby. A way to burn energy and clear my head. I've always hated running, but I forced myself to keep going, and now I look forward to it. It's weird.

The key clicks as I turn it in my mailbox to check for another pink envelope. Like I have every single day for the past two weeks.

I burned off enough steam during my run that I've convinced myself already that I won't be seeing one today. Which makes the sight of it in the slot so much better.

I don't even wait until I get up to my unit to rip the envelope open. I'm too fucking excited.

This time I see a hot-pink flower that's all fuzzy in the middle. I definitely dig the color. I swap it for the note, smiling like a maniac before I've even read it.

Monkey Flower

That fuzzy part in the middle is called a stigma. Apparently, it's the female reproductive organ. These flowers have especially sensitive stigmas, and they think that might help with pollination. I still think about that little whimpering noise you make. Reminds me of you.

I bark out a laugh. *Fucking perv.* I smile at the note the entire ride up in the elevator and into my unit. I smile all the way into the shower. It's not until the water scalds my skin that I let my tears pour out and wash down the drain.

I miss him.

Finals are upon me, and I'm stoked. Like actually excited to prove how good I am at this. I'm at the top of my class and not slowing down. What started out as a semester of me feeling scared and alone has turned into one of the best times of my life. I'm learning. I'm making new friends who don't know me from Adam. They don't know my brother. They don't know my reputation from high school. They don't know Griffin. The experience just wouldn't have been the same had I lived in Ruby Creek and commuted every day. I'd have dragged a little bit of baggage out this way with me every day.

But now I just get to be Nadia Dalca. The girl who wants to be a doctor of veterinary medicine.

I've been asked out a couple of times, and I've kindly declined. I don't even have to think about it. Are Griffin and I torturing ourselves and each other by taking this self-imposed time-out? Absolutely. But I know in my heart I needed this. I told him I didn't expect him to wait for me, which is true. But I try not to think about that.

Not waiting for him just feels wrong.

And I know in my bones that we aren't done.

Especially when I get home from my last exam and find another baby-pink envelope waiting for me. This time I race up to my condo to open it in the privacy of my space. I plop myself down onto my bed and really savor opening this envelope.

I realize that I don't know how many of the wildflower-themed notes he might send. He might stop one day. He might move on. He *should* move on. I would never expect him to sit around twiddling his thumbs, waiting for me.

But the insecure girl inside me desperately wants him to be okay with waiting for me.

I drag it out of the envelope. This time I'm met with spiky red and yellow flowers at the top of tall green stalks.

Paintbrush

Hummingbirds depend on these alpine wildflowers. The nectar sustains them as they migrate. These flowers keep them going, keep them moving forward in their lives without even trying. Just by being themselves. These flowers are the reason the hummingbirds survive. Reminds me of you.

My eyes burn, but I don't cry. Because his message isn't lost on me. I'm what's keeping him going, and that motivates me more than anything he could have told me. Blinking rapidly, I put everything back in the envelope and tuck it into my bedside table with the rest of his notes. Then I go to my desk, crack my books, and get to studying. I focus on the task before me, but still…

I miss him.

***

My brother and Mira took off for a tropical vacation over Christmas. Hawaii. They begged me to come with them, but the thought of taking that particular vacation with their little family and without Griffin felt like more than I could bear. I've waited this long to take that vacation. When I do it, I want it to be perfect. As perfect as that day in the field.

Plus, one of my professors offered a student placement at their prestigious vet clinic in the city over the holidays. And by prestigious, I mean working overnight shifts so the other vets and techs get their holidays off. No one wanted it—surprise, surprise—except me.

My memories of Christmas growing up aren't warm and fuzzy, so I guess I'll work my ass off and run myself into the ground in celebration. At least it'll look good on my résumé. And it seemed like the perfect way to pass the time between term one and term two.

On Christmas Eve, I sit at the emergency vet clinic, taking care of other people's furry family members surrounded by employees I don't know. It's my doing, but I miss my family and friends something fierce. I miss my horse. I've gone back on the weekends to see him and cashed in on my riding lessons from Violet and Billie. I'm getting pretty good.

When I go back, I avoid town and hole up on my brother's farm, not wanting to run into anyone. I spend hours grooming Cowboy to a perfect gloss, dreaming of the day I'll be able to ride him. I massage him. I cuddle him. I tell him all my most embarrassing secrets.

If Cowboy were here right now, I'd tell him I was secretly hoping Griffin would reach out to me for Christmas. I told Griffin I wanted a clean break, but I thought he might send me a text message or something. *Something.*

According to Violet, who has reached out to me more than ever since I left, Griffin will be picking Cowboy up and taking him to his place to start his training in the new year. I've learned so much about rehabilitating racehorses since Griffin bought him for me, and I can see myself doing this over and over again with other horses in the future. Ones who need a second shot at life—a fresh start.

Kindred spirits.

I'm at the front desk watching the clock on the wall move toward midnight. The ticking sound is almost hypnotic in the otherwise quiet clinic. All the staff has warned me Christmas is a real shit show. And that starts in the middle of the night usually with people's pets who have eaten something they shouldn't have.

So I soak up the peace while I can, watching Christmas Eve melt into Christmas Day. At a few minutes past midnight, the front door jangles, and a tired-looking man walks through.

He holds up a pale-pink envelope and says, "Is Nadia Dalca here?"

I point at my chest, right where my heart is rushing uncontrollably. "That's me."

He smiles briefly and drops the envelope down on the countertop between us. "Merry Christmas."

"Merry Christmas," I say, unable to pull my attention from the best gift I could have asked for.

When I open the envelope, I see small blue and purple almost-spherical petals growing along a tall stem in a spear-like shape. I recognize them from the field at Griffin's house.

Arctic Lupin

These wildflowers produce a neurotoxin called sparteine. In the afternoon, they produce nearly five times the concentration they do at night. It's a defensive tactic against the grazing patterns of the snowshoe hare. Smart as fuck. Reminds me of you.

Sitting here, holding this note from one of the most profoundly thoughtful men I've ever had the pleasure of meeting, I feel distinctly *not* smart. Smart girls wouldn't leave someone like this behind.

What if I made the wrong choice? The question has crossed my mind more than once.

I tuck the envelope into my purse beneath the desk, and then I lock myself in the bathroom and let myself shed tears for one minute. I actually set a timer. And then I take a deep, deep breath and walk back out to the front desk and prepare myself to save some lives.

Because I am smart. Smart enough to know I'm here to work hard and prove to myself that I can do this life on my own if I need to. That I don't toss away every hope and dream for a man. I'll always wonder if I'm capable of it if I don't do this. He knows it, and I know it too.

Still, with every note he sends, I fall more deeply in love with him. The distance. The space. The unwavering understanding. It just makes me love him harder.

I miss him.

It's spring break, and a good chunk of my classmates are heading south for a vacation. But partying at a resort isn't my scene. One of the things I've learned living away is that certain settings work for me and my past trauma while others do not. Big loud parties with heavy drinking will never be my happy place. People inevitably try to push alcohol on me, and having to turn them down over and over inevitably gets awkward.

And annoying.

Every party I've been to in the past few months has just proved that there is a limit to what I have in common with people my age. It's why I've joined a study group of "mature students." Or that's the running joke.

Marni is a mom of three who has stayed home for the past several years. Jin is already a medical doctor but has found his bedside manner may be more well suited to animals. His intensely literal persona cracks me up. And Erin has been a vet tech for over a decade. She's spent years thinking she'd like to be the doctor in the room but was constantly told by her shitty husband she couldn't. That it was too expensive. That she was too old.

She ditched him and went back to school. I admire her fiercely. Needless to say, all the people who have become my real friends at school went back to their families for spring break. So here I am, doing the same. Hefting a suitcase out of my car and dragging it up the front steps of my brother's house at Cascade Acres.

Stefan throws the front door open and rushes out to take my bag. Ever the gentleman. "Little sister." He slings an arm over my shoulder. "Nice to have you home."

Home. I love this place. But it doesn't feel like home. A cozy little house in the mountains overlooking a rocky cliff and surrounded by wildflowers is what my mind conjures up when I hear the word. But the only reason that place feels like home is because of the man who lives there.

The one who lives rent-free in my head and heart. The one who makes me smile and cry all at once. Anywhere with him would feel like home.

"Nice to be here." I drop my head on my brother's shoulder and smile. "I've missed you, Stef."

"Ah, you're just saying that. We both know I annoy you a little bit. It's almost like you've been avoiding me these days."

Not you, your best friend.

I chuckle. "A little bit. It's part of your charm."

He gives me a gentle shove just before we hit the stairs. "You love me."

"You know it," I reply, meaning it.

When we get to the top of the stairs, just in front of my bedroom, he stops behind me and I turn to face him, wondering why he isn't keeping up.

"I love you too. You know that?" He swallows, looking a little nervous.

"I know." I smile and nod, eyes searching his face for some clue where this sudden seriousness is coming from.

"I feel like I owe you an apology. I feel like I overstepped." My heart thuds heavily against my ribs, and the color drains from my face. "I feel like I forced you and Griffin apart without really understanding."

My mouth is dry as I suck in a deep breath. "Understanding what?"

He nods his head toward my bedroom, his expression almost stricken. "You've got mail."

I turn, peering into the room. The bed is made perfectly. And on one pillow lies a pale-pink envelope.

One hand falls across my chest, and when I look back at my brother, he winks before heading back down the stairs.

Suitcase forgotten in the hallway, I walk into the room and sit gingerly on the edge of the bed before picking up the envelope.

I haven't gotten one since Christmas but avoided thinking about why. Avoided thinking that he has probably moved on like I told him to.

When I peel it open, what looks like pure yellow daisies stare back at me.

Mountain Arnica

Used for healing cuts and bruises. Considered a love charm in some cultures. Reminds me of another wildflower I know who heals a bruised heart and wounded soul so fucking effortlessly—my love charm. My reason.

If you ever need some mountain arnica of your own, you can find these in the field where I fell. Cowboy is here too. We're waiting for you.

In the field where he fell. The property between this one and Gold Rush Ranch? Where he first told me he loved me?

I'm back out the door and racing down the stairs before I even settle in.

My brother calls out, "See you tomorrow!" as I blow straight back out the front door and hop in my car, the small sheet of paper still pressed between my clammy fingers and the steering wheel as I speed down the back roads, trying to remember where the access is for that property.

Things are greening up in the valley. It's pretty much the definition of spring out my window. Bright greens, flowers blooming, pollen floating in the air. When I finally find the back road I think will take me closest, I gun it down to the spot where the trail we'd been on that day spat us out.

It's not until I throw my vehicle in park that I look out over the picturesque valley where Griffin told me the words I've spent my entire life desperate to hear.

And I sob, slapping a hand over my mouth in shock. Because the entire thing is full of wildflowers. A mosaic of bright spring colors. White. Pink. Red. Orange. Blue. Yellow.

Every single kind of flower he sent me in his notes.

On the top of the hill overlooking the field is a silver trailer and a pretty new barn. Small and picturesque. Blue and white. Freshly painted.

I'm certain I see my shiny, dark bay horse grazing up there behind a bright-white fence.

Without another thought, I'm out of my car, ducking through the fence and walking through the field of flowers with my stomach in my throat.

And my heart in my hand.

CHAPTER 40

Griffin

I KNOW NADIA IS GETTING HOME TODAY AT SOME POINT, BUT I'M not positive when. Which is why I'm sitting on the steps of the Airstream trailer I've been living in, staring at the freshly paved driveway on what was formerly a completely untouched piece of land.

Basically, I'm stressing the fuck out. I chuck a stick and watch Tripod rip after it with a gleeful bark. And I wait.

For her.

Earlier today, Stefan let me up to her room to put the final envelope on her pillow, and then he told me not to let her walk out of my life again. He's been a steadfast friend these past several months. He's watched me crumble over my life, my career, and his sister.

He's watched me be heartsick with every ounce of my being and hasn't shied away a single time. He visited me in rehab. He took care of my horse for me that month. And he gives me updates on his sister that definitely don't fall neatly into the "clean break" category.

I didn't *need* his approval to love her. But knowing he supports us definitely feels good.

It's been six months since Nadia walked away from me. And they have been hands down the most agonizing months of my life but also the most enlightening.

I finally got the support I've always known I needed but avoided addressing.

I finally had a reason.

Tripod drops the stick at my feet and then bounces on the spot, tongue lolling and black button eyes bulging in anticipation of my next toss. But then his focus shifts, and he bounds past me, yapping like a goddamn squeaky toy. As I follow the sound, I do a double take. My stomach flips, like I just dropped off the highest point of a roller coaster.

She came.

I unfold myself from the aluminum steps, heart thudding loudly in the cage of my chest. Pre–Super Bowl jitters have nothing on this. All the words I've wanted to say to her for the past half year are at the tip of my tongue, but when I take her in, every one of them dies on my lips.

I stand and face her as she walks in my direction wearing a simple gray T-shirt dress and leather jacket, head swiveling around the property. She looks older somehow, more mature, more self-assured. More at peace. There's a security in her movements that wasn't there before.

She leaves me breathless.

"Griffin?" She finally reaches the top of the hill and comes to stand mere meters away. Her voice quavers as she glances up at me, and I cram my hands into the pockets of my jeans to keep from rushing forward and touching her. I ache to touch her in a way I didn't know was possible. To slip her hair behind her ear, to brush my nose against the tip of hers, and then to tuck her under my chin. "I came as soon as I got your note."

She fits so perfectly there. And I hope with every ounce of my being that she still feels the same.

"Hi, Wildflower."

Her lips roll together, her lashes blinking just a little too quickly. "You look good."

I swallow and let my gaze scour her appreciatively. In a way that makes color streak across her cheeks before I respond, "I feel good."

She nods. "Are you divorced now?"

"As single as they come."

A small, satisfied smile tugs at her lips. Giving me a little taste of hope. "What is this?" She clears her throat as she turns away, eyes scouring the field of wildflowers. She only turns back at Tripod's insistence. He's pawing at her legs, ready to burst with excitement, and when she finally pets him, his little eyes flutter shut in pleasure.

And I'm momentarily jealous of a fucking dog.

"It's… um. Well, walk with me. I'll show you." I wave a hand over my shoulder and turn away, both hating not seeing her and feeling relieved by not having to look at her for a moment. I'm staring down at my boots when I see her white sneakers fall into step next to them.

Here at the top of the hill, flat green fields stretch out on both sides of the barn and paddocks. It's the perfect spot to build. Flat and at no risk of flooding.

We walk down the driveway, the silence between us practically brimming with questions. Usually, she would fill this space with adorable ramblings, but I think she might be speechless right now. For the briefest of moments, her pinky finger hooks through mine, like she just can't help herself. But when I turn to look at her, she drops it and pushes her chin down.

"Is this all new?" she finally blurts out as we approach the end of the driveway.

"Yeah. It's… well, it's partly therapy. Figured out I'm happiest and healthiest when I'm working with my hands."

I peek at her again from beneath the brim of my favorite hat. The one my granddad bought for me at my first rodeo. It was too big at the time, and I didn't find it again until after his death. It's funny how something you didn't even know you had can come to mean so much to you.

We approach the front gate along the main road. "I sort of thought you might come through this way."

She hits me with a nervous smile, palms rubbing against her dress. "I only remembered that one spot."

I clear my throat, trying not to blow this. "Right." I take a few more steps and then turn to face her, waving her ahead to join me. She regards me somewhat quizzically but does as I've asked.

"Like I was saying. This place is partly therapy." She turns to face the sign at the front gate, and her hand shoots up over her mouth on a strangled gasp.

"But it's mostly for you."

The sign reads *Wildflower Racehorse Rescue*.

"Griffin." All I can see is her back, the way her shoulders squeeze up tight around her ears as both hands come to cup her cheeks. I can hear her sniffle, but it's been so long that I don't know what's appropriate. I don't know if she wants me to touch her.

"Do you like it? I made it at rehab."

"Do I like it?" She turns on me slowly, looking absolutely floored.

"The sign. I made the sign myself. Art therapy. Carved it. Painted it. I tried to use all the colors of the flowers I sent you."

Tears streak down her face, and she goes pale, like she's seen a ghost. *Great, she hates it.* Figures. I try to do something romantic and fail miserably.

She steps up to the sign where it's mounted on two thick posts. Her manicured fingers trace the flowers I painted there before she turns to glance back up the hill. "And the barn?"

I scrub a hand across my beard. "Built that too. It's been keeping me busy. That's why I haven't written lately. Didn't want to bother you." She stares at me blankly, so I just keep talking. "I wasn't sure what color you'd want it to be, so I just went with white because I thought it would be fresh and crisp. But it looked too plain. Didn't suit you, so I added the blue tin roof and trim. We can change it."

I'm rambling.

She blinks at me, hands sinking down to her throat. "Change it?"

My tongue darts out over my lip. Her responses are making me nervous. I wasn't sure how she'd react, but standing there vacantly repeating my words back to me wasn't something I accounted for.

"Yeah. Whatever you think. I just want you to love it. There's room over there to build a house. I just didn't want to start that without your input. My plan was to have it overlooking the wildflowers." I kick at the ground and peer up at her nervously. "I'm really blowing it here, aren't I? I made a lot of assumptions. I know. If you're over me, I'll just—"

Her voice cuts me off. "Griffin. This is..." She looks around, mouth opening and closing as she searches for the words. Her arms flop down at her sides, and she finally gazes into my eyes, gifting me with a clear view of those beautiful whiskey irises. "This is too much."

I just chuckle. She has no idea. Not a fucking clue.

"This isn't enough, Nadia. To repay you for the way you've brought me back? It will never be enough. I'll spend the rest of my goddamn life repaying the favor, and I'll do it with a smile. This place is yours whenever you want it. With me. Without me. No strings attached. I want you to have it. I want to see you spread your wings and soar. To see all your dreams come true." I pause, sucking in a deep, centering breath, and then I forge ahead like I planned. "But right now, I'm going to beg you to give me another shot. Before? That was a false start. This? This is a clean slate. I want all your right nows. All your tomorrows. I want it all with you."

She sobs and shakes her head helplessly, but I don't stop.

"I've made a lot of mistakes in my life. But you're not one of them. You're the happiest accident I've ever known. The very best decision I've ever made. My reason."

With two swift steps, she crashes into me, arms snaking around my ribs and hands grappling with my jean jacket, tugging me as tight against her as she can. I soften, wrapping my arms around her and letting the warmth of her seep into me.

I release a sigh I've been holding for six months.

She nuzzles against me, the dampness of her tears soaking through my shirt. She hiccups, and I press my cheek onto the crown of her head, tucking her in right where I've dreamed of having her. She still smells like sweet roses, and I let my eyes flutter shut as I soak her in.

She pulls back to look up at me, eyes glistening, heart-shaped lips quivering as she finally speaks. "For six months, I've gone without you. And do you know what I've learned?"

I blink rapidly, squeezing her again just to make sure she's real. "What's that?"

"I can do anything I set my mind to without you." She pauses and licks her lips nervously. "But I don't want to." Her head shakes in disbelief as she carries on. "Get over you? Are you out of your mind? I'll *never* get over you. I have missed you every single day, Griffin Sinclaire. I've ached for you. Never let me walk away again. Tie me up, lock me down, keep me forever. I only ever want to do this life with you."

The air between us crackles, and I don't hesitate. I drop my head and claim those pretty lips, savoring the delicious little whimpering noise she makes when I do. Swallowing the words I so desperately needed to hear.

"I can do that," I murmur, letting my hands roam her body, like I almost can't believe she's here. That this is real.

"Your notes kept me going."

"Then I'll keep writing them. I'll write you notes for the rest of my life if it makes you happy."

She gives me a shy smile from beneath her wet lashes. "Thank you for waiting for me."

I clear my throat. Preparing myself to hand my heart over on a platter. "I'd do that for the rest of my life too if you wanted me to."

She tugs me close, brushing the tip of her nose against mine like she always does. "I love the blue roof, Griffin. I love this place. I love how hard you've worked. On yourself and on this home for us. But more than anything, I love *you.*"

A genuine smile touches my lips, hearing the words that she's never gifted me before. I never really cared. I'd have spent my life loving her whether or not she loved me back. But hearing her say it feels better than I could have imagined. Earning the love of a woman like Nadia Dalca is no easy feat, but she's been worth every challenge.

She always will be.

"I love you too, Wildflower."

Her sigh is wistful, satisfied. "Good, can we be done waiting now?" She trails her fingers through my beard, and when I offer her a decisive nod, she guides me back down to her, hands winding around my neck and tugging at my hair.

And we stand there, wrapped up in each other at the entrance to what I hope is the rest of our lives together. Because I let her walk away from me once before, but this time I'm never letting her go.

EPILOGUE

Griffin

THREE YEARS LATER

I'M SITTING IN THE MOST UNCOMFORTABLE FOLDING CHAIR OF all time. But I don't give a flying fuck because I got here early enough to get a front-row seat to my girl's graduation. I'm about to be dating a doctor.

Talk about overachieving.

And fuck, I've never been happier to be overachieving in my life.

The rows in front of the temporary stage they've set up down by Emerald Lake start to fill, and I get some dirty looks for the number of seats I've blocked off in the front row. But ask me if I care.

Eventually, music plays through the big speakers, and butterflies dance in my stomach. She did it. I'm so goddamn proud of her it makes the bridge of my nose sting.

When we first got back together, she spent the last two months of her semester living close to campus in her apartment. She wanted to move in with me right away, but I convinced her to finish the year out strong. And she did, and then we spent the weekends together fucking like rabbits during her study breaks.

Then that summer, we got to work on *our* property. Something that still sounds like music to my ears. We designed a small simple house and put a blue tin roof on it. A rancher with huge banks of windows looking out over the valley that bursts with wildflowers every summer.

She told me it was a waste of a field. But I reminded her of all the incredible things those wildflowers can do. She just rolled her eyes at me, but I don't care. I get to see them out my window every day. I get to walk through them with *her*, and life doesn't get any better than that.

I train my horses and work on our farm, and she goes to school. Until today. Today that ends, and she gets to bring some horses of her own back to the property. She'll rehabilitate them at our place and still put some hours in with Mira at Gold Rush Ranch. She has a whole plan, and I'm just lucky enough to be here and stand witness to it all coming together for her.

But first, I've got a surprise of my own.

"Hey, man." Stefan slaps my shoulder, and I stand to hug Mira. The rest of the Gold Rush crew filters in behind them. Billie, Vaughn, Violet, Cole, Hank, Trixie. Even my parents, Joan and Doug, are here, positively beaming like she's their own. Everyone who loves her is here to watch her walk across that stage today—the family she chose.

The group chats as they find their seats, but my knee bounces as I stare at the stage. My heart is about ready to burst for the woman I love. And when the ceremony starts, everyone else falls away for me. My sole focus is on the podium, front and center. And when they get to the *D* last names and a girl who shines from the inside walks out in her blue gown to accept a diploma, I let out a loud, borderline-inappropriate whistle.

Nadia's eyes find mine instantly, and we share a look, like we both know how huge this day is. And I fully intend to celebrate the hell out of her once I rip that gown off.

As soon as she clears the stage, Stefan squeezes my shoulder. "Go. Get out of here!"

I give my best friend a mischievous grin, a punch to the shoulder, and then duck out of the ceremony.

I walk behind the stage, and my eye is drawn to where she's hugging a friend, blissfully happy. I shove my hands into the pockets of my slacks and let her have her moment, soaking her up, watching from afar.

But like always, she knows I'm looking, and her head turns in my direction. Within moments, the rest of her follows as she jogs across the staging area toward me with an infectious smile on her face. Once she's close enough, she launches herself into my arms, and I lift her off the ground, spinning her around.

"I did it! I really did it." I feel her breath against the shell of my ear as she nuzzles against me, happiness radiating off her in waves.

"Always knew you would, Wildflower." Because I did. I knew she was remarkable from the first moment I laid eyes on her.

When I place her gently back down on the ground, she whispers in my ear. "You know how there was a vote on if you looked better in jeans or football tights?"

I grunt and roll my eyes, which makes her laugh.

Her top teeth sink into her bottom lip, and she reaches up to trace the seam of my mouth with her pink manicured finger as her eyes rake over my body with a hell of a lot of appreciation. "I think you might look the most fuckable in a suit."

I scoff. “Watch your mouth, Dr. Dalca.”

“Or what?” She gives my tie a light tug and arches a brow. *Okay, my girl is ready to celebrate.*

I reach into my jacket pocket and pull out two airline tickets. “Or I won’t want to go on a tropical vacation to Costa Rica with you.”

Her jaw drops. “You didn’t!”

I shrug, feeling really fucking smug about this surprise. Surprising her has become one of my new favorite pastimes. “I did. It was the last thing on your bucket list. It felt incomplete. We leave in a few hours.”

She holds a hand up, shaking her head with disbelief. “First of all, it’s a to-do list.”

“Semantics.” I turn away, heading to the parking lot. “Keep up, Wildflower. I don’t want to miss our flight.”

She hustles to keep up with me. “Second of all, *my* list felt incomplete to *you*?”

I promised myself I’d complete that list four years ago. Seemed about time. I glance down at her out of the corner of my eye, noting the amusement stamped on her face. “Yeah. And I just added something.”

Two somethings.

She snorts. “*You* added something to *my* list?”

“Yeah. Join the Mile High Club.”

And say yes when your boyfriend gets down on one knee and begs you to be Dr. Sinclaire for the rest of your life.

“I’m actually good with that addition. Dirty bathrooms are kind of our thing.”

I bark out a laugh and reach for her hand, rubbing the spot where the ring I picked out for her will go. I’m taking her on a well-earned tropical vacation, and while we're there, I plan to make her mine once and for all.

My girl. My reason. My Wildflower.

Forever.

Nadia

TWO YEARS LATER

I'M WARM FROM THE TIPS OF MY TOES RIGHT TO THE TOP OF MY head. Deliciously warm. Incredibly sated. Blissfully happy.

This is perfection. The hot sun warming my bones, the smell of sand and sea water floating on the breeze, and the sound of laughter rolling along with the crashing of the waves.

Heaven.

We come every year for Christmas now, and it never gets old. The same beach where he proposed is now our family vacation destination. And each year he continues to get down on one knee and asks me to marry him.

Again.

And now I laugh because we already are married.

"I'll never stop asking," he'll say, right before I fall into the sand and maul him like a teenager.

We did the same thing last night. We stayed up way too late reenacting the proposal night. Which is why I'm here, dozing like a cat in the sun. Sated.

The only thing that could make this better is having a pineapple sparkling water in my hand. But I am seriously not about to complain. I hardly entertain the thought because this life is just too good to be true. More than I ever envisioned for myself.

I sigh deeply and drift off softly, turning myself over to the utter peace I'm feeling inside. A peace that is somewhat new. It used to be borderline uncomfortable for me to feel so at ease, but I've come around to it. To feeling like it isn't just fleeting. To feeling like it might really be here to stay.

A slow, full smile stretches across my face when I feel it. The press of lips against my swollen belly. The rasp of calloused fingers along the inside of my knee.

I moan when cold glass presses and slides against the full curve of my breast.

"Have I told you how fucking beautiful you look all laid out in the sun with my baby growing inside you?" Griffin's voice rumbles across me, making my stomach flip and goose-flesh race out over my bare skin. His possessive streak has come on full force since we found out we have a baby on the way.

I didn't think my smile could get any bigger, but it does. My eyes flutter open, and I take in the delicious man kneeling in the sand beside me. I feel like a beached whale on a chaise longue, but what he sees is *fucking beautiful.*

"It's just because my tits are about to explode out of this triangle top," I chuckle, letting a hand trail down his arm, nail dancing over the outline of the ink there. The spot where he added a traditional-style tattoo.

A heart with a banner that reads *Nadia*.

When he told me he had a spot picked out to have a matching one done for our baby, I cried. Which doesn't count for much. I cry a lot these days. It's the hormones, and Griffin knows it. But he smiles softly and wraps me in his big arms anyway, tucks me right under his chin where I belong.

"I mean… I'm not mad about them. But then I'm a big fan at any size."

"Even when they're saggy?" I quirk a brow, eyeing up the drink in his hand.

He just scoffs. "Please. We both know I'm going to be saggy way before you."

I giggle. "We can be saggy together."

"You won't be saggy. I'll be way overachieving. I already am."

I roll my eyes and slap him across the chest playfully. "Stop insulting my taste in men, Sinclaire. You're one of those people who just gets better with age. It's annoying, if I'm being honest. Do you know how many steps my skin care routine is? And then you wash your face with shampoo and look like *that.*"

He just chuckles with a cocky, panty-melting smirk and holds the glass in his hand up to me in a cheers motion. "Like a fine wine, Wildflower."

I give him another eye roll. "What is that?" I point at it, watching a droplet of condensation trickling down the outside.

"The closest thing I could get you to your favorite drink. Soda water with a splash of pineapple juice. I walked to all the bars on this resort to check, but this was the best I could do."

I feel the bridge of my nose start to tingle as I take the glass. Then my eyes start to burn. *Fuck.* I blink quickly and look away over the sand toward the tall net set up near the water.

Billie and Vaughn are facing off in a vicious match of beach volleyball. Billie made Stefan be on her team, but he's proving to be really rather useless. He can't stop laughing at the jabs flying back and forth between the other couple. Mira is all focus though, so she and Vaughn are kicking their asses. The tension is about to boil over. Billie is a terrible loser.

A watery chuckle escapes me as I carry on, avoiding looking at my husband.

Hank and Trixie are elbow-deep in the sand, building an epic sandcastle with Silas and the twins. And then down in the water Cole is teaching his brood of children, all three of them, how to snorkel while Violet sits on the wet sand, trailing her fingers through it drawing looping patterns with a serene smile on her face.

Which is exactly why she isn't prepared when her huge husband yanks her over his shoulder and tosses her into the water to the delighted tune of hysterical squealing from their kids.

The sight before me is really, really not helping with the tears. In fact, I feel one slip out and trail down my cheek.

Griffin's hand cups the base of my skull and turns me back to him, his deep, dark eyes anchoring me like they always do.

"Happy tears or sad tears?" he asks, his hand rubbing gently over my stomach.

We both startle when baby aims a perfect kick at his palm, but I don't look away from my husband.

I can't. Since the first day I saw him he's been with me. In my head, my heart, my spirit. I know in my bones that the two of us were meant to be. It was fate.

His gaze traces where he has his hand placed protectively over *us*, and the look on his face is so full of love and wonder that it makes my chest ache. And the tears fall.

"The happiest tears," I say as I lean forward to touch the tip of my nose to his.

He kisses me then, and it's just as good as the first time.

It always is.

It always will be.

BILLIE AND VAUGHN'S WEDDING

Vaughn

We're finally settled in our spots on the airplane.

In coach. On a public flight. Even though my family's company owns a jet and we could have flown back to Ontario for our wedding in total luxury.

Billie said that private jets are "pretentious" and "bad for the environment."

So here we are.

All six foot two of me is cramped into a seat that makes me feel like a pretzel, the length of my femurs angled awkwardly toward my fiancée. Especially since she insisted on taking the window seat.

She'd smirked and dove into the bank of three seats, like she knew I'd be crowded in the middle and was amused anyway.

My lips tug up at the memory. She might be the love of my life, but she's never going to stop picking on me.

And I wouldn't have it any other way.

The flight attendants start going through their spiel, and my eyes drop down, landing on the knee pressed up against mine that won't stop bouncing.

Since we left the farm, Billie has fallen quiet, which is concerning if you know her and her endless chatter. And with only a week to go before our wedding, it definitely has some alarm bells ringing for me.

I drape my palm over her knee and give her a gentle squeeze. "Babe. You okay?"

She flashes me a tight smile. "Yeah. All good." Then she turns her head to look back out the window onto the dark tarmac, all deep blues and flashing lights as the ground crew begins to guide us out for an overnight flight to Ontario, where her parents and brother live.

I rub my thumb in a small circle on her knee, hoping I can soothe her into a calmer state. But the jiggling knee continues up into the sky and is soon joined by the sound of her teeth biting down on a nail as she stares through the small round window. Something her mom, Miranda, expressly wrote in an email to keep her from doing. *So her nails will look good on her wedding day.* I had rolled my eyes and brushed the comment off because I know exactly what type of people the Farringtons are—I know how to deal with them. And in the interest of not squaring off with my future in-laws, my strategy is to ignore their shitty remarks for as long as possible.

Billie needs me to shield her from them—from the life she ran from—and I'm happy to do it. I'll save my temper for when I really need it. And after being the go-between for the past several months, I'm well aware that there is a time when I'm going to need it.

Her mother and I have taken over the wedding planning. Billie wanted no part of the process. She told me she trusts me to plan the perfect wedding and that so long as I'm there at the end of the aisle, she doesn't care about the rest.

But watching her curl in on herself now, I have to wonder if that's really the case.

I turn toward her, blocking out the woman dozing in the aisle seat with the bulk of my frame. My hand finds Billie's chin, turning her toward me as I lean in close.

Her amber eyes are wide—wild almost.

"Talk to me," I demand as she nibbles at her bottom lip and scans my face.

With a ragged sigh, she softens, leaning her forehead against my lips. "I'm scared. I'm stressed. I really don't want to go back home. It's been over a decade since I've seen them in person, and I..." She shakes her head and looks up momentarily, like she might find the right words written on the ceiling of the airplane somewhere.

I fucking *hate* seeing her like this. My happy, snarky, inappropriate girl. The woman who brings grown men to their knees with the size of her attitude. I hate knowing that people she hasn't had contact with in years can do this to her from the other side of the country.

"There's a big part of me that doesn't want to see them again. I'm not the girl they remember. I'll never be her again. But I almost want to go just to prove that to them. I know their love is conditional. I know that if I'm not the perfect little well-bred doll they want me to be, they'll have something to say about it."

Let them fucking try.

"I mean, hey. At least you picked a man they approve of," I joke, trailing my fingers over her cheekbone as she rolls her eyes.

"That's even worse! You're like my mom's wet dream. If she could have arranged a marriage, she'd have picked someone with your *credentials* or whatever other dumb fucking word she'd have for it."

She groans before giggling quietly and nuzzling into my neck. The sound of her light laughter eases the anxiety coiled in my chest. The tip of her nose trails over my throat as her lips press against my collarbone, just above the V neckline of my T-shirt. And that has all the blood in my body rushing to my cock—like always.

"You know what I don't give a flying fuck about, Billie?"

"Careful. They'll want you to call me Wilhelmina while we're there putting on the show."

I cup the back of her skull, weave my fingers into her silky chestnut hair, and tip her face up to mine again. "We're not putting on a show, Billie. I'll call you what I want, when I want. Because this wedding is about *us*. It's you and me and the rest of our lives together. The thing I don't give a fuck about is your parents or whatever anyone else thinks. Do you understand me? Your home is with *me*, not with them."

My fingers pulse and my teeth grind at the mere thought of these people ruining this experience for her. At how they jerk her around. If I let it, it could send me into an absolute rage. So when she nods her understanding, I kiss her. Hard.

I kiss her with all I've got. When I tug on her hair, she whimpers, and I use that moment to slide my tongue into her mouth, swallowing the noise. Our lips move against each other with a fervor that is probably not appropriate for a public flight.

But I don't give a flying fuck about that either.

I pull back, breathing heavily and trying to ignore how uncomfortably I've swollen in my jeans. The points of her nipples pressing against the thin material of Billie's shirt tell me she's feeling much the same.

I drag my lips against the shell of her ear to distract her further. She shivers, and my voice comes out all gravelly when I say, "Tell me you don't want this and I'll turn around, take you home, fuck your brains out, and marry you at city hall. Hell, I'll marry you in a back alley with the rats as our witnesses. I'll marry you anyplace, anytime."

A saucy smile plays on her full lips when I take in her face. She takes a hold of my free hand and pulls it against the warm apex of her thighs. Her tongue darts out to wet her lips when she whispers back, "The rats do sound cute, but I'm thinking less about that and more about riding your fingers right now, Boss Man."

This. This is my girl.

I glance over my shoulder at the woman beside us. Noise-cancelling headphones on. Eyes closed. Good enough.

Then I reach beneath the seat in front of me, grab my leather jacket, and toss it over my fiancée's lap. Within moments, she has her jeans undone and I'm sliding a hand into her lace panties, tracing my fingers over her slick pussy.

"So ready for me," I whisper.

"What can I say? I love it when you use your serious boardroom voice." Her head tips back and her lashes flutter shut on a breathless sigh when I slide one finger inside her.

We stay close together and speak in hushed tones, hidden in our own little corner under the dim light of a night flight.

"Legs wider."

She responds instantly, slender fingers wrapping around my forearm as her nails dig in.

"What a good fucking girl you are." I press a kiss to the column of her neck and add a second finger, smiling devilishly when I feel her grind down on my hand.

"Vaughn…"

"I love the sound of my name on your lips, Billie."

Her eyes flutter open, suddenly less playful than before. I stroke into her slowly and get lost in the glowing depth of her feline eyes. The ones that caught me in a stranglehold on day one and haven't let me go since. The ones I'm going to spend the rest of my life looking into.

"I love you, Vaughn."

"I love you too. Always have, always will. No matter what." I thrust in harder, and a moan escapes her. I cup her cheek and press my thumb against her lips, reveling in the way she always responds to me. "Shh. I don't want the entire plane to hear you come all over my hand."

And then I get to work, watching my future wife fall apart in my arms.

Best sight in the world.

Billie

Usually, I like cream in my coffee. But in the presence of Miranda and Victor Farrington, I think I'd trade my cream for whiskey. Baileys isn't even strong enough to get me through this breakfast.

When the server walks past with a fresh pot of coffee, I flag him down.

"Wilhelmina, really. You'll be all jittery if you drink more coffee," my mother interjects primly, dabbing at her lipstick, the kind that doesn't come off even if you rub hand sanitizer on it or whatever.

I smile wanly in her direction. "Good point." Then I turn back to the server, who is pouring out a steaming stream of lifeblood into the too-small cup on a saucer in front of me. "Can I also grab a shot of Jack Daniel's? You know"—I roll my eyes in my mother's direction—"to help with the jitters."

My brother, Rich, makes a strangled snorting noise as he shoves his napkin up against his mouth to keep from spewing his coffee everywhere.

"Richard!" my mother scolds him while my father looks on impassively. Emotionless, as usual.

"Actually, make that two shots of Jack. Little Dickie here could use a drink." I grin at my big brother, and my heart twists in my chest. We've always gotten along, but the distance I've created between my parents and myself has kept him away too. He's chasing his politician goals, following in our father's footsteps. And unlike me, he's not quite as keen to rock the boat.

I miss him.

Vaughn raises his hand from beside me. "Why not make it three, friend?"

I smile at my fiancé, my rock. What the fuck would I do without him?

"It's a bit early for drinking, wouldn't you say, Wilhelmina?"

I can see my mother's eyes pinching as she looks around the opulent dining room at their country club. Like she's worried someone might see us having whiskey with breakfast and start talking shit.

I hope they do.

You think she'd be immune after the scandal she and my father have endured, but instead they do this really cool thing where they pretend like nothing happened. Gotta love it.

My eyes bug out when my dad pipes up. "Ah, what the hell. Make it four."

"Victor!" My mother looks downright scandalized. Almost more than when a video of her husband, the prime minister of Canada at that time, snorting coke off a hooker's ass made the rounds.

I almost suggest we do that next. Instead, I bite my tongue hard enough to taste blood.

"Why don't we talk more about the ceremony, Miranda?" Vaughn redirects her with something akin to dangling a bone in front of a dog. She loves this bone. She's going to take it and run.

My wedding has become her wedding.

I know I told Vaughn I didn't care. But what I meant is that the wedding itself doesn't matter to me. I meant *don't make a big deal about it*. But instead my mother got her meddling fingers into the process and turned it into some sort of social calendar event for her and her tennis friends.

And now I hate it.

I hate that *my* special day has become more about her than me. But the date is too close to do anything about it now. I'll grin and bear it. Because in the grand scheme of things, it really doesn't matter. It's not a day I've dreamed of since I was a child, so it shouldn't matter this much. I'm being petty. It's one little day in a big long series of days I plan to spend with Vaughn.

On the West Coast.

Away from my parents and their fake elitist bullshit.

"Yes, well. That's a great idea."

My mom bats her lashes at Vaughn, and I roll my eyes dramatically enough that she sees it. Her lips pinch together in disapproval, and I start to mentally count how many days I have left in this godforsaken city.

"So after Victor walks her down the aisle—"

"Whoa." I hold my hand up to interrupt her. "No. Hank is walking me down the aisle." I don't miss the flash of hurt on my father's face, but he also doesn't say anything. Not much to say after he dragged me around on his apology tour and trotted me out in front of the press to make himself look better.

Classic Victor.

I'm not sure I'll ever truly forgive him. And he's never apologized or really even reached out to me personally, so I haven't exactly been given the opportunity. He's not a mean man, but he's not a good one either.

Not like Hank.

"Wilhelmina, don't be ridiculous." My mother rolls her eyes right back at me, and it incenses me.

Vaughn cuts in, gaze narrowing viciously. "You'll mind your words, Miranda. That's my wife you're talking to."

I'm not his wife yet, but when he says it, butterflies riot in my stomach. It sounds so good. I want that so badly.

The server returns with our shots, interrupting the tense moment. He places them down, and when he leaves, I flatten my hands on the table and lean across it toward my mother. I can feel all eyes at the table on me, but I'm not backing down.

I haven't been under her perfectly manicured thumb for *years*. I'm not going to let her squash me now.

"I'm not being ridiculous. My name is Billie. And that"—I point at my dad—"is my absentee father who had nothing to do with my life until he needed me to salvage his reputation. Hank will walk me down the aisle. This is not up for discussion. This is *my* wedding, something you seem to have lost sight of. Pick the cake you want. Pick the colors you want. But *this*? This is not negotiable." I reach for a glass of the amber liquid and throw it back. The burn makes my eyes water as I push to stand. "This has really been swell, everything I dreamed it would be. I'm going back to my hotel room for a nap. I didn't sleep much on the plane, and I'm not all that great at playing charades with you lot."

I look down at Vaughn, who has leaned back in his chair and steepled his hands beneath his chin. He's looking at my mother like he wishes he could disintegrate her on the spot. There's an angry flush on his cheeks, the only outward clue that he's ready to explode.

"Vaughn?" I ask with a quirk of my head.

"I'll catch up." He smiles at me, but it's feral, cruel. And suddenly I almost feel bad for my parents. Because I know that my future husband is about to eviscerate them.

I roll my lips together, momentarily thinking of all the ways I'm going to thank him later. For once, I'm happy to let someone take care of me. I need it. Leaning down, I brush a quick kiss to his lips.

Then I turn and flip my parents off. Because my maturity does in fact know some bounds.

And with that, I storm out of the restaurant and hail a cab back to our hotel.

Billie

"Billie."

I feel gentle fingers combing through my hair and smile. This is a good dream.

"Billie. Sweetheart. You have to get up now."

"Not yet," I murmur and snuggle deeper into the down duvet.

"I let you sleep as long as I could. But we need to go."

My eyes flutter open, and I look up into the face of the man I've been obsessed with for the past couple of years. Dark eyes, dark brows, darker hair pushed back in the perfect McDreamy swoop. *Goddamn, is he pretty.*

"Where are we going?" I sigh sleepily, still staring at him like he hung the fucking moon.

"Home. *Our* home."

I blink rapidly. "But…" I look around the room, awareness seeping from every corner. "We just got here. Did I sleep through the wedding?" I joke.

"No. Because it's tonight. In Ruby Creek."

I shoot up, and his hand falls from my hair. "What?"

"We're not getting married here. We're not getting married with these people speaking to you that way. I won't stand for it. We're doing this our own way. You and me."

My throat dries out as I swallow desperately and stare down at this beautiful, kindhearted man crouched beside the bed.

I'm in utter disbelief.

"But… you've spent months planning this with Miranda."

"You think I give a shit about a woman who insults you the way she does? She doesn't deserve to be at our wedding."

Tears sting my eyes, and my voice croaks when I whisper his name.

He just smiles softly and brushes his lips against the corner of my mouth. He wipes away a tear and tucks a stray piece of hair behind my ear. "No time for tears, Mowgli. The jet is waiting for us."

"Vaughn Harding. You did not."

"I did. We're getting out of here as quickly as possible. And if I have to charter a flight to do it, then I will. Because you're worth it." He squeezes my leg firmly. "Up we get. Rich will be waiting for us already."

"My brother? Dick?"

"Yes. What do you call him? Little Dickie? Well, Little Dickie wanted to come. Said he wouldn't miss it. He told me right after he finished laughing over the dressing down I gave your parents at the country club." He winks.

Shit disturber. God, do I love this man.

I shoot out of bed to pull my things together and realize he's packed us up. Our bags are set by the door. "You did everything?"

He just tugs me under his arm and presses a reverent kiss against my hair. "You were snoring so sweetly."

A laugh bubbles up out of me, and I slap him across the chest. "I thought you said I *purr*?"

"That does sound more ladylike, doesn't it?"

"Dick." I laugh, reaching for my bag. But he just swats my hand away and takes them both.

"Let's go. We've got a wedding to attend. I'm going to make you Mrs. Harding tonight."

The smile on his face is downright contagious.

I swing the door open for him, and we head into the hallway. "I can't believe we're taking a private jet. It's so pretentious."

I snuggle into him, feeling inexplicably safe and precious pushed up against his body. Like he's chosen me. Again.

"If getting you home as quickly as possible so I can marry you tonight makes me pretentious, then I'll happily be pretentious."

Over and over again.

Vaughn

Billie was whisked away by Mira and Violet to get ready the moment we got back. Which is how I find myself down at the pasture with Cole and Stefan Dalca.

The pasture where she threw a horse cookie at me. The pasture where we sat and had coffee every morning and got to know each other. The pasture where DD brought us together in the most unexpected way possible.

This is where it all started.

And staring at it now, lit with hundreds of candles, it strikes me that this is the most perfect place to make it all official.

"You two are some seriously romantic motherfuckers. This looks amazing."

Cole just grunts and crosses his arms with a small smirk. Stefan slaps me on the back with a wide grin. "Had to make it up to you. I did kind of break you up that one time, remember?"

I just raise a brow at him and chuckle. That water is so far under the bridge, it's not even funny. I was happy to welcome him into the fold. He has become one of my best friends. "You're going to make an adorable flower girl, Stef."

"I don't mind prancing down the path dropping rose petals. I'm not above that." He laughs. And it's funny because I know he would do it too.

A light jangling sound has me turning to see Trixie, Hank's partner, walking down toward the paddock wearing some sort of caftan-looking thing and an awful lot of silver jewelry. I know it's her because I can smell the patchouli.

She smiles at us, and her eyes crinkle deeply. The lines are proof of years spent smiling. And around Trixie, you can't help but smile. She's eccentric, a hippie, my brother's therapist, and apparently also licensed to marry people.

It's just obscure enough to not surprise me at all where this woman is concerned.

She claps her hands together dramatically. "Okay! Are we ready, boys?" Her chin juts out in the direction of the white pergola they've moved into the paddock. "How are we doing this? Is everyone standing up there? Just the two of you? What's the plan?"

I almost laugh. This morning, we were discussing the intricacies of a wedding neither of us wanted with an almost sleep-inducing level of detail. And now we're here, winging it. And I love it.

This is us.

Messy, funny, unscripted. We always have been. I think we always will be.

"Just the two of us," I reply. And when she gestures for me to follow her, I do.

The guys take a seat in the plastic folding chairs they've lined up. A far cry from the gold chairs Miranda was planning at the country club. As if chairs matter in the face of spending the rest of my life with a woman like Billie.

Mira and Violet walk up with Rich, all three with shit-eating grins on their faces. Like everyone and their dog knows this is far and away a better wedding. It feels natural, cozy. It feels like home. Here at the farm where my father and grandfather loved to spend their time. Under the starlit sky, tucked beneath the watchful shadows of the Cascade Mountains behind us.

It's perfect.

And when I look up to see Billie wearing an elegant lace dress and a wide smile, arm linked through Hank's, I know we made the right choice.

I was right to choose her.

That knowledge settles in my bones as I watch her walk down the candlelit path to only the sound of crickets chirping in the fields.

Her head swivels as she takes in the setting. Her eyes water, but her smile grows.

She is breathtaking.

And she's mine.

When they draw near, Hank wraps her in a tight, heartfelt hug and whispers something in her ear. She laughs. But they both come away teary-eyed.

The older man reaches forward and shakes my hand firmly. "Your dad. Your grandfather. They'd be proud of you, son."

I nod, feeling suddenly choked up.

Hank just smiles and squeezes my hand harder. "Take good care of her."

"I promise," I say, meaning it.

And Hank chuckles good-naturedly, shaking his head as he backs away from us. "Good luck. You're gonna need it."

At that, everyone laughs. It's no secret that Billie and I enjoy needling each other. And she can give as good as she gets. It's one of my favorite things about her.

She steps up in front of me, lacing her fingers through mine, and looks up into my eyes. Hair undone and flowing around her shoulders. Loose curls matching her untamed personality. Nothing like the tight twist her mother had planned.

She looks perfect. Perfectly *her*.

"Okay!" Trixie begins. "We are gathered here today…"

I should probably be paying closer attention, but I get lost in Billie's eyes. The golds, the greens, the warm tones. It strikes me that I'm one lucky motherfucker to get to stare into them for the rest of my life.

She gives me a shy smile and silently mouths, *I love you*.

And I just smile back, shaking my head. Because I almost can't believe it.

These people. This place. This woman. Marrying her standing in the exact spot we fell in love. What could be better?

Author Note

I would like to note that Griffin's brain injury resulted in what is called neurogenic stuttering. It is not common and varies in how it manifests or heals. I understand that no two traumatic brain injuries are the same and that every person's experience with them will differ. This story tells but one fictional character's experience, and I hope you all loved him as much as I do.

A special thank you to C.F. for taking the time to chat with me about living with a speech impediment and being available to bounce ideas off of. Your feedback was invaluable.

Acknowledgments

My first series. Complete. I almost can't believe it! About a year ago I decided to hit publish on my first book, and I just can't believe where that one click has taken me.

I can genuinely say that writing has changed my life. In so many ways. The friendships, the independence, the sense of accomplishment—I'm just overwhelmed that I'm here and that this is my life. Pinch me!

If you've followed along with my journey, thank you. From the bottom of my heart, thank you. And if you're new to my books, welcome! It's so good to have you all here.

Of course, books wouldn't happen without an incredible supporting cast. So here I go.

To my husband, who laughs at me when I leave everything to do with publishing a book to the last moment. You know me well, and you love me for it. You prop me up when I need it the most, and I love you for that. Thank you.

To my son, who is mad that Gold Rush Ranch is coming to an end and who likes *Off to the Races* the best because the title is in blue. I love you for all your opinions. You make me laugh every day.

To my editor, Paula. You are a gift. Seriously. Never leave me. I will cry.

Krista Callaghan, YOU KEEP ME SANE. I would honestly be lost without you. Please also never leave me.

Brandi and Shannon, thank you for your kind words and for finding aaallll the missing commas. This would be a mess without your eagle eyes.

My beta readers, Lena, Amy, Amber, and Kylie, thank you for reading my rough draft with so much love and patience. Your feedback is invaluable.

My ARC and street team members, I am absolutely overwhelmed by all of your support! I'm so lucky to know you all and be on the receiving end of your support.

Finally, Melanie Harlow, my blurb-helper and back-patter. Thank you for your endless support and thoughtful feedback.

The Elsie Silver Saloon

Come hang out in The Saloon on Facebook and interact with Elsie! Early announcements, exclusive excerpts, bonus giveaways, and general book boyfriend chitchat all happen here.

Take me to The Saloon!

facebook.com/groups/elsiesilversaloon

Read the other books in the Gold Rush Ranch series now!

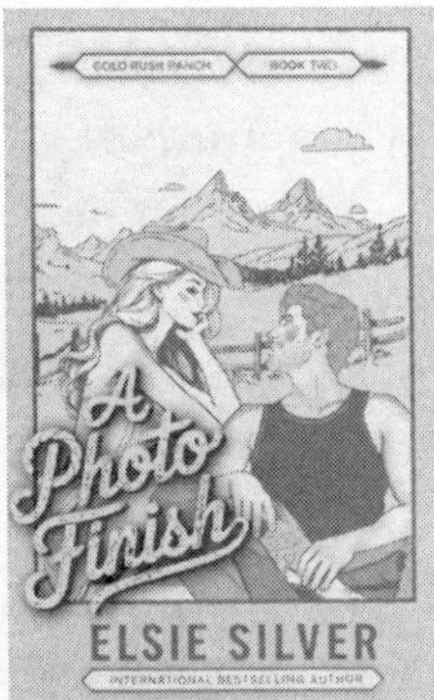

About the Author

Elsie Silver is a Canadian author of sassy, sexy, small-town romance who loves a good book boyfriend and the strong heroines who bring them to their knees. She lives just outside Vancouver, British Columbia, with her husband, son, and three dogs, and has been voraciously reading romance books since before she was probably supposed to.

She loves cooking and trying new foods, traveling, and spending time with her boys—especially outdoors. Elsie has also become a big fan of her quiet five o'clock mornings, which is when most of her writing happens. It's during this time that she can sip a cup of hot coffee and dream up a fictional world full of romantic stories to share with her readers.

Website: elsiesilver.com
Facebook: authorelsiesilver
Instagram: @authorelsiesilver
TikTok: @authorelsiesilver